THE GOOD STUFF

THE GOOD STUFF

Adventure SF in the Grand Tradition

The Good Old Stuff
The Good New Stuff

Edited by
GARDNER DOZOIS

FANTASY

THE GOOD OLD STUFF Copyright © 1998 by Gardner Dozois
Publishing History: St. Martin's/Griffin trade paperback, November 1998

THE GOOD NEW STUFF Copyright © 1999 by Gardner Dozois
Publishing History: St. Martin's/Griffin trade paperback, January 1999

First SFBC Science Fiction Printing: January 1999

Published by arrangement with:
St. Martin's Press
175 Fifth Avenue
New York, NY 10010

Visit The SFBC online at *http://www.sfbc.com*

ISBN # 0-7394-0044-4

PRINTED IN THE UNITED STATES OF AMERICA.

CONTENTS

CONTENTS

THE
GOOD OLD
STUFF

For Janet Kagan and Bob Walters—
who like the good old stuff.

CONTENTS

I would like to thank the following people for their help and support on this project:

Susan Casper, Janet Kagan, Barry N. Malzberg, Darrell Schweitzer, Virginia Kidd, Vaughne Lee Hansen, Kirby Mc-Cauley, Kay McCauley, Ralph M. Vicinanza, Chris Lotts, Richard Curtis, Ginjer Buchanan, Jennifer Uram, Mark Mc-Cloud, Eleanor Wood, Ashley D. Grayson, Dan Hooker, Gordon R. Dickson, David W. Wixon, Poul Anderson, Brian W. Aldiss, L. Sprague de Camp, Catherine Crook de Camp and, of course, special thanks to my own editor on this project, Gordon Van Gelder.

PREFACE

We say, in short, that we grew from the pulps to *Astounding*, and from *Astounding* into our present enlightenment. These are lies. We read the pulps and *ASF* simultaneously and with equal voracity, they were two sides of the one coin, and our special relationship with the pulps was more intriguing, racier, and in some ways more genuine, while our relationship with *Astounding* was respectable. And our present enlightenment, which will no doubt dim in the hindsight of years to come, derives not linearly from *ASF* but from a complex action of the love/hate relationship between the pulps and "modern science fiction" within ourselves.

—Algis Budrys, *The Magazine of Fantasy & Science Fiction,* January 1977

Science fiction can be a window on worlds we'd never otherwise see and people and creatures we'd never otherwise know, it can provide us with insights into the inner workings of our society that are difficult to gain in any other way, grant us perspectives into social mores and human nature itself mostly otherwise unreachable; it can be an invaluable tool with which to take preconceived notions and received wisdom to pieces and reassemble them into something new, it can prepare us for the inevitable and sometimes dismaying changes ahead of us, helping to buffer us against the winds of Future Shock; it can be terrifying and cautionary, it can be chastening and angry, it can be sad and elegiac, it can be wise and profound—but sometimes it's just *fun.*

Sometimes it's "just" pure entertainment. Sometimes it's an *adventure*—the sort of adventure unavailable anywhere else, where new worlds open up before us to be discovered and explored, and monstrous new threats undreamed of on our familiar Earth loom up and confront us at every step.

Fun is a concept not much talked about in our harried, hurried, anxious, serious-minded—if not downright grim—society these days, where everyone is constantly and apprehensively looking over their shoulder for a stock market crash, a nuclear attack, an asteroid impact, Ebola, El Niño, global warming, the destruction of the ozone layer, acid rain, cancer-causing agents in the food, Mad Cow Disease, microwave radiation, desertification, kidnappers from Flying Saucers, insane dictators, sinister government conspiracies, corporate downsizing, and all the other Dooms that daily hang suspended over our heads on the thinnest of threads. Fun, in fact, is often looked at as a shameful indulgence that should not be bothered with when there are More Important things to confront.

But nobody, no matter how intense and dedicated and committed, can be serious *all* the time. Sometimes, you've got to relax and enjoy yourself.

The same is true of science fiction as a genre, no matter how serious-minded and substantial and profound it gets—sometimes the writers turn one out just for fun, a fast-paced, no-holds-barred, flat-out *adventure* story, pure entertainment, with any more serious implications or troubling social issues—and they *do* get raised, even in the most seemingly insubstantial of tales—largely left to be dealt with in the subtext . . . the *fore*ground of such stories being occupied with action, wonder, color, and—another almost outmoded concept—adventure.

These are the kind of stories people are talking about when they say "they don't write 'em like that anymore." Well, yes, they *do,* actually, as I hope to demonstrate in the follow-up anthology to the one you're now holding in your hand, *The Good New Stuff,* due out early next year. For *this* book, though, it seemed worthwhile, in a day when adventure SF—even if it *is* still around—is the least talked-about and critically evaluated of the different types of science fiction, and perhaps the least esteemed, to give you a book of some of the classic SF adventure stories. These stories still hold up *as* adventures, as fresh and exciting and entertaining as anything being written today, but also they're seminal stories that helped to shape the field, and they hold within them the seeds of much later work and of much work yet to come.

As with my other retrospective anthologies, *Modern Classics of Science Fiction, Modern Classic Short Novels of Science Fiction,* and *Modern Classics of Fantasy,* a big part of my motivation for putting this anthology together was to battle the loss of historical memory in the genre, which seems to be accelerating all the time, so that now even stuff published as recently as the early '80s seems to already be out-of-print and forgotten. The shelf life for books is so short now, and things come back into print so rarely once they go *out* of it (and back-issue copies of magazines and second-hand copies of old books are so difficult to find, even in SF speciality bookstores and dealer's rooms at SF conventions), that many younger readers have probably never had a chance to read the stories here, even those stories that were famous in their day, even the Hugo-winners; many younger readers may not have even heard of the *authors* whose work is assembled here, something that I've discovered, to my dismay, in talking to bright and literate young readers who consider themselves hardcore SF fans and yet have never heard of Cordwainer Smith or Alfred Bester or Fritz Leiber or Leigh Brackett or James Schmitz or Murray Leinster or A. E. van Vogt (and even most young readers who *have* heard of them, have never *read* anything by them). This book, and similar books, and the re-issues of classic work that *do* occasionally still appear from publishers such as NESFA Press and Tor and Tachyon Press and White Wolf, are bandages on a gaping wound—but, alas, at the moment, they seem to be the best remedy that can be applied.

I've found, to my surprise, that many people don't seem to *care* whether the old stuff is available or not, or whether they've read it or not. The attitude seems to be that nothing that wasn't in print five years ago is worth bothering with anyway. Who cares whether a bunch of moldy old pulp stories are available to be read?

Unfortunately, to feel that way is to assign huge chunks of the genre's history to the dumpster—and to be ignorant of the past means that you can't even understand (or appreciate) the *present,* let alone have the slightest idea where you're going in the future, or why.

Besides, I don't happen to think that these old stories are moldy—in fact, I think that most readers will get as much or more entertainment value out of this book as they would out of any modern volume. Old wine may not necessarily always be the best—but it's not always vinegar, either.

As usual with these retrospective anthologies, though, once I actually sat down to put it together, I found that there were many more stories that I would have *liked* to use than I had *room* to use. Winnowing-screens were clearly called for.

Ever since the specific *science fiction* adventure story began to precipitate out from the larger and older tradition of the generalized pulp adventure story, the form that slowly emerged as being most specific to science fiction, (differentiating it from the kind of Lost World/Lost Race adventure that went all the way back into the middle of the 19th Century—it was usually different in tone as well from the more solemn, slower-paced, Visit To A Future Society story popular with Hugo Gernsback and other editors, which, especially after Wells, tended toward Utopian polemic and ran to guided tours of the Great Steam Grommet Works) was the *Space* Adventure story.

Although the SF adventure story has always had—and still has—other branches as well, the Space Adventure story or the Space Opera remains to this day probably the most characteristic sort of SF adventure tale. Thus that's the kind of story I've primarily stuck with for this anthology (although I've also included a story that takes place on an Alternate Earth, as well as a story that takes place in a devastated Future Earth after a nuclear holocaust, and I'd like to pretend piously that I did it to be inclusive and to cover all the bases, but really, truth be known, it was just because they were such good stories, and had affected me so powerfully as a kid, that I couldn't resist them). I also decided that, however adventure-driven it was, the story *also* had to qualify as genuine science fiction, by the aesthetic standards and the standards of scientific knowledge of its time; I didn't want the stereotypical "Bat Durston" stories, where a cowboy story is retold as a science fiction story by the simple expedient of swapping the term

"horse" for "spaceship" and "six-gun" for "blaster," and so forth; this requirement also omitted much of the stuff from the *Weird Tales* of the '30s and the
Planet Stories of the '40s, which were just horror stories or sword & sorcery
tales recast as science fiction in a similarly naive one-for-one way. So Planetary
Romances, Other World Adventures, Space Adventure, and Space Opera were
acceptable only if they were *more* than translated versions of standard boiler-
plate adventure stories common to other pulp genres, if they had some quality
of vision or invention or intent that solidly centered them as adventures germane
to *science fiction,* stories that wouldn't be possible—with the same kind of impact, anyway—if translated to other forms.

(Of course these judgment calls are subjective. I believe that I can discern
subtle differences in flavor between the Space Adventure, the Space Opera, the
Planetary Romance, and the tale of off-Earth Other World adventure— later on,
in the next volume, I'll claim to be able to discern differences in flavor between cyberpunk, hard science fiction, radical hard science fiction, and the New
Baroque Space Opera as well—just as I can discern differences between Vanilla,
French Vanilla, Vanilla Fudge, and Chocolate Chip ice-cream, but the differences in flavor are subtle, hard to articulate, and, in the end, what tastes like
Vanilla to me might taste like Chocolate Chip to you.)

Even after making these decisions, though, the potential stories I wanted to
use outweighed the room available for them by a factor of three or four. If I'd
been editing the multi-dimensional, infinitely expandable ideal edition of this
anthology, I'd have gladly put all of them in, and so been able to cover the entire development of the space adventure tale with something like the kind of
completeness it deserves, starting all the way back in the Superscience days of
the '20s and '30s. Unfortunately, out here in the real world, this volume could
only contain a certain finite amount of material, so something else had to go.
More winnowing-screens were called for, and I had further decisions to make—
some fairly Draconian decisions, at that—as to what historical periods I was
going to cover in this book, and which periods I was *not* going to cover.

In order to make these decisions more understandable, we should really
pause here for a comprehensive history of the development of the genre space
adventure tale, from its beginnings in the Gernsback *Amazing Stories* of the late
'20s all the way through to the '90s, but we don't have room for that. Suffice it
to say—in a brutally compressed and distorted version of the truth, with no al-
lowance made for dozens of exceptions and contradictions—that by the time the
earliest of the stories collected here saw print, after World War II, science fiction
had passed through what is sometimes referred to retroactively as the "Superscience" era of the '20s and '30s, the first great Age of the Space Opera, when
writers such as E. E. "Doc" Smith, Ray Cummings, Raymond Z. Gallun, Edmond Hamilton, John W. Campbell, Jack Williamson, Clifford D. Simak, and
others greatly widened the stage upon which the science fiction adventure story

could be played; before E. E. Smith, for instance, SF writers rarely ventured outside of the solar system for settings for their stories, but by the end of the "Superscience" era, the rest of the Galaxy—and, indeed, the rest of the universe—was their playground. They also increased both the permissible scope for an adventure and the size of the stakes at risk; it was not for nothing that Edmond Hamilton, for instance, was referred to as "World-Wrecker" or "Planet-Buster" Hamilton, and the space fleets of immense mile-long space-dreadnoughts armed with awesome world-shattering super-scientific weapons that have continued to prowl through deep space throughout all of the subsequent history of science fiction (and on out of the print media and onto television and movie screens, and onto computer monitors in the form of space-adventure computer games) were first launched on their paper voyages in the pages of the pulp magazines of the '20s and '30s.

By 1948, though—which is when the earliest story here, A. E. van Vogt's "The Rull," appeared—we'd *also* gone through the Campbellian revolution in science fiction, when the new editor of *Astounding* magazine, John W. Campbell, had, by sheer force of will (aided by the example of radical new writers such as Robert A. Heinlein and Isaac Asimov), changed the consensus definition of what a "good" science fiction story should be like, downplaying and devaluing the more garish and melodramatic lowest-common-denominator pulp stuff in favor of better-written, more thoughtful material that actually made a stab at rigor and scientific possibility, the aim being to produce the "kind of story that could be printed in a magazine of the year two thousand A.D." as a contemporary story of the day, a story with "no gee-whiz," where the author would "just take the technology for granted." (There would be exceptions, of course, and much adventure stuff, including some rather garish Space Opera, continued to appear in *Astounding*—and later, *Analog,* after the magazine changed its name . . . a move that in itself was symbolic of Campbell's desire to move away from pulpishness and toward respectability and unsmiling polemic purpose—throughout Campbell's lifetime; but that was the often-stated goal. And, in spite of Campbell's occasional seduction by fast-paced widescreen adventure stories too juicy to resist—such as Frank Herbert's *Dune,* which, in spite of some canny ideas about the nature of society that were just the sort of thing that Campbell liked, was fundamentally a baroque Space Opera on a scale not seen since the Superscience era—that was the direction in which he consciously tried to steer the magazine.)

One result of the Campbellian revolution—an ironic one, since Campbell himself was one of the most widescreen planet-busters of the "Superscience" era—was to make the Space Adventure tale or the Space Opera somewhat *declassé:* outmoded, outdated, passed-by, no longer the arena where the Cutting Edge work of the day was being done. The very term "Space Opera"—coined in 1941 by Wilson Tucker (on the model of the older, and also negative, terms

"Soap Opera" and "Horse Opera") to describe the "hacky, grinding, stinking, outworn, spaceship yarn"—has a derisive edge to it, a disapproving edge that has stuck with the term ever since. Even today, Space Opera has a raffish, slightly disreputable, Not Quite Nice, disapproved-of outlaw tang to it—so that people who *like* Space Opera are often just the faintest bit hang-dog or shame-faced about admitting it, as if they've been caught in a Guilty Pleasure, something we like even though we know it's Bad for us, and probably not Politically Correct, like admitting to binging on potato chips or Chocolate Chip Cookie Dough ice cream, or being caught out ordering a junk-food hamburger for dinner instead of a healthy Chef's salad, or watching *Gunsmoke* reruns instead of *Masterpiece Theater.* (Ironically, it may be this very whiff of Beyond-The-Pale that has attracted new writers, seeking for a chance to run up the pirate flag and be Outlaws, to the form in the '80s and the '90s.)

The effect of the Campbellian revolution was exacerbated in the beginning of the decade of the '50s by the founding of two *new* major SF magazines, *Galaxy* and *The Magazine of Fantasy & Science Fiction,* whose editors would push the accepted model for the science fiction story even further in the direction of psychological and sociological maturity and literary sophistication of style and conceptualization, sometimes further than Campbell himself was willing to go—and would also therefore push it even further away from the familiar pulp adventure tale, which as a result became even more *declassé.*

Another ironic effect of all this, the Campbellian revolution followed by the launching of *Galaxy* and *F&SF,* was that literary standards went up throughout the field, even at magazines such as *Planet Stories* and *Thrilling Wonder Stories* and *Startling Stories,* whose readers now *also* wanted to get a product that was better written line-by-line . . . so that even in the pulp adventure market, a clumsy and poorly written story that would have been accepted without question in 1935 might have more difficulty getting into print in 1955—and the level of craft needed to get an adventure story into one of the mainline magazines such as *Astounding* or *Galaxy* or *F&SF* rose sharply. The literary ante had been upped, permanently, for the entire genre, low-end as well as high-end. (And some of the stuff those "low-end" markets would publish as the SF adventure story struggled to evolve, work by Jack Vance, Ray Bradbury, Charles Harness, Theodore Sturgeon, and others, although not widely accepted at the time, would in retrospect look just as good if not better than much of the more "respectable" fare offered by the mainline magazines.)

This helped me set one parameter for the book. I didn't want a book comprised of dusty museum pieces, literary curiosities so out-of-date in terms of style and aesthetics that they could only be enjoyed through a lens of nostalgia; I wanted a book that contemporary readers could *enjoy,* stories that would be as vivid and entertaining to today's readers as anything else they can find on the bookstore shelves—and that meant that a certain median level of line-by-line craft was essential. The blunt truth is, many of the classic stories of the '20s and '30s, although they contain the seeds of much later work within them, are so poorly written line-by-line (and so dated stylistically even when they aren't clumsy) that they are opaque and impenetrable to many modern readers. So I decided that I would omit coverage here of the "Superscience" era of the '30s (already heavily covered anyway in anthologies such as Isaac Asimov's *Before the Golden Age* and Damon Knight's *Science Fiction of the Thirties*), and concentrate on work published after World War II instead, a period of swift change and forced evolution in the magazine market, when many of the aesthetic lessons of the Campbellian revolution had already been absorbed and applied. Besides, "after World War II" made a neat and symbolically obvious starting point—the science fiction scenes before the war and after the war were radically different, and even some of the authors who had been publishing pre-war, such as Jack Williamson and Clifford D. Simak, would change their styles and approaches radically after the war.

Deciding to start after World War II set one limiting parameter, but that still left almost fifty years to cover until the present day, too much territory to cover adequately in one volume. The book would have to be broken into two volumes, and was, with the upcoming volume to be called *The Good New Stuff.* But the question still remained: where to break it?

The SF adventure story, and particularly those specialized forms known as the Space Adventure and Space Opera, underwent hothouse forced evolution in the '50s and in the early and mid-'60s. In retrospect this time might be seen as the second great Age of the Space Opera, although that fact is often obscured by the attention paid—both then and now—to the work being done outside the compress of the Space Adventure, especially by the *Galaxy* writers. And yet, during those years, writers such as Poul Anderson and Jack Vance and James H. Schmitz were at their most prolific, L. Sprague de Camp was publishing his tales of the Viagens Interplanetarias, Cordwainer Smith was producing the best of his Instrumentality stories, Brian W. Aldiss was helping to invent the modern science-fantasy form with the outrageous and gorgeously colored adventures (loudly attacked at the time for not being scientifically plausible—as indeed they were *not,* although to protest that is almost to miss the point) of his "Hothouse" series, Robert A. Heinlein was (with mixed success) diluting the Space Adventure story to make it acceptable to the readers of *The Saturday Evening Post,* while, at the same time, with his so-called "juvenile" novels—actually Young Adult novels, by today's classification system—he was addicting whole new generations of readers to that form (as was Andre Norton), Hal Clement was turning out his two best books—both vivid otherworld adventures—*Mission of Gravity* and *Cycle of Fire* . . . and Alfred Bester was raising the stakes for baroque Space Opera in 1956 with *The Stars My Destination* (still one of the most influential SF novels ever written, and a story that was no more typical of

H. L. Gold's *Galaxy*, where the emphasis was usually on biting social satire, than Frank Herbert's "Dune" stories were of *Analog*—it's hard to resist a good adventure story!), just as Frank Herbert would raise them again, at least in terms of the complexity of the social background—Bester had more headlong momentum and bravura—in *Dune*.

By the mid-'60s, there would even be a magazine again that specialized—although in a defacto way—in ripsnorting adventure tales (*Thrilling Wonder Stories, Planet Stories,* and *Startling Stories* had all disappeared at the end of the '50s, along with more than forty other titles that had appeared during the genre's short-lived '50s Boom), Frederik Pohl's *Worlds of If* magazine. Although designed as a second-string back-up magazine in which to dump stuff that was good but not good *enough* for Pohl's front-line magazine, *Galaxy*—it was *"Galaxy's* remainder outlet,"* to use Pohl's own blunt phrase—*Worlds of If* always seemed much livelier and looser and more entertaining to me than its somewhat gray older sister, and, somewhat to Pohl's annoyance, it kept winning the Hugo Award for Best Magazine instead of the more "respectable" *Galaxy.* In addition to much memorable work off the mainline of the development of the Space Adventure by Harlan Ellison, Samuel R. Delany, James Tiptree, Jr., Robert Silverberg, Philip K. Dick, R. A. Lafferty, and others, Pohl's *Worlds of If* also published Larry Niven's early "Known Space" stories and Fred Saberhagen's long sequence of "Berserker" stories, and started something of a mini-boom in the even-more-specialized form of the "Interstellar Espionage" story, a form Keith Laumer started out *satirizing* in his "Retief" stories—although later Retief stories more-or-less became the very thing they'd originally been mocking, with perhaps a slight satirical edge maintained—which quickly became one of the most popular series to appear in *If.* They were later joined by similar series—without the satire—by C. C. MacApp and others; some of Saberhagen's "Berserker" stories can also be seen as falling into this category. This form was also popular elsewhere in the SF world of the mid-'60s, with Poul Anderson's "Dominic Flandry" series and Jack Vance's Demon Princes novels only the most prominent examples, and it's tempting to wonder, considering the timing, whether Ian Fleming's James Bond novels, then on the bestseller charts, weren't really the hidden influence here.

A good argument could be made, though, that by the mid-'60s the true home of Space Opera in the United States was not in any of the magazines anyway, but rather at Ace Books, especially the Ace Doubles line, which in addition to returning almost all of Edgar Rice Burroughs's work to print, produced under the editorship of Donald A. Wollheim a long sequence of cheaply priced (affordable even to teenagers! A key point), garish-looking paperback editions of adventure books by Poul Anderson, John Brunner, Andre Norton, Jack Vance, Gordon R. Dickson, Tom Purdom, Kenneth Bulmer, G. C. Edmondson, Keith Laumer, A. Bertram Chandler, Marion Zimmer Bradley, Avram Davidson, and dozens of other authors—including, in the late '60s, innovative Space Opera work by brand-new writers such as Samuel R. Delany and Ursula K. Le Guin.

However, by the late '60s and early '70s, perhaps because of the prominence of the "New Wave" revolution in SF, which concentrated both on introspective, stylistically "experimental" work and work with more immediate sociological and political "relevance" to the tempestuous social scene of the day (critics like Aldiss would call for more stories dealing with the Vietnam War, the "youth movement," the ecology, the sexual revolution, the psychedelic scene, and so forth, while, in England, Michael Moorcock would utter his famous demand for work with "real drugs, real sex, really shocking ideas about society"), perhaps because of scientific proof that the other planets of the solar system were not likely abodes for life of *any* sort, let alone oxygen-breathing humanoid natives that you could have swordfights with and/or fall in love with, perhaps because the now more-widely-understood limitations of Einsteinian relativity had come to make even the less flamboyant idea of far-flung interstellar empires seem improbable at best (there were those, even SF writers, who said that the whole idea of interstellar *flight* itself was wishful nonsense, forget about interstellar empires!), science fiction as a genre was turning away from the Space Adventure tale, which now became even more outmoded and *declassé* than it had been before.

Stalwarts such as Poul Anderson and Jack Vance and Larry Niven continued to soldier on (and there would be one last seminal book published in the '60s, coming out right at the end of the decade, Samuel R. Delany's *Nova*—a book which, although its influence was not immediately apparent, clearly had immense impact on the later Space Opera work of the new writers of the '80s and '90s), but there would be less Space Adventure stuff written in the following ten years or so than in any other comparable period in SF history. The generation of new writers who would come to prominence in the late '60s and early '70s would write almost none of it, for instance. By far the majority of work published during this period was set on Earth, often in the near future. Even the solar system had been largely deserted as a setting for stories, let alone the distant stars.

Not until the late '70s and early '80s would new writers such as John Varley, George R. R. Martin, Bruce Sterling, Michael Swanwick, and others, begin to grow interested in the Space Adventure again. By the '90s, a whole new boom in Baroque Space Opera would be underway, fueled by authors such as Iain M. Banks, Dan Simmons, Paul J. McAuley, Orson Scott Card, Vernor Vinge, Stephen Baxter, Stephen R. Donaldson, Alexander Jablokov, Charles Sheffield, Peter F. Hamilton, and a dozen others, ushering in the third great Age of Space Opera.

But that's clearly territory for *The Good New Stuff.* It became obvious that the natural breaking point for this volume was the beginning of the '70s, with the Space Adventure tale just about to fade into an interregnum . . . and that's where I've ended it. The follow-up volume, *The Good New Stuff*, due out in January of 1999, will take up the story after the interregnum, in the mid-'70s.

It's hard to deny that another of my major reasons for putting this anthology together was a nostalgic one. Just xeroxing the stories from crumbling old magazines and paperback collections, looking at the lurid covers and the garish pulp blurbs, having the cheap ink rub off on my fingers, smelling that curiously unique and instantly identifiable smell of old, brittle, yellowing paper, provided me with a nostalgic rush of such intensity that I was often able to remember where I was and what I was doing when I read the story for the first time thirty or more years before—and actually *reading* the stories again filled me with a much greater rush of images, outlandish settings, bizarre characters, strange creatures, odd concepts, vivid color, wild action.

But reading these stories again—as I had to read them over and over again to prepare this book for publication—I was struck by how well most of them hold up, even by today's standards. There isn't a story here that I wouldn't buy today, if it were somehow crossing my desk for the first time. So I don't think that this book is *merely* an aging reader's nostalgia trip, although it is inarguably *also* that. I think that these stories, like all good stories, are timeless. And I hope that this book—no doubt long out-of-print by then, sitting in a dusty heap in some secondhand book store, perhaps battered and coverless, waiting to be discovered by someone restless or bored enough to dust it off and pick it up—will still be offering its store of entertainment and wonder to new readers fifty years from *now*.

So sit back in a comfortable chair, break out the potato chips and ice cream (or a snifter of fine brandy, if you'd rather), and enjoy. Few—if any—adventure stories ever written in any genre are better than the ones you are about to read, forged in the crucible of a market where stories competed with each other on the basis of how exciting they were, and didn't get bought if they *weren't* exciting.

This is the Good Old Stuff. Have fun.

—Gardner Dozois

A. E. van Vogt

THE RULL

A. E. van Vogt was one of the first genre writers ever to publish an actual science fiction *book,* at a time when science fiction as a commercial publishing category did not yet exist, and almost all SF writers—even later giants such as Robert A. Heinlein—were able to publish novels *only* as serials in science fiction magazines. It's indicative of the prestige and popularity that van Vogt could claim at the time that he was one of the first authors to whom publishers would turn when taking the first tentative steps toward establishing science fiction as a viable publishing category—which makes it all the more ironic that his work is all but forgotten today by most readers in the genre that he helped to shape.

Van Vogt's stories were more complex, ornate, and recomplicated than the work of many of his predecessors from the Superscience days of the '30s—his most famous piece of writing advice is that you should throw a new idea into a story every five hundred words, a theory he seems to have consciously tried to apply in his own work. Van Vogt upped the stakes for Space Opera in the late '40s and early and mid-'50s with work like *The Voyage of the Space Beagle, The Weapon Shops of Isher, The World of Null-A, Slan,* and *The War Against the Rull,* increasing the Imagination Ante you had to come up with in order to sit down at the high-stakes table and play with the Big Boys, much as Alfred Bester and Jack Vance would do toward the end of the '50s, Cordwainer Smith and Frank Herbert would do in the mid-'60s, and Samuel R. Delany would do in the late '60s. Nobody, however, with the possible exception of the Bester of *The Stars My Destination* (who was himself clearly influenced by van Vogt), ever came close to matching van Vogt for headlong, breakneck pacing, or for the electric, crackling, paranoid tension with which he was capable of suffusing his work . . . as should be more than evident in the story that follows, which gives us one of the classic SF situations: a man pitted against an alien in a situation where there is no escape and to lose the struggle is to die, and where *both* adversaries are willing to do whatever it takes in order to *win* . . .

Van Vogt is the author of 65 books, including, in addition to those named above, *The Empire of the Atom, The Wizard of Linn, The Players of Null-A, Null-A Three, The Book of Ptath, The Weapon Makers, The House That Stood Still, Masters of Time, The Universe Makers, Quest for the Future, Computerworld,* and *The Silkie,* among many others. In 1996, he was honored with a long-overdue Grandmaster Nebula Award for Life Achievement. Most of van Vogt's work is long out-of-print and usually unfindable, but by the time you read these words, a reprint of one of his best-known novels, *Slan,* should be available as a trade paperback from Tor, and *The Voyage of the Space Beagle*—a landmark volume that, among other distinctions, was one of the chief inspirations for the original *Star Trek* series and was a seminal influence on the movie *Alien* as well—should be available as part of a three-novel omnibus volume (matched with novels by Poul Anderson and Barry N. Malzberg) from White Wolf Borealis called *Three in Space: White Wolf Rediscovery Trio #2*. We can only hope that more of van Vogt's books will come back into print again in the days ahead. (I myself would particularly like to see *The War Against the Rull*—one of my favorite van Vogt books—and back in print again, although a good historical case could be made for reprinting a half-dozen other van Vogt titles as well.)

1

Trevor Jamieson saw the other space boat out of the corner of his eye. He was sitting in a hollow about a dozen yards from the edge of the precipice, and some score of feet from the doorway of his own lifeboat. He had been intent on his survey book, annotating a comment beside the voice graph, to the effect that Laertes III was so close to the invisible dividing line between Earth-controlled and Rull-controlled space that its prior discovery by man was in itself a major victory in the Rull-human war.

He had written: "The fact that ships based on this planet could strike at several of the most densely populated areas of the galaxy, *Rull* or *human,* gives it an AA priority on all available military equipment. Preliminary defense units should be set up on Mount Monolith, where I am now, within three weeks. . . ."

It was at that point that he saw the other boat, above and somewhat to his left, approaching the tableland. He glanced up at it, and froze where he was, torn between two opposing purposes. His first impulse, to run for the lifeboat, yielded to the realization that the movement would be seen instantly by the electronic reflexes of the other ship. For a moment, then, he had the dim hope that, if he remained quiet enough, neither he nor his ship would be observed.

Even as he sat there, perspiring with indecision, his tensed eyes noted the Rull markings and the rakish design of the other vessel. His vast knowledge of things Rull enabled him to catalogue it instantly as a survey craft.

A *survey* craft. The Rulls had discovered the Laertes sun.

The terrible potentiality was that, behind this small craft, might be fleets of battleships, whereas he was alone. His own lifeboat had been dropped by the *Orion* nearly a parsec away, while the big ship was proceeding at antigravity speeds. That was to insure that Rull energy tracers did not record its passage through this area of space. The *Orion* was to head for the nearest base, load up with planetary defense equipment, and then return. She was due in ten days.

Ten days. Jamieson groaned inwardly and drew his legs under him and clenched his hand about the survey book. But still the possibility that his ship, partially hidden under a clump of trees, might escape notice if *he* remained quiet, held him there in the open. His head tilted up, his eyes glared at the alien, and his brain willed it to turn aside. Once more, while he waited, the implications of the disaster that could be here struck deep.

The Rull ship was a hundred yards away now and showed no signs of changing its course. In seconds it would cross the clump of trees, which half hid the lifeboat.

In a spasm of movement, Jamieson launched himself from his chair. With complete abandon, he dived for the open doorway of his machine. As the door clanged behind him, the boat shook as if it had been struck by a giant. Part of the ceiling sagged; the floor heaved under him, and the air grew hot and suffocating. Gasping, Jamieson slid into the control chair and struck the main emergency switch. The rapid-fire blasters huzzaed into automatic firing positions and let go with a hum and a deep-throated *ping*. The refrigerators whined with power; a cold blast of air blew at his body. The relief was so quick that a second passed before Jamieson realized that the atomic engines had failed to respond. And that the lifeboat, which should have already been sliding into the air, was still lying inert in an exposed position.

Tense, he stared into the visiplates. It took a moment to locate the Rull ship. It was at the lower edge of one plate, tumbling slowly out of sight beyond a clump of trees a quarter of a mile away. As he watched, it disappeared; and then the crash of the landing came clear and unmistakable from the sound board in front of him.

The relief that came was weighted with an awful reaction. Jamieson sank into the cushions of the control chair, weak from the narrowness of his escape. The weakness ended abruptly as a thought struck him. There had been a sedateness about the way the enemy ship fell. *The crash hadn't killed the Rulls aboard.* He was alone in a damaged lifeboat on an impassable mountain with one or more of the most remorseless creatures ever spawned. For ten days he must fight in the hope that man would still be able to seize the most valuable planet discovered in half a century.

Jamieson opened the door and went out onto the tableland. He was still trembling with reaction, but it was rapidly growing darker and there was no time to waste. He walked quickly to the top of the nearest hillock a hundred feet away, taking the last few feet on his hands and knees. Cautiously, he peered over the rim. Most of the mountaintop was visible. It was a rough oval some eight hundred yards wide at its narrowest, a wilderness of scraggly brush and upjutting rock, dominated here and there by clumps of trees. There was not a movement to be seen, and not a sign of the Rull ship. Over everything lay an atmosphere of desolation, and the utter silence of an uninhabited wasteland.

The twilight was deeper now that the sun had sunk below the southwest precipice. And the deadly part was that, to the Rulls, with their wider vision and more complete equipment, the darkness would mean nothing. All night long he would have to be on the defensive against beings whose nervous systems outmatched his in every function except, possibly, intelligence. On that level, and that alone, human beings claimed equality. The very comparison made him realize how desperate his situation was. He needed an advantage. If he could get to the Rull wreck and cause them some kind of damage before it got pitch-dark, before they recovered from the shock of the crash, that alone might make the difference between life and death for him.

It was a chance he had to take. Hurriedly, Jamieson backed down the hillock and, climbing to his feet, started along a shallow wash. The ground was rough with stone and projecting edges of rock and the gnarled roots and tangle of hardy growth. Twice he fell, the first time gashing his right hand. It slowed him mentally and physically. He had never before tried to make speed over the pathless wilderness of the tableland. He saw that in ten minutes he had covered a distance of no more than a few hundred yards. He stopped. It was one thing to be bold on the chance of making a vital gain. It was quite another to throw away his life on a reckless gamble. The defeat would not be his alone but man's.

As he stood there he grew aware of how icy cold it had become. A chilling wind from the east had sprung up. By midnight the temperature would be zero. He began to retreat. There were several defenses to rig up before night; and he had better hurry. An hour later, when the moonless darkness lay heavily over the mountain of mountains, Jamieson sat tensely before his visiplates. It was going to be a long night for a man who dared not sleep. Somewhere about the middle of it, Jamieson saw a movement at the remote perimeter of his all-wave vision plate. Finger on blaster control, he waited for the object to come into sharper focus. It never did. The cold dawn found him weary but still alertly watching for an enemy that was acting as cautiously as he himself. He began to wonder if he had actually seen anything.

Jamieson took another antisleep pill and made a more definite examination of the atomic motors. It didn't take long to verify his earlier diagnosis. The basic gravitation pile had been thoroughly frustrated. Until it could be reactivated on the *Orion,* the motors were useless. The conclusive examination braced him. He was committed irrevocably to this deadly battle of the tableland. The idea that had been turning over in his mind during the night took on new meaning. This was the first time in his knowledge that a Rull and a human being had faced each other on a limited field of action, where neither was a prisoner. The great battles in space were ship against ship and fleet against fleet. Survivors either escaped or were picked up by overwhelming forces.

Unless he was bested before he could get organized, here was a priceless opportunity to try some tests on the Rulls—and without delay. Every moment of daylight must be utilized to the uttermost limit.

Jamieson put on his special "defensive" belts and went outside. The dawn was brightening minute by minute; and the vistas that revealed themselves with each increment of light-power held him, even as he tensed his body for the fight ahead. Why, he thought, in sharp, excited wonder, this is happening on the strangest mountain ever known.

Mount Monolith stood on a level plain and reared up precipitously to a height of eight thousand two hundred feet. The most majestic pillar in the known universe, it easily qualified as one of the hundred nature wonders of the galaxy.

He had walked the soil of planets a hundred thousand light-years from Earth, and the decks of great ships that flashed from the eternal night into the blazing brightness of suns red and suns blue, suns yellow and white and orange and violet, suns so wonderful and different that no previous imaginings could match the reality.

Yet, here he stood on a mountain on far Laertes, one man compelled by circumstances to pit his cunning against one or more of the supremely intelligent Rull enemy.

Jamieson shook himself grimly. It was time to launch his attack—and discover the opposition that could be mustered against him. That was Step One, and the important point about it was to insure that it wasn't also Step Last. By the time the Laertes sun peered palely over the horizon that was the northeast cliff's edge, the assault was under way. The automatic defensors, which he had set up the night before, moved slowly from point to point ahead of the mobile blaster. He cautiously saw to it that one of the three defensors also brought up his rear. He augmented that basic protection by crawling from one projecting rock after another. The machines he manipulated from a tiny hand control, which was connected to the visiplates that poked out from his headgear just above his eyes. With tensed eyes, he watched the wavering needles that would indicate movement or that the defensor screens were being subjected to energy opposition.

Nothing happened. As he came within sight of the Rull craft, Jamieson halted, while he seriously pondered the problem of no resistance. He didn't like it. It was possible that all the Rulls aboard had been killed, but he doubted it.

Bleakly he studied the wreck through the telescopic eyes of one of the defensors. It lay in a shallow indentation, its nose buried in a wall of gravel. Its lower plates were collapsed versions of the original. His single energy blast of the day before, completely automatic though it had been, had really dealt a smashing blow to the Rull ship.

The over-all effect was of lifelessness. If it were a trick, then it was a very skillful one. Fortunately, there were tests he could make, not final but evidential and indicative.

The echoless height of the most unique mountain ever discovered hummed with the fire sound of the mobile blaster. The noise grew to a roar as the unit's pile warmed to its task and developed its maximum kilocurie of activity. Under that barrage, the hull of the enemy craft trembled a little and changed color slightly, but that was all. After ten minutes, Jamieson cut the power and sat baffled and indecisive.

The defensive screens of the Rull ship were full on. Had they gone on automatically after his first shot of the evening before? Or had they been put up deliberately to nullify just such an attack as this? He couldn't be sure. That was the trouble; he had no positive knowledge.

The Rull could be lying inside dead. (Odd, how he was beginning to think in terms of one rather than several, but the degree of caution being used by the opposition—if opposition existed—matched his own, and indicated the caution of an individual moving against unknown odds.) It could be wounded and incapable of doing anything against him. It could have spent the night marking up the tableland with nerve control lines— he'd have to make sure he never looked directly at the ground—or it could simply be waiting for the arrival of the greater ship that had dropped it onto the planet.

Jamieson refused to consider that last possibility. That way was death, without qualification of hope. Frowning, he studied the visible damage he had done to the ship. All the hard metals had held together, so far as he could see, but the whole bottom of the ship was dented to a depth that varied from one to four feet. Some radiation must have got in, and the question was, what would it have damaged? He had examined dozens of captured Rull survey craft, and if this one ran to the pattern, then in the front would be the control center, with a sealed-off blaster chamber. In the rear the engine room, two storerooms, one for fuel and equipment, the other for food and—

For food. Jamieson jumped, and then with wide eyes noted how the food section had suffered greater damage than any other part of the ship. Surely, surely, some radiation must have got into it, poisoning it, ruining it, and instantly putting the Rull, with his swift digestive system, into a deadly position.

Jamieson sighed with the intensity of his hope and prepared to retreat. As he turned away, quite incidentally, accidentally, he glanced at the rock behind which he had shielded himself from possible direct fire. Glanced at it and saw the lines on it. Intricate lines, based on a profound and inhuman study of human neurons. He recognized them for what they were and stiffened in horror. He thought, Where—*where* am I being directed?

That much had been discovered after his return from Mira 23, with his report of how he had been apparently, instantly, hypnotized; the lines impelled movement to somewhere. Here, on this fantastic mountain, it could only be to a cliff. But which one?

With a desperate will, he fought to retain his senses a moment longer. He strove to see the lines again. He saw, briefly, flashingly, five wavering verticals and above them three lines that pointed east with their wavering ends. The pressure built up inside him, but still he fought to keep his thoughts self-motivated. Fought to remember if there were any wide ledges near the top of the east cliff. There were. He recalled them in a final agony of hope. There, he thought, that one, that one. Let me fall on that one. He strained to hold the ledge image he wanted and to repeat, many times, the command that might save his life. His last dreary thought was that here was the answer to his doubts. The Rull *was* alive. Blackness came like a curtain of pure essence of night.

2

From the far galaxy had he come, a cold, remorseless leader of leaders, the *yeli,* Meesh, the Iin of Ria, the high Aaish of Yeel. And other titles, and other positions, and power. Oh, the power that he had, the power of death, the power of life and the power of the Leard ships.

He had come in his great anger to discover what was wrong. Many years before, the command had been given: Expand into the Second Galaxy. Why were they-who-could-not-be-more-perfect so slow in carrying out these instructions? What was the nature of the two-legged creatures whose multitudinous ships, impregnable planetary bases and numerous allies had fought those-who-possessed-Nature's-supreme-nervous-system to an impasse?

"Bring me a live human being!"

The command echoed to the ends of Riatic space. It produced a dull survivor of an Earth cruiser, a sailor of low degree with an I.Q. of ninety-six, and a fear index of two hundred and seven. The creature made vague efforts to kill himself, and squirmed on the laboratory tables, and finally escaped into death when the scientists were still in the beginning of the experiments which *he* had ordered to be performed before his own eyes.

"Surely this is not the enemy."

"Sire, we capture so few that are alive. Just as we have conditioned our own, so do they seem to be conditioned to kill themselves in case of capture."

"The environment is wrong. We must create a situation where the captured does not know himself to be a prisoner. Are there any possibilities?"

"The problem will be investigated."

He had come, as the one who would conduct the experiment, to the sun where a man had been observed seven periods before. The man was in a small craft—as the report put it—"which was precipitated suddenly out of subspace and fell toward this sun. The fact that it used no energy aroused the suspicions of our observing warship, which might otherwise have paid no attention to so small a machine. And so, because an investigation was made immediately, we have a new base possibility, and of course an ideal situation for the experiment."

The report continued: "No landings have been made yet, as you instructed; so far as we know, our presence is not suspected. It may be assumed that there was an earlier human landing on the third planet, for the man quickly made that curious mountaintop his headquarters. It will be ideal for your purposes."

A battle group patrolled the space around the sun. But *he* came down in a small ship, and because he had contempt for his enemy, he had flown in over the mountains, fired his disabling blast at the ship on the ground—and then was struck by a surprisingly potent return blast that sent his machine spinning to a crash. Death almost came in those seconds. But he crawled out of his control chair, shocked but still alive. With thoughtful eyes, he assessed the extent of the disaster that had befallen him. He had issued commands that he would call when he wanted them to return. But he could not call. The radio was shattered beyond repair. He had an uneasy sensation when he discovered that his food was poisoned.

Swiftly, he stiffened to the necessity of the situation. The experiment would go on, with one proviso. When the need for food became imperative, he would kill the man, and so survive until the commanders of the ships grew alarmed and came down to see what had happened.

He spent part of the sunless period exploring the cliff's edge. Then he hovered on the perimeter of the man's defensor energies, studying the lifeboat and pondering the possible actions the other might take against him. Finally, with a tireless patience, he examined the approaches to his own ship. At key points, he drew the lines-that-could-seize-the-minds-of-men. There was satisfaction, shortly after the sun came up, in seeing the enemy "caught" and "compelled." The satisfaction had but one drawback. He could not take the advantage of the situation that he wanted. The difficulty was that the man's blaster had been left focused on his main airlock. It was not emitting energy, but the Rull did not doubt that it would fire automatically if the door opened.

What made the situation serious was that, when he tried the emergency exit, it was jammed. It hadn't been. With the forethought of his kind, he had tested it immediately after the crash. Then, it opened. Now it didn't. The ship, he decided, must have settled while he was out during the sunless period. Actually, the reason for what had happened didn't matter. What counted was that he was locked in just when he wanted to be outside. It was not as if he had definitely decided to destroy the man immediately. If capturing him meant gaining control of his food supply, then it would be unnecessary to give him death. It was important to be able to make the decision, however, while the man was helpless. And the further possibility that the *elled* fall might kill him made the *yeli* grim. He didn't like accidents to disturb his plans.

From the beginning the affair had taken a sinister turn. He had been caught up by forces beyond his control, by elements of space and time which he had always taken into account as being theoretically possible, but he had never considered them as having personal application.

That was for the depths of space where the Leard ships fought to extend the frontiers of the perfect ones. Out there lived alien creatures that had been spawned by Nature before the ultimate nervous system was achieved. All those aliens must die because they were now unnecessary, and because, existing, they might accidentally discover means of upsetting the balance of Yeelian life. In civilized Ria accidents were forbidden.

The Rull drew his mind clear of such weakening thoughts. He decided against trying to open the emergency door. Instead, he turned his blaster against a crack in the hard floor. The frustrators blew their gases across the area where he had worked, and the suction pumps caught the swirling radioactive stuff and drew it into a special chamber. But the lack of an open door as a safety valve made the work dangerous. Many times he paused while the air was cleansed, so that he could come out again from the frustrating chamber to which he retreated whenever the heat made his nerves tingle—a more reliable guide than any instrument that had to be watched.

The sun was past the meridian when the metal plate finally lifted clear and gave him an opening into the gravel and rock underneath. The problem of tunneling out into the open was easy except that it took time and physical effort. Dusty and angry and hungry, the Rull emerged from the hole near the center of the clump of trees beside which his craft had fallen.

His plan to conduct an experiment had lost its attraction. He had obstinate qualities in his nature, but he reasoned that this situation could be reproduced for him on a more civilized level. No need to take risks or to be uncomfortable. He would kill the man and chemically convert him to food until the ships came down to rescue him. With hungry gaze, he searched the ragged, uneven east cliff, peering down at the ledges, crawling swiftly along until he had virtually circumvented the tableland. He found nothing he could be sure about. In one or two places the ground looked lacerated as by the passage of a body, but the most intensive examination failed to establish that anyone had actually been there.

Somberly, the Rull glided toward the man's lifeboat. From a safe distance, he examined it. The defense screens were up, but he couldn't be sure they had been put up before the attack of the morning, or had been raised since then, or had come on automatically at his approach. He couldn't be sure. That was the trouble. Everywhere on the tableland around him was a barrenness, a desolation unlike anything he had ever known. The man could be dead, his smashed body lying at the remote bottom of the mountain. He could be inside the ship badly injured; he had, unfortunately, *had* time to get back to the safety of his craft. Or he could be waiting inside, alert, aggressive, and conscious of his enemy's uncertainty, determined to take full advantage of that uncertainty.

The Rull set up a watching device that would apprise him when the door opened. Then he returned to the tunnel that led into his ship, laboriously crawled through it, and settled himself to wait out the emergency. The hunger in him was an expanding force, hourly taking on a greater urgency. It was time to stop moving around. He would need all his energy for the crisis. The days passed.

Jamieson stirred in an effluvium of pain. At first it seemed allenveloping, a mist of anguish that bathed him in sweat from head to toe. Gradually, then, it localized in the region of his lower left leg. The pulse of the pain made a rhythm in his nerves. The minutes lengthened into an hour, and then he finally thought, Why, I've got a sprained ankle! There was more to it than that, of course. The pressure that had driven him here oppressed his life force. How long he lay there, partly conscious, was not clear, but when he finally opened his eyes, the sun was still shining on him, though it was almost directly overhead.

He watched it with the mindlessness of a dreamer as it withdrew slowly past the edge of the overhanging precipice. It was not until the shadow of the cliff suddenly plopped across his face that he started to full consciousness with a sudden memory of deadly danger. It took a while for him to shake the remnants of the effect of the nerve lines from his brain. And, even as it was fading, he sized up, to some extent, the difficulties of his position. He saw that he had tumbled over the edge of a cliff to a steep slope. The angle of descent of the slope was a sharp fifty-five degrees, and what had saved him was that his body had been caught in the tangled growth near the edge of the greater precipice beyond. His foot must have twisted in those roots and been sprained.

As he finally realized the nature of his injuries, Jamieson braced up. He was safe. In spite of having suffered an accidental defeat of major proportions, his intense concentration on this slope, his desperate will to make *this* the place where he must fall, had worked out. He began to climb. It was easy enough on the slope, steep as it was; the ground was rough, rocky and scraggly with brush. It was when he came to the ten-foot overhanging cliff that his ankle proved what an obstacle it could be. Four times he slid back reluctantly; and then, on the fifth try, his fingers, groping, caught an unbreakable root. Triumphantly, he dragged himself to the safety of the tableland.

Now that the sound of his scraping and struggling was gone, only his heavy breathing broke the silence of the emptiness. His anxious eyes studied the uneven terrain. The tableland spread before him with not a sign of a moving figure anywhere. To one side, he could see his lifeboat. Jamieson began to crawl toward it, taking care to stay on rock as much as possible. What had happened to the Rull he did not know. And since, for several days, his ankle would keep him inside his ship, he might as well keep his enemy guessing during that time.

It was getting dark, and he was inside the ship, when a peevish voice said in his ear, "When do we go home? When do I eat again?"

It was the Ploian, with his perennial question about returning to Ploia. Jamieson shrugged aside his momentary feeling of guilt. He had forgotten all about his companion these many hours.

As he "fed" the being, he thought, not for the first time, How could he explain the Rull-human war to this untutored mind? More important, how could he explain his present predicament?

Aloud, he said, "Don't you worry. You stay with me, and I'll see that you get home." That—plus the food—seemed to satisfy the being.

For a time, then, Jamieson considered how he might use the Ploian against the Rull. But the fact was that his principal ability was not needed. There was no point in letting a starving Rull discover that his human opponent had a method of scrambling the electrical system of his ship.

3

Jamieson lay in his bunk thinking. He could hear the beating of his heart. There were the occasional sounds when he dragged himself out of bed. The radio, when he turned it on, was dead—no static, not even the fading in and out of a wave. At this colossal distance, even subspace radio was impossible. He listened on all the more active Rull wave lengths. But the silence was there too. Not that they would be broadcasting if they were in the vicinity. He was cut off here in this tiny ship on an uninhabited planet, with useless motors. He tried not to think of it like that. Here, he told himself, is the opportunity of a lifetime for an experiment. He warmed to the idea as a moth to flame. Live Rulls were hard to get hold of. And here was an ideal situation. *We're prisoners, both of us.* That was the way he tried to picture it. Prisoners of an environment and, therefore, in a curious fashion, prisoners of each other. Only each was free of the conditioned need to kill himself.

There were things a man might discover. The great mysteries—as far as men were concerned—that motivated Rull actions. Why did they want to destroy other races totally? Why did they needlessly sacrifice valuable ships in attacking Earth machines that ventured into their sectors of space when they knew that the intruders would leave in a few weeks anyway?

The potentialities of this fight of man against Rull on a lonely mountain exhilarated Jamieson as he lay on his bunk, scheming, turning the problem over in his mind. There were times during those dog days when he crawled over to the control chair and peered for an hour at a stretch into the visiplates. He saw the tableland and the vista of distance beyond it. He saw the sky of Laertes III, pale orchid in color, silent and lifeless. He saw the prison. Caught here, he thought bleakly. Trevor Jamieson, whose quiet voice in the scientific council chambers of Earth's galactic empire spoke with considerable authority—that Jamieson was here, alone, lying in a bunk, waiting for a leg to heal, so that he might conduct an experiment with a Rull. It seemed incredible. But he grew to believe it as the days passed.

On the third day, he was able to move around sufficiently to handle a few heavy objects. He began work immediately on the light-screen. On the fifth day it was finished. Then the story had to be recorded. That was easy. Each sequence had been so carefully worked out in bed that it flowed from his mind onto the visiwire.

He set it up about two hundred yards from the lifeboat, behind a screening of trees. He tossed a can of food a dozen feet to one side of the screen.

The rest of the day dragged. It was the sixth day since the arrival of the Rull, the fifth since he had sprained his ankle. Came the night.

4

A gliding shadow, undulating under the starlight of Laertes III, the Rull approached the screen the man had set up. How bright it was, shining in the darkness of the tableland, a blob of light in a black universe of uneven ground and dwarf shrubbery. When he was a hundred feet from the light, he sensed the food—and realized that here was a trap. For the Rull, six days without food had meant a stupendous loss of energy, visual blackouts on a dozen color levels, a dimness of life-force that fitted with the shadows, not the sun. That inner world of disjointed nervous systems was like a rundown battery, with a score of organic "instruments" disconnecting one by one as the energy level fell. The *yeli* recognized dimly, but with a savage anxiety, that the keenest edges of that nervous system might never be fully restored. Speed was essential. A few more steps downward, and then the old, old conditioning of mandatory self-inflicted death would apply even to the high Aaish of the Yeel.

The reticulated body grew quiet. The visual centers which were everywhere accepted light on a narrow band from the screen. From beginning to end, he watched the story as it unfolded, and then watched it again, craving repetition with all the ardor of a primitive.

The picture began in deep space with the man's lifeboat being dropped from a launching lock of a battleship. It showed the battleship going to a military base, and there taking on supplies and acquiring a vast fleet of reinforcements, and then starting on the return journey. The scene switched to the lifeboat dropping down on Laertes III, showed everything that had subsequently happened, suggested the situation was dangerous to them both—and pointed out the only safe solution. The final sequence of each showing of the story was of the Rull approaching the can, to the left of the screen, and opening it. The method was shown in detail, as was the visualization of the Rull busily eating the food inside. Each time that sequence drew near, a tenseness came over the Rull, a will to make the story real. But it was not until the seventh showing had run its course that he glided forward, closing the last gap between himself and the can. It was a trap, he knew, perhaps even death—it didn't matter. To live, he had to take the chance. Only by this means, by risking what was in the can, could he hope to remain alive for the necessary time.

How long it would take for the commanders cruising up there in the black of space—how long it would be before they would decide to supersede his command, he didn't know. But they would come. Even if they waited until the enemy ships arrived before they dared to act against his strict orders, they would come. At that point they could come down without fear of suffering from his ire. Until then he would need all the food he could get. Gingerly, he extended a sucker and activated the automatic opener of the can.

It was shortly after four in the morning when Jamieson awakened to the sound of an alarm ringing softly. It was still pitch-dark outside—the Laertes day was twenty-six side-real hours long, and dawn was still three hours away. He did not get up at once. The alarm had been activated by the opening of the can of food. It continued to ring for a full fifteen minutes, which was just about perfect. The alarm was tuned to the electronic pattern emitted by the can, once it was opened, and so long as any food remained in it. The lapse of time involved fitted with the capacity of one of the Rull mouths in absorbing three pounds of treated food. For fifteen minutes, accordingly, a member of the Rull race, man's mortal enemy, had been subjected to a pattern of mental vibrations corresponding to its own thoughts. It was a pattern to which the nervous systems of other Rulls had responded in laboratory experiments. Unfortunately, those others had killed themselves on awakening, and so no definite results had been proved. But it had been established by the ecphoriometer that the unconscious and not the conscious mind was affected. It was the beginning of hypnotic indoctrination and control.

Jamieson lay in bed, smiling quietly to himself. He turned over finally to go back to sleep, and then he realized how excited he was. It was the greatest moment in the history of Rull-human warfare. Surely he wasn't going to let it pass unremarked. He climbed out of bed and poured himself a drink.

The attempt of the Rull to attack him through his unconscious mind had emphasized his own possible actions in that direction. Each race had discovered some of the weaknesses of the other. Rulls used their knowledge to exterminate. Man tried for communication and hoped for association. Both were ruthless, murderous, pitiless in their methods. Outsiders sometimes had difficulty distinguishing one from the other. But the difference in purpose was as great as the difference between black and white, the absence, as compared to the presence, of light. There was only one trouble with the immediate situation. Now that the Rull had food, he might develop a few plans of his own.

Jamieson returned to bed and lay staring into the darkness. He did not underrate the resources of the Rull, but since he had decided to conduct an experiment, no chances must be considered too great. He turned over finally and slept the sleep of a man determined that things were working in his favor.

Morning. Jamieson put on his cold-proof clothes and went out into the chilly dawn. Again he savored the silence and the atmosphere of isolated grandeur. A strong wind was blowing from the east, and there was an iciness in it that stung his face. He forgot that. There were things to do on this morning of mornings. He would do them with his usual caution.

Paced by defensors and the mobile blaster, he headed for the metal screen. It stood in open high ground, where it would be visible from a dozen different hiding places, and so far as he could see it was undamaged. He tested the automatic mechanism, and for good measure ran the picture through one showing.

He had already tossed another can of food in the grass near the screen, and he was turning away when he thought, That's odd. The metal framework looks as if it's been polished.

He studied the phenomenon in a de-energizing mirror and saw that the metal had been covered with a clear varnish-like substance. A dreadful sickness came over him as he recognized it. He decided in agony: If the cue is not to fire at all, I won't do it. I'll fire even if the blaster turns on me.

He scraped some of the "varnish" into a receptacle and began his retreat to the lifeboat. He was thinking violently: Where does he get all this stuff? That isn't part of the equipment of a survey craft.

The first suspicion was on him that what was happening was not just an accident. He was pondering the vast implications of that when off to one side he saw the Rull. For the first time, in his many days on the tableland, he saw the Rull.

What's the cue?

Memory of purpose came to the Rull shortly after he had eaten. It was a dim memory at first, but it grew stronger. It was not the only sensation of his returning energy. His visual centers interpreted more light. The starlit tableland grew brighter, not as bright as it could be for him, by a large percentage, but the direction was up instead of down. He felt unutterably fortunate that it was no worse.

He had been gliding along the edge of the precipice. Now he paused to peer down. Even with his partial light vision, the view was breathtaking. There was distance below and distance afar. From a spaceship, the effect of height was minimized. But gazing down that wall of gravel into those depths was a different experience. It emphasized how greatly he had suffered, how completely he had been caught by an accident. And it reminded him of what he had been doing before the hunger. He turned instantly away from the cliff and hurried to where the wreckage of his ship had gathered dust for days—bent and twisted wreckage, half buried in the hard ground of Laertes III. He glided over the dented plates inside to one in which he had the day before sensed a quiver of anti-gravity oscillation—tiny, potent, tremendous minutiae of oscillation, capable of being influenced.

The Rull worked with intensity and purposefulness. The plate was still firmly attached to the frame of the ship. And the first job, the extremely difficult job, was to tear it completely free. The hours passed.

With a tearing sound, the hard plate yielded to the slight rearrangement of its nucleonic structure. The shift was infinitesimal, partly because the directing nervous energy of his body was not at norm and partly because it was calculated to be small. There was such a thing as releasing energy enough to blow up a mountain.

Not, he discovered finally, that there was any danger in this plate. He found that out the moment he crawled onto it. The sensation of power that pulsed from it was so slight that, briefly, he doubted that it would lift from the ground. But it did. The test run lasted seven feet and gave him his measurement of the limited force he had available. Enough for an attack only.

There were no doubts in his mind. The experiment was over. His only purpose must be to kill the man, and the question was, how could he insure that the man did not kill him while he was doing it? The varnish!

He applied it painstakingly, dried it with a drier, and then, picking up the plate again, he carried it on his back to the hiding place he wanted. When he had buried it and himself under the dead leaves of a clump of brush, he grew calmer. He recognized that the veneer of his civilization was off. It shocked him, but he did not regret it. In giving him the food, the two-legged being was obviously doing something to him. Something dangerous. The only answer to the entire problem of the experiment of the tableland was to deal death without delay. He lay tense, ferocious, beyond the power of any vagrant thoughts, waiting for the man to come.

What happened then was as desperate a venture as Jamieson had seen in Service. Normally, he would have handled it expertly. But he was watching intently—for the paralysis to strike him. The paralysis that was of the varnish. And so, it was the unexpected normal act that confused him. The Rull flew out of a clump of trees mounted on the antigravity plate. The surprise of that was so great that it almost succeeded. The plates had been drained of all such energies, according to his tests, the first morning. Yet here was one alive again and light again with the special antigravity lightness which Rull scientists had brought to the peak of perfection.

The action of movement through space toward him was, of course, based on the motion of the planet as it turned on its axis. The speed of the attack, starting as it did from zero, did not come near the eight-hundred-mile-an-hour velocity of the spinning planet, but it was swift enough. The apparition of metal and reticulated Rull body charged at him through the air. And even as he drew his weapon and fired at it, he had a choice to make, a restraint to exercise: *Do not kill!*

That was hard, oh, hard. The necessity imposed a limitation so stern that during the second it took him to adjust, the Rull came to within ten feet of him. What saved him was the pressure of the air on the metal plate. The air tilted it like the wing of a plane becoming air-borne. He fired his irresistible weapon at the bottom of the metal plate, seared it, and deflected it to a crash landing in a clump of bushes twenty feet to his right. Jamieson was deliberately slow in following up his success. When he reached the bushes, the Rull was fifty feet beyond them and disappearing into a clump of trees. He did not pursue it or fire a second time. Instead, he gingerly pulled the Rull antigravity plate out of the brush and examined it.

The question was, how had the Rull degravitized it without the elaborate machinery necessary? And if it were capable of creating such a "parachute" for itself why hadn't it floated down to the forest far below, where food would be available and where it would be safe from its human enemy? One question was answered the moment he lifted the antigravity plate. It was about normal weight, its energy apparently exhausted after traveling less than a hundred feet. It had obviously never been capable of making the mile-and-a-half trip to the forest and plain below.

Jamieson took no chances. He dropped the plate over the nearest precipice and watched it fall into distance. He was back in the lifeboat when he remembered the "varnish." There had been no cue; not yet. He tested the scraping he had brought with him. Chemically, it turned out to be simple resin, used to make varnishes. Atomically, it was stabilized. Electronically, it transformed light into energy on the vibration level of human thought. It was alive all right. But what was the recording? He made a graph of every material and energy level, for comparison purposes. As soon as he had established that it had been altered on the electronic level—which had been obvious but which, still, had to be proved—he recorded the images on a visiwire. The result was a hodgepodge of dreamlike fantasies.

Symbols. He took down his book, *Symbol Interpretations of the Unconscious,* and found the cross-reference: "Inhibitions Mental." On the referred page and line, he read, "Do not kill!"

"Well, I'll be . . ." Jamieson said aloud into the silence of the lifeboat interior. "That's what happened."

He was relieved, and then not so relieved. It had been his personal intention not to kill at this stage. But the Rull hadn't known that. By working such a subtle inhibition, it had dominated the attack even in defeat. That was the trouble. So far he had gotten out of situations but had created no successful ones in retaliation. He had a hope, but that wasn't enough.

He must take no more risks. Even his final experiment must wait until the day the *Orion* was due to arrive. Human beings were just a little too weak in certain directions. Their very life cells had impulses which could be stirred by the cunning and the remorseless. He did not doubt that, in the final issue, the Rull would try to stir him toward self-destruction.

5

On the ninth night, the day before the *Orion* was due, Jamieson refrained from putting out a can of food. The following morning he spent half an hour at the radio trying to contact the battleship. He made a point of broadcasting a detailed account of what had happened so far, and he described what his plans were, including his intention of testing the Rull to see if it had suffered any injury from its period of hunger.

Subspace was totally silent. Not a pulse of vibration answered his call. He finally abandoned the attempt to establish contact and went outside and swiftly set up the instruments he would need for his experiment. The tableland had the air of a deserted wilderness. He tested his equipment, then looked at his watch. It was eleven minutes to noon. Suddenly jittery, he decided not to wait the extra minutes. He walked over, hesitated, and then pressed a button. From a source near the screen, a rhythm on a very high energy level was being broadcast. It was a variation of the rhythm pattern to which the Rull had been subjected for four nights. Slowly Jamieson retreated toward the lifeboat. He wanted to try again to contact the *Orion.* Looking back, he saw the Rull glide into the clearing and head straight for the source of the vibration. As Jamieson paused involuntarily, fascinated, the main alarm system of the lifeboat went off with a roar. The sound echoed with an alien eeriness on the wings of the icy wind that was blowing, and it acted like a cue. His wrist radio snapped on, synchronizing automatically with the powerful radio in the lifeboat.

A voice said urgently, "Trevor Jamieson, this is the *Orion*. We heard your earlier calls but refrained from answering. An entire Rull fleet is cruising in the vicinity of the Laertes sun. In approximately five minutes, an attempt will be made to pick you up. Meanwhile, *drop everything.*"

Jamieson dropped. It was a physical movement, not a mental one. Out of the corner of one eye, even as he heard his own radio, he saw a movement in the sky: two dark blobs that resolved into vast shapes. There was a roar as the Rull super-battleships flashed by overhead. A cyclone followed their passage that nearly tore him from the ground, where he clung desperately to the roots of intertwining brush. At top speed, obviously traveling under gravitonic power, the enemy warships made a sweeping turn and came back toward the tableland. Jamieson expected death momentarily, but the fire flashed past; then the thunder of the released energies rolled toward him, a colossal sound, almost yet not quite submerging his awareness of what had happened. His lifeboat! They had fired at his lifeboat.

He groaned as he pictured it destroyed in one burst of intolerable flame. And then there was no time for thought of anguish.

A third warship came into view, but, as Jamieson strained to make out its contours, it turned and fled.

His wrist radio clicked on. "Cannot help you now. Save yourself. Our four accompanying battleships and attendant squadrons will engage the Rull fleet, and try to draw them toward our larger battle group cruising near the star, Bianca, and then re———"

A flash of fire in the distant sky ended the message. It was a full minute before the cold air of Laertes III echoed to the remote burst of the broadside. The sound died slowly, reluctantly, as if little overtones of it were clinging to each molecule of air. The silence that settled finally was, strangely, not peaceful, but a fateful, quiescent stillness, alive with unmeasurable threat.

Shakily, Jamieson climbed to his feet. It was time to assess the immediate danger that had befallen him. The greater danger he dared not even think about. He headed first for his lifeboat. He didn't have to go all the way. The entire section of the cliff had been sheared away. Of the ship, there was no sign. He had expected it, but the shock of the reality was numbing. He crouched like an animal and stared up into the sky. Not a movement was there, not a sound came out of it, except the sound of the east wind. He was alone in a universe between heaven and earth, a human being poised at the edge of an abyss.

Into his mind, tensely waiting, pierced a sharp understanding. The Rull ships had flown once over the mountain to size up the situation on the tableland and then had tried to destroy him. Equally disturbing and puzzling was the realization that battleships of the latest design were taking risks to defend his opponent on this isolated mountain.

He'd have to hurry. At any moment they might risk one of their destroyers in a rescue landing. As he ran, he felt himself one with the wind. He knew that feeling, that sense of returning primitiveness during moments of excitement. It was like that in battles, and the important thing was to yield one's whole body and soul to it. There was no such thing as fighting efficiently with half your mind or half your body. All was demanded.

He expected falls, and he had them. Each time he got up, almost unaware of the pain, and ran on again. He arrived bleeding, almost oblivious to a dozen cuts. And the sky remained silent.

From the shelter of a line of brush, he peered at the Rull. The captive Rull, *his* Rull to do with as he pleased. To watch, to force, to educate—the fastest education in the history of the world. There wasn't any time for a leisurely exchange of information. From where he lay, he manipulated the controls of the screen.

The Rull had been moving back and forth in front of the screen. Now it speeded up, then slowed, then speeded up again, according to his will.

Nearly a thousand years before, in the twentieth century, the classic and timeless investigation had been made of which this was one end result. A man called Pavlov fed a laboratory dog at regular intervals, to the accompaniment of the ringing of a bell. Soon the dog's digestive system responded as readily to the ringing of the bell without the food as to the food and the bell together. Pavlov himself did not, until late in his life, realize the most important reality behind his conditioning process. But what began on that remote day ended with a science that could brainwash animals and aliens—and men—almost at will. Only the Rulls baffled the master experimenters in the later centuries when it was an exact science. Defeated by the will to death of all the Rull captives, the scientists foresaw the doom of Earth's galactic empire unless some beginning could be made in penetrating the minds of Rulls. It was his desperate bad luck that he had no time for penetrations. There was death here for those who lingered.

But even the bare minimum of what he had to do would take time. Back and forth, back and forth; the rhythm of obedience had to be established. The image of the Rull on the screen was as lifelike as the original. It was three-dimensional, and its movements were like those of an automaton: Basic nerve centers were affected. The Rull could no more help falling into step than it could resist the call of the food impulse. After it had followed that mindless pattern for fifteen minutes, changing pace at his direction, Jamieson started the Rull and its image climbing trees. Up, then down again, half a dozen times. At that point, Jamieson introduced an image of himself.

Tensely, with one eye on the sky and one on the scene before him, he watched the reactions of the Rull. When, after a few minutes, he substituted himself for his image, he was satisfied that this Rull had temporarily lost its normal hate and suicide conditioning when it saw a human being.

Now that he had reached the stage of final control, he hesitated. It was time to make his tests. Could he afford the time? He realized that he had to. This opportunity might not occur again in a hundred years.

When he finished the tests twenty-five minutes later, he was pale with excitement. He thought, This is it. We've got it. He spent ten precious minutes broadcasting his discovery by means of his wrist radio—hoping that the transmitter on his lifeboat had survived its fall down the mountain—and was rebroadcasting the message out through subspace. There was not a single answer to his call, however, during the entire ten minutes.

Aware that he had done what he could, Jamieson headed for the cliff's edge he had selected as a starting point. He looked down and shuddered, then remembered what the *Orion* had said: "An entire Rull fleet cruising . . ."

Hurry!

He lowered the Rull to the first ledge. A moment later he fastened the harness around his own body and stepped into space. Sedately, with easy strength, the Rull gripped the other end of the rope and lowered him down to the ledge beside it. They continued on down and down. It was hard work although they used a very simple system. A long plastic line spanned the spaces for them. A metal climbing rod held position after position while the rope did its work.

On each ledge, Jamieson burned the rod at a downward slant into solid rock. The rope slid through an arrangement of pulleys in the metal as the Rull and he, in turn, lowered to ledges farther down. The moment they were both safely in the clear of one ledge, Jamieson would explode the rod out of the rock, and it would drop down ready for use again. The day sank toward darkness like a restless man into sleep. Jamieson's whole being filled with the melancholy of the fatigue that dragged at his muscles.

He could see that the Rull was growing more aware of him. It still cooperated, but it watched him with intent eyes each time it swung him down. The conditioned state was ending. The Rull was emerging from its trance. The process should be complete before night.

There was a time, then, when Jamieson despaired of getting down before the shadows fell. He had chosen the western, sunny side for that fantastic descent down a sheer, brown and black cliff like no other in the known worlds of space. He watched the Rull with quick, nervous glances during the moments when they were together on a ledge.

At 4:00 P.M. Jamieson had to pause again for a rest. He walked to the side of the ledge away from the Rull and sank down on a rock. The sky was silent and windless now, a curtain drawn across the black space above, concealing what must already be the greatest Rull-human battle in ten years. It was a tribute to the five Earth battleships that no Rull ship had yet attempted to rescue the Rull on the tableland. Possibly, of course, they didn't want to give away the presence of one of their own kind.

Jamieson gave up the futile speculation. Wearily, he compared the height of the cliff above with the depth that remained below. He estimated they had come two thirds of the distance. He saw that the Rull had turned to face the valley. Jamieson turned and gazed with it. The scene, even from this reduced elevation, was still spectacular. The forest began a quarter of a mile from the bottom of the cliff, and it almost literally had no end. It rolled up over the hills and down into the shallow valleys. It faltered at the edge of a broad river, then billowed out again, and climbed the slopes of mountains that sprawled mistily in the distance.

Time to get going again. At twenty-five minutes after six, they reached a ledge a hundred and fifty feet above the uneven plain. The distance strained the capacity of the rope, but the initial operation of lowering the Rull to freedom and safety was achieved without incident. Jamieson gazed down curiously at the creature. What would it do now that it was in the clear?

It merely waited. Jamieson stiffened. He was not taking any such chance as that. He waved imperatively at the Rull and took out his blaster. The Rull backed away, but only into the safety of a group of rocks. Blood-red, the sun was sinking behind the mountains. Darkness moved over the land. Jamieson ate his dinner, and as he was finishing, he saw a movement below. He watched as the Rull glided along close to the foot of the precipice, until it disappeared beyond an outjut of the cliff.

Jamieson waited briefly, then swung out on the rope. The descent strained his strength, but there was solid ground at the bottom. Three quarters of the way down, he cut his finger on a section of the rope that was unexpectedly rough. When he reached the ground, he noticed that his finger was turning an odd gray. In the dimness, it looked strange and unhealthy. As he stared at it, the color drained from his face. He thought in bitter anger. The Rull must have smeared it on the rope on the way down.

A pang went through his body and was followed instantly by a feeling of rigidity. With a gasp, he clutched at his blaster, intending to kill himself. His hand froze in mid-air. He toppled stiffly, unable to break his fall. There was the shock of contact with the hard ground, then unconsciousness.

The will to death is in all life. Every organic cell ecphorizes the inherited engrams of its inorganic origin. The pulse of life is a squamous film superimposed on an underlying matter so intricate in its delicate balancing of different energies that life itself is but a brief, vain straining against that balance. For an instant of eternity a pattern is attempted. It takes many forms, but these are apparent. The real shape is always a time and not a space shape. And that shape is a curve. Up and then down. Up from darkness into the light, then down again into the blackness.

The male salmon sprays his mist of milt onto the eggs of the female. And instantly he is seized with a mortal melancholy. The male bee collapses from the embrace of the queen he has won, back into that inorganic mold from which he climbed for one single moment of ecstasy. In man, the fateful pattern is impressed time and again into numberless ephemeral cells, but only the pattern endures.

The sharp-minded Rull scientists, probing for chemical substances that would shock man's system into its primitive forms, had, long before, found the special secret of man's will to death.

The *yeli*, Meesh, gliding toward Jamieson, did not think of the process. He had been waiting for the opportunity. It had occurred. Briskly, he removed the man's blaster; then he searched for the key to the lifeboat. Then he carried Jamieson a quarter of a mile around the base of the cliff to where the man's ship had been catapulted by the blast from the Rull warships. Five minutes later the powerful radio inside was broadcasting on Rull wave lengths an imperative command to the Rull fleet.

Dimness. Inside and outside his skin. Jamieson felt himself at the bottom of a well, peering out of night into twilight. As he lay, a pressure of something swelled around him, lifted him higher and higher, and nearer to the mouth of the well. He struggled the last few feet, a distinct mental effort, and looked over the edge. Consciousness.

He was lying on a raised table inside a room which had several large mouselike openings at the floor level, openings that led to other chambers. Doors, he identified, odd-shaped, alien, unhuman. Jamieson cringed with the stunning shock of recognition. He was inside a Rull warship.

He could not decide if the ship were in motion, but he guessed that it was. The Rull would not linger in the vicinity of a planet.

He was able to turn his head, and he saw that nothing material held him. Of such things he knew as much as any Rull, so in an instant he had located the source of gravitonic beams that interlaced across him.

The discovery was of abstract value, he realized bitterly. He began to nerve himself, then, for the kind of death that he could expect. Torture by experiment.

Nerving himself was a simple procedure. It had been discovered that if a man could contemplate every possible type of torture, and what he would do while it was occurring, and became angry rather than afraid, he could maintain himself to the very edge of death with a minimum of pain.

Jamieson was hurriedly cataloguing the types of torture he might receive when a plaintive voice said into his ear, "Let's go home, huh?"

It took a moment to recover; it took seconds to consider that the Ploian was probably invulnerable to energy blasts such as had been dealt his lifeboat by the Rull warship. And at least a minute went by before Jamieson said in a low voice, "I want you to do something for me."

"Of course."

"Go into that box over there and let the energy flow through you."

"Oh, goody. I've been wanting to go in there."

An instant later the electric source of the gravitonic beams was obviously rechanneled. For Jamieson was able to sit up. He moved hastily away from the box and called, "Come out."

It required several calls to attract the Ploian's attention. Then Jamieson asked, "Have you looked this ship over?"

"Yes," the Ploian replied.

"Is there a section through which all the electric energy is channeled?"

"Yes."

Jamieson drew a deep breath. "Go into it and let the energy flow through you. Then come back here."

"Oh, you're so good to me," the Ploian responded.

Jamieson took the precaution of hastily finding a nonmetallic object to stand on. He was barely in a safe position when a hundred thousand volts crackled from every metal plate.

"What now?" said the Ploian two minutes later.

"Look the ship over and see if any Rulls are alive."

Almost instantly, Jamieson was informed that about a hundred Rulls were still alive. From the reports of the Ploian, the survivors were already staying away from contact with metal surfaces. Jamieson accepted the information thoughtfully. Then he described the radio equipment to the Ploian, and finished, "Whenever anyone attempts to use this equipment, you go inside it and let the electricity flow through you—understand?"

The Ploian agreed to do this, and Jamieson added, "Report back to me periodically, but only at times when no one is trying to use the radio. And don't go into the main switchboard without my permission."

"Consider it done," the Ploian said.

Five minutes later the Ploian located Jamieson in the weapon room. "Somebody tried to use the radio just now; but he gave up finally, and went away."

"Fine," said Jamieson. "Keep watch—and listen—and join me as soon as I'm through here."

Jamieson proceeded on the positive assumption that he had one decisive advantage over the Rull survivors: he knew when it was safe to touch metal. They would have to rig up elaborate devices before they could dare move.

In the weapon control room he worked with energy cutting tools, hurriedly but effectively. His purpose: to make certain that the gigantic blasters could not be fired until the weapon control wiring was totally repaired.

That job done, he headed for the nearest lifeboat. The Ploian joined him as he was edging his way through an opening.

"There're some Rulls that way," the Ploian warned. "Better go this way."

They finally entered a Rull lifeboat without mishap. A few minutes later Jamieson launched the small craft, but five days went by before they were picked up.

The high Aaish of Yeell was not on the ship to which Jamieson had been taken as a captive. And so he was not among the dead, and, indeed, did not learn of the escape of the prisoner for some time. When the information was finally brought to him, his staff took it for granted that he would punish the Rull survivors of the wrecked battleship.

Instead, he said thoughtfully, "So that was the enemy? A very powerful being."

He silently considered the week of anguish he had endured. He had recovered almost all of his perceptive powers—so he was able to have a very unusual thought for an individual of his high estate.

He said, using the light-wave communicator, "I believe that this is the first time that a Prime Leader has visited the battlefront. Is this not correct?"

It was correct. A Super-General had come from rear headquarters to the "front lines." Top brass had come out of the sheltered and protected home planet and risked a skin so precious that all of Ria shuddered anxiously when the news was released.

The greatest Rull continued his speculations: "It would seem to me that we have not received the most accurate intelligence about human beings. There appears to have been an attempt to underestimate their abilities, and while I commend the zeal and courage of such attempts, my reaction is that this war is not likely to be successful in any decisive way.

It is therefore my conclusion that the Central Council reexamine the motives for the continuation of the battle effort. I do not foresee an immediate disengagement, but it might well be that the fighting could gradually dissipate, as we assume a defensive position in this area of space, and perhaps turn our attention to other galaxies."

Far away, across light-years of space, Jamieson was reporting to an august body, the Galactic Convention:

"I feel that this was a Very Important Person among the Rulls; and, since I had him under complete hypnosis for some time, I think we should have a favorable reaction. I told him that the Rulls were underestimating human beings, and that the war would not be successful, and I suggested that they turn their attention to other galaxies."

Years were to pass before men would finally be certain that the Rull-human war was over. At the moment, the members of the convention were fascinated by the way in which a mind-reading baby ezwal had been used to contact an invisible Ploian; and of how this new ally had been the means of a human being escaping from a Rull battleship with such vital information as Jamieson had brought with him.

It was justification for all the hard years and patient effort that men had devoted to a policy of friendship with alien races. By an overwhelming majority the convention created for Jamieson a special position which would be called: Administrator of Races.

He would return to Carson's Planet as the ultimate alien authority, not only for ezwals, but as it turned out, the wording of his appointment was later interpreted to mean that he was Man's negotiator with the Rull.

While these matters developed, the galactic-wide Rull-human war ended.

James H. Schmitz

THE SECOND NIGHT OF SUMMER

Although he lacked van Vogt's paranoid tension and ornately Byzantine plots, the late James H. Schmitz was considerably better at *people* than van Vogt was, crafting even his villains as complicated, psychologically complex, and non-stereotypical characters, full of surprising quirks and behaviors that you didn't see in a lot of other Space Adventure stuff. And his universes, although they come with their own share of monsters and sinister menaces, seem as if they would be more pleasant places in which to live than most Space Opera universes, places where you could have a viable, ordinary, and decent life once the plot was through requiring you to battle for existence against some Dread Implacable Monster; Schmitz even has sympathy for the *monsters,* who are often seen in the end not to be monsters at all, but rather creatures with agendas and priorities and points-of-view of their own, from which perspectives their actions are justified and sometimes admirable—a tolerant attitude almost unique amidst the Space Adventure tales of the day, most of which were frothingly xenophobic.

Similarly, Schmitz was decades ahead of the curve in his portrayal of female characters—years before the Women's Movement of the '70s would come along to raise the consciousness of SF writers (or attempt to), Schmitz was not only frequently using women as the heroines in swashbuckling tales of interplanetary adventure—itself almost unheard of at the time—but he was also treating them as the total equal of the male characters, every bit as competent and brave and smart (and ruthless, when needs be), without saddling them with any of the "female weaknesses"—like an inclination to faint or cower under extreme stress, and/or seek protection behind the muscular frame of the Tough Male Hero) that would mar the characterization of women by some writers for years to come. (The Schmitz Woman, for instance, is every bit as tough and competent as the Heinlein Woman—who, to be fair, isn't prone to fainting in a crisis either—but *without* her annoying tendency to think that nothing in the universe is as important as marrying Her Man and settling down to have as many babies as possible.) In the vivid and suspenseful story that follows, for instance, the hero of the piece is not only a woman, but an *old* woman, named Grandma Wannattel—a choice that most adventure writers wouldn't even make *now,* in 1998, let alone in 1950, which is when Schmitz made it!

The novel *The Witches of Karres* is usually thought of as Schmitz's best work, but I myself am fond of the "Vega" stories—one of which is "The Second Night of Summer"—which were collected in the book *Agent of Vega,* a book that is long out-of-print, alas, but one which—if you can find it—delivers as pure a jolt of Widescreen Space Opera Sense Of Wonder as can be found anywhere. Also atypically among writers of Space Adventure, Schmitz did most of his best work at short lengths, most of it for *Astounding* (and later for *Analog,* after the magazine had changed its name) and for *Galaxy,* including such memorable stories as "Grandpa," "Balanced Ecology," "Lion Loose . . .," "Greenface," "The Searcher," "The Winds of Time," "The Custodians," and dozens of others, plus a large number of stories about the adventures of a PSI-powered teenager, Telzey Amberdon. Schmitz's stories have been collected in *A Nice Day For Screaming and Other Tales of The Hub, A Pride of Monsters,* and, most recently, the posthumous collection *The Best of James H. Schmitz;* the "Telzey Amberdon" stories have been collected in *The Universe Against Her* and *The Telzey Toy.* Schmitz's other books include *The Demon Breed, A Tale of Two Clocks,* and *The Eternal Frontiers.*

Most of Schmitz's work is out-of-print, although copies of *The Witches of Karres* still show up in used bookstores with some frequency. Your best choice of sampling his work would probably be his most recent book, published in 1991, *The Best of James H. Schmitz,* which does contain several of his best stories—you could try ordering it from the publisher, NESFA Press (NESFA PRESS, P.O. Box 809, Framingham, MA 97101-0203; www.nesfa.org), although I have no idea whether they have any left in stock or not; the price *was* $18.95, but you'd better write first and ask for information.

On the night after the day that brought summer officially to the land of Wend, on the planet of Noorhut, the shining lights were seen again in the big hollow at the east end of Grimp's father's farm.

Grimp watched them for more than an hour from his upstairs room. The house was dark, but an occasional murmur of voices floated up to him through the windows below. Everyone in the farmhouse was looking at the lights.

On the other farms around and in the village, which was over a hill and another two miles up the valley, every living soul who could get within view of the hollow was probably doing the same. For a time, the agitated yelling of the Village Guardian's big pank-hound had sounded clearly over the hill, but he had quieted down then very suddenly—or had *been* quieted down, more likely, Grimp suspected. The Guardian was dead-set against anyone making a fuss about the lights—and that included the pank-hound, too.

There was some excuse for the pank-hound's excitement, though. From the window, Grimp could see there were a lot more lights tonight than had turned up in previous years—big, brilliant-blue bubbles, drifting and rising and falling silently all about the hollow. Sometimes one would lift straight up for several hundred feet, or move off over the edge of the hollow for about the same distance, and hang there suspended for a few minutes, before floating back to the others. That was as far as they ever went away from the hollow.

There was, in fact, no need for the Halpa detector-globes to go any farther than that to get the information wanted by those who had sent them out, and who were listening now to the steady flow of brief reports, in some Halpa equivalent of human speech-thought, coming back to them through the globes:

"No signs of hostile activity in the vicinity of the break-through point. No weapons or engines of power within range of detection. The area shows no significant alterations since the last investigation. Sharp curiosity among those who observe us consciously—traces of alarm and suspicion. But no overt hostility."

The reports streamed on without interruption, repeating the same bits of information automatically and incessantly, while the globes floated and dipped soundlessly above and about the hollow.

Grimp continued to watch them, blinking sleepily now and then, until a spreading glow over the edge of the valley announced that Noorhut's Big Moon was coming up slowly, like a Planetary Guardian, to make its own inspection of the lights. The globes began to dim out then, just as they always had done at moonrise in the preceding summers; and even before the top rim of the Big Moon's yellow disk edged over the hills, the hollow was completely dark.

Grimp heard his mother starting up the stairs. He got hurriedly into bed. The show was over for the night and he had a lot of pleasant things to think about before he went to sleep.

Now that the lights had showed up, his good friend Grandma Erisa Wannattel and her patent-medicine trailer were sure to arrive, too. Sometime late tomorrow afternoon, the big draft-trailer would come rolling up the valley road from the city. For that was what Grandma Wannattel had done the past four summers—ever since the lights first started appearing above the hollow for the few nights they were to be seen there each year. And since four years were exactly half of Grimp's whole life, that made Grandma's return a mathematical certainty for him.

Other people, of course, like the Village Guardian, might have a poor opinion of Grandma, but just hanging around her and the trailer and the gigantic, exotic-looking rhinocerine pony that pulled it was, in Grimp's opinion, a lot better even than going to the circus.

And vacations started the day after tomorrow! The whole future just now, in fact, looked like one good thing after another, extending through a vista of summery infinities.

Grimp went to sleep happily.

· · ·

At about the same hour, though at a distance greater than Grimp's imagination had stretched as yet, eight large ships came individually out of the darkness between the stars that was their sea, and began to move about Noorhut in a carefully timed pattern of orbits. They stayed much too far out to permit any instrument of space-detection to suspect that Noorhut might be their common center of interest.

But that was what it was. Though the men who crewed the eight ships bore the people of Noorhut no ill will, hardly anything could have looked less promising for Noorhut than the cargo they had on board.

Seven of them were armed with a gas which was not often used any more. A highly volatile lethal catalyst, it sank to the solid surface of a world over which it was freed and spread out swiftly there to the point where its presence could no longer be detected by any chemical means. However, its effect of drawing the final breath almost imperceptibly out of all things that were oxygen-breathing was not noticeably reduced by diffusion.

The eighth ship was equipped with a brace of torpedoes, which were normally released some hours after the gas-carriers dispersed their invisible death. They were quite small torpedoes, since the only task remaining for them would be to ignite the surface of the planet that had been treated with the catalyst.

All those things might presently happen to Noorhut. But they would happen only if a specific message was flashed from it to the circling squadron—the message that Noorhut already was lost to a deadly foe who must, at any cost now, be prevented from spreading out from it to other inhabited worlds.

Next afternoon, right after school, as Grimp came expectantly around the bend of the road at the edge of the farm, he found the village policeman sitting there on a rock, gazing tearfully down the road.

"Hello, Runny," said Grimp, disturbed. Considered in the light of gossip he'd overheard in the village that morning, this didn't look so good for Grandma. It just didn't look good.

The policeman blew his nose on a handkerchief he carried tucked into the front of his uniform, wiped his eyes, and gave Grimp an annoyed glance.

"Don't *you* call me Runny, Grimp!" he said, replacing the handkerchief. Like Grimp himself and most of the people on Noorhut, the policeman was brown-skinned and dark-eyed, normally a rather good-looking young fellow. But his eyes were swollen and red-rimmed now; and his nose, which was a bit larger than average, anyway, was also red and swollen and undeniably runny. He had hay-fever bad.

Grimp apologized and sat down thoughtfully on the rock beside the policeman, who was one of his numerous cousins. He was about to mention that he had overheard Vellit using the expression when she and the policeman came through the big Leeth-flower orchard above the farm the other evening—at a much less leisurely rate than was their custom there. But he thought better of it. Vellit was the policeman's girl for most of the year, but she broke their engagement regularly during hay-fever season and called him cousin instead of dearest.

"What are you doing here?" Grimp asked bluntly instead.

"Waiting," said the policeman.

"For what?" said Grimp, with a sinking heart.

"Same individual you are, I guess," the policeman told him, hauling out the handkerchief again. He blew. "This year she's going to go right back where she came from or get pinched."

"Who says so?" scowled Grimp.

"The Guardian, that's who," said the policeman. "That good enough for you?"

"He can't do it!" Grimp said hotly. "It's our farm and she's got all her licenses."

"He's had a whole year to think up a new list she's got to have," the policeman informed him. He fished in the breastpocket of his uniform; pulled out a folded paper and opened it. "He put thirty-four items down here I got to check—she's bound to miss on one of them."

"It's a dirty trick!" said Grimp, rapidly scanning as much as he could see of the list.

"Let's us have more respect for the Village Guardian, Grimp!" the policeman said warningly.

"Uh-huh," muttered Grimp. "Sure . . ." If Runny would just move his big thumb out of the way. But what a list! Trailer; rhinocerine pony (beast, heavy draft, imported); patent medicines; household utensils; fortune-telling; pets; herbs; miracle-healing—

The policeman looked down, saw what Grimp was doing and raised the paper out of his line of vision. "That's an official document," he said, warding Grimp off with one hand and tucking the paper away with the other. "Let's us not get our dirty hands on it."

Grimp was thinking fast. Grandma Wannattel did have framed licenses for some of the items he'd read hanging around inside the trailer, but certainly not thirty-four of them.

"Remember that big skinless werret I caught last season?" he asked.

The policeman gave him a quick glance, looked away again and wiped his eyes thoughtfully. The season on werrets would open the following week and he was as ardent a fisherman as anyone in the village—

and last summer Grimp's monster werret had broken a twelve-year record in the valley.

"Some people," Grimp said idly, staring down the valley road to the point where it turned into the woods, "would sneak after a person for days who's caught a big werret, hoping he'd be dumb enough to go back to that pool."

The policeman flushed and dabbed the handkerchief gingerly at his nose.

"Some people would even sit in a haystack and use spyglasses, even when the hay made them sneeze like crazy," continued Grimp quietly.

The policeman's flush deepened. He sneezed.

"But a person isn't that dumb," said Grimp. "Not when he knows there's anyway two werrets there six inches bigger than the one he caught."

"Six inches?" the policeman repeated a bit incredulously—eagerly.

"Easy," nodded Grimp. "I had a look at them again last week."

It was the policeman's turn to think. Grimp idly hauled out his slingshot, fished a pebble out of his small-pebble pocket and knocked the head off a flower twenty feet away. He yawned negligently.

"You're pretty good with that slingshot," the policeman remarked. "You must be just about as good as the culprit that used a slingshot to ring the fire-alarm signal on the defense unit bell from the top of the school house last week."

"That'd take a pretty good shot," Grimp admitted.

"And who then," continued the policeman, "dropped pepper in his trail, so the pank-hound near coughed off his head when we started to track him. The Guardian," he added significantly, "would like to have a clue about that culprit, all right."

"Sure, sure," said Grimp, bored. The policeman, the Guardian, and probably even the pank-hound, knew exactly who the culprit was; but they wouldn't be able to prove it in twenty thousand years. Runny just had to realize first that threats weren't going to get him anywhere near a record werret.

Apparently, he had; he was settling back for another bout of thinking. Grimp, interested in what he would produce next, decided just to leave him to it. . . .

Then Grimp jumped up suddenly from the rock.

"There they are!" he yelled, waving the slingshot.

A half-mile down the road, Grandma Wannattel's big, silvery trailer had come swaying out of the woods behind the rhinocerine pony and turned up toward the farm. The pony saw Grimp, lifted its head, which was as long as a tall man, and bawled a thunderous greeting. Grandma

Wannattel stood up on the driver's seat and waved a green silk handkerchief.

Grimp started sprinting down the road.

The werrets should turn the trick—but he'd better get Grandma informed, just the same, about recent developments here, before she ran into Runny.

Grandma Wannattel flicked the pony's horny rear with the reins just before they reached the policeman, who was waiting at the side of the road with the Guardian's check-list unfolded in his hand.

The pony broke into a lumbering trot, and the trailer swept past Runny and up around the bend of the road, where it stopped well within the boundaries of the farm. They climbed down and Grandma quickly unhitched the pony. It waddled, grunting, off the road and down into the long, marshy meadow above the hollow. It stood still there, cooling its feet.

Grimp felt a little better. Getting the trailer off community property gave Grandma a technical advantage. Grimp's people had a favorable opinion of her, and they were a sturdy lot who enjoyed telling off the Guardian any time he didn't actually have a law to back up his orders. But on the way to the farm, she had confessed to Grimp that, just as he'd feared, she didn't have anything like thirty-four licenses. And now the policeman was coming up around the bend of the road after them, blowing his nose and frowning.

"Just let me handle him alone," Grandma told Grimp out of the corner of her mouth.

He nodded and strolled off into the meadow to pass the time with the pony. She'd had a lot of experience in handling policemen.

"Well, well, young man," he heard her greeting his cousin behind him. "That looks like a bad cold you've got."

The policeman sneezed.

"Wish it were a cold," he said resignedly. "It's hay-fever. Can't do a thing with it. Now I've got a list here—"

"Hay-fever?" said Grandma. "Step up into the trailer a moment. We'll fix that."

"About this list—" began Runny, and stopped. "You think you got something that would fix it?" he asked skeptically. "I've been to I don't know how many doctors and they didn't help any."

"Doctors!" said Grandma. Grimp heard her heels click up the metal steps that led into the back of the trailer. "Come right in, won't take a moment."

"Well—" said Runny doubtfully, but he followed her inside.

Grimp winked at the pony. The first round went to Grandma.

"Hello, pony," he said.

His worries couldn't reduce his appreciation of Grandma's fabulous draft-animal. Partly, of course, it was just that it was such an enormous beast. The long, round barrel of its body rested on short legs with wide, flat feet which were settled deep in the meadow's mud by now. At one end was a spiky tail, and at the other a very big, wedge-shaped head, with a blunt, badly chipped horn set between nose and eyes. From nose to tail and all around, it was covered with thick, rectangular, horny plates, a mottled green-brown in color.

Grimp patted its rocky side affectionately. He loved the pony most for being the ugliest thing that had ever showed up on Noorhut. According to Grandma, she had bought it from a bankrupt circus which had imported it from a planet called Treebel; and Treebel was supposed to be a world full of hot swamps, inexhaustibly explosive volcanoes and sulphurous stenches.

One might have thought that after wandering around melting lava and under rainfalls of glowing ashes for most of its life, the pony would have considered Noorhut pretty tame. But though there wasn't much room for expression around the solid slab of bone supporting the horn, which was the front of its face, Grimp thought it looked thoroughly contented with its feet sunk out of sight in Noorhut's cool mud.

"You're a big fat pig!" he told it fondly.

The pony slobbered out a long, purple tongue and carefully parted his hair.

"Cut it out!" said Grimp. "Ugh!"

The pony snorted, pleased, curled its tongue about a huge clump of weeds, pulled them up and flipped them into its mouth, roots, mud and all. It began to chew.

Grimp glanced at the sun and turned anxiously to study the trailer. If she didn't get rid of Runny soon, they'd be calling him back to the house for supper before he and Grandma got around to having a good talk. And they weren't letting him out of doors these evenings, while the shining lights were here.

He gave the pony a parting whack, returned quietly to the road and sat down out of sight near the back door of the trailer, where he could hear what was going on.

". . . so about the only thing the Guardian could tack on you now," the policeman was saying, "would be a Public Menace charge. If there's any trouble about the lights this year, he's likely to try that. He's not a bad Guardian, you know, but he's got himself talked into thinking you're sort of to blame for the lights showing up here every year."

Grandma chuckled. "Well, I try to get here in time to see them every summer," she admitted. "I can see how that might give him the idea."

"And of course," said the policeman, "we're all trying to keep it quiet about them. If the news got out, we'd be having a lot of people coming here from the city, just to look. No one but the Guardian minds you being here, only you don't want a lot of city people tramping around your farms."

"Of course not," agreed Grandma. "And I certainly haven't told anyone about them myself."

"Last night," the policeman added, "everyone was saying there were twice as many lights this year as last summer. That's what got the Guardian so excited."

Chafing more every minute, Grimp had to listen then to an extended polite argument about how much Runny wanted to pay Grandma for her hay-fever medicines, while she insisted he didn't owe her anything at all. In the end, Grandma lost and the policeman paid up—much too much to take from any friend of Grimp's folks, Grandma protested to the last. And then, finally, that righteous minion of the law came climbing down the trailer steps again, with Grandma following him to the door.

"How do I look, Grimp?" he beamed cheerfully as Grimp stood up.

"Like you ought to wash your face sometime," Grimp said tactlessly, for he was fast losing patience with Runny. But then his eyes widened in surprise.

Under a coating of yellowish grease, Runny's nose seemed to have returned almost to the shape it had out of hay-fever season, and his eyelids were hardly puffed at all! Instead of flaming red, those features, furthermore, now were only a delicate pink in shade. Runny, in short, was almost handsome again.

"Pretty good, eh?" he said. "Just one shot did it. And I've only got to keep the salve on another hour. Isn't that right, Grandma?"

"That's right," smiled Grandma from the door, clinking Runny's money gently out of one hand into the other. "You'll be as good as new then."

"Permanent cure, too," said Runny. He patted Grimp benevolently on the head. "And next week we go werret-fishing, eh, Grimp?" he added greedily.

"I guess so," Grimp said, with a trace of coldness. It was his opinion that Runny could have been satisfied with the hay-fever cure and forgotten about the werrets.

"It's a date!" nodded Runny happily and took his greasy face whistling down the road. Grimp scowled after him, half-minded to reach for the slingshot then and there and let go with a medium stone at the lower rear of the uniform. But probably he'd better not.

"Well, that's that," Grandma said softly.

At that moment, up at the farmhouse, a cow horn went "Whoop-whoop!" across the valley.

"Darn," said Grimp. "I knew it was getting late, with him doing all that talking! Now they're calling me to supper." There were tears of disappointment in his eyes.

"Don't let it fuss you, Grimp," Grandma said consolingly. "Just jump up in here a moment and close your eyes."

Grimp jumped up into the trailer and closed his eyes expectantly.

"Put out your hands," Grandma's voice told him.

He put out his hands, and she pushed them together to form a cup. Then something small and light and furry dropped into them, caught hold of one of Grimp's thumbs, with tiny, cool fingers, and chittered.

Grimp's eyes popped open.

"It's a lortel!" he whispered, overwhelmed.

"It's for you!" Grandma beamed.

Grimp couldn't speak. The lortel looked at him from a tiny, black, human face with large blue eyes set in it, wrapped a long, furry tail twice around his wrist, clung to his thumb with its fingers, and grinned and squeaked.

"It's wonderful!" gasped Grimp. "Can you really teach them to talk?"

"Hello," said the lortel.

"That's all it can say so far," Grandma said. "But if you're patient with it, it'll learn more."

"I'll be patient," Grim promised, dazed. "I saw one at the circus this winter, down the valley at Laggand. They said it could talk, but it never said anything while I was there."

"Hello!" said the lortel.

"Hello!" gulped Grimp.

The cow horn whoop-whooped again.

"I guess you'd better run along to supper, or they might get mad," said Grandma.

"I know," said Grimp. "What does it eat?"

"Bugs and flowers and honey and fruit and eggs, when it's wild. But you just feed it whatever you eat yourself."

"Well, good-by," said Grimp. "And golly—thanks, Grandma."

He jumped out of the trailer. The lortel climbed out of his hand, ran up his arm and sat on his shoulder, wrapping its tail around his neck.

"It knows you already," Grandma said. "It won't run away."

Grimp reached up carefully with his other hand and patted the lortel.

"I'll be back early tomorrow," he said. "No school. . . . They won't let me out after supper as long as those lights keep coming around."

The cow horn whooped for the third time, very loudly. This time it meant business.

"Well, good-by," Grimp repeated hastily. He ran off, the lortel hanging on to his shirt collar and squeaking.

Grandma looked after him and then at the sun, which had just touched the tops of the hills with its lower rim.

"Might as well have some supper myself," she remarked, apparently to no one in particular. "But after that I'll have to run out the go-buggy and create a diversion."

Lying on its armor-plated belly down in the meadow, the pony swung its big head around toward her. Its small yellow eyes blinked questioningly.

"What makes you think a diversion will be required?" Its voice asked into her ear. The ability to produce such ventriloquial effects was one of the talents that made the pony well worth its considerable keep to Grandma.

"Weren't you listening?" she scolded. "That policeman told me the Guardian's planning to march the village's defense unit up to the hollow after supper, and start them shooting at the Halpa detector-globes as soon as they show up."

The pony swore an oath meaningless to anyone who hadn't been raised on the planet Treebel. It stood up, braced itself, and began pulling its feet out of the mud in a succession of loud, sucking noises.

"I haven't had an hour's straight rest since you talked me into tramping around with you eight years ago!" it complained.

"But you've certainly been seeing life, like I promised," Grandma smiled.

The pony slopped in a last, enormous tongueful of wet weeds. "That I have!" it said, with emphasis.

It came chewing up to the road.

"I'll keep a watch on things while you're having your supper," it told her.

As the uniformed twelve-man defense unit marched in good order out of the village, on its way to assume a strategic position around the hollow on Grimp's father's farm, there was a sudden, small explosion not very far off.

The Guardian, who was marching in the lead with a gun over his shoulder and the slavering pank-hound on a leash, stopped short. The unit broke ranks and crowded up behind him.

"What was that?" the Guardian inquired.

Everybody glanced questioningly around the rolling green slopes of the valley, already darkened with evening shadows. The pank-hound sat down before the Guardian, pointed its nose at the even darker shadows in the woods ahead of them and growled.

"Look!" a man said, pointing in the same direction.

A spark of bright green light had appeared on their path, just where it entered the woods. The spark grew rapidly in size, became as big as a human head—then bigger! Smoky green streamers seemed to be pouring out of it. . . .

"I'm going home right now," someone announced at that point, sensibly enough.

"Stand your ground!" the Guardian ordered, conscious of the beginnings of a general withdrawal movement behind him. He was an old soldier. He unslung his gun, cocked it and pointed it. The pank-hound got up on his six feet and bristled.

"Stop!" the Guardian shouted at the green light.

It expanded promptly to the size of a barrel, new streamers shooting out from it and fanning about like hungry tentacles.

He fired.

"*Run!*" everybody yelled then. The pank-hound slammed backward against the Guardian's legs, upsetting him, and streaked off after the retreating unit. The green light had spread outward jerkily into the shape of something like a many-armed, writhing starfish, almost the size of the trees about it. Deep, hooting sounds came out of it as it started drifting down the path toward the Guardian.

He got up on one knee and, in a single drumroll of sound, emptied all thirteen charges remaining in his gun into the middle of the starfish. It hooted more loudly, waved its arms more wildly, and continued to advance.

He stood up quickly then, slung the gun over his shoulder and joined the retreat. By the time the unit reached the first houses of the village, he was well up in the front ranks again. And a few minutes later, he was breathlessly organizing the local defenses, employing the tactics that had shown their worth in the raids of the Laggand Bandits nine years before.

The starfish, however, was making no attempt to follow up the valley people's rout. It was still on the path at the point where the Guardian had seen it last, waving its arms about and hooting menacingly at the silent trees.

"That should do it, I guess," Grandma Wannattel said. "Before the first projection fizzles out, the next one in the chain will start up where they can see it from the village. It ought to be past midnight before any-one starts bothering about the globes again. Particularly since there aren't going to be any globes around tonight—that is, if the Halpa attack-schedule has been correctly estimated."

"I wish we were safely past midnight right now," the rhinocerine pony worriedly informed her. Its dark shape stood a little up the road from the trailer, outlined motionlessly like a ponderous statue against the red evening sky. Its head was up; it looked as if it were listening. Which it was, in its own way—listening for any signs of activity from the hollow.

"No sense getting anxious about it," Grandma remarked. She was perched on a rock at the side of the road, a short distance from the pony, with a small black bag slung over her shoulder. "We'll wait here another hour till it's good and dark and then go down to the hollow. The break-through might begin a couple of hours after that."

"It *would* have to be us again!" grumbled the pony. In spite of its size, its temperament was on the nervous side. And while any compan-ion of Zone Agent Wannattel was bound to run regularly into situations that were far from soothing, the pony couldn't recall any previous ex-perience that had looked as extremely unsoothing as the prospects of the night-hours ahead. On far-off Vega's world of Jeltad, in the planning offices of the Department of Galactic Zones, the decision to put Noorhut at stake to win one round in mankind's grim war with the alien and mysterious Halpa might have seemed as distressing as it was un-avoidable. But the pony couldn't help feeling that the distress would have become a little more acute if Grandma's distant employers had happened to be standing right here with the two of them while the crit-ical hours approached.

"I'd feel a lot better myself if Headquarters hadn't picked us for this particular operation," Grandma admitted. "Us and Noorhut. . . ."

Because, by what was a rather singular coincidence, considering how things stood there tonight, the valley was also Grandma's home. She had been born, quite some while before, a hundred and eighty miles farther inland, at the foot of the dam of the great river Wend, which had given its name to the land, and nowadays supplied it with almost all its required power.

Erisa Wannattel had done a great deal of traveling since she first be-came aware of the fact that her varied abilities and adventuresome nature needed a different sort of task to absorb them than could be found on Noorhut, which was progressing placidly up into the final stages of a rounded and balanced planetary civilization. But she still liked to con-sider the Valley of the Wend as her home and headquarters, to which she returned as often as her work would permit. Her exact understanding of the way people there thought about things and did things also made them easy for her to manipulate; and on occasion that could be very useful.

In most other places, the means she had employed to turn the Guardian and his troop back from the hollow probably would have started a panic or brought armed ships and radiation guns zooming up for the kill within minutes. But the valley people had considered it just another local emergency. The bronze alarm bell in the village had pronounced a state of siege, and cow horns passed the word up to the outlying farms. Within minutes, the farmers were pelting down the roads to the village with their families and guns; and, very soon afterward, everything quieted down again. Guard lines had been set up by then, with the women and children quartered in the central buildings, while the armed men had settled down to watching Grandma's illusion projections—directional video narrow beams—from the discreet distance marked by the village boundaries.

If nothing else happened, the people would just stay there till morning and then start a cautious investigation. After seeing mysterious blue lights dancing harmlessly over Grimp's farm for four summers, this section of Wend was pretty well conditioned to fiery apparitions. But even if they got too adventurous, they couldn't hurt themselves on the projections, which were designed to be nothing but very effective visual displays.

What it all came to was that Grandma had everybody in the neighborhood rounded up and immobilized where she wanted them.

In every other respect, the valley presented an exceptionally peaceful twilight scene to the eye. There was nothing to show that it was the only present point of contact between forces engaged in what was probably a war of intergalactic proportions—a war made wraithlike but doubly deadly by the circumstance that, in over a thousand years, neither side had found out much more about the other than the merciless and devastating finality of its forms of attack. There never had been any actual battles between Mankind and the Halpa, only alternate and very thorough massacres—all of them, from Mankind's point of view, on the wrong side of the fence.

The Halpa alone had the knowledge that enabled them to reach their human adversary. That was the trouble. But, apparently, they could launch their attacks only by a supreme effort, under conditions that existed for periods of less than a score of years, and about three hundred years apart as Mankind measured time.

It was hard to find any good in them, other than the virtue of persistence. Every three hundred years, they punctually utilized that brief period to execute one more thrust, carefully prepared and placed, and carried out with a dreadfully complete abruptness, against some new point of human civilization—and this time the attack was going to come through on Noorhut.

"Something's starting to move around in that hollow!" the pony announced suddenly. "It's not one of their globe-detectors."

"I know," murmured Grandma. "That's the first of the Halpa themselves. They're going to be right on schedule, it seems. But don't get nervous. They can't hurt anything until their transmitter comes through and revives them. We've got to be particularly careful now not to frighten them off. They seem to be even more sensitive to emotional tensions in their immediate surroundings than the globes."

The pony made no reply. It knew what was at stake and why eight big ships were circling Noorhut somewhere beyond space-detection tonight. It knew, too, that the ships would act only if it was discovered that Grandma had failed. But—

The pony shook its head uneasily. The people on Treebel had never become civilized to the point of considering the possibility of taking calculated risks on a planetary scale—not to mention the fact that the lives of the pony and of Grandma were included in the present calculation. In the eight years it had been accompanying her on her travels, it had developed a tremendous respect for Erisa Wannattel's judgment and prowess. But, just the same, frightening the Halpa off, if it still could be done, seemed like a very sound idea right now to the pony.

As a matter of fact, as Grandma well knew, it probably could have been done at this stage by tossing a small firecracker into the hollow. Until they had established their planetary foothold, the Halpa took extreme precautions. They could spot things in the class of radiation weapons a hundred miles away, and either that or any suggestion of local aggressiveness or of long-range observation would check the invasion attempt on Noorhut then and there.

But one of the principal reasons she was here tonight was to see that nothing *did* happen to stop it. For this assault would only be diverted against some other world then, and quite probably against one where the significance of the spying detector-globes wouldn't be understood before it was too late. The best information system in the Galaxy couldn't keep more than an insignificant fraction of its population on the alert for dangers like that—

She bounced suddenly to her feet and, at the same instant, the pony swung away from the hollow toward which it had been staring. They both stood for a moment then, turning their heads about, like baffled hounds trying to fix a scent on the wind.

"It's Grimp!" Grandma exclaimed.

The rhinocerine pony snorted faintly. "Those are his thought images, all right," it agreed. "He seems to feel you need protection. Can you locate him?"

"Not yet," said Grandma anxiously. "Yes, I can. He's coming up through the woods on the other side of the hollow, off to the left. The little devil!" She was hustling back to the trailer. "Come on, I'll have to ride you there. I can't even dare use the go-buggy this late in the day."

The pony crouched beside the trailer while she quickly snapped on its saddle from the top of the back steps. Six metal rings had been welded into the horny plates of its back for this purpose, so it was a simple job. Grandma clambered aloft, hanging onto the saddle's hand-rails.

"Swing wide of the hollow!" she warned. "This could spoil everything. But make all the noise you want. The Halpa don't care about noise as such—it has to have emotional content before they get interested—and the quicker Grimp spots us, the easier it will be to find him."

The pony already was rushing down into the meadow at an amazing rate of speed—it took a lot of very efficient muscle to drive as heavy a body as that through the gluey swamps of Treebel. It swung wide of the hollow and of what it contained, crossed a shallow bog farther down the meadow with a sound like a charging torpedo-boat, and reached the woods.

It had to slow down then, to avoid brushing off Grandma.

"Grimp's down that slope somewhere," Grandma said. "He's heard us."

"They're making a lot of noise!" Grimp's thought reached them suddenly and clearly. He seemed to be talking to someone. "But we're not scared of them, are we?"

"Bang-bang!" another thought-voice came excitedly.

"It's the lortel," Grandma and the pony said together.

"That's the stuff!" Grimp resumed approvingly. "We'll sling-shoot them all if they don't watch out. But we'd better find Grandma soon."

"Grimp!" shouted Grandma. The pony backed her up with a roaring call.

"Hello?" came the lortel's thought.

"Wasn't that the pony?" asked Grimp. "All right—let's go that way."

"Here we come, Grimp!" Grandma shouted as the pony descended the steep side of a ravine with the straightforward technique of a rock-slide.

"That's Grandma!" thought Grimp. "Grandma!" he yelled. "Look out! There's monsters all around!"

"What you missed!" yelled Grimp, dancing around the pony as Grandma Wannattel scrambled down from the saddle. "There's monsters all around the village and the Guardian killed one and I slingshot another till he fizzled out and I was coming to find you—"

"Your mother will be worried!" began Grandma as they rushed into each other's arms.

"No," grinned Grimp. "All the kids are supposed to be sleeping in the school house and she won't look there till morning and the schoolteacher said the monsters were all"—he slowed down cautiously—"ho-lucy-nations. But he wouldn't go look when the Guardian said they'd show him one. He stayed right in bed. But the Guardian's all right—he killed one and I slingshot another and the lortel learned a new word. Say 'bang-bang,' lortel!" he invited.

"Hello!" squeaked the lortel.

"Aw," said Grimp disappointedly. "He can say it, though. And I've come to take you to the village so the monsters don't get you. Hello, pony!"

"Bang-bang," said the lortel, distinctly.

"See?" cried Grimp. "He isn't scared at all—he's a real brave lortel! If we see some monsters don't you get scared either, because I've got my slingshot," he said, waving it blood-thirstily, "and two back pockets still full of medium stones. The way to do it is to kill them all!"

"It sounds like a pretty good idea, Grimp," Grandma agreed. "But you're awfully tired now."

"No, I'm not!" Grimp said surprised. His right eye sagged shut and then his left; and he opened them both with an effort and looked at Grandma.

"That's right," he admitted. "I am . . ."

"In fact," said Grandma, "you're asleep!"

"No, I'm n———" objected Grimp. Then he sagged toward the ground, and Grandma caught him.

"In a way I hate to do it," she panted, wrestling him aboard the pony which had lain down and flattened itself as much as it could to make it easier. "He'd probably enjoy it. But we can't take a chance. He's a husky little devil, too," she groaned, giving a final boost, "and those ammunition pockets don't make him any lighter!" She clambered up again herself and noticed that the lortel had transferred itself to her coat collar.

The pony stood up cautiously.

"Now what?" it said.

"Might as well go straight to the hollow," said Grandma, breathing hard. "We'll probably have to wait around there a few hours, but if we're careful it won't do any harm."

"Did you find a good deep pond?" Grandma asked the pony a little later, as it came squishing up softly through the meadow behind her to join her at the edge of the hollow.

"Yes," said the pony. "About a hundred yards back. That should be close enough. How much more waiting do you think we'll have to do?"

Grandma shrugged carefully. She was sitting in the grass with what, by daylight, would have been a good view of the hollow below. Grimp was asleep with his head on her knees; and the lortel, after catching a few bugs in the grass and eating them, had settled down on her shoulder and dozed off too.

"I don't know," she said. "It's still three hours till Big Moonrise, and it's bound to be some time before then. Now you've found a waterhole, we'll just stay here together and wait. The one thing to remember is not to let yourself start getting excited about them."

The pony stood huge and chunky beside her, its forefeet on the edge of the hollow, staring down. Muddy water trickled from its knobby flanks. It had brought the warm mud-smells of a summer pond back with it to hang in a cloud about them.

There was vague, dark, continuous motion at the bottom of the hollow. A barely noticeable stirring in the single big pool of darkness that filled it.

"If I were alone," the pony said, "I'd get out of here! I know when I ought to be scared. But you've taken psychological control of my reactions, haven't you?"

"Yes," said Grandma. "It'll be easier for me, though, if you help along as much as you can. There's really no danger until their transmitter has come through."

"Unless," said the pony, "they've worked out some brand-new tricks in the past few hundred years."

"There's that," Grandma admitted. "But they've never tried changing their tricks on us yet. If it were *us* doing the attacking, we'd vary our methods each time, as much as we could. But the Halpa don't seem to think just like we do about anything. They wouldn't still be so careful if they didn't realize they were very vulnerable at this point."

"I hope they're right about that!" the pony said briefly.

Its head moved then, following the motion of something that sailed flutteringly out of the depths of the hollow, circled along its far rim, and descended again. The inhabitants of Treebel had a much deeper range of dark-vision than Grandma Wannattel, but she was also aware of that shape.

"They're not much to look at," the pony remarked. "Like a big, dark rag of leather, mostly."

"Their physical structure is believed to be quite simple," Grandma agreed slowly. The pony was tensing up again, and it was best to go on talking to it, about almost anything at all. That always helped, even though the pony knew her much too well by now to be really fooled by such tricks.

"Many very efficient life-forms aren't physically complicated, you know," she went on, letting the sound of her voice ripple steadily into its mind. "Parasitical types, particularly. It's pretty certain, too, that the Halpa have the hive-mind class of intelligence, so what goes for the nerve-systems of most of the ones they send through to us might be nothing much more than secondary reflex-transmitters. . . ."

Grimp stirred in his sleep at that point and grumbled. Grandma looked down at him. "You're sound asleep!" she told him severely, and he was again.

"You've got plans for that boy, haven't you?" the pony said, without shifting its gaze from the hollow.

"I've had my eye on him," Grandma admitted, "and I've already recommended him to Headquarters for observation. But I'm not going to make up my mind about Grimp till next summer, when we've had more time to study him. Meanwhile, we'll see what he picks up naturally from the lortel in the way of telepathic communication and sensory extensions. I think Grimp's the kind we can use."

"He's all right," the pony agreed absently. "A bit murderous, though, like most of you. . . ."

"He'll grow out of it!" Grandma said, a little annoyedly, for the subject of human aggressiveness was one she and the pony argued about frequently. "You can't hurry developments like that along too much. All of Noorhut should grow out of that stage, as a people, in another few hundred years. They're about at the turning-point right now—"

Their heads came up together, then, as something very much like a big, dark rag of leather came fluttering up from the hollow and hung in the dark air above them. The representatives of the opposing powers that were meeting on Noorhut that night took quiet stock of one another for a moment.

The Halpa was about six foot long and two wide, and considerably less than an inch thick. It held its position in the air with a steady, rippling motion, like a bat the size of a man. Then, suddenly, it extended itself with a snap, growing taut as a curved sail.

The pony snorted involuntarily. The apparently featureless shape in the air turned towards it and drifted a few inches closer. When nothing more happened, it turned again and fluttered quietly back down into the hollow.

"Could it tell I was scared?" the pony asked uneasily.

"You reacted just right," Grandma said soothingly. "Startled suspi-

cion at first, and then just curiosity, and then another start when it made
that jump. It's about what they'd expect from creatures that would be
hanging around the hollow now. We're like cows to them. They can't tell
what things are by their looks, like we do—"

But her tone was thoughtful, and she was more shaken than she
would have cared to let the pony notice. There had been something inde-
scribably menacing and self-assured in the Halpa's gesture. Almost certainly, it had only been trying to draw a reaction of hostile intelligence
from them, probing, perhaps, for the presence of weapons that might be
dangerous to its kind.

But there was a chance—a tiny but appalling chance—that the things
had developed some drastically new form of attack since their last break-
through, and that they already were in control of the situation. . . .

In which case, neither Grimp nor anyone else on Noorhut would be
doing any more growing-up after tomorrow.

Each of the eleven hundred and seventeen planets that had been lost
to the Halpa so far still traced a fiery, forbidding orbit through space—
torn back from the invaders only at the cost of depriving it, by humanity's
own weapons, of the conditions any known form of life could tolerate.

The possibility that this might also be Noorhut's future had loomed
as an ugly enormity before her for the past four years. But of the nearly
half a hundred worlds which the Halpa were found to be investigating
through their detector-globes as possible invasion points for this period,
Noorhut finally had been selected by Headquarters as the one where local
conditions were most suited to meet them successfully. And that meant in
a manner which must include the destruction of their only real invasion
weapon, the fabulous and mysterious Halpa Transmitter. Capable as they
undoubtedly were, they had shown in the past that they were able or willing to employ only one of those instruments for each period of attack.
Destroying the transmitter meant therefore that humanity would gain a
few more centuries to figure out a way to get back at the Halpa before a
new attempt was made.

So on all planets but Noorhut the detector-globes had been encouraged carefully to send back reports of a dangerously alert and well-armed
population. On Noorhut, however, they had been soothed along . . . and
just as her home-planet had been chosen as the most favorable point of
encounter, so was Erisa Wannattel herself selected as the agent most
suited to represent humanity's forces under the conditions that existed
there.

Grandma sighed gently and reminded herself again that Headquarters
was as unlikely to miscalculate the overall probability of success as it was
to select the wrong person to achieve it. There was only the tiniest, the

most theoretical, of chances that something might go wrong and that she would end her long career with the blundering murder of her own home-world.

But there was that chance.

"There seem to be more down there every minute!" the pony was saying.

Grandma drew a deep breath.

"Must be several thousand by now," she acknowledged. "It's getting near breakthrough time, all right, but those are only the advance forces." She added, "Do you notice anything like a glow of light down there, to-wards the center?"

The pony stared a moment. "Yes," it said. "But I would have thought that was way under the red for you. Can you see it?"

"No," said Grandma. "I get a kind of feeling, like heat. That's the transmitter beginning to come through. I think we've got them!"

The pony shifted its bulk slowly from side to side.

"Yes," it said resignedly, "or they've got us."

"Don't think about that," Grandma ordered sharply and clamped one more mental lock shut on the foggy, dark terrors that were curling and writhing under her conscious thoughts, threatening to emerge at the last moment and paralyze her actions.

She had opened her black bag and was unhurriedly fitting together something composed of a few pieces of wood and wire, and a rather heavy, stiff spring. . . .

"Just be ready," she added.

"I've been ready for an hour," said the pony, shuffling its feet unhap-pily.

They did no more talking after that. All the valley had become quiet about them. But slowly the hollow below was filling up with a black, stir-ring, slithering tide. Bits of it fluttered up now and then like strips of black smoke, hovered a few yards above the mass and settled again.

Suddenly, down in the center of the hollow, there was something else.

The pony had seen it first, Grandma Wannattel realized. It was star-ing in that direction for almost a minute before she grew able to distin-guish something that might have been a group of graceful miniatures spires. Semi-transparent in the darkness, four small domes showed at the corners, with a larger one in the center. The central one was about twenty feet high and very slender.

The whole structure began to solidify swiftly. . . .

The Halpa Transmitter's appearance of crystalline slightness was perhaps the most mind-chilling thing about it. For it brought instantly a jarring sense of what must be black distance beyond all distances, reaching back unimaginably to its place of origin. In that unknown somewhere, a prodigiously talented and determined race of beings had labored for human centuries to prepare and point some stupendous gun . . . and were able then to bridge the vast interval with nothing more substantial than this dark sliver of glass that had come to rest suddenly in the valley of the Wend.

But, of course, the Transmitter was all that was needed; its deadly poison lay in a sluggish, almost inert mass about it. Within minutes from now, it would waken to life, as similar transmitters had wakened on other nights on those lost and burning worlds. And in much less than minutes after that, the Halpa invaders would be hurled by their slender machine to every surface section of Noorhut—no longer inert, but quickened into a ravening, almost indestructible form of vampiric life, dividing and subdividing in its incredibly swift cycle of reproduction, fastening to feed anew, growing and dividing again—

Spreading, at that stage, much more swiftly than it could be exterminated by anything but the ultimate weapons!

The pony stirred suddenly, and she felt the wave of panic roll up in it.

"It's the Transmitter, all right," Grandma's thought reached it quickly. "We've had two descriptions of it before. But we can't be sure it's *here* until it begins to charge itself. Then it lights up—first at the edges, and then at the center. Five seconds after the central spire lights up, it will be energized too much to let them pull it back again. At least, they couldn't pull it back after that, the last time they were observed. And then we'd better be ready—"

The pony had been told all that before. But as it listened it was quieting down again.

"And you're going to go on sleeping!" Grandma Wannattel's thought told Grimp next. "No matter what you hear or what happens, you'll sleep on and know nothing at all any more until I wake you up. . . ."

Light surged up suddenly in the Transmitter—first into the four outer spires, and an instant later into the big central one, in a sullen red glow. It lit the hollow with a smoky glare. The pony took two startled steps backwards.

"Five seconds to go!" whispered Grandma's thought. She reached into her black bag again and took out a small plastic ball. It reflected the light from the hollow in dull crimson gleamings. She let it slip down carefully inside the shaftlike frame of the gadget she had put together of wood and wire. It clicked into place there against one end of the compressed spring.

Down below, they lay now in a blanket fifteen feet thick over the wet ground, like big, black, water-sogged leaves swept up in circular piles about the edges of the hollow. The tops and sides of the piles were stirring and shivering and beginning to slide down toward the Transmitter.

". . . five, and go!" Grandma said aloud. She raised the wooden catapult to her shoulder.

The pony shook its blunt-horned head violently from side to side, made a strangled, bawling sound, surged forward and plunged down the steep side of the hollow in a thundering rush.

Grandma aimed carefully and let go.

The blanket of dead-leaf things was lifting into the air ahead of the pony's ground-shaking approach in a weightless, silent swirl of darkness which instantly blotted both the glowing Transmitter and the pony's shape from sight. The pony roared once as the blackness closed over it. A second later, there was a crash like the shattering of a hundred-foot mirror—and at approximately the same moment, Grandma's plastic ball exploded somewhere in the center of the swirling swarm.

Cascading fountains of white fire filled the whole of the hollow. Within the fire, a dense mass of shapes fluttered and writhed frenziedly like burning rags. From down where the fire boiled fiercest rose continued sounds of brittle substances suffering enormous violence. The pony was trampling the ruined Transmitter, making sure of its destruction.

"Better get out of it!" Grandma shouted anxiously. "What's left of that will all melt now anyway!"

She didn't know whether it heard her or not. But a few seconds later, it came pounding up the side of the hollow again. Blazing from nose to rump, it tramped past Grandma, plunged through the meadow behind her, shedding white sheets of fire that exploded the marsh grass in its tracks, and hurled itself headlong into the pond it had selected previously. There was a great splash, accompanied by sharp hissing noises. Pond and pony vanished together under billowing clouds of steam.

"That was pretty hot!" its thought came to Grandma.

She drew a deep breath.

"Hot as anything that ever came out of a volcano!" she affirmed. "If you'd played around in it much longer, you'd have fixed up the village with roasts for a year."

"I'll just stay here for a while, till I've cooled off a bit," said the pony.

Grandma found something strangling her then, and discovered it was the lortel's tail. She unwound it carefully. But the lortel promptly reanchored itself with all four hands in her hair. She decided to leave it there. It seemed badly upset.

Grimp, however, slept on. It was going to take a little maneuvering to get him back into the village undetected before morning, but she would figure that out by and by. A steady flow of cool night-air was being drawn past them into the hollow now and rising out of it again in boiling, vertical columns of invisible heat. At the bottom of the deluxe blaze she'd lit down there, things still seemed to be moving about—but very slowly. The Halpa were tough organisms, all right, though not nearly so tough, when you heated them up with a really good incendiary, as were the natives of Treebel.

She would have to make a final check of the hollow around dawn, of course, when the ground should have cooled off enough to permit it—but her century's phase of the Halpa War did seem to be over. The defensive part of it, at any rate—

Wet, munching sounds from the pond indicated the pony felt comfortable enough by now to take an interest in the parboiled vegetation it found floating around it. Everything had turned out all right.

So she settled down carefully on her back in the long marsh grass without disturbing Grimp's position too much, and just let herself faint for a while.

By sunrise, Grandma Wannattel's patent-medicine trailer was nine miles from the village and rolling steadily southwards up the valley road through the woods. As usual, she was departing under a cloud.

Grimp and the policeman had showed up early to warn her. The Guardian was making use of the night's various unprecedented disturbances to press through a vote on a Public Menace charge against Grandma in the village; and since everybody still felt rather excited and upset, he had a good chance just now of getting a majority.

Grimp had accompanied her far enough to explain that this state of affairs wasn't going to be permanent. He had it all worked out.

Runny's new immunity to hay-fever had brought him and the pretty Vellit to a fresh understanding overnight; they were going to get married five weeks from now. As a married man, Runny would then be eligible for the post of Village Guardian at the harvest elections—and between Grimp's cousins and Vellit's cousins, Runny's backers would just about control the vote. So when Grandma got around to visiting the valley again next summer, she needn't worry any more about police interference or official disapproval. . . .

Grandma had nodded approvingly. That was about the kind of neighborhood politics she'd begun to play herself at Grimp's age. She was pretty sure by now that Grimp was the one who eventually would become her successor, and the Guardian not only of Noorhut and the star-system to which Noorhut belonged, but of a good many other star-systems besides. With careful schooling, he ought to be just about ready for the job by the time she was willing, finally, to retire.

An hour after he had started back to the farm, looking suddenly a little forlorn, the trailer swung off the valley road into a narrow forest path. Here the pony lengthened its stride, and less than five minutes later they entered a curving ravine, at the far end of which lay something that Grimp would have recognized instantly, from his one visit to the nearest port city, as a small spaceship.

A large round lock opened soundlessly in its side as they approached. The pony came to a stop. Grandma got down from the driver's seat and unhitched it. The pony walked into the lock, and the trailer picked its wheels off the ground and floated in after it. Grandma Wannattel walked in last, and the lock closed quietly on her heels.

The ship lay still a moment longer. Then it was suddenly gone. Dead leaves went dancing for a while about the ravine, disturbed by the breeze of its departure.

In a place very far away—so far that neither Grimp nor his parents nor anyone in the village except the schoolteacher had ever heard of it—a set of instruments began signalling for attention. Somebody answered them.

Grandma's voice announced distinctly:

"This is Zone Agent Wannattel's report of the successful conclusion of the Halpa operation on Noorhut—"

High above Noorhut's skies, eight great ships swung instantly out of their watchful orbits about the planet and flashed off again into the blackness of the boundless space that was their sea and their home.

L. Sprague de Camp

THE GALTON WHISTLE

L. Sprague de Camp is a seminal figure, one whose career spans almost the entire development of modern SF and fantasy. Much of the luster of the "Golden Age" of *Astounding* during the late '30s and the '40s is due to the presence in those pages of de Camp, along with his great contemporaries Robert A. Heinlein, Theodore Sturgeon, and A. E. van Vogt. At the same time, for *Astounding*'s sister fantasy magazine, *Unknown,* he helped to create a whole new modern style of fantasy writing—funny, whimsical, and irreverent—of which he is still the most prominent practitioner. (De Camp's stories for *Unknown* are among the best short fantasies ever written, and include such classics as "The Wheels of If," "Nothing in the Rules," "The Hardwood Pile," and—written in collaboration with Fletcher Pratt—the famous "Harold Shea" stories that would later be collected as *The Complete Enchanter*.) In science fiction, he is the author of *Lest Darkness Fall,* in my opinion one of the three or four best Alternate Worlds novels ever written (it was reprinted in 1996, by Baen Books, bound in a package with David Drake's *To Bring the Light*), as well as the at-the-time highly controversial novel (although it now looks rather tame) *Rogue Queen,* and a body of expertly-crafted short fiction such as "Judgment Day," "Divide and Rule," "A Gun for Dinosaur," and "Aristotle and the Gun."

De Camp may be primarily known today as a humorist, perhaps best remembered for the *Unknown* stories and the "Howard Shea" saga, but everything he writes has a strong element of fast-paced adventure to it—just as even the most headlong and swashbuckling of his adventure tales contains a generous portion of wry humor. His greatest contribution to the evolution of the Space Opera is the "Viagens Interplanetarias"—which means "interplanetary tours" in Portuguese, the language of the dominant political and economic power of de Camp's future Earth, Brazil—sequence of stories and novels (sometimes also referred to as the "Krishna" series, after the name of the alien planet on which many of them take place), detailing the intricate and sometimes contentious interrelations that develop between Earthmen and the intelligent native species who inhabit the nearby regions of space. Intelligence is a quality that suffuses every de Camp story, just as surely as does humor—de Camp's Space Opera is just *smarter* than that of most of his contemporaries: you can see that a very shrewd mind is working out the background details and structure of what such an interstellar society would be like, and the consequences that would inevitably result, insisting on logic, rigor, and consistency even within the framework of the Interplanetary Swashbuckler (there's no such thing as Faster Than Light travel in the Viagens universe, for instance—and *that* generates some inevitable and surprising consequences that few other authors writing a Space Adventure tale would have bothered to deal with . . .). The intelligence of the conceptualization that went into the background of the Viagens stories shows up everywhere, not least in de Camp's prediction that Brazil would be the dominant power on Earth by the middle of the 21st Century, the old superpowers having by then exhausted and bankrupted themselves—a prediction considered to be wild and extravagantly unlikely when de Camp made it back in the '50s, but one which seems increasingly credible these days, and one which makes the Viagens stories still look remarkably contemporary, in spite of being almost half a century old. Nor, in spite of all the intellectual rigor that went into them, are they the least bit solemn or slow—instead, they remain among the most colorful and vivid stories of Interplanetary Adventure ever written: as the sly and suspenseful story that follows will amply demonstrate.

The Viagens Interplanetarias stories were assembled in the landmark collection *The Continent Makers and Other Tales of the Viagens* (long out of print, alas, but it can be found in many libraries). The Viagens or "Krishna" novels, some of them recently reissued, include *The Hand of Zei, The Tower of Zanid, The Queen of Zamba, The Virgin of Zesh, The Prisoner of Zhamanak,* and *The Hostage of Zir.* The single best of these novels, in my opinion, is *The Hand of Zei,* which makes a good entry-point into the series, and which is still often findable in secondhand bookstores. De Camp has continued to produce an occasional "Krishna" novel well into the '90s, the most recent of which are *The Bones of Zora, The Stones of Nomuru,* and *The Swords of Zinjahan,* all written in collaboration with his wife, Catherine Crook de Camp.

De Camp's other books include *The Glory That Was, The Great Fetish,* and *The Reluctant King;* with Fletcher Pratt, in addition to the "Harold Shea" books, *The Carnelian Cube, The Land of Unreason,* and the collection *Tales from Gavagan's Bar;* with Catherine Crook de Camp, in addition to their collaborative "Krishna" novels, *The Incorporated Knight* and *The Pixilated Peeress;* de Camp has also written a number of "Conan" novels in posthumous collaboration with the late Robert E. Howard. He has also written a long sequence of critically-acclaimed historical novels, including *The Bronze God of Rhodes, An Elephant for Aristotle, The Dragon of the Ishtar Gate,* and *The Arrows of Hercules,* as well as a number of nonfiction books on scientific and technical topics, literary biographies such as his painstaking examination of the life of H. P. Lovecraft, *Lovecraft: A Biography,* and *Dark Valley Destiny: The Life of Robert E. Howard,* and critical/biographical studies of fantasy and fantasy writers such as *Literary Swordsmen and Sorcerers.* As editor, his anthologies include *Swords & Sorcery, The Spell of Seven, The Fantastic Swordsmen,* and *Warlocks and Warriors.* His short fiction has been collected in *The Best of L. Sprague de Camp, A Gun for Dinosaur, The Purple Pterodactyls,* and *Rivers in Time.* De Camp has won the Grandmaster Nebula Award, and the Gandalf or Grandmaster of Fantasy Award, as well as the prestigious Life Achievement Award given by the World Fantasy Convention. In 1997, he won a Hugo Award for his autobiography, *Time and Change.* He and his wife live in Texas.

Adrian Frome regained consciousness to the sound of harsh Dzlieri consonants. When he tried to move, he found he was tied to a tree by creepers, and that the Vishnuvan centaurs were cavorting around him, fingering weapons and gloating.

"I think," said one, "that if we skinned him carefully and rolled him in salt . . ."

Another said: "Let us rather open his belly and draw forth his guts little by little. Flaying is too uncertain; Earthmen often die before one is half done."

Frome saw that his fellow-surveyors had indeed gone, leaving nothing but two dead zebras (out of the six they had started out with) and some smashed apparatus. His head ached abominably. Quinlan must have conked him from behind while Hayataka was unconscious, and then packed up and shoved off, taking his wounded chief but leaving Frome.

The Dzlieri yelled at one another until one said: "A pox on your fancy slow deaths! Let us stand off and shoot him, thus ridding ourselves of him and bettering our aim at once. Archers first. What say you?"

The last proposal carried. They spread out as far as the dense vegetation allowed.

The Dzlieri were not literally centaurs in the sense of looking like handsome Greek statues. If you imagine the front half of a gorilla mounted on the body of a tapir you will have a rough idea of their looks. They had large mobile ears, a caricature of a human face covered with red fur, four-fingered hands, and a tufted tail. Still, the fact that they were equipped with two arms and four legs apiece made people who found the native name hard call them centaurs, though the sight of them would have scared Pheidias or Praxiteles out of his wits.

"Ready?" said the archery enthusiast. "Aim low, for his head will make a fine addition to our collection if you spoil it not."

"Wait," said another. "I have a better thought. One of their missionaries told me a Terran legend of a man compelled by his chief to shoot a fruit from the head of his son. Let us therefore . . ."

"No! For then you will surely spoil his head!" And the whole mob was yelling again.

Lord, thought Frome, how they talk! He tested his bonds, finding that someone had done a good job of tying him up. Although badly frightened, he pulled himself together and put on a firm front: "I say, what are you chaps up to?"

They paid him no heed until the William Tell party carried the day and one of them, with a trader's stolen rifle slung over his shoulder, approached with a fruit the size of a small pumpkin.

Frome asked: "Does that gun of yours shoot?"

"Yes," said the Dzlieri. "I have bullets that fit, too!"

Frome doubted this, but said: "Why not make a real sporting event of it? Each of us put a fruit on our heads and the other try to shoot it off?"

The Dzlieri gave the gargling sound that passed for laughter. "So you can shoot us, eh? How stupid you think we are?"

Frome, thinking it more tactful not to say, persisted with the earnestness of desperation: "Really, you know, it'll only make trouble if you kill me, whereas if you let me go . . ."

"Trouble we fear not," roared the fruit-bearer, balancing the fruit on Frome's head. "Think you we should let go such a fine head? Never have we seen an Earthman with yellow hair on head and face."

Frome cursed the coloration that he had always been rather proud of hitherto, and tried to compose more arguments. It was hard to think in the midst of this deafening racket.

The pseudo-pumpkin fell off with a thump. The Dzlieri howled, and he who had placed it came back and belted Frome with a full-armed slap across the face. "That will teach you to move your head!" Then he tied it fast with a creeper that went over the fruit and under Frome's chin.

Three Dzlieri had been told off to loose the first flight.

"Now look here, friends," said Frome, "you know what the Earthmen can do if they—"

T-twunk! The bowstrings snapped; the arrows came on with a sharp whistle. Frome heard a couple hit. The pumpkin jerked, and he became aware of a sharp pain in his left ear. Something sticky dripped onto his bare shoulder.

The Dzlieri shouted. "Etsnoten wins the first round!"

"Was that not clever, to nail his ear to the tree?"

"Line up for the next flight!"

"Hoy!" Hooves drummed and more Dzlieri burst into view. "What is this?" asked one in a crested brass helmet.

They explained, all jabbering at once.

"So," said the helmeted one, whom the others addressed as Mishinatven. (Frome realized that this must be the insurgent chief who had seceded from old Kamatobden's rule. There had been rumors of war . . .) "The other Earthman knocked him witless, bound him, and left him for us, eh? After slaying our fellows there in the brush?" He pointed to the bodies of the two Dzlieri that had fallen to the machine-gun in the earlier skirmish.

Mishinatven then addressed Frome in the Brazilo-Portuguese of the spaceways, but very brokenly: "Who—you? What—name?"

"I speak Dzlieri," said Frome. "I'm Frome, one of the survey-party from Bembom. Your folk attacked us without provocation this morning as we were breaking camp, and wounded our chief."

"Ah. One of those who bounds and measures our country to take it from us?"

"No such thing at all. We only wish . . ."

"No arguments. I think I will take you to God. Perhaps you can add to our store of the magical knowledge of the Earthmen. For instance, what are these?" Mishinatven indicated the rubbish left by Quinlan.

"That is a thing for talking over distances. I fear it's broken beyond repair. And that's a device for telling direction, also broken. That—" (Mishinatven had pointed to the radar-target, an aluminum structure something like a kite and something like a street-sign) "is—uh—a kind of totem-pole we were bringing to set up on Mount Ertma."

"Why? That is my territory."

"So that by looking at it from Bembom with our radar—you know what radar is?"

"Certainly; a magic eye for seeing through fog. Go on."

"So you see, old fellow, by looking at this object with the radar from Bembom we could tell just how far and in what direction Mount Ertma was, and use this information in our maps."

Mishinatven was silent, then said: "This is too complicated for me. We must consider the deaths of my two subjects against the fact that they were head-hunting, which God has forbidden. Only God can settle this question." He turned to the others. "Gather up these things and bring them to Amnairad for salvage." He wrenched out the arrow that had pierced Frome's ear and cut the Earthman's bonds with a short hooked sword like an oversized linoleum-knife. "Clamber to my back and hold on."

Although Frome had ridden zebras over rough country (the Viagens Interplanetarias having found a special strain of Grévy's zebra, the big one with narrow stripes on the rump, best for travel on Vishnu where mechanical transport was impractical) he had never experienced anything like this wild bareback ride. At least he was still alive, and hoped to learn who "God" was. Although Mishinatven had used the term *gimoa-brtsqun,* "supreme spirit," the religion of the Dzliéri was demonology and magic of a low order, without even a centaur-shaped creator-god to head its pantheon. Or, he thought uneasily, by "taking him to God" did they simply mean putting him to death in some formal and complicated manner?

Well, even if the survey was washed up for the time being, perhaps he could learn something about the missing missionary and the trader. He had come out with Hayataka, the chief surveyor, and Pete Quinlan, a new man with little background and less manners. He and Quinlan had gotten on each other's nerves, though Frome had tried to keep things smooth. Hayataka, despite his technical skill and experience, was too mild and patient a little man to keep such an unruly subordinate as Quinlan in line.

First the Dzlieri guide had run off, and Quinlan had begun making homesick noises. Hayataka and Frome, however, had agreed to try for Mount Ertma by travelling on a magnetic bearing, though cross-country travel on this steaming soup kettle of a planet with its dense jungle and almost constant rain was far from pleasant.

They had heard of the vanished Earthfolk yesterday when Quinlan had raised Comandante Silva himself on the radio: ". . . and when you get into the Dzlieri country, look for traces of Sirat Mongkut and Elena Millán. Sirat Mongkut is an entrepreneur dealing mainly in scrap-metals with the Dzlieri, and has not been heard of for a Vishnuvan year. Elena Millán is a Cosmotheist missionary who has not been heard of in six weeks. If they're in trouble, try to help them and get word to us . . ."

After signing off, Quinlan had said: "Ain't that a hell of a thing, now? As if the climate and bugs and natives wasn't enough, it's hunting a couple of fools we are. What was that first name? It don't sound like any Earthly name I ever heard."

Hayataka answered: "Sirat Mongkut. He's a Thai—what you would call a Siamese."

Quinlan laughed loudly. "You mean a pair of twins joined together?"

Then this morning a party of Dzlieri, following the forbidden old custom of hunting heads, had rushed the camp. They had sent a javelin through both Hayataka's calves and mortally wounded the two zebras before Frome had knocked over two and scattered the rest with the light machine-gun.

Quinlan, however, had panicked and run. Frome, trying to be fair-minded, couldn't blame the lad too much; he'd panicked on his first trail-trip himself. But when Quinlan had slunk back, Frome, furious, had promised him a damning entry in his fitness report. Then they had bound Hayataka's wounds and let the chief surveyor put himself out with a trance-pill while they got ready to retreat to Bembom.

Quinlan must have brooded over his blighted career, slugged Frome, and left him for the Dzlieri, while he hauled his unconscious supervisor back to Bembom.

After a couple of hours of cross-country gallop, the party taking Frome to Amnairad began to use roads. Presently they passed patches of clearings where the Dzlieri raised the pushball-sized lettuce-like plants they ate. Then they entered a "town," which to human eyes looked more like a series of corrals with stables attached. This was Amnairad. Beyond loomed Mount Ertma, its top hidden in the clouds. Frome was surprised to see a half-dozen zebras in one of the enclosures; that meant men.

At the center of this area they approached a group of "buildings"—

inclosed structures made of poles with sheets of matting stretched between them. Up to the biggest structure the cavalcade cantered. At the entrance a pair of Dzlieri, imposing in helmets, spears, and shields, blocked the way.

"Tell God we have something for him," said Mishinatven.

One of the guards went into the structure and presently came out again. "Go on in," he said. "Only you and your two officers, Mishinatven. And the Earthman."

As they trotted through the maze of passages, Frome heard the rain on the matting overhead. He noted that the appointments of this odd place seemed more civilized than one would expect of Dzlieri, who, though clever in some ways, seemed too impulsive and quarrelsome to benefit from civilizing influences. They arrived in a room hung with drapes, of native textiles and decorated with groups of crossed Dzlieri weapons: bows, spears and the like.

"Get off," said Mishinatven. "God, this is an Earthman named Frome we found in the woods. Frome, this is God."

Frome watched Mishinatven to see whether to prostrate himself on the pounded-clay floor or what. But as the Dzlieri took the sight of his deity quite casually, Frome turned to the short, burly man with the flat Mongoloid face, wearing a pistol and sitting in an old leather armchair of plainly human make.

Frome nodded, saying: "Delighted to meet you, God old thing. Did your name used to be—uh—Sirat Mongkut before your deification?"

The man smiled faintly, nodded, and turned his attention to the three Dzlieri, who were all trying to tell the story of finding Frome and shouting each other down.

Sirat Mongkut straightened up and drew from his pocket a small object hung round his neck by a cord: a brass tube about the size and shape of a cigarette. He placed one end of this in his mouth and blew into it, his yellow face turning pink with effort. Although Frome heard no sound, the Dzlieri instantly fell silent. Sirat put the thing back in his pocket, the cord still showing, and said in Portuguese:

"Tell us how you got into that peculiar predicament, Senhor Frome."

Unable to think of any lie that would serve better than simple truth, Frome told Sirat of his quarrel with Quinlan and its sequel.

"Dear, dear," said Sirat. "One would almost think you two were a pair of my Dzlieri. I am aware, however, that such antipathies arise among Earthmen, especially when a few of them are confined to enforced propinquity for a considerable period. What would your procedure be if I released you?"

"Try to beat my way back to Bembom, I suppose. If you could lend me a Grévy and some rations. . . ."

Sirat shook his head, still smiling like a Cheshire-cat. "I fear that is not within the bourne of practicability. But why are you in such a hurry to get back? After the disagreement of which you apprised me, your welcome will hardly be fraternal; your colleague will have reported his narrative in a manner to place you in the worst possible light."

"Well, what then?" said Frome, thinking that the entrepreneur must have swallowed a dictionary in his youth. He guessed that Sirat was determined not to let him go, but on the contrary might want to use him. While Frome had no intention of becoming a renegade, it wouldn't hurt to string him along until he learned what was up.

Sirat asked: "Are you a college-trained engineer?"

Frome nodded. "University of London; Civil Engineering."

"Can you run a machine-shop?"

"I'm not an expert machinist, but I know the elements. Are you hiring me?"

Sirat smiled. "I perceive you usually anticipate me by a couple of steps. That is, roughly, the idea I had in mind. My Dzlieri are sufficiently clever metal-workers but lack the faculty of application; moreover I find it difficult to elucidate the more complicated operations to organisms from the pre-machine era. And finally, Senhor, you arrive at an inopportune time, when I have projects under way news of which I do not desire to have broadcast. Do you comprehend?"

Frome at once guessed Sirat was violating Interplanetary Council Regulation No. 368, Section 4, Sub-section 26, Paragraph 15, which forbade imparting technical information to intelligent but backward and warlike beings like the Dzlieri without special permission. This was something Silva should know about. All he said, though, was:

"I'll see what I can do."

"Good." Sirat rose. "I will patch up your ear and then show you the shop myself. Accompany us, Mishinatven."

The Siamese led the way through the maze of mat-lined passages and out. The "palace" was connected by a breezeway with a smaller group of structures in which somebody was banging on an anvil; somebody was using a file; somebody was pumping the bellows of a simple forge.

In a big room several Dzlieri were working on metal parts with homemade tools, including a crank-operated lathe and boring-mill. In one corner rose a pile of damaged native weapons and tools. As his gaze roamed the room, Frome saw a rack holding dozens of double-barrelled guns.

Sirat handed one to Frome. "Two-centimeter smooth-bores, of the simplest design. My Dzlieri are not yet up to complicated automatic actions, to say nothing of shock-guns and paralyzers and such complex weapons. That is why the guns they expropriate from traders seldom remain long in use. They will not clean guns, nor believe that each gun requires appropriate ammunition. Therefore the guns soon get out of order and they are unable to effect repairs. But considering that we are not yet up to rifling the barrels, and that vision is limited in the jungle, one of these with eight-millimeter buckshot is quite as effective as an advanced gun.

"Now," he continued, "I contemplate making you my shop foreman. You will first undergo a training-course by working in each department in turn for a few days. As for your loyalty—I trust to your excellent judgment not to attempt to depart from these purlieus. You shall start in the scrap-sorting department today, and when you have completed your stint, Mishinatven will escort you to your quarters. As my Dzlieri have not yet evolved a monetary economy, you will be recompensed in copper ingots. Lastly, I trust I shall have the gratification of your companionship for the evening repast tonight?"

The scrap-sorting room was full of piles of junk, both of human and of native origin. Idznamen, the sorter, harangued Frome on such elementary matters as how to tell brass from iron. When Frome impatiently said: "Yes, yes, I know that," Idznamen glowered and went right on. Meanwhile Frome was working up a state of indignation. An easy-going person most of the time, he was particular about his rights, and now was in a fine fury over the detention of him, a civil servant of the mighty Viagens, by some scheming renegade.

During the lecture Frome prowled, turning over pieces of junk. He thought he recognized a motor-armature that had vanished from Bembom recently. Then there was a huge copper kettle with a hole in its bottom. Finally he found the remains of the survey-party's equipment, including the radar-target.

Hours later, tired and dirty, he was dismissed and taken by Mishinatven to a small room in this same building. Here he found a few simple facilities for washing up. He thought he should mow the incipient yellow beard in honor of dining with God, but Mishinatven did not know what a razor was. The Dzlieri hung around, keeping Frome in sight. Evidently Sirat was taking no chances with his new associate.

At the appointed time, Mishinatven led him to the palace and into Sirat's dining-room, which was fixed up with considerable elegance. Besides a couple of Dzlieri guards, two people were there already: Sirat Mongkut and a small dark girl, exquisitely formed but clad in a severely plain Earthly costume—much more clothes than human beings normally wore on this steaming planet.

Sirat said: "My dear, allow me to present Senhor Adrian Frome; Senhor, I have the ineffable pleasure of introducing Senhorita Elena Millán. Will you partake of a drink?" he added, offering a glass of *moikhada*.

"Righto," said Frome, noticing that Sirat already held one but that Miss Millán did not.

"It is contrary to her convictions," said Sirat. "I hope to cure her of such unwarranted extremism, but it consumes time. Now narrate your recent adventures to us again."

Frome obliged.

"What a story!" said Elena Millán. "So that handsome North European coloring of yours was almost your death! You Northerners ought to stick to the cold planets like Ganesha. Not that I believe Junqueiros's silly theory of the superiority of the Mediterranean race."

"He might have a point as far as Vishnu is concerned," said Frome. "I do notice that the climate seems harder on people like Van der Gracht and me than on natives of tropical countries like Mehtalal. But perhaps I'd better dye my hair black to discourage these chaps from trying to collect my head as a souvenir."

"Truly I regret the incident," said Sirat. "But perhaps it is a fortunate misfortune. Is there not an English proverb about ill winds? Now, as you observe, I possess a skilled mechanic and another human being with whom to converse. You have no conception of the *ennui* of seeing nobody but extraterrestrials."

Frome watched them closely. So this was the missing missionary! At least she had a friendly smile and a low sweet voice. Taking the bull by the horns he asked:

"How did Miss Millán get here?"

Elena Millán spoke: "I was travelling with some Dzlieri into Mishinatven's territory, when a monster attacked my party and ate one of them. I should have been eaten, too, had not Mr. Sirat come along and shot the beast. And now . . ."

She looked at Sirat, who said with his usual smile: "And now she finds it difficult to accustom herself to the concept of becoming the foundress of a dynasty."

"What?" said Frome.

"Oh, have I not enlightened you? I am imbued with considerable ambitions—exalted, I think, is the word I want. Nothing that need involve me with Bembom, I trust, but I hope before many years have elapsed to bring a sizable area under my sovereignty. I already rule Mishinatven's people for all practical purposes, and within a few weeks I propose to have annexed old Kamatobden's as well. Then for the tribe of Romeli living beyond Bembom . . ." He referred to the other intelligent species of the planet, six-limbed ape-like beings who quarreled constantly with the Dzlieri.

"You see yourself as a planetary emperor?" said Frome. This should certainly be reported back to his superiors at Bembom without delay!

Sirat made a deprecating motion. "I should not employ so extravagant a term—at least not yet. It is a planet of large land area. But—you comprehend the general idea. Under unified rule I could instill real culture into the Dzlieri and Romeli, which they will never attain on a basis of feuding tribes." He chuckled. "A psychologist once asserted that I had a power-complex because of my short stature. Perhaps he was correct; but is that any pretext for neglecting to put this characteristic to good use?"

"And where does Miss Millán come in?" asked Frome.

"My dear Frome! These primitives can comprehend the dynastic principle, but are much too backward for your recondite democratic ideals, as the failure of attempts to teach the representative government has amply demonstrated. Therefore we must have a dynasty, and I have elected Miss Millán to assist me in founding it."

Elena's manner changed abruptly and visibly. "I never shall," she said coldly. "If I ever marry, it will be because the Cosmos has infused my spiritual self with a Ray of its Divine Love."

Frome choked on his drink, wondering how such a nice girl could talk such tosh.

Sirat smiled. "She will alter her mind. She does not know what is beneficial for her, poor infant."

Elena said: "He walks in the darkness of many lives' accumulated karma, Mr. Frome, and so cannot understand spiritual truths."

Sirat grinned broadly. "Just a benighted old ignoramus. I suppose, my love, you would find our guest more amenable to your spiritual suasion?"

"Judging by the color of his aura, yes." (Frome glanced nervously about.) "If his heart were filled with Cosmic Love, I could set his feet on the Seven-Fold Path to Union with the Infinite."

Frome almost declared he wouldn't stand by and see an Earthwoman put under duress—not while he had his health—but thought better of it. Such an outburst would do more harm than good. Still, Adrian Frome had committed himself mentally to helping Elena, for while he affected a hardboiled attitude towards women, he was secretly a sentimental softhead towards anything remotely like a damsel in distress.

Sirat said: "Let us discuss less rarefied matters. How are affairs proceeding at Bembom, Mr. Frome? The information brought hither by my Dzlieri is often garbled in transit."

After that the meal went agreeably enough. Frome found Sirat Mongkut, despite his extraordinarily pedantic speech, a shrewd fellow with a good deal of charm, though obviously one who let nothing stand in his way. The girl, too, fascinated him. She seemed to be two different people—one, a nice normal girl whom he found altogether attractive; the other, a priestess of the occult who rather frightened him.

When Sirat dismissed his guests, a Dzlieri escorted each of them out of the room. Mishinatven saw to it that Frome was safely in bed (Frome had to move the bed a couple of times to avoid the drip of rain-water through the mat ceiling) before leaving him. As for Adrian Frome, he was too tired to care whether they mounted guard over him or not.

During the ensuing days Frome learned more of the workings of the shop and revived his familiarity with the skills that make a metal-worker. He also got used to being tailed by Mishinatven or some other Dzlieri. He supposed he should be plotting escape, and felt guilty because he had not been able to devise any clever scheme for doing so. Sirat kept his own person guarded, and Frome under constant surveillance.

And assuming Frome could give his guards the slip, what then? Even if the Dzlieri failed to catch him in his flight (as they probably would) or if he were not devoured by one of the carnivores of the jungle, without a compass, he would get hopelessly lost before he had gone one kilometer and presently die of the deficiency-diseases that always struck down Earthmen who tried to live on an exclusively Vishnuvan diet.

Meanwhile he liked the feeling of craftsmanship that came from exercising his hands on the tough metals, and found the other human beings agreeable to know.

One evening Sirat said: "Adrian, I should like you to take tomorrow off to witness some exercises I am planning."

"Glad to," said Frome. "You coming, Elena?"

She said: "I prefer not to watch preparations for the crime of violence."

Sirat laughed. "She still thinks she can convert the Dzlieri to pacifism. You might as well instruct a horse to perform on the violin. She tried it on Chief Kamatobden and he thought her simply deranged."

"I shall yet bring enlightenment to these strayed souls," she said firmly.

The exercises took place in a large clearing near Amnairad. Sirat sat on a saddled zebra watching squadrons of Dzlieri maneuver at breakneck speed with high precision: some with native weapons, some with the new shotguns. A troop of lancers would thunder across the field in line abreast; then a square of musketeers would run onto the field, throw themselves down behind stumps and pretend to fire, and then leap up and scatter into the surrounding jungle, to reassemble elsewhere. There was some target practice like trapshooting, but no indiscriminate firing; Sirat kept the ammunition for his new guns locked up and doled it out only for specific actions.

Frome did not think Sirat was in a position to attack Bembom—yet. But he could certainly make a sweep of the nearby Vishnuvan tribes, whose armies were mere yelling mobs by comparison with his. And then . . . Silva *must* be told about this.

Sirat seemed to be controlling the movements in the field, though he neither gestured nor spoke. Frome worked his way close enough to the *renegado* to see that he had the little brass tube in his mouth and was going through the motions of blowing into it. Frome remembered: a Galton whistle, of course! It gave out an ultrasonic blast above the limits of human hearing, and sometimes people back on Earth called their dogs with them. The Dzlieri must have a range of hearing beyond 20,000 cycles per second.

At dinner that night he asked Sirat about this method of signalling.

Sirat answered: "I thought you would so conjecture. I have worked out a system of signals, something like Morse. There is no great advantage in employing the whistle against hostile Dzlieri, since they can perceive it also; but with human beings or Romeli . . . For instance, assume some ill-intentioned Earthman were to assault me in my quarters when my guards were absent? A blast would bring them running without the miscreant's knowing I had called.

"That reminds me," continued the adventurer, "tomorrow I desire you to commence twenty more of these, for my subordinate officers. I have decided to train them in the use of the device as well. And I must request haste, since I apprehend major movements in the near future."

"Moving against Kamatobden, eh?" said Frome.

"You may think so if you wish. Do not look so fearful, Elena; I will take good care of myself. Your warrior shall return."

Maybe, thought Frome, that's what she's scared of.

Frome looked over the Galton whistle Sirat had left with him. He now ran the whole shop and knew where he could lay hands on a length of copper tubing (probably once the fuel-line of a helicopter) that should do for the duplication of the whistle.

With the help of one of the natives he completed the order by nightfall, plus one whistle the Dzlieri had spoiled. Sirat came over from the palace and said: "Excellent, my dear Adrian. We shall go far together. You must pardon my not inviting you to dine with me tonight, but I am compelled to confer with my officers. Will you and Miss Millán carry on in the regular dining-room in my absence?"

"Surely, Dom Sirat," said Frome. "Glad to."

Sirat wagged a forefinger. "However, let me caution you against exercising your charm too strongly on my protégée. An inexperienced girl like that might find a tall young Englishman glamorous, and the results would indubitably be *most* deplorable for all concerned."

When the time came, he took his place opposite Elena Millán at the table. She said: "Let us speak English, since some of our friends here" (she referred to the ubiquitous Dzlieri guards) "know a little Portuguese, too. Oh, Adrian, I'm so afraid!"

"Of what; Sirat? What's new?"

"He has been hinting that if I didn't fall in with his dynastic plans, he would compel me. You know what that means."

"Yes. And you want me to rescue you?"

"I—I should be most grateful if you could. While we are taught to resign ourselves to such misfortunes, as things earned in earlier incarnations, I don't think I could bear it. I should kill myself."

Frome pondered. "D'you know when he's planning this attack?"

"He leaves the day after tomorrow. Tomorrow night the Dzlieri will celebrate."

That meant a wild orgy, and Sirat might well take the occasion to copy his subjects. On the other hand, the confusion afforded a chance to escape.

"I'll try to cook up a scheme," he told her.

Next day Frome found his assistants even more restless and insubordinate than usual. About noon they walked out for good. "Got to get ready for the party!" they shouted. "To hell with work!"

Mishinatven had vanished, too. Frome sat alone, thinking. After a while he wandered around the shop, handling pieces of material. He noticed the spoilt Galton whistle lying where he had thrown it the day before; the remaining length of copper tubing from which he had made the whistles; the big copper kettle he had never gotten around either to scrapping or to fixing. Slowly an idea took shape.

He went to the forge-room and started the furnace up again. When he had a hot fire, he brazed a big thick patch over the hole in the kettle, on the inside where it would take pressure. He tested the kettle for leakage and found none. Then he sawed a length off the copper tube and made another Galton whistle, using the spoilt one as a model.

In the scrap-sorting room he found a length of plastic which he made into a sealing-ring or gasket to go between the kettle and its lid. He took off the regular handle of the kettle, twisted a length of heavy wire into a shorter bail, and installed it so that it pressed the lid tightly down against the gasket. Finally he made a little conical adapter of sheet-copper and brazed it to the spout of the kettle, and brazed the whistle to the adapter. He then had an air-tight kettle whose spout ended in the whistle.

Then it was time for dinner.

Sirat seemed in a rollicking good humor and drank more moikhada than usual.

"Tomorrow," he said, "tomorrow we cast the die. What was that ancient European general who remarked about casting the die when crossing a river? Napoleon? Anyway, let us drink to tomorrow!" He raised his goblet theatrically. "Will you not weaken, Elena? Regrettable; you do not know what you miss. Come, let us fall upon the provender, lest my cook decamp to the revellers before we finish."

From outside came Dzlieri voices in drunken song, and sounds of a fight. The high shriek of a female Dzlieri tore past the palace, followed by the laughter and hoofbeats of a male in pursuit.

These alarming sounds kept the talk from reaching its usual brilliance. When the meal was over, Sirat said:

"Adrian, you must excuse me; I have a portentous task to accomplish. Please return to your quarters. Not you, Elena; kindly remain where you are."

Frome looked at the two of them, then at the guards, and went. In passing through the breezeway he saw a mob of Dzlieri dancing around a bonfire. The palace proper seemed nearly deserted.

Instead of going to his room he went into the machine-shop. He lit a cresset to see by, took the big copper kettle out to the pump, and half filled it with several liters of water. Then he staggered back into the shop and heaved the kettle up on top of the forge. He clamped the lid on, stirred the coals, and pumped the bellows until he had a roaring fire.

He hunted around the part of the shop devoted to the repair of tools and weapons until he chose a big spear with a three-meter shaft and a broad keen-edged half-meter head. Then he went back to the forge with it.

After a long wait, a faint curl of water-vapor appeared in the air near the spout of the kettle. It grew to a long plume, showing that steam was shooting out fast. Although Frome could hear nothing, he could tell by touching a piece of metal to the spout that the whistle was vibrating at a tremendous frequency.

Remembering that ultrasonics have directional qualities, Frome slashed through the matting with the broad blade of the spear until the forge-room lay open to view in several directions. Then he went back into the palace.

By now he knew the structure well. Towards the center of the maze Sirat had his private suite: a sitting-room, bedroom, and bath. The only way into this suite was through an always-guarded door into the sitting-room.

Frome walked along the hallway that ran beside the suite and around the corner to the door into the sitting-room. He listened, ear to the matting. Although it was hard to hear anything over the racket outside, he thought he caught sounds of struggle within. And from up ahead came Dzlieri voices.

He stole to the bend in the corridor and heard: ". . . surely some demon must have sent this sound to plague us. In truth it makes my head ache to the splitting-point!"

"It is like God's whistle," said the other voice, "save that it comes not from God's chambers, and blows continually. Try stuffing a bit of this into your ears."

The first voice (evidently that of one of the two regular guards) said: "It helps a little; remain you here on guard while I seek the medicine-man."

"That I will, but send another to take your place, for God will take it amiss if he finds but one of us here. And hasten, for the scream drives me to madness!"

Dzlieri hooves departed. Frome grinned in his whiskers. He might take a chance of attacking the remaining guard, but if the fellow's ears were plugged there was a better way. Sirat would have closed off his bedroom from the sitting-room by one of those curtains of slats that did duty for doors.

Frome retraced his steps until he was sure he was opposite the bedroom. Then he thrust his spear into the matting, slashed downward, and pushed through the slit into a bedroom big enough for basketball.

Sirat Mongkut looked up from what he was doing. He had tied Elena's wrists to the posts at the head of the bed, so that she lay supine, and now, despite her struggles, was tying one of her ankles to one of the posts at the foot. Here was a conqueror who liked to find his dynasties in comfort.

"Adrian!" cried Elena.

Sirat's hand flashed to his hip—and came away empty. Frome's biggest gamble had paid off: he assumed that just this once Sirat might have discarded his pistol. Frome had planned, if he found Sirat armed, to throw the spear at him; now he could take the surer way.

He gripped the big spear in both hands, like a bayonetted rifle, and ran towards Sirat. The stocky figure leaped onto the bed and then to the floor on the far side, fumbling for his whistle. Frome sprang onto the bed in pursuit, but tripped on Elena's bound ankle and almost sprawled head-long. By the time he recovered he had staggered nearly the width of the room. Meanwhile Sirat, having avoided Frome's rush, put his whistle to his mouth, and his broad cheeks bulged with blowing.

Frome gathered himself for another charge. Sirat blew and blew, his expression changing from confidence to alarm as nobody came. Frome knew that no Dzlieri in the neighborhood could hear the whistle over the continuous blast of the one attached to the kettle. But Sirat, unable to hear ultrasonics, did not know his signals were jammed.

As Frome started towards him again, Sirat threw a chair. It flew with deadly force; part of it gave Frome's knuckles a nasty rap while another part smote him on the forehead, sending him reeling back. Sirat darted across the room again on his short legs and tore from the wall one of those groups of native weapons he ornamented his palace with.

Down with a clatter came the mass of cutlery: a pair of crossed battle-axes, a gisarme, and a brass buckler. By the time Frome, having re-covered from the impact of the chair, came up, Sirat had possessed him-self of the buckler and one of the axes. He whirled and brought up the buckler just in time to ward off a lunge of the spear. Then he struck out with his ax and spun himself half around as he met only empty air. Frome, seeing the blow coming, had leaped back.

Sirat followed, striking out again and again. Frome gave ground, afraid to parry for fear of having his spear ruined, then drove Sirat back again by jabs at his head, legs, and exposed arm. They began to circle, the spearpoint now and then clattering against the shield. Frome found that he could hold Sirat off by his longer reach, but could not easily get past the buckler. Round they went, *clank! clank!*

Sirat was slow for a second and Frome drove the spearpoint into his right thigh, just above the knee . . . But the thrust, not centered, inflicted only a flesh-wound and a great rip in Sirat's pants. Sirat leaped forward, whirling his ax, and drove Frome back almost to the wall before the lat-ter stopped him with his thrusts.

They circled again. Then came a moment when Sirat was between Frome and the door to the sitting-room. Quick as a flash Sirat threw his ax at Frome, dropped his shield, turned, and ran for the curtained door, calling "Help!"

Frome dodged the ax, which nevertheless hit him a jarring blow in the shoulder. As he recovered, he saw Sirat halfway to safety, hands out to wrench the curtain aside. He could not possibly catch the Siamese before the latter reached the sitting-room and summoned his delinquent guards to help him.

Frome threw his spear like a javelin. The shaft arced through the air and the point entered Sirat's broad back. In it went. And in, until half its length was out of sight.

Sirat fell forward, face down, clutching at the carpet and gasping. Blood ran from his mouth.

Frome strode over to where the would-be emperor lay and wrenched out the spear. He held it poised, ready to drive home again, until Sirat ceased to move. He was almost sorry . . . But there was no time for Hamlet-like attitudes; he wiped the blade on Sirat's clothes, carried it over to the bed, and sawed through Elena's bonds with the edge. Without waiting for explanations he said:

"If we're quick, we may get away before they find out. That is, if the guards haven't heard the noise in here."

"They will think it was he and I," she replied. "Before he dragged me in here he told them not to come in, no matter what they heard, unless he whistled for them."

"Serves him right. I'm going down-street to get some of his zebras. Where's that bloody gun of his?"

"In that chest," she said, pointing. "He locked it in there, I suppose because he was afraid I'd snatch it and shoot him—as though I could kill any sentient being."

"How do we get into—" Frome began, and stopped as he saw that the chest had a combination lock. "I fear we don't. How about his ammunition-chest in the storeroom?"

"That has a combination lock, too."

"Tamates!" growled Frome. "It looks as though we'd have to start out without a gun. While I'm gone, try to collect a sack of tucker from the kitchen, and whatever else looks useful." And out he went through the slit.

Outside the palace, he took care to saunter as if on legitimate business. The Dzlieri, having cast off what few inhibitions they normally possessed, were too far gone in their own amusements to pay him much heed, though one or two roared greetings at him.

Catching the zebras, though, was something else. The animals dodged around the corral, evading with ease his efforts to seize their bridles. Finally he called to a Dzlieri he knew:

"Mzumelitsen, lend a hand, will you? God wants a ride."

"Wait till I finish what I am doing," said the Dzlieri.

Frome waited until Mzumelitsen finished what he was doing and came over to help collect three zebras. Once caught, the animals followed Frome back to the palace tamely enough. He hitched them to the rail in the rear and went into the machine-shop, where he rummaged until he found a machete and a hatchet. He also gathered up the radar-target, which looked still serviceable if slightly battered.

When he got back he found that Elena had acquired a bag of food, a supply of matches, and a few other items. These they loaded on one of the zebras, and the other two they saddled.

When they rode out of Amnairad, the Dzlieri celebration was still in its full raucous swing.

Next day they were beginning to raise the lower slopes of the foothills of Mount Ertma when Frome held up a hand and said: "Listen!"

Through the muffling mass of the Vishnuvan jungle they heard loud Dzlieri voices. Then the sound of bodies moving along the trail came to their ears.

Frome exchanged one look with Elena and they broke into a gallop.

The pursuers must have been coming fast also, for the sounds behind became louder and louder. Frome caught a glimpse of the gleam of metal behind them. Whoops told them the Dzlieri had seen them, too.

Frome said: "You go on; I'll lead them off the trail and lose them."

"I won't! I won't desert you—"

"Do as I say!"

"But—"

"Go on!" he yelled so fiercely that she went. Then he sat waiting until they came into sight, fighting down his own fears, for he had no illusions about being able to "lose" the Dzlieri in their native jungle.

They poured up the trail towards him with triumphant screams. If he only had a gun . . . At least they did not seem to have any, either. They had only a few guns that would shoot (not counting the shotguns, whose shells were still locked up) and would have divided into many small parties to scour the trails leading out from their center.

Frome turned the zebra's head off into the jungle. Thank the gods the growth was thinner here than lower down, where the jungle was practically impassable off the trails.

He kicked his mount into an irregular run and vainly tried to protect his face from the lashing branches. Thorns ripped his skin and a trunk gave his right leg a brutal blow. As the Dzlieri bounded off the trail after him, he guided his beast in a wide semicircle around them to intersect the trail again behind his pursuers.

When he reached the trail, and could keep his eyes open again, he saw that the whole mob was crowding after him and gaining, led by

Mishinatven. As the trail bent, Sirat's lieutenant cut across the corner and hurled himself back on the path beside the Earthman. Frome felt for his machete, which had been slapping against his left leg. The Dzlieri thundered at him from the right, holding a javelin up for a stab.

"Trickster! Deicide!" screamed Mishinatven, and thrust. Frome slashed through the shaft. As they galloped side by side, the point grazed Frome's arm and fell to the ground.

Mishinatven swung the rest of the shaft and whacked Frome's shoulders. Frome slashed back; heard the clang of brass as the Dzlieri brought up his buckler. Mishinatven dropped the javelin and snatched out his short sword. Frome parried the first cut and, as Mishinatven recovered, struck at the Dzlieri's sword-hand and felt the blade bite bone. The sword spun away.

Frome caught the edge of the buckler with his left hand, pulled it down, and hacked again and again until the brass was torn from his grip by the fall of his foe.

The others were still coming. Looking back, Frome saw that they halted when they came to their fallen leader.

Frome pulled on his reins. The best defense is a bloody strong attack. If he charged them now . . . He wheeled the zebra and went for them at a run, screeching and whirling his bloody blade.

Before he could reach them, they scattered into the woods with cries of despair. He kept right on through the midst of them and up the long slope until they were far behind and the exhaustion of his mount forced him to slow down.

When he finally caught up with Elena Millán, she looked at him with horror. He wondered why until he realized that with blood all over he must be quite a sight.

They made the last few kilometers on foot, leading their zebras zigzag among the immense boulders that crested the peak and beating the beasts to make them buck-jump up the steep slopes. When they arrived at the top, they tied the beasts to bushes and threw themselves down to rest.

Elena said: "Thank the Cosmos that's over! I could not have gone on much further."

"We're not done yet," said Frome. "When we get our breath we'll have to set up the target."

"Are we safe here?"

"By no means. Those Dzlieri will go back to Amnairad and fetch the whole tribe, then they'll throw a cordon around the mountain to make sure we shan't escape. We can only hope the target brings a rescue in time."

Presently he forced himself to get up and go to work again. In half an hour, with Elena's help, the radar target was up on its pole, safely guyed against the gusts.

Then Adrian Frome flopped down again. Elena said: "You poor creature! You're all over bruises."

"Don't I know it! But it might have been a sight worse."

"Let me at least wash those scratches, lest you get infected."

"That's all right; Vishnuvan germs don't bother Earthfolk. Oh, well, if you insist . . ." His voice trailed off sleepily.

He woke up some hours later to find that Elena had gotten a fire going despite the drizzle and had a meal laid out.

"Blind me, what have we here?" he exclaimed. "I say, you're the sort of trail-mate to have!"

"That is nothing. It's you who are wonderful. And to think I've always been prejudiced against blond men, because in Spanish novels the villain is always pictured as a blond!"

Frome's heart, never so hard as he made it out to be, was full to overflowing. "Perhaps this isn't the time to say this but—uh—I'm not a very spiritual sort of bloke, but I rather love you, you know."

"I love you too. The Cosmos has sent a love-ray . . ."

"*Oi!*" It was a jarring reminder of that other Elena. "That's enough of that, my girl. Come here."

She came.

When Peter Quinlan got back to Bembom with the convalescing Hayataka, Comandante Silva listened eagerly to Quinlan's story until he came to his flight from Mishinatven's territory.

". . . after we started," said Quinlan, "while Hayataka was still out, they attacked again. I got three, but not before they had killed Frome with javelins. After we beat them off I buried—"

"Wait! You say Frome was killed?"

"*Pois sim.*"

"And you came right back here, without going to Ertma?"

"Naturally. What else could I do?"

"Then who set up the radar target on the mountain?"

"*What?*"

"Why yes. We sent up our radars on the ends of the base-line yesterday, and the target showed clearly on the scopes."

"I don't understand," said Quinlan.

"Neither do I, but we'll soon find out. *Amigo,*" he said to the sergeant Martins, "tell the aviation group to get the helicopter ready to fly to Mount Ertma, at once."

When the pilot homed on the radar target, he came out of the clouds to see a kite-like polygonal structure gleaming with a dull gray aluminum finish on top of a pole on the highest peak of Mount Ertma. Beside the pole were two human beings sitting on a rock and three tethered zebras munching the herbage.

The human beings leaped to their feet and waved wildly. The pilot brought his aircraft around, tensely guiding it through gusts that threatened to dash it against the rocks, and let the rope-ladder uncoil through the trapdoor. The man leaped this way and that, like a fish jumping for a fly, as the ladder whipped about him. Finally he caught it.

Just then a group of Dzlieri came out of the trees. They pointed and jabbered and ran towards the people whipping out javelins.

The smaller of the two figures was several rungs up the ladder when the larger one, who had just begun his ascent, screamed up over the whirr of the rotor-blades and the roar of the wind:

"Straight up! Quick!"

More Dzlieri appeared—scores of them—and somewhere a rifle barked. The pilot (just as glad it was not he dangling from an aircraft bucking through a turbulent overcast) canted his blades and rose until the clouds closed in below.

The human beings presently popped into the cabin, gasping from their climb. They were a small dark young woman and a tall man with a centimeter of butter-colored beard matted with dried blood. Both were nearly naked save for tattered canvas boots and a rag or two elsewhere, and were splashed with half-dried mud. The pilot recognized Adrian Frome, the surveyor.

"Home, Jayme," said Frome.

Frome, cleaned, shaved and looking his normal self once more except for a notch in his left ear, sat down across the desk from Silva, who said: "I cannot understand why you ask for a transfer to Ganesha now of all times. You're the hero of Bembom. I can get you a permanent P-5 appointment; perhaps even a P-6. Quinlan will be taken to Krishna for trial; Hayataka is retiring on his pension; and I shall be hard up for surveyors. So why must you leave?"

Frome smiled a wry, embarrassed smile. "You'll manage, *chefe.* You still have Van der Gracht and Mehtalal, both good men. But I'm quite determined, and I'll tell you why. When Elena and I got to the top of that mountain we were in a pretty emotional state, and what with one thing and another, and not having seen another human female for weeks, I asked her to marry me and she accepted."

Silva's eyebrows rose. "Indeed! My heartiest congratulations! But what has that to do with—"

"Wait till you hear the rest! At first everything was right as rain. She claimed it was the first time she'd been kissed, and speaking as a man of some experience I suppose it was. However, she soon began telling me *her* ideas. In the first place this was to be a purely spiritual marriage, the purpose of which was to put my feet on the sevenfold path of enlightenment so I could be something better than a mere civil engineer in my next incarnation—a Cosmotheist missionary, for example. Now I ask you!

"Well, at first I thought that was just a crochet I'd get her over in time; after all we don't let our women walk over us the way the Americans do. But then she started preaching Cosmotheism to me. And during the two and a half days we were up there, I'll swear she didn't stop talking five minutes except when she was asleep. The damndest rot you ever heard—rays and cosmic love and vibrations and astral planes and so on. I was never so bored in my life."

"I know," said Silva. He too had suffered.

"So," concluded Frome, "about that time I began wishing I could give her back to Sirat Mongkut. I was even sorry I'd killed the blighter. Although he'd have caused no end of trouble if he'd lived, he was a likeable sort of scoundrel at that. So here I am with one unwanted fiancée, and I just *can't* explain the facts of life to her. She once said as a joke that I'd be better off on Ganesha, and damned if I don't think she was right. Now if you'll just indorse that application . . . Ah, *muito obrigado,* Senhor Augusto! If I hurry I can just catch the ship to Krishna. Cheerio!"

Jack Vance

THE NEW PRIME

Much as SF authors writing today about phenomonology or the nature of reality write inevitably in the shadow of Philip K. Dick, so writers describing distant worlds and alien societies with strange alien customs write in the shadow of Jack Vance. No one in the history of the field has brought more intelligence, imagination, or inexhaustible fertility of invention to that theme than Vance, a fertility which shows no sign of slackening even here at the end of the '90s, with recent books such as *Night Lamp* being as richly and lushly imaginative as the stuff he was writing in the '50s; even ostensible potboilers such as his *Planet of Adventure* series are full of vivid and richly portrayed alien societies, and bizarre and often profoundly disturbing insights into the ways in which human psychology might be altered by immersion in alien values and cultural systems. No one is better than Vance is at delivering that quintessential "sense of wonder" that is at the heart of science fiction, and reading him has left me a legacy of evocative images that will stay with me forever.

Like his colleagues L. Sprague de Camp and Fritz Leiber, Vance has produced some of the very best work of the last fifty years in several different genres, and is of immense evolutionary importance to the development both of modern fantasy *and* of modern science fiction. In fantasy, his classic novel *The Dying Earth*—together with the related "Cugel the Clever" stories, collected in *The Eyes of the Overworld, Cugel's Saga,* and *Rhialto the Marvellous*—would have enormous impact on future generations of fantasy writers. (It could be argued—and has been—that these works are actually science fiction—or at least a hybrid form called "science fantasy"—rather than fantasy, taking place in a future so many millions of years from now that technology has indeed become indistinguishable from magic, as per Arthur C. Clarke's famous dictum. These arguments are not without merit, and are hard to refute—nevertheless, for anyone who has kept an eye on the fantasy genre over the last few decades, or ever read a slushpile, Vance's influence on the fantasy field is hard to deny, no matter what hairs taxonomists split.) In the same way, his most famous SF novels—*The Dragon Masters, The Last Castle, Big Planet, Emphyrio,* the five-volume "Demon Princes" series (the best known of which are *The Star King* and *The Killing Machine*), *Blue World, The Anome, The Languages of Pao,* among many others—have had a widespread impact on generations of science fiction writers. And his effect on the specialized form of Space Adventure or Space Opera (as differentiated from science fiction in general) is immense—with the possible exception of Poul Anderson, nobody has written more of that sort of work, or written at such a consistently high level of quality, as has Jack Vance.

Born in San Francisco in 1920, Vance served throughout World War II in the U.S. Merchant Navy. Most of the individual stories that would later be melded into his first novel, *The Dying Earth,* were written while Vance was at sea—he was unable to sell them, a problem he would also have with the book itself, the market for fantasy being almost non-existent at the time. *The Dying Earth* was eventually published in an obscure edition in 1950 by a small semi-professional press, went out of print almost immediately, and remained out of print for more than a decade thereafter. Nevertheless, it became an underground cult classic, and its effect on future generations of writers, both in and out of the fantasy genre, is incalculable: for one example out of many, *The Dying Earth* is a major influence on Gene Wolfe's *The Book of the New Sun* (Wolfe has said, for instance, that *The Book of Gold* which is mentioned by Severian is supposed to be *The Dying Earth*).

In SF, especially during the '50s and '60s, Vance was sometimes criticized for not being "rigorous" enough in his writing, for turning out Space Opera rather than "real" science fiction; I suspect this is one of the things that largely kept him out of *Astounding,* the leading market of his day (most of his work for *Astounding* would be rather bland by Vance's standards, only one story there, the later novella "The Miracle Workers," being full-throated Vancian Future Baroque—a somewhat atypical style for *Astounding,* and I can't help but wonder if John W. Campbell took the story mostly because it deals fairly centrally with psionics, a pet Campbellian topic of the time). Instead, he had to sell the bulk of his work to lower-paying "salvage" markets such as *Thrilling Wonder Stories* and *Startling Stories,* the last resort for a story before you relegated it to the trunk. Certainly it's true that there are few hard-science restraints on his fictional settings, where people in tiny personal spaceships zip easily and effortlessly across immense gulfs of space, vast powers and potencies are manipulated, and the universe is full to bursting with both strange alien races *and* curiously mutated variations on the normal human stock (this is one of Vance's major themes, in fact: how plastic and changeable the stuff of human nature is, how what we think of as "humanity" itself can be shaped and molded like wax, under the proper sort of environmental pressures, often with profoundly disturbing results), and there is little in his work that resembles either the broad social satire popular in *Galaxy* magazine at the time under H. L. Gold or the sober speculations about the impact of scientific advancement on current human society that was *Astounding*'s preferred stock-in-trade. The irony is that, in retrospect, the stuff he was writing for those lowly "salvage markets" seems just as significant—if not *more* significant—as most of the stuff that was appearing in the more-respectable magazines, ostensibly at the forefront of the field.

In fact, Vance would do some of his best early work for magazines such as *Thrilling Wonder Stories* and *Startling Stories* and the short-lived *Worlds Beyond* in the mid '50s—"The Five Gold Bands," "Abercrombie Station," "The Houses of Izam," "The Kokod Warriors" and the other "Magnus Ridolph" stories, and the magazine version of "Big Planet," among others.

The story that follows, "The New Prime," one of Vance's best from that period, is yet another demonstration of the ease and fertility of his imagination; instead of settling for *one* background for the story, as most writers would have done, Vance—glorying in his strength and inventiveness—gives us *five* instead, each as rich, evocative, and ornate as the others—and each capable, in the hands of an ordinary writer, of having served as the background for an entire novel all by itself. Vance, though, as you will see, is no ordinary writer . . .

By the late '50s and early '60s, Vance was doing some of his best work, and some of the best work of the period, most of it by this time for the new Pohl *Galaxy* and for *F&SF*—"The Men Return," the underrated *The Languages of Pao* (one of only a handful of books even today to deal with semantics as a science; Delany *Babel-17* and Ian Watson's *The Embedding* are two later examples), the wonderful *The Star King* and *The Killing Machine* (two of the best hybrids of SF and the mystery/espionage novel ever written), "Green Magic," *The Blue World,* "The Dragon Master," "The Last Castle," and many others. Throughout the '70s and into the '80s, he would continue to produce a steady stream of memorable work, including the brilliant *Emphyrio, The Anome, Trullion: Alastor 2262,* the "Planet of Adventure" series, *The Face, The Book of Dreams,* and at least a dozen others.

By the '90s, ironically enough, the erosion of the midlist by a changing publishing environment had driven Vance, once the King of the Paperback Shelves, out of mass-market altogether. Although much of Vance's work *is* still in print, it's largely available as expensive hardcovers from small-press specialty publishers such as Underwood-Miller (now known just as Charles F. Miller, after the business partnership split up), who've made something of a pocket industry out of reprinting Vance novels (contact them at Charles F. Miller, 708 Westover Drive, Lancaster, PA 17601, for a listing of Vance titles available); this is an ironic turnaround from the old days, when almost nothing by Vance was available in a hardcover edition, but almost all of his titles were available in paperback—now, it's just the reverse! Recently, Tor has been bringing some of Vance's novels back into print in omnibus trade paperback editions, reprinting his "Demon Princess" series, for instance, in two omnibus volumes, and collecting three of his "Alastor" novels in the omnibus *Alastor*—the recent *Night Lamp* is also available as a trade paperback—and this may be the best and most cost-effective place to sample his work, although some of Vance's old mass-market paperbacks still turn up fairly often in used-book stores.

Vance has won two Hugo Awards, a Nebula Award, two World Fantasy Awards (one the prestigious Life Achievement Award), a Grandmaster Nebula Award for Life Achievement, and the Edgar Award for best mystery novel. His other books include *The Palace of Love, City of the Chasch, The Dirdir, The Pnume, The Gray Prince, The Brave Free Men, Space Opera, Showboat World, Marune: Alastor 933, Wyst: Alastor 1716, Lyonesse, The Green Pearl, Madouc, Araminta Station, Ecce and Olde Earth,* and *Throy,* among many others. His short fiction has been collected in *Eight Fantasms and Magics, The Best of Jack Vance, Green Magic, Lost Moons, The Complete Magnus Ridolph, The World Between and Other Stories, The Dark Side of the Moon,* and *The Narrow Land.* His most recent books are the novels *Night Lamp* and *Ports of Call.*

Music, carnival lights, the slide of feet on waxed oak, perfume, muffled talk and laughter.

Arthur Caversham of twentieth-century Boston felt air along his skin, and discovered himself to be stark naked.

It was at Janice Paget's coming-out party: three hundred guests in formal evening-wear surrounded him.

For a moment he felt no emotion beyond vague bewilderment. His presence seemed the outcome of logical events, but his memory was fogged and he could find no definite anchor of certainty.

He stood a little apart from the rest of the stag line, facing the red and gold calliope where the orchestra sat. The buffet, the punch bowl, the champagne wagons, tended by clowns, were to his right; to the left, through the open flap of the circus tent, lay the garden, now lit by strings of colored lights, red, green, yellow, blue, and he caught a glimpse of a merry-go-round across the lawn.

Why was he here? He had no recollection, no sense of purpose. . . . The night was warm; the other young men in the full-dress suits must feel rather sticky, he thought. . . . An idea tugged at a corner of his mind. There was a significant aspect of the affair that he was overlooking.

He noticed that the young men nearby had moved away from him. He heard chortles of amusement, astonished exclamations. A girl dancing past saw him over the arm of her escort; she gave a startled squeak, jerked her eyes away, giggling and blushing.

Something was wrong. These young men and women were startled and amazed by his naked skin to the point of embarrassment. The gnaw of urgency came closer to the surface. He must do something. Taboos felt with such intensity might not be violated without unpleasant consequences; such was his understanding. He was lacking garments; these he must obtain.

He looked about him, inspecting the young men who watched him with ribald delight, disgust, or curiosity. To one of these latter he addressed himself.

"Where can I get some clothing?"

The young man shrugged. "Where did you leave yours?"

Two heavyset men in dark blue uniforms entered the tent; Arthur Caversham saw them from the corner of his eye, and his mind worked with desperate intensity.

This young man seemed typical of those around him. What sort of appeal would have meaning for him? Like any other human being, he could be moved to action if the right chord were struck. By what method could he be moved?

Sympathy?

Threats?

The prospect of advantage or profit?

Caversham rejected all of these. By violating the taboo he had forfeited his claim to sympathy. A threat would excite derision, and he had

no profit or advantage to offer. The stimulus must be more devious. . . .
He reflected that young men customarily banded together in secret societies. In the thousand cultures he had studied this was almost infallibly
true. Long-houses, drug-cults, tongs, instruments of sexual initiation—
whatever the name, the external aspects were near-identical: painful initiation, secret signs and passwords, uniformity of group conduct,
obligation to service. If this young man were a member of such an association, he might react to an appeal to this group-spirit.

Arthur Caversham said, "I've been put in this taboo situation by the
brotherhood; in the name of the brotherhood, find me some suitable garments."

The young man stared, taken aback. "Brotherhood? . . . You mean
fraternity?" Enlightenment spread over his face. "Is this some kind of
hell-week stunt?" He laughed. "If it is, they sure go all the way."

"Yes," said Arthur Caversham. "My fraternity."

The young man said, "This way, then—and hurry, here comes the
law. We'll take off under the tent. I'll lend you my topcoat till you make
it back to your house."

The two uniformed men, pushing quietly through the dancers, were
almost upon them. The young man lifted the flap of the tent, Arthur
Caversham ducked under, his friend followed. Together they ran through
the many-colored shadows to a little booth painted with gay red and
white stripes that was near the entrance to the tent.

"You stay back, out of sight," said the young man. "I'll check out my
coat."

"Fine," said Arthur Caversham.

The young man hesitated. "What's your house? Where do you go to
school?"

Arthur Caversham desperately searched his mind for an answer. A
single fact reached the surface.

"I'm from Boston."

"Boston U? Or MIT? Or Harvard?"

"Harvard."

"Ah." The young man nodded. "I'm Washington and Lee myself.
What's your house?"

"I'm not supposed to say."

"Oh," said the young man, puzzled but satisfied. "Well—just a
minute. . . ."

Bearwald the Halforn halted, numb with despair and exhaustion. The
remnants of his platoon sank to the ground around him, and they stared
back to where the rim of the night flickered and glowed with fire. Many

villages, many wood-gabled farmhouses had been given the torch, and the Brands from Mount Medallion reveled in human blood.

The pulse of a distant drum touched Bearwald's skin, a deep *thrumm-thrumm-thrumm,* almost inaudible. Much closer he heard a hoarse human cry of fright, then exultant killing-calls, not human. The Brands were tall, black, man-shaped but not men. They had eyes like lamps of red glass, bright white teeth, and tonight they seemed bent on slaughtering all the men of the world.

"Down," hissed Kanaw, his right arm-guard, and Bearwald crouched. Across the flaring sky marched a column of tall Brand warriors, rocking jauntily, without fear.

Bearwald said suddenly, "Men—we are thirteen. Fighting arm to arm with these monsters we are helpless. Tonight their total force is down from the mountain; the hive must be near deserted. What can we lose if we undertake to burn the home-hive of the Brands? Only our lives, and what are these now?"

Kanaw said, "Our lives are nothing; let us be off at once."

"May our vengeance be great," said Broctan the left arm-guard. "May the home-hive of the Brands be white ashes this coming morn. . . ."

Mount Medallion loomed overhead; the oval hive lay in Pangborn Valley. At the mouth of the valley, Bearwald divided the platoon into two halves, and placed Kanaw in the van of the second. "We move silently twenty yards apart; thus if either party rouses a Brand, the other may attack from the rear and so kill the monster before the vale is roused. Do all understand?"

"We understand."

"Forward then, to the hive."

The valley reeked with an odor like sour leather. From the direction of the hive came a muffled clanging. The ground was soft, covered with runner moss; careful feet made no sound. Crouching low, Bearwald could see the shapes of his men against the sky—here indigo with a violent rim. The angry glare of burning Echevasa lay down the slope to the south.

A sound. Bearwald hissed, and the columns froze. They waited. *Thud-thud-thud-thud* came the steps—then a hoarse cry of rage and alarm.

"Kill, kill the beast!" yelled Bearwald.

The Brand swung his club like a scythe, lifting one man, carrying the body around with the after-swing. Bearwald leapt close, struck with his blade, slicing as he hewed; he felt the tendons part, smelled the hot gush of Brand blood.

The clanging had stopped now, and Brand cries carried across the night.

"Forward," panted Bearwald. "Out with your tinder, strike fire to the hive. Burn, burn, burn. . . ."

Abandoning stealth he ran forward; ahead loomed the dark dome. Immature Brands came surging forth, squeaking and squalling, and with them came the genetrices—twenty-foot monsters crawling on hands and feet, grunting and snapping as they moved.

"Kill!" yelled Bearwald the Halforn. "Kill! Fire, fire, fire!"

He dashed to the hive, crouched, struck spark to tinder, puffed. The rag, soaked with saltpeter, flared; Bearwald fed it straw, thrust it against the hive. The reed-pulp and withe crackled.

He leapt up as a horde of young Brands darted at him. His blade rose and fell; they were cleft, no match for his frenzy. Creeping close came the great Brand genetrices, three of them, swollen of abdomen, exuding an odor vile to his nostrils.

"Out with the fire!" yelled the first. "Fire, out. The Great Mother is tombed within; she lies too fecund to move. . . . Fire, woe, destruction!" And they wailed, "Where are the mighty? Where are our warriors?"

Thrumm-thrumm-thrumm came the sound of skindrums. Up the valley rolled the echo of hoarse Brand voices.

Bearwald stood with his back to the blaze. He darted forward, severed the head of a creeping genetrix, jumped back. . . . Where were his men? "Kanaw!" he called. "Laida! Theyat! Gyorg! Broctan!"

He craned his neck, saw the flicker of fires. "Men! Kill the creeping mothers!" And leaping forward once more, he hacked and hewed, and another genetrix sighed and groaned and rolled flat.

The Brand voices changed to alarm; the triumphant drumming halted; the thud of footsteps came loud.

At Bearwald's back the hive burnt with a pleasant heat. Within came a shrill keening, a cry of vast pain.

In the leaping blaze he saw the charging Brand warriors. Their eyes glared like embers, their teeth shone like white sparks. They came forward, swinging their clubs, and Bearwald gripped his sword, too proud to flee.

After grounding his air sled Ceistan sat a few minutes inspecting the dead city Therlatch: a wall of earthen brick a hundred feet high, a dusty portal, and a few crumbled roofs lifting above the battlements. Behind the city the desert spread across the near, middle, and far distance to the hazy shapes of the Allune Mountains at the horizon, pink in the light of the twin suns Mig and Pag.

Scouting from above he had seen no sign of life, nor had he expected any, after a thousand years of abandonment. Perhaps a few sand-crawlers wallowed in the heat of the accident bazaar. Otherwise the streets would feel his presence with great surprise.

Jumping from the air sled, Ceistan advanced toward the portal. He passed under, stood looking right and left with interest. In the parched air the brick buildings stood almost eternal. The wind smoothed and rounded all harsh angles; the glass had been cracked by the heat of day and chill of night; heaps of sand clogged the passageways.

Three streets led away from the portal and Ceistan could find nothing to choose between them. Each was dusty, narrow, and each twisted out of his line of vision after a hundred yards.

Ceistan rubbed his chin thoughtfully. Somewhere in the city lay a brassbound coffer, containing the Crown and Shield Parchment. This, according to tradition, set a precedent for the fiefholder's immunity from energy-tax. Glay, who was Ceistan's liege-lord, having cited the parchment as justification for his delinquency, had been challenged to show validity. Now he lay in prison on charge of rebellion, and in the morning he would be nailed to the bottom of an air sled and sent drifting into the west, unless Ceistan returned with the parchment.

After a thousand years, there was small cause for optimism, thought Ceistan. However, the lord Glay was a fair man and he would leave no stone unturned. . . . If it existed, the chest presumably would lie in state, in the town's Legalic, or the Mosque, or in the Hall of Relics, or possibly in the Sumptuar. He would search all of these, allowing two hours per building; the eight hours so used would see the end to the pink daylight.

At random he entered the street in the center and shortly came to a plaza at whose far end rose the Legalic, the Hall of Records and Decisions. At the façade Ceistan paused, for the interior was dim and gloomy. No sound came from the dusty void save the sigh and whisper of the dry wind. He entered.

The great hall was empty. The walls were illuminated with frescoes of red and blue, as bright as if painted yesterday. There were six to each wall, the top half displaying a criminal act and the bottom half the penalty.

Ceistan passed through the hall, into the chambers behind. He found but dust and the smell of dust. Into the crypts he ventured, and these were lit by embrasures. There was much litter and rubble, but no brass coffer.

Up and out into the clean air he went, and strode across the plaza to the Mosque, where he entered under the massive architrave.

The Nunciator's Confirmatory lay wide and bare and clean, for the tessellated floor was swept by a powerful draft. A thousand apertures opened from the low ceiling, each communicating with a cell overhead; thus arranged so that the devout might seek counsel with the Nunciator as he passed below without disturbing their attitudes of supplication. In the center of the pavilion a disk of glass roofed a recess. Below was a coffer and in the coffer rested a brass-bound chest. Ceistan sprang down the steps in high hopes.

But the chest contained jewels—the tiara of the Old Queen, the chest vellopes of the Gonwand Corps, the great ball, half emerald, half ruby, which in the ancient ages was rolled across the plaza to signify the passage of the old year.

Ceistan tumbled them all back in the coffer. Relics on this planet of dead cities had no value, and synthetic gems were infinitely superior in luminosity and water.

Leaving the Mosque, he studied the height of the suns. The zenith was past, the moving balls of pink fire leaned to the west. He hesitated, frowning and blinking at the hot earthen walls, considering that not impossibly both coffer and parchment were fable, like so many others regarding dead Therlatch.

A gust of wind swirled across the plaza and Ceistan choked on a dry throat. He spat, and an acrid taste bit his tongue. An old fountain opened in the wall nearby; he examined it wistfully, but water was not even a memory along these dead streets.

Once again he cleared his throat, spat, turned across the city toward the Hall of Relics.

He entered the great nave, past square pillars built of earthen brick. Pink shafts of light struck down from the cracks and gaps in the roof, and he was like a midge in the vast space. To all sides were niches cased in glass, and each held an object of ancient reverence: the armor in which Plange the Forewarned led the Blue Flags; the coronet of the First Serpent; an array of antique Padang skulls; Princess Thermosteraliam's bridal gown of woven cobweb palladium, as fresh as the day she wore it; the original Tablets of Legality; the great conch throne of an early dynasty; a dozen other objects. But the coffer was not among them.

Ceistan sought for entrance to a possible crypt, but except where the currents of dusty air had channeled grooves in the porphyry, the floor was smooth.

Out once more into the dead streets, and now the suns had passed behind the crumbled roofs, leaving the streets in magenta shadow.

With leaden feet, burning throat, and a sense of defeat, Ceistan turned to the Sumptuar, on the citadel. Up the wide steps, under the verdigris-fronted portico into a lobby painted with vivid frescoes. These depicted the maidens of ancient Therlatch at work, at play, amid sorrow and joy; slim creatures with short, black hair and glowing ivory skin, as graceful as water vanes, as round and delectable as chermoyan plums. Ceistan passed through the lobby with many side-glances, reflecting that these ancient creatures of delight were now the dust he trod under his feet.

He walked down a corridor which made a circuit of the building, and from which the chambers and apartments of the Sumptuar might be entered. The wisps of a wonderful rug crunched under his feet, and the walls displayed moldy tatters, once tapestries of the finest weave. At the entrance to each chamber a fresco pictured the Sumptuar maiden and the sign she served; at each of these chambers Ceistan paused, made a quick investigation, and so passed on to the next. The beams slanting in through the cracks served him as a gauge of time, and they flattened ever more toward the horizontal.

Chamber after chamber after chamber. There were chests in some, altars in others, cases of manifestos, triptychs, and fonts in others. But never the chest he sought.

And ahead was the lobby where he had entered the building. Three more chambers were to be searched, then the light would be gone.

He came to the first of these, and this was hung with a new curtain. Pushing it aside, he found himself looking into an outside court, full in the long light of the twin suns. A fountain of water trickled down across steps of apple-green jade into a garden as soft and fresh and green as any in the north. And rising in alarm from a couch was a maiden, as vivid and delightful as any in the frescoes. She had short, dark hair, a face as pure and delicate as the great white frangipani she wore over her ear.

For an instant Ceistan and the maiden stared eye to eye; then her alarm faded and she smiled shyly.

"Who are you?" Ceistan asked in wonder. "Are you a ghost or do you live here in the dust?"

"I am real," she said. "My home is to the south, at the Palram Oasis, and this is the period of solitude to which all maidens of the race submit when aspiring for Upper Instruction. . . . So without fear may you come beside me, and rest, and drink of fruit wine and be my companion through the lonely night, for this is my last week of solitude and I am weary of my aloneness."

Ceistan took a step forward, then hesitated. "I must fulfill my mission. I seek the brass coffer containing the Crown and Shield Parchment. Do you know of this?"

She shook her head. "It is nowhere in the Sumptuar." She rose to her feet, stretching her ivory arms as a kitten stretches. "Abandon your search, and come let me refresh you."

Ceistan looked at her, looked up at the fading light, looked down the corridor to the two doors yet remaining. "First I must complete my search; I owe duty to my lord Glay, who will be nailed under an air sled and sped west unless I bring him aid."

The maiden said with a pout, "Go then to your dusty chamber; and go with a dry throat. You will find nothing, and if you persist so stubbornly, I will be gone when you return."

"So let it be," said Ceistan.

He turned away, marched down the corridor. The first chamber was bare and dry as a bone. In the second and last, a man's skeleton lay tumbled in a corner; this Ceistan saw in the last rosy light of the twin suns.

There was no brass coffer, no parchment. So Glay must die, and Ceistan's heart hung heavy.

He returned to the chamber where he had found the maiden, but she had departed. The fountain had been stopped, and moisture only filmed the stones.

Ceistan called, "Maiden, where are you? Return; my obligation is at an end. . . ."

There was no response.

Ceistan shrugged, turned to the lobby and so outdoors, to grope his way through the deserted twilight street to the portal and his air sled.

Dobnor Daksat became aware that the big man in the embroidered black cloak was speaking to him.

Orienting himself to his surroundings, which were at once familiar and strange, he also became aware that the man's voice was condescending, supercilious.

"You are competing in a highly advanced classification," he said. "I marvel at your . . . ah, confidence." And he eyed Daksat with a gleaming and speculative eye.

Daksat looked down at the floor, frowned at the sight of his clothes. He wore a long cloak of black-purple velvet, swinging like a bell around his ankles. His trousers were of scarlet corduroy, tight at the waist, thigh, and calf, with a loose puff of green cloth between calf and ankle. The clothes were his own, obviously: they looked wrong and right at once, as did the carved gold knuckle-guards he wore on his hands.

The big man in the dark cloak continued speaking, looking at a point over Daksat's head, as if Daksat were nonexistent.

"Clauktaba has won Imagist honors over the years. Bel-Washab was the Korsi Victor last month; Tol Morabait is an acknowledged master of the technique. And then there is Ghisel Ghang of West Ind, who knows no peer in the creation of fire-stars, and Pulakt Havjorska, the Champion of the Island Realm. So it becomes a matter of skepticism whether you, new, inexperienced, without a fund of images, can do more than embarrass us all with your mental poverty."

Daksat's brain was yet wrestling with his bewilderment, and he could feel no strong resentment at the big man's evident contempt. He said, "Just what is all this? I'm not sure that I understand my position."

The man in the black cloak inspected him quizzically. "So, now you commence to experience trepidation? Justly, I assure you." He sighed, waved his hands. "Well, well—young men will be impetuous, and perhaps you have formed images you considered not discreditable. In any event, the public eye will ignore you for the glories of Clauktaba's geometrics and Ghisel Ghang's star-bursts. Indeed, I counsel you, keep your images small, drab, and confined; you will so avoid the faults of bombast and discord. . . . Now, it is time to go to your Imagicon. This way, then. Remember, grays, browns, lavenders, perhaps a few tones of ocher and rust; then the spectators will understand that you compete for the schooling alone, and do not actively challenge the masters. This way then. . . ."

He opened a door and led Dobnor Daksat up a stair and so out into the night.

They stood in a great stadium, facing six great screens forty feet high. Behind them in the dark sat tier upon tier of spectators—thousands and thousands, and their sounds came as a soft crush. Daksat turned to see them, but all their faces and their individualities had melted into the entity as a whole.

"Here," said the big man, "this is your apparatus. Seat yourself and I will adjust the ceretemps."

Daksat suffered himself to be placed in a heavy chair, so soft and deep that he felt himself to be floating. Adjustments were made at his head and neck and the bridge of his nose. He felt a sharp prick, a pressure, a throb, and then a soothing warmth. From the distance, a voice called out over the crowd:

"Two minutes to gray mist! Two minutes to gray mist! Attend, Imagists, two minutes to gray mist!"

The big man stooped over him. "Can you see well?"

Daksat raised himself a trifle. "Yes . . . all is clear."

"Very well. At 'gray mist,' this little filament will glow. When it dies, then it is your screen, and you must imagine your best."

The far voice said, "One minute to gray mist! The order is Pulakt Havjorska, Tol Morabait, Ghisel Ghang, Dobnor Daksat, Clauktaba, and Bel-Washab. There are no handicaps; all colors and shapes are permitted. Relax then, ready your lobes, and now—gray mist!"

The light glowed on the panel of Daksat's chair, and he saw five of the six screens light to a pleasant pearl-gray, swirling a trifle as if agitated, excited. Only the screen before him remained dull. The big man, who stood behind him, reached down, prodded. "Gray mist, Daksat; are you deaf and blind?"

Daksat thought gray mist, and instantly his screen sprang to life, displaying a cloud of silver-gray, clean and clear.

"Humph," he heard the big man snort. "Somewhat dull and without interest—but I suppose good enough. . . . See how Cluktaba's rings with hints of passion already, quivers with emotion."

And Daksat, noting the screen to his right, saw this to be true. The gray, without actually displaying color, flowed and filmed as if suppressing a vast flood of light.

Now, to the far left, on Pulakt Havjorska's screen, color glowed. It was a gambit image, modest and restrained—a green jewel dripping a rain of blue and silver drops which struck a black ground and disappeared in little orange explosions.

Then Tol Morabait's screen glowed: a black and white checkerboard with certain of the squares flashing suddenly green, red, blue, and yellow—warm, searching colors, pure as shafts from a rainbow. The image disappeared in a flush mingled of rose and blue.

Ghisel Ghang wrought a circle of yellow which quivered, brought forth a green halo, which in turn bulged giving rise to a larger band of brilliant black and white. In the center formed a complex kaleidoscopic pattern. The pattern suddenly vanished in a brilliant flash of light; on the screen for an instant or two appeared the identical pattern in a complete new suit of colors. A ripple of sound from the spectators greeted this *tour de force*.

The light on Daksat's panel died. Behind him he felt a prod. "Now."

Daksat eyed the screen and his mind was blank of ideas. He ground his teeth. Anything. Anything. A picture . . . he imagined a view across the meadowlands beside the River Melramy.

"Hm," said the big man behind him. "Pleasant. A pleasant fantasy, and rather original."

Puzzled, Daksat examined the picture on the screen. So far as he could distinguish, it was an uninspired reproduction of a scene he knew well. Fantasy? Was that what was expected? Very well, he'd produce fantasy. He imagined the meadows glowing, molten, white-hot. The vegetation, the old cairns slumped into a viscous seethe. The surface smoothed, became a mirror which reflected the Copper Crags.

Behind him the big man grunted. "A little heavy-handed, that last, and thereby you destroyed the charming effect of those unearthly colors and shapes. . . ."

Daksat slumped back in his chair, frowning, eager for his turn to come again.

Meanwhile Clauktaba created a dainty white blossom with purple stamens on a green stalk. The petals wilted, the stamens discharged a cloud of swirling yellow pollen.

Then Bel-Washab, at the end of the line, painted his screen a luminous underwater green. It rippled, bulged, and a black irregular blot marred the surface. From the center of the blot seeped a trickle of hot gold that quickly meshed and veined the black blot.

Such was the first passage.

There was a pause of several seconds. "Now," breathed the voice behind Daksat, "now the competition begins."

On Pulakt Havjorska's screen appeared an angry sea of color: waves of red, green, blue, an ugly mottling. Dramatically, a yellow shape appeared at the lower right, vanquished the chaos. It spread over the screen, the center went lime-green. A black shape appeared split, bowed softly and easily to both sides. Then turning, the two shapes wandered into the background, twisting, bending with supple grace. Far down a perspective they merged, darted forward like a lance, spread out into a series of lances, formed a slanting pattern of slim black bars.

"Superb!" hissed the big man. "The timing, so just, so exact!"

Tol Morabait replied with a fuscous brown field threaded with crimson lines and blots. Vertical green hatching formed at the left, strode across the screen to the right. The brown field pressed forward, bulged through the green bars, pressed hard, broke, and segments flitted forward to leave the screen. On the black background behind the green hatching, which now faded, lay a human brain, pink, pulsing. The brain sprouted six insectlike legs, scuttled crabwise back into the distance.

Ghisel Ghang brought forth one of his fire-bursts—a small pellet of bright blue exploding in all directions, the tips working and writhing through wonderful patterns in the five colors, blue, violet, white, purple, and light green.

Dobnor Daksat, rigid as a bar, sat with hands clenched and teeth grinding into teeth. Now! Was not his brain as excellent as those of the far lands? Now!

On the screen appeared a tree, conventionalized in greens and blues, and each leaf was a tongue of fire. From these fire wisps of smoke arose on high to form a cloud which worked and swirled, then emptied a cone of rain about the tree. The flames vanished and in their places appeared starshaped white flowers. From the cloud came a bolt of lightning, shattering the tree to agonized fragments of glass. Another bolt into the brittle heap and the screen exploded in a great gout of white, orange, and black.

The voice of the big man said doubtfully, "On the whole, well done, but mind my warning, and create more modest images, since—"

"Silence!" said Dobnor Daksat in a harsh voice.

So the competition went, round after round of spectacles, some sweet as canmel honey, others as violent as the storms that circle the poles. Color strove with color, patterns evolved and changed, sometimes in glorious cadence, sometimes in the bitter discord necessary to the strength of the image.

And Daksat built dream after dream, while his tension vanished, and he forgot all save the racing pictures in his mind and on the screen, and his images became as complex and subtle as those of the masters.

"One more passage," said the big man behind Daksat, and now the imagists brought forth the master-dreams: Pulakt Havjorska, the growth and decay of a beautiful city; Tol Morabait, a quiet composition of green and white interrupted by a marching army of insects who left a dirty wake, and who were joined in battle by men in painted leather armor and tall hats, armed with short swords and flails. The insects were destroyed and chased off the screen; the dead warriors became bones and faded to twinkling blue dust. Ghisel Ghang created three fire-bursts simultaneously, each different, a gorgeous display.

Daksat imagined a smooth pebble, magnified it to a block of marble, chipped it away to create the head of a beautiful maiden. For a moment she stared forth and varying emotions crossed her face—joy at her sudden existence, pensive thought, and at last fright. Her eyes turned milky opaque blue, the face changed to a laughing sardonic mask, black-cheeked with a fleering mouth. The head tilted, the mouth spat into the air. The head flattened into a black background, the drops of spittle shone like fire, became stars, constellations, and one of these expanded, became a planet with configurations dear to Daksat's heart. The planet hurtled off into darkness, the constellations faded. Dobnor Daksat relaxed. His last image. He sighed, exhausted.

The big man in the black cloak removed the harness in brittle silence. At last he asked, "The planet you imagined in that last screening, was that a creation or a remembrance of actuality? It was none of our system here, and it rang with the clarity of truth."

Dobnor Daksat stared at him, puzzled, and the words faltered in his throat. "But it is—home! This world! Was it not this world?"

The big man looked at him strangely, shrugged, turned away. "In a moment now the winner of the contest will be made known and the jeweled brevet awarded."

The day was gusty and overcast, the galley was low and black, manned by the oarsmen of Belaclaw. Ergan stood on the poop, staring across the two miles of bitter sea to the coast of Racland, where he knew the sharp-faced Racs stood watching from the headlands.

A gout of water erupted a few hundred yards astern.

Ergan spoke to the helmsman. "Their guns have better range than we bargained for. Better stand offshore another mile and we'll take our chances with the current."

Even as he spoke, there came a great whistle and he glimpsed a black pointed projectile slanting down at him. It struck the waist of the galley, exploded. Timber, bodies, metal flew everywhere, and the galley laid its broken back into the water, doubled up and sank.

Ergan, jumping clear, discarded his sword, casque, and greaves almost as he hit the chill gray water. Gasping from the shock, he swam in circles, bobbing up and down in the chop; then, finding a length of timber, he clung to it for support.

From the shores of Racland a longboat put forth and approached, bow churning white foam as it rose and fell across the waves. Ergan turned loose the timber and swam as rapidly as possible from the wreck. Better drowning than capture; there would be more mercy from the famine-fish that swarmed the waters than from the pitiless Racs.

So he swam, but the current took him to the shore, and at last, struggling feebly, he was cast upon a pebbly beach.

Here he was discovered by a gang of Rac youths and marched to a nearby command post. He was tied and flung into a cart and so conveyed to the city Korsapan.

In a gray room he was seated facing an intelligence officer of the Rac secret police, a man with the gray skin of a toad, a moist gray mouth, eager, searching eyes.

"You are Ergan," said the officer. "Emissary to the Bargee of Salomdek. What was your mission?"

Ergan stared back eye to eye, hoping that a happy and convincing response would find his lips. None came, and the truth would incite an immediate invasion of both Belaclaw and Salomdek by the tall, thin-headed Rac soldiers, who wore black uniforms and black boots.

Ergan said nothing. The officer leaned forward. "I ask you once more; then you will be taken to the room below." He said "Room Below" as if the words were capitalized, and he said it with soft relish.

Ergan, in a cold sweat, for he knew of the Rac torturers, said, "I am not Ergan; my name is Ervard; I am an honest trader in pearls."

"This is untrue," said the Rac. "Your aide was captured, and under the compression pump he blurted up your name with his lungs."

"I am Ervard," said Ergan, his bowels quaking.

The Rac signaled. "Take him to the Room Below."

A man's body, which has developed nerves as outposts against danger, seems especially intended for pain, and cooperates wonderfully with the craft of the torturer. These characteristics of the body had been studied by the Rac specialists, and other capabilities of the human nervous system had been blundered upon by accident. It had been found that certain programs of pressure, heat, strain, friction, torque, surge, jerk, sonic and visual shock, vermin, stench, and vileness created cumulative effects, whereas a single method, used to excess, lost its stimulation thereby.

All this lore and cleverness was lavished upon Ergan's citadel of nerves, and they inflicted upon him the entire gamut of pain: the sharp twinges, the dull, lasting joint-aches which groaned by night, the fiery flashes, the assaults of filth and lechery, together with shocks of occasional tenderness when he would be allowed to glimpse the world he had left.

Then back to the Room Below.

But always: "I am Ervard the trader." And always he tried to goad his mind over the tissue barrier to death, but always the mind hesitated at the last toppling step, and Ergan lived.

The Racs tortured by routine, so that the expectation, the approach of the hour, brought as much torment as the act itself. And then the heavy, unhurried steps outside the cell, the feeble thrashing around to evade, the harsh laughs when they cornered him and carried him forth, and the harsh laughs when three hours later they threw him sobbing and whimpering back to the pile of straw that was his bed.

"I am Ervard," he said, and trained his mind to believe that this was the truth, so that never would they catch him unaware. "I am Ervard! I am Ervard, I trade in pearls!"

He tried to strangle himself on straw, but a slave watched always, and this was not permitted.

He attempted to die by self-suffocation, and would have been glad to succeed, but always as he sank into blessed numbness, so did his mind relax and his motor nerves take up the mindless business of breathing once more.

He ate nothing, but this meant little to the Racs, as they injected him full of tonics, sustaining drugs, and stimulants, so that he might always be keyed to the height of his awareness.

"I am Ervard," said Ergan, and the Racs gritted their teeth angrily. The case was now a challenge; he defied their ingenuity, and they puzzled long and carefully upon refinements and delicacies, new shapes to the iron tools, new types of jerk ropes, new directions for the strains and pressures. Even when it was no longer important whether he was Ergan or Ervard, since war now raged, he was kept and maintained as a problem, an ideal case; so he was guarded and cosseted with even more than usual care, and the Rac torturers mulled over their techniques, making changes here, improvements there.

Then one day the Belaclaw galleys landed and the feather-crested soldiers fought past the walls of Korsapan.

The Racs surveyed Ergan with regret. "Now we must go, and still you will not submit to us."

"I am Ervard," croaked that which lay on the table. "Ervard the trader."

A splintering crash sounded overhead.

"We must go," said the Racs. "Your people have stormed the city. If you tell the truth, you may live. If you lie, we kill you. So there is your choice. Your life for the truth."

"The truth?" muttered Ergan. "It is a trick—" And then he caught the victory chant of the Belaclaw soldiery. "The truth? Why not? . . . Very well." And he said, "I am Ervard," for now he believed this to be the truth.

Galactic Prime was a lean man with reddish-brown hair, sparse across a fine arch of skull. His face, undistinguished otherwise, was given power by great dark eyes flickering with a light like fire behind smoke. Physically, he had passed the peak of his youth; his arms and legs were thin and loose-jointed; his head inclined forward as if weighted by the intricate machinery of his brain.

Arising from the couch, smiling faintly, he looked across the arcade to the eleven Elders. They sat at a table of polished wood, backs to a wall festooned with vines. They were grave men, slow in their motions, and their faces were lined with wisdom and insight. By the ordained system, Prime was the executive of the universe, the Elders the deliberative body, invested with certain restrictive powers.

"Well?"

The Chief Elder without haste raised his eyes from the computer. "You are the first to arise from the couch."

Prime turned a glance up the arcade, still smiling faintly. The others lay variously: some with arms clenched, rigid as bars; others huddled in fetal postures. One had slumped from the couch half to the floor; his eyes were open, staring at remoteness.

Prime returned his gaze to the Chief Elder, who watched him with detached curiosity. "Has the optimum been established?"

The Chief Elder consulted the computer. "Twenty-six thirty-seven is the optimum score."

Prime waited, but the Chief Elder said no more. Prime stepped to the alabaster balustrade beyond the couches. He leaned forward, looked out across the vista—miles and miles of sunny haze, with a twinkling sea in the distance. A breeze blew past his face, ruffling the scant russet strands of his hair. He took a deep breath, flexed his fingers and hands, for the memory of the Rac torturers was still heavy on his mind. After a moment he swung around, leaned back, resting his elbows upon the balustrade. He glanced once more down the line of couches; there were still no signs of vitality from the candidates.

"Twenty-six thirty-seven," he muttered. "I venture to estimate my own score at twenty-five ninety. In the last episode I recall an incomplete retention of personality."

"Twenty-five seventy-four," said the Chief Elder. "The computer judged Bearwald the Halforn's final defiance of the Brand warriors unprofitable."

Prime considered. "The point is well made. Obstinacy serves no purpose unless it advances a predetermined end. It is a flaw I must seek to temper." He looked along the line of Elders, from face to face. "You make no enunciations, you are curiously mute."

He waited; the Chief Elder made no response.

"May I inquire the high score?"

"Twenty-five seventy-four."

Prime nodded. "Mine."

"Yours is the high score," said the Chief Elder.

Prime's smile disappeared: a puzzled line appeared across his brow. "In spite of this, you are still reluctant to confirm my second span of authority; there are still doubts among you."

"Doubts and misgivings," replied the Chief Elder.

Prime's mouth pulled in at the corners, although his brows were still raised in polite inquiry. "Your attitude puzzles me. My record is one of selfless service. My intelligence is phenomenal, and in this final test, which I designed to dispel your last doubts, I attained the highest score. I have proved my social intuition and flexibility, my leadership, devotion to duty, imagination, and resolution. In every commensurable aspect, I fulfill best the qualifications for the office I hold."

The Chief Elder looked up and down the line of his fellows. There were none who wished to speak. The Chief Elder squared himself in his chair, sat back.

"Our attitude is difficult to represent. Everything is as you say. Your intelligence is beyond dispute, your character is exemplary, you have served your term with honor and devotion. You have earned our respect, admiration, and gratitude. We realize also that you seek this second term from praise-worthy motives: you regard yourself as the man best able to coordinate the complex business of the galaxy."

Prime nodded grimly. "But you think otherwise."

"Our position is perhaps not quite so blunt."

"Precisely what is your position?" Prime gestured along the couches.

"Look at these men. They are the finest of the galaxy. One man is dead. That one stirring on the third couch has lost his mind; he is a lunatic. The others are sorely shaken. And never forget that this test has been expressly designed to measure the qualities essential to the Galactic Prime."

"This test has been of great interest to us," said the Chief Elder mildly. "It has considerably affected our thinking."

Prime hesitated, plumbing the unspoken overtones of the words. He came forward, seated himself across from the line of Elders. With a narrow glance he searched the faces of the eleven men, tapped once, twice, three times with his fingertips on the polished wood, leaned back in the chair.

"As I have pointed out, the test has gauged each candidate for the exact qualities essential to the optimum conduct of office, in this fashion: Earth of the twentieth century is a planet of intricate conventions; on Earth the candidate, as Arthur Caversham, is required to use his social intuition—a quality highly important in this galaxy of two billion suns. On Belotsi, Bearwald the Halforn is tested for courage and the ability to conduct positive action. At the dead city Therlatch on Praesepe Three, the candidate, as Ceistan, is rated for devotion to duty, and as Dobnor Daksat at the Imagicon on Staff, his creative conceptions are rated against the most fertile imaginations alive. Finally as Ergan, on Chankozar, his will, persistence, and ultimate fiber are explored to their extreme limits.

"Each candidate is placed in the identical set of circumstances by a trick of temporal, dimensional, and cerebroneural meshing, which is rather complicated for the present discussion. Sufficient that each candidate is objectively rated by his achievements, and that the results are commensurable."

He paused, looked shrewdly along the line of grave faces. "I must emphasize that although I myself designed and arranged the test, I thereby gained no advantage. The mnemonic synapses are entirely disengaged from incident to incident, and only the candidate's basic personality acts. All were tested under precisely the same conditions. In my opinion the scores registered by the computer indicate an objective and reliable index of the candidate's ability for the highly responsible office of Galactic Executive."

The Chief Elder said, "The scores are indeed significant."

"Then—you approve my candidacy?"

The Chief Elder smiled. "Not so fast. Admittedly you are intelligent, admittedly you have accomplished much during your term as Prime. But much remains to be done."

"Do you suggest that another man would have achieved more?"

The Chief Elder shrugged. "I have no conceivable way of knowing. I point out your achievements, such as the Glenart civilization, the Dawn Time on Masilis, the reign of King Karal on Aevir, the suppression of the Arkid Revolt. There are many such examples. But there are also short-comings: the totalitarian governments on Earth, the savagery on Belotsi and Chankozar, so pointedly emphasized in your test. Then there is the decadence of the planets in the Eleven Hundred Ninth Cluster, the rise of the priest-kings on Fiir, and much else."

Prime clenched his mouth and the fires behind his eyes burnt more brightly.

The Chief Elder continued. "One of the most remarkable phenomena of the galaxy is the tendency of humanity to absorb and manifest the personality of the Prime. There seems to be a tremendous resonance which vibrates from the brain of the Prime through the minds of man from Center to the outer fringes. It is a matter which should be studied, analyzed, and subjected to control. The effect is as if every thought of the Prime is magnified a billion-fold, as if every mood sets the tone for a thousand civilizations, every facet of his personality reflects in the ethics of a thousand cultures."

Prime said tonelessly, "I have remarked this phenomenon and have thought much on it. Prime's commands are promulgated in such a way as to exert subtle rather than overt influence; perhaps here is the background of the matter. In any event, the fact of this influence is even more reason to select for the office a man of demonstrated virtue."

"Well put," said the Chief Elder. "Your character is indeed beyond reproach. However, we of the Elders are concerned by the rising tide of authoritarianism among the planets of the galaxy. We suspect that this principle of resonance is at work. You are a man of intense and indomitable will, and we feel that your influence has unwittingly prompted an irruption of autarchies."

Prime was silent a moment. He looked down the line of couches where the other candidates were recovering awareness. They were men of various races: a pale Northkin of Palast, a stocky red Hawolo, a gray-haired gray-eyed Islander from the Sea Planet—each the outstanding man of the planet of his birth. Those who had returned to consciousness sat quietly, collecting their wits, or lay back on the couch, trying to expunge the test from their minds. There had been a toll taken: one lay dead, another bereft of his wits crouched whimpering beside his couch.

The Chief Elder said, "The objectionable aspects of your character are perhaps best exemplified by the test itself."

Prime opened his mouth; the Chief Elder held up his hand. "Let me speak; I will try to deal fairly with you. When I am done, you may say your say.

"I repeat that your basic direction is displayed by the details of the test that you devised. The qualities you measured were those which you considered the most important: that is, those ideals by which you guide your own life. This arrangement I am sure was completely unconscious, and hence completely revealing. You conceive the essential characteristics of the Prime to be social intuition, aggressiveness, loyalty, imagination, and dogged persistence. As a man of strong character you seek to exemplify these ideals in your own conduct; therefore it is not at all surprising that in this test, designed by you, with a scoring system calibrated by you, your score should be highest.

"Let me clarify the idea by an analogy. If the Eagle were conducting a test to determine the King of Beasts, he would rate all the candidates on their ability to fly; necessarily he would win. In this fashion the Mole would consider ability to dig important; by his system of testing *he* would inevitably emerge King of Beasts."

Prime laughed sharply, ran a hand through his sparse red-brown locks. "I am neither Eagle nor Mole."

The Chief Elder shook his head. "No. You are zealous, dutiful, imaginative, indefatigable—so you have demonstrated, as much by specifying tests for these characteristics as by scoring high in these same tests. But conversely, by the very absence of other tests you demonstrate deficiencies in your character."

"And these are?"

"Sympathy. Compassion. Kindness." The Chief Elder settled back in his chair. "Strange. Your predecessor two times removed was rich in these qualities. During his term, the great humanitarian systems based on the idea of human brotherhood sprang up across the universe. Another example of resonance—but I digress."

Prime said with a sardonic twitch of his mouth, "May I ask this: have you selected the next Galactic Prime?"

The Chief Elder nodded. "A definite choice has been made."

"What was his score in the test?"

"By your scoring system—seventeen eighty. He did poorly as Arthur Caversham; he tried to explain the advantages of nudity to the policeman. He lacked the ability to concoct an instant subterfuge; he has little of your quick craft. As Arthur Caversham he found himself naked. He is sincere and straightforward, hence tried to expound the positive motivations for his state, rather than discover the means to evade the penalties."

"Tell me more about this man," said Prime shortly.

"As Bearwald the Halform, he led his band to the hive of the Brands on Mount Medallion, but instead of burning the hive, he called forth to the queen, begging her to end the useless slaughter. She reached out from the doorway, drew him within and killed him. He failed—but the computer still rated him highly on his forthright approach.

"At Therlatch, his conduct was as irreproachable as yours, and at the Imagicon his performance was adequate. Yours approached the brilliance of the Master Imagists, which is high achievement indeed.

"The Rac tortures are the most trying element of the test. You knew well you could resist limitless pain; therefore you ordained that all other candidates must likewise possess this attribute. The new Prime is sadly deficient here. He is sensitive, and the idea of one man intentionally inflicting pain upon another sickens him. I may add that none of the candidates achieved a perfect count in the last episode. Two others equaled your score—"

Prime evinced interest. "Which are they?"

The Chief Elder pointed them out—a tall hard-muscled man with rock-hewn face standing by the alabaster balustrade gazing moodily out across the sunny distance, and a man of middle age who sat with his legs folded under him, watching a point three feet before him with an expression of imperturbable placidity.

"One is utterly obstinate and hard," said the Chief Elder. "He refused to say a single word. The other assumes an outer objectivity when unpleasantness overtakes him. Others among the candidates fared not so well; therapy will be necessary in almost all cases."

Their eyes went to the witless creature with vacant eyes who padded up and down the aisle, humming and muttering quietly to himself.

"The tests were by no means valueless," said the Chief Elder. "We learned a great deal. By your system of scoring, the competition rated you most high. By other standards which we Elders postulated, your place was lower."

With a tight mouth, Prime inquired, "Who is this paragon of altruism, kindliness, sympathy, and generosity?"

The lunatic wandered close, fell on his hands and knees, crawled whimpering to the wall. He pressed his face to the cool stone, stared blankly up at Prime. His mouth hung loose, his chin was wet, his eyes rolled apparently free of each other.

The Chief Elder smiled in great compassion; he stroked the mad creature's head. "This is he. Here is the man we select."

The old Galactic Prime sat silent, mouth compressed, eyes burning like far volcanoes.

At his feet the new Prime, Lord of Two Billion Suns, found a dead leaf, put it into his mouth and began to chew.

C. M. Kornbluth

THAT SHARE OF GLORY

The late C. M. Kornbluth first started selling stories as a teenage prodigy in 1940, making his first sale to *Super Science Stories,* and wrote vast amounts of pulp fiction under many different pseudonyms in the years before World War II, most of it unknown today. Only after the war, in the booming SF scene of the early '50s, did Kornbluth begin to attract some serious attention. As a writer, C. M. Kornbluth first came to widespread prominence with a series of novels written in collaboration with Frederik Pohl, including *The Space Merchants* (one of the most famous SF novels of the '50s), *Gladiator-at-Law* (a book that comes to seem less and less like a satire every time you turn on your television set), *Search the Sky,* and *Wolfbane* (perhaps the best of the Pohl/Kornbluth novels, and decades ahead of its time in its depiction of humans forced to function as plug-in component parts in an organic alien computer); he also produced two fairly routine novels in collaboration with Judith Merril as "Cyril Judd," *Outpost Mars* and *Gunner Cade,* that were moderately well-received at the time but largely forgotten today, as well as two long-forgotten mainstream novels in collaboration with Pohl. As a solo writer—in addition to several mainstream novels under different pseudonyms—he produced three interesting but largely unsuccessful novels (*Not This August,* a Cold War saga about the military conquest of the United States by the USSR, *The Syndic,* a caustic but ultimately somewhat lightweight *Galaxy*-style satire of a future America run by gangsters, and, the weakest of the lot, *Takeoff,* a then-theoretical novel about the conquest of space), but they had little impact on the SF world of the day.

What *did* have a powerful impact on the SF world, though, was Kornbluth's short fiction. Kornbluth was a master of the short story, working with a sophistication, maturity, elegance, and grace rarely seen in the genre, then or now. He was one of those key authors—one also thinks of Damon Knight, Theodore Sturgeon, Alfred Bester, Algis Budrys, and a few others—who were busy in the '50s redefining what you could do with the instrument known as the science fiction short story, and greatly expanding its range. In the years before his tragically early death in 1958 (on his way in to Manhattan for a meeting in which he was going to be offered the editorship of *The Magazine of Fantasy & Science Fiction,* by the way; now *there's* an interesting basis for an Alternate Worlds scenario! One wonders what stories he would have bought, and what effect his editorship would have had on the evolution of SF . . .), Kornbluth created some of the best short work of the '50s, including the classic "The Little Black Bag," "The Marching Morons," "Shark Ship," "Two Dooms," "The Mindworm," "Gomez," "The Last Man Left in the Bar," "The Advent on Channel Twelve," "Ms. Found in a Chinese Fortune Cookie," "With These Hands," and dozens of others . . .

. . . Including the hugely entertaining story that follows, a somewhat atypical story for Kornbluth—for the fact is that, except for this one famous story (and one or two other exceptions, such as the much weaker "The Slave"), Kornbluth rarely wrote straightforward adventure stories, under the Kornbluth byline anyway, especially Space Adventure stories of the swashbuckling, hard-nosed, rapacious, fast-paced sort that follows, where sharp-eyed cool-headed entrepreneurs haggle and brawl and wheel-and-deal their way across the Universe, out-thinking their adversaries and out-*tricking* them when backed into a corner. "That Share of Glory," in fact, is such a perfect *Astounding* story, so much the Platonic Ideal of what a story for John Campbell's *Astounding* of that period should be like, that I can't help but wonder if Kornbluth's tongue wasn't in his cheek when he wrote it, or if he wasn't deliberately (with the cool-eyed calculation of the characters in the story) writing stuff that he knew would "push Campbell's buttons," a popular game among writers of the day. Even if one or both of those things are true, though, it hardly matters—Kornbluth may have told his friends or even himself that that's what he was doing, but there's too much conviction in his voice here, and he does too good a job, for me to believe that he didn't like the stuff himself, whatever he may have claimed that he'd *rather* drink instead. For all of the cynical, jaded facade that he was famous for projecting, nobody but a True Believer at heart, one who somewhere, down deep, still thrilled to the dream of venturing out among the wonders and terrors of deep space, out to the unknown stars, could possibly have written the adventure that follows . . .

Kornbluth won no major awards during his lifetime, but "The Meeting," a story of his completed from a partial draft by Pohl years after his death, won a Hugo Award in 1972. Kornbluth's solo short work was collected in *The Explorers, A Mile Beyond the Moon, The Marching Morons, Thirteen O'Clock and Other Zero Hours,* and *The Best of C. M. Kornbluth.* Pohl and Kornbluth's collaborative short work has been collected in *The Wonder Effect, Critical Mass, Before the Universe,* and *Our Best.* Until recently, I would have said that everything by Kornbluth was long out of print, but, fortunately, NESFA Press published a massive retrospective Kornbluth collection in 1996, *His Share of Glory: The Complete Short Fiction of C. M. Kornbluth* (NESFA Press, P.O. Box 809, Framingham, MA 07101-0203, www.nesfa.org $27.00), a collection which, true to its name, assembles almost everything Kornbluth ever wrote under his own name, and one which belongs in every serious SF reader's library.

Young Alen, one of a thousand in the huge refectory, ate absent-mindedly as the reader droned into the perfect silence of the hall. Today's lesson happened to be a word list of the Thetis VIII planet's seagoing folk.

"*Tlon*—a ship," droned the reader.

"*Rtlo*—some ships, number unknown.

"*Long*—some ships, number known, always modified by cardinal.

"*Ongr*—a ship in a collection of ships, always modified by ordinal.

"*Ngrt*—first ship in a collection of ships; an exception to *ongr.*"

A lay brother tiptoed to Alen's side. "The Rector summons you," he whispered.

Alen had no time for panic, though that was the usual reaction to a summons from the Rector to a novice. He slipped from the refectory, stepped onto the northbound corridor and stepped off at his cell, a minute later and a quarter mile farther on. Hastily, but meticulously, he changed from his drab habit to the heraldic robes in the cubicle with its simple stool, washstand, desk, and paperweight or two. Alen, a levelheaded young fellow, was not aware that he had broken any section of the Order's complicated Rule, but he was aware that he could have done so without knowing it. It might, he thought, be the last time he would see the cell.

He cast a glance which he hoped would not be the final one over it; a glance which lingered a little fondly on the reel rack where were stowed: *Nicholson on Martian Verbs, The New Oxford Venusian Dictionary,* the ponderous six-reeler *Deutsche-Ganymedische Konversasionslexikon* published long ago and far away in Leipzig. The later works were there, too: *The Tongues of the Galaxy—an Essay in Classification, A Concise Grammar of Cephean, The Self-Pronouncing Vegan II Dictionary*—scores of them, and, of course, the worn reel of old Machiavelli's *The Prince.*

Enough of that! Alen combed out his small, neat beard and stepped onto the southbound corridor. He transferred to an eastbound at the next intersection and minutes later was before the Rector's lay secretary.

"You better review your Lyran irregulars," said the secretary disrespectfully. "There's a trader in there who's looking for a cheap herald on a swindling trip to Lyra VI." Thus unceremoniously did Alen learn that he was not to be ejected from the Order but that he was to be elevated to Journeyman. But as a herald should, he betrayed no sign of his immense relief. He did, however, take the secretary's advice and sensibly reviewed his Lyran.

While he was in the midst of a declension which applied only to inanimate objects, the voice of the Rector—and what a mellow voice it was!—floated through the secretary's intercom.

"Admit the novice, Alen," said the Master Herald.

A final settling of his robes and the youth walked into the Rector's huge office, with the seal of the Order blazing in diamonds above his desk. There was a stranger present; presumably the trader—a blackbearded fellow whose rugged frame didn't carry his Vegan cloak with ease.

Said the Rector: "Novice, this is to be the crown of your toil if you are acceptable to—?" He courteously turned to the trader, who shrugged irritably.

"It's all one to me," growled the blackbeard. "Somebody cheap, somebody who knows the cant of the thievish Lyran gem peddlers, above all, somebody *at once.* Overhead is devouring my flesh day by day as the ship waits at the field. And when we are spaceborne, my imbecile crew will doubtless waste liter after priceless liter of my fuel. And when we land the swindling Lyrans will without doubt make my ruin complete by tricking me even out of the minute profit I hope to realize. Good Master Herald, let me have the infant cheap and I'll bid you good day."

The Rector's shaggy eyebrows drew down in a frown. "Trader," he said sonorously, "our mission of galactic utilitarian culture is not concerned with your margin of profit. I ask you to test this youth and, if you find him able, to take him as your Herald on your voyage. He will serve you well, for he has been taught that commerce and words, its medium, are the unifying bonds which will one day unite the cosmos into a single humankind. Do not conceive that the College and Order of Heralds is a mere aid to you in your commercial adventure."

"Very well," growled the trader. He addressed Alen in broken Lyran: "Boy, how you make up Vegan stones of three fires so Lyran women like, come buy, buy again?"

Alen smoothly replied: "The Vegan triple-fire gem finds most favor on Lyra and especially among its women when set in a wide glass anklet if large, and when arranged in the Lyran 'lucky five' pattern in a glass thumb ring if small." He was glad, very glad, he had come across—and as a matter of course memorized, in the relentless fashion of the Order— a novel which touched briefly on the Lyran jewel trade.

The trader glowered and switched to Cephean—apparently his native tongue. "That was well-enough said, Herald. Now tell me whether you've got guts to man a squirt in case we're intercepted by the thieving so-called Customs collectors of Eyolf's Realm between here and Lyra?"

Alen knew the Rector's eyes were on him. "The noble mission of our Order," he said, "forbids me to use any weapon but the truth in furthering cosmic utilitarian civilization. No, master trader, I shall not man one of your weapons."

The trader shrugged. "So I must take what I get. Good Master Herald, make me a price."

The Rector said casually: "I regard this chiefly as a training mission for our novice; the fee will be nominal. Let us say twenty-five per cent of your net as of blastoff from Lyra, to be audited by Journeyman-Herald Alen."

The trader's howl of rage echoed in the dome of the huge room. "It's not fair!" he roared. "Who but you thievish villains with your Order and your catch-'em-young and your years of training can learn the tongues of the galaxy? What chance has a decent merchant busy with profit and loss got to learn the cant of every race between Sirius and the Coalsack? It's not fair! It's not fair and I'll say so until my dying breath!"

"Die outside if you find our terms unacceptable," said the Rector. "The Order does not haggle."

"Well I know it," sighed the trader brokenly. "I should have stuck to my own system and my good father's pump-flange factory. But no! I had to pick up a bargain in gems on Vega! Enough of this—bring me your contract and I'll sign it."

The Rector's shaggy eyebrows went up. "There is no contract," he said. "A mutual trust between Herald and trader is the cornerstone upon which cosmos-wide amity and understanding will be built."

"At twenty-five per cent for an unlicked pup," muttered blackbeard to himself in Cephean.

None of his instructors had played Polonius as Alen, with the seal of the Journeyman-Herald on his brow, packed for blastoff and vacated his cell. He supposed they knew that twenty years of training either had done their work or had not.

The trader taking Alen to the field where his ship waited was less wise. "The secret of successful negotiation," he weightily told his Herald, "is to yield willingly. This may strike you as a paradox, but it is the veritable key to my success in maintaining the profits of my good father's pump-flange trade. The secret is to yield with rueful admiration of your opponent—but *only in unimportant details*. Put up a little battle about delivery date or about terms of credit and then let him have his way. But you never give way a hair's breadth on your asking price unless—"

Alen let him drivel on as they drove through the outer works of the College. He was glad the car was open. For the first time he was being accorded the doffed hat that is the due of Heralds from their inferiors in the Order, and the grave nod of salutation from equals. Five-year-old postulants seeing his brow seal tugged off their headgear with comical celerity; fellow novices, equals a few hours before, uncovered as though he were the Rector himself.

The ceremonial began to reach the trader. When, with a final salutation, a lay warder let them through the great gate of the curtain wall, he said with some irritation, "They appear to hold you in high regard, boy."

"I am better addressed as Herald," said Alen composedly.

"A plague descend on the College and Order! Do you think I don't know my manners? Of course, I call a Herald 'Herald,' but we're going to be cooped up together and you'll be working for me. What'll happen to ship's discipline if I have to kowtow to you?"

"There will be no problem," said Alen.

Blackbeard grunted and trod fiercely on the accelerator.

"That's my ship," he said at length. *"Starsong.* Vegan registry—it may help passing through Eyolf's Realm, though it cost me overmuch in bribes. A crew of eight, lazy, good-for-nothing wastrels—Agh! Can I believe my eyes?" The car jammed to a halt before the looming ship, and blackbeard was up the ladder and through the port in a second. Settling his robes, Alen followed.

He found the trader fiercely denouncing his chief engineer for using space drive to heat the ship; he had seen the faint haze of a minimum exhaust from the stern tubes.

"For that, dolt," screamed blackbeard, "we have a thing known as electricity. Have you by chance ever heard of it? Are you aware that a chief engineer's responsibility is the efficient and *economical* operation of his ship's drive mechanism?"

The chief, a cowed-looking Cephean, saw Alen with relief and swept off his battered cap. The Herald nodded gravely and the trader broke off in irritation. "We need none of that bowing and scraping for the rest of the voyage," he declared.

"Of course not, sir," said the chief. "O'course not. I was just welcoming the Herald aboard. Welcome aboard, Herald. I'm Chief Elwon, Herald. And I'm glad to have a Herald with us." A covert glance at the trader. *"I've* voyaged with Heralds and without, and I don't mind saying I feel safer indeed with you aboard."

"May I be taken to my quarters?" asked Alen.

"Your—" began the trader, stupefied.

The chief broke in, "I'll fix you a cabin, Herald. We've got some bulkheads I can rig aft for a snug little space, not roomy, but the best a little ship like this can afford."

The trader collapsed into a bucket seat as the chief bustled aft and Alen followed.

"Herald," the chief said with some embarrassment after he had collared two crewmen and set them to work, "you'll have to excuse our good master trader. He's new to the interstar lanes and he doesn't exactly know the jets yet. Between us we'll get him squared away."

Alen inspected the cubicle run up for him—a satisfactory enclosure affording him the decent privacy he rated. He dismissed the chief and the crewmen with a nod and settled himself on the cot.

Beneath the iron composure in which he had been trained, he felt scared and alone. Not even old Machiavelli seemed to offer comfort or council: "There is nothing more difficult to take in hand, more perilous to conduct, or more uncertain in its success, than to take the lead in the introduction of a new order of things," said Chapter Six.

But what said Chapter Twenty-Six? "Where the willingness is great, the difficulties cannot be great."

Starsong was not a happy ship. Blackbeard's nagging stinginess hung over the crew like a thundercloud, but Alen professed not to notice. He walked regularly fore and aft for two hours a day greeting the crew members in their various native tongues and then wrapping himself in the reserve the Order demanded—though he longed to salute them man-to-man, eat with them, gossip about their native planets, the past misdeeds that had brought them to their berths aboard the miserly *Starsong,* their hopes for the future. The Rule of the College and Order of Heralds decreed otherwise. He accepted the uncoverings of the crew with a nod and tried to be pleased because they stood in growing awe of him that ranged from Chief Elwon's lively appreciation of a Herald's skill to Wiper Jukkl's superstitious reverence. Jukkl was a low-browed specimen from a planet of the decadent Sirius system. He outdid the normal slovenliness of an all-male crew on a freighter—a slovenliness in which Alen could not share. Many of his waking hours were spent in his locked cubicle burnishing his metal and cleaning and pressing his robes. A Herald was never supposed to suggest by his appearance that he shared mortal frailties.

Blackbeard himself yielded a little, to the point of touching his cap sullenly. This probably was not so much awe at Alen's studied manner as respect for the incisive, lightning-fast job of auditing the Herald did on the books of the trading venture—absurdly complicated books with scores of accounts to record a simple matter of buying gems cheap on Vega and chartering a ship in the hope of selling them dearly on Lyra. The complicated books and overlapping accounts did tell the story, but they made it very easy for an auditor to erroneously read a number of costs as far higher than they actually were. Alen did not fall into the trap.

On the fifth day after blastoff, Chief Elwon rapped, respectfully but urgently, on the door of Alen's cubicle.

"If you please, Herald," he urged, "could you come to the bridge?"

Alen's heart bounded in his chest, but he gravely said, "My meditation must not be interrupted. I shall join you on the bridge in ten minutes." And for ten minutes he methodically polished a murky link in the massive gold chain that fastened his boat-cloak—the "meditation." He donned the cloak before stepping out; the summons sounded like a full-dress affair in the offing.

The trader was stamping and fuming. Chief Elwon was riffling through his spec book unhappily. Astrogator Hufner was at the plot computer running up trajectories and knocking them down again. A quick glance showed Alen that they were all high-speed trajectories in the evasive-action class.

"Herald," said the trader grimly, "we have broken somebody's detector bubble." He jerked his thumb at a red-lit signal. "I expect we'll be overhauled shortly. Are you ready to earn your twenty-five per cent of the net?"

Alen overlooked the crudity. "Are you rigged for color video, merchant?" he asked.

"We are."

"Then I am ready to do what I can for my client."

He took the communicator's seat, stealing a glance in the still-blank screen. The reflection of his face was reassuring, though he wished he had thought to comb his small beard.

Another light flashed on, and Hufner quit the operator to study the detector board. "Big, powerful, and getting closer," he said tersely. "Scanning for us with directionals now. Putting out plenty of energy—"

The loudspeaker of the ship-to-ship audio came to life.

"What ship are you?" it demanded in Vegan. "We are a Customs cruiser of the Realm of Eyolf. What ship are you?"

"Have the crew man the squirts," said the trader softly to the chief.

Elwon looked at Alen, who shook his head. "Sorry, sir," said the engineer apologetically. "The Herald—"

"We are the freighter *Starsong*, Vegan registry," said Alen into the audio mike as the trader choked. "We are carrying Vegan gems to Lyra."

"They're on us," said the astrogator despairingly, reading his instruments. The ship-to-ship video flashed on, showing an arrogant, square-jawed face topped by a battered naval cap.

"Lyra indeed? We have plans of our own for Lyra. You will heave to—" began the officer in the screen, before he noted Alen. "My pardon, Herald," he said sardonically. "Herald, will you please request the ship's master to heave to for boarding and search? We wish to assess and collect Customs duties. You are aware, of course, that your vessel is passing through the Realm."

The man's accented Vegan reeked of Algol IV. Alen switched to that obscure language to say, "We were not aware of that. Are you aware that there is a reciprocal trade treaty in effect between the Vegan system and the Realm which specifies that freight in Vegan bottoms is dutiable only when consigned to ports in the Realm?"

"You speak Algolian, do you? You Heralds have not been underrated, but don't plan to lie your way out of this. Yes, I am aware of some such agreement as you mentioned. We shall board you, as I said, and assess and collect duty in kind. If, regrettably, there has been any mistake, you are of course free to apply to the Realm for reimbursement. Now, heave to!"

"I have no intentions of lying. I speak the solemn truth when I say that we shall fight to the last man any attempt of yours to board and loot us."

Alen's mind was racing furiously through the catalog of planetary folkways the Rule had decreed that he master. Algol IV—some ancestor worship; veneration of mother; hand-to-hand combat with knives; complimentary greeting, "May you never strike down a weaker foe"; folk-hero Gaarek unjustly accused of slaying a cripple and exiled but it was an enemy's plot—

A disconcerted shadow was crossing the face of the officer as Alen improvised: "You will, of course, kill us all. But before this happens I shall have messaged back to the College and Order of Heralds the facts in the case, with a particular request that your family be informed. Your name, I think, will be remembered as long as Gaarek's—though not in the same way, of course; the Algolian whose hundred-man battle cruiser wiped out a virtually unarmed freighter with a crew of eight."

The officer's face was dark with rage. "You devil!" he snarled. "Leave my family out of this! I'll come aboard and fight you man-to-man if you have the stomach for it!"

Alen shook his head regretfully. "The Rule of my Order forbids recourse to violence," he said. "Our only permissible weapon is the truth."

"We're coming aboard," said the officer grimly. "I'll order my men not to harm your people. We'll just be collecting customs. If your people shoot first, my men will be under orders to do nothing more than disable them."

Alen smiled and uttered a sentence or two in Algolian.

The officer's jaw dropped and he croaked, after a pause, "I'll cut you to ribbons. You can't say that about my mother, you—" and he spewed back some of the words Alen had spoken.

"Calm yourself," said the Herald gravely. "I apologize for my disgusting and unheraldic remarks. But I wished to prove a point. You would have killed me if you could; I touched off a reaction which had been planted in you by your culture. I will be able to do the same with the men of yours who come aboard. For every race of man there is the intolerable insult that must be avenged in blood.

"Send your men aboard under orders not to kill if you wish; I shall goad them into a killing rage. We shall be massacred, yours will be the blame and you will be disgraced and disowned by your entire planet." Alen hoped desperately that the naval crews of the Realm were, as reputed, a barbarous and undisciplined lot—

Evidently they were, and the proud Algolian dared not risk it. In his native language he spat again, "You devil!" and switched back into Vegan. "Freighter *Starsong*," he said bleakly, "I find that my space fix was in error and that you are not in Realm territory. You may proceed."

The astrogator said from the detector board, incredulously, "He's disengaging. He's off us. He's accelerating. Herald, *what* did you say to him?"

But the reaction from blackbeard was more gratifying. Speechless, the trader took off his cap. Alen acknowledged the salute with a grave nod before he started back to his cubicle. It was just as well, he reflected, that the trader didn't know his life and his ship had been unconditionally pledged in a finish fight against a hundred-man battle cruiser.

Lyra's principal spaceport was pocked and broken, but they made a fair-enough landing. Alen, in full heraldic robes, descended from *Starsong* to greet a handful of port officials.

"Any metals aboard?" demanded one of them.

"None for sale," said the Herald. "We have Vegan gems, chiefly triple-fire." He knew that the dull little planet was short of metals and, having made a virtue of necessity, was somehow prejudiced against their import.

"Have your crew transfer the cargo to the Customs shed," said the port official studying *Starsong*'s papers. "And all of you wait there."

All of them—except Alen—lugged numbered sacks and boxes of gems to the low brick building designated. The trader was allowed to pocket a handful for samples before the shed was sealed—a complicated business. A brick was mortared over the simple ironwood latch that closed the ironwood door, a pat of clay was slapped over the brick, and the port seal stamped in it. A mechanic with what looked like a pottery blowtorch fed by powdered coal played a flame on the clay seal until it glowed orange-red and that was that.

"Herald," said the port official, "tell the merchant to sign here and make his fingerprints."

Alen studied the document; it was a simple identification form. Blackbeard signed with the reed pen provided and fingerprinted the document. After two weeks in space he scarcely needed to ink his fingers first.

"Now tell him that we'll release the gems on his written fingerprinted order to whatever Lyran citizens he sells to. And explain that this roundabout system is necessary to avoid metal smuggling. Please remove *all* metal from your clothes and stow it on your ship. Then we will seal that, too, and put it under guard until you are ready to take off. We regret that we will have to search you before we turn you loose, but we can't afford

to have our economy disrupted by irresponsible introduction of metals."
Alen had not realized it was that bad.

After the thorough search that extended to the confiscation of forgotten
watches and pins, the port officials changed a sheaf of the trader's uranium-
backed Vegan currency into Lyran legal tender based on man-hours. Blackbeard made a partial payment to the crew, told them to have a good liberty
and check in at the port at sunset the next day for probable takeoff.

Alen and the trader were driven to town in an unlikely vehicle whose
power plant was a pottery turbine. The driver, when they were safely out
on the open road, furtively asked whether they had any metal they wanted
to discard.

The trader asked sharply in his broken Lyran: "What you do you get
metal? Where sell, how use?"

The driver, following a universal tendency, raised his voice and
lapsed into broken Lyran himself to tell the strangers: "Black market science men pay much, much for little bit metal. Study, use build. Politicians
make law no metal, what I care politicians? But you no tell, gentlemen?"

"We won't tell," said Alen. "But we have no metal for you."

The driver shrugged.

"Herald," said the trader, "what do you make of it?"

"I didn't know it was a political issue. We concern ourselves with the
basic patterns of a people's behavior, not the day-to-day expressions of
the patterns. The planet's got no heavy metals, which means there were
no metals available to the primitive Lyrans. The lighter metals don't
occur in native form or in easily split compounds. They proceeded along
the ceramic line instead of the metallic line and appear to have done quite
well for themselves up to a point. No electricity, of course, no aviation
and no space flight."

"And," said the trader, "naturally the people who make these buggies
and that blowtorch we saw are scared witless that metals will be imported
and put them out of business. So naturally they have laws passed pro-
hibiting it."

"Naturally," said the Herald, looking sharply at the trader. But blackbeard was back in character a moment later. "An outrage," he growled.
"Trying to tell a man what he can and can't import when he sees a decent
chance to make a bit of profit."

The driver dropped them at a boardinghouse. It was half-timbered
construction, which appeared to be swankier than the more common
brick. The floors were plate glass, roughened for traction. Alen got them
a double room with a view.

"What's that thing?" demanded the trader, inspecting the view.

The thing was a structure looming above the slate and tile roofs of the town—a round brick tower for its first twenty-five meters and then wood for another fifteen. As they studied it, it pricked up a pair of ears at the top and began to flop them wildly.

"Semaphore," said Alen.

A minute later blackbeard piteously demanded from the bathroom, *"How* do you make water come out of the tap? I touched it all over but nothing happened."

"You have to turn it," said Alen, demonstrating. "And that thing—you pull it sharply down, hold it, and then release."

"Barbarous," muttered the trader. "Barbarous."

An elderly maid came in to show them how to string their hammocks and ask if they happened to have a bit of metal to give her for a souvenir. They sent her away and, rather than face the public dining room, made a meal from their own stores and turned in for the night.

It's going well, though Alen drowsily; going very well indeed.

He awoke abruptly, but made no move. It was dark in the double room, and there were stealthy, furtive little noises nearby. A hundred thoughts flashed through his head of Lyran treachery and double-dealing. He lifted his eyelids a trifle and saw a figure silhouetted against the faint light of the big window. If a burglar, he was a clumsy one.

There was a stirring from the other hammock, the trader's. With a subdued roar that sounded like "Thieving villains!" blackbeard launched himself from the hammock at the intruder. But his feet tangled in the hammock cords and he belly-flopped on the floor.

The burglar, if it was one, didn't dash smoothly and efficiently for the door. He straightened himself against the window and said resignedly, "You need not fear. I will make no resistance."

Alen rolled from the hammock and helped the trader to his feet. "He said he doesn't want to fight," he told the trader.

Blackbeard seized the intruder and shook him like a rat. "So the rogue is a coward too!" he boomed. "Give us a light, Herald."

Alen uncovered the slow-match, blew it to a flame, squeakily pumped up a pressure torch until a jet of pulverized coal sprayed from its nozzle and ignited it. A dozen strokes more and there was enough heat feeding back from the jet to maintain the pressure cycle.

Through all of this the trader was demanding in his broken Lyran, "What make here, thief? What reason thief us room?"

The Herald brought the hissing pressure lamp to the window. The intruder's face was not the unhealthy, neurotic face of a criminal. Its thin lines told of discipline and thought.

"What did you want here?" asked Alen.

"Metal," said the intruder simply. "I thought you might have a bit of iron."

It was the first time a specific metal had been named by any Lyran. He used, of course, the Vegan word for iron.

"You are particular," remarked the Herald. "Why iron?"

"I have heard that it possesses certain properties—perhaps you can tell me before you turn me over to the police. Is it true, as we hear, that a mass of iron whose crystals have been aligned by a sharp blow will strongly attract another piece of iron with a force related to the distance between them?"

"It is true," said the Herald, studying the man's face. It was lit with excitement. Deliberately Alen added, "This alignment is more easily and uniformly ejected by placing the mass of iron in an electric field—that is, a space surrounding the passage of an electron stream through a conductor." Many of the words he used had to be Vegan; there were no Lyran words for "electric," "electron," or "conductor."

The intruder's face fell. "I have tried to master the concept you refer to," he admitted. "But it is beyond me. I have questioned other interstar voyagers and they have touched on it; but I cannot grasp it— But thank you, sir; you have been very courteous. I will trouble you no further while you summon the watch."

"You give up too easily," said Alen. "For a scientist, much too easily. If we turn you over to the watch, there will be hearings and testimony and whatnot. Our time is limited here on your planet; I doubt that we can spare any for your legal processes."

The trader let go of the intruder's shoulder and grumbled, "Why you no ask we have iron, I tell you no. Search, search, take all metal away. We no police you. I sorry hurted you arms. Here for you." Blackbeard brought out a palmful of his sample gems and picked out a large triple-fire stone. "You not be angry me," he said, putting it in the Lyran's hand.

"I can't—" said the scientist.

Blackbeard closed his fingers over the stone and growled, "I give, you take. Maybe buy iron with, eh?"

"That's so," said the Lyran. "Thank you both, gentlemen. Thank you—"

"You go," said the trader. "You go, we sleep again."

The scientist bowed with dignity and left their room.

"Gods of space," swore the trader. "To think that Jukkl, the *Star-song*'s wiper, knows more about electricity and magnetism than a brainy fellow like that."

"And they are the key to physics," mused Alen. "A scientist here is dead-ended forever, because their materials are all insulators! Glass, clay, glaze, wood."

"Funny, all right," yawned blackbeard. "Did you see me collar him once I got on my feet? Sharp, eh? Good night, Herald." He gruntingly hauled himself into the hammock again, leaving Alen to turn off the hissing light and cover the slow-match with its perforated lid.

They had roast fowl of some sort or other for breakfast in the public dining room. Alen was required by his Rule to refuse the red wine that went with it. The trader gulped it approvingly. "A sensible, though backward people," he said. "And now if you'll inquire of the management where the thievish jewel buyers congregate, we can get on with our business and perhaps be off by dawn tomorrow."

"So quickly?" asked Alen, almost forgetting himself enough to show surprise.

"My charter on *Starsong,* good Herald—thirty days to go, but what might not go wrong in space? And then there would be penalties to mulct me of whatever minute profit I may realize."

Alen learned that Gromeg's Tavern was the gem mart and they took another of the turbine-engined cabs through the brick-paved streets.

Gromeg's was a dismal, small-windowed brick barn with heavyset men lounging about, an open kitchen at one end and tables at the other. A score of smaller, sharp-faced men were at the tables, sipping wine and chatting.

"I am Journeyman-Herald Alen," announced Alen clearly, "with Vegan gems to dispose of."

There was a silence of elaborate unconcern, and then one of the dealers spat and grunted, "Vegan gems. A drug on the market. Take them away, Herald."

"Come, master trader," said Alen in the Lyran tongue. "The gem dealers of Lyra do not want your wares." He started for the door.

One of the dealers called languidly, "Well, wait a moment. I have nothing better to do; since you've come all this way, I'll have a look at your stuff."

"You honor us," said Alen. He and blackbeard sat at the man's table. The trader took out a palmful of samples, counted them meaningfully, and laid them on the boards.

"Well," said the gem dealer, "I don't know whether to be amused or insulted. I am Garthkint, the gem dealer—not a retailer of *beads.* However, I have no hard feelings. A drink for your frowning friend, Herald? I know you gentry don't indulge." The drink was already on the table, brought by one of the hulking guards.

Alen passed Garthkint's own mug of wine to the trader, explaining politely: "In my master trader's native Cepheus it is considered honorable for the guest to sip the drink his host laid down and none other. A charming custom, is it not?"

"Charming, though unsanitary," muttered the gem dealer—and he did not touch the drink he had ordered for blackbeard.

"I can't understand a word either of you is saying—too flowery. Was this little rat trying to drug me?" demanded the trader in Cephean.

"No," said Alen. "Just trying to get you drunk." To Garthkint in Lyran, he explained, "The good trader was saying that he wishes to leave at once. I was agreeing with him."

"Well," said Garthkint, "perhaps I can take a couple of your gauds. For some youngster who wishes a cheap ring."

"He's getting to it," Alen told the trader.

"High time," grunted blackbeard.

"The trader asks me to inform you," said Alen, switching back to Lyran, "that he is unable to sell in lots smaller than five hundred gems."

"A compact language, Cephean," said Garthkint, narrowing his eyes.

"Is it not?" Alen blandly agreed.

The gem dealer's forefinger rolled an especially fine three-fire stone from the little pool of gems on the table. "I suppose," he said grudgingly, "that this is what I must call the best of the lot. What, I am curious to know, is the price you would set for five hundred equal in quality and size to this poor thing?"

"This," said Alen, "is the good trader's first venture to your delightful planet. He wishes to be remembered and welcomed all of the many times he anticipates returning. Because of this he has set an absurdly low price, counting good will as more important than a prosperous voyage. Two thousand Lyran credits."

"Absurd," snorted Garthkint. "I cannot do business with you. Either you are insanely rapacious or you have been pitifully misguided as to the value of your wares. I am well known for my charity; I will assume that the latter is the case. I trust you will not be too downcast when I tell you that five hundred of these muddy, undersized out-of-round objects are worth no more than two hundred credits."

"If you are serious," said Alen with marked amazement, "we would not dream of imposing on you. At the figure you mention, we might as well not sell at all but return with our wares to Cepheus and give these gems to children in the streets for marbles. Good gem trader, excuse us for taking up so much of your time and many thanks for your warm hospitality in the matter of the wine." He switched to Cephean and said:

"We're dickering now. Two thousand and two hundred. Get up; we're going to start to walk out."

"What if he lets us go?" grumbled blackbeard, but he did heave himself to his feet and turn to the door as Alen rose.

"My trader echoes my regrets," the Herald said in Lyran. "Farewell."

"Well, stay a moment," said Garthkint. "I am well known for my soft heart toward strangers. A charitable man might go as high as five hundred and absorb the inevitable loss. If you should return some day with a passable lot of *real* gems, it would be worth my while for you to remember who treated you with such benevolence and give me fair choice."

"Noble Lyran," said Alen, apparently almost overcome. "I shall not easily forget your combination of acumen and charity. It is a lesson to traders. It is a lesson to me. I shall *not* insist on two thousand. I shall cut the throat of my trader's venture by reducing his price to eighteen hundred credits, though I wonder how I shall dare tell him of it."

"What's going on now?" demanded blackbeard.

"Five hundred and eighteen hundred," said Alen. "We can sit down again."

"Up, down—up, down," muttered the trader.

They sat, and Alen said in Lyran: "My trader unexpectedly endorses the reduction. He says, 'Better to lose some than all'—an old proverb in the Cephean tongue. And he forbids any further reduction."

"Come, now," wheedled the gem dealer. "Let us be men of the world about this. One must give a little and take a little. Everybody knows he can't have his own way forever. I shall offer a good, round eight hundred credits and we'll close on it, eh? Pilquis, fetch us a pen and ink!" One of the burly guards was right there with an inkpot and a reed pen. Garthkint had a Customs form out of his tunic and was busily filling it in to specify the size, number, and fire of gems to be released to him.

"What's it now?" asked blackbeard.

"Eight hundred."

"Take it!"

"Garthkint," said Alen regretfully, "you heard the firmness and decision in my trader's voice? What can I do? I am only speaking for him. He is a hard man but perhaps I can talk him around later. I offer you the gems at a ruinous fifteen hundred credits."

"Split the difference," said Garthkint resignedly.

"Done at eleven-fifty," said Alen.

That blackbeard understood. "Well done!" he boomed at Alen and took a swig at Garthkint's wine cup. "Have him fill in 'Sack eighteen' on his paper. It's five hundred of that grade."

The gem dealer counted out twenty-three fifty-credit notes and blackbeard signed and fingerprinted the release.

"Now," said Garthkint, "you will please remain here while I take a trip to the spaceport for my property." Three or four of the guards were suddenly quite close.

"You will find," said Alen dryly, "that our standard of commercial morality is no lower than yours."

The dealer smiled politely and left.

"Who will be the next?" asked Alen of the room at large.

"I'll look at your gems," said another dealer, sitting at the table.

With the ice breaking down, the transactions went quicker. Alen had disposed of a dozen lots by the time their first buyer returned.

"It's all right," he said. "We've been tricked before, but your gems are as represented. I congratulate you, Herald, on driving a hard, fair bargain."

"That means," said Alen regretfully, "that I should have asked for more." The guards were once more lounging in corners and no longer seemed so menacing.

They had a midday meal and continued to dispose of their wares. At sunset Alen held a final auction to clean up the odd lots that remained over and was urged to stay to dinner.

The trader, counting a huge wad of the Lyran manpower-based notes, shook his head. "We should be off before dawn, Herald," he told Alen. "Time is money, time is money."

"They are very insistent."

"And I am very stubborn. Thank them and let us be on our way before anything else is done to increase my overhead."

Something did turn up—a city watchman with a bloody nose and split lip.

He demanded of the Herald, "Are you responsible for the Cephean maniac known as Elwon?"

Garthkint glided up to mutter in Alen's ear, "Beware how you answer!"

Alen needed no warning. His grounding included Lyran legal concepts—and on the backward little planet touched with many relics of feudalism, "responsible" covered much territory.

"What has Chief Elwon done?" he parried.

"As you see," the watchman glumly replied, pointing to his wounds. "And the same to three others before we got him out of the wrecked wine shop and into the castle. Are you responsible for him?"

"Let me speak with my trader for a moment. Will you have some wine meantime?" He signaled and one of the guards brought a mug.

"Don't mind if I do. I can use it," sighed the watchman.

"We are in trouble," said Alen to blackbeard. "Chief Elwon is in the castle—prison—for drunk and disorderly conduct. You as his master are considered responsible for his conduct under Lyran law. You must pay his fines or serve his penalties. Or you can disown him, which is considered dishonorable but sometimes necessary. For paying his fine or serving his time you have a prior lien on his services, without pay—but of course that's unenforceable off Lyra."

Blackbeard was sweating a little. "Find out from the policeman how long all this is likely to take. I don't want to leave Elwon here and I do want us to get off as soon as possible. Keep him occupied, now, while I go about some business."

The trader retreated to a corner of the darkening barnlike tavern, beckoning Garthkint and a guard with him as Alen returned to the watchman.

"Good keeper of the peace," he said, "will you have another?"

He would.

"My trader wishes to know what penalties are likely to be levied against the unfortunate Chief Elwon."

"Going to leave him in the lurch, eh?" asked the watchman a little belligerently. "A fine master you have!"

One of the dealers at the table indignantly corroborated him. "If you foreigners aren't prepared to live up to your obligations, why did you come here in the first place? What happens to business if a master can send his man to steal and cheat and then say, 'Don't blame *me*—it was *his* doing!' "

Alen patiently explained, "On other planets, good Lyrans, the tie of master and man is not so strong that a man would obey if he were ordered to go and steal or cheat."

They shook their heads and muttered. It was unheard of.

"Good watchman," pressed the Herald, "my trader does not *want* to disown Chief Elwon. Can you tell me what recompense would be necessary—and how long it would take to manage the business?"

The watchman started on a third cup which Alen had unostentatiously signaled for. "It's hard to say," he told the Herald weightily. "For my damages, I would demand a hundred credits at least. The three other members of the watch battered by your lunatic could ask no less. The wine shop suffered easily five hundred credits' damage. The owner of it was beaten, but that doesn't matter, of course."

"No imprisonment?"

"Oh, a flogging, of course." Alen started before he recalled that the "flogging" was a few half-hearted symbolic strokes on the covered shoulders with a light cane. "But no imprisonment. His Honor, Judge Krarl, does not sit on the night bench. Judge Krarl is a newfangled reformer, stranger. He professes to believe that mulcting is unjust—that it makes it easy for the rich to commit crime and go scot-free."

"But doesn't it?" asked Alen, drawn off course in spite of himself. There was pitying laughter around him.

"Look you," a dealer explained kindly. "The good watchman suffers battery, the mad Cephean or his master is mulcted for damages, the watchman is repaid for his injuries. What kind of justice is it to the watchman if the mad Cephean is locked away in a cell, unfined?"

The watchman nodded approvingly. "Well said," he told the dealer. "Luckily we have on the night bench a justice of the old school, His Honor, Judge Treel. Stern, but fair. You should hear him! 'Fifty credits! A hundred credits and the lash! Robbed a ship, eh? Two thousand credits!' " He returned to his own voice and said with awe, "For a murder, he never assesses less than *ten thousand credits!*"

And if the murderer couldn't pay, Alen knew, he became a "public charge," "responsible to the state"—that is, a slave. If he could pay, of course, he was turned loose.

"And His Honor, Judge Treel," he pressed, "is sitting tonight? Can we possibly appear before him, pay the fines, and be off?"

"To be sure, stranger. I'd be a fool if I waited until morning, wouldn't I?" The wine had loosened his tongue a little too far and he evidently realized it. "Enough of this," he said. "Does your master honorably accept responsibility of the Cephean? If so, come along with me, the two of you, and we'll get this over with."

"Thanks, good watchman. We are coming."

He went to blackbeard, now alone in his corner, and said, "It's all right. We can pay off—about a thousand credits—and be on our way."

The trader muttered darkly, "Lyran jurisdiction or not, it's coming out of Elwon's pay. The bloody fool!"

They rattled through the darkening streets of the town in one of the turbine-powered wagons, the watchman sitting up front with the driver and the trader and the Herald behind.

"Something's burning," said Alen to the trader, sniffing the air.

"This stinking buggy—" began blackbeard. "Oops," he said, interrupting himself and slapping at his cloak.

"Let me, trader," said Alen. He turned back the cloak, licked his thumb, and rubbed out a crawling ring of sparks spreading across a few centimeters of the cloak's silk lining. And he looked fixedly at what had started the little fire. It was an improperly covered slow-match protruding from a holstered device that was unquestionably a hand weapon.

"I bought it from one of their guards while you were parleying with the policeman," explained blackbeard embarrassedly. "I had a time making him understand. That Garthkint fellow helped." He fiddled with the perforated cover of the slow-match, screwing it on more firmly.

"A pitiful excuse for a weapon," he went on, carefully arranging his cloak over it. "The trigger isn't a trigger and the thumb safety isn't a safety. You pump the trigger a few times to build up pressure, and a little air squirts out to blow the match to life. Then you uncover the match and pull back the cocking piece. This levers a dart into the barrel. *Then* you push the thumb safety which puffs coal dust into the firing chamber and also swivels down the slow-match onto a touch-hole. *Poof,* and away goes the dart if you didn't forget any of the steps or do them in the wrong order. Luckily, I also got a knife."

He patted the nape of his neck and said, "That's where they carry 'em here. A little sheath between the shoulder blades—wonderful for a fast draw-and-throw, though it exposes you a little more than I like when you reach. The knife's black glass. Splendid edge and good balance.

"And the thieving Lyrans knew they had me where it hurt. Seven thousand, five hundred credits for the knife and gun—if you can call it that—and the holsters. By rights I should dock Elwon for them, the bloody fool. Still, it's better to buy his way out and leave no hard feelings behind us, eh, Herald?"

"Incomparably better," said Alen. "And I am amazed that you even entertain the idea of an armed jail-delivery. What if Chief Elwon had to serve a few days in a prison? Would that be worse than forever barring yourself from the planet and blackening the names of all traders with Lyra? Trader, do not hope to put down the credits that your weapons cost you as a legitimate expense of the voyage. I will not allow it when I audit your books. It was a piece of folly on which you spent personal funds, as far as the College and Order of Heralds is concerned."

"Look here," protested blackbeard. "You're supposed to be spreading utilitarian civilization, aren't you? What's utilitarian about leaving one of my crewmen here?"

Alen ignored the childish argument and wrapped himself in angry silence. As to civilization, he wondered darkly whether such a trading voyage and his part in it were relevant at all. Were the slanders true? Was the College and Order simply a collection of dupes headed by cynical oldsters greedy for luxury and power?

Such thoughts hadn't crossed his mind in a long time. He'd been too busy to entertain them, cramming his head with languages, folkways, mores, customs, underlying patterns of culture, of hundreds of galactic peoples—and for what? So that this fellow could make a profit and the College and Order take a quarter of that profit. If civilization was to come to Lyra, it would have to come in the form of metal. If the Lyrans didn't want metal, *make* them take it.

What did Machiavelli say? "The chief foundations of all states are good laws and good arms; and as there cannot be good laws where the state is not well-armed, it follows that where they are well-armed, they have good laws." It was odd that the teachers had slurred over such a seminal idea, emphasizing instead the spiritual integrity of the weaponless College and Order—or was it?

The disenchantment he felt creeping over him was terrifying.

"The castle," said the watchman over his shoulder, and their wagon stopped with a rattle before a large but unimpressive brick structure of five stories.

"You wait," the trader told the driver after they got out. He handed him two of his fifty-credit bills. "You wait, you get many, many more money. You understand, wait?"

"I wait plenty much," shouted the driver delightedly. "I wait all night, all day. You wonderful master. You great, great master, I wait—"

"All right," growled the trader, shutting him off. "You wait."

The watchman took them through an entrance hall lit by hissing pressure lamps and casually guarded by a few liveried men with truncheons. He threw open the door of a medium-sized, well-lit room with a score of people in it, looked in, and uttered a despairing groan.

A personage on a chair that looked like a throne said sharply, "Are those the star travelers? Well, don't just stand there. Bring them in!"

"Yes, Your Honor, Judge Krarl," said the watchman unhappily.

"It's the wrong judge!" Alen hissed at the trader. "This one gives out jail sentences!"

"Do what you can," said blackbeard grimly.

The watchman guided them to the personage in the chair and indicated a couple of low stools, bowed to the chair, and retired to stand at the back of the room.

"Your Honor," said Alen, "I am Journeyman-Herald Alen, Herald for the trading voyage—"

"Speak when you're spoken to," said the judge sharply. "Sir, with the usual insolence of wealth you have chosen to keep us waiting. I do not take this personally; it might have happened to Judge Treel, whom—to your evident dismay—I am replacing because of a sudden illness, or to any other member of the bench. But as an insult to our justice, we cannot overlook it. Sir, consider yourself reprimanded. Take your seats. Watchman, bring in the Cephean."

"Sit down," Alen murmured to the trader. "This is going to be bad."

A watchman brought in Chief Elwon, bleary-eyed, tousled, and sporting a few bruises. He gave Alen and the trader a shamefaced grin as his guard sat him on a stool beside them. The trader glared back.

Judge Krarl mumbled perfunctorily: "Let battle be joined among the several parties in this dispute let no man question our impartial awarding of the victory speak now if you yield instead to our judgment. *Well?* Speak up, you watchmen!"

The watchman who had brought the Herald and the trader started and said from the back of the room, "I yield instead to Your Honor's judgment."

Three other watchmen and a battered citizen, the wine-shop keeper, mumbled in turn, "I yield instead to Your Honor's judgment."

"Herald, speak for the accused," snapped the judge.

Well, thought Alen, I can try. "Your Honor," he said, "Chief Elwon's master does not yield to Your Honor's judgment. He is ready to battle the other parties in the dispute or their masters."

"What insolence is this?" screamed the judge, leaping from his throne. "The barbarous customs of other worlds do not prevail in this court! Who spoke of battle—" He shut his mouth with a snap, evidently abruptly realizing that *he* had spoken of battle, in an archaic phrase that harked back to the origins of justice on the planet. The judge sat down again and told Alen, more calmly, "You have mistaken a mere formality. The offer was not made in earnest." Obviously, he didn't like the sound of that himself, but he proceeded, "Now say 'I yield instead to Your Honor's judgment,' and we can get on with it. For your information, trial by combat has not been practiced for many generations on our enlightened planet."

Alen said politely, "Your Honor, I am a stranger to many of the ways of Lyra, but our excellent College and Order of Heralds instructed me well in the underlying principles of your law. I recall that one of your most revered legal maxims declares: 'The highest crime against man is murder; the highest crime against man's society is breach of promise.' "

Purpling, the judge snarled, "Are you presuming to bandy law with me, you slippery-tongued foreigner? Are you presuming to accuse me of the high crime of breaking my promise? For your information, a promise consists of an offer to do, or refrain from doing, a thing in return for a consideration. There must be the five elements of promiser, promisee, offer, substance, and consideration."

"If you will forgive a foreigner," said Alen, suddenly feeling the ground again under his feet, "I maintain that you offered the parties in the dispute your services in awarding the victory."

"An empty argument," snorted the judge. "Just as an offer with substance from somebody to nobody for a consideration is no promise, or an offer without substance from somebody to somebody for a consideration is no promise, so my offer was no promise, for there was no consideration involved."

"Your Honor, must the consideration be from the promisee to the promiser?"

"Of course not. A third party may provide the consideration."

"Then I respectfully maintain that your offer was a promise, since a third party, the government, provided you with the considerations of salary and position in return for offering your services to the disputants."

"Watchmen, clear the room of disinterested persons," said the judge hoarsely. While it was being done, Alen swiftly filled in the trader and Chief Elwon. Blackbeard grinned at the mention of a five-against-one battle royal, and the engineer looked alarmed.

When the doors closed leaving the nine of them in privacy, the judge said bitterly, "Herald, where did you learn such devilish tricks?"

Alen told him: "My College and Order instructed me well. A similar situation existed on a planet called England during an age known as the Victorious. Trial by combat had long been obsolete, there as here, but had never been declared so—there as here. A litigant won a hopeless lawsuit by publishing a challenge to his opponent and appearing at the appointed place in full armor. His opponent ignored the challenge and so lost the suit by default. The English dictator, one Disraeli, hastily summoned his parliament to abolish trial by combat."

"And so," mused the judge, "I find myself accused in my own chamber of high crime if I do not permit you five to slash away at each other and decide who won."

The wine-shop keeper began to blubber that he was a peaceable man and didn't intend to be carved up by that blackbearded, bloodthirsty star traveler. All he wanted was his money.

"Silence!" snapped the judge. "Of course there will be no combat. Will you, shopkeeper, and you, watchmen, withdraw if you receive satisfactory financial settlements?"

They would.

"Herald, you may dicker with them."

The four watchmen stood fast by their demand for a hundred credits apiece, and got it. The terrified shopkeeper regained his balance and demanded a thousand. Alen explained that his black-bearded master from a rude and impetuous world might be unable to restrain his rage when he, Alen, interpreted the demand and, ignoring the consequences, might beat him, the shopkeeper, to a pulp. The asking price plunged to a reasonable five hundred, which was paid over. The shopkeeper got the judge's permission to leave and backed out, bowing.

"You see, trader," Alen told blackbeard, "that it was needless to buy weapons when the spoken word—"

"And now," said the judge with a sneer, "we are easily out of *that* dilemma. Watchmen, arrest the three star travelers and take them to the cages."

"Your Honor!" cried Alen, outraged.

"Money won't get you out of *this* one. I charge you with treason."

"The charge is obsolete—" began the Herald hotly, but he broke off as he realized the vindictive strategy.

"Yes, it is. And one of its obsolete provisions is that treason charges must be tried by the parliament at a regular session, which isn't due for two hundred days. You'll be freed and I may be reprimanded, but by my head, for two hundred days you'll regret that you made a fool of *me*. Take them away."

"A trumped-up charge against us. Prison for two hundred days," said Alen swiftly to the trader as the watchmen closed in.

"Why buy weapons?" mocked the blackbeard, showing his teeth. His left arm whipped up and down, there was a black streak through the air— and the judge was pinned to his throne with a black glass knife through his throat and the sneer of triumph still on his lips.

The trader, before the knife struck, had the clumsy pistol out, with the cover off the glowing match and the cocking piece back. He must have pumped and cocked it under his cloak, thought Alen numbly as he told the watchmen, without prompting, "Get back against the wall and turn around." They did. They wanted to live, and the grinning blackbeard who had made meat of the judge with a flick of the arm was a terrifying figure.

"Well done, Alen," said the trader. "Take their clubs, Elwon. Two for you, two for the Herald. Alen, don't argue! I had to kill the judge before he raised an alarm—nothing but death will silence his breed. You may have to kill too before we're out of this. Take the clubs." He passed the clumsy pistol to Chief Elwon and said, "Keep it on their backs. The thing that looks like a thumb safety is a trigger. Put a dart through the first one who tries to make a break. Alen, tell the fellow on the end to turn around and come to me slowly."

Alen did. Blackbeard swiftly stripped him, tore and knotted his clothes into ropes and bound and gagged him. The others got the same treatment in less than ten minutes.

The trader holstered the gun and rolled the watchmen out of the line of sight from the door of the chamber. He recovered his knife and wiped it on the judge's shirt. Alen had to help him prop the body behind the throne's high back.

"Hide those clubs," blackbeard said. "Straight faces. Here we go."

They went out, single file, opening the door only enough to pass. Alen, last in line, told one of the liveried guards nearby, "His honor, Judge Krarl, does not wish to be disturbed."

"That's news?" asked the tipstaff sardonically. He put his hand on the Herald's arm. "Only yesterday he gimme a blast when I brought him a mug of water he asked me for himself. An outrageous interruption, he called me, and he asked for the water himself. What do you think of that?"

"Terrible," said Alen hastily. He broke away and caught up with the trader and the engineer at the entrance hall. Idlers and loungers were staring at them as they headed for the waiting wagon.

"I wait!" the driver told them loudly. "I wait long, much. You pay more, more?"

"We pay more," said the trader. "You start."

The driver brought out a smoldering piece of punk, lit a pressure torch, lifted the barn-door section of the wagon's floor to expose the pottery turbine and preheated it with the torch. He pumped squeakily for minutes, spinning a flywheel with his other hand, before the rotor began to turn on its own. Down went the hatch, up onto the seats went the passengers.

"The spaceport," said Alen. With a slate-pencil screech the driver engaged his planetary gear and they were off.

Through it all, blackbeard had ignored frantic muttered questions from Chief Elwon, who had wanted nothing to do with murder, especially of a judge. "You sit up there," growled the trader, "and every so often you look around and see if we're being followed. Don't alarm the driver. And if we get to the spaceport and blast off without any trouble, keep your story to yourself." He settled down in the back seat with Alen and maintained a gloomy silence. The young Herald was too much in awe of this stranger, so suddenly competent in assorted forms of violence, to question him.

They did get to the spaceport without trouble, and found the crew in the Customs shed, emptied of the gems by dealers with releases. They had built a fire for warmth.

"We wish to leave immediately," said the trader to the port officer. "Can you change my Lyran currency?"

The officer began to sputter apologetically that it was late and the vault was sealed for the night—

"That's all right. We'll change it on Vega. It'll get back to you. Call off your guards and unseal our ship."

They followed the port officer to *Starsong*'s dim bulk out on the field. The officer cracked the seal on her with his club in the light of a flaring pressure lamp held by one of the guards.

Alen was sweating hard through it all. As they started across the field he had seen what looked like two closely spaced green stars low on the horizon toward town suddenly each jerk up and toward each other in minute arcs. The semaphore!

The signal officer in the port administration building would be watching too—but nobody on the field, preoccupied with the routine of departure, seemed to have noticed.

The lights flipped this way and that. Alen didn't know the code and bitterly regretted the lack. After some twenty signals the lights flipped to the "rest" position again as the port officer was droning out a set of take-off regulations: bearing, height above settled areas, permissible atomic fuels while in atmosphere—Alen saw somebody start across the field to-ward them from the administration building. The guards were leaning on their long, competent looking weapons.

Alen inconspicuously detached himself from the group around *Star-song* and headed across the dark field to meet the approaching figure. Nearing it, he called out a low greeting in Lyran, using the noncom-to-officer military form.

"Sergeant," said the signal officer quietly, "go and draw off the men a few meters from the star travelers. Tell them the ship mustn't leave, that they're to cover the foreigners, and shoot if—"

Alen stood dazedly over the limp body of the signal officer. And then he quickly hid the bludgeon again and strolled back to the ship, wonder-ing whether he'd cracked the Lyran's skull.

The port was open by then and the crew filing in. He was last. "Close it fast," he told the trader. "I had to—"

"I saw you," grunted blackbeard. "A semaphore message?" He was working as he spoke, and the metal port closed.

"Astrogator and engineer, take over," he told them.

"All hands to their bunks," ordered Astrogator Hufner. "Blast off im-mediate."

Alen took to his cubicle and strapped himself in. Blastoff deafened him, rattled his bones, and made him thoroughly sick as usual. After what seemed like several wretched hours, they were definitely space-borne under smooth acceleration, and his nausea subsided.

Blackbeard knocked, came in, and unbuckled him.

"Ready to audit the books of the voyage?" asked the trader.

"No," said Alen feebly.

"It can wait," said the trader. "The books are the least important part, anyway. We have headed off a frightful war."

"War? We have?"

"War between Eyolf's Realm and Vega. It is the common gossip of chancelleries and trade missions that both governments have cast longing eyes on Lyrane, that they have plans to penetrate its economy by supplying metals to the planet without metals—by force, if need be. Alen, we have removed the pretext by which Eyolf's Realm and Vega would have attempted to snap up Lyrane and inevitably have come into conflict. Lyra is getting its metal now, and without imperialist entanglements."

"I saw none," the Herald said blankly.

"You wondered why I was in such haste to get off Lyra, and why I wouldn't leave Elwon there. It is because our Vegan gems were most unusual gems. I am not a technical man, but I understand they are actual gems which were treated to produce a certain effect at just about this time."

Blackbeard glanced at his wrist chronometer and said dreamily, "Lyra is getting metal. Wherever there is one of our gems, pottery is decomposing into its constituent aluminum, silicon, and oxygen. Flukes and glazes are decomposing into calcium, zinc, barium, potassium, chromium, *and iron*. Buildings are crumbling, pants are dropping as ceramic belt-buckles disintegrate—"

"It means chaos!" protested Alen.

"It means civilization and peace. An ugly clash was in the making." Blackbeard paused and added deliberately, "Where neither their property nor their honor is touched, most men live content."

The Prince, Chapter Nineteen. You are—"

"There was another important purpose to the voyage," said the trader, grinning. "You will be interested in this." He handed Alen a document which, unfolded, had the seal of the College and Order at its head.

Alen read in a daze, "Examiner Nineteen to the Rector—final clearance of Novice—"

He lingered pridefully over the paragraph that described how he had "with coolness and great resource" foxed the battle cruiser of the Realm, "adapting himself readily in a delicate situation requiring not only physical courage but swift recall, evaluation, and application of a minor planetary culture."

Not so pridefully he read, ". . . inclined toward pomposity of manner somewhat ludicrous in one of his years, though not unsuccessful in dominating the crew by his bearing—"

And, ". . . highly profitable disposal of our gems; a feat of no mean importance since the College and Order must, after all, maintain itself."

And, ". . . cleared the final and crucial hurdle with some mental turmoil if I am any judge, but did clear it. After some twenty years of indoctrination in unrealistic nonviolence, the youth was confronted with a situation where nothing but violence would serve, correctly evaluated this, and applied violence in the form of a truncheon to the head of a Lyran signal officer, thereby demonstrating an ability to learn and common sense as precious as it is rare."

And, finally, simply, "Recommended for training."

"Training?" gasped Alen. "You mean there's more?"

"Not for most, boy. Not for most. The bulk of us are what we seem to be: oily, gun-shy, indispensable adjuncts to trade who feather our nest with percentages. We need those percentages and we need gun-shy Heralds."

Alen recited slowly, "Among other evils which being unarmed brings you, it causes you to be despised."

"Chapter Fourteen," said blackbeard mechanically. "We leave such clues lying by their bedsides for twenty years, and they never notice them. For the few of us who do—more training."

"Will I learn to throw a knife like you?" asked Alen, repelled and fascinated at once by the idea.

"On your own time, if you wish. Mostly it's ethics and morals so you'll be able to weigh the values of such things as knife-throwing."

"Ethics! Morals!"

"We started as missionaries, you know."

"Everybody knows that. Buth the Great Utilitarian Reform—"

"Some of us," said blackbeard dryly, "think it was neither great, utilitarian, nor a reform."

It was a staggering idea. "But we're spreading utilitarian civilization!" protested Alen. "Or if we're not, what's the sense of it all?"

Blackbeard told him, "We have our different motives. One is a sincere utilitarian; another is a gamber—happy when he's in danger and his pulses are pounding. Another is proud and likes to trick people. More than a few conceive themselves as servants of mankind. I'll let you rest for a bit now." He rose.

"But you?" asked Alen hesitantly.

"Me? You will find me in Chapter Twenty-Six," grinned blackbeard. "And perhaps you'll find someone else." He closed the door behind him.

Alen ran through the chapter in his mind, puzzled, until—that was it.

It had a strange and inevitable familiarity to it as if he had always known that he would be saying it aloud, welcomingly, in this cramped cubicle aboard a battered starship:

"God is not willing to do everything, and thus take away our free will and that share of glory which belongs to us."

Leigh Brackett

THE LAST DAYS OF SHANDAKOR

For some unknown reason—they don't grow up with a "boy's adventure" tradition of Young Adult literature to inspire them, perhaps? They're more thoughtful and/or emotionally mature than the men are? Market forces (i.e., male editors) discourage them from writing it? Sunspot cycles?—straightforward adventure SF, especially the space adventure tale—and *especially* Space Opera—has been largely a male domain. There were exceptions then (C. L. Moore, Katherine MacLean, Andre Norton) and there are exceptions now (C. J. Cherryh, Eleanor Arnason, Janet Kagan, Lois Mc-Master Bujold), but it remains more true than not; certainly male would be the way to bet if you were uncertain of the gender of a particular Space Opera writer. Even today, when some of the Biggest Names in mainline science fiction are women, there are far more men writing that specialized sub-variety known as Space Opera than there are women—and the situation was even more lopsided in the '40s and '50s.

One of the most obvious "exceptions" to the rule was the late Leigh Brackett. Even in the male-dominated world of the adventure pulps of the '40s and '50s, testosterone-drenched venues such as *Planet Stories, Thrilling Wonder Stories,* and *Startling Stories,* where it was taken for granted that the reading audience was primarily composed of equally testosterone-drenched teenage boys, and even in an era where women were expected to stay safely in the kitchen and away from the typewriter keys, nobody could doubt that Leigh Brackett had earned the right to sit at the high-stakes table with The Men. In fact, her stuff was more popular with the readers than the work of most of her male compatriots, and ultimately more influential than almost anything else that appeared in those adventure pulps, with the possible exception of the work of Ray Bradbury and Jack Vance. There is little doubt that she was the Queen of the Planetary Romance during this period, especially as, by the mid-'40s, C. L. Moore—her major competitor for the title, whose work for magazines such as *Weird Tales* in the '30s had always had one foot in the horror genre anyway—had moved away from the adventure pulps and into more respectable mainline science fiction work for *Astounding* (except for the occasional collaboration with her husband Henry Kuttner, where her contribution was often hidden by the work appearing under his solo byline).

Brackett sold her first story in 1940, and by the late '40s and 'early '50s had become one of the mainstays of magazines such as *Planet Stories, Startling Stories, Astonishing Stories,* and *Thrilling Wonder Stories,* particularly *Planet Stories,* where much of her best work appeared. Although her best novel by a considerable margin is the mature, thoughtful *The Long Tomorrow,* one of the best SF novels of any sort of the '50s, that was an atypical work for her. More typical of her output, and more popular, were her series of stories about the savage, swashbuckling, half-feral Eric John Stark—

a sort of Conan of the Spaceways, with a touch of Tarzan of Mercury thrown in—that appeared in the magazines and were later expanded into books such as *The Secret of Sinharat* and *People of the Talisman*. Other novels in a similar richly romantic vein included *The Sword of Rhiannon* and *The Nemesis from Terra*. She also wrote more standard interstellar Space Operas, including *The Starmen of Llyrdis, The Big Jump,* and *Alpha Centauri—or Die!,* which are competent, but lack the extravagant color and lush romanticism of her sword-and-planet work.

Brackett's autumnal vision of a decadent, dying Mars, the abode of Lost Cities and attenuated, hypercivilized Elder Races on the brink of extinction, is one of the three most influential conceptualizations of the Red Planet in science fiction, ranking only behind Edgar Rice Burroughs's Barsoom and the Mars of Ray Bradbury's *The Martian Chronicles*. (Burroughs's Mars strongly influenced both Brackett and Bradbury, but although their visions of Mars are clearly similar—close cousins at least, if not blood brothers—it's an open question how much influence was swapped between Brackett and Bradbury, or who influenced *whom*—they were close working colleagues, critiquing each others stories, as early as 1941, and their Martian stories were published roughly contemporaneously, often in the same magazines.) It's hard to sort out whether later influences on the Martian story are coming from Burroughs, Brackett, or Bradbury, and any such judgments must remain subjective to some degree, but I think I can see the influence of Brackett's Mars in particular on Roger Zelazny's famous story "A Rose for Ecclesiastes," and perhaps even on Robert A. Heinlein's Mars in *Red Planet* and *Stranger in a Strange Land*. Her influence on Ursula K. Le Guin is clear, as well as on writers of the '70s such as John Varley and George R. R. Martin and Elizabeth A. Lynn, and has probably continued on down to the '90s in the work of later writers such as Eleanor Arnason (although, with writers of newer generations, you have to take into consideration the possibility that that influence is filtered *through* Le Guin's work, which had an immense impact, rather than directly derived).

Brackett's vision of Mars was never expressed in any clearer or more concentrated form than in the intense, brooding, melancholy story that follows, in which a well-meaning Earthman inadvertently ushers in the last days of an immensely ancient civilization . . .

By the mid 1950s, Brackett had drifted away from science fiction and into crime novels, which subsequently led to her writing scripts for television and for movies such as *Rio Bravo, El Dorado, Hatari!, Rio Lobo,* and *The Long Goodbye*. (Legend has it that after reading her novel *No Good From a Corpse,* Howard Hawks told an assistant to "get me that guy Brackett" to work with William Faulkner on her first major film, the 1946 classic *The Big Sleep*.) In the mid-1970s, she briefly returned to science fiction with an attempt to revive her old series hero, Eric John Stark, in the novels *The Ginger Star, The Hounds of Skaith,* and *The Reavers of Skaith,* but by then space probes had determined that none of the planets in the solar system were likely abodes for life, and she felt constrained to abandon the Mars, Venus, and Mercury that had been the settings for her earlier stories and set Stark's new adventures on the planets of distant stars instead. Somehow it was just not the same; the innocent exuberance of her earlier work was gone, and the series faltered and died after three volumes. At about the same time, she edited an anthology of stories drawn from *Planet Stories* magazine, *The Best of Planet Stories No. 1,* which, as the name implies, was supposed to be the first in a series of similar anthologies, but that series died as well, never reaching a second volume. Her last work with any significant impact on science fiction was the screenplay for the immensely successful movie *The Empire Strikes Back,* for which she received in 1980 a posthumous Hugo, her only major award. Her many short stories, which is where she did most of her best work (with the significant exception of *The Long Tomorrow*) have been assembled in the collections *The Coming of the Terrans, The Halfling and Other Stories,* and, most recently (1977), *The Best of Leigh Brackett.* Almost all of Brackett's work is out-of-print.

1

He came alone into the wineshop, wrapped in a dark red cloak, with the cowl drawn over his head. He stood for a moment by the doorway and one of the slim dark predatory women who live in those places went to him, with a silvery chiming from the little bells that were almost all she wore.

I saw her smile up at him. And then, suddenly, the smile became fixed and something happened to her eyes. She was no longer looking at the cloaked man but through him. In the oddest fashion—it was as though he had become invisible.

She went by him. Whether she passed some word along or not I couldn't tell but an empty space widened around the stranger. And no one looked at him. They did not avoid looking at him. They simply refused to see him.

He began to walk slowly across the crowded room. He was very tall and he moved with a fluid, powerful grace that was beautiful to watch. People drifted out of his way, not seeming to, but doing it. The air was thick with nameless smells, shrill with the laughter of women.

Two tall barbarians, far gone in wine, were carrying on some inter-tribal feud and the yelling crowd had made room for them to fight. There was a silver pipe and a drum and a double-banked harp making old wild music. Lithe brown bodies leaped and whirled through the laughter and the shouting and the smoke.

The stranger walked through all this, alone, untouched, unseen. He passed close to where I sat. Perhaps because I, of all the people in that place, not only saw him but stared at him, he gave me a glance of black eyes from under the shadow of his cowl—eyes like blown coals, bright with suffering and rage.

I caught only a glimpse of his muffled face. The merest glimpse—but that was enough. *Why did he have to show his face to me in that wineshop in Barrakesh?*

He passed on. There was no space in the shadowy corner where he went but space was made, a circle of it, a moat between the stranger and the crowd. He sat down. I saw him lay a coin on the outer edge of the table. Presently a serving wench came up, picked up the coin and set down a cup of wine. But it was as if she waited on an empty table.

I turned to Kardak, my head drover, a Shunni with massive shoulders and uncut hair braided in an intricate tribal knot. "What's all that about?" I asked.

Kardak shrugged. "Who knows?" He started to rise. "Come, Jon-Ross. It is time we got back to the Serai."

"We're not leaving for hours yet. And don't lie to me, I've been on Mars a long time. What is that man? Where does he come from?"

Barrakesh is the gateway between north and south. Long ago, when there were oceans in equatorial and southern Mars, when Valkis and Jekkara were proud seats of empire and not thieves' dens, here on the edge of the northern Drylands the great caravans had come and gone to Barrakesh for a thousand thousand years. It is a place of strangers.

In the time-eaten streets of rock you see tall Keshi hillmen, nomads from the high plains of Upper Shun, lean dark men from the south who barter away the loot of forgotten tombs and temples, cosmopolitan sophisticates up from Kahora and the trade cities, where there are space-ports and all the appurtenances of modern civilization.

The red-cloaked stranger was none of these.

A glimpse of a face—I am a planetary anthropologist. I was supposed to be charting Martian ethnology and I was doing it on a fellowship grant I had wangled from a Terran university too ignorant to know that the vastness of Martian history makes such a project hopeless.

I was in Barrakesh, gathering an outfit preparatory to a year's study of the tribes of Upper Shun. And suddenly there had passed close by me a man with golden skin and un-Martian black eyes and a facial structure that belonged to no race I knew. I have seen the carven faces of fauns that were a little like it.

Kardak said again, "It is time to go, JonRoss!"

I looked at the stranger, drinking his wine in silence and alone. "Very well, *I'll* ask him."

Kardak sighed. "Earthmen," he said, "are not given much to wisdom." He turned and left me.

I crossed the room and stood beside the stranger. In the old courteous High Martian they speak in all the Low-Canal towns I asked permission to sit.

Those raging, suffering eyes met mine. There was hatred in them, and scorn, and shame. "What breed of human are you?"

"I am an Earthman."

He said the name over as though he had heard it before and was trying to remember. "Earthman. Then it is as the winds have said, blowing across the desert—that Mars is dead and men from other worlds defile her dust." He looked out over the wineshop and all the people who would not admit his presence. "Change," he whispered. "Death and change and the passing away of things."

The muscles of his face drew tight. He drank and I could see now that he had been drinking for a long time, for days, perhaps for weeks. There was a quiet madness on him.

"Why do the people shun you?"

"Only a man of Earth would need to ask," he said and made a sound of laughter, very dry and bitter.

I was thinking, *A new race, an unknown race!* I was thinking of the fame that sometimes comes to men who discover a new thing, and of a Chair I might sit in at the University if I added one bright unheard-of piece of the shadowy mosaic of Martian history. I had had my share of wine and a bit more. That Chair looked a mile high and made of gold.

The stranger said softly, "I go from place to place in this wallow of Barrakesh and everywhere it is the same. I have ceased to be." His white teeth glittered for an instant in the shadow of the cowl. "They were wiser than I, my people. When Shandakor is dead, we are dead also, whether our bodies live or not."

"Shandakor?" I said. It had a sound of distant bells.

"How should an Earthman know? Yes, Shandakor! Ask of the men of Kesh and the men of Shun! Ask the kings of Mekh, who are half around the world! Ask of all the men of Mars—they have not forgotten Shandakor! But they will not tell you. It is a bitter shame to them, the memory and the name."

He stared out across the turbulent throng that filled the room and flowed over to the noisy street outside. "And I am here among them—lost."

"Shandakor is dead?"

"Dying. There were three of us who did not want to die. We came south across the desert—one turned back, one perished in the sand, I am here in Barrakesh." The metal of the wine-cup bent between his hands.

I said, "And you regret your coming."

"I should have stayed and died with Shandakor. I know that now. But I cannot go back."

"Why not?" I was thinking how the name John Ross would look, inscribed in golden letters on the scroll of the discoverers.

"The desert is wide, Earthman. Too wide for one alone."

And I said, "I have a caravan. I am going north tonight."

A light came into his eyes, so strange and deadly that I was afraid. "No," he whispered. *"No!"*

I sat in silence, looking out across the crowd that had forgotten me as well, because I sat with the stranger. *A new race, an unknown city. And I was drunk.*

After a long while the stranger asked me, "What does an Earthman want in Shandakor?"

I told him. He laughed. "You study men," he said and laughed again, so that the red cloak rippled.

"If you want to go back I'll take you. If you don't, tell me where the city lies and I'll find it. Your race, your city, should have their place in history."

He said nothing but the wine had made me very shrewd and I could guess at what was going on in the stranger's mind. I got up.

"Consider it," I told him. "You can find me at the serai by the northern gate until the lesser moon is up. Then I'll be gone."

"Wait." His fingers fastened on my wrist. They hurt. I looked into his face and I did not like what I saw there. But, as Kardak had mentioned, I was not given much to wisdom.

The stranger said, "Your men will not go beyond the Wells of Karthedon."

"Then we'll go without them."

A long long silence. Then he said, "So be it."

I knew what he was thinking as plainly as though he had spoken the words. He was thinking that I was only an Earthman and that he would kill me when we came in sight of Shandakor.

2

The caravan tracks branch off at the Wells of Karthedon. One goes westward into Shun and one goes north through the passes of Outer Kesh. But there is a third one, more ancient than the others. It goes toward the east and it is never used. The deep rock wells are dry and the stone-built shelters have vanished under the rolling dunes. It is not until the track begins to climb the mountains that there are even memories.

Kardak refused politely to go beyond the Wells. He would wait for me, he said, a certain length of time, and if I came back we would go on into Shun. If I didn't—well, his full pay was left in charge of the local headman. He would collect it and go home. He had not liked having the stranger with us. He had doubled his price.

In all that long march up from Barrakesh I had not been able to get a word out of Kardak or the men concerning Shandakor. The stranger had not spoken either. He had told me his name—Corin—and nothing more. Cloaked and cowled he rode alone and brooded. His private devils were still with him and he had a new one now—impatience. He would have ridden us all to death if I had let him.

So Corin and I went east alone from Karthedon, with two led animals and all the water we could carry. And now I could not hold him back.

"There is no time to stop," he said. "The days are running out. There is no time!"

When we reached the mountains we had only three animals left and when we crossed the first ridge we were afoot and leading the one remaining beast which carried the dwindling water skins.

We were following a road now. Partly hewn and partly worn it led up and over the mountains, those naked leaning mountains that were full of silence and peopled only with the shapes of red rock that the wind had carved.

"Armies used to come this way," said Corin. "Kings and caravans and beggars and human slaves, singers and dancing girls and the embassies of princes. This was the road to Shandakor."

And we went along it at a madman's pace.

The beast fell in a slide of rock and broke its neck and we carried the last water skin between us. It was not a heavy burden. It grew lighter and then was almost gone.

One afternoon, long before sunset, Corin said abruptly, "We will stop here."

The road went steeply up before us. There was nothing to be seen or heard. Corin sat down in the drifted dust. I crouched down too, a little distance from him. I watched him. His face was hidden and he did not speak.

The shadows thickened in that deep and narrow way. Overhead the strip of sky flared saffron and then red—and then the bright cruel stars came out. The wind worked at its cutting and polishing of stone, muttering to itself, an old and senile wind full of dissatisfaction and complaint. There was the dry faint click of falling pebbles.

The gun felt cold in my hand, covered with my cloak. I did not want to use it. But I did not want to die here on this silent pathway of vanished armies and caravans and kings.

A shaft of greenish moonlight crept down between the walls. Corin stood up.

"Twice now I have followed lies. Here I am met at last by truth."

I said, "I don't understand you."

"I thought I could escape the destruction. That was a lie. Then I thought I could return to share it. That too was a lie. Now I see the truth.

Shandakor is dying. I fled from that dying, which is the end of the city and the end of my race. The shame of flight is on me and I can never go back."

"What will you do?"

"I will die here."

"And I?"

"Did you think," asked Corin softly, "that I would bring an alien creature in to watch the end of Shandakor?"

I moved first. I didn't know what weapons he might have, hidden under that dark red cloak. I threw myself over on the dusty rock. Something went past my head with a hiss and a rattle and a flame of light and then I cut the legs from under him and he fell down forward and I got on top of him, very fast.

He had vitality. I had to hit his head twice against the rock before I could take out of his hands the vicious little instrument of metal rods. I threw it far away. I could not feel any other weapons on him except a knife and I took that, too. Then I got up.

I said, "I will carry you to Shandakor."

He lay still, draped in the tumbled folds of his cloak. His breath made a harsh sighing in his throat. "So be it." And then he asked for water.

I went to where the skin lay and picked it up, thinking that there was perhaps a cupful left. I didn't hear him move. What he did was done very silently with a sharp-edged ornament. I brought him the water and it was already over. I tried to lift him up. His eyes looked at me with a curiously brilliant look. Then he whispered three words, in a language I didn't know, and died. I let him down again.

His blood had poured out across the dust. And even in the moonlight I could see that it was not the color of human blood.

I crouched there for a long while, overcome with a strange sickness. Then I reached out and pushed that red cowl back to bare his head. It was a beautiful head. I had never seen it. If I had, I would not have gone alone with Corin into the mountains. I would have understood many things if I had seen it and not for fame nor money would I have gone to Shandakor.

His skull was narrow and arched and the shaping of the bones was very fine. On that skull was a covering of short curling fibers that had an almost metallic luster in the moonlight, silvery and bright. They stirred under my hand, soft silken wires responding of themselves to an alien touch. And even as I took my hand away the luster faded from them and the texture changed.

When I touched them again they did not stir. Corin's ears were pointed and there were silvery tufts on the tips of them. On them and on his forearms and his breast were the faint, faint memories of scales, a powdering of shining dust across the golden skin. I looked at his teeth and they were not human either.

I knew now why Corin had laughed when I told him that I studied men.

It was very still. I could hear the falling of pebbles and the little stones that rolled all lonely down the cliffs and the shift and whisper of dust in the settling cracks. The Wells of Karthedon were far away. Too far by several lifetimes for one man on foot with a cup of water.

I looked at the road that went steep and narrow on ahead. I looked at Corin. The wind was cold and the shaft of moonlight was growing thin. I did not want to stay alone in the dark with Corin.

I rose and went on along the road that led to Shandakor.

It was a long climb but not a long way. The road came out between two pinnacles of rock. Below that gateway, far below in the light of the little low moons that pass so swiftly over Mars, there was a mountain valley.

Once around that valley there were great peaks crowned with snow and crags of black and crimson where the flying lizards nested, the hawk-lizards with the red eyes. Below the crags there were forests, purple and green and gold, and a black tarn deep on the valley floor. But when I saw it it was dead. The peaks had fallen away and the forests were gone and the tarn was only a pit in the naked rock.

In the midst of that desolation stood a fortress city.

There were lights in it, soft lights of many colors. The outer walls stood up, black and massive, a barrier against the creeping dust, and within them was an island of life. The high towers were not ruined. The lights burned among them and there was movement in the streets.

A living city—and Corin had said that Shandakor was almost dead.

A rich and living city. I did not understand. But I knew one thing. Those who moved along the distant streets of Shandakor were not human.

I stood shivering in that windy pass. The bright towers of the city beckoned and there was something unnatural about all lightlife in the deathly valley. And then I thought that human or not the people of Shandakor might sell me water and a beast to carry it and I could get away out of these mountains, back to the Wells.

The road broadened, winding down the slope. I walked in the middle of it, not expecting anything. And suddenly two men came out of nowhere and barred the way.

I yelled. I jumped backward with my heart pounding and the sweat pouring off me. I saw their broadswords glitter in the moonlight. And they laughed.

They were human. One was a tall red barbarian from Mekh, which lay to the east half around Mars. The other was a leaner browner man

from Taarak, which was farther still. I was scared and angry and astonished and I asked a foolish question.

"What are you doing *here?*"

"We wait," said the man of Taarak. He made a circle with his arm to
take in all the darkling slopes around the valley. "From Kesh and Shun,
from all the countries of the Norlands and the Marches men have come,
to wait. And you?"

"I'm lost," I said. "I'm an Earthman and I have no quarrel with anyone." I was still shaking but now it was with relief. I would not have to
go to Shandakor. If there was a barbarian army gathered here it must have
supplies and I could deal with them.

I told them what I needed. "I can pay for them, pay well."

They looked at each other.

"Very well. Come and you can bargain with the chief."

They fell in on either side of me. We walked three paces and then I
was on my face in the dirt and they were all over me like two great wild-
cats. When they were finished they had everything I owned except the
few articles of clothing for which they had no use. I got up again, wiping
the blood from my mouth.

"For an outlander," said the man of Mekh, "you fight well." He
chinked my money-bag up and down in his palm, feeling the weight of it,
and then he handed me the leather bottle that hung at his side. "Drink,"
he told me. "That much I can't deny you. But our water must be carried
a long way across these mountains and we have none to waste on Earthmen."

I was not proud. I emptied his bottle for him. And the man of Taarak
said, smiling, "Go on to Shandakor. Perhaps they will give you water."

"But you've taken all my money!"

"They are rich in Shandakor. They don't need money. Go ask them
for water."

They stood there, laughing at some secret joke of their own, and I
did not like the sound of it. I could have killed them both and danced on
their bodies but they had left me nothing but my bare hands to fight with.
So presently I turned and went on and left them grinning in the dark behind me.

The road led down and out across the plain. I could feel eyes watching me, the eyes of the sentinels on the rounding slopes, piercing the dim
moonlight. The walls of the city began to rise higher and higher. They hid
everything but the top of one tall tower that had a queer squat globe on top
of it. Rods of crystal projected from the globe. It revolved slowly and the
rods sparkled with a sort of white fire that was just on the edge of seeing.

A causeway lifted toward the Western Gate. I mounted it, going very slowly, not wanting to go at all. And now I could see that the gate was open. *Open*—and this was a city under siege!

I stood still for some time, trying to puzzle out what meaning this might have—an army that did not attack and a city with open gates. I could not find a meaning. There were soldiers on the walls but they were lounging at their ease under the bright banners. Beyond the gate many people moved about but they were intent on their own affairs. I could not hear their voices.

I crept closer, closer still. Nothing happened. The sentries did not challenge me and no one spoke.

You know how necessity can force a man against his judgment and against his will?

I entered Shandakor.

3

There was an open space beyond the gate, a square large enough to hold an army. Around its edges were the stalls of merchants. Their canopies were of rich woven stuffs and the wares they sold were such things as have not been seen on Mars for more centuries than men can remember.

There were fruits and rare furs, the long-lost dyes that never fade, furnishings carved from vanished woods. There were spices and wines and exquisite cloths. In one place a merchant from the far south offered a ceremonial rug woven from the long bright hair of virgins. And it was new.

These merchants were all human. The nationalities of some of them I knew. Others I could guess at from traditional accounts. Some were utterly unknown.

Of the throngs that moved about among the stalls, quite a number were human also. There were merchant princes come to barter and there were companies of slaves on their way to the auction block. But the others . . .

I stayed where I was, pressed into a shadowy corner by the gate, and the chill that was on me was not all from the night wind.

The golden-skinned silver-crested lords of Shandakor I knew well enough from Corin. I say lords because that is how they bore themselves, walking proudly in their own place, attended by human slaves. And the humans who were not slaves made way for them and were most deferential as though they knew that they were greatly favored to be allowed inside the city at all. The women of Shandakor were very beautiful, slim golden sprites with their bright eyes and pointed ears.

And there were others. Slender creatures with great wings, some who were lithe and furred, some who were hairless and ugly and moved with a sinuous gliding, some so strangely shaped and colored that I could not even guess at their possible evolution.

The lost races of Mars. The ancient races, of whose pride and power nothing was left but the half-forgotten tales of old men in the farthest corners of the planet. Even I, who had made the anthropological history of Mars my business, had never heard of them except as the distorted shapes of legend, as satyrs and giants used to be known on Earth.

Yet here they were in gorgeous trappings, served by naked humans whose fetters were made of precious metals. And before them too the merchants drew aside and bowed.

The lights burned, many-colored—not the torches and cressets of the Mars I knew but cool radiances that fell from crystal globes. The walls of the buildings that rose around the market-place were faced with rare veined marbles and the fluted towers that crowned them were inlaid with turquoise and cinnabar, with amber and jade and the wonderful corals of the southern oceans.

The splendid robes and the naked bodies moved in a swirling pattern about the square. There was buying and selling and I could see the mouths of the people open and shut. The mouths of the women laughed. But in all that crowded place there was no sound. No voice, no scuff of sandal, no chink of mail. There was only silence, the utter stillness of deserted places.

I began to understand why there was no need to shut the gates. No superstitious barbarian would venture himself into a city peopled by living phantoms.

And I—I was civilized. I was, in my non-mechanical way, a scientist. And had I not been trapped by my need for water and supplies I would have run away right out of the valley. But I had no place to run to and so I stayed and sweated and gagged on the acrid taste of fear.

What were these creatures that made no sound? Ghosts—images—dreams? The human and the non-human, the ancient, the proud, the lost and forgotten who were so insanely present—did they have some subtle form of life I knew nothing about? Could they see me as I saw them? Did they have thought and volition of their own?

It was the solidity of them, the intense and perfectly prosaic business in which they were engaged. Ghosts do not barter. They do not hang jeweled necklets upon their women nor argue about the price of a studded harness.

The solidity and the silence—that was the worst of it. If there had been one small living sound . . .

A dying city, Corin had said. *The days are running out.* What if they had run out? What if I were here in this massive pile of stone with all its countless rooms and streets and galleries and hidden ways, alone with the lights and the soundless phantoms?

Pure terror is a nasty thing. I had it then.

I began to move, very cautiously, along the wall. I wanted to get away from that market-place. One of the hairless gliding non-humans was bartering for a female slave. The girl was shrieking. I could see every drawn muscle in her face, the spasmodic working of her throat. Not the faintest sound came out.

I found a street that paralleled the wall. I went along it, catching glimpses of people—human people—inside the lighted buildings. Now and then men passed me and I hid from them. There was still no sound. I was careful how I set my feet. Somehow I had the idea that if I made a noise something terrible would happen.

A group of merchants came toward me. I stepped back into an archway and suddenly from behind me there came three spangled women of the serais. I was caught.

I did not want those silent laughing women to touch me. I leaped back toward the street and the merchants paused, turning their heads. I thought that they had seen me. I hesitated and the women came on. Their painted eyes shone and their red lips glistened. The ornaments on their bodies flashed. They walked straight into me.

I made noise then, all I had in my lungs. And the women passed through me. They spoke to the merchants and the merchants laughed. They went off together down the street. They hadn't seen me. They hadn't heard me. And when I got in their way I was no more than a shadow. They passed through me.

I sat down on the stones of the street and tried to think. I sat for a long time. Men and women walked through me as through the empty air. I sought to remember any sudden pain, as of an arrow in the back that might have killed me between two seconds, so that I hadn't known about it. It seemed more likely that I should be the ghost than the other way around.

I couldn't remember. My body felt solid to my hands as did the stones I sat on. They were cold and finally the cold got me up and sent me on again. There was no reason to hide any more. I walked down the middle of the street and I got used to not turning aside.

I came to another wall, running at right angles back into the city. I followed that and it curved around gradually until I found myself back at the market-place, at the inner end of it. There was a gateway, with the main part of the city beyond it, and the wall continued. The non-humans passed back and forth through the gate but no human did except the slaves. I realized then that all this section was a ghetto for the humans who came to Shandakor with the caravans.

I remembered how Corin had felt about me. And I wondered— granted that I were still alive and that some of the people of Shandakor were still on the same plane as myself—how they would feel about me if I trespassed in their city.

There was a fountain in the market-place. The water sprang up sparkling in the colored light and filled a wide basin of carved stone. Men and women were drinking from it. I went to the fountain but when I put my hands in it all I felt was a dry basin filled with dust. I lifted my hands and let the dust trickle from them. I could see it clearly. But I saw the water too. A child leaned over and splashed it and it wetted the garments of the people. They struck the child and he cried and there was no sound.

I went on through the gate that was forbidden to the human race.

The avenues were wide. There were trees and flowers, wide parks and garden villas, great buildings as graceful as they were tall. A wise proud city, ancient in culture but not decayed, as beautiful as Athens but rich and strange, with a touch of the alien in every line of it. Can you think what it was like to walk in that city, among the silent throngs that were not human—to see the glory of it, that was not human either?

The towers of jade and cinnabar, the golden minarets, the lights and the colored silks, the enjoyment and the strength. And the people of Shandakor! No matter how far their souls have gone they will never forgive me.

How long I wandered I don't know. I had almost lost my fear in wonder at what I saw. And then, all at once in that deathly stillness, I heard a sound—the quick, soft scuffing of sandaled feet.

4

I stopped where I was, in the middle of a plaza. The tall silver-crested ones drank wine under canopies of dusky blooms and in the center a score of winged girls as lovely as swans danced a slow strange measure that was more like flight than dancing. I looked all around. There were many people. How could you tell which one had made a noise?

Silence.

I turned and ran across the marble paving. I ran hard and then suddenly I stopped again, listening. *Scuff-scuff*—no more than a whisper, very light and swift. I spun around but it was gone. The soundless people walked and the dancers wove and shifted, spreading their white wings.

Someone was watching me. Some one of those indifferent shadows was not a shadow.

I went on. Wide streets led off from the plaza. I took one of them. I tried the trick of shifting pace and two or three times I caught the echo of other steps than mine. Once I knew it was deliberate. Whoever followed me slipped silently among the noiseless crowd, blending with them, protected by them, only making a show of footsteps now and then to goad me.

I spoke to that mocking presence. I talked to it and listened to my own voice ringing hollow from the walls. The groups of people ebbed and flowed around me and there was no answer.

I tried making sudden leaps here and there among the passersby with my arms outspread. But all I caught was empty air. I wanted a place to hide and there was none.

The street was long. I went its length and the someone followed me. There were many buildings, all lighted and populous and deathly still. I thought of trying to hide in the buildings but I could not bear to be closed in between walls with those people who were not people.

I came into a great circle, where a number of avenues met around the very tall tower I had seen with the revolving globe on top of it. I hesitated, not knowing which way to go. Someone was sobbing and I realized that it was myself, laboring to breathe. Sweat ran into the corners of my mouth and it was cold, and bitter.

A pebble dropped at my feet with a brittle *click*.

I bolted out across the square. Four or five times, without reason, like a rabbit caught in the open, I changed course and fetched up with my back against an ornamental pillar. From somewhere there came a sound of laughter.

I began to yell. I don't know what I said. Finally I stopped and there was only the silence and the passing throngs, who did not see nor hear me. And now it seemed to me that the silence was full of whispers just below the threshold of hearing.

A second pebble clattered off the pillar above my head. Another stung my body. I sprang away from the pillar. There was laughter and I ran.

There were infinities of streets, all glowing with color. There were many faces, strange faces, and robes blown out on a night wind, litters with scarlet curtains and beautiful cars like chariots drawn by beasts. They flowed past me like smoke, without sound, without substance, and the laughter pursued me, and I ran.

Four men of Shandakor came toward me. I plunged through them *but their bodies opposed mine, their hands caught me and I could see their eyes, their black shining eyes, looking at me. . . .*

I struggled briefly and then it was suddenly very dark.

The darkness caught me up and took me somewhere. Voices talked far away. One of them was a light young shiny sort of voice. It matched the laughter that had haunted me down the streets. I hated it.

I hated it so much that I fought to get free of the black river that was carrying me. There was a vertiginous whirling of light and sound and stubborn shadow and then things steadied down and I was ashamed of myself for having passed out.

I was in a room. It was fairly large, very beautiful, very old, the first place I had seen in Shandakor that showed real age—Martian age, that runs back before history had begun on Earth. The floor, of some magnificent somber stone the color of a moonless night, and the pale slim pillars that upheld the arching roof all showed the hollowings and smoothnesses of centuries. The wall paintings had dimmed and softened and the rugs that burned in pools of color on that dusky floor were worn as thin as silk.

There were men and women in that room, the alien folk of Shandakor. But these breathed and spoke and were alive. One of them, a girl-child with slender thighs and little pointed breasts, leaned against a pillar close beside me. Her black eyes watched me, full of dancing lights. When she saw that I was awake again she smiled and flicked a pebble at my feet.

I got up. I wanted to get that golden body between my hands and make it scream. And she said in High Martian, "Are you a human? I have never seen one before close to."

A man in a dark robe said, "Be still, Duani." He came and stood before me. He did not seem to be armed but others were and I remembered Corin's little weapon. I got hold of myself and did none of the things I wanted to do.

"What are you doing here?" asked the man in the dark robe.

I told him about myself and Corin, omitting only the fight that he and I had had before he died, and I told him how the hillmen had robbed me.

"They sent me here," I finished, "to ask for water."

Someone made a harsh humorless sound. The man before me said, "They were in a jesting mood."

"Surely you can spare some water and a beast!"

"Our beasts were slaughtered long ago. And as for water . . ." He paused, then asked bitterly, "Don't you understand? We are dying here of thirst!"

I looked at him and at the she-imp called Duani and the others. "You don't show any signs of it," I said.

"You saw how the human tribes have gathered like wolves upon the hills. What do you think they wait for? A year ago they found and cut the buried aqueduct that brought water into Shandakor from the polar cap. All they needed then was patience. And their time is very near. The store we had in the cisterns is almost gone."

A certain anger at their submissiveness made me say, "Why do you stay here and die like mice bottled up in a jar? You could have fought your way out. I've seen your weapons."

"Our weapons are old and we are very few. And suppose that some of us did survive—tell me again, Earthman, how did Corin fare in the world of men?" He shook his head. "Once we were great and Shandakor was mighty. The human tribes of half a world paid tribute to us. We are only the last poor shadow of our race but we will not beg from men!"

"Besides," said Duani softly, "where else could we live but in Shandakor?"

"What about the others?" I asked. "The silent ones."

"They are the past," said the dark-robed man and his voice rang like a distant flare of trumpets.

Still I did not understand. I did not understand at all. But before I could ask more questions a man came up and said, "Rhul, he will have to die."

The tufted tips of Duani's ears quivered and her crest of silver curls came almost erect.

"No, Rhul!" she cried. "At least not right away."

There was a clamor from the others, chiefly in a rapid angular speech that must have predated all the syllables of men. And the one who had spoken before to Rhul repeated, "He will have to die! He has no place here. And we can't spare water."

"I'll share mine with him," said Duani, "for a while."

I didn't want any favors from her and said so. "I came here after supplies. You haven't any, so I'll go away again. It's as simple as that." I couldn't buy from the barbarians, but I might make shift to steal.

Rhul shook his head. "I'm afraid not. We are only a handful. For years our single defense has been the living ghosts of our past who walk the streets, the shadows who man the walls. The barbarians believe in enchantments. If you were to enter Shandakor and leave it again alive the barbarians would know that the enchantment cannot kill. They would not wait any longer."

Angrily, because I was afraid, I said, "I can't see what difference that would make. You're going to die in a short while anyway."

"But in our own way, Earthman, and in our own time. Perhaps, being human, you can't understand that. It is a question of pride. The oldest race of Mars will end well, as it began."

He turned away with a small nod of the head that said *kill him*—as easily as that. And I saw the ugly little weapons rise.

5

There was a split second then that seemed like a year. I thought of many things but none of them were any good. It was a devil of a place to die without even a human hand to help me under. And then Duani flung her arms around me.

"You're all so full of dying and big thoughts!" she yelled at them. "And you're all paired off or so old you can't do anything but think! What about *me?* I don't have anyone to talk to and I'm sick of wandering alone, thinking how I'm going to die! Let me have him just for a little while? I told you I'd share my water."

On Earth a child might talk that way about a stray dog. And it is written in an old Book that a live dog is better than a dead lion. I hoped they would let her keep me.

They did. Rhul looked at Duani with a sort of weary compassion and lifted his hand. "Wait," he said to the men with the weapons. "I have thought how this human may be useful to us. We have so little time left now that it is a pity to waste any of it, yet much of it must be used up in tending the machine. He could do that labor—and a man can keep alive on very little water."

The others thought that over. Some of them dissented violently, not so much on the grounds of water as that it was unthinkable that a human should intrude on the last days of Shandakor. Corin had said the same thing. But Rhul was an old man. The tufts of his pointed ears were colorless as glass and his face was graven deep with years and wisdom had distilled in him its bitter brew.

"A human of our own world, yes. But this man is of Earth and the men of Earth will come to be the new rulers of Mars as we were the old. And Mars will love them no better than she did us because they are as alien as we. So it is not unfitting that he should see us out."

They had to be content with that. I think they were already so close to the end that they did not really care. By ones and twos they left as though already they had wasted too much time away from the wonders that there were in the streets outside. Some of the men still held the weapons on me and others went and brought precious chains such as the human slaves had worn—shackles, so that I should not escape. They put them on me and Duani laughed.

"Come," said Rhul, "and I will show you the machine."

He led me from the room and up a winding stair. There were tall embrasures and looking through them I discovered that we were in the base of the very high tower with the globe. They must have carried me back to it after Duani had chased me with her laughter and her pebbles. I looked out over the glowing streets, so full of splendor and of silence, and asked Rhul why there were no ghosts inside the tower.

"You have seen the globe with the crystal rods?"

"Yes."

"We are under the shadow of its core. There had to be some retreat for us into reality. Otherwise we would lose the meaning of the dream."

The winding stair went up and up. The chain between my ankles clattered musically. Several times I tripped on it and fell.

"Never mind," Duani said. "You'll grow used to it."

We came at last into a circular room high in the tower. And I stopped and stared.

Most of the space in that room was occupied by web of metal girders that supported a great gleaming shaft. The shaft disappeared upward through the roof. It was not tall but very massive, revolving slowly and quietly. There were traps, presumably for access to the offset shaft and the cogs that turned it. A ladder led to a trap in the roof.

All the visible metal was sound with only a little surface corrosion. What the alloy was I don't know and when I asked Rhul he only smiled rather sadly. "Knowledge is found," he said, "only to be lost again. Even we of Shandakor forget."

Every bit of that enormous structure had been shaped and polished and fitted into place by hand. Nearly all the Martian peoples work in metal. They seem to have a genius for it and while they are not and apparently never have been mechanical, as some of our races are on Earth, they find many uses for metal that we have never thought of.

But this before me was certainly the high point of the metalworkers' craft. When I saw what was down below, the beautifully simple power plant and the rotary drive set-up with fewer moving parts than I would have thought possible, I was even more respectful. "How old is it?" I asked and again Rhul shook his head.

"Several thousand years ago there is a record of the yearly Hosting of the Shadows and it was not the first." He motioned me to follow him up the ladder, bidding Duani sternly to remain where she was. She came anyway.

There was a railed platform open to the universe and directly above it swung the mighty globe with its crystal rods that gleamed so strangely. Shandakor lay beneath us, a tapestry of many colors, bright and still, and out along the dark sides of the valley the tribesmen waited for the light to die.

"When there is no one left to tend the machine it will stop in time and then the men who have hated us so long will take what they want of Shandakor. Only fear has kept them out this long. The riches of half a world flowed through these streets and much of it remained."

He looked up at the globe. "Yes," he said, "we had knowledge. More, I think, than any other race of Mars."

"But you wouldn't share it with the humans."

Rhul smiled. "Would you give little children weapons to destroy you? We gave men better ploughshares and brighter ornaments and if they invented a machine we did not take it from them. But we did not tempt and burden them with knowledge that was not their own. They were content to make war with sword and spear and so they had more pleasure and less killing and the world was not torn apart."

"And you—how did you make war?"

"We defended our city. The human tribes had nothing that we coveted, so there was no reason to fight them except in self-defense. When we did we won." He paused. "The other non-human races were more stupid or less fortunate. They perished long ago."

He turned again to his explanations of the machine. "It draws its power directly from the sun. Some of the solar energy is converted and stored within the globe to serve as the light-source. Some is sent down to turn the shaft."

"What if it should stop," Duani said, "while we're still alive?" She shivered, looking out over the beautiful streets.

"It won't—not if the Earthman wishes to live."

"What would I have to gain by stopping it?" I demanded.

"Nothing. And that," said Rhul, "is why I trust you. As long as the globe turns you are safe from the barbarians. After we are gone you will have the pick of the loot of Shandakor."

How I was going to get away with it afterward he did not tell me.

He motioned me down the ladder again but I asked him, "What *is* the globe, Rhul? How does it make the—the Shadows?"

He frowned. "I can only tell you what has become, I'm afraid, mere traditional knowledge. Our wise men studied deeply into the properties of light. They learned that light has a definite effect upon solid matter and they believed, because of that effect, that stone and metal and crystalline things retain a 'memory' of all that they have 'seen.' Why this should be I do not know."

I didn't try to explain to him the quantum theory and the photoelectric effect nor the various experiments of Einstein and Millikan and the men who followed them. I didn't know them well enough myself and the old High Martian is deficient in such terminology.

I only said, "The wise men of my world also know that the impact of light tears away tiny particles from the substance it strikes."

I was beginning to get a glimmering of the truth. Light-patterns "cut" in the electrons of metal and stone—sound-patterns cut in unlikely looking mediums of plastic, each needing only the proper "needle" to recreate the recorded melody or the recorded picture.

"They constructed the globe," said Rhul. "I do not know how many generations that required nor how many failures they must have had. But they found at last the invisible light that makes the stones give up their memories."

In other words they had found their needle. What wave-length or combination of wave-lengths in the electromagnetic spectrum flowed out from those crystal rods, there was no way for me to know. But where they probed the walls and the paving blocks of Shandakor they scanned the hidden patterns that were buried in them and brought them forth again in form and color—as the electron needle brings forth whole symphonies from a little ridged disc.

How they had achieved sequence and selectivity was another matter. Rhul said something about the "memories" having different lengths. Perhaps he meant depth of penetration. The stones of Shandakor were ages old and the outer surfaces would have worn away. The earliest impressions would be gone altogether or at least have become fragmentary and extremely shallow.

Perhaps the scanning beams could differentiate between the overlapping layers of impressions by that fraction of a micron difference in depth. Photons only penetrate so far into any given substance but if that substance is constantly growing less in thickness the photons would have the effect of going deeper. I imagine the globe was accurate in centuries or numbers of centuries, not in years.

However it was, the Shadows of a golden past walked the streets of Shandakor and the last men of the race waited quietly for death, remembering their glory.

Rhul took me below again and showed me what my tasks would be, chiefly involving a queer sort of lubricant and a careful watch over the power leads. I would have to spend most of my time there but not all of it. During the free periods, Duani might take me where she would.

The old man went away. Duani leaned herself against a girder and studied me with intense interest. "How are you called?" she asked.

"John Ross."

"JonRoss," she repeated and smiled. She began to walk around me, touching my hair, inspecting my arms and chest, taking a child's delight in discovering all the differences there were between herself and what we call a human. And that was the beginning of my captivity.

6

There were days and nights, scant food and scanter water. There was Duani. And there was Shandakor. I lost my fear. And whether I lived to occupy the Chair or not, this was something to have seen.

Duani was my guide. I was tender of my duties because my neck depended on them but there was time to wander in the streets, to watch the crowded pageant that was not and sense the stillness and the desolation that were so cruelly real.

I began to get the feel of what this alien culture had been like and how it had dominated half a world without the need of conquest.

In a Hall of Government, built of white marble and decorated with wall friezes of austere magnificence, I watched the careful choosing and the crowning of a king. I saw the places of learning. I saw the young men trained for war as fully as they were instructed in the arts of peace. I saw the pleasure gardens, the theaters, the forums, the sporting fields—and I saw the places of work, where the men and women of Shandakor coaxed beauty from their looms and forges to trade for the things they wanted from the human world.

The human slaves were brought by their own kind to be sold, and they seemed to be well treated, as one treats a useful animal in which one has invested money. They had their work to do but it was only a small part of the work of the city.

The things that could be had nowhere else on Mars—the tools, the textiles, the fine work in metal and precious stones, the glass and porcelain—were fashioned by the people of Shandakor and they were proud of their skill. Their scientific knowledge they kept entirely to themselves, except what concerned agriculture or medicine or better ways of building drains and houses.

They were the lawgivers, the teachers. And the humans took all they would give and hated them for it. How long it had taken these people to attain such a degree of civilization Duani could not tell me. Neither could old Rhul.

"It is certain that we lived in communities, had a form of civil government, a system of numbers and written speech, before the human tribes. There are traditions of an earlier race than ours, from whom we learned these things. Whether or not this is true I do not know."

In its prime Shandakor had been a vast and flourishing city with countless thousands of inhabitants. Yet I could see no signs of poverty or crime. I couldn't even find a prison.

"Murder was punishable by death," said Rhul, "but it was most infrequent. Theft was for slaves. We did not stoop to it." He watched my face, smiling a little acid smile. "That startles you—a great city without suffering or crime or places of punishment."

I had to admit that it did. "Elder race or not, how did you manage to do it? I'm a student of cultures, both here and on my own world. I know all the usual patterns of development and I've read all the theories about them—but Shandakor doesn't fit any of them."

Rhul's smile deepened. "You are human," he said. "Do you wish the truth?"

"Of course."

"Then I will tell you. We developed the faculty of reason."

For a moment I thought he was joking. "Come," I said, "man is a reasoning being—on Earth the only reasoning being."

"I do not know of Earth," he answered courteously. "But on Mars man has always said, 'I reason, I am above the beasts because I reason.' And he has been very proud of himself because he could reason. It is the mark of his humanity. Being convinced that reason operates automatically within him he orders his life and his government upon emotion and superstition.

"He hates and fears and believes, not with reason but because he is told to by other men or by tradition. He does one thing and says another and his reason teaches him no difference between fact and falsehood. His bloodiest wars are fought for the merest whim—and that is why we did not give him weapons. His greatest follies appear to him the highest wisdom, his basest betrayals become noble acts—and that is why we could not teach him justice. We learned to reason. Man only learned to talk."

I understood then why the human tribes had hated the men of Shandakor. I said angrily, "Perhaps that is so on Mars. But only reasoning minds can develop great technologies and we humans of Earth have outstripped yours a million times. All right, you know or knew some things we haven't learned yet, in optics and some branches of electronics and perhaps in metallurgy. But . . ."

I went on to tell him all the things we had that Shandakor did not. "You never went beyond the beast of burden and the simple wheel. We achieved flight long ago. We have conquered space and the planets. We'll go on to conquer the stars!"

Rhul nodded. "Perhaps we were wrong. We remained here and conquered ourselves." He looked out toward the slopes where the barbarian army waited and he sighed. "In the end it is all the same."

Days and nights and Duani, bringing me food, sharing her water, asking questions, taking me through the city. The only thing she would not show me was something they called the Place of Sleep. "I shall be there soon enough," she said and shivered.

"How long?" I asked. It was an ugly thing to say.

"We are not told. Rhul watches the level in the cisterns and when it's time . . ." She made a gesture with her hands. "Let us go up on the wall."

We went up among the ghostly soldiery and the phantom banners. Outside there were darkness and death and the coming of death. Inside there were light and beauty, the last proud blaze of Shandakor under the shadow of its doom. There was an eerie magic in it that had begun to tell on me. I watched Duani. She leaned against the parapet, looking outward. The wind ruffled her silver crest, pressed her garments close against her body. Her eyes were full of moonlight and I could not read them. Then I saw that there were tears.

I put my arm around her shoulders. She was only a child, an alien child, not of my race or breed . . .

"JonRoss."

"Yes?"

"There are so many things I will never know."

It was the first time I had touched her. Those curious curls stirred under my fingers, warm and alive. The tips of her pointed ears were soft as a kitten's.

"Duani."

"What?"

"I don't know . . ."

I kissed her. She drew back and gave me a startled look from those black brilliant eyes and suddenly I stopped thinking that she was a child and I forgot that she was not human and—I didn't care.

"Duani, listen. You don't have to go to the Place of Sleep."

She looked at me, her cloak spread out upon the night wind, her hands against my chest.

"There's a whole world out there to live in. And if you aren't happy there I'll take you to my world, to Earth. There isn't any reason why you have to die!"

Still she looked at me and did not speak. In the streets below the silent throngs went by and the towers glowed with many colors. Duani's gaze moved slowly to the darkness beyond the wall, to the barren valley and the hostile rocks.

"No."

"Why not? Because of Rhul, because of all this talk of pride and race?"

"Because of truth. Corin learned it."

I didn't want to think about Corin. "He was alone. You're not. You'd never be alone."

She brought her hands up and laid them on my cheeks very gently. "That green star, that is your world. Suppose it were to vanish and you were the last of all the men of Earth. Suppose you lived with me in Shandakor forever—would you not be alone?"

"It wouldn't matter if I had you."

She shook her head. "It would matter. And our two races are as far apart as the stars. We would have nothing to share between us."

Remembering what Rhul had told me I flared up and said some angry things. She let me say them and then she smiled. "It is none of that, Jon-Ross." She turned to look out over the city. "This is my place and no other. When it is gone I must be gone too."

Quite suddenly I hated Shandakor.

I didn't sleep much after that. Every time Duani left me I was afraid she might never come back. Rhul would tell me nothing and I didn't dare to question him too much. The hours rushed by like seconds and Duani was happy and I was not. My shackles had magnetic locks. I couldn't break them and I couldn't cut the chains.

One evening Duani came to me with something in her face and in the way she moved that told me the truth long before I could make her put it into words. She clung to me, not wanting to talk, but at last she said, "Today there was a casting of lots and the first hundred have gone to the Place of Sleep."

"It is the beginning, then."

She nodded. "Every day there will be another hundred until all are gone."

I couldn't stand it any longer. I thrust her away and stood up. "You know where the 'keys' are. Get these chains off me!"

She shook her head. "Let us not quarrel now, JonRoss. Come. I want to walk in the city."

We had quarreled more than once, and fiercely. She would not leave Shandakor and I couldn't take her out by force as long as I was chained. And I was not to be released until everyone but Rhul had entered the Place of Sleep and the last page of that long history had been written.

I walked with her among the dancers and the slaves and the bright-cloaked princes. There were no temples in Shandakor. If they worshipped anything it was beauty and to that their whole city was a shrine. Duani's eyes were rapt and there was a remoteness on her now.

I held her hand and looked at the towers of turquoise and cinnabar, the pavings of rose quartz and marble, the walls of pink and white and deep red coral, and to me they were hideous. The ghostly crowds, the mockery of life, the phantom splendors of the past were hideous, a drug, a snare.

"The faculty of reason!" I thought and saw no reason in any of it.

I looked up to where the great globe turned and turned against the sky, keeping these mockeries alive. "Have you ever seen the city as it is— without the Shadows?"

"No. I think only Rhul, who is the oldest, remembers it that way. I think it must have been very lonely. Even then there were less than three thousand of us left."

It must indeed have been lonely. They must have wanted the Shadows as much to people the empty streets as to fend off the enemies who believed in magic.

I kept looking at the globe. We walked for a long time. And then I said, "I must go back to the tower."

She smiled at me very tenderly. "Soon you will be free of the tower— and of these." She touched the chains. "No, don't be sad, JonRoss. You will remember me and Shandakor as one remembers a dream." She held up her face, that was so lovely and so unlike the meaty faces of human women, and her eyes were full of somber lights. I kissed her and then I caught her up in my arms and carried her back to the tower.

In that room, where the great shaft turned, I told her, "I have to tend the things below. Go up onto the platform, Duani, where you can see all Shandakor. I'll be with you soon."

I don't know whether she had some hint of what was in my mind or whether it was only the imminence of parting that made her look at me as she did. I thought she was going to speak but she did not, climbing the ladder obediently. I watched her slender golden body vanish upward. Then I went into the chamber below.

There was a heavy metal bar there that was part of a manual control for regulating the rate of turn. I took it off its pin. Then I closed the simple switches on the power plant. I tore out all the leads and smashed the connections with the bar. I did what damage I could to the cogs and the offset shaft. I worked very fast. Then I went up into the main chamber again. The great shaft was still turning but slowly, ever more slowly.

There was a cry from above me and I saw Duani. I sprang up the ladder, thrusting her back onto the platform. The globe moved heavily of its own momentum. Soon it would stop but the white fires still flickered in the crystal rods. I climbed up onto the railing, clinging to a strut. The chains on my wrists and ankles made it hard but I could reach. Duani tried to pull me down. I think she was screaming. I hung on and smashed the crystal rods with the bar, as many as I could.

There was no more motion, no more light. I got down on the platform again and dropped the bar. Duani had forgotten me. She was looking at the city.

The lights of many colors that had burned there were burning still but they were old and dim, cold embers without radiance. The towers of jade and turquoise rose up against the little moons and they were broken and cracked with time and there was no glory in them. They were desolate and very sad. The night lay clotted around their feet. The streets, the plazas and the market-squares were empty, their marble paving blank and bare. The soldiers had gone from the walls of Shandakor, with their banners and their bright mail, and there was no longer any movement anywhere within the gates.

Duani let out one small voiceless cry. And as though in answer to it, suddenly from the darkness of the valley and the slopes beyond there rose a thin fierce howling as of wolves.

"Why?" she whispered. *"Why?"* She turned to me. Her face was pitiful. I caught her to me.

"I couldn't let you die! Not for dreams and visions, nothing. Look, Duani. Look at Shandakor." I wanted to force her to understand. "Shandakor is broken and ugly and forlorn. It is a dead city—but you're alive. There are many cities but only one life for you."

Still she looked at me and it was hard to meet her eyes. She said, "We knew all that, JonRoss."

"Duani, you're a child, you've only a child's way of thought. Forget the past and think of tomorrow. We can get through the barbarians. Corin did. And after that . . ."

"And after that you would still be human—and I would not."

From below us in the dim and empty streets there came a sound of lamentation. I tried to hold her but she slipped out from between my hands. "And I am glad that you are human," she whispered. "You will never understand what you have done."

And she was gone before I could stop her, down into the tower.

I went after her. Down the endless winding stairs with my chains clattering between my feet, out into the streets, the dark and broken and deserted streets of Shandakor. I called her name and her golden body went before me, fleet and slender, distant and more distant. The chains dragged upon my feet and the night took her away from me.

I stopped. The whelming silence rushed smoothly over me and I was bitterly afraid of this dark dead Shandakor that I did not know. I called again to Duani and then I began to search for her in the shattered shadowed streets. I know now how long it must have been before I found her.

For when I found her, she was with the others. The last people of Shandakor, the men and the women, the women first, were walking silently in a long line toward a low flat-roofed building that I knew without telling was the Place of Sleep.

They were going to die and there was no pride in their faces now. There was a sickness in them, a sickness and a hurt in their eyes as they moved heavily forward, not looking, not wanting to look at the sordid ancient streets that I had stripped of glory.

"Duani!" I called, and ran forward but she did not turn in her place in the line. And I saw that she was weeping.

Rhul turned toward me, and his look had a weary contempt that was bitterer than a curse. "Of what use, after all, to kill you now?"

"But I did this thing! *I* did it!"

"You are only human."

The long line shuffled on and Duani's little feet were closer to that final doorway. Rhul looked upward at the sky. "There is still time before the sunrise. The women at least will be spared the indignity of spears."

"Let me go with her!"

I tried to follow her, to take my place in line. And the weapon in Rhul's hand moved and there was the pain and I lay as Corin had lain while they went silently on into the Place of Sleep.

The barbarians found me when they came, still half doubtful, into the city after dawn. I think they were afraid of me. I think they feared me as a wizard who had somehow destroyed all the folk of Shandakor.

For they broke my chains and healed my wounds and later they even gave me out of the loot of Shandakor the only thing I wanted—a bit of porcelain, shaped like the head of a young girl.

I sit in the Chair that I craved at the University and my name is written on the roll of the discoverers. I am eminent, I am respectable—I, who murdered the glory of a race.

Why didn't I go after Duani into the Place of Sleep? I could have crawled! I could have dragged myself across those stones. And I wish to God I had. I wish that I had died with Shandakor!

Murray Leinster

EXPLORATION TEAM

"Murray Leinster" was one of the writing names used by the late William Fitzger-ald Jenkins, who also wrote as "Will F. Jenkins" and employed another half-dozen pseudonyms. Although he wrote copiously in many other fields, turning out millions of words of pulp stories, little of it other than the science fiction work he produced as Murray Leinster is known today—and, in fact, little outside of his SF work gained much attention even *during* his lifetime. As Murray Leinster, though, Jenkins had a pro-found and lasting effect on the development of modern science fiction.

"Leinster" sold his first SF story to *Argosy* in 1919, had work published in Hugo Gernsback's *Amazing* during the '20s, and went on to be one of the mainstays of John W. Campbell's "Golden Age" *Astounding* in the '40s and '50s, where most of his best work appeared. Most of Leinster's novels are heavily dated and long forgotten—one of the few figures of the day who made his reputation almost entirely on his short fic-tion, he was somehow never able to make much of an impact with his novels, which were widely regarded as inferior to his short work even during his working lifetime—but the best of his short stories remain fresh and powerful today. In his short work, Leinster more or less invented several subgenres still active today: for instance, he is credited with writing one of the first Alternate History stories, "Sideways In Time," and one of the earliest First Contact stories, the famous "First Contact," and both stories still hold up as among the best treatments of their subjects. Also among his most famous stories is the taut, suspenseful, and scary tale that follows, "Exploration Team," which won Leinster his only Hugo Award in 1956, and which is practically the model of how to write an intricate and intelligent adventure set on an alien world, a story which has been an influence on—if not indeed the inspiration for—countless other stories and novels, as well as television shows and movies, over the years. Nobody before Lein-ster had ever written the tale of Terran explorers battling a hostile alien planet any bet-ter than he wrote it here—and, you know what? Forty years later, nobody has done it any better *yet.*

Leinster's best novel is probably *The Wailing Asteroid,* above-average among Leinster novels for imagination and evocativeness, with some quirky detail work that holds up fairly well. His other novels include *The Pirates of Zan, The Forgotten Planet, The Greks Bring Gifts,* and *The War with the Gizmos.* "Exploration Team" was collected, with other Survey Team stories, as *Colonial Survey,* one of his best collections. His "Med Service" series—not as successful as his Survey Team stories, but still of inter-est—was collected in *S.O.S. from Three Worlds* and *Doctor to the Stars;* there were also two Med Service novels, *The Mutant Weapon* and *This World Is Taboo.* Other Leinster collections include *Monsters and Such* and *The Best of Murray Leinster.*

Almost all of Leinster's books are long out-of-print, and almost impossible to find;

you probably have the best chance of finding *The Best of Murray Leinster,* published in 1978, in a used-book store, but even that's rather unlikely these days. Fortunately, NESFA Press has just brought out a big retrospective anthology of his work, *First Contacts: The Essential Murray Leinster* (NESFA Press, P.O. Box 809, Framingham, MA 07101-0203, $27), which features most of his best stories. Buy it while you still can, since much of this work is unfindable anywhere else.

A multi-talented man, Will Jenkins, the person behind the Murray Leinster mask, was a successful inventor as well as an author, having created, among other things, a front-projection method for filming backgrounds still used in the film industry today, where it is known as the "Leinster Projector." During World War II, he also came up with an ingenious method for disguising the wake left by submarine periscopes that probably saved the lives of thousands of submarine sailors over the course of the war. He died in 1975.

I

The nearer moon went by overhead. It was jagged and irregular in shape, and was probably a captured asteroid. Huyghens had seen it often enough, so he did not go out of his quarters to watch it hurtle across the sky with seemingly the speed of an atmosphere-flier, occulting the stars as it went. Instead, he sweated over paper work, which should have been odd because he was technically a felon and all his labors on Loren Two felonious. It was odd, too, for a man to do paper work in a room with steel shutters and a huge bald eagle—untethered—dozing on a three-inch perch set in the wall. But paper work was not Huyghens' real task. His only assistant had tangled with a night-walker and the furtive Kodius Company ships had taken him away to where Kodius Company ships came from. Huyghens had to do two men's work in loneliness. To his knowledge, he was the only man in this solar system.

Below him, there were snufflings. Sitka Pete got up heavily and padded to his water pan. He lapped the refrigerated water and sneezed violently. Sourdough Charley waked and complained in a rumbling growl. There were divers other rumblings and mutterings below. Huyghens called reassuringly, "Easy there!" and went on with his work. He finished a climate report, and fed figures to a computer, and while it hummed over them he entered the inventory totals in the station log, showing what supplies remained. Then he began to write up the log proper.

"Sitka Pete," he wrote, *"has apparently solved the problem of killing individual sphexes. He has learned that it doesn't do to hug them and that his claws can't penetrate their hide—not the top hide, anyhow. Today Semper notified us that a pack of sphexes had found the scent-trail to the*

station. Sitka hid downwind until they arrived. Then he charged from the rear and brought his paws together on both sides of a sphex's head in a terrific pair of slaps. It must have been like two twelve-inch shells arriving from opposite directions at the same time. It must have scrambled the sphex's brains as if they were eggs. It dropped dead. He killed two more with such mighty pairs of wallops. Sourdough Charley watched, grunting, and when the sphexes turned on Sitka, he charged in his turn. I, of course, couldn't shoot too close to him, so he might have fared badly but that Faro Nell came pouring out of the bear quarters to help. The diversion enabled Sitka Pete to resume the use of his new technic, towering on his hind legs and swinging his paws in the new and grisly fashion. The fight ended promptly. Semper flew and screamed above the scrap, but as usual did not join in. Note: Nugget, the cub, tried to mix in but his mother cuffed him out of the way. Sourdough and Sitka ignored him as usual. Kodius Champion's genes are sound!"

The noises of the night went on outside. There were notes like organ tones—song lizards. There were the tittering giggling cries of nightwalkers—not to be tittered back at. There were sounds like tack hammers, and doors closing, and from every direction came noises like hiccups in various keys. These were made by the improbable small creatures which on Loren Two took the place of insects.

Huyghens wrote out:

"Sitka seemed ruffled when the fight was over. He painstakingly used his trick on every dead or wounded sphex, except those he'd killed with it, lifting up their heads for his pile-driver-like blows from two directions at once, as if to show Sourdough how it was done. There was much grunting as they hauled the carcasses to the incinerator. It almost seemed—"

The arrival bell clanged, and Huyghens jerked up his head to stare at it. Semper, the eagle, opened icy eyes. He blinked.

Noises. There was a long, deep, contented snore from below. Something shrieked, out in the jungle. Hiccups. Clatterings, and organ notes—

The bell clanged again. It was a notice that a ship aloft somewhere had picked up the beacon beam—which only Kodius Company ships should know about—and was communicating for a landing. But there shouldn't be any ships in this solar system just now! This was the only habitable planet of the sun, and it had been officially declared uninhabitable by reason of inimical animal life. Which meant sphexes. Therefore no colony was permitted, and the Kodius Company broke the law. And there were few graver crimes than unauthorized occupation of a new planet.

The bell clanged a third time. Huyghens swore. His hand went out to cut off the beacon—but that would be useless. Radar would have fixed it and tied it in with physical features like the nearby sea and the Sere Plateau. The ship could find the place, anyhow, and descend by daylight.

"The devil!" said Huyghens. But he waited yet again for the bell to ring. A Kodius Company ship would double-ring to reassure him. But there shouldn't be a Kodius Company ship for months.

The bell clanged singly. The space phone dial flickered and a voice came out of it, tinny from stratospheric distortion:

"Calling ground! Calling ground! Crete Line ship Odysseus *calling ground on Loren Two. Landing one passenger by boat. Put on your field lights."*

Huyghens' mouth dropped open. A Kodius Company ship would be welcome. A Colonial Survey ship would be extremely unwelcome, because it would destroy the colony and Sitka and Sourdough and Faro Nell and Nugget—and Semper—and carry Huyghens off to be tried for unauthorized colonization and all that it implied.

But a commercial ship, landing one passenger by boat— There was simply no circumstances under which that would happen. Not to an unknown, illegal colony. Not to a furtive station!

Huyghens flicked on the landing-field lights. He saw the glare in the field outside. Then he stood up and prepared to take the measures required by discovery. He packed the paper work he'd been doing into the disposal safe. He gathered up all personal documents and tossed them in. Every record, every bit of evidence that the Kodius Company maintained this station went into the safe. He slammed the door. He touched his finger to the disposal button, which would destroy the contents and melt down even the ashes past their possible use for evidence in court.

Then he hesitated. If it were a Survey ship, the button had to be pressed and he must resign himself to a long term in prison. But a Crete Line ship—if the space phone told the truth—was not threatening. It was simply unbelievable.

He shook his head. He got into travel garb and armed himself. He went down into the bear quarters, turning on lights as he went. There were startled snufflings and Sitka Pete reared himself very absurdly to a sitting position to blink at him. Sourdough Charley lay on his back with his legs in the air. He'd found it cooler, sleeping that way. He rolled over with a thump. He made snorting sounds which somehow sounded cordial. Faro Nell padded to the door of her separate apartment—assigned her so that Nugget would not be underfoot to irritate the big males.

Huyghens, as the human population of Loren Two, faced the work force, fighting force, and—with Nugget—four-fifths of the terrestrial nonhuman population of the planet. They were mutated Kodiak bears, descendants of the Kodius Champion for whom the Kodius Company was named. Sitka Pete was a good twenty-two hundred pounds of lumbering, intelligent carnivore. Sourdough Charley would weigh within a hundred pounds of that figure. Faro Nell was eighteen hundred pounds of female charm—and ferocity. Then Nugget poked his muzzle around his mother's furry rump to see what was toward, and he was six hundred pounds of ursine infancy. The animals looked at Huyghens expectantly. If he'd had Semper riding on his shoulder, they'd have known what was expected of them.

"Let's go," said Huyghens. "It's dark outside, but somebody's coming. And it may be bad!"

He unfastened the outer door of the bear quarters. Sitka Pete went charging clumsily through it. A forthright charge was the best way to develop any situation—if one was an oversized male Kodiak bear. Sourdough went lumbering after him. There was nothing hostile immediately outside. Sitka stood up on his hind legs—he reared up a solid twelve feet—and sniffed the air. Sourdough methodically lumbered to one side and then the other, sniffing in his turn. Nell came out, nine-tenths of a ton of daintiness, and rumbled admonitorily at Nugget, who trailed her closely. Huyghens stood in the doorway, his night-sighted gun ready. He felt uncomfortable at sending the bears ahead into a Loren Two jungle at night. But they were qualified to scent danger, and he was not.

The illumination of the jungle in a wide path toward the landing field made for weirdness in the look of things. There were arching giant ferns and columnar trees which grew above them, and the extraordinary lanceolate underbrush of the jungle. The flood lamps, set level with the ground, lighted everything from below. The foliage, then, was brightly lit against the black night-sky—brightly lit enough to dim-out the stars. There were astonishing contrasts of light and shadow everywhere.

"On ahead!" commanded Huyghens, waving. "Hup!"

He swung the bear-quarters door shut. He moved toward the landing field through the lane of lighted forest. The two giant male Kodiaks lumbered ahead. Sitka Pete dropped to all fours and prowled. Sourdough Charley followed closely, swinging from side to side. Huyghens came alertly behind the two of them, and Faro Nell brought up the rear with Nugget following her closely.

It was an excellent military formation for progress through dangerous jungle. Sourdough and Sitka were advance-guard and point, respectively, while Faro Nell guarded the rear. With Nugget to look after, she was especially alert against attack from behind. Huyghens was, of course, the striking force. His gun fired explosive bullets which would discourage even sphexes, and his night-sight—a cone of light which went on when he took up the trigger-slack—told exactly where they would strike. It was not a sportsmanlike weapon, but the creatures of Loren Two were not sportsmanlike antagonists. The night-walkers, for example— But night-walkers feared light. They attacked only in a species of hysteria if it were too bright.

Huyghens moved toward the glare at the landing field. His mental state was savage. The Kodius Company station on Loren Two was completely illegal. It happened to be necessary, from one point of view, but it was still illegal. The tinny voice on the space phone was not convincing, in ignoring that illegality. But if a ship landed, Huyghens could get back to the station before men could follow, and he'd have the disposal safe turned on in time to protect those who'd sent him here.

But he heard the faraway and high harsh roar of a landing-boat rocket—not a ship's bellowing tubes—as he made his way through the unreal-seeming brush. The roar grew louder as he pushed on, the three big Kodiaks padding here and there, sniffing thoughtfully, making a perfect defensive-offensive formation for the particular conditions of this planet.

He reached the edge of the landing field, and it was blindingly bright, with the customary divergent beams slanting skyward so a ship could check its instrument landing by sight. Landing fields like this had been standard, once upon a time. Nowadays all developed planets had landing grids—monstrous structures which drew upon ionospheres for power and lifted and drew down star ships with remarkable gentleness and unlimited force. This sort of landing field would be found where a survey-team was at work, or where some strictly temporary investigation of ecology or bacteriology was under way, or where a newly authorized colony had not yet been able to build its landing grid. Of course it was unthinkable that anybody would attempt a settlement in defiance of the law!

Already, as Huyghens reached the edge of the scorched open space, the night-creatures had rushed to the light like moths on Earth. The air was misty with crazily gyrating, tiny flying things. They were innumerable and of every possible form and size, from the white midges of the night and multi-winged flying worms to those revoltingly naked-looking larger creatures which might have passed for plucked flying monkeys if they had not been carnivorous and worse. The flying things soared and whirred and danced and spun insanely in the glare. They made peculiarly plaintive humming noises. They almost formed a lamp-lit ceiling over the cleared space. They did hide the stars. Staring upward, Huyghens could just barely make out the blue-white flame of the space-boat's rocket through the fog of wings and bodies.

• • •

The rocket-flame grew steadily in size. Once, apparently, it tilted to adjust the boat's descending course. It went back to normal. A speck of incandescence at first, it grew until it was like a great star, and then a more-than-brilliant moon, and then it was a pitiless glaring eye. Huyghens averted his gaze from it. Sitka Pete sat lumpily—more than a ton of him—and blinked wisely at the dark jungle away from the light. Sourdough ignored the deepening, increasing rocket roar. He sniffed the air delicately. Faro Nell held Nugget firmly under one huge paw and licked his head as if tidying him up to be seen by company. Nugget wriggled.

The roar became that of ten thousand thunders. A warm breeze blew outward from the landing-field. The rocket boat hurled downward, and its flame touched the mist of flying things, and they shriveled and burned and were hot. Then there were churning clouds of dust everywhere, and the center of the field blazed terribly—and something slid down a shaft of fire, and squeezed it flat, and sat on it—and the flame went out. The rocket boat sat there, resting on its tail fins, pointing toward the stars from which it came.

There was a terrible silence after the tumult. Then, very faintly, the noises of the night came again. There were sounds like those of organ pipes, and very faint and apologetic noises like hiccups. All these sounds increased, and suddenly Huyghens could hear quite normally. Then a side-port opened with a quaint sort of clattering, and something unfolded from where it had been inset into the hull of the space boat, and there was a metal passageway across the flame-heated space on which the boat stood.

A man came out of the port. He reached back in and shook hands very formally. He climbed down the ladder rungs to the walkway. He marched above the steaming baked area, carrying a traveling bag. He reached the end of the walk and stepped gingerly to the ground. He moved hastily to the edge of the clearing. He waved to the space boat. There were ports. Perhaps someone returned the gesture. The walkway folded briskly back up to the hull and vanished in it. A flame exploded into being under the tail fins. There were fresh clouds of monstrous, choking dust and a brightness like that of a sun. There was noise past the possibility of endurance. Then the light rose swiftly through the dust cloud, and sprang higher and climbed more swiftly still. When Huyghens' ears again permitted him to hear anything, there was only a diminishing mutter in the heavens and a small bright speck of light ascending to the sky and swinging eastward as it rose to intercept the ship which had let it descend.

The night noises of the jungle went on. Life on Loren Two did not need to heed the doings of men. But there was a spot of incandescence in the day-bright clearing, and a short, brisk man looked puzzledly about him with a traveling bag in his hand.

Huyghens advanced toward him as the incandescence dimmed. Sourdough and Sitka preceded him. Faro Nell trailed faithfully, keeping a maternal eye on her offspring. The man in the clearing stared at the parade they made. It would be upsetting, even after preparation, to land at night on a strange planet, and to have the ship's boat and all links with the rest of the cosmos depart, and then to find one's self approached—it might seem stalked—by two colossal male Kodiak bears, with a third bear and cub behind them. A single human figure in such company might seem irrelevant.

The new arrival gazed blankly. He moved, startled. Then Huyghens called:

"Hello, there! Don't worry about the bears! They're friends!"

Sitka reached the newcomer. He went warily downwind from him and sniffed. The smell was satisfactory. Man-smell. Sitka sat down with the solid impact of more than a ton of bear-meat landing on packed dirt. He regarded the man amiably. Sourdough said *"Whoosh!"* and went on to sample the air beyond the clearing. Huyghens approached. The newcomer wore the uniform of the Colonial Survey. That was bad. It bore the insignia of a senior officer. Worse.

"Hah!" said the just-landed man. "Where are the robots? What in all the nineteen hells are these creatures? Why did you shift your station? I'm Roane, here to make a progress report on your colony."

Huyghens said:

"What colony?"

"Loren Two Robot Installation—" Then Roane said indignantly, "Don't tell me that that idiot skipper dropped me at the wrong place! This is Loren Two, isn't it? And this is the landing field. But where are your robots? You should have the beginning of a grid up! What the devil's happened here and what are these beasts?"

Huyghens grimaced.

"This," he said politely, "is an illegal, unlicensed settlement. I'm a criminal. These beasts are my confederates. If you don't want to associate with criminals you needn't, of course, but I doubt if you'll live till morning unless you accept my hospitality while I think over what to do about your landing. In reason, I ought to shoot you."

Faro Nell came to a halt behind Huyghens, which was her proper post in all out-door movement. Nugget, however, saw a new human. Nugget was a cub, and, therefore, friendly. He ambled forward ingratiatingly. He was four feet high at the shoulders, on all fours. He wriggled bashfully as he approached Roane. He sneezed, because he was embarrassed.

His mother overtook him swiftly and cuffed him to one side. He wailed. The wail of a six-hundred-pound Kodiak bear-cub is a remarkable sound. Roane gave ground a pace.

"I think," he said carefully, "that we'd better talk things over. But if this is an illegal colony, of course you're under arrest and anything you say will be used against you."

Huyghens grimaced again.

"Right," he said. "But now if you'll walk close to me, we'll head back to the station. I'd have Sourdough carry your bag—he likes to carry things—but he may need his teeth. We've half a mile to travel." He turned to the animals. "Let's go!" he said commandingly. "Back to the station! Hup!"

Grunting, Sitka Pete arose and took up his duties as advanced point of a combat team. Sourdough trailed, swinging widely to one side and another. Huyghens and Roane moved together. Faro Nell and Nugget brought up the rear. Which, of course, was the only relatively safe way for anybody to travel on Loren Two, in the jungle, a good half mile from one's fortresslike residence.

But there was only one incident on the way back. It was a nightwalker, made hysterical by the lane of light. It poured through the underbrush, uttering cries like maniacal laughter.

Sourdough brought it down, a good ten yards from Huyghens. When it was all over, Nugget bristled up to the dead creature, uttering cub-growls. He feigned to attack it.

His mother whacked him soundly.

II

There were comfortable, settling-down noises below. The bears grunted and rumbled, but ultimately were still. The glare from the landing field was gone. The lighted lane through the jungle was dark again. Huyghens ushered the man from the space boat up into his living quarters. There was a rustling stir, and Semper took his head from under his wing. He stared coldly at the two humans. He spread monstrous, seven-foot wings and fluttered them. He opened his beak and closed it with a snap.

"That's Semper," said Huyghens. "Semper Tyrannis. He's the rest of the terrestrial population here. Not being a fly-by-night sort of creature, he didn't come out to welcome you."

Roane blinked at the huge bird, perched on a three-inch-thick perch set in the wall.

"An eagle?" he demanded. "Kodiak bears—mutated ones you say, but still bears—and now an eagle? You've a very nice fighting unit in the bears."

"They're pack animals, too," said Huyghens. "They can carry some hundreds of pounds without losing too much combat efficiency. And there's no problem of supply. They live off the jungle. Not sphexes, though. Nothing will eat a sphex, even if it can kill one."

He brought out glasses and a bottle. He indicated a chair. Roane put down his traveling bag. He took a glass.

"I'm curious," he observed. "Why Semper Tyrannis? I can under-stand Sitka Pete and Sourdough Charley as names. The home of their an-cestors makes them fitting. But why Semper?"

"He was bred for hawking," said Huyghens. "You sic a dog on some-thing. You sic Semper Tyrannis. He's too big to ride on a hawking glove, so the shoulders of my coats are padded to let him ride there. He's a fly-ing scout. I've trained him to notify us of sphexes, and in flight he carries a tiny television camera. He's useful, but he hasn't the brains of the bears."

Roane sat down and sipped at his glass.

"Interesting . . . very interesting! But this is an illegal settlement. I'm a Colonial Survey officer. My job is reporting on progress according to plan, but nevertheless I have to arrest you. Didn't you say something about shooting me?"

Huyghens said doggedly:

"I'm trying to think of a way out. Add up all the penalties for illegal colonization and I'd be in a very bad fix if you got away and reported this set-up. Shooting you would be logical."

"I see that," said Roane reasonably. "But since the point has come up—I have a blaster trained on you from my pocket."

Huyghens shrugged.

"It's rather likely that my human confederates will be back here be-fore your friends. You'd be in a very tight fix if my friends came back and found you more or less sitting on my corpse."

Roane nodded.

"That's true, too. Also it's probable that your fellow terrestrials wouldn't co-operate with me as they have with you. You seem to have the whip hand, even with my blaster trained on you. On the other hand, you could have killed me quite easily after the boat left, when I'd first landed. I'd have been quite unsuspicious. So you may not really intend to mur-der me."

Huyghens shrugged again.

"So," said Roane, "since the secret of getting along with people is that of postponing quarrels—suppose we postpone the question of who kills whom? Frankly, I'm going to send you to prison if I can. Unlawful colonization is very bad business. But I suppose you feel that you have to do something permanent about me. In your place I probably should, too. Shall we declare a truce?"

Huyghens indicated indifference. Roane said vexedly:

"Then I do! I have to! So—"

He pulled his hand out of his pocket and put a pocket blaster on the table. He leaned back, defiantly.

"Keep it," said Huyghens. "Loren Two isn't a place where you live long unarmed." He turned to a cupboard. "Hungry?"

"I could eat," admitted Roane.

Huyghens pulled out two mealpacks from the cupboard and inserted them in the readier below. He set out plates.

"Now—what happened to the official, licensed, authorized colony here?" asked Roane briskly. "License issued eighteen months ago. There was a landing of colonists with a drone fleet of equipment and supplies. There've been four ship-contacts since. There should be several thousand robots being industrious under adequate human supervision. There should be a hundred-mile-square clearing, planted with food plants for later human arrivals. There should be a landing grid at least half-finished. Obviously there should be a space beacon to guide ships to a landing. There isn't. There's no clearing visible from space. That Crete Line ship has been in orbit for three days, trying to find a place to drop me. Her skipper was fuming. Your beacon is the only one on the planet, and we found it by accident. What happened?"

Huyghens served the food. He said dryly:

"There could be a hundred colonies on this planet without any one knowing of any other. I can only guess about your robots, but I suspect they ran into sphexes."

Roane paused, with his fork in his hand.

"I read up on this planet, since I was to report on its colony. A sphex is part of the inimical animal life here. Cold-blooded belligerent carnivore, not a lizard but a genus all its own. Hunts in packs. Seven to eight hundred pounds, when adult. Lethally dangerous and simply too numerous to fight. They're why no license was ever granted to human colonists. Only robots could work here, because they're machines. What animal attacks machines?"

Huyghens said:

"What machine attacks animals? The sphexes wouldn't bother robots, of course, but would robots bother the sphexes?"

Roane chewed and swallowed.

"Hold it! I'll agree that you can't make a hunting-robot. A machine
can discriminate, but it can't decide. That's why there's no danger of a
robot revolt. They can't decide to do something for which they have no
instructions. But this colony was planned with full knowledge of what robots can and can't do. As ground was cleared, it was enclosed in an electric fence which no sphex could touch without frying."

Huyghens thoughtfully cut his food. After a moment:

"The landing was in the wintertime," he observed. "It must have
been, because the colony survived a while. And at a guess, the last ship-
landing was before thaw. The years are eighteen months long here, you
know."

Roane admitted:

"It was in winter that the landing was made. And the last ship-landing
was before spring. The idea was to get mines in operation for material,
and to have ground cleared and enclosed in sphex-proof fence before the
sphexes came back from the tropics. They winter there, I understand."

"Did you ever see a sphex?" Huyghens asked. Then added, "No, of
course not. But if you took a spitting cobra and crossed it with a wildcat,
painted it tan-and-blue and then gave it hydrophobia and homicidal
mania at once—why you might have one sphex. But not the race of
sphexes. They can climb trees, by the way. A fence wouldn't stop them."

"An electrified fence," said Roane. "Nothing could climb that!"

"No one animal," Huyghens told him. "But sphexes are a race. The
smell of one dead sphex brings others running with blood in their eyes.
Leave a dead sphex alone for six hours and you've got them around by
the dozen. Two days and there are hundreds. Longer, and you've got
thousands of them! They gather to caterwaul over their dead pal and hunt
for whoever or whatever killed him."

He returned to his meal. A moment later he said:

"No need to wonder what happened to your colony. During the winter the robots burned out a clearing and put up an electrified fence according to the book. Come spring, the sphexes came back. They're
curious, among their other madnesses. A sphex would try to climb the
fence just to see what was behind it. He'd be electrocuted. His carcass
would bring others, raging because a sphex was dead. Some of them
would try to climb the fence—and die. And their corpses would bring
others. Presently the fence would break down from the bodies hanging on
it, or a bridge of dead beasts' carcasses would be built across it—and
from as far downwind as the scent carried there'd be loping, raging,

scent-crazed sphexes racing to the spot. They'd pour into the clearing through or over the fence, squalling and screeching for something to kill. I think they'd find it."

Roane ceased to eat. He looked sick.

"There were . . . pictures of sphexes in the data I read. I suppose that would account for . . . everything."

He tried to lift his fork. He put it down again.

"I can't eat," he said abruptly.

Huyghens made no comment. He finished his own meal, scowling. He rose and put the plates into the top of the cleaner. There was a whirring. He took them out of the bottom and put them away.

"Let me see those reports, eh?" he asked dourly. "I'd like to see what sort of a set-up they had—those robots."

Roane hesitated and then opened his traveling bag. There was a microviewer and reels of films. One entire reel was labeled "Specifications for Construction, Colonial Survey," which would contain detailed plans and all requirements of material and workmanship for everything from desks, office, administrative personnel, for use of, to landing grids, heavy-gravity planets, lift-capacity one hundred thousand Earth-tons. But Huyghens found another. He inserted it and spun the control swiftly here and there, pausing only briefly at index frames until he came to the section he wanted. He began to study the information with growing impatience.

"Robots, robots, robots!" he snapped. "Why don't they leave them where they belong—in cities to do the dirty work, and on airless planets where nothing unexpected ever happens! Robots don't belong in new colonies! Your colonists depended on them for defense! Dammit, let a man work with robots long enough and he thinks all nature is as limited as they are! This is a plan to set up a controlled environment! On Loren Two! Controlled environment—" He swore, luridly. "Complacent, idiotic, desk-bound half-wits!"

"Robots are all right," said Roane. "We couldn't run civilization without them."

"But you can't tame a wilderness with 'em!" snapped Huyghens. "You had a dozen men landed, with fifty assembled robots to start with. There were parts for fifteen hundred more—and I'll bet anything I've got that the ship-contacts landed more still."

"They did," admitted Roane.

"I despise 'em," growled Huyghens. "I feel about 'em the way the old Greeks and Romans felt about slaves. They're for menial work—the sort of work a man will perform for himself, but that he won't do for another man for pay. Degrading work!"

"Quite aristocratic!" said Roane with a touch of irony. "I take it that robots clean out the bear quarters downstairs."

"No!" snapped Huyghens. "I do! They're my friends! They fight for me! They can't understand the necessity and no robot would do the job right!"

He growled, again. The noises of the night went on outside. Organ tones and hiccupings and the sound of tack hammers and slamming doors. Somewhere there was a singularly exact replica of the discordant squeaking of a rusty pump.

"I'm looking," said Huyghens at the micro-viewer, "for the record of their mining operations. An open-pit operation wouldn't mean a thing. But if they had driven a tunnel, and somebody was there supervising the robots when the colony was wiped out, there's an off-chance he survived a while."

Roane regarded him with suddenly intent eyes.

"And—"

"Dammit," snapped Huyghens, "if so I'll go see! He'd . . . they'd have no chance at all, otherwise. Not that the chance is good in any case!"

Roane raised his eyebrows.

"I'm a Colonial Survey officer," he said. "I've told you I'll send you to prison if I can. You've risked the lives of millions of people, maintaining non-quarantined communication with an unlicensed planet. If you did rescue somebody from the ruins of the robot colony, does it occur to you that they'd be witnesses to your unauthorized presence here?"

Huyghens spun the viewer again. He stopped. He switched back and forth and found what he wanted. He muttered in satisfaction: "They did run a tunnel!" Aloud he said, "I'll worry about witnesses when I have to."

He pushed aside another cupboard door. Inside it were the odds and ends a man makes use of to repair the things about his house that he never notices until they go wrong. There was an assortment of wires, transistors, bolts, and similar stray items that a man living alone will need. When to his knowledge he's the only inhabitant of a solar system, he especially needs such things.

"What now?" asked Roane mildly.

"I'm going to try to find out if there's anybody left alive over there. I'd have checked before if I'd known the colony existed. I can't prove they're all dead, but I may prove that somebody's still alive. It's barely two weeks' journey away from here! Odd that two colonies picked spots so near!"

He absorbedly picked over the oddments he'd selected. Roane said vexedly:

"Confound it! How can you check whether somebody's alive some hundreds of miles away—when you didn't know he existed half an hour ago?"

Huyghens threw a switch and took down a wall panel, exposing electronic apparatus and circuits behind. He busied himself with it.

"Ever think about hunting for a castaway?" he asked over his shoulder. "There's a planet with some tens of millions of square miles on it. You know there's a ship down. You've no idea where. You assume the survivors have power—no civilized man will be without power very long, so long as he can smelt metals!—but making a space beacon calls for high-precision measurements and workmanship. It's not to be improvised. So what will your ship-wrecked civilized man do, to guide a rescue ship to the one or two square miles he occupies among some tens of millions on the planet?"

Roane fretted visibly.

"What?"

"He's had to go primitive, to begin with," Roane explained. "He cooks his meat over a fire, and so on. He has to make a strictly primitive signal. It's all he can do without gauges and micrometers and very special tools. But he can fill all the planet's atmosphere with a signal that searchers for him can't miss. You see?"

Roane thought irritably. He shook his head.

"He'll make," said Huyghens, "a spark transmitter. He'll fix its output at the shortest frequency he can contrive—it'll be somewhere in the five-to-fifty-meter wave-band, but it will tune very broad—and it will be a plainly human signal. He'll start it broadcasting. Some of those frequencies will go all around the planet under the ionosphere. Any ship that comes in under the radio roof will pick up his signal, get a fix on it, move and get another fix, and then go straight to where the castaway is waiting placidly in a hand-braided hammock, sipping whatever sort of drink he's improvised out of the local vegetation."

Roane said grudgingly:

"Now that you mention it, of course—"

"My space phone picks up microwaves," said Huyghens, "I'm shifting a few elements to make it listen for longer stuff. It won't be efficient, but it will pick up a distress signal if one's in the air. I don't expect it, though."

He worked. Roane sat still a long time, watching him. Down below, a rhythmic sort of sound arose. It was Sourdough Charley, snoring. He lay on his back with his legs in the air. He'd discovered that he slept cooler that way. Sitka Peter grunted in his sleep. He was dreaming. In the general room of the station Semper, the eagle, blinked his eyes rapidly and then tucked his head under a gigantic wing and went to sleep. The noises of the Loren Two jungle came through the steel-shuttered windows. The nearer moon—which had passed overhead not long before the ringing of the arrival bell—again came soaring over the eastern horizon. It sped across the sky at the apparent speed of an atmosphere-flier. Overhead, it could be seen to be a jagged irregular mass of rock or metal, plunging blindly about the great planet forever.

Inside the station, Roane said angrily:

"See here, Huyghens! You've reason to kill me. Apparently you don't intend to. You've excellent reason to leave that robot colony strictly alone. But you're preparing to help, if there's anybody alive to need it. And yet you're a criminal—and I mean a criminal! There've been some ghastly bacteria exported from planets like Loren Two! There've been plenty of lives lost in consequence, and you're risking more! Why do you do it? Why do you do something that could produce monstrous results to other beings?"

Huyghens grunted.

"You're only assuming there are no sanitary and quarantine precautions taken in my communications. As a matter of fact, there are. They're taken, all right! As for the rest, you wouldn't understand."

"I don't understand," snapped Roane, "but that's no proof I can't! Why are you a criminal?"

Huyghens painstakingly used a screwdriver inside the wall panel. He delicately lifted out a small electronic assembly. He carefully began to fit in a spaghettied new assembly with larger units.

"I'm cutting my amplification here to hell-and-gone," he observed, "but I think it'll do. I'm doing what I'm doing," he added calmly, "I'm being a criminal because it seems to me befitting what I think I am. Everybody acts according to his own real notion of himself. You're a conscientious citizen, and a loyal official, and a well-adjusted personality. You consider yourself an intelligent rational animal. But you don't act that way! You're reminding me of my need to shoot you or something similar, which a merely rational animal would try to make me forget. You happen, Roane, to be a man. So am I. But I'm aware of it. Therefore, I deliberately do things a merely rational animal wouldn't, because they're my notion of what a man who's more than a rational animal should do."

He very carefully tightened one small screw after another. Roane said annoyedly:

"Oh. Religion."

"Self-respect," corrected Huyghens. "I don't like robots. They're too much like rational animals. A robot will do whatever it can that its supervisor requires it to do. A merely rational animal will do whatever it can that circumstances require it to do. I wouldn't like a robot unless it had some idea of what was befitting it and would spit in my eye if I tried to make it do something else. The bears downstairs, now— They're no robots! They are loyal and honorable beasts, but they'd turn and tear me to bits if I tried to make them do something against their nature. Faro Nell would fight me and all creation together, if I tried to harm Nugget. It would be unintelligent and unreasonable and irrational. She'd lose out and get killed. But I like her that way! And I'll fight you and all creation when you make me try to do something against my nature. I'll be stupid and unreasonable and irrational about it." Then he grinned over his shoulder. "So will you. Only you don't realize it."

He turned back to his task. After a moment he fitted a manual-control knob over a shaft in his haywire assembly.

"What did somebody try to make you do?" asked Roane shrewdly. "What was demanded of you that turned you into a criminal? What are you in revolt against?"

Huyghens threw a switch. He began to turn the knob which controlled the knob of his makeshift-modified receiver.

"Why," he said amusedly, "when I was young the people around me tried to make me into a conscientious citizen and a loyal employee and a well-adjusted personality. They tried to make me into a highly intelligent rational animal and nothing more. The difference between us, Roane, is that I found it out. naturally, I rev—"

He stopped short. Faint, crackling, crisp frying sounds came from the speaker of the space phone now modified to receive what once were called short waves.

Huyghens listened. He cocked his head intently. He turned the knob very, very slowly. Then Roane made an arrested gesture, to call attention to something in the sibilant sound. Huyghens nodded. He turned the knob again, with infinitesimal increments.

Out of the background noise came a patterned mutter. As Huyghens shifted the tuning, it grew louder. It reached a volume where it was unmistakable. It was a sequence of sounds like discordant buzzing. There were three half-second buzzings with half-second pauses between. A two-second pause. Three full-second buzzings with half-second pauses between. Another two-second pause and three half-second buzzings, again. Then silence for five seconds. Then the pattern repeated.

"The devil!" said Huyghens. "That's a human signal! Mechanically made, too! In fact, it used to be a standard distress-call. It was termed an S O S, though I've no idea what that meant. Anyhow, somebody must have read old-fashioned novels, some time, to know about it. And so someone is still alive over at your licensed, but now smashed-up, robot colony. And they're asking for help. I'd say they're likely to need it."

He looked at Roane.

"The intelligent thing to do is sit back and wait for a ship—either of my friends or yours. A ship can help survivors or castaways much better than we can. A ship can even find them more easily. But maybe time is important to the poor devils! So I'm going to take the bears and see if I can reach them. You can wait here, if you like. What say? Travel on Loren Two isn't a picnic! I'll be fighting nearly every foot of the way. There's plenty of 'inimical animal life' here!"

Roane snapped angrily:

"Don't be a fool! Of course I'm coming! What do you take me for? And two of us should have four times the chance of one!"

Huyghens grinned.

"Not quite. You forget Sitka Pete and Sourdough Charley and Faro Nell. There'll be five of us if you come, instead of four. And, of course, Nugget has to come—and he'll be no help—but Semper may make up for him. You won't quadruple our chances, Roane, but I'll be glad to have you if you want to be stupid and unreasonable and not at all rational—and come along."

III

There was a jagged spur of stone looming precipitously over a river-valley. A thousand feet below, a broad stream ran westward to the sea. Twenty miles to the east, a wall of mountains rose sheer against the sky. Its peaks seemed to blend to a remarkable evenness of height. There was rolling, tumbled ground between for as far as the eye could see.

A speck in the sky came swiftly downward. Great pinions spread, and flapped, and icy eyes surveyed the rocky space. With more great flappings, Semper the eagle came to ground. He folded his huge wings and turned his head jerkily, his eyes unblinking. A tiny harness held a miniature camera against his chest. He strutted over the bare stone to the highest point. He stood there, a lonely and arrogant figure in the vastness.

There came crashings and rustlings, and then snuffling sounds. Sitka Pete came lumbering out into the clear space. He wore a harness too, and a pack. The harness was complex, because it had not only to hold a pack in normal travel, but, when he stood on his hind legs, it must not hamper the use of his forepaws in combat.

He went cagily all over the open area. He peered over the edge of the spur's farthest tip. He prowled to the other side and looked down. He scouted carefully. Once he moved close to Semper and the eagle opened his great curved beak and uttered an indignant noise. Sitka paid no attention.

He relaxed, satisfied. He sat down untidily, his hind legs sprawling. He wore an air approaching benevolence as he surveyed the landscape about and below him.

More snufflings and crashings. Sourdough Charley came into view with Huyghens and Roane behind him. Sourdough carried a pack, too. Then there was a squealing and Nugget scurried up from the rear, impelled by a whack from his mother. Faro Nell appeared, with the carcass of a staglike animal lashed to her harness.

"I picked this place from a space photo," said Huyghens, "to make a directional fix from. I'll get set up."

He swung his pack from his shoulders to the ground. He extracted an obviously self-constructed device which he set on the ground. It had a whip aerial, which he extended. Then he plugged in a considerable length of flexible wire and unfolded a tiny, improvised directional aerial with an even tinier booster at its base. Roane slipped his pack from his shoulders and watched. Huyghens slipped headphones over his ears. He looked up and said sharply:

"Watch the bears, Roane. The wind's blowing up the way we came. Anything that trails us—sphexes, for example—will send its scent on before. The bears will tell us."

He busied himself with the instruments he'd brought. He heard the hissing, frying, background noise which could be anything at all except a human signal. He reached out and swung the small aerial around. Rasping, buzzing tones came in, faintly and then loudly. This receiver, though, had been made for this particular wave band. It was much more efficient than the modified space phone had been. It picked up three short buzzes, three long ones, and three short ones again. Three dots, three dashes, and three dots. Over and over again. S O S. S O S. S O S.

Huyghens took a reading and moved the directional aerial a carefully measured distance. He took another reading. He shifted it yet again and again, carefully marking and measuring each spot and taking notes of the instrument readings. When he finished, he had checked the direction of the signal not only by loudness but by phase—he had as accurate a fix as could possibly be had with portable apparatus.

Sourdough growled softly. Sitka Pete whiffed the air and arose from his sitting position. Faro Nell whacked Nugget, sending him whimpering to the farthest corner of the flea place. She stood bristling, facing downhill the way they'd come.

"Damn!" said Huyghens.

He got up and waved his arm at Semper, who had turned his head at the stirrings. Semper squawked in a most un-eaglelike fashion and dived off the spur and was immediately fighting the down-draught beyond it. As Huyghens reached his weapon, the eagle came back overhead. He went magnificently past, a hundred feet high, careening and flapping in the tricky currents. He screamed, abruptly, and circled and screamed again. Huyghens swung a tiny vision plate from its strap to where he could look into it. He saw, of course, what the little camera on Semper's chest could see—reeling, swaying terrain as Semper saw it, though without his breadth of field. There were moving objects to be seen through the shifting trees. Their coloring was unmistakable.

"Sphexes," said Huyghens dourly. "Eight of them. Don't look for them to follow our track, Roane. They run parallel to a trail on either side. That way they attack in breadth and all at once when they catch up. And listen! The bears can handle anything they tangle with! It's our job to pick off the loose ones! And aim for the body! The bullets explode."

He threw off the safety of his weapon. Faro Nell, uttering thunderous growls, went padding to a place between Sitka Pete and Sourdough. Sitka glanced at her and made a whuffing noise, as if derisive of her blood-curdling sounds. Sourdough grunted in a somehow solid fashion. He and Sitka moved farther away from Nell to either side. They would cover a wider front.

There was no other sign of life than the shrillings of the incredibly tiny creatures which on this planet were birds, and Faro Nell's deep-bass, raging growls, and then the click of Roane's safety going off as he got ready to use the weapon Huyghens had given him.

Semper screamed again, flapping low above the treetops, following parti-colored, monstrous shapes beneath.

Eight blue-and-tan fiends came racing out of the underbrush. They had spiny fringes, and horns, and glaring eyes, and they looked as if they had come straight out of hell. On the instant of their appearance they leaped, emitting squalling, spitting squeals that were like the cries of fighting tomcats ten thousand times magnified. Huyghens' rifle cracked, and its sound was wiped out in the louder detonation of its bullet in sphexian flesh. A tan-and-blue monster tumbled over, shrieking. Faro Nell charged, the very impersonation of white-hot fury. Roane fired, and his bullet exploded against a tree. Sitka Pete brought his massive forepaws in a clapping, monstrous ear-boxing motion. A sphex died.

Then Roane fired again. Sourdough Charley whuffed. He fell forward upon a spitting bi-colored fiend, rolled him over, and raked with his hind claws. The belly-hide of the sphex was tenderer than the rest. The creature rolled away, snapping at its own wounds. Another sphex found itself shaken loose from the tumult about Sitka Pete. It whirled to leap on him from behind—and Huyghens fired very coldly—and two plunged upon Faro Nell and Roane blasted one and Faro Nell disposed of the other in truly awesome fury. Then Sitka Pete heaved himself erect—seeming to drip sphexes—and Sourdough waddled over and pulled one off and killed it and went back for another. And both rifles cracked together and there was suddenly nothing left to fight.

The bears prowled from one to another of the corpses. Sitka Pete rumbled and lifted up a limp head. Crash! Then another. He went over the lot, whether or not they showed signs of life. When he had finished, they were wholly still.

Semper came flapping down out of the sky. He had screamed and fluttered overhead as the fight went on. Now he landed with a rush. Huyghens went soothingly from one bear to another, calming them with his voice. It took longest to calm Faro Nell, licking Nugget with impassioned solicitude and growling horribly as she licked.

"Come along, now," said Huyghens, when Sitka showed signs of intending to sit down again. "Heave these carcasses over a cliff. Come along! Sitka! Sourdough! Hup!"

He guided them as the two big males somewhat fastidiously lifted up the nightmarish creatures they and the guns together had killed, and carried them to the edge of the spur of stone. They let the dead beasts go bouncing and sliding down into the valley.

"That," said Huyghens, "is so their little pals will gather round them and caterwaul their woe where there's no trail of ours to give them ideas. If we'd been near a river, I'd have dumped them in to float downriver and gather mourners wherever they stranded. Around the station I incinerate them. If I had to leave them, I'd make tracks away. About fifty miles upwind would be a good idea."

He opened the pack Sourdough carried and extracted giant sized swabs and some gallons of antiseptic. He tended the three Kodiaks in turn, swabbing not only the cuts and scratches they'd received, but deeply soaking their fur where there could be suspicion of spilled sphex blood.

"This antiseptic deodorizes, too," he told Roane. "Or we'd be trailed by any sphex who passed to leeward of us. When we start off, I'll swab the bears' paws for the same reason."

Roane was very quiet. He'd missed his first shot with a bullet-firing weapon—a beam hasn't the stopping-power of an explosive bullet—but he'd seemed to grow savagely angry with himself. The last few seconds of the fight, he'd fired very deliberately and every bullet hit. Now he said bitterly:

"If you're instructing me so I can carry on should you be killed, I doubt that it's worth while!"

Huyghens felt in his pack and unfolded the enlargements he'd made of the space photos of this part of the planet. He carefully oriented the map with distant landmarks. He drew a painstakingly accurate line across the photo.

"The S O S signal comes from somewhere close to the robot colony," he reported. "I think a little to the south of it. Probably from a mine they'd opened up, on the far side—of course—of the Sere Plateau. See how I've marked this map? Two fixes, one from the station and one from here. I came away off-course to get a fix here so we'd have two position-lines to the transmitter. The signal could have come from the other side of the planet. But it doesn't."

"The odds would be astronomical against other castaways," protested Roane.

"No-o-o-o," said Huyghens. "Ships have been coming here. To the robot-colony. One could have crashed. And I have friends, too."

He repacked his apparatus and gestured to the bears. He led them beyond the scene of combat and very carefully swabbed off their paws, so they could not possibly leave a trail of sphex-blood scent behind them. He waved Semper, the eagle, aloft.

"Let's go," he told the Kodiaks. "Yonder! Hup!"

The party headed downhill and into the jungle again. Now it was Sourdough's turn to take the lead, and Sitka Pete prowled more widely behind him. Faro Nell trailed the men, with Nugget. She kept an extremely sharp eye upon the cub. He was a baby, still. He only weighed six hundred pounds. And of course she watched against danger from the rear.

Overhead, Semper fluttered and flew in giant circles and spirals, never going very far away. Huyghens referred constantly to the screen which showed what the air-borne camera saw. The image tilted and circled and banked and swayed. It was by no means the best air-reconnaissance that could be imagined. But it was the best that would work. Presently Huyghens said:

"We swing to the right, here. The going's bad straight ahead, and it looks like a pack of sphexes has killed and is feeding."

Roane was upset. He was dissatisfied with himself. So he said:

"It's against reason for carnivores to be as thick as you say! There has to be a certain amount of other animal life for every meat-eating beast! Too many of them would eat all the game and starve!"

"They're gone all winter," explained Huyghens, "which around here isn't as severe as you might think. And a good many animals seem to breed just after the sphexes go south. Also, the sphexes aren't around all the warm weather. There's a sort of peak, and then for a matter of weeks you won't see a one of them, and suddenly the jungle swarms with them again. Then, presently, they head south. Apparently they're migratory in some fashion, but nobody knows." He said dryly: "There haven't been many naturalists around on this planet. The animal life is inimical."

Roane fretted. He was a senior officer in the Colonial Survey, and he was accustomed to arrival at a partly or completely-finished colonial set-up, and to pass upon the completion or non-completion of the planned installation as designed. Now he was in an intolerably hostile environment, depending upon an illegal colonist for his life, engaged upon a demoralizingly indefinite enterprise—because the mechanical spark-signal could be working long after its constructors were dead—and his ideas about a number of matters were shaken. He was alive, for example, because of three giant Kodiak bears and a bald eagle. He and Huyghens could have been surrounded by ten thousand robots, and they'd have been killed. Sphexes and robots would have ignored each other, and sphexes would have made straight for the men, who'd have had less than four seconds in which to discover for themselves that they were attacked, prepare to defend themselves, and kill eight sphexes.

Roane's convictions as a civilized man were shaken. Robots were marvelous contrivances for doing the expected: accomplishing the planned; coping with the predicted. But they also had defects. Robots could only follow instructions—if this thing happens, do this, if that thing happens do that. But before something else, neither this nor that, robots were helpless. So a robot civilization worked only in an environment where nothing unanticipated ever turned up, and human supervisors never demanded anything unexpected. Roane was appalled. He'd never encountered the truly unpredictable before in all his life and career.

He found Nugget, the cub, ambling uneasily in his wake. The cub flattened his ears miserably when Roane glanced at him. It occurred to the man that Nugget was receiving a lot of disciplinary thumpings from Faro Nell. He was knocked about physically, pretty much as Roane was being knocked about psychologically. His lack of information and unfitness for independent survival in this environment was being hammered into him.

"Hi, Nugget," said Roane ruefully. "I feel just about the way you do!"

Nugget brightened visibly. He frisked. He tended to gambol. He looked very hopefully up into Roane's face—and he stood four feet high at the shoulder and would overtop Roane if he stood erect.

Roane reached out and patted Nugget's head. It was the first time in all his life that he'd ever petted an animal.

He heard a snuffling sound behind him. Skin crawled at the back of his neck. He whirled.

Faro Nell regarded him—eighteen hundred pounds of she-bear only ten feet away and looking into his eyes. For one panicky instant Roane went cold all over. Then he realized that Faro Nell's eyes were not burning. She was not snarling. She did not emit those blood-curdling sounds which the bare prospect of danger to Nugget had produced up on the rocky spur. She looked at him blandly. In fact, after a moment she swung off on some independent investigation of a matter that had aroused her curiosity.

The traveling party went on, Nugget frisking beside Roane and tending to bump into him out of pure cub-clumsiness. Now and again he looked adoringly at Roane, in the instant and overwhelming affection of the very young.

Roane trudged on. Presently he glanced behind again. Faro Nell was now ranging more widely. She was well satisfied to have Nugget in the immediate care of a man. From time to time he got on her nerves.

A little while later, Roane called ahead.

"Huyghens! Look here! I've been appointed nursemaid to Nugget!"

Huyghens looked back.

"Oh, slap him a few times and he'll go back to his mother."

"The devil I will!" said Roane querulously. "I like it!"

The traveling party went on.

When night fell, they camped. There could be no fire, of course, because all the minute night-things about would come eagerly to dance in the glow. But there could not be darkness, equally, because night-walkers hunted in the dark. So Huyghens set out the barrier lamps which made a wall of twilight about their halting place, and the staglike creature Faro Nell had carried became their evening meal. Then they slept—at least the men did—and the bears dozed and snorted and waked and dozed again. But Semper sat immobile with his head under his wing on a tree limb. And presently there was a glorious cool hush and all the world glowed in morning light diffused through the jungle by a newly risen sun. And they arose, and traveled again.

This day they stopped stock-still for two hours while sphexes puzzled over the trail the bears had left. Huyghens discoursed calmly on the need for an anti-scent, to be used on the boots of men and the paws of bears, which would make the following of their trails unpopular with sphexes. And Roane seized upon the idea and absorbedly suggested that a sphex-repellent odor might be worked out, which would make a human revolting to a sphex. If that were done—why—humans could go freely about unmolested.

"Like stink-bugs," said Huyghens, sardonically. "A very intelligent idea! Very rational! You can feel proud!"

And suddenly Roane, very obscurely, was not proud of the idea at all.

They camped again. On the third night they were at the base of that remarkable formation, the Sere Plateau, which from a distance looked like a mountain-range but was actually a desert tableland. And it was not reasonable for a desert to be raised high, while lowlands had rain, but on the fourth morning they found out why. They saw, far, far away, a truly monstrous mountain-mass at the end of the long-way expanse of the plateau. It was like the prow of a ship. It lay, so Huyghens observed, directly in line with the prevailing winds, and divided them as a ship's prow divides the waters. The moisture-bearing air-currents flowed beside the plateau, not over it, and its interior was pure sere desert in the unscreened sunshine of high altitudes.

It took them a full day to get halfway up the slope. And here, twice as they climbed, Semper flew screaming over aggregations of sphexes to one side of them or the other. These were much larger groups than Huyghens had ever seen before—fifty to a hundred monstrosities together, where a dozen was a large hunting-pack elsewhere. He looked in the screen which showed him what Semper saw, four to five miles away. The sphexes padded uphill toward the Sere Plateau in a long line. Fifty—sixty—seventy tan-and-azure beasts out of hell.

"I'd hate to have that bunch jump us," he said candidly to Roane. "I don't think we'd stand a chance."

"Here's where a robot tank would be useful," Roane observed.

"Anything armored," conceded Huyghens. "One man in an armored station like mine would be safe. But if he killed a sphex he'd be besieged. He'd have to stay holed up, breathing the smell of dead sphex, until the odor had gone away. And he mustn't kill any others or he'd be besieged until winter came."

Roane did not suggest the advantages of robots in other directions. At that moment, for example, they were working their way up a slope which averaged fifty degrees. The bears climbed without effort despite their burdens. For the men it was infinite toil. Semper, the eagle, manifested impatience with bears and men alike, who crawled so slowly up an incline over which he soared.

He went ahead up the mountainside and teetered in the air-currents at the plateau's edge. Huyghens looked in the visionplate by which he reported.

"How the devil," panted Roane—they had stopped for a breather, and the bears waited patiently for them—"do you train bears like these? I can understand Semper."

"I don't train them," said Huyghens, staring into the plate. "They're mutations. In heredity the sex-linkage of physical characteristics is standard stuff. But there's been some sound work done on the gene-linkage of psychological factors. There was need, on my home planet, for an animal who could fight like a fiend, live off the land, carry a pack and get along with men at least as well as dogs do. In the old days they'd have tried to breed the desired physical properties into an animal who already had the personality they wanted. Something like a giant dog, say. But back home they went at it the other way about. They picked the wanted physical characteristics and bred for the personality—the psychology. The job got done over a century ago—a Kodiak bear named Kodius Champion was the first real success. He had everything that was wanted. These bears are his descendants."

"They look normal," commented Roane.

"They are!" said Huyghens warmly. "Just as normal as an honest dog! They're not trained, like Semper. They train themselves!" He looked back into the plate in his hands, which showed the ground five and six and seven thousand feet higher. "Semper, now, is a trained bird without too much brains. He's educated—a glorified hawk. But the bears want to get along with men. They're emotionally dependent on us! Like dogs. Semper's a servant, but they're companions and friends. He's trained, but they're loyal. He's conditioned. They love us. He'd abandon me if he ever realized he could—he thinks he can only eat what men feed him. But the bears wouldn't want to. They like us. I admit that I like them. Maybe because they like me."

Roane said deliberately:

"Aren't you a trifle loose-tongued, Huyghens? I'm a Colonial Survey officer. I have to arrest you sooner or later. You've told me something that will locate and convict the people who set you up here. It shouldn't be hard to find where bears were bred for psychological mutations, and where a bear named Kodius Champion left descendants! I can find out where you came from now, Huyghens!"

Huyghens looked up from the plate with its tiny swaying television image, relayed from where Semper floated impatiently in mid-air.

"No harm done," he said amiably. "I'm a criminal there, too. It's officially on record that I kidnapped these bears and escaped with them. Which, on my home planet, is about as heinous a crime as a man can commit. It's worse than horse-theft back on Earth in the old days. The kin and cousins of my bears are highly thought of. I'm quite a criminal, back home."

Roane stared.

"Did you steal them?" he demanded.

"Confidentially," said Huyghens, "no. But prove it!" Then he said: "Take a look in this plate. See what Semper can see up at the plateau's edge."

Roane squinted aloft, where the eagle flew in great sweeps and dashes. Somehow, by the experience of the past few days, Roane knew that Semper was screaming fiercely as he flew. He made a dart toward the plateau's border.

Roane looked at the transmitter picture. It was only four inches by six, but it was perfectly without grain and in accurate color. It moved and turned as the camera-bearing eagle swooped and circled. For an instant the screen showed the steeply sloping mountainside, and off at one edge the party of men and bears could be seen as dots. Then it swept away and showed the top of the plateau.

There were sphexes. A pack of two hundred trotted toward the desert interior. They moved at leisure, in the open. The viewing camera reeled, and there were more. As Roane watched and as the bird flew higher, he could see still other sphexes moving up over the edge of the plateau from a small erosion-defile here and another one there. The Sere Plateau was alive with the hellish creatures. It was inconceivable that there should be game enough for them to live on. They were visible as herds of cattle would be visible on grazing planets.

It was simply impossible.

"Migrating," observed Huyghens. "I said they did. They're headed somewhere. Do you know, I doubt that it would be healthy for us to try to cross the plateau through such a swarm of sphexes?"

Roane swore, in abrupt change of mood.

"But the signal's still coming through! Somebody's alive over at the robot colony! Must we wait till the migration's over?"

"We don't know," Huyghens pointed out, "that they'll stay alive. They may need help badly. We have to get to them. But at the same time—"

He glanced at Sourdough Charley and Sitka Pete, clinging patiently to the mountainside while the men rested and talked. Sitka had managed to find a place to sit down, though one massive paw anchored him in his place.

Huyghens waved his arm, pointing in a new direction.

"Let's go!" he called briskly. "Let's go! Yonder! Hup!"

IV

They followed the slopes of the Sere Plateau, neither ascending to its level top—where sphexes congregated—nor descending into the foothills where sphexes assembled. They moved along hillsides and mountain-flanks which sloped anywhere from thirty to sixty degrees, and they did not cover much distance. They practically forgot what it was to walk on level ground. Semper, the eagle, hovered overhead during the daytime, not far away. He descended at nightfall for his food from the pack of one of the bears.

"The bears aren't doing too well for food," said Huyghens dryly. "A ton of bear needs a lot to eat. But they're loyal to us. Semper hasn't any loyalty. He's too stupid. But he's been conditioned to think that he can only eat what men feed him. The bears know better, but they stick to us regardless. I rather like these bears."

It was the most self-evident of understatements. This was at an encampment on the top of a massive boulder which projected from a mountainous stony wall. This was six days from the start of their journey. There was barely room on the boulder for all the party. And Faro Nell fussily insisted that Nugget should be in the safest part, which meant near the mountain-flank. She would have crowded the men outward, but Nugget whimpered for Roane. Wherefore, when Roane moved to comfort him, Faro Nell contentedly drew back and snorted at Sitka and Sourdough and they made room for her near the edge.

It was a hungry camp. They had come upon tiny rills upon occasion, flowing down the mountain side. Here the bears had drunk deeply and the men had filled canteens. But this was the third night, and there had been no game at all. Huyghens made no move to bring out food for Roane or himself. Roane made no comment. He was beginning to participate in the relationship between bears and men, which was not the slavery of the bears but something more. It was two-way. He felt it.

"It would seem," he said fretfully, "that since the sphexes don't seem to hunt on their way uphill, that there should be some game. They ignore everything as they file uphill."

This was true enough. The normal fighting formation of sphexes was line abreast, which automatically surrounded anything which offered to flee and outflanked anything which offered fight. But here they ascended the mountain in long lines, one after the other, following apparently long-established trails. The wind blew along the slopes and carried scent only sidewise. But the sphexes were not diverted from their chosen paths. The long processions of hideous blue-and-tawny creatures—it was hard to think of them as natural beasts, male and female and laying eggs like reptiles on other planets—simply climbed.

"There've been other thousands of beasts before them," said Huyghens. "They must have been crowding this way for days or even weeks. We've seen tens of thousands in Semper's camera. They must be uncountable, altogether. The first-comers ate all the game there was, and the last-comers have something else on whatever they use for minds."

Roane protested: "But so many carnivores in one place is impossible! I know they are here, but they can't be!"

"They're cold-blooded," Huyghens pointed out. "They don't burn food to sustain body-temperature. After all, lots of creatures go for long periods without eating. Even bears hibernate. But this isn't hibernation—or estivation, either."

He was setting up the radiation-wave receiver in the darkness. There was no point in attempting a fix here. The transmitter was on the other side of the Sere Plateau, which inexplicably swarmed with the most ferocious and deadly of all the creatures of Loren Two. The men and bears would commit suicide by crossing here.

But Huyghens turned on the receiver. There came the whispering, scratchy sound of background-noise. Then the signal. Three dogs, three dashes, three dots. Three dots, three dashes, three dots. It went on and on and on. Huyghens turned it off. Roane said:

"Shouldn't we have answered that signal before we left the station? To encourage them?"

"I doubt they have a receiver," said Huyghens. "They won't expect an answer for months, anyhow. They'd hardly listen all the time, and if they're living in a mine-tunnel and trying to sneak out for food to stretch their supplies—why, they'll be too busy to try to make complicated recorders or relays."

Roane was silent for a moment or two.

"We've got to get food for the bears," he said presently. "Nugget's weaned, and he's hungry."

"We will," Huyghens promised. "I may be wrong, but it seems to me that the number of sphexes climbing the mountain is less than yesterday and the day before. We may have just about crossed the path of their migration. They're thinning out. When we're past their trail, we'll have to look out for night-walkers and the like again. But I think they wiped out all animal life on their migration-route."

He was not quite right. He was waked in darkness by the sound of slappings and the grunting of bears. Feather-light puffs of breeze beat upon his face. He struck his belt-lamp sharply and the world was hidden by a whitish film which snatched itself away. Something flapped. Then he saw the stars and the emptiness on the edge of which they camped. Then big white things flapped toward him.

Sitka Pete whuffed mightily and swatted. Faro Nell grunted and swung. She caught something in her claws. She crunched. The light went off as Huyghens realized. Then he said:

"Don't shoot, Roane!" He listened, and heard the sounds of feeding in the dark. It ended. "Watch this!" said Huyghens.

The belt-light came on again. Something strangely-shaped and pallid like human skin reeled and flapped crazily toward him. Something else. Four. Five—ten—twenty—more . . .

A huge hairy paw reached up into the light-beam and snatched a flying thing out of it. Another great paw. Huyghens shifted the light and the three great Kodiaks were on their hind legs, swatting at creatures which flittered insanely, unable to resist the fascination of the glaring lamp. Because of their wild gyrations it was impossible to see them in detail, but they were those unpleasant night-creatures which looked like plucked flying monkeys but were actually something quite different.

The bears did not snarl or snap. They swatted, with a remarkable air of businesslike competence and purpose. Small mounds of broken things built up about their feet.

Suddenly there were no more. Huyghens snapped off the light. The bears crunched and fed busily in the darkness.

"Those things are carnivores *and* blood-suckers, Roane," said Huyghens calmly. "They drain their victims of blood like vampire bats—they've some trick of not waking them—and when they're dead the whole tribe eats. But bears have thick furs, and they wake when they're touched. And they're omnivorous—they'll eat anything but sphexes, and like it. You might say that those night-creatures came to lunch. But they stayed. They are it—for the bears, who are living off the country as usual."

Roane uttered a sudden exclamation. He made a tiny light, and blood flowed down his hand. Huyghens passed over his pocket kit of antiseptic and bandages. Roane stanched the bleeding and bound up his hand. Then he realized that Nugget chewed on something. When he turned the light, Nugget swallowed convulsively. It appeared that he had caught and devoured the creature which had drawn blood from Roane. But Roane had lost none to speak of, at that.

In the morning they started along the sloping scarp of the plateau once more. During the morning, Roane said painfully:

"Robots wouldn't have handled those vampire-things, Huyghens."

"Oh, they could be built to watch for them," said Huyghens, tolerantly. "But you'd have to swat for yourself. I prefer the bears."

He led the way on. Here their jungle-formation could not apply. On a steep slope the bears ambled comfortably, the tough pads of their feet holding fast on the slanting rock, but the men struggled painfully. Twice Huyghens halted to examine the ground about the mountains' bases through binoculars. He looked encouraged as they went on. The monstrous peak which was like the bow of a ship at the end of the Sere Plateau was visibly nearer. Toward midday, indeed, it looked high above the horizon, no more than fifteen miles away. And at midday Huyghens called a final halt.

"No more congregations of sphexes down below," he said cheerfully, "and we haven't seen a climbing line of them in miles." The crossing of a sphex-trail meant simply waiting until one party had passed, and then crossing before another came in view. "I've a hunch we've crossed their migration-route. Let's see what Semper tells us!"

He waved the eagle aloft. And Semper, like all creatures other than men, normally functioned only for the satisfaction of his appetite, and then tended to loaf or sleep. He had ridden the last few miles perched on Sitka Pete's pack. Now he soared upward and Huyghens watched in the small vision-plate.

Semper went soaring—and the image on the plate swayed and turned and turned—and in minutes was above the plateau's edge. And here there was some vegetation and the ground rolled somewhat, and there were even patches of brush. But as Semper towered higher still, the inner desert appeared. But nearby it was clear of beasts. Only once, when the eagle banked sharply and the camera looked along the long dimension of the plateau, did Huyghens see any sign of the blue-and-tan beasts. There he saw what looked like masses amounting to herds. But, of course, carnivores do not gather in herds.

"We go straight up," said Huyghens in satisfaction. "We cross the plateau here—and we can edge downwind a bit, even. I think we'll find something interesting on our way to your robot colony."

He waved to the bears to go ahead uphill.

They reached the top hours later—barely before sunset. And they saw game. Not much, but game at the grassy, brushy border of the desert. Huyghens brought down a shaggy ruminant which surely would not live on a desert. When night fell there was an abrupt chill in the air. It was much colder than night-temperatures on the slopes. The air was thin. Roane thought confusedly and presently guessed at the cause. In the lee of the prow-mountain the air was calm. There were no clouds. The ground radiated its heat to empty space. It could be bitterly cold in the nighttime, here.

"And hot by day," Huyghens agreed when he mentioned it. "The sunshine's terrifically hot where the air is thin, but on most mountains there's wind. By day, here, the ground will tend to heat up like the surface of a planet without atmosphere. It may be a hundred and forty or fifty degrees on the sand at midday. But it should be cold at night."

It was. Before midnight Huyghens built a fire. There could be no danger of night-walkers where the temperature dropped to freezing.

In the morning the men were stiff with cold, but the bears snorted and moved about briskly. They seemed to revel in the morning chill. Sitka and Sourdough Charley, in fact, became festive and engaged in a mock fight, whacking each other with blows that were only feigned, but would have crushed in the skull of any man. Nugget sneezed with excitement as he watched them. Faro Nell regarded them with female disapproval.

They went on. Semper seemed sluggish. After a single brief flight he descended and rode on Sitka's pack, as on the previous day. He perched there, surveying the landscape as it changed from semi-arid to pure desert in their progress. His air was arrogant. But he would not fly. Soaring birds do not like to fly when there are no winds to make currents of which to take advantage. On the way, Huyghens painstakingly pointed out to Roane exactly where they were on the enlarged photograph taken from space, and the exact spot from which the distress-signal seemed to come.

"You're doing it in case something happens to you," said Roane. "I admit it's sense, but—what could I do to help those survivors even if I got to them, without you?"

"What you've learned about sphexes would help," said Huyghens. "The bears would help. And we left a note back at my station. Whoever grounds at the landing field back there—and the beacon's working again—will find instructions to come to the place we're trying to reach."

Roane plodded alongside him. The narrow non-desert border of the Sere Plateau was behind them, now. They marched across powdery desert sand.

"See here," said Roane. "I want to know something! You tell me you're listed as a bear-thief on your home planet. You tell me it's a lie—to protect your friends from prosecution by the Colonial Survey. You're on your own, risking your life every minute of every day. You took a risk in not shooting me. Now you're risking more in going to help men who'd have to be witnesses that you were a criminal. What are you doing it for?"

Huyghens grinned.

"Because I don't like robots. I don't like the fact that they're subduing men—making men subordinate to them."

"Go on," insisted Sourdough. "I don't see why disliking robots should make you a criminal. Nor men subordinating themselves to robots, either!"

"But they are," said Huyghens mildly. "I'm a crank, of course. But—I live like a man on this planet. I go where I please and do what I please. My helpers, the bears, are my friends. If the robot colony had been a success, would the humans in it have lived like men? Hardly! They'd have to live the way the robots let them! They'd have to stay inside a fence the robots built. They'd have to eat foods that robots could raise, and no others. Why—a man couldn't move his bed near a window, because if he did the house-tending robots couldn't work! Robots would serve them—the way the robots determined—but all they'd get out of it would be jobs servicing the robots!"

Roane shook his head.

"As long as men want robot service, they have to take the service that robots can give. If you don't want those services—"

"I want to decide what I want," said Huyghens, again mildly, "instead of being limited to choose among what I'm offered. On my home planet we halfway tamed it with dogs and guns. Then we developed the bears, and we finished the job with them. Now there's population-pressure and the room for bears and dogs—and men—is dwindling. More and more people are being deprived of the power of decision, and being allowed only the power of choice among the things robots allow. The more we depend on robots, the more limited those choices become. We don't want our children to limit themselves to wanting what robots can provide! We don't want them shriveling to where they abandon everything robots can't give—or won't! We want them to be men—and women. Not damned automatons who live *by* pushing robot-controls so they can live *to* push robot-controls. If that's not subordination to robots—"

"It's an emotional argument," protested Roane. "Not everybody feels that way."

"But I feel that way," said Huyghens. "And so do a lot of others. This is a big galaxy and it's apt to contain some surprises. The one sure thing about a robot and a man who depends on them is that they can't handle the unexpected. There's going to come a time when we need men who can. So on my home planet, some of us asked for Loren Two, to colonize. It was refused—too dangerous. But men can colonize anywhere if they're men. So I came here to study the planet. Especially the sphexes. Eventually, we expected to ask for a license again, with proof that we could handle even those beasts. I'm already doing it in a mild way. But the Survey licensed a robot colony—and where is it?"

Roane made a sour face.

"You picked the wrong way to go about it, Huyghens. It was illegal. It is. It was the pioneer spirit, which is admirable enough, but wrongly directed. After all, it was pioneers who left Earth for the stars. But—"

Sourdough raised up on his hind legs and sniffed the air. Huyghens swung his rifle around to be handy. Roane slipped off the safety-catch of his own. Nothing happened.

"In a way," said Roane vexedly, "you're talking about liberty and freedom, which most people think is politics. You say it can be more. In principle, I'll concede it. But the way you put it, it sounds like a freak religion."

"It's self-respect," corrected Huyghens.

"You may be—"

Faro Nell growled. She bumped Nugget with her nose, to drive him closer to Roane. She snorted at him. She trotted swiftly to where Sitka and Sourdough faced toward the broader, sphex-filled expanse of the Sere Plateau. She took up her position between them.

Huyghens gazed sharply beyond them and then all about.

"This could be bad!" he said softly. "But luckily there's no wind. Here's a sort of hill. Come along, Roane!"

He ran ahead, Roane following and Nugget plumping heavily with him. They reached the raised place—actually a mere hillock no more than five or six feet above the surrounding sand, with a distorted cactuslike growth protruding from the ground. Huyghens stared again. He used his binoculars.

"One sphex," he said curtly. "Just one! And it's out of all reason for a sphex to be alone! But it's not rational for them to gather in hundreds of thousands, either!" He wetted his finger and held it up. "No wind at all."

He used the binoculars again.

"It doesn't know we're here," he added. "It's moving away. Not another one in sight—" He hesitated, biting his lips. "Look here, Roane! I'd like to kill that one lone sphex and find out something. There's a fifty per cent chance I could find out something really important. But—I might have to run. If I'm right—" Then he said grimly, "It'll have to be done quickly. I'm going to ride Faro Nell—for speed. I doubt Sitka or Sourdough would stay behind. But Nugget can't run fast enough. Will you stay here with him?"

Roane drew in his breath. Then he said calmly:

"You know what you're doing. Of course."

"Keep your eyes open. If you see anything, even at a distance, shoot and we'll be back—fast! Don't wait until something's close enough to hit. Shoot the instant you see anything—if you do!"

Roane nodded. He found it peculiarly difficult to speak again. Huyghens went over to the embattled bears. He climbed up on Faro Nell's back, holding fast by her shaggy fur.

"Let's go!" he snapped. "That way! Hup!"

The three Kodiaks plunged away at a dead run, Huyghens lurching and swaying on Faro Nell's back. The sudden rush dislodged Semper from his perch. He flapped wildly and got aloft. Then he followed effortfully, flying low.

It happened very quickly. A Kodiak bear can travel as fast as a race horse on occasion. These three plunged arrow-straight for a spot perhaps half a mile distant, where a blue-and-tawny shape whirled to face them. There was the crash of Huyghens' weapon from where he rode on Faro Nell's back—the explosion of the weapon and the bullet was one sound. The somehow unnatural spiky monster leaped and died.

Huyghens jumped down from Faro Nell. He became feverishly busy at something on the ground—where the parti-colored sphex had fallen. Semper banked and whirled and came down to the ground. He watched, with his head on one side.

Roane stared, from a distance. Huyghens was doing something to the dead sphex. The two male bears prowled about. Faro Nell regarded Huyghens with intense curiosity. Back at the hillock, Nugget whimpered a little. Roane patted him roughly. Nugget whimpered more loudly. In the distance, Huyghens straightened up and took three steps toward Faro Nell. He mounted. Sitka turned his head back toward Roane. He seemed to see or sniff something dubious. He reared upward. He made a noise, apparently, because Sourdough ambled to his side. The two great beasts began to trot back. Semper flapped wildly and—lacking wind—lurched crazily in the air. He landed on Huyghens' shoulder and his talons clung there.

Then Nugget howled hysterically and tried to swarm up Roane, as a cub tries to swarm up the nearest tree in time of danger. Roane collapsed, and the cub upon him—and there was a flash of stinking scaly hide, while the air was filled with the snarling, spitting squeals of a sphex in full leap. The beast had overjumped, aiming at Roane and the cub while both were upright and arriving when they had fallen. It went tumbling.

Roane heard nothing but the fiendish squalling, but in the distance Sitka and Sourdough were coming at rocketship speed. Faro Nell let out a roar and fairly split the air. And then there was a furry cub streaking toward her, bawling, while Roane rolled to his feet and snatched up his gun. He raged through pure instinct. The sphex crouched to pursue the cub and Roane swung his weapon as a club. He was literally too close to shoot— and perhaps the sphex had only seen the fleeing bear-cub. But he swung furiously.

And the sphex whirled. Roane was toppled from his feet. An eight-hundred-pound monstrosity straight out of hell—half wildcat and half spitting cobra with hydrophobia and homicidal mania added—such a monstrosity is not to be withstood when in whirling its body strikes one in the chest.

That was when Sitka arrived, bellowing. He stood on his hind legs, emitting roars like thunder, challenging the sphex to battle. He waddled forward. Huyghens arrived, but he could not shoot with Roane in the sphere of an explosive bullet's destructiveness. Faro Nell raged and snarled, torn between the urge to be sure that Nugget was unharmed, and the frenzied fury of a mother whose offspring has been endangered.

Mounted on Faro Nell, with Semper clinging idiotically to his shoulder, Huyghens watched helplessly as the sphex spat and squalled at Sitka, having only to reach out one claw to let out Roane's life.

V

They got away from there, though Sitka seemed to want to lift the limp carcass of his victim in his teeth and dash it repeatedly to the ground. He seemed doubly raging because a man—with whom all Kodius Champion's descendants had an emotional relationship—had been mishandled. But Roane was not grievously hurt. He bounced and swore as the bears raced for the horizon. Huyghens had flung him up on Sourdough's pack and snapped for him to hold on. He bumped and chattered furiously:

"Dammit, Huyghens! This isn't right! Sitka got some deep scratches! That horror's claws may be poisonous!"

But Huyghens snapped, "Hup! Hup!" to the bears, and they continued their race against time. They went on for a good two miles, when Nugget wailed despairingly of his exhaustion and Faro Nell halted firmly to nuzzle him.

"This may be good enough," said Huyghens. "Considering that there's no wind and the big mass of beasts is down the plateau and there were only those two around here. Maybe they're too busy to hold a wake, even! Anyhow—"

He slid to the ground and extracted the antiseptic and swabs.

"Sitka first," snapped Roane. "I'm all right!"

Huyghens swabbed the big bear's wounds. They were trivial, because Sitka Pete was an experienced sphex-fighter. Then Roane grudgingly let the curiously-smelling stuff—it reeked of ozone—be applied to the slashes on his chest. He held his breath as it stung. Then he said dourly:

"It was my fault, Huyghens. I watched you instead of the landscape. I couldn't imagine what you were doing."

"I was doing a quick dissection," Huyghens told him. "By luck, that first sphex was a female, as I hoped. And she was just about to lay her eggs. Ugh! And now I know why the sphexes migrate, and where, and how it is that they don't need game up here."

He slapped a quick bandage on Roane. He led the way eastward, still putting distance between the dead sphexes and his party. It was a crisp walk, only, but Semper flapped indignantly overhead, angry that he was not permitted to ride again.

"I'd dissected them before," said Huyghens. "Not enough's been known about them. Some things needed to be found out if men were ever to be able to live here."

"With bears?" asked Roane ironically.

"Oh, yes," said Huyghens. "But the point is that sphexes come to the desert here to breed—to mate and lay their eggs for the sun to hatch. It's a particular place. Seals return to a special place to mate—and the males at least don't eat for weeks on end. Salmon return to their native streams to spawn. They don't eat, and they die afterward. And eels—I'm using Earth examples, Roane—travel some thousands of miles to the Sargasso to mate and die. Unfortunately, sphexes don't appear to die, but it's clear that they have an ancestral breeding place and that they come here to the Sere Plateau to deposit their eggs!"

Roane plodded onward. He was angry: angry with himself because he hadn't taken elementary precautions; because he'd felt too safe, as a man in a robot-served civilization forms the habit of doing; because he hadn't used his brain when Nugget whimpered, in even a bear-cub's awareness that danger was near.

"And now," Huyghens added, "I need some equipment that the robot colony had. With it, I think we can make a start toward making this a planet that men can live like men on!"

Roane blinked.

"What's that?"

"Equipment," said Huyghens impatiently. "It'll be at the robot colony. Robots were useless because they wouldn't pay attention to sphexes. They'd still be. But take out the robot controls and the machines will do! They shouldn't be ruined by a few months' exposure to weather!"

Roane marched on and on. Presently he said:

"I never thought you'd want anything that came from that colony, Huyghens!"

"Why not?" demanded Huyghens impatiently. "When men make machines do what they want, that's all right. Even robots—when they're where they belong. But men will have to handle flame-casters in the job I want them for. There have to be some, because there was a hundred-mile clearing to be burned off. And Earth-sterilizers—intended to kill the seeds of any plants that robots couldn't handle. We'll come back up here, Roane, and at the least we'll destroy the spawn of these infernal beasts! If we can't do more than that—just doing that every year will wipe out the race in time. There are probably other hordes than this, with other breeding places. But we'll find them, too. We'll make this planet into a place where men from my world can come—and still be men!"

Roane said sardonically:

"It was sphexes that beat the robots. Are you sure you aren't planning to make this world safe for robots?"

Huyghens laughed shortly.

"You've only seen one night-walker," he said. "And how about those things on the mountain-slope—which would have drained you of blood and then feasted? Would you care to wander about this planet with only a robot bodyguard, Roane? Hardly! Men can't live on this planet with only robots to help them—and stop them from being fully men! You'll see!"

They found the colony after only ten days more of travel and after many sphexes and more than a few staglike creatures and shaggy ruminants had fallen to their weapons and the bears. But first they found the survivors of the colony.

There were three of them, hard-bitten and bearded and deeply embittered. When the electrified fence went down, two of them were away at a mine-tunnel, installing a new control-panel for the robots who worked in it. The third was in charge of the mining operation. They were alarmed by the stopping of communication with the colony and went back in a tank-truck to find out what had happened, and only the fact that they were unarmed saved them. They found sphexes prowling and caterwauling about the fallen colony, in numbers they still did not wholly believe. And the sphexes smelled men inside the armored vehicle, but couldn't break in. In turn, the men couldn't kill them, or they'd have been trailed to the mine and besieged there for as long as they could kill an occasional monster.

The survivors stopped all mining—of course—and tried to use remote-controlled robots for revenge and to get supplies for them. Their mining-robots were not designed for either task. And they had no weapons. They improvised miniature throwers of burning rocket-fuel, and they sent occasional prowling sphexes away screaming with scorched hides. But this was useful only because it did not kill the beasts. And it cost fuel. In the end they barricaded themselves and used the fuel only to keep a spark-signal going against the day when another ship came to seek the colony. They stayed in the mine as in a prison, on short rations, waiting without real hope. For diversion they could only contemplate the mining-robots they could not spare fuel to run and which could not do anything but mine.

When Huyghens and Roane reached them, they wept. They hated robots and all things robotic only a little less than they hated sphexes. But Huyghens explained, and armed them with weapons from the packs of the bears, and they marched to the dead colony with the male Kodiaks as point and advance-guard, and with Faro Nell bringing up the rear. They killed sixteen sphexes on the way. In the now overgrown clearing there were four more. In the shelters of the colony they found only foulness and the fragments of what had been men. But there was some food—not much, because the sphexes clawed at anything that smelled of men, and had ruined the plastic packets of radiation-sterilized food. But there were some supplies in metal containers which were not destroyed.

And there was fuel, which men could dispense when they got to the control-panels of the equipment. There were robots everywhere, bright and shining and ready for operation, but immobile, with plants growing up around and over them.

They ignored those robots. But lustfully they fueled tracked flame-casters—adapting them to human rather than robot operation—and the giant soil-sterilizer which had been built to destroy vegetation that robots could not be made to weed out or cultivate. And they headed back for the Sere Plateau, burning-eyed and filled with hate.

But Nugget became a badly spoiled bear-cub, because the freed men approved passionately of anything that would even grow up to kill sphexes. They petted him to excess, when they camped.

And they reached the plateau by a sphex-trail to the top. And Semper scouted for sphexes, and the giant Kodiaks disturbed them and the sphexes came squalling and spitting to destroy them—and while Roane and Huyghens fired steadily, the great machines swept up with their special weapons. The Earth-sterilizer, it was found, was deadly against animal life as well as seeds, when its diathermic beam was raised and aimed. But it had to be handled by a man. No robot could decide just when it was to be used, and against what target.

Presently the bears were not needed, because the scorched corpses of sphexes drew live ones from all parts of the plateau even in the absence of noticeable breezes. The official business of the sphexes was presumably finished, but they came to caterwaul and seek vengeance—which they did not find. Presently the survivors of the robot colony drove machines—as men needed to do, here—in great circles around the hugest heap of slaughtered fiends, destroying new arrivals as they came. It was such a killing as men had never before made on any planet, but there would not be many left of the sphex-horde which had bred in this particular patch of desert. There might be other hordes elsewhere, and other breeding places, but the normal territory of this mass of monsters would see few of them this year.

Or next year, either. Because the soil-sterilizer would go over the dug-up sand where the sphex-spawn lay hidden for the sun to hatch. And the sun would never hatch them.

But Huyghens and Roane, by that time, were camped on the edge of the plateau with the Kodiaks. They were technically upwind from the scene of slaughter—and somehow it seemed more befitting for the men of the robot colony to conduct it. After all, it was those men whose companions had been killed.

There came an evening when Huyghens amiably cuffed Nugget away from where he sniffed too urgently at a stag-steak cooking on the campfire. Nugget ambled dolefully behind the protecting form of Roane and sniveled.

"Huyghens," said Roane painfully, "we've got to come to a settlement of our affairs. I'm a Colonial Survey officer. You're an illegal colonist. It's my duty to arrest you."

Huyghens regarded him with interest.

"Will you offer me lenience if I tell on my confederates," he asked mildly, "or may I plead that I can't be forced to testify against myself?"

Roane said vexedly:

"It's irritating! I've been an honest man all my life, but—I don't believe in robots as I did, except in their place. And their place isn't here. Not as the robot colony was planned, anyhow. The sphexes are nearly wiped out, but they won't be extinct and robots can't handle them. Bears and men will have to live here or—the people who do will have to spend their lives behind sphex-proof fences, accepting only what robots can give them. And there's much too much on this planet for people to miss it! To live in a robot-managed controlled environment on a planet like Loren Two wouldn't . . . it wouldn't be self-respecting!"

"You wouldn't be getting religious, would you?" asked Huyghens dryly. "That was your term for self-respect before."

Semper, the eagle, squawked indignantly as Sitka Pete almost stepped on him, approaching the fire. Sitka Pete sniffed, and Huyghens spoke to him sharply, and he sat down with a thump. He remained sitting in an untidy lump, looking at the steak and drooling.

"You don't let me finish!" protested Roane querulously. "I'm a Colonial Survey officer, and it's my job to pass on the work that's done on a planet before any but the first-landed colonists may come there to live. And of course to see that specifications are followed. Now—the robot colony I was sent to survey was practically destroyed. As designed, it wouldn't work. It couldn't survive."

Huyghens grunted. Night was falling. He turned the meat over the fire.

"Now, in emergencies," said Roane carefully, "colonists have the right to call on any passing ship for aid. Naturally! So— I've always been an honest man before, Huyghens—my report will be that the colony as designed was impractical, and that it was overwhelmed and destroyed except for three survivors who holed up and signaled for help. They did, you know!"

"Go on," grunted Huyghens.

"So," said Roane querulously, "it just happened—just happened, mind you—that a ship with you and Sitka and Sourdough and Faro Nell on board—and Nugget and Semper, too, of course—picked up the distress-call. So you landed to help the colonists. And you did. That's the story. Therefore it isn't illegal for you to be here. It was only illegal for you to be here when you were needed. But we'll pretend you weren't."

Huyghens glanced over his shoulder in the deepening night. He said calmly:

"I wouldn't believe that if I told it myself. Do you think the Survey will?"

"They're not fools," said Roane tartly. "Of course they won't! But when my report says that because of this unlikely series of events it is practical to colonize the planet, whereas before it wasn't—and when my report proves that a robot colony alone is stark nonsense, but that with bears and men from your world added, so many thousand colonists can be received per year— And when that much is true, anyhow—"

Huyghens seemed to shake a little as a dark silhouette against the flames. A little way off, Sourdough sniffed the air hopefully. With a bright light like the fire, presently naked-looking flying things might appear to be slapped down out of the air. They were succulent—to a bear.

"My reports carry weight," insisted Roane. "The deal will be offered, anyhow! The robot colony organizers will have to agree or they'll have to fold up. It's true! And your people can hold them up for nearly what terms they choose."

Huyghens' shaking became understandable. It was laughter.

"You're a lousy liar, Roane," he said, chuckling. "Isn't it unintelligent and unreasonable and irrational to throw away a lifetime of honesty just to get me out of a jam? You're not acting like a rational animal, Roane. But I thought you wouldn't, when it came to the point."

Roane squirmed.

"That's the only solution I can think of. But it'll work."

"I accept it," said Huyghens, grinning. "With thanks. If only because it means another few generations of men living like men on a planet that is going to take a lot of taming. And—if you want to know—because it keeps Sourdough and Sitka and Nell and Nugget from being killed because I brought them here illegally."

Something pressed hard against Roane. Nugget, the cub, pushed urgently against him in his desire to get closer to the fragrantly cooking meat. He edged forward. Roane toppled from where he squatted on the ground. He sprawled. Nugget sniffed luxuriously.

"Slap him," said Huyghens. "He'll move back."

"I won't!" said Roane indignantly from where he lay. "I won't do it! He's my friend!"

Poul Anderson

THE SKY PEOPLE

Poul Anderson has been one of the stalwarts of adventure SF writing for more than fifty years now, and has probably written more of it, at a level of quality that's not only consistent but extremely high, than any other writer—in fact, if any writer of the post–World War II generation deserves the title Father Of Modern Space Opera, it would have to be Anderson; only Jack Vance has produced a body of work extensive and memorable enough to rival his claim on that title. And, like Vance, Anderson is still producing first-rate work well into the '90s, work which holds up admirably in terms of imagination and scope in head-to-head competition with the work of any of the Young Turks on the current scene; his 1995 story "Genesis," for instance, is a Modern Space Opera as complex, inventive, and scientifically up-to-date as anything being turned out by writers younger than him by decades (many of whom weren't even born when he started writing), and could validly have been included in the follow-up anthology to *this* anthology, *The Good New Stuff.*

Anderson had trained to be a scientist, taking a degree in physics from the University of Minnesota, but the writing life proved to be more seductive, and he never did get around to working in his original field of choice. Instead, the sales mounted steadily, until by the late '50s and early '60s he may have been one of the most prolific writers in the genre, and by the mid '60s was also on his way to becoming one of the most honored and respected writers in the genre as well. At one point during this period (in addition to non-related work, and lesser series such as the "Hoka" stories he was writing in collaboration with Gordon R. Dickson), Anderson was running three of the most popular and prestigious series in science fiction *all at the same time:* the "Technic History" series detailing the exploits of the wily trader Nicholas van Rijn (which includes novels such as *The Man Who Counts, The Trouble Twisters, Satan's World, Mirkheim, The People of the Wind,* and collections such as *Trader to the Stars* and *The Earth Book of Stormgate*); the extremely popular series relating the adventures of interstellar secret agent Dominic Flandry, probably the most successful attempt to cross SF with the spy thriller, next to Jack Vance's "Demon Princes" novels (the Flandry series includes novels such as *A Circus of Hells, The Rebel Worlds, The Day of Their Return, Flandry of Terra, A Knight of Ghosts and Shadows, A Stone in Heaven,* and *The Game of Empire,* and collections such as *Agent of the Terran Empire*); and, my own personal favorite, a series that took us along on assignment with the agents of the Time Patrol (including the collections *The Guardians of Time, Time Patrolman, The Shield of Time,* and *The Time Patrol*).

It's hard to convey a sense of how astonishing this was, especially in the somewhat more limited compress of the science fiction world of the day. It's as if you should find out that the most popular and high-selling series on the B. Dalton's bestseller list,

Isaac Asimov's *Robot* novels, say, and Orson Scott Card's *Ender* series, and Anne Mc-
Caffery's *Dragonrider* books, were actually all being written by the *same person.*

The effect was staggering—and when you add to it the impact of the best of Anderson's non-series novels, work such as *Brain Wave, Three Hearts and Three Lions, The
Night Face, The Enemy Stars,* and *The High Crusade,* all of which was being published
in *addition* to the series books, it becomes clear that Anderson dominated the late
'50s and the pre-New Wave '60s in a way that only Robert A. Heinlein, Isaac Asimov,
and Arthur C. Clarke could rival. And, like them, he remained an active and dominant
figure right through the '70s and '80s as well, and is still turning up on bestseller lists
almost to the end of the decade of the '90s.

Almost any of the best stories from any of Anderson's major series would have
been an appropriate choice for this anthology; one of his "Time Patrol" stories was an
early favorite in the running, and there were exploits of Dominic Flandry or Nicholas
van Rijn that would have served equally as well, as would some of his non-series work.
I kept coming back to the big, vivid, and powerful novella that follows, though—an
evocative story full of color and action that, in spite of all the swordplay and swashbuckling, also examines a subtle point with a good deal of profundity: just what *is* civilization, anyway? And are you sure you'll recognize it when you *see* it . . . ?

In the course of his 51-year career, Poul Anderson has published over a hundred
books (in several different fields, as Anderson has written historical novels, fantasies,
and mysteries, in addition to SF), sold hundreds of short pieces to every conceivable
market, and won seven Hugo Awards, three Nebula Awards, and the Tolkein Memorial Award. In 1998 he was presented with the Grandmaster Nebula Award for life
achievement. His other books include *Tau Zero, Orion Shall Rise, The Broken Sword,
The Boat of a Million Years,* and *Harvest of Stars.* His short work has been collected in
*The Queen of Air and Darkness and Other Stories, Guardians of Time, The Earth Book
of Stormgate, Fantasy, The Unicorn Trade* (with Karen Anderson), *Past Times, Time Patrolman,* and *Explorations.* His most recent books are the novels *The Stars Are Also Fire*
and *The Fleet of Stars.* Anderson lives in Orinda, California, with his wife and fellow
writer, Karen.

I

The rover fleet got there just before sunrise. From its height, five
thousand feet, the land was bluish gray, smoked with mists. Irrigation
canals caught the first light as if they were full of mercury. Westward the
ocean gleamed, its far edge dissolved into purple and a few stars.

Loklann sunna Holber leaned over the gallery rail of his flagship and
pointed a telescope at the city. It sprang to view as a huddle of walls, flat
roofs, and square watchtowers. The cathedral spires were tinted rose by a
hidden sun. No barrage balloons were aloft. It must be true what rumor
said, that the Perio had abandoned its outlying provinces to their fate. So
the portable wealth of Meyco would have flowed into S' Antón, for safe-

keeping—which meant that the place was well worth a raid. Loklann grinned.

Robra sunna Stam, the *Buffalo*'s mate, spoke. "Best we come down to about two thousand," he suggested. "To make sure the men aren't blown sideways, to the wrong side of the town walls."

"Aye." The skipper nodded his helmeted head. "Two thousand, so be it."

Their voices seemed oddly loud up here, where only the wind and a creak of rigging had broken silence. The sky around the rovers was dusky immensity, tinged red gold in the east. Dew lay on the gallery deck. But when the long wooden horns blew signals, it was somehow not an interruption, nor was the distant shouting of orders from other vessels, thud of crew feet, clatter of windlasses and hand-operated compressor pumps. To a Sky Man, those sounds belonged in the upper air.

Five great craft spiraled smoothly downward. The first sunrays flashed off gilt figureheads, bold on sharp gondola prows, and rioted along the extravagant designs painted on gas bags. Sails and rudders were unbelievably white across the last western darkness.

"Hullo, there," said Loklann. He had been studying the harbor through his telescope. "Something new. What could it be?"

He offered the tube to Robra, who held it to his remaining eye. Within the glass circle lay a stone dock and warehouses, centuries old, from the days of the Perio's greatness. Less than a fourth of their capacity was used now. The normal clutter of wretched little fishing craft, a single coasting schooner . . . and yes, by Oktai the Stormbringer, a monster thing, bigger than a whale, seven masts that were impossibly tall!

"I don't know." The mate lowered the telescope. "A foreigner? But where from? Nowhere in this continent—"

"I never saw any arrangement like that," said Loklann. "Square sails on the topmasts, fore-and-aft below." He stroked his short beard. It burned like spun copper in the morning light; he was one of the fair-haired blue-eyed men, rare even among the Sky People and unheard of elsewhere. "Of course," he said, "we're no experts on water craft. We only see them in passing." A not unamiable contempt rode his words: sailors made good slaves, at least, but naturally the only fit vehicle for a fighting man was a rover abroad and a horse at home.

"Probably a trader," he decided. "We'll capture it if possible."

He turned his attention to more urgent problems. He had no map of S' Antón, had never even seen it before. This was the farthest south any Sky People had yet gone plundering, and almost as far as any had ever visited; in bygone days aircraft were still too primitive and the Perio too strong. Thus Loklann must scan the city from far above, through drifting

white vapors, and make his plan on the spot. Nor could it be very complicated, for he had only signal flags and a barrel-chested hollerer with a
megaphone to pass orders to the other vessels.

"That big plaza in front of the temple," he murmured. "Our contingent will land there. Let the *Stormcloud* men tackle that big building east
of it . . . see . . . it looks like a chief's dwelling. Over there, along the north
wall, typical barracks and parade ground—*Coyote* can deal with the soldiers. Let the *Witch of Heaven* men land on the docks, seize the seaward
gun emplacements and that strange vessel, then join the attack on the garrison. *Fire Elk*'s crew should land inside the east city gate and send a detachment to the south gate, to bottle in the civilian population. Having
occupied the plaza, I'll send reinforcements wherever they're needed. All
clear?"

He snapped down his goggles. Some of the big men crowding about
him wore chain armor, but he preferred a cuirass of hardened leather,
Mong style; it was nearly as strong and a lot lighter. He was armed with
a pistol, but had more faith in his battle ax. An archer could shoot almost
as fast as a gun, as accurately—and firearms were getting fabulously expensive to operate as sulfur sources dwindled.

He felt a tightness which was like being a little boy again, opening
presents on Midwinter Morning. Oktai knew what treasures he would
find, of gold, cloth, tools, slaves, of battle and high deeds and eternal
fame. Possibly death. Someday he was sure to die in combat; he had sacrificed so much to his josses, they wouldn't grudge him war-death and a
chance to be reborn as a Sky Man.

"Let's go!" he said.

He sprang up on a gallery rail and over. For a moment the world pin-
wheeled; now the city was on top and now again his *Buffalo* streaked
past. Then he pulled the ripcord and his harness slammed him to steadiness. Around him, air bloomed with scarlet parachutes. He gauged the
wind and tugged a line, guiding himself down.

II

Don Miwel Carabán, calde of S' Antón d' Inio, arranged a lavish
feast for his Maurai guests. It was not only that this was a historic occasion, which might even mark a turning point in the long decline. (Don
Miwel, being that rare combination, a practical man who could read,
knew that the withdrawal of period troops to Brasil twenty years ago was
not a "temporary adjustment." They would never come back. The outer
provinces were on their own.) But the strangers must be convinced that
they had found a nation rich, strong, and basically civilized, that it was

worthwhile visiting the Meycan coasts to trade, ultimately to make alliance against the northern savages.

The banquet lasted till nearly midnight. Though some of the old irrigation canals had choked up and never been repaired, so that cactus and rattlesnake housed in abandoned pueblos, Meyco Province was still fertile. The slant-eyed Mong horsemen from Tekkas had killed off innumerable peons when they raided five years back; wooden pitchforks and obsidian hoes were small use against saber and arrow. It would be another decade before population had returned to normal and the periodic famines resumed. Thus Don Miwel offered many courses, beef, spiced ham, olives, fruits, wines, nuts, coffee, which last the Sea People were unfamiliar with and didn't much care for, et cetera. Entertainment followed—music, jugglers, a fencing exhibition by some of the young nobles.

At this point the surgeon of the *Dolphin,* who was rather drunk, offered to show an Island dance. Muscular beneath tattoos, his brown form went through a series of contortions which pursed the lips of the dignified Dons. Miwel himself remarked, "It reminds me somewhat of our peons' fertility rites," with a strained courtesy that suggested to Captain Ruori Rangi Lohannaso that peons had an altogether different and not very nice culture.

The surgeon threw back his queue and grinned. "Now let's bring the ship's wahines ashore to give them a real hula," he said in Maurai-Ingliss.

"No," answered Ruori. "I fear we may have shocked them already. The proverb goes, 'When in the Solomon Islands, darken your skin.' "

"I don't think they know how to have any fun," complained the doctor.

"We don't yet know what the taboos are," warned Ruori. "Let us be as grave, then, as these spike-bearded men, and not laugh or make love until we are back on shipboard among our wahines."

"But it's stupid! Shark-toothed Nan eat me if I'm going to—"

"Your ancestors are ashamed," said Ruori. It was about as sharp a rebuke as you could give a man whom you didn't intend to fight. He softened his tone to take out the worst sting, but the doctor had to shut up. Which he did, mumbling an apology and retiring with his blushes to a dark corner beneath faded murals.

Ruori turned back to his host. "I beg your pardon, S'ñor," he said, using the local tongue. "My men's command of Spañol is even less than my own."

"Of course." Don Miwel's lean black-clad form made a stiff little bow. It brought his sword up, ludicrously, like a tail. Ruori heard a smothered snort of laughter from among his officers. And yet, thought the captain, were long trousers and ruffled shirt any worse than sarong, sandals, and clan tattoos? Different customs, no more. You had to sail the Maurai Federation, from Awaii to his own N'Zealann and west to Mlaya, before you appreciated how big this planet was and how much of it a mystery.

"You speak our language most excellently, S'ñor," said Doñita Tresa Carabán. She smiled. "Perhaps better than we, since you studied texts centuries old before embarking, and the Spañol has changed greatly since."

Ruori smiled back. Don Miwel's daughter was worth it. The rich black dress caressed a figure as good as any in the world; and, while the Sea People paid less attention to a woman's face, he saw that hers was proud and well formed, her father's eagle beak softened to a curve, luminous eyes and hair the color of midnight oceans. It was too bad these Meycans—the nobles, at least—thought a girl should be reserved solely for the husband they eventually picked for her. He would have liked her to swap her pearls and silver for a lei and go out in a ship's canoe, just the two of them, to watch the sunrise and make love.

However—

"In such company," he murmured, "I am stimulated to learn the modern language as fast as possible."

She refrained from coquetting with her fan, a local habit the Sea People found alternately hilarious and irritating. But her lashes fluttered. They were very long, and her eyes, he saw, were gold-flecked green. "You are learning cab'llero manners just as fast, S'ñor," she said.

"Do not call our language 'modern,' I pray you," interrupted a scholarly-looking man in a long robe. Ruori recognized Bispo Don Carlos Ermosillo, a high priest of that Esu Carito who seemed cognate with the Maurai Lesu Haristi. "Not modern, but corrupt. I too have studied ancient books, printed before the War of Judgment. Our ancestors spoke the true Spañol. Our version of it is as distorted as our present-day society." He sighed. "But what can one expect, when even among the well born, not one in ten can write his own name?"

"There was more literacy in the high days of the Perio," said Don Miwel. "You should have visited us a hundred years ago, S'ñor Captain, and seen what our race was capable of."

"Yet what was the Perio itself but a successor state?" asked the Bispo bitterly. "It unified a large area, gave law and order for a while, but what did it create that was new? Its course was the same sorry tale as a thousand kingdoms before, and therefore the same judgment has fallen on it."

Doñita Tresa crossed herself. Even Ruori, who held a degree in engineering as well as navigation, was shocked. "Not atomics?" he exclaimed.

"What? Oh. The old weapons, which destroyed the old world. No, of course not." Don Carlos shook his head. "But in our more limited way, we have been as stupid and sinful as the legendary forefathers, and the results have been parallel. You may call it human greed or el Dío's punishment as you will; I think the two mean much the same thing."

Ruori looked closely at the priest. "I should like to speak with you further, S'ñor," he said, hoping it was the right title. "Men who know history, rather than myth, are rare these days."

"By all means," said Don Carlos. "I should be honored."

Doñita Tresa shifted on light, impatient feet. "It is customary to dance," she said.

Her father laughed. "Ah, yes. The young ladies have been getting quite impatient, I am sure. Time enough to resume formal discussions tomorrow, S'ñor Captain. Now let the music begin."

He signalled. The orchestra struck up. Some instruments were quite like those of the Maurai, others wholly unfamiliar. The scale itself was different. . . . They had something like it in Stralia, but—a hand fell on Ruori's arm. He looked down at Tresa. "Since you do not ask me to dance," she said, "may I be so immodest as to ask you?"

"What does 'immodest' mean?" he inquired.

She blushed and tried to explain, without success. Ruori decided it was another local concept which the Sea People lacked. By that time the Meycan girls and their cavaliers were out on the ballroom floor. He studied them for a moment. "The motions are unknown to me," he said, "but I think I could soon learn."

She slipped into his arms. It was a pleasant contact, even though nothing would come of it. "You do very well," she said after a minute. "Are all your folk so graceful?"

Only later did he realize that was a compliment for which he should have thanked her; being an Islander, he took it at face value as a question and replied, "Most of us spend a great deal of time on the water. A sense of balance and rhythm must be developed or one is likely to fall into the sea."

She wrinkled her nose. "Oh, stop," she laughed. "You're as solemn as S' Osé in the cathedral."

Ruori grinned back. He was a tall young man, brown as all his race but with the gray eyes which many bore in memory of Ingliss ancestors. Being a N'Zealanner, he was not tattooed as lavishly as some Federation men. On the other hand, he had woven a whalebone filigree into his queue, his sarong was the finest batik, and he had added thereto a fringed shirt. His knife, without which a Maurai felt obscenely helpless, was in contrast: old, shabby until you saw the blade, a tool.

"I must see this god, S' Osé," he said. "Will you show me? Or no. I would not have eyes for a mere statue."

"How long will you stay?" she asked.

"As long as we can. We are supposed to explore the whole Meycan coast. Hitherto the only Maurai contact with the Merikan continent has been one voyage from Awaii to Calforni. They found desert and a few savages. We have heard from Okkaidan traders that there are forests still farther north, where yellow and white men strive against each other. But what lies south of Calforni was unknown to us until this expedition was sent out. Perhaps you can tell us what to expect in Su-Merika."

"Little enough by now," she sighed, "even in Brasil."

"Ah, but lovely roses bloom in Meyco."

Her humor returned. "And flattering words in N'Zealann," she chuckled.

"Far from it. We are notoriously straightforward. Except, of course, when yarning about voyages we have made."

"What yarns will you tell about this one?"

"Not many, lest all the young men of the Federation come crowding here. But I will take you aboard my ship, Doñita, and show you to the compass. Thereafter it will always point toward S' Antón d' Inio. You will be, so to speak, my compass rose."

Somewhat to his surprise, she understood, and laughed. She led him across the floor, supple between his hands.

Thereafter, as the night wore on, they danced together as much as decency allowed, or a bit more, and various foolishness which concerned no one else passed between them. Toward sunrise the orchestra was dismissed and the guests, hiding yawns behind well-bred hands, began to take their departure.

"How dreary to stand and receive farewells," whispered Tresa. "Let them think I went to bed already." She took Ruori's hand and slipped behind a column and thence out onto a balcony. An aged serving woman, stationed to act as duenna for couples that wandered thither, had wrapped up in her mantle against the cold and fallen asleep. Otherwise the two were alone among jasmines. Mists floated around the palace and blurred the city; far off rang the *"Todos buen"* of pikemen tramping the outer walls. Westward the balcony faced darkness, where the last stars glittered. The seven tall topmasts of the Maurai *Dolphin* caught the earliest sun and glowed.

Tresa shivered and stood close to Ruori. They did not speak for a while.

"Remember us," she said at last, very low. "When you are back with your own happier people, do not forget us here."

"How could I?" he answered, no longer in jest.

"You have so much more than we," she said wistfully. "You have told me how your ships can sail unbelievably fast, almost into the wind. How your fishers always fill their nets, how your whale ranchers keep herds that darken the water, how you even farm the ocean for food and fiber and . . ." She fingered the shimmering material of his shirt. "You told me this was made by craft out of fishbones. You told me that every family has its own spacious house and every member of it, almost, his own boat . . . that even small children on the loneliest island can read, and have printed books . . . that you have none of the sicknesses which destroy us . . . that no one hungers and all are free—oh, do not forget us, you on whom el Dío has smiled!"

She stopped, then, embarrassed. He could see how her head lifted and nostrils dilated, as if resenting him. After all, he thought, she came from a breed which for centuries had given, not received, charity.

Therefore he chose his words with care. "It has been less our virtue than our good fortune, Doñita. We suffered less than most in the War of Judgment, and our being chiefly Islanders prevented our population from outrunning the sea's rich ability to feed us. So we—no, we did not retain any lost ancestral arts. There are none. But we did re-create an ancient attitude, a way of thinking, which has made the difference—science."

She crossed herself. "The atom!" she breathed, drawing from him.

"No, no, Doñita," he protested. "So many nations we have discovered lately believe science was the cause of the old world's ruin. Or else they think it was a collection of cut-and-dried formulas for making tall buildings or talking at a distance. But neither is true. The scientific method is only a means of learning. It is a . . . a perpetual starting afresh. And that is why you people here in Meyco can help us as much as we can help you, why we have sought you out and will come knocking hopefully at your doors again in the future."

She frowned, though something began to glow within her. "I do not understand," she said.

He cast about for an example. At last he pointed to a series of small holes in the balcony rail. "What used to be here?" he asked.

"Why . . . I do not know. It has always been like that."

"I think I can tell you. I have seen similar things elsewhere. It was a wrought-iron grille. But it was pulled out a long time ago and made into weapons or tools. No?"

"Quite likely," she admitted. "Iron and copper have grown very scarce. We have to send caravans across the whole land, to Támico ruins, in great peril from bandits and barbarians, to fetch our metal. Time was when there were iron rails within a kilometer of this place. Don Carlos has told me."

He nodded. "Just so. The ancients exhausted the world. They mined the ores, burned the oil and coal, eroded the land, until nothing was left. I exaggerate, of course. There are still deposits. But not enough. The old civilization used up the capital, so to speak. Now sufficient forest and soil have come back that the world could try to reconstruct machine culture—except that there aren't enough minerals and fuels. For centuries men had been forced to tear up the antique artifacts, if they were to have any metal at all. By and large, the knowledge of the ancients hasn't been lost; it has simply become unusable, because we are so much poorer than they."

He leaned forward, earnestly. "But knowledge and discovery do not depend on wealth," he said. "Perhaps because we did not have much metal to cannibalize in the Islands, we turned elsewhere. The scientific method is just as applicable to wind and sun and living matter as it was to oil, iron, or uranium. By studying genetics we learned how to create seaweeds, plankton, fish that would serve our purposes. Scientific forest management gives us adequate timber, organic-synthesis bases, some fuel. The sun pours down energy which we know how to concentrate and use. Wood, ceramics, even stone can replace metal for most purposes. The wind, through such principles as the airfoil or the Venturi law or the Hilsch tube, supplies force, heat, refrigeration; the tides can be harnessed. Even in its present early stage, paramathematical psychology helps control population, as well as—no, I am talking like an engineer now, falling into my own language. I apologize.

"What I wanted to say was that if we can only have the help of other people, such as yourselves, on a worldwide scale, we can match our ancestors, or surpass them . . . not in their ways, which were often short-sighted and wasteful, but in achievements uniquely ours. . . ."

His voice trailed off. She wasn't listening. She stared over his head, into the air, and horror stood on her face.

Then trumpets howled on battlements, and the cathedral bells crashed to life.

"What the nine devils!" Ruori turned on his heel and looked up. The zenith had become quite blue. Lazily over S' Antón floated five orca shapes. The new sun glared off a jagged heraldry painted along their flanks. He estimated dizzily that each of them must be three hundred feet long.

Blood-colored things petaled out below them and drifted down upon the city.

"The Sky People!" said a small broken croak behind him. "Sant'sima Marí, pray for us now!"

III

Loklann hit flagstones, rolled over, and bounced to his feet. Beside him a carved horseman presided over fountain waters. For an instant he admired the stone, almost alive; they had nothing like that in Canyon, Zona, Corado, any of the mountain kingdoms. And the temple facing this plaza was white skywardness.

The square had been busy, farmers and handicrafters setting up their booths for a market day. Most of them scattered in noisy panic. But one big man roared, snatched a stone hammer, and dashed in his rags to meet Loklann. He was covering the flight of a young woman, probably his wife, who held a baby in her arms. Through the shapeless sack dress Loklann saw that her figure wasn't bad. She would fetch a price when the Mong slave dealer next visited Canyon. So could her husband, but there wasn't time now, still encumbered with a chute. Loklann whipped out his pistol and fired. The man fell to his knees, gaped at the blood seeping between fingers clutched to his belly, and collapsed. Loklann flung off his harness. His boots thudded after the woman. She shrieked when fingers closed on her arm and tried to wriggle free, but the brat hampered her. Loklann shoved her toward the temple. Robra was already on its steps.

"Post a guard!" yelled the skipper. "We may as well keep prisoners in here, till we're ready to plunder it."

An old man in priest's robes tottered to the door. He held up one of the cross-shaped Meycan josses, as if to bar the way. Robra brained him with an ax blow, kicked the body off the stairs, and urged the woman inside.

It sleeted armed men. Loklann winded his oxhorn bugle, rallying them. A counterattack could be expected any minute. . . . Yes, now.

A troop of Meycan cavalry clanged into view. They were young, proud-looking men in baggy pants, leather breastplate and plumed helmet, blowing cloak, fire-hardened wooden lances but steel sabres—very much like the yellow nomads of Tekkas, whom they had fought for centuries. But so had the Sky People. Loklann pounded to the head of his line, where his standard bearer had raised the Lightning Flag. Half the *Buffalo*'s crew fitted together sections of pike tipped with edged ceramic, grounded the butts, and waited. The charge crested upon them. Their pikes slanted down. Some horses spitted themselves, others reared back screaming. The pikemen jabbed at their riders. The second paratroop line stepped in, ax and sword and hamstringing knife. For a few minutes murder boiled. The Meycans broke. They did not flee, but they retreated in confusion. And then the Canyon bows began to snap.

Presently only dead and hurt cluttered the square. Loklann moved briskly among the latter. Those who weren't too badly wounded were hustled into the temple. Might as well collect all possible slaves and cull them later.

From afar he heard a dull boom. "Cannon," said Robra, joining him. "At the army barracks."

"Well, let the artillery have its fun, till our boys get in among 'em," said Loklann sardonically.

"Sure, sure." Robra looked nervous. "I wish they'd let us hear from them, though. Just standing around here isn't good."

"It won't be long," predicted Loklann.

Nor was it. A runner with a broken arm staggered to him. "*Storm-cloud,*" he gasped. "The big building you sent us against . . . full of swordsmen. . . . They repulsed us at the door—"

"Huh! I thought it was only the king's house," said Loklann. He laughed. "Well, maybe the king was giving a party. Come on, then, I'll go see for myself. Robra, take over here." His finger swept out thirty men to accompany him. They jogged down streets empty and silent except for their bootfalls and weapon-jingle. The housefolk must be huddled terrified behind those blank walls. So much the easier to corral them later, when the fighting was done and the looting began.

A roar broke loose. Loklann led a dash around a last corner. Opposite him he saw the palace, an old building, red-tiled roof and mellow walls and many glass windows. The *Stormcloud* men were fighting at the main door. Their dead and wounded from the last attack lay thick.

Loklann took in the situation at a glance. "It wouldn't occur to those lardheads to send a detachment through some side entrance, would it?" he groaned. "Jonak, take fifteen of our boys and batter in a lesser door and hit the rear of that line. The rest of you help me keep it busy meanwhile."

He raised his red-spattered ax. "A Canyon!" he yelled. "A Canyon!" His followers bellowed behind him and they ran to battle.

The last charge had reeled away bloody and breathless. Half a dozen Meycans stood in the wide doorway. They were nobles: grim men with goatees and waxed mustaches, in formal black, red cloaks wrapped as shields on their left arms and long slim swords in their right hands. Behind them stood others, ready to take the place of the fallen.

"A Canyon!" shouted Loklann as he rushed.

"*Quel Dío wela!*" cried a tall grizzled Don. A gold chain of office hung around his neck. His blade snaked forth.

Loklann flung up his ax and parried. The Don was fast, riposting with a lunge that ended on the raider's breast. But hardened six-ply leather turned the point. Loklann's men crowded on either side, reckless of thrusts, and hewed. He struck the enemy sword; it spun from the owner's grasp. *"Ah, no, Don Miwel!"* cried a young person beside the calde. The older man snarled, threw out his hands, and somehow clamped them on Loklann's ax. He yanked it away with a troll's strength. Loklann stared into eyes that said death. Don Miwel raised the ax. Loklann drew his pistol and fired point blank.

As Don Miwel toppled, Loklann caught him, pulled off the gold chain, and threw it around his own neck. Straightening, he met a savage thrust. It glanced off his helmet. He got his ax back, planted his feet firmly, and smote.

The defending line buckled.

Clamor lifted behind Loklann. He turned and saw weapons gleam beyond his own men's shoulders. With a curse he realized—there had been more people in the palace than these holding the main door. The rest had sallied out the rear and were now on his back!

A point pierced his thigh. He felt no more than a sting, but rage flapped black before his eyes. "Be reborn as the swine you are!" he roared. Half unaware, he thundered loose, cleared a space for himself, lurched aside and oversaw the battle.

The newcomers were mostly palace guards, judging from their gaily striped uniforms, pikes, and machetes. But they had allies, a dozen men such as Loklann had never seen or heard of. Those had the brown skin and black hair of Injuns, but their faces were more like a white man's; intricate blue designs covered their bodies, which were clad only in wraparounds and flower wreaths. They wielded knives and clubs with wicked skill.

Loklann tore his trouser leg open to look at his wound. It wasn't much. More serious was the beating his men were taking. He saw Mork sunna Brenn rush, sword uplifted, at one of the dark strangers, a big man who had added a rich-looking blouse to his skirt. Mork had killed four men at home for certain, in lawful fights, and nobody knew how many abroad. The dark man waited, a knife between his teeth, hands hanging loose. As the blade came down, the dark man simply wasn't there. Grinning around his knife, he chopped at the sword wrist with the edge of a hand. Loklann distinctly heard bones crack. Mork yelled. The foreigner hit him in the Adam's apple. Mork went to his knees, spat blood, caved in, and was still. Another Sky Man charged, ax aloft. The stranger again evaded the weapon, caught the moving body on his hip, and helped it along. The Sky Man hit the pavement with his head and moved no more.

Now Loklann saw that the newcomers were a ring around others who did not fight. Women. By Oktai and man-eating Ulagu, these bastards were leading out all the women in the palace! And the fighting against them had broken up; surly raiders stood back nursing their wounds.

Loklann ran forward. "A Canyon! A Canyon!" he shouted.

"Ruori Rangi Lohannaso," said the big stranger politely. He rapped a string of orders. His party began to move away.

"Hit them, you scum!" bawled Loklann. His men rallied and straggled after. Rearguard pikes prodded them back. Loklann led a rush to the front of the hollow square.

The big man saw him coming. Gray eyes focused on the calde's chain and became full winter. "So you killed Don Miwel," said Ruori in Spañol. Loklann understood him, having learned the tongue from prisoners and concubines during many raids further north. "You lousy son of a skua."

Loklann's pistol rose. Ruori's hand blurred. Suddenly the knife stood in the Sky Man's right biceps. He dropped his gun. "I'll want that back!" shouted Ruori. Then, to his followers: "Come, to the ship."

Loklann stared at blood rivering down his arm. He heard a clatter as the refugees broke through the weary Canyon line. Jonak's party appeared in the main door—which was now empty, its surviving defenders having left with Ruori.

A man approached Loklann, who still regarded his arm. "Shall we go after 'em, Skipper?" he said, almost timidly. "Jonak can lead us after 'em."

"No," said Loklann.

"But they must be escorting a hundred women. A lot of young women too."

Loklann shook himself, like a dog coming out of a deep cold stream. "No. I want to find the medic and get this wound stitched. Then we'll have a lot else to do. We can settle with those outlanders later, if the chance comes. Man, we've a city to sack!"

IV

There were dead men scattered on the wharves, some burned. They looked oddly small beneath the warehouses, like rag dolls tossed away by a weeping child. Cannon fumes lingered to bite nostrils.

Atel Hamid Seraio, the mate, who had been left aboard the *Dolphin* with the enlisted crew, led a band to meet Ruori. His salute was in the Island manner, so casual that even at this moment several of the Meycans looked shocked. "We were about to come for you, Captain," he said.

Ruori looked toward that forest which was the *Dolphin*'s rig. "What happened here?" he asked.

"A band of those devils landed near the battery. They took the emplacements while we were still wondering what it was all about. Part of them went off toward that racket in the north quarter, I believe where the army lives. But the rest of the gang attacked us. Well, with our gunwale ten feet above the dock, and us trained to repel pirates, they didn't have much luck. I gave them a dose of flame."

Ruori winced from the blackened corpses. Doubtless they had deserved it, but he didn't like the idea of pumping flaming blubber oil across live men.

"Too bad they didn't try from the seaward side," added Atel with a sigh. "We've got such a lovely harpoon catapult. I used one like it years ago off Hinja, when a Sinese buccaneer came too close. His junk sounded like a whale."

"Men aren't whales!" snapped Ruori.

"All right, Captain, all right, all right." Atel backed away from his violence, a little frightened. "No ill-speaking meant."

Ruori recollected himself and folded his hands. "I spoke in needless anger," he said formally. "I laugh at myself."

"It's nothing, Captain. As I was saying, we beat them off and they finally withdrew. I imagine they'll bring back reinforcements. What shall we do?"

"That's what I don't know," said Ruori in a bleak tone. He turned to the Meycans, who stood with stricken, uncomprehending faces. "Your pardon is prayed, Dons and Doñitas," he said in Spañol. "He was only relating to me what had happened."

"Don't apologize!" Tresa Carabán spoke, stepping out ahead of the men. Some of them looked a bit offended, but they were too tired and stunned to reprove her forwardness, and to Ruori it was only natural that a woman act as freely as a man. "You saved our lives, Captain. More than our lives."

He wondered what was worse than death, then nodded. Slavery, of course—ropes and whips and a lifetime's unfree toil in a strange land. His eyes dwelt upon her, the long hair disheveled past smooth shoulders, gown ripped, weariness and a streak of tears across her face. He wondered if she knew her father was dead. She held herself straight and regarded him with an odd defiance.

"We are uncertain what to do," he said awkwardly. "We are only fifty men. Can we help your city?"

A young nobleman, swaying on his feet, replied: "No. The city is done. You can take these ladies to safety, that is all."

Tresa protested: "You are not surrendering already, S'ñor Dónoju!"

"No, Doñita," the young man breathed. "But I hope I can be shriven before returning to fight, for I am a dead man."

"Come aboard," said Ruori curtly.

He led the way up the gangplank. Liliu, one of the ship's five wahines, ran to meet him. She threw arms about his neck and cried, "I feared you were slain!"

"Not yet." Ruori disengaged her as gently as possible. He noticed Tresa standing stiff, glaring at them both. Puzzlement came—did these curious Meycans expect a crew to embark on a voyage of months without taking a few girls along? Then he decided that the wahines' clothing, being much like his men's, was against local mores. To Nan with their silly prejudices. But it hurt that Tresa drew away from him.

The other Meycans stared about them. Not all had toured the ship when she first arrived. They looked in bewilderment at lines and spars, down fathoms of deck to the harpoon catapult, capstans, bowsprit, and back at the sailors. The Maurai grinned encouragingly. Thus far most of them looked on this as a lark. Men who skindove after sharks, for fun, or who sailed outrigger canoes alone across a thousand ocean miles to pay a visit, were not put out by a fight.

But they had not talked with grave Don Miwel and merry Don Wan and gentle Bispo Ermosillo, and then seen those people dead on a dance floor, thought Ruori in bitterness.

The Meycan women huddled together, ladies and servants, to weep among each other. The palace guards formed a solid rank around them. The nobles, and Tresa, followed Ruori up on the poop deck.

"Now," he said, "let us talk. Who are these bandits?"

"The Sky People," whispered Tresa.

"I can see that." Ruori cocked an eye on the aircraft patrolling overhead. They had the sinister beauty of as many barracuda. Here and there columns of smoke reached toward them. "But who are they? Where from?"

"They are Nor-Merikans," she answered in a dry little voice, as if afraid to give it color. "From the wild highlands around the Corado River, the Grand Canyon it has cut for itself—mountaineers. There is a story that they were driven from the eastern plains by Mong invaders, a long time ago; but as they grew strong in the hills and deserts, they defeated some Mong tribes and became friendly with others. For a hundred years they have harried our northern borders. This is the first time they have ventured so far south. We never expected them—I suppose their spies learned most of our soldiers are along the Río Gran, chasing a rebel force. They sailed southwesterly, above our land—" She shivered.

The young Dónoju spat. "They are heathen dogs! They know nothing but to rob and burn and kill!" He sagged. "What have we done that they are loosed on us?"

Ruori rubbed his chin thoughtfully. "They can't be quite such savages," he murmured. "Those blimps are better than anything my own Federation has tried to make. The fabric . . . some tricky synthetic? It must be, or it wouldn't contain hydrogen any length of time. Surely they don't use helium! But for hydrogen production on that scale, you need industry. A good empirical chemistry, at least. They might even electrolyze it . . . good Lesu!"

He realized he had been talking to himself in his home language. "I beg your pardon," he said. "I was wondering what we might do. This ship carried no flying vessels."

Again he looked upward. Atel handed him his binoculars. He focused on the nearest blimp. The huge gas bag and the gondola beneath—itself as big as many a Maurai ship—formed an aerodynamically clean unit. The gondola seemed to be light, woven cane about a wooden frame, but strong. Three-fourths of the way up from its keel a sort of gallery ran clear around, on which the crew might walk and work. At intervals along the rail stood muscle-powered machines. Some must be for hauling, but others suggested catapults. Evidently the blimps of various chiefs fought each other occasionally, in the northern kingdoms. That might be worth knowing. The Federation's political psychologists were skilled at the divide-and-rule game. But for now . . .

The motive power was extraordinarily interesting. Near the gondola bows two lateral spars reached out for some fifty feet, one above the other. They supported two pivoted frames on either side, to which square sails were bent. A similar pair of spars pierced the after hull: eight sails in all. Shark-fin control surfaces were braced to the gas bag. A couple of small retractable windwheels, vaned and pivoted, jutted beneath the gondola, evidently serving the purpose of a false keel. Sails and rudders were trimmed by lines running through block and tackle to windlasses on the gallery. By altering their set, it should be possible to steer at least several points to windward. And, yes, the air moved in different directions at different levels. A blimp could descend by pumping out cells in its gas bag, compressing the hydrogen into storage tanks; it could rise by reinflating or by dropping ballast (though the latter trick would be reserved for home stretches, when leakage had depleted the gas supply). Between sails, rudders, and its ability to find a reasonably favoring wind, such a blimp could go roving across several thousand miles, with a payload of several tons. Oh, a lovely craft!

Ruori lowered his glasses. "Hasn't the Perio built any air vessels, to fight back?" he asked.

"No," mumbled one of the Meycans. "All we ever had was balloons. We don't know how to make a fabric which will hold the lifting-gas long enough, or how to control the flight. . . ." His voice trailed off.

"And being a nonscientific culture, you never thought of doing systematic research to learn those tricks," said Ruori.

Tresa, who had been staring at her city, whirled about upon him. "It's easy for you!" she screamed. "You haven't stood off Mong in the north and Raucanians in the south for century after century. You haven't had to spend twenty years and ten thousand lives making canals and aqueducts, so a few less people would starve. You aren't burdened with a peon majority who can only work, who cannot look after themselves because they have never been taught how because their existence is too much of a burden for our land to afford it. It's easy for you to float about with your shirtless doxies and poke fun at us! What would you have done, S'ñor Almighty Captain?"

"Be still," reproved young Dónoju. "He saved our lives."

"So far!" she said, through teeth and tears. One small dancing shoe stamped the deck.

For a bemused moment, irrelevantly, Ruori wondered what a doxie was. It sounded uncomplimentary. Could she mean the wahines? But was there a more honorable way for a woman to earn a good dowry than by hazarding her life, side by side with the men of her people, on a mission of discovery and civilization? What did Tresa expect to tell her grandchildren about on rainy nights?

Then he wondered further why she should disturb him. He had noticed it before, in some of the Meycans, an almost terrifying intensity between man and wife, as if a spouse were somehow more than a respected friend and partner. But what other relationship was possible? A psychological specialist might know; Ruori was lost.

He shook an angry head, to clear it, and said aloud: "This is no time for inurbanity." He had to use a Spañol word with not quite the same connotation. "We must decide. Are you certain we have no hope of repelling the pirates?"

"Not unless S' Antón himself passes a miracle," said Dónoju in a dead voice.

Then, snapping erect: "There is only a single thing you can do for us, S'ñor. If you will leave now, with the women—there are high-born ladies among them, who must not be sold into captivity and disgrace. Bear them south to Port Wanawato, where the calde will look after their welfare."

"I do not like to run off," said Ruori, looking at the men fallen on the wharf.

"S'ñor, these are *ladies!* In el Dío's name, have mercy on them!"

Ruori studied the taut, bearded faces. He did owe them a great deal of hospitality, and he could see no other way he might ever repay it. "If you wish," he said slowly. "What of yourselves?"

The young noble bowed as if to a king. "Our thanks and prayers will go with you, my lord Captain. We men, of course, will now return to battle." He stood up and barked in a parade-ground voice: "Atten-tion! Form ranks!"

A few swift kisses passed on the main deck, and then the men of Meyco had crossed the gangplank and tramped into their city.

Ruori beat a fist on the taffrail. "If we had some way," he mumbled. "If I could do something." Almost hopefully: "Do you think the bandits might attack us?"

"Only if you remain here," said Tresa. Her eyes were chips of green ice. "Would to Marí you had not pledged yourself to sail!"

"If they come after us at sea—"

"I do not think they will. You carry a hundred women and a few trade goods. The Sky People will have their pick of ten thousand women, as many men, and our city's treasures. Why should they take the trouble to pursue you?"

"Aye . . . aye. . . ."

"Go," she said. "You dare not linger."

Her coldness was like a blow. "What do you mean?" he asked. "Do you think the Maurai are cowards?"

She hesitated. Then, in reluctant honesty: "No."

"Well, why do you scoff at me?"

"Oh, go away!" She knelt by the rail, bowed head in arms, and surrendered to herself.

Ruori left her and gave his orders. Men scrambled into the rigging. Furled canvas broke loose and cracked in a young wind. Beyond the jetty, the ocean glittered blue, with small whitecaps; gulls skimmed across heaven. Ruori saw only the glimpses he had had before, as he led the retreat from the palace.

A weaponless man, his head split open. A girl, hardly twelve years old, who screamed as two raiders carried her into an alley. An aged man fleeing in terror, zigzagging, while four archers took potshots at him and howled laughter when he fell transfixed and dragged himself along on his hands. A woman sitting dumb in the street, her dress torn, next to a baby whose brains had been dashed out. A little statue in a niche, a holy image, a faded bunch of violets at its feet, beheaded by a casual war-hammer. A house that burned, and shrieks from within.

Suddenly the aircraft overhead were not beautiful.

To reach up and pull them out of the sky!

Ruori stopped dead. The crew surged around him. He heard a short-haul chantey, deep voices vigorous from always having been free and well fed, but it echoed in a far corner of his brain.

"Casting off," sang the mate.

"Not yet! Not yet! Wait!"

Ruori ran toward the poop, up the ladder and past the steersman to Doñita Tresa. She had risen again, to stand with bent head past which the hair swept to hide her countenance.

"Tresa," panted Ruori. "Tresa, I've an idea. I think—there may be a chance—perhaps we can fight back after all."

She raised her eyes. Her fingers closed on his arm till he felt the nails draw blood.

Words tumbled from him. "It will depend . . . on luring them . . . to us. At least a couple of their vessels . . . must follow us . . . to sea. I think then—I'm not sure of the details, but it may be . . . we can fight . . . even drive them off—"

Still she stared at him. He felt a hesitation. "Of course," he said, "we may lose the fight. And we do have the women aboard."

"If you lose," she asked, so low he could scarcely hear it, "will we die or be captured?"

"I think we will die."

"That is well." She nodded. "Yes. Fight, then."

"There is one thing I am unsure of. How to make them pursue us." He paused. "If someone were to let himself . . . be captured by them—and told them we were carrying off a great treasure—would they believe that?"

"They might well." Life had come back to her tones, even eagerness. "Let us say, the calde's hoard. None ever existed, but the robbers would believe my father's cellars were stuffed with gold."

"Then someone must go to them." Ruori turned his back to her, twisted his fingers together and slogged toward a conclusion he did not want to reach. "But it could not be just anyone. They would club a man in among the other slaves, would they not? I mean, would they listen to him at all?"

"Probably not. Very few of them know Spañol. By the time a man who babbled of treasure was understood, they might be halfway home." Tresa scowled. "What shall we do?"

Ruori saw the answer, but could not get it past his throat.

"I am sorry," he mumbled. "My idea was not so good after all. Let us be gone."

The girl forced her way between him and the rail to stand in front of him, touching as if they danced again. Her voice was altogether steady. "You know a way."

"I do not."

"I have come to know you well, in one night. You are a poor liar. Tell me."

He looked away. Somehow, he got out: "A woman—not any woman, but a very beautiful one—would she not soon be taken to their chief?"

Tresa stood aside. The color drained from her cheeks.

"Yes," she said at last. "I think so."

"But then again," said Ruori wretchedly, "she might be killed. They do much wanton killing, those men. I cannot let anyone who was given into my protection risk death."

"You heathen fool," she said through tight lips. "Do you think the chance of being killed matters to me?"

"What else could happen?" he asked, surprised. And then: "Oh, yes, of course, the woman would be a slave if we lost the battle afterward. Though I should imagine, if she is beautiful, she would not be badly treated."

"And is that all you—" Tresa stopped. He had never known it was possible for a smile to show pure hurt. "Of course. I should have realized. Your people have your own ways of thinking."

"What do you mean?" he fumbled.

A moment more she stood with clenched fists. Then, half to herself: "They killed my father; yes, I saw him dead in the doorway. They would leave my city a ruin peopled by corpses."

Her head lifted. "I will go," she said.

"You?" He grabbed her shoulders. "No, surely not you! One of the others—"

"Should I send anybody else? I am the calde's daughter."

She pulled herself free of him and hurried across the deck, down the ladder toward the gangway. Her gaze was turned from the ship. A few words drifted back. "Afterward, if there is an afterward, there is always the convent."

He did not understand. He stood on the poop, staring after her and abominating himself until she was lost to sight. Then he said, "Cast off," and the ship stood out to sea.

V

The Meycans fought doggedly, street by street and house by house, but in a couple of hours their surviving soldiers had been driven into the northeast corner of S' Antón. They themselves hardly knew that, but a Sky chief had a view from above; a rover was now tethered to the cathedral, with a rope ladder for men to go up and down, and the companion vessel, skeleton crewed, brought their news to it.

"Good enough," said Loklann. "We'll keep them boxed in with a quarter of our force. I don't think they'll sally. Meanwhile the rest of us can get things organized. Let's not give these creatures too much time to hide themselves and their silver. In the afternoon, when we're rested, we can land parachuters behind the city troops, drive them out into our lines and destroy them."

He ordered the *Buffalo* grounded, that he might load the most precious loot at once. The men, by and large, were too rough—good lads, but apt to damage a robe or a cup or a jeweled cross in their haste; and sometimes those Meycan things were too beautiful even to give away, let alone sell.

The flagship descended as far as possible. It still hung at a thousand feet, for hand pumps and aluminum-alloy tanks did not allow much hydrogen compression. In colder, denser air it would have been suspended even higher. But ropes snaked from it to a quickly assembled ground crew. At home there were ratcheted capstans outside every lodge, enabling as few as four women to bring down a rover. One hated the emergency procedure of bleeding gas, for the Keepers could barely meet demand, in spite of a new sunpower unit added to their hydroelectric station, and charged accordingly. (Or so the Keepers said, but perhaps they were merely taking advantage of being inviolable, beyond any kings, to jack up prices. Some chiefs, including Loklann, had begun to experiment with hydrogen production for themselves, but it was a slow thing to puzzle out an art that even the Keepers only half understood.)

Here, strong men replaced machinery. The *Buffalo* was soon pegged down in the cathedral plaza, which it almost filled. Loklann inspected each rope himself. His wounded leg ached, but not too badly to walk on. More annoying was his right arm, which hurt worse from stitches than from the original cut. The medic had warned him to go easy with it. That meant fighting left-handed, for the story should never be told that Loklann sunna Holber stayed out of combat. However, he would only be half himself.

He touched the knife which had spiked him. At least he'd gotten a fine steel blade for his pains. And . . . hadn't the owner said they would meet again, to settle who kept it? There were omens in such words. It could be a pleasure to reincarnate that Ruori.

"Skipper. Skipper, sir."

Loklann glanced about. Yuw Red-Ax and Allan sunna Rickar, men of his lodge, had hailed him. They grasped the arms of a young woman in black velvet and silver. The beweaponed crowd, moiling about, was focusing on her; raw whoops lifted over the babble.

"What is it?" said Loklann brusquely. He had much to do.

"This wench, sir. A looker, isn't she? We found her down near the waterfront."

"Well, shove her into the temple with the rest till—oh." Loklann rocked back on his heels, narrowing his eyes to meet a steady green glare. She was certainly a looker.

"She kept hollering the same words over and over: *'Shef, rey, ombro gran.'* I finally wondered if it didn't mean 'chief,' " said Yuw, "and then when she yelled 'khan' I was pretty sure she wanted to see you. So we didn't use her ourselves," he finished virtuously.

"Aba tu Español?" said the girl.

Loklann grinned. "Yes," he replied in the same language, his words heavily accented but sufficient. "Well enough to know you are calling me 'thou.' " Her pleasantly formed mouth drew into a thin line. "Which means you think I am your inferior—or your god, or your beloved."

She flushed, threw back her head (sunlight ran along crow's-wing hair) and answered: "You might tell these oafs to release me."

Loklann said the order in Angliz. Yuw and Aalan let go. The marks of their fingers were bruised into her arms. Loklann stroked his beard. "Did you want to see me?" he asked.

"If you are the leader, yes," she said. "I am the calde's daughter, Doñita Tresa Carabán." Briefly, her voice wavered. "That is my father's chain of office you are wearing. I came back on behalf of his people, to ask for terms."

"What?" Loklann blinked. Someone in the warrior crowd laughed.

It must not be in her to beg mercy, he thought; her tone remained brittle. "Considering your sure losses if you fight to a finish, and the chance of provoking a counterattack on your homeland, will you not accept a money ransom and a safe-conduct, releasing your captive and ceasing your destruction?"

"By Oktai," murmured Loklann. "Only a woman could imagine we—" He stopped. "Did you say you came back?"

She nodded. "On the people's behalf. I know I have no legal authority to make terms, but in practice—"

"Forget that!" he rapped. "Where did you come back from?"

She faltered. "That has nothing to do with—"

There were too many eyes around. Loklann bawled orders to start systematic plundering. He turned to the girl. "Come aboard the airship," he said. "I want to discuss this further."

Her eyes closed, for just a moment, and her lips moved. Then she looked at him—he thought of a cougar he had once trapped—and she said in a flat voice: "Yes. I do have more arguments."

"Any woman does," he laughed, "but you better than most."

"Not that!" she flared. "I meant—no. Marí, pray for me." As he pushed a way through his men, she followed him.

They went past furled sails, to a ladder let down from the gallery. A hatch stood open to the lower hull, showing storage space and leather fetters for slaves. A few guards were posted on the gallery deck. They leaned on their weapons, sweating from beneath helmets, swapping jokes; when Loklann led the girl by, they yelled good-humored envy.

He opened a door. "Have you ever seen one of our vessels?" he asked. The upper gondola contained a long room, bare except for bunk frames on which sleeping bags were laid. Beyond, a series of partitions defined cabinets, a sort of galley, and at last, in the very bow, a room for maps, tables, navigation instruments, speaking tubes. Its walls slanted so far outward that the glazed windows would give a spacious view when the ship was aloft. On a shelf, beneath racked weapons, sat a small idol, tusked and four-armed. A pallet was rolled on the floor.

"The bridge," said Loklann. "Also the captain's cabin."

He gestured at one of four wicker chairs, lashed into place. "Be seated, Doñita. Would you like something to drink?"

She sat down but did not reply. Her fists were clenched on her lap. Loklann poured himself a slug of whiskey and tossed off half at a gulp. "Ahhh! Later we will get some of your own wine for you. It is a shame you have no art of distilling here."

Desperate eyes lifted to him, where he stood over her. "S'ñor," she said, "I beg of you, in Carito's name—well, in your mother's, then—spare my people."

"My mother would laugh herself ill to hear that," he said. Leaning forward: "See here, let us not spill words. You were escaping, but you came back. Where were you escaping to?"

"I—does that matter?"

Good, he thought, she was starting to crack. He hammered: "It does. I know you were at the palace this dawn. I know you fled with the dark foreigners. I know their ship departed an hour ago. You must have been on it, but left again. True?"

"Yes." She began to tremble.

He sipped molten fire and asked reasonably: "Now, tell me, Doñita, what you have to bargain with. You cannot have expected we would give up the best part of our booty and a great many valuable slaves for a mere safe-conduct. All the Sky kingdoms would disown us. Come, now, you must have more to offer, if you hope to buy us off."

"No . . . not really—"

His hand exploded against her cheek. Her head jerked from the blow. She huddled back, touching the red mark, as he growled: "I have no time for games. Tell me! Tell me this instant what thought drove you back here from safety, or down in the hold you go. You'd fetch a good price when the traders next visit Canyon. Many homes are waiting for you: a woods runner's cabin in Orgon, a Mong khan's yurt in Tekkas, a brothel as far east as Chai Ka-Go. Tell me now, truly, what you know, and you will be spared that much."

She looked downward and said raggedly: "The foreign ship is loaded with the calde's gold. My father had long wanted to remove his personal treasure to a safer place than this, but dared not risk a wagon train across country. There are still many outlaws between here and Fortlez d' S' Ernán; that much loot would tempt the military escort itself to turn bandit. Captain Lohannaso agreed to carry the gold by sea to Port Wanawato, which is near Fortlez. He could be trusted because his government is anxious for trade with us; he came here officially. The treasure had already been loaded. Of course, when your raid came, the ship also took those women who had been at the palace. But can you not spare them? You'll find more loot in the foreign ship than your whole fleet can lift."

"By Oktai!" whispered Loklann.

He turned from her, paced, finally stopped and stared out the window. He could almost hear the gears turn in his head. It made sense. The palace had been disappointing. Oh, yes, a lot of damask and silverware and what not, but nothing like the cathedral. Either the calde was less rich than powerful, or he concealed his hoard. Loklann had planned to torture a few servants and find out which. Now he realized there was a third possibility.

Better interrogate some prisoners anyway, to make sure—no, no time. Given a favoring wind, that ship could outrun any rover without working up a sweat. It might already be too late to overhaul. But if not—h'm. Assault would be no cinch. That lean, pitching hull was a small target for paratroopers, and with rigging in the way . . . Wait. Bold men could always find a road. How about grappling to the upper works? If the strain tore the rigging loose, so much the better: a weighted rope would then give a clear slideway to the deck. If the hooks held, though, a storming party could nevertheless go along the lines, into the topmasts. Doubtless the sailors were agile too, but had they ever reefed a rover sail in a Merikan thunderstorm, a mile above the earth?

He could improvise as the battle developed. At the very least, it would be fun to try. And at most, he might be reborn a world conqueror, for such an exploit in this life.

He laughed aloud, joyously. "We'll do it!"

Tresa rose. "You will spare the city?" she whispered hoarsely.

"I never promised any such thing," said Loklann. "Of course, the ship's cargo will crowd out most of the stuff and people we might take otherwise. Unless, hm, unless we decide to sail the ship to Calforni, loaded, and meet it there with more rovers. Yes, why not?"

"You oathbreaker," she said, with a hellful of scorn.

"I only promised not to sell you," said Loklann. His gaze went up and down here. "And I won't."

He took a stride forward and gathered her to him. She fought, cursing; once she managed to draw Ruori's knife from his belt; but his cuirass stopped the blade.

Finally he rose. She wept at his feet, her breast marked red by her father's chain. He said more quietly, "No, I will not sell you, Tresa. I will keep you."

VI

"Blimp ho-o-o!"

The lookout's cry hung lonesome for a minute between wind and broad waters. Down under the mainmast, it seethed with crewmen running to their posts.

Ruori squinted eastward. The land was a streak under cumulus clouds, mountainous and blue-shadowed. It took him a while to find the enemy, in all that sky. At last the sun struck them. He lifted his binoculars. Two painted killer whales lazed his way, slanting down from a mile altitude.

He sighed. "Only two," he said.

"That may be more than plenty for us," said Atel Hamid. Sweat studded his forehead.

Ruori gave his mate a sharp look. "You're not afraid of them, are you? I daresay that's been one of their biggest assets, superstition."

"Oh, no, Captain. I know the principle of buoyancy as well as you do. But those people are tough. And they're not trying to storm us from a dock this time; they're in their element."

"So are we." Ruori clapped the other man's back. "Take over. Tanaroa knows what's going to happen, but use your own judgment if I'm spitted."

"I wish you'd let me go," protested Atel. "I don't like being safe here. It's what can happen aloft that worries me."

"You won't be too safe for your liking." Ruori forced a grin. "And somebody has to steer this tub home to hand in those lovely reports to the Geoethnic Research Endeavor."

He swung down the ladder to the main deck and hurried to the mainmast shrouds. His crew yelled around him, weapons gleamed. The two big box kites quivered, taut canvas, lashed to a bollard and waiting. Ruori wished there had been time to make more.

Even as it was, though, he had delayed longer than seemed wise, first heading far out to sea and then tacking slowly back, to make the enemy search for him while he prepared. (Or planned, for that matter. When he dismissed Tresa, his ideas had been little more than a conviction that he could fight.) Assuming they were lured after him at all, he had risked their losing patience and going back to the land. For an hour, now, he had dawdled under mainsail, genoa, and a couple of flying jibs, hoping the Sky People were lubbers enough not to find that suspiciously little canvas for this good weather.

But here they were, and here was an end to worry and remorse on a certain girl's behalf. Such emotions were rare in an Islander; and to find himself focusing them thus on a single person, out of earth's millions, had been horrible. Ruori swarmed up the ratlines, as if he fled something.

The blimps were still high, passing overhead on an upper-level breeze. Down here was almost a straight south wind. The aircraft, unable to steer really close-hauled, would descend when they were sea-level upwind of him. Regardless, estimated a cold part of Ruori, the *Dolphin* could avoid their clumsy rush.

But the *Dolphin* wasn't going to.

The rigging was now knotted with armed sailors. Ruori pulled himself onto the mainmast crosstrees and sat down, casually swinging his legs. The ship heeled over in a flaw and he hung above greenish-blue, white-streaked immensity. He balanced, scarcely noticing, and asked Hiti: "Are you set?"

"Aye." The big harpooner, his body a writhe of tattoos and muscles, nodded a shaven head. Lashed to the fid where he squatted was the ship's catapult, cocked and loaded with one of the huge irons that could kill a sperm whale at a blow. A couple more lay alongside in their rack. Hiti's two mates and four deckhands poised behind him, holding the smaller harpoons—mere six-foot shafts—that were launched from a boat by hand. The lines of all trailed down the mast to the bows.

"Aye, let 'em come now." Hiti grinned over his whole round face. "Nan eat the world, but this'll be something to make a dance about when we come home!"

"If we do," said Ruori. He touched the boat ax thrust into his loincloth. Like a curtain, the blinding day seemed to veil a picture from home, where combers broke white under the moon, longfires flared on a beach and dancers were merry, and palm trees cast shadows for couples who stole away. He wondered how a Meycan calde's daughter might like it . . . if her throat had not been cut.

"There's a sadness on you, Captain," said Hiti.

"Men are going to die," said Ruori.

"What of it?" Small kindly eyes studied him. "They'll die willing, if they must, for the sake of the song that'll be made. You've another trouble than death."

"Let me be!"

The harpooner looked hurt, but withdrew into silence. Wind streamed and the ocean glittered.

The aircraft steered close. They would approach one on each side. Ruori unslung the megaphone at his shoulder. Atel Hamid held the *Dolphin* steady on a broad reach.

Now Ruori could see a grinning god at the prow of the starboard airship. It would pass just above the topmasts, a little to windward. . . . Arrows went impulsively toward it from the yardarms, without effect, but no one was excited enough to waste a rifle cartridge. Hiti swiveled his catapult. "Wait," said Ruori. "We'd better see what they do."

Helmeted heads appeared over the blimp's gallery rail. A man stepped up—another, another, at intervals; they whirled triple-clawed iron grapnels and let go. Rutor saw one strike the foremast, rebound, hit a jib. . . . The line to the blimp tautened and sang but did not break; it was of leather. . . . The jib ripped, canvas thundered, struck a sailor in the belly and knocked him from his yard. . . . The man recovered to straighten out and hit the water in a clean dive. Lesu grant he lived. . . . The grapnel bumped along, caught the gaff of the fore-and-aft mainsail, wood groaned. . . . The ship trembled as line after line snapped tight.

She leaned far over, dragged by leverage. Her sails banged. No danger of capsizing—yet—but a mast could be pulled loose. And now, over the gallery rail and seizing a rope between hands and knees, the pirates came. Whooping like boys, they slid down to the grapnels and clutched after any rigging that came to hand.

One of them sprang monkeylike onto the mainmast gaff, below the crosstrees. A harpooner's mate cursed, hurled his weapon, and skewered the invader. "Belay that!" roared Hiti. "We need those irons!"

Ruori scanned the situation. The leeward blimp was still maneuvering in around its mate, which was being blown to port. He put the megaphone to his mouth and a solar-battery amplifier cried for him: "Hear this! Hear this! Burn that second enemy now, before he grapples! Cut the lines to the first one and repel all boarders!"

"Shall I fire?" called Hiti. "I'll never have a better target."

"Aye."

The harpooner triggered his catapult. It unwound with a thunder noise. Barbed steel smote the engaged gondola low in a side, tore through, and ended on the far side of interior planking.

"Wind 'er up!" bawled Hiti. His own gorilla hands were already on a crank lever. Somehow two men found space to help him.

Ruori slipped down the futtock shrouds and jumped to the gaff. Another pirate had landed there and a third was just arriving, two more aslide behind him. The man on the spar balanced barefooted, as good as any sailor, and drew a sword. Ruori dropped as the blade whistled, caught a mainsail grommet one-handed, and hung there, striking with his boat ax at the grapnel line. The pirate crouched and stabbed at him. Ruori thought of Tresa, smashed his hatchet into the man's face, and flipped him off, down to the deck. He cut again. The leather was tough, but his blade was keen. The line parted and whipped away. The gaff swung free, almost yanking Ruori's fingers loose. The second Sky Man toppled, hit a cabin below and spattered. The men on the line slid to its end. One of them could not stop; the sea took him. The other was smashed against the masthead as he pendulumed.

Ruori pulled himself back astride the gaff and sat there awhile, heaving air into lungs that burned. The fight ramped around him, on shrouds and spars and down on the decks. The second blimp edged closer.

Astern, raised by the speed of a ship moving into the wind, a box kite lifted. Atel sang a command and the helmsman put the rudder over. Even with the drag on her, the *Dolphin* responded well; a profound science of fluid mechanics had gone into her design. Being soaked in whale oil, the kite clung to the gas bag for a time—long enough for "messengers" of burning paper to whirl up its string. It burst into flame.

The blimp sheered off, the kite fell away, its small gunpowder load exploded harmlessly. Atel swore and gave further orders. The *Dolphin* tacked. The second kite, already aloft and afire, hit target. It detonated.

Hydrogen gushed out. Sudden flames wreathed the blimp. They seemed pale in the sun-dazzle. Smoke began to rise, as the plastic between gas cells disintegrated. The aircraft descended like a slow meteorite to the water.

Its companion vessel had no reasonable choice but to cast loose unsevered grapnels, abandoning the still outnumbered boarding party. The captain could not know that the *Dolphin* had only possessed two kites. A few vengeful catapult bolts spat from it. Then it was free, rapidly falling astern. The Maurai ship rocked toward an even keel.

The enemy might retreat or he might plan some fresh attack. Ruori did not intend that it should be either. He megaphoned: "Put about! Face that scum-gut!" and led a rush down the shrouds to a deck where combat still went on.

For Hiti's gang had put three primary harpoons and half a dozen lesser ones into the gondola.

Their lines trailed in tightening catenaries from the blimp to the capstan in the bows. No fear now of undue strain. The *Dolphin,* like any

Maurai craft, was meant to live off the sea as she traveled. She had dragged right whales alongside; a blimp was nothing in comparison. What counted was speed, before the pirates realized what was happening and found ways to cut loose.

"Tohiha, hioha, itoki, itoki!" The old canoe chant rang forth as men tramped about the capstan. Ruori hit the deck, saw a Canyon man fighting a sailor, sword against club, and brained the fellow from behind as he would any other vermin. (Then he wondered, dimly shocked, what made him think thus about a human being.) The battle was rapidly concluded; the Sky Men faced hopeless odds. But half a dozen Federation people were badly hurt. Ruori had the few surviving pirates tossed into a lazaret, his own casualties taken below to anesthetics and antibiotics and cooing Doñitas. Then, quickly, he prepared his crew for the next phase.

The blimp had been drawn almost to the bowsprit. It was canted over so far that its catapults were useless. Pirates lined the gallery deck, howled and shook their weapons. They outnumbered the *Dolphin* crew by a factor of three or four. Ruori recognized one among them—the tall yellow-haired man who had fought him outside the palace; it was a somehow eerie feeling.

"Shall we burn them?" asked Atel.

Ruori grimaced. "I suppose we have to," he said. "Try not to ignite the vessel itself. You know we want it."

A walking beam moved up and down, driven by husky Islanders. Flame spurted from a ceramic nozzle. The smoke and stench and screams that followed, and the things to be seen when Ruori ordered cease fire, made the hardest veteran of corsair patrol look a bit ill. The Maurai were an unsentimental folk, but they did not like to inflict pain.

"Hose," rasped Ruori. The streams of water that followed were like some kind of blessing. Wicker that had begun to burn hissed into charred quiescence.

The ship's grapnels were flung. A couple of cabin boys darted past grown men to be first along the lines. They met no resistance on the gallery. The uninjured majority of pirates stood in a numb fashion, their armament at their feet, the fight kicked out of them. Jacob's ladders followed the boys; the *Dolphin* crew swarmed aboard the blimp and started collecting prisoners.

A few Sky Men lurched from behind a door, weapons aloft. Ruori saw the tall fair man among them. The man drew Ruori's dagger, left-handed, and ran toward him. His right arm seemed nearly useless. "A Canyon, a Canyon!" he called, the ghost of a war cry.

Ruori sidestepped the charge and put out a foot. The blond man tripped. As he fell, the hammer of Ruori's ax clopped down, catching him on the neck. He crashed, tried to rise, shuddered, and lay twitching.

"I want my knife back." Ruori squatted, undid the robber's tooled leather belt, and began to hogtie him.

Dazed blue eyes looked up with a sort of pleading. "Are you not going to kill me?" mumbled the other in Spañol.

"Haristi, no," said Ruori, surprised. "Why should I?"

He sprang erect. The last resistance had ended; the blimp was his. He opened the forward door, thinking the equivalent of a ship's bridge must lie beyond it.

Then for a while he did not move at all, nor did he hear anything but the wind and his own blood.

It was Tresa who finally came to him. Her hands were held out before her, like a blind person's, and her eyes looked through him. "You are here," she said, flat and empty voiced.

"Doñita," stammered Ruori. He caught her hands. "Doñita, had I known you were aboard, I would never have . . . have risked—"

"Why did you not burn and sink us, like that other vessel?" she asked. "Why must this return to the city?"

She wrenched free of him and stumbled out onto the deck. It was steeply tilted, and bucked beneath her. She fell, picked herself up, walked with barefoot care to the rail and stared out across the ocean. Her hair and torn dress fluttered in the wind.

VII

There was a great deal of technique to handling an airship. Ruori could feel that the thirty men he had put aboard this craft were sailing it as awkwardly as possible. An experienced Sky Man would know what sort of thermal and downdrafts to expect, just from a glance at land or water below; he could estimate the level at which a desired breeze was blowing, and rise or fall smoothly; he could even beat to windward, though that would be a slow process much plagued by drift.

Nevertheless, an hour's study showed the basic principles. Ruori went back to the bridge and gave orders in the speaking tube. Presently the land came nearer. A glance below showed the *Dolphin,* with a cargo of war captives, following on shortened sail. He and his fellow aeronauts would have to take a lot of banter about their celestial snail's pace. Ruori did not smile at the thought or plan his replies, as he would have done yesterday. Tresa sat so still behind him.

"Do you know the name of this craft, Doñita?" he asked, to break the silence.

"He called it *Buffalo*," she said, remote and uninterested.

"What's that?"

"A sort of wild cattle."

"I gather, then, he talked to you while cruising in search of me. Did he say anything else of interest?"

"He spoke of his people. He boasted of the things they have which we don't . . . engines, powers, alloys . . . as if that made them any less a pack of filthy savages."

At least she was showing some spirit. He had been afraid she had started willing her heart to stop; but he remembered he had seen no evidence of that common Maurai practice here in Meyco.

"Did he abuse you badly?" he asked, not looking at her.

"You would not consider it abuse," she said violently. "Now leave me alone, for mercy's sake!" He heard her go from him, through the door to the after sections.

Well, he thought, after all, her father was killed. That would grieve anyone, anywhere in the world, but her perhaps more than him. For a Meycan child was raised solely by its parents; it did not spend half its time eating or sleeping or playing with any casual relative, like most Island young. So the immediate kin would have more psychological significance here. At least, this was the only explanation Ruori could think of for the sudden darkness within Tresa.

The city hove into view. He saw the remaining enemy vessels gleam above. Three against one . . . yes, today would become a legend among the Sea People, if he succeeded. Ruori knew he should have felt the same reckless pleasure as a man did surfbathing, or shark fighting, or sailing in a typhoon, any breakneck sport where success meant glory and girls. He could hear his men chant, beat war-drum rhythms out with hands and stamping feet. But his own heart was Antarctic.

The nearest hostile craft approached. Ruori tried to meet it in a professional way. He had attired his prize crew in captured Sky outfits. A superficial glance would take them for legitimate Canyonites, depleted after a hard fight for the captured Maurai ship at their heels.

As the northerners steered close in the leisurely airship fashion, Ruori picked up his speaking tube. "Steady as she goes. Fire when we pass abeam."

"Aye, aye," said Hiti.

A minute later the captain heard the harpoon catapult rumble. Through a port he saw the missile strike the enemy gondola amidships. "Pay out line," he said. "We want to hold her for the kite, but not get burned ourselves."

"Aye, I've played swordfish before now." Laughter bubbled in Hiti's tones.

The foe sheered, frantic. A few bolts leaped from its catapults; one struck home, but a single punctured gas cell made slight difference. "Put about!" cried Ruori. No sense in presenting his beam to a broadside. Both craft began to drift downwind, sails flapping. "Hard alee!" The *Buffalo* became a drogue, holding its victim to a crawl. And here came the kite prepared on the way back. This time it included fish hooks. It caught and held fairly on the Canyonite bag. "Cast off!" yelled Ruori. Fire whirled along the kite string. In minutes it had enveloped the enemy. A few parachutes were blown out to sea.

"Two to go," said Ruori, without any of his men's shouted triumph.

The invaders were no fools. Their remaining blimps turned back over the city, not wishing to expose themselves to more flame from the water. One descended, dropped hawsers, and was rapidly hauled to the plaza. Through his binoculars, Ruori saw armed men swarm aboard it. The other, doubtless with a mere patrol crew, maneuvered toward the approaching *Buffalo*.

"I think that fellow wants to engage us," warned Hiti. "Meanwhile number two down yonder will take on a couple of hundred soldiers, then lay alongside us and board."

"I know," said Ruori. "Let's oblige them."

He steered as if to close with the sparsely manned patroller. It did not avoid him, as he had feared it might; but then, there was a compulsive bravery in the Sky culture. Instead, it maneuvered to grapple as quickly as possible. That would give its companion a chance to load warriors and rise. It came very near.

Now to throw a scare in them, Ruori decided. "Fire arrows," he said. Out on deck, hardwood pistons were shoved into little cylinders, igniting tinder at the bottom; thus oil-soaked shafts were kindled. As the enemy came in range, red comets began to streak from the *Buffalo* archers.

Had his scheme not worked, Ruori would have turned off. He didn't want to sacrifice more men in hand-to-hand fighting; instead, he would have tried seriously to burn the hostile airship from afar, though his strategy needed it. But the morale effect of the previous disaster was very much present. As blazing arrows thunked into their gondola, a battle tactic so two-edged that no northern crew was even equipped for it, the Canyonites panicked and went over the side. Perhaps, as they parachuted down, a few noticed that no shafts had been aimed at their gas bag.

"Grab fast!" sang Ruori. "Douse any fires!"

Grapnels thumbed home. The blimps rocked to a relative halt. Men leaped to the adjacent gallery; bucketsful of water splashed.

"Stand by," said Ruori. "Half our boys on the prize. Break out the lifelines and make them fast."

He put down the tube. A door squeaked behind him. He turned, as Tresa reentered the bridge. She was still pale, but she had combed her hair, and her head was high.

"Another!" she said with a note near joy. "Only one of them left!"

"But it will be full of their men." Ruori scowled. "I wish now I had not accepted your refusal to go aboard the *Dolphin*. I wasn't thinking clearly. This is too hazardous."

"Do you think I care for that?" she said. "I am a Carabán."

"But I care," he said.

The haughtiness dropped from her; she touched his hand, fleetingly, and color rose in her cheeks. "Forgive me. You have done so much for us. There is no way we can ever thank you."

"Yes, there is," said Ruori.

"Name it."

"Do not stop your heart just because it has been wounded."

She looked at him with a kind of sunrise in her eyes.

His boatswain appeared at the outer door. "All set, Captain. We're holding steady at a thousand feet, a man standing by every valve these two crates have got."

"Each has been assigned a particular escape line?"

"Aye." The boatswain departed.

"You'll need one too. Come." Ruori took Tresa by the hand and led her onto the gallery. They saw sky around them, a breeze touched their faces and the deck underfoot moved like a live thing. He indicated many light cords from the *Dolphin*'s store, bowlined to the rail. "We aren't going to risk parachuting with untrained men," he said. "But you've no experience in skinning down one of these. I'll make you a harness which will hold you safely. Ease yourself down hand over hand. When you reach the ground, cut loose." His knife slashed some pieces of rope and he knotted them together with a seaman's skill. When he fitted the harness on her, she grew tense under his fingers.

"But I am your friend," he murmured.

She eased. She even smiled, shakenly. He gave her his knife and went back inboard.

And now the last pirate vessel stood up from the earth. It moved near; Ruori's two craft made no attempt to flee. He saw sunlight flash on edged metal. He knew they had witnessed the end of their companion craft and would not be daunted by the same technique. Rather, they would close in, even while their ship burned about them. If nothing else, they could kindle him in turn and then parachute to safety. He did not send arrows.

When only a few fathoms separated him from the enemy, he cried: "Let go the valves!"

Gas whoofed from both bags. The linked blimps dropped.

"Fire!" shouted Ruori. Hiti aimed his catapult and sent a harpoon with anchor cable through the bottom of the attacker. "Burn and abandon!"

Men on deck touched off oil which other men splashed from jars. Flames sprang high.

With the weight of two nearly deflated vessels dragging it from below, the Canyon ship began to fall. At five hundred feet the tossed lifelines draped across flat rooftops and trailed in the streets. Ruori went over the side. He scorched his palms going down.

He was not much too quick. The harpooned blimp released compressed hydrogen and rose to a thousand feet with its burden, seeking sky room. Presumably no one had yet seen that the burden was on fire. In no case would they find it easy to shake or cut loose from one of Hiti's irons.

Ruori stared upward. Fanned by the wind, the blaze was smokeless, a small fierce sun. He had not counted on his fire taking the enemy by total surprise. He had assumed they would parachute to earth, where the Meycans could attack. Almost, he wanted to warn them.

Then flame reached the remaining hydrogen in the collapsed gas bags. He heard a sort of giant gasp. The topmost vessel became a flying pyre. The wind bore it out over the city walls. A few antlike figures managed to spring free. The parachute of one was burning.

"Sant'sima Marí," whispered a voice, and Tresa crept into Ruori's arms and hid her face.

VIII

After dark, candles were lit throughout the palace. They could not blank the ugliness of stripped walls and smoke-blackened ceilings. The guards-men who lined the throne room were tattered and weary. Nor did S' Antón itself rejoice, yet. There were too many dead.

Ruori sat throned on the calde's dais, Tresa at his right and Páwolo Dónoju on his left. Until a new set of officials could be chosen, these must take authority. The Don sat rigid, not allowing his bandaged head to droop; but now and then his lids grew too heavy to hold up. Tresa watched enormous-eyed from beneath the hood of a cloak wrapping her. Ruori sprawled at ease, a little more happy now that the fighting was over.

It had been a grim business, even after the heartened city troops had sallied and driven the surviving enemy before them. Too many Sky Men fought till they were killed. The hundreds of prisoners, mostly from the first Maurai success, would prove a dangerous booty; no one was sure what to do with them.

"But at least their host is done for," said Dónoju.

Ruori shook his head. "No, S'ñor. I am sorry, but you have no end in sight. Up north are thousands of such aircraft, and a strong hungry people. They will come again."

"We will meet them, Captain. The next time we shall be prepared. A larger garrison, barrage balloons, fire kites, cannons that shoot upward, perhaps a flying navy of our own . . . we can learn what to do."

Tresa stirred. Her tone bore life again, though a life which hated. "In the end, we will carry the war to them. Not one will remain in all the Corado highlands."

"No," said Ruori. "That must not be."

Her head jerked about; she stared at him from the shadow of her hood. Finally she said, "True, we are bidden to love our enemies, but you cannot mean the Sky People. They are not human!"

Ruori spoke to a page. "Send for the chief prisoner."

"To hear our judgment on him?" asked Dónoju. "That should be done formally, in public."

"Only to talk with us," said Ruori.

"I do not understand you," said Tresa. Her words faltered, unable to carry the intended scorn. "After everything you have done, suddenly there is no manhood in you."

He wondered why it should hurt for her to say that. He would not have cared if she had been anyone else.

Loklann entered between two guards. His hands were tied behind him and dried blood was on his face, but he walked like a conqueror under the pikes. When he reached the dais, he stood, legs braced apart, and grinned at Tresa.

"Well," he said, "so you find these others less satisfactory and want me back."

She jumped to her feet and screamed: "Kill him!"

"No!" cried Ruori.

The guardsmen hesitated, machetes half drawn. Ruori stood up and caught the girl's wrists. She struggled, spitting like a cat. "Don't kill him, then," she agreed at last, so thickly it was hard to understand. "Not now. Make it slow. Strangle him, burn him alive, toss him on your spears—"

Ruori held fast till she stood quietly.

When he let go, she sat down and wept.

Páwolo Dónoju said in a voice like steel: "I believe I understand. A fit punishment must certainly be devised."

Loklann spat on the floor. "Of course," he said. "When you have a man bound, you can play any number of dirty little games with him."

"Be still," said Ruori. "You are not helping your own cause. Or mine."

He sat down, crossed his legs, laced fingers around a knee, and gazed before him, into the darkness at the hall's end. "I know you have suffered from this man's work," he said carefully. "You can expect to suffer more from his kinfolk in the future. They are a young race, heedless as children, even as your ancestors and mine were once young. Do you think the Perio was established without hurt and harm? Or, if I remember your history rightly, that the Spañol people were welcomed here by the Inios? That the Ingliss did not come to N'Zealann with slaughter, and that the Maurai were not formerly cannibals? In an age of heroes, the hero must have an opponent.

"Your real weapon against the Sky People is not an army, sent to lose itself in unmapped mountains. . . . Your priests, merchants, artists, craftsmen, manners, fashions, learning—there is the means to bring them to you on their knees, if you will use it."

Loklann started. "You devil," he whispered. "Do you actually think to convert us to . . . a woman's faith and a city's cage?" He shook back his tawny mane and roared till the walls rung. "No!"

"It will take a century or two," said Ruori.

Don Páwolo smiled in his young scanty beard. "A refined revenge, S'ñor Captain," he admitted.

"Too refined!" Tresa lifted her face from her hands, gulped after air, held up claw-crooked fingers and brought them down as if into Loklann's eyes. "Even if it could be done," she snarled, "even if they did have souls, what do we want with them, or their children or grandchildren . . . they who murdered our babies today? Before almighty Dío—I am the last Carabán and I will have my following to speak for me in Meyco—there will never be anything for them but extermination. We can do it, I swear. Many Tekkans would help, for plunder. I shall yet live to see your home burning, you swine, and your sons hunted with dogs."

She turned frantically toward Ruori. "How else can our land be safe? We are ringed in by enemies. We have no choice but to destroy them, or they will destroy us. And we are the last Merikan civilization."

She sat back and shuddered. Ruori reached over to take her hand. It felt cold. For an instant, unconsciously, she returned the pressure, then jerked away.

He sighed in his weariness.

"I must disagree," he said. "I am sorry. I realize how you feel."

"You do not," she said through clamped jaws. "You cannot."

"But after all," he said, forcing dryness, "I am not just a man with human desires. I represent my government. I must return to tell them what is here, and I can predict their response.

"They will help you stand off attack. That is not an aid you can refuse, is it? The men who will be responsible for Meyco are not going to decline our offer of alliance merely to preserve a precarious independence of action, whatever a few extremists may argue for. And our terms will be most reasonable. We will want little more from you than a policy working toward conciliation and close relations with the Sky People, as soon as they have tired of battering themselves against our united defense."

"What?" said Loklann. Otherwise the chamber was very still. Eyes gleamed white from the shadows of helmets, toward Ruori.

"We will begin with you," said the Maurai. "At the proper time, you and your fellows will be escorted home. Your ransom will be that your nation allow a diplomatic and trade mission to enter."

"No," said Tresa, as if speech hurt her throat. "Not him. Send back the others if you must, but not him—to boast of what he did today."

Loklann grinned again, looking straight at her. "I will," he said.

Anger flicked in Ruori, but he held his mouth shut.

"I do not understand," hesitated Don Páwolo. "Why do you favor these animals?"

"Because they are more civilized than you," said Ruori.

"What?" The noble sprang to his feet, snatching for his sword. Stiffly, he sat down again. His tone froze over. "Explain yourself, S'ñor."

Ruori could not see Tresa's face, in the private night of her hood, but he felt her drawing farther from him than a star. "They have developed aircraft," he said, slumping back in his chair, worn out and with no sense of victory; *O great creating Tanaroa, grant me sleep this night!*

"But—"

"That was done from the ground up," explained Ruori, "not as a mere copy of ancient techniques. Beginning as refugees, the Sky People created an agriculture which can send warriors by the thousands from what was desert, yet plainly does not require peon hordes. On interrogation I have learned that they have sunpower and hydroelectric power, a synthetic chemistry of sorts, a well-developed navigation with the mathematics which that implies, gunpowder, metallurgics, aerodynamics. . . . Yes, I daresay it's a lopsided culture, a thin layer of learning above a largely illiterate mass. But even the mass must respect technology, or it would never have been supported to get as far as it has.

"In short," he sighed, wondering if he could make her comprehend, "the Sky People are a scientific race—the only one besides ourselves which we Maurai have yet discovered. And that makes them too precious to lose.

"You have better manners here, more humane laws, higher art, broader vision, every traditional virtue. But you are not scientific. You use rote knowledge handed down from the ancients. Because there is no more fossil fuel, you depend on muscle power; inevitably, then, you have a peon class, and always will. Because the iron and copper mines are exhausted, you tear down old ruins. In your land I have seen no research on wind power, sun power, the energy reserves of the living cell—not to mention the theoretical possibility of hydrogen fusion without a uranium primer. You irrigate the desert at a thousand times the effort it would take to farm the sea, yet have never even tried to improve your fishing techniques. You have not exploited the aluminum which is still abundant in ordinary clays, not sought to make it into strong alloys; no, your farmers use tools of wood and volcanic glass.

"Oh, you are neither ignorant nor superstitious. What you lack is merely the means of gaining new knowledge. You are a fine people; the world is the sweeter for you; I love you as much as I loathe this devil before us. But ultimately, my friends, if left to yourselves, you will slide gracefully back to the Stone Age."

A measure of strength returned. He raised his voice till it filled the hall. "The way of the Sky People is the rough way outward, to the stars. In that respect—and it overrides all others—they are more akin to us Maurai than you are. We cannot let our kin die."

He sat then, in silence, under Loklann's smirk and Dónoju's stare. A guardsman shifted on his feet, with a faint squeak of leather harness.

Tresa said at last, very low in the shadows: "That is your final word, S'ñor?"

"Yes," said Ruori. He turned to her. As she leaned forward, the hood fell back a little, so that candlelight touched her. And the sight of green eyes and parted lips gave him back his victory.

He smiled. "I do not expect you will understand at once. May I discuss it with you again, often? When you have seen the Islands, as I hope you will—"

"You *foreigner!*" she screamed.

Her hand cracked on his cheek. She rose and ran down the dais steps and out of the hall.

Gordon R. Dickson

THE MAN IN THE MAILBAG

Gordon R. Dickson is probably best known for his ambitious "Childe Cycle"—more commonly referred to as the "Dorsai" series—which largely focuses on the history of a race of interstellar mercenary soldiers (the Dorsai) as they work their destiny out against a complex Future History of warring planets and philosophies. But in his forty-eight-year career, Dickson's written just about every kind of science fiction that it's possible to write, from broad slapstick social comedies to broodingly introspective psychological studies, as well as a fair amount of fantasy. The "Childe Cycle" consists of the controversial *Soldier, Ask Not* (considered by many to be an "answer" to Robert A. Heinlein's *Starship Troopers*), *No Room For Man, The Far Call, The Tactics of Mistake, Dorsai!, The Spirit of Dorsai, Young Bleys,* and, most recently, *The Final Encyclopedia* and *The Chantry Guild;* the Dorsai short stories have been collected in *Lost Dorsai.* He won a Hugo Award in 1965 for the short novel version of "Soldier, Ask Not," a Nebula Award in 1966 for "Call Him Lord," and another two Hugo Awards in 1981 for "Lost Dorsai" and "The Cloak and the Staff." His other books include *Arcturus Landing, The Alien Way, Sleepwalker's World, The Last Master, Hour of the Horde, Way of the Pilgrim, Wolf and Iron, Timestorm, Wolfling, The Pritcher Mass, The Space Swimmers,* and a series of fantasy novels that include *The Dragon and the George, The Dragon Knight,* and *The Dragon on the Border.* His most recent novel is *The Dragon and the Djinn.* Dickson's many short stories have been assembled in the collections *In Iron Years, The Book of Gordon R. Dickson, None But Man, Love Not Human, Beginnings, Ends, Invaders!, Mindspan, The Earth Lords, Foreward!, The Man From Earth, Steel Brother,* and others. His long series of comic "Hoka" stories, written with Poul Anderson, have been assembled in the collections *Hoka!* and *Earthman's Burden;* there is also a "Hoka" novel, *Star Prince Charlie.* The story that follows, "The Man in the Mailbag," was later expanded into the novel *Special Delivery,* which was followed by a sequel, *Spacepaw.*

Although they frequently contain a strong element of physical action, Dickson's stories are usually thoughtful and thought-provoking as well, sometimes even somber, revolving around the changes in philosophies and ethics and social codes necessary to ensure humanity's survival in the complex and rapidly evolving social environments we'll have to deal with in the future.

Sometimes, though (the series of "Hoka" stories he wrote in collaboration with Poul Anderson also come to mind), he writes one just for the *fun* of it. And few stories then or now have been as purely entertaining as the fast and funny tale that follows (although, come to think of it, all that speculation about social codes and the most effective way to adapt your behavior in order to manipulate the society you're dealing with is still *there,* afterall, just played in a slightly different key), dealing with the misadventures of a hapless Earthman who must somehow find a way to cope with the huge, boisterous, furry, cantankerous Dilbians, even if he has to literally *kill* himself trying—an outcome which, alas, looks all too *likely.* . . .

The Right Honorable Joshua Guy, Ambassador Plenipotentiary to Dilbia, was smoking tobacco in a pipe. The fumes from it made John Tardy cough and strangle—or, at least, so it seemed.

"Sir?" wheezed John Tardy.

"Sorry," said Joshua, knocking the pipe out in an ashtray where the coals continued to smolder only slightly less villainously than before. "Thought you heard me the first time. I said that naturally as soon as we knew you were being assigned to the job, we let out word that you were deeply attached to the girl."

"To—" John gulped air. Both men were talking Dilbian, to exercise the command of the language John had had hypnoed into him on his way here from the Belt Stars, and the Dilbian nickname for the missing Earthian female sociologist came from his lips automatically—"this Greasy Face?"

"Miss Ty Lamorc," nodded Joshua, smoothly slipping into Basic and then out again. "Greasy Face, if you prefer. By the by, you mustn't go taking all these Dilbian names at face value. The two old gentlemen you're going to meet—Daddy Shaking Knees and Two Answers—aren't what they might sound like. Daddy Shaking Knees got his name from holding up one end of a timber one day in an emergency—after about forty-five minutes, someone noticed his knees beginning to tremble. And Two Answers is a tribute to the Dilbian who can come up with more than one answer to a problem."

About to ask Joshua about his own Dilbian nickname of Little Bite, John Tardy shifted to safe ground. "What about this Schlaff fellow who—"

"Heiner Schlaff," interrupted Joshua Guy, frowning, "made a mistake. You'd think anyone would know better than to lose his head when a Dilbian picks him up. After the first time one picked up Heinie, he wasn't able to step out onto the street without some Dilbian lifting him up to hear him yell for help. The Squeaking Squirt, they called him—very bad for Earth-Dilbian relations." He looked severely at John. "I don't expect anything like that from you." The ambassador's eye seemed to weigh John's chunky body and red hair.

"No, no," said John hastily.

"Decathlon winner in the Olympics four years back, weren't you?"

"Yes," said John. "But what I really want is to get on an exploration team to one of the new planets. I'm a fully qualified biochemist and—"

"I read your file. Well," Joshua Guy said, "do a good job here and who knows?" He glanced out the window beside him at the sprawling log buildings of the local Dilbian town of Humrog, framed against the native conifers and the mountain peaks beyond. "But it's your physical condition that'll count. You understand *why* you have to go it alone, don't you?"

"They told me back on Earth. But if you can add anything—"

"Headquarters never understands the fine points of these situations," said Joshua, almost cheerfully. "To put it tersely—we want to make friends with these Dilbians. They're the race nearest to ours in intelligence that we've run across so far. They'd make fine partners. Unfortunately we don't seem to be able to impress them very much."

"Size?" asked John Tardy.

"Well, yes—size is probably the biggest stumbling block. The fact that we're about lap-dog proportions in relation to them. But it shows up even more sharply in a cultural dissimilarity. They don't give a hang for our mechanical gimmicks and they're all for personal honor and a healthy outdoors life." He looked at John. "You'll say, of course, why not a show of force?"

"I should think—" began John.

"But we don't want to fight them—we want to make friends with them. Let me give you an Earth-type analogy. For centuries, humans have been able to more or less tame most of the smaller wild animals. The large ones, however, being unused to knuckling under to anyone—"

Beep! signaled the annunciator on Joshua's desk.

"Ah, they're here now." Joshua Guy rose. "We'll go into the reception room. Now remember that Boy-Is-She-Built is old Shaking Knees' daughter. It was the fact that the Streamside Terror wanted her that caused all this ruckus and ended up with the Terror's kidnapping Ty Lamorc."

He led the way through the door into the next room. John Tardy followed, his head, in spite of the hypno training, still spinning a little with the odd Dilbian names—in particular Boy-Is-She-Built, the Basic translation of which was only a pale shadow of its Dilbian original. While not by any means a shy person, John rather hesitated to look a father in the eye and refer to the female child of his old age as—further reflections were cut short as he entered the room.

"Ah, there, Little Bite!" boomed the larger of the two black-furred monsters awaiting them. The one who spoke stood well over two and a half meters in height—at least eight feet tall. "This the new one? Two Answers and I came right over to meet him. Kind of bright-colored on top, isn't he?"

John Tardy blinked. But Joshua Guy answered equably enough.

"Some of us have that color hair back home," he said. "This is John Tardy—John, meet Shaking Knees. And the quiet one is Two Answers."

"Quiet!" roared the other Dilbian, bursting into gargantuan roars of laughter. "Me *quiet!* That's good!" He bellowed his merriment.

John stared. In spite of the hypno training, he could not help comparing these two to a couple of very large bears who had stood up on their hind legs and gone on a diet. They were leaner than bears—though leanness is relative when you weigh upward of a thousand pounds—and longer-legged. Their noses were more pug, their lower jaws more humanlike than ursinoid in the way of chin. But their complete coat of thick black hair and their bearishness of language and actions made the comparison almost inevitable—though in fact their true biological resemblance was closer to the humans themselves.

"Haven't laughed like that since old Souse Nose fell in the beer vat!" snorted Two Answers, gradually getting himself under control. "All right, Bright Top, what've you got to say for yourself? Think you can take the Streamside Terror with one hand tied behind your back?"

"I'm here," said John Tardy, "to bring back—er—Greasy Face, and—"

"Streamside won't just hand her over. Will he, Knees?" Two Answers jogged his companion with a massively humorous elbow.

"Not that boy!" Shaking Knees shook his head. "Little Bite, I ought never have let you talk me out of a son-in-law like that. Tough? Rough? Tricky? My little girl'd do all right with a buck like that."

"I merely," demurred Joshua, "suggested you make them wait a bit. Boy-Is-She-Built is still rather young—"

"And, boy, is she built!" said Shaking Knees in a tone of fond, fatherly pride. "Still, it's hard to see how she could do much better." He peered suddenly at Joshua. "You wouldn't have something hidden between your paws on this?"

Joshua Guy spread his hands in a wounded manner. "Would I risk one of my own people? Maybe two? All to start something that would make the Terror mad enough to steal Greasy to pay me back?"

"Guess not," admitted Shaking Knees. "But you Shorties are shrewd little characters." His words rang with honest admiration.

"Thanks. The same to you," said Joshua. "Now about the Terror—"

"He headed west through the Cold Mountains," replied Two Answers. "He was spotted yesterday a half-day's hike north, pointed toward

Sour Ford and the Hollows. He probably nighted at Brittle Rock Inn there."

"Good," said Joshua. "We'll have to find a guide for my friend here."

"Guide? Ho!" chortled Shaking Knees. "Wait'll you see what *we* got for you." He shouldered past Two Answers, opened the door and bellowed, "Bluffer! Come on in!"

There was a moment's pause, and then a Dilbian even leaner and taller than Shaking Knees shoved his way into the room, which, with this new Dilbian addition, became decidedly crowded.

"There you are," said Shaking Knees, waving a prideful paw. "What more could you want? Walk all day, climb all night, and start out fresh next morning after breakfast. Little Bite, meet the Hill Bluffer!"

"That's me!" boomed the newcomer, rattling the walls. "Anything on two feet walk away from me? Not over solid ground or living rock! When I look at a hill, it knows it's beat, and it lays out flat for my trampling feet!"

"Very good," said Joshua dryly. "But I don't know about my friend here keeping up if you can travel like that."

"Keep up? Hah!" guffawed Shaking Knees. "No, no, Little Bite— don't you recognize the Bluffer here? He's the postman. We're going to mail this half-pint friend of yours to the Terror. Only way. Cost you five kilos of nails."

"Nobody stops the mail," put in the Hill Bluffer.

"Hmm," said Joshua. He glanced at John Tardy. "Not a bad suggestion. The only thing is how you plan to carry him—"

"Who? Him?" boomed the Bluffer, focusing on John. "Why, I'll handle him like he was a week-old pup. I'll wrap him in some real soft straw and tuck him in the bottom of my mailbag and—"

"Hold it," interrupted Joshua. "That's just what I was afraid of. If you're going to carry him, you'll have to do it humanely."

"I won't wear it!" the Hill Bluffer was still roaring, two hours later. The cause of his upset, a system of straps and pads arranged into a rough saddlebag that would ride between his shoulders and bear John, lay on the crushed rock of Humrog's main street. A few Dilbian bystanders had gathered to watch and their bass-voiced comments were not of the sort to bring the Hill Bluffer to a more reasonable frame of mind.

"Listen, you tad!" Shaking Knees was beginning to get a little hot under the neck-fur himself. "This is your mother's uncle's first cousin speaking. You want me to speak to the great-grandfathers of your clan—"

"Arright—arright—arright!" snarled the Hill Bluffer. "Buckle me up in the obscenity thing!"

"That's better!" growled Shaking Knees, simmering down as John

Tardy and Joshua Guy went to work to put the saddle on. "Not that I blame you, but—"

"Don't feel so bad at that," said the Hill Bluffer sulkily, wriggling his shoulders under the straps in experimental fashion.

"You'll find it," grunted Joshua, tugging on a strap, "easier to carry than your regular bag."

"That's not the point," groused the Hill Bluffer. "A postman's got dignity. He just don't wear—" He exploded suddenly at a snickering onlooker. *"What's so funny, you? Want to make something out of it? Just say the—"*

"I'll take care of him!" roared Shaking Knees, rolling forward. "What's wrong with you, Split Nose?"

The Dilbian addressed as Split Nose swallowed his grin rather hastily as the Humrog village chief took a hand in the conversation.

"Just passing by," he growled defensively, backing out of the crowd.

"Well, just pass on, friend, pass on!" boomed Shaking Knees. He was rewarded by a hearty laugh from the crowd, and Split Nose rolled off down the street with every indication his hairy ears were burning.

John had taken advantage of this little by-play to mount into the saddlebag. The Hill Bluffer grunted in surprise and looked back at him.

"You're light enough," he said. "How is it? All right back there?"

"Feels fine," said John, unsuspecting.

"Then so long, everybody!" boomed the Hill Bluffer, and, without further warning, barreled off down the main street in the direction of the North Trail, the Cold Mountains and the elusive but dangerous Streamside Terror.

Had it not been for the hypno training, John Tardy would not have been able to recognize this fast and unexpected start for the Dilbian trick it was. He realized instantly, however, that the Hill Bluffer, having lost his enthusiasm for the job at first sight of the harness which was to carry John, was attempting a little strategy to get out of it. Outright refusal to carry John was out of the question, but if John should object to the unceremoniousness of his departure, the Bluffer would be perfectly justified—by Dilbian standards—if he threw up his hands and refused to deliver a piece of mail that insisted on imposing conditions on him. John shut his mouth and hung on.

All the same, it was awkward. John had intended to work out a plan of action with Joshua Guy before he left. Well, there was always the wrist-phone. He would call Joshua at the first convenient opportunity.

Meanwhile, it was developing that the Hill Bluffer had not exaggerated his ability to cover ground. One moment they were on the main street of Humrog, and the next upon a mountain trail, green pinelike branches whipping by as John Tardy plunged and swayed to the Hill Bluffer's motion like a man on the back of an elephant. It was no time for abstract thought. John clung to the straps before him, meditating rather bitterly on that natural talent of his for athletics which had got him into this, when by all rights he should be on an exploration team on one of the frontier planets right now. He was perfectly qualified, but just because of that decathlon win . . .

He continued to nurse his grievances for something better than an hour, when he was suddenly interrupted by the Hill Bluffer's grunting and slowing down. Peering forward over the postman's shoulder, John discovered another Dilbian who had just stepped out of the woods before them. The newcomer was on the shaggy side. He carried an enormous triangular-headed axe and had some native herbivore roughly the size and shape of a musk-ox slung casually over one shoulder.

"Hello, woodsman," said the Hill Bluffer, halting.

"Hello, postman." The other displayed a gap-toothed array of fangs in a grin. "Got some mail for me?"

"You!" the Hill Bluffer snorted.

"Not so funny. I could get mail," growled the other. He peered around at John. "So that's the Half Pint Posted."

"Oh?" said the Hill Bluffer. "Who told you?"

"The Cobbly Queen, that's who!" retorted the other, curling the right side of his upper lip in the native equivalent of a wink. John Tardy, recalling the Cobblies were the Dilbian equivalent of fairies, brownies, or what-have-you, peered at the woodsman to see if he was serious. John decided he wasn't. Which still left the problem of how he had recognized John.

Remembering the best Dilbian manners were made of sheer brass, John Tardy horned in on the conversation.

"Who're you?" he demanded of the woodsman.

"So it talks, does it?" The woodsman grinned. "They call me Tree Weeper, Half Pint. Because I chop them down, you see."

"Who told you about me?"

"Oh, that'd be telling," grinned Tree Weeper. "Say, you know why they call him the Streamside Terror, Half Pint? It's on account of he likes to fight alongside a stream, pull the other feller in and drown him."

"I know," said John shortly.

"Do you now?" said the other. "Well, it ought to be something to watch. Good going to you, Half Pint, and you too, postman. Me for home."

He turned away into the brush alongside the trail and it swallowed him up. The Hill Bluffer took up his route again without a word.

"Friend of yours?" inquired John, when it became apparent the Hill Bluffer was not going to comment on the meeting.

"Friend?" the Hill Bluffer snorted angrily. *"I'm* a public official!"

"I just thought—" said John. "He seemed to know things."

"That hill hopper! Somebody ahead of us told him!" growled the Bluffer. But he fell unaccountably silent after that and said no more for the next three hours, until—the two of them having left Humrog a couple of hours past noon—they pulled up in the waning sunlight before the roadside inn at Brittle Rock, where they would spend the night.

The first thing John Tardy did, after working some life back into his legs, was to stroll off to the limits of the narrow, rocky ledge on which the inn stood—Brittle Rock was hardly more than a wide spot in the narrow mountain gorge up which their road ran—and put in a call to Joshua Guy with the phone on his wrist. As soon as Joshua got on the beam, John relievedly explained the reason behind his call. It did not go over, apparently, very well.

"Instructions?" floated the faintly astonished voice of the ambassador out of the receiver. "What instructions?"

"The ones you were going to give me. Before I took off so suddenly—"

"But there's absolutely nothing I can tell you," interrupted Joshua. "You've had your hypno training. It's up to you. Find the Terror and get the girl back. You'll have to figure out your own means, my dear fellow."

"But—" John stopped, staring helpless at the phone.

"Well, good luck, then. Call me tomorrow. Call me anytime."

"Thanks," said John.

"Not at all. Luck. Good-by."

"Good-by."

John Tardy clicked off the phone and walked somberly back to the inn. Inside its big front door, he found a wide common room filled with tables and benches. The Hill Bluffer, to the amusement of a host of other travelers, was arguing with a female Dilbian wearing an apron.

"How the unmentionable should *I* know what to feed him?" the Hill Bluffer was bellowing. "Give him some meat, some beer—anything!"

"But you haven't had the children dragging in pets like I have. Feed one the wrong thing and it dies. And then they cry their little hearts—"

"Talking about me?" John Tardy broke in.

"Oh!" gasped the female, glancing down and retreating half a step. "It talks!"

"Didn't I say he did?" demanded the Bluffer. "Half Pint, what kind of stuff do you eat?"

John fingered the four-inch tubes of food concentrate at his waist. Dilbian food would not poison him, though he could expect little nourishment from it, and a fair chance of an allergic reaction from certain fruits and vegetables. Bulk was all he needed to supplement the concentrates.

"Just give me a little beer," he said.

The room buzzed approval. This little critter, they seemed to feel, could not be too alien if he liked to drink. The female brought him a wastebasket-sized wooden mug that had no handles and smelled like the most decayed of back-lot breweries. John took a cautious sip and held the bitter, sour, flat-tasting liquid in his mouth for an indecisive moment.

He swallowed manfully. The assembled company gave vent to rough-voiced approval, then abruptly turned their attention elsewhere. Looking around, he saw that the Hill Bluffer had gone off somewhere. John climbed up on a nearby bench and got to work on his food concentrates.

After finishing these, he continued to sit where he was for the better part of an hour, but the Hill Bluffer did not return. Struck by a sudden thought, John Tardy climbed down and went back toward the kitchen of the inn. Pushing his way through a hide curtain, he found himself in it—a long room with a stone fire-trough down the center, carcasses hanging from overhead beams, and a dozen or so Dilbians of both sexes equally immersed in argument and the preparation of food and drink. Among them was the female who had brought John the beer.

He stepped into her path as she headed for the front room with a double handful of full mugs.

"Eeeeek!" she exclaimed, or the Dilbian equivalent, stopping so hastily she spilled some of the beer. "There's a good little Shorty," she said in a quavering, coaxing tone. "Good Shorty. Go back now."

"Was the Terror really here last night?" John asked.

"He stopped to pick up some meat and beer, but I didn't see him," she said. "I've no time for hill-and-alley brawlers. Now shoo!"

John Tardy shooed.

As he was heading back to his bench, however, he felt himself scooped up from behind. Looking back over his shoulder, he saw he was being carried by a large male Dilbian with a pouch hanging from one shoulder. This individual carried him to a table where three other Dilbians sat and dropped him on it. John Tardy instinctively got to his feet.

"There he be," said the one who had picked him up. "A genuine Shorty."

"Give him some beer," suggested one with a scar on his face, who was seated at the table.

They did. John prudently drank some.

"Don't hold much," commented one of the others at the table, examining the mug John had set down after what had been actually a very healthy draft for a human. "I wonder if he—"

"Couldn't. Not at that size," replied the one with the pouch. "He's chasing that female Shorty, though. You reckon—?"

Scarface regretted that they did not have the Shorty female there at the moment. Her presence, in his opinion, would have provided the opportunity for interesting and educative experimentation.

"Go to hell!" said John in Basic. He then made the most forceful translation he could manage in Dilbian.

"Tough character!" said the pouched one, and they all laughed. "Better not get tough with me, though."

He made a few humorous swipes at John's red head that would have split it on contact. They laughed again.

"I wonder," said Scarface, "can he do tricks?"

"Sure," John answered promptly. He left his still-ful mug of beer. "Watch. I take a firm grip, rock back, and—" He spun suddenly on one heel, sloshing a wave of beer into their staring faces. Then he was off the table and dodging among Dilbian and table legs toward the front entrance. The rest of the guests, roaring with laughter, made no attempt to halt him. He ducked into the outer darkness.

Fumbling in the gloom, he made his way around the side of the inn and dropped down on a broken keg he found there. He was just making up his mind to stay there until the Hill Bluffer came and found him, when the back kitchen door opened and closed very softly, off to his left.

He slipped off the keg into deeper shadow. He had caught just a glimpse out of the corner of his eye, but he had received the impression of a Dilbian female in the doorway. There was no sound now.

He began to creep backward. Dilbia's one moon was not showing over these latitudes at this season of the year, and the starlight gave only a faint illumination. He stumbled suddenly over the edge of an unseen slope and froze, remembering the cliff edge overhanging the gorge below.

A faint reek of the Dilbian odor came to his nostrils—and a sound of sniffing. Dilbians were no better than human when it came to a sense of smell, but each had a perceptible odor to the nostrils of the other—an odor partly dependent on diet, partly on a differing physiological makeup. The odor John Tardy smelled was part-pine, part-musk.

The sniffing ceased. John held his breath, waiting for it to start again.

The pressure built up in his chest, and finally he was forced to exhale. He turned his head slowly from side to side.

Silence.

Only the inner creak of his tense neck muscles turning. There! Was that something? John began to creep back along the edge beside him.

There was a sudden rush, a rearing up of some huge dark shape in the darkness before him. He dodged, felt himself slipping on the edge, and something smashed like a falling wall against the side of his head, and he went whirling down and away into star-shot darkness.

He opened his eyes to bright sunlight.

The sun, just above the mountain peaks, was shining right in his eyes. He blinked and started to roll over, out of its glare, into—

—And grabbed in a sudden cold sweat for the stubby trunk of a dwarf tree growing right out of the cliffside.

For a second then, he hung there, sweating and looking down. He lay on a narrow ledge and the gorge was deep below. How deep, he did not stop to figure. It was deep enough.

He twisted around and looked up the distance of a couple of meters to the ledge on which the inn was built. It was not far. He could climb it. After a little while, with his heart in his throat, John Tardy did.

When he came back around the front of the inn, in the morning sunlight, it was to find the Bluffer orating at a sort of open-air meeting, with the four who had harried John standing hangdog between two axemen and before an elderly Dilbian judgelike on a bench.

"—the mail!" the Hill Bluffer was roaring. "The mail is sacred! Anyone daring to lay fist upon the mail in transit—"

John, tottering forward, put an end to the trial in progress.

Later on, after washing his slight scalp-wound and having taken on some more food concentrates and flat beer for breakfast, John Tardy climbed back up on the Bluffer's back and they were under way once more. Their route today led from Brittle Rock through the mountains to Sour Ford and the Hollows. The Hollows, John had learned, was clan-country for the Terror, and their hope was to catch him before he reached it. The trail now led across swinging rope suspension bridges and along narrow cuts in the rock—all of which the Hill Bluffer took not only with the ease of one well accustomed to them, but with the abstraction of one lost in deep thought.

"Hey!" said John, at last.

"Huh? What?" grunted the Hill Bluffer, coming to suddenly.

"Tell me something," said John, reaching out for anything to keep his carrier awake. "How'd the ambassador get the name Little Bite?"

"You don't know that?" exclaimed the Hill Bluffer. "I thought you Shorties all knew. Well, it was old Hammertoes down at Humrog."

The Bluffer chuckled. "Got drunk and all worked up about Shorties. 'Gimme the good old days,' he said, and went down to just make an example of Little Bite—Shorty One, we called him then. He pushes the door open far as it'll go, but Little Bite's got it fixed to only open part way. So there's Hammertoes, with only one arm through the door, feeling around and hollering, 'All right, Shorty! You can't get away! I'll get you—' when Little Bite picks up something sharp and cuts him a couple times across the knuckles. Old Hammertoes yells bloody murder and yanks his hand back. Slam goes the door."

The Hill Bluffer chortled to himself. "Then old Hammertoes comes back uptown, sucking his knuckles. 'What happened?' says everybody. 'Nothing,' says Hammertoes. 'Something must've happened—look at your hand,' everybody says. 'I tell you nothing happened!' yells Hammertoes. 'He wouldn't let me in where I could grab hold of him, so I come away. And as for my hand, that's got nothing to do with it. He didn't hurt my hand hardly at all. He just give it a little bite!' "

The Hill Bluffer's laughter rolled like thunder between the mountain walls. "Old Hammertoes never did live that down. Every time since, whenever he goes to give somebody a hard time, they all tell him, 'Look out, Hammertoes, or I'm liable to give you a little bite!' "

John Tardy found himself laughing. Possibly it was the time and place of the telling, possibly the story, but he could see the situation in his mind's eye and it was funny.

"You know," said the Bluffer over one furry shoulder when John stopped laughing, "you're not bad for a Shorty." He fell silent, appeared to wrestle with himself for a moment, then came to a stop and sat down in a convenient wide spot on the trail.

"Get off," he said. "Come around where I can talk to you."

John complied. He found himself facing the seated Dilbian, their heads about on a level. Behind the large, black-furred skull, a few white clouds floated in the high blue sky.

"You know," the Bluffer said, "the Streamside Terror's mug's been spilled."

"Spilled?" echoed John—then remembered this as a Dilbian phrase expressing loss of honor. "By me? He's never even seen me."

"By Little Bite," the Bluffer said. "But Little Bite's a Guest in Humrog and the North Country. The Terror couldn't call him to account personally for speaking against Shaking Knees giving the Terror Boy-Is-She-Built. He had to do something, though, so he took Greasy Face."

"Oh," said John.

"So you got to fight the Terror if you want Greasy back."

"Fight?" John blurted.

"Man's got his pride," said the Bluffer. "That's why I can't figure you out. I mean you aren't bad for a Shorty. You got guts—like with those drunks last night. But you fighting the Terror—I mean *hell!"* said the Bluffer, in deeply moved tones.

Silently, John Tardy found himself in full agreement with the postman.

"So what're you going to do when you meet Streamside?"

"Well," said John, rather inadequately, "I don't exactly know—"

"Well," growled the Bluffer in his turn, "not my problem. Get on." John went around behind his furry back. "Oh, by the way, know who it was tried to pitch you over the cliff?"

"Who?" asked John.

"The Cobbly Queen—Boy-Is-She-Built!" translated the Bluffer as John looked blank. "She heard about you and got ahead of us somehow . . ." The Bluffer's voice trailed off into a mutter. "If they're thinking of monkeying with the mail . . ."

John paid no attention. He had his own fish to fry, and very fishy indeed they smelled just at the moment. Swaying on top of the enormous back as they took off again, he found himself scowling over the situation. Headquarters had said nothing about his being expected to fight some monstrous free-style scrapper of an alien race—a sort of gargantuan Billy the Kid with a number of kills to his credit. Joshua Guy had not mentioned it. Just what was going on here, anyway?

Abruptly casting aside the security regulation that recommended a "discreet" use of the instrument, John lifted the wrist that bore his wristphone to his lips.

"Josh—" he began, and suddenly checked. A fine trickle of sweat ran coldly down his spine.

The phone was gone.

He had the rest of the morning to ponder this new development in the situation, and a good portion of the afternoon. He might have continued indefinitely if it had not been for a sudden interruption in their journey.

They had crossed a number of spidery suspension bridges during the course of the day, and now they had come to another one, somewhat longer than any met so far. If this had been the only difference, John might have been left to his thoughts. But this bridge was different.

Somebody had fixed it so they couldn't get across.

It happened that their end of the bridge had its anchors sunk in a rock face a little back and some seven or eight meters above their heads. All that had been done, simply enough, was to tighten the two main support cables at the far end. The sag of the span had straightened out, lifting the near end up above them, out of reach.

The Hill Bluffer bellowed obscenely across the gap. There was no response from the windlass on the far side, or the small hut beyond.

"What's happened?" John Tardy asked.

"I don't know," said the Bluffer, suddenly thoughtful. "It isn't supposed to be rucked up except at night, to keep people from sneaking over and not paying toll."

He reached as high as he could, but his fingertips fell far short.

"Lift me up," suggested John.

They tried it, but even upheld by the ankles, at the full stretch of the Bluffer's arms, John was rewarded only by a throat-squeezing view of the Knobby River below.

"It'll take five days to go around by Slide Pass," growled the Bluffer, putting John down.

John went over to examine the rock face. What he discovered about it did not make him happy, though perhaps it should have. It was climbable. Heart tucked in throat, he began to go up it.

"Hey! Where're you going?" bellowed the Hill Bluffer.

John did not answer. He needed his breath; anyway, his destination was obvious. The climb up the rock was not bad for someone who had had some mountain experience, but a reaction set in when he wrapped his arms around the rough six-inch cable. He inched his way upward and got on top, both arms and both legs wrapped around the cable, and began a worm-creep toward the bridge end, floating on nothingness at a rather remarkable distance—seen from this angle—ahead of him.

It occurred to him, after he had slowly covered about a third of the cable-distance in this fashion, that a real hero in a place like this should stand up and tightrope-walk to the bridge proper. This, in addition to impressing the Bluffer, would shorten the suspense considerably. John Tardy concluded he must be a conservative and went on crawling.

Eventually he reached the bridge, crawled out on it and lay panting for a while, then got up and crossed the gorge. At the far end, he knocked loose the lock on the windlass with a heavy rock, and the bridge banged down into position, raising a cloud of dust.

Through this same cloud of dust, the Hill Bluffer was shortly to be seen advancing with a look of grim purpose. He stalked past John and entered the hut—from which subsequently erupted thunderous crashes, thuds and roars.

John Tardy looked about for a place of safety. He had never seen two

Dilbians fight, but it was only too apparent now what was going on in-side.

He was still looking around, however, when the sound ceased abruptly and the Hill Bluffer emerged, dabbing at a torn ear.

"Old slaver-tongue," he growled. *"She* got at him."

"Who?" asked John.

"Boy-Is-She-Built. Well, mount up, Half Pint. Oh, by the way, that was pretty good."

"Good? What was?"

"Climbing across the bridge that way. Took guts. Well, let's go."

John climbed back up into his saddlebag and thought heavily.

"You didn't kill him?" he asked, as they started out once more.

"Who? Old Winch Rope? Just knocked a little sense into him. Hell, there's got to be somebody to work the bridge. Hang on now. It's all downhill from here and it'll be twilight before we hit the ford."

It was indeed twilight before they reached their stopping place at Sour Ford. John Tardy, who had been dozing, awoke with a jerk and sat up in his saddle, blinking.

In the fading light, they stood in a large, grassy clearing semicircled by forest. Directly before them was a long low log building, and behind it a smooth-flowing river with its farther shore shrouded in tree shadow and the approaching dusk.

"Get down," said the Bluffer.

Stiffly, John Tardy descended, stamped about to restore his circula-tion, and followed the Bluffer's huge bulk through the hide-curtain of the doorway to the building's oil-lamp lit interior.

John discovered a large room like that at the Brittle Rock Inn—but one that was cleaner, airier, and filled with travelers a good deal less noisy and drunken. Gazing around for the explanation behind this differ-ence, John caught sight of a truly enormous Dilbian, grizzled with age and heavy with fat, seated like a patriarch in a huge chair behind a table at the room's far end.

John and the Bluffer found a table and set about eating. But as soon as they were through, the postman led John up to the patriarch.

"One Man," said the Bluffer in a respectful voice, "this here's the Half Pint Posted."

John Tardy blinked. Up close, One Man had turned out to be even more awe-inspiring than he had seemed from a distance. He over-flowed the carved chair he sat in, and the graying fur on top of his head all but brushed against a polished staff of hardwood laid crosswise on pegs driven into the wall two meters above the floor. His massive fore-arms and great pawlike hands were laid out on the table before him like swollen clubs of bone and muscle. But his face was almost Biblically serene.

"Sit down," he rumbled in a voice so deep it sounded like a great drum sounding far off somewhere in a woods. "I've wanted to see a Shorty. You're my Guest, Half Pint, for as long as you wish. Anyone tell you about me?"

"I'm sorry—" began John.

"Never mind." The enormous head nodded mildly. "They call me One Man, Half Pint, because I once held blood feud all by myself—being an orphan—with a whole clan. And won." He looked calmly at John. "What you might call an impossible undertaking."

"Some of them caught him on a trail once," put in the Hill Bluffer. "He killed all three."

"That was possible," murmured One Man. His eyes were still on John. "Tell me, Half Pint, what are you Shorties doing here, anyhow?"

"Well—" John blinked. "I'm looking for Greasy Face—"

"I mean the entire lot of you," One Man said. "There must be some plan behind it. Nobody asked you all here, you know."

"Well—" said John again, rather lamely, and proceeded to try an explanation. It did not seem to go over very well, a technological civilization being hard to picture with the Dilbian vocabulary.

One Man nodded when John Tardy was through. "I see. If that's the case, what makes you think we ought to like you Shorties?"

"Ought to?" said John, jolted into a reactive answer, for he did not have red hair for nothing. "You don't ought to! It's up to you."

One Man nodded. "Pass me my stick," he said.

One of the Dilbians standing around took down the staff from its pegs and passed it to him. He laid it on the table before him—a young post ten centimeters in thickness—grasping it with fists held over two meters apart.

"No one's ever been able to do this but me," he said.

Without lifting his fists from contact with the table, he rotated them to the outside. The staff sprang upward in the center like a bow, and snapped.

"Souvenir for you," said One Man, handing the pieces to John. "Good night."

He closed his eyes and sat as if dozing. The Bluffer tapped John on a shoulder and led him away, off to their sleeping quarters.

Once in the inn dormitory, however, John found himself totally unable to sleep. He had passed from utter bone-weariness into a sort of feverish wide-awakeness, through which the little episode with One Man buzzed and circled like a persistently annoying fly.

What had been the point of all that talk and wood-breaking?

Suddenly and quietly, John sat up. Beside him, on his heap of soft branches, the Bluffer slept without stirring, as did the rest of the dormitory inhabitants. A single lamp burned high above, hanging from the rooftree. By its light, John got out and examined the broken pieces of wood. There was a little node or knot visible just at the point of breakage. A small thing, but—

John frowned. He seemed surrounded by mysteries. The more he thought of it, the more certain he was that One Man had been attempting to convey some message to him. What was it? For that matter, what was going on between humans and Dilbians, and what had his mission to rescue Greasy Face to do with the business of persuading the recalcitrant Dilbians into a partnership? If that was indeed the aim, as Joshua Guy had said.

John swung out of the pile of boughs and to his feet. One Man, he decided, owed him a few more—and plainer—answers.

He went softly down the length of the dormitory and through the door into the common room of the inn.

There were few Dilbians about—they went early to bed. And One Man was also nowhere to be seen. He had not come into the dormitory, John knew. So either he had separate quarters, or else he had stepped outside for some reason . . .

John Tardy crossed the room and slipped out through the inn entrance. He paused to accustom his eyes to the darkness and moved off from the building to get away from the window light. Slowly the night took shape around him, the wide face of the river running silver-dark in the faint light of the stars, and the clearing pooled in gloom.

He circled cautiously around the inn to its back. Unlike Brittle Rock, the backyard here was clear of rubbish, sloping gradually to the river. It was given over to smaller huts and outbuildings. Among these the darkness was more profound and he felt his way cautiously.

Groping about in this fashion, quietly, but with some small, unavoidable noise, he saw a thin blade of yellow light. It cut through the parting of two leather curtains in the window of a hut close by him. He stepped eagerly toward it, about to peer through the crack, when, from deep wall shadow, a hand reached out and took his arm.

"Do you *want* to get yourself killed?" hissed a voice.

And, of course, it was human. And, of course, it spoke in Basic.

Whoever had hold of him drew him deeper into the shadow and away from the building where they stood. They came to another hut whose door stood ajar on an interior blackness, and John was led into this darkness. The hand let go of his arm. The door closed softly. There was a scratch, a sputter, and an animal-oil lamp burst into light within the place.

John squinted against the sudden illumination. When he could see again, he found himself looking into the face of one of the best-looking young women he had ever seen.

She was a good fifteen centimeters shorter than he, but at first glance looked taller by reason of her slim outline in the tailored coveralls she wore. To John Tardy, after two days of Dilbians, she looked tiny—fragile. Her chestnut hair swept back in two wide wings on each side of her head. Her eyes were green above sharply marked cheekbones that gave her face a sculptured look. Her nose was thin, her lips firm rather than full, and her small chin was determined.

John blinked. "Who—?"

"I'm Ty Lamorc," she whispered fiercely. "Keep your voice down!"

"Ty Lamorc? *You?*"

"Yes, yes!" she said impatiently. "Now—"

"Are y-you sure?" stammered John. "I mean—"

"Who were you expecting to run into way out here in—oh, I see!" She glared at him. "It's that Greasy Face name the Dilbians gave me. You were expecting some horror."

"Certainly not," said John stoutly.

"Well, for your information, they just happened to see me putting on makeup one day. That's where the name came from."

"Well, naturally. I didn't think it was because—"

"I'll bet! Anyway, never mind that now. The point is, what are *you* doing out here? Do you *want* to get knocked on the head?"

"Who'd knock—" John Tardy stiffened. "The Terror's here!"

"No, no!" She sounded annoyed. "Boy-Is-She-Built is."

"Oh." John frowned. "You know, I still don't get it—her angle on all this, I mean."

"She loves him, of course," said Ty Lamorc. "Actually, they make an ideal couple, by Dilbian standards. Now let's get you back to the inn before she catches you. She won't follow you in there. You're a Guest."

"Now wait—" John took a deep breath. "This is silly. I came out here to find you. I've found you. Let's head back right now. Not to Humrog—"

"You don't," interrupted Ty with feeling, "understand a blasted thing about these people, Half Pint—I mean, Tardy."

"John."

"John, you don't understand the situation. The Streamside Terror left me here with Boy-Is-She-Built because I was slowing him down. That

Hill Bluffer of yours is too fast for him, and he wanted to be sure to be in his own clan-country before you caught up with him, in case there would be—" her voice faltered a little—"repercussions to what happens when you meet. It's all a matter of honor, and that's the point. *You're a piece of mail, John.* Don't you understand? The Hill Bluffer's honor is involved, too."

"Oh," said John. He was silent for a while. "You mean he'd insist on delivering me?"

"What do you think?"

"I see." John was silent again. "Well, to blazes with it," he said at last. "Maybe we can make it across a bridge and cut the ropes and get away from it all. We can't leave you here."

Ty Lamorc did not reply at once. When she did, it was with a pat on his arm.

"You're nice," she said softly. "I'll remember that. Now get back to the inn." And then she had blown out the lamp and he could hear her go.

Next morning, One Man was still nowhere to be seen. Nor, in the half hour that elapsed before they got going, did John Tardy catch any glimpse of Ty, or a female Dilbian who might be Boy-Is-She-Built. He mounted into the Hill Bluffer's mailbag with his mind still engrossed by the happenings of the night before, and it continued to be engrossed as they began their third day of journey.

They were descending now into a country of lower altitudes, though they were still in hill country. The ground was more gently hollowed and crested, and several new varieties of trees appeared.

But John had no time to consider this. He rode through the cool hours of the morning and into noon's heat still trying to find a common solution to the riddles that occupied his mind—about One Man, about the abduction of Ty Lamorc, and about his own peculiar lack of briefing.

"Tell me," said John finally to the Hill Bluffer, "is it a fact no other Dilbian could break that stick of One Man's that same way?"

"Nobody ever can," replied the Bluffer, as they rounded a small hill and plunged through a thin belt of trees. "Nobody ever will."

"Well, you know," said John, "back where I come from, we have a trick with something called a phone directory—"

He stopped. For the Hill Bluffer himself had stopped, with a jolt that almost pitched John from the mailbag. John sat up, looked around the Dilbian's head—and stared.

They had passed through the woods. They had emerged into a small valley in which a cluster of buildings stood in the brown color of their peeled and weathered logs, haphazardly about a stream that ran the valley's length. Beyond these houses there was a sort of natural amphitheater made by a curved indentation of the far rock wall of the valley. Past this the path went when it emerged from between the buildings and plunged into the trees again.

However, none of this claimed John's attention after the first second. He blinked, instead, at a living wall of five large Dilbians with axes.

"Who do you think you're stopping?" bellowed the Hill Bluffer.

"Clan Hollows' in full meeting," responded the central axeman. "The Great-Grandfathers want to see you both. You come with us."

The axemen formed around the Bluffer and John. They led off down and through the village and beyond to the amphitheater that was swarming with Dilbians of all ages. Several hundred of them were there, and more accumulating, below a ledge of rock where six ancient Dilbians sat.

"This is the mail!" stormed the Hill Bluffer as soon as they were close. "Listen, you Clan Hollows—"

"Be quiet, postman!" snapped the old Dilbian at the extreme right of the line as it faced John and the Bluffer. "Your honor will be guarded. Call the meeting."

"Great-Grandfathers of Clan Hollows, sitting in judgment upon a point of honor!" chanted a young Dilbian standing just below the ledge. He repeated the cry six times.

There was a stir in the crowd. Looking around, John saw Ty Lamorc. With her was a plump young female that was most likely Boy-Is-She-Built. Boy-Is-She-Built was currently engaged in herding Ty to the foot of the ledge. She accomplished this and immediately began talking.

"I'm Boy-Is-She-Built," she announced.

"We know you," said the Great-Grandfather on the right end.

"I'm speaking here for the Streamside Terror, who's waiting over at Glenn Hollow for the Shorty known as the Half Pint Posted. That Shorty over there. His mug has been spilled—the Terror's, I mean. This Shorty belongs to him—the male over there, I mean. Not that this female Shorty here with me doesn't belong to him, too. He took her fair and square, and it serves those Shorties right. After all, nobody has more honor than the Terror—"

"That's enough," said the judge. "We will decide—"

"I should think you wouldn't even have to call a meeting over it. After all, it's perfectly plain—"

"I said *that's enough!* Be quiet, female!" roared the end judge.

"Well?" interjected one of the other judges testily. "We've heard the arguments. The Shorties are both here. What's left to say?"

"Can I speak?" boomed a new voice, and the crowd parted to let One Man come up before the ledge of rock. The Great-Grandfathers thawed visibly as only great men can in the company of their peers.

"One Man is always welcome to speak," piped an ancient who had not spoken before, and whose voice, with age, had risen almost to the pitch of a human baritone.

"Thank you," said One Man. He raised his head and his voice rose with it, carrying easily out over the assembled Dilbians. "Just think this over. That's what I've got to say. Think deep about it—because it may be Clan Hollows' decision here is going to be binding on just about every-body—us and Shorties alike."

He waved to the judges and went back into the crowd.

"Thanks, One Man," said the right-end judge. "Now, having heard from everybody important who had something to say, here's our opinion. This is a matter concerning the honor of the Streamside Terror—"

"How about me?" roared the Hill Bluffer. "The mail must—"

"Hold your jaw about the mail!" snapped the right-end judge. "As I was saying, Terror's mug was spilled by the Guest in Humrog. Quite properly, the Terror then spilled the mug of the Guest by stealing off one of the Guest's household. This by itself is a dispute between individuals not touching Clan Hollows. But now here comes along a Shorty who wants to fight Terror for the stolen Shorty. And the question is, can Clan Hollows honorably allow the Terror to do so?"

He paused for a moment, as if to let the point sink in on the crowd.

"For us to do this in honor," he continued, "the combat mentioned must be a matter of honor. And this point arises—is honor possible be-tween a man and a Shorty? We Great-Grandfathers have sat up a full night finding an answer, and to do so we have had to ask ourselves, 'What *is* a Shorty?' That is, is it the same thing as us, a being capable of having honor and suffering its loss?"

He paused again. The crowd muttered its interest.

"A knotty question," said the spokesman, with a touch of compla-cency in his voice. "But your Great-Grandfathers have settled it."

The crowd murmured this time in admiration.

"What makes honor?" demanded the spokesman rhetorically. "Honor is a matter of rights—rights violated and rights protected. Have the Short-ies among us had any rights? Guest-rights, only. Failing Guest-rights, can one imagine a Shorty defending and maintaining its rights in our world?"

A chortle broke out in the crowd and spread through its listening ranks at the picture conjured up.

"Silence!" snapped another of the judges. "This is *not* a house-raising."

The crowd went silent.

"Your display of bad manners," said the right-end judge severely, "has pointed up the same conclusion we came to—by orderly process of discussion. It is ridiculous to suppose a Shorty existing as an honor-bound equal in our world. Accordingly, the rules of honor are not binding. Both Shorties here will be returned unharmed to the Guest in Humrog. The Terror has lost no honor. The matter is closed."

He stood up. So did the other five Great-Grandfathers.

"This meeting," he said, "is ended."

"Not yet it isn't!" bellowed the Hill Bluffer.

He plunged forward to the edge of the rock bench, hauling John Tardy along by the slack in John's jacket.

"What do you all know about Shorties?" he demanded. "I've seen this one in action. When a bunch of drunks at Brittle Rock tried to make him do tricks like a performing animal, he fooled them all and got away. How's that for defending his honor? On our way here, the Knobby Gorge Bridge was cranked up out of our reach. He risked his neck climbing up to get it down again, so's not to be slowed in getting his paws on the Terror. How's that for a willingness to defend his rights? I say this Shorty here's as good as some of us any day. Maybe he isn't any bigger'n a two-year-old baby," roared the Hill Bluffer, "but I'm here today to tell you he's all guts!"

He spun on John. "How about it, Shorty? You want Greasy Face handed back to you like scraps from a plate—"

John's long cogitations at last paid off. These and something just witnessed in the Clan Meeting had thrown the switch he had been hunting for.

"Show me that skulking Terror!" he shouted.

The words had barely passed his lips when he felt himself snatched up. The free air whistled past his face. The Hill Bluffer had grabbed him in two huge hands and was now running toward the far woods with him, like a football player with a ball. A roar of voices followed them; looking back, John saw the whole of Clan Hollows in pursuit.

John blinked. He was being jolted along at something like fifty kilometers an hour, and the crowd was coming along behind at the same rate. Or were they? For a long second, John hesitated, then allowed himself to recognize the inescapable fact. All praise to the postman—the Bluffer was outrunning them!

John felt the thrill of competition in his own soul. He and the Hill Bluffer might be worlds apart biologically, but, by heaven, when it came to real competition . . .

Abruptly, the shadow of the further forest closed about them. The Hill Bluffer ran on dropped needles from the conifers, easing to a lope. John Tardy climbed over his shoulder into the mailbag and hung on.

The forest muffled the roar of pursuit. They descended one side of a small hollow and, coming up the other, the Bluffer dropped to his usual ground-eating walk. On the next downslope, he ran again. And so he continued, alternating his pace as the ground shifted.

"How far to the Terror?" asked John.

"Glen Hollow," puffed the Hill Bluffer. He gave the answer in Dilbian units that worked out to just under eight kilometers.

About ten minutes later, they broke through a small fringe of trees to emerge over the lip of a small cuplike valley containing a meadow split by a stream which, in the meadow's center, spread into a pool. The pool was a good fifty meters across and showed the sort of color that indicates a fair depth. By the poolside, a male Dilbian was just looking up at the sound of their approach.

John leaned forward and said quietly to the Hill Bluffer, "Put me down by the deepest part of the water." Reaching to his waist, he loosened the buckle of the belt threaded through the loops on his pants.

The Hill Bluffer grunted and continued his descent. At the water's margin, some dozen meters from the waiting Dilbian, he stopped.

"Hello, postman," said the Dilbian.

"Hello, Terror," answered the Bluffer. "Mail."

The Terror looked curiously past the Bluffer's head at John.

"So that's the Half Pint Posted, is it?" he said. "They let you come?"

"No, we just came," said the Bluffer.

While the Terror stared at John Tardy, John had been examining the Terror. The other Dilbian did not, at first glance, seem to live up to his reputation. He was big, but nowhere near the height of the Hill Bluffer, nor the awe-inspiring massiveness of One Man. John noted, however, with an eye which had judged physical capabilities among his own race, the unusually heavy boning of the other's body, the short, full neck, and, more revealing than any of these, the particularly *poised* balance exhibited by the Terror's thick body.

John Tardy threw one quick glance at the water alongside and slid down from the Bluffer's back. The Bluffer moved off and, with no attempt at the amenities, the Streamside Terror charged.

John turned and dived deep into the pool.

He expected the Terror to follow him immediately, reasoning the other was too much the professional fighter to take chances, even with a Shorty. And, indeed, the water-shock of the big body plunging in after John made him imagine the Terror's great clawed hands all but scratching at his heels. John stroked desperately for depth and distance. He did have a strategy of battle, but it all depended on time and elbow room. He changed direction underwater, angled up to the surface, and, flinging the water from his eyes with a jerk of his head, looked around him.

The Terror, looking the other way, had just broken water four meters off.

John dived again and proceeded to get rid of boots, pants and jacket. He came up again practically under the nose of the Terror and was forced to dive once more. But this time, as he went down, he trailed from one fist the belt he had taken from his trousers, waving in the water like a dark stem of weed.

Coming up the third time at a fairly safe distance, John discovered the Terror had spotted him and was coming after him. John grinned to himself and dove, as if to hide again. But under the water he changed direction and swam directly at his opponent. He saw the heavy legs and arms churning toward him overhead. They moved massively but relatively slowly through the water, and in this he saw the final proof he needed. He had guessed that, effective as the Terror might be against other Dilbians, in the water his very size made him slow and clumsy in comparison to a human—in possibly all but straightaway swimming.

Now John let his opponent pass him overhead. Then, as it went by, he grabbed the foot. And pulled.

The Terror instinctively checked and dived. John, flung surfaceward, let go and dived—this time behind and above the Dilbian. He saw the great back, the churning arms, and then, as the Terror turned once more toward the surface, John closed in, passing the belt around the thick neck and twisting its leather length tight.

At this the Terror, choking, should have headed toward the surface, giving John a chance to breathe. The Dilbian did, John got his breath—and there the battle departed from John's plan entirely.

John had simply failed to give his imagination full rein. He had, in spite of himself, been thinking of the Dilbian in human terms—as a very big man, a man with vast but not inconceivable strength. It is not inconceivable to strangle a giant man with a belt. But how conceivable is it to strangle a grizzly?

John was all but out of reach, stretched at arm's-length by his grip on the belt, trailing like a lamprey attached to a lake trout. But now and then the Terror's huge hand, beating back at him through the water, brushed against him. Only brushed—but each impact slammed John about like a chip in the water. His head rang. The water roared about him. His shoulder numbed to a blow and his ribs gave to another.

His senses began to fog; and he tightened his grip on the belt—for it was, in the end, kill or be killed. If he did not do for the Terror, there was no doubt the Terror would . . . do for . . . him . . .

Choking and gasping, he found his hands no longer on the belt, but clawing at the grassy edge of the pond. Hands were helping him. He pulled himself up on the slippery margin. His knees found solid ground. He coughed water and was suddenly, ungracefully sick. Then he blacked out.

He came around after an indeterminate time to find his head in some-one's lap. He blinked upward and a blur of color slowly turned into the face of Ty Lamorc, very white and taut—and crying.

"What?" he croaked.

"Oh, shut up!" she said. She was wiping his damp face with a rag of cloth that was nearly as wet as he was.

"No—" he managed. "I mean—what're *you* doing here?" He tried to sit up.

"Lie down!"

"I'm all right—I think." He struggled into sitting position. The whole area of Glen Hollow, he saw, was aswarm with Dilbians. A short way off, a knot of them were gathered on the pool-bank around something.

"What—?" he began.

"The Terror, Half Pint," said a familiar voice, and he looked up at the looming figure of the Hill Bluffer, mountainous from this angle. "He's still out. It's your fight, all right." He went off, and they could hear him informing the other group down the bank that the Shorty was up and talking.

John Tardy looked at Ty.

"What happened?" he asked.

"They had to pull him out. You made it to shore by yourself." She found a handkerchief somewhere, wiped her eyes and blew her nose vigorously. "You were wonderful."

"Wonderful?" said John, still too groggy for subtlety. "I was out of my head to even think of it!" He felt his ribs gingerly. "I better get back to Humrog and have an X-ray of this side."

"Oh, are your ribs broken?"

"Maybe just bruised. Wow!" said John, coming on an especially tender spot.

"Oh!" wept Ty. "You might have been killed! And it's all my fault!"

"Your fault?" said John. He spotted the massive figure of One Man breaking away from the group around the fallen Terror and hissed quickly at her. "Hurry. Help me up." She assisted him clumsily to his feet. "Tell me, did they find anything around the Terror's neck when they pulled him out?"

She stared at him and wiped her eyes. "Why, no. What should they find around his neck?"

"Nothing," whispered John. "Well!" he said as One Man rolled up to a halt before them. "What do *you* think of the situation?"

"I think, Half Pint," said One Man, "that it's all very interesting. Very interesting indeed. I think you Shorties may be getting a few takers now on this business of going off into the sky and learning things."

"You do, eh? How about you, for one?"

"No-o," said One Man slowly. "No, I don't think me. I'm a little too old to jump at new things that quick. Some of the young ones'll be ready, though. The Terror, for one, possibly. He's quite a bright lad, you know. Of course, now that you've done the preliminary spadework, I may put in a good word for you people here and there."

"Mighty nice of you—*now*," said John, a little bitterly.

"Nothing wins like a winner, Half Pint," rumbled One Man. "You Shorties should have known that. Matter of fact, I'm surprised it took you so long to show some common sense. You just don't come in and sit down at a man's table and expect him to take your word for it that you're one of the family. As I said to you once before, who asked you Shorties to come here, anyway, in the first place? And what made you think we had to like you? What if, when you were a lad, some new kid moved into your village? He was half your size, but he had a whole lot of shiny new playthings you didn't have, and he came up and tapped you on the shoulder and said, 'C'mon, from now on we'll play *my* sort of game!' How'd you think *you'd* have felt?"

He eyed John shrewdly out of his hairy face.

"I see," said John, after a moment. "Then why'd you help me?"

"Me? Help you? I was as neutral as they come. What're you talking about?"

"We've got something back home called a phone directory—a book like those manuals Little Bite has down at Humrog. It's about this thick—" he measured with thumb and forefinger. "And for one of us Shorties, you'd say it was a physical impossibility to pick it up and tear it in two. But some of us can do it." He eyed One Man. "Of course, there's a trick to it."

"Well, now," said One Man judiciously, "I can believe it. Directories, thick sticks, or first-class hill-and-alley scrappers—there's a trick to handle almost any of them. Not that I'd ever favor a Shorty over any of us in the long run—don't get that idea." He looked around them. The Streamside Terror was being helped out of the Glen and most of the crowd was already gone. "We'll have to get together for a chat one of these days, Half Pint. Well, see you in the near future, Shorties."

John Tardy wiped a damp nose with the back of his hand and stared after One Man. Then he turned to Ty Lamorc.

"Now," he said, "what'd you mean—it was all your fault?"

"It was," she said miserably. "It was all my idea. Earth knew we weren't getting through to the Dilbians, so they sent me out. And I—" she gulped—"I recommended they send out a man who conformed as nearly as possible to the Dilbian psychological profile and we'd get him mixed up in a Dilbian emotional situation—to convince them we weren't the utter little aliens we seemed to be. They've got a very unusual culture here. They really have. I never thought Boy-Is-She-Built would catch up with you and nearly kill you and take your wrist-phone away. You were supposed to be able to stay in contact with Joshua Guy so he could always rescue you from the other end."

"I see. And why," queried John, very slowly and patiently, "did you decide not to let *me* in on what was going on?"

"Because," she wailed, "I thought it would be better for you to react like the Dilbians in a natural, extroverted, uncerebral way!"

"I see," said John again. They were still standing beside the pool. He picked her up—she was quite light and slender—and threw her in. There was a shriek and a satisfying splash. John turned and walked off.

After half a dozen steps, he slowed down, turned and went back. She was clinging to the bank.

"Here," he said gruffly, extending his hand.

"Thag you," she said humbly, with her nose full of water, as he hauled her out.

Cordwainer Smith

MOTHER HITTON'S LITTUL KITTONS

The late Cordwainer Smith—in "real" life Dr. Paul M. A. Linebarger, scholar, states-man, and author of the definitive text (still taught from today) on the art of psycho-logical warfare—was a writer of enormous talents who, from 1948 until his untimely death in 1966, produced a double-handful of some of the best short fiction this genre has ever seen—"Alpha Ralpha Boulevard," "A Planet Named Shayol," "On the Storm Planet," "The Ballad of Lost C'Mell," "The Dead Lady of Clown Town," "The Game of Rat and Dragon," "Drunkboat," "The Lady Who Sailed *The Soul,*" "Under Old Earth," "Scan-ners Live in Vain"—as well as a large number of lesser, but still fascinating, stories, all twisted and blended and woven into an interrelated tapestry of incredible lushness and intricacy. Smith created a baroque cosmology unrivaled even today for its scope and complexity: a millennia-spanning Future History, logically outlandish and elegantly strange, set against a vivid, richly-colored, mythically-intense universe where animals assume the shape of men, vast planoform ships whisper through multidimensional space, immense sick sheep are the most valuable objects in the universe, immortality can be bought, and the mysterious Lords of the Instrumentality rule a hunted Earth too old for history . . .

It is a cosmology that looks as evocative and bizarre today in the 1990s as it did in the 1960s—certainly for sheer sweep and daring of conceptualization, in its vision of how different and *strange* the future will be, it rivals any contemporary vision con-jured up by Young Turks such as Bruce Sterling and Greg Bear, and I suspect that it is timeless. It certainly upped the ante for complexity for the Space Adventure, much as A. E. van Vogt had done in the early '50s: after Smith's exotic landscapes and societies and people, the Space Opera scenarios of most other writers seemed flat, dull, and routine by comparison.

Here Smith takes us along on a thief's desperate quest to steal eternal life, with all the money in the world for forfeit, and only the childish-sounding "littul kittons" to bar the way . . .

Cordwainer Smith's books include the novel *Norstrilia* and the collections *Space Lords*—one of the landmark collections of the genre—*The Best of Cordwainer Smith, Quest of the Three Worlds, Stardreamer, You Will Never Be the Same,* and *The Instru-mentality of Mankind.* As Felix C. Forrest, he wrote two mainstream novels, *Ria* and *Car-ola,* and as Carmichael Smith he wrote the thriller *Atomsk.*

His most recent book is the posthumous collection *The Rediscovery of Man: The Complete Short Science Fiction of Cordwainer Smith* (NESFA Press, P.O. Box 809, Framingham, MA 07101-0203, www.nesfa.org, $24.95), a huge book which collects almost all of his short fiction, and which will certainly stand as one of the very best collections of the decade—and a book which belongs in every complete science fiction collection.

> Poor communications deter theft;
> good communications promote theft;
> perfect communications stop theft.
>
> —Van Braam

1

The moon spun. The woman watched. Twenty-one facets had been polished at the moon's equator. Her function was to arm it. She was Mother Hitton, the weapons mistress of Old North Australia.

She was a ruddy-faced, cheerful blonde of indeterminate age. Her eyes were blue, her bosom heavy, her arms strong. She looked like a mother, but the only child she had ever had died many generations ago. Now she acted as mother to a planet, not to a person; the Norstrilians slept well because they knew she was watching. The weapons slept their long, sick sleep.

This night she glanced for the two-hundredth time at the warning bank. The bank was quiet. No danger lights shone. Yet she felt an enemy out somewhere in the universe—an enemy waiting to strike at her and her world, to snatch at the immeasurable wealth of the Norstrilians—and she snorted with impatience. *Come along, little man,* she thought. *Come along, little man, and die. Don't keep me waiting.*

She smiled when she recognized the absurdity of her own thought.

She waited for him.

And he did not know it.

He, the robber, was relaxed enough. He was Benjacomin Bozart, and was highly trained in the arts of relaxation.

No one at Sunvale, here on Ttiollé, could suspect that he was a senior warden of the Guild of Thieves, reared under the light of the starry-violet star. No one could smell the odor of Viola Siderea upon him. "Viola Siderea," the Lady Ru had said, "was once the most beautiful of worlds and it is now the most rotten. Its people were once models for mankind, and now they are thieves, liars and killers. You can smell their souls in the open day." The Lady Ru had died a long time ago. She was much respected, but she was wrong. The robber did not smell to others at all. He knew it. He was no more "wrong" than a shark approaching a school of cod. Life's nature is to live, and he had been nurtured to live as he had to live—by seeking prey.

How else could he live? Viola Siderea had gone bankrupt a long time ago, when the photonic sails had disappeared from space and the planoforming ships began to whisper their way between the stars. His ancestors had been left to die on an off-trail planet. They refused to die. Their ecology shifted and they became predators upon man, adapted by time and genetics to their deadly tasks. And he, the robber, was champion of all his people—the best of their best.

He was Benjacomin Bozart.

He had sworn to rob Old North Australia or to die in the attempt, and he had no intention of dying.

The beach at Sunvale was warm and lovely. Ttiollé was a free and casual transit planet. His weapons were luck and himself: he planned to play both well.

The Norstrilians could kill.

So could he.

At this moment, in this place, he was a happy tourist at a lovely beach. Elsewhere, elsewhen, he could become a ferret among conies, a hawk among doves.

Benjacomin Bozart, thief and warden. He did not know that someone was waiting for him. Someone who did not know his name was prepared to waken death, just for him. He was still serene.

Mother Hitton was not serene. She sensed him dimly but could not yet spot him.

One of her weapons snored. She turned it over.

A thousand stars away, Benjacomin Bozart smiled as he walked toward the beach.

2

Benjacomin felt like a tourist. His tanned face was tranquil. His proud, hooded eyes were calm. His handsome mouth, even without its charming smile, kept a suggestion of pleasantness at its corners. He looked attractive without seeming odd in the least. He looked much younger than he actually was. He walked with springy, happy steps along the beach of Sunvale.

The waves rolled in, white-crested, like the breakers of Mother Earth. The Sunvale people were proud of the way their world resembled Manhome itself. Few of them had ever seen Manhome, but they had all heard a bit of history and most of them had a passing anxiety when they thought of the ancient government still wielding political power across the depth of space. They did not like the old Instrumentality of Earth, but they respected and feared it. The waves might remind them of the pretty side of Earth; they did not want to remember the not-so-pretty side.

This man was like the pretty side of old Earth. They could not sense the power within him. The Sunvale people smiled absently at him as he walked past them along the shoreline.

The atmosphere was quiet and everything around him serene. He turned his face to the sun. He closed his eyes. He let the warm sunlight beat through his eyelids, illuminating him with its comfort and its reassuring touch.

Benjacomin dreamed of the greatest theft that any man had ever planned. He dreamed of stealing a huge load of the wealth from the richest world that mankind had ever built. He thought of what would happen when he would finally bring riches back to the planet of Viola Siderea where he had been reared. Benjacomin turned his face away from the sun and languidly looked over the other people on the beach.

There were no Norstrilians in sight yet. They were easy enough to recognize. Big people with red complexions; superb athletes and yet, in their own way, innocent, young and very tough. He had trained for this theft for two hundred years, his life prolonged for the purpose by the Guild of Thieves on Viola Siderea. He himself embodied the dreams of his own planet, a poor planet once a crossroads of commerce, now sunken to being a minor outpost for spoliation and pilferage.

He saw a Norstrilian woman come out from the hotel and go down to the beach. He waited, and he looked, and he dreamed. He had a question to ask and no adult Australian would answer it.

"Funny," thought he, "that I call them 'Australians' even now. That's the old, old Earth name for them—rich, brave, tough people. Fighting children standing on half the world . . . and now they are the tyrants of all mankind. They hold the wealth. They have the santaclara, and other people live or die depending upon the commerce they have with the Norstrilians. But I won't. And my people won't. We're men who are wolves to man."

Benjacomin waited gracefully. Tanned by the light of many suns, he looked forty though he was two hundred. He dressed casually, by the standards of a vacationer. He might have been an intercultural salesman, a senior gambler, an assistant starport manager. He might even have been a detective working along the commerce lanes. He wasn't. He was a thief. And he was so good a thief that people turned to him and put their property in his hands because he was reassuring, calm, gray-eyed, blondhaired. Benjacomin waited. The woman glanced at him, a quick glance full of open suspicion.

What she saw must have calmed her. She went on past. She called back over the dune, "Come on, Johnny, we can swim out here." A little boy, who looked eight or ten years old, came over the dune top, running toward his mother.

Benjacomin tensed like a cobra. His eyes became sharp, his eyelids narrowed.

This was the prey. Not too young, not too old. If the victim had been too young he wouldn't know the answer; if the victim were too old it was no use taking him on. Norstrilians were famed in combat; adults were mentally and physically too strong to warrant attack.

Benjacomin knew that every thief who had approached the planet of the Norstrilians—who had tried to raid the dream world of Old North Australia—had gotten out of contact with his people and had died. There was no word of any of them.

And yet he knew that hundreds of thousands of Norstrilians must know *the* secret. They now and then made jokes about it. He had heard these jokes when he was a young man, and now he was more than an old man without once coming near the answer. Life was expensive. He was well into his third lifetime and the lifetimes had been purchased honestly by his people. Good thieves all of them, paying out hard-stolen money to obtain the medicine to let their greatest thief remain living. Benjacomin didn't like violence. But when violence prepared the way to the greatest theft of all time, he was willing to use it.

The woman looked at him again. The mask of evil which had flashed across his face faded into benignity; he calmed. She caught him in that moment of relaxation. She liked him.

She smiled and, with that awkward hesitation so characteristic of the Norstrilians, she said, "Could you mind my boy a bit while I go in the water? I think we've seen each other here at the hotel."

"I don't mind," said he. "I'd be glad to. Come here, son."

Johnny walked across the sunlight dunes to his own death. He came within reach of his mother's enemy.

But the mother had already turned.

The trained hand of Benjacomin Bozart reached out. He seized the child by the shoulder. He turned the boy toward him, forcing him down. Before the child could cry out, Benjacomin had the needle into him with the truth drug.

All Johnny reacted to was pain, and then a hammerblow inside his own skull as the powerful drug took force.

Benjacomin looked out over the water. The mother was swimming. She seemed to be looking back at them. She was obviously unworried. To her, the child seemed to be looking at something the stranger was showing him in a relaxed, easy way.

"Now, sonny," said Benjacomin, "tell me, what's the outside defense?"

The boy didn't answer.

"What is the outer defense, sonny? What is the outer defense?" repeated Benjacomin. The boy still didn't answer.

Something close to horror ran over the skin of Benjacomin Bozart as he realized that he had gambled his safety on this planet, gambled the plans themselves for a chance to break the secret of the Norstrilians.

He had been stopped by simple, easy devices. The child had already been conditioned against attack. Any attempt to force knowledge out of the child brought on a conditioned reflex of total muteness. The boy was literally unable to talk.

Sunlight gleaming on her wet hair, the mother turned around and called back, "Are you all right, Johnny?"

Benjacomin waved to her instead. "I'm showing him my pictures, ma'am. He likes 'em. Take your time." The mother hesitated and then turned back to the water and swam slowly away.

Johnny, taken by the drug, sat lightly, like an invalid, on Benjacomin's lap.

Benjacomin said, "Johnny, you're going to die now and you will hurt terribly if you don't tell me what I want to know." The boy struggled weakly against his grasp. Benjacomin repeated. "I'm going to hurt you if you don't tell me what I want to know. What are the outer defenses? What are the outer defenses?"

The child struggled and Benjacomin realized that the boy was putting up a fight to comply with the orders, not a fight to get away. He let the child slip through his hands and the boy put out a finger and began writing on the wet sand. The letters stood out.

A man's shadow loomed behind them.

Benjacomin, alert, ready to spin, kill or run, slipped to the ground beside the child and said, "That's a jolly puzzle. That is a good one. Show me some more." He smiled up at the passing adult. The man was a stranger. The stranger gave him a very curious glance which became casual when he saw the pleasant face of Benjacomin, so tenderly and so agreeably playing with the child.

The fingers were still making the letters in the sand.

There stood the riddle in letters: MOTHER HITTON'S LITTUL KITTONS.

The woman was coming back from the sea, the mother with questions. Benjacomin stroked the sleeve of his coat and brought out his second needle, a shallow poison which it would take days or weeks of laboratory work to detect. He thrust it directly into the boy's brain, slipping the needle up behind the skin at the edge of the hairline. The hair shadowed the tiny prick. The incredibly hard needle slipped under the edge of the skull. The child was dead.

Murder was accomplished. Benjacomin casually erased the secret from the sand. The woman came nearer. He called to her, his voice full of pleasant concern, "Ma'am, you'd better come here, I think your son has fainted from the heat."

He gave the mother the body of her son. Her face changed to alarm. She looked frightened and alert. She didn't know how to meet this.

For a dreadful moment she looked into his eyes.

Two hundred years of training took effect . . . She saw nothing. The murderer did not shine with murder. The hawk was hidden beneath the dove. The heart was masked by the trained face.

Benjacomin relaxed in professional assurance. He had been prepared to kill her too, although he was not sure that he could kill an adult, female Norstrilian. Very helpfully said he, "You stay here with him. I'll run to the hotel and get help. I'll hurry."

He turned and ran. A beach attendant saw him and ran toward him. "The child's sick," he shouted. He came to the mother in time to see blunt, puzzled tragedy on her face and with it, something more than tragedy: doubt.

"He's not sick," said she. "He's dead."

"He can't be." Benjacomin looked attentive. He felt attentive. He forced the sympathy to pour out of his posture, out of all the little muscles of his face. "He can't be. I was talking to him just a minute ago. We were doing little puzzles in the sand."

The mother spoke with a hollow, broken voice that sounded as though it would never find the right chords for human speech again, but would go on forever with the ill-attuned flats of unexpected grief. "He's dead," she said. "You saw him die and I guess I saw him die, too. I can't tell what's happened. The child was full of santaclara. He had a thousand years to live but now he's dead. What's your name?"

Benjacomin said, "Eldon. Eldon the salesman, ma'am. I live here lots of times."

3

"Mother Hitton's littul kittons. Mother Hitton's littul kittons."

The silly phrase ran in his mind. Who was Mother Hitton? Who was she the mother of? What were *kittons?* Were they a misspelling for "kittens?" Little cats? Or were they something else?

Had he killed a fool to get a fool's answer?

How many more days did he have to stay there with the doubtful, staggered woman? How many days did he have to watch and wait? He wanted to get back to Viola Siderea; to take the secret, bad as it was, for his people to study. Who was Mother Hitton?

He forced himself out of his room and went downstairs.

The pleasant monotony of a big hotel was such that the other guests looked interestedly at him. He was the man who had watched while the child died on the beach.

Some lobby-living scandalmongers that stayed there had made up fantastic stories that he had killed the child. Others attacked the stories, saying they knew perfectly well who Eldon was. He was Eldon the salesman. It was ridiculous.

People hadn't changed much, even though the ships with the Go-captains sitting at their hearts whispered between the stars, even though people shuffled between worlds—when they had the money to pay their passage back and forth—like leaves falling in soft, playful winds. Benjacomin faced a tragic dilemma. He knew very well that any attempt to decode the answer would run directly into the protective devices set up by the Norstrilians.

Old North Australia was immensely wealthy. It was known the length and breadth of all the stars that they had hired mercenaries, defensive spies, hidden agents and alerting devices.

Even Manhome—Mother Earth herself, whom no money could buy—was bribed by the drug of life. An ounce of the santaclara drug, reduced, crystallized and called "stroon," could give forty to sixty years of life. Stroon entered the rest of the Earth by ounces and pounds, but it was refined back on North Australia by the ton. With treasure like this, the Norstrilians owned an unimaginable world whose resources overreached all conceivable limits of money. They could buy anything. They could pay with other peoples' lives.

For hundreds of years they had given secret funds to buying foreigners' services to safeguard their own security.

Benjacomin stood there in the lobby: "Mother Hitton's littul kittons."

He had all the wisdom and wealth of a thousand worlds stuck in his mind but he didn't dare ask anywhere as to what it meant.

Suddenly he brightened.

He looked like a man who had thought of a good game to play, a pleasant diversion to be welcomed, a companion to be remembered, a new food to be tasted. He had had a very happy thought.

There was one source that wouldn't talk. The library. He could at least check the obvious, simple things, and find out what there was already in the realm of public knowledge concerning the secret he had taken from the dying boy.

His own safety had not been wasted, Johnny's life had not been thrown away, if he could find any one of the four words as a key. *Mother* or *Hitton* or *Littul,* in its special meaning, or *Kitton.* He might yet break through to the loot of Norstrilia.

He swung jubilantly, turning on the ball of his right foot. He moved lightly and pleasantly toward the billiard room, beyond which lay the library. He went in.

This was a very expensive hotel and very old-fashioned. It even had books made out of paper, with genuine bindings. Benjacomin crossed the room. He saw that they had the *Galactic Encyclopedia* in two hundred volumes. He took down the volume headed "Hi-Hi." He opened it from the rear, looking for the name "Hitton" and there it was. "Hitton, Benjamin—pioneer of old North Australia. Said to be originator of part of the defense system. Lived A.D. 10719–17213." That was all. Benjacomin moved among the books. The word "kittons" in that peculiar spelling did not occur anywhere, neither in the encyclopedia nor in any other list maintained by the library. He walked out and upstairs, back to his room.

"Littul" had not appeared at all. It was probably the boy's own childish mistake.

He took a chance. The mother, half blind with bewilderment and worry, sat in a stiff-backed chair on the edge of the porch. The other women talked to her. They knew her husband was coming. Benjacomin went up to her and tried to pay his respects. She didn't see him.

"I'm leaving now, ma'am. I'm going on to the next planet, but I'll be back in two or three subjective weeks. And if you need me for urgent questions, I'll leave my addresses with the police here."

Benjacomin left the weeping mother.

Benjacomin left the quiet hotel. He obtained a priority passage.

The easy-going Sunvale Police made no resistance to his demand for a sudden departure visa. After all, he had an identity, he had his own funds, and it was not the custom of Sunvale to contradict its guests. Benjacomin went on the ship and as he moved toward the cabin in which he could rest for a few hours, a man stepped up beside him. A youngish man, hair parted in the middle, short of stature, gray of eyes.

This man was the local agent of the Norstrilian secret police.

Benjacomin, trained thief that he was, did not recognize the policeman. It never occurred to him that the library itself had been attuned and that the word "kittons" in the peculiar Norstrilian spelling was itself an alert. Looking for that spelling had set off a minor alarm. He had touched the trip-wire.

The stranger nodded. Benjacomin nodded back. "I'm a traveling man, waiting over between assignments. I haven't been doing very well. How are you making out?"

"Doesn't matter to me. I don't earn money; I'm a technician. Liverant is the name."

Benjacomin sized him up. The man was a technician all right. They shook hands perfunctorily. Liverant said, "I'll join you in the bar a little later. I think I'll rest a bit first."

They both lay down then and said very little while the momentary flash of planoform went through the ship. The flash passed. From books and lessons they knew that the ship was leaping forward in two dimensions while, somehow or other, the fury of space itself was fed into the computers—and that these in turn were managed by the Go-captain who controlled the ship.

They knew these things but they could not feel them. All they felt was the sting of a slight pain.

The sedative was in the air itself, sprayed in the ventilating system. They both expected to become a little drunk.

The thief Benjacomin Bozart was trained to resist intoxication and bewilderment. Any sign whatever that a telepath had tried to read his mind would have been met with fierce animal resistance, implanted in his unconscious during early years of training. Bozart was not trained against deception by a technician; it never occurred to the Thieves' Guild back on Viola Siderea that it would be necessary for their own people to resist deceivers. Liverant had already been in touch with Norstrilia—Norstrilia whose money reached across the stars, Norstrilia who had alerted a hundred thousand worlds against the mere thought of trespass.

Liverant began to chatter. "I wish I could go further than this trip. I wish that I could go to Olympia. You can buy anything in Olympia."

"I've heard of it," said Bozart. "It's sort of a funny trading planet with not much chance for businessmen, isn't it?"

Liverant laughed and his laughter was merry and genuine. "Trading? They don't trade. They swap. They take all the stolen loot of a thousand worlds and sell it over again and they change and they paint it and they mark it. That's their business there. The people are blind. It's a strange world, and all you have to do is to go in there and you can have anything you want. Man," said Liverant, "what I could do in a year in that place! Everybody is blind except me and a couple of tourists. And there's all the wealth that everybody thought he's mislaid, half the wrecked ships, the forgotten colonies (they've all been cleaned out) and bang! it all goes to Olympia."

Olympia wasn't really that good and Liverant didn't know why it was his business to guide the killer there. All he knew was that he had a duty and the duty was to direct the trespasser.

Many years before either man was born the code word had been planted in directories, in books, in packing cases and invoices: *Kittons* misspelled. This was the cover name for the outer moon of Norstrilian defense. The use of the cover name brought a raging alert ready into action, with systemic nerves as hot and quick as incandescent tungsten wire.

By the time that they were ready to go to the bar and have refreshments, Benjacomin had half forgotten that it was his new acquaintance who had suggested Olympia rather than another place. He had to go to Viola Siderea to get the credits to make the flight to take the wealth, to win the world of Olympia.

4

At home on his native planet Bozart was a subject of a gentle but very sincere celebration.

The elders of the Guild of Thieves welcomed him. They congratulated him. "Who else could have done what you've done, boy? You've made the opening move in a brand new game of chess. There has never been a gambit like this before. We have a name; we have an animal. We'll try it right here." The Thieves' Council turned to their own encyclopedia. They turned through the name "Hitton" and then found the reference "kitton." None of them knew that a false lead had been planted there—by an agent in their world.

The agent, in his turn, had been seduced years before, debauched in the middle of his career, forced into temporary honesty, blackmailed and sent home. In all the years that he had waited for a dreaded countersign— a countersign which he himself never knew to be an extension of Norstrilian intelligence—he never dreamed that he could pay his debt to the outside world so simply. All they had done was to send him one page to add to the encyclopedia. He added it and then went home, weak with exhaustion. The years of fear and waiting were almost too much for the thief. He drank heavily for fear that he might otherwise kill himself. Meanwhile, the pages remained in order, including the new one, slightly altered for his colleagues. The encyclopedia indicated the change like any normal revision, though the whole entry was new and falsified:

Beneath this passage one revision ready. Dated 24th year of second issue.

The reported "Kittons" of Norstrilia are nothing more than the use of organic means to induce the disease in Earth-mutated sheep which produces a virus in its turn, refinable as the santaclara drug. The term "Kittons" enjoyed a temporary vogue as a refer-

ence term both to the disease and to the destructibility of the
disease in the event of external attack. This is believed to have
been connected with the career of Benjamin Hitton, one of the
original pioneers of Norstrilia.

The Council of Thieves read it and the Chairman of the Council said,
"I've got your papers ready. You can go try them now. Where do you want
to go? Through Neuhamburg?"

"No," said Benjacomin. "I thought I'd try Olympia."

"Olympia's all right," said the chairman. "Go easy. There's only one
chance in a thousand you'll fail. But if you do, we might have to pay
for it."

He smiled wryly and handed Benjacomin a blank mortgage against
all the labor and all the property of Viola Siderea.

The Chairman laughed with a sort of snort. "It'd be pretty rough on
us if you had to borrow enough on the trading planet to force us to become honest—and then lost out anyhow."

"No fear," said Benjacomin. "I can cover that."

There are some worlds where all dreams die, but square-clouded
Olympia is not one of them. The eyes of men and women are bright on
Olympia, for they see nothing.

"Brightness was the color of pain," said Nachtigall, "when we could
see. If thine eye offend thee, pluck thyself out, for the fault lies not in the
eye but in the soul."

Such talk was common in Olympia, where the settlers went blind a
long time ago and now think themselves superior to sighted people.
Radar wires tickle their living brains; they can perceive radiation as well
as can an animal-type man with little aquariums hung in the middle of his
face. Their pictures are sharp, and they demand sharpness. Their buildings soar at impossible angles. Their blind children sing songs as the tailored climate proceeds according to the numbers, geometrical as a
kaleidoscope.

There went the man, Bozart himself. Among the blind his dreams
soared, and he paid money for information which no living person had
ever seen.

Sharp-clouded and aqua-skied, Olympia swam past him like another
man's dream. He did not mean to tarry there, because he had a rendezvous with death in the sticky, sparky space around Norstrilia.

Once in Olympia, Benjacomin went about his arrangements for the
attack on Old North Australia. On his second day on the planet he had
been very lucky. He met a man named Lavender and he was sure he had

heard the name before. Not a member of his own Guild of Thieves, but a daring rascal with a bad reputation among the stars.

It was no wonder that he had found Lavender. His pillow had told him Lavender's story fifteen times during his sleep in the past week. And, whenever he dreamed, he dreamed dreams which had been planted in his mind by the Norstrilian counterintelligence. They had beaten him in getting to Olympia first and they were prepared to let him have only that which he deserved. The Norstrilian Police were not cruel, but they were out to defend their world. And they were also out to avenge the murder of a child.

The last interview which Benjacomin had with Lavender in striking a bargain before Lavender agreed was a dramatic one.

Lavender refused to move forward.

"I'm not going to jump off anywhere. I'm not going to raid anything. I'm not going to steal anything. I've been rough, of course I have. But I don't get myself killed and that's what you're bloody well asking for."

"Think of what we'll have. The wealth. I tell you, there's more money here than anything else anybody's ever tried."

Lavender laughed. "You think I haven't heard that before? You're a crook and I'm a crook. I don't do anything that's speculation. I want my hard cash down. I'm a fighting man and you're a thief and I'm not going to ask you what you're up to . . . but I want my money first."

"I haven't got it," said Benjacomin.

Lavender stood up.

"Then you shouldn't have talked to me. Because it's going to cost you money to keep me quiet whether you hire me or not."

The bargaining process started.

Lavender looked ugly indeed. He was a soft, ordinary man who had gone to a lot of trouble to become evil. Sin is a lot of work. The sheer effort it requires often shows in the human face.

Bozart stared him down, smiling easily, not even contemptuously.

"Cover me while I get something from my pocket," said Bozart.

Lavender did not even acknowledge the comment. He did not show a weapon. His left thumb moved slowly across the outer edge of his hand. Benjacomin recognized the sign, but did not flinch.

"See," he said. "A planetary credit."

Lavender laughed. "I've heard that, too."

"Take it," said Bozart.

The adventurer took the laminated card. His eyes widened. "It's real," he breathed. "It is real." He looked up, incalculably more friendly. "I never even saw one of these before. What are your terms?"

Meanwhile the bright, vivid Olympians walked back and forth past them, their clothing all white and black in dramatic contrast. Unbeliev-able geometric designs shone on their cloaks and their hats. The two bar-gainers ignored the natives. They concentrated on their own negotiations.

Benjacomin felt fairly safe. He placed a pledge of one year's service of the entire planet of Viola Siderea in exchange for the full and unqual-ified services of Captain Lavender, once of the Imperial Marines Internal Space Patrol. He handed over the mortgage. The year's guarantee was written in. Even on Olympia there were accounting machines which re-layed the bargain back to Earth itself, making the mortgage a valid and binding commitment against the whole planet of thieves.

"This," thought Lavender, "was the first step of revenge." After the killer had disappeared his people would have to pay with sheer honesty. Lavender looked at Banjacomin with a clinical sort of concern.

Benjacomin mistook his look for friendliness and Benjacomin smiled his slow, charming, easy smile. Momentarily happy, he reached out his right hand to give Lavender a brotherly solemnification of the bargain. The men shook hands, and Bozart never knew with what he shook hands.

5

"Gray lay the land oh. Gray grass from sky to sky. Not near the weir, dear. Not a mountain, low or high—only hills and gray gray. Watch the dappled, dimpled twinkles blooming on the star bar.

"That is Norstrilia.

"All the muddy gubbery is gone—all the work and the waiting and the pain.

"Beige-brown sheep lie on blue-gray grass while the clouds rush past, low overhead, like iron pipes ceilinging the world.

"Take your pick of sick sheep, man, it's the sick that pays. Sneeze me a planet, man, or cough me up a spot of immortality. If it's barmy there, where the noddies and the trolls like you live, it's too right here.

"That's the book, boy.

"If you haven't seen Norstrilia, you haven't seen it. If you did see it, you wouldn't believe it.

"Charts call it Old North Australia."

Here in the heart of the world was the farm which guarded the world. This was the Hitton place.

Towers surrounded it, and wires hung between the towers, some of them drooping crazily and some gleaming with the sheen not shown by any other metal made by men from Earth. Within the towers there was open land. And within the open land there were twelve thousand hectares of concrete. Radar reached down to within millimeter smoothness of the surface of the concrete and the other radar threw patterns back and forth, down through molecular thinness. The farm went on. In its center there was a group of buildings. That was where Katherine Hitton worked on the task which her family had accepted for the defense of her world.

No germ came in, no germ went out. All the food came in by space transmitter. Within this, there lived animals. The animals depended on her alone. Were she to die suddenly, by mischance or as a result of an attack by one of the animals, the authorities of her world had complete facsimiles of herself with which to train new animal tenders under hypnosis.

This was a place where the gray wind leapt forward released from the hills, where it raced across the gray concrete, where it blew past the radar towers. The polished, faceted, captive moon always hung due overhead. The wind hit the buildings, themselves gray, with the impact of a blow, before it raced over the open concrete beyond and whistled away into the hills.

Outside the buildings, the valley had not needed much camouflage. It looked like the rest of Norstrilia. The concrete itself was tinted very slightly to give the impression of poor, starved, natural soil. This was the farm, and this the woman. Together they were the outer defense of the richest world mankind had ever built.

Katherine Hitton looked out the window and thought to herself, "Forty-two days before I go to market and it's a welcome day that I get there and hear the jig of a music."

Oh, to walk on market day,
And see my people proud and gay!

She breathed deeply of the air. She loved the gray hills—though in her youth she had seen many other worlds. And then she turned back into the building to the animals and the duties which awaited her. She was the only Mother Hitton and these were her littul kittons.

She moved among them. She and her father had bred them from Earth mink, from the fiercest, smallest, craziest little minks that had ever been shipped out from Manhome. Out of these minks they had made their lives to keep away other predators who might bother the sheep on whom the stroon grew. But these minks were born mad.

Generations of them had been bred psychotic to the bone. They lived only to die and they died so that they could stay alive. These were the kittons of Norstrilia. Animals in whom fear, rage, hunger and sex were utterly intermixed; who could eat themselves or each other; who could eat their young, or people, or anything organic; animals who screamed with murder-lust when they felt love; animals born to loathe themselves with a fierce and livid hate and who survived only because their waking moments were spent on couches, strapped tight, claw by claw, so that they could not hurt each other or themselves. Mother Hitton let them waken only a few moments in each lifetime. They bred and killed. She wakened them only two at a time.

All that afternoon she moved from cage to cage. The sleeping animals slept well. The nourishment ran into their blood streams; they lived sometimes for years without awaking. She bred them when the males were only partly awakened and the females aroused only enough to accept her veterinary treatments. She herself had to pluck the young away from their mothers as the sleeping mothers begot them. Then she nourished the young through a few happy weeks of kittonhood, until their adult natures began to take, their eyes ran red with madness and heat and their emotions sounded in the sharp, hideous, little cries they uttered through the building; and the twisting of their neat, furry faces, the rolling of their crazy, bright eyes and the tightening of their sharp, sharp claws.

She woke none of them this time. Instead, she tightened them in their straps. She removed the nutrients. She gave them delayed stimulus medicine which would, when they were awakened, bring them suddenly full waking with no lulled stupor first.

Finally, she gave herself a heavy sedative, leaned back in a chair and waited for the call which would come.

When the shock came and the call came through, she would have to do what she had done thousands of times before.

She would ring an intolerable noise through the whole laboratory.

Hundreds of the mutated minks would awaken. In awakening, they would plunge into life with hunger, with hate, with rage and with sex; plunge against their straps; strive to kill each other, their young, themselves, her. They would fight everything and everywhere, and do everything they could to keep going.

She knew this.

In the middle of the room there was a tuner. The tuner was a direct, emphatic relay, capable of picking up the simpler range of telepathic communications. Into this tuner went the concentrated emotions of Mother Hitton's littul kittons.

The rage, the hate, the hunger, the sex were all carried far beyond the limits of the tolerable, and then all were thereupon amplified. And then the waveband on which this telepathic control went out was amplified, right there beyond the studio, on the high towers that swept the mountain ridge, up and beyond the valley in which the laboratory lay. And Mother Hitton's moon, spinning geometrically, bounced the relay into a hollow englobement.

From the faceted moon, it went to the satellites—sixteen of them, apparently part of the weather control system. These blanketed not only space, but nearby subspace. The Nostrilians had thought of everything.

The short shocks of an alert came from Mother Hitton's transmitter bank.

A call came. Her thumb went numb.

The noise shrieked.

The mink awakened.

Immediately, the room was full of chattering, scraping, hissing, growling and howling.

Under the sound of the animal voices, there was the other sound: a scratchy, snapping sound like hail falling on a frozen lake. It was the individual claws of hundreds of mink trying to tear their way through metal panels.

Mother Hitton heard a gurgle. One of the minks had succeeded in tearing its paw loose and had obviously started to work on its own throat. She recognized the tearing fur, the ripping of veins.

She listened for the cessation of that individual voice, but she couldn't be sure. The others were making too much noise. One mink less.

Where she sat, she was partly shielded from the telepathic relay, but not altogether. She herself, old as she was, felt queer wild dreams go through her. She thrilled with hate as she thought of beings suffering out beyond her—suffering terribly, since they were not masked by the built-in defenses of the Norstrilian communications system.

She felt the wild throb of long-forgotten lust.

She hungered for things she had not known she remembered. She went through the spasms of fear that the hundreds of animals expressed.

Underneath this, her sane mind kept asking, "How much longer can I take it? How much longer must I take it? Lord God, be good to your people here on this world! Be good to poor old me."

The green light went on.

She pressed a button on the other side of her chair. The gas hissed in. As she passed into unconsciousness, she knew that her kittons passed into instant unconsciousness too.

She would waken before they did and then her duties would begin: checking the living ones, taking out the one that had clawed out its own throat, taking out those who had died of heart attacks, re-arranging them, dressing their wounds, treating them alive and asleep—asleep and happy—breeding, living in their sleep—until the next call should come to waken them for the defense of the treasures which blessed and cursed her native world.

6

Everything had gone exactly right. Lavender had found an illegal planoform ship. This was no inconsequential accomplishment, since planoform ships were very strictly licensed and obtaining an illegal one was a chore on which a planet full of crooks could easily have worked a lifetime.

Lavender had been lavished with money—Benjacomin's money.

The honest wealth of the thieves' planet had gone in and had paid the falsifications and great debts, imaginary transactions that were fed to the computers for ships and cargoes and passengers that would be almost untraceably commingled in the commerce of ten thousand worlds.

"Let him pay for it," said Lavender, to one of his confederates, an apparent criminal who was also a Norstrilian agent. "This is paying good money for bad. You better spend a lot of it."

Just before Benjacomin took off Lavender sent on an additional message.

He sent it directly through the Go-captain, who usually did not carry messages. The Go-captain was a relay commander of the Norstrilian fleet, but he had been carefully ordered not to look like it.

The message concerned the planoform license—another twenty-odd tablets of stroon which could mortgage Viola Siderea for hundreds upon hundreds of years. The captain said: "I don't have to send that through. The answer is yes."

Benjacomin came into the control room. This was contrary to regulations, but he had hired the ship to violate regulations.

The captain looked at him sharply. "You're a passenger, get out."

Benjacomin said: "You have my little yacht on board. I am the only man here outside of your people."

"Get out. There's a fine if you're caught here."

"It does not matter," Benjacomin said. "I'll pay it."

"You will, will you?" said the Captain. "You would not be paying twenty tablets of stroon. That's ridiculous. Nobody could get that much stroon."

Benjacomin laughed, thinking of the thousands of tablets he would soon have. All he had to do was to leave the planoform ship behind, strike once, go past the kittons and come back.

His power and his wealth came from the fact that he knew he could now reach it. The mortgage of twenty tablets of stroon against this planet was a low price to pay if it would pay off at thousands to one. The Captain replied: "It's not worth it, it just is not worth risking twenty tablets for your being here. But I can tell you how to get inside the Norstrilian communications net if that is worth twenty-seven tablets."

Benjacomin went tense.

For a moment he thought he might die. All this work, all this training—the dead boy on the beach, the gamble with the credit, and now this unsuspected antagonist!

He decided to face it out. "What do you know?" said Benjacomin.

"Nothing," said the Captain.

"You said 'Norstrilia.' "

"That I did," said the Captain.

"If you said Norstrilia, you must have guessed it. Who told you?"

"Where else would a man go if you look for infinite riches? If you get away with it. Twenty tablets is nothing to a man like you."

"It's two hundred years' worth of work from three hundred thousand people," said Benjacomin grimly.

"When you get away with it, you will have more than twenty tablets, and so will your people."

And Benjacomin thought of the thousands and thousands of tablets. "Yes, that I know."

"If you don't get away with it, you've got the card."

"That's right. All right. Get me inside the net. I'll pay the twenty-seven tablets."

"Give me the card."

Benjacomin refused. He was a trained thief, and he was alert to thievery. Then he thought again. This was the crisis of his life. He had to gamble a little on somebody.

He had to wager the card. "I'll mark it and then I'll give it back to you." Such was his excitement that Benjacomin did not notice that the card went into a duplicator, that the transaction was recorded, that the message went back to Olympic Center, that the loss and the mortgage against the planet of Viola Siderea should be credited to certain commercial agencies in Earth for three hundred years to come.

Benjacomin got the card back. He felt like an honest thief.

If he did die, the card would be lost and his people would not have to pay. If he won, he could pay that little bit out of his own pocket.

Benjacomin sat down. The Go-captain signalled to his pinlighters. The ship lurched.

For half a subjective hour they moved, the Captain wearing a helmet of space upon his head, sensing and grasping and guessing his way, stepping stone to stepping stone, right back to his home. He had to fumble the passage, or else Benjacomin might guess that he was in the hands of double agents.

But the captain was well trained. Just as well trained as Benjacomin. Agents and thieves, they rode together.

They planoformed inside the communications net. Benjacomin shook hands with them. "You are allowed to materialize as soon as I call."

"Good luck, Sir," said the Captain.

"Good luck to me," said Benjacomin.

He climbed into his space yacht. For less than a second in real space, the gray expanse of Norstrilia loomed up. The ship which looked like a simple warehouse disappeared into planoform, and the yacht was on its own.

The yacht dropped.

As it dropped, Benjacomin had a hideous moment of confusion and terror.

He never knew the woman down below but she sensed him plainly as he received the wrath of the much-amplified kittons. His conscious mind quivered under the blow. With a prolongation of subjective experience which made one or two seconds seem like months of hurt drunken bewilderment, Benjacomin Bozart swept beneath the tide of his own personality. The moon relay threw minkish minds against him. The synapses of his brain re-formed to conjure up might-have-beens, terrible things that never happened to any man. Then his knowing mind whited out in an overload of stress.

His subcortical personality lived on a little longer.

His body fought for several minutes. Mad with lust and hunger, the body arched in the pilot's seat, the mouth bit deep into his own arm. Driven by lust, the left hand tore at his face, ripping out his left eyeball. He screeched with animal lust as he tried to devour himself . . . not entirely without success.

The overwhelming telepathic message of Mother Hitton's littul kittons ground into his brain.

The mutated minks were fully awake.

The relay satellites had poisoned all the space around him with the craziness to which the minks were bred.

Bozart's body did not live long. After a few minutes, the arteries were open, the head slumped forward and the yacht was dropping helplessly toward the warehouses which it had meant to raid. Norstrilian police picked it up.

The police themselves were ill. All of them were ill. All of them were white-faced. Some of them had vomited. They had gone through the edge of the mink defense. They had passed through the telepathic band at its thinnest and weakest point. This was enough to hurt them badly.

They did not want to know.

They wanted to forget.

One of the younger policemen looked at the body and said, "What on earth could do that to a man?"

"He picked the wrong job," said the police captain.

The young policeman said: "What's the wrong job?"

"The wrong job is trying to rob us, boy. We are defended, and we don't want to know how."

The young policeman, humiliated and on the verge of anger, looked almost as if he would defy his superior, while keeping his eyes away from the body of Benjacomin Bozart.

The older man said: "It's all right. He did not take long to die and this is the man who killed the boy Johnny, not very long ago."

"Oh, him? So soon?"

"We brought him." The old police officer nodded. "We let him find his death. That's how we live. Tough, isn't it?"

The ventilators whispered softly, gently. The animals slept again. A jet of air poured down on Mother Hitton. The telepathic relay was still on. She could feel herself, the sheds, the faceted moon, the little satellites. Of the robber there was no sign.

She stumbled to her feet. Her raiment was moist with perspiration. She needed a shower and fresh clothes . . .

Back at Manhome, the Commercial Credit Circuit called shrilly for human attention. A junior subchief of the Instrumentality walked over to the machine and held out his hand.

The machine dropped a card neatly into his fingers.

He looked at the card.

"Debit Viola Siderea—credit Earth Contingency—subcredit Norstrilian account—four hundred million man megayears."

Though all alone, he whistled to himself in the empty room. "We'll all be dead, stroon or no stroon, before they finish paying that!" He went off to tell his friends the odd news.

The machine, not getting its card back, made another one.

Brian W. Aldiss

A KIND OF ARTISTRY

In many ways, Brian W. Aldiss was the *enfant terrible* of the late '50s, exploding into the science fiction world and shaking it up with the ferocious verve and pyrotechnic verbal brilliance of stories like "Poor Little Warrior," "Outside," "The New Father Christmas," "Who Can Replace a Man?", "A Kind of Artistry," and "Old Hundredth," and with the somber beauty and unsettling poetic vision—in the main, of a world where Mankind signally has *not* triumphantly conquered the universe, as the Campbellian dogma of the time insisted that he would—of his classic novels *Starship* and *The Long Afternoon of Earth* (*Non-Stop* and *Hothouse* respectively, in Britain). All this made him one of the most controversial writers of the day . . . and, some years later, he'd be one of the most controversial figures of the New Wave era as well, shaking up the SF world of the mid-'60s in an even more dramatic and drastic fashion with the ferociously Joycean "acid-head war" stories that would be melded into *Barefoot in the Head*, with the irreverent *Cryptozoic!*, and with his surrealistic anti-novel *Report on Probability A*.

But Aldiss has never been willing to work any one patch of ground for very long. By 1976, he had worked his way through two controversial British mainstream bestsellers—*The Hand-Reared Boy* and *A Soldier Erect*—and the strange transmuted Gothic of *Frankenstein Unbound*, and gone on to produce a lyrical masterpiece of science-fantasy, *The Malacia Tapestry*, one of his best books, and certainly one of the best novels of the '70s. Ahead, in the decade of the '80s, was the monumental accomplishment of his *Helliconia* trilogy—*Helliconia Spring*, *Helliconia Summer*, and *Helliconia Winter*—and by the end of that decade only the grumpiest of reactionary critics could deny that Aldiss was one of the true giants of the field, a figure of artistic complexity and amazing vigor, as much on the Cutting Edge in the '90s as he had been in the '50s.

Although his restless, ambitious work, always evolving and looking for new horizons to pioneer, has often taken him far from the purview of the standard SF adventure tale, Aldiss has clearly retained a deep fondness for Space Opera of the most primordial, planet-busting, swashbuckling sort. As an editor, he has produced some of the key retrospective anthologies of the form, including *Space Opera, Space Odysseys, Evil Earths, All About Venus,* and the two-volume *Galactic Empires.* As a writer, although it's a bit off the mainline of development for Space Opera, Aldiss's monumental *The Long Afternoon of Earth* remains one of the classic visions of the distant future of Earth, and certainly is a foundation-stone of the subgenre of science-fantasy, which is at least cousin-germane to Space Opera, and sometimes close enough that any perceivable differences between the two are almost subliminal. (Few SF writers have ever had the imagination, poetic skills, and visionary scope to write convincingly about the *really* far future—once you have mentioned Olaf Stapledon, Clark Ashton Smith, Jack Vance, Gene Wolfe, Cordwainer Smith, Michael Moorcock, and M. John Harrison, you have almost exhausted the roster of authors who have handled the theme with any kind of evocativeness or complexity—but Aldiss has almost made a specialty of it, also handling the theme with grace and a wealth of poetic imagination in stories like "Old Hundredth," "The Worm That Flies," and "Full Sun," as well as the novels of the "Helliconia" trilogy, and handling a related theme with similar excellence in *The Malacia Tapestry* as well.)

Oddly, though, one of his most lasting impacts on the space adventure tale was with the elegant and evocative little story that follows, which was not only cited by Roger Zelazny as a direct inspiration for his own story "The Doors of His Face, the Lamps of His Mouth," but whose influence was still showing up decades later in works such as Michael Bishop's "The White Otters of Childhood" and Michael Swanwick's *Stations of the Tide,* and no doubt in many other places where it hasn't yet been detected . . .

Brian W. Aldiss has been publishing science fiction for nearly forty years, and has more than two dozen books to his credit *The Long Afternoon of Earth* won a Hugo Award in 1962. "The Saliva Tree" won a Nebula Award in 1965, and Aldiss's novel *Starship* won the Prix Jules Verne in 1977. He took another Hugo Award in 1987 for his critical study of science fiction, *Trillion Year Spree,* written with David Wingrove. His other books include *An Island Called Moreau, Graybeard, Enemies of the System, A Rude Awakening, Life in the West, Forgotten Life, Remembrance Day,* and *Dracula Unbound,* and a memoir, *Bury My Heart at W. H. Smith's.* His short fiction has been collected in *Space, Time, and Nathaniel, Who Can Replace a Man?, New Arrivals, Old Encounters, Galaxies Like Grains of Sand, Seasons in Flight,* and *A Tupolev Too Far.* His many anthologies include *The Penguin Science Fiction Omnibus,* and, with Harry Harrison, *Decade: The 1940s, Decade: The 1950s,* and *Decade: The 1960s.* His latest books include the novel *Somewhere East of Life,* and a collection *Common Clay: 20-Odd Stories.* Due out shortly is his memoir, *In the Twinkling of an Eye.*

I

A giant rising from the fjord, from the grey arm of sea in the fjord, could have peered over the crown of its sheer cliffs and discovered Endehaaven there on the edge, sprawling at the very start of the island.

Derek Flamifew Ende saw much of this sprawl from his high window; indeed, a growing ill-ease, apprehensions of a quarrel, forced him to see everything with particular clarity, just as a landscape takes on an intense actinic visibility before a thunderstorm. Although he was warmseeing with his face, yet his eye vision wandered over the estate.

All was bleakly neat at Endehaaven—as I should know, for its neat-ness is my care. The gardens are made to support evergreens and shrubs that never flower; this is My Lady's whim, that likes a sobriety to match the furrowed brow of the coastline. The building, gaunt Endehaaven itself, is tall and lank and severe; earlier ages would have found its structure impossible: for its thousand built-in paragravity units ensure the support of masonry the mass of which is largely an illusion.

Between the building and the fjord, where the garden contrived itself into a parade, stood My Lady's laboratory, and My Lady's pets—and, indeed, My Lady herself at this time, her long hands busy with the minicoypu and the agoutinis. I stood with her, attending the animals' cages or passing her instruments or stirring the tanks, doing always what she asked. And the eyes of Derek Ende looked down on us; no, they looked down on her only.

Derek Flamifew Ende stood with his face over the receptor bowl, reading the message from Star One. It played lightly over his countenance and over the boscises of his forehead. Though he stared down across that achingly familiar stage of his life outside, he still warmsaw the communication clearly. When it was finished, he negated the receptor, pressed his face to it, and flexed his message back.

"I will do as you message, Star One. I will go at once to Festi XV in the Veil Nebula and enter liason with the being you call the Cliff. If possible I will also obey your order to take some of its substance to Pyrylyn. Thank you for your greetings; I return them in good faith. Good-bye."

He straightened and massaged his face: warmlooking over great light distances was always tiring, as if the sensitive muscles of the countenance knew that they delivered up their tiny electrostatic charges to parsecs of vacuum, and were appalled. Slowly his boscises also relaxed, as slowly he gathered together his gear. It would be a long flight to the Veil, and the task that had been set him would daunt the stoutest heart on Earth; yet it was for another reason he lingered: before he could be away, he had to say a farewell to his Mistress.

Dilating the door, he stepped out into the corridor, walked along it with a steady tread—feet covering mosaics of a pattern learnt long ago in his childhood—and walked into the paragravity shaft. Moments later, he was leaving the main hall, approaching My Lady as she stood gaunt, with her rodents scuttling at beast level before her and Vatna Jokull's heights rising behind her, gray with the impurities of distance.

"Go indoors and fetch me the box of name rings, Hols," she said to me; so I passed him, My Lord, as he went to her. He noticed me no more than he noticed any of the other parthenos.

When I returned, she had not turned towards him, though he was speaking urgently to her.

"You know I have my duty to perform, Mistress," I heard him saying. "Nobody else but a normal-born Earthborn can be entrusted with this sort of task."

"This sort of task! The galaxy is loaded inexhaustibly with such tasks! You can excuse yourself forever with such excursions."

He said to her remote back, pleadingly: "You can't talk of them like that. You know of the nature of the Cliff—I told you all about it. You know this isn't an excursion: it requires all the courage I have. And you know that only Earthborns, for some reason, have such courage . . . Don't you, Mistress?"

Although I had come up to them, threading my subservient way between cage and tank, they noticed me not enough even to lower their voices. My Lady stood gazing at the grey heights inland, her countenance as formidable as they; one boscis twitched as she said, "You think you are so big and brave, don't you?"

Knowing the power of sympathetic magic, she never spoke his name when she was angry; it was as if she wished him to disappear.

"It isn't that," he said humbly. "Please be reasonable, Mistress; you know I must go; a man cannot be forever at home. Don't be angry."

She turned to him at last.

Her face was high and stern; it did not receive. Yet she had a beauty of some dreadful kind I cannot describe, if weariness and knowledge can together knead beauty. Her eyes were as grey and distant as the frieze of snow-covered volcano behind her, O My Lady! She was a century older than Derek: though the difference showed not in her skin—which would stay fresh yet a thousand years—but in her authority.

"I'm not angry. I'm only hurt. You know how you have the power to hurt me."

"Mistress—," he said, taking a step toward her.

"Don't touch me," she said. "Go if you must, but don't make a mockery of it by touching me."

He took her elbow. She held one of the minicoypus quiet in the crook of her arm—animals were always docile at her touch—and strained it closer.

"I don't mean to hurt you, Mistress. You know we owe allegiance to Star One; I must work for them, or how else do we hold this estate? Let me go for once with an affectionate parting."

"Affection! You go off and leave me alone with a handful of parthenos and you talk of affection! Don't pretend you don't rejoice to get away from me. You're tired of me, aren't you?"

Wearily he said, as if nothing else would come, "It's not that . . ."

"You see! You don't even attempt to sound sincere. Why don't you go? It doesn't matter what happens to me."

"Oh, if you could only hear your own self-pity."

Now she had a tear on the icy slope of one cheek. Turning, she flashed it for his inspection.

"Who else should pity me? You don't, or you wouldn't go away from me as you do. Suppose you got killed by this Cliff, what will happen to me?"

"I shall be back, Mistress," he said. "Never fear."

"It's easy to say. Why don't you have the courage to admit that you're only too glad to leave me?"

"Because I'm not going to be provoked into a quarrel."

"Pah, you sound like a child again. You won't answer, will you? Instead you're going to run away, evading your responsibilities."

"I'm not running away!"

"Of course you are, whatever you pretend. You're just immature."

"I'm not, I'm not! And I'm not running away! It takes real courage to do what I'm going to do."

"You think so well of yourself!"

He turned away then, petulantly, without dignity. He began to head towards the landing platform. He began to run.

"Derek!" she called.

He did not answer.

She took the squatting minicoypu by the scruff of its neck. Angrily she flung it into the nearby tank of water. It turned into a fish and swam down into the depths.

II

Derek journeyed toward the Veil Nebula in his fast lightpusher. Lonely it sailed, a great fin shaped like an archer's bow, barnacled all over with the photon cells that sucked its motive power from the dense and dusty emptiness of space. Midway along the trailing edge was the blister in which Derek lay, senseless over most of his voyage.

He woke in the therapeutic bed, called to another resurrection day that was no day, with gentle machine hands easing the stiffness from his muscles. Soup gurgled in a retort, bubbling up towards a nipple only two inches from his mouth. He drank. He slept again, tired from his long inactivity.

When he woke again, he climbed slowly from the bed and exercised for fifteen minutes. Then he moved forward to the controls. My friend Jon was there.

"How is everything?" Derek asked.

"Everything is in order, My Lord," Jon replied. "We are swinging into the orbit of Festi XV now." He gave the coordinates and retired to eat. Jon's job was the loneliest any partheno could have. We are hatched according to strictly controlled formulae, without the inbred organisations of DNA that assure true Earthborns of their amazing longevity; five more long hauls and Jon will be old and worn out, fit only for the transmuter.

Derek sat at the controls. Did he see, superimposed on the face of Festi, the face he loved and feared? I think he did. I think there were no swirling clouds for him that could erase the clouding of her brow.

Whatever he saw, he settled the lightpusher into a fast low orbit about the desolate planet. The sun Festi was little more than a blazing point some eight hundred million miles away. Like the riding light of a ship it bobbed above a turbulent sea of cloud as they went in.

For a long while, Derek sat with his face in a receptor bowl, checking ground heats far below. Since he was dealing with temperatures approaching absolute zero, this was not simple; yet when the Cliff moved into a position directly below, there was no mistaking its bulk; it stood out as clearly on his senses as if outlined on a radar screen.

"There she goes!" Derek exclaimed.

Jon had come forward again. He fed the time coordinates into the lightpusher's brain, waited, and read off the time when the Cliff would be below them again.

Nodding, Derek began to prepare to jump. Without haste, he assumed his special suit, checking each item as he took it up, opening the paragravs until he floated, then closing them again, clicking down every snap-fastener until he was entirely encased.

"395 seconds to next zenith, My Lord," Jon said.

"You know all about collecting me?"

"Yes, sir."

"I shall not activate the radio beacon till I'm back in orbit."

"I fully understand, sir."

"Right. I'll be moving."

A little animated prison, he walked ponderously into the air lock.

Three minutes before they were next above the Cliff, Derek opened the outer door and dived into the sea of cloud. A brief blast of his suit jets set him free from the lightpusher's orbit. Cloud engulfed him like death as he fell.

The twenty surly planets that swung round Festi held only an infinitesimal fraction of the mysteries of the galaxy. Every globe in the universe huddled its own secret purpose to itself. On some of those globes, as on Earth, the purpose manifested itself in a type of being that could shape itself, burst into the space lanes, and rough-hew its aims in a civilized extra-planetary environment. On others, the purpose remained aloof and dark; only Earthborns, weaving their obscure patterns of will and compulsion, challenged those alien beings, to wrest from them new knowledge that might be added to the pool of the old.

All knowledge has its influence. Over the millennia since interstellar flight had become practicable, mankind was insensibly moulded by its own findings; together with its lost innocence, its genetic stability went out of the galactic window. As man fell like rain over other planets, so his strain lost its original hereditary design: each center of civilization bred new ways of thought, of feeling, of shape—of life. Only on old Earth itself did man still somewhat resemble the men of prestellar days.

That was why it was an Earthborn who dived head-first to meet an entity called the Cliff.

The Cliff had destroyed each of the few spaceships or lightpushers that had landed on its desolate globe. After long study of the being from safe orbits, the wise men of Star One evolved the theory that it destroyed any considerable source of power, as a man will swat a buzzing fly. Derek Ende, going along with no powering but his suit motors, would be safe— or so the theory went.

Riding down on the paragravs, he sank more and more slowly into planetary night. The last of the cloud was whipped from about his shoulders and a high wind thrummed and whistled round the supporters of his suit. Beneath him, the ground loomed. So as not to be blown across it, he speeded his rate of fall; next moment he sprawled full length on Festi XV. For a while he lay there, resting and letting his suit cool.

The darkness was not complete. Though almost no solar light touched this continent, green flares grew from the earth, illuminating its barren contours. Wishing to accustom his eyes to the gloom, he did not switch on his head, shoulder, stomach, or hand lights.

Something like a stream of fire flowed to his left. Because its radiance was poor and guttering, it confused itself with its own shadows, so that the smoke it gave off, distorted into bars by the bulk of the 4G planet, appeared to roll along its course like burning tumbleweed. Further off were larger sources of fire, impure ethane and methane most probably, burning with a sound that came like frying steak to Derek's ears, and spouting upwards with an energy that licked the lowering cloud race with blue light. At another point, blazing on an eminence, a geyser of flame wrapped itself in a thickly swirling mantle of brown smoke, a pall that spread upwards as slowly as porridge. Elsewhere, a pillar of white fire burnt without motion or smoke; it stood to the right of where Derek lay, like a floodlit sword in its perfection.

He nodded approval to himself. His drop had been successfully placed. This was the Region of Fire, where the Cliff lived.

To lie there was content enough, to gaze on a scene never closely viewed by man fulfillment enough—until he realised that a wide segment of landscape offered not the slightest glimmer of illumination. He looked into it with a keen warmsight, and found it was the Cliff.

The immense bulk of the thing blotted out all lights from the ground and rose to eclipse the cloud over its crest.

At the mere sight of it, Derek's primary and secondary hearts began to beat out a hastening pulse of awe. Stretched flat on the ground, his paragravs keeping him level to 1G, he peered ahead at it; he swallowed to clear his choked throat; his eyes strained through the mosaic of dull light in an effort to define the Cliff.

One thing was sure: it was large! He cursed that although photosistors allowed him to use his warmsight on objects beyond the suit he wore, this sense was distorted by the eternal firework display. Then in a moment of good seeing he had an accurate fix: the Cliff was three quarters of a mile away! From first observations, he had thought it to be no more than a hundred yards distant.

Now he knew how large it was. It was enormous!

Momentarily he gloated. The only sort of tasks worth being set were impossible ones. Star One's astrophysicists held the notion that the Cliff was in some sense aware, so they required Derek to take them a pound of its flesh. How do you carve a being the size of a small moon?

All the time he lay there, the wind jarred along the veins and supporters of his suit. Gradually, it occurred to Derek that the vibration he felt from this constant motion was changed. It carried a new note and a new strength. He looked about, placed his gloved hand outstretched on the ground.

The wind was no longer vibrating. It was the earth that shook, Festi itself that trembled. The Cliff was moving!

When he looked back up at it with both his senses, he saw which way it headed. Jarring steadily, it bore down on him.

"If it has intelligence, then it will reason—if it has detected me—that I am too small to offer it harm. So it will offer me none and I have nothing to fear," Derek told himself. The logic did not reassure him.

An absorbent pseudopod, activated by a simple humidity gland in the brow of his helmet, slid across his forehead and removed the sweat that formed there.

Visibility fluttered like a rag in a cellar. The slow forward surge of the Cliff was still something Derek sensed rather than saw. Now the rolling mattresses of cloud blotted the thing's crest, as it in its turn eclipsed the fountains of fire. To the jar of its approach even the marrow of Derek's bones raised a response.

Something else also responded.

The legs of Derek's suit began to move. The arms moved. The body wriggled.

Puzzled, Derek stiffened his legs. Irresistibly, the knees of the suit hinged, forcing his own to do likewise. And not only his knees: his arms too, stiffly though he braced them on the ground before him, were made to bend to the whim of the suit. He could not keep still without breaking bones.

Thoroughly alarmed he lay there, flexing contortedly to keep rhythm with his suit, performing the gestures of an idiot.

As if it had suddenly learnt to crawl, the suit began to move forward. It shuffled forward over the ground; Derek inside went willy-nilly with it.

One ironic thought struck him. Not only was the mountain coming to Mohammed; Mohammed was perforce going to the mountain . . .

III

Nothing he could do checked his progress; he was no longer master of his movements; his will was useless. With the realisation rode a sense of relief. His Mistress could hardly blame him for anything that happened now.

Through the darkness he went on hands and knees, blundering in the direction of the on-coming Cliff, prisoner in an animated prison.

The only constructive thought that came to him was that his suit had somehow become subject to the Cliff. How, he did not know or try to guess. He crawled. He was almost relaxed now, letting his limbs move limply with the suit movements.

Smoke furled him about. The vibrations ceased, telling him that the Cliff was stationary again. Raising his head, he could see nothing but smoke—produced perhaps by the Cliff's mass as it scraped over the ground. When the blur parted, he glimpsed only darkness. The thing was directly ahead!

He blundered on. Abruptly he began to climb, still involuntarily aping the movements of his suit.

Beneath him was a doughy substance, tough yet yielding. The suit worked its way heavily upwards at an angle of something like sixty-five degrees; the stiffeners creaked, the paragravs throbbed. He was ascending the Cliff.

By this time there was no doubt in Derek's mind that the thing possessed what might be termed volition, if not consciousness. It possessed too a power no man could claim: it could impart that volition to an inanimate object like his suit. Helpless inside it, he carried his considerations a stage further. This power to impart volition seemed to have a limited range: otherwise the Cliff would surely not have bothered to move its gigantic mass at all, but would have forced the suit to traverse all the distance between them. If this reasoning were sound, then the lightpusher was safe from capture in orbit.

The movement of his arms distracted him. His suit was tunneling. Giving it no aid, he lay and let his hands make swimming motions. If it was going to bore into the Cliff, then he could only conclude he was about to be digested: yet he stilled his impulse to struggle, knowing that struggle was fruitless.

Thrusting against the doughy stuff, the suit burrowed into it and made a sibilant little world of movement and friction which stopped directly it stopped, leaving Derek embedded in the most solid kind of isolation.

To ward off growing claustrophobia, he attempted to switch on his headlight; his suit arms remained so stiff he could not bend them enough to reach the toggle. All he could do was lie there helplessly in his shell and stare into the featureless darkness of the Cliff.

But the darkness was not entirely featureless. His ears detected a constant *slither* along the outside surfaces of his suit. His warmsight discerned a meaningless pattern beyond his helmet. Though he focussed his boscises, he could make no sense of the pattern; it had neither symmetry nor meaning for him . . .

Yet for his body it seemed to have some meaning. Derek felt his limbs tremble, was aware of pulses and phantom impressions within himself that he had not known before. The realisation percolated through to him that he was in touch with powers of which he had no cognisance— and, conversely, that something was in touch with him that had no cognisance of his powers.

An immense heaviness overcame him. The forces of life laboured within him. He sensed more vividly than before the vast bulk of the Cliff. Thought it was dwarfed by the mass of Festi XV, it was as large as a good-sized asteroid . . . He could picture an asteroid, formed from a jetting explosion of gas on the face of Festi the sun. Half-solid, half-molten, it swung about its parent on an eccentric orbit. Cooling under an interplay of pressures, its interior crystallised into a unique form. So, with its sur-

face semi-plastic, it existed for many millions of years, gradually accumulating an electrostatic charge that poised . . . and waited . . . and
brewed the life acids about its crystalline heart.

Festi was a stable system, but once in every so many thousands of
millions of years, the giant first, second, and third planets achieved peri-
helion with the sun and with each other simultaneously. This happened
coincidentally with the asteroid's nearest approach; it was wrenched from
its orbit and all but grazed the three lined-up planets. Vast electrical and
gravitational forces were unleashed. The asteroid glowed: and woke to
consciousness. Life was not born on it: it was born to life, born in one cat-
aclysmic clash!

Before it had more than mutely swallowed the sad-sharp-sweet sensation of consciousness, it was in trouble. Plunging away from the sun on
its new course, it found itself snared in the gravitational pull of the 4G
planet, Festi XV. It knew no shaping force but gravity; gravity was to it
all that oxygen was to cellular life on Earth; yet it had no wish to exchange its flight for captivity; yet it was too puny to resist. For the first
time, the asteroid recognised that its consciousness had a use, in that it
could to some extent control its environment outside itself. Rather than
risk being broken up in Festi's orbit, it sped inwards, and by retarding its
own fall performed its first act of volition, an act that brought it down
shaken but entire on the planet's surface.

For an immeasurable period, the asteroid—but now it was the Cliff—
lay in the shallow crater formed by its impact, speculating without
thought. It knew nothing except the inorganic scene about it, and could
visualise nothing else, but that scene it knew well. Gradually it came to
some kind of terms with the scene. Formed by gravity, it used gravity as
thoughtlessly as a man uses breath; it began to move other things, and it
began to move itself.

That it should be other than alone in the universe had never occurred
to the Cliff. Now it knew there was other life, it accepted the fact. The
other life was not as it was; that it accepted. The other life had its own requirements; that it accepted. Of questions, of doubt, it did not know. It
had a need; so did the other life; they should both be accommodated, for
accommodation was the adjustment to pressure, and that response it com-
prehended.

Derek Ende's suit began to move again under external volition. Carefully it worked its way backwards. It was ejected from the Cliff. It lay still.

Derek himself lay still. He was barely conscious.

In a half daze, he was piecing together what had happened.

The Cliff had communicated with him; if he ever doubted that, the
evidence of it lay clutched in the crook of his left arm.

"Yet it did not—yet it could not communicate with me!" he murmured. But it had communicated: he was still faint with the burden of it.

The Cliff had nothing like a brain. It had not "recognised" Derek's brain. Instead, it had communicated with the only part of him it could recognise; it had communicated direct to his cell organisation, and in particular probably to those cytoplasmic structures, the mitochondria, the power sources of the cell. His brain had been by-passed, his own cells had taken in the information offered.

He recognised his feeling of weakness. The Cliff had drained him of power. Even that could not drain his feeling of triumph. For the Cliff had taken information even as it gave it. The Cliff had learnt that other life existed in other parts of the universe.

Without hesitation, without debate, it had given a fragment of itself to be taken to those other parts of the universe. Derek's mission was completed.

In the Cliff's gesture, Derek read one of the deepest urges of living things: the urge to make an impression on another living thing. Smiling wryly, he pulled himself to his feet.

He was alone in the Region of Fire. The occasional mournful flame still confronted its surrounding dark, but the Cliff had disappeared; he had lain on the threshold of consciousness longer than he thought. He looked at his chronometer, to find it was high time he moved towards his rendezvous with the lightpusher. Stepping up his suit heating to combat the cold that began to seep through his bones, he revved up the paragrav unit and rose. The noisome clouds came down and engulfed him; Festi was lost to view. Soon he had risen beyond cloud or atmosphere.

Under Jon's direction, the space craft homed onto Derek's radio beacon. After a few tricky minutes, they matched velocities and Derek climbed aboard.

"Are you all right?" the partheno asked, as his master staggered into a flight seat.

"Fine—just weak. I'll tell you all about it as I do a report on spool for Pyrylyn. They're going to be pleased with us."

He produced a yellowy grey blob of matter that had expanded to the size of a large turkey and held it out to Jon.

"Don't touch this with your bare hands. Put it in one of the low-temperature lockers under 4Gs. It's a little souvenir from Festi XV."

IV

The Eyebright in Pynnati, one of Pyrylyn's capital cities, was where you went to enjoy yourself on the most lavish scale possible. This was where Derek Ende's hosts took him, with Jon in self-effacing attendance.

They lay in a nest of couches which slowly revolved, giving them a full view of other dance and couch parties. The room itself moved. Its walls were transparent; through them could be seen an ever-changing view as the room slid up and down and about the great metal framework of the Eyebright. First they were on the outside of the structure, with the bright night lights of Pynnati winking up at them as if intimately involved in their delight. Then they slipped inwards in the slow evagination of the building, to be surrounded by other pleasure rooms, their revelers clearly visible as they moved grandly up or down or along.

Uneasily, Derek lay on his couch. A vision of his Mistress's face was before him; he could imagine how she would treat all this harmless festivity: with cool contempt. His own pleasure was consequently reduced to ashes.

"I suppose you'll be moving back to Earth as soon as possible?"

"Eh?" Derek grunted.

"I said, I supposed you would soon be going home again." The speaker was Belix Ix Sappose, Chief Administrator of High Gee Research at Star One; as Derek's host of the evening, he lay next to him.

"I'm sorry, Belix, yes—I shall have to head back for home soon."

"No 'have to' about it. You have discovered an entirely new life form; we can now attempt communication with the Festi XV entity, with goodness knows what extension of knowledge. The government can easily show its gratitude by awarding you any sort of post here you care to name: I am not without influence in that respect, as you are aware. I don't imagine that Earth in its senescent stage has much to offer a man of your calibre."

Derek thought of what it had to offer. He was bound to it. These decadent people did not understand how anything could be binding.

"Well, what do you say, Ende? I'm not speaking idly." Belix Ix Sappose tapped his antler system impatiently.

"Er . . . Oh, they will discover a great deal from the Cliff. That doesn't concern me. My part of the work is over. I'm just a field worker, not an intellectual."

"You don't reply to my suggestion."

He looked at Belix with only slight vexation. Belix was an unglaat, one of a species that had done as much as any to bring about the peaceful concourse of the galaxy. His backbone branched into an elaborate antler system, from which six sloe-dark eyes surveyed Derek with un-blinking irritation. Other members of the party, including Jupkey, Belix's female, were also looking at him.

"I must get back to Earth soon," Derek said. What had Belix said? Offered some sort of post? Restlessly he shifted on his couch, under pres-sure as always when surrounded by people he knew none too well.

"You are bored, Mr. Ende."

"No, not at all. My apologies, Belix. I'm overcome as always by the luxury of Eyebright. I was watching the nude dancers."

"I fear you are bored."

"Not at all, I assure you."

"May I get you a woman?"

"No, thank you."

"A boy, perhaps?"

"No, thank you."

"Have you ever tried the flowering asexuals from the Cphids?"

"Not at present, thank you."

"Then perhaps you will excuse us if Jupkey and I remove our clothes and join the dance," Belix said stiffly.

As they moved out onto the dance floor to greet the strepent trum-pets, Derek heard Jupkey say something of which he caught only the words "arrogant Earthborn." His eyes met Jon's; he saw that the partheno had overheard also.

In an instinctive dismissive gesture of his left hand, Derek revealed his mortification. He rose and began to pace round the room. Often he shouldered his way through a knot of naked dancers, ignoring their com-plaints.

At one of the doors, a staircase was floating by. He stepped onto it to escape from the crowds.

Four young women were passing down the stairs. They were gaily dressed, with sonant-stones pulsing on their costumes. In their faces youth kept its lantern, lighting them as they laughed and chattered. Derek stopped and beheld the girls. One of them he recognised. Instinctively he called her name: "Eva!"

She had already seen him. Waving her companions on, she came back to him, dancing up the intervening steps.

"So the brave Earthborn climbs once more the golden stairs of Pyn-nati! Well, Derek Ende, your eyes are as dark as ever, and your brow as high!"

As he looked at her, the strepent trumpets were in tune for him for the first time that evening, and his delight rose up in his throat.

"Eva! . . . And your eyes as bright as ever . . . And you have no man with you."

"The powers of coincidence work on your behalf." She laughed—yes, he remembered that sound!—and then said more seriously, "I heard you were here with Belix Sappose and his female; so I was making the grandly foolish gesture of coming to see you. You remember how devoted I am to foolish gestures."

"So foolish?"

"Probably. You have less change in you, Derek Ende, than the core of Pyrylyn. To suppose otherwise is foolish, to know how unalterable you are and still to see you doubly foolish."

He took her hand, beginning to lead her up the staircase; the rooms moving by them on either side were blurs to his eyes.

"Must you still bring up that old charge, Eva?"

"It lies between us; I do not have to touch it. I fear your unchangeability because I am a butterfly against your grey castle."

"You are beautiful, Eva, so beautiful!—And may a butterfly not rest unharmed on a castle wall?" He fitted into her allusive way of speech with difficulty.

"Walls! I cannot bear your walls, Derek! Am I a bulldozer that I should want to come up against walls? To be either inside or outside them is to be a prisoner."

"Let us not quarrel until we have found some point of agreement," he said. "Here are the stars. Can't we agree about them?"

"If we are both indifferent to them," she said, looking out and impudently winding his arm about her. The staircase had reached the zenith of its travels and moved slowly sideways along the upper edge of Eyebright. They stood on the top step with night flashing their images back at them from the glass.

Eva Coll-Kennerley was a human, but not of Earthborn stock. She was a velure, born on the y-cluster worlds of the dense Third Arm of the galaxy, and her skin was richly covered with the brown fur of her kind. Her mercurial talents were employed in the same research department that enjoyed Belix Sappose's more sober ones; Derek had met her there on an earlier visit to Pyrylyn. Their love had been an affair of swords.

He looked at her now and touched her and could say not one word for himself. When she flashed a liquid eye at him, he essayed an awkward smile.

"Because I am oriented like a compass towards strong men, my lavish offer to you still holds good. Is it not bait enough?"

"I don't think of you as a trap, Eva."

"Then for how many more centuries are you going to refrigerate your nature on Earth? You still remain faithful, if I recall your euphemism for slavery, to your Mistress, to her cold lips and locked heart?"

"I have no choice!"

"Ah yes, my debate on that motion was defeated: and more than once. Is she still pursuing her researches into the transmutability of species?"

"Oh yes, indeed. The mediaeval idea that one species can turn into another was foolish in the Middle Ages; now, with the gradual accumulation of cosmic radiation in planetary bodies, it is correct to a certain definable extent. She is endeavouring to show that cellular bondage can be—"

"Yes, yes, and this serious talk is an eyesore in Eyebright! You are locked away, Derek, doing your sterile deeds of heroism and never entering the real world. If you imagine you can live with her much longer and then come to me, you are mistaken. Your walls grow higher about your ears every century, till I cannot, cannot—oh, it's the wrong metaphor!—cannot scale you!"

Even in his pain, the texture of her fur was joy to his warm-sight. Helplessly he shook his head in an effort to shake her clattering words away.

"Look at you being big and brave and silent even now! You're so arrogant," she said—and then, without perceptible change of tone, "because I still love the bit of you inside the castle, I'll make once more my monstrous and petty offer to you."

"No, please, Eva!—"

"But yes! Forget this tedious bondage of Earth, forget this ghastly matriarchy, live here with me. I don't want you forever. You know I am a eudemonist and judge by standards of pleasure—our liaison need be only for a century or two. In that time, I will deny you nothing your senses may require."

"Eva!"

"After that, our demands will be satisfied. You may then go back to the Lady Mother of Endehaaven for all I care."

"Eva, you know how I spurn this belief, this eudemonism."

"Forget your creed! I'm asking you nothing difficult. Who are you to haggle? Am I fish, to be bought by the kilo, this bit selected, this rejected?"

He was silent.

"You don't really need me," he said at last. "You have everything already: beauty, wit, sense, warmth, feeling, balance, comfort. *She* has nothing. She is shallow, haunted, cold—oh, she needs me, Eva . . ."

"You are apologising for yourself, not her."

She had already turned with the supple movement of a velure and was running down the staircase. Lighted chambers drifted up about them like bubbles.

His laboured attempt to explain his heart turned to exasperation. He ran down after her, grasping her arm.

"Listen to me, will you, damn you!"

"Nobody in Pyrylyn would listen to such masochistic nonsense as yours! You are an arrogant fool, Derek, and I am a weak-willed one. Now release me!"

As the next room came up, she jumped through its entrance and disappeared into the crowd.

V

Not all the drifting chambers of Eyebright were lighted. Some pleasures come more delightfully with the dark, and these pleasures were coaxed and cossetted into fruition in shrouded halls where illumination cast only the gentlest ripple on the ceiling and the gloom was sensuous with ylang-ylang and other perfumes. Here Derek found a place to weep.

Sections of his life slid before him as if impelled by the same mechanisms that moved Eyebright. Always, one presence was there.

Angrily he related to himself how he always laboured to satisfy her—yes, in every sphere laboured to satisfy her! And how when that satisfaction was accorded him it came as though riven from her, as a spring sometimes trickles down the split face of a rock. Undeniably there was satisfaction for him in drinking from that cool source—but no, where was the satisfaction when pleasure depended on such extreme disciplining and subduing of himself?

Mistress, I love and hate your needs!

And the discipline had been such . . . so long, also . . . that now when he might enjoy himself far from her, he could scarcely strike a trickle from his own rock. He had walked here before, in this city where the hedonists and eudemonists reigned, walked among the scents of pleasure, walked among the ioblepharous women, the beautiful guests and celebrated beauties, with My Lady away in him, feeling that she showed even on his countenance. People spoke to him: somehow he replied. They manifested gaiety: he tried to do so. They opened to him: he attempted a response. All the time, he hoped they would understand that his arrogance masked only shyness—or did he hope that it was his shyness which masked arrogance? He did not know.

Who could presume to know? The one quality holds much of the other. Both refuse to come forward and share.

He roused from his meditation knowing that Eva Coll-Kennerley was again somewhere near. She had not left the building, then! She was seeking him out!

Derek half-rose from his position in a shrouded alcove. He was baffled to think how she could have traced him here. On entering Eyebright, visitors were given sonant-stones, by which they could be traced from room to room; but judging that nobody would wish to trace him, Derek had switched his stone off even before leaving Belix Sappose's party.

He heard Eva's voice, its unmistakable overtones not near, not far . . .

"You find the most impenetrable bushels to hide your light under . . ."

He caught no more. She had sunk down among tapestries with someone else. She was not after him at all! Waves of relief and regret rolled over him . . . and when he paid attention again, she was speaking his name.

With shame on him, like a wolf creeping towards a camp fire, he crouched forward to listen. At once his warmsight told him to whom Eva spoke. He recognised the pattern of the antlers; Belix was there, with Jupkey sprawled beside him on some elaborate kind of bed.

". . . useless to try again. Derek is too far entombed within himself," Eva said.

"Entombed rather within his conditioning," Belix said. "We found the same. It's conditioning, my dear."

"However he became entombed, I still admire him enough to want to understand him." Eva's voice was a note or two astray from its usual controlled timbre.

"Look at it scientifically," Belix said, with the weighty inflections of a man about to produce truth out of a hat. "Earth is the last bastion of a bankrupt culture. The Earthborns number less than a couple of millions now. They disdain social graces and occasions. They are served by parthenogenically bred slaves, all of which are built on the same controlled genetic formula. They are inbred. In consequence, they have become practically a species apart. You can see it all in friend Ende. As I say, he's entombed in his conditioning. A tragedy, Eva, but you must face up to it."

"You're probably right, you pontifical old pop," Jupkey said lazily. "Who but an Earthborn would do what Derek did on Festi?"

"No, no!" Eva said. "Derek's ruled by a woman, not by conditioning. He's—"

"In Ende's case they are one and the same thing, my dear, believe me. Consider Earth's social organisation. The partheno slaves have replaced all but a comparative handful of true Earthborns. That handful has parcelled out Earth into great estates which it holds by a sinister matriarchalism."

"Yes, I know, but Derek—"

"Derek is caught in the system. The Earthborns had fallen into a mating pattern for which there is no precedent. The sons of a family marry their mothers, not only to perpetuate their line but because the productive Earthborn female is scarce now that Earth itself is senescent. This is what the Endes have done; this is what Derek Ende has done. His 'mistress' is both mother and wife to him. Given the factor of longevity as well—well, naturally you ensure an excessive emotional rigidity that almost nothing can break. Not even you, my sweet-coated Eva!"

"He was on the point of breaking tonight!"

"I doubt it," Belix said. "Ende may want to get away from his claustrophobic home, but the same forces that drive him off will eventually lure him back."

"I tell you he was on the point of breaking—only I broke first."

"Well, as Teer Ruche said to me many centuries ago, only a pleasure-hater knows how to shape a pleasure-hater. I would say you were lucky he did not break; you would only have had a baby on your hands."

Her answering laugh did not ring true.

"My Lady of Endehaaven, then, must be the one to do it. I will never try again—though he seems under too much stress to stand for long. Oh, it's really immoral! He deserves better!"

"A moral judgement from you, Eva!" Jupkey exclaimed amusedly to the fragrant gloom.

"My advice to you, Eva, is to forget all about the poor fellow. Apart from anything else, he is barely articulate—which would not suit you for a season."

The unseen listener could bear no more. A sudden rage—as much against himself for hearing as against them for speaking—burst over him, freeing him to act. Straightening up, he seized the arm of the couch on which Belix and Jupkey nestled, wildly supposing he could tip them onto the floor.

Too late, his warmsight warned him of the real nature of the couch. Instead of tipping, it swivelled, sending a wave of liquid over him. The two unglaats were lying in a warm bath scented with ylang-ylang and other essences.

Jupkey squealed in anger and fright. Kicking out, she caught Derek on the shin with a hoof; he slipped in the oily liquid and fell. Belix, unaided by warmsight, jumped out of the bath, entangled himself with Derek's legs, and also fell.

Eva was shouting for lights. Other occupants of the hall cried back that darkness must prevail at all costs.

Picking himself up—leaving only his dignity behind—Derek ran for the exit, abandoning the confusion to sort itself out as it would.

Burningly, disgustedly, he made his way dripping from Eyebright. The hastening footsteps of Jon followed him like an echo all the way to the space field.

Soon he would be back at Endehaaven. Though he would always be a failure in his dealings with other humans, there at least he knew every inch of his bleak allotted territory.

Envoi

Had there been a spell over all Endehaaven, it could have been no quieter when My Lord Derek Ende arrived home."

I informed My Lady of the moment when his lightpusher arrived and rode at orbit. In the receptor bowl I watched him and Jon come home, cutting north west across the emaciated wilds of Europe, across Denmark, over the Shetlands, the Faroes, the sea, alighting by the very edge of the island, by the fjord with its silent waters.

All the while the wind lay low as if under some stunning malediction, and none of our tall trees stirred.

"Where is my Mistress, Hols?" Derek asked me, as I went to greet him and assist him out of his suit.

"She asked me to tell you that she is confined to her chambers and cannot see you, My Lord."

He looked me in the eyes as he did so rarely.

"Is she ill?"

"No."

Without waiting to remove his suit, he hurried on into the building.

Over the next two days, he was about but little, preferring to remain in his room. Once he wandered among the experimental tanks and cages. I saw him net a fish and toss it into the air, watching it while it struggled into new form and flew away until it was lost in a jumbled background of cumulus; but it was plain he was less interested in the riddles of stress and transmutation than in the symbolism of the carp's flight.

Mostly he sat compiling the spools on which he imposed the tale of his life. All one wall was covered with files full of these spools: the arrested drumbeats of past centuries. From the later spools I have secretly compiled this record; for all his unspoken self-pity, he never knew the sickness of merely observing.

We parthenos will never understand the luxuries of a divided mind. Surely suffering as much as happiness is a kind of artistry?

On the day that he received a summons from Star One to go upon another quest for them, Derek met My Lady in the Blue Corridor.

"It is good to see you about again, Mistress," he said, kissing her cheek.

She stroked his hair. On her nervous hand she wore one ring with an amber stone; her gown was of olive and umber.

"I was very upset to have you go away from me. The Earth is dying, Derek, and I fear its loneliness. You have left me alone too much. However, I have recovered myself and am glad to see you back."

"You know I am glad to see you. Smile for me and come outside for some fresh air. The sun is shining."

"It's so long since it shone. Do you remember how once it always shone? I can't bear to quarrel any more. Take my arm and be kind to me."

"Mistress, I always wish to be kind to you. And I have all sorts of things to discuss with you. You'll want to hear what I have been doing, and—"

"You won't leave me any more?"

He felt her hand tighten on his arm. She spoke very loudly.

"That was one of the things I wished to discuss—later," he said. "First let me tell you about the wonderful life form with which I made contact on Festi."

As they left the corridor and descended the paragravity shaft, My Lady said wearily, "I suppose that's a polite way of telling me that you are bored here."

He clutched her hands as they floated down. Then he released them and clutched her face instead.

"Understand this, Mistress mine, I love you and want to serve you. You are in my blood; wherever I go I never can forget you. My dearest wish is to make you happy—this you must know. But equally you must know that I have needs of my own."

Grumpily she said, withdrawing her face, "Oh, I know that all right. And I know those needs will always come first with you. Whatever you say or pretend, you don't care a rap about me. You make that all too clear."

She moved ahead of him, shaking off the hand he put on her arm. He had a vision of himself running down a golden staircase and stretching out that same detaining hand to another girl. The indignity of having to repeat oneself, century after century.

"You're lying! You're faking! You're being cruel!" he said.

Gleaming, she turned.

"Am I? Then answer me this—aren't you already planning to leave Endehaaven and me soon?"

He smote his forehead.

He said inarticulately, "Look, you must try to stop this recrimination. Yes, yes, it's true I am thinking . . . But I have to—I reproach myself. I could be kinder. But you shut yourself away when I come back, you don't welcome me—"

"Trust you to find excuses rather than face up to your own nature," she said contemptuously, walking briskly into the garden. Amber and olive and umber, and sable of hair, she walked down the path, her outlines sharp in the winter air; in the perspectives of his mind she did not dwindle.

For some minutes he stood in the threshold, immobilized by antagonistic emotions.

Finally he pushed himself out into the sunlight.

She was in her favourite spot by the fjord, feeding an old badger from her hand. Only her increased attention to the badger suggested that she heard him approach.

His boscises twitched as he said, "If you will forgive a cliché, I apologise."

"I don't mind what you do."

Walking backwards and forwards behind her, he said, "When I was away, I heard some people talking. On Pyrylyn this was. They were discussing the mores of our matrimonial system."

"It's no business of theirs."

"Perhaps not. But what they said suggested a new line of thought to me."

She put the old badger back in his cage without comment.

"Are you listening, Mistress?"

"Do go on."

"Try to listen sympathetically. Consider all the history of galactic exploration—or even before that, consider the explorers of Earth in the pre-space age, men like Shackleton and so on. They were brave men, of course, but wouldn't it be strange if most of them only ventured where they did because the struggle at home was too much for them?"

He stopped. She had turned to him; the half-smile was whipped off his face by her look of fury.

"And you're trying to tell me that that's how you see yourself—a martyr? Derek, how you must hate me! Not only do you go away, you secretly blame me because you go away. It doesn't matter that I tell you a thousand times I want you here—no, it's all my fault! I drive you away! That's what you tell your charming friends on Pyrylyn, isn't it? Oh, how you must hate me!"

Savagely he grasped her wrists. She screamed to me for aid and struggled. I came near but halted, playing my usual impotent part. He swore at her, bellowed for her to be silent, whereupon she cried the louder, shaking furiously in his arms.

He struck her across the face.

At once she was quiet. Her eyes closed: almost, it would seem, in ecstasy. Standing there, she had the pose of a woman offering herself.

"Go on, hit me! You want to hit me!" she whispered.

With the words, with the look of her, he too was altered. As if realising for the first time her true nature, he dropped his fists and stepped back, staring at her sick-mouthed. His heel met no resistance. He twisted suddenly, spread out his arms as if to fly, and fell over the cliff edge.

Her scream pursued him down.

Even as his body hit the water of the fjord, it began to change. A flurry of foam marked some sort of painful struggle beneath the surface. Then a seal plunged into view, dived below the next wave, and swam towards open sea over which already a freshening breeze blew.

H. Beam Piper

GUNPOWDER GOD

A former detective for the Pennsylvania Railroad, the late H. Beam Piper made his first sale in 1947, to *Astounding,* and soon became a robust player in the booming SF scene of the '50s. In the years to come, he would become a mainstay of *Astounding,* with which magazine he was strongly associated, and where much of his best work (such as the classic story "Omnilingual") appeared, but he also sold widely to other magazines of the day such as *Amazing, Future, Weird Tales,* and *Fantastic Universe.* By the late '50s, as the market for SF novels rapidly expanded, he was primarily writing novels, some of them fix-ups assembled from his magazine work, some of them original.

Piper's work was solidly in the adventure tradition of the day—although usually more in the tradition of *Astounding,* where adventure was always mated with serious social/political speculation, than in the more flamboyant, swashbuckling, sword-and-planet interplanetary Romance tradition of *Planet Stories* or *Thrilling Wonder Stories,* or with the planet-busting Superscience Space Opera of the '30s—with only one or two of his later works, produced toward the end of his life, straying into somewhat different territory. His two major series were the "Terro-Human" stories—which explore the rise and fall of interstellar empires and politics in a complex future history scenario rather reminiscent of Asimov's "Foundation" future history, although different in tone, closer to what we would today call "libertarian" in outlook and philosophy, more concerned with politics, economics, and military campaigns, than was Asimov's; perhaps closer in tone to Poul Anderson's contemporaneous "Technic History" cycle—and the more colorful and freewheeling "Paratime Police" stories; both series have been continued after Piper's death by other writers, although not with the conviction that Piper himself brought to them.

Most of Piper's Terro-Human novels, such as *Space Viking, Four-Day Planet,* and *The Cosmic Computer,* are competent but rather routine Space Opera, as were his first two novels, written with John R. McGuire, *Crisis in 2140* and *A Planet for Texans* (the last later reissued as *Lonestar Planet*). Although technically also in the "Terro-Human" sequence, Piper later moved away from straightforward Space Opera and into more thoughtful territory, and broke some intriguing new ground, with his two best novels, *Little Fuzzy* and *Fuzzy Sapiens* (later reissued in an omnibus collection as *The Fuzzy Papers,* and followed much later by a long-lost and posthumously published third "Fuzzy" novel, *Fuzzies and Other People*), which revolve around intelligently argued courtroom battles (as well as the usual *Astounding*-style behind-the-scenes political intrigues and Dirty Tricks) waged to prove that the native Fuzzies inhabiting a Terran-colonized planet are intelligent, sentient beings, and deserve the same legal rights as humans, including protection from exploitation and the destruction of their habitats and lifeways by a rapacious mining corporation. This was fairly radical stuff in 1962, when science fiction was much more likely to take the side of the calvary or of the intrepid white settlers than of the Indians lurking in ambush over the hill, or of the Kiplingesque colonial administrators rather than that of the downtrodden native sepoys they rule, and has even more relevance today than it had then, making the Fuzzy novels surprisingly germane and up-to-date in sensibility. (If the Fuzzies seem familiar to you the first time you encounter them, it may be because they are very probably [at least one of] the inspirations for a race of little, fuzzy, cute—but warlike—tribal people in a famous blockbuster SF movie of the 1980s; but if there *was* influence, keep in mind that the movie got them from Piper, not the other way around.)

The Fuzzy novels are substantial enough to make me wonder what kind of books Piper would have written in the '70s and '80s, if he had lived to produce them. Unfortunately, he did not—in 1964, despondent over mounting debts and what he considered the failure of his writing career, he picked up a gun (ironic, since he was an enthusiastic gun collector) and shot and killed himself, just as Alice Sheldon would do—driven by different devils—a little more than twenty years later. A final, bitter irony is that there was a big revival of interest in Piper's work in the late '70s and early '80s, with all of his books coming back into print and proving successful enough with readers that new books in both the Fuzzy and the broader Terro-Human series were commissioned to be written by other authors—but by then Piper was long dead, and received no benefit from the Phoenix-like rebirth of a career that he'd thought was over back in 1964.

Little Fuzzy may be Piper's best book, but his most *entertaining* book by far, and my own personal favorite, is the Alternate History novel *Lord Kalvin of Otherwhen,* assembled from the story that follows, "Gunpowder God," plus two sequels, from the pages of *Astounding,* and published in 1965, after Piper's death. Again, Piper was ahead of the curve here, publishing an Alternate History novel long before Alternate History novels became the rage, as they are in today's publishing scene—and although *Lord Kalvin of Otherwhen* was not the first Alternate History novel (being proceeded by de Camp's *Lest Darkness Fall,* and Ward Moore's *Bring the Jubilee,* among others), it remains one of the best of them, and can be seen to have had an influence on the work of future writers such as R. Garcia y Robertson and G. David Nordley, and particularly on the Alternate History work of Harry Turtledove. I think it holds up well in comparison to the other novels being published today in the Alternate History miniboom, and, if re-issued, would probably prove to be as popular with today's readers—publishers take note!

"Gunpowder God," the story that follows, is the first and most self-contained of the Lord Kalvin stories, and as an inventive, action-packed, and relentlessly fast-paced adventure tale grounded in a thorough knowledge of history and the potential social consequences of isolated technological breakthroughs, is just as fresh and effective as anything being written today, more than thirty years later.

Piper never saw a short-story collection published in his lifetime, but his short work was posthumously assembled in the early '80s in the collections *Paratime, Foundation, Empire,* and *The Worlds of H. Beam Piper.* His other works include the omnibus volume *Four-Day Planet/Lonestar Planet,* and a mystery novel, *Murder in the Gun Room.* I think most of Piper's work is again out-of-print here in the late '90s, but the books re-issued during the revival of interest in his work in the '80s, mostly from Ace and Baen, may still be findable in used-book stores and SF convention huckster rooms.

Tortha Karf, Chief of Paratime Police, told himself to stop fretting. Only two hundred odd days till Year-End Day, and then, precisely at midnight, he would rise from this chair and Verkan Vall would sit down in it, and after that he would be free to raise grapes and lemons and wage guerrilla war against the rabbits on the island of Sicily, which he owned on one uninhabited Fifth Level time-line. He wondered how long it would take Vall to become as tired of the chief's seat as he was now.

Vall was tired of it already, in anticipation. He'd never wanted to be chief; prestige and authority meant little to him, and freedom much. It was a job somebody had to do, though, and it was the job for which he had been trained, so Vall would take it, and do it, he suspected, better than he himself had done. The job, policing a near-infinity of different worlds, each one of which was this same planet, Earth, would be safe in the hands of Verkan Vall.

Twelve thousand years ago, facing extinction on an exhausted planet, the First Level race had discovered the existence of a second, lateral dimension of time, and a means of physical transposition to and from the worlds of alternate probability parallel to their own. So the conveyers had gone out by stealth, to bring back wealth in abundance to First Level Home Time-Line, a little from here, a little from there, never enough to be missed.

It all had to be policed. Some Paratimers were unscrupulous in dealing with outtime peoples—he'd have retired five years ago, but for the discovery of a huge paratemporal slave trade, only recently smashed. More often, by somebody's bad luck or indiscretion, the Paratime Secret would be endangered, and that had to be preserved at any cost. Not merely the technique of paratemporal transposition, that went without comment, but the very existence of a race possessing it. If for no other reason, and there were many others, it would be utterly immoral to make any outtime people live with the knowledge that there were among them aliens indistinguishable from themselves, watching and exploiting. So there was the Paratime Police.

Second Level; it had been civilized almost as long as the First, but there had been long Dark-Age interludes. Except for paratemporal transposition, it almost equaled First. Third Level civilization was more recent, but still of respectable antiquity. Fourth Level had started late and

advanced slowly; some Fourth Level genius was inventing agriculture
when the coal-burning steam engine was obsolescent on the Third. And
Fifth Level—on a few time-lines, subhuman brutes, fireless and speechless, were using stones to crack nuts and each other's head; on most of it
nothing even humanoid had evolved.

Fourth Level was the big one. The others had devolved from low-
probability genetic accidents; Fourth had been the maximum probability. It
was divided into many sectors and subsectors, on most of which civilization had first appeared in the Nile and Tigris-Euphrates valleys, and, later,
on the Indus and the Yangtze. Europo-American Sector; they might have to
pull out of that entirely, that would be Chief Verkan's decision. Too many
thermonuclear weapons and too many competing national sovereignties,
always a disaster-fraught combination. That had happened all over Third
Level within Home Time-Line experience. Alexandrian-Roman, off to a
fine start with the pooling of Greek theory and Roman engineering ability,
and then, a thousand years ago, two half-forgotten religions had been rummaged out of the dustbin and their respective proselytes had begun mas-
sacring each other. They were still at it, with pikes and matchlocks, having
lost the ability to make anything better. Europo-American would come to
that, if its competing politico-economic sectarians kept on. Sino-Hindic,
that wasn't a civilization, was a bad case of cultural paralysis. Indo-
Turanian, about where Europo-American had been a thousand years ago.

And Aryan-Oriental; the Aryan migration of three thousand years
ago, instead of moving west and south as on most sectors, had rolled east
into China.

And Aryan-Transpacific, there was one to watch. An off-shoot of
Aryan-Oriental; the conquerors of Japan had sailed north and east along
the Kuriles and Aleutians, and then spread south and east over North
America, bringing with them horses and cattle and iron-working skills,
exterminating the Amerinds, splitting into diverse peoples and cultures.
There was a civilization along the Pacific coast, and nomads on the plains
herding bison and cross-breeding them with Asian cattle, another civilization in the Mississippi Valley, and one around the Great Lakes. And a
new one, only four centuries old, on the Atlantic seaboard and back in the
Appalachians.

The technological level was about that of Europe in the Middle Ages,
a few subsectors slightly higher. But they were going forward. Things, he
thought, were about ripe to happen on Aryan-Transpacific.

Well, let Chief Verkan watch that.

She tried to close her mind to the voices around her, and stared at the
map between the two candlesticks on the table. There was Tarr-Hostigos

overlooking the gap, just a tiny fleck of gold on the parchment, but she could see it all in her mind, the walls, the outer bailey, the citadel and the keep, the watchtower pointing a blunt finger skyward. Below, the little Darro glinted, flowing north to join the Listra and, with it, the broad Athan to the north and east. The town of Hostigos, white walls and slate roofs and busy streets; the checkerboard of fields and forests.

A voice, louder and harsher than the others, brought her back to reality.

"He'll do nothing? What in Dralm's name is a Great King for but to keep the peace?"

She looked along the table, from one to another of them. The speaker for the peasants, at the foot, uncomfortable in his feast-day clothes and ill at ease seated among his betters, the speakers for the artisans and the merchants and the townsfolk, the lesser family members, the sworn landholders. Chartiphon, the captain-in-chief, his blond beard streaked with gray like the gray lead-splashes on his gilded breastplate, his long sword on the table in front of him. Old Xentos, the cowl of his priestly robe thrown back from his snowy head, his blue eyes troubled. And her father, Prince Ptosphes of Hostigos, beside whom she sat at the table-head, his mouth tight between pointed mustache and pointed beard. How long it had been since she had seen a smile on her father's lips!

Xentos passed a hand negatively in front of his face.

"The Great King, Kaiphranos, said that it was every prince's duty to guard his own realm; that it was for Prince Ptosphes to keep raiders out of Hostigos."

"Well, great Dralm, didn't you tell him it wasn't just bandits?" the other voice bullyragged. "They're Nostori soldiers; it's war! Gormoth of Nostor means to take all Hostigos, as his grandfather took Sevenhills Valley after the traitor we don't name sold him Tarr-Dombra!"

That was a part of the map her eyes had shunned, the bowl valley to the east, where Dombra Gap split the mountains. It was from thence the Nostori raiders came.

"And what hope have we from Styphon's House?" her father asked. He knew the answer; he wanted them all to hear it at first hand.

"Chartiphon spoke with them," Xentos said. "The priests of Styphon hold no speech with priests of other gods."

"The archpriest wouldn't talk to me," Chartiphon said. "Only one of the upper priests. He took our offerings and said that he would pray to Styphon for us. When I asked for fireseed, he would give us none."

"None at all?" somebody cried. "Then we are under the ban!"

Her father rapped with the pommel of his poignard.

"You've heard the worst, now," he said. "What's in your minds to do? You first, Phosg."

The peasant leader rose awkwardly, cleared his throat.

"Lord, my cottage is as dear to me as this fine castle is to you," he said. "I'll fight for mine as you would for yours."

There was a quick mutter of approval along the table. The others spoke in their turns, a few tried to make speeches. Chartiphon said only: "Fight. What else?"

"Submission to evil is the worst of all sins," Xentos said. "I am a priest of Dralm, and Dralm is a god of peace, but I say, fight with Dralm's blessing."

"Rylla?" her father asked.

"Better die in armor than live in chains," she said. "When the time comes, I will be in armor with the rest of you."

Her father nodded. "I expect no less from any of you." He rose, and all with him. "I thank you all. At sunset, we dine together; until then, servants will attend you. Now, if you please, leave me with my daughter. Xentos, you and Chartiphon stay."

There was a scrape of chairs, a shuffle of feet going out, a murmur of voices in the hall before the door closed. Chartiphon had begun to fill his stubby pipe.

"Sarrask of Sask won't aid us, of course," her father said.

"Sarrask of Sask's a fool," Chartiphon said shortly. "He should know that when Gormoth's conquered Hostigos, his turn will come next."

"He knows it," Xentos said calmly. "He'll try to strike before Gormoth does. But even if he wanted to, he'd not aid us. Not even King Kaiphranos dares aid those whom the priests of Styphon would destroy."

"They want that land in Wolf Valley, for a temple farm," she said slowly. "I know that would be bad, but—"

"Too late," Xentos told her. "Styphon's House is determined upon our destruction, as a warning to others." He turned to her father. "And it was on my advice, Lord, that you refused them."

"I'd have refused against your advice. I swore long ago that Styphon's House should never come into Hostigos while I lived, and by Dralm neither shall they! They come into a princedom, they build a temple, they make a temple farm, and make slaves of the peasants on it. They tax the prince, and force him to tax the people till nobody has anything left. Look at that temple farm in Sevenhills Valley."

"Yes, you'd hardly believe it," Chartiphon said. "They make the peasants on the farms around cart in their manure, till they have none left for their own fields. Dralm only knows what they do with it." He puffed at his pipe. "I wonder why they want Wolf Valley."

"There's something there that makes the water of those springs taste and smell badly," she considered.

"Sulfur," Xentos said. "But why do they want sulfur?"

Corporal Calvin Morrison, Pennsylvania State Police, crouched in the brush at the edge of the old field and looked across the brook at the farmhouse two hundred yards away, scabrous with peeling yellow paint and festooned by a sagging porchroof. A few white chickens pecked disinterestedly in the littered barnyard; there was no other sign of life, but he knew that there was a man inside. A man with a rifle, who would use it; he had murdered once, broken jail, would murder again.

He looked at his watch; the minute hand was squarely on the nine. Jack French and Steve Kovac would be starting down from the road above where they had left the car. He rose, unsnapping the retaining-strap of his holster.

"I'm starting. Watch that middle upstairs window."

"I'm watching," a voice behind assured him. A rifle action clattered softly as a cartridge went into the chamber. "Luck."

He started forward across the weed-grown field. He was scared, as scared as he'd been the first time, back in '52 in Korea, but there was nothing to do about that. He just told his legs to keep moving, knowing that in a few moments he wouldn't have time to be scared. He was almost to the little brook, his hand close to the butt of his Colt, when it happened.

There was a blinding flash, followed by a moment's darkness. He thought he'd been shot; by pure reflex, the .38-special was in his hand. Then, all around him, a flickering iridescence of many colors glowed, in a perfect hemisphere thirty feet across and fifteen high, and in front of him was an oval desk or cabinet, with an instrument panel over it, and a swivel chair from which a man was turning and rising. Young, well-built; wore loose green trousers and black ankle boots and a pale green shirt; a shoulder holster under his left arm, a weapon in his hand.

He was sure it was a weapon, though it looked more like an electric soldering iron, with two slender metal rods instead of a barrel, joined at the front in a blue ceramic knob. It was probably something that made his own Official Police look like a kid's cap pistol, and it was coming up fast to line on him.

He fired, holding the trigger back to keep the hammer down on the fired chamber, and threw himself down, hearing something fall with a crash, landing on his left hand and his left hip and rolling, until the nacreous dome was gone from around him and he bumped hard against something. For a moment, he lay still, then rose to his feet, letting out the trigger of the Colt.

What he'd bumped into was a tree. That wasn't right, there'd been no trees around, nothing but brush. And this tree, and the others, were huge, great columns rising to support a green roof through which only stray gleams of sunlight leaked. Hemlocks, must have been growing here while Columbus was conning Isabella into hocking her jewelry. Come to think of it, there was a stand of trees like this in Alan Seeger Forest. Maybe that was where he was.

He wondered how he was going to explain this.

"While approaching the house," he began aloud and in a formal tone, "I was intercepted by a flying saucer, the operator of which threatened me with a ray pistol. I defended myself with my revolver, firing one round—"

No. That wouldn't do, at all.

He swung out the cylinder of his Colt, ejecting the fired round and replacing it. Then he looked around, and started in the direction of where the farmhouse ought to be, coming to the little brook and jumping across.

Verkan Vall watched the landscape flicker outside the almost invisible shimmer of the transportation field. The mountains stayed the same, but from one time-line to another there was a good deal of randomness about which tree grew where. Occasionally there were glimpses of open country and buildings and installations, the Fifth Level bases his people had established. The red light overhead winked off and on, and each time it went off, a buzzer sounded. The dome of the conveyer became a solid iridescence, and then a cold, inert metal mesh. The red light came on and stayed on. He was picking up the sigma-ray needler from the desk in front of him and holstering it when the door slid open and a lieutenant of Paratime Police looked in.

"Hello, Chief's Assistant. Any trouble?"

In theory, the Ghaldron-Hesthor transposition field was impenetrable from the outside, but in practice, especially when two conveyers going in opposite paratemporal directions interpenetrated, it would go weak, and outside objects, sometimes alive and hostile, would intrude. That was why Paratimers kept weapons at hand, and why conveyers were checked immediately on emergence; it was also why some Paratimers didn't make it home.

"Not this trip. My rocket ready?"

"Yes, sir. Be a little delay about an aircar for the rocketport." The lieutenant stepped inside, followed by a patrolman, who began taking the transportation record tape and the photo-film record out of the cabinet. "They'll call you when it's in."

He and the lieutenant strolled outside into the noise and color of the conveyer-head rotunda. He got out his cigarette case and offered it; the lieutenant flicked his lighter. They had only taken a few first puffs when another conveyer quietly materialized in a vacant space nearby. A couple of Paracops strolled over as the door opened, drawing their needlers. One peeped inside, then holstered his weapon and snatched a radio phone from his belt; the other entered cautiously. Throwing away his cigarette, he strode toward the newly arrived conveyer, the lieutenant following.

The chair was overturned; a Paracop, his tunic off and his collar open, lay on the floor, a needler a few inches from his outstretched hand. His shirt, pale green, was dark with blood. The lieutenant, without touching him, looked at him.

"Still alive," he said. "Bullet, or sword-thrust?"

"Bullet; I can smell nitro powder." Then he saw the hat lying on the floor, and stepped around the fallen man. Two men were coming in with an antigrav stretcher; they and the patrolmen got the wounded man onto it. "Look at this, lieutenant."

The lieutenant glanced at the hat. It was gray felt, wide-brimmed, the crown peaked with four indentations.

"Fourth Level," he said. "Europo-American."

He picked it up, glancing inside. The sweatband was lettered in gold, JOHN B. STETSON COMPANY. PHILADELPHIA, PA., and, hand-inked, *Cpl. Calvin Morrison, Penna. State Police,* and a number.

"I know that outfit," the lieutenant said. "Good men, every bit as good as ours."

"One was a split second better than one of ours." He got out his cigarette case. "Lieutenant, this is going to be a real baddie. This pickup's going to be missed, and the people who'll miss him will be one of the ten best constabulary organizations in the world on their time-line. They won't be put off with the sort of lame-brained explanations that usually get by on Europo-American. They'll want factual proof and physical evidence. And we'll have to find where he came out. A man who can beat a Paracop to the draw won't sink into obscurity on any time-line. He's going to kick up a fuss that'll have to be smoothed over."

"I hope he doesn't come out on a next-door time-line and turn up at a duplicate of his own police post, where a duplicate of himself is on duty. With identical fingerprints," the lieutenant said. "That would kick up a small fuss."

"Wouldn't it?" He went to the cabinet and took out the synchronized transposition record and photo film. "Have that rocket held; I'll want it after a while. But I'm going over these myself. I'm going to make this operation my own personal baby."

Calvin Morrison dangled black-booted legs over the edge of the low cliff and wished, again, that he hadn't lost his hat. He knew exactly where he was, he was on the little cliff, not more than a big outcrop, above the road where they'd left the car, but there was no road under it now, nor ever had been. And there was a hemlock four feet at the butt growing right where the farmhouse ought to be, and no trace of the stone foundations of it or the barn. But the really permanent features, the Bald Eagles to the north and Nittany Mountain to the south, were exactly as they should be.

That flash and momentary darkness could have been subjective; put that in the unproven column. He was sure the strangely beautiful dome of shimmering light had been real, and so had the oval desk and the instrument panel and the man with the odd weapon. And there was certainly nothing subjective about all this virgin forest where farmlands ought to be.

He didn't for an instant consider questioning either his senses or his sanity; neither did he indulge in dirty language like "incredible," or "impossible." Extraordinary; now there was a good word. He was quite sure that something extraordinary had happened to him. It seemed to break into two parts: (One), the dome of pearly light and what had happened inside it, and, (Two), emerging into this same-but-different place.

What was wrong with both was anachronism, and the anachronisms were mutually contradictory. None of (One) belonged in 1964 or, he suspected, for many centuries to come. None of (Two) belonged in 1964, either, or at any time within two centuries in the past. His pipe had gone out; for a while he forgot to relight it, while tossing those two facts back and forth. Then he got out his lighter and thumbed it, and then buttoned it back in his pocket.

In spite—no, because—of his clergyman father's insistence that he study for and enter the Presbyterian ministry, he was an agnostic. Agnosticism, to him, was refusal either to accept or reject without factual proof. A good philosophy for a cop, by the way. Well, he wasn't going to reject the possibility of time machines; not after having been shanghaied out of his own time in one. Whenever he was, it wasn't the Twentieth Century, and he was never going to get back to it. He made up his mind on that once and for all.

Climbing down from the low cliff, he went to the little brook, and followed it to where it joined a larger stream, just as he knew it would. A bluejay made a fuss at his approach. Two deer ran in front of him. A small black bear regarded him with suspicion and hastened away. Now, if he could find some Indians who wouldn't throw tomahawks first and ask questions afterward . . .

A road dipped to cross the stream. For a moment, he accepted that, then caught his breath. A real, wheel-rutted road! And brown horse-droppings in it; they were the most beautiful things he had seen since he came into this here-and-now. They meant that he hadn't beaten Columbus here, after all. He'd have trouble giving a plausible account of himself, but at least he could do it in English. Maybe he was even in time to get into the Civil War. He waded through the ford and started west along the road, toward where Bellefonte ought to be.

The sun went down in front of him. By now, the big hemlocks were gone, lumbered off, and there was a respectable second growth, mostly hardwoods. Finally, in the dusk, he smelled turned earth beside the road. It was full dark before he saw a light ahead.

The house was only a dim shape, the light came from narrow horizontal windows near the roof. Behind, he thought he could make out stables and, by his nose, pigpens. Two dogs ran into the road and began whauff-whauffing in front of him. "Hello, in there!" he called. Through the open windows he heard voices, a man's, a woman's, another man's. He called again. A bar scraped, and the door swung in. A woman, heavy-bodied, in a dark dress, stood aside for him to enter.

It was all one big room, lighted by one candle on a table and one on the mantel and by the fire on the hearth. Double-deck bunks along one wall, table spread with a meal. There were three men and another woman beside the one who had admitted him, and from the corner of his eye he could see children peering around a door that seemed to open into a shed annex. One of the men, big and blond-bearded, stood with his back to the fire, with something that looked like a short gun in his hands. No it wasn't, either; it was a crossbow, bent and quarrel in place.

The other men were younger, the crossbowman's sons for a guess; they were bearded, too, though one's beard was only a fuzz. They all wore short-sleeved jerkins of leather and cross-gartered hose. One of the younger men had a halberd and the other an axe. The older woman spoke in a whisper to the younger; she went through the door, pushing the children ahead of her.

He lifted his hands pacifically as he entered. "I'm a friend," he said. "I'm going to Bellefonte; how far is it?"

The man with the crossbow said something. The man with the halberd said something. The woman replied. The youth with the axe said something, and they all laughed.

"My name's Calvin Morrison. Corporal, Pennsylvania State Police."
Hell, they wouldn't know the State Police from the Swiss Marines. "Am
I on the road to Bellefonte?"

More back-and-forth. They weren't talking Pennsylvania Dutch, he
was sure of that. Maybe Polish; no, he'd heard enough of that to recognize, if he couldn't understand, it. He looked around, while they argued,
and saw, in the far corner left of the fireplace, three images on a shelf. He
meant to get a closer look at them. Roman Catholics used images, so did
Greek Catholics, and he could tell the difference.

The man with the crossbow laid his weapon down, but kept it bent
and loaded, and spoke slowly and distinctly. It was no language he had
ever heard before. He replied just as distinctly in English. They all looked
at one another, passing their hands in front of their faces in bafflement.
Finally, by signs, they invited him to sit down and eat, and the children,
six of them, trooped in.

The meal was roast ham, potatoes and succotash. The eating tools
were knives and a few horn spoons; the men used their sheath knives. He
took out his jackknife, a big switchblade he'd taken off an arrest he'd
made. It caused a sensation, and he had to demonstrate it several times.
There was also elderberry wine, strong but not particularly good. Then
they left the table for the women to clear, and the men filled pipes from
a tobacco jar on the mantel, offering it to him. He filled his pipe and
lighted it, as they did theirs, with a twig at the fire. Stepping back, he got
a look at the images.

The central figure was an elderly man in a white robe, with a blue
eight-pointed star on the breast. He was flanked, on one side, by a seated
female figure, exaggeratedly pregnant, crowned with a grain, and holding
a cornstalk, and, on the other, by a masculine figure in a male shirt, with
a spiked mace. The only really unusual thing about him was that he had
the head of a wolf. Father-god, fertility-goddess, war-god; no, this gang
weren't Catholics, Greek, Roman or any other kind. He bowed to the central figure, touching his forehead, and repeated the gesture to the other
two. There was a gratified murmur behind him; anybody could see he
wasn't any heathen. Then he sat down on a chest against the wall.

They hadn't re-barred the door. The children had been chased back
into the shed after the meal. Nobody was talking, everybody was listening. Now that he remembered, there had been a vacant place at the table.
They'd sent one of the youngsters off with a message. As soon as he finished his pipe, he pocketed it, and unobtrusively unsnapped the strap of
his holster. It might have been half an hour before he heard galloping
hoofs down the road. He affected not to hear; so did everybody else. The

older man moved over to where he had put down his crossbow; his elder son got the halberd and a rag as though to polish the blade. The horses clattered to a stop outside, accoutrements jingled. The dogs set up a frantic barking. He slipped the .38 out and cocked it.

The youngest man went to the door. Before he could touch it, it flew open in his face, knocking him backward, and a man—bearded face under a high-combed helmet, steel breastplate, black and orange scarf—burst in, swinging a long sword. Everybody in the room shouted in alarm; this wasn't what they'd been expecting, at all. There was another helmeted head behind the first man, and the muzzle of a short musket. Outside, a shot boomed and one of the dogs howled.

He rose from the chest and shot the man with the sword. Half-cocking with the double action and thumbing the hammer the rest of the way, he shot the man with the musket. The musket went off into the ceiling. A man behind caught a crossbow quarrel through the forehead and pitched forward on top of the other two, dropping a long pistol unfired.

Shifting the Colt to his left hand, he caught up the sword the first man had dropped. It was lighter than it looked, and beautifully balanced. He tramped over the bodies in the doorway, to be confronted by another swordsman outside. For a few moments they cut and parried, and then he drove his point into his opponent's unarmored face and tugged his blade free. The man in front of him went down. The boy who had been knocked down had gotten hold of the dropped pistol and fired it, hitting a man who was holding a clump of horses in the road. The older son dashed out with his halberd, chopping a man down. The father had gotten hold of the musket and ammunition, and was ramming a charge into it.

Driving the point of the sword into the ground, he holstered the .38-special; as one of the loose horses dashed past, he caught the reins and stopped it, vaulting into the saddle. Then, stooping, he retrieved his sword, thankful that even in a motorized age the State Police insisted on teaching their men to ride. The fight was over, at least here. Six attackers were down, presumably dead. The other two were galloping away. Five loose horses milled about, and the two young men were trying to catch them. The older man, priming the pan of the gun, came outside, looking around.

This had only been a sideshow fight, though. The main event was half a mile down the road, where he could hear shots, yells, and screams, and where a sudden orange glare mounted into the night. He was wondering just what he'd cut himself into when the fugitives began streaming up the road. He had no trouble identifying them as such; he'd seen enough of that in Korea. Another fire was blazing up beside the first one.

Some of them had weapons, spears and axes, a few bows, and he saw one big musket. His bearded host shouted at them, and they stopped.

"What's going on, down there?" he demanded loudly.

Babble answered him. One or two tried to push past; he hit at them with his flat, cursing them luridly. The words meant nothing, but the tone did. That had worked for him in Korea, too. They all stopped, in a clump; a few cheered. Many were women and children, and not all the men were armed. Call it twenty effectives. The bodies in the road were quickly stripped of weapons; out of the corner of his eye he saw the two women of the house passing things out the door. Four of the riderless horses had been caught and mounted. More fugitives came up, saw what was going on, and joined.

"All right!" he bawled. "You guys want to live forever?" He swung his sword to include all of them, then stabbed down the road with it. "Let's go!"

A cheer went up, and as he started his horse the whole mob poured after him, shouting. They met more fugitives, who stopped, saw that a counterattack had been organized, if that were the word for it, and joined. The firelight was brighter, half a dozen houses must be burning now, but the shooting had stopped. Nobody left to shoot at, he supposed.

Then, when they were halfway to the burning village, there was a blast of forty or fifty shots in less than ten seconds, and more yelling, much of it in alarm. More shots, and then mounted men began streaming up the road; this was a rout. Everybody with guns or bows let fly at them. A horse went down, and another had its saddle emptied. Considering how many shots it had taken for one casualty in Korea, that wasn't bad. He stood up in his stirrups, which were an inch or so too short for him as it was, and yelled, *"Chaaarge!"*—like Teddy, in "Arsenic and Old Lace."

A man coming in the opposite direction aimed a cut at his bare head. He parried and thrust, his point glanced from a breastplate, and before he could recover the other's horse had carried him past and among the spears and pitchforks behind. Then he was trading thrusts for cuts with another rider, wondering if none of these imbeciles ever heard that a sword had a point. By this time, the road for a hundred yards ahead, and the open field on the left, was a swirl of horsemen, chopping and firing at each other.

He got his point in under his opponent's armpit, almost had the sword wrenched from his hand, and then saw another rider coming at him, unarmored and wearing a wide hat and a cloak, aiming a pistol almost as long as the arm that held it. He urged his horse forward, swinging back for a cut at the weapon, and knew that he wouldn't make it. *O.K., Cal; your luck's run out.* There was an upflash from the pan of the pistol, a belch of flame from the muzzle, and something sledged him in the chest.

He hung onto consciousness long enough to kick his feet free of the stirrups. In that last moment, he was aware that the rider who had shot him had been a young girl.

Vekan Vall put the lighter down on the desk and took the cigarette from his mouth. Tortha Karf leaned back in the chair in which he, himself, would be sitting all too soon.

"We had one piece of luck, right at the start. The time-line is one we've already penetrated. One of our people, in a newspaper office in Philadelphia, that's the nearest large city, reported the disappearance. The press associations have it already, there's nothing we can do about that."

"Well, just what did happen, on the pickup time-line?"

"This Corporal Morrison and three other State Policemen were closing in on a house in which a wanted criminal was hiding. Morrison and another man were in front; the other two were coming in from behind. Morrison started forward, his companion covering for him with a rifle. This other man is the nearest to a witness there is, and he was watching the front of the house and was only marginally aware of Morrison. He heard the other two officers pounding on the back door and demanding admittance, and then the man they were after burst out the front door with a rifle in his hands. Morrison's companion shouted at him to halt; the criminal raised his rifle, and the State Police officer shot him, killing him instantly.

"Then, he says, he realized that Morrison was nowhere in sight. He called to him, without answer. The man they were after was dead, he wouldn't run off, so all three of them hunted for Morrison for almost half an hour. Then they took the body in to the county seat and had to go through a lot of formalities, and it was evening before they were back at their substation. A local reporter happened to be there at the time. He got the story, including the disappearance of Morrison, phoned it to his paper, and the press associations got it from there. Now the State Police refuse to discuss, and are even trying to deny, the disappearance."

"They believe their man lost his nerve, bolted, and is now ashamed to come back," Tortha Karf said. "Naturally they wouldn't want anything like that getting out. Are you going to use that line?"

He nodded. "The hat he lost in the conveyer. It will be planted about a mile from the scene, along a stream. Then one of our people will catch a local, preferably a boy of twelve or so, give him a hypno-injection, and instruct him to find the hat and take it to the State Police. The reporter responsible for the original news break will be notified by anonymous phone call. Later, there will be the usual spate of rumors of Morrison having been seen in all sorts of unlikely places."

"How about his family?"

"We're in luck there, too. Unmarried, parents both dead, only a few relatives with whom he didn't maintain contact."

"That's good. How about the exit?"

"We have that approximated; Aryan-Transpacific. We're not quite sure even of the sector, because the transposition field was weak for several thousand parayears and we can't determine the instant he broke out of the conveyer. It'll be thirty or forty days before we have it pinpointed. We have one positive indication to look for at the scene."

The chief nodded. "The empty cartridge?"

"Yes. He used a revolver, they don't eject automatically. As soon as he was out and no longer immediately threatened, he would open his revolver, remove the empty, and replace it. I'm as sure of that as though I saw him do it. We may not be able to find it, but if we do, it'll be positive proof."

He woke, in bed under soft covers, and for a moment lay with his eyes closed. There was a clicking sound near him, and from a distance an anvil rang, and there was shouting. Then he opened his eyes. He was in a fairly large room, paneled walls and a painted ceiling; two windows on one side, both open, and nothing but blue sky visible through them. A woman, stout and gray-haired, sat under one, knitting. His boots stood beside a chest across the room, and on its top were piled his clothes and his belt and revolver. A long unsheathed sword with a swept handguard and a copper pommel leaned against the wall by the boots. His body was stiff and sore, and his upper torso was swathed in bandages.

The woman looked up quickly as he stirred, then put down her knitting and rose, going to a table and pouring water for him. Pitcher and cup were silver, elaborately chased. He took the cup, drank, and handed it back, thanking her. She replaced it on the table and went out.

He wasn't a prisoner, the presence of the sword and revolver proved that. This was the crowd that had surprised the raiders at the village. That whole business had been a piece of luck for him. He ran a hand over his chin and estimated about three days' growth of stubble. His fingernails had grown enough since last trimmed to confirm that. He'd have a nasty hole in his chest, and possibly a broken rib.

The woman returned, accompanied by a man in a cowled blue robe with an eight-pointed white star on his breast. Reversed colors from the image at the peasant's farm; a priest, doubling as doctor. The man laid a hand on his brow, felt his pulse, and spoke in a cheerfully optimistic tone; the bedside manner seemed to be a universal constant. With the woman's help, he changed the bandages and smeared the wound with ointment.

The woman took out the old bandages and returned with a steaming bowl. It was turkey broth, with finely minced meat in it. While he was finishing it, two more visitors entered.

One was robed like the doctor, his cowl thrown back. He had white hair, and a good face, gentle and pleasant. His companion was a girl with blond hair cut in what would be a page-boy bob in the Twentieth Century; she had blue eyes and red lips and an impudent tilty little nose dusted with golden freckles. She wore a jerkin of something like brown suede, stitched with gold thread, a yellow under-tunic with long sleeves and a high neck, knit hose and thigh-length boots. There was a gold chain around her neck, and a gold-hilted dagger on her belt. He began to laugh when he saw her; they'd met before.

"You shot me!" he accused, then aimed an imaginary pistol, said, "Bang!" and pointed to his chest.

She said something to the older priest, he replied, and she said something to him, pantomiming shame and sorrow, covering her face with one hand and winking at him over it. When he laughed, she laughed with him. Perfectly natural mistake, she hadn't known which side he was on. The two priests held a lengthy colloquy, and the younger brought him about four ounces of something in a tumbler. It tasted alcoholic and medicinally bitter. They told him, by signs, to go to sleep, and went out, all but the gray-haired woman, who went back to her chair and her knitting. He dozed off.

Late in the afternoon he woke briefly. Outside, somebody was drilling troops. Tramping feet, a voice counting cadence, long-drawn preparatory commands, sharp commands, of execution, clattering equipment. That was another universal constant. He smiled; he wasn't going to have much trouble finding a job, here-and-now, whenever now was.

It wasn't the past. Penn's Colony had never been like this. It was more like Sixteenth Century Europe, but no Sixteenth Century cavalryman, who was as incompetent a swordsman as that gang he'd been fighting, would have lived to wear out his first pair of issue boots. And two years in college and a lot of independent reading had given him at least a nodding acquaintance with most of the gods of his own history, and none, back to Egypt and Sumeria, had been like that trio on the peasant's shrine shelf.

So it was the future. A far future, maybe a thousand years later than 1964, A.D.; a world devastated by atomic wars, blasted back to the Stone Age, and then bootstrap-lifted to something like the end of the Middle Ages. That wasn't important, though. Now was when he was, and now was when he was stuck.

Make the best of it, Cal. You're a soldier; you just got re-assigned, that's all.

He went back to sleep.

The next morning, after breakfast, he sign-talked the woman watching over him to bring him his tunic, and got out his pipe and tobacco and lighter from the pockets. She brought him a stool to set beside the bed to put things on. The badge on the tunic breast was twisted and lead-splotched; that was why he was still alive.

The old priest and the girl were in, an hour later. This time, she was wearing a red and gray knit frock that could have gone into Bergdorf Goodman's window with a $200 price-tag any day, but the dagger she wore with it wasn't exactly Fifth Avenue. They greeted him, then pulled chairs up beside the bed and got to business.

First they taught him words for "You," and "Me," and "He," and "She," and names. The girl was Rylla. The old priest was Xentos. The younger priest, who came in to see his patient, was Mytron. Calvin Morrison puzzled them; evidently they didn't have surnames here-and-now. They settled for calling him Kalvan. They had several shingle-sized boards of white pine, and sticks of charcoal, to draw pictures. Rylla smoked a pipe, with a small stone bowl and a cane stem, which she carried on her belt along with her dagger. His lighter intrigued her, and she showed him her own. It was a tinderbox, the flint held down by a spring against a semicircular striker which was pushed by hand and returned for another push by a spring. With a spring to drive the striker instead of returning it, it would have done for a gunlock. By noon, they were able to tell him that he was their friend, and he was able to tell Rylla he didn't blame her for shooting him in the skirmish on the road.

They were back in the afternoon, accompanied by a gentleman with a gray mustache and imperial, wearing a garment like a fur-collared bathrobe, with a sword-belt over it. He had a large gold chain around his neck. His name was Ptosphes, and after much pantomime and picture-writing it emerged that he was Rylla's father, that he was Prince of this place, and that this place was Hostigos. Rylla's mother was dead. The raiders with whom he had fought had come from a place called Nostor, to the north and east, ruled by a Prince Gormoth. Gormoth was not well thought of in Hostigos.

The next day, he was up in a chair, and they began giving him solid food, and wine. The wine was excellent; so was the tobacco they gave him. He decided he was going to like it, here-and-now. Rylla was in at least twice a day, sometimes alone, sometimes with Xentos, and sometimes with a big man with a graying beard, Chartiphon, who seemed to be Ptosphes' top soldier. He always wore a sword, and often an ornate but battered steel back-and-breast. Sometimes he visited alone, and occasionally accompanied by a younger officer, a cavalryman named Harmakros. Harmakros had been in the skirmish at the raided village, but Rylla had been in command.

"The gods," he explained, "did not give Prince Ptosphes a son. A Prince should have a son, to rule after him, so the Princess Rylla must be a son to him."

The gods, he thought, ought to be persuaded to furnish Ptosphes with a son-in-law, named Calvin Morrison, no, Kalvan. He made up his mind to give the gods a hand on that.

Chartiphon showed him a map, elaborately illuminated on parchment. Hostigos appeared to be all of Centre and Union counties, a snip of Clinton south and west of where Lock Haven ought to be, and southeastern Lycoming, east of the West Branch, which was the Athan, and south of the Bald Eagles, the Mountains of Hostigos. Nostor was the West Branch Valley from above Lock Haven to the forks of the river, and it obtruded south into Hostigos through Ante's Gap, Dombra Gap, to take in Nippenose, Sevenhills Valley. To the west, all of Blair County, and parts of Huntington and Bedford, was the Princedom of Sask, ruled by Prince Sarrask. Sarrask was no friend; Gormoth was an open enemy.

On a bigger map, he saw that all Pennsylvania and Maryland, Delaware and the southern half of New Jersey, was the Great Kingdom of Hos-Harphax, ruled from Harphax City at the mouth of the Susquehanna by King Kaiphranos. Ptosphes, Gormoth, Sarrask and a dozen other princes were his nominal subjects. Judging from what he had seen on the night of his advent here-and-now, Kaiphranos' authority would be maintained for about one day's infantry march around his capital and ignored elsewhere.

He had a suspicion that Hostigos was in a bad squeeze, between Nostor and Sask. Something was bugging these people. Too often, while laughing with him—she was teaching him to read and write, now, and that was fun—Rylla would remember something she wanted to forget, and then her laughter would be strained. Chartiphon was always preoccupied; occasionally he'd forget, for a moment, what he was talking about. And he never saw Ptosphes smile.

Xentos showed him a map of the world. The world, it seemed, was not round, but flat like a pancake. Hudson's Bay was in the exact center, North America was shaped rather like India, Florida ran almost due east and Cuba north and south. The West Indies were a few random spots to show that the mapmaker had heard about them from somebody. Asia was

THE GOOD STUFF

attached to North America, but it was still blank. An illimitable ocean
stretched around the perimeter. Europe, Africa and South America simply
weren't. Xentos wanted him to show the country from which he had
come. He put his finger down on central Pennsylvania's approximate location. Xentos thought he misunderstood.

"No, Kalvan. This is your home now, and we want you to stay with
us, but where is the country you came from?"

"Here," he insisted. "But at another time, a thousand years from now.
I had an enemy, an evil sorcerer. Another sorcerer, who was my friend,
put a protection on me that I might not be slain by sorcery, so my enemy
twisted time around me and hurled me far into the past, before my first
known ancestor had been born, and now here I am and here I must stay."

Xentos' hand made a quick circle around the white star on his breast,
and he muttered rapidly. Another universal constant.

"What a terrible fate!"

"Yes. I do not like to speak of it, but it was right that you should
know. You may tell Prince Ptosphes and Princess Rylla and Chartiphon,
but beg them not to speak of it to me. I must forget my old life and make
a new one in this time. You may tell the others merely that I come from a
far country. From here." He indicated the approximate location of Korea.
"I was there, once, fighting in a great war."

"Ah; I knew you had been a warrior." Xentos hesitated, then asked:
"Do you know sorcery?"

"No. My father was a priest, as you are, and wished me to become a
priest also, and our priest hated sorcery. But I knew that I would never be
a good priest, so when this war came, I left my studies and went to fight.
Afterward, I was a warrior in my own country, to keep the peace."

Xentos nodded. "If one cannot be a good priest, one should not be a
priest at all, and to be a good warrior is almost as good. Tell me, what
gods did your people worship?"

"Oh, we had many gods. There was Conformity, and Authority, and
Opinion. And there was Status, whose symbols were many and who rode
in the great chariot Cadillac, which was almost a god itself. And there
was Atombomb, the dread Destroyer, who would someday end the
world. For myself, I worshiped none of them. Tell me about your gods,
Xentos."

Then he filled his pipe and lit it with the tinderbox he had learned to
use in place of his now fuelless Zippo. He didn't need to talk any more;
Xentos was telling him about his own god, Dralm, and about Yirtta the
All-Mother, and wolf-headed Galzar the god of battle, and Tranth the
lame craftsman—funny how often craftsman-gods were lame—and about
all the others.

"And Styphon," he added grudgingly. "Styphon is an evil god, and evil men serve him, and are given great wealth and power."

After that, he noticed a subtle change in manner toward him. He caught Rylla looking at him in wondering pity. Chartiphon merely clasped his hand and said, "You'll like it here with us, Kalvan." Prince Ptosphes hemmed and hawed, and said: "Xentos tells me there are things you don't want to talk about, Kalvan. Nobody will mention them to you, ever. We're all happy to have you with us. Stay, and make this your home."

The others treated him with profound respect. They'd been told that he was a prince from a distant land, driven from his throne by treason. They gave him clothes, more than he had ever owned before, and weapons. Rylla gave him a pair of her own pistols, one of which had wounded him in the skirmish. They were two feet long, but lighter than his .38 Colt, the barrels almost paper-thin at the muzzles. They had locks operating on the same principle as the tinderboxes, and Rylla's name was inlaid in gold on the butts. They gave him another, larger room, and a body servant.

As soon as he was able to walk unaided, he went outside to watch the troops being drilled. They had no uniforms except scarves or sashes of Ptosphes' colors, red and blue. The infantry wore leather or canvas jacks sewn with metal plates, and helmets not unlike the one he'd worn in Korea. Some had pikes, some halberds, and some hunting spears, and many had scythe blades with the tangs straightened out, on eight-foot shafts. Foot movements were simple and uncomplicated; the squad was unknown, and they maneuvered by platoons of forty or fifty.

A few of the firearms were huge fifteen-pound muskets, aimed and fired from rests. Most were lighter, arquebuses, calivers, and a miscellany of hunting guns. There would be two or three musketeers and a dozen calivermen or arquebusiers to each spear-and-scythe platoon. There were also archers and crossbowmen. The cavalry were good; they wore cuirasses and high-combed helmets, and were armed with swords and pistols and either lances or short musketoons. The artillery was laughable; wrought-iron six- to twelve-pounders, hand-welded tubes strengthened with shrunk-on bands, without trunnions. They were mounted on four-wheel carts. He made up his mind to do something about that.

He also noticed that while the archers and crossbowmen practiced constantly, not a single practice shot was fired with any firearm.

He took his broadsword to the castle bladesmith and wanted it ground down into a rapier. The bladesmith thought he was crazy. He called in a cavalry lieutenant and demonstrated with a pair of wooden practice swords. Immediately, the lieutenant wanted a rapier, too. The blacksmith promised to make both of them real rapiers. By the next evening, his own was finished.

"You have enemies on both sides, Nostor and Sask, and that's not good," he said one evening as he and Ptosphes and Rylla and Xentos and Chartiphon sat over a flagon of wine in the Prince's study. "You've made me one of you. Now tell me what I can do to help."

"Well, Kalvan," Ptosphes said, "you could better tell us that. You know many things we don't. The thrusting sword"—he glanced down admiringly at his own new rapier—"and what you told Chartiphon about mounting cannon. What else can you give us to help fight our enemies?"

"Well, I can't teach you to make weapons like that six-shooter of mine, or ammunition for it." He tried, as simply as possible, to explain about machine industry and mass production; they only stared in uncomprehending wonder. "I can show you things you don't know but can do with the tools you have. For instance, we cut spiral grooves in the bores of our guns to make the bullets spin. Grooved guns will shoot harder, farther and straighter than smoothbores. I can show your gunsmiths how to do that with guns you already have. And there's another thing." He mentioned never having seen any practice firing. "You have very little powder, fireseed, you call it. Is that it?"

"We haven't enough in Hostigos to fire all the cannon of this castle once," Chartiphon said. "And we can't get any. The priests of Styphon will give us none, and they send cart after cart of it to Nostor."

"You mean, you get fireseed from the priests of Styphon? Can't you get it from anybody else, or make your own?"

They all looked at him, amazed that he didn't know any better.

"Only Styphon's House can make fireseed, and that by Styphon's aid," Xentos said. "That was what I meant when I said that Styphon gives his servants great wealth, and power even over the Great Kings."

He gave Styphon's House the grudging respect any good cop gives a really smart crook. Styphon's House had a real racket. No wonder this country was a snakepit of warring princes and barons. Styphon's House wanted it that way; it kept them in the powder business. He set down his goblet and laughed.

"You think nobody can make fireseed but Styphon's House?" he demanded. "Why, in my time, even the children could do that." Well, children who got as far as high school chemistry; he'd almost gotten expelled, once. "I can make fireseed, right here on this table!"

Ptosphes threw back his head and laughed. Just a trifle hysterically, but it was the first time he'd ever heard the Prince laugh. Chartiphon banged a fist on the table and shouted, "Ha, Gormoth! Now see how soon your head goes up over your own gate!" And no War Crimes foolishness about it, either. Rylla flung her arms around him. "Kalvan! You really and truly can?"

"But it is only by the power of Styphon . . ." Xentos began.

"Styphon's a big fake; his priests are a pack of impudent swindlers. You want to see me make fireseed? Get Mytron in here; he has everything I need in his dispensary. I want sulfur, he has that, and saltpeter, he has that." Mytron gives sulfur mixed with honey for colds; saltpeter was supposed to cool the blood. "And charcoal, and a couple of brass mortars and pestles, and a flour-screen, and balance-scales."

"Go on, man; hurry!" Ptosphes cried. "Bring him anything he wants."

Xentos went out. He asked for a pistol, and Ptosphes brought one from a closet behind him. He opened the pan and dumped out the priming on a sheet of parchment, touching it off with a lighted splinter. It scorched the parchment, which it shouldn't have, and left too much black residue. Styphon wasn't a very honest powdermaker; he cheapened his product with too much charcoal and not enough saltpeter. Xentos returned, accompanied by Mytron; the two priests carried jars, and a bucket of charcoal, and the other things. Xentos seemed dazed; Mytron was scared and trying not to show it.

He put Mytron to work grinding charcoal in one mortar and Xentos to grinding saltpeter in the other. The sulfur was already pulverized. Screening each, he mixed them in a dry goblet, saltpeter .75, charcoal .15, sulfur .10; he had to think a little to remember that.

"But it's just dust," Chartiphon objected.

"Yes. The mixture has to be moistened, worked into a dough, pressed into cakes and dried, and then ground and sieved. We can't do all that now, but this will flash. Look."

He primed the pistol with a pinch of it, aimed at a half burned log in the fireplace, and squeezed. The pistol roared and kicked. Ptosphes didn't believe in reduced charges, that was for sure. Outside, somebody shouted, feet pounded, and the door flew open. A guard with a halberd looked in.

"The Lord Kalvan is showing us something with a pistol," Ptosphes said. "There may be more shots; nobody is to worry."

"All right," he said, when the guard closed the door. "Now we see how it fires." He poured in about forty grains, wadded it with a bit of rag, and primed it, handing it to Rylla. "You fire. This is a great moment in the history of Hostigos. I hope."

She pushed down the striker, aimed into the fireplace and squeezed. The report wasn't quite as loud, but it did fire. They tried it with a bullet, which went into the log half an inch. He laid the pistol on the table. The room was full of smoke, and they were all coughing, but nobody cared. Chartiphon went to the door and bawled into the hall for more wine.

"But you said no prayers," Mytron faltered. "You just made fireseed. Just like cooking soup."

"That's right. And soon everybody will make fireseed."

And when that day comes, the priests of Styphon will be out on the sidewalk beating a drum for pennies. Chartiphon wanted to know how soon they would be able to march on Nostor.

"It will take more fireseed than Kalvan can make here on this table," Ptosphes told him. "We will need saltpeter, and charcoal, and sulfur. We will have to teach people how to get these things, and grind and mix them. We will need things we don't have, and tools to make them. And nobody knows all this but Kalvan, and there is only one of him."

Well, glory be, Ptosphes had gotten something from the lecture on production, if nobody else had.

"Mytron knows a few things, I think. Where did you get the sulfur and the saltpeter?" he asked the doctor-priest.

Mytron had downed his first goblet of wine at one gulp. He had taken three to the second; now he was working his way down the third and coming out of shock nicely. It was about as he thought. The saltpeter was found in crude lumps under manure piles and refined; the sulfur was gotten by evaporating water from the sulfur springs in Sugar Valley, Wolf Valley here-and-now. For some reason, mention of this threw both Ptosphes and Chartiphon into a fury. He knew how to extract both, on a quart-jar scale. He was a trifle bewildered when told how much would be needed for military purposes.

"But this'll take time," Chartiphon objected. "And as soon as Gormoth hears about it, he'll attack, before we can get any made."

"Don't let him hear about it. Clamp down the security." He had to explain that. "Cavalry patrols, on all the roads and trails out of Hostigos; let anybody in, but don't let anybody out. And here's another thing. I'll have to give orders, and people won't like them. Will I be obeyed?"

"By anybody who wants to keep his head on his shoulders," Ptosphes said. "You speak with my voice."

"And with mine, Lord Kalvan!" Chartiphon was on his feet, extending his sword for him to touch the hilt. "I am at your orders; you command here."

They gave him a room inside the main gateway of the citadel, across from the guardroom, a big flagstone-floored place with the indefinable but unmistakable flavor of a police court. The walls were white plaster, he could write and draw diagrams on them with charcoal. Paper was unknown, here-and-now. He decided to do something about that, after the war. It was a wonder these people had gotten as far as they had without it. Rylla attached herself to him as adjutant. He gathered in Mytron and the chief priest of Tranth, all the master-artisans in Tarr-Hostigos and some from Hostigo Town, a couple of Chartiphon's officers, and some soldiers to carry messages.

Charcoal was going to be easy, there was plenty of that. For sulfur evaporation he'd need big pans, and sheet iron, larger than a breastplate or a cooking pan—all unavailable. There were bog-iron mines over in Bald Eagle, Listra Valley, and ironworks, but no rolling mill. They'd have to beat sheet iron out by hand in two-foot squares and weld them together like a patch quilt. Saltpeter could be accumulated from all over. Manure piles, at least one to a farm, were the best source, and stables, cellars, underground drains. He set up a saltpeter commission, headed by one of Chartiphon's officers, with authority to go anywhere and enter anything, to hang any subordinate who abused that authority out of hand, and to deal just as summarily with anybody who tried to obstruct.

Mobile units, oxcarts loaded with caldrons, tubs, tools and the like, to go from farm to farm. Peasant women to be collected and taught to leach nitrated soil and purify nitrates.

Grinding mills; there was plenty of water power, and the water wheel was known, here-and-now. Gristmills could be converted. Special grinding equipment, designing of. Sifting screens, cloth. Mixing machines, big casks with counter-rotating paddle wheels inside. Presses to squeeze dough into cakes. Mills to grind caked powder; he spent considerable thought on a set of regulations to prevent anything from striking a spark around them, with bloodthirsty enforcement threats.

During the morning, he ground up the cake he'd made the night before, running it through a couple of sieves to FFFg fineness. A hundred-grain charge in one of the big eight-bore muskets drove the two-ounce ball an inch deeper into a log than an equal charge of Styphon's Best, and fouled the bore much less.

By noon, he was almost sure that most of his War Production Board understood most of what he'd told them. In the afternoon, there was a meeting in the outer bailey of as many of the people who would be working on the Fireseed Project as could be collected. There was an invocation of Dralm by Xentos. Ptosphes spoke, bearing down heavily on the fact that the Lord Kalvan had full authority and would be backed to the limit, by the headsman if necessary. Chartiphon made a speech, picturing the howling wilderness they were going to make of Nostor. He made a speech, himself, emphasizing that there was nothing whatever of a supernatural nature about fireseed. The meeting then broke up into small groups, everybody having his own job explained to him. He was kept running back and forth from one to another to explain to the explainers.

In the evening, they had a feast. By that time, he and Rylla had gotten a rough table of organization charcoaled onto the wall in his headquarters.

Of the next four days, he spent eighteen hours of each in that room, talking to five or six hundred people. The artisans, who had a guild organization, objected to peasants invading their crafts. The masters complained that the apprentices and young journeymen were becoming intractable, which meant that they had started thinking for themselves. The peasants objected to having their dunghills forked down and the ground under them dug up, and to being put to unaccustomed work. The landlords objected to having the peasants taken from the fields, and predicted that the year's crop would be lost.

"Don't worry about that," he told them. "If we win, we'll eat Gormoth's crops. If we lose, we'll all be too dead to eat."

And the Iron Curtain went down. Itinerant pack traders and wagoners began to collect in Hostigos Town, trapped for the duration. Sooner or later, Gormoth and Sarrask would start wondering why nobody was leaving Hostigos, and send spies in through the woods to find out. Organize some counterespionage; get a few spies of his own into both princedoms.

By the fifth day, the sulfur-evaporation plant was operating, and saltpeter production had started, only a few pounds of each, but that would increase rapidly. He put Mytron in charge of the office, and went out to supervise mill construction. It was at this time that he began wearing armor, at least six and often eight hours a day—helmet over a padded coif, with a band of fine-linked mail around his throat and under his chin, steel back-and-breast over a quilted arming-doublet with mail sleeves, mail under the arms, and a mail skirt to below his hips, and double leather hose with mail between. The whole panoply weighed close to forty pounds, and his life was going to depend on accustoming himself to it.

Verkan Vall watched Tortha Karf spin the empty cartridge on the top of his desk. It was a very valuable empty cartridge; it had cost over ten thousand man-hours of crawling on hands and knees and pawing among dead hemlock needles, not counting transposition time.

"A marvel you found it, Vall. Aryan-Transpacific?"

"Oh, yes. We were sure of that from the first. Styphon's House subsector." He gave the numerical designation of the exact time-line.

"Styphon's House. That's that gunpowder theocracy, isn't it?"

That was it. At one time, Styphon had been a minor god of healing. Still was, on most of Aryan-Transpacific. But, three hundred years ago, on one time-line, a priest of Styphon, trying to concoct a new remedy for something, had mixed a batch of saltpeter, charcoal and sulfur—fortunately for him, a small batch—and put it on the fire. For fifty years, the mixture had been a temple miracle, and then its propellant properties were discovered, and Styphon had gone out of medical practice and into the munitions business. The powder had been improved by priestly researchers; weapons to use it were designed. Now no king or prince without gunpowder stood a chance against one with it. No matter who sat on any throne, Styphon's House was his master, because Styphon's House could throw him off it at will.

"I wonder if this Morrison knows how to make gunpowder," Tortha Karf said.

"I'll find that out. I'm going out there myself."

"You don't have to, you know. You have hundreds of men who could do that."

He shook his head obstinately. "After Year-End Day, I'm going to be chained to that chair of yours. But until then, I'm going to work outtime as much as I can." He leaned over to the map-screen and twiddled the selector until he had the Great Kingdom of Hos-Harphax. "I'm going in about here," he said. "I'll be a pack trader, they go anywhere without question. I'll have a saddle horse and three pack horses, with loads of appropriate merchandise. That's in the adjoining princedom of Sask. I'll travel slowly, to let word travel ahead of me. I may even hear something about this Morrison before I enter Hostigos."

"What'll you do when you find him?"

He shrugged. "That will depend on what he's doing, and particularly how he's accounting for himself. I don't want to, the man's a police officer like ourselves, but I'm afraid I'm going to have to kill him. He knows too much."

"What does he know, Vall?"

"First, he's seen the inside of a conveyer. He knows that it was something completely alien to his own culture and technology. Then, he knows that he was shifted in time, because he wasn't shifted to another place, and he will recognize that the conveyer was the means affecting that shift. From that, he will deduce a race of time-travelers.

"Now, he knows enough of the history of his own time-line to know that he wasn't shifted into the past. And he will also know he wasn't shifted into the future. That's all limestone country, where he was picked up and dropped, and on his own time-line it's been quarried extensively for the past fifty or more years. Traces of those operations would remain for tens of thousands of years, and he will find none of them. So what does that leave?"

"A lateral shift, and people who travel laterally in time," the chief said. "Why, that's the Paratime Secret itself."

There would be a feast at Tarr-Hostigos that evening. All morning cattle and pigs, lowing and squealing, had been driven in and slaughtered. Woodcutters' axes thudded for the roasting pits, casks of wine came up from the cellars. He wished the fireseed mills were as busy as the castle kitchens and bakeries. A whole day's production shot to hell. He said as much to Rylla.

"But, Kalvan, they're all so happy." She was pretty excited about it, herself. "And they've worked so hard."

He had to grant that, and maybe the morale gain would offset a day's work lost. And they had a full hundredweight of fireseed, fifty percent better than Styphon's Best, and half of it made in the last two days.

"It's been so long since anybody had anything to be happy about. When we had feasts, everybody would get drunk as soon as they could, to keep from thinking about what was coming. And now, maybe it won't come at all."

And now, they were all drunk on a hundred pounds of black powder. Five thousand arquebus rounds at the most. They'd have to do better than twenty-five pounds a day; have to get it up to a hundred. Mixing, caking and grinding was the bottleneck, that meant still more mill machinery, and there weren't enough men able to build it. It would mean stopping work on the rifling machinery, and on the carriages and limbers for the light four-pounders the ironworks were turning out.

It would take a year to build the sort of army he wanted, and Gormoth or Nostor would attack in two months at most.

He brought that up, that afternoon, at General Staff meeting. Like rifling and trunnions on cannon and teaching swordsmen to use the point, that was new for here-and-now. You just hauled a lot of peasants together and armed them, that was Organization. You picked a march-route, that was Strategy. You lined up your men somehow and shot or hit anybody in front of you, that was Tactics. And Intelligence was something mounted scouts, if any, brought in at the last moment from a mile ahead. It cheered him to recall that that would be Gormoth's idea of the Art of War. Why, with ten thousand men Gustavus Adolphus or the Duke of Parma or Gonzalo de Córdoba could have gone through all five of these Great Kingdoms like a dose of croton oil.

Ptosphes and Rylla were present *ex officio* as Prince and Heiress-Apparent. The Lord Kalvan was Commander-in-Chief. Chartiphon was

Field Marshal and Chief of Operations. Harmakros was G-2, an elderly infantry captain was drillmaster, paymaster, quartermaster, inspector-general and head of the draft board. A civilian merchant, who wasn't losing any money on it, was in charge of supply and procurement. Xentos, who was Ptosphes' chancellor as well as chief ecclesiastic, attended to political matters, and also fifth-column activities, another of Lord Kalvan's marvelous new ideas, mainly because he was in touch with the priests of Dralm in Nostor and Sask, all of whom hated Styphon's House beyond expression.

The first blaze of optimism had died down, he was glad to observe. Chartiphon was grumbling:

"We have three thousand at most; Gormoth has ten thousand, six thousand mercenaries and four thousand of his own people. Making our own fireseed gives us a chance, which we didn't have before, but that's all."

"Two thousand of his own people," somebody said. "He won't take the peasants out of the fields."

"Then he'll attack earlier," Ptosphes said. "While our peasants are getting the harvest in."

He looked at the map painted on one of the walls. Gormoth could invade up the Listra Valley, but that would only give him half of Hostigos—less than that. The whole line of the Mountains of Hostigos was held at every gap except one. Dombra Gap, guarded by Tarr-Dombra, lost by treachery three quarters of a century ago, and Sevenhills Valley behind it.

"We'll have to take Tarr-Dombra and clean Sevenhills Valley out," he said.

Everybody stared at him. It was Chartiphon who first found his voice.

"Man! You never saw Tarr-Dombra, or you wouldn't talk like that. It's smaller than Tarr-Hostigos, but it's even stronger."

"That's right," the retread captain who was G-1 and part of G-4 supported him.

"Do the Nostori think it can't be taken, too?" he asked. "Then it can be. Prince, have you plans of the castle?"

"Oh, yes. On a big scroll, in one of my coffers. It was my grandfather's, and we always hoped . . ."

"I'll want to see them. Later will do. Do you know of any changes made on it since?"

Not on the outside, at least. He asked about the garrison; five hundred, Harmakros thought. A hundred regular infantry of Gormoth's, and four hundred cavalry for patrolling around the perimeter of Sevenhills

Valley. They were mercenaries, and they were the ones who had been
raiding into Hostigos.

"Then stop killing raiders who can be taken alive. Prisoners can be
made to talk." The Geneva Convention was something else unknown
here-and-now. He turned to Xentos. "Is there a priest of Dralm in Sevenhills Valley? Can you get in touch with him, and will he help us? Explain
that this is a war against Styphon's House."

"He knows that, and he will help, as he can. But he can't get into
Tarr-Dombra. There is a priest of Galzar there for the mercenaries, and a
priest of Styphon for the lord of the castle. Among the Nostori, Dralm is
but a god for the peasants."

That rankled. Yes, the priests of Dralm would help.

"All right. But he can talk to people who can get in, can't he? And he
can send messages, and organize an espionage apparatus among his peasants. I want to know everything that can be found out, no matter how trivial. Particularly, I want to know the guard-routine at the castle, and how
it's supplied. And I want it observed all the time; Harmakros, you find
men to do that. I take it we can't storm the place, or you'd have done that
long ago. Then we'll have to surprise it."

Verkan the pack trader went up the road, his horse plodding unhurriedly and the pack horses on the lead-line trailing behind. He was hot
and sticky under his steel back-and-breast, and sweat ran down his cheeks
from under his helmet into his new beard, but nobody ever saw an unarmed pack trader, so he had to endure it. They were local-made, from an
adjoining near-identical time-line, and so were his clothes, his sword, the
carbine in the saddle sheath, his horse gear, and the loads of merchandise,
all except a metal coffer on top of one pack load.

Reaching the brow of the hill, he started down the other side, and as
he did he saw a stir in front of a thatched and whitewashed farm cottage.
Men mounting horses; glints of armor, and red-and-blue Hostigi colors.
Another cavalry post, the third he'd passed since crossing the border from
Sask. The other two had ignored him, but this crowd meant to stop him.
Two had lances, the third a musketoon, and the fourth, who seemed to be
in command, had his holsters open and his right hand on his horse's neck.

He reined in his horse; the pack horses came to a well-trained stop.

"Good cheer, soldiers," he greeted.

"Good cheer, trader," the man with his hand close to his pistol-butt
replied. "From Sask?"

"Sask last. From Ulthor, this trip; Grefftscharr by birth." Ulthor was
the lake port to the northwest; Grefftscharr was the kingdom around the
Great Lakes. "I'm for Agrys City."

One of the troopers laughed. The sergeant asked: "Have you any fire-seed?"

"About twenty charges." He touched the flask on his belt. "I tried to get some in Sask, but when the priests of Styphon heard that I was coming through Hostigos they'd give me none."

"I know; we're under the ban, here." It did not seem to distress him greatly. "But I'm afraid you'll not see Agrys soon. We're on the edge of war with Nostor, and the Lord Kalvan wants no tales carried, so he's ordered that no one may leave Hostigos."

He cursed; that was expected of him.

"I'd feel ill-used, too, in your place," the sergeant sympathized, "but when princes and lords order, commonfolk obey. It won't be so bad, though. You can get good prices in Hostigos Town or at Tarr-Hostigos, and then, if you know a skilled trade, you can find work at good wages. Or you might take the colors. You're well armed and horsed; the Lord Kalvan welcomes all such."

"The Lord Kalvan? I thought Ptosphes was Prince of Hostigos."

"Why, so he is, Dralm guard him, but the Lord Kalvan, Dralm guard him, too, is the war leader. It's said he's a prince himself, from a far land. It's also said that he's a sorcerer, but that I doubt."

Ah, yes; the stranger prince from afar. And among these people, Corporal Calvin Morrison—he willed himself no longer to think of the man as anything but the Lord Kalvan—would be suspected of sorcery. He chatted pleasantly with the sergeant and the troopers, asking about inns, about prices being paid for things, all the questions a wandering trader would ask, then bade them good luck and rode on. He passed other farms along the road. At most of them, work was going on; men were forking down dunghills and digging under them, fires burned, and caldrons steamed over them. He added that to the cheerfulness with which the sergeant and his men had accepted the ban of Styphon's House.

Styphon, it seemed, had acquired a competitor.

Hostigos Town spread around a low hill and a great spring as large as a small lake, facing the mountains which, on the Europo-American Sector, had been quarried into sheer cliffs. The Lord Kalvan wouldn't fail to notice that. Above the gap stood a strong castle; that would be Tarr-Hostigos, *tarr* meant castle, or stronghold. The streets were crowded with carts and wagons; the artisans' quarter was noisy with the work of smiths and joiners. He found the Sign of the Red Halberd, the inn the sergeant had commended to him. He put up his horses and safe-stowed the packs, all but his personal luggage, his carbine, and the metal coffer. A servant carried the former; he took the coffer over one shoulder and followed to the room he had been given.

When he was alone, he set the coffer down. It was an almost featureless block of bronze, without visible lock or hinges, only two bright steel ovals on the top. Pressing his thumbs to these, he heard a slight click as the photoelectric lock inside responded to his thumbprint patterns. The lid opened. Inside were four globes of gleaming coppery mesh, a few small instruments with dials and knobs, and a little sigma-ray needler, a ladies' model, small enough to be covered by his hand, but as deadly as the big one he usually carried. It was silent, and it killed without trace that any autopsy would reveal.

There was also an antigrav unit, attached to the bottom of the coffer; it was on, the tiny pilot light glowed red. When he switched it off, the floor boards under the coffer creaked. Lined with collapsed metal, it now weighed over half a ton. He pushed down the lid, which only his thumbprints could open, and heard the lock click.

The common room downstairs was crowded and noisy. He found a vacant place at one of the long tables and sat down. Across from him, a man with a bald head and a small straggling beard grinned at him.

"New fish in the net?" he asked. "Welcome. Where from?"

"Ulthor, with three horse loads. My name's Verkan."

"Mine's Skranga." The bald man was from Agrys City.

"They took them all, fifty of them. Paid me less than I asked, but more than I thought they would, so I guess I got a fair price. I had four Trygathi herders, they're all in the cavalry, now. I'm working in the fireseed mill."

"The what?" He was incredulous. "You mean these people make their own fireseed? But nobody but the priests of Styphon can do that."

Skranga laughed. "That's what I thought, when I came here, but anybody can do it. No more trick than boiling soap. See, they get saltpeter from under dunghills, and . . ."

He detailed the process, step by step. The man facing him joined the conversation; he even understood, dimly, the theory. The charcoal was what burned, the sulfur was the kindling, and the saltpeter made the air to blow up the fire and blow the bullet out of the gun. And there was no secrecy about it, at least inside Hostigos. Except for keeping the news out of Nostor until he had enough fireseed for a war, the Lord Kalvan simply didn't care.

"I bless Dralm for bringing me into this," the horse trader said. "When people can leave here, I'm going some place and start making fireseed myself. Why, I'll be rich in a few years, and so can you."

He finished his meal, said he had to return to work, and left. A cavalry officer who had been sitting a few places down the table picked up his cup and flagon and took the vacant seat.

"You just came in?" he asked. "From Nostor?"

"No, from Sask." The answer seemed to disappoint the cavalryman; he went into the Ulthor-Grefftscharr story again. "How long will I be kept from going on?"

"Till we fight the Nostori and beat them. What do the Saski think we're doing here?"

"Waiting to have your throats cut. They don't know anything about your making fireseed."

The officer laughed. "Ha! Some of them'll get theirs cut, if Prince Sarrask doesn't mind his step. You say you have three horseloads of Grefftscharr wares; any weapons?"

"Some sword blades. Some daggers, a dozen gunlocks, three good shirts of rivet-link mail, bullet molds. And brassware, and jewelry, of course."

"Well, take your loads up to Tarr-Hostigos. They have a little fair each evening in the outer bailey, you can sell anything you have. Go early. Use my name"—he gave it—"and speak to Captain Harmakros. He'll be glad of any news you have."

He re-packed his horses, when he had eaten, and led them up the road to the castle above the gap. Along the wall of the outer bailey, inside the gate, were workshops, all busy. One thing he noticed was a gun carriage for a light fieldpiece being put together, not a little cart, but two big wheels and a trail, to be hauled with a limber. The gun for it was the sort of wrought-iron four-pounder normal for this sector, but it had trunnions, which was not. The Lord Kalvan, again.

Like all the local gentry, Captain Harmakros wore a small neat beard. His armor was rich but well battered, but the long rapier on his belt was new. He asked a few questions, then listened to a detailed account of what Verkan the trader had seen and heard in Sask; the mercenary companies Sarrask had hired, the names of the captains, their strength and equipment.

"You've kept your eyes open and your wits about you," he commented. "I wish you'd come through Nostor instead. Were you ever a soldier?"

"All traders are soldiers, in their own service."

"Yes, well when you've sold your loads, you'll be welcome in ours. Not as a common trooper, as a scout. You want to sell your pack horses, too? We'll give you your own price for them."

"If I sell my loads, yes."

"You'll have no trouble doing that. Stay about, have your meals with the officers here. We'll find something for you."

He had some tools, for both wood and metal work. He peddled them among the artisans, for a good price in silver and a better one in information. Beside cannon with trunnions on regular field-carriages, Kalvan had introduced rifling in small arms. Nobody knew whence Kalvan had come, but they knew it had been a great distance.

The officers with whom he ate listened avidly to what he had to tell about his observations in Sask. Nostor first, and then Sask, seemed to be the schedule. When they talked about the Lord Kalvan, the coldest expressions were of deep respect, and shaded up to hero-worship. But they knew nothing about him before the night he had appeared at a peasant's cottage and rallied a rabble fleeing from a raided village.

He sold the mail and sword blades and gunlocks as a lot to one of the officers; the rest of the stuff he spread to offer to the inmates of the castle. He saw the Lord Kalvan strolling through the crowd, in full armor and wearing a rapier and a Colt .38 Special on his belt. He had grown a small beard since the photograph the Paratime Police had secured on Europo-American had been taken. Clinging to his arm was a beautiful blond girl in male riding dress; Prince Ptosphes' daughter Rylla, he was told. He had already heard the story of how she had shot him by mistake in a skirmish and brought him to Tarr-Hostigos to be cared for. The happy possessiveness with which she held his arm, and the tenderness with which he looked at her, made him smile. Then the smile froze on his lips and died in his eyes as he wondered what Kalvan had told her privately.

Returning to the Red Halberd, he spent some time and money in the taproom. Everybody, as far as he could learn, seemed satisfied that Kalvan had come, with or without divine guidance, to Hostigos in a perfectly normal manner. Finally he went to his room.

Pressing his thumbs to the sensitized ovals, he opened the coffer and lifted out one of the gleaming copper-mesh balls. It opened at pressure on a small stud; he drew out a wire with a mouthpiece attached, and spoke for a long time into it.

"So far," he concluded, "there seems to be no question of anything paranormal about the man in anybody's mind. I have not yet made any contacts with anybody who would confide in me to the contrary. I have been offered an opportunity to take service under him as a scout; I intend doing this. Some assistance can be given me in carrying out this work. I will find a location for a conveyer-head; this will have to be somewhere in the woods near Hostigos Town. I will send a ball through when I do. Verkan Vall, ending communication."

Then he set the timer of the transposition field generator and switched on the antigrav unit. Carrying the ball to the open window, he released it. It rose quickly into the night, and then, high above, among the many visible stars, there was an instant's flash. It could have been a meteor.

Kalvan sat on a rock under a tree, wishing that he could smoke, and knowing that he was beginning to be scared. He cursed mentally. It didn't mean anything, as soon as things got started he'd forget to be scared, but it always happened before, and he hated it. It was quiet on the mountain top, even though there were two hundred men sitting or squatting or lying around him, and another five hundred, under Chartiphon and Prince Ptosphes, five hundred yards behind. There were fifty more a hundred yards ahead, a skirmish-line of riflemen. Now there was a new word in the here-and-now military lexicon. They were the first riflemen on any battlefield in the history of here-and-now. A few of the rifles were big fifteen- to twenty-pound muskets, eight- to six-bore; mostly they were calivers, sixteen- and twenty-bore, the size and weight of a Civil War musket. They were commanded by the Grefftscharr trader, Verkan. There had been objection to giving an outland stranger so important a command; he had informed the objectors, stiffly, that he had been an outland stranger himself only recently.

Out in front of Verkan's line, in what the defenders of Tarr-Dombra thought was cleared ground, were fifteen sharp-shooters. They all had big-bore muskets, rifled and fitted with peep-sights, zeroed in for just that range. The condition of that supposedly cleared approach was the most promising thing about the whole operation. The trees had been felled and the stumps rooted out, but the Nostori thought Tarr-Dombra couldn't be taken and that nobody would try to take it, so they'd gone slack. There were bushes all over it up to a man's waist, and many of them were high enough to hide behind standing up.

His men were hard enough to see even in the open. The helmets have been carefully rusted, so had the body-armor and every gun-barrel or spearhead. Nobody wore anything but green or brown, most of them had bits of greenery fastened to their helmets and clothes. The whole operation, with over twelve hundred men, had been rehearsed a dozen times, each time some being eliminated until they were down to eight hundred of the best.

There was a noise, about what a feeding wild-turkey would make, in front of him, and then a voice said, "Lord Kalvan!" It was Verkan, the Grefftscharrer. He had a rifle in his hand, and wore a dirty green-gray hooded smock; his sword and belt were covered with green and brown rags.

"I never saw you till you spoke," he commented.

"The wagons are coming. They're around the top switch-back, now."

He nodded. "We start, then." His mouth was dry. What was that thing in "For Whom the Bell Tolls" about spitting to show you weren't afraid? He couldn't do that, now. He nodded to the boy squatting beside him; he picked up his arquebus and started back toward where Ptosphes and Chartiphon had the main force.

And Rylla! He cursed vilely, in English; there was no satisfaction in taking the name of Dralm in vain, or blaspheming Styphon. She'd announced that she was coming along. He'd told her she was doing nothing of the sort. So had her father, and so had Chartiphon. She'd thrown a tantrum; thrown other things, too. In the end, she had come along. He was going to have his hands full with that girl, when he married her.

"All right," he said softly. "Let's go earn our pay."

The men on either side of him rose, two spears or scythe-blade things to every arquebus, though some of the spearmen had pistols in their belts. He and Verkan went ahead, stopping at the edge of the woods, where the riflemen crouched behind trees, and looked across the open four hundred yards at Tarr-Dombra, the castle that couldn't be taken, its limestone walls rising beyond the chasm that had been quarried straight across the mountain top. The drawbridge was down and the portcullis was up, a few soldiers in black and orange scarves—his old college colors, he oughtn't to shoot them—loitering in the gateway. A few more kept perfunctory watch from the battlements.

Chartiphon and Ptosphes brought their men, one pike to every three calivers and arquebuses, up with a dreadful crashing and clattering that almost stood his hair on end under his helmet and padded coif, but nobody at the castle seemed to have heard it. Chartiphon wore a long sack, with neck and arm holes, over his cuirass, and what looked like a well-used dishrag wrapped around his helmet. Ptosphes was in brown, with browned armor, so was Rylla. They all looked to the left, where the road came up the side and onto the top of the mountain.

Four cavalrymen, black-and-orange scarves and lance-pennons, came into view. They were only fake Princeton men; he hoped they'd remember to tear that stuff off before some other Hostigi shot them. A long ox-wagon followed, piled high with hay and eight Hostigi infantrymen under it, then two more cavalrymen in false Nostori colors, another wagon, and six more cavalry. Two more wagons followed.

The first four cavalrymen clattered onto the drawbridge and spoke to the guards at the gate, then rode through. Two of the wagons followed. The third rumbled onto the drawbridge and stopped directly under the portcullis. That was the one with the log framework on top and the log slung underneath. The driver must have cut the strap that held that up, jamming the wagon. The fourth wagon, the one loaded to the top of the bed with rocks, stopped on the outer end of the drawbridge, weighting it down. A pistol banged inside the gate, and another; there were shouts of "Hostigos! Hostigos!" The hay seemed to explode off the two wagons in sight as men piled out of them.

He blew his Pennsylvania State Police whistle, and half a dozen big elephant-size muskets bellowed, from places he'd have sworn there had been nobody at all. Verkan's rifle platoon began firing, sharp whip-crack reports like none of the smoothbores. He hoped they were remembering to patch their bullets; that was something new to them. Then he blew his whistle twice and started running forward.

The men who had been showing themselves on the walls were all gone; a musket-shot or so showed that the snipers hadn't gotten all of them. He ran past a man with a piece of fishnet over his helmet, stuck full of oak twigs, who was ramming a musket. Gray powder-smoke hung in the gateway, and everybody who had been outside had gotten in. Yells of "Hostigo!" and "Nostor!" and shots and blade-clashing from within. He broke step and looked back; his two hundred were pouring after him, keeping properly spaced out, the arquebusiers not firing. All the shooting was coming from where Chartiphon—and Rylla, he hoped—had formed a line two hundred yards from the walls and were plastering the battlements, firing as rapidly as they could reload. A cannon went off above when he was almost at the end of the drawbridge, and then, belatedly, the portcullis came down to stop seven feet from the ground on the top of the log framework hidden under the hay on the third wagon.

All six of the oxen on the last wagon were dead; the drivers had been furnished short-handle axes for that purpose. The oxen on the portcullis-stopper had also been killed. The gate towers on both sides had already been taken. There were black-and-orange scarves lying where they had been ripped off, and more on corpses. But shots were beginning to come from the citadel, across the outer bailey, and a mob of Nostori were pouring out from its gate. This, he thought, was the time to expend some .38's.

Feet apart, left hand on hip, he aimed and emptied the Colt, killing six men with six shots, timed-fire rate. He'd done just as well at that range on silhouette targets many a time; that was all this was. They were the front six; the men behind them stopped momentarily, and then the men behind swept around him, arquebuses banging and pikemen and halberdiers running forward. He holstered the empty Colt, he only had eight rounds left, now, and drew his rapier and poignard. Another cannon on the outside wall thundered; he hoped Rylla and Chartiphon hadn't been in front of it. Then he was fighting his way through the citadel gate.

Behind, in the outer bailey, something beside "Nostor!" and "Hostigos!" was being shouted. It was:

"Mercy, comrade! Mercy; I yield!"

He heard more of that as the morning passed. Before noon, the Nostori garrison had either been given mercy or hadn't needed it. There had only been those two cannon-shots, though between them they had killed and wounded fifty men. Nobody was crazy enough to attack Tarr-Dombra, so they'd left the cannon empty, and had only been given time to load and fire two. He doubted if they'd catch Gormoth with his panzer down again.

The hardest fighting was inside the citadel. He ran into Rylla there, with Chartiphon trying to keep up with her. There was a bright scar on her browned helmet and blood on her sword; she was laughing happily. He expected that taking the keep would be even bloodier work, but as soon as they had the citadel it surrendered. By that time he had used up all his rounds for the Colt.

They hauled down Gormoth's black flag with the orange lily and ran up Ptosphes' halberd-head, blue on red. They found four huge bombards, throwing hundred-pound stone cannon balls, and handspiked them around to bear on the little town of Dyssa, at the mouth of Pine Creek, Gorge River here-and-now, and fired one round from each to announce that Tarr-Dombra was under new management. They set the castle cooks to work cutting up and roasting the oxen from the two rear wagons. Then they turned their attention to the prisoners herded in the inner bailey.

First, there were the mercenaries. They would enter the service of Ptosphes, though they could not be used against Nostor until their captain's terms of contract with Gormoth had run out. They would be sent to the Sask border. Then, there were Gormoth's own troops. They couldn't be used at all, but they could be put to work, as long as they were given soldiers' pay and soldierly treatment. Then, there was the governor of the castle, a Count Pheblon, cousin to Prince Gormoth, and his officers. They would be released, on oath to send their ransoms in silver to Hostigos. The priest of Galzar elected to go to Hostigos with his parishioners.

As for the priest of Styphon, Chartiphon wanted him questioned under torture, and Ptosphes thought he ought merely to be beheaded on the spot.

"Send him to Nostor with Pheblon," Kalvan said. "With a letter for his high priest—no, for the Supreme Priest, Styphon's Voice. Tell Styphon's Voice that we make our own fireseed, that we will teach everybody to make it, and that we will not rest until Styphon's House is utterly destroyed."

Everybody, including those who had been making suggestions for novel and interesting ways of putting the priest to death, shouted in delight.

"And send Gormoth a copy of the letter, and a letter offering him peace and friendship. Tell him we'll teach his soldiers how to make fireseed, and they can make it in Nostor when they're sent home."

"Kalvan!" Ptosphes almost howled. "What god has addled your wits? Gormoth's our enemy!"

"Anybody who can make fireseed will be our enemy, because Styphon's House will be his. If Gormoth doesn't realize that now, he will soon enough."

Verkan the Grefftscharr trader commanded the party that galloped back to Hostigos with the good news—Tarr-Dombra taken, with over two hundred prisoners, a hundred and fifty horses, four tons of fireseed, twenty cannon. And Sevenhills Valley was part of Hostigos again. Harmakros had destroyed a company of mercenary cavalry, killing twenty and capturing the rest, and he had taken Styphon's temple farm, a richly productive nitriary, freeing the slaves and butchering the priests and the guards. And the once persecuted priest of Dralm had gathered all the peasants for a thanksgiving, telling them that the Hostigi came not as conquerors but as liberators.

He seemed to recall having heard that before, on a number of paratemporal areas, including Calvin Morrison's own.

He also brought copies of the letters Prince Ptosphes had written, or, more likely, which Kalvan had written and Ptosphes had signed, to the Supreme Priest of Styphon and to Prince Gormoth. Dropping a couple of troopers in the town to spread the good news, he rode up to the castle and reported to Xentos. It took a long time to tell the old priest-chancellor the whole story, counting interruptions while Xentos told Dralm about it. When he got away, he was immediately dragged into the officers' hall, where a wine barrel had been tapped. By the time he got back to the Red Halberd in Hostigo Town, it was after dark, and everybody was roaring drunk, and somebody had a little two-pounder in the street and was wasting fireseed that could have been better used to kill Gormoth's soldiers. The bell at the town hall, which had begun ringing while he was riding in through the castle gate, was still ringing.

Going up to his room, he opened the coffer and got out another of the copper balls, putting it under his cloak. He rode a mile out of town, tied his horse in the brush, and made his way to where a single huge tree rose above the scrub oak. Speaking into the ball, he activated and released it. Then he got out his cigarettes and sat down under the tree to wait for the half hour it would take the message-ball to reach Fifth Level Police Terminal Time-Line, and the half hour it would take a mobile antigrav conveyer to come in.

The servant brought him the things, one by one, and Lord Kalvan laid them on the white sheet spread on the table top. The whipcord breeches; he left the billfold in the hip pocket. He couldn't spend United States currency here, and his identity cards belonged to another man, who didn't exist here-and-now. The shirt, torn and bloodstained; the tunic with the battered badge that had saved his life. The black boots, one on either side; the boots they made here were softer and more comfortable. The Sam Browne belt, with the holster and the empty-looped cartridge-carrier and the handcuffs in their pouch. Anybody you needed handcuffs on, here-and-now, you just shot or knocked on the head. The Colt Official Police; he didn't want to part with that, even if there were no more cartridges for it, but the rest of this stuff would seem meaningless without it. He slipped it into the holster, and then tossed the blackjack on top of the pile.

The servant wrapped them and carried the bundle out. There goes Calvin Morrison, he thought; long live Lord Kalvan of Hostigos. Tomorrow, at the thanksgiving service before the feast, these things would be deposited as a votive offering in the temple of Dralm. That had been Xentos' idea, and he had agreed at once. Beside being a general and an ordnance engineer and an industrialist, he had to be a politician, and politicians can't slight their constituents' religion. He filled a goblet from a flagon on the smaller table and sat down, stretching his legs. Unchilled white wine was a crime against nature; have to do something about refrigeration—after the war, of course.

That mightn't be too long, either. They'd already unsealed the frontiers, and the transients who had been blockaded in would be leaving after the feast. They all knew that anybody could make fireseed, and most of them knew how. That fellow they'd gotten those Trygath horses from; he'd had a few words with him, and he was going to Nostor. So were half a dozen agents to work with Xentos' fifth column. Gormoth would begin making his own fireseed, and that would bring him under the ban of Styphon's House.

Gormoth wouldn't think of that. All he wanted was to conquer Hostigos, and without the help of Styphon's House, he couldn't. He couldn't anyhow, now that he had lost his best invasion-route. Two days after Tarr-Dombra had fallen, he'd had two thousand men at the mouth of Gorge

River and lost at least three hundred by cannon fire trying to cross the Athan before his mercenary captains had balked, and the night after that Harmakros had come out of McElhattan Gap, Vrylos Gap, with two hundred cavalry and raided western Nostor, burning farms and villages and running off horses and cattle, devastating everything to the end of Listra Valley.

Maybe they'd thrown Gormoth off until winter. That would mean, till next spring. They didn't fight wars in the winter, here-and-now; against mercenary union rules. By then, he should have a real army, trained in new tactics he'd dredged from what he remembered of Sixteenth and Seventeenth Century history. Four or five batteries of little four-pounders, pieces and caissons each drawn by four horses, and as mobile as cavalry. And plenty of rifles, and men trained to use them. And get rid of all these bear spears and scythe blade things, and substitute real eighteen-foot Swiss pikes; they'd hold off cavalry.

Styphon's House was the real enemy. Beat Gormoth once, properly, and he'd stay beaten, and Sarrask of Sask was only a Mussolini to Gormoth's Hitler. But Styphon's House was big; it spread over all five Great Kingdoms, from the mouth of the St. Lawrence to the Gulf of Mexico.

Big but vulnerable, and he knew the vulnerable point. Styphon wasn't a popular god as, say, Dralm was; that was why Xentos' fifth column was building strength in Nostor. Styphon's House had ignored the people and even the minor nobility, and ruled by pressure on the Great Kings and their subject princes, and as soon as they could make their own powder, they'd turn on Styphon's House, and their people with them. This wasn't a religious war, like the ones in the Sixteenth and Seventeenth Centuries in his own former history. It was just a job of racket-busting.

He set down the goblet and rose, throwing off the light robe, and began to dress for dinner. For a moment, he wondered whether the Democrats or the Republicans would win the election this year—he was sure it was the same year, now, in a different dimension of time—and how the Cold War and the Space Race were coming along.

Verkan Vall, his story finished, relaxed in his chair. There was no direct light on this terrace, only a sky-reflection from the city lights below, so dim that the tips of their cigarettes glowed visibly. There were four of them: the Chief of Paratime Police, the Director of the Paratime Commission, the Chairman of the Paratemporal Board of Trade, and Chief's Assistant Verkan Vall, who would be chief in another hundred days.

"You took no action about him?" the director asked.

"None at all. The man's no threat to the Paratime Secret. He knows he isn't in his own past, and from things he ought to find and hasn't he knows he isn't in his own future. So he knows he's in the corresponding present in a second time dimension, and he knows that somebody else is able to travel laterally in time. I grant that. But he's keeping it to himself. On Aryan-Transpacific, in the idiom of his original time-line, he has it made. He won't take any chances on unmaking it.

"Look what he has that the Europo-American Sector could never give him. He is a great nobleman; they're out of fashion on Europo-American, where the Common Man is the ideal. He's going to marry a beautiful princess, that's even out of fashion for children's fairy tales. He's a sword-swinging soldier of fortune, and they've vanished from his own nuclear-weapons world. He's in command of a good little army, and making a better one out of it, and he has a cause worth fighting for. Any speculations about what space-time continuum he's in he'll keep inside his own skull.

"Look at the story he put out. He told Xentos that he had been thrown into the past from a time in the far future by sorcery. Sorcery, on that time-line, is a perfectly valid scientific explanation of anything. Xentos, with his permission, passed the story on, under oath of secrecy, to Ptosphes, Rylla, and Chartiphon. The story they gave out is that he's an exiled prince from a country outside local geographical knowledge. Regular defense in depth, all wrapped around the real secret, and everybody has an acceptable explanation."

"How'd you get it, then?" the Board Chairman asked.

"From Xentos, at the feast. I got him into a theological discussion, and slipped some hypno truth-drug into his wine. He doesn't remember, now, that he told me."

"Well, nobody else on that time-line'll get it that way," the Commission director agreed. "But didn't you take a chance getting those things of Morrison's out of the temple? Was that necessary?"

"No. We ran a conveyer in the night of the feast, when the temple was empty. The next morning, the priests all cried, 'A miracle! Dralm has accepted the offering!' I was there and saw it. Morrison doesn't believe that, he thinks some of these pack traders who left Hostigos the next morning stole the stuff. I know Harmakros' cavalrymen were stopping people and searching wagons and packs. Publicly, of course, he has to believe in the miracle.

"As to the necessity, yes. This stuff will be found on Morrison's original time-line, first the clothing, with the numbered badge still on the tunic, and, later, in connection with some crime we'll arrange for the purpose, the revolver. They won't explain anything, they'll make more of a mystery, but it will be a mystery in normal terms of what's locally accepted as possible."

"Well, this is all very interesting," the Trade Board chairman said, "but what have I to do with it, officially?"

"Trenth, you disappoint me," the Commission director said. "This Styphon's House racket is perfect for penetration of that subsector, and in a couple of centuries it'll be a very valuable subsector to have penetrated. We'll just move in on Styphon's House, and take it over, the way we did the Yat-Zar temples on the Hulgun Sector, and build that up to general economic and political control."

"You'll have to stay off Morrison's time-line, though," Tortha Karf said.

"You certainly will!" He was vehement about it. "We'll turn that time-line over to the University, here, for study, and quarantine it absolutely to everybody else. And about five adjoining time-lines, for control study. You know what we have here?" He was becoming excited about it. "We have the start of an entirely new subsector, and we have the divarication point absolutely identified, the first time we've been able to do that except from history. Now, here; I've already established myself with those people as Verkan the Grefftscharr trader. I'll get back, now and then, about as frequently as plausible for traveling by horse, and set up a trading depot. A building big enough to put a conveyer head into . . ."

Tortha Karf began laughing. "I knew it," he said. "You'd find some way!"

"All right. We all have hobbies; yours is fruit-growing and rabbit-hunting on Fifth Level Sicily. Well, my hobby farm is going to be the Kalvan Subsector, Fourth Level Aryan-Transpacific. I'm only a hundred and twenty years old, now. In a couple of centuries, when I'm ready to retire . . ."

Ursula K. Le Guin

SEMLEY'S NECKLACE

Ursula K. Le Guin is so universally respected as a writer these days, and so honored as one of science fiction's most profound thinkers and complex and subtle artists, that it's sometimes forgotten that when she first appeared, the writer that she was most often compared to was Leigh Brackett—indeed, she was referred to on at least one occasion as "the New Leigh Brackett." It's often also forgotten these days that her first few books—*Rocannon's World,* the strongly van Vogtian *City of Illusions,* and her best early book, the underrated and still largely overlooked (even by Le Guin fans) *Planet of Exile*—were published by Ace as pulp-adventure Space Opera of the most basic, lowest-common-denominator sort (much as Samuel R. Delany's first books were also being published as stock Space Opera, at about the same time, by the same publishing house), with garish pulp covers and lurid pulp blurbs such as "Wherever he went, his super-science made him a legendary figure!" and "Was he a human meteor or a time-bomb from the stars?"

As it turned out, Le Guin had a greater destiny to fulfill than to become merely the new Queen Of The Space-Ways—but although she became more than that, and explored literary territories far beyond the purview of Space Opera, the New Leigh Brackett lurks somewhere in her still, a vital component of her artistic makeup. Indeed, her recent return to the star-spanning, Hainish-settled interstellar community known as the Ekumen (the fictional universe that provided the setting for those early novels) in stories such as "Forgiveness Day" and "A Woman's Liberation" and "Another Story" demonstrates that she can *still* spin a tale of Interplanetary Adventure and Intrigue as fast-paced and compelling and compulsively readable as any ever produced by anyone anywhere . . . with the additional benefit of being able to explore politics, human sexuality, competing social modes and models for civilization, and the fundamental questions of life, death, and moral responsibility, perhaps a bit more fully and more complexly than that early Le Guin of the garish Ace Doubles would have been allowed to do. But then, one thing she has in common with Brackett, and perhaps the thing that made critics compare Le Guin to her in the first place, is that Le Guin rarely if ever forgets about Story, and the fact that the deep heart of any story is provided by the *people* who live *in* it. A lesson she already knew well at the very beginning of her career, as the haunting and yet suspenseful story that follows, one of her first sales, demonstrates very well . . .

Ursula K. Le Guin is probably one of the best-known writers in the world today. Her famous novel *The Left Hand of Darkness* may have been the most influential SF novel of its decade, and shows every sign of becoming one of the enduring classics of the genre—even ignoring the rest of Le Guin's work, the impact of this one novel alone on future SF and future SF writers would be incalculably strong. (Her 1968 fantasy novel, *A Wizard of Earthsea,* would be almost as influential on future generations of High Fantasy writers.) *The Left Hand of Darkness* won both the Hugo and Nebula Awards, as did Le Guin's monumental novel *The Dispossessed* a few years later. Her novel *Tehanu* won her another Nebula in 1990, and she has also won three other Hugo Awards and two Nebula Awards for her short fiction, as well as the National Book Award for children's literature for her novel *The Farthest Shore,* part of her acclaimed Earthsea trilogy. Her other novels include *The Lathe of Heaven, The Beginning Place, A Wizard of Earthsea, The Tombs of Atuan, Tehanu, Searoad,* and the controversial multimedia novel *Always Coming Home.* She has had six collections: *The Wind's Twelve Quarters, Orsinian Tales, The Compass Rose, Buffalo Gals and Other Animal Presences, A Fisherman of the Inland Sea,* and her most recent book, *Four Ways to Forgiveness.*

How can you tell the legend from the fact on these worlds that lie so many years away?—planets without names, called by their people simply The World, planets without history, where the past is the matter of myth, and a returning explorer finds his own doings of a few years back have become the gestures of a god. Unreason darkens that gap of time bridged by our lightspeed ships, and in the darkness uncertainty and disproportion grow like weeds.

In trying to tell the story of a man, an ordinary League scientist, who went to such a nameless half-known world not many years ago, one feels like an archaeologist amid millennial ruins, now struggling through choked tangles of leaf, flower, branch and vine to the sudden bright geometry of a wheel or a polished cornerstone, and now entering some commonplace, sunlit doorway to find inside it the darkness, the impossible flicker of a flame, the glitter of a jewel, the half-glimpsed movement of a woman's arm.

How can you tell fact from legend, truth from truth?

Through Rocannon's story the jewel, the blue glitter seen briefly, returns. With it let us begin, here:

Galactic Area 8, No. 62: FOMALHAUT II.
High-Intelligence Life Forms: Species Contacted:
Species I.
  A. Gdemiar (singular Gdem): Highly intelligent, fully hominoid nocturnal troglodytes, 120–135 cm. in height, light skin, dark head-hair. When contacted these cave-dwellers possessed a rigidly stratified oligarchic urban society modified by partial colonial telepathy, and a technologically oriented Early Steel culture. Technology en-

hanced to Industrial, Point C, during League Mission of 252–254. In 254 an Automatic Drive ship (to-from New South Georgia) was presented to oligarchs of the Kiriensea Area community. Status C-Prime.

B. Fiia (singular Fian): Highly intelligent, fully hominoid, diurnal, av. ca. 130 cm. in height, observed individuals generally light in skin and hair. Brief contacts indicated village and nomadic communal societies, partial colonial telepathy, also some indication of short-range TK. The race appears a-technological and evasive, with minimal and fluid culture-patterns. Currently untaxable. Status E-Query.

Species II.

Liuar (singular Liu): Highly intelligent, fully hominoid, diurnal, av. height above 170 cm., this species possesses a fortress/village, clan-descent society, a blocked technology (Bronze), and feudal-heroic culture. Note horizontal social cleavage into a pseudo-races: (a) Ol-gyior, "midmen," light-skinned and dark-haired; (b) Angyar, "lords," very tall, dark-skinned, yellow-haired—

"That's her," said Rocannon, looking up from the *Abridged Handy Pocket Guide to Intelligent Life-forms* at the very tall, dark-skinned, yellow-haired woman who stood halfway down the long museum hall. She stood still and erect, crowned with bright hair, gazing at something in a display case. Around her fidgeted four uneasy and unattractive dwarves.

"I didn't know Fomalhaut II had all those people besides the trogs," said Ketho, the curator.

"I didn't either. There are even some 'Unconfirmed' species listed here, that they never contacted. Sounds like time for a more thorough survey mission to the place. Well, now at least we know what she is."

"I wish there were some way of knowing *who* she is. . . ."

She was of an ancient family, a descendant of the first kings of the Angyar, and for all her poverty her hair shone with the pure, steadfast gold of her inheritance. The little people, the Fiia, bowed when she passed them, even when she was a barefoot child running in the fields, the light and fiery comet of her hair brightening the troubled winds of Kirien.

She was still very young when Durhal of Hallan saw her, courted her, and carried her away from the ruined towers and windy halls of her childhood to his own high home. In Hallan on the mountainside there was no comfort either, though splendor endured. The windows were unglassed, the stone floors bare; in coldyear one might wake to see the night's snow in long, low drifts beneath each window. Durhal's bride stood with narrow bare feet on the snowy floor, braiding up the fire of her hair and laughing at her young husband in the silver mirror that hung in their room. That mirror, and his mother's bridal-gown sewn with a thousand tiny crystals, were all his wealth. Some of his lesser kinfolk of Hallan still possessed wardrobes of brocaded clothing, furniture of gilded wood, silver harness for their steeds, armor and silver mounted swords, jewels and jewelry—and on these last Durhal's bride looked enviously, glancing back at a gemmed coronet or a golden brooch even when the wearer of the ornament stood aside to let her pass, deferent to her birth and marriage-rank.

Fourth from the High Seat of Hallan Revel sat Durhal and his bride Semley, so close to Hallanlord that the old man often poured wine for Semley with his own hand, and spoke of hunting with his nephew and heir Durhal, looking on the young pair with a grim, unhopeful love. Hope came hard to the Angyar of Hallan and all the Western Lands, since the Starlords had appeared with their houses that leaped about on pillars of fire and their awful weapons that could level hills. They had interfered with all the old ways and wars, and though the sums were small there was terrible shame to the Angyar in having to pay a tax to them, a tribute for the Starlords' war that was to be fought with some strange enemy, somewhere in the hollow places between the stars, at the end of years. "It will be your war too," they said, but for a generation now the Angyar had sat in idle shame in their revel-halls, watching their double swords rust, their sons grow up without ever striking a blow in battle, their daughters marry poor men, even midmen, having no dowry of heroic loot to bring a noble husband. Hallanlord's face was bleak when he watched the fair-haired couple and heard their laughter as they drank bitter wine and joked together in the cold, ruinous, resplendent fortress of their race.

Semley's own face hardened when she looked down the hall and saw, in seats far below hers, even down among the halfbreeds and the midmen, against white skins and black hair, the gleam and flash of precious stones. She herself had brought nothing in dowry to her husband, not even a silver hairpin. The dress of a thousand crystals she had put away in a chest for the wedding-day of her daughter, if daughter it was to be.

It was, and they called her Haldre, and when the fuzz on her little brown skull grew longer it shone with steadfast gold, the inheritance of the lordly generations, the only gold she would ever possess. . . .

Semley did not speak to her husband of her discontent. For all his gentleness to her, Durhal in his pride had only contempt for envy, for vain wishing, and she dreaded his contempt. But she spoke to Durhal's sister Durossa.

"My family had a great treasure once," she said. "It was a necklace all of gold, with the blue jewel set in the center—sapphire?"

Durossa shook her head, smiling, not sure of the name either. It was late in warmyear, as these Northern Angyar called the summer of the eight-hundred-day year, beginning the cycle of months anew at each equinox; to Semley it seemed an outlandish calendar, a mid-mannish reckoning. Her family was at an end, but it had been older and purer than the race of any of these northwestern marchlanders, who mixed too freely with the Olgyior. She sat with Durossa in the sunlight on a stone window-seat high up in the Great Tower, where the older woman's apartment was. Widowed young, childless, Durossa had been given in second marriage to Hallanlord, who was her father's brother. Since it was a kinmarriage and a second marriage on both sides she had not taken the title of Hallanlady, which Semley would some day bear; but she sat with the old lord in the High Seat and ruled with him his domains. Older than her brother Durhal, she was fond of his young wife, and delighted in the bright-haired baby Haldre.

"It was bought," Semley went on, "with all the money my forebear Leynen got when he conquered the Southern Fiefs—all the money from a whole kingdom, think of it, for one jewel! Oh, it would outshine anything here in Hallan, surely, even those crystals like koob-eggs your cousin Issar wears. It was so beautiful they gave it a name of its own; they called it the Eye of the Sea. My great-grandmother wore it."

"You never saw it?" the older woman asked lazily, gazing down at the green mountainslopes where long, long summer sent its hot and restless winds straying among the forests and whirling down white roads to the seacoast far away.

"It was lost before I was born."

"No, my father said it was stolen before the Starlords ever came to our realm. He wouldn't talk of it, but there was an old midwoman full of tales who always told me the Fiia would know where it was."

"Ah, the Fiia I should like to see!" said Durossa. "They're in so many songs and tales; why do they never come to the Western Lands?"

"Too high, too cold in winter, I think. They like the sunlight of the valleys of the south."

"Are they like the Clayfolk?"

"Those I've never seen; they keep away from us in the south. Aren't they white like midmen, and misformed? The Fiia are fair; they look like children, only thinner, and wiser. Oh, I wonder if they know where the necklace is, who stole it and where he hid it! Think, Durossa—if I could come into Hallan Revel and sit down by my husband with the wealth of a kingdom round my neck, and outshine the other women as he outshines all men!"

Durossa bent her head above the baby, who sat studying her own brown toes on a fur rug between her mother and aunt. "Semley is foolish," she murmured to the baby; "Semley who shines like a falling star, Semley whose husband loves no gold but the gold of her hair. . . ."

And Semley, looking out over the green slopes of summer toward the distant sea, was silent.

But when another coldyear had passed, and the Starlords had come again to collect their taxes for the war against the world's end—this time using a couple of dwarfish Clayfolk as interpreters, and so leaving all the Angyar humiliated to the point of rebellion—and another warmyear too was gone, and Haldre had grown into a lovely, chattering child, Semley brought her one morning to Durossa's sunlit room in the tower. Semley wore an old cloak of blue, and the hood covered her hair.

"Keep Haldre for me these few days, Durossa," she said, quick and calm. "I'm going south to Kirien."

"To see your father?"

"To find my inheritance. Your cousins of Harget Fief have been taunting Durhal. Even that halfbreed Parna can torment him, because Parna's wife has a satin coverlet for her bed, and a diamond earring, and three gowns, the dough-faced black-haired trollop! while Durhal's wife must patch her gown—"

"Is Durhal's pride in his wife, or what she wears?"

But Semley was not to be moved. "The Lords of Hallan are becoming poor men in their own hall. I am going to bring my dowry to my lord, as one of my lineage should."

"Semley! Does Durhal know you're going?"

"My return will be a happy one—that much let him know," said young Semley, breaking for a moment into her joyful laugh; then she bent to kiss her daughter, turned, and before Durossa could speak, was gone like a quick wind over the floors of sunlit stone.

Married women of the Angyar never rode for sport, and Semley had not been from Hallan since her marriage; so now, mounting the high saddle of a windsteed, she felt like a girl again, like the wild maiden she had been, riding half-broken steeds on the north wind over the fields of Kirien. The beast that bore her now down from the hills of Hallan was of finer breed, striped coat fitting sleek over hollow, buoyant bones, green eyes slitted against the wind, light and mighty wings sweeping up and down to either side of Semley, revealing and hiding, revealing and hiding the clouds above her and the hills below.

On the third morning she came to Kirien and stood again in the ruined courts. Her father had been drinking all night, and, just as in the old
days, the morning sunlight poking through his fallen ceilings annoyed
him, and the sight of his daughter only increased his annoyance. "What
are you back for?" he growled, his swollen eyes glancing at her and away.
The fiery hair of his youth was quenched, grey strands tangled on his
skull. "Did the young Halla not marry you, and you've come sneaking
home?"

"I am Durhal's wife. I came to get my dowry, father."

The drunkard growled in disgust; but she laughed at him so gently
that he had to look at her again, wincing.

"Is it true, father, that the Fiia stole the necklace Eye of the Sea?"

"How do I know? Old tales. The thing was lost before I was born, I
think. I wish I never had been. Ask the Fiia if you want to know. Go to
them, go back to your husband. Leave me alone here. There's no room at
Kirien for girls and gold and all the rest of the story. The story's over
here; this is the fallen place, this is the empty hall. The sons of Leynen all
are dead, their treasures are all lost. Go on your way, girl."

Grey and swollen as the web-spinner of ruined houses, he turned and
went blundering toward the cellars where he hid from daylight.

Leading the striped windsteed of Hallan, Semley left her old home
and walked down the steep hill, past the village of the midmen, who
greeted her with sullen respect, on over fields and pastures where the
great, wing-clipped, half-wild herilor grazed, to a valley that was green
as a painted bowl and full to the brim with sunlight. In the deep of the
valley lay the village of the Fiia, and as she descended leading her steed
the little, slight people ran up toward her from their huts and gardens,
laughing, calling out in faint, thin voices.

"Hail Halla's bride, Kirienlady, Windborne, Semley the Fair!"

They gave her lovely names and she liked to hear them, minding not
at all their laughter; for they laughed at all they said. That was her own
way, to speak and laugh. She stood tall in her long blue cloak among their
swirling welcome.

"Hail Lightfolk, Sundwellers, Fiia friends of men!"

They took her down into the village and brought her into one of their
airy houses, the tiny children chasing along behind. There was no telling
the age of a Fian once he was grown; it was hard even to tell one from
another and be sure, as they moved about quick as moths around a candle, that she spoke always to the same one. But it seemed that one of them
talked with her for a while, as the others fed and petted her steed, and
brought water for her to drink, and bowls of fruit from their gardens of

little trees. "It was never the Fiia that stole the necklace of the Lords of Kirien!" cried the little man. "What would the Fiia do with gold, Lady? For us there is sunlight in warmyear, and in coldyear the remembrance of sunlight; the yellow fruit, the yellow leaves in endseason, the yellow hair of our lady of Kirien; no other gold."

"Then it was some midman stole the thing?"

Laughter ran long and faint about her. "How would a midman dare? O Lady of Kirien, how the great jewel was stolen no mortal knows, not man nor midman nor Fian nor any among the Seven Folk. Only dead minds know how it was lost, long ago when Kireley the Proud whose great-granddaughter is Semley walked alone by the caves of the sea. But it may be found perhaps among the Sunhaters."

"The Clayfolk?"

A louder burst of laughter, nervous.

"Sit with us, Semley, sunhaired, returned to us from the north." She sat with them to eat, and they were as pleased with her graciousness as she with theirs. But when they heard her repeat that she would go to the Clayfolk to find her inheritance, if it was there, they began not to laugh; and little by little there were fewer of them around her. She was alone at last with perhaps the one she had spoken with before the meal. "Do not go among the Clayfolk, Semley," he said, and for a moment her heart failed her. The Fian, drawing his hand down slowly over his eyes, had darkened all the air about them. Fruit lay ash-white on the plate; all the bowls of clear water were empty.

"In the mountains of the far land the Fiia and the Gdemiar parted. Long ago we parted," said the slight, still man of the Fiia. "Longer ago we were one. What we are not, they are. What we are, they are not. Think of the sunlight and the grass and the trees that bear fruit, Semley; think that not all roads that lead down lead up as well."

"Mine leads neither down nor up, kind host, but only straight on to my inheritance. I will go to it where it is, and return with it."

The Fian bowed, laughing a little.

Outside the village she mounted her striped windsteed, and, calling farewell in answer to their calling, rose up into the wind of afternoon and flew southwestward toward the caves down by the rocky shores of Kiriensea.

She feared she might have to walk far into those tunnel-caves to find the people she sought, for it was said the Clayfolk never came out of their caves into the light of the sun, and feared even the Greatstar and the moons. It was a long ride; she landed once to let her steed hunt tree-rats while she ate a little bread from her saddle-bag. The bread was hard and dry by now and tasted of leather, yet kept a faint savor of its making, so that for a moment, eating it alone in a glade of the southern forests, she heard the quiet tone of a voice and saw Durhal's face turned to her in the light of the candles of Hallan. For a while she sat daydreaming of that stern and vivid young face, and of what she would say to him when she came home with a kingdom's ransom around her neck: "I wanted a gift worthy of my husband, Lord. . . ." Then she pressed on, but when she reached the coast the sun had set, with the Greatstar sinking behind it. A mean wind had come up from the west, starting and gusting and veering, and her windsteed was weary fighting it. She let him glide down on the sand. At once he folded his wings and curled his thick, light limbs under him with a thrum of purring. Semley stood holding her cloak close at her throat, stroking the steed's neck so that he flicked his ears and purred again. The warm fur comforted her hand, but all that met her eyes was grey sky full of smears of cloud, grey sea, dark sand. And then running over the sand a low, dark creature—another—a group of them, squatting and running and stopping.

She called aloud to them. Though they had not seemed to see her, now in a moment they were all around her. They kept a distance from her windsteed; he had stopped purring, and his fur rose a little under Semley's hand. She took up the reins, glad of his protection but afraid of the nervous ferocity he might display. The strange folk stood silent, staring, their thick bare feet planted in the sand. There was no mistaking them: they were the height of the Fiia and in all else a shadow, a black image of those laughing people. Naked, squat, stiff, with lank hair and grey-white skins, dampish-looking like the skins of grubs; eyes like rocks.

"You are the Clayfolk?"

"Gdemiar are we, people of the Lords of the Realms of Night." The voice was unexpectedly loud and deep, and rang out pompous through the salt, blowing dusk; but, as with the Fiia, Semley was not sure which one had spoken.

"I greet you, Nightlords. I am Semley of Kirien, Durhal's wife of Hallan. I come to you seeking my inheritance, the necklace called Eye of the Sea, lost long ago."

"Why do you seek it here, Angya? Here is only sand and salt and night."

"Because lost things are known of in deep places," said Semley, quite ready for a play of wits, "and gold that came from earth has a way of going back to the earth. And sometimes the made, they say, returns to the maker." This last was a guess; it hit the mark.

"It is true the necklace Eye of the Sea is known to us by name. It was made in our caves long ago, and sold by us to the Angyar. And the blue stone came from the Clayfields of our kin to the east. But these are very old tales, Angya."

"May I listen to them in the places where they are told?"

The squat people were silent a while, as if in doubt. The grey wind blew by over the sand, darkening as the Greatstar set; the sound of the sea loudened and lessened. The deep voice spoke again: "Yes, lady of the Angyar. You may enter the Deep Halls. Come with us now." There was a changed note in his voice, wheedling. Semley would not hear it. She followed the Claymen over the sand, leading on a short rein her sharp-taloned steed.

At the cave-mouth, a toothless, yawning mouth from which a stinking warmth sighed out, one of the Claymen said, "The air-beast cannot come in."

"Yes," said Semley.

"No," said the squat people.

"Yes. I will not leave him here. He is not mine to leave. He will not harm you, so long as I hold his reins."

"No," deep voices repeated; but others broke in, "As you will," and after a moment of hesitation they went on. The cave-mouth seemed to snap shut behind them, so dark was it under the stone. They went in single file, Semley last.

The darkness of the tunnel lightened, and they came under a ball of weak white fire hanging from the roof. Farther on was another, and another; between them long black worms hung in festoons from the rock. As they went on these fire-globes were set closer, so that all the tunnel was lit with a bright, cold light.

Semley's guides stopped at a parting of three tunnels, all blocked by doors that looked to be of iron. "We shall wait, Angya," they said, and eight of them stayed with her, while three others unlocked one of the doors and passed through. It fell to behind them with a clash.

Straight and still stood the daughter of the Angyar in the white, blank light of the lamps; her windsteed crouched beside her, flicking the tip of his striped tail, his great folded wings stirring again and again with the checked impulse to fly. In the tunnel behind Semley the eight Claymen squatted on their hams, muttering to one another in their deep voices, in their own tongue.

The central door swung clanging open. "Let the Angya enter the Realm of Night!" cried a new voice, booming and boastful. A Clayman who wore some clothing on his thick grey body stood in the doorway, beckoning to her. "Enter and behold the wonders of our lands, the marvels made by hands, the works of the Nightlords!"

Silent, with a tug at her steed's reins, Semley bowed her head and followed him under the low doorway made for dwarfish folk. Another glaring tunnel stretched ahead, dank walls dazzling in the white light, but, instead of a way to walk upon, its floor carried two bars of polished iron stretching off side by side as far as she could see. On the bars rested some kind of cart with metal wheels. Obeying her new guide's gestures, with no hesitation and no trace of wonder on her face, Semley stepped into the cart and made the windsteed crouch beside her. The Clayman got in and sat down in front of her, moving bars and wheels about. A loud grinding noise arose, and a screaming of metal on metal, and then the walls of the tunnel began to jerk by. Faster and faster the walls slid past, till the fireglobes overhead ran into a blur, and the stale warm air became a foul wind blowing the hood back off her hair.

The cart stopped. Semley followed the guide up basalt steps into a vast anteroom and then a still vaster hall, carved by ancient waters or by the burrowing Clayfolk out of the rock, its darkness that had never known sunlight lit with the uncanny cold brilliance of the globes. In grilles cut in the walls huge blades turned and turned, changing the stale air. The great closed space hummed and boomed with noise, the loud voices of the Clayfolk, the grinding and shrill buzzing and vibration of turning blades and wheels, the echoes and re-echoes of all this from the rock. Here all the stumpy figures of the Claymen were clothed in garments imitating those of the Starlords—divided trousers, soft boots, and hooded tunics—though the few women to be seen, hurrying servile dwarves, were naked. Of the males many were soldiers, bearing at their sides weapons shaped like the terrible light-throwers of the Starlords, though even Semley could see these were merely shaped iron clubs. What she saw, she saw without looking. She followed where she was led, turning her head neither to left nor right. When she came before a group of Claymen who wore iron circlets on their black hair her guide halted, bowed, boomed out, "The High Lords of the Gdemiar!"

There were seven of them, and all looked up at her with such arrogance on their lumpy grey faces that she wanted to laugh.

"I come among you seeking the lost treasure of my family, O Lords of the Dark Realm," she said gravely to them. "I seek Leynen's prize, the Eye of the Sea." Her voice was faint in the racket of the huge vault.

"So said our messengers, Lady Semley." This time she could pick out the one who spoke, one even shorter than the others, hardly reaching Semley's breast, with a white, fierce face. "We do not have this thing you seek."

"Once you had it, it is said."

"Much is said, up there where the sun blinks."

"And words are borne off by the winds, where there are winds to blow. I do not ask how the necklace was lost to us and returned to you, its makers of old. Those are old tales, old grudges. I only seek to find it now. You do not have it now; but it may be you know where it is."

"It is not here."

"Then it is elsewhere."

"It is where you cannot come to it. Never, unless we help you."

"Then help me. I ask this as your guest."

"It is said, *The Angyar take; the Fiia give; the Gdemiar give and take.* If we do this for you, what will you give us?"

"My thanks, Nightlord."

She stood tall and bright among them, smiling. They all stared at her with a heavy, grudging wonder, a sullen yearning.

"Listen, Angya, this is a great favor you ask of us. You do not know how great a favor. You cannot understand. You are of a race that will not understand, that cares for nothing but wind-riding and crop-raising and sword-fighting and shouting together. But who made your swords of the bright steel? We, the Gdemiar! Your lords come to us here and in the Clayfields and buy their swords and go away, not looking, not understanding. But you are here now, you will look, you can see a few of our endless marvels, the lights that burn forever, the car that pulls itself, the machines that make our clothes and cook our food and sweeten our air and serve us in all things. Know that all these things are beyond your understanding. And know this: we, the Gdemiar, are the friends of those you call the Starlords! We came with them to Hallan, to Reohan, to Hul-Orren, to all your castles, to help them speak to you. The lords to whom you, the proud Angyar, pay tribute, are our friends. They do us favors as we do them favors! Now, what do your thanks mean to us?"

"That is your question to answer," said Semley, "not mine. I have asked my question. Answer it, Lord."

For a while the seven conferred together, by word and silence. They would glance at her and look away, and mutter and be still. A crowd grew around them, drawn slowly and silently, one after another till Semley was encircled by hundreds of the matted black heads, and all the great booming cavern floor was covered with people, except a little space directly around her. Her windsteed was quivering with fear and irritation too long controlled, and his eyes had gone very wide and pale, like the eyes of a steed forced to fly at night. She stroked the warm fur of his head, whispering, "Quietly now, brave one, bright one, windlord. . . ."

"Angya, we will take you to the place where the treasure lies." The Clayman with the white face and iron crown had turned to her once more. "More than that we cannot do. You must come with us to claim the necklace where it lies, from those who keep it. The air-beast cannot come with you. You must come alone."

"How far a journey, Lord?"

His lips drew back and back. "A very far journey, Lady. Yet it will last only one long night."

"I thank you for your courtesy. Will my steed be well cared for this night? No ill must come to him."

"He will sleep till you return. A greater windsteed you will have ridden, when you see that beast again! Will you not ask where we take you?"

"Can we go soon on this journey? I would not stay long away from my home."

"Yes. Soon." Again the grey lips widened as he stared up into her face.

What was done in those next hours Semley could not have retold; it was all haste, jumble, noise, strangeness. While she held her steed's head a Clayman stuck a long needle into the golden-striped haunch. She nearly cried out at the sight, but her steed merely twitched and then, purring, fell asleep. He was carried off by a group of Clayfolk who clearly had to summon up their courage to touch his warm fur. Later on she had to see a needle driven into her own arm—perhaps to test her courage, she thought, for it did not seem to make her sleep; though she was not quite sure. There were times she had to travel in the rail-carts, passing iron doors and vaulted caverns by the hundred and hundred; once the rail-cart ran through a cavern that stretched off on either hand measureless into the dark, and all that darkness was full of great flocks of herilor. She could hear their cooing, husky calls, and glimpse the flocks in the front-lights of the cart; then she saw some more clearly in the white light, and saw that they were all wingless, and all blind. At that she shut her eyes. But there were more tunnels to go through, and always more caverns, more grey lumpy bodies and fierce faces and booming boasting voices, until at last they led her suddenly out into the open air. It was full night; she raised her eyes joyfully to the stars and the single moon shining, little Heliki brightening in the west. But the Clayfolk were all about her still, making her climb now into some new kind of cart or cave, she did not know which. It was small, full of little blinking lights like rushlights, very narrow and shining after the great dank caverns and the starlit night. Now another needle was stuck in her, and they told her she would have to be tied down in a sort of flat chair, tied down head and hand and foot.

"I will not," said Semley.

But when she saw that the four Claymen who were to be her guides let themselves be tied down first, she submitted. The others left. There was a roaring sound, and a long silence; a great weight that could not be seen pressed upon her. Then there was no weight; no sound; nothing at all.

"Am I dead?" asked Semley.

"Oh no, Lady," said a voice she did not like.

Opening her eyes, she saw the white face bent over her, the wide lips pulled back, the eyes like little stones. Her bonds had fallen away from her, and she leaped up. She was weightless, bodiless; she felt herself only a gust of terror on the wind.

"We will not hurt you," said the sullen voice or voices. "Only let us touch you, Lady. We would like to touch your hair. Let us touch your hair. . . ."

The round cart they were in trembled a little. Outside its one window lay blank night, or was it mist, or nothing at all? One long night, they had said. Very long. She sat motionless and endured the touch of their heavy grey hands on her hair. Later they would touch her hands and feet and arms, and once her throat: at that she set her teeth and stood up, and they drew back.

"We have not hurt you, Lady," they said. She shook her head.

When they bade her, she lay down again in the chair that bound her down; and when light flashed golden, at the window, she would have wept at the sight, but fainted first.

"Well," said Rocannon, "now at least we know what she is."

"I wish there were some way of knowing *who* she is," the curator mumbled. "She wants something we've got here in the Museum, is that what the trogs say?"

"Now, don't call 'em trogs," Rocannon said conscientiously; as a hilfer, an ethnologist of the High Intelligence Life-forms, he was supposed to resist such words. "They're not pretty, but they're Status C Allies. . . . I wonder why the Commission picked them to develop? Before even contacting all the HILF species? I'll bet the survey was from Centaurus— Centaurans always like nocturnals and cave dwellers. I'd have backed Species II, here, I think."

"The troglodytes seem to be rather in awe of her."

"Aren't you?"

Ketho glanced at the tall woman again, then reddened and laughed. "Well, in a way. I never saw such a beautiful alien type in eighteen years here on New South Georgia. I never saw such a beautiful woman anywhere, in fact. She looks like a goddess." The red now reached the top of his bald head, for Ketho was a shy curator, not given to hyperbole. But Rocannon nodded soberly, agreeing.

"I wish we could talk to her without those tr—Gdemiar as interpreters. But there's no help for it." Rocannon went toward their visitor, and when she turned her splendid face to him he bowed down very deeply, going right down to the floor on one knee, his head bowed and his eyes shut. This was what he called his All-Purpose Intercultural Curtsey, and he performed it with some grace. When he came erect again the beautiful woman smiled and spoke.

"She say, Hail, Lord of Stars," growled one of her squat escorts in Pidgin-Galactic.

"Hail, Lady of the Angyar," Rocannon replied. "In what way can we of the Museum serve the lady?"

Across the troglodytes' growling her voice ran like a brief silver wind.

"She say, Please give her necklace which treasure her blood-kinforebears long long."

"Which necklace?" he asked, and understanding him, she pointed to the central display of the case before them, a magnificent thing, a chain of yellow gold, massive but very delicate in workmanship, set with one big hot-blue sapphire. Rocannon's eyebrows went up, and Ketho at his shoulder murmured, "She's got good taste. That's the Fomalhaut Necklace—famous bit of work."

She smiled at the two men, and again spoke to them over the heads of the troglodytes.

"She say, O Starlords, Elder and Younger Dwellers in House of Treasures, this treasure her one. Long long time. Thank you."

"How did we get the thing, Ketho?"

"Wait; let me look it up in the catalogue. I've got it here. Here. It came from these trogs—trolls—whatever they are: Gdemiar. They have a bargain-obsession, it says; we had to let 'em buy the ship they came here on, an AD-4. This was part payment. It's their own handiwork."

"And I'll bet they can't do this kind of work anymore, since they've been steered to Industrial."

"But they seem to feel the thing is hers, not theirs or ours. It must be important, Rocannon, or they wouldn't have given up this time-span to her errand. Why, the objective lapse between here and Fomalhaut must be considerable!"

"Several years, no doubt," said the hilfer, who was used to star-jumping. "Not very far. Well, neither the *Handbook* nor the *Guide* gives me enough data to base a decent guess on. These species obviously haven't been properly studied at all. The little fellows may be showing her simple courtesy. Or an interspecies war may depend on this damn sapphire. Perhaps her desire rules them, because they consider themselves totally inferior to her. Or despite appearances she may be their prisoner, their decoy. How can we tell? . . . Can you give the thing away, Ketho?"

"Oh, yes. All the Exotica are technically on loan, not our property, since these claims come up now and then. We seldom argue. Peace above all, until the War comes. . . ."

"Then I'd say give it to her."

Ketho smiled. "It's a privilege," he said. Unlocking the case, he lifted out the great golden chain; then, in his shyness, he held it out to Rocannon, saying, "You give it to her."

So the blue jewel first lay, for a moment, in Rocannon's hand.

His mind was not on it; he turned straight to the beautiful, alien woman, with his handful of blue fire and gold. She did not raise her hands to take it, but bent her head, and he slipped the necklace over her hair. It lay like a burning fuse along her golden-brown throat. She looked up from it with such pride, delight, and gratitude in her face that Rocannon stood wordless, and the little curator murmured hurriedly in his own language, "You're welcome, you're very welcome." She bowed her golden head to him and to Rocannon. Then, turning, she nodded to her squat guards—or captors?—and, drawing her worn blue cloak about her, paced down the long hall and was gone. Ketho and Rocannon stood looking after her.

"What I feel . . ." Rocannon began.

"Well?" Ketho inquired hoarsely, after a long pause.

"What I feel sometimes is that I . . . meeting these people from worlds we know so little of, you know, sometimes . . . that I have as it were blundered through the corner of a legend, or a tragic myth, maybe, which I do not understand. . . ."

"Yes," said the curator, clearing his throat. "I wonder . . . I wonder what her name is."

Semley the Fair, Semley the Golden, Semley of the Necklace. The Clayfolk had bent to her will, and so had even the Starlords in that terrible place where the Clayfolk had taken her, the city at the end of the night. They had bowed to her, and given her gladly her treasure from amongst their own.

But she could not yet shake off the feeling of those caverns about her where rock lowered overhead, where you could not tell who spoke or what they did, where voices boomed and grey hands reached out— Enough of that. She had paid for the necklace; very well. Now it was hers. The price was paid, the past was the past.

Her windsteed had crept out of some kind of box, with his eyes filmy and his fur rimed with ice, and at first when they had left the caves of the Gdemiar he would not fly. Now he seemed all right again, riding a smooth south wind through the bright sky toward Hallan. "Go quick, go quick," she told him, beginning to laugh as the wind cleared away her mind's darkness. "I want to see Durhal soon, soon. . . ."

And swiftly they flew, coming to Hallan by dusk of the second day. Now the caves of the Clayfolk seemed no more than last year's nightmare, as the steed swooped with her up the thousand steps of Hallan and across the Chasmbridge where the forests fell away for a thousand feet. In the gold light of evening in the flightcourt she dismounted and walked up the last steps between the stiff carven figures of heroes and the two gatewards, who bowed to her, staring at the beautiful, fiery thing around her neck.

In the Forehall she stopped a passing girl, a very pretty girl, by her looks one of Durhal's close kin, though Semley could not call to mind her name. "Do you know me, maiden? I am Semley, Durhal's wife. Will you go tell the Lady Durossa that I have come back?"

For she was afraid to go on in and perhaps face Durhal at once, alone; she wanted Durossa's support.

The girl was gazing at her, her face very strange. But she murmured, "Yes, Lady," and darted off toward the Tower.

Semley stood waiting in the gilt, ruinous hall. No one came by; were they all at table in the Revel-hall? The silence was uneasy. After a minute Semley started toward the stairs to the Tower. But an old woman was coming to her across the stone floor, holding her arms out, weeping.

"O Semley, Semley!"

She had never seen the grey-haired woman, and shrank back.

"But Lady, who are you?"

"I am Durossa, Semley."

She was quiet and still, all the time that Durossa embraced her and wept, and asked if it were true the Clayfolk had captured her and kept her under a spell all these long years, or had it been the Fiia with their strange arts? Then, drawing back a little, Durossa ceased to weep.

"You're still young, Semley. Young as the day you left here. And you wear round your neck the necklace. . . ."

"I have brought my gift to my husband Durhal. Where is he?"

"Durhal is dead."

Semley stood unmoving.

"Your husband, my brother, Durhal Hallanlord was killed seven years ago in battle. Nine years you had been gone. The Starlords came no more. We fell to warring with the Eastern Halls, with the Angyar of Log and Hul-Orren. Durhal, fighting, was killed by a midman's spear, for he had little armor for his body, and none at all for his spirit. He lies buried in the fields above Orren Marsh."

Semley turned away. "I will go to him, then," she said, putting her hand on the gold chain that weighed down her neck. "I will give him my gift."

"Wait, Semley! Durhal's daughter, your daughter, see her now, Haldre the Beautiful!"

It was the girl she had first spoken to and sent to Durossa, a girl of nineteen or so, with eyes like Durhal's eyes, dark blue. She stood beside Durossa, gazing with those steady eyes at this woman Semley who was her mother and was her own age. Their age was the same, and their gold hair, and their beauty. Only Semley was a little taller, and wore the blue stone on her breast.

"Take it, take it. It was for Durhal and Haldre that I brought it from the end of the long night!" Semley cried this aloud, twisting and bowing her head to get the heavy chain off, dropping the necklace so it fell on the stones with a cold, liquid clash. "O take it, Haldre!" she cried again, and then, weeping aloud, turned and ran from Hallan, over the bridge and down the long, broad steps, and, darting off eastward into the forest of the mountainside like some wild thing escaping, was gone.

Fritz Leiber

MOON DUEL

With a fifty-year career that stretched from the "Golden Age" *Astounding* of the 1940s to the beginning of the '90s, the late Fritz Leiber was an indispensable figure in the development of modern science fiction, fantasy, and horror. It is impossible to imagine what those genres would be like today without him, except to say that they would be poorer for it. Probably no other figure of his generation (with the possible exception of L. Sprague de Camp) wrote in as many different genres as Leiber, or was as important as he was to the development of each. Leiber was one of the fathers of modern "heroic fantasy," and his long sequence of stories about Fafhrd and the Gray Mouser remains one of the most complex and intelligent bodies of work in the entire subgenre of "Sword & Sorcery" (which term Leiber himself is usually credited with coining). He may also be one of the best—if not *the* best—writers of the supernatural horror tale since Lovecraft and Poe, and was writing updated "modern" or "urban" horror stories like "Smoke Ghost" and the classic *Conjure Wife* long before the work of Stephen King engendered the Big Horror Boom of the middle 1970s and brought that form to wide popular attention.

Leiber was also a towering Ancestral Figure in science fiction as well, having been one of the major writers of both Campbell's "Golden Age" *Astounding* of the '40s— with works like *Gather, Darkness*—and H.L. Gold's *Galaxy* in the '50s—with works like the classic "Coming Attraction" and the superb novel *The Big Time,* which still holds up as one of the best SF novels *ever* written—and *then* going on to contribute a steady stream of superior fiction to the magazines and anthologies of the '60s, the '70s, and the '80s, as well as powerful novels such as *The Wanderer* and *Our Lady of Darkness. The Big Time* won a well-deserved Hugo in 1959, and Leiber also won a slew of other awards: all told, six Hugos and four Nebulas, plus three World Fantasy Awards—one of them the prestigious Life Achievement Award—and a Grandmaster of Fantasy Award.

Leiber's relationship with Space Opera or the Space Adventure tale was complex and contradictory. His *homage* to Space Opera, the Hugo-winning novel *The Wanderer*—where attractive, seductive, (and rather dominatrix-like) alien Tiger Women in a planet-sized spaceship stop off in our solar system just long enough to demolish our moon for fuel, with disastrous consequences for the Earth—shows a genuine fondness and nostalgia for the form . . . but, at the same time, he used stock Space Opera clichés cunningly, to sharp satiric effect, in stories such as "The Secret Songs"—where a drug-dependant young husband, high on barbiturates and paraldehyde, hallucinates that he is being put to a nightly series of pulp-adventure space-operaish "tests" by his "mentor," a Wise Old Crocodile From Beyond the Magnellanic Clouds—in a manner that seems to signify that he may have grown rather tired of the Interplanetary

Adventure and impatient with its limitations (which was not an isolated opinion among the more intellectual writers of his day, just as it would not be among the radical new writers of the generation just about to rise to prominence—most of them strongly influenced by Leiber—who would collectively produce less adventure SF, particularly Space Opera, than any other comparable generational group of authors). At the very least, when Leiber dabbled in Space Adventure, he insisted on doing something *new*—and often bizarre—with it, as in "A Pail of Air" or the surreal "The Big Trek." So it will come as no surprise that the Moon that Leiber takes us to in the sly and incisive story that follows is not quite like any *other* writer's conception of the place, or that the adventure that we have there is a quirky and surprising one, with unexpected consequences for even the simplest of actions . . .

Fritz Leiber's other books include *The Green Millennium, A Spectre Is Haunting Texas, The Big Engine,* and *The Silver Eggheads,* the collections *The Best of Fritz Leiber, The Book of Fritz Leiber, The Change War, Night's Dark Agents, Heroes and Horrors, The Mind Spider,* and *The Ghost Light,* and the seven volumes of Fafhrd-Gray Mouser stories. Much of this work is out of print, but the Fafhrd-Gray Mouser stories are now being reissued in massive omnibus editions by White Wolf Borealis, the first two of which are *Ill Met in Lankhmar* and *Lean Times in Lankhmar;* the most recent such volume is *Return to Lankhmar.*

First hint I had we'd been spotted by a crusoe was a little *tick* coming to my moonsuit from the miniradar Pete and I were gaily heaving into position near the east end of Gioja crater to scan for wrecks, trash, and nodules of raw metal.

Then came a *whish* which cut off the instant Pete's hand lost contact with the squat instrument. His gauntlet, silvery in the raw low polar sunlight, drew away very slowly, as if he'd grown faintly disgusted with our activity. My gaze kept on turning to see the whole shimmering back of his helmet blown off in a gorgeous sickening brain-fog and blood-mist that was already falling in the vacuum as fine red snow.

A loud *tock* then and glove-sting as the crusoe's second slug hit the miniradar, but my gaze had gone back to the direction Pete had been facing when he bought it—in time to see the green needle-flash of the crusoe's gun in a notch in Gioja's low wall, where the black of the shadowed rock met the gem-like starfields along a jagged border. I unslung my Swift* as I dodged a long step to the side and squeezed off three shots. The first two shells must have traveled a touch too high, but the third made a beautiful fleeting violet

---

* All-purpose vacuum rifle named for the .22 cartridge which as early as 1940 was being produced by Winchester, Remington, and Norma with factory loads giving it a muzzle velocity of 4,140 feet, almost a mile, a second.

globe at the base of the notch. It didn't show me a figure, whole or shattered, silvery or otherwise, on the wall or atop it, but then some crusoes are camouflaged like chameleons and most of them move very fast.

Pete's suit was still falling slowly and stiffly forward. Three dozen yards beyond was a wide black fissure, though exactly how wide I couldn't tell because much of the opposite lip merged into the shadow of the wall. I scooted toward it like a rat toward a hole. On my third step, I caught up Pete by his tool belt and oxy tube while his falling front was still inches away from the powdered pumice, and I heaved him along with me. Some slow or over-drilled part of my brain hadn't yet accepted he was dead.

Then I began to skim forward, inches above the ground myself, kicking back against rocky outcrops thrusting up through the dust—it was like fin-swimming. The crusoe couldn't have been expecting this nut stunt, by which I at least avoided the dreamy sitting-duck slowness of safer, higher-bounding moon-running, for there was a green flash behind me and hurtled dust faintly pittered my soles and seat. He hadn't been leading his target enough. Also, I knew now he had shells as well as slugs.

I was diving over the lip three seconds after skoot-off when Pete's boot caught solidly against a last hooky outcrop. The something in my brain was still stubborn, for I clutched him like clamps, which made me swing around with a jerk. But even that was lucky, for a bright globe two yards through winked on five yards ahead like a mammoth firefly's flash, but not quite as gentle, for the invisible rarified explosion-front hit me hard enough to *boom* my suit and make the air inside slap me. Now I knew he had metal-proximity fuses on some of his shells too—they must be very good at mini-stuff on his home planet.

The tail of the pale green flash showed me the fissure's bottom a hundred yards straight below and all dust, as ninety percent of them are— pray God the dust was deep. I had time to thumb Extreme Emergency to the ship for it to relay automatically to Circumluna. Then the lip had cut me off from the ship and I had lazily fallen out of the glare into the blessed blackness, the dial lights in my helmet already snapped off—even they might make enough glow for the crusoe to aim by. The slug had switched off Pete's.

Ten, twelve seconds to fall and the opposite lip wasn't cutting off the notched crater wall. I could feel the crusoe's gun trailing me down—he'd know moon-G, sticky old five-foot. I could feel his tentacle or finger or claw or ameboid bump tightening on the trigger or button or what. I shoved Pete away from me, parallel to the fissure wall, as hard as I could. Three more seconds, four, and my suit *boomed* again and I was walloped as another green flash showed me the smooth-sifted floor moving up and beginning to hurry a little. This flash was a hemisphere, not a globe—it had burst against the wall—but if there were any rock fragments they missed me. And it exactly bisected the straight line between me and Pete's silvery coffin. The crusoe knew his gun and his Luna—I really admired him, even if my shove had pushed Pete and me, action and reaction, just enough out of the target path. Then the fissure lip had cut the notch and I was readying to land like a three-legged crab, my Swift reslung, my free hand on my belted dust-shoes.

Eleven seconds' fall on Luna is not much more than two on earth, but either are enough to build up a velocity of over fifty feet a second. The dust jarred me hard, but thank God there were no reefs in it. It covered at least all the limbs and front of me, including my helmet-front—my dial lights, snapped on again, showed a grayness fine-grained as flour.

The stuff resisted like flour, too, as I unbelted my dust-shoes. Using them for a purchase, I pulled my other arm and helmet-front free. The stars looked good, even gray-dusted. With a hand on each shoe, I dragged out my legs and, balancing gingerly on the slithery stuff, got each of my feet snapped to a shoe. Then I raised up and switched on my headlight. I hated that. I no more wanted to do it than a hunted animal wants to break twigs or show itself on the skyline, but I knew I had exactly as long to find cover as it would take the crusoe to lope from the notch to the opposite lip of the fissure. Most of them lope very fast, they're that keen on killing.

Well, we started the killing, I reminded myself. *This time I'm the quarry.*

My searchlight made a perverse point of hitting Pete's shimmering casket, spread-eagled, seven-eighths submerged, like a man floating on his back. I swung the beam steadily. The opposite wall was smooth except for a few ledges and cracks and there wasn't any overhang to give a man below cover from someone on top.

But a section of the wall on my side, not fifty yards away, was hugely pocked with holes and half-bubbles where the primeval lava had foamed high and big against the feeble plucking of lunar gravity. I aimed myself at the center of that section and started out. I switched off my headlight and guided myself by the wide band of starfields.

You walk dust-shoes with much the same vertical lift and low methodical forward swing as snowshoes. It was nostalgic, but hunted animals have no time for memory-delicatessen.

Suddenly there was more and redder brightness overhead than the stars. A narrow ribbon of rock along the top of the opposite wall was glaringly bathed in orange, while the rim peaks beyond glowed faintly, like smoldering volcanoes. Light from the orange ribbon bounced down into my fissure, caroming back and forth between the walls until I could dimly see again the holes I was headed for.

The crusoe had popped our ship—both tanks, close together, so that the sun-warmed gasses, exploding out into each other, burned like a hundred torches. The oxyaniline lasted until I reached the holes. I crawled through the biggest. The fading glow dimly and fleetingly showed a rock-bubble twelve feet across with another hole at the back of it. The stuff looked black, felt rough yet diamond-hard. I risked a look behind me.

The ribbon glow was darkest red—the skeleton of our ship still aglow. The ribbon flashed green in the middle—a tiny venomous dagger—and then a huge pale green firefly winked where Pete lay. He'd saved me a fourth time.

I had barely pushed sideways back when there was another of those winks just outside my hole, this one glaringly bright, its front walloping me. I heard through the rock faint *tings* of fragments of Pete's suit hitting the wall, but they may have been only residual ringings, from the nearer blast, in my suit or ears.

I scrambled through the back door in the bubble into a space which I made out by crawling to be a second bubble, resembling the first even to having a back door. I went through that third hole and turned around and rested my Swift's muzzle on the rough-scooped threshold. Since the crusoe lived around here, he'd know the territory better wherever I went. Why retreat farther and get lost? My dial lights showed that about a minute and a half had gone by since Pete bought it. Also, I wasn't losing pressure and I had oxy and heat for four hours—Circumluna would be able to deliver a rescue force in half that time, if my message had got through and if the crusoe didn't scupper them too. Then I got goosy again about the glow of the dial lights and snapped them off. I started to change position and was suddenly afraid the crusoe might already be trailing me by my transmitted sounds through the rock, and right away I held stock still and started to listen for *him*.

No light, no sound, a ghost-fingered gravity—it was like being tested for sanity-span in an anechoic chamber. Almost at once dizziness and the sensory mirages started to come, swimming in blue and burned and moaning from the peripheries of my senses—even waiting in ambush for a crusoe wouldn't stop them; I guess I wanted them to come. So though straining every sense against the crusoe's approach, I had at last to start thinking about him.

It's strange that men should have looked at the moon for millennia and never guessed it was exactly what it looked like: a pale marble graveyard for living dead men, a Dry Tortuga of space where the silver ships from a million worlds marooned their mutineers, their recalcitrants, their criminals, their lunatics. Not on fertile warm-blanketed earth with its quaint adolescent race, which such beings might harm, but on the great silver rock of earth's satellite, to drag out their solitary furious lives, each with his suit and gun and lonely hut or hole, living by recycling his wastes; recycling, too, the bitter angers and hates and delusions which had brought him there. As many as a thousand of them, enough to mine the moon for meals and fuel-gases and to reconquer space and perhaps become masters of earth—had they chosen to cooperate. But their refusal to cooperate was the very thing for which they'd been marooned, and besides that they were of a half thousand different galactic breeds. And so although they had some sort of electronic or psionic or what-not grapevine—at least what happened to one maroon became swiftly known to the others—each of them remained a solitary Friday-less Robinson Crusoe, hence the name.

I risked flashing my time dial. Only another thirty seconds gone. At this rate it would take an eternity for the two hours to pass before I could expect aid *if* my call had got through, while the crusoe— As my senses screwed themselves tighter to their task, my thoughts went whirling off again.

Earthmen shot down the first crusoe they met—in a moment of fumbling panic and against all their training. Ever since then the crusoes have shot first, or tried to, ignoring our belated efforts to communicate.

I brooded for what I thought was a very short while about the age-old problem of a universal galactic code, yet when I flashed my time dial again, seventy minutes had gone somewhere.

That really froze me. He'd had time to stalk and kill me a dozen times—he'd had time to go home and fetch his dogs!—my senses couldn't be *that* good protection with my mind away. Why even now, straining them in my fear, all I got was my own personal static: I heard my heart pounding, my blood roaring, I think for a bit I heard the Brownian movement of the air molecules against my eardrums.

What I hadn't been doing, I told myself, was thinking about the crusoe in a systematic way.

He had a gun like mine and at least three sorts of ammo.

He'd made it from notch to fissure-lip in forty seconds or less—he must be a fast loper, whatever number feet; he might well have a jet unit.

And he'd shot at the miniradar ahead of me. Had he thought it a communicator?—a weapon?—*or some sort of robot as dangerous as a man . . . ?*

My heart had quieted, my ears had stopped roaring, and in that instant I heard through the rock the faintest *scratching*.

Scratch-scratch, scratch-scratch, scratch, scratch, scratch it went, each time a little louder.

I flipped on my searchlight and there coming toward me across the floor of the bubble outside mine was a silver spider as wide as a platter with four opalescent eyes and a green-banded body. Its hanging jaws were like inward-curving notched scissor blades.

I fired by automatism as I fell back. The spider's bubble was filled with violet glare instantly followed by green. I was twice walloped by explosion-fronts and knocked down.

That hardly slowed me a second. The same flashes had shown me a hole in the top of my bubble and as soon as I'd scrambled to my feet I leaped toward it.

I did remember to leap gently. My right hand caught the black rim of the hole and it didn't break off and I drew myself up into the black bubble above. It had no hole in the top, but two high ones in the sides, and I went through the higher one.

I kept on that way. The great igneous bubbles were almost uniform. I always took the highest exit. Once I got inside a bubble with no exit and had to backtrack. After that I scanned first. I kept my searchlight on.

I'd gone through seven or seventeen bubbles before I could start to think about what had happened.

That spider had almost certainly not been my crusoe—or else there was a troop of them dragging a rifle like an artillery piece. And it hadn't likely been an hitherto-unknown, theoretically impossible, live vacuum-arthropod—or else the exotic biologists were in for a great surprise and I'd been right to wet my pants. No, it had most likely been a tracking or tracking-and-attack robot of some sort. Eight legs are a useful number, likewise eight hands. Were the jaws for cutting through suit armor? Maybe it was a robot pet for a lonely being. Here, Spid!

The second explosion? Either the crusoe had fired into the chamber from the other side, or else the spider had carried a bomb to explode when it touched me. Fine use to make of a pet! I giggled. I was relieved, I guess, to think it likely that the spider had been "only" a robot.

Just then—I was in the ninth or nineteenth bubble—the inside of my helmet misted over everywhere. I was panting and sweating and my dehumidifier had overloaded. It was as if I were in a real peasouper of a fog. I could barely make out the black loom of the wall behind me. I switched out my headlight. My time dial showed seventy-two minutes gone. I switched it off and then I did a queer thing.

I leaned back very carefully until as much of my suit as possible touched rock. Then I measuredly thumped the rock ten times with the butt of my Swift and held very still.

Starting with ten would mean we were using the decimal system. Of course there were other possibilities, but . . .

Very faintly, coming at the same rate as mine, I heard six thuds.

What constant started with six? If he'd started with three, I'd have given him one, and so on through a few more places of pi. Or if with one, I'd have given him four—and then started to worry about the third and fourth places in the square root of two. I might take his signal for the beginning of a series with the interval of minus four and rap him back two, but then how could he rap me minus two? Oh why hadn't I simply started rapping out primes? Of course all the integers, in fact all the real numbers, from thirty-seven through forty-one had square roots beginning with six, but which one . . . ?

Suddenly I heard a scratching . . .

My searchbeam was on again, my helmet had unmisted, my present bubble was empty.

Just the same I scuttled out of it, still trending upward where I could. But now the holes wouldn't trend that way. They kept going two down for one up and the lines of bubbles zigzagged. I wanted to go back, but then I might hear the scratching. Once the bubbles started getting smaller. It was like being in solid black suds. I lost any sense of direction. I began to lose the sense of up-down. What's moon-gravity to the numbness of psychosis? I kept my searchlight on although I was sure the glow it made must reach ten bubbles away. I looked all around every bubble before I entered it, especially the overhang just above the entry hole.

Every once in a while I would hear somebody saying Six! Six? Six! like that and then very rapidly seven-eight-nine-five-four-three-two-one-naught. How would you rap naught in the decimal system? That one I finally solved: you'd rap ten.

Finally I came into a bubble that had a side-hole four feet across and edged at the top with diamonds. Very fancy. Was this the Spider Princess' boudoir? There was also a top hole but I didn't bother with that—it had no decor. I switched off my searchlight and looked out the window without exposing my head. The diamonds were stars. After a bit I made out what I took to be the opposite lip of the fissure I'd first dove in, only about one hundred feet above me. The rim-wall beyond looked vaguely familiar, though I wasn't sure about the notch. My time dial said one hundred eighteen minutes gone as I switched it off. Almost time to start hoping for rescue. Oh great!—with their ship a sitting duck for the crusoe they wouldn't be expecting. I hadn't signaled a word besides Extreme Emergency.

I moved forward and sat in the window, one leg outside, my Swift under my left arm. I plucked a flash grenade set for five seconds from my belt, pulled the fuse and tossed it across the fissure, almost hard enough to reach the opposite wall.

I looked down, my Swift swinging like my gaze.

The fissure lit up like a boulevard. Across from me I knew the flare was dropping dreamily, but I wasn't looking that way. Right below me, two hundred feet down, I saw a transparent helmet with something green and round and crested inside and with shoulders under it.

Just then I heard the *scratching* again, quite close.

I fired at once. My shell made a violet burst and raised a fountain of dust twenty feet from the crusoe. I scrambled back into my bubble, switching on my searchlight. Another spider was coming in on the opposite side, its legs moving fast. I jumped for the top-hole and grabbed its rim with my free hand. I'd have dropped my Swift if I'd needed my other hand, but I didn't. As I pulled myself up and through, I looked down and saw the spider straight below me eyeing me with its uptilted opalescent eyes and doubling its silver legs. Then it straightened its legs and sprang up toward me, not very fast but enough against Luna's feeble gravitational tug to put it into this upper room with me. I knew it mustn't touch me and I mustn't touch it by batting at it. I had started to shift the explosive shell in my gun for a slug, and its green-banded body was growing larger, when there was a green blast in the window below and its explosion-front, *booming* my suit a little, knocked the spider aside and out of sight before it made it through the trap door of my new bubble. Yet the spider didn't explode, if that was what had happened to the first one; at any rate there was no second green flash.

My new bubble had a top hole too and I went through it the same way I had the last. The next five bubbles were just the same too. I told myself that my routine was getting to be like that of a circus acrobat—except who stages shows inside black solidity?—except the gods maybe with the dreams they send us. The lava should be transparent, so the rim-wall peaks could admire.

At the same time I was thinking how if the biped humanoid shape is a good one for medium-size creatures on any planet, why so the spider shape is a good one for tiny creatures and apt to turn up anywhere and be copied in robots too.

The top hole in the sixth bubble showed me the stars, while one half of its rim shone white with sunlight.

Panting, I lay back against the rock. I switched off my searchlight. I didn't hear any scratching.

The stars. The stars were energy. They filled the universe with light, except for hidey holes and shadows here and there.

Then the number came to me. With the butt of my Swift I rapped out five. No answer. No scratching either. I rapped out five again.

Then the answer came, ever so faintly. Five knocked back at me.

Six five five—Planck's Constant, the invariant quantum of energy. Oh, it should be to the minus 29th power, of course, but I couldn't think how to rap that and, besides, the basic integers were all that mattered.

I heard the *scratching . . .*

I sprang and caught the rim and lifted myself into the glaring sunlight . . . and stopped with my body midway.

Facing me a hundred feet away, midway through another top-hole— he must have come very swiftly by another branch of the bubble ladder— he'd know the swiftest ones—was my green-crested crusoe. His face had a third eye where a man's nose would be, which with his crest made him look like a creature of mythology. We were holding our guns vertically.

We looked like two of the damned, half out of their holes in the floor of Dante's hell.

I climbed very slowly out of my hole, still pointing my gun toward the zenith. So did he.

We held very still for a moment. Then with his gun butt he rapped out ten. I could both see and also hear it through the rock.

I rapped out three. Then, as if the black bubble-world were one level of existence and this another, I wondered why we were going through this rigamarole. We each knew the other had a suit and a gun (and a lonely hole?) and so we knew we were both intelligent and knew math. So why was our rapping so precious?

He raised his gun—I think to rap out one, to start off pi.

But I'll never be sure, for just then there were two violet bursts, close together, against the fissure wall, quite close to him.

He started to swing the muzzle of his gun toward me. At least I think he did. He must know violet was the color of my explosions. I know I thought someone on my side was shooting. And I must have thought he was going to shoot me—because a violet dagger leaped from my Swift's muzzle and I felt its sharp recoil and then there was a violet globe where he was standing and moments later some fragment *twinged* lightly against my chest—a playful ironic tap.

He was blown apart pretty thoroughly, all his constants scattered, including—I'm sure—Planck's.

It was another half hour before the rescue ship from Circumluna landed. I spent it looking at earth low on the horizon and watching around for the spider, but I never saw it. The rescue party never found it either, though they made quite a hunt—with me helping after I'd rested a bit and had my batteries and oxy replenished. Either its power went off when its master died, or it was set to "freeze" then, or most likely go into a "hide" behavior pattern. Likely it's still out there waiting for an incautious earthman, like a rattlesnake in the desert or an old, forgotten land mine.

I also figured out, while waiting in Gioja crater, there near the north pole on the edge of Shackleton crater, the only explanation I've ever been able to make, though it's something of a whopper, of the two violet flashes which ended my little mathematical friendship-chant with the crusoe. They were the first two shells I squeezed off at him—the ones that skimmed the notch. They had the velocity to orbit Luna, and the time they took—two hours and five minutes—was right enough.

Oh, the consequences of our past actions!

Roger Zelazny

THE DOORS OF HIS FACE,
THE LAMPS OF HIS MOUTH

Like a number of other writers, the late Roger Zelazny began publishing in 1962 in the pages of Cele Goldsmith's *Amazing*. This was the so-called "Class of '62," whose membership also included Thomas M. Disch, Keith Laumer, and Ursula K. Le Guin. Everyone in that "class" would eventually achieve prominence, but some of them would achieve it faster than others, and Zelazny's subsequent career would be one of the most meteoric in the history of SF. The first Zelazny story to attract wide notice was "A Rose for Ecclesiastes," published in 1963 (it was later selected by vote of the SFWA membership to have been one of the best SF stories of all time). By the end of that decade, he had won two Nebula Awards and two Hugo Awards and was widely regarded as one of the two most important American SF writers of the '60s (the other was Samuel R. Delany). His famous novel *Lord of Light* may have been one of the most popular, widely acclaimed, and hugely influential novels of that whole era. By the end of the '70s, although his critical acceptance as an important science fiction writer had dimmed, his long series of novels about the enchanted land of Amber—beginning with *Nine Princes in Amber*—had made him one of the most popular and best-selling fantasy writers of our time, and inspired the founding of worldwide fan clubs and fanzines.

Zelazny's early novels, such as *This Immortal* and *The Dream Masters,* were, on the whole, well-received, but it was the strong and stylish short work he published in magazines like *F&SF* and *Amazing* and *Worlds of If* throughout the middle years of the decade of the 1960s that electrified the genre, and it was these early stories—stories like "This Moment of the Storm," "The Graveyard Heart," "He Who Shapes," "The Keys to December," "For a Breath I Tarry," and "This Mortal Mountain,"—that established Zelazny as a giant of the field, and that many consider to be his best work. These stories are still amazing for their invention and elegance and verve, for their good-natured effrontery and easy ostentation, for the risks Zelazny took in pursuit of eloquence without ruffling a hair, the grace and nerve he displayed as he switched from high-flown pseudo-Spenserian to wisecracking Chandlerian slang to vivid prose-poetry to Hemingwayesque starkness in the course of only a few lines—and for the way he made it all look easy and effortless, the same kind of illusion Fred Astaire used to generate when he danced.

Unlike some of his peers, Zelazny's fondness for fast-paced adventure writing never faded, which may be one reason for the dimming of his critical reputation in the '70s, as he continued to turn out what were dismissed as "routine Space Adventures" by hostile critics during a period that demanded more "serious" and "ambitious" work by its writers. Zelazny's work was *never* "routine," however—some of his books of this period *were* rather weak by his own standards, but in even the weakest of them, you could count on inventiveness, vivid color, scope, intricate plotting, quirky characters . . . and, of course, plenty of action.

One of the inspirations for the famous story that follows, as well as for the even more famous "A Rose for Ecclesiastes," is clearly a loving nostalgia for the era of the pulp adventure story that was then widely supposed to be ending. By the time Zelazny wrote this story, he knew perfectly well that Venus was probably *not* an Earth-like planet girded by vast seas full of immense swimming dinosaur-like creatures, just as he knew that in all likelihood there were no canals and decadent, dying, ancient races of intelligent beings on Mars—so that these stories, which still feature the lushly romantic pulp version of those planets that had been popularized in tales from *Planet Stories* and *Thrilling Wonder Stories* decades before, can be seen as an homage, a deliberate act of retro nostalgia for those beloved worlds, written in the last possible tick of time before the hardest of hard proof—the actual *visitation* of those planets by exploring space probes, only a few years later—would come along to make those garish, melodramatic, and gorgeously colored pulp visions of what Venus and Mars were like totally untenable. For a long time after this, it was considered to be no longer possible to write an adventure story or a Planetary Romance set on any of the planets of the solar system—which were now considered to be just sterile, lifeless balls of rock (especially after the first Viking lander mission in 1976 had found no trace of life in the soil of Mars), as unromantic and uninteresting and drab as a parking lot, settings that offered few opportunities for stories at all, let alone for John Carter-like swashbuckling—and indeed, few stories set on any planet of the solar system except for the Earth were written for the next decade. It wasn't until late in the '70s and the early '80s that new generations of writers would come along who began to find the solar system romantic and evocative *just as it was,* and began to write stories, even lush adventure stories, once again set on planets such as Venus and Mars. So even though Zelazny almost certainly intended "The Doors of His Face, the Lamps of His Mouth" to be a Farewell to Fantastic Venus (to paraphrase an Aldiss anthology title), he was being premature—within another decade or so, writers would be back exploring Venus again; thanks to the notion of terraforming, even the *seas* of Venus would be back in some stories—although the monstrous, mountain-like Inky remains, so far, unique to the vivid story that follows.

Zelazny won another Nebula and Hugo Award in 1976 for his novella "Home Is the Hangman," another Hugo in 1986 for his novella "24 Views of Mt. Fuji, by Hokusai," and a final Hugo in 1987 for his story "Permafrost." His other books include, in addition to the multi-volume *Amber* series, the novels *This Immortal, The Dream Master, Isle of the Dead, Jack of Shadows, Eye of Cat, Doorways in the Sand, Today We Choose Faces, Bridge of Ashes, To Die in Italbar,* and *Roadmarks,* and the collections *Four For Tomorrow, The Doors of His Face, the Lamps of His Mouth and Other Stories, The Last Defender of Camelot,* and *Frost and Fire.* Among his last books are two collaborative novels, *A Farce to Be Reckoned With,* with Robert Sheckley, and *Wilderness,* with Gerald Hausman, and, as editor, two anthologies, *Wheel of Fortune* and *Warriors of Blood and Dream.* Zelazny died—a tragically untimely death—in 1995.

A collaborative novel with Jane Lindskold, *Donnerjack,* was published recently, and another posthumous collaboration. Zelazny's completion of an unfinished Alfred Bester novel entitled *Psychoshop,* has just been published.

I'm a baitman. No one is born a baitman, except in a French novel where everyone is. (In fact, I think that's the title, *We Are All Bait,* Pfft!) How I got that way is barely worth telling and has nothing to do with neo-exes, but the days of the beast deserve a few words, so here they are.

The Lowlands of Venus lie between the thumb and forefinger of the continent known as Hand. When you break into Cloud Alley it swings its silverblack bowling ball toward you without a warning. You jump then, inside that firetailed tenpin they ride you down in, but the straps keep you from making a fool of yourself. You generally chuckle afterwards, but you always jump first.

Next, you study Hand to lay its illusion and the two middle fingers become dozen-ringed archipelagoes as the outers resolve into greengray peninsulas; the thumb is too short, and curls like the embryo tail of Cape Horn.

You suck pure oxygen, sigh possibly, and begin the long topple to the Lowlands.

There, you are caught like an infield fly at the Lifeline landing area—so named because of its nearness to the great delta in the Eastern Bay—located between the first peninsula and "thumb." For a minute it seems as if you're going to miss Lifeline and wind up as canned seafood, but afterwards—shaking off the metaphors—you descend to scorched concrete and present your middle-sized telephone directory of authorizations to the short, fat man in the gray cap. The papers show that you are not subject to mysterious inner rottings and etcetera. He then smiles you a short, fat, gray smile and motions you toward the bus which hauls you to the Reception Area. At the R.A. you spend three days proving that, indeed, you are not subject to mysterious inner rottings and etcetera.

Boredom, however, is another rot. When your three days are up, you generally hit Lifeline hard, and it returns the compliment as a matter of reflex. The effects of alcohol in variant atmospheres is a subject on which the connoisseurs have written numerous volumes, so I will confine my remarks to noting that a good binge is worthy of at least a week's time and often warrants a lifetime study.

I had been a student of exceptional promise (strictly undergraduate) for going on two years when the *Bright Water* fell through our marble ceiling and poured its people like targets into the city.

Pause. The Worlds Almanac re Lifeline: ". . . Port city on the eastern coast of Hand. Employees of the Agency for Non-terrestrial Research compromise approximately 85% of its 100,000 population (2010 Census). Its other residents are primarily personnel maintained by several industrial corporations engaged in basic research. Independent marine biologists, wealthy fishing enthusiasts, and waterfront entrepreneurs make up the remainder of its inhabitants."

I turned to Mike Dabis, a fellow entrepreneur, and commented on the lousy state of basic research.

"Not if the mumbled truth be known."

He paused behind his glass before continuing the slow swallowing process calculated to obtain my interest and a few oaths, before he continued.

"Carl," he finally observed, poker playing, "they're shaping Tensquare."

I could have hit him. I might have refilled his glass with sulfuric acid and looked on with glee as his lips blackened and cracked. Instead, I grunted a noncommittal.

"Who's fool enough to shell out fifty grand a day? ANR?"

He shook his head.

"Jean Luharich," he said, "the girl with the violet contacts and fifty or sixty perfect teeth. I understand her eyes are really brown."

"Isn't she selling enough face cream these days?"

He shrugged.

"Publicity makes the wheels go 'round. Luharich Enterprises jumped sixteen points when she picked up the Sun Trophy. You ever play golf on Mercury?"

I had, but I overlooked it and continued to press.

"So she's coming here with a blank check and a fishhook?"

"*Bright Water,* today," he nodded. "Should be down by now. Lots of cameras. She wants an Ikky, bad."

"Hmm," I hmmed. "How bad?"

"Sixty day contract, Tensquare. Indefinite extension clause. Million and a half deposit," he recited

"You seem to know a lot about it."

"I'm Personal Recruitment. Luharich Enterprises approached me last month. It helps to drink in the right places.

"Or own them." He smirked, after a moment.

I looked away, sipping my bitter brew. After awhile I swallowed several things and asked Mike what he expected to be asked, leaving myself open for his monthly temperance lecture.

"They told me to try getting you," he mentioned. "When's the last time you sailed?"

"Month and a half ago. The *Corning.*"

"Small stuff," he snorted. "When have you been under, yourself?"

"It's been awhile."

"It's been over a year, hasn't it? That time you got cut by the screw, under the *Dolphin?*"

I turned to him.

"I was in the river last week, up at Angleford where the currents are strong. I can still get around."

"Sober," he added.

"I'd stay that way," I said, "on a job like this."

A doubting nod.

"Straight union rates. Triple time for extraordinary circumstances," he narrated. "Be at Hangar Sixteen with your gear, Friday morning, five hundred hours. We push off Saturday, daybreak."

"You're sailing?"

"I'm sailing."

"How come?"

"Money."

"Ikky guano."

"The bar isn't doing so well and baby needs new minks."

"I repeat—"

". . . And I want to get away from baby, renew my contact with basics—fresh air, exercise, make cash. . . ."

"All right, sorry I asked."

I poured him a drink, concentrating on H_2SO_4, but it didn't transmute. Finally I got him soused and went out into the night to walk and think things over.

Around a dozen serious attempts to land *Ichthyform Leviosaurus Levianthus,* generally known as "Ikky," had been made over the past five years. When Ikky was first sighted, whaling techniques were employed. These proved either fruitless or disastrous, and a new procedure was inaugurated. Tensquare was constructed by a wealthy sportsman named Michael Jandt, who blew his entire roll on the project.

After a year on the Eastern Ocean, he returned to file bankruptcy. Carlton Davits, a playboy fishing enthusiast, then purchased the huge raft and laid a wake for Ikky's spawning grounds. On the nineteenth day out he had a strike and lost one hundred and fifty bills' worth of untested gear, along with one *Ichthyform Levianthus.* Twelve days later, using tripled lines, he hooked, narcotized, and began to hoist the huge beast. It awakened then, destroyed a control tower, killed six men, and worked general hell over five square blocks of Tensquare. Carlton was left with partial hemiplegia and a bankruptcy suit of his own. He faded into waterfront atmosphere and Tensquare changed hands four more times, with less spectacular but equally expensive results.

Finally, the big raft, built only for one purpose, was purchased at auction by ANR for "marine research." Lloyd's still won't insure it, and the only marine research it has ever seen is an occasional rental at fifty bills a day—to people anxious to tell Leviathan fish stories. I've been baitman on three of the voyages, and I've been close enough to count Ikky's fangs on two occasions. I want one of them to show my grandchildren, for personal reasons.

I faced the direction of the landing area and resolved a resolve.

"You want me for local coloring, gal. It'll look nice on the feature page and all that. But clear this—If anyone gets you an Ikky, it'll be me. I promise."

I stood in the empty Square. The foggy towers of Lifeline shared their mists.

Shoreline a couple eras ago, the western slope above Lifeline stretches as far as forty miles inland in some places. Its angle of rising is not a great one, but it achieves an elevation of several thousand feet before it meets the mountain range which separates us from the Highlands. About four miles inland and five hundred feet higher than Lifeline are set most of the surface airstrips and privately owned hangars. Hangar Sixteen houses Cal's Contract Cab, hop service, shore to ship. I do not like Cal, but he wasn't around when I climbed from the bus and waved to a mechanic.

Two of the hoppers tugged at the concrete, impatient beneath flywing haloes. The one on which Steve was working belched deep within its barrel carburetor and shuddered spasmodically.

"Bellyache?" I inquired.

"Yeah, gas pains and heartburn."

He twisted setscrews until it settled into an even keening, and turned to me.

"You're for out?"

I nodded.

"Tensquare. Cosmetics. Monsters. Stuff like that."

He blinked into the beacons and wiped his freckles. The temperature was about twenty, but the big overhead spots served a double purpose.

"Luharich," he muttered. "Then you *are* the one. There's some people want to see you."

"What about?"

"Cameras. Microphones. Stuff like that."

"I'd better stow my gear. Which one am I riding?"

He poked the screwdriver at the other hopper.

"That one. You're on video tape now, by the way. They wanted to get you arriving."

He turned to the hangar, turned back.

"Say 'cheese.' They'll shoot the close-ups later."

I said something other than "cheese." They must have been using telelens and been able to read my lips, because that part of the tape was never shown.

I threw my junk in the back, climbed into a passenger seat, and lit a cigarette. Five minutes later, Cal himself emerged from the office Quonset, looking cold. He came over and pounded on the side of the hopper. He jerked a thumb back at the hangar.

"They want you in there!" he called through cupped hands. "Interview!"

"The show's over!" I yelled back. "Either that, or they can get themselves another baitman!"

His rustbrown eyes became nailheads under blond brows and his glare a spike before he jerked about and stalked off. I wondered how much they had paid him to be able to squat in his hangar and suck juice from his generator.

Enough, I guess, knowing Cal. I never liked the guy, anyway.

Venus at night is a field of sable waters. On the coasts, you can never tell where the sea ends and the sky begins. Dawn is like dumping milk into an inkwell. First, there are erratic curdles of white, then streamers. Shade the bottle for a gray colloid, then watch it whiten a little more. All of a sudden you've got day. Then start heating the mixture.

I had to shed my jacket as we flashed out over the bay. To our rear, the skyline could have been under water for the way it waved and rippled in the heatfall. A hopper can accommodate four people (five, if you want to bend Regs and underestimate weight), or three passengers with the sort of gear a baitman uses. I was the only fare, though, and the pilot was like his machine. He hummed and made no unnecessary noises. Lifeline turned a somersault and evaporated in the rear mirror at about the same time Tensquare broke the fore-horizon. The pilot stopped humming and shook his head.

I leaned forward. Feelings played flopdoodle in my guts. I knew every bloody inch of the big raft, but the feelings you once took for granted change when their source is out of reach. Truthfully, I'd had my doubts I'd ever board the hulk again. But now, now I could almost believe in predestination. There it was!

A tensquare football field of a ship. A-powered. Flat as a pancake, except for the plastic blisters in the middle and the "Rooks" fore and aft, port and starboard.

The Rook towers were named for their corner positions—and any two can work together to hoist, co-powering the graffles between them. The graffles—half gaff, half grapple—can raise enormous weights to near water level; their designer had only one thing in mind, though, which accounts for the gaff half. At water level, the Slider has to implement elevation for six to eight feet before the graffles are in a position to push upward, rather than pulling.

The Slider, essentially, is a mobile room—a big box capable of moving in any of Tensquare's crisscross groovings and "anchoring" on the strike side by means of a powerful electromagnetic bond. Its winches could hoist a battleship the necessary distance, and the whole craft would tilt, rather than the Slider come loose, if you want any idea of the strength of that bond.

The Slider houses a section operated control indicator which is the most sophisticated "reel" ever designed. Drawing broadcast power from the generator beside the center blister, it is connected by shortwave with the sonar room, where the movements of the quarry are recorded and repeated to the angler seated before the section control.

The fisherman might play his "lines" for hours, days even, without seeing any more than metal and an outline on the screen. Only when the beast is graffled and the extensor shelf, located twelve feet below waterline, slides out for support and begins to aid the winches, only then does the fisherman see his catch rising before him like a fallen Seraph. Then, as Davits learned, one looks into the Abyss itself and is required to act. He didn't, and a hundred meters of unimaginable tonnage, undernarcotized and hurting, broke the cables of the winch, snapped a graffle, and took a half-minute walk across Tensquare.

We circled till the mechanical flag took notice and waved us on down. We touched beside the personnel hatch and I jettisoned my gear and jumped to the deck.

"Luck," called the pilot as the door was sliding shut. Then he danced into the air and the flag clicked blank.

I shouldered my stuff and went below.

Signing in with Malvern, the de facto captain, I learned that most of the others wouldn't arrive for a good eight hours. They had wanted me alone at Cal's so they could pattern the pub footage along twentieth-century cinema lines.

Open: landing strip, dark. One mechanic prodding a contrary hopper. Stark-o-vision shot of slow bus pulling in. Heavily dressed baitman descends, looks about, limps across field. Close-up: he grins. Move in for words: "Do you think this is the time? The time he *will* be landed?" Embarrassment, taciturnity, a shrug. Dub something—"I see. And why do you think Miss Luharich has a better chance than any of the others? It is because she's better equipped? [Grin.] Because more is known now about the creature's habits than when you were out before? Or is it because of her will to win, to be a champion? Is it any one of these things, or is it all of them?" Reply: "Yeah, all of them." "—Is that why you signed on with her? Because your instincts say, 'This one will be it'?" Answer: "She pays union rates. I couldn't rent that damned thing myself. And I want in." Erase. Dub something else. Fadeout as he moves toward hopper, etcetera.

"Cheese," I said, or something like that, and took a walk around Tensquare, by myself.

I mounted each Rook, checking out the controls and the underwater video eyes. Then I raised the main lift.

Malvern had no objections to my testing things this way. In fact, he encouraged it. We had sailed together before and our positions had even been reversed upon a time. So I wasn't surprised when I stepped off the lift into the Hopkins Locker and found him waiting. For the next ten minutes we inspected the big room in silence, walking through its copper coil chambers soon to be Arctic.

Finally, he slapped a wall.

"Well, will we fill it?"

I shook my head.

"I'd like to, but I doubt it. I don't give two hoots and a damn who gets credit for the catch, so long as I have a part in it. But it won't happen. That gal's an egomaniac. She'll want to operate the Slider, and she can't."

"You ever meet her?"

"Yeah."

"How long ago?"

"Four, five years."

"She was a kid then. How do you know what she can do now?"

"I know. She'll have learned every switch and reading by this time. She'll be up on all theory. But do you remember one time we were together in the starboard Rook, forward, when Ikky broke water like a porpoise?"

"How could I forget?"

"Well?"

He rubbed his emery chin.

"Maybe she can do it, Carl. She's raced torch ships and she's scubaed in bad waters back home." He glanced in the direction of invisible Hand. "And she's hunted in the Highlands. She might be wild enough to pull that horror into her lap without flinching.

". . . For John Hopkins to foot the bill and shell out seven figures for the corpus," he added. "That's money, even to a Luharich."

I ducked through a hatchway.

"Maybe you're right, but she was a rich witch when I knew her."

"And she wasn't blonde," I added, meanly.

He yawned.

"Let's find breakfast."

We did that.

When I was young I thought that being born a sea creature was the finest choice Nature could make for anyone. I grew up on the Pacific coast and spent my summers on the Gulf or the Mediterranean. I lived months of my life negotiating coral, photographing trench dwellers, and playing tag with dolphins. I fished everywhere there are fish, resenting the fact that they can go places I can't. When I grew older I wanted bigger fish, and there was nothing living that I knew of, excepting a Sequoia, that came any bigger than Ikky. That's part of it. . . .

I jammed a couple of extra rolls into a paper bag and filled a thermos with coffee. Excusing myself, I left the galley and made my way to the Slider berth. It was just the way I remembered it. I threw a few switches and the shortwave hummed.

"That you, Carl?"

"That's right, Mike. Let me have some juice down here, you double-crossing rat."

He thought it over, then I felt the hull vibrate as the generators cut in. I poured my third cup of coffee and found a cigarette.

"So why am I a double-crossing rat this time?" came his voice again.

"You knew about the cameramen at Hangar Sixteen?"

"Yes."

"Then you're a double-crossing rat. The last thing I want is publicity. 'He who fouled up so often before is ready to try it, nobly once more.' I can read it now."

"You're wrong. The spotlight's only big enough for one, and she's prettier than you."

My next comment was cut off as I threw the elevator switch and the elephant ears flapped above me. I rose, settling flush with the deck. Retracting the lateral rail, I cut forward into the groove. Amidships, I stopped at a juncture, dropped the lateral, and retracted the longitudinal rail.

I slid starboard, midway between the Rooks, halted, and threw on the coupler.

I hadn't spilled a drop of coffee.

"Show me pictures."

The screen glowed. I adjusted and got outlines of the bottom.

"Okay."

I threw a Status Blue switch and he matched it. The light went on. The winch unlocked. I aimed out over the waters, extended the arm, and fired a cast.

"Clean one," he commented.

"Status Red. Call strike." I threw a switch.

"Status Red."

The baitman would be on his way with this, to make the barbs tempting.

It's not exactly a fishhook. The cables bear hollow tubes; the tubes convey enough dope for any army of hopheads; Ikky takes the bait, dangled before him by remote control, and the fisherman rams the barbs home.

My hands moved over the console, making the necessary adjustments. I checked the narco-tank reading. Empty. Good, they hadn't been filled yet. I thumbed the Inject button.

"In the gullet," Mike murmured.

I released the cables. I played the beast imagined. I let him run, swinging the winch to stimulate his sweep.

I had an air conditioner on and my shirt off and it was still uncomfortably hot, which is how I knew that morning had gone over into noon. I was dimly aware of the arrivals and departures of the hoppers. Some of the crew sat in the "shade" of the doors I had left open, watching the operation. I didn't see Jean arrive or I would have ended the session and gotten below.

She broke my concentration by slamming the door hard enough to shake the bond.

"Mind telling me who authorized you to bring up the Slider?" she asked.

"No one," I replied. I'll take it below now."

"Just move aside."

I did, and she took my seat. She was wearing brown slacks and a baggy shirt and she had her hair pulled back in a practical manner. Her cheeks were flushed, but not necessarily from the heat. She attacked the panel with a nearly amusing intensity that I found disquieting.

"Status Blue," she snapped, breaking a violet fingernail on the toggle.

I forced a yawn and buttoned my shirt slowly. She threw a side glance my way, checked the registers, and fired a cast.

I monitored the lead on the screen. She turned to me for a second.

"Status Red," she said levelly.

I nodded my agreement.

She worked the winch sideways to show she knew how. I didn't doubt she knew how and she didn't doubt that I didn't doubt, but then—

"In case you're wondering," she said, "you're not going to be anywhere near this thing. You were hired as a baitman, remember? Not a Slider operator! A baitman! Your duties consist of swimming out and setting the table for our friend the monster. It's dangerous, but you're getting well paid for it. Any questions?"

She squashed the Inject button and I rubbed my throat.

"Nope," I smiled, "but I am qualified to run that thingamajigger— and if you need me I'll be available, at union rates."

"Mister Davits," she said, "I don't want a loser operating this panel."

"Miss Luharich, there has never been a winner at this game."

She started reeling in the cable and broke the bond at the same time, so that the whole Slider shook as the big yo-yo returned. We skidded a couple of feet backward. She raised the laterals and we shot back along the groove. Slowing, she transferred rails and we jolted to a clanging halt, then shot off at a right angle. The crew scrambled away from the hatch as we skidded onto the elevator.

"In the future, Mister Davits, do not enter the Slider without being ordered," she told me.

"Don't worry. I won't even step inside if I am ordered," I answered. "I signed on as a baitman. Remember? If you want me in here, you'll have to *ask* me."

"That'll be the day," she smiled.

I agreed, as the doors closed above us. We dropped the subject and headed in our different directions after the Slider came to a halt in its berth. She did say "good day," though, which I thought showed breeding as well as determination, in reply to my chuckle.

Later that night Mike and I stoked our pipes in Malvern's cabin. The winds were shuffling waves, and a steady spattering of rain and hail overhead turned the deck into a tin roof.

"Nasty," suggested Malvern.

I nodded. After two bourbons the room had become a familiar woodcut, with its mahogany furnishings (which I had transported from Earth long ago on a whim) and the dark walls, the seasoned face of Malvern, and the perpetually puzzled expression of Dabis set between the big pools of shadow that lay behind chairs and splashed in cornets, all cast by the tiny table light and seen through a glass, brownly.

"Glad I'm in here."

"What's it like underneath on a night like this?"

I puffed, thinking of my light cutting through insides of a black diamond, shaken slightly. The meteor-dart of a suddenly illuminated fish, the swaying of grotesque ferns, like nebulae—shadow, then green, then gone—swam in a moment through my mind. I guess it's like a spaceship would feel, if a spaceship could feel, crossing between worlds—and quiet, uncannily, preternaturally quiet; and peaceful as sleep.

"Dark," I said, "and not real choppy below a few fathoms."

"Another eight hours and we shove off," commented Mike.

"Ten, twelve days, we should be there," noted Malvern.

"What do you think Ikky's doing?"

"Sleeping on the bottom with Mrs. Ikky if he has any brains."

"He hasn't. I've seen ANR's skeletal extrapolation from the bones that have washed up—"

"Hasn't everyone?"

". . . Fully fleshed, he'd be over a hundred meters long. That right, Carl?"

I agreed.

". . . Not much of a brain box, though, for his bulk."

"Smart enough to stay out of our locker."

Chuckles, because nothing exists but this room, really. The world outside is an empty, sleet drummed deck. We lean back and make clouds.

"Boss lady does not approve of unauthorized fly fishing."

"Boss lady can walk north till her hat floats."

"What did she say in there?"

"She told me that my place, with fish manure, is on the bottom."

"You don't Slide?"

"I bait."

"We'll see."

"That's all I do. If she wants a Slideman she's going to have to ask nicely."

"You think she'll have to?"

"I think she'll have to."

"And if she does, can you do it?"

"A fair question," I puffed. "I don't know the answer, though."

I'd incorporate my soul and trade forty percent of the stock for the answer. I'd give a couple years off my life for the answer. But there doesn't seem to be a lineup of supernatural takers, because no one knows.

Supposing when we get out there, luck being with us, we find ourselves an Ikky? Supposing we succeed in baiting him and get lines on him. What then? If we get him shipside, will she hold on or crack up? What if she's made of sterner stuff than Davits, who used to hunt sharks with poison-darted air pistols? Supposing she lands him and Davits has to stand there like a video extra.

Worse yet, supposing she asks for Davits and he still stands there like a video extra or something else—say, some yellowbellied embodiment named Cringe?

It was when I got him up above the eight-foot horizon of steel and looked out at all that body, sloping on and on till it dropped out of sight like a green mountain range . . . And that head. Small for the body, but still immense. Fat, craggy, with lidless roulettes that had spun black and red since before my forefathers decided to try the New Continent. And swaying.

Fresh narco-tanks had been connected. It needed another shot, fast. But I was paralyzed.

It had made a noise like God playing a Hammond organ. . . .

And looked at me!

I don't know if seeing is even the same process in eyes like those. I doubt it. Maybe I was just a gray blur behind a black rock, with the plexi-reflected sky hurting its pupils. But it fixed on me. Perhaps the snake doesn't really paralyze the rabbit, perhaps it's just that rabbits are cowards by constitution. But it began to struggle and I still couldn't move, fascinated.

Fascinated by all that power, by those eyes, they found me there fif-teen minutes later, a little broken about the head and shoulders, the Inject still unpushed.

And I dream about those eyes. I want to face them once more, even if their finding takes forever. I've got to know if there's something inside me that sets me apart from a rabbit, from notched plates of reflexes and instincts that always fall apart in exactly the same way whenever the proper combination is spun.

Looking down, I noticed that my hand was shaking. Glancing up, I noticed that no one else was noticing.

I finished my drink and emptied my pipe. It was late and no song-birds were singing.

I sat whittling, my legs hanging over the aft edge, the chips spinning down into the furrow of our wake. Three days out. No action.

"You!"

"Me?"

"You."

Hair like the end of the rainbow, eyes like nothing in nature, fine teeth.

"Hello."

"There's a safety rule against what you're doing, you know."

"I know. I've been worrying about it all morning."

A delicate curl climbed my knife then drifted out behind us. It settled into the foam and was plowed under. I watched her reflection in my blade, taking a secret pleasure in its distortion.

"Are you baiting me?" she finally asked.

I heard her laugh then, and turned, knowing it had been intentional.

"What, me?"

"I could push you off from here, very easily."

"I'd make it back."

"Would you push me off, then—some dark night, perhaps?"

"They're all dark, Miss Luharich. No, I'd rather make you a gift of my carving."

She seated herself beside me then, and I couldn't help but notice the dimples in her knees. She wore white shorts and a halter and still had an offworld tan to her which was awfully appealing. I almost felt a twinge of guilt at having planned the whole scene, but my right hand still blocked her view of the wooden animal.

"Okay, I'll bite. What have you got for me?"

"Just a second. It's almost finished."

Solemnly, I passed her the wooden jackass I had been carving. I felt a little sorry and slightly jackass-ish myself, but I had to follow through. I always do. The mouth was split into a braying grin. The ears were upright.

She didn't smile and she didn't frown. She just studied it.

"It's very good," she finally said, "like most things you do—and appropriate, perhaps."

"Give it to me." I extended a palm.

She handed it back and I tossed it out over the water. It missed the white water and bobbed for awhile like a pigmy seahorse.

"Why did you do that?"

"It was a poor joke. I'm sorry."

"Maybe you are right, though. Perhaps this time I've bitten off a little too much."

I snorted.

"Then why not do something safer, like another race?"

She shook her end of the rainbow.

"No. It has to be an Ikky."

"Why?"

"Why did you want one so badly that you threw away a fortune?"

"Many reasons," I said. "An unfrocked analyst who held black therapy sessions in his basement once told me, 'Mister Davits, you need to reinforce the image of your masculinity by catching one of every kind of fish in existence.' Fish are a very ancient masculinity symbol, you know. So I set out to do it. I have one more to go. Why do you want to reinforce *your* masculinity?"

"I don't," she said. "I don't want to reinforce anything but Luharich Enterprises. My chief statistician once said, 'Miss Luharich, sell all the cold cream and face powder in the System and you'll be a happy girl. Rich, too.' And he was right. I am the proof. I can look the way I do and do anything, and I sell most of the lipstick and face powder in the System—but I have to be *able* to do anything."

"You do look cool and efficient," I observed.

"I don't feel cool," she said, rising. "Let's go for a swim."

"May I point out that we are making pretty good time?"

"If you want to indicate the obvious, you may. You said you could make it back to the ship, unassisted. Change your mind?"

"No."

"Then get us two scuba outfits and I'll race you under Tensquare."

"I'll win, too," she added.

I stood and looked down at her, because that usually makes me feel superior to women.

"Daughter of Lir, eyes of Picasso," I said, "you've got yourself a race. Meet me at the forward Rook, starboard, in ten minutes."

"Ten minutes," she agreed.

And ten minutes it was. From the center blister to the Rook took maybe two of them, with the load I was carrying. My sandals grew very hot and I was glad to shuck them for flippers when I reached the comparative cool of the corner.

We slid into harnesses and adjusted our gear. She had changed into a trim one-piece green job that made me shade my eyes and look away, then look back again.

I fastened a rope ladder and kicked it over the side. Then I pounded on the wall of the Rook.

"Yeah?"

"You talk to the port Rook, aft?" I called.

"They're all set up," came the answer. "There's ladders and draglines all over that end."

"You sure you want to do this?" asked the sunburnt little gink who was her publicity man, Anderson yclept.

He sat beside the Rook in a deckchair, sipping lemonade through a straw.

"It might be dangerous," he observed, sunken-mouthed. (His teeth were beside him, in another glass.)

"That's right," she smiled. "It *will* be dangerous. Not overly, though."

"Then why don't you let me get some pictures? We'd have them back to Lifeline in an hour. They'd be in New York by tonight. Good copy."

"No," she said, and turned away from both of us.

She raised her hands to her eyes.

"Here, keep these for me."

She passed him a box full of her unseeing, and when she turned back to me they were the same brown that I remembered.

"Ready?"

"No," I said, tautly. "Listen carefully, Jean. If you're going to play this game there are a few rules. First," I counted, "we're going to be directly beneath the hull, so we have to start low and keep moving. If we bump the bottom, we could rupture an air tank. . . ."

She began to protest that any moron knew that and I cut her down.

"Second," I went on, "there won't be much light, so we'll stay close together, and we will *both* carry torches."

Her wet eyes flashed.

"I dragged you out of Govino without—"

Then she stopped and turned away. She picked up a lamp.

"Okay. Torches. Sorry."

". . . And watch out for the drive-screws," I finished. "There'll be strong currents for at least fifty meters behind them."

She wiped her eyes again and adjusted the mask.

"All right, let's go."

We went.

She led the way, at my insistence. The surface layer was pleasantly warm. At two fathoms the water was bracing; at five it was nice and cold. At eight we let go the swinging stairway and struck out. Tensquare sped forward and we raced in the opposite direction, tattooing the hull yellow at ten-second intervals.

The hull stayed where it belonged, but we raced on like two darkside satellites. Periodically, I tickled her frog feet with my light and traced her antennae of bubbles. About a five meter lead was fine; I'd beat her in the home stretch, but I couldn't let her drop behind yet.

Beneath us, black. Immense. Deep. The Mindanao of Venus, where eternity might eventually pass the dead to a rest in cities of unnamed fishes. I twisted my head away and touched the hull with a feeler of light; it told me we were about a quarter of the way along.

I increased my beat to match her stepped-up stroke, and narrowed the distance which she had suddenly opened by a couple meters. She sped up again and I did, too. I spotted her with my beam.

She turned and it caught on her mask. I never knew whether she'd been smiling. Probably. She raised two fingers in a V-for-Victory and then cut ahead at full speed.

I should have known. I should have felt it coming. It was just a race to her, something else to win. Damn the torpedoes!

So I leaned into it, hard. I don't shake in the water. Or, if I do it doesn't matter and I don't notice it. I began to close the gap again.

She looked back, sped on, looked back. Each time she looked it was nearer, until I'd narrowed it down to the original five meters.

Then she hit the jatoes.

That's what I had been fearing. We were about half-way under and she shouldn't have done it. The powerful jets of compressed air could easily rocket her upward into the hull, or tear something loose if she allowed her body to twist. Their main use is in tearing free from marine plants or fighting bad currents. I had wanted them along as a safety measure, because of the big suck-and-pull windmills behind.

She shot ahead like a meteorite, and I could feel a sudden tingle of perspiration leaping to meet and mix with the churning waters.

I swept ahead, not wanting to use my own guns, and she tripled, quadrupled the margin.

The jets died and she was still on course. Okay, I was an old fuddy-duddy. She *could* have messed up and headed toward the top.

I plowed the sea and began to gather back my yardage, a foot at a time. I wouldn't be able to catch her or beat her now, but I'd be on the ropes before she hit deck.

Then the spinning magnets began their insistence and she wavered. It was an awfully powerful drag, even at this distance. The call of the meat grinder.

I'd been scratched up by one once, under the *Dolphin,* a fishing boat of the middle-class. I *had* been drinking, but it was also a rough day, and the thing had been turned on prematurely. Fortunately, it was turned off in time, also, and a tendon-stapler made everything good as new, except in the log, where it only mentioned that I'd been drinking. Nothing about it being off-hours when I had a right to do as I damn well pleased.

She had slowed to half her speed, but she was still moving crosswise, toward the port, aft corner. I began to feel the pull myself and had to slow down. She'd made it past the main one, but she seemed too far back. It's hard to gauge distances under water, but each red beat of time told me I was right. She was out of danger from the main one, but the smaller port screw, located about eighty meters in, was no longer a threat but a certainty.

She had turned and was pulling away from it now. Twenty meters separated us. She was standing still. Fifteen.

Slowly, she began a backward drifting. I hit my jatoes, aiming two meters behind her and about twenty back of the blades.

Straightline! Thankgod! Catching, softbelly, leadpipe on shoulder SWIMLIKEHELL! maskcracked, not broke though AND UP!

We caught a line and I remember brandy.

Into the cradle endlessly rocking I spit, pacing. Insomnia tonight and left shoulder sore again, so let it rain on me—they can cure rheumatism. Stupid as hell. What I said. In blankets and shivering. She: "Carl, I can't say it." Me: "Then call it square for that night in Govino, Miss Luharich. Huh?" She: nothing. Me: "Any more of that brandy?" She: "Give me another, too." Me: sounds of sipping. It had only lasted three months. No alimony. Many $ on both sides. Not sure whether they were happy or not. Wine-dark Aegean. Good fishing. Maybe he should have spent more time on shore. Or perhaps she shouldn't have. Good swimmer, though. Dragged him all the way to Vido to wring out his lungs. Young. Both. Strong. Both. Rich and spoiled as hell. Ditto. Corfu should have brought them closer. Didn't. I think that mental cruelty was a trout. He wanted to go to Canada. She: "Go to hell if you want!" He: "Will you go along?" She: "No." But she did, anyhow. Many hells. Expensive. He lost a monster or two. She inherited a couple. Lot of lightning tonight. Stupid as hell. Civility's the coffin of a conned soul. By whom?—Sounds like a bloody neo-ex. . . . But I hate you, Anderson, with your glass full of teeth and her new eyes. . . . Can't keep this pipe lit, keep sucking tobacco. Spit again!

Seven days out and the scope showed Ikky.

Bells jangled, feet pounded, and some optimist set the thermostat in the Hopkins. Malvern wanted me to sit out, but I slipped into my harness and waited for whatever came. The bruise looked worse than it felt. I had exercised every day and the shoulder hadn't stiffened on me.

A thousand meters ahead and thirty fathoms deep, it tunneled our path. Nothing showed on the surface.

"Will we chase him?" asked an excited crewman.

"Not unless she feels like using money for fuel." I shrugged.

Soon the scope was clear, and it stayed that way. We remained on alert and held our course.

I hadn't said over a dozen words to my boss since the last time we went drowning together, so I decided to raise the score.

"Good afternoon," I approached. "What's new?"

"He's going north-northeast. We'll have to let this one go. A few more days and we can afford some chasing. Not yet."

Sleek head . . .

I nodded. "No telling where this one's headed."

"How's your shoulder?"

"All right. How about you?"

Daughter of Lir . . .

"Fine. By the way, you're down for a nice bonus."

Eyes of perdition!

"Don't mention it," I told her back.

Later that afternoon, and appropriately, a storm shattered. (I prefer "shattered" to "broke." It gives a more accurate idea of the behavior of tropical storms on Venus and saves lots of words.) Remember that inkwell I mentioned earlier? Now take it between thumb and forefinger and hit its side with a hammer. Watch your self! Don't get splashed or cut—

Dry, then drenched. The sky one million bright fractures as the hammer falls. And sounds of breaking.

"Everyone below?" suggested loudspeakers to the already scurrying crew.

Where was I? Who do you think was doing the loudspeaking?

Everything loose went overboard when the water got to walking, but by then no people were loose. The Slider was the first thing below decks. Then the big lifts lowered their shacks.

I had hit it for the nearest Rook with a yell the moment I recognized the pre-brightening of the holocaust. From there I cut in the speakers and spent half a minute coaching the track team.

Minor injuries had occurred, Mike told me over the radio, but nothing serious. I, however, was marooned for the duration. The Rooks do not lead anywhere; they're set too far out over the hull to provide entry downwards, what with the extensor shelves below.

So I undressed myself of the tanks which I had worn for the past several hours, crossed my flippers on the table, and leaned back to watch the hurricane. The top was black as the bottom and we were in between, and somewhat illuminated because of all that flat, shiny space. The waters above didn't rain down—they just sort of got together and dropped.

The Rooks were secure enough—they'd weathered any number of these onslaughts—it's just that their positions gave them a greater arc of rise and descent when Tensquare makes like the rocker of a very nervous grandma. I had used the belts from my rig to strap myself into the bolted-down chair, and I removed several years in purgatory from the soul of whoever left a pack of cigarettes in the table drawer.

I watched the water make teepees and mountains and hands and trees until I started seeing faces and people. So I called Mike.

"What are you doing down there?"

"Wondering what you're doing up there," he replied. "What's it like?"

"You're from the Midwest, aren't you?"

"Yeah."

"Get bad storms out there?"

"Sometimes."

"Try to think of the worst one you were ever in. Got a slide rule handy?"

"Right here."

"Then put a one under it, imagine a zero or two following after, and multiply the thing out."

"I can't imagine the zeros."

"Then retain the multiplicand—that's all you can do."

"So what are you doing up there?"

"I've strapped myself in the chair. I'm watching things roll around the floor right now."

I looked up and out again. I saw one darker shadow in the forest.

"Are you praying or swearing?"

"Damned if I know. But if this were the Slider—if only this were the Slider!"

"He's out there?"

I nodded, forgetting that he couldn't see me.

Big, as I remembered him. He'd only broken surface for a few moments, to look around. *There is no power on Earth that can be compared with him who was made to fear no one.* I dropped my cigarette. It was the same as before. Paralysis and an unborn scream.

"You all right, Carl?"

He had looked at me again. Or seemed to. Perhaps that mindless brute had been waiting half a millenium to ruin the life of a member of the most highly developed species in business. . . .

"You okay?"

. . . Or perhaps it had been ruined already, long before their encounter, and theirs was just a meeting of beasts, the stronger bumping the weaker aside, body to psyche. . . .

"Carl, dammit! Say something!"

He broke again, this time nearer. Did you ever see the trunk of a tornado? It seems like something alive, moving around in all that dark. Nothing has a right to be so big, so strong, and moving. It's a sickening sensation.

"Please answer me."

He was gone and did not come back that day. I finally made a couple of wisecracks at Mike, but I held my next cigarette in my right hand.

The next seventy or eighty thousand waves broke by with a monotonous similarity. The five days that held them were also without distinction. The morning of the thirteenth day out, though, our luck began to rise. The bells broke our coffee-drenched lethargy into small pieces, and we dashed from the galley without hearing what might have been Mike's finest punchline.

"Aft!" cried someone. "Five hundred meters!"

I stripped to my trunks and started buckling. My stuff is always within grabbing distance.

I flipflopped across the deck, girding myself with a deflated squiggler.

"Five hundred meters, twenty fathoms!" boomed the speakers.

The big traps banged upward and the Slider grew to its full height, m'lady at the console. It rattled past me and took root ahead. Its one arm rose and lengthened.

I breasted the Slider as the speakers called, "Four-eighty, twenty!"

"Status Red!"

A belch like an emerging champagne cork and the line arced high over the waters.

"Four-eighty, twenty!" it repeated, all Malvern and static. "Baitman, attend!"

I adjusted my mask and hand-over-handed it down the side. Then warm, then cool, then away.

Green, vast, down. Fast. This is the place where I am equal to a squiggler. If something big decides a baitman looks tastier than what he's carrying, then irony colors his title as well as the water about it.

I caught sight of the drifting cables and followed them down. Green to dark green to black. It had been a long cast, too long. I'd never had to follow one this far down before. I didn't want to switch on my torch.

But I had to.

Bad! I still had a long way to go. I clenched my teeth and stuffed my imagination into a straightjacket.

Finally the line came to an end.

I wrapped one arm about it and unfastened the squiggler. I attached it, working as fast as I could, and plugged in the little insulated connections which are the reason it can't be fired with the line. Ikky could break them, but by then it wouldn't matter.

My mechanical eel hooked up, I pulled its section plugs and watched it grow. I had been dragged deeper during this operation, which took about a minute and a half. I was near—too near—to where I never wanted to be.

Loathe as I had been to turn on my light, I was suddenly afraid to turn it off. Panic gripped me and I seized the cable with both hands. The squiggler began to glow, pinkly. It started to twist. It was twice as big as I am and doubtless twice as attractive to pink squiggler-eaters. I told myself this until I believed it, then I switched off my light and started up.

If I bumped into something enormous and steel-hided my heart had orders to stop beating immediately and release me—to dart fitfully forever along Acheron, and gibbering.

Ungibbering, I made it to green water and fled back to the nest.

As soon as they hauled me aboard I made my mask a necklace, shaded my eyes, and monitored for surface turbulence. My first question, of course, was: "Where is he?"

"Nowhere," said a crewman; "we lost him right after you went over. Can't pick him up on the scope now. Musta dived."

"Too bad."

The squiggler stayed down, enjoying its bath. My job ended for the time being, I headed back to warm my coffee with rum.

From behind me, a whisper: "Could you laugh like that afterwards?"

Perceptive Answer: "Depends on what he's laughing at."

Still chuckling, I made my way into the center blister with two cupfuls.

"Still hell and gone?"

Mike nodded. His big hands were shaking, and mine were steady as a surgeon's when I set down the cups.

He jumped as I shrugged off the tanks and looked for a bench.

"Don't drip on that panel! You want to kill yourself and blow expensive fuses?"

I toweled down, then settled down to watching the unfilled eye on the wall. I yawned happily; my shoulder seemed good as new.

The little box that people talk through wanted to say something, so Mike lifted the switch and told it to go ahead.

"Is Carl there, Mister Dabis?"

"Yes, ma'am."

"Then let me talk to him."

Mike motioned and I moved.

"Talk," I said.

"Are you all right?"

"Yes, thanks. Shouldn't I be?"

"That was a long swim. I—I guess I overshot my cast."

"I'm happy," I said. "More triple-time for me. I really clean up on that hazardous duty clause."

"I'll be more careful next time," she apologized. "I guess I was too eager. Sorry—" Something happened to the sentence, so she ended it there, leaving me with half a bagful of replies I'd been saving.

I lifted the cigarette from behind Mike's ear and got a light from the one in the ashtray.

"Carl, she was being nice," he said, after turning to study the panels.

"I know," I told him. "I wasn't."

"I mean, she's an awfully pretty kid, pleasant. Head-strong and all that. But what's she done to you?"

"Lately?" I asked.

He looked at me, then dropped his eyes to his cup.

"I know it's none of my bus—" he began.

"Cream and sugar?"

Ikky didn't return that day, or that night. We picked up some Dixieland out of Lifeline and let the muskrat ramble while Jean had her supper sent to the Slider. Later she had a bunk assembled inside. I piped in "Deep Water Blues" when it came over the air and waited for her to call up and cuss us out. She didn't, though, so I decided she was sleeping.

Then I got Mike interested in a game of chess that went on until daylight. It limited conversation to several "checks," one "checkmate," and a "damn!" Since he's a poor loser it also effectively sabotaged subsequent talk, which was fine with me. I had a steak and fried potatoes for breakfast and went to bed.

Ten hours later someone shook me awake and I propped myself on one elbow, refusing to open my eyes.

"Whassamadder?"

"I'm sorry to get you up," said one of the younger crewmen, "but Miss Luharich wants you to disconnect the squiggler so we can move on."

I knuckled open one eye, still deciding whether I should be amused.

"Have it hauled to the side. Anyone can disconnect it."

"It's at the side now, sir. But she said it's in your contract and we'd better do things right."

"That's very considerate of her. I'm sure my Local appreciates her remembering."

"Uh, she also said to tell you to change your trunks and comb your hair, and shave, too. Mister Anderson's going to film it."

"Okay. Run along; tell her I'm on my way—and ask if she has some toenail polish I can borrow."

I'll save on details. It took three minutes in all, and I played it properly, even pardoning myself when I slipped and bumped into Anderson's white tropicals with the wet squiggler. He smiled, brushed it off; she smiled, even though Luharich Complectacolor couldn't completely mask the dark circles under her eyes; and I smiled, waving to all our fans out there in videoland. —Remember, Mrs. Universe, you, too, can look like a monster-catcher. Just use Luharich face cream.

I went below and made myself a tuna sandwich, with mayonnaise.

Two days like icebergs—bleak, blank, half-melting, all frigid, mainly out of sight, and definitely a threat to peace of mind—drifted by and were good to put behind. I experienced some old guilt feelings and had a few disturbing dreams. Then I called Lifeline and checked my bank balance.

"Going shopping?" asked Mike, who had put the call through for me.

"Going home," I answered.

"Huh?"

"I'm out of the baiting business after this one, Mike. The Devil with Ikky! The Devil with Venus and Luharich Enterprises! And the Devil with you!"

Up eyebrows.

"What brought that on?"

"I waited over a year for this job. Now that I'm here, I've decided the whole thing stinks."

"You knew what it was when you signed on. No matter what else you're doing, you're selling face cream when you work for face cream sellers."

"Oh, that's not what's biting me. I admit the commercial angle irritates me, but Tensquare has always been a publicity spot, ever since the first time it sailed."

"What, then?"

"Five or six things, all added up. The main one being that I don't care any more. Once it meant more to me than anything else to hook that critter, and now it doesn't. I went broke on what started out as a lark and I wanted blood for what it cost me. Now I realize that maybe I had it coming. I'm beginning to feel sorry for Ikky."

"And you don't want him now?"

"I'll take him if he comes peacefully, but I don't feel like sticking out my neck to make him crawl into the Hopkins."

"I'm inclined to think it's one of the four or five other things you said you added."

"Such as?"

He scrutinized the ceiling.

I growled.

"Okay, but I won't say it, not just to make you happy you guessed right."

He, smirking: "That look she wears isn't just for Ikky."

"No good, no good." I shook my head. "We're both fission chambers by nature. You can't have jets on both ends of the rocket and expect to go anywhere—what's in the middle just gets smashed."

"That's how it *was*. None of my business, of course—"

"Say that again and you'll say it without teeth."

"Any day, big man"—he looked up—"any place . . ."

"So go ahead. Get it said!"

"She doesn't care about that bloody reptile, she came here to drag you back where you belong. You're not the baitman this trip."

"Five years is too long."

"There must be something under that cruddy hide of yours that people like," he muttered, "or I wouldn't be talking like this. Maybe you remind us humans of some really ugly dog we felt sorry for when we were kids. Anyhow, someone wants to take you home and raise you—also, something about beggars not getting menus."

"Buddy," I chuckled, "do you know what I'm going to do when I hit Lifeline?"

"I can guess."

"You're wrong. I'm torching it to Mars, and then I'll cruise back home, first class. Venus bankruptcy provisions do not apply to Martian trust funds, and I've still got a wad tucked away where moth and corruption enter not. I'm going to pick up a big old mansion on the Gulf and if you're ever looking for a job you can stop around and open bottles for me."

"You are a yellowbellied fink," he commented.

"Okay," I admitted, "but it's her I'm thinking of, too."

"I've heard the stories about you both," he said. "So you're a heel and a goofoff and she's a bitch. That's called compatibility these days. I dare you, baitman, try keeping something you catch."

I turned.

"If you ever want that job, look me up."

I closed the door quietly behind me and left him sitting there waiting for it to slam.

The day of the beast dawned like any other. Two days after my gutless flight from empty waters I went down to rebait. Nothing on the scope. I was just making things ready for the routine attempt.

I hollered a "good morning" from outside the Slider and received an answer from inside before I pushed off. I had reappraised Mike's words, sans sound, sans fury, and while I did not approve of their sentiment or significance, I had opted for civility anyhow.

So down, under, and away. I followed a decent cast about two hundred-ninety meters out. The snaking cables burned black to my left and I paced their undulations from the yellowgreen down into the darkness. Soundless lay the wet night, and I bent my way through it like a cock-eyed comet, bright tail before.

I caught the line, slick and smooth, and began baiting. An icy world swept by me then, ankles to head. It was a draft, as if some one had opened a big door beneath me. I wasn't drifting downwards that fast either.

Which meant that something might be moving up, something big enough to displace a lot of water. I still didn't think it was Ikky. A freak current of some sort, but not Ikky. Ha!

I had finished attaching the leads and pulled the first plug when a big, rugged, black island grew beneath me. . . .

I flicked the beam downward. His mouth was opened.

I was rabbit.

Waves of the death-fear passed downward. My stomach imploded. I grew dizzy.

Only one thing, and one thing only. Left to do. I managed it, finally. I pulled the rest of the plugs.

I could count the scaly articulations ridging his eyes by then.

The squiggler grew, pinked into phosphorescence . . . squiggled!

Then my lamp. I had to kill it, leaving just the bait before him.

One glance back as I jammed the jatoes to life.

He was so near that the squiggler reflected on his teeth, in his eyes. Four meters, and I kissed his lambent jowls with two jets of backwash as I soared. Then I didn't know whether he was following or halted. I began to black out as I waited to be eaten.

The jatoes died and I kicked weakly.

Too fast, I felt a cramp coming on. One flick of the beam, cried rabbit. One second, to know . . .

Or end things up, I answered. No, rabbit, we don't dart before hunters. Stay dark.

Green waters finally, to yellowgreen, then top.

Doubling, I beat off toward Tensquare. The waves from the explosion behind pushed me on ahead. The world closed in, and a screamed, "He's alive!" in the distance.

A giant shadow and a shock wave. The line was alive, too. Happy Fishing Grounds. Maybe I did something wrong. . . .

Somewhere Hand was clenched. What's bait?

THE GOOD STUFF

• • •

A few million years. I remember starting out as a one-celled organism and painfully becoming an amphibian, then an air-breather. From somewhere high in the treetops I heard a voice.

"He's coming around."

I evolved back into homosapience, then a step further into a hangover.

"Don't try to get up yet."

"Have we got him?" I slurred.

"Still fighting, but he's hooked. We thought he took you for an appetizer."

"So did I."

"Breathe some of this and shut up."

A funnel over my face. Good. Lift your cups and drink. . . .

"He was awfully deep. Below scope range. We didn't catch him till he started up. Too late, then."

I began to yawn.

"We'll get you inside now."

I managed to uncase my ankle knife.

"Try it and you'll be minus a thumb."

"You need rest."

"Then bring me a couple more blankets. I'm staying."

I fell back and closed my eyes.

Someone was shaking me. Gloom and cold. Spotlights bled yellow on the deck. I was in a jury-rigged bunk, bulked against the center blister. Swaddled in wool, I still shivered.

"It's been eleven hours. You're not going to see anything now."

I tasted blood.

"Drink this."

Water. I had a remark but I couldn't mouth it.

"Don't ask how I feel," I croaked. "I know that comes next, but don't ask me. Okay?"

"Okay. Want to go below now?"

"No. Just get me my jacket."

"Right here."

"What's he doing?"

"Nothing. He's deep, he's doped but he's staying down."

"How long since last time he showed?"

"Two hours, about."

"Jean?"

"She won't let anyone in the Slider. Listen, Mike says come on in. He's right behind you in the blister."

I sat up and turned. Mike was watching. He gestured; I gestured back.

I swung my feet over the edge and took a couple of deep breaths. Pains in my stomach. I got to my feet and made it into the blister.

"Howza gut?" queried Mike.

I checked the scope. No Ikky. Too deep.

"You buying?"

"Yeah, coffee."

"Not coffee."

"You're ill. Also, coffee is all that's allowed in here."

"Coffee is a brownish liquid that burns your stomach. You have some in the bottom drawer."

"No cups. You'll have to use a glass."

"Tough."

He poured.

"You do that well. Been practicing for that job?"

"What job?"

"The one I offered you—"

A bolt on the scope!

"Rising, ma'am! Rising!" he yelled into the box.

"Thanks, Mike. I've got it in here," she crackled.

"Jean!"

"Shut up! She's busy!"

"Was that Carl?"

"Yeah," I called. "Talk later," and I cut it.

Why did I do that?

"Why did you do that?"

I didn't know.

"I don't know."

Damned echoes! I got up and walked outside.

Nothing. Nothing.

Something?

Tensquare actually rocked! He must have turned when he saw the hull and started downward again. White water to my left, and boiling. An endless spaghetti of cable roared hotly into the belly of the deep.

I stood awhile, then turned and went back inside.

Two hours sick. Four, and better.

"The dope's getting to him."

"Yeah."

"What about Miss Luharich?"

"What about her?"

"She must be half dead."

"Probably."

"What are you going to do about it?"

"She signed the contract for this. She knew what might happen. It did."

"I think you could land him."

"So do I."

"So does she."

"Then let her ask me."

Ikky was drifting lethargically, at thirty fathoms.

I took another walk and happened to pass behind the Slider. She wasn't looking my way.

"Carl, come in here!"

Eyes of Picasso, that's what, and a conspiracy to make me Slide . . .

"Is that an order?"

"Yes—No! Please."

I dashed inside and monitored. He was rising.

"Push or pull?"

I slammed the "wind" and he came like a kitten.

"Make up your own mind now."

He balked at ten fathoms.

"Play him?"

"No!"

She wound him upwards—five fathoms, four . . .

She hit the extensors at two, and they caught him. Then the graffles.

Cries without and a heat lightning of flashbulbs.

The crew saw Ikky.

He began to struggle. She kept the cables tight, raised the graffles . . .

Up.

Another two feet and the graffles began pushing.

Screams and fast footfalls.

Giant beanstalk in the wind, his neck, waving. The green hills of his shoulders grew.

"He's big, Carl!" she cried.

And he grew, and grew, and grew uneasy . . .

"Now!"

He looked down.

He looked down, as the god of our most ancient ancestors might have looked down. Fear, shame, and mocking laughter rang in my head. Her head, too?

"Now!"

She looked up at the nascent earthquake.

"I can't!"

It was going to be so damnably simple this time, now the rabbit had died. I reached out.

I stopped.

"Push it yourself."

"I can't. You do it. Land him, Carl!"

"No. If I do, you'll wonder for the rest of your life whether you could have. You'll throw away your soul finding out. I know you will, because we're alike, and I did it that way. Find out now!"

She stared.

I gripped her shoulders.

"Could be that's me out there," I offered. "I am a green sea serpent, a hateful, monstrous beast, and out to destroy you. I am answerable to no one. Push the Inject."

Her hand moved to the button, jerked back.

"Now!"

She pushed it.

I lowered her still form to the floor and finished things up with Ikky.

It was a good seven hours before I awakened to the steady, sea-chewing grind of Tensquare's blades.

"You're sick," commented Mike.

"How's Jean?"

"The same."

"Where's the best?"

"Here."

"Good." I rolled over. ". . . Didn't get away this time."

So that's the way it was. No one is born a baitman, I don't think, but the rings of Saturn sing epithalamium the sea-beast's dower.

James Tiptree, Jr.

MOTHER IN THE SKY WITH DIAMONDS

As most of you probably know by now, multiple Hugo- and Nebula- winning author James Tiptree, Jr.—at one time a figure reclusive and mysterious enough to be regarded as the B. Traven of science fiction—was actually the pseudonym of the late Dr. Alice Bradley Sheldon, a semi-retired experimental psychologist who also wrote occasionally under the name of Raccoona Sheldon. Dr. Sheldon's tragic death in 1987 put an end to "both" authors' careers, but, before that, she had won two Nebula and two Hugo Awards as Tiptree, won another Nebula Award as Raccoona Sheldon, and established herself, under whatever name, as one of the best writers in SF.

Although "Tiptree" published two reasonably well-received novels—*Up the Walls of the World* and *Brightness Falls From the Air*—she was, like Damon Knight and Theodore Sturgeon (two writers she aesthetically resembled, and by whom she was strongly influenced) more comfortable with the short story, and more effective with it. She wrote some of the very best short stories of the '70s: "The Screwfly Solution," "The Girl Who Was Plugged In," "The Women Men Don't See," "Beam Us Home," "And I Awoke and Found Me Here on the Cold Hill's Side," "I'm Too Big But I Love to Play," "The Man Who Walked Home," "Slow Music," "Her Smoke Rose Up Forever." Already it's clear that these are stories that will last. They—and a dozen others almost as good—show that Alice Sheldon was simply one of the best short-story writers to work in the genre in our times. In fact, with her desire for a high bit-rate, her concern for societal goals, her passion for the novel and the unexpected, her taste for extrapolation, her experimenter's interest in the reactions of people to supernormal stimuli and bizarre situations, her fondness for the apocalyptic, her love of color and sweep and dramatic action, and her preoccupation with the mutability of time and the vastness of space, Alice Sheldon was a natural SF writer. I doubt that she would have been able to realize her particular talents as fully in any other genre, and she didn't even seem particularly interested in trying. At a time when many other SF writers would be just as happy—or happier—writing "mainstream" fiction, and chaffed at the artistic and financial restrictions of the genre, what *she* wanted to be was a *science fiction writer;* that was *her* dream, and her passion.

Sheldon clearly loved space adventure and Space Opera, even of the most basic, junk-food, lowest-common-denominator sort—the kind of stuff you consume with guilty pleasure although you know it is Bad for you, and is probably clogging your arteries—and worked variations on slambang space adventure motifs into many of her stories and both of her novels, although often they were played in a discordant, somber—sometimes unrelievedly bleak—minor key, with lots of curious fluting and eccentric fingerings. (In the '80s, toward the end of her life, she would make a deliberately "retro" attempt to write Nostalgic Space Opera with tales like "The Only Neat Thing To Do" and "Collision," later collected in *The Starry Rift.* Although they contain much excellent material, the tone of these stories is perhaps too self-conscious to match the power of her earlier, less mannered, more naive and genuine—if sometimes considerably rawer and clumsier—explorations of the form.) Tiptree's considerable impact on future generations of science fiction writers was especially pronounced on the cyberpunks—with stories like "The Girl Who Was Plugged In" directly ancestral to that form—but I think that she had a good deal of impact on the future evolution of the space adventure tale as well. For instance, although it's not one of her better-known stories, rarely if ever remarked on by critics, I think that I can see the footprints of "Mother in the Sky with Diamonds" on a lot of subsequent work, from John Varley's stuff a few years later, to Bruce Sterling's early Shaper/Mechanist stories such as "Swarm," and on to the Modern Baroque Space Opera of the '90s.

It's an inelegant story in some ways, so jammed with new ideas and packed with plot that it's almost claustrophobic, a sweaty, dense, exhausting read, brutally and ruthlessly paced, with no changes of mood or breathing spaces, that might have worked better as a novella (John W. Campbell reportedly referred to this story as a "condensed novel" in his rejection letter—and he was probably right about that, anyway). But look at the *thinking* that's going on in the background, as Sheldon reinvents the familiar Asteroid Belt civilization of past science fiction from top to bottom, replacing it with a bizarre and fascinating society of her own, featuring remote-controlled cyborg slaves, biologically-altered people adapted for living in space, spaceships made of monomolecular bubbles of "quasi-living cytoplasm," degenerate drug-runners, and, most importantly, an entire psychological set radically different both from our own and from that of the Asteroid Belt-dwellers of earlier science fiction stories. You're going to see these tropes show up again and again in the science fiction of the '80s and '90s, as will, increasingly, the idea that the people who live in the future will be *different* from you and me, with different perspectives, goals, and ethics, shaped by technology and the social changes driven by that technology, and by new environments. In a brutally compressed context of less than 10,000 words, this little story contains within it many of the seeds that will blossom and cross-fertilize and mutate into a rich crop of Story in the years to come . . .

As James Tiptree, Jr., Alice Sheldon also published nine short-story collections: *Ten-Thousand Light Years from Home, Warm Worlds and Otherwise, Star Songs of an Old Primate, Out of the Everywhere, Tales of the Quintana Roo, Byte Beautiful, The Starry Rift,* the posthumously published *Crown of Stars,* and the recent retrospective collection *Her Smoke Rose Up Forever.*

"Signal coming in now, 'Spector."

The Coronis operator showed the pink of her tongue to the ugly man waiting in the Belt patrolboat, half a mega-mile downstream. *All that feky old hair, too,* she thought. *Yick.* She pulled in her tongue and said sweetly, "It's from—oh—Franchise Twelve."

The man in the patrolboat looked uglier. His name was Space Safety Inspector Gollem and his stomach hurt.

The news that a Company inspector was in pain would have delighted every mollysquatter from Deimos to the Rings. The only surprise would be the notion that Inspector Gollem had a stomach instead of a Company contract tape. Gollem? All the friends Gollem had could colonize a meson and he knew it.

His stomach was used to that, though. His stomach was even getting used to working for Coronis Mutual, and he still hoped it might manage to survive his boss, Quine.

What was murdering him by inches was the thing he had hidden out beyond Franchise Fourteen on the edge of Coronis sector.

He scowled at the screen where Quine's girl was logging in the grief for his next patrol. Having a live girl-girl for commo was supposed to be good for morale. It wasn't doing one thing for Gollem. He knew what he looked like and his stomach knew what the flash from Twelve could be.

When she threw it on the screen he saw it was a bogy complaint, all right. Ghost signals on their lines.

Oh, no. Not again.

Not when he had it all fixed.

Franchise Twelve was West Hem Chemicals, an itchy outfit with a jillabuck of cyborgs. They would send out a tracker if he didn't get over there soon. But how? He had just come that way, he was due upstream at Franchise One.

"Reverse patrol," he grunted. "Starting Franchise Fourteen. Purpose, uh, unscheduled recheck of aggregation shots in Eleven plus expedited service to West Hem. Allocate two units additional power."

She logged it in; it was all right with her if Gollem started with spacerot.

He cut channel and coded in the new course, trying not to think about the extra power he would have to justify to Quine. If anyone ever got into his console and found the bugger bypass on his log he would be loading ore with electrodes in his ears.

He keyed his stomach a shot of Vageez and caught an error in his code which he corrected with no joy. Most Belters took naturally to the new cheap gee-cumulator drive. Gollem loathed it. Sidling around arsy-versy instead of *driving* the can where you wanted to go. The old way, the real way.

I'm the last machine freak, he thought. A godlost dinosaur in space . . .

But a dinosaur would have had more sense than to get messed up with a dead girl.

And *Ragnarok.*

His gee-sum index was wobbling up the scale, squeezing him retrograde in a field stress-node—he hoped. He slapped away a pod of the new biomonitor they had put in his boat and took a scan outside before his screens mushed. Always something to see in the Belts. This time it was a storm of little crescents trailing him, winking as the gravel tumbled.

In the sky with diamonds . . .

From *Ragnarok's* big ports you could see into naked space. That was the way they liked it, once. His Iron Butterfly. He rubbed his beard, figuring: five hours to *Ragnarok,* after he checked the squatternest in Fourteen.

The weathersignal showed new data since he'd coded in the current field vortices and fronts. He tuned up, wondering what it must be like to live under weather made of gales of gas and liquid water. He had been raised on Luna.

The flash turned out to be a couple of rogue males coming in from Big J's orbit. Jup stirred up a rock now and then. This pair read like escaped Trojans, estimated to node downstream in Sector Themis. Nothing in that volume except some new medbase. His opposite number there was a gigglehead named Hara who was probably too busy peddling mutant phage to notice them go by. A pity, Trojans were gas-rich.

Feeding time. He opened a pack of Ovipuff and tuned up his music. *His* music. Old human power music from the frontier time. Not for Gollem, the new subliminal biomoans. He dug it hard, the righteous electronic decibels. Chomping the paste with big useless teeth, the cabin pounding.

I can't get no—satisFACTION!

The biomonitor was shrinking in its pods. Good. Nobody asked you into Gollem's ship, you sucking symbiote.

The beat helped. He started through his exercises. Not to let himself go null-gee like Hara. Like them all now. Spacegrace? Shit. His unfashionable body bucked and strained.

A gorilla, no wonder his own mother had taken one look and split. *Two thousand light-years from home . . .* what home for Gollem? Ask Quine, ask the Company. The Companies owned space now.

It was time to brake into Fourteen.

Fourteen was its usual disorderly self, a giant spawn of mollybubbles hiding an aggregate of rock that had been warped into synch long before his time. The first colonists had done it with reaction engines. Tough. Now a kid with a gee-cumulator could true an orbit.

Fourteen had more bubbles every time he passed—and more kids.

The tissue tanks that paid the franchise were still clear but elsewhere the bubbles were layers deep, the last ones tethered loose. Running out of rock for their metabolite to work on. Gollem hassled them about that every time he passed.

"Where are your rock nudgers?" he asked now when the squatterchief came on his screen.

"Soon, soon, 'Spector Gollem." The squatterchief was a slender skinhead with a biotuner glued to one ear.

"The Company will cancel, Juki. Coronis Mutual won't carry you on policyholder status if you don't maintain insurable life-support."

Juki smiled, manipulated the green blob. They were abandoning the rocks all right, drifting off into symbiotic spacelife. Behind Juki he saw a couple of the older chiefs.

"You can't afford to cut the services the Company provides," he told them angrily. Nobody knew better than Gollem how minimal those services were, but without them, what? "Get some rock."

He couldn't use any more time here.

As he pulled away he noticed one of the loose bubbles was a sick purple. Not his concern and not enough time.

Cursing, he eased alongside and cautiously slid his lock probes into the monomolecular bubbleskin. When the lock opened a stink came in. He grabbed his breather and kicked into the foul bubble. Six or seven bodies were floating together in the middle like a tangle of yellow wires.

He jerked one out, squirted oxy at its face. It was a gutbag kid, a born null-gee. When his eyes fanned open Gollem pushed him at the rotting metabolite core.

"You were feeding it phage." He slapped the boy. "Thought it would replicate, didn't you? You poisoned it."

The boy's eyes crossed, then straightened. Probably didn't get a word, the dialect of Fourteen was drifting fast. Maybe some of them truly were starting to communicate symbiotically. Vegetable ESP.

He pushed the boy back into the raft and knocked the dead metabolite through the waster. The starved molly-bubble wall was pitted with necrosis, barely holding. He flushed his CO_2 tank over it and crawled back to his boat for a spare metabolite core. When he got back the quasi-living cytoplasm of the bubbleskin was already starting to clear. It would regenerate itself if they didn't poison it again with a CO_2-binding mutant. That was the way men built their spacehomes now, soft heterocatalytic films that ran on starlight, breathed human wastes.

Gollem rummaged through the stirring bodies until he found a bag of phage between a woman and her baby. She whimpered when he jerked it loose. He carried it back to his boat and pulled carefully away, releasing a flow of nutrient gel to seal his probe-hole. The mollybubble would heal itself.

At last he was clear for *Ragnarok*.

He punched course for Twelve and then deftly patched in the log bypass and set his true trajectory. The log would feed from his cache of duplicates, another item nobody had better find. Then he logged in the expendables he'd just used, padding it a piece as always. Embezzlement. His stomach groaned.

He tuned up a rock storm to soothe it. There was an old poem about a man with a dead bird tied around his neck. Truly he had his dead bird. All the good things were dead, the free wild human things. He felt like a specter, believe it. A dead one hanging in from the days when men rode machines to the stars and the algae stayed in pans. Before they cooked up all the metabolizing Martian macromolecules that quote, tamed space, unquote. Tame men, women and kids breathing through 'em, feeding off 'em, navigating and computing and making music with 'em—mating with them, maybe!

Steppenwolf growled, worried the biomonitor. His metal-finder squealed.

Ragnarok!

Time shivered and the past blazed on his screens. He let himself have one quick look.

The great gold-skinned hull floated in the starlight, edged with diamonds against the tiny sun. The last Argo, the lonesomest Conestoga of them all. *Ragnarok*. Huge, proud, ungainly star machine, blazoned with the symbols of the crude technology that had blasted man to space. *Ragnarok* that opened the way to Saturn and beyond. A human fist to the gods. Drifting now a dead hulk, lost in the sea she'd conquered. Lost and forgotten to all but Gollem the specter.

No time now to suit up and prowl over and around her, to pry and tinker with her archaic fitments. The pile inside her was long dead and cold. He dared not even try to start it, a thing like that would set off every field-sounder in the zone. Quine's stolen power in her batteries was all that warmed her now.

Inside her also was his dead bird.

He coasted into the main lock, which he had adapted to his probe. Just as he hit he thought he glimpsed a new bubble firming up in the storage cluster he had hung on *Ragnarok's* freightlock. What had Topanga been up to?

The locks meshed with a soul-satisfying clang of metal and he cycled through, eye to eye with the two old monster suits that hung in *Rag-*

narok's lock. Unbelievable, so cumbersome. How ever had they done it? He kicked up through dimness to the bridge.

For one moment his girl was there.

The wide ports were a wheeling maze of starlight and fire-studded shadows. She sat in the command couch, gazing out. He saw her pure, fierce profile, the hint of girl-body in the shadows. Star-hungry eyes.

Then the eyes slid around and the lights came up. His star girl vanished into the thing that had killed her.

Time.

Topanga was an old, sick, silly woman in a derelict driveship.

She smiled at him from the wreckage of her face.

"Golly? I was remembering—" What an instrument it was still, that husky voice in the star haze. The tales it had spun for him over the years. She had not always been like this. When he had first found her, adrift and ill—she had still been Topanga then. The last one left.

"You were using the caller. Topanga, I warned you they were too close. Now they've picked you up."

"I wasn't sending, Golly." Eerie blue, the wide old eyes reminded him of a place he had never seen.

He began to check the telltales he had hung on her console leads. Hard to believe those antiques were still operational. Completely inorganic, a ton of solid-state circuitry. Topanga claimed she couldn't activate it, but when she had had her first crazy fit he had found out otherwise. He'd had her parked in Four then, in a clutch of spacejunk. She started blasting the bands with docking signals to men twenty years dead. Company salvage had nearly blown her out of space before he got there—he'd had to fake a collision to satisfy Quine.

A telltale was hot.

"Topanga. Listen to me. West Hem Chemicals are sending a hunter out to find you. You were jamming their miners. Don't you know what they'll do to you? The best—the very best you'll get is a geriatric ward. Needles. Tubes. Doctors ordering you around, treating you like a thing. They'll grab *Ragnarok* for a space trophy. Unless they blast you first."

Her face crumpled crazily.

"I can take care of myself. I'll turn the lasers on 'em."

"You'd never see them." He glared at the defiant ghost. He could do anything he wanted here, what was stopping him? "Topanga, I'm going to kill that caller. It's for your own good."

She stuck up her ruined chin, the wattles waving.

"I'm not afraid of them."

"You have to be afraid of a jerry ward. You want to end as a mess of tubing, under the gees? I'm going to dismantle it."

"No, Golly, no!" Her stick arms drummed in panic, trailing skin. "I won't touch it, I'll remember. Don't leave me helpless. Oh, please don't."

Her voice broke and so did his stomach. He couldn't look at it, this creature that had eaten his girl. Topanga inside there somewhere, begging for freedom, for danger. Safe, helpless, gagged? No.

"If I nudge you out of West Hem's range you'll be in three others. Topanga, baby, I can't save you one more time."

She had gone limp now, shrouded in the Martian oxy-blanket he had brought her. He caught a blue gleam under the shadows and his stomach squirted bile. Let go, witch. Die before you kill me too.

He began to code in the gee-sum unit he had set up here. It was totally inadequate for *Ragnarok's* mass but he could overload it for a nudge. He would stabilize her on his next pass-by, if only he could find her without wasting too much power.

From behind him came a husky whisper. "Strange to be old—" Ghost of a rich girl's laugh. "Did I ever tell you about the time the field shifted, on Tethys?"

"You told me."

Ragnarok was stirring.

"Stars," she said dreamily. "Hart Crane was the first space poet. Listen. *Stars scribble on our eyes the frosty sagas, the gleaming cantos of unvanquished space. O silver sinewy—*"

Gollem heard the hull clang.

Someone was trying to sneak out of *Ragnarok.*

He launched himself down-shaft to the freightlock, found it cycling and jacknifed back to get out through his boat at the main lock. Too late. As he sprang into his cabin the screens showed a strange pod taking off from behind that new bubble.

Dummy, dummy—

He suited up and scrambled out across *Ragnarok's* hull. The new bubble was still soft, mostly nutri-gel. Pushing his face into it he cracked his breather.

He came back to Topanga in a blue rage.

"You are letting a phage-runner park on *Ragnarok.*"

"Oh, was that Leo?" She laughed vaguely. "He's a courier from the next zone—Themis, isn't it? He calls by sometimes. He's been beautiful to me, Golly."

"He is a stinking phage-runner and you know it. You were covering for him." Gollem was sick. The old Topanga would have put "Leo" out the trash hole. "Not phage. Not phage on top of everything, Topanga."

Her ancient eyelids fell. "Let it be, Golly. I'm alone so long," she whispered. "You leave me for so long."

Her withered paw groped out, seeking him. Brown-spotted, criss-crossed with reedy pulses. Knobs, strings. Where were the hands of the girl who had held the camp on Tethys?

He looked up at the array of holographs over the port and saw her. The camera had caught her grinning up at black immensity, the wild light of Saturn's rings reflected in her red-gold hair. . . .

"Topanga, old mother," he said painfully.

"Don't call me mother, you plastic spacepig!" she blazed. Her carcass jerked out of the pilot couch and he had to web her back, hating to touch her. A quarter-gee would break these sticks. "I should be dead," she mumbled. "It won't be long, you'll be rid of me."

Ragnarok was set now, he could go.

"Maintain, spacer, maintain," he told her heartily. His stomach knew what lay ahead. None of it was any good.

As he left he heard her saying brightly, "Gimbals, check," to her dead computer.

He took off high-gain for Franchise Twelve and West Hem. Just as he had the log tied back into real time his caller bleeped. The screen stayed blank.

"Identify."

"Been waitin' on you, Gollem." A slurred tenor; Gollem's beard twitched.

"One freakin' fine ship." The voice chuckled. "Main-mouth by Co'o-nis truly flash that ship."

"Stay off *Ragnarok* if you want to keep your air," Gollem told the phage-runner.

The voice giggled again. "My pa'tners truly grieve on that, 'Spector." There was a click and he heard his own voice saying, "Topanga, baby, I can't save you one more time."

"Deal, 'Spector, deal. Why we flash on war?"

"Blow your clobbing tapes," Gollem said tiredly. "You can't run me like you run Hara."

" 'Panga," the invisible Leo said reflectively. "Freakin' fine old fox. She tell I fix her wire fire?"

Gollem cut channel.

The phager must have made a circuit smoke to win her trust. Gollem's stomach wept acid. So vulnerable. An old sick eagle dead in space and the rats have found her. . . .

They wouldn't quit, either. *Ragnarok* had air, water, power. Transmitters. Maybe they were using her caller, maybe she'd been telling the truth. They could take over. Shove her out through the lock. . . .

Gollem's hand hovered over his console.

If he turned back now his log would blow it all. And for what? No, he decided. They'll wait, they'll sniff around first. They want to take me too. They want to see how much squeeze they have. Pray they don't find out.

He had to get some power somewhere and jump *Ragnarok* out. How, how? Like trying to hide Big Jup.

He noticed that he had punched the biomonitor into a sick yellow blob and hurled it across the cabin. . . . How much longer could he cool Coronis?

Right on cue, his company hotline blatted.

"Why aren't you at Franchise Two, Gollem?"

It was mainmouth Quine himself. Gollem took a deep breath and repeated his course reversal plan, watching Quine's little snout purse up.

"After this clear with me. Now hear this, Gollem," Quine leaned back in his bioflex, pink and plump. Coronis was no hardship station. "I don't know what you think you're into with Franchise Three but I want it stopped. The miners are yelling and our Company won't tolerate it."

Gollem shook his shaggy head like a dazed bull. Franchise Three? Oh yeah, the heavy metal-mining outfit.

"They're overloading their tractor beams for hot extraction," he told Quine. "It's in my report. If they keep it up they'll have one bloody hashup. And they won't be covered because their contract annex specifies the load limits."

Quine's jowls twitched ominously. "Gollem. Again I warn you. It is not your role to interpret the contract to the policyholder. If the miners choose to get their ore out faster by abrogating their contract that's their decision. Your job is to report the violation, not to annoy them with technicalities. Right now they are very angry with *you*. And I trust you don't imagine that our Company"—reverent pause—"appreciates your initiative?"

Gollem made an inarticulate noise in his throat. He should be used to this. Coronis wanted its piece quickly *and* it wanted to avoid paying compensation when the thing blew. The miners got paid by the shuttle load and most of them couldn't tell a contract annex from a flush valve. By the time they found out they'd be dead.

"Another item." Quine was watching him. "You may be getting some noise from Themis sector. They seemed to be all sweated up about a bit of rock."

"You mean those Trojans?" Gollem was puzzled. "What's there?"

"Have you been talking to Themis?"

"No."

"Very well. You will not, repeat not, deviate from your patrol. You are on a very thin line with us, Gollem. If your log shows anything *whatever* in connection with Themis you're out of the Company and there will be a lien against you for your overdrawn pension. *And* there will be no transport rights. Do I make myself clear?"

Gollem cut channel. When he could control his hands he punched Weather for the updated rogue orbits. Both rocks were now computed to node in sector Themis, but well clear of Themis main. He frowned. Who was hurting? His ephemeris showed only the new medbase in the general volume, listed as Nonaffiliated, no details. It seemed to be clear, too. If that polluted Hara . . .

Gollem grunted. He understood now. Quine was hoping for some hassle in Themis which might persuade Ceres Control to reassign part of that sector to him. And the medbase wasn't Company, it was expendable for publicity purposes. Truly fine, he thought. Much gees for Quine if it works.

He was coming into West Hem Chemicals. Before he could signal, his audio cut loose with curses from the cyborg chief. Gollem swerved to minimize his intrusion on their body lines and the chief cooled down enough to let him report that he had killed their bogy.

"It was an old field-sounder," Gollem lied. Had they identified *Ragnarok?*

"Slope out. Go." The old cyborg op couldn't care less. He had electrode jacks all over his skull and his knuckles sprouted wires. Much as Gollem loved metal, this was too much. He backed out as gingerly as he could. The men—or maybe the creatures—in there were wired into the controls of robot refining plants on all the nearby rocks, and he was hashing across their neural circuit. Wouldn't be surprising if they fired on him one day.

His next stop was the new aggregation franchise in Eleven. It was a slow-orbit complex on the rim of the Kirkwood Gap, a touchy location to work. If they started losing rocks they could spread chaos in the zone.

Aggregation meant power units, lots of them. Gollem began figuring *Ragnarok's* parameters. His stomach also began to gripe him; the outfit that had leased Eleven had big plans for a self-sustaining colony on a slim budget. They needed those units to bring in gas-rich rocks.

When he got inside Gollem saw they had other problems too.

"We've computed for two-sigma contingency," the Eleven chief repeated tiredly. They were standing beside a display tank showing the projected paths of the rocks they intended to blast.

"Not enough," Gollem told him. "Your convergence-point is smeared the hell all over. You lose a big one and it'll plow right into Ten."

"But Franchise Ten isn't occupied," the chief protested.

"Makes no difference. Why do you think you got this franchise

THE GOOD OLD STUFF

cheap? The Company's delighted to have you aggregating this lode, they're just waiting for you to lose one rock so they can cancel and resell your franchise. I can't certify your operation unless you recompute."

"But that means buying computer input from Ceres Main!" he yelped. "We can't afford it."

"You should have looked at the instability factors before you signed," Gollem said woodenly. He was wishing the chief didn't have all his hair; it would be easier to do this to a skinhead.

"At least let me bring in the rocks we have armed," the chief was pleading.

"How many one-gee units have you got out there?" Gollem pointed.

"Twenty-one."

"I'll take six of them and certify you. That's cheaper than recomputing."

The chief's jaw sagged, clenched in a snarl.

"You polluted bastard!"

Suddenly there was a squeal behind them and the commo op tore off her earphones. The chief reached over and flicked on the speaker, filling the bubble with an all-band blare. For a minute Gollem thought it was a flare-front, and then he caught the human scream.

"MAYDAY! MA-A-Y-DAY-AAY! GO-OLLEE—"

Oh no! Oh Jesus, no. He slammed down the speaker, the sweat starting out all over him.

"What in space—" the chief began.

"Old beacon in the Gap." Gollem bunted through them. "I have to go kill it."

He piled into his boat and threw in the booster. No time for power units now. That yell meant Topanga was in real trouble, she wasn't calling dead men.

If he tied in the spare booster he could override the field-forms for a straighter course. Strictly *verboten*. He did so and then opened his commo channels. Topanga wasn't there.

Fire? Collision? More like, Leo and friends had made their move.

He hurtled downstream in a warp of wasted power, his hands mechanically tuning the board in hopes of pulling in some phagers' signals, something. He picked up only far-off mining chatter and a couple of depot ops asking each other what the Mayday was. Someone in Sector Themis was monotonously calling Inspector Hara. As usual Hara wasn't answering, there was only the automatic standby from Themis main. Gollem cursed them all impartially, trying to make his brain yield a plan.

Why would the phagers move in on *Ragnarok* so fast? Not their style, confrontation. If he blew they'd lose the ship, they'd have to cope with a new inspector. Why risk it when they had him by the handle already?

Maybe they figured it was no risk. Gollem's fist pounded on the tuner in a heavy rhythm. *Paint it black.* . . . But they have to keep her alive till I get there. They want me.

What to do? Would they believe a threat to call Ceres Control? Don't bother to answer. They know as well as I do that a Company bust would end with Topanga in a gerry ward, *Ragnarok* in Quine's trophy park and Gollem in a skull-cage. . . . How to break Topanga loose from them? If I try to jive along the first thing they'll do will be to shoot us both up on phage. Addiction dose. *Why, why did I leave her there alone?*

He was going around this misery orbit for the nth time when he noticed the Themis voice had boosted gain and was now trying to reach Coronis, his home base. Correction, Quine's home base. No answer.

Against his stomach's advice he tuned it up.

"Medbase Themis to Coronis main, emergency. Please answer, Coronis. Medbase Themis calling Coronis, emergency, please—"

The woman was clearly no commo op.

Finally Quine's girl chirped: "Medbase Themis, you are disturbing our traffic. Please damp your signal."

"Coronis, this is an emergency. We need help—we're going to get hit!"

"Medbase Themis, contact your sector safety patrol officer, we have no out-of-sector authorization. You are disturbing our traffic."

"Our base won't answer! We have to have help, we have casualties—"

A male voice cut in. "Coronis, put me through to your chief at once. This is a medical priority."

"Medbase Themis, Sector Chief Quine is outstation at present. We are in freight shuttle assembly for the trans-Mars window, please stand by until after launch."

"But—"

"Coronis out."

Gollem grimaced, trying to picture Quine going outstation.

He went back to pounding on his brain. The Themis woman went on calling. "We are in an impact path, we need power to move. If anyone can help us please come in. Medbase Themis—"

He cut her off. One *Ragnarok* was enough and his was just ahead now.

There was a faint chance they weren't expecting him so soon. He powered down and drifted. As his screens cleared he saw a light move in the bubbles behind the freightlock.

His one possible break, if they hadn't yet moved that phage inboard.

He grabbed the wrecking laser controls and kicked the patrolboat straight at *Ragnarok's* main lock. The laser beam fanned over the bubbles, two good slices before he had to brake. The crash sent him into his boards. The docking probes meshed and he sprang headfirst into *Ragnarok's* lock. As it started to cycle he burned the override, setting off alarms all over the ship. Then he was through and caroming up the shaft. Among the hoots he could hear more clanging. Phagers were piling out through the freightlock to save their bubbles. If he could get to the bridge first he could lock them out.

He twisted, kicked piping and shot into the bridge, his arm aimed at the emergency hatch-lock lever. It hadn't been used for decades—he nearly broke his wrist, yanking the lever against his own inertia and was rewarded by the sweet grind of lock toggles far below.

Then he turned to the command couch where Topanga should be and saw he was too late.

She was there all right, both hands to her neck and her eyes rolling. Behind her a lank hairless figure was holding a relaxed pose, in his fist a wirenoose leading around Topanga's throat.

"Truly fine, 'Spector." The phager grinned.

For a second Gollem wondered if Leo hadn't noticed the hand-laser Gollem pointed. Then he saw that the phagehead was holding a welder against Topanga's side. Its safety sleeve was off.

"Deal, Gollyboy. Deal the fire down."

No way. After a minute Gollem sent his weapon drifting by Leo's arm. Leo didn't take the bait.

"Open up." The phager jerked his chin at the hatch lever and Topanga gave a bubbling whine.

When Gollem opened the hatch the game would be over all the way. He hung frozen, his coiled body sensing for solidity behind him, measuring the spring.

The phager jerked the wire. Topanga's arms flailed. One horrible eye rolled at Gollem. A spark in there, trying to say no.

"You're killing her. Then I tear your head off and throw you out the waster."

The phager giggled. "Why you flash on killin'?" Suddenly he twisted Topanga upside down, feet trailing out toward Gollem. She kicked feebly. Weird, her bare feet were like a girl's.

"Open up."

When Gollem didn't move the phager's arm came out in a graceful swing, his fingers flaring. The welding arc sliced, retraced, sliced again as Topanga convulsed. One girlish foot floated free, trailing droplets.

Gollem saw a white stick pointing at him out of the blackened stump. Topanga was quiet now.

"Way to go." The phager grinned. "Truly tough old bird. Open up."

"Turn her loose. Turn her loose. I'll open."

"Open now." The welder moved again.

Suddenly Topanga made a weak twist, scrabbling at Leo's groin. The phager's head dipped.

Gollem drove inside his arm, twisted it against momentum. The welder rocketed out around the cabin while he and the phager thrashed around each other, blinded by Topanga's robe. The phager had a knife now but he couldn't get braced. Gollem felt legs lock his waist and took advantage of it to push Topanga away. When the scene cleared he clamped the phager to him and began savagely to collect on his investment in muscle-building.

Just as he was groping for the wire to tie up the body something walloped him back of the ear and the lights went out.

He came to with Topanga yelling, "Val, Val! I've got em!"

She was hanging on the console in her hair using both hands to point an ancient Thunderbolt straight at him. The muzzle yawned smoke a foot from his beard.

"Topanga, it's me—Golly. Wake up, spacer, let me tie him up."

"Val?" A girl laughing, screaming. "I'm going to finish the murdering mothers, Val!"

Valentine Orlov, her husband, had been in the snows of Ganymede for thirty years.

"Val is busy, Topanga," Gollem said gently. He was hearing hull noises he didn't like. "Val sent me to help you. Put the jolter down spacegirl. Help me tie up this creep. They're trying to steal my boat."

He hadn't had time to lock it, he remembered now.

Topanga stared at him.

"And why do I often meet your visage here?" she croaked. *"Your eyes like unwashed platters—"*

Then she fainted and he flung himself downshaft to the lock.

His patrolboat was swinging away. Tethered to it was the phage-runners' pod.

He was stranded on *Ragnarok*.

Rage exploded him back to the bridge consoles. He managed to send one weak spit from *Ragnarok's* lasers after them as they picked up gees. Futile. Then he pulled the phager's head over his knee and clouted it and turned to setting up Topanga with an i.v. in her old cobweb veins. How in hell had those claws held a jolter? He wrapped a gel sheath over her burns, grinding his jaw to still the uproar in his stomach. He completed his cleaning by towing the phager and the foot to the waste lock.

With one hand on the cycle button he checked frowning. He could use some information from Leo—what were they into in his patrol sector?

Then his head came together and his fist crunched the eject. *His* patrol sector?

If the Companies ever got their hands on him he'd spend the rest of his life with his brains wired up, paying for that patrolboat. If he were lucky. No way, no where to go. The Companies owned space. Truly he was two thousand light-years from home now—on a dead driveship.

Dead?

Gollem threw back his lank hair and grinned. *Ragnarok* had a rich ecosystem, he'd seen to that. Nobody but the phagers knew she was here and he could hold them out for a while. Long enough, maybe, to see if he could coax some power out of that monster-house without waking up the sector. Suddenly he laughed out loud. Rusty shutter sliding in his mind, letting in glory.

"Man, man!" he muttered and stuck his head into the regeneration chamber to check the long trays of culture stretching away under the lights.

It took him a minute to understand what was wrong.

No wonder the phagers came back so fast, no wonder he was laughing like a dummy. They'd seeded the whole works with phage culture. A factory. The first trays were near sporing, the air was ropy. He hauled them out, inhaled a clean lungful and jettisoned the ripe trays.

Then he crawled back in to search. On every staging the photosynthetic algae were starting to clump, coagulating to the lichen-like symbiote that was phage. Not one clean tray.

In hours *Ragnarok* would have no more air.

But he and Topanga wouldn't care. They'd be through the walls in phagefreak long before.

He was well and truly shafted now.

He flushed some oxy into the ventilators and kicked back to the bridge. Get some clean metabolite or die.

Who would give him air? Even if he could move *Ragnarok,* the company depots and franchises would be alerted. He might just as well signal Coronis and give himself up. Maybe Quine wouldn't bother to reach him and Topanga in time. Maybe better so. Wards. Wires.

Topanga groaned. Gollem felt her temples. Hot as plasma, old ladies with a leg shortened shouldn't play war. He rummaged out biogens, marveling at the vials, ampoules, tabs, hyposprays. Popping who knew what to keep alive. Contraband she and Val had picked up in the old free days, her hoard would stock a . . .

Wait a minute.

Medbase Themis.

He tuned up *Ragnarok's* board. The Themis woman was still calling, low and hoarse. He cranked the antennae for the narrowest beam he could get.

"Medbase Themis, do you read?"

"Who are you? Who's there?" She was startled out of her code book.

"This is a spacesweep mission. I have a casualty."

"Where—" The male voice took over.

"This is Chief Medic Kranz, spacer. You can bring in your casualty but we have a rogue headed through our space with a gravel cloud. If we can't get power to move the station in about thirty hours we'll be holed out. Can you help us?"

"You can have what I've got. Check coordinates."

The woman choked up on the decimals. No use telling them he couldn't do them any good. The gee-sum unit he had in *Ragnarok* wouldn't nudge that base in time for Halley's comet. And *Ragnarok's* drive—if it worked it would be like trying to wipe your eye with a blowtorch.

But their air could help *him.*

The drive. He bounced down the engineway, knowing the spring in his muscles was partly phage. Only partly. A thousand times he had come this way, a thousand times torn himself away from temptation. Gleefully now he began to check out the circuits he had traced, restored the long-pulled fuses. There was a sealed hypergolic reserve for ignition. A stupefying conversion process, a plumber's nightmare of heat-exchangers and back-cycling. Crazy, wasteful, dangerous. Enough circuitry to wire the Belt. Unbelievable it had carried man to Saturn, more unbelievable it would work today.

He clanked the rod controls. No telling what had crystallized. The converter fuel chutes jarred out thirty years' accumulated dust. The ignition reserve was probably only designed for one emergency firing. Would he be able to ignite again to brake? Learn as you go. One thing sure, when that venerable metal volcano burst to life every board from here to Coronis would be lit.

When he got back to the bridge Topanga was whispering.

"We left the haven hanging in the night— O thou steel cognizance whose leap commits—"

"Pray it leaps," he told her and began setting course, double-checking everything because of the phagemice running in the shadows. He wrapped Topanga's webs.

He started the ignition train.

The subsonic rumble that grew through *Ragnarok* filled him with terror and delight. He threw himself into the webs, wishing he had said something, counted down maybe. Blastoff. *Go.* The rumble bloomed into an oremill roar. Gees smashed down on him. Everything in the cabin started raining on the deck. The web gave sideways and the roar wound up in a scream that parted his brain and then dwindled into silence.

When he struggled back to the board he found the burn had cut right. *Ragnarok* was barreling toward Themis. He saw Topanga's eyes open.

"Where are we headed?" She sounded sane as soap.

"I'm taking you over to the next sector, Themis. We need metabolite, oxygen. The phagers ruined your regenerators."

"Themis?"

"There's a medbase there. They'll give us some."

Mistake.

"Oh, no—no!" She struggled up. "No, Golly! I won't go to a hospital—don't let them take me!"

"You're not going to a hospital, Topanga. You're going to stay right here in the ship while I go in for the cores. They'll never know about you. We'll be out of there in minutes."

No use.

"God hate you, Gollem." She made an effort to spit. "You're trying to trap me. I know you! Never let me free. You won't bury me here, Gollem. Rot in Moondome with your ugly cub—I'm going to Val!"

"Cool, spacer, you're yawning." He got some tranks into her finally and went back to learning *Ragnarok.* The phage was getting strong now. When he looked up the holographs were watching him drive their ship. The old star heroes. Val Orlov, Fitz, Hannes, Mura, all the great ones. Sometimes only a grin behind a gold-washed headplate, a name on a suit beside some mad hunk of machine. Behind them, spacelost wildernesses lit by unknown moons. All alive, all so young. There was Topanga with her arm around that other spacegirl, the dark Russian one who was still orbiting Io. They grinned past him, bright and living.

When they start talking, we've had it. . . .

He set the gyros to crank *Ragnarok* into what he hoped was attitude for the retro burn. If he could trust the dials, there was enough ignition for braking and for one last burn to get out of there. But where would he go from Medbase? Into the sky with diamonds . . .

He heard himself humming and decided to lock the whole thing into autopilot. No matter what shape that computer was in it would be saner than he was.

Have you seen your mother, baby, standing in the shadows? . . .

When he began hearing the Stones he went down and threw out half the trays. The three remaining oxy tanks struck him as hilarious. He cracked one.

The oxy sobered him enough to check the weather signal. The Medbase woman was still trying to raise Themis Main. He resisted the impulse to enlighten her about the Companies and concentrated on the updated orbits of the Trojan rogues. He saw now what had Medbase sweating. The lead rogue would miss them by megamiles but it was massive enough to have stirred up a lot of gravel. The small rogue behind was sweeping up a tail. The rock itself would go by far off—but that gravel cloud would rip their bubbles to shreds.

He had to get in there and out again fast.

He sniffed some more oxy and computed the rogue orbits on a worst-contingency basis. It looked O.K.—for him. His stomach flinched; even under phage it had an idea what it was going to be like when those medics found out they were wasted.

He saw Topanga grinning. The phage was doing her more good than the tranks.

"Not to worry, star girl. Golly won't let 'em get you."

"Air." She was trying to point to life-support, which had long since gone red.

"I know, spacer. We're getting air at Medbase."

She gave him a strange un-Topanga smile. "Whatever you say, little Golly." Whispering hoarsely, "I know—you've been beautiful—"

Her hand reached, burning. This he positively could not take. Too bad his music was gone.

"Give us verses as we go, star girl."

But she was too weak.

"Read me—"

Her scanner was full of it.

"In oil-rinsed circles of blind ecstasy." Hard to dig, until the strobing letters suddenly turned to music in his throat. *"Man hears himself an engine in a cloud!"* he chanted, convoyed by ghosts.

"—What marathons new-set among the stars! . . . The soul, by naphtha fledged into new reaches, already knows the closer clasp of Mars—"

. . . It was indeed fortunate, he discovered, that he had set the autopilot and stayed suited up.

His first clear impression of Medbase was a chimpanzee's big brown eyes staring into his under a flashprobe. He jerked away, found himself peeled and tied on a table. The funny feeling was the luxury of simulated gravity. The chimpanzee turned out to be a squat little type in med-whites, who presently freed him.

"I told you he wasn't a phager." It was the woman's voice.

Craning, Gollem saw she was no girl-girl and had a remarkable absence of chin. The chimpanzee eventually introduced himself as Chief Medic Kranz.

"What kind of ship *is* that?" the woman asked as he struggled into his suit.

"A derelict," he told them. "Phagerunners were using it. My teammate's stoned. All he needs is air."

"The power units," said Kranz. "I'll help you bring them over."

"No need for you to go in—I've got them ready to go. Just give me a couple of metabolite cores to take back to start the air cleaning."

Unsuspicious, Kranz motioned the woman to show the way to their stores. Gollem saw that their base was one big cheap bubble behind a hard-walled control module. The molly hadn't even seamed together under the film; a couple of pebbles would finish them. The ward had twenty-odd burn cases in cocoons. Themis didn't bother much with burns.

An old spacerat minus a lot of his original equipment came wambling over to open up. Gollem loaded as much metabolite as he could carry and headed for the lock. At the port the woman grabbed his arm.

"You *will* help us?" Her eyes were deep green. Gollem concentrated on her chin.

"Be right back." He cycled out.

Ragnarok was on a tether he didn't recall securing. He scrambled over, found the end fouled in the lock toggles. If there had been tumble—bye-bye.

When he got inside he heard Topanga's voice. He hustled up the shaft.

Once again he was too late.

While he'd been in the stores unsuspicious Chief Medic Kranz had suited up and beat him into *Ragnarok*.

"This is a very sick woman, spacer," he informed Gollem.

"The legal owner of this derelict, doctor. I'm taking her to Coronis Base."

"I'm taking her into my ward right now. We have the facilities. Get those power units."

He could see Topanga's eyes close.

"She doesn't wish to be hospitalized."

"She's in no condition to decide that," Kranz snapped.

The metabolite was on board. Doctor Chimpanzee Kranz appeared to have elected himself a driveship ride to nowhere. Gollem began drifting toward the ignition panel, beside Topanga's web.

"I guess you're right, sir. I'll help you prepare her and we'll take her in."

But Kranz's little hand had a little stungun in it.

"The power units, spacer." He waved Gollem toward the shaft.

There weren't any power units.

Gollem backed into the metabolite, watching for the stunner to waver. It didn't. There was only one chance left, if you could call it a chance.

"Topanga, this good doctor is going to take you into his hospital," he said loudly. "He wants you where he can take good care of you."

One of Topanga's eyelids wrinkled, sagged down again. An old, battered woman. No chance.

"Can you handle her, doctor?"

"Get that power *now.*" Kranz snapped the safety off.

Gollem nodded sourly and started downshaft as slowly as he could. Kranz came over to watch him, efficiently out of reach. What now? Gollem couldn't reach the ignition circuits from here even if he knew how to short them.

Just as he turned around to look for something to fake a power cell it happened.

A whomp like an imploding mollybubble smacked into the shaft. Chief Medic Kranz sailed down in a slow cartwheel.

"Good girl!" Gollem yelled. "You got him!" He batted the stunner out of Kranz' limp glove and kicked upward. When his head cleared the shaft he found he was looking into the snout of Topanga's jolter.

"Get out of my ship," she rasped. "You lying suitlouse. And take your four-eyed, needle-sucking friend with you!"

"Topanga, it's me—it's Golly—"

"I know who you are," she said coldly. "You'll never trap me."

"Topanga!" he cried. A bolt went by his ear, rocking him.

"Out!" She was leaning down the shaft, squeezing on the jolter.

Gollem backed slowly down, collecting Kranz. The witch figure above him streamed biotape and bandages, the hair that once shone red standing up like white fire. She must be breathing pure phage, he thought.

Can't last long. All I have to do is go slow.

"Out!" She screamed. Then he saw she had Kranz's oxy tube clamped under one arm. This seemed to be his day for underestimating people.

"Topanga," he began to plead and had to dodge another jolt-bolt. She couldn't go on missing forever. He decided to haul Kranz out and cut back into the ship through the emergency port. He recalled seeing a welding torch in the medbase port rack.

He boosted Kranz along the tether and into the med-base lock. The woman was waiting on the other side. As the port opened he pushed Kranz at her and grabbed the welder. The chinless wonder learned fast— she flung herself on the welder and started to wrestle. There was solid woman-muscle under her whites, but he got a fist where her jaw should have been and threw himself back into the lock.

As it started to cycle he realized she had probably saved his life.

The outer lock had a viewport through which he could see *Ragnarok's* vents. The starfield behind them was dissolving.

He let out an inarticulate groan and slammed the reverse cycle to let himself back into Medbase. As soon as it cracked he bolted through, carrying the medics to the deck. The port behind him lit up like a solar flare.

They all stared at the silent torrent of flame pouring out of *Ragnarok.* Then she was moving, faster, faster yet. The jetstream swung and the port went black.

"It's burning! Get the foam!"

Kranz grabbed a sealant cannister and they raced to the edge of the hard-wall area, where *Ragnarok's* exhaust had seared the bubble. When the burns were sealed the ship was a dwindling firetail among the stars.

"Topanga doesn't like hospitals," Gollem told them.

"The power units!" Kranz said urgently. "Call her back!"

They were pushing Gollem toward the commo board.

"No way. She just blew the last ignition charge. Where she's headed now she goes."

"What do you mean? To Coronis?"

"Never." He rubbed his shaggy head. "I—I don't recall exactly. Mars, maybe the sun."

"With the power units that would have saved these people." Kranz's face had the expression he probably used on gangrene. "Thanks to you. I suggest that you remove yourself from my sight for the remainder of our joint existence."

"There never were any power units," Gollem said, starting to go out. "The phagers got my boat and you saw for yourself what the drive was like. Her acceleration would have broken you apart."

The woman followed him out.

"Who was she, spacer?"

"Topanga Orlov," Gollem said painfully. "Val Orlov's wife. They were the first Saturn mission. That was their ship, *Ragnarok*. She was holed up in my sector."

"You just wanted air."

Gollem nodded.

They were by the base display tank. The computer was running a real-time display of the uncoming Trojans. The green blip was Medbase and the red blip with the smear was the smaller Trojan and attendant gravel tail. He studied the vectors. No doubt.

It was now dark-period. Sleep time coming up. The people here might eat breakfast, but for true they wouldn't eat lunch. By noon or thereabouts Medbase ould be organic enrichment on a swarm of space ice.

So would ex-Inspector Gollem.

The two medics went out on the wards and Kranz unbent enough to accept Gollem's offer to man the commo board. The spacer wobbled in to watch him. The sight of *Ragnarok's* blast-out had lit his fires.

Gollem taped a routine red-call and began to hunt across the bands. The old man mumbled about ships. Nobody was answering, nobody would. Once Gollem thought he heard an echo from Topanga, but it was nothing. Her oxy must be long gone by now, he thought. A mad old phage-ghost on her last trip. Where had he computed her to? He seemed to recall something about Mars. At least they wouldn't end in some trophy-hunter's plastic park.

"You know what they got in them cocoons? Squatters!" The old man squinted out of his good side to see how Gollem took this. "Skinheads. Freaks 'n' crotties. Phagers, even. Medics, they don't care." He sighed, scratched his burned skin with his stump. "Grounders. They won't last out here."

"Too right," Gollem agreed. "Like maybe tomorrow." That tickled the old man.

Toward midnight Kranz took over. The woman brought in some hot redeye. Gollem started to refuse and then realized his stomach wasn't hurting any more. Nothing to worry about now. He sipped the stimulant. The woman was looking at a scanner.

"She was beautiful," she murmured.

"Knock it off, Anna," Kranz snapped.

She went on scanning and suddenly caught her breath.

"Your name. It's Gollem, isn't it?"

Gollem nodded and got up to go look at the tank.

Presently the woman Anna came out after him and looked at the tank, too. The old spacer was asleep in the corner.

"Topanga was married to a George Gollem once," Anna said quietly. "They had a son. On Luna."

Gollem took the scanner cartridge out of her hand and flipped it into the wastechute. She said nothing more. They both watched the tank for a while. Gollem noticed that her eyes were almost good enough to make up for her chin. She didn't look at him. The tank didn't change.

Around four she went in and took over from Kranz and the men settled down to wait.

"Medbase Themis calling, please come in. Medbase Themis calling anyone," the woman whispered monotonously.

Kranz went out. It seemed a lot of work to breathe.

Suddenly Kranz snapped his fingers from the next room. Gollem went to him.

"Look."

They hung over the tank. The red smear was closer to the green blip. Between them was a yellow spark.

"What is that?"

Gollem shrugged. "A rock."

"Impossible, we scan-swept that area a dozen times."

"No mass," Gollem frowned. "It's a tank ghost."

Kranz began systematically flushing the computer input checks. The woman left the board and came to lean over the tank. Gollem watched absently, his brain picking at phage-warped memories. Something about the computer.

On impulse he went to the commo board and ran the receiver through its limits. All he got was a blast of squeals and whistles, the stress-front of the incoming rocks.

"What is it?" Anna's eyes were phosphorescent.

"Nothing."

Kranz finished his checks. The yellow ghost stayed in, sidling toward the red smear. If that were a rock, and it had about a hundred times more mass than it could have, it just might deflect the Trojan's gravel swarm. But it didn't.

Gollem played monotonously with the board. The old spacer snored. The minutes congealed. Kranz shook himself, took Anna out to tour the wards. When they came back they stopped at the tank.

The whatever-it-was stayed in, closing on the Trojan.

Sometime in the unreal dimlight hours Gollem caught it, wavering on a gale of space noise:

"I have contact! Val! I'm coming—"

They crowded around him as he coaxed the tuners but there was nothing there. Presently a ripple of relays tripped off in the next room and they all ran to the tank. It was dead; the computer had protected itself against an induction overload.

They never knew exactly what happened.

"It's possible," Gollem admitted to them. It was long after noon when they decided to eat.

"While we were on the way here I know I computed that Trojan all the way to Medbase, before that I got really bombed. Maybe I threw a bridge into the course computer, maybe it was already in. Say she took off with no course setting. Those old mechs are set to hunt. It's possible it inverted and boosted straight back out that trajectory to the rock."

"But your ship had no mass," Kranz objected.

"That thing was a space-scoop feeding a monster drive. The pile dampers were cheese. *Ragnarok* could have scooped herself solid right through the gravel cloud and blown as she hit the Trojan. You could get a pocket sun."

They went over it again at dark-period. And again later while he and Anna looked at nothing in particular out the ports. A long time after that he showed her a script he'd fixed for the wall of Medbase Free Enclave:

Launched in abyssal cupolas of space
Toward endless terminas, Easters of speeding light—
Vast engines outward veering with seraphic grace
On clarion cylinders pass out of sight.

Recommended Reading

There has been so much adventure SF of one sort or another published over the years that making a definitive list of novels and collections is almost impossible; I'm not even going to try—for suggestions, read the Preface, and the storynotes for the individual authors. Making a list of anthologies is almost as difficult, since a great many anthologies will contain one or two such stories even when that sort of material isn't the major emphasis of the book.

Here's a quick and inadequate list, though, of some of the major anthologies that emphasize adventure work from the '30s, '40s, '50s, and '60s. Most of the SF magazines, *Astounding/Analog, Galaxy, Worlds of If, The Magazine of Fantasy & Science Fiction,* have a number of "Best of" collections, too many to list individually, though I have listed a few of them below that arbitrarially strike me as functioning as more generally retrospective overviews. Anthologies are listed alphabetically by the name of the editor:

Ackermanthology, Forrest J. Ackerman
All About Venus, Brian W. Aldiss
Evil Earths, Brian W. Aldiss
Galactic Empires, Volumes 1–2, Brian W. Aldiss
Space Oddessys, Brian W. Aldiss
Space Opera, Brian W. Aldiss
Spectrum, volumes 1–4, Kingsley Amis and Robert Conquest
Before the Golden Age, Isaac Asimov
The Hugo Winners, volumes 1 & 2, Isaac Asimov (the other volumes of
    Hugo-winners are valuable as well, but the first two are the best for
    older work)
*The Mammoth Book of Classic Science Fiction: Short Novels of the
    1930s* (in the U.S. as *Great Tales of Classic Science Fiction*), Isaac
    Asimov, Martin H. Greenberg, and Charles G. Waugh
*The Mammoth Book of Golden Age Science Fiction: Short Novels of the
    1940s,* Isaac Asimov, Martin H. Greenberg, and Charles G. Waugh
*The Mammoth Book of Vintage Science Fiction: Short Novels of the
    1950s,* Isaac Asimov, Martin H. Greenberg, and Charles G. Waugh
*The Mammoth Book of New World Science Fiction: Great Short Novels
    of the 1960s,* Isaac Asimov, Martin H. Greenberg, and Charles G.
    Waugh

Wonderful Worlds of Science Fiction 1: Intergalactic Empires, Isaac Asimov, Martin H. Greenberg, and Charles G. Waugh

(Asimov and Greenberg also edited a long-running series—24 volumes, too many to individually list here—called *Isaac Asimov Presents the Great SF Stories,* which gives a year-by-year overview, starting with 1939 and ending with 1962)

The Best Science Fiction Stories, 1949–1954, Everett F. Bleiler & T. E. Dikty

Year's Best Science Fiction Novels, 1952–1954

The Best from Planet Stories No. 1, Leigh Brackett

A Treasury of Great Science Fiction, volumes 1 & 2, Anthony Boucher

The Science Fiction Hall of Fame, volume 2, Ben Bova

The Astounding Science Fiction Anthology, John W. Campbell

The Big Book of Science Fiction, Groff Conklin

The Omnibus of Science Fiction, Groff Conklin

Seven Trips Through Time and Space, Groff Conklin

A Treasury of Science Fiction, Groff Conklin

Modern Classics of Science Fiction, Gardner Dozois

Modern Classic Short Novels of Science Fiction, Gardner Dozois

The Magazine of Fantasy & Science Fiction, a 30 Year Retrospective, Edward L. Ferman

The Best from the Magazine of Fantasy & Science Fiction: A 45th Anniversary Anthology, Edward L. Ferman and Kristine Kathryn Rusch

Science Fiction of the '50s, Martin H. Greenberg and Joseph Olander

The Road to Science Fiction, volumes 1–4, James Gunn

Astounding, Harry Harrison

Ascent of Wonder, David G. Hartwell

A Science Fiction Century, David G. Hartwell

Visions of Wonder, David G. Hartwell

A World Treasury of Science Fiction, David G. Hartwell

Adventures in Time and Space, Raymond J. Healy and J. Francis McComas

Mars, We Love You, Jane Hipolito and Willis E. McNelly

First Step Outward, Robert Hoskins

The Stars Around Us, Robert Hoskins

One Hundred Years of Science Fiction, Damon Knight

A Science Fiction Argosy, Damon Knight

Science Fiction of the Thirties, Damon Knight

Worlds To Come, Damon Knight

The End of Summer: Science Fiction of the Fifties, Barry N. Malzberg and Bill Pronzini

SF: The Best of the Best, Judith Merril

The Year's Best S-F, volumes 1–12, Judith Merril
Galaxy: Thirty Years of Innovative Science Fiction, Frederik Pohl, Martin H. Greenberg, and Joseph Olander
The Great Science Fiction Series, Frederik Pohl, Martin H. Greenberg, and Joseph Olander
Worlds of If: A Retrospective Anthology, Frederik Pohl, Martin H. Greenberg, and Joseph Olander
Yesterday's Tomorrows, Frederik Pohl
Alpha, volumes 1–9, Robert Silverberg
The Arbor House Treasury of Great Science Fiction Short Novels, Robert Silverberg and Martin H. Greenberg
The Arbor House Treasury of Modern Science Fiction, Robert Silverberg and Martin H. Greenberg
The Arbor House Treasury of Science Fiction Masterpieces, Robert Silverberg and Martin H. Greenberg
Deep Space, Robert Silverberg
The Ends of Time, Robert Silverberg
Explorers of Space, Robert Silverberg
Great Short Novels of Science Fiction, Robert Silverberg
Invaders from Space, Robert Silverberg
The Mirror of Infinity, Robert Silverberg
A Century of Science Fiction 1950–1959, Robert Silverberg
Robert Silverberg's Worlds of Wonder, Robert Silverberg
The Science Fiction Hall of Fame, Volume 1, Robert Silverberg
Adventures on Other Planets, Donald A. Wollheim
More Adventures on Other Planets, Donald A. Wollheim
Swordsmen in the Sky, Donald A. Wollheim

Libraries may still be your best bet for finding many of these titles, although, alas, libraries don't carry as many old titles as they did twenty years ago (try a university library, if you have one near you, preferably one with a science fiction collection). If libraries and regular used-book stores fail you, try science fiction specialty stores and the dealer's rooms at science fiction conventions. If they fail you as well, as they may, then you have no choice but to mail-order. We've mentioned the addresses of NESFA Press and Charles L. Miller in the storynotes. Some of the biggest mail-order services are Barry R. Levin, 720 Santa Monica Blvd., Santa Monica CA, 90401-2602; Robert A. Madle, 44606 Bestor Drive, Rockville MD 20853; Greg Ketter, DreamHaven Books, 912 West Lake Street, Minneapolis, MN 55408; Lloyd Currey, Box 187, Elizabethtown, NY 12932; and Mark V. Ziesing, P.O. Box 97, Shingletown CA 96088, all of whom publish catalogs periodically. Listings for other mail-order dealers can usually be found in the classified ads of the news magazine *Locus* (Locus Publications, P.O. Box 13305, Oakland CA 94661—$43 for a 12-issue subscription in the U.S. via periodical mail; $53 for a first-class subscription in the U.S.)

On the Internet, try Amazon.com or abebooks.com, among other services.

THE
GOOD NEW
STUFF

For Isabella Marie Amelio Casper—
the good new stuff.

CONTENTS

PREFACE

"They don't write 'em like that anymore," you often hear people say, talking about fast-paced, no-holds-barred, flat-out *adventure* stories, stories drenched with color, wonder, and action, stories that take us to far worlds for adventures of a sort that could not be encountered on our familiar, present-day Earth, stories that bring us face-to-face with strange dangers and even stranger wonders—but, actually, they *do* still write stories like that!

Yes, they really do. Don't listen to the voices that say you can't find anything like that anymore—they're the voices of people so lost in nostalgia for the stories of their youth that they can't look around them and see what's happening right in front of their own eyes. If they did look around, they'd find that the space adventure story is not only alive and well here at the end of the nineties, it's flourishing.

As I hope to demonstrate in this anthology, you can still find science fiction adventure stories today every bit as wild and woolly and mind-blowing as anything from the old pulp days, stories as full of swashbuckling action, dash, and élan as any of the Planetary Romances from the old *Planet Stories* and *Thrilling Wonder Stories,* stories just as full of cosmic sweep and scale and grandeur and the immense, sun-shattering, planet-busting clash of titanic forces in conflict as anything from the old "Superscience" days of the thirties when Edmond Hamilton was earning his nickname of "World-Wrecker Hamilton" (except with much more accurate, up-to-date, cutting-edge science!).

Adventure writing is not the only sort of science fiction there is, of course, or the only thing science fiction does well, and never has been. Science fiction can be serious-minded and substantial and profound; it can be a window on worlds we'd never otherwise see and people and creatures we'd never otherwise know; it can provide us with insights into the inner workings of our society that are difficult to gain in any other way, grant us perspectives into social mores and human nature itself mostly otherwise unreachable; it can be an invaluable tool with which to take preconceived notions and received wisdom to pieces and reassemble them into something new; it can prepare us for the inevitable and sometimes dismaying changes ahead of us, helping to buffer us against the winds of Future Shock—but sometimes it's just *fun.* Sometimes it's "just" pure entertainment (with any more serious implications or troubling social issues—and they do get raised, even in the most seemingly insubstantial of stories—largely left to be dealt with in the subtext), adventure writing as vivid and entertaining as any that has ever been written in any genre anywhere.

Although adventure writing is often looked down on by critics (it's hard even to think of the phrase *adventure writing* without automatically adding the prefix *mere,* since that's the way it's almost always referred to) or ignored completely, it's no more but certainly no less valid and valuable than any other kind of science fiction. It's something that's always been part of the palette of the science fiction genre as well, ever since the days of Hugo Gernsback's *Amazing Stories* in the late twenties, when the specific *science fiction* adventure story began to precipitate out from the larger and older tradition of the generalized pulp adventure story—often Lost World/Lost Race tales—that goes all the way back into the middle of the nineteenth century. (Although the SF adventure story has always had—and still has—other branches as well, the Space Adventure story or the Space Opera, of one subvariety or another, remains to this day probably the most characteristic sort of SF adventure tale, the form that slowly emerged as being most specific to science fiction, and that's the kind of story I've primarily stuck with for this anthology.)

The previous anthology in this series, *The Good Old Stuff,* published in 1998, traced the development of the genre space adventure tale, from its beginnings in the Gernsback magazines through the "Superscience" era of the thirties and early forties (the First Great Age of the Space Opera, when writers such as E. E. "Doc" Smith, Ray Cummings, Raymond Z. Gallun, Edmond Hamilton, John W. Campbell Jr., Jack Williamson, Clifford D. Simak, and others developed and refined a form of adventure tale specific to science fiction), and on through the years from the mid-forties to the mid-sixties, the Second Great Age of the Space Opera, when writers such as A. E. van Vogt, L. Sprague de Camp, James H. Schmitz, Murray Leinster, Leigh Brackett, Jack Vance, Poul Anderson, Gordon R. Dickson, and H. Beam Piper would add an increased social-political sophistication and an increase in line-by-line writing craft to the form, a trend taken to new heights of complexity, flamboyance, and vividness by writers such as Cordwainer Smith, Alfred Bester, Frank Herbert, Robert A. Heinlein, Brian W. Aldiss, Larry Niven, Ursula K. Le Guin, Roger Zelazny, Samuel R. Delany, James Tiptree, Jr., and many others.

By the late sixties and early seventies, however, perhaps because of the prominence of the "New Wave" revolution in SF, which concentrated both on introspective, stylistically "experimental" work and work with more immediate sociological and political "relevance" to the tempestuous social scene of the day, perhaps because of scientific proof that the other planets of the solar system were not likely abodes for life (and so, it seemed, not interesting settings for adventure stories), perhaps because the now more widely understood limitations of Einsteinian relativity had come to make the idea of far-flung interstellar empires seem improbable at best, science fiction as a genre was tending to turn away from the Space Adventure tale. Although it would never disappear completely, it had become widely regarded as outmoded and déclassé; the radical new writers of the generation just about to rise to prominence would collectively produce less adventure SF, particularly Space Opera, than any other comparable generational group of authors, and there would be less Space Adventure stuff written in the following ten years or so than in any other comparable period in SF history. By far the majority of work published during this period would be set on Earth, often in the near future—even the solar system had been largely deserted as a setting for stories, let alone the distant stars. Although stalwarts such as Poul Anderson and Jack Vance and Larry Niven continued to soldier on throughout those years, it was a common—and frequently expressed—opinion that Space Opera was dead.

But by the late seventies and early eighties, new writers such as John Varley, George R.R. Martin, Bruce Sterling, Michael Swanwick, Vernor Vinge, and others would begin to become interested in the Space Adventure again, reinvented to better fit the aesthetic style and tastes of the day. And by the nineties, a whole new boom in Baroque Space Opera would be under way, on both sides of the Atlantic (there are some slight but perceptible differences in flavor between the New British Space Opera and the New American Space Opera, although they clearly are responses to the same evolutionary impetus—and, as was also true of the New Wave, which also manifested itself in slightly different forms on either side of the ocean, the similarities are far more significant than the differences are), fueled by authors such as Iain M. Banks, Dan Simmons, Orson Scott Card, C. J. Cherryh, Gregory Benford, Greg Bear, Colin Greenland, Paul J. McAuley, Alexander Jablokov, Stephen Baxter, Walter Jon Williams, Stephen R. Donaldson, John Barnes, Lois McMaster Bujold, Charles Sheffield, Eleanor Arnason, Peter F. Hamilton, and a dozen others, ushering in the Third Great Age of Space Opera.

Which brings us into the territory of the book you hold in your hands, *The Good New Stuff.*

Even having decided on the territory that I would cover in this volume, though (the mid-seventies to the present day), I found, as is usually the case with these retrospective anthologies, that there were many more stories that I would have liked to use than I had room to use. Some arbitrary decisions clearly needed to be made to winnow the mass of potential stories down to a usable number, and, arbitrarily, I made them.

Most of these judgment calls are subjective, again as always. While there's often plenty of action in a William Gibson story, for instance, action alone is not the only criterion, and somehow Cyberpunk doesn't *feel* like adventure writing to me—too intense, too noir-ish, too gloomy (plus the fact that almost all cyberpunk writing, or the bulk of it, anyway, takes place on Earth in the relatively near future). So, arbitrarily, I decided to omit Cyberpunk stories from consideration, although it cost me first-rate authors from Gibson to Pat Cadigan to Lewis Shiner (Bruce Sterling gets in, but for his earlier, more Space Opera-ish work, not his later cyberpunk and post-cyberpunk stuff). Similarly, Military SF, although concerned largely with the exploits of Space Mercenaries and usually chockablock with battle scenes, doesn't feel right to me either—too narrowly specialized, and too often easily recognized as only Horatio Hornblower stories "translated" into science fiction terms, or thinly disguised recastings of Vietnam War or World War II scenarios. Lucius Shepard's stuff always has strong action elements, but it's usually on the borderland of horror fiction as well, or at least partakes of that aesthetic tone, and again that was not the "flavor" I was subjectively groping for (and again, the vast majority of Shepard's stories take place on Earth, or in interconnecting fantasy realms). So all of that was out as well.

The last major judgment call I made was even more subjective. Parallel with the new boom in Space Opera has been a boom in the "Hard Science" story, also reinvented to fit the styles and prejudices of the times better, and although there are many similarities between the two forms, and the reader who likes one is at least fairly likely to like the other, and although the situation is complicated by the fact that many authors have a foot in both camps, sometimes producing one kind of thing and sometimes another, I still thought that I could discern enough differences between the two styles to assign writers, arbitrarily, to one camp or the other. Stephen Baxter, Greg Egan, Greg Benford, Brian Stableford, and Paul J. McAuley, for instance, all write some of the hardest SF around, but somehow *some* of what Baxter and Benford and McAuley are doing strikes me as being legitimately classifiable as Space Opera, while what Egan and Stableford are doing does not. So no Egan or Stableford, even though they're excellent writers, and Egan in particular may be one of the best new writers of the nineties. (It's hard to articulate exactly what I'm instinctively basing this decision on, except perhaps a vague feeling that Space Opera or Space Adventure needs a quality of flamboyance, exaggeration, scope, swagger, outrageousness, overheatedness, perhaps even lurid excess—an over-the-top quality that the cool, mannered, cerebral, tightly controlled work of Egan and Stableford doesn't have.)

Some other decisions made themselves for me. Some of the major players in the current subgenre of the New Space Opera, such as Iain M. Banks and Colin Greenland, for instance, write almost no short fiction at all, and while others, such as Orson Scott Card, Dan Simmons, Stephen Donaldson, and C. J. Cherryh, do occasionally write short fiction, almost none of it is in the Space Adventure mode (almost all of Cherryh's short work is fantasy, for instance, as is the bulk of Donaldson's, while most of Simmons's is horror, and so on). And the practical difficulties involved in the assembling of an anthology necessitated the omission of still other stories, those, say, which had recently appeared in a competing anthology, or those for which the reprint rights were either encumbered or priced too high for me to be able to afford them on the limited budget I had to work with.

Even with all of those winnowing screens in place, I was still left with a mass of material too large to use. The constraints of a technically feasible book length dictated the omission of other stories, but I could easily have produced an anthology twice the length of this one, with little or no discernable letdown in quality, and I would have if I could have.

There are a *lot* of good new stories of this sort out there, and if you like this book, I urge you to go and seek them out on your own. They're not hard to find, believe me, in spite of what "they" say. All you have to do is open your eyes and look around you.

So, then, this is the Good New Stuff. Enjoy!

John Varley

GOODBYE, ROBINSON CRUSOE

John Varley appeared on the SF scene in 1974, and by the end of 1976—in what was a meteoric rise to prominence even for a field known for meteoric rises—he was already being recognized as one of the hottest new writers of the seventies. His first story, "Picnic on Nearside," appeared in 1974 in *The Magazine of Fantasy & Science Fiction,* and was followed by as concentrated an outpouring of first-rate stories as the genre has ever seen, stories such as "Retrograde Summer," "In the Bowl," "Gotta Sing, Gotta Dance," "In the Hall of the Mountain King," "Equinoctial," "The Black Hole Passes," "Overdrawn at the Memory Bank," "The Phantom of Kansas," and many others: smart, bright, fresh, brash, audacious, effortlessly imaginative stories that seemed to suddenly shake the field out of its uneasy slumber like a wake-up call from a brand-new trumpet. It's hard to think of a group of short stories that has had a greater, more concentrated impact on the field, with the exception of Robert Heinlein's early work for John W. Campbell's *Astounding,* or perhaps Roger Zelazny's early stories in the mid-sixties (maybe a better example anyway, since, although Heinlein has always been one of Varley's major influences, his early Eight Worlds stuff in some ways had more in common with Zelazny, if only in that quality of good-natured effrontery and easy ostentation, and the almost insolent you-ain't-seen-*nothing*-yet ease and fecundity of his invention). By 1978, largely because of Varley's work, it would be possible for Algis Budrys to say (in the introduction to Varley's first collection, appropriately enough), "There is beginning to be, in other words, yet another new SF: vigorous, relevant, richer than ever"—a statement that would have been inconceivable a few years before, in the dull gray doldrums that had been left behind after the ferocious tempest of the New Wave Era had blown itself out and died away to stillness.

Varley was one of the first new writers to become interested in the solar system again, after several years in which it had been largely abandoned as a setting for stories because the space probes of the late sixties and early seventies had "proved" that it was nothing but an "uninteresting" collection of balls of rock and ice, with no available abodes for life—dull as a supermarket parking lot. Instead, Varley seemed to find the solar system lushly romantic *just as it was,* lifeless balls of rock and all (and this was even before the later Pioneer probes to the Jupiter and Saturn systems had proved the solar system to be a lot more surprising than people thought that it was). He makes this obvious in "In the Bowl," where he specifically invokes the richly romantic Venus of the *Planet Stories* days (and of Heinlein's *Between Planets,* which is even more specifically referenced), describing the human settlements of Venus as places of "steamy swamps and sleazy hotels" where you can "hunt the prehistoric monsters that wallow in the field marshes that are just a swamp-buggy ride out of town," or rub shoulders in the teeming streets with the "eight-legged dragons with eyestalks" who go lumbering by . . . and then, when the tourists go home, they *shut all that off,* all the *Planet Stories* dreams that are just there to amuse the rubes, and then "the place reverts to an ordinary cluster of silvery domes sitting in darkness and eight-hundred-degree temperature." The remarkable thing here, the revolutionary thing, is that Varley finds Venus *more* romantic once the pulp *Planet Stories* dreams are switched off and you're left with the uncompromising reality of Venus to deal with instead—finds it more romantic *because* it's an airless hellhole of eight-hundred-degree temperature and deadly crushing pressure, completely and totally unlike the Earth, instead of the ersatz copy of Earth in the dinosaur age that had been the dream of earlier writers. This is an aesthetic shift in perception that will go ringing on down through the eighties and nineties in the work of writers such as G. David Nordley, Stephen Baxter, and a dozen others.

This perceptual shift was common to all his early stories, which share a common setting in which humankind has been forcibly exiled from the Earth and forced to live instead on the other planets of the solar system—but where the children of those outcasts have adapted so well that they've made a virtue of necessity, and actually *enjoy* living in hostile environments such as Venus or Mercury or the Moon, something that's made clear and explicit in stories such as "Retrograde Summer," among others. They've become new people, different in values from their parents, just as Varley himself was different in values even from his biggest role model (although there are echoes in his work of Zelazny, James Tiptree, Jr., Samuel R. Delany, and Larry Niven as well), Robert A. Heinlein. I always felt that Varley had made this explicit in his very first story, "Picnic on Nearside," when the young Varley Individuals (children by today's standards, although fully mature and sexually active) find what I take to be the last Heinlein Individual living as a hermit on the other side of the Moon, a crusty, competent, self-sufficient, ferociously independent, politically and sexually conservative, somewhat paranoid individual whom the children regard with affection and a certain degree of respect, but who also seems to them outmoded and out of touch and faintly pathetic, and whose problems and ultimate demise are caused by his own stubbornness and inability to compromise, and by the obsolete social attitudes that he is unable to change or even suspect that he should change. This always struck me as a highly significant moment in genre history. The Varley Individuals had won, not by fighting, not by Campbell-esque political Dirty Tricks, but simply because they *were* new people, with new attitudes that made the old ones obsolete. From now on the future would belong to them and *their* children, not to the Heinlein Individual, who had owned it for more than thirty years.

Varley often uses children as protagonists of his Eight Worlds stories, in fact. As in the one that follows, one of the best but also one of the lesser-known of those stories, in which he demonstrates that when you become a man, it's time to put away childish things—but that sometimes doing that can be very hard indeed.

Varley somehow never had as great an impact with his novels as he did with his short fiction, with the possible exception of his first novel, *Ophiuchi Hotline.* His other novels include the somewhat disappointing "Gaean" trilogy, consisting of *Titan, Wizard,* and *Demon,* and a novelization of one of his own short stories that was also made into a movie, *Millennium;* he has also published four collections,

The Persistence of Vision, The Barbie Murders, Picnic on Nearside, and *Blue Champagne.*

In the eighties, Varley moved away from the print world to produce a number of screenplays for Hollywood producers, most of which were never produced. He produced one last significant story, 1984's "Press Enter ■," which won him both the Hugo and the Nebula Award. (He also won a Hugo in 1982 for his story "The Pusher," and a Hugo and a Nebula in 1979 for his novella "The Persistence of Vision.") After "Press Enter ■," little was heard from Varley in the genre until the publication of a major new novel, *Steel Beach,* in 1992, which was successful commercially, but received a lukewarm reception from many critics. Since then he has been largely silent, but that may be about to change; a new novel, *The Golden Globe,* has just been published, and another book, *Irontown Blues,* has already been announced.

It was summer, and Piri was in his second childhood. First, second; who counted? His body was young. He had not felt more alive since his original childhood back in the spring, when the sun drew closer and the air began to melt.

He was spending his time at Rarotonga Reef, in the Pacifica disneyland. Pacifica was still under construction, but Rarotonga had been used by the ecologists as a testing ground for the more ambitious barrier-type reef they were building in the south, just off the "Australian" coast. As a result, it was more firmly established than the other biomes. It was open to visitors, but so far only Piri was there. The "sky" disconcerted everyone else.

Piri didn't mind it. He was equipped with a brand-new toy: a fully operational imagination, a selective sense of wonder that allowed him to blank out those parts of his surroundings that failed to fit with his current fantasy.

He awoke with the tropical sun blinking in his face through the palm fronds. He had built a rude shelter from flotsam and detritus on the beach. It was not to protect him from the elements. The disneyland management had the weather well in hand; he might as well have slept in the open. But castaways *always* build some sort of shelter.

He bounced up with the quick alertness that comes from being young and living close to the center of things, brushed sand from his naked body, and ran for the line of breakers at the bottom of the narrow strip of beach.

His gait was awkward. His feet were twice as long as they should have been, with flexible toes that were webbed into flippers. Dry sand showered around his legs as he ran. He was brown as coffee and cream, and hairless.

Piri dived flat to the water, sliced neatly under a wave, and paddled out to waist-height. He paused there. He held his nose and worked his arms up and down, blowing air through his mouth and swallowing at the same time. What looked like long, hairline scars between his lower ribs came open. Red-orange fringes became visible inside them, and gradually lowered. He was no longer an air-breather.

He dived again, mouth open, and this time he did not come up. His esophagus and trachea closed and a new valve came into operation. It would pass water in only one direction, so his diaphragm now functioned as a pump pulling water through his mouth and forcing it out through the gill-slits. The water flowing through this lower chest area caused his gills to engorge with blood, turning them purplish-red and forcing his lungs to collapse upward into his chest cavity. Bubbles of air trickled out his sides, then stopped. His transition was complete.

The water seemed to grow warmer around him. It had been pleasantly cool; now it seemed no temperature at all. It was the result of his body temperature lowering in response to hormones released by an artificial gland in his cranium. He could not afford to burn energy at the rate he had done in the air; the water was too efficient a coolant for that. All through his body arteries and capillaries were constricting as parts of him stabilized at a lower rate of function.

No naturally evolved mammal had ever made the switch from air to water breathing, and the project had taxed the resources of bio-engineering to its limits. But everything in Piri's body was a living part of him. It had taken two full days to install it all.

He knew nothing of the chemical complexities that kept him alive where he should have died quickly from heat loss or oxygen starvation. He knew only the joy of arrowing along the white sandy bottom. The water was clear, blue-green in the distance.

The bottom kept dropping away from him, until suddenly it reached for the waves. He angled up the wall of the reef until his head broke the surface, climbed up the knobs and ledges until he was standing in the sunlight. He took a deep breath and became an air-breather again.

The change cost him some discomfort. He waited until the dizziness and fit of coughing had passed, shivering a little as his body rapidly underwent a reversal to a warm-blooded economy.

It was time for breakfast.

He spent the morning foraging among the tidepools. There were dozens of plants and animals that he had learned to eat raw. He ate a great deal, storing up energy for the afternoon's expedition on the outer reef.

Piri avoided looking at the sky. He wasn't alarmed by it; it did not disconcert him as it did the others. But he had to preserve the illusion that he was actually on a tropical reef in the Pacific Ocean, a castaway, and not a vacationer in an environment bubble below the surface of Pluto.

Soon he became a fish again, and dived off the sea side of the reef.

The water around the reef was oxygen-rich from the constant wave action. Even here, though, he had to remain in motion to keep enough water flowing past his external gill fringes. But he could move more slowly as he wound his way down into the darker reaches of the sheer reef face. The reds and yellows of his world were swallowed by the blues and greens and purples. It was quiet. There were sounds to hear, but his ears were not adapted to them. He moved slowly through shafts of blue light, keeping up the bare minimum of water flow.

He hesitated at the ten-meter level. He had thought he was going to his Atlantis Grotto to check out his crab farm. Then he wondered if he ought to hunt up Ocho the Octopus instead. For a panicky moment he was afflicted with the bane of childhood: an inability to decide what to do with himself. Or maybe it was worse, he thought. Maybe it was a sign of growing up. The crab farm bored him, or at least it did today.

He waffled back and forth for several minutes, idly chasing the tiny red fish that flirted with the anemones. He never caught one. This was no good at all. Surely there was an adventure in this silent fairyland. He had to find one.

An adventure found him, instead. Piri saw something swimming out in the open water, almost at the limits of his vision. It was long and pale, an attenuated missile of raw death. His heart squeezed in panic, and he scuttled for a hollow in the reef.

Piri called him the Ghost. He had seen him many times in the open sea. He was eight meters of mouth, belly and tail: hunger personified. There were those who said the great white shark was the most ferocious carnivore that ever lived. Piri believed it.

It didn't matter that the Ghost was completely harmless to him. The Pacifica management did not like having its guests eaten alive. An adult could elect to go into the water with no protection, providing the necessary waivers were on file. Children had to be implanted with an equalizer. Piri had one, somewhere just below the skin of his left wrist. It was a sonic generator, set to emit a sound that would mean terror to any predator in the water.

The Ghost, like all the sharks, barracudas, morays, and other predators in Pacifica, was not like his cousins who swam the seas of Earth. He had been cloned from cells stored in the Biological Library on Luna. The library had been created two hundred years before as an insurance policy against the extinction of a species. Originally, only endangered species were filed, but for years before the Invasion the directors had been trying to get a sample of everything. Then the Invaders had come, and Lunarians were too busy surviving without help from Occupied Earth to worry about the library. But when the time came to build the disneylands, the library had been ready.

By then, biological engineering had advanced to the point where many modifications could be made in genetic structure. Mostly, the disneyland biologists had left nature alone. But they had changed the predators. In the Ghost, the change was a mutated organ attached to the brain that responded with a flood of fear when a supersonic note was sounded.

So why was the Ghost still out there? Piri blinked his nictating membranes, trying to clear his vision. It helped a little. The shape looked a bit different.

Instead of moving back and forth, the tail seemed to be going up and down, perhaps in a scissoring motion. Only one animal swims like that. He gulped down his fear and pushed away from the reef.

But he had waited too long. His fear of the Ghost went beyond simple danger, of which there was none. It was something more basic, an unreasoning reflex that prickled his neck when he saw that long white shape. He couldn't fight it, and didn't want to. But the fear had kept him against the reef, hidden, while the person swam out of reach. He thrashed to catch up, but soon lost track of the moving feet in the gloom.

He had seen gills trailing from the sides of the figure, muted down to a deep blue-black by the depths. He had the impression that it was a woman.

Tongatown was the only human habitation on the island. It housed a crew of maintenance people and their children, about fifty in all, in grass huts patterned after those of South Sea natives. A few of the buildings concealed elevators that went to the underground rooms that would house the tourists when the project was completed. The shacks would then go at a premium rate, and the beaches would be crowded.

Piri walked into the circle of firelight and greeted his friends. Nighttime was party time in Tongatown. With the day's work over, everybody gathered around the fire and roasted a vat-grown goat or lamb. But the real culinary treats were the fresh vegetable dishes. The ecologists were still working out the kinks in the systems, controlling blooms, planting more of failing species. They often produced huge excesses of edibles that would have cost a fortune on the outside. The workers took some of the excess for themselves. It was understood to be a fringe benefit of the job. It was hard enough to find people who could stand to stay under the Pacifica sky.

"Hi, Piri," said a girl. "You meet any pirates today?" It was Harra, who used to be one of Piri's best friends but had seemed increasingly remote over the last year. She was wearing a hand-made grass skirt and a lot of flowers, tied into strings that looped around her body. She was fifteen now, and Piri was . . . but who cared? There were no seasons here, only days. Why keep track of time?

Piri didn't know what to say. The two of them had once played together out on the reef. It might be Lost Atlantis, or Submariner, or Reef Pirates; a new plot line and cast of heroes and villains every day. But her question had held such thinly veiled contempt. Didn't she care about the Pirates anymore? What was the matter with her?

She relented when she saw Piri's helpless bewilderment.

"Here, come on and sit down. I saved you a rib." She held out a large chunk of mutton.

Piri took it and sat beside her. He was famished, having had nothing all day since his large breakfast.

"I thought I saw the Ghost today," he said, casually.

Harra shuddered. She wiped her hands on her thighs and looked at him closely.

"Thought? You thought you saw him?" Harra did not care for the Ghost. She had cowered with Piri more than once as they watched him prowl.

"Yep. But I don't think it was really him."

"Where was this?"

"On the sea side, down about, oh, ten meters. I think it was a woman."

"I don't see how it could be. There's just you and—and Midge and Darvin with—did this woman have an air tank?"

"Nope. Gills. I saw that."

"But there's only you and four others here with gills. And I know where they all were today."

"You used to have gills," he said, with a hint of accusation.

She sighed. "Are we going through that again? I *told* you, I got tired of the flippers. I wanted to move around the *land* some more."

"I can move around the land," he said, darkly.

"All right, all right. You think I deserted you. Did you ever think that you sort of deserted *me?*"

Piri was puzzled by that, but Harra had stood up and walked quickly away. He could follow her, or he could finish his meal. She was right about the flippers. He was no great shakes at chasing anybody.

Piri never worried about anything for too long. He ate, and ate some more, long past the time when everyone else had joined together for the dancing and singing. He usually hung back, anyway. He could sing, but dancing was out of his league.

Just as he was leaning back in the sand, wondering if there were any more corners he could fill up—perhaps another bowl of that shrimp teriyaki?—Harra was back. She sat beside him.

"I talked to my mother about what you said. She said a tourist showed up today. It looks like you were right. It was a woman, and she was amphibious."

Piri felt a vague unease. One tourist was certainly not an invasion, but she could be a harbinger. And amphibious. So far, no one had gone to that expense except for those who planned to live here for a long time. Was his tropical hideout in danger of being discovered?

"What—what's she doing here?" He absently ate another spoonful of crab cocktail.

"She's looking for *you*," Harra laughed, and elbowed him in the ribs. Then she pounced on him, tickling his ribs until he was howling in helpless glee. He fought back, almost to the point of having the upper hand, but she was bigger and a little more determined. She got him pinned, showering flower petals on him as they struggled. One of the red flowers from her hair was in her eye, and she brushed it away, breathing hard.

"You want to go for a walk on the beach?" she asked.

Harra was fun, but the last few times he'd gone with her she had tried to kiss him. He wasn't ready for that. He was only a kid. He thought she probably had something like that in mind now.

"I'm too full," he said, and it was almost the literal truth. He had stuffed himself disgracefully, and only wanted to curl up in his shack and go to sleep.

Harra said nothing, just sat there getting her breathing under control. At last she nodded, a little jerkily, and got to her feet. Piri wished he could see her face to face. He knew something was wrong. She turned from him and walked away.

Robinson Crusoe was feeling depressed when he got back to his hut. The walk down the beach away from the laughter and singing had been a lonely one. Why had he rejected Harra's offer of companionship? Was it really so bad that she wanted to play new kinds of games?

But no, damn it. She wouldn't play his games, why should he play hers?

After a few minutes of sitting on the beach under the crescent moon, he got into character. Oh, the agony of being a lone castaway, far from the company of fellow creatures, with nothing but faith in God to sustain oneself. Tomorrow he would read from the scriptures, do some more exploring along the rocky north coast, tan some goat hides, maybe get in a little fishing.

With his plans for the morrow laid before him, Piri could go to sleep, wiping away a last tear for distant England.

The ghost woman came to him during the night. She knelt beside him in the sand. She brushed his sandy hair from his eyes and he stirred in his sleep. His feet thrashed.

He was churning through the abyssal deeps, heart hammering, blind to everything but internal terror. Behind him, jaws yawned, almost touching his toes. They closed with a snap.

He sat up woozily. He saw rows of serrated teeth in the line of breakers in front of him. And a tall, white shape in the moonlight dived into a curling breaker and was gone.

"Hello."

Piri sat up with a start. The worst thing about being a child living alone on an island—which, when he thought about it, was the sort of thing every child dreamed of—was not having a warm mother's breast to cry on when you had nightmares. It hadn't affected him much, but when it did, it was pretty bad.

He squinted up into the brightness. She was standing with her head blocking out the sun. He winced, and looked away, down to her feet. They were webbed, with long toes. He looked a little higher. She was nude, and quite beautiful.

"Who . . . ?"

"Are you awake now?" She squatted down beside him. Why had he expected sharp, triangular teeth? His dreams blurred and ran like watercolors in the rain, and he felt much better. She had a nice face. She was smiling at him.

He yawned, and sat up. He was groggy, stiff, and his eyes were coated with sand that didn't come from the beach. It had been an awful night.

"I think so."

"Good. How about some breakfast?" She stood, and went to a basket on the sand.

"I usually—" but his mouth watered when he saw the guavas, melons, kippered herring, and the long brown loaf of bread. She had butter, and some orange marmalade. "Well, maybe just a—" and he had bitten into a succulent slice of melon. But before he could finish it, he was seized by an even stronger urge. He got to his feet and scuttled around the palm tree with the waist-high dark stain and urinated against it.

"Don't tell anybody, huh?" he said, anxiously.

She looked up. "About the tree? Don't worry."

He sat back down and resumed eating the melon. "I could get in a lot of trouble. They gave me a thing and told me to use it."

"It's all right with me," she said, buttering a slice of bread and handing it to him. "Robinson Crusoe never had a portable EcoSan, right?"

"Right," he said, not showing his surprise. How did she know *that?*

Piri didn't know quite what to say. Here she was, sharing his morning, as much a fact of life as the beach or the water.

"What's your name?" It was as good a place to start as any.

"Leandra. You can call me Lee."

"I'm—"

"Piri. I heard about you from the people at the party last night. I hope you don't mind me barging in on you like this."

He shrugged, and tried to indicate all the food with the gesture. "Anytime," he said, and laughed. He felt good. It was nice to have someone friendly around after last night. He looked at her again, from a mellower viewpoint.

She was large; quite a bit taller than he was. Her physical age was around thirty, unusually old for a woman. He thought she might be closer to sixty or seventy, but he had nothing to base it on. Piri himself was in his nineties, and who could have known that? She had the slanting eyes that were caused by the addition of transparent cyclids beneath the natural ones. Her hair grew in a narrow band, cropped short, starting between her eyebrows and going over her head to the nape of her neck. Her ears were pinned efficiently against her head, giving her a lean, streamlined look.

"What brings you to Pacifica?" Piri asked.

She reclined on the sand with her hands behind her head, looking very relaxed.

"Claustrophobia." She winked at him. "Not really. I wouldn't survive long in Pluto with *that*." Piri wasn't even sure what it was, but he smiled as if he knew. "Tired of the crowds. I heard that people couldn't enjoy themselves here, what with the sky, but I didn't have any trouble when I visited. So I bought flippers and gills and decided to spend a few weeks skin-diving by myself."

Piri looked at the sky. It was a staggering sight. He'd grown used to it, but knew that it helped not to look up more than he had to.

It was an incomplete illusion, all the more appalling because the half of the sky that had been painted was so very convincing. It looked like it really was the sheer blue of infinity, so when the eye slid over to the unpainted overhanging canopy of rock, scarred from blasting, painted with gigantic numbers that were barely visible from twenty kilometers below—one could almost imagine God looking down through the blue opening. It loomed, suspended by nothing, gigatons of rock hanging up there.

Visitors to Pacifica often complained of headaches, usually right on the crown of the head. They were cringing, waiting to get conked.

"Sometimes I wonder how *I* live with it," Piri said.

She laughed. "It's nothing for me. I was a space pilot once."

"Really?" This was catnip to Piri. There's nothing more romantic than a space pilot. He had to hear stories.

The morning hours dwindled as she captured his imagination with a series of tall tales he was sure were mostly fabrication. But who cared? Had he come to the South Seas to hear of the mundane? He felt he had met a kindred spirit, and gradually, fearful of being laughed at, he began to tell her stories of the Reef Pirates, first as wishful wouldn't-it-be-fun-if's, then more and more seriously as she listened intently. He forgot her age as he began to spin the best of the yarns he and Harra had concocted.

It was a tacit conspiracy between them to be serious about the stories, but that was the whole point. That was the only way it would work, as it had worked with Harra. Somehow, this adult woman was interested in playing the same games he was.

Lying in his bed that night, Piri felt better than he had for months, since before Harra had become so distant. Now that he had a companion, he realized that maintaining a satisfying fantasy world by yourself is hard work. Eventually you need someone to tell the stories to, and to share in the making of them.

They spent the day out on the reef. He showed her his crab farm, and introduced her to Ocho the Octopus, who was his usual shy self. Piri suspected the damn thing only loved him for the treats he brought.

She entered into his games easily and with no trace of adult condescension. He wondered why, and got up the courage to ask her. He was afraid he'd ruin the whole thing, but he had to know. It just wasn't normal.

They were perched on a coral outcropping above the high tide level, catching the last rays of the sun.

"I'm not sure," she said. "I guess you think I'm silly, huh?"

"No, not exactly that. It's just that most adults seem to, well, have more 'important' things on their minds." He put all the contempt he could into the word.

"Maybe I feel the same way you do about it. I'm here to have fun. I sort of feel like I've been reborn into a new element. It's *terrific* down there, you know that. I just didn't feel like I wanted to go into that world alone. I was out there yesterday . . ."

"I thought I saw you."

"Maybe you did. Anyway, I needed a companion, and I heard about you. It seemed like the polite thing to, well, not to ask you to be my guide, but sort of fit myself into your world. As it were." She frowned, as if she felt she had said too much. "Let's not push it, all right?"

"Oh, sure. It's none of my business."

"I like you, Piri."

"And I like you. I haven't had a friend for . . . too long."

That night at the luau, Lee disappeared. Piri looked for her briefly, but was not really worried. What she did with her nights was her business. He wanted her during the days.

As he was leaving for his home, Harra came up behind him and took his hand. She walked with him for a moment, then could no longer hold it in.

"A word to the wise, old pal," she said. "You'd better stay away from her. She's not going to do you any good."

"What are you talking about? You don't even know her."

"Maybe I do."

"Well, do you or don't you?"

She didn't say anything, then sighed deeply.

"Piri, if you do the smart thing you'll get on that raft of yours and sail to Bikini. Haven't you had any . . . feelings about her? Any premonitions or anything?"

"I don't know what you're talking about," he said, thinking of sharp teeth and white death.

"I think you do. You have to, but you won't face it. That's all I'm saying. It's not my business to meddle in your affairs."

"I'll say it's not. So why did you come out here and put this stuff in my ear?" He stopped, and something tickled at his mind from his past life, some earlier bit of knowledge, carefully suppressed. He was used to it. He knew he was not really a child, and that he had a long life and many experiences stretching out behind him. But he didn't think about it. He hated it when part of his old self started to intrude on him.

"I think you're jealous of her," he said, and knew it was his old, cynical self talking. "She's an adult, Harra. She's no threat to you. And, hell, I know what you've been hinting at these last months. I'm not ready for it, so leave me alone. I'm just a kid."

Her chin came up, and the moonlight flashed in her eyes.

"You idiot. Have you looked at yourself lately? You're not Peter Pan, you know. You're growing up. You're damn near a man."

"That's not true." There was panic in Piri's voice. "I'm only . . . well, I haven't exactly been counting, but I can't be more than nine, ten years—"

"Shit. You're as old as I am, and I've had breasts for two years. But

I'm not out to cop you. I can cop with any of seven boys in the village younger than you are, but not you." She threw her hands up in exasperation and stepped back from him. Then, in a sudden fury, she hit him on the chest with the heel of her fist. He fell back, stunned at her violence.

"She *is* an adult," Harra whispered through her teeth. "That's what I came here to warn you against. *I'm* your friend, but you don't know it. Ah, what's the use? I'm fighting against that scared old man in your head, and he won't listen to me. Go ahead, go with her. But she's got some surprises for you."

"What? What surprises?" Piri was shaking, not wanting to listen to her. It was a relief when she spat at his feet, whirled, and ran down the beach.

"Find out for yourself," she yelled back over her shoulder. It sounded like she was crying.

That night, Piri dreamed of white teeth, inches behind him, snapping.

But morning brought Lee, and another fine breakfast in her bulging bag. After a lazy interlude drinking coconut milk, they went to the reef again. The pirates gave them a rough time of it, but they managed to come back alive in time for the nightly gathering.

Harra was there. She was dressed as he had never seen her, in the blue tunic and shorts of the reef maintenance crew. He knew she had taken a job with the disneyland and had been working days with her mother at Bikini, but had not seen her dressed up before. He had just begun to get used to the grass skirt. Not long ago, she had been always nude like him and the other children.

She looked older somehow, and bigger. Maybe it was just the uniform. She still looked like a girl next to Lee. Piri was confused by it, and his thoughts veered protectively away.

Harra did not avoid him, but she was remote in a more important way. It was like she had put on a mask, or possibly taken one off. She carried herself with a dignity that Piri thought was beyond her years.

Lee disappeared just before he was ready to leave. He walked home alone, half hoping Harra would show up so he could apologize for the way he'd talked to her the night before. But she didn't.

He felt the bow-shock of a pressure wave behind him, sensed by some mechanism he was unfamiliar with, like the lateral line of a fish, sensitive to slight changes in the water around him. He knew there was something behind him, closing the gap a little with every wild kick of his flippers.

It was dark. It was always dark when the thing chased him. It was not the wispy, insubstantial thing that darkness was when it settled on the night air, but the primal, eternal night of the depths. He tried to scream with his mouth full of water, but it was a dying gurgle before it passed his lips. The water around him was warm with his blood.

He turned to face it before it was upon him, and saw Harra's face corpse-pale and glowing sickly in the night. But no, it wasn't Harra, it was Lee, and her mouth was far down her body, rimmed with razors, a gaping crescent hole in her chest. He screamed again—

And sat up.

"What? Where are you?"

"I'm right here, it's going to be all right." She held his head as he brought his sobbing under control. She was whispering something but he couldn't understand it, and perhaps wasn't meant to. It was enough. He calmed down quickly, as he always did when he woke from nightmares. If they hung around to haunt him, he never would have stayed by himself for so long.

There was just the moonlit paleness of her breast before his eyes and the smell of skin and sea water. Her nipple was wet. Was it from his tears? No, his lips were tingling and the nipple was hard when it brushed against him. He realized what he had been doing in his sleep.

"You were calling for your mother," she whispered, as though she'd read his mind. "I've heard you shouldn't wake someone from a nightmare. It seemed to calm you down."

"Thanks," he said quietly. "Thanks for being here, I mean."

She took his cheek in her hand, turned his head slightly, and kissed him. It was not a motherly kiss, and he realized they were not playing the same game. She had changed the rules on him.

"Lee . . ."

"Hush. It's time you learned."

She eased him onto his back, and he was overpowered with *deja vu.* Her mouth worked downward on his body and it set off chains of associations from his past life. He was familiar with the sensation. It had happened to him often in his second childhood. Something would happen that had happened to him in much the same way before and he would remember a bit of it. He had been seduced by an older woman the first time he was young. She had taught him well, and he remembered it all but didn't want to remember. He was an experienced lover and a child at the same time.

"I'm not old enough," he protested, but she was holding in her hand the evidence that he was old enough, had been old enough for several years. *I'm fourteen years old,* he thought. How could he have kidded himself into thinking he was ten?

"You're a strong young man," she whispered in his ear. "And I'm going to be very disappointed if you keep saying that. You're not a child anymore, Piri. Face it."

"I . . . I guess I'm not."

"Do you know what to do?"

"I think so."

She reclined beside him, drew her legs up. Her body was huge and ghostly and full of limber strength. She would swallow him up, like a shark. The gill slits under her arms opened and shut quickly with her breathing, smelling of salt, iodine, and sweat.

He got on his hands and knees and moved over her.

He woke before she did. The sun was up: another warm, cloudless morning. There would be two thousand more before the first scheduled typhoon.

Piri was a giddy mixture of elation and sadness. It was sad, and he knew it already, that his days of frolicking on the reef were over. He would still go out there, but it would never be the same.

Fourteen years old! Where had the years gone? He was nearly an adult. He moved away from the thought until he found a more acceptable one. He was an adolescent, and a very fortunate one to have been initiated into the mysteries of sex by this strange woman.

He held her as she slept, spooned cozily back to front with his arms around her waist. She had already been playmate, mother, and lover to him. What else did she have in store?

But he didn't care. He was not worried about anything. He already scorned his yesterdays. He was not a boy, but a youth, and he remembered from his other youth what that meant and was excited by it. It was a time of sex, of internal exploration and the exploration of others. He would pursue these new frontiers with the same single-mindedness he had shown on the reef.

He moved against her, slowly, not disturbing her sleep. But she woke as he entered her and turned to give him a sleepy kiss.

They spent the morning involved in each other, until they were content to lie in the sun and soak up heat like glossy reptiles.

"I can hardly believe it," she said. "You've been here for . . . how long? With all these girls and women. And I know at least one of them was interested."

He didn't want to go into it. It was important to him that she not find out he was not really a child. He felt it would change things, and it was not fair. Not fair at all, because it *had* been the first time. In a way he could never have explained to her, last night had been not a rediscovery but an entirely new thing. He had been with many women and it wasn't as if he couldn't remember it. It was all there, and what's more, it showed up in his lovemaking. He had not been the bumbling teenager, had not needed to be told what to do.

But it was *new*. That old man inside had been a spectator and an invaluable coach, but his hardened viewpoint had not intruded to make last night just another bout. It had been a first time, and the first time is special.

When she persisted in her questions he silenced her in the only way he knew, with a kiss. He could see he had to rethink his relationship to her. She had not asked him questions as a playmate, or a mother. In the one role, she had been seemingly as self-centered as he, interested only in the needs of the moment and her personal needs above all. As a mother, she had offered only wordless comfort in a tight spot.

Now she was his lover. What did lovers do when they weren't making love?

They went for walks on the beach, and on the reef. They swam together, but it was different. They talked a lot.

She soon saw that he didn't want to talk about himself. Except for the odd question here and there that would momentarily confuse him, throw him back to stages of his life he didn't wish to remember, she left his past alone.

They stayed away from the village except to load up on supplies. It was mostly his unspoken wish that kept them away. He had made it clear to everyone in the village many years ago that he was not really a child. It had been necessary to convince them that he could take care of himself on his own, to keep them from being overprotective. They would not spill his secret knowingly, but neither would they lie for him.

So he grew increasingly nervous about his relationship with Lee, founded as it was on a lie. If not a lie, then at least a withholding of the facts. He saw that he must tell her soon, and dreaded it. Part of him was convinced that her attraction to him was based mostly on age difference.

Then she learned he had a raft, and wanted to go on a sailing trip to the edge of the world.

Piri did have a raft, though an old one. They dragged it from the bushes that had grown around it since his last trip and began putting it into shape. Piri was delighted. It was something to do, and it was hard work. They didn't have much time for talking.

It was a simple construction of logs lashed together with rope. Only an insane sailor would put the thing to sea in the Pacific Ocean, but it was safe enough for them. They knew what the weather would be, and the reports were absolutely reliable. And if it came apart, they could swim back.

All the ropes had rotted so badly that even gentle wave action would have quickly pulled it apart. They had to be replaced, a new mast erected, and a new sailcloth installed. Neither of them knew anything about sailing, but Piri knew that the winds blew toward the edge at night and away from it during the day. It was a simple matter of putting up the sail and letting the wind do the navigating.

He checked the schedule to be sure they got there at low tide. It was a moonless night, and he chuckled to himself when he thought of her reaction to the edge of the world. They would sneak up on it in the dark, and the impact would be all the more powerful at sunrise.

But he knew as soon as they were an hour out of Rarotonga that he had made a mistake. There was not much to do there in the night but talk.

"Piri, I've sensed that you don't want to talk about certain things."

"Who? Me?"

She laughed into the empty night. He could barely see her face. The stars were shining brightly, but there were only about a hundred of them installed so far, and all in one part of the sky.

"Yeah, you. You won't talk about yourself. It's like you grew here, sprang up from the ground like a palm tree. And you've got no mother in evidence. You're old enough to have divorced her, but you'd have a guardian somewhere. Someone would be looking after your moral upbringing. The only conclusion is that you don't need an education in moral principles. So you've got a co-pilot."

"Um." She had seen through him. Of course she would have. Why hadn't he realized it?

"So you're a clone. You've had your memories transplanted into a new body, grown from one of your own cells. How old are you? Do you mind my asking?"

"I guess not. Uh . . . what's the date?"

She told him.

"And the year?"

She laughed, but told him that, too.

"Damn. I missed my one-hundredth birthday. Well, so what? It's not important. Lee, does this change anything?"

"Of course not. Listen, I could tell the first time, that first night together. You had that puppy-dog eagerness, all right, but you knew how to handle yourself. Tell me: what's it like?"

"The second childhood, you mean?" He reclined on the gently rocking raft and looked at the little clot of stars. "It's pretty damn great. It's like living in a dream. What kid hasn't wanted to live alone on a tropic isle? I can, because there's an adult in me who'll keep me out of trouble. But for the last seven years I've been a kid. It's you that finally made me grow up a little, maybe sort of late, at that."

"I'm sorry. But it felt like the right time."

"It was. I was afraid of it at first. Listen, I *know* that I'm really a hundred years old, see? I know that all the memories are ready for me when I get to adulthood again. If I think about it, I can remember it all as plain as anything. But I haven't wanted to, and in a way, I still don't want to. The memories are suppressed when you opt for a second childhood instead of being transplanted into another full-grown body."

"I know."

"Do you? Oh, yeah. Intellectually. So did I, but I didn't understand what it meant. It's a nine- or ten-year holiday, not only from your work, but from yourself. When you get into your nineties, you might find that you need it."

She was quiet for a while, lying beside him without touching.

"What about the reintegration? Is that started?"

"I don't know. I've heard it's a little rough. I've been having dreams about something chasing me. That's probably my former self, right?"

"Could be. What did your older self do?"

He had to think for a moment, but there it was. He'd not thought of it for eight years.

"I was an economic strategist."

Before he knew it, he found himself launching into an explanation of offensive economic policy.

"Did you know that Pluto is in danger of being gutted by currency transfers from the Inner Planets? And you know why? The speed of light, that's why. Time lag. It's killing us. Since the time of the Invasion of Earth it's been humanity's idea—and a good one, I think—that we should stand together. Our whole cultural thrust in that time has been toward a total economic community. But it won't work at Pluto. Independence is in the cards."

She listened as he tried to explain things that only moments before he would have had trouble understanding himself. But it poured out of him like a breached dam, things like inflation multipliers, futures buying on the oxygen and hydrogen exchanges, phantom dollars and their manipulation by central banking interests, and the invisible drain.

"Invisible drain? What's that?"

"It's hard to explain, but it's tied up in the speed of light. It's an economic drain on Pluto that has nothing to do with real goods and services, or labor, or any of the other traditional forces. It has to do with the fact that any information we get from the Inner Planets is already at least nine hours old. In an economy with a stable currency—pegged to gold, for instance, like the classical economies on Earth—it wouldn't matter much, but it would still have an effect. Nine hours can make a difference in prices, in futures, in outlook on the markets. With a floating exchange medium, one where you need the hourly updates on your credit meter to know what your labor input will give you in terms of material output— your personal financial equation, in other words—and the inflation multiplier is something you simply *must* have if the equation is going to balance and you're not going to be wiped out, then time is really of the essence. We operate at a perpetual disadvantage on Pluto in relation to the Inner Planet money markets. For a long time it ran on the order of point three percent leakage due to outdated information. But the inflation multiplier has been accelerating over the years. Some of it's been absorbed by the fact that we've been moving closer to the I.P.; the time lag has been getting shorter as we move into summer. But it can't last. We'll reach the inner point of our orbit and the effects will really start to accelerate. Then it's war."

"War?" She seemed horrified, as well she might be.

"War, in the economic sense. It's a hostile act to renounce a trade agreement, even if it's bleeding you white. It hits every citizen of the Inner Planets in the pocketbook, and we can expect retaliation. We'd be introducing instability by pulling out of the Common Market."

"How bad will it be? Shooting?"

"Not likely. But devastating enough. A depression's no fun. And they'll be planning one for us."

"Isn't there any other course?"

"Someone suggested moving our entire government and all our corporate headquarters to the Inner Planets. It could happen, I guess. But who'd feel like it was ours? We'd be a colony, and that's a worse answer than independence, in the long run."

She was silent for a time, chewing it over. She nodded her head once; he could barely see the movement in the darkness.

"How long until the war?"

He shrugged. "I've been out of touch. I don't know how things have been going. But we can probably take it for another ten years or so. Then we'll have to get out. I'd stock up on real wealth if I were you. Canned goods, air, water, so forth. I don't think it'll get so bad that you'll need those things to stay alive by consuming them. But we may get to a semi-barter situation where they'll be the only valuable things. Your credit meter'll laugh at you when you punch a purchase order, no matter how much work you've put into it."

The raft bumped. They had arrived at the edge of the world.

They moored the raft to one of the rocks on the wall that rose from the open ocean. They were five kilometers out of Rarotonga. They waited for some light as the sun began to rise, then started up the rock face.

It was rough: blasted out with explosives on this face of the dam. It went up at a thirty-degree angle for fifty meters, then was suddenly level and smooth as glass. The top of the dam at the edge of the world had been smoothed by cutting lasers into a vast table top, three hundred kilometers long and four kilometers wide. They left wet footprints on it as they began the long walk to the edge.

They soon lost any meaningful perspective on the thing. They lost sight of the sea-edge, and couldn't see the dropoff until they began to near it. By then, it was full light. Timed just right, they would reach the edge when the sun came up and they'd really have something to see.

A hundred meters from the edge when she could see over it a little, Lee began to unconsciously hang back. Piri didn't prod her. It was not something he could force someone to see. He'd reached this point with others, and had to turn back. Already, the fear of falling was building up. But she came on, to stand beside him at the very lip of the canyon.

Pacifica was being built and filled in three sections. Two were complete, but the third was still being hollowed out and was not yet filled with water except in the deepest trenches. The water was kept out of this section by the dam they were standing on. When it was completed, when all the underwater trenches and mountain ranges and guyots and slopes had been built to specifications, the bottom would be covered with sludge and ooze and the whole wedge-shaped section flooded. The water came from liquid hydrogen and oxygen on the surface, combined with the limitless electricity of fusion powerplants.

"We're doing what the Dutch did on Old Earth, but in reverse," Piri pointed out, but he got no reaction from Lee. She was staring, spellbound, down the sheer face of the dam to the apparently bottomless trench below. It was shrouded in mist, but seemed to fall off forever.

"It's eight kilometers deep," Piri told her. "It's not going to be a regular trench when it's finished. It's there to be filled up with the remains of this dam after the place has been flooded." He looked at her face, and didn't bother with more statistics. He let her experience it in her own way.

The only comparable vista on a human-inhabited planet was the Great Rift Valley on Mars. Neither of them had seen it, but it suffered in comparison to this because not all of it could be seen at once. Here, one could see from one side to the other, and from sea level to a distance equivalent to the deepest oceanic trenches on Earth. It simply fell away beneath them and went straight down to nothing. There was a rainbow beneath their feet. Off to the left was a huge waterfall that arced away from the wall in a solid stream. Tons of overflow water went through the wall, to twist, fragment, vaporize and blow away long before it reached the bottom of the trench.

Straight ahead of them and about ten kilometers away was the mountain that would become the Okinawa biome when the pit was filled. Only the tiny, blackened tip of the mountain would show above the water.

Lee stayed and looked at it as long as she could. It became easier the longer one stood there, and yet something about it drove her away. The scale was too big, there was no room for humans in that shattered world. Long before noon, they turned and started the long walk back to the raft.

She was silent as they boarded, and set sail for the return trip. The winds were blowing fitfully, barely billowing the sail. It would be another hour before they blew very strongly. They were still in sight of the dam wall.

They sat on the raft, not looking at each other.

"Piri, thanks for bringing me here."

"You're welcome. You don't have to talk about it."

"All right. But there's something else I have to talk about. I . . . I don't know where to begin, really."

Piri stirred uneasily. The earlier discussion about economics had disturbed him. It was part of his past life, a part that he had not been ready to return to. He was full of confusion. Thoughts that had no place out here in the concrete world of wind and water were roiling through his brain. Someone was calling to him, someone he knew but didn't want to see right then.

"Yeah? What is it you want to talk about?"

"It's about—" she stopped, seemed to think it over. "Never mind. It's not time yet." She moved close and touched him. But he was not interested. He made it known in a few minutes, and she moved to the other side of the raft.

He lay back, essentially alone with his troubled thoughts. The wind gusted, then settled down. He saw a flying fish leap, almost passing over the raft. There was a piece of the sky falling through the air. It twisted and turned like a feather, a tiny speck of sky that was blue on one side and brown on the other. He could see the hole in the sky where it had been knocked loose.

It must be two or three kilometers away. No, wait, that wasn't right.

The top of the sky was twenty kilometers up, and it looked like it was falling from the center. How far away were they from the center of Pacifica? A hundred kilometers?

A piece of the sky?

He got to his feet, nearly capsizing the raft.

"What's the matter?"

It was *big*. It looked large even from this far away. It was the dreamy tumbling motion that had deceived him.

"The sky is . . ." he choked on it, and almost laughed. But this was no time to feel silly about it. "The sky is falling, Lee." How long? He watched it, his mind full of numbers. Terminal velocity from that high up, assuming it was heavy enough to punch right through the atmosphere . . . over six hundred meters per second. Time to fall, seventy seconds. Thirty of those must already have gone by.

Lee was shading her eyes as she followed his gaze. She still thought it was a joke. The chunk of sky began to glow red as the atmosphere got thicker.

"Hey, it really is falling," she said. "Look at that."

"It's big. Maybe one or two kilometers across. It's going to make quite a splash, I'll bet."

They watched it descend. Soon it disappeared over the horizon, picking up speed. They waited, but the show seemed to be over. Why was he still uneasy?

"How many tons in a two-kilometer chunk of rock, I wonder?" Lee mused. She didn't look too happy, either. But they sat back down on the raft, still looking in the direction where the thing had sunk into the sea.

Then they were surrounded by flying fish, and the water looked crazy. The fish were panicked. As soon as they hit they leaped from the water again. Piri felt rather than saw something pass beneath them. And then, very gradually, a roar built up, a deep bass rumble that soon threatened to turn his bones to powder. It picked him up and shook him, and left him limp on his knees. He was stunned, unable to think clearly. His eyes were still fixed on the horizon, and he saw a white fan rising in the distance in silent majesty. It was the spray from the impact, and it was still going up.

"Look up there," Lee said, when she got her voice back. She seemed as confused as he. He looked where she pointed and saw a twisted line crawling across the blue sky. At first he thought it was the end of his life, because it appeared that the whole overhanging dome was fractured and about to fall in on them. But then he saw it was one of the tracks that the sun ran on, pulled free by the rock that had fallen, twisted into a snake of tortured metal.

"The dam!" he yelled. "The dam! We're too close to the dam!"

"What?"

"The bottom rises this close to the dam. The water here isn't that deep. There'll be a wave coming, Lee, a big wave. It'll pile up here."

"Piri, the shadows are moving."

"Huh?"

Surprise was piling on surprise too fast for him to cope with it. But she was right. The shadows were moving. But *why?*

Then he saw it. The sun was setting, but not by following the tracks that led to the concealed opening in the west. It was falling through the air, having been shaken loose by the rock.

Lee had figured it out, too.

"What is that thing?" she asked. "I mean, how big is it?"

"Not too big, I heard. Big enough, but not nearly the size of that chunk that fell. It's some kind of fusion generator. I don't know what'll happen when it hits the water."

They were paralyzed. They knew there was something they should do, but too many things were happening. There was not time to think it out.

"Dive!" Lee yelled. "Dive into the water!"

"What?"

"We have to dive and swim away from the dam, and down as far as we can go. The wave will pass over us, won't it?"

"I don't know."

"It's all we can do."

So they dived. Piri felt his gills come into action, then he was swimming down at an angle toward the dark-shrouded bottom. Lee was off to his left, swimming as hard as she could. And with no sunset, no warning, it got black as pitch. The sun had hit the water.

He had no idea how long he had been swimming when he suddenly felt himself pulled upward. Floating in the water, weightless, he was not well equipped to feel accelerations. But he did feel it, like a rapidly rising elevator. It was accompanied by pressure waves that threatened to burst his eardrums. He kicked and clawed his way downward, not even knowing if he was headed in the right direction. Then he was falling again.

He kept swimming, all alone in the dark. Another wave passed, lifted him, let him down again. A few minutes later, another one, seeming to come from the other direction. He was hopelessly confused. He suddenly felt he was swimming the wrong way. He stopped, not knowing what to do. Was he pointed in the right direction? He had no way to tell.

He stopped paddling and tried to orient himself. It was useless. He felt surges, and was sure he was being tumbled and buffeted.

Then his skin was tingling with the sensation of a million bubbles crawling over him. It gave him a handle on the situation. The bubbles would be going up, wouldn't they? And they were traveling over his body from belly to back. So down was that way.

But he didn't have time to make use of the information. He hit something hard with his hip, wrenched his back as his body tried to tumble over in the foam and water, then was sliding along a smooth surface. It felt like he was going very fast, and he knew where he was and where he was heading and there was nothing he could do about it. The tail of the wave had lifted him clear of the rocky slope of the dam and deposited him on the flat surface. It was now spending itself, sweeping him along to the edge of the world. He turned around, feeling the sliding surface beneath him with his hands, and tried to dig in. It was a nightmare; nothing he did had any effect. Then his head broke free into the air.

He was still sliding, but the huge hump of the wave had dissipated itself and was collapsing quietly into froth and puddles. It drained away with amazing speed. He was left there, alone, cheek pressed lovingly to the cold rock. The darkness was total.

He wasn't about to move. For all he knew, there was an eight-kilometer drop just behind his toes.

Maybe there would be another wave. If so, this one would crash down on him instead of lifting him like a cork in a tempest. It should kill him instantly. He refused to worry about that. All he cared about now was not slipping any further.

The stars had vanished. Power failure? Now they blinked on. He raised his head a little, in time to see a soft, diffused glow in the east. The moon was rising, and it was doing it at breakneck speed. He saw it rotate from a thin crescent configuration to bright fullness in under a minute. Someone was still in charge, and had decided to throw some light on the scene.

He stood, though his knees were weak. Tall fountains of spray far away to his right indicated where the sea was battering at the dam. He was about in the middle of the tabletop, far from either edge. The ocean was whipped up as if by thirty hurricanes, but he was safe from it at this distance unless there were another tsunami yet to come.

The moonlight turned the surface into a silver mirror, littered with flopping fish. He saw another figure get to her feet, and ran in that direction.

The helicopter located them by infrared detector. They had no way of telling how long it had been. The moon was hanging motionless in the center of the sky.

They got into the cabin, shivering.

The helicopter pilot was happy to have found them, but grieved over other lives lost. She said the toll stood at three dead, fifteen missing and presumed dead. Most of these had been working on the reefs. All the land surface of Pacifica had been scoured, but the loss of life had been minimal. Most had had time to get to an elevator and go below or to a helicopter and rise above the devastation.

From what they had been able to find out, heat expansion of the crust had moved farther down into the interior of the planet than had been expected. It was summer on the surface, something it was easy to forget down here. The engineers had been sure that the inner surface of the sky had been stabilized years ago, but a new fault had been opened by the slight temperature rise. She pointed up to where ships were hovering like fireflies next to the sky, playing searchlights on the site of the damage. No one knew yet if Pacifica would have to be abandoned for another twenty years while it stabilized.

She set them down on Rarotonga. The place was a mess. The wave had climbed the bottom rise and crested at the reef, and a churning hell of foam and debris had swept over the island. Little was left standing except the concrete blocks that housed the elevators, scoured of their decorative camouflage.

Piri saw a familiar figure coming toward him through the wreckage that had been a picturesque village. She broke into a run, and nearly bowled him over, laughing and kissing him.

"We were sure you were dead," Harra said, drawing back from him as if to check for cuts and bruises.

"It was a fluke, I guess," he said, still incredulous that he had survived. It had seemed bad enough out there in the open ocean; the extent of the disaster was much more evident on the island. He was badly shaken to see it.

"Lee suggested that we try to dive under the wave. That's what saved us. It just lifted us up, then the last one swept us over the top of the dam and drained away. It dropped us like leaves."

"Well, not quite so tenderly in my case," Lee pointed out. "It gave me quite a jolt. I think I might have sprained my wrist."

A medic was available. While her wrist was being bandaged, she kept looking at Piri. He didn't like the look.

"There's something I'd intended to talk to you about on the raft, or soon after we got home. There's no point in your staying here any longer anyway, and I don't know where you'd go."

"No!" Harra burst out. "Not yet. Don't tell him anything yet. It's not fair. Stay away from him." She was protecting Piri with her body, from no assault that was apparent to him.

"I just wanted to—"

"No, no. Don't listen to her, Piri. Come with me." She pleaded with the other woman. "Just give me a few hours alone with him; there's some things I never got around to telling him."

Lee looked undecided, and Piri felt mounting rage and frustration. He had known things were going on around him. It was mostly his own fault that he had ignored them, but now he had to know. He pulled his hand free from Harra and faced Lee.

"Tell me."

She looked down at her feet, then back to his eyes.

"I'm not what I seem, Piri. I've been leading you along, trying to make this easier for you. But you still fight me. I don't think there's any way it's going to be easy."

"No!" Harra shouted again.

"What are you?"

"I'm a psychiatrist. I specialize in retrieving people like you, people who are in a mental vacation mode, what you call 'second childhood.' You're aware of all this, on another level, but the child in you has fought it at every stage. The result has been nightmares—probably with me as the focus, whether you admitted it or not."

She grasped both his wrists, one of them awkwardly because of her injury.

"Now listen to me." She spoke in an intense whisper, trying to get it all out before the panic she saw in his face broke free and sent him running. "You came here for a vacation. You were going to stay ten years, growing up and taking it easy. That's all over. The situation that prevailed when you left is now out of date. Things have moved faster than you believed possible. You had expected a ten-year period after your return to get things in order for the coming battles. That time has evaporated. The Common Market of the Inner Planets has fired the first shot. They've instituted a new system of accounting and it's locked into their computers and running. It's aimed right at Pluto, and it's been working for a month now. We cannot continue as an economic partner to the C.M.I.P., because from now on every time we sell or buy or move money the inflationary multiplier is automatically juggled against us. It's all perfectly legal by all existing treaties, and it's necessary to their economy. But it ignores our time-lag disadvantage. We have to consider it as a hostile act, no matter what the intent. You have to come back and direct the war, Mister Finance Minister."

The words shattered what calm Piri had left. He wrenched free of her hands and turned wildly to look all around him. Then he sprinted down the beach. He tripped once over his splay feet, got up without ever slowing, and disappeared.

Harra and Lee stood silently and watched him go.

"You didn't have to be so rough with him," Harra said, but knew it wasn't so. She just hated to see him so confused.

"It's best done quickly when they resist. And he's all right. He'll have a fight with himself, but there's no real doubt of the outcome."

"So the Piri I know will be dead soon?"

Lee put her arm around the younger woman.

"Not at all. It's a reintegration, without a winner or a loser. You'll see." She looked at the tear-streaked face.

"Don't worry. You'll like the older Piri. It won't take him any time at all to realize that he loves you."

He had never been to the reef at night. It was a place of furtive fish, always one step ahead of him as they darted back into their places of concealment. He wondered how long it would be before they ventured out in the long night to come. The sun might not rise for years.

They might never come out. Not realizing the changes in their environment, night fish and day fish would never adjust. Feeding cycles would be disrupted, critical temperatures would go awry, the endless moon and lack of sun would frustrate the internal mechanisms, bred over billions of years, and fish would die. It had to happen.

The ecologists would have quite a job on their hands.

But there was one denizen of the outer reef that would survive for a long time. He would eat anything that moved and quite a few things that didn't, at any time of the day or night. He had no fear, he had no internal clocks dictating to him, no inner pressures to confuse him except the one overriding urge to attack. He would last as long as there was anything alive to eat.

But in what passed for a brain in the white-bottomed torpedo that was the Ghost, a splinter of doubt had lodged. He had no recollection of similar doubts, though there had been some. He was not equipped to remember, only to hunt. So this new thing that swam beside him, and drove his cold brain as near as it could come to the emotion of anger, was a mystery. He tried again and again to attack it, then something would seize him with an emotion he had not felt since he was half a meter long, and fear would drive him away.

Piri swam along beside the faint outline of the shark. There was just enough moonlight for him to see the fish, hovering at the ill-defined limit of his sonic signal. Occasionally, the shape would shudder from head to tail, turn toward him, and grow larger. At these times Piri could see nothing but a gaping jaw. Then it would turn quickly, transfix him with that bottomless pit of an eye, and sweep away.

Piri wished he could laugh at the poor, stupid brute. How could he have feared such a mindless eating machine?

Good-bye, pinbrain. He turned and stroked lazily toward the shore. He knew the shark would turn and follow him, nosing into the interdicted sphere of his transponder, but the thought did not impress him. He was without fear. How could he be afraid, when he had already been swallowed into the belly of his nightmare? The teeth had closed around him, he had awakened, and remembered. And that was the end of his fear.

Good-bye, tropical paradise. You were fun while you lasted. Now I'm a grownup, and must go off to war.

He didn't relish it. It was a wrench to leave his childhood, though the time had surely been right. Now the responsibilities had descended on him, and he must shoulder them. He thought of Harra.

"Piri," he told himself, "as a teenager, you were just too dumb to live."

Knowing it was the last time, he felt the coolness of the water flowing over his gills. They had served him well, but had no place in his work. There was no place for a fish, and no place for Robinson Crusoe.

Good-bye, gills.

He kicked harder for the shore and came to stand, dripping wet, on the beach. Harra and Lee were there, waiting for him.

George R.R. Martin

THE WAY OF CROSS AND DRAGON

Born in Bayonne, New Jersey, George R.R. Martin made his first sale in 1971, and soon established himself as one of the most popular SF writers of the seventies. He quickly became a mainstay of the Ben Bova *Analog* with stories such as "With Morning Comes Mistfall," "And Seven Times Never Kill Man," "The Second Kind of Loneliness," "The Storms of Windhaven" (in collaboration with Lisa Tuttle, and later expanded by them into the novel *Windhaven*), "Override," and others, although he also sold to *Amazing, Fantastic, Galaxy, Orbit,* and other markets. One of his *Analog* stories, the striking novella "A Song for Lya," won him his first Hugo Award in 1974.

By the end of the seventies, he had reached the height of his influence as a science fiction writer, and was producing his best work in that category with stories such as the famous "Sandkings," his best-known story, which won both the Nebula and the Hugo in 1980, "The Way of Cross and Dragon," which won a Hugo Award in the same year (making Martin the first author ever to receive two Hugo Awards for fiction in the same year), "Bitterblooms," "The Stone City," "Starlady," and others. These stories would be collected in *Sandkings,* one of the strongest collections of the period. By now he had mostly moved away from *Analog,* although he would have a long sequence of stories about the droll interstellar adventures of Haviland Tuf (later collected in *Tuf Voyaging*) running throughout the eighties in the Stanley Schmidt *Analog,* as well as a few strong individual pieces such as the novella "Nightflyers"—most of his major work of the late seventies and early eighties, though, would appear in *Omni.* The late seventies also saw the publication of his memorable novel *Dying of the Light,* his only solo SF novel.

By the early middle years of the eighties, though, Martin's career was turning in other directions, directions that would take him far from the kind of career path that might have been forecast for him in the seventies. Horror was starting to burgeon then as a separate publishing category, in the early and middle eighties, and that was the direction in which Martin moved at first, with what was until recently probably his best-known novel, 1982's *Fevre Dream,* an intelligent and suspenseful horror novel set in a vividly realized historical milieu, still one of the best of modern vampire novels. His next horror novel, though, the big, ambitious *Armageddon Rag,* a rock 'n' roll horror apocalypse, was a severe commercial disappointment, and would pretty much bring Martin's career as a horror writer to an end, although he'd later win the Bram Stoker Award for his horror story "The Pear-Shaped Man" and the World Fantasy Award for his werewolf novella "The Skin Trade." Increasingly, though, he'd turn away from the print world altogether, and move into the world of television instead, becoming a story editor on the new *Twilight Zone* series in the mid eighties, and later becoming a producer on the fantasy series *Beauty and the Beast.*

Highly successful as a writer/story editor/producer in the television world, Martin had little contact with the print world throughout the mid-eighties (although he did win another Nebula in 1985 for his story "Portraits of His Children") and throughout most of the decade of the nineties, except as editor of the long-running *Wild Cards* shared-world anthologies, which reached nine volumes before the series faltered in the late nineties. By then, soured on the television business by the failure of his still-born series *Doorways* to make it onto the air, Martin returned to the print world with the publication in 1996 of the immensely popular and successful fantasy novel *A Game of Thrones,* one of 1996's best-selling genre titles. A free-standing novella taken from that work, "Blood of the Dragon," won Martin another Hugo Award in 1997, the novel is on this year's Nebula final ballot as I type these words, and two further books in the *Thrones* series are planned. It's clear that Martin has returned to the print world with a bang, and I hope he stays here this time (in fact, what I'd like to see him write next is a new *science fiction* novel).

Martin has always been a richly romantic writer, clearly a direct descendant of the old *Planet Stories* tradition, probably influenced by Leigh Brackett in particular, although you can see strong traces of writers such as Jack Vance and Roger Zelazny in his work as well. In spite of long being a mainstay of *Analog,* science and technology play little real part in his work, where the emphasis is on color, adventure, exoticism, and lush romance, in a universe crowded and jostling both with alien races and human societies that have evolved toward strangeness in isolation, and where the drama is often generated by the inability of one of these cultures to understand clearly the psychology and values and motivations of another. As is evident in the story that follows, a powerful and exotic study of the future of religion, and of a very special kind of heresy.

George R.R. Martin's other books include the collections *A Song for Lya, Songs of Stars and Shadows, Songs the Dead Men Sing, Nightflyers,* and *Portraits of His Children.* In addition to the *Wild Cards* series, he's also the editor of the five-volume *New Voices* series, and of *The Science Fiction Weight-Loss Book,* edited with Isaac Asimov and Martin H. Greenberg. He lives in Santa Fe, New Mexico.

"Heresy," he told me. The brackish waters of his pool sloshed gently. "Another one?" I said wearily. "There are so many these days."

My Lord Commander was displeased by that comment. He shifted position heavily, sending ripples up and down the pool. One broke over the side, and a sheet of water slid across the tiles of the receiving chamber. My boots were soaked yet again. I accepted that philosophically. I had worn my worst boots, well aware that wet feet are among the inescapable consequences of paying call on Torgathon Nine-Klariis Tûn, elder of the ka-Thane people, and also Archbishop of Vess, Most Holy Father of the Four Vows, Grand Inquisitor of the Order Militant of the

Knights of Jesus Christ, and councillor to His Holiness, Pope Daryn XXI of New Rome.

"Be there as many heresies as stars in the sky, each single one is no less dangerous, Father," the Archbishop said solemnly. "As Knights of Christ, it is our ordained task to fight them one and all. And I must add that this new heresy is particularly foul."

"Yes, my Lord Commander," I replied. "I did not intend to make light of it. You have my apologies. The mission to Finnegan was most taxing. I had hoped to ask you for a leave of absence from my duties. I need rest, a time for thought and restoration."

"Rest?" The Archbishop moved again in his pool; only a slight shift of his immense bulk, but it was enough to send a fresh sheet of water across the floor. His black, pupilless eyes blinked at me. "No, Father, I am afraid that is out of the question. Your skills and your experience are vital to this new mission." His bass tones seemed then to soften somewhat. "I have not had time to go over your reports on Finnegan," he said. "How did your work go?"

"Badly," I told him, "though I think that ultimately we will prevail. The Church is strong on Finnegan. When our attempts at reconciliation were rebuffed, I put some standards into the right hands, and we were able to shut down the heretics' newspaper and broadcast facilities. Our friends also saw to it that their legal actions came to nothing."

"That is not *badly,*" the Archbishop said. "You won a considerable victory for the Lord."

"There were riots, my Lord Commander," I said. "More than a hundred of the heretics were killed, and a dozen of our own people. I fear there will be more violence before the matter is finished. Our priests are attacked if they so much as enter the city where the heresy has taken root. Their leaders risk their lives if they leave that city. I had hoped to avoid such hatreds, such bloodshed."

"Commendable, but not realistic," said Archbishop Torgathon. He blinked at me again, and I remembered that among people of his race, that was a sign of impatience. "The blood of martyrs must sometimes be spilled, and the blood of heretics as well. What matters it if a being surrenders his life, so long as his soul is saved?"

"Indeed," I agreed. Despite his impatience, Torgathon would lecture me for another hour if given a chance. That prospect dismayed me. The receiving chamber was not designed for human comfort, and I did not wish to remain any longer than necessary. The walls were damp and moldy, the air hot and humid and thick with the rancid-butter smell characteristic of the ka-Thane. My collar was chafing my neck raw, I was sweating beneath my cassock, my feet were thoroughly soaked, and my stomach was beginning to churn. I pushed ahead to the business at hand. "You say this new heresy is unusually foul, my Lord Commander?"

"It is," he said.

"Where has it started?"

"On Arion, a world some three weeks distance from Vess. A human world entirely. I cannot understand why you humans are so easily corrupted. Once a ka-Thane has found the faith, he would scarcely abandon it."

"That is well known," I said politely. I did not mention that the number of ka-Thane to find the faith was vanishingly small. They were a slow, ponderous people, and most of their vast millions showed no interest in learning any ways other than their own, nor in following any creed but their own ancient religion. Torgathon Nine-Klariis Tûn was an anomaly. He had been among the first converts almost two centuries ago, when Pope Vidas L had ruled that non-humans might serve as clergy. Given his great lifespan and the iron certainty of his belief, it was no wonder that Torgathon had risen as far as he had, despite the fact that less than a thousand of his race had followed him into the Church. He had at least a century of life remaining to him. No doubt he would someday be Torgathon Cardinal Tûn, should he squelch enough heresies. The times are like that.

"We have little influence on Arion," the Archbishop was saying. His arms moved as he spoke, four ponderous clubs of mottled green-gray flesh churning the water, and the dirty white cilia around his breathing hole trembled with each word. "A few priests, a few churches, and some believers, but no power to speak of. The heretics already outnumber us on this world. I rely on your intellect, your shrewdness. Turn this calamity into an opportunity. This heresy is so spurious that you can easily disprove it. Perhaps some of the deluded will turn to the true way."

"Certainly," I said. "And the nature of this heresy? What must I disprove?" It is a sad indication of my own troubled faith to add that I did not really care. I have dealt with too many heresies. Their beliefs and their questionings echo in my head and trouble my dreams at night. How can I be sure of my own faith? The very edict that had admitted Torgathon into the clergy had caused a half-dozen worlds to repudiate the Bishop of New Rome, and those who had followed that path would find a particularly ugly heresy in the massive naked (save for a damp Roman collar) alien who floated before me, who wielded the authority of the Church in four great webbed hands. Christianity is the greatest single human religion, but that means little. The non-Christian outnumber us five-to-one, and there are well over seven hundred Christian sects, some almost as large as the One True Interstellar Catholic Church of Earth and the Thousand Worlds. Even Daryn XXI, powerful as he is, is only one of seven to claim the title of Pope. My own belief was once strong, but I have moved too long among heretics and non-believers. Now even my prayers do not make the doubts go away. So it was that I felt no horror—only a sudden intellectual interest—when the Archbishop told me the nature of the heresy on Arion.

"They have made a saint," he said, "out of Judas Iscariot."

As a senior in the Knights Inquisitor, I command my own starship, which it pleases me to call the *Truth of Christ.* Before the craft was assigned to me, it was named the *Saint Thomas,* after the apostle, but I did not consider a saint notorious for doubting to be an appropriate patron for a ship enlisted in the fight against heresy.

I have no duties aboard the *Truth,* which is crewed by six brothers and sisters of the Order of Saint Christopher the Far-Travelling, and captained by a young woman I hired away from a merchant trader. I was therefore able to devote the entire three-week voyage from Vess to Arion to a study of the heretical Bible, a copy of which had been given to me by the Archbishop's administrative assistant. It was a thick, heavy, handsome book, bound in dark leather, its pages tipped with gold leaf, with many splendid interior illustrations in full color with holographic enhancement. Remarkable work, clearly done by someone who loved the all-but-forgotten art of bookmaking. The paintings reproduced inside—the originals, I gathered, were to be found on the walls of the House of Saint Judas on Arion—were masterful, if blasphemous, as much high art as the Tammerwens and RoHallidays that adorn the Great Cathedral of Saint John on New Rome.

Inside, the book bore an imprimatur indicating that it had been approved by Lukyan Judasson, First Scholar of the Order of Saint Judas Iscariot.

It was called *The Way of Cross and Dragon.*

I read it as the *Truth of Christ* slid between the stars, at first taking copious notes to better understand the heresy I must fight, but later simply absorbed by the strange, convoluted, grotesque story it told. The words of text had passion and power and poetry.

Thus it was that I first encountered the striking figure of Saint Judas Iscariot, a complex, ambitious, contradictory, and altogether extraordinary human being.

He was born of a whore in the fabled ancient city-state of Babylon on the same day that the savior was born in Bethlehem, and he spent his childhood in the alleys and gutters, selling his own body when he had to, pimping when he was older. As a youth he began to experiment with the dark arts, and before the age of twenty he was a skilled necromancer.

That was when he became Judas the Dragon-Tamer, the first and only man to bend to his will the most fearsome of God's creatures, the great winged fire-lizards of Old Earth. The book held a marvelous painting of Judas in some great dank cavern, his eyes aflame as he wields a glowing lash to keep a mountainous green-gold dragon at bay. Beneath his arm is a woven basket, its lid slightly ajar, and the tiny scaled heads of three dragon chicks are peering from within. A fourth infant dragon is crawling up his sleeve. That was in the first chapter of his life.

In the second, he was Judas the Conqueror, Judas the Dragon-King, Judas of Babylon, the Great Usurper. Astride the greatest of his dragons, with an iron crown on his head and a sword in his hand, he made Babylon the capital of the greatest empire Old Earth had ever known, a realm that stretched from Spain to India. He reigned from a dragon throne amid the Hanging Gardens he had caused to be constructed, and it was there he sat when he tried Jesus of Nazareth, the troublemaking prophet who had been dragged before him bound and bleeding. Judas was not a patient man, and he made Christ bleed still more before he was through was Him. And when Jesus would not answer his questions, Judas contemptuously had Him cast back out into the streets. But first, he ordered his guards to cut off Christ's legs. "Healer," he said, "heal thyself."

Then came the Repentance, the vision in the night, and Judas Iscariot gave up his crown, his dark arts, and his riches to follow the man he had crippled. Despised and taunted by those he had tyrannized, Judas became the Legs of the Lord, and for a year carried Jesus on his back to the far corners of the realm he once ruled. When Jesus did finally heal Himself, then Judas walked at his side, and from that time forth he was Jesus' trusted friend and counselor, the first and foremost of the Twelve. Finally, Jesus gave Judas the gift of tongues, recalled and sanctified the dragons that Judas had sent away, and sent his disciple forth on a solitary ministry across the oceans, "to spread My Word where I cannot go."

There came a day when the sun went dark at noon and the ground trembled, and Judas swung his dragon around on ponderous wings and flew back across the raging seas. But when he reached the city of Jerusalem, he found Christ dead on the cross.

In that moment his faith faltered, and for the next three days the Great Wrath of Judas was like a storm across the ancient world. His dragons razed the Temple in Jerusalem, drove the people forth from the city, and struck as well at the great seats of power in Rome and Babylon. And when he found the others of the Twelve and questioned them and learned of how the one named Simon-called-Peter had three times betrayed the Lord, he strangled Peter with his own hands and fed the corpse to his dragons. Then he sent those dragons forth to start fires throughout the world, funeral pyres for Jesus of Nazareth.

And Jesus rose on the third day, and Judas wept, but his tears could not turn Christ's anger, for in his wrath he had betrayed all of Christ's teachings.

So Jesus called back the dragons, and they came, and everywhere the fires went out. And from their bellies he called forth Peter and made him whole again, and gave him dominion over the Church.

Then the dragons died, and so too did all dragons everywhere, for they were the living sigil of the power and wisdom of Judas Iscariot, who had sinned greatly. And He took from Judas the gift of tongues and the power of healing He had given, and even his eyesight, for Judas had acted as a blind man (there was a fine painting of the blinded Judas weeping over the bodies of his dragons). And He told Judas that for long ages he would be remembered only as Betrayer, and people would curse his name, and all that he had been and done would be forgotten.

But then, because Judas had loved Him so, Christ gave him a boon: an extended life, during which he might travel and think on his sins and finally come to forgiveness. Only then might he die.

And that was the beginning of the last chapter in the life of Judas Iscariot. But it was a very long chapter indeed. Once dragon-king, once the friend of Christ, now he was only a blind traveler, outcast and friendless, wandering all the cold roads of the Earth, living still when all the cities and people and things he had known were dead. Peter, the first Pope and ever his enemy, spread far and wide the tale of how Judas had sold Christ for thirty pieces of silver, until Judas dared not even use his true name. For a time he called himself just Wandering Ju', and afterward many other names. He lived more than a thousand years and became a preacher, a healer, and a lover of animals, and was hunted and persecuted when the Church that Peter had founded became bloated and corrupt. But he had a great deal of time, and at last he found wisdom and a sense of peace, and finally, Jesus came to him on a long-postponed deathbed and they were reconciled, and Judas wept once again. Before he died, Christ promised that he would permit a few to remember who and what Judas had been, and that with the passage of centuries the news would spread, until finally Peter's Lie was displaced and forgotten.

Such was the life of St. Judas Iscariot, as related in *The Way of Cross and Dragon*. His teachings were there as well and the apocryphal books he had allegedly written.

When I had finished the volume, I lent it to Arla-k-Bau, the captain of the *Truth of Christ*. Arla was a gaunt, pragmatic woman of no particular faith, but I valued her opinion. The others of my crew, the good sisters and brothers of Saint Christopher, would only have echoed the Archbishop's religious horror.

"Interesting," Arla said when she returned the book to me.

I chuckled. "Is that all?"

She shrugged. "It makes a nice story. An easier read than your Bible, Damien, and more dramatic as well."

"True," I admitted. "But it's absurd. An unbelievable tangle of doctrine, apocrypha, mythology, and superstition. Entertaining, yes, certainly. Imaginative, even daring. But ridiculous, don't you think? How can you credit dragons? A legless Christ? Peter being pieced together after being devoured by four monsters?"

Arla's grin was taunting. "Is that any sillier than water changing into wine, or Christ walking on the waves, or a man living in the belly of a fish?" Arla-k-Bau liked to jab at me. It had been a scandal when I selected a nonbeliever as my captain, but she was very good at her job, and I liked her around to keep me sharp. She had a good mind, Arla did, and I valued that more than blind obedience. Perhaps that was a sin in me.

"There is a difference," I said.

"Is there?" she snapped back. Her eyes saw through my masks. "Ah, Damien, admit it. You rather liked this book."

I cleared my throat. "It piqued my interest," I acknowledged. I had to justify myself. "You know the kind of matter I deal with ordinarily. Dreary little doctrinal deviations; obscure quibblings on theology somehow blown all out of proportion; bald-faced political maneuverings designed to set some ambitious planetary bishop up as a new pope, or wrest some concession or other from New Rome or Vess. The war is endless, but the battles are dull and dirty. They exhaust me spiritually, emotionally, physically. Afterward I feel drained and guilty." I tapped the book's leather cover. "This is different. The heresy must be crushed, of course, but I admit that I am anxious to meet this Lukyan Judasson."

"The artwork is lovely as well," Arla said, flipping through the pages of *The Way of Cross and Dragon* and stopping to study one especially striking plate—Judas weeping over his dragons, I think. I smiled to see that it had affected her as much as me. Then I frowned.

That was the first inkling I had of the difficulties ahead.

So it was that the *Truth of Christ* came to the porcelain city Ammadon on the world of Arion, where the Order of Saint Judas Iscariot kept its House.

Arion was a pleasant, gentle world, inhabited for these past three centuries. Its population was under nine million; Ammadon, the only real city, was home to two of those millions. The technological level was medium high, but chiefly imported. Arion had little industry and was not an innovative world, except perhaps artistically. The arts were quite important here, flourishing and vital. Religious freedom was a basic tenet of the society, but Arion was not a religious world either, and the majority of the populace lived devoutly secular lives. The most popular religion was Aestheticism, which hardly counts as a religion at all. There were also Taoists, Erikaners, Old True Christers, and Children of the Dreamer, plus adherents of a dozen lesser sects.

And finally there were nine churches of the One True Interstellar Catholic faith. There had been twelve. The other three were now houses of Arion's fastest-growing faith, the Order of Saint Judas Iscariot, which also had a dozen newly built churches of its own.

The Bishop of Arion was a dark, severe man with close-cropped black hair who was not at all happy to see me. "Damien Har Veris!" he exclaimed with some wonderment when I called on him at his residence. "We have heard of you, of course, but I never thought to meet or host you. Our numbers here are small."

"And growing smaller," I said, "a matter of some concern to my Lord Commander, Archbishop Torgathon. Apparently you are less troubled, Excellency, since you did not see fit to report the activities of this sect of Judas worshippers."

He looked briefly angry at the rebuke, but quickly swallowed his temper. Even a bishop can fear a Knight Inquisitor. "We are concerned, of course," he said. "We do all we can to combat the heresy. If you have advice that will help us, I will be glad to listen."

"I am an Inquisitor of the Order Militant of the Knights of Jesus Christ," I said bluntly. "I do not give advice, Excellency. I take action. To that end I was sent to Arion, and that is what I shall do. Now, tell me what you know about this heresy, and this First Scholar, this Lukyan Judasson."

"Of course, Father Damien," the Bishop began. He signaled for a servant to bring us a tray of wine and cheese, and began to summarize the short but explosive history of the Judas cult. I listened, polishing my nails on the crimson lapel of my jacket until the black paint gleamed brilliantly, interrupting from time to time with a question. Before he had half finished, I was determined to visit Lukyan personally. It seemed the best course of action.

And I had wanted to do so all along.

Appearances were important on Arion, I gathered, and I deemed it necessary to impress Lukyan with myself and my station. I wore my best

---

---

boots—sleek, dark hand-made boots of Roman leather that had never seen the inside of Torgathon's receiving chamber—and a severe black suit with deep burgundy lapels and stiff collar. Around my neck was a splendid crucifix of pure gold; my collarpin was a matching golden sword, the sigil of the Knights Inquisitor. Brother Denis carefully painted my nails, all black as ebon, and darkened my eyes as well, and used a fine white powder on my face. When I glanced in the mirror, I frightened even myself. I smiled, but only briefly. It ruined the effect.

I walked to the House of Saint Judas Iscariot. The streets of Ammadon were wide and spacious and golden, lined by scarlet trees called whisperwinds whose long, drooping tendrils did indeed seem to whisper secrets to the gentle breeze. Sister Judith came with me. She is a small woman, slight of build even in the cowled coveralls of the Order of Saint Christopher. Her face is meek and kind, her eyes wide and youthful and innocent. I find her useful. Four times now she has killed those who attempted to assault me.

The House itself was newly built. Rambling and stately, it rose from amid gardens of small bright flowers and seas of golden grass; the gardens were surrounded by a high wall. Murals covered both the outer wall around the property and the exterior of the building itself. I recognized a few of them from *The Way of Cross and Dragon,* and stopped briefly to admire them before walking through the main gate. No one tried to stop us. There were no guards, not even a receptionist. Within the walls, men and women strolled languidly through the flowers, or sat on benches beneath silverwoods and whisperwinds.

Sister Judith and I paused, then made our way directly to the House itself.

We had just started up the steps when a man appeared from within, and stood waiting in the doorway. He was blond and fat, with a great wiry beard that framed a slow smile, and he wore a flimsy robe that fell to his sandaled feet. On the robe were dragons, dragons bearing the silhouette of a man holding a cross.

When I reached the top of the steps, he bowed to me. "Father Damien Har Veris of the Knights Inquisitor," he said. His smile widened. "I greet you in the name of Jesus, and in the name of Saint Judas. I am Lukyan."

I made a note to myself to find out which of the Bishop's staff was feeding information to the Judas cult, but my composure did not break. I have been a Knight Inquisitor for a long, long time. "Father Lukyan Mo," I said, taking his hand. "I have questions to ask of you." I did not smile.

He did. "I thought you might," he said.

Lukyan's office was large but spartan. Heretics often have a simplicity that the officers of the true Church seem to have lost. He did have one indulgence, however. Dominating the wall behind his desk console was the painting I had already fallen in love with: the blinded Judas weeping over his dragons.

Lukyan sat down heavily and motioned me to a second chair. We had left Sister Judith outside in the waiting chamber. "I prefer to stand, Father Lukyan," I said, knowing it gave me an advantage.

"Just Lukyan," he said. "Or Luke, if you prefer. We have little use for hierarchy here."

"You are Father Lukyan Mo, born here on Arion, educated in the seminary on Cathaday, a former priest of the One True Interstellar Catholic Church of Earth and the Thousand Worlds," I said. "I will address you as befits your station, Father. I expect you to reciprocate. Is that understood?"

"Oh, yes," he said amiably.

"I am empowered to strip you of your right to perform the sacraments, to order you shunned and excommunicated for this heresy you have formulated. On certain worlds I could even order your death."

"But not on Arion," Lukyan said quickly. "We're very tolerant here. Besides, we outnumber you." He smiled. "As for the rest, well, I don't perform those sacraments much anyway, you know. Not for years. I'm First Scholar now. A teacher, a thinker. I show others the way, help them find the faith. Excommunicate me if it will make you happy, Father Damien. Happiness is what all of us seek."

"You have given up the faith, then, Father Lukyan," I said. I deposited my copy of *The Way of Cross and Dragon* on his desk. "But I see you have found a new one." Now I did smile, but it was all ice, all menace, all mockery. "A more ridiculous creed I have yet to encounter. I suppose you will tell me that you have spoken to God, that he trusted you with this new revelation, so that you might clear the good name, such that it is, of Holy Judas?"

Now Lukyan's smile was very broad indeed. He picked up the book and beamed at me. "Oh, no," he said. "No, I made it all up."

That stopped me. "What?"

"I made it all up," he repeated. He hefted the book fondly. "I drew on many sources, of course, especially the Bible, but I do think of *Cross and Dragon* as mostly my own work. It's rather good, don't you agree? Of course, I could hardly put my name on it, proud as I am of it, but I did include my imprimatur. Did you notice that? It was the closest I dared come to a byline."

I was speechless only for a moment. Then I grimaced. "You startle me," I admitted. "I expected to find an inventive madman, some poor self-deluded fool, firm in his belief that he had spoken to God. I've dealt with such fanatics before. Instead I find a cheerful cynic who has invented a religion for his own profit. I think I prefer the fanatics. You are beneath contempt, Father Lukyan. You will burn in hell for eternity."

"I doubt it," Lukyan said, "but you do mistake me, Father Damien. I am no cynic, nor do I profit from my dear Saint Judas. Truthfully, I lived more comfortably as a priest of your own Church. I do this because it is my vocation."

I sat down. "You confuse me," I said. "Explain."

"Now I am going to tell you the truth," he said. He said it in an odd way, almost as a cant. "I am a Liar," he added.

"You want to confuse me with a child's paradoxes," I snapped.

"No, no," he smiled. "A *Liar.* With a capital. It is an organization, Father Damien. A religion, you might call it. A great and powerful faith. And I am the smallest part of it."

"I know of no such church," I said.

"Oh, no, you wouldn't. It's secret. It has to be. You can understand that, can't you? People don't like being lied to."

"I do not like being lied to," I said.

Lukyan looked wounded. "I told you this would be the truth, didn't I? When a Liar says that, you can believe him. How else could we trust each other?"

"There are many of you?" I asked. I was starting to think that Lukyan was a madman after all, as fanatical as any heretic, but in a more complex way. Here was a heresy within a heresy, but I recognized my duty: to find the truth of things, and set them right.

"Many of us," Lukyan said, smiling. "You would be surprised, Father Damien, really you would. But there are some things I dare not tell you."

"Tell me what you dare, then."

"Happily," said Lukyan Judasson. "We Liars, like those of all other religions, have several truths we take on faith. Faith is always required. There are some things that cannot be proven. We believe that life is worth living. That is an article of faith. The purpose of life is to live, to resist death, perhaps to defy entropy."

"Go on," I said, interested despite myself.

"We also believe that happiness is a good, something to be sought after."

"The Church does not oppose happiness," I said dryly.

"I wonder," Lukyan said. "But let us not quibble. Whatever the Church's position on happiness, it does preach belief in an afterlife, in a supreme being and a complex moral code."

"True."

"The Liars believe in no afterlife, no God. We see the universe as it *is,* Father Damien, and these naked truths are cruel ones. We who believe in life, and treasure it, will die. Afterward there will be nothing, eternal emptiness, blackness, nonexistence. In our living there has been no purpose, no poetry, no meaning. Nor do our deaths possess these qualities. When we are gone, the universe will not long remember us, and shortly it will be as if we had never lived at all. Our worlds and our universe will not long outlive us. Ultimately, entropy will consume all, and our puny efforts cannot stay that awful end. It will be gone. It has never been. It has never mattered. The universe itself is doomed, transient, uncaring."

I slid back in my chair, and a shiver went through me as I listened to poor Lukyan's dark words. I found myself fingering my crucifix. "A bleak philosophy," I said, "as well as a false one. I have had that fearful vision myself. I think all of us do, at some point. But it is not so, Father. My faith sustains me against such nihilism. It is a shield against despair."

"Oh, I know that, my friend, my Knight Inquisitor," Lukyan said. "I'm glad to see you understand so well. You are almost one of us already."

I frowned.

"You've touched the heart of it," Lukyan continued. "The truths, the great truths—and most of the lesser ones as well—they are unbearable for most men. We find our shield in faith. Your faith, my faith, any faith. It doesn't matter, so long as we *believe,* really and truly believe, in whatever lie we cling to." He fingered the ragged edges of his great blond beard. "Our psychs have always told us that believers are the happy ones, you know. They may believe in Christ or Buddha or Erika Stormjones, in reincarnation or immortality or nature, in the power of love or the platform of a political faction, but it all comes to the same thing. They believe. They are happy. It is the ones who have seen truth who despair, and kill themselves. The truths are so vast, the faiths so little, so poorly made, so riddled with error and contradiction that we see around them and through them, and then we feel the weight of darkness upon us, and can no longer be happy."

I am not a slow man. I knew, by then, where Lukyan Judasson was going. "Your Liars invent faiths."

He smiled. "Of all sorts. Not only religious. Think of it. We know truth for the cruel instrument it is. Beauty is infinitely preferable to truth. We invent beauty. Faiths, political movements, high ideals, belief in love and fellowship. All of them are lies. We tell those lies, among others, endless others. We improve on history and myth and religion, make each more beautiful, better, easier to believe in. Our lies are not perfect, of course. The truths are too big. But perhaps someday we will find one great lie that all humanity can use. Until then, a thousand small lies will do."

"I think I do not care for your Liars very much," I said with a cold, even fervor. "My whole life has been a quest for truth."

Lukyan was indulgent. "Father Damien Har Veris, Knight Inquisitor, I know you better than that. You are a Liar yourself. You do good work. You ship from world to world, and on each you destroy the foolish, the rebels, the questioners who would bring down the edifice of the vast lie that you serve."

"If my lie is so admirable," I said, "then why have you abandoned it?"

"A religion must fit its culture and society, work with them, not against them. If there is conflict, contradiction, then the lie breaks down, and the faith falters. Your Church is good for many worlds, Father, but not for Arion. Life is too kind here, and your faith is stern. Here we love beauty, and your faith offers too little. So we have improved it. We studied this world for a long time. We know its psychological profile. Saint Judas will thrive here. He offers drama, and color, and much beauty—the aesthetics are admirable. His is a tragedy with a happy ending, and Arion dotes on such stories. And the dragons are a nice touch. I think your own Church ought to find a way to work in dragons. They are marvelous creatures."

"Mythical," I said.

"Hardly," he replied. "Look it up." He grinned at me. "You see, really, it all comes back to faith. Can you really know what happened three thousand years ago? You have one Judas, I have another. Both of us have books. Is yours true? Can you really believe that? I have been admitted only to the first circle of the order of Liars, so I do not know all our secrets, but I know that we are very old. It would not surprise me to learn that the gospels were written by men very much like me. Perhaps there never was a Judas at all. Or a Jesus."

"I have faith that that is not so," I said.

"There are a hundred people in this building who have a deep and very real faith in Saint Judas, and the way of cross and dragon," Lukyan said. "Faith is a very good thing. Do you know that the suicide rate on Arion has decreased by almost a third since the Order of Saint Judas was founded?"

I remember rising slowly from my chair. "You are fanatical as any heretic I have ever met, Lukyan Judasson," I told him. "I pity you the loss of your faith."

Lukyan rose with me. "Pity yourself, Damien Har Veris," he said. "I have found a new faith and a new cause, and I am a happy man. You, my dear friend, are tortured and miserable."

"That is a lie!" I am afraid I screamed.

"Come with me," Lukyan said. He touched a panel on his wall, and the great painting of Judas weeping over his dragons slid up out of sight. There was a stairway leading down into the ground. "Follow me," he said.

In the cellar was a great glass vat full of pale green fluid, and in it a thing was floating, a thing very like an ancient embryo, aged and infantile at the same time, naked, with a huge head and a tiny atrophied body. Tubes ran from its arms and legs and genitals, connecting it to the machinery that kept it alive.

When Lukyan turned on the lights, it opened its eyes. They were large and dark and they looked into my soul.

"This is my colleague," Lukyan said, patting the side of the vat, "Jon Azure Cross, a Liar of the fourth circle."

"And a telepath," I said with a sick certainty. I had led pogroms against other telepaths, children mostly, on other worlds. The Church teaches that the psionic powers are one of Satan's traps. They are not mentioned in the Bible. I have never felt good about those killings.

"The moment you entered the compound, Jon read you and notified me," Lukyan said. "Only a few of us know that he is here. He helps us lie most efficiently. He knows when faith is true, and when it is feigned. I have an implant in my skull. Jon can talk to me at all times. It was he who initially recruited me into the Liars. He knew my faith was hollow. He felt the depth of my despair."

Then the thing in the tank spoke, its metallic voice coming from a speaker-grill in the base of the machine that nurtured it. *"And I feel yours, Damien Har Veris, empty priest. Inquisitor, you have asked too many questions. You are sick at heart, and tired, and you do not believe. Join us, Damien. You have been a Liar for a long, long time!"*

For a moment I hesitated, looking deep into myself, wondering what it was I *did* believe. I searched for my faith—the fire that had once sustained me, the certainty in the teachings of the Church, the presence of Christ within me. I found none of it, none. I was empty inside, burned out, full of questions and pain. But as I was about to answer Jon Azure Cross and the smiling Lukyan Judasson, I found something else, something I *did* believe in, had always believed in.

Truth.

I believed in truth, even when it hurt.

"He is lost to us," said the telepath with the mocking name of Cross.

Lukyan's smile faded. "Oh, really? I had hoped you would be one of us, Damien. You seemed ready."

I was suddenly afraid, and I considered sprinting up the stairs to Sister Judith. Lukyan had told me so very much, and now I had rejected them.

The telepath felt my fear. *"You cannot hurt us, Damien,"* it said. *"Go in peace. Lukyan has told you nothing."*

Lukyan was frowning. "I told him a good deal, Jon," he said.

"Yes. But can he trust the words of such a Liar as you?" The small misshapen mouth of the thing in the vat twitched in a smile, and its great eyes closed, and Lukyan Judasson sighed and led me up at the stairs.

It was not until some years later that I realized it was Jon Azure Cross who was lying, and the victim of his lie was Lukyan. I *could* hurt them. I did.

It was almost simple. The Bishop had friends in government and media. With some money in the right places, I made some friends of my own. Then I exposed Cross in his cellar, charging that he had used his psionic powers to tamper with the minds of Lukyan's followers. My friends were receptive to the charges. The guardians conducted a raid, took the telepath Cross into custody, and later tried him.

He was innocent, of course. My charge was nonsense; human telepaths can read minds in close proximity, but seldom anything more. But they are rare, and much feared, and Cross was hideous enough so that it was easy to make him a victim of superstition. In the end, he was acquitted, but he left the city Ammadon and perhaps Arion itself, bound for regions unknown.

But it had never been my intention to convict him. The charge was enough. The cracks began to show in the lie that he and Lukyan had built together. Faith is hard to come by, and easy to lose. The merest doubt can begin to erode even the strongest foundation of belief.

The Bishop and I labored together to sow further doubts. It was not as easy as I might have thought. The Liars had done their work well. Ammadon, like most civilized cities, had a great pool of knowledge, a computer system that linked the schools and universities and libraries together, and made their combined wisdom available to any who needed it.

But when I checked, I soon discovered that the histories of Rome and Babylon had been subtly reshaped, and there were three listings for Judas Iscariot—one for the betrayer, one for the saint, and one for the conqueror-king of Babylon. His name was also mentioned in connection with the Hanging Gardens, and there is an entry for a so-called "Codex Judas."

And according to the Ammadon library, dragons became extinct on Old Earth around the time of Christ.

We finally purged all those lies, wiped them from the memories of the computers, though we had to cite authorities on a half-dozen non-Christian worlds before the librarians and academics would credit that the differences were anything more than a question of religious preference. By then the Order of Saint Judas had withered in the glare of exposure. Lukyan Judasson had grown gaunt and angry, and at least half of his churches had closed.

The heresy never died completely, of course. There are always those who believe no matter what. And so to this day *The Way of Cross and Dragon* is read on Arion, in the porcelain city Ammadon, amid murmuring whisperwinds.

Arla-k-Bau and the *Truth of Christ* carried me back to Vess a year after my departure, and Archbishop Torgathon finally gave me the rest I had asked for, before sending me out to fight still other heresies. So I had my victory, and the Church continued on much as before, and the Order of Saint Judas Iscariot was crushed and diminished. The telepath Jon Azure Cross had been wrong, I thought then. He had sadly underestimated the power of a Knight Inquisitor.

Later, though, I remembered his words.

You cannot hurt us, Damien.

Us?

The Order of Saint Judas? Or the Liars?

He lied, I think, deliberately, knowing I would go forth and destroy the way of cross and dragon, knowing too that I could not touch the Liars, would not even dare mention them. How could I? Who would believe it? A grand star-spanning conspiracy as old as history? It reeks of paranoia, and I had no proof at all.

The telepath lied for Lukyan's benefit, so that he would let me go. I am certain of that now. Cross risked much to snare me. Failing, he was willing to sacrifice Lukyan Judasson and his lie, pawns in some greater game.

So I left, and carried within me the knowledge that I was empty of faith but for a blind faith in truth, a truth I could no longer find in my Church.

I grew certain of that in my year of rest, which I spent reading and studying on Vess and Cathaday and Celia's World. Finally I returned to the Archbishop's receiving room, and stood again before Torgathon Nine-Klariis Tûn in my very worst pair of boots. "My Lord Commander," I said to him, "I can accept no further assignments. I ask that I be retired from active service."

"For what cause?" Torgathon rumbled, splashing feebly.

"I have lost the faith," I said to him, simply.

He regarded me for a long time, his pupilless eyes blinking. At last he said, "Your faith is a matter between you and your confessor. I care only about your results. You have done good work, Damien. You may not retire, and we will not allow you to resign."

The truth will set us free.

But freedom is cold and empty and frightening, and lies can often be warm and beautiful.

Last year the Church finally granted me a new and better ship. I named this one *Dragon*.

Dubuque, Iowa.
December, 1978

Bruce Sterling

SWARM

One of the most powerful and innovative new talents to enter SF in recent years, a man with a rigorously worked-out and aesthetically convincing vision of what the future may have in store for humanity, Bruce Sterling as yet may still be better known to the cognoscente than to the SF-reading population at large, in spite of a recent Hugo win. If you look behind the scenes, though, you will find him everywhere, and he had almost as much to do—as writer, critic, propagandist, aesthetic theorist, and tireless polemicist—with the shaping and evolution of SF in the eighties and nineties as Michael Moorcock did with the shaping of SF in the sixties; it is not for nothing that many of the other writers of the eighties and nineties refer to him, half ruefully, half admiringly, as "Chairman Bruce."

Sterling published his first story in 1976, in an obscure anthology of stories by Texas writers called *Lone Star Universe,* and followed it up in 1977 with his first novel, *Involution Ocean.* Neither story nor novel attracted much attention, nor would his second novel, *The Artificial Kid,* in 1980—indeed, both novels remain fundamentally unread even today, although, in retrospect, *The Artificial Kid* is interesting, if for nothing else because it is clearly an early cyberpunk work; at the time the few critics who mentioned it seemed to be puzzled by it, and dismissed it as a grotesque curiosity. Although Sterling would later produce much better work, both novels are still readable, and in some ways closer to the canons of traditional adventure fiction than some of his more mature later work. They're also interesting because some of Sterling's influences show up more clearly there than they do elsewhere. William Gibson has referred to *The Artificial Kid* as being like "a Jack Vance novel, but with a protagonist who seemed to be compounded of equal parts Bruce Lee, Iggy Pop, and Johnny Rotten," but both that novel and *Involution Ocean* demonstrate as well a heady stew of (sometimes only partially digested) influences from writers as diverse as Melville, Dickens, the J. G. Ballard of the "Vermilion Sands" stories, Harlan Ellison, and Jules Verne, as well as from a number of other pop culture sources, many of them not only outside the SF genre but outside the print genre altogether. Perhaps most noticeably, the strong influence of the early work of Samuel R. Delany can be seen—Sterling's Artificial Kid is clearly a variant of the Magic Kid character (to borrow Algis Budrys's useful critical phrase) who figures in most of Delany's early work, and it's easy to picture him strolling into Sterling's novel for a side gig after working a day job in *The Einstein Intersection* or *The Jewels of Aptor.*

Sterling's early work raised hardly a ripple in the gunmetal-placid surface of the SF world of the late seventies, though. Like many another new writer of the day, Sterling would have to wait for "steam engine time," for the revolutionary surge of new creative energy that would sweep into the field around 1982, before his work was suddenly accessible to, and ready to be appreciated by, the SF readership. And like many another new writer, he first caught on with his short fiction, attracting interest and acclaim with a series of stories he published in the middle eighties in places like *The Magazine of Fantasy & Science Fiction, Omni,* and *Universe.*

The first such story was the one that follows, "Swarm," published in 1982 in *F&SF.* It was clear at once that this was something new; although there were still recognizable influences on Sterling's new work—A. E. van Vogt, Charles Harness, Alfred Bester, Cordwainer Smith, Larry Niven, Olaf Stapledon, along with echoes of Delany and James Tiptree, Jr.—he had integrated those influences better, melded them successfully to produce a strong and individual new voice of his own. With his usual flair for the vivid phrase, Sterling himself has said of "Swarm" that "with that story, I finally gnawed my way through the insulation and got my teeth set into the buzzing copper wire."

"Swarm" was followed in the next three years by a string of other "Shaper/Mechanist" stories such as "Cicada Queen," "Spider Rose," and "Sunken Gardens," all set against the backdrop of Sterling's exotic Shaper/Mechanist future, a complex and disturbing future where warring political factions struggle to control the shape of human destiny and the nature of humanity itself. Although there were only a few "Shaper/Mechanist" stories, they rank among the strongest work of the decade, and had a disproportionate impact on the SF scene of the day, being especially influential on other new writers and authors-in-the-egg

The Shaper/Mechanist vision of the future would reach its purest expression in his landmark 1985 novel *Schismatrix,* a vivid, complex, chewy meditation on cultural evolution, Stapledonian and yet buzzing with paranoid energy and tension, something like what you might get if Alfred Bester and A. E. van Vogt had collaborated to write *Last and First Men.*

(Shaper/Mechanist stories were far from all that Sterling produced in the eighties, although much of his other work takes us far enough away from the adventure tradition to be outside the purview of this book. With only the partial exception of the Shaper/Mechanist series, though, no two stories by Sterling are ever much alike in tone or setting or style; there is so much difference between the Sterling of "Dinner in Audoghast" and the Sterling of "The Beautiful and the Sublime" and the Sterling of "Green Days in Brunei" and the Sterling of "Flowers of Edo" and the Sterling of "Dori Bangs" that they might as well all be different individual writers—which makes their influence on later work more difficult to spot.)

Sterling would spend the rest of the eighties up to his hips in blood as one of the chief antagonists in the newly launched Cyberpunk War in SF, editing the influential anthology *Mirrorshades: The Cyberpunk Anthology,* writing fierce manifestos and letters, and relentlessly hyping cyberpunk in his agitprop organ, *Cheap Truth,* almost certainly the most influential, admired, and loathed critical magazine of the decade, even though it was only a shoddy-looking photocopied fanzine sent out to a reader list—selected personally by Sterling—of only a few hundred people. What would be obscured by all the fierce polemics and bitter infighting was the fact that Sterling was undoubtedly the best new hard-science writer of the decade, rivaled for the title only by Greg Bear. Ironically, the traditional hard science audience, centered now around *Analog* and Jim Baen's *Far Frontiers,* would be put off by Sterling's political stance and by the punk flavor of his work, and would have nothing to do with him, while he would receive most of his support outside of his own core clique from the leftist literary intellectuals like John Kessel that *Cheap Truth* would devote a good deal of its energy to attacking.

Toward the end of the eighties and the beginning of the nineties, Sterling would publish two more novels, a somewhat overblown "steampunk" novel in collaboration with William Gibson, *The Difference Engine,* and a complex political future thriller, *Islands in the Net.* Perhaps because of backlash from the Cyberpunk Wars, *Islands in the Net* would be largely ignored, although it was more mature and thoughtful than his earlier work, with more fully rounded and more psychologically complex characters. After this, perhaps partially as a result, Sterling retreated into the "New Journalism" for a couple of years, making a major impact with his first (and, so far, only) nonfiction book, a study of First Amendment issues in the world of computer networking, *The Hacker Crackdown: Law and Disorder on the Electronic Frontier,* as well as with a series of articles for *Wired* magazine that made him one of that magazine's big guns (ironically, he may have a bigger reputation as a journalist, especially with the Internet crowd, than he does as a science fiction writer).

In the mid-nineties, after the dust settled and the Cyberpunk Wars had retreated into memory (to the point that critics are now beginning to speak about "post-cyberpunk" work), Sterling returned to the field with two of his best books, *Heavy Weather* and *Holy Fire* (with *Holy Fire* in particular providing as complex, detailed, and fully realized a vision of what the future might actually be like as any that science fiction as a genre has to offer), and a handful of new short stories such as "Sacred Cow" and "Deep Eddy," one of which, "Bicycle Repairman," finally earned him a long-overdue Hugo in 1997.

Sterling is still a young writer by any reasonable definition of the term, and—unless he gets hit by a truck or snuffed by one of the Russian mafia types and computer criminals he hangs out with in his capacity as a hip techno-journalist—will probably keep on growing and evolving well into the next century. Already, his influence has been profound. Although widely recognized as one of the two main "cyberpunk" works, *Schismatrix* was overshadowed at the time by William Gibson's first novel, *Neuromancer,* a more accessible book that would have a powerful and immediate impact on much subsequent SF. I've heard critics say that it was odd that *Schismatrix* didn't have a greater impact . . . but, in fact, its impact may ultimately turn out to be as large as that of *Neuromancer*—it's just taken longer to show up. If you want to know where all of *Schismatrix*'s influence went, all you have to do is look at some of the recent works of the New Baroque Space Opera, especially British Space Opera, being written by people such as Iain M. Banks, Colin Greenland, Stephen Baxter, Paul J. McAuley, Alastair Reynolds, and Peter F. Hamilton. In fact, on the British side of the Atlantic, at least, I'd have to say that *Schismatrix* has probably had more influence on the development of the New Space Opera than any other single book, with the exception of Samuel R. Delany's *Nova.* It would be very interesting to see Sterling himself return to the Baroque Space Opera somewhere down the road, and I hope he does.

Sterling's other books include the collections *Crystal Express* and *Globalhead.* His most recent book is the omnibus collection (it contains the novel *Schismatrix* as well as the rest of his Shaper/Mechanist stories) *Schismatrix Plus*. He lives with his family in Austin, Texas. His latest novel, *Distraction,* is due out soon.

"I will miss your conversation during the rest of the voyage," the alien said.

Captain-Doctor Simon Afriel folded his jeweled hands over his gold-embroidered waistcoat. "I regret it also, ensign," he said in the alien's own hissing language. "Our talks together have been very useful to me. I would have paid to learn so much, but you gave it freely."

"But that was only information," the alien said. He shrouded his bead-bright eyes behind thick nictitating membranes. "We Investors deal in energy, and precious metals. To prize and pursue mere knowledge is an immature racial trait." The alien lifted the long ribbed frill behind his pinhole-sized ears.

"No doubt you are right," Afriel said, despising him. "We humans are as children to other races, however; so a certain immaturity seems natural to us." Afriel pulled off his sunglasses to rub the bridge of his nose. The starship cabin was drenched in searing blue light, heavily ultraviolet. It was the light the Investors preferred, and they were not about to change it for one human passenger.

"You have not done badly," the alien said magnanimously. "You are the kind of race we like to do business with: young, eager, plastic, ready for a wide variety of goods and experiences. We would have contacted you much earlier, but your technology was still too feeble to afford us a profit."

"Things are different now," Afriel said. "We'll make you rich."

"Indeed," the Investor said. The frill behind his scaly head flickered rapidly, a sign of amusement. "Within two hundred years you will be wealthy enough to buy from us the secret of our starflight. Or perhaps your Mechanist faction will discover the secret through research."

Afriel was annoyed. As a member of the Reshaped faction, he did not appreciate the reference to the rival Mechanists. "Don't put too much stock in mere technical expertise," he said. "Consider the aptitude for languages we Shapers have. It makes our faction a much better trading partner. To a Mechanist, all Investors look alike."

The alien hesitated. Afriel smiled. He had appealed to the alien's personal ambition with his last statement, and the hint had been taken. That was where the Mechanists always erred. They tried to treat all Investors consistently, using the same programmed routines each time. They lacked imagination.

Something would have to be done about the Mechanists, Afriel thought. Something more permanent than the small but deadly confrontations between isolated ships in the Asteroid Belt and the ice-rich Rings of Saturn. Both factions maneuvered constantly, looking for a decisive stroke, bribing away each other's best talent, practicing ambush, assassination, and industrial espionage.

Captain-Doctor Simon Afriel was a past master of these pursuits. That was why the Reshaped faction had paid the millions of kilowatts necessary to buy his passage. Afriel held doctorates in biochemistry and alien linguistics, and a master's degree in magnetic weapons engineering. He was thirty-eight years old and had been Reshaped according to the state of the art at the time of his conception. His hormonal balance had been altered slightly to compensate for long periods spent in free-fall. He had no appendix. The structure of his heart had been redesigned for greater efficiency, and his large intestine had been altered to produce the vitamins normally made by intestinal bacteria. Genetic engineering and rigorous training in childhood had given him an intelligence quotient of one hundred and eighty. He was not the brightest of the agents of the Ring Council, but he was one of the most mentally stable and the best trusted.

"It seems a shame," the alien said, "that a human of your accomplishments should have to rot for two years in this miserable, profitless outpost."

"The years won't be wasted," Afriel said.

"But why have you chosen to study the Swarm? They can teach you nothing, since they cannot speak. They have no wish to trade, having no tools or technology. They are the only spacefaring race that is essentially without intelligence."

"That alone should make them worthy of study."

"Do you seek to imitate them, then? You would make monsters of yourselves." Again the ensign hesitated. "Perhaps you could do it. It would be bad for business, however."

There came a fluting burst of alien music over the ship's speakers, then a screeching fragment of Investor language. Most of it was too high-pitched for Afriel's ears to follow.

The alien stood, his jeweled skirt brushing the tips of his clawed bird-like feet. "The Swarm's symbiote has arrived," he said.

"Thank you," Afriel said. When the ensign opened the cabin door, Afriel could smell the Swarm's representative; the creature's warm yeasty scent had spread rapidly through the starship's recycled air.

Afriel quickly checked his appearance in a pocket mirror. He touched powder to his face and straightened the round velvet hat on his shoulder-length reddish-blond hair. His earlobes glittered with red impact-rubies, thick as his thumbs' ends, mined from the Asteroid Belt. His knee-length coat and waistcoat were of gold brocade; the shirt beneath was of dazzling fineness, woven with red-gold thread. He had dressed to impress the Investors, who expected and appreciated a prosperous look from their customers. How could he impress this new alien? Smell, perhaps. He freshened his perfume.

Beside the starship's secondary airlock, the Swarm's symbiote was chittering rapidly at the ship's commander. The commander was an old and sleepy Investor, twice the size of most of her crewmen. Her massive head was encrusted in a jeweled helmet. From within the helmet her clouded eyes glittered like cameras.

The symbiote lifted on its six posterior legs and gestured feebly with its four clawed forelimbs. The ship's artificial gravity, a third again as strong as Earth's, seemed to bother it. Its rudimentary eyes, dangling on stalks, were shut tight against the glare. It must be used to darkness, Afriel thought.

The commander answered the creature in its own language. Afriel grimaced, for he had hoped that the creature spoke Investor. Now he would have to learn another language, a language designed for a being without a tongue.

After another brief interchange the commander turned to Afriel. "The symbiote is not pleased with your arrival," she told Afriel in the Investor language. "There has apparently been some disturbance here involving humans, in the recent past. However, I have prevailed upon it to admit you to the Nest. The episode has been recorded. Payment for my diplomatic services will be arranged with your faction when I return to your native star system."

"I thank Your Authority," Afriel said. "Please convey to the symbiote my best personal wishes, and the harmlessness and humility of my intentions—" He broke off short as the symbiote lunged toward him, biting him savagely in the calf of his left leg. Afriel jerked free and leapt backward in the heavy artificial gravity, going into a defensive position. The symbiote had ripped away a long shred of his pants leg; it now crouched quietly, eating it.

"It will convey your scent and composition to its nest-mates," said the commander. "This is necessary. Otherwise you would be classed as an invader, and the Swarm's warrior caste would kill you at once."

Afriel relaxed quickly and pressed his hand against the puncture wound to stop the bleeding. He hoped that none of the Investors had noticed his reflexive action. It would not mesh well with his story of being a harmless researcher.

"We will reopen the airlock soon," the commander said phlegmatically, leaning back on her thick reptilian tail. The symbiote continued to munch the shred of cloth. Afriel studied the creature's neckless segmented head. It had a mouth and nostrils; it had bulbous atrophied eyes on stalks; there were hinged slats that might be radio receivers, and two parallel ridges of clumped wriggling antennae, sprouting among three chitinous plates. Their function was unknown to him.

The airlock door opened. A rush of dense, smoky aroma entered the departure cabin. It seemed to bother the half-dozen Investors, who left rapidly. "We will return in six hundred and twelve of your days, as by our agreement," the commander said.

"I thank Your Authority," Afriel said.

"Good luck," the commander said in English. Afriel smiled.

The symbiote, with a sinuous wriggle of its segmented body, crept into the airlock. Afriel followed it. The airlock door shut behind them. The creature said nothing to him but continued munching loudly. The second door opened, and the symbiote sprang through it, into a wide, round stone tunnel. It disappeared at once into the gloom.

Afriel put his sunglasses into a pocket of his jacket and pulled out a pair of infrared goggles. He strapped them to his head and stepped out of the airlock. The artificial gravity vanished, replaced by the almost imperceptible gravity of the Swarm's asteroid nest. Afriel smiled, comfortable for the first time in weeks. Most of his adult life had been spent in freefall, in the Shapers' colonies in the Rings of Saturn.

Squatting in a dark cavity in the side of the tunnel was a disk-headed furred animal the size of an elephant. It was clearly visible in the infrared of its own body heat. Afriel could hear it breathing. It waited patiently until Afriel had launched himself past it, deeper into the tunnel. Then it took its place in the end of the tunnel, puffing itself up with air until its swollen head securely plugged the exit into space. Its multiple legs sank firmly into sockets in the walls.

The Investors' ship had left. Afriel remained here, inside one of the millions of planetoids that circled the giant star Betelgeuse in a girdling ring with almost five times the mass of Jupiter. As a source of potential wealth it dwarfed the entire solar system, and it belonged, more or less, to the Swarm. At least, no other race had challenged them for it within the memory of the Investors.

Afriel peered up the corridor. It seemed deserted, and without other bodies to cast infrared heat, he could not see very far. Kicking against the wall, he floated hesitantly down the corridor.

He heard a human voice. "Dr. Afriel!"

"Dr. Mirny!" he called out. "This way!"

He first saw a pair of young symbiotes scuttling toward him, the tips of their clawed feet barely touching the walls. Behind them came a woman wearing goggles like his own. She was young, and attractive in the trim, anonymous way of the genetically reshaped.

She screeched something at the symbiotes in their own language, and they halted, waiting. She coasted forward, and Afriel caught her arm, expertly stopping their momentum.

"You didn't bring any luggage?" she said anxiously.

He shook his head. "We got your warning before I was sent out. I have only the clothes I'm wearing and a few items in my pockets."

She looked at him critically. "Is that what people are wearing in the Rings these days? Things have changed more than I thought."

Afriel glanced at his brocaded coat and laughed. "It's a matter of policy. The Investors are always readier to talk to a human who looks ready to do business on a large scale. All the Shapers' representatives dress like this these days. We've stolen a jump on the Mechanists; they still dress in those coveralls."

He hesitated, not wanting to offend her. Galina Mirny's intelligence was rated at almost two hundred. Men and women that bright were sometimes flighty and unstable, likely to retreat into private fantasy worlds or become enmeshed in strange and impenetrable webs of plotting and rationalization. High intelligence was the strategy the Shapers had chosen in the struggle for cultural dominance, and they were obliged to stick to it, despite its occasional disadvantages. They had tried breeding the Superbright—those with quotients over two hundred—but so many had defected from the Shapers' colonies that the faction had stopped producing them.

"You wonder about my own clothing," Mirny said.

"It certainly has the appeal of novelty," Afriel said with a smile.

"It was woven from the fibers of a pupa's cocoon," she said. "My original wardrobe was eaten by a scavenger symbiote during the troubles last year. I usually go nude, but I didn't want to offend you by too great a show of intimacy."

Afriel shrugged. "I often go nude myself, I never had much use for clothes except for pockets. I have a few tools on my person, but most are of little importance. We're Shapers, our tools are here." He tapped his head. "If you can show me a safe place to put my clothes . . ."

She shook her head. It was impossible to see her eyes for the goggles, which made her expression hard to read. "You've made your first mistake, Doctor. There are no places of our own here. It was the same mistake the Mechanist agents made, the same one that almost killed me as well. There is no concept of privacy or property here. This is the Nest. If you seize any part of it for yourself—to store equipment, to sleep in, whatever—then you become an intruder, an enemy. The two Mechanists—a man and a woman—tried to secure an empty chamber for their computer lab. Warriors broke down their door and devoured them. Scavengers ate their equipment, glass, metal, and all."

Afriel smiled coldly. "It must have cost them a fortune to ship all that material here."

Mirny shrugged. "They're wealthier than we are. Their machines, their mining. They meant to kill me, I think. Surreptitiously, so the warriors wouldn't be upset by a show of violence. They had a computer that was learning the language of the springtails faster than I could."

"But you survived," Afriel pointed out. "And your tapes and reports—especially the early ones, when you still had most of your equipment—were of tremendous interest. The Council is behind you all the way. You've become quite a celebrity in the Rings, during your absence."

"Yes, I expected as much," she said.

Afriel was nonplused. "If I found any deficiency in them," he said carefully, "it was in my own field, alien linguistics." He waved vaguely at the two symbiotes who accompanied her. "I assume you've made great progress in communicating with the symbiotes, since they seem to do all the talking for the Nest."

She looked at him with an unreadable expression and shrugged. "There are at least fifteen different kinds of symbiotes here. Those that accompany me are called the springtails, and they speak only for themselves. They are savages, Doctor, who received attention from the Investors only because they can still talk. They were a spacefaring race once, but they've forgotten it. They discovered the Nest and they were absorbed, they became parasites." She tapped one of them on the head. "I tamed these two because I learned to steal and beg food better than they can. They stay with me now and protect me from the larger ones. They are jealous, you know. They have only been with the Nest for perhaps ten thousand years and are still uncertain of their position. They still think, and wonder sometimes. After ten thousand years there is still a little of that left to them."

"Savages," Afriel said. "I can well believe that. One of them bit me while I was still aboard the starship. He left a lot to be desired as an ambassador."

"Yes, I warned him you were coming," said Mirny. "He didn't much like the idea, but I was able to bribe him with food. . . . I hope he didn't hurt you badly."

"A scratch," Afriel said. "I assume there's no chance of infection."

"I doubt it very much. Unless you brought your own bacteria with you."

"Hardly likely," Afriel said, offended. "I have no bacteria. And I wouldn't have brought microorganisms to an alien culture anyway."

Mirny looked away. "I thought you might have some of the special genetically altered ones. . . . I think we can go now. The springtail will have spread your scent by mouth-touching in the subsidiary chamber, ahead of us. It will be spread throughout the Nest in a few hours. Once it reaches the Queen, it will spread very quickly."

She jammed her feet against the hard shell of one of the young springtails and launched herself down the hall. Afriel followed her. The air was warm and he was beginning to sweat under his elaborate clothing, but his antiseptic sweat was odorless.

They exited into a vast chamber dug from the living rock. It was arched and oblong, eighty meters long and about twenty in diameter. It swarmed with members of the Nest.

There were hundreds of them. Most of them were workers, eighty-legged and furred, the size of Great Danes. Here and there were members of the warrior caste, horse-sized furry monsters with heavy fanged heads the size and shape of overstuffed chairs.

A few meters away, two workers were carrying a member of the sensor caste, a being whose immense flattened head was attached to an atrophied body that was mostly lungs. The sensor had great platelike eyes, and its furred chitin sprouted long coiled antennae that twitched feebly as the workers bore it along. The workers clung to the hollowed rock of the chamber walls with hooked and suckered feet.

A paddle-limbed monster with a hairless, faceless head came sculling past them, through the warm reeking air. The front of its head was a nightmare of sharp grinding jaws and blunt armored acid spouts. "A tunneler," Mirny said. "It can take us deeper into the Nest—come with me." She launched herself toward it and took a handhold on its furry, segmented back. Afriel followed her, joined by the two immature springtails, who clung to the thing's hide with their forelimbs. Afriel shuddered at the warm, greasy feel of its rank, damp fur. It continued to scull through the air, its eight fringed paddle feet catching the air like wings.

"There must be thousands of them," Afriel said.

"I said a hundred thousand in my last report, but that was before I had fully explored the Nest. Even now there are long stretches I haven't seen. They must number close to a quarter of a million. This asteroid is about the size of the Mechanists' biggest base—Ceres. It still has rich veins of carbonaceous material. It's far from mined out."

Afriel closed his eyes. If he was to lose his goggles, he would have to feel his way, blind, through these teeming, twitching, wriggling thousands. "The population's still expanding, then?"

"Definitely," she said. "In fact, the colony will launch a mating swarm soon. There are three dozen male and female alates in the chambers near the Queen. Once they're launched, they'll mate and start new Nests. I'll take you to see them presently." She hesitated. "We're entering one of the fungal gardens now."

One of the young springtails quietly shifted position. Grabbing the tunneler's fur with its forelimbs, it began to gnaw on the cuff of Afriel's pants. Afriel kicked it soundly, and it jerked back, retracting its eyestalks.

When he looked up again, he saw that they had entered a second chamber, much larger than the first. The walls around, overhead, and below were buried under an explosive profusion of fungus. The most common types were swollen barrellike domes, multibranched massed thickets, and spaghettilike tangled extrusions that moved very slightly in the faint and odorous breeze. Some of the barrels were surrounded by dim mists of exhaled spores.

"You see those caked-up piles beneath the fungus, its growth medium?" Mirny said.

"Yes."

"I'm not sure whether it is a plant form or just some kind of complex biochemical sludge," she said. "The point is that it grows in sunlight, on the outside of the asteroid. A food source that grows in naked space! Imagine what that would be worth, back in the Rings."

"There aren't words for its value," Afriel said.

"It's inedible by itself," she said. "I tried to eat a very small piece of it once. It was like trying to eat plastic."

"Have you eaten well, generally speaking?"

"Yes. Our biochemistry is quite similar to the Swarm's. The fungus itself is perfectly edible. The regurgitate is more nourishing, though. Internal fermentation in the worker hind-gut adds to its nutritional value."

Afriel stared. "You grow used to it," Mirny said. "Later I'll teach you how to solicit food from the workers. It's a simple matter of reflex tapping—it's not controlled by pheromones, like most of their behavior." She brushed a long lock of clumped and dirty hair from the side of her face. "I hope the pheromonal samples I sent back were worth the cost of transportation."

"Oh, yes," said Ariel. "The chemistry of them was fascinating. We managed to synthesize most of the compounds. I was part of the research team myself." He hesitated. How far did he dare trust her? She had not been told about the experiment he and his superiors had planned. As far as Mirny knew, he was a simple, peaceful researcher, like herself. The Shapers' scientific community was suspicious of the minority involved in military work and espionage.

As an investment in the future, the Shapers had sent researchers to each of the nineteen alien races described to them by the Investors. This had cost the Shaper economy many gigawatts of precious energy and tons of rare metals and isotopes. In most cases, only two or three researchers could be sent; in seven cases, only one. For the Swarm, Galina Mirny had been chosen. She had gone peacefully, trusting in her intelligence and her good intentions to keep her alive and sane. Those who had sent her had not known whether her findings would be of any use or importance. They had only known that it was imperative that she be sent, even alone, even ill-equipped, before some other faction sent their own people and possibly discovered some technique or fact of overwhelming importance. And Dr. Mirny had indeed discovered such a situation. It had made her mission into a matter of Ring security. That was why Afriel had come.

"You synthesized the compounds?" she said. "Why?"

Afriel smiled disarmingly. "Just to prove to ourselves that we could do it, perhaps."

She shook her head. "No mind-games, Dr. Afriel, please. I came this far partly to escape from such things. Tell me the truth."

Afriel stared at her, regretting that the goggles meant he could not meet her eyes. "Very well," he said. "You should know, then, that I have been ordered by the Ring Council to carry out an experiment that may endanger both our lives."

Mirny was silent for a moment. "You're from Security, then?"

"My rank is captain."

"I knew it. . . . I knew it when those two Mechanists arrived. They were so polite, and so suspicious—I think they would have killed me at once if they hadn't hoped to bribe or torture some secret out of me. They scared the life out of me, Captain Afriel. . . . You scare me, too."

"We live in a frightening world, Doctor. It's a matter of faction security."

"Everything's a matter of faction security with your lot," she said. "I shouldn't take you any farther, or show you anything more. This Nest, these creatures—they're not *intelligent,* Captain. They can't think, they can't learn. They're innocent, primordially innocent. They have no knowledge of good and evil. They have no knowledge of *anything.* The last thing they need is to become pawns in a power struggle within some other race, light-years away."

The tunneler had turned into an exit from the fungal chambers and was paddling slowly along in the warm darkness. A group of creatures like gray, flattened basketballs floated by from the opposite direction. One of them settled on Afriel's sleeve, clinging with frail whiplike tentacles. Afriel brushed it gently away, and it broke loose, emitting a stream of foul reddish droplets.

"Naturally I agree with you in principle, Doctor," Afriel said smoothly. "But consider these Mechanists. Some of their extreme factions are already more than half machine. Do you expect humanitarian motives from them? They're cold, Doctor—cold and soulless creatures who can cut a living man or woman to bits and never feel their pain. Most of the other factions hate us. They call us racist supermen. Would you rather that one of these cults do what we must do, and use the results against us?"

"This is double-talk." She looked away. All around them workers laden down with fungus, their jaws full and guts stuffed with it, were spreading out into the Nest, scuttling alongside them or disappearing into branch tunnels departing in every direction, including straight up and straight down. Afriel saw a creature much like a worker, but with only six legs, scuttle past in the opposite direction, overhead. It was a parasite mimic. How long, he wondered, did it take a creature to evolve to look like that?

"It's no wonder that we've had so many defectors, back in the Rings," she said sadly. "If humanity is so stupid as to work itself into a corner like you describe, then it's better to have nothing to do with them. Better to live alone. Better not to help the madness spread."

"That kind of talk will only get us killed," Afriel said. "We owe an allegiance to the faction that produced us."

"Tell me truly, Captain," she said. "Haven't you ever felt the urge to leave everything—everyone—all your duties and constraints, and just go somewhere to think it all out? Your whole world, and your part in it? We're trained so hard, from childhood, and so much is demanded from us. Don't you think it's made us lose sight of our goals, somehow?"

"We live in space," Afriel said flatly. "Space is an unnatural environment, and it takes an unnatural effort from unnatural people to prosper there. Our minds are our tools, and philosophy has to come second. Naturally I've felt those urges you mention. They're just another threat to guard against. I believe in an ordered society. Technology has unleashed tremendous forces that are ripping society apart. Some one faction must arise from the struggle and integrate things. We Shapers have the wisdom and restraint to do it humanely. That's why I do the work I do." He hesitated. "I don't expect to see our day of triumph. I expect to die in some brush-fire conflict, or through assassination. It's enough that I can foresee that day."

"But the arrogance of it, Captain!" she said suddenly. "The arrogance of your little life and its little sacrifice! Consider the Swarm, if you really want your humane and perfect order. Here it is! Where it's always warm and dark, and it smells good, and food is easy to get, and everything is endlessly and perfectly recycled. The only resources that are ever lost are the bodies of the mating swarms, and a little air. A Nest like this one could last unchanged for hundreds of thousands of years. Hundreds . . . of thousands . . . of years. Who, or what, will remember us and our stupid faction in even a thousand years?"

Afriel shook his head. "That's not a valid comparison. There is no such long view for us. In another thousand years we'll be machines, or gods." He felt the top of his head; his velvet cap was gone. No doubt something was eating it by now.

The tunneler took them deeper into the asteroid's honeycombed free-fall maze. They saw the pupal chambers, where pallid larvae twitched in swaddled silk; the main fungal gardens; the graveyard pits, where winged workers beat ceaselessly at the soupy air, feverishly hot from the heat of decomposition. Corrosive black fungus ate the bodies of the dead into coarse black powder, carried off by blackened workers themselves three-quarters dead.

Later they left the tunneler and floated on by themselves. The woman moved with the ease of long habit; Afriel followed her, colliding bruisingly with squeaking workers. There were thousands of them, clinging to ceiling, walls, and floor, clustering and scurrying at every conceivable angle.

Later still they visited the chamber of the winged princes and princesses, an echoing round vault where creatures forty meters long hung crooked-legged in midair. Their bodies were segmented and metallic, with organic rocket nozzles on their thoraxes, where wings might have been. Folded along their sleek backs were radar antennae on long sweeping booms. They looked more like interplanetary probes under construction than anything biological. Workers fed them ceaselessly. Their bulging spiracled abdomens were full of compressed oxygen.

Mirny begged a large chunk of fungus from a passing worker, deftly tapping its antennae and provoking a reflex action. She handed most of the fungus to the two springtails, which devoured it greedily and looked expectantly for more.

Afriel tucked his legs into a free-fall lotus position and began chewing with determination on the leathery fungus. It was tough, but tasted good, like smoked meat—a delicacy he had tasted only once. The smell of smoke meant disaster in a Shaper's colony.

Mirny maintained a stony silence. "Food's no problem," Afriel said. "Where do we sleep?"

She shrugged. "Anywhere . . . there are unused niches and tunnels here and there. I suppose you'll want to see the Queen's chamber next."

"By all means."

"I'll have to get more fungus. The warriors are on guard there and have to be bribed with food."

She gathered an armful of fungus from another worker in the endless stream, and they moved on. Afriel, already totally lost, was further confused in the maze of chambers and tunnels. At last they exited into an immense lightless cavern, bright with infrared heat from the Queen's monstrous body. It was the colony's central factory. The fact that it was made of warm and pulpy flesh did not conceal its essentially industrial nature. Tons of predigested fungal pap went into the slick blind jaws at one end. The rounded billows of soft flesh digested and processed it, squirming, sucking, and undulating, with loud machinelike churnings and gurglings. Out of the other end came an endless conveyorlike blobbed stream of eggs, each one packed in a thick hormonal paste of lubrication. The workers avidly licked the eggs clean and bore them off to nurseries. Each egg was the size of a man's torso.

The process went on and on. There was no day or night here in the lightless center of the asteroid. There was no remnant of a diurnal rhythm in the genes of these creatures. The flow of production was as constant and even as the working of an automated mine.

"This is why I'm here," Afriel murmured in awe. "Just look at this, Doctor. The Mechanists have cybernetic mining machinery that is generations ahead of ours. But here—in the bowels of this nameless little world, is a genetic technology that feeds itself, maintains itself, runs itself, efficiently, endlessly, mindlessly. It's the perfect organic tool. The faction that could use these tireless workers could make itself an industrial titan. And our knowledge of biochemistry is unsurpassed. We Shapers are just the ones to do it."

"How do you propose to do that?" Mirny asked with open skepticism. "You would have to ship a fertilized queen all the way to the solar system. We could scarcely afford that, even if the Investors would let us, which they wouldn't."

"I don't need an entire Nest," Afriel said patiently. "I only need the genetic information from one egg. Our laboratories back in the Rings could clone endless numbers of workers."

"But the workers are useless without the Nest's pheromones. They need chemical cues to trigger their behavior modes."

"Exactly," Afriel said. "As it so happens, I possess those pheromones, synthesized and concentrated. What I must do now is test them. I must prove that I can use them to make the workers do what I choose. Once

I've proven it's possible, I'm authorized to smuggle the genetic information necessary back to the Rings. The Investors won't approve. There are, of course, moral questions involved, and the Investors are not genetically advanced. But we can win their approval back with the profits we make. Best of all, we can beat the Mechanists at their own game."

"You've carried the pheromones here?" Mirny said. "Didn't the Investors suspect something when they found them?"

"Now it's you who has made an error," Afriel said calmly. "You assume that the Investors are infallible. You are wrong. A race without curiosity will never explore every possibility, the way we Shapers did." Afriel pulled up his pants cuff and extended his right leg. "Consider this varicose vein along my shin. Circulatory problems of this sort are common among those who spend a lot of time in free-fall. This vein, however, has been blocked artificially and treated to reduce osmosis. Within the vein are ten separate colonies of genetically altered bacteria, each one specially bred to produce a different Swarm pheromone."

He smiled. "The Investors searched me very thoroughly, including X-rays. But the vein appears normal to X-rays, and the bacteria are trapped within compartments in the vein. They are indetectable. I have a small medical kit on my person. It includes a syringe. We can use it to extract the pheromones and test them. When the tests are finished—and I feel sure they will be successful, in fact I've staked my career on it—we can empty the vein and all its compartments. The bacteria will die on contact with air. We can refill the vein with the yolk from a developing embryo. The cells may survive during the trip back, but even if they die, they can't rot inside my body. They'll never come in contact with any agent of decay. Back in the Rings, we can learn to activate and suppress different genes to produce the different castes, just as is done in nature. We'll have millions of workers, armies of warriors if need be, perhaps even organic rocketships, grown from altered alates. If this works, who do you think will remember me then, eh? Me and my arrogant little life and little sacrifice?"

She stared at him; even the bulky goggles could not hide her new respect and even fear. "You really mean to do it, then."

"I made the sacrifice of my time and energy. I expect results, Doctor."

"But it's kidnapping. You're talking about breeding a slave race."

Afriel shrugged, with contempt. "You're juggling words, Doctor. I'll cause this colony no harm. I may steal some of its workers' labor while they obey my own chemical orders, but that tiny theft won't be missed. I admit to the murder of one egg, but that is no more a crime than a human abortion. Can the theft of one strand of genetic material be called 'kidnapping'? I think not. As for the scandalous idea of a slave race—I reject it out of hand. These creatures are genetic robots. They will no more be slaves than are laser drills or cargo tankers. At the very worst, they will be our domestic animals."

Mirny considered the issue. It did not take her long. "It's true. It's not as if a common worker will be staring at the stars, pining for its freedom. They're just brainless neuters."

"Exactly, Doctor."

"They simply work. Whether they work for us or the Swarm makes no difference to them."

"I see that you've seized on the beauty of the idea."

"And if it worked," Mirny said, "If it worked, our faction would profit astronomically."

Afriel smiled genuinely, unaware of the chilling sarcasm of his expression. "And the personal profit, Doctor . . . the valuable expertise of the first to exploit the technique." He spoke gently, quietly. "Ever see a nitrogen snowfall on Titan? I think a habitat of one's own there—larger, much larger than anything possible before . . . A genuine city, Galina, a place where a man can scrap the rules and discipline that madden him . . ."

"Now it's you who are talking defection, Captain-Doctor."

Afriel was silent for a moment, then smiled with an effort. "Now you've ruined my perfect reverie," he said. "Besides, what I was describing was the well-earned retirement of a wealthy man, not some self-indulgent hermitage . . . there's a clear difference." He hesitated. "In any case, may I conclude that you're with me in this project?"

She laughed and touched his arm. There was something uncanny about the small sound of her laugh, drowned by a great organic rumble from the Queen's monstrous intestines. . . . "Do you expect me to resist your arguments for two long years? Better that I give in now and save us friction."

"Yes."

"After all, you won't do any harm to the Nest. They'll never know anything has happened. And if their genetic line is successfully reproduced back home, there'll never be any reason for humanity to bother them again."

"True enough," said Afriel, though in the back of his mind he instantly thought of the fabulous wealth of Betelgeuse's asteroid system. A day would come, inevitably, when humanity would move to the stars en masse, in earnest. It would be well to know the ins and outs of every race that might become a rival.

"I'll help you as best I can," she said. There was a moment's silence. "Have you seen enough of this area?"

"Yes." They left the Queen's chamber.

"I didn't think I'd like you at first," she said candidly. "I think I like you better now. You seem to have a sense of humor that most Security people lack."

"It's not a sense of humor," Afriel said sadly. "It's a sense of irony disguised as one."

There were no days in the unending stream of hours that followed. There were only ragged periods of sleep, apart at first, later together, as they held each other in free-fall. The sexual feel of skin and body became an anchor to their common humanity, a divided, frayed humanity so many light-years away that the concept no longer had any meaning. Life in the warm and swarming tunnels was the here and now; the two of them were like germs in a bloodstream, moving ceaselessly with the pulsing ebb and flow. Hours stretched into months, and time itself grew meaningless.

The pheromonal tests were complex, but not impossibly difficult. The first of the ten pheromones was a simple grouping stimulus, causing large numbers of workers to gather as the chemical was spread from palp to palp. The workers then waited for further instructions; if none were forthcoming, they dispersed. To work effectively, the pheromones had to be given in a mix, or series, like computer commands; number one, grouping, for instance, together with the third pheromone, a transferral order, which caused the workers to empty any given chamber and move its effects to another. The ninth pheromone had the best industrial possibilities; it was a building order, causing the workers to gather tunnelers and dredgers and set them to work. Others were annoying; the tenth pheromone provoked grooming behavior, and the workers' furry palps stripped off the remaining rags of Afiel's clothing. The eighth pheromone sent the workers off to harvest material on the asteroid's surface, and in their eagerness to observe its effects the two explorers were almost trapped and swept off into space.

The two of them no longer feared the warrior caste. They knew that a dose of the sixth pheromone would send them scurrying off to defend the eggs, just as it sent the workers to tend them. Mirny and Afriel took advantage of this and secured their own chambers, dug by chemically hijacked workers and defended by a hijacked airlock guardian. They had their own fungal gardens to refresh the air, stocked with the fungus they liked best, and digested by a worker they kept drugged for their own food use. From constant stuffing and lack of exercise the worker had swollen up into its replete form and hung from one wall like a monstrous grape.

Afriel was tired. He had been without sleep recently for a long time;

how long, he didn't know. His body rhythm had not adjusted as well as Mirny's, and he was prone to fits of depression and irritability that he had to repress with an effort. "The Investors will be back sometime," he said. "Sometime soon."

Mirny was indifferent. "The Investors," she said, and followed the remark with something in the language of the springtails, which he didn't catch. Despite his linguistic training, Afriel had never caught up with her in her use of the springtails' grating jargon. His training was almost a liability; the springtail language had decayed so much that it was a pidgin tongue, without rules or regularity. He knew enough to give them simple orders, and with his partial control of the warriors he had the power to back it up. The springtails were afraid of him, and the two juveniles that Mirny had tamed had developed into fat, overgrown tyrants that freely terrorized their elders. Afriel had been too busy to seriously study the springtails or the other symbiotes. There were too many practical matters at hand.

"If they come too soon, I won't be able to finish my latest study," she said in English.

Afriel pulled off his infrared goggles and knotted them tightly around his neck. "There's a limit, Galina," he said, yawning. "You can only memorize so much data without equipment. We'll just have to wait quietly until we can get back. I hope the Investors aren't shocked when they see me. I lost a fortune with those clothes."

"It's been so dull since the mating swarm was launched. If it weren't for the new growth in the alates' chamber, I'd be bored to death." She pushed greasy hair from her face with both hands. "Are you going to sleep?"

"Yes, if I can."

"You won't come with me? I keep telling you that this new growth is important. I think it's a new caste. It's definitely not an alate. It has eyes like an alate, but it's clinging to the wall."

"It's probably not a Swarm member at all, then," he said tiredly, humoring her. "It's probably a parasite, an alate mimic. Go on and see it, if you want to. I'll be here waiting for you."

He heard her leave. Without his infrareds on, the darkness was still not quite total; there was a very faint luminosity from the steaming, growing fungus in the chamber beyond. The stuffed worker replete moved slightly on the wall, rustling and gurgling. He fell asleep.

When he awoke, Mirny had not yet returned. He was not alarmed. First, he visited the original airlock tunnel, where the Investors had first left him. It was irrational—the Investors always fulfilled their contracts—

but he feared that they would arrive someday, become impatient, and leave without him. The Investors would have to wait, of course. Mirny could keep them occupied in the short time it would take him to hurry to the nursery and rob a developing egg of its living cells. It was best that the egg be as fresh as possible.

Later he ate. He was munching fungus in one of the anterior chambers when Mirny's two tamed springtails found him. "What do you want?" he asked in their language.

"Food-giver no good," the larger one screeched, waving its forelegs in brainless agitation. "Not work, not sleep."

"Not move," the second one said. It added hopefully, "Eat it now?"

Afriel gave them some of his food. They ate it, seemingly more out of habit than real appetite, which alarmed him. "Take me to her," he told them.

The two springtails scurried off; he followed them easily, adroitly dodging and weaving through the crowds of workers. They led him several miles through the network, to the alates' chamber. There they stopped, confused. "Gone," the large one said.

The chamber was empty. Afriel had never seen it empty before, and it was very unusual for the Swarm to waste so much space. He felt dread. "Follow the food-giver," he said. "Follow the smell."

The springtails snuffled without much enthusiasm along one wall; they knew he had no food and were reluctant to do anything without an immediate reward. At last one of them picked up the scent, or pretended to, and followed it up across the ceiling and into the mouth of a tunnel.

It was hard for Afriel to see much in the abandoned chamber; there was not enough infrared heat. He leapt upward after the springtail.

He heard the roar of a warrior and the springtail's choked-off screech. It came flying from the tunnel's mouth, a spray of clotted fluid bursting from its ruptured head. It tumbled end over end until it hit the far wall with a flaccid crunch. It was already dead.

The second springtail fled at once, screeching with grief and terror. Afriel landed on the lip of the tunnel, sinking into a crouch as his legs soaked up momentum. He could smell the acrid stench of the warrior's anger, a pheromone so thick that even a human could scent it. Dozens of other warriors would group here within minutes, or seconds. Behind the enraged warrior he could hear workers and tunnelers shifting and cementing rock.

He might be able to control one enraged warrior, but never two, or twenty. He launched himself from the chamber wall and out an exit.

He searched for the other springtail—he felt sure he could recognize it, since it was so much bigger than the others—but he could not find it. With its keen sense of smell, it could easily avoid him if it wanted to.

Mirny did not return. Uncountable hours passed. He slept again. He returned to the slates' chamber; there were warriors on guard there, warriors that were not interested in food and brandished their immense serrated fangs when he approached. They looked ready to rip him apart; the faint reek of aggressive pheromones hung about the place like a fog. He did not see any symbiotes of any kind on the warriors' bodies. There was one species, a thing like a huge tick, that clung only to warriors, but even the ticks were gone.

He returned to his chambers to wait and think. Mirny's body was not in the garbage pits. Of course, it was possible that something else might have eaten her. Should he extract the remaining pheromone from the spaces in his vein and try to break into the alates' chamber? He suspected that Mirny, or whatever was left of her, was somewhere in the tunnel where the springtail had been killed. He had never explored that tunnel himself. There were thousands of tunnels he had never explored.

He felt paralyzed by indecision and fear. If he was quiet, if he did nothing, the Investors might arrive at any moment. He could tell the Ring Council anything he wanted about Mirny's death; if he had the genetics with him, no one would quibble. He did not love her; he respected her, but not enough to give up his life, or his faction's investment. He had not thought of the Ring Council in a long time, and the thought sobered him. He would have to explain his decision. . . .

He was still in a brown study when he heard a whoosh of air as his living airlock deflated itself. Three warriors had come for him. There was no reek of anger about them. They moved slowly and carefully. He knew better than to try to resist. One of them seized him gently in its massive jaws and carried him off.

It took him to the slates' chamber and into the guarded tunnel. A new, large chamber had been excavated at the end of the tunnel. It was filled almost to bursting by a black-spattered white mass of flesh. In the center of the soft speckled mass were a mouth and two damp, shining eyes, on stalks. Long tendrils like conduits dangled, writhing, from a clumped ridge above the eyes. The tendrils ended in pink, fleshy plug-like clumps.

One of the tendrils had been thrust through Mirny's skull. Her body hung in midair, limp as wax. Her eyes were open, but blind.

Another tendril was plugged into the braincase of a mutated worker. The worker still had the pallid tinge of a larva; it was shrunken and deformed, and its mouth had the wrinkled look of a human mouth. There was a blob like a tongue in the mouth, and white ridges like human teeth. It had no eyes.

It spoke with Mirny's voice. "Captain-Doctor Afriel . . ."

"Galina . . ."

"I have no such name. You may address me as Swarm."

Afriel vomited. The central mass was an immense head. Its brain almost filled the room.

It waited politely until Afriel had finished.

"I find myself awakened again," Swarm said dreamily. "I am pleased to see that there is no major emergency to concern me. Instead it is a threat that has become almost routine." It hesitated delicately. Mirny's body moved slightly in midair; her breathing was inhumanly regular. The eyes opened and closed. "Another young race."

"What are you?"

"I am the Swarm. That is, I am one of its castes. I am a tool, an adaptation; my specialty is intelligence. I am not often needed. It is good to be needed again."

"Have you been here all along? Why didn't you greet us? We'd have dealt with you. We meant no harm."

The wet mouth on the end of the plug made laughing sounds. "Like yourself, I enjoy irony," it said. "It is a pretty trap you have found yourself in, Captain-Doctor. You meant to make the Swarm work for you and your race. You meant to breed us and study us and use us. It is an excellent plan, but one we hit upon long before your race evolved."

Stung by panic, Afriel's mind raced frantically. "You're an intelligent being," he said. "There's no reason to do us any harm. Let us talk together. We can help you."

"Yes," Swarm agreed. "You will be helpful. Your companion's memories tell me that this is one of those uncomfortable periods when galactic intelligence is rife. Intelligence is a great bother. It makes all kinds of trouble for us."

"What do you mean?"

"You are a young race and lay great stock by your own cleverness," Swarm said. "As usual, you fail to see that intelligence is not a survival trait."

Afriel wiped sweat from his face. "We've done well," he said. "We came to you, and peacefully. You didn't come to us."

"I refer to exactly that," Swarm said urbanely. "This urge to expand, to explore, to develop, is just what will make you extinct. You naively suppose that you can continue to feed your curiosity indefinitely. It is an old story, pursued by countless races before you. Within a thousand years—perhaps a little longer—your species will vanish."

"You intend to destroy us, then? I warn you it will not be an easy task—"

"Again you miss the point. Knowledge is power! Do you suppose that fragile little form of yours—your primitive legs, your ludicrous arms and hands, your tiny, scarcely wrinkled brain—can *contain* all that power? Certainly not! Already your race is flying to pieces under the impact of your own expertise. The original human form is becoming obsolete. Your own genes have been altered, and you, Captain-Doctor, are a crude experiment. In a hundred years you will be a relic. In a thousand years you will not even be a memory. Your race will go the same way as a thousand others."

"And what way is that?"

"I do not know." The thing on the end of the Swarm's arm made a chuckling sound. "They have passed beyond my ken. They have all discovered something, learned something, that has caused them to transcend my understanding. It may be that they even transcend *being*. At any rate, I cannot sense their presence anywhere. They seem to do nothing, they seem to interfere in nothing; for all intents and purposes, they seem to be dead. Vanished. They may have become gods, or ghosts. In either case, I have no wish to join them."

"So then—so then you have—"

"Intelligence is very much a two-edged sword, Captain-Doctor. It is useful only up to a point. It interferes with the business of living. Life, and intelligence, do not mix very well. They are not at all closely related, as you childishly assume."

"But you, then—you are a rational being—"

"I am a tool, as I said." The mutated device on the end of its arm made a sighing noise. "When you began your pheromonal experiments, the chemical imbalance became apparent to the Queen. It triggered certain genetic patterns within her body, and I was reborn. Chemical sabotage is a problem that can best be dealt with by intelligence. I am a brain replete, you see, specially designed to be far more intelligent than any young race. Within three days I was fully self-conscious. Within five days I had deciphered these markings on my body. They are the genetically encoded history of my race . . . within five days and two hours I recognized the problem at hand and knew what to do. I am now doing it. I am six days old."

"What is it you intend to do?"

"Your race is a very vigorous one. I expect it to be here, competing with us, within five hundred years. Perhaps much sooner. It will be necessary to make a thorough study of such a rival. I invite you to join our community on a permanent basis."

"What do you mean?"

"I invite you to become a symbiote. I have here a male and a female, whose genes are altered and therefore without defects. You make a perfect breeding pair. It will save me a great deal of trouble with cloning."

"You think I'll betray my race and deliver a slave species into your hands?"

"Your choice is simple, Captain-Doctor. Remain an intelligent, living being, or become a mindless puppet, like your partner. I have taken over all the functions of her nervous system; I can do the same to you."

"I can kill myself."

"That might be troublesome, because it would make me resort to developing a cloning technology. Technology, though I am capable of it, is painful to me. I am a genetic artifact; there are fail-safes within me that prevent me from taking over the Nest for my own uses. That would mean falling into the same trap of progress as other intelligent races. For similar reasons, my life span is limited. I will live for only a thousand years, until your race's brief flurry of energy is over and peace resumes once more."

"Only a thousand years?" Afriel laughed bitterly. "What then? You kill off my descendants, I assume, having no further use for them."

"No. We have not killed any of the fifteen other races we have taken for defensive study. It has not been necessary. Consider that small scavenger floating by your head, Captain-Doctor, that is feeding on your vomit. Five hundred million years ago its ancestors made the galaxy tremble. When they attacked us, we unleashed their own kind upon them. Of course, we altered our side, so that they were smarter, tougher, and, naturally, totally loyal to us. Our Nests were the only world they knew, and they fought with a valor and inventiveness we never could have matched. . . . Should your race arrive to exploit us, we will naturally do the same."

"We humans are different."

"Of course."

"A thousand years here won't change us. You will die and our descendants will take over this Nest. We'll be running things, despite you, in a few generations. The darkness won't make any difference."

"Certainly not. You don't need eyes here. You don't need anything."

"You'll allow me to stay alive? To teach them anything I want?"

"Certainly, Captain-Doctor. We are doing you a favor, in all truth. In a thousand years your descendants here will be the only remnants of the human race. We are generous with our immortality; we will take it upon ourselves to preserve you."

"You're wrong, Swarm. You're wrong about intelligence, and you're wrong about everything else. Maybe other races would crumble into parasitism, but we humans are different."

"Certainly. You'll do it, then?"

"Yes. I accept your challenge. And I will defeat you."

"Splendid. When the Investors return here, the springtails will say that they have killed you, and will tell them to never return. They will not return. The humans should be the next to arrive."

"If I don't defeat you, they will."

"Perhaps." Again it sighed. "I'm glad I don't have to absorb you. I would have missed your conversation."

Michael Swanwick

THE BLIND MINOTAUR

One of the most popular and respected of all the new writers who entered the field in the eighties, Michael Swanwick made his debut in 1980 with two strong and compelling stories, "The Feast of St. Janis" and "Ginnungagap," both of which were Nebula Award finalists that year, and which were both selected either for a Best of the Year anthology or for that year's annual Nebula Awards volume—as auspicious a debut as anyone has ever made.

He stayed in the public eye, and on major award ballots, throughout the rest of the eighties with intense and powerful stories such as "Mummer Kiss," "The Man Who Met Picasso," "Trojan Horse," "Dogfight" (written with William Gibson), "Covenant of Souls," "The Dragon Line," "Snow Angels," "A Midwinter's Tale," and many others—all of which earned him a reputation as one of the most powerful and consistently inventive short-story writers of his generation. Nor has his output of short fiction slackened noticeably in the nineties, in spite of a burgeoning career as a novelist, and recent years have seen the appearance of major Swanwick stories such as "The Edge of the World," "The Changeling's Tale," "Griffin's Egg," "Cold Iron," and "The Dead," which was on the final Hugo ballot in 1997 and is on the Nebula final ballot as I type these words in 1998; he remains one of SF's most prolific writers at short lengths, writing and selling seven or eight new stories in 1997 alone, for instance. By the end of the nineties, his short work had won him several *Asimov's* Reader's Awards, a Sturgeon Award, and the World Fantasy Award (for his bizarre and powerful after-death fantasy "Radio Waves").

At first, his reputation as a novelist lagged behind his reputation as a short-story writer, with his first novel, *In the Drift*—published in 1985 as part of Terry Carr's resurrected Ace Specials line, along with first novels by William Gibson, Kim Stanley Robinson, and Lucius Shepard—largely ignored by critics, and panned by some of them. His second novel, though, the critically acclaimed *Vacuum Flowers,* caused a stir, and his third and perhaps best-known novel, *Stations of the Tide,* established him firmly among the vanguard of the hot novelists of the nineties; *Stations of the Tide* won him a Nebula Award in 1991. His next novel, *The Iron Dragon's Daughter,* a finalist for both the World Fantasy Award *and* the Arthur C. Clarke Award (a unique distinction!), explored new literary territory on the ambiguous borderland of science fiction and fantasy, and has been hailed by some critics as the first example of an as yet still nascent subgenre called "Hard Fantasy" (sort of a mix between the Dickensian sensibilities of "steampunk," high-tech science fiction, and traditional Tolkienesque fantasy). His most recent novel, *Jack Faust,* a sly reworking of the Faust legend that explores the unexpected impact of technology on society, blurs genre boundaries even more, and has garnered rave reviews from nearly every source from *The Washington Post* to *Interzone.*

Swanwick is a chameleonic writer, difficult to pin down as belonging firmly to one aesthetic camp or another. He writes everything from hard-science to Tolkienesque fantasy, but puts his own unique spin on everything he writes. During the eighties, during the Cyberpunk Wars, most critics included him in the cyberpunk camp, although the cyberpunks themselves never really seemed to accept him as One of Them, in spite of his famous collaboration with Gibson on "Dogfight," and in spite of the fact that *Vacuum Flowers* is usually listed as part of the cyberpunk canon by outside critics who are not themselves cyberpunks—and indeed, whatever it was that he was doing that made him appear to some to be writing cyberpunk, he was doing it on his own in stories such as "Ginnungagap"—published in 1980—before the cyberpunks themselves were publishing much that looked like cyberpunk, certainly long before the publication of Gibson's *Neuromancer* in 1985. So it was a matter of convergent evolution rather than influence, I think, as far as Swanwick's relationship to cyberpunk is concerned. Similarly, Swanwick is now widely accepted as having written one of the two main "Post-Cyberpunk" works with *Stations of the Tide* (the other is Neal Stephenson's *Snow Crash*)—but if you go back and look at works such as "Ginnungagap," you can see that he was writing stuff that resembles "post-cyberpunk" *then,* before the Cyberpunk Revolution had even really gotten under way. So pinning him down to one of these categories is rather like trying to catch fog in a net.

This is not to say that there are no influences on his work. I think that recognizable traces of the influence of the work of writers such as Jack Vance, Cordwainer Smith, Brian W. Aldiss, Philip K. Dick, Howard Waldrop, Walter M. Miller, Jr., and Roger Zelazny can be seen in Swanwick's work, and perhaps even the influence of John Varley, although Varley started publishing only a few years before Swanwick himself did (influences turn over *fast* in the science fiction field!). Another big influence on Swanwick, as on Sterling, was clearly the early work of Samuel R. Delany; this is especially clear with the evocative story that follows, "The Blind Minotaur," which rings with strong echoes of Delany's work, particularly *The Einstein Intersection*—although, as always, Swanwick has changed the melody line and the orchestration and the fingering to make the material uniquely his own.

Although Swanwick's last few novels seem to be taking him away from science fiction (and perhaps even away from conventional genre fantasy toward that vaguely defined territory that might be described as "American Magic Realism," or perhaps "Postmodernism"), I don't think he will ever entirely abandon the field (at least some of his short fiction remains solidly centered here, and, in fact, falls under the heading of "hard science"), and it will be interesting to see what he produces the next time he returns to it at novel length. Like Sterling, Swanwick is also still a young writer by any reasonable definition, and I have a feeling he will be one of the factors shaping the evolution of SF well into the next century.

Swanwick's other books include the novella-length *Griffin's Egg,* one of the most brilliant and compelling of modern-day Moon-colony stories. His short fiction has been assembled in *Gravity's Angels* and in a collection of his collaborative short work with other writers, *Slow Dancing Through Time.* His most recent books are a collection of critical articles, *The Postmodern Archipelago,* and a new collection, *A Geography of Unknown Lands.* Swanwick lives in Philadelphia with his wife, Marianne Porter, and their son, Sean.

It was late afternoon when the blinded Minotaur was led through the waterfront. He cried openly, without shame, lost in his helplessness.

The sun cast shadows as crisp and black as an obsidian knife. Fisherfolk looked up from their nets or down from the masts of their boats, mild sympathy in their eyes. But not pity; memory of the Wars was too fresh for that. They were mortals and not subject to his tragedy.

Longshoremen stepped aside, fell silent at the passing of this shaggy bull-headed man. Offworld tourists stared down from their restaurant balconies at the serenely grave little girl who led him by the hand.

His sight stolen away, a new universe of sound, scent, and touch crashed about the Minotaur. It threatened to swallow him up, to drown him in its complexity.

There was the sea, always the sea, its endless crash and whisper on the beach, and quicker irregular slap at the docks. The sting of salt on his tongue. His callused feet fell clumsily on slick cobblestones, and one staggered briefly into a shallow puddle, muddy at its bottom, heated piss-warm by the sun.

He smelled creosoted pilings, exhaust fumes from the great shuttles bellowing skyward from the Starport, a horse sweating as it clipclopped by, pulling a groaning cart that reeked of the day's catch. From a nearby garage, there was the *snap* and ozone crackle of an arc-welding rig. Fishmongers' cries and the creaking of pitch-stained tackle overlaid rattling silverware from the terrace cafés, and fan-vented air rich with stews and squid and grease. And, of course, the flowers the little girl—was she really his daughter?—held crushed to her body with one arm. And the feel of her small hand in his, now going slightly slippery with sweat, but still cool, yes, and innocent.

This was not the replacement world spoken of and promised to the blind. It was chaotic and bewildering, rich and contradictory in detail. The universe had grown huge and infinitely complex with the dying of the light, and had made him small and helpless in the process.

The girl led him away from the sea, to the shabby buildings near the city's hot center. They passed through an alleyway between crumbling sheetbrick walls—he felt their roughness graze lightly against his flanks—and through a small yard ripe with fermenting garbage. The Minotaur stumbled down three wooden steps and into a room that smelled of sad, ancient paint. The floor was slightly gritty underfoot.

She walked him around the room. "This was built by expatriate Centaurimen," she explained. "So it's laid out around the kitchen in the center, *my* space to this side"—she let go of him briefly, rattled a vase, adding her flowers to those he could smell as already present, took his hand again—"and yours to this side."

He let himself be sat down on a pile of blankets, buried his head in his arms while she puttered about, raising a wall, laying out a mat for him under the window. "We'll get you some cleaner bedding in the morning, okay?" she said. He did not answer. She touched a cheek with her tiny hand, moved away.

"Wait," he said. She turned, he could hear her. "What—what is your name?"

"Yarrow," she said.

He nodded, curled about himself.

By the time evening had taken the edge off the day, the Minotaur was cried out. He stirred himself enough to strip off his loincloth and pull a sheet over himself, and tried to sleep.

Through the open window the night city was coming to life. The Minotaur shifted as his sharp ears picked up drunken laughter, the calls of streetwalkers, the wail of jazz saxophone from a folk club, and music of a more contemporary nature, hot and sinful.

His cock moved softly against one thigh, and he tossed and turned, kicking off the crisp sheet (it was linen, and it had to be white), agonized, remembering similar nights when he was whole.

The city called to him to come out and prowl, to seek out women who were heavy and slatternly in the *tavernas,* cool and crisp in white, gazing out from the balconies of their husbands' *casavillas.* But the power was gone from him. He was no longer that creature that, strong and confident, had quested into the night. He twisted and turned in the warm summer air.

One hand moved down his body, closed about his cock. The other joined it. Squeezing tight his useless eyes, he conjured up women who had opened to him, coral-pink and warm, as beautiful as orchids. Tears rolled down his shaggy cheeks.

He came with great snorts and grunts.

Later he dreamed of being in a cool white *casavilla* by the sea, salt breeze wafting in through open windowspaces. He knelt at the edge of a bed and wonderingly lifted the sheet—it billowed slightly as he did—

from his sleeping lover. Crouching before her naked body, his face was gentle as he marveled at her beauty.

It was strange to wake to darkness. For a time he was not even certain he *was* awake. And this was a problem, this unsureness, that would haunt him for all his life. Today, though, it was comforting to think it all a dream, and he wrapped the uncertainty around himself like a cloak.

The Minotaur found a crank recessed into the floor, and lowered the wall. He groped his way to the kitchen, and sat by the cookfire.

"You jerked off three times last night," Yarrow said. "I could hear you." He imagined that her small eyes were staring at him accusingly. But apparently not, for she took something from the fire, set it before him, and innocently asked, "When are you going to get your eyes replaced?"

The Minotaur felt around for the platedough, and broke off a bit from the edge. "Immortals don't heal," he mumbled. He dipped the fragment into the paste she ladled onto the dough's center, stirred it about, let the bread drop. "New eyes would be rejected, didn't your mother tell you that?"

She chose not to answer. "While you were asleep, a newshawk came snooping around with that damned machine grafted to his shoulder. I told him he had the wrong place." Then, harshly, urgently, "Why won't they just leave you *alone?*"

"I'm an immortal," he said. "I'm not supposed to be left alone." Her mother really *should* have explained all this, if she was really what she claimed to be. Perhaps she wasn't; he would have sworn he had never bedded another of his kind, had in fact scrupulously avoided doing so. It was part of the plan of evasion that had served him well for so many years, and yet ended with his best friend dying in the sand at his feet.

Yarrow put some fragment of foodstuff in his hand, and he automatically placed it in his mouth. It was gummy and tasteless, and took forever to disappear. She was silent until he swallowed, and then asked, "Am I going to die?"

"What kind of question is that?" he asked angrily.

"Well, I just thought—my mother said that I was an immortal like her, and I thought . . . Isn't an immortal supposed to be someone who never dies?"

He opened his mouth to tell her that her mother should be hung up by her hair   and in that instant the day became inarguably, inalterably real. He wanted to cling to the possibility that it was all a dream for just a while longer, but it was gone. Wearily, he said, "Yarrow, I want you to go get me a robe. And a stick"—he raised a hand above his head—"so high. Got that?"

"Yes, but—"

"Go!"

A glimmering of his old presence must have still clung to him, for the child obeyed. The Minotaur leaned back, and—involuntarily—was flooded with memories.

He was young, less than a year released from the crèche by gracious permission of the ministries of the Lords. The Wars were less than a year away, but the Lords had no way of knowing that—the cabarets were full, and the starlanes swollen with the fruits of a thousand remarkable harvests. There had never been such a rich or peaceful time.

The Minotaur was drunk, and at the end of his nightly round of bars. He had wound up in a *taverna* where the patrons removed their shirts to dance and sweet-smelling sweat glistened on their chests. The music was fast and heavy and sensual. Women eyed him as he entered, but could not politely approach him, for he still wore his blouse.

He bellied up to the bar, and ordered a jarful of the local beer. The barkeep frowned when he did not volunteer money, but that was his right as an immortal.

Crouched on their ledge above the bar, the musicians were playing hot and furious. The Minotaur paid them no attention. Nor did he notice the Harlequin, limbs long and impossibly thin, among them, nor how the Harlequin's eyes followed his every move.

The Minotaur was entranced by the variety of women in the crowd, the differences in their movements. He had been told that one could judge how well a woman made love by how well she danced, but it seemed to him, watching, that there must be a thousand styles of making love, and he would be hard put to choose among them, were the choice his.

One woman with flashing brown feet stared at him, ignoring her partner. She wore a bright red skirt that flew up to her knees when she whirled around, and her nipples were hard and black. He smiled in friendly cognizance of her glance, and her answering grin was a razor-crisp flash of teeth that took his breath away, a predatory look that said: *You're* mine *tonight.*

Laughing, the Minotaur flung his shirt into the air. He plunged into the dancers and stooped at the woman's feet. In a rush he lifted her into the air, away from her partner, one hand closing about her ankles, the other supporting her by the small of her back. She gasped, and laughed, and balanced herself, so that he could remove one hand and lift her still higher, poised with one foot on the palm of his great hairy hand.

"I am strong!" he shouted. The crowd—even the woman's abandoned partner—cheered and stamped their feet. The Harlequin stepped up the band. The woman lifted her skirts and kicked her free leg high, so that one toe grazed the ceiling beams. She threw her head back and laughed.

The dancers swirled about them. For a single pure moment, life was bright and full and good. And then . . .

A touch of cool air passed through the crowd. A chance movement, a subtle shifting of colors, brought the Minotaur's eyes around to the door. A flash of artificial streetlight dazzled and was gone as the door swung shut.

The Woman entered.

She was masked in silver filigree, and her breasts were covered. Red silk washed from shoulder to ankle, now caressing a thigh, now releasing it. Her eyes were a drenched, saturated green. She walked with a sure and sensual authority, knowing the dancers would part for her. No one could mistake her for a mortal.

The Minotaur was stunned. Chemical and hormonal balances shifted in preparation for the bonding to come. Nerveless, his arms fell to his sides. With an angry squawk, the woman he had hoisted into the air leapt, arms waving, to avoid falling. The Minotaur did not notice. He stepped forward, eyes wide and helpless, toward the immortal.

The silver mask headed straight for him. Green eyes mocked, challenged, promised.

Behind him, unnoticed, the Harlequin slipped to the floor. He wrapped long fingers lovingly around a length of granite pipe, and brought it down, fast and surprisingly forcefully, into the back of the Minotaur's neck.

Bright shards of light flashed before the Minotaur's eyes. The dance floor washed out and faded to white. He fell.

At the Minotaur's direction, Yarrow led him out to the bluffs on the outskirts of the city. There was a plaza there, overlooking the ocean. He sent the child away.

Though his every bone protested, he slowly crouched, and then carefully spread out a small white cloth before him. He was a beggar now.

Salt breezes gusted up from the ocean, and he could feel the cobalt sky above, and the cool cumulus clouds that raced across the sun. There were few passersby, mostly dirt farmers who were not likely to be generous. Perhaps once an hour a small ceramic coin fell on his cloth.

But that was how he preferred it. He had no interest in money, was a beggar only because his being demanded a role to play. He had come to remember, and to prepare himself for death by saying farewell to the things of life.

Times had changed. There was a stone altar set in the center of this very plaza where children had been sacrificed. He had seen it himself, the young ones taken from their homes or schooling-places by random selection of the cruel Lords. They had shrieked like stuck pigs when the gold-masked priests raised their bronze knives to the noonday sun. The crowds were always large at these events. The Minotaur was never able to determine whether the parents were present or not.

This was only one of the means the Lords had of reminding their subjects that to be human was often painful or tragic.

"Let's not sleep the day away, eh? Time to start rehearsing."

The Minotaur awoke to find himself sprawled on the wooden floor of a small caravan. The Harlequin, sitting cross-legged beside him, thrust a jar of wine into his hand.

Groggily, the Minotaur focused his eyes on the Harlequin. He reached for the man's neck, only to find one hand taken up by the wine-jar. He squinted at it. The day was already hot, and his throat as dry as the Severna. His body trembled from the aftereffects of its raging hormonal storm. He lifted the wine to his lips.

Chemical imbalances shifted, found a new equilibrium.

"Bravo!" The Harlequin hauled the Minotaur to his feet, clapped him on the back. "We'll be famous friends, you and I. With luck, we may even keep each other alive, eh?"

It was a new idea to the Minotaur, and a disquieting, perhaps even blasphemous, one. But he grinned shyly, and dipped his head. He *liked* the little fellow. "Sure," he said.

The sun was setting. The Minotaur felt the coolness coming off of the sea, heard the people scurrying to their homes. He carefully tied the ceramics into his cloth, and knotted it onto his belt. He stood, leaning wearily on his staff. Yarrow had not yet come for him, and he was glad; he hoped she had gone off on her own, forgotten him, left him behind forever. But the city's rhythms demanded that he leave, though he had nowhere to go, and he obeyed.

He went down into the city, taking the turns by random whim. He could not be said to be lost, for one place was as good as another to him.

It was by mistake, though, that he found himself in a building whose doors were never shut, whose windows were not shuttered. He had entered, thinking the way yet another alley. No doors barred progress down halls or into rooms. Still, he felt closed in. The corridors smelled—there was the male stench and the female, and intermingled with them, almost overpowering, an insect smell, the odor of something large and larval.

He stopped. Things stirred about him. There was the pat of bare feet on stone, the slow breathing of many people, and—again—a sluggish movement of creatures larger than anything smelling thus should be. People were gathering; twelve, eighteen, more. They surrounded him. He could tell they were all naked, for there was not the whisper of cloth on cloth. Some walked as if they had almost forgotten how. In the distance, he thought he could hear someone crawling.

"*Who are you?*" Panic touched him lightly; sourceless, pure.

"Whrrarrwr," began one of the people. He stopped, swallowed, tried again. "Why are you in the Hive?" His voice sounded forced, as if he were unused to speech. "Why are you here? You are a creature of the old days, of the Lords. This is no place for you."

"I took a wrong turn," the Minotaur said simply. Then, when there was no reply, "Who are you people? Why do you cohabit with insects?"

Someone coughed and sputtered and made hacking noises. A second joined her, making the same sounds, and then others, and yet more. With a start, the Minotaur realized they were laughing at him. "Is it religious or political?" he demanded. "Are you seeking transcendence?"

"We are trying to become victims," the speaker said. "Does that help you understand?" He was growing angry. "How can we explain ourselves to you, Old Fossil? You never performed a free act in your life."

Some whim, then, of internal chemistry made him want these strangers, these creatures, to understand him. It was the same compulsion that had forced him to empty himself to the newshawks before Yarrow appeared to lead him out of the arena.

"I had a friend, another immortal," the Minotaur said. "Together, we cheated the patterning instinct by making our own pattern, a safe, strong one, we were like"—his short, powerful fingers joined, closing around the staff, intermeshing—"like *this,* you see. And it worked, it worked for years. It was only when our predators worked *within* the patterns we formed that we were destroyed." The words gushed out, and he trembled as the hormones that might give him the power to explain *almost* keyed in.

But the communards did not want to understand. They closed in on him, their laughter growing sharper, with more of a bark, more of a bite to it. Their feeble footsteps paltered closer, and behind them the chitinous whine grew louder, was joined by that of more insects, and more, until all the world seemed to buzz. The Minotaur flinched back.

And then they seemed to hesitate in confusion. They milled about uncertainly for a moment, then parted, and quick, small footsteps passed through them, ran to his side. A cool, smooth hand took his.

"Come home with me," Yarrow said. And he followed.

He dreamed of the arena that night, of the hot white sands underfoot that drank up his friend's blood. The Harlequin's body lay limp at his feet, and the bronze knife was as heavy as guilt in his hands.

It was as if his eyes had opened, as if he were seeing clearly for the first time. He stared around the encircling bleachers, and every detail burned into his brain.

The people were graceful and well-dressed; they might almost have been the old Lords, deposed these many years ago in violent public revulsion. The Woman sat ringside. Her silver mask rested lightly on the lip of the white limestone wall, beside a small bowl of orange ices. She held a spoon in her hand, cocked lightly upward.

The Minotaur stared into her blazing green eyes, and read in them a fierce triumph, an obscene gloating, a very specific and direct lust. She had hunted him out of hiding, stripped him of his protection, and chivvied him into the open. She had forced him to rise to his destiny. To enter the arena.

Try though he might, the Minotaur could not awaken. If he had not known all this to be a dream, he would have gone mad.

Waking, he found himself already dressed, the last bit of breakfast in his hand. He dropped it, unnerved by this transition. Yarrow was cleaning the kitchen walls, singing an almost tuneless made-up song under her breath.

"Why aren't you out being taught?" he demanded, trying to cover over his unease with words. She stopped singing. "Well? Answer me!"

"I'm learning from you," she said quietly.

"Learning what?" She did not answer. "Learning how to tend to a cripple? Or maybe how a beggar lives? Hey? What could you possibly learn from me?"

She flung a wet cloth to the floor. "You won't tell me anything," she cried. "I ask you and you won't tell me."

"Go home to your mother," he said.

"I can't." She was crying now. "She told me to take care of you. She said not to come back until my task was done."

The Minotaur bowed his head. Whatever else she might or might not be, the mother had the casual arrogance of an immortal. Even he could be surprised by it.

"Why won't you tell me anything?"

"Go and fetch me my stick."

Bleak plains dominated the southern continent, and the Minotaur came to know them well. The carnival worked the long route, the four-year circuit of small towns running up the coast and then inland to the fringes of the Severna Desert.

Creeping across the plains, the carnival was small, never more than eight hands of wagons and often fewer. But when the paper lanterns had been lit, the fairway laid out, the holographic-woven canvases blazing neon-bright, they created a fantasy city that stretched to the edge of forever.

The Minotaur grunted. Muscles glistening, he bent the metal bar across his chest. Portions of the audience were breathing heavily.

It was the last performance of the evening. Outside the hot, crowded tent, the fairgoers were thinning, growing quieter. The Minotaur was clad only in a stained white loincloth. He liked to have room to sweat.

Applause. He threw the bar to the stage and shouted: "My last stunt! I'll need five volunteers!" He chose the four heaviest, and the one who blushed most prettily. Her he helped up on the stage, and set in the middle of the lifting bench, a pair of hefty *bouergers* to either side.

The Minotaur slid his head under the bench. His face emerged between the young woman's legs, and she shrieked and drew them up on the bench. The audience howled. He rolled his eyes, flared his nostrils. And indeed, she did have a pleasant scent.

He dug into the stage with naked toes, placed his hands carefully. With a grunt, the Minotaur lifted the bench a handsbreath off the floor. It wobbled slightly, and he shifted his weight in compensation. A surge— he was crouching.

Sweat poured down the Minotaur's face, and ran in rivulets from his armpits. The tent was saturated with the sweet smell, redolent with his pheromones. He felt a light touch on his muzzle. The woman on the bench had reached down to caress his nose with quick, shy fingertips. The Minotaur quirked a half-grin on one side of his mouth.

By the tent flap, the Harlequin lounged on a wooden crate, cleaning his toenails with a knife. They had a date with a sculptor in town after the show.

The Minotaur awoke suddenly, reached out and touched the cloth laid out before him. There was nothing on it, though he distinctly remembered having heard ceramics fall earlier. He swept his hands in great arcs in the dust, finding nothing.

Snickers and derisive jeers sounded from the stone in the plaza's center. Small feet scurried away—children running to deliver the swag to their masters. "Little snots," the Minotaur grumbled. They were an ever-present nuisance, like sparrows. He fell back into his daydreaming.

The sculptor had had stone jugs of wine sent up. By orgy's end they were empty, and the women lay languid on the sheets of their couches. They all stared upward, watching the bright explosions in space, like slow-blossoming flowers. "What do they hope to accomplish, these rebels?" the Minotaur asked wonderingly. "I can see no pattern to their destruction."

"Why should a man like you—a *real* man—look any higher than his waist?" the sculptor asked coarsely. He laid a hand on the Minotaur's knee. His lady of the moment laughed throatily, reached back over her head to caress his beard.

"I'd just like to know."

The Harlequin had been perched on the wall. He leapt down now, and tossed the Minotaur his clothes. "Time we went home," he said.

The streets were dark and still, but there were people in the shadows, silently watching the skies. The sidestreet cabarets were uncharacteristically crowded. They stopped in several on their way back to the carnival.

The Minotaur was never sure at exactly what point they picked up the woman with skin the color of orange brick. She was from offworld, she said, and needed a place to hide. Her hands were callused and beautiful from work. The Minotaur liked her strong, simple dignity.

Back at the carnival, the Harlequin offered their wagon, and the woman refused. The Minotaur said that he would sleep on the ground, it didn't bother him, and she changed her mind.

Still, he was not surprised when, sometime later, she joined him under the wagon.

The sun hot on his forehead, the Minotaur again dreamed of the arena. He did not relive the murder—that memory had been driven from his mind, irretrievably burned away, even in dream. But he remembered the killing rage that drove the knife upward, the insane fury that propelled his hand. And afterward he stood staring into the Woman's eyes.

Her eyes were as green as oceans, and as complex, but easy to read for all that. The lusts and rages, and fears and evil, grasping desire that had brought them all to this point—they were all there, and they were . . . insignificant. For the true poisoned knowledge was that she was lost in her own chemical-hormonal storm, her body trembling almost imperceptibly, all-but-invisible flecks of foam on her lips. She had run not only him, but herself as well, to the blind end of a tangled and malignant fate. She was as much a puppet as he or the Harlequin.

There, on the burning sands, he tore out his eyes.

The newshawks vaulted the fence to get at him. His drama completed, he was fair game. They probed, scanned, recorded—prodded to find the least significant detail of a story that might be told over campfires a thousand years hence, in theatrical productions on worlds not yet discovered, in uninvented media, or possibly merely remembered in times of stress. Trying to get in on a story that might have meaning to the human race as it grew away from its homeworld, forgot its origins, expanded and evolved and changed in ways that could not be predicted or prepared for.

They questioned the Minotaur for hot grueling hours. The corpse of his friend began to rot, or perhaps that was only olfactory hallucination, a side effect of his mind telling his body that it had no further purpose. He felt dizzy and without hope, and he *could not* express his grief, *could not* cry, *could not* scream or rage or refuse their questions or even move away until they were done with him.

And then a cool hand slipped into his, and tugged him away. A small voice said, "Come home, Papa," and he went.

Yarrow was screaming. The Minotaur awoke suddenly, on his feet and slashing his stick before him, back and forth in pure undirected reaction. "Yarrow?" he cried.

"No!" the child shrieked in anger and panic. Someone slapped her face so hard she fell. The sound echoed from the building walls. "Fuckpigs!" she swore from the ground.

The Minotaur lurched toward her, and someone tripped him up, so that he crashed onto the road. He heard a rib crack. He felt a trickle of blood from one nostril. And he heard laughter, the laughter of madwomen. And under that he heard the creaking of leather harness, the whirring of tiny pumps, the metal snicks of complex machinery.

There was no name for them, these madwomen, though their vice was not rare. They pumped themselves full of the hormone drugs that had once been the exclusive tools of the Lords, but they used them randomly, to no purpose. Perhaps—the Minotaur could not imagine, did not care—they enjoyed the jolts of power and importance, of sheer godlike caprice.

He was on his feet. The insane ones—there were three, he could tell by their sick laughter—ignored him. "What are you doing?" he cried. "Why are you doing it?" They were dancing, arms linked, about the huddled child. She was breathing shallowly, like a hypnotized animal.

"Why?" asked the one. "Why do you ask why?" and convulsed in giggles.

"We are all frogs!" laughed the second.

Yarrow lay quietly now, intimidated not so much by the women's hyperadrenal strength as by the pattern of victim laid out for her. There were microtraces of hormones in the air, leaks from the chemical pumps.

"She has interesting glands," said the third. "We can put their secretions to good use."

The Minotaur roared and rushed forward. They yanked the stick from his hand and broke it over his head. He fell against the altar stone, hard, nearly stunning himself.

"We need to use that stone," said a madwoman. And when he did not move away, said, "Well, we'll wait."

But again the Minotaur forced himself to stand. He stepped atop the stone. Something profound was happening deep within him, something beyond his understanding. Chemical keys were locking into place, hormones shifting into balance. Out of nowhere his head was filled with eloquence.

"Citizens!" he cried. He could hear the people at their windows, in their doorways, watching and listening, though with no great interest. They had not interfered to save Yarrow. The Lords would have interfered, and human society was still in reaction to the rule of the Lords. "Awake! Your freedom is being stolen from you!"

A lizard, startled, ran over the Minotaur's foot, as quick and soft as a shiver. The words poured from him in a cold fever, and he could hear the householders straighten, lean forward, step hesitantly out onto the cobblestones. "No one is above you now," he shouted. "But I still see the dead hands of the Lords on your shoulders."

That got to them—he could smell their anger. His throat was dry, but he dared not spare the time to cough. His head was light, and a cool breeze stirred his curls. He spoke, but did not listen to the words.

Yarrow was lost, somewhere on the plaza. As he spoke, the Minotaur listened for her, sniffed the air, felt for vibrations through the stone—and could not find her. "Inaction is a greater tyrant than error ever was!" he cried, listening to heads nodding agreement with the old familiar homily. He could hear the frantic hopping motions the madwomen made, forward and back again, baffled and half-fascinated by the hormones he was generating, by the cadences and odd rhythms of his words.

The speech was a compulsion, and the Minotaur paid it no more mind than he did to the sliding of muscles under skin that went into his gestures, some wide and sweeping, others short and blunt. A whiff of girlish scent finally located Yarrow, not two arm's lengths away, but he could not go to her. The words would not release him, not until he had spoken them all.

And when, finally, he lowered his arms, the plaza was filled with people, and the madwomen's harnesses had been ripped from them, the drug pumps smashed underfoot, their necks snapped quickly and without malice.

He turned to Yarrow, offered his hand. "Come," he said. "It's time to go home."

The Minotaur lay belly-down on the earth under the wagon. He stared down his muzzle at a slice of early-morning sky framed by two wheel spokes. The clouds of energy were still slowly dissipating. "I'd love to go out there," he said. "To see other worlds."

The orange-skinned woman scratched him above the ears, at the base of his small ivory horns. Her hands were strong and sure. "They couldn't refuse you passage. What's stopping you?"

He nodded upward. "He gets sick—I'd have to go alone."

A triceratops beetle crept laboriously past his nose. He exhaled sharply, trying to turn it over, failed. "You two are inseparable, aren't you?" the woman asked.

The beetle was getting away. He snorted sharply again, twice. "I guess."

"Won't he be upset that I chose you over him?"

It took the Minotaur a moment to puzzle out her meaning. "Ah! You mean—I see. Good joke, very good joke!" He laughed without taking his eyes away from the beetle, watched it escape into the grass. "No, the Harlequin doesn't know that women are important."

It did not take long to gather belongings: the Minotaur had none and Yarrow few. "You can find your mother?" he asked her. They left the door open behind them, an old Centaurimen custom at final partings.

"I can always find my mother," Yarrow said.

"Good." Still, he did not let her go. He led her by the hand back along the waterfront. There, among the sounds and smells, the subliminal tastes and touches that had grown familiar to him, he leaned forward to kiss her tenderly on the cheeks and forehead.

"Good-bye," he said. "I am proud that you are my daughter."

Yarrow did not move away. There was a slight tremble in her voice when she spoke. "You still haven't *told* me anything."

"Ah," the Minotaur said. For a moment he was silent, mentally cataloging what she would need to know. The history of the Lords, to begin with. Their rise to power, how they had shaped and orchestrated the human psyche, and why they thought the human race had to be held back. She needed to know of the crèches, of their bioprogramming chemicals, and of those immortals released from them who had gone on to become legend. She needed to know everything about the immortals, in fact, for the race had been all but exterminated in the Wars. And how the Lords had endured as long as they had. How their enemies had turned their toys against them. All the history of the Wars. It would not be a short telling.

"Sit down," he commanded. There, in the center of the thoroughfare, he sat, and Yarrow followed.

The Minotaur opened his mouth to speak. At the sound of his words, resonant and deep, people would stop to listen for the briefest second . . . for just a moment longer . . . they would sit down in the road. The hormonal combinations that enforced strictest truth before the newshawks were to be in his voice, but combined with the strong eloquence of earlier in the day. He would speak plainly, with a fine parsimony of syllables. He would speak in strict accord with the ancient oratorical traditions. He would speak with tongues of fire.

The waterfront would fill and then overflow as people entered and did not leave, as they joined the widening circle of hushed listeners, as the fisherfolk came up from their boats and down from their masts, the boy prostitutes came out from the brothels, the offworld *tourista* joined with the kitchen help to lean over the edges of their terraces.

In future years this same telling, fined down and refined, elaborated and simplified, would become the epic that was to mark this age—his age—as great for its genesis. But what was to come in just a moment was only a first draft. A prototype. A seed. But it was to be beautiful and moving beyond all possible imagining of its listeners, for it was new, an absolutely new word, a clear new understanding. It was to sum up an age that most people did not realize was over.

"Listen," said the Minotaur.

He spoke.

Vernor Vinge

THE BLABBER

Born in Waukesha, Wisconsin, Vernor Vinge now lives in San Diego, California, where he is an associate professor of math sciences at San Diego State University. He sold his first story, "Apartness," to *New Worlds* in 1965; it immediately attracted a good deal of attention, was picked up for Donald A. Wollheim and Terry Carr's collaborative *World's Best Science Fiction* anthology the following year, and still strikes me as one of the strongest stories of that entire period, holding up well even in comparison with more famous stories also reprinted in that same anthology, such as Clarke's "Sunjammer" or Ellison's " 'Repent, Harlequin!' Said the Ticktockman." Since this impressive debut, he has become a frequent contributor to *Analog;* he has also sold to *Orbit, Far Frontiers, If, Stellar,* and other markets. His novella "True Names" was a finalist for both the Nebula and Hugo awards in 1981, his novel *A Fire Upon the Deep,* one of the most epic and sweeping of modern Space Operas, won him a Hugo Award in 1993, and these days Vinge is regarded as one of the best of the new breed of American "hard science" writers, along with people such as Charles Sheffield and Greg Bear.

Vinge is not a prolific writer, although the few stories he does produce usually have a strong impact on the field. "True Names," for instance, is famous in Internet circles and among computer enthusiasts well outside of the usual limits of the genre, and is cited by some as having been the *real* progenitor of cyberpunk rather than William Gibson's "Burning Chrome" or *Neuromancer.* Certainly, at the very least, it can be said to have prefigured many of the tropes of "cyberspace" before Gibson got there, although it lacks the aesthetic/political "punk" flavor of Gibson's work, as well as the intensely romantic and attractive archetype of the Gibson Hero, an alienated hacker/cowboy who must go down the Mean Streets of the future all alone—both elements which helped to make Gibson's stuff the cult favorite that it became. "True Names" has an even better claim to being one of the first Virtual Reality stories and, as such, the progenitor of a host of "computer gaming/VR" stories that would follow in years to come.

Adventure elements have always been strong in Vinge's work, from "Apartness" through such stories as "The Barbarian Princess," "Gemstone," and "Grimm's World" (later expanded into the novel *Tatja Grimm's World*), on to novels such as *The Witling* and *A Fire Upon the Deep.* Seldom has he—or anybody else—put everything together better, though, than in the fast-paced, colorful, highly inventive novella that follows, "The Blabber." The influence of Robert A. Heinlein is strong and obvious here—in fact, the story is in part an undisguised homage to Heinlein's *The Star Beast,* which novel is specifically invoked in the text—although traces of the influence of Larry Niven, Poul Anderson, Charles Harness, and perhaps Roger Zelazny (whose influence shows up even more clearly in "True Names," I think) can be discerned as well. Although consciously modeled on the plot of *The Star Beast,* Vinge does some exciting new things with this familiar story, as well as a lot of shrewd and radical new thinking about what interstellar societies would *really* be like, thinking that prefigures his well-known speculations about "The Singularity" (the point waiting ahead for us all where technological change speeds up to *such* a degree that society becomes incomprehensible even to the people living in it)—and thinking that would perhaps have as great an impact (although a largely unacknowledged one) on future Space Adventure stories as "True Names" had had on the Virtual Reality tale.

Vinge's other books include the well-received novels *The Peace War* and *Marooned in Realtime,* Hugo finalists, which have been released in an omnibus volume as *Across Realtime,* and two short-story collections, *True Names and Other Dangers,* and *Threats and Other Promises.* He has not published a new novel since *A Fire Upon the Deep,* but the current word is that a new novel entitled *A Deepness in the Sky* will be out soon. His fans wait eagerly for it—as do I.

Some dreams take a long time in dying. Some get a last-minute reprieve . . . and that can be even worse.

It was just over two klicks from the Elvis revival to the center of campus. Hamid Thompson took the long way, across the Barker's stubbly fields and through the Old Subdivision. Certainly the Blabber preferred that route. She raced this way and that across Ham's path, rooting at roach holes, and covertly watching the birds that swooped close on her seductive calls. As usual, her stalking was more for fun than food. When a bird came within striking distance, the Blab's head would flick up, touching the bird with her nose, blasting it with a peal of human laughter. The Blab hadn't taken this way in some time; all the birds in her regular haunts had wised up, and were no fun anymore.

When they reached the rock bluffs behind the subdivision, there weren't any more roach holes, and the birds had become cautious. Now the Blab walked companionably beside him, humming in her own way: scraps of Elvis overlaid with months-old news commentary. She went a minute or two in silence . . . listening? Contrary to what her detractors might say, she could be both awake and silent for hours at a time—but even then Hamid felt an occasional buzzing in his head, or a flash of pain. The Blab's tympana could emit across a two hundred kilohertz band, which meant that most of her mimicry was lost on human ears.

They were at the crest of the bluff. "Sit down, Blab. I want to catch my breath." *And look at the view . . . And decide what in heaven's name I should do with you and with me.*

The bluffs were the highest natural viewpoints in New Michigan province. The flatlands that spread around them were pocked with ponds, laced with creeks and rivers, the best farmland on the continent. From orbit, the original colonists could find no better. Water landings would have been easier, but they wanted the best odds on long-term survival. Thirty klicks away, half hidden by gray mist, Hamid could see the glassy streaks that marked the landing zone. The history books said it took three years to bring down the people and all the salvage from the greatship. Even now the glass was faintly radioactive, one cause for the migration across the isthmus to Westland.

Except for the forest around those landing strips, and the old university town just below the bluff, most everything in this direction was farmland, unending squares of brown and black and gray. The year was well into autumn and the last of the Earth trees had given up their colored leaves. The wind blowing across the plains was chill, leaving a crispness in his nose that promised snow someday soon. Halloween was next week. Halloween indeed. *I wonder if in Man's thirty thousand years, there has ever been a celebration of that holiday like we'll be seeing next week.* Hamid resisted the impulse to look back at Marquette. Ordinarily it was one of his favorite places: the planetary capital, population four hundred thousand, a real city. As a child, visiting Marquette had been like a trip to some far star system. But now reality had come, and the stars were so *close. . . .* Without turning, he knew the position of every one of the Tourist barges. They floated like colored balloons above the city, yet none massed less than a thousand tonnes. And those were their *shuttles.* After the Elvis revival, Halloween was the last big event on the Marquette leg of the Tour. Then they would be off to Westland, for more semi-fraudulent peeks at Americana.

Hamid crunched back in the dry moss that cushioned the rock. "Well, Blabber, what should I do? Should I sell you? We could both make it Out There if I did."

The Blabber's ears perked up. "Talk? Converse? Disgust?" She settled her forty kilo bulk next to him, and nuzzled her head against his chest. The purring from her foretympanum was like some transcendental cat. The sound was pink noise, buzzing through his chest and shaking the rock they sat on. There were few things she enjoyed more than a good talk with a peer. Hamid stroked her black and white pelt. "I said, should I sell you?"

The purring stopped, and for a moment the Blab seemed to give the matter thoughtful consideration. Her head turned this way and that, bobbing—a good imitation of a certain prof at the University. She rolled her big dark eyes at him, "Don't rush me! I'm thinking. I'm thinking." She licked daintily at the sleek fur at the base of her throat. And for all Hamid knew, she really seemed to try to understand . . . and sometimes she almost made sense. Finally she shut her mouth and began talking.

"Should I sell you? Should I sell you?" The intonation was still Hamid's but she wasn't imitating his voice. When they talked like this, she typically sounded like an adult human female (and a very attractive one, Hamid thought). It hadn't always been that way. When she had been a pup and he a little boy, she'd sounded to him like another little boy. The strategy was clear: she understood the type of voice he most likely wanted to hear. Animal cunning? "Well," she continued, "*I* know what I think. Buy, don't sell. And always get the best price you can."

She often came across like that: oracular. But he had known the Blab all his life. The longer her comment, the less she understood it. In this case . . . Ham remembered his finance class. That was before he got his present apartment, and the Blab had hidden under his desk part of the semester. (It had been an exciting semester for all concerned.) "Buy, don't sell." That was a quote, wasn't it, from some nineteenth-century tycoon?

She blabbered on, each sentence having less correlation with the question. After a moment, Hamid grabbed the beast around the neck, laughing and crying at the same time. They wrestled briefly across the rocky slope, Hamid fighting at less than full strength, and the Blab carefully keeping her talons retracted. Abruptly he was on his back and the Blab was standing on his chest. She held his nose between the tips of her long jaws. "Say Uncle! Say Uncle!" she shouted.

The Blabber's teeth stopped a couple of centimeters short of the end of her snout, but the grip was powerful; Hamid surrendered immediately. The Blab jumped off him, chuckling triumph, then grabbed his sleeve to help him up. He stood up, rubbing his nose gingerly. "Okay, monster, let's get going." He waved downhill, toward Ann Arbor Town.

"Ha, ha! For sure. Let's get going!" The Blab danced down the rocks faster than he could hope to go. Yet every few seconds the creature paused an instant, checking that he was still following. Hamid shook his head, and started down. Damned if he was going to break a leg just to keep up with her. Whatever her homeworld, he guessed that winter around Marquette was the time of year most homelike for the Blab. Take her coloring: stark black and white, mixed in wide curves and swirls. He'd seen that pattern in pictures of ice pack seals. When there was snow on the ground, she was practically invisible.

She was fifty meters ahead of him now. From this distance, the Blab could almost pass for a dog, some kind of greyhound maybe. But the paws were too large, and the neck too long. The head looked more like a seal's than a dog's. Of course, she could bark like a dog. But then, she could also sound like a thunderstorm, and make something like human conversation—all at the same time. There was only one of her kind in all Middle America. This last week, he'd come to learn that her kind were almost as rare Out There. A Tourist wanted to buy her . . . and Tourists could pay with coin what Hamid Thompson had sought for more than half his twenty years.

Hamid desperately needed some good advice. It had been five years since he'd asked his father for help; he'd be damned if he did so now. That left the University, and Lazy Larry. . . .

By Middle American standards, Ann Arbor Town was *ancient*. There were older places: out by the landing zone, parts of Old Marquette still stood. School field trips to those ruins were brief—the prefab quonsets were mildly radioactive. And of course there was individual buildings in the present-day capital that went back almost to the beginning. But much of the University in Ann Arbor dated from just after those first permanent structures: the University had been a going concern for 190 years.

Something was up today, and it had nothing to do with Hamid's problems. As they walked into town, a couple of police helicopters swept in from Marquette, began circling the school. On the ground, some of Ham's favorite back ways were blocked off by University safety patrols. No doubt it was Tourist business. He might have to come in through the Main Gate, past the Math Building. *Yuck.* Even after ten years he loathed that place: his years as a supposed prodigy; his parents forcing him into math classes he just wasn't bright enough to handle; the tears and anger at home, till he finally convinced them that he was not the boy they thought.

They walked around the Quad, Hamid oblivious to the graceful buttresses, the ivy that meshed stone walls into the flute trees along the street. That was all familiar . . . what was new was all the Federal cop cars. Clusters of students stood watching the cops, but there was no riot in the air. They just seemed curious. Besides, the Feds had never interfered on campus before.

"Keep quiet, okay?" Hamid muttered.

"Sure, sure." The Blab scrunched her neck back, went into her doggie act. At one time they had been notorious on campus, but he had dropped out that summer, and people had other things on their minds today. They walked through the main gate without comment from students or cops.

The biggest surprise came when they reached Larry's slummy digs at Morale Hall. Morale wasn't old enough to be historic; it was old enough to be in decay. It had been an abortive experiment in brick construction.

The clay had cracked and rotted, leaving gaps for vines and pests. By now it was more a reddish mound of rubble than a habitable structure. This was where the University Administration stuck tenured faculty in greatest disfavor; the Quad's Forgotten Quarter . . . but not today. Today the cop cars were piled two deep in the parking areas, and there were shotgun-toting guards at the entrance!

Hamid walked up the steps. He had a sick feeling that Lazy Larry might be the hardest prof in the world to see today. On the other hand, working with the Tourists meant Hamid saw some of these security people every day.

"Your business, sir?" Unfortunately, the guard was no one he recognized.

"I need to see my advisor . . . Professor Fujiyama." Larry had never been his advisor, but Hamid was looking for advice.

"Um." The cop flicked on his throat mike. Hamid couldn't hear much, but there was something about "that black and white off-planet creature." Over the last twenty years, you'd have to have been living in a cave never to see anything about the Blabber.

A minute passed, and an older officer stepped through the doorway. "Sorry, son, Mr. Fujiyama isn't seeing any students this week. Federal business."

Somewhere a funeral dirge began playing. Hamid tapped the Blab's forepaw with his foot; the music stopped abruptly. "Ma'am, it's not school business." Inspiration struck: why not tell something like the truth? "It's about the Tourists and my Blabber."

The senior cop sighed. "That's what I was afraid you'd say. Okay, come along." As they entered the dark hallway, the Blabber was chuckling triumph. Someday the Blab would play her games with the wrong people and get the crap beat out of her, but apparently today was not that day.

They walked down two flights of stairs. The lighting got even worse, half-dead fluorescents built into the acoustic tiling. In places the wooden stairs sagged elastically under their feet. There were no queues of students squatting before any of the doors, but the cops hadn't cleared out the faculty: Hamid heard loud snoring from one of the offices. The Forgotten Quarter—Morale Hall in particular—was a strange place. The one thing the faculty here had in common was that they had been an unbearable pain in the neck to someone. That meant that both the most incompetent and the most brilliant were jammed into these tiny offices.

Larry's office was in the sub-basement, at the end of a long hall. Two more cops flanked the doorway, but otherwise it was as Hamid remembered it. There was a brass nameplate: "Professor L. Lawrence Fujiyama,

Department of Transhuman Studies." Next to the nameplate, a sign boasted implausible office hours. In the center of the door was the picture of a piglet and the legend: "If a student appears to need help, then appear to give him some."

The police officer stood aside as they reached the door; Hamid was going to have to get in under his own power. Ham gave the door a couple of quick knocks. There was the sound of footsteps, and the door opened a crack. "What's the secret password?" came Larry's voice.

"Professor Fujiyama, I need to talk to—"

"That's not it!" The door was slammed loudly in Hamid's face.

The senior cop put her hand on Hamid's shoulder. "Sorry, son. He's done that to bigger guns than you."

He shrugged off her hand. Sirens sounded from the black and white creature at his feet. Ham shouted over the racket, "Wait! It's me, Hamid Thompson! From your Transhume 201."

The door came open again. Larry stepped out, glanced at the cops, then looked down at the Blabber. "Well, why didn't you say so? Come on in." As Hamid and the Blab scuttled past him, Larry smiled innocently at the Federal officer. "Don't worry, Susie, this is official business."

Fujiyama's office was long and narrow, scarcely an aisle between deep equipment racks. Larry's students (those who dared these depths) doubted the man could have survived on Old Earth before electronic datastorage. There must be tonnes of junk squirreled away on those shelves. The gadgets stuck out this way and that into the aisle. The place was a museum—perhaps literally; one of Larry's specialties was archeology. Most of the machines were dead, but here and there something clicked, something glowed. Some of the gadgets were Rube Goldberg jokes, some were early colonial prototypes . . . and a few were from Out There. Steam and water pipes covered much of the ceiling. The place reminded Hamid of the inside of a submarine.

At the back was Larry's desk. The junk on the table was balanced precariously high: a display flat, a beautiful piece of night black statuary. In Transhume 201, Larry had described his theory of artifact management: Last-In-First-Out, and every year buy a clean bed sheet, date it, and lay it over the previous layer of junk on your desk. Another of Lazy Larry's jokes, most had thought. But there really *was* a bed sheet peeking out from under the mess.

Shadows climbed sharp and deep from the lamp on Larry's desk. The cabinets around him seemed to lean inwards. The open space between them was covered with posters. Those posters were one small reason Larry was down here: ideas to offend every sensible faction of society. A pile of . . . something . . . lay on the visitor's chair. Larry slopped it onto the floor and motioned Hamid to sit.

"Sure, I remember you from Transhume. But why mention that? You own the Blabber. You're Huss Thompson's kid." He settled back in his chair.

I'm not Huss Thompson's kid! Aloud, "Sorry, that was all I could think to say. This is about my Blabber, though. I need some advice."

"Ah!" Fujiyama gave his famous polliwog smile, somehow innocent and predatory at the same time. "You came to the right place. I'm full of it. But I heard you had quit school, gone to work at the Tourist Bureau."

Hamid shrugged, tried not to seem defensive. "Yeah. But I was already a senior, and I know more American Thought and Lit than most graduates . . . and the Tourist caravan will only be here another half year. After that, how long till the next? We're showing them everything I could imagine they'd want to see. In fact, we're showing them more than there really *is* to see. It could be a hundred years before anyone comes down here again."

"Possibly, possibly."

"Anyway, I've learned a lot. I've met almost half the Tourists. But . . ."
There were ten million people living on Middle America. At least a million had a romantic yearning to get Out There. At least ten thousand would give everything they owned to leave the Slow Zone, to live in a civilization that spanned thousands of worlds. For the last ten years, Middle America had known of the Caravan's coming. Hamid had spent most of those years—half his life, all the time since he got out of math—preparing himself with the skills that could buy him a ticket Out.

Thousands of others had worked just as hard. During the last decade, every department of American Thought and Literature on the planet had been jammed to the bursting point. And more had been going on behind the scenes. The government and some large corporations had had secret programs that weren't revealed till just before the Caravan arrived. Dozens of people had bet on the long shots, things that no one else thought the Outsiders might want. Some of those were fools: the world-class athletes, the chess masters. They could never be more than eighth rate in the vast populations of the Beyond. No, to get a ride you needed something that was odd . . . Out There. Besides the Old Earth angle, there weren't many possibilities—though that could be approached in surprising ways: there was Gilli Weinberg, a bright but not brilliant ATL student. When the Caravan reached orbit, she bypassed the Bureau, announced herself to the Tourists as a genuine American cheerleader and premier courtesan. It was a ploy pursued less frankly and less successfully by others of both sexes. In Gilli's case, it had won her a ticket Out. The big laugh was that her sponsor was one of the few non-humans in the Caravan, a Lothlrimarre slug who couldn't survive a second in an oxygen atmosphere.

"I'd say I'm on good terms with three of the Outsiders. But there are at least five Tour Guides that can put on a better show. And you know the Tourists managed to revive four more corpsicles from the original Middle America crew. Those guys are sure to get tickets Out, if they want 'em." Men and women who had been adults on Old Earth, two thousand light-years away and twenty thousand years ago. It was likely that Middle America had no more valuable export this time around. "If they'd just come a few years later, after I graduated . . . maybe made a name for myself."

Larry broke into the self-pitying silence. "You never thought of using the Blabber as your ticket Out?"

"Off and on." Hamid glanced down at the dark bulk that curled around his feet. The Blab was *awfully* quiet.

Larry noticed the look. "Don't worry. She's fooling with some ultrasound imagers I have back there." He gestured at the racks behind Hamid, where a violet glow played hopscotch between unseen gadgets. The boy smiled, "We may have trouble getting her out of here." He had several ultrasonic squawkers around the apartment, but the Blab rarely got to play with high-resolution equipment. "Yeah, right at the beginning, I tried to interest them in the Blab. Said I was her trainer. They lost interest as soon as they saw she couldn't be native to Old Earth. . . . These guys are *freaks,* Professor! You could rain transhuman treasure on 'em, and they'd call it spit! But give 'em Elvis Presley singing Bruce Springsteen and they build you a spaceport on Selene!"

Larry just smiled, the way he did when some student was heading for academic catastrophe. Hamid quieted, "Yeah, I know. There are good reasons for some of the strangeness." Middle America had nothing that would interest anybody rational from Out There. They were stuck nine light-years inside the Slow Zone: commerce was hideously slow and expensive. Middle American technology was obsolete and—considering their location—it could never amount to anything competitive. Hamid's unlucky world had only one thing going for it. It was a direct colony of Old Earth, and one of the first. Their greatship's tragic flight had lasted twenty thousand years, long enough for the Earth to become a legend for much of humankind.

In the Beyond, there were millions of solar systems known to bear human-equivalent intelligences. Most of these could be in more or less instantaneous communication with one another. In that vastness humanity was a speck—perhaps four thousand worlds. Even on those, interest in a first-generation colony within the Slow Zone was near zero. But with four thousand worlds, that was enough: here and there was a rich eccentric, a historical foundation, a religious movement—all strange enough to undertake a twenty-year mission into the Slowness. So Middle America should be glad for these rare mixed nuts. Over the last hundred years there had been occasional traders and a couple of Tourists caravans. That commerce had raised the Middle American standard of living substantially. More important to many—including Hamid—it was almost their only peephole on the universe beyond the Zone. In the last century, two hundred Middle Americans had escaped to the Beyond. The early ones had been government workers, commissioned scientists. The Feds' investment had not paid off: of all those who left, only five had returned. Larry Fujiyama and Hussein Thompson were two of those five.

"Yeah, I guess I knew they'd be fanatics. But most of them aren't even much interested in accuracy. We make a big thing of representing twenty-first-century America. But we both know what that was like: heavy industry moving up to Earth orbit, five hundred million people still crammed into North America. At best what we have here is like mid-twentieth-century America—or even earlier. I've worked very hard to get our past straight. But except for a few guys I really respect, anachronism doesn't seem to bother them. It's like just being here with us is the big thing."

Larry opened his mouth, seemed on the verge of providing some insight. Instead he smiled, shrugged. (One of his many mottos was, "If you didn't figure it out yourself, you don't understand it.")

"So after all these months, where did you dig up the interest in the Blabber?"

"It was the slug, the guy running the Tour. He just mailed me that he had a party who wanted to buy. Normally, this guy haggles. He—wait, you know him pretty well, don't you? Well, he just made a flat offer. A payoff to the Feds, transport for me to Lothlrimarre," that was the nearest civilized system in the Beyond, "and some ftl privileges beyond that."

"And you kiss your pet goodbye?"

"Yeah. I made a case for them needing a handler: me. That's not just bluff, by the way. We've grown up together. I can't imagine the Blab accepting anyone without lots of help from me. But they're not interested. Now, the slug claims no harm is intended her, but . . . do you believe him?"

"Ah, the slug's slime is generally clean. I'm sure he doesn't know of any harm planned . . . and he's straight enough to do at least a little checking. Did he say who wanted to buy?"

"Somebody—something named Ravna&Tines." He passed Larry a flimsy showing the offer. Ravna&Tines had a logo: it looked like a stylized claw. "There's no Tourist registered with that name."

Larry nodded, copied the flimsy to his display flat: "I know. Well, let's see. . . ." He puttered around for a moment. The display was a lecture model, with imaging on both sides. Hamid could see the other was searching internal Federal databases. Larry's eyebrows rose. "Hm*hm!* Ravna&Tines arrived just last week. It's not part of the Caravan at all."

"A solitary trader . . ."

"Not only that. It's been hanging out past the Jovians—at the slug's request. The Federal space net got some pictures." There was a fuzzy image of something long and wasp-waisted, typical of the Outsiders' ramscoop technology. But there were strange fins—almost like the wings on a sailplane. Larry played some algorithmic game with the display and the image sharpened. "Yeah. Look at the aspect ratio on those fins. This guy is carrying high-performance ftl gear. No good down here of course, but hot stuff across an enormous range of environment . . ." he whistled a few bars of Nightmare Waltz. "I think we're looking at a High Trader."

Someone from the Transhuman Spaces.

Almost every university on Middle America had a Department of Transhuman Studies. Since the return of the five, it had been a popular thing to do. Yet most people considered it a joke. Transhume was generally the bastard child of Religious Studies and an Astro or Computer Science department, the dumping ground for quacks and incompetents. Lazy Larry had founded the department at Ann Arbor—and spent much class time eloquently proclaiming its fraudulence. Imagine, trying to study what lay *beyond* the Beyond! Even the Tourists avoided the topic. Transhuman Space existed—perhaps it included most of the universe—but it was a tricky, risky, ambiguous thing. Larry said that its reality drove most of the economics of the Beyond . . . but that all the theories about it were rumors at tenuous second hand. One of his proudest claims was that he raised Transhuman Studies to the level of palm reading.

Yet now . . . apparently a trader had arrived that regularly penetrated the Transhuman Reaches. If the government hadn't sat on the news, it would have eclipsed the Caravan itself. And *this* was what wanted the Blab. Almost involuntarily, he reached down to pet the creature. "Y-you don't think there could really be anybody transhuman on that ship?" An hour ago he had been agonizing about parting with the Blab; that might be nothing compared to what they really faced.

For a moment he thought Larry was going to shrug the question off. But the older man sighed. "If there's anything we've got right it's that no transhuman can think at these depths. Even in the Beyond, they'd die or fragment or maybe cyst. I think this Ravna&Tines must be a human-equivalent intellect, but it could be a lot more dangerous than the average Outsider . . . the tricks it would know, the gadgets it would have." His voice drifted off; he stared at the forty-centimeter statue perched on his desk. It was lustrous green, apparently cut from a flawless block of jade. *Green? Wasn't it black a minute ago?*

Larry's gaze snapped up to Hamid. "Congratulations. Your problem is a lot more interesting than you thought. Why would any Outsider want the Blab, much less a High Trader?"

". . . Well, her kind must be rare. I haven't talked to any Tourist who recognized the race."

Lazy Larry just nodded. Space is deep. The Blab might be from somewhere else in the Slow Zone.

"When she was a pup, lots of people studied her. You saw the articles. She has a brain as big as a chimp, but most of it's tied up in driving her tympana and processing what she hears. One guy said she's the ultimate in verbal orientation—all mouth and no mind."

"Ah! A student!"

Hamid ignored the Larryism. "Watch this." He patted the Blab's shoulder.

She was slow in responding; that ultrasound equipment must be fascinating. Finally she raised her head. "What's up?" The intonation was natural, the voice a young woman's.

"Some people think she's just a parrot. She can play things back better than a high-fidelity recorder. But she also picks up favorite phrases, and uses them in different voices—and almost appropriately. . . . Hey, Blab. What's that?" Hamid pointed at the electric heater that Larry had propped by his feet. The Blab stuck her head around the corner of the desk, saw the cherry glowing coils. This was not the sort of heater Hamid had in his apartment.

"What's that . . . that . . ." The Blab extended her head curiously toward the glow. She was a bit too eager; her nose bumped the heater's safety grid. *"Hot!"* She jumped back, her nose tucked into her neck fur, a foreleg extended toward the heater. "Hot! Hot!" She rolled onto her haunches, and licked tentatively at her nose. "Jeeze!" She gave Hamid a look that was both calculating and reproachful.

"Honest, Blab, I didn't think you would touch it. . . . She's going to get me for this. Her sense of humor extends only as far as ambushes, but it can be pretty intense."

"Yeah. I remember the Zoo Society's documentary on her." Fujiyama was grinning broadly. Hamid had always thought that Larry and the Blab had kindred humors. It even seemed that the animal's cackling became like the old man's after she attended a couple of his lectures.

Larry pulled the heater back and walked around the desk. He hunched down to the Blab's eye level. He was all solicitude now, and a good thing: he was looking into a mouth full of sharp teeth, and somebody was playing the Timebomb Song. After a moment, the music stopped and she shut her mouth. "I can't believe there isn't human equivalence hiding here somewhere. Really. I've had freshmen who did worse at the start of the semester. How could you get this much verbalization without intelligence to benefit from it?" He reached out to rub her shoulders. "You got sore shoulders, Baby? Maybe little hands ready to burst out?"

The Blab cocked her head. "I like to soar."

Hamid had thought long about the Heinlein scenario; the science fiction of Old Earth was a solid part of the ATL curriculum. "If she is still a child, she'll be dead before she grows up. Her bone calcium and muscle strength have deteriorated about as much as you'd expect for a thirty-year-old human."

"Hm. Yeah. And we know she's about your age." Twenty. "I suppose she could be an ego frag. But most of those are brain-damaged transhumans, or obvious constructs." He went back behind his desk, began whistling tunelessly. Hamid twisted uneasily in his chair. He had come for advice. What he got was news that they were in totally over their heads. He shouldn't be surprised; Larry was like that. "What we need is a whole lot more information."

"Well, I suppose I could flat-out demand the slug tell me more. But I don't know how I can force any of the Tourists to help me."

Larry waved breezily. "That's not what I meant. Sure, I'll ask the Lothlrimarre about it. But basically the Tourists are at the end of a nine light-year trip to nowhere. Whatever libraries they have are like what you would take on a South Seas vacation—and out of date, to boot. . . . And of course the federal government of Middle America doesn't know what's coming off to begin with. Heh, heh. Why else do they come to me when they're really desperate? . . . No, what we need is direct access to library resources Out There."

He said it casually, as though he were talking about getting an extra telephone, not solving Middle America's greatest problem. He smiled complacently at Hamid, but the boy refused to be drawn in. Finally, "Haven't you wondered why the campus—Morale Hall, in particular—is crawling with cops?"

"Yeah." *Or I would have, if there weren't lots else on my mind.*

"One of the more serious Tourists—Skandr Vrinimisrinithan—brought along a genuine transhuman artifact. He's been holding back on it for months, hoping he could get what he wants other ways. The Feds—I'll give 'em this—didn't budge. Finally he brought out his secret weapon. It's in this room right now."

Ham's eyes were drawn to the stone carving (now bluish green) that sat on Larry's desk. The old man nodded. "It's an ansible."

"Surely they don't call it that!"

"No. But that's what it is."

"You mean, all these years, it's been a lie that ftl won't work in the Zone?" *You mean I've wasted my life trying to suck up to these Tourists?*

"Not really. Take a look at this thing. See the colors change. I swear its size and mass do, too. This is a real transhuman artifact. Not an intellect, of course, but not some human design manufactured in Transhuman space. Skandr claims—and I believe him—that no other Tourist has one."

A transhuman artifact. Hamid's fascination was tinged with fear. This was something one heard of in the theoretical abstract, in classes run by crackpots.

"Skandr claims this gadget is 'aligned' on the Lothlrimarre commercial outlet. From there we can talk to any registered address in the Beyond."

"Instantaneously." Hamid's voice was very small.

"Near enough. It would take a while to reach the universal event horizon; there are some subtle limitations if you're moving at relativistic speeds."

"And the catch?"

Larry laughed. "Good man. Skandr admits to a few. This thing won't work more than ten light years into the Zone. I'll bet there aren't twenty worlds in the Galaxy that could benefit from it—but we are *definitely* on one. The trick sucks enormous energy. Skandr says that running this baby will dim our sun by half a percent. Not noticeable to the guy in the street, but it could have long-term bad effects." There was a short silence; Larry often did that after a cosmic understatement. "And from your standpoint, Hamid, there's one big drawback. The mean bandwidth of this thing is just under a six bits per minute."

"Huh? Ten seconds to send a single bit?"

"Yup. Skandr left three protocols at the Lothlrimarre end: ASCII, a Hamming map to a subset of English, and an AI scheme that guesses what you'd say if you used more bits. The first is Skandr's idea of a joke, and I wouldn't trust the third more than wishful thinking. But with the Hamming map, you could send a short letter—say five hundred English words—in a day. It's full-duplex, so you might get a good part of your answer in that time. Neat, huh? Anyway, it beats waiting twenty years."

Hamid guessed it would be the biggest news since first contact, one hundred years ago. "So . . . uh, why did they bring it to you, Professor?"

Larry looked around his hole of an office, smiling wider and wider. "Heh, heh. It's true, our illustrious planetary president is one of the five; he's been Out There. But I'm the only one with real friends in the Beyond. You see, the Feds are very leery of this deal. What Skandr wants in return is most of our zygote bank. The Feds banned any private sale of human zygotes. It was a big moral thing: 'no unborn child sold into slavery or worse.' Now they're thinking of doing it themselves. They really *want* this ansible. But what if it's a fake, just linked up to some fancy database on Skandr's ship? Then they've lost some genetic flexibility, and maybe they've sold some kids into hell—and got nothing but a colorful trinket for their grief.

"So. Skandr's loaned them the thing for a week, and the Feds loaned it to me—with close to *carte blanche.* I can call up old friends, exchange filthy jokes, let the sun go dim doing it. After a week, I report on whether the gadget is really talking to the Outside."

Knowing you, "I bet you have your own agenda."

"Sure. Till you showed up the main item was to check out the foundation that sponsors Skandr, see if they're as clean as he says. Now . . . well, your case isn't as important morally, but it's very interesting. There should be time for both. I'll use Skandr's credit to do some netstalking, see if I can find *anyone* who's heard of Blabbers, or this Ravna&Tines."

Hamid didn't have any really close friends. Sometimes he wondered if that was another penalty of his strange upbringing, or if he was just naturally unlikable. He had come to Fujiyama for help all right, but all he'd been expecting was a round of prickly questions that eventually brought *him* to some insight. Now he seemed to be on the receiving end of a favor of world-shaking proportions. It made him suspicious and very grateful all at once. He gabbled some words of abject gratitude.

Larry shrugged. "It's no special problem for me. I'm curious, and this week I've got the *means* to satisfy my curiosity." He patted the ansible. "There's a real favor I can do though: so far, Middle America has been cheated occasionally, but no Outsider has used force against us. That's one good thing about the Caravan system: it's to the Tourists' advantage to keep each other straight. Ravna&Tines may be different. If this is really a High Trader, it might just make a grab for what it wants. If I were you, I'd keep close to the Blabber. . . . And I'll see if the slug will move one of the Tourist barges over the campus. If you stay in this area, not much can happen without them knowing.

"Hey, see what a help I am? I did nothing for your original question, and now you have a whole, ah, shipload of new things to worry about. . . ."

He leaned back, and his voice turned serious. "But I don't have much to say about your original question, Hamid. If Ravna&Tines turn out to be decent, you'll still have to decide for yourself about giving up the Blab. I bet every critter that thinks it thinks—even the transhumans—worry about how to do right for themselves and the ones they love. I—uh, oh damn! Why don't you ask your pop, why don't you ask Hussein about these things? The guy has been heartbroken since you left."

Ham felt his face go red. Pop had never had much good to say about Fujiyama. Who'd have guessed the two would talk about him? If Hamid had known, he'd never have come here today. He felt like standing up, screaming at this old man to mind his own business. Instead, he shook his head and said softly, "It's kind of personal."

Larry looked at him, as if wondering whether to push the matter. One word, and Ham knew that all the pain would come pouring out. But after a moment, the old man sighed. He looked around the desk to where the Blab lay, eyeing the heater. "Hey, Blabber. You take good care of this kid."

The Blab returned his gaze. "Sure, sure," she said.

Hamid's apartment was on the south side of campus. It was large and cheap, which might seem surprising so near the oldest university around, and just a few kilometers south of the planetary capital. The back door opened on kilometers of forested wilderness. It would be a long time before there was any land development immediately south of here. The original landing zones were just twenty klicks away. In a bad storm there might be a little hot stuff blown north. It might be only fifty percent of natural background radiation, but with a whole world to colonize, why spread towns toward the first landings?

Hamid parked the commons bicycle in the rack out front, and walked quietly around the building. Lights were on upstairs. There were the usual motorbikes of other tenants. *Something* was standing in back, at the far end of the building. Ah. A Halloween scarecrow.

He and the Blab walked back to his end. It was past twilight and neither moon was in the sky. The tips of his fingers were chilled to numbness. He stuck his hands in his pockets, and paused to look up. The starships of the Caravan were in synch orbit at this longitude. They formed a row of bright dots in the southern sky. Something dark, too regular to be a cloud hung almost straight overhead. That must be the protection Larry had promised.

"I'm hungry."

"Just a minute and we'll go in."

"Okay." The Blab leaned companionably against his leg, began humming. She looked fat now, but it was just her fur, all puffed out. These temperatures were probably the most comfortable for her. He stared across the star fields. *God, how many hours have I stood like this, wondering what all those stars mean?* The Big Square was about an hour from setting. The fifth brightest star in that constellation was Lothlrimarre's sun. At Lothlrimarre and beyond, faster than light travel was possible—even for twenty-first-century Old Earth types. If Middle America were just ten more light years farther out from the galactic center, Hamid would have had all the Beyond as his world.

His gaze swept back across the sky. Most everything he could see there would be in the Slow Zone. It extended four thousand light years inward from here, if the Outsiders were to be believed. Billions of star systems, millions of civilizations—trapped. Most would never know about the outside.

Even the Outsiders had only vague information about the civilizations down here in the Slow Zone. Greatships, ramscoops, they all must be invented here again and again. Colonies spread, knowledge gained, most often lost in the long slow silence. What theories the Slow Zone civilizations must have for why nothing could move faster than light—even in the face of superluminal events seen at cosmic distances. What theories they must have to explain why human-equivalent intelligence was the highest ever found and ever created. Those ones deep inside, they might at times be the happiest of all, their theories assuring them they were at the top of creation. If Middle America were only a hundred light years further down, Hamid would never know the truth. He would love this world, and the spreading of civilization upon it.

Hamid's eye followed the Milky Way to the western horizon. The glow wasn't really brighter there than above, but he knew his constellations. He was looking at the galactic center. He smiled wanly. In twentieth-century science fiction, those star clouds were imagined as the homes of "elder races," godlike intellects. . . . But the Tourists call those regions of the galaxy, the Depths. The Unthinking Depths. Not only was ftl impossible there, but so was sentience. So they guessed. They couldn't know for sure. The fastest round-trip probe to the edge of the Depths took about ten thousand years. Such expeditions were rare, though some were well documented.

Hamid shivered, and looked back at the ground. Four cats sat silently just beyond the lawn, watching the Blab. "Not tonight, Blab," he said, and the two of them went indoors.

The place looked undisturbed: the usual mess. He fixed the Blab her dinner and heated some soup for himself.

"Yuck. This stuff tastes like *shit!*" The Blab rocked back on her haunches and made retching sounds. Few people have their own childhood obnoxiousness come back to haunt them so directly as Hamid Thompson did. He could remember using exactly those words at the dinner table. Mom should have stuffed a sock down his throat.

Hamid glanced at the chicken parts. "Best we can afford, Blab." He was running his savings down to zero to cover the year of the Tourists. Being a guide was such a plum that no one thought to pay for it.

"Yuck." But she started nibbling.

As Ham watched her eat, he realized that one of his problems was solved. If Ravna&Tines wouldn't take him as the Blab's "trainer," they could hike back to the Beyond by themselves. Furthermore, he'd want better evidence from the slug—via the ansible he could get assurances directly from Lothlrimarre—that Ravna&Tines could be held to promises. The conversation with Larry had brought home all the nightmare fears, the fears that drove some people to demand total rejection of the Caravan. Who knew what happened to those that left with Outsiders? Almost all Middle American knowledge of the Beyond came from less than thirty starships, less than a thousand strangers. Strange strangers. If it weren't for the five who came back, there would be zero corroboration. Of those five . . . well, Hussein Thompson was a mystery even to Hamid: seeming kind, inside a vicious mercenary. Lazy Larry was a mystery, too, a cheerful one who made it clear that you better think twice about what folks tell you. But one thing came clear from all of them: space is deep. There were millions of civilized worlds in the Beyond, thousands of star-spanning empires. In such vastness, there could be no single notion of law and order. Cooperation and enlightened self-interest were common, but . . . nightmares lurked.

So what if Ravna&Tines turned him down, or couldn't produce credible assurances? Hamid went into the bedroom, and punched up the news, let the color and motion wash over him. Middle America was a beautiful world, still mostly empty. With the agrav plates and the room-temperature fusion electrics that the Caravan had brought, life would be more exciting here then ever before. . . . In twenty or thirty years there would likely be another caravan. If he and the Blab were still restless—well, there was plenty of time to prepare. Larry Fujiyama had been forty years old when he went Out.

Hamid sighed, happy with himself for the first time in days.

The phone rang just as he finished with the news. The name of the incoming caller danced in red letters across the news display: *Ravna.* No location or topic. Hamid swallowed hard. He bounced off the bed, turned the phone pickup to look at a chair in an uncluttered corner of the room, and sat down there. Then he accepted the call.

Ravna was human. And female. "Mr. Hamid Thompson, please."

"T-that's me." *Curse the stutter.*

For an instant there was no reaction. Then a quick smile crossed her face. It was not a friendly smile, more like a sneer at his nervousness. "I call to discuss the animal. The Blabber, you call it. You have heard our offer. I am prepared to improve upon it." As she spoke, the Blab walked into the room and across the phone's field of view. Her gaze did not waver. Strange. He could see that the video transmit light was on next to the screen. The Blab began to hum. A moment passed and *then* she reacted, a tiny start of surprise.

"What is your improvement?"

Again, a half-second pause. Ravna&Tines were a lot nearer than the Jovians tonight, though apparently still not at Middle America. "We possess devices that allow faster than light communication to a world in the . . . Beyond. Think on what this access means. With this, if you stay on Middle America, you will be the richest man on the planet. If you choose to accept passage Out, you will have the satisfaction of knowing you have moved your world a good step out of the darkness."

Hamid found himself thinking faster than he ever had outside of a Fujiyama oral exam. There were plenty of clues here. Ravna's English was more fluent than most Tourists', but her pronunciation was awful. Human but awful: her vowel stress was strange to the point of rendering her speech unintelligible, and she didn't voice things properly: "pleess" instead "pleez," "chooss" instead of "chooz."

At the same time, he had to make sense of what she was saying and decide the correct response. Hamid thanked God he already knew about ansibles. "Miss Ravna, I agree. That is an improvement. Nevertheless, my original requirement stands. I must accompany my pet. Only I know her needs." He cocked his head. "You could do worse than have an expert on call."

As he spoke, her expression clouded. Rage? She seemed hostile toward him *personally.* But when he finished, her face was filled with an approximation of a friendly smile. "Of course, we will arrange that also. We had not realized earlier how important this is to you."

Jeeze. Even I can lie better than that! This Ravna was used to getting her own way without face-to-face lies, or else she had real emotional problems. Either way: "And since you and I are scarcely equals, we also need to work something out with the Lothlrimarre that will put a credible bond on the agreement."

Her poorly constructed mask slipped. "That is absurd." She looked at something off camera. "The Lothlrimarre knows nothing of us. . . . I will try to satisfy you. But know this, Hamid Thompson: I am the congenial, uh, *humane* member of my team. Mr. Tines is very impatient. I try to restrain him, but if he becomes enough desperate . . . things could happen that would hurt us all. Do you understand me?"

First a lie, and now chainsaw subtlety. He fought back a smile. *Careful. You might be mistaking raw insanity for bluff and bluster.* "Yes, Miss Ravna, I do understand, and your offer is generous. But . . . I need to think about this. Can you give me a bit more time?" *Enough time to complain to the Tour Director.*

"Yes. One hundred hours should be feasible."

After she rang off, Hamid sat for a long time, staring sightlessly at the dataset. What *was* Ravna? Through twenty thousand years of colonization, on worlds far stranger than Middle America, the human form had drifted far. Cross fertility existed between most of Earth's children, though they differed more from one another than had races on the home planet. Ravna looked more like an Earth human than most of the Tourists. Assuming she was of normal height, she could almost have passed as an American of Middle East descent: sturdy, dark-skinned, black-haired. There were differences. Her eyes had epicanthic folds, and the irises were the most intense violet he had ever seen. Still, all that was trivial compared to her manner.

Why hadn't she been receiving Hamid's video? Was she blind? She didn't seem so otherwise; he remembered her looking at things around her. Perhaps she was some sort of personality simulator. That had been a standard item in American science fiction at the end of the twentieth century; the idea passed out of fashion when computer performance seemed to top out in the early twenty-first. But things like that should be possible in the Beyond, and certainly in Transhuman Space. They wouldn't work very well down here, of course. Maybe she was just a graphical front end for whatever Mr. Tines was.

Somehow, Hamid thought she was real. She certainly had a human effect on him. Sure she had a good figure, obvious under soft white shirt and pants. And sure, Hamid had been girl crazy the last five years. He was so horny most of the time, it felt good just to ogle femikins in downtown Marquette stores. But for all-out sexiness, Ravna wasn't *that* spectacular. She had nothing on Gilli Weinberg or Skandr Vrinimisrinithan's wife. Yet, if he had met her at school, he would have tried harder to gain her favor than he had Gilli's . . . and that was saying *a lot.*

Hamid sighed. That probably just showed that *he* was nuts.

"I wanna go out." The Blab rubbed her head against his arm. Hamid realized he was sweating even though the room was chill.

"God, not tonight, Blab." He realized that there was a lot of bluff in Ravna&Tines. At the same time, it was clear they were the kind who might just *grab* if they could get away with it.

"I wanna go out!" Her voice came louder. The Blab spent many nights outside, mainly in the forest. That made it easier to keep her quiet when she was indoors. For the Blab, that was a chance to play with her pets: the cats—and sometimes the dogs—in the neighborhood. There had been a war when he and the Blab first arrived here. Pecking orders had been abruptly revised, and two of the most ferocious dogs had just disappeared. What was left was very strange. The cats were fascinated by the Blab. They hung around the yard just for a glimpse of her. When she was here they didn't even fight among themselves. Nights like tonight were the best. In a couple of hours both Selene and Diana would rise, the silver moon and the gold. On nights like this, when gold and silver lay between deep shadows, Hamid had seen her pacing through the edge of the forest, followed by a dozen faithful retainers.

But, *"Not tonight, Blab!"* There followed a major argument, the Blabber blasting rock music and kiddie shows at high volume. The noise wasn't the loudest she could make. That would have been physically painful to Ham. No, this was more like a cheap music player set way high. Eventually it would bring complaints from all over the apartment building. Fortunately for Hamid, the nearest rooms were unoccupied just now.

After twenty minutes of din, Hamid twisted the fight into a "game of humans." Like many pets, the Blab thought of herself as a human being. But unlike a cat or a dog or even a parrot, she could do a passable job of imitating one. The trouble was, she couldn't always find people with the patience to play along.

They sat across from each other at the dinette table, the Blab's forelegs splayed awkwardly across its surface. Hamid would start with some question—it didn't matter the topic. The Blab would nod wisely, ponder a reply. With most abstractions, anything she had to say was nonsense, meaningful only to tea-leaf readers or wishful thinkers. Never mind that. In the game, Hamid would respond with a comment, or laugh if the Blab seemed to be in a joke-telling behavior. The pacing, the intonation—they were all perfect for real human dialog. If you didn't understand English, the game would have sounded like two friends having a good time.

"How about an imitation, Blab? Joe Ortega. President Ortega. Can you do that?"

"Heh, heh." That was Lazy Larry's cackle. "Don't rush me. I'm thinking. I'm thinking!" There were several types of imitation games. For instance, she could speak back Hamid's words instantly, but with the voice of some other human. Using that trick on a voice-only phone was probably her favorite game of all, since her audience really *believed* she was a person. What he was asking for now was almost as much fun, if the Blab would play up to it.

She rubbed her jaw with a talon, "Ah yes." She sat back pompously, almost slid onto the floor before she caught herself. "We must all work together in these exciting times." That was from a recent Ortega speech, a simple playback. But even when she got going, responding to Hamid's questions, adlibbing things, she was still a perfect match for the President of Middle America. Hamid laughed and laughed. Ortega was one of the five who came back, not a very bright man but self-important and ambitious. It said something that even his small knowledge of the Outside was enough to propel him to the top of the world state. The five were very big fish in a very small pond—that was how Larry Fujiyama put it.

The Blab was an enormous show-off, and was quickly carried away by her own wit. She began waving her forelegs around, lost her balance and fell off the chair. "Oops!" She hopped back on the chair, looked at Hamid—and began laughing herself. The two were in stitches for almost half a minute. This had happened before; Hamid was sure the Blab could not appreciate humor above the level of pratfalls. Her laughter was imitation for the sake of congeniality, for the sake of being a person. "Oh, God!" She flopped onto the table, "choking" with mirth, her forelegs across the back of her neck as if to restrain herself.

The laughter died away to occasional snorts, and then a companionable silence. Hamid reached across to rub the bristly fur that covered the Blab's forehead tympanum. "You're a good kid, Blab."

The dark eyes opened, turned up at him. Something like a sigh escaped her, buzzing the fur under his palm. "Sure, sure," she said.

Hamid left the drapes partly pulled, and a window pane cranked open where the Blab could sit and look out. He lay in the darkened bedroom and watched her silhouette against the silver and gold moonlight. She had her nose pressed up to the screen. Her long neck was arched to give both her head and shoulder tympana a good line on the outside. Every so often her head would jerk a few millimeters, as if something very interesting had just happened outside.

The loudest sound in the night was faint roach racket, out by the forest. The Blab was being very quiet—in the range Hamid could hear—and he was grateful. She really was a good kid.

He sighed and pulled the covers up to his nose. It had been a long day, one where life's problems had come out ahead.

He'd be very careful the next few days; no trips away from Marquette and Ann Arbor, no leaving the Blab unattended. At least the slug's protection looked solid. *I better tell Larry about the second ansible, though.* If Ravna&Tines just went direct to the government with it . . . that might be the most dangerous move of all. For all their pious talk and restrictions on private sales, the Feds would sell their own grandmothers if they thought it would benefit the Planetary Interest. Thank God they already had an ansible—or almost had one.

Funny. After all these years and all the dreams, that it was the Blab the Outsiders were after. . . .

Hamid was an adopted child. His parents had told him that as soon as he could understand the notion. And somewhere in those early years, he had guessed the truth . . . that his father had brought him in . . . from the Beyond. Somehow Huss Thompson had kept that fact secret from the public. Surely the government knew, and cooperated with him. In those early years—before they forced him into Math—it had been a happy secret for him; he thought he had all his parents' love. Knowing that he was really from Out There had just given substance to what most well-loved kids believe anyway—that somehow they are divinely special. His secret dream had been that he was some Outsider version of an exiled prince. And when he grew up, when the next ships from the Beyond came down . . . he would be called to his destiny.

Starting college at age eight had just seemed part of that destiny. His parents had been so confident of him, even though his tests results were scarcely more than bright normal. . . . That year had been the destruction of innocence. He wasn't a genius, no matter how much his parents insisted. The fights, the tears, their insistence. In the end, Mom had left Hussein Thompson. Not till then did the man relent, let his child return to normal schools. Life at home was never the same. Mom's visits were brief, tense . . . and rare. But it wasn't for another five years that Hamid learned to hate his father. The learning had been an accident, a conversation overheard. Hussein had been *hired* to raise Hamid as he had, to push him into school, to twist and ruin him. The old man had never denied the boy's accusations. His attempts to "explain" had been vague mumbling . . . worse than lies. . . . If Hamid was a prince, he must be a very hated one indeed.

The memories had worn deep grooves, ones he often slid down on his way to sleep. . . . But tonight there was something new, something ironic to the point of magic. All these years . . . it had been the Blab who was the lost princeling . . . !

There was a hissing sound. Hamid struggled toward wakefulness, fear and puzzlement playing through his dreams. He rolled to the edge of the bed and forced his eyes to see. Only stars shone through the window. The Blab. She wasn't sitting at the window screen anymore. She must be having one of her nightmares. They were rare, but spectacular. One winter's night Hamid had been wakened by the sounds of a full-scale thunderstorm. This was not so explosive, but . . .

He looked across the floor at the pile of blankets that was her nest. Yes. She was there, and facing his way.

"Blab? It's okay, baby."

No reply. Only the hissing, maybe louder now. *It wasn't coming from the Blab.* For an instant his fuzzy mind hung in a kind of mouse-and-snake paralysis. Then he flicked on the lights. No one here. The sound was from the dataset; the picture flat remained dark. *This is crazy.*

"Blab?" He had never seen her like this. Her eyes were open wide, rings of white showing around the irises. Her forelegs reached beyond the blankets. The talons were extended and had slashed deep into the plastic flooring. A string of drool hung from her muzzle.

He got up, started toward her. The hissing formed a voice, and the voice spoke. "I want her. Human, I want her. And I will have her." Her, the Blab.

"How did you get access? You have no business disturbing us." Silly talk, but it broke the nightmare spell of this waking.

"My name is Tines." Hamid suddenly remembered the claw on the Ravna&Tines logo. Tines. Cute. "We have made generous offers. We have been patient. That is past. I will have her. If it means the death of all you m-meat animals, so be it. But I *will* have her."

The hissing was almost gone now, but the voice still sounded like something from a cheap synthesizer. The syntax and accent were similar to Ravna's. They were either the same person, or they had learned English from the same source. Still, Ravna had seemed angry. Tines sounded flat-out nuts. Except for the single stutter over "meat," the tone and pacing were implacable. And that voice gave away more than anything yet about why the Outsider wanted his pet. There was a *hunger* in its voice, a lust to feed or to rape.

Hamid's rage climbed on top of his fear. "Why don't you just go screw yourself, comic monster! We've got *protection,* else you wouldn't come bluffing—"

"Bluffing! *Bluffiiyowru*—" the words turned into choked gobbling sounds. Behind him, Hamid heard the Blab scream. After a moment the noises faded. "I do not bluff. Hussein Thompson has this hour learned what I do with those who cross me. You and all your people will also die unless you deliver her to me. I see a ground car parked by your . . . house. Use it to take her east fifty kilometers. Do this within one hour, or learn what Hussein Thompson learned—that *I do not bluff.*" And Mr. Tines was gone.

It has *to be a bluff! If Tines has that power why not wipe the Tourists from the sky and just grab the Blab?* Yet they were so stupid about it. A few smooth lies a week ago, and they might have gotten everything without a murmur. It was as if they couldn't imagine being disobeyed—or were desperate beyond reason.

Hamid turned back to the Blab. As he reached to stroke her neck, she twisted, her needle-toothed jaws clicking shut on his pyjama sleeve. "Blab!"

She released his sleeve, and drew back into the pile of blankets. She was making whistling noises like the time she got hit by a pickup trike. Hamid's father guessed those must be true Blabber sounds, like human sobs or chattering of teeth. He went to his knees and made comforting noises. This time she let him stroke her neck. He saw that she had wet her bed. The Blab had been toilet trained as long as he had. Bluff or not, this had thoroughly terrified her. Tines claimed he could kill everyone. Hamid remembered the ansible, a god-damned telephone that could dim the sun.

Bluff or madness?

He scrambled back to his dataset, and punched up the Tour Director's number. Pray the slug was accepting more than mail tonight. The ring pattern flashed twice, and then he was looking at a panorama of cloud tops and blue sky. It might have been an aerial view of Middle America, except that as you looked downwards the clouds seemed to extend forever, more and more convoluted in the dimness. This was a picture clip from the ten-bar level over Lothlrimarre. No doubt the slug chose it to soothe human callers, and still be true to the nature of his home world— a subjovian thirty thousand kilometers across.

For five seconds they soared through the canyons of cloud. *Wake up, damn you!*

The picture cleared and he was looking at a human—Larry Fujiyama! Lazy Larry did not look surprised to see him. "You got the right number, kid. I'm up here with the slug. There have been developments."

Hamid gaped for an appropriate reply, and the other continued. "Ravna&Tines have been all over the slug since about midnight. Threats and promises, mostly threats since the Tines critter took their comm. . . . I'm sorry about your dad, Hamid. We should've thought to—"

"What?"

"Isn't that what you're calling about? . . . Oh. It's been on the news. Here—" The picture dissolved into a view from a news chopper flying over eastern Michigan farmland. It took Hamid a second to recognize the hills. This was near the Thompson spread, two thousand klicks east of

Marquette. It would be past sunup there. The camera panned over a familiar creek, the newsman bragging how On-Line News was ahead of the first rescue teams. They crested a range of hills and . . . where were the trees? Thousands of black lines lay below, trunks of blown-over trees, pointing inevitably inward, toward the center of the blast. The newsman babbled on about the meteor strike and how fortunate it was that ground zero was in a lake valley, how only one farm had been affected. Hamid swallowed. That farm . . . was Hussein Thompson's. The place they lived after Mom left. Ground zero itself was obscured by rising steam—all that was left of the lake. The reporter assured his audience that the crater consumed all the land where the farm buildings had been.

The news clip vanished. "It was no Middle American nuke, but it wasn't natural, either," said Larry. "A lighter from Ravna&Tines put down there two hours ago. Just before the blast, I got a real scared call from Huss, something about 'the tines' arriving. I'll show it to you if—"

"No!" Hamid gulped. "No," he said more quietly. How he had hated Hussein Thompson; how he had loved his father in the years before. Now he was gone, and Hamid would never get his feelings sorted out. "Tines just called me. He said he killed my—Hussein." Hamid played back the call. "Anyway, I need to talk to the slug. Can he protect me? Is Middle America really in for it if I refuse the Tines thing?"

For once Larry didn't give his "you figure it" shrug. "It's a mess," he said. "And sluggo's waffling. He's around here somewhere. Just a sec—" More peaceful cloud-soaring. Damn, damn, damn. Something bumped gently into the small of his back. The Blab. The black and white neck came around his side. The dark eyes looked up at him. "What's up?" she said quietly.

Hamid felt like laughing and crying. She was very subdued, but at least she recognized him now. "Are you okay, Baby?" he said. The Blabber curled up around him, her head stretched out on his knee.

On the dataset, the clouds parted and they were looking at both Larry Fujiyama and the slug. Of course, they were not in the same room; that would have been fatal to both. The Lothlrimarre barge was a giant pressure vessel. Inside, pressure and atmosphere were just comfy for the slug—about a thousand bars of ammonia and hydrogen. There was a terrarium for human visitors. The current view showed the slug in the foreground. Part of the wall behind him was transparent, a window into the terrarium. Larry gave a little wave, and Hamid felt himself smiling. No question who was in a zoo.

"Ah, Mr. Thompson. I'm glad you called. We have a very serious problem." The slug's English was perfect, and though the voice was artificial, he sounded like a perfectly normal Middle American male. "Many problems would be solved if you could see your way clear to give—"

"No." Hamid's voice was flat. "N-not while I'm alive, anyway. This is no business deal. You've heard the threats, and you saw what they did to my father." The slug had been his ultimate employer these last six months, someone rarely spoken to, the object of awe. None of that mattered now. "You've always said the first responsibility of the Tour Director is to see that no party is abused by another. I'm asking you to live up to that."

"Um. Technically, I was referring to you Middle Americans and the Tourists in my caravan. I know I have the power to make good on my promises with them. . . . But we're just beginning to learn about Ravna&Tines. I'm not sure it's reasonable to stand up against them." He swiveled his thousand-kilo bulk toward the terrarium window. Hamid knew that under Lothlrimarre gravity, the slug would have been squashed into the shape of a flatworm, with his manipulator fringe touching the ground. At one gee, he looked more like an overstuffed silk pillow, fringed with red tassles. "Larry has told me about Skandr's remarkable Slow Zone device. I've heard of such things. They are *very* difficult to obtain. A single one would have more than financed my caravan. . . . And to think that Skandr pleaded his foundation's poverty in begging passage. . . . Anyway, Larry has been using the 'ansible' to ask about what your Blabber really is."

Larry nodded. "Been at it since you left, Hamid. The machine's down in my office, buzzing away. Like Skandr says, it is aligned on the commercial outlet at Lothlrimarre. From there I have access to the Known Net. Heh, heh. Skandr left a *sizable* credit bond at Lothlrimarre. I hope he and Ortega aren't too upset by the phone bill I run up testing this gadget for them. I described the Blab, and put out a depth query. There are a million subnets, all over the Beyond, searching their databases for anything like the Blab. I—" His happy enthusiasm wavered, "Sluggo thinks we've dug up a reference to the Blabber's race. . . ."

"Yes, and it's frightening, Mr. Thompson." It was no surprise that none of the Tourists had heard of a blabber. The only solid lead coming back to Larry had been from halfway around the galactic rim, a nook in the Beyond that had only one occasional link with the rest of the Known Net. That far race had no direct knowledge of the Blabbers. But they heard rumors. From a thousand light-years below them, deep within the Slow Zone, there came stories . . . of a race matching the Blab's appearance. The race was highly intelligent, and had quickly developed the relativistic transport that was the fastest thing inside the Zone. They colonized a vast sphere, held an empire of ten thousand worlds—all without ftl. And the tines—the name seemed to fit—had not held their empire through the power of brotherly love. Races had been exterminated, planets busted with relativistic kinetic energy bombs. The tines' technology had been about as advanced and deadly as could exist in the Zone. Most of their volume was a tomb now, their story whispered through centuries of slow flight toward the Outside.

"Wait, wait. Prof Fujiyama told me the ansible's bandwidth is a tenth of a bit per second. You've had less than twelve hours to work this question. How can you possibly know all this?"

Larry looked a little embarrassed—a first as far as Hamid could remember. "We've been using the AI protocol I told you about. There's massive interpolation going on at both ends of our link to Lothlrimarre."

"I'll bet!"

"Remember, Mr. Thompson, the data compression applies only to the first link in the chain. The Known Net lies in the Beyond. Bandwidth and data integrity are very high across most of its links."

The slug sounded very convinced. But Hamid had read a lot about the Known Net; the notion was almost as fascinating as ftl travel itself. There was no way a world could have a direct link with all others—partly because of range limitations, mainly because of the *number* of planets involved. Similarly, there was no way a single "phone company" (or even ten thousand phone companies!) could run the thing. Most likely, the information coming to them from around the galaxy had passed through five or ten intermediate hops. The intermediates—not to mention the race on the far rim—were likely nonhuman. Imagine asking a quesiton in English to someone who also speaks Spanish, and that person asking the question in Spanish to someone who understands Spanish and passes the question on in German. This was a million times worse. Next to some of the creatures Out There, the slug could pass for human!

Hamid said as much. "F-furthermore, even if this *is* what the sender meant, it could still be a lie! Look at what local historians did to Richard the Third, or Mohamet Rose."

Lazy Larry smiled his polliwog smile, and Hamid realized they must have been arguing about this already. Larry put in, "There's also this, sluggo: the nature of the identification. The tines must have something like hands. See any on Hamid's Blabber?"

The slug's scarlet fringe rippled three quick cycles. Agitation? Dismissal? "The text is still coming in. But I have a theory. You know, Larry, I've always been a great student of sex. I may be a 'he' only by courtesy, but I think sex is fascinating. It's what makes the 'world go around' for so many races." Hamid suddenly understood Gilli Weinberg's success. "So. Grant me my expertise. My guess is the tines exhibit *extreme* sexual dimorphism. The males' forepaws probably are hands. No doubt it's the males who are the killers. The females—like the Blab—are by contrast friendly, mindless creatures."

The Blab's eyes rolled back to look at Hamid. "Sure, sure," she murmured. The accident of timing was wonderful, seeming to say *who is this clown?*

The slug didn't notice. "This may even explain the viciousness of the male. Think back to the conversation Mr. Thompson had. These creatures seem to regard their own females as property to exploit. Rather the ultimate in sexism." Hamid shivered. That *did* ring a bell. He couldn't forget the *hunger* in the tines's voice.

"Is this the long way to tell me you're not going to protect us?"

The slug was silent for almost fifteen seconds. Its scarlet fringe waved up and down the whole time. Finally: "Almost, I'm afraid. My caravan customers haven't heard this analysis, just the threats and the news broadcasts. Nevertheless, they are tourists, not explorers. They demand that I refuse to let you aboard. Some demand that we leave your planet immediately. . . . How secure is this line, Larry?"

Fujiyama said, "Underground fiberoptics, and an encrypted laser link. Take a chance, sluggo."

"Very well. Mr. Thompson, there is what you can expect from me: I can stay over the city, and probably defend against direct kidnapping—that unless I see a planetbuster coming. I doubt very much they have that set up, but if they do—well, I don't think even you would want to keep your dignity at the price of a relativistic asteroid strike.

"I can *not* come down to pick you up. That would be visible to all, a direct violation of my customers' wishes. On the other hand," there was another pause, and his scarlet fringe whipped about even faster than before, "if you should appear, uh, up here, I would take you aboard my barge. Even if this were noticed, it would be a *fait accompli.* I could hold off my customers, and likely our worst fate would be a premature and unprofitable departure from Middle America."

"T-that's very generous." *Unbelievably so.* The slug was thought to be an honest fellow—but a very hard trader. Even Hamid had to admit that the claim on the slug's honor was tenuous here, yet he was risking a twenty-year mission for it.

"Of course, *if* we reach that extreme, I'll want a few years of your time once we reach the Outside. My bet is that hard knowledge about your Blabber might make up for the loss of everything else."

A day ago, Hamid would have quibbled about contracts and assurances. Today, well, the alternative was Ravna&Tines. . . . With Larry as witness, they settled on two years indenture and a pay scale.

Now all he and the Blab had to do was figure how to climb five thousand meters straight up. There was one obvious way:

It was Dave Larson's car, but Davey owed him. Hamid woke his neighbor, explained that the Blab was sick and had to go into Marquette. Fifteen minutes later, Hamid and the Blab were driving through Ann Arbor Town. It was a Saturday, and barely into morning twilight; he had the road to himself. He'd half expected the place to be swarming with cops and military. If Ravna&Tines ever guessed how easy it was to intimidate Joe Ortega . . . If the Feds knew exactly what was going on, they'd turn the Blab over to Tines in an instant. But apparently the government was simply confused, lying low, hoping it wouldn't be noticed till the big boys upstairs settled their arguments. The farm bombing wasn't in the headline list anymore. The Feds were keeping things quiet, thereby confining the mindless panic to the highest circles of government.

The Blab rattled around the passenger side of the car, alternately leaning on the dash and sniffing in the bag of tricks that Hamid had brought. She was still subdued, but riding in a private auto was a novelty. Electronics gear was cheap, but consumer mechanicals were still at a premium. And without a large highway system, cars would never be the rage they had been on Old Earth; most freight transport was by rail. A lot of this would change because of the Caravan. They brought one hundred thousand agrav plates—enough to revolutionize transport. Middle America would enter the Age of the Aircar—and for the first time surpass the homeworld. So saith Joe Ortega.

Past the University, there was a patch of open country. Beyond the headlights, Hamid caught glimpses of open fields, a glint of frost. Hamid looked up nervously every few seconds. Selene and Diana hung pale in the west. Scattered clouds floated among the Tourist barges, vague grayness in the first light of morning. No intruders, but three of the barges were gone, presumably moved to orbit. The Lothlrimarre vessel floated just east of Marquette, over the warehouse quarter. It looked like the slug was keeping his part of the deal.

Hamid drove into downtown Marquette. Sky signs floated brightly amid the two-hundred-storey towers, advertising dozens of products— some of which actually existed. Light from discos and shopping malls flooded the eight-lane streets. Of course the place was deserted; it was Saturday morning. Much of the business section was like this—a reconstruction of the original Marquette as it had been on Earth in the middle of the twenty-first century. That Marquette had sat on the edge of an enormous lake, called Superior. Through that century, as Superior became the splash-down point for heavy freight from space, Marquette had become one of the great port cities of Earth, the gateway to the solar system. The Tourists said it was legend, ur-mother to a thousand worlds.

Hamid turned off the broadway, down an underground ramp. The Marquette of today was for show, perhaps one percent the area of the original, with less than one percent the population. But from the air it looked good, the lights and bustle credible. For special events, the streets could be packed with a million people—everyone on the continent that could be spared from essential work. And the place wasn't really a fraud; the Tourists knew this was a reconstruction. The point was, it was an *authentic* reconstruction, as could only be done by a people one step from the original source—that was the official line. And in fact, the people of Middle America had made enormous sacrifices over almost twenty years to have this ready in time for the Caravan.

The car rental was down a fifteen-storey spiral, just above the train terminal. *That* was for real, though the next arrival was a half hour away. Hamid got out, smelling the cool mustiness of the stone cavern, hearing only the echoes of his own steps. Millions of tonnes of ceramic and stone stood between them and the sky. Even an Outsider couldn't see through that . . . he hoped. One sleepy-eyed attendant watched him fill out the forms. Hamid stared at the display, sweating even in the cool; would the guy in back notice? He almost laughed at the thought. His first sally into crime was the least of his worries. If Ravna&Tines were plugged into the credit net, then in a sense they really *could* see down here—and the bogus number Larry had supplied was all that kept him invisible.

They left in a Millennium Commander, the sort of car a Tourist might use to bum around in olden times. Hamid drove north through the underground, then east, and when finally they saw open sky again, they were driving south. Ahead was the warehouse district . . . and hanging above it, the slug's barge, its spheres and cupolas green against the brightening sky. So huge. It looked near, but Hamid knew it was a good five thousand meters up.

A helicopter might be able to drop someone on its topside, or maybe land on one of the verandas—though it would be a tight fit under the overhang. But Hamid couldn't fly a chopper, and wasn't even sure how to rent one at this time of day. No, he and the Blab were going to try something a lot more straightforward, something he had done every couple of weeks since the Tourists arrived.

They were getting near the incoming lot, where Feds and Tourists held payments-to-date in escrow. Up ahead there would be cameras spotted on the roofs. He tinted all but the driver-side window, and pushed down on the Blab's shoulders with his free hand. "Play hide for a few minutes."

"Okay."

Three hundred meters more and they were at the outer gate. He saw the usual three cops out front, and a fourth in an armored box to the side. If Ortega was feeling the heat, it could all end right here.

They looked *real* nervous, but they spent most of their time scanning the sky. They knew something was up, but they thought it was out of their hands. They took a quick glance at the Millennium Commander and waved him through. The inner fence was almost as easy, though here he had to enter his Guide ID. . . . If Ravna&Tines were watching the nets, Hamid and the Blab were running on borrowed time now.

He pulled into the empty parking lot at the main warehouse, choosing a slot with just the right position relative to the guard box. "Keep quiet a little while, Blab," he said. He hopped out and walked across the gravel yard. Maybe he should move faster, as if panicked? But no, the guard had already seen him. *Okay, play it cool.* He waved, kept walking. The glow of morning was already dimming the security lamps that covered the lot. No stars shared the sky with the clouds and the barges.

It was kind of a joke that merchandise from the Beyond was socked away here. The warehouse was big, maybe two hundred meters on a side, but an old place, sheet plastic and aging wood timbers.

The armored door buzzed even before Hamid touched it. He pushed his way through. "Hi, Phil."

Luck! The other guards must be on rounds. Phil Lucas was a friendly sort, but not too bright, and not very familiar with the Blab. Lucas sat in the middle of the guard cubby, and the armored partition that separated him from the visitor trap was raised. To the left was a second door that opened into the warehouse itself. "Hi, Ham." The guard looked back at him nervously. "Awful early to see you."

"Yeah. Got a little problem. There's a Tourist out in the Commander." He waved through the armored window. "He's drunk out of his mind. I need to get him Upstairs and quietly."

Phil licked his lips. "Christ. Everything happens at once. Look, I'm sorry, Ham. We've got orders from the top at Federal Security: nothing comes down, nothing goes up. There's some kind of a ruckus going on amongst the Outsiders. If they start shooting, we want it to be at each other, not us."

"That's the point. We think this fellow is part of the problem. If we can get him back, things should cool off. You should have a note on him. It's Antris ban Reempt."

"Oh. *Him.*" Ban Reempt was the most obnoxious Tourist of all. If he'd been an ordinary Middle American, he would have racked up a century of jail time in the last six months. Fortunately, he'd never killed anyone, so his antics were just barely ignorable. Lucas pecked at his dataset. "No, we don't have anything."

"Nuts. Everything stays jammed unless we can get this guy Upstairs," Hamid paused judiciously, as if giving the matter serious thought. "Look, I'm going back to the car, see if I can call somebody to confirm this."

Lucas was dubious. "Okay, but it's gotta be from the top, Ham."

"Right."

The door buzzed open, and Hamid was jogging back across the parking lot. Things really seemed on track. Thank God he'd always been friendly with the cops running security here. The security people regarded most of the Guides as college-trained snots—and with some reason. But Hamid had had coffee with these guys more than once. He knew the system . . . he knew the incoming phone number for security confirmations.

Halfway across the lot, Hamid suddenly realized that he didn't have the shakes anymore. The scheme, the adlibbing, it almost seemed normal—a skill he'd never guessed he had. Maybe that's what desperation does to a fellow. . . . Somehow this was almost fun.

He pulled open the car door. "Back! Not yet." He pushed the eager Blab onto the passenger seat. "Big game, Blab." He rummaged through his satchel, retrieved the two comm sets. One was an ordinary head and throat model, the other had been modified for the Blab. He fastened the mike under the collar of his windbreaker. The earphone shouldn't be needed, but it was small; he put it on, turned the volume down. Then he strapped the other commset around the Blab's neck, turned off *its* mike, and clipped the receiver to her ear. "The game, Blab: Imitation. Imitation." He patted the commset on her shoulder. The Blab was fairly bouncing around the Commander's cab. "For sure. Sure, sure! Who, who?"

"Joe Ortega. Try it: 'We must all pull together . . .' "

The words came back from the Blab as fast as he spoke them, but changed into the voice of the Middle American President. He rolled down the driver-side window; this worked best if there was eye contact. Besides, he might need her out of the car. "Okay. Stay here. I'll go get us the sucker." She rattled his instructions back in pompous tones.

One last thing: He punched a number into the car phone, and set its timer and no video option. Then he was out of the car, jogging back to the guard box. This sort of trick had worked often enough at school. Pray that it would work now. Pray that she wouldn't ad lib.

He turned off the throat mike as Lucas buzzed him back into the visitor trap. "I got to the top. Someone—maybe even the Chief of Federal Security—will call back on the Red Line."

Phil's eyebrows went up. "That would do it." Hamid's prestige had just taken a giant step up.

Hamid made a show of impatient pacing about the visitor trap. He stopped at the outer door with his back to the guard. Now he really *was* impatient. Then the phone rang, and he heard Phil pick it up.

"Escrow One, Agent Lucas speaking, Sir!"

From where he was standing, Hamid could see the Blab. She was in the driver's seat, looking curiously at the dash phone. Hamid turned on the throat mike and murmured, "Lucas, this is Joseph Stanley Ortega."

Almost simultaneously, "Lucas, this is Joseph Stanley Ortega," came from the phone behind him. The words were weighted with all the importance Hamid could wish, and something else: a furtiveness not in the public speeches. That was probably because of Hamid's original delivery, but it didn't sound too bad.

In any case, Phil Lucas was impressed. "Sir!"

"Agent Lucas, we have a problem." Hamid concentrated on his words, and tried to ignore the Ortega echo. For him, that was the hardest part of the trick, especially when he had to speak more than a brief sentence. "There could be nuclear fire, unless the Tourists cool off. I'm with the National Command Authorities in deep shelter: it's that serious." Maybe that would explain why there was no video.

Phil's voice quavered. "Yes, sir." *He* wasn't in deep shelter.

"Have you verified—" *clicket* "—my ID?" The click was in Hamid's earphone; he didn't hear it on the guard's set. A loose connection in the headpiece?

"Yes, sir. I mean . . . just one moment." Sounds of hurried keyboard tapping. There should be no problem with a voiceprint match, and Hamid needed things nailed tight to bring this off. "Yes, sir, you're fine. I mean—"

"Good. Now listen carefully: The guide, Thompson, has a Tourist with him. We need that Outsider returned, *quickly and quietly.* Get the lift ready, and keep everybody clear of these two. If Thompson fails, millions may die. Give him whatever he asks for." Out in the car, the Blab was having a high old time. Her front talons were hooked awkwardly over the steering wheel. She twisted it back and forth, "driving" and "talking" at the same time: the apotheosis of life—to be taken for a person by real people!

"Yes, sir!"

"Very well. Let's—" *clicket-click* "—get moving on this." And on that last click, the Ortega voice was gone. *God damned cheapjack comm-set!*

Lucas was silent a moment, respectfully waiting for his President to continue. Then, "Yes, sir. What must we do?"

Out in the Millennium Commander, the Blab was the picture of consternation. She turned toward him, eyes wide. *What do I say now?* Hamid repeated this line, as loud as he dared. No Ortega. *She can't hear anything I'm saying!* He shut off his mike.

"Sir? Are you still there?"

"Line must be dead," Hamid said casually, and gave the Blab a little wave to come running.

"Phone light says I still have a connection, Ham. . . . Mr. President, can you hear me? You were saying what we must do. Mr. President?"

The Blab didn't recognize his wave. Too small. He tried again. She tapped a talon against her muzzle. *Blab! Don't ad lib!* "Well, uh," came Ortega's voice, "don't rush me. I'm thinking. I'm thinking! . . . We must all pull together or else millions may die. Don't you think? I mean, it makes sense—", which it did not, and less so by the second. Lucas was making "uh huh" sounds, trying to fit reason on the Blabber. His tone was steadily more puzzled, even suspicious.

No help for it. Hamid slammed his fist against the transp armor, and waved wildly to the Blab. *Come here!* Ortega's voice died in midsyllable. He turned to see Lucas staring at him, surprise and uneasiness on his face. "Something's going on here, and I don't like it—" Somewhere in his mind, Phil had figured out he was being taken, yet the rest of him was carried forward by the inertia of the everyday. He leaned over the counter, to get Hamid's line of view on the lot.

The original plan was completely screwed, yet strangely he felt no panic, no doubt; there were still options: Hamid smiled—and jumped across the counter, driving the smaller man into the corner of wall and counter. Phil's hand reached wildly for the tab that would bring the partition down. Hamid just pushed him harder against the wall . . . and grabbed the guard's pistol from its holster. He jammed the barrel into the other's middle. "Quiet down, Phil."

"Son of a bitch!" But the other stopped struggling. Hamid heard the Blab slam into the outer door.

"Okay. Kick the outside release." The door buzzed. A moment later, the Blab was in the visitor trap, bouncing around his legs.

"Heh heh heh! That was good. That was really good!" The cackle was Lazy Larry's but the voice was still Ortega's.

"Now buzz the inner door." The other gave his head a tight shake. Hamid punched Lucas's gut with the point of the pistol. *"Now!"* For an instant, Phil seemed frozen. Then he kneed the control tab, and the inner door buzzed. Hamid pushed it ajar with his foot, then heaved Lucas away from the counter. The other bounced to his feet, his eyes staring at the muzzle of the pistol, his face very pale. *Dead men don't raise alarums.* The thought was clear on his face.

Hamid hesitated, almost as shocked by his success as Lucas was. "Don't worry, Phil." He shifted his aim and fired a burst over Lucas's shoulder . . . into the warehouse security processor. Fire and debris flashed back into the room—and now alarms sounded everywhere.

He pushed through the door, the Blab close behind. The armor clicked shut behind them; odds were it would stay locked now that the security processor was down. Nobody in sight, but he heard shouting. Hamid ran down the aisle of upgoing goods. They kept the agrav lift at the back of the building, under the main ceiling hatch. Things were definitely not going to plan, but if the lift was there, he could still—

"There he is!"

Hamid dived down an aisle, jigged this way and that between pallets . . . and then began walking very quietly. He was in the downcoming section now, surrounded by the goods that had been delivered thus far by the Caravan. These were the items that would lift Middle America beyond Old Earth's twenty-first century. Towering ten meters above his head were stacks of room-temperature fusion electrics. With them— and the means to produce more—Middle America could trash its methanol economy and fixed fusion plants. Two aisles over were the raw agrav units. These looked more like piles of fabric than anything high-tech. Yet the warehouse lifter was built around one, and with them Middle America would soon make aircars as easily as automobiles.

Hamid knew there were cameras in the ceiling above the lights. Hopefully they were as dead as the security processor. Footsteps one aisle over. Hamid eased into the dark between two pallets. Quiet, quiet. The Blab didn't feel like being quiet. She raced down the aisle ahead of him, raking the spaces between the pallets with a painfully loud imitation of his pistol. They'd see her in a second. He ran the other direction a few meters, and fired a burst into the air.

"Jesus! How many did asshole Lucas let in?" Someone very close replied, "That's still low-power stuff." Much quieter: "We'll show these guys some firepower." Hamid suddenly guessed there were only two of them. And with the guard box jammed, they might be trapped in here till the alarm brought guards from outside.

He backed away from the voices, continued toward the rear of the warehouse.

"Boo!" The Blab was on the pallets above him, talking to someone on the ground. Explosive shells smashed into the fusion electrics around her. The sounds bounced back and forth through the warehouse. Whatever it was, it was a cannon compared to his pistol. No doubt it was totally unauthorized for indoors, but that did Hamid little good. He raced forward, heedless of the destruction. "Get down!" he screamed at the pallets. A bundle of shadow and light materialized in front of him and streaked down the aisle.

A second roar of cannon fire, tearing through the space where he had just been. But something else was happening now. Blue light shone from somewhere in the racks of fusion electrics, sending brightness and crisp shadows across the walls ahead. It felt like someone had opened a furnace door behind him. He looked back. The blue was spreading, an arc-welder light that promised burns yet unfelt. He looked quickly away, afterimages dancing on his eyes, afterimages of the pallet shelves *sagging* in the heat.

The autosprinklers kicked on, an instant rainstorm. But this was a fire that water would not quench—and might even fuel. The water exploded into steam, knocking Hamid to his knees. He bounced up sprinting, falling, sprinting again. The agrav lift should be around the next row of pallets. In the back of his mind, something was analyzing the disaster. That explosive cannon fire had started things, a runaway melt in the fusion electrics. They were supposedly safer than meth engines—but they could melt down. This sort of destruction in a Middle American nuclear plant would have meant rad poisoning over a continent. But the Tourists claimed their machines melted clean—shedding low-energy photons and an enormous flood of particles that normal matter scarcely responded to. Hamid felt an urge to hysterical laughter; Slow Zone astronomers light-years away might notice this someday, a wiggle on their neutrino scopes, one more datum for their flawed cosmologies.

There was lightning in the rainstorm now, flashes between the pallets and across the aisle—into the raw agrav units. The clothlike material jerked and rippled, individual units floating upwards. Magic carpets released by a genie.

Then giant hands clapped him, sound that was pain, and the rain was gone, replaced by a hot wet wind that swept around and up. Morning light shown through the steamy mist. The explosion had blasted open the roof. A rainbow arced across the ruins. Hamid was crawling now. Sticky wet ran down his face, dripped redly on the floor. The pallets bearing the fusion electrics had collapsed. Fifteen meters away, molten plastic slurried atop flowing metal.

He could see the agrav lift now, what was left of it. The lift sagged like an old candle in the flow of molten metal. So. No way up. He pulled himself back from the glare, and leaned against the stacked agravs. They slid and vibrated behind him. The cloth was soft, yet it blocked the heat, and some of the noise. The pinkish blue of a dawn sky shown through the last scraps of mist. The Lothlrimarre barge hung there, four spherical pressure vessels embedded in intricate ramps and crenellations.

Jeeze. Most of the warehouse roof was just . . . gone. A huge tear showed through the far wall. *There!* The two guards. They were facing away from him, one half leaning on the other. Chasing him was very far from their minds at the moment. They were picking their way through the jumble, trying to get out of the warehouse. Unfortunately, a rivulet of silver metal crossed their path. One false step and they'd be ankle deep in the stuff. But they were lucky, and in fifteen seconds passed from sight around the outside of the building.

No doubt he could get out that way, too. . . . But that wasn't why he was here. Hamid struggled to his feet, and began shouting for the Blab. The hissing, popping sounds were loud, but not like before. If she were conscious, she'd hear him. He wiped blood from his lips and limped along the row of agrav piles. *Don't die, Blab. Don't die.*

There was motion everywhere. The piles of agravs had come alive. The top ones simply lifted off, tumbled upwards, rolling and unrolling. The lower layers strained and jerked. Normal matter might not notice the flood of never-never particles from the melt-down; the agravs were clearly not normal. Auras flickered around the ones trapped at the bottom. But this was not the eye-sizzling burn of the fusion electrics. This was a soft thing, an awakening rather than an explosion. Hamid's eyes were caught on the rising. Hundreds of them just floating off, gray and russet banners in the morning light. He leaned back. Straight up, the farthest ones were tiny specks against the blue. *Maybe—*

Something banged into his legs, almost dumping him back on the floor. "Wow. So loud." The Blab had found *him!* Hamid knelt and grabbed her around the neck. She looked fine! A whole lot better than he did anyway. Like most smaller animals, she could take a lot of bouncing around. He ran his hands down her shoulders. There were some nicks, a spattering of blood. And she looked subdued, not quite the hellion of before. "Loud. Loud," she kept saying.

"I know, Blab. But that's the worst." He looked back into the sky. At the rising agravs . . . at the Lothlrimarre barge. *It would be crazy to try . . .* but he heard sirens outside.

He patted the Blab, then stood and clambered up the nearest pile of agravs. The material, hundreds of separate units piled like blankets, gave beneath his boots like so much foam rubber. He slid back a ways after each step. He grabbed at the edges of the units above him, and pulled himself near the top. He wanted to test one that was free to rise. Hamid grabbed the top layer, already rippling in an unsensed wind. He pulled out his pocket knife, and slashed at the material. It parted smoothly, with the resistance of heavy felt. He ripped off a strip of the material, stuffed it in his pocket, then grabbed again at the top layer. The unit fluttered in his hands, a four-meter square straining for the sky. It slowly tipped him backwards. His feet left the pile. It was rising as fast as the unloaded ones!

"Wait for me! Wait!" The Blab jumped desperately at his boots. Two meters up, three meters. Hamid gulped, and let go. He crashed to the concrete, lay stunned for a moment, imagining what would have happened if he'd dithered an instant longer. . . . Still. He took the scrap of agrav from his pocket, stared at it as it tugged on his fingers. There was a pattern in the reddish-gray fabric, intricate and recursive. The Tourists said it was in a different class from the fusion electrics. The electrics involved advanced technology, but were constructable within the Slow Zone. Agrav, on the other hand . . . the effect could be explained in theory, but its practical use depended on instant-by-instant restabilization at atomic levels. The Tourists claimed there were billions of protein-sized processors in the fabric. This was an import—not just from the Beyond—but from Transhuman Space. Till now, Hamid had been a skeptic. Flying was such a prosaic thing. But . . . these things had no simple logic. They were more like living creatures, or complex control systems. They seemed a lot like the "smart matter" Larry claimed was common in Transhuman technology.

Hamid cut the strip into two different-sized pieces. The cut edges were smooth, quite unlike cuts in cloth or leather. He let the fragments go. . . . They drifted slowly upwards, like leaves on a breeze. But after a few seconds, the large one took the lead, falling higher and higher above the smaller. *I could come down just by trimming the fabric!* And he remembered how the carpet had drifted sideways, in the direction of his grasp.

The sirens were louder. He looked at the pile of agravs. Funny. A week ago he had been worried about flying commercial air to Westland. "You want games, Blab? This is the biggest yet."

He climbed back up the pile. The top layer was just beginning to twitch. They had maybe thirty seconds, if it was like the others. He pulled the fabric around him, tying it under his arms. "Blab! Get your ass up here!"

She came, but not quite with the usual glee. Things had been rough this morning—or maybe she was just brighter than he was. He grabbed her, and tied the other end of the agrav under her shoulders. As the agrav twitched toward flight, the cloth seemed to shrink. He could still cut the fabric, but the knots were tight. He grabbed the Blab under her hind quarters, and drew her up to his chest—just like Pop used to do when the Blab was a pup. Only now, she was big. Her forelegs stuck long over his shoulders.

The fabric came taut around his armpits. Now he was standing. Now—his feet left the pile. He looked *down* at the melted pallets, the silver metal rivers that dug deep through the warehouse floor. The Blab was making the sounds of a small boy crying.

They were through the roof. Hamid shuddered as the morning chill turned his soaked clothing icy. The sun was at the horizon, its brilliance no help against the cold. Shadows grew long and crisp from the buildings. The guts of the warehouse lay open below them; from here it looked dark, but lightning still flickered. More reddish-gray squares floated up from the ruins. In the gravel lot fronting the warehouse, there were fire trucks and armored vehicles. Men ran back and forth from the guard box. A squad was moving around the side of the building. Two guys by the armored cars pointed at him, and others just stopped to stare. A boy and his not-dog, swinging beneath a wrong-way parachute. He'd seen enough Feds 'n' Crooks to know they could shoot him down easily, any number of ways. One of the figures climbed into the armored car. If they were half as trigger happy as the guards inside the warehouse . . .

Half a minute passed. The scene below could fit between his feet now. The Blab wasn't crying anymore, and he guessed the chill was no problem for her. The Blab's neck and head extended over his shoulder. He could feel her looking back and forth. "Wow," she said softly. "Wow."

Rockabye baby. They swung back and forth beneath the agrav. Back and forth. The swings were getting wider each time! In a sickening whirl, the sky and ground traded places. He was buried head first in agrav fabric. He struggled out of the mess. They weren't hanging below the agrav now, they were *lying* on top of it. This was crazy. How could it be stable with them on top? In a second it would dump them back under. He held tight to the Blab . . . but no more swinging. It was as if the hanging-down position had been the unstable one. More evidence that the agrav was smart matter, its processors using underlying nature to produce seemingly unnatural results.

The damn thing really was a flying carpet! Of course, with all the knots, the four-meter square of fabric was twisted and crumpled. It looked more like the Blab's nest of blankets back home than the flying carpets of fantasy.

The warehouse district was out of sight beneath the carpet. In the spaces around and above them, dozens of agravs paced him—some just a few meters away, some bare specks in the sky. Westwards, they were coming even with the tops of the Marquette towers: brown and ivory walls, vast mirrors of windows reflecting back the landscape of morning. Southwards, Ann Arbor was a tiny crisscross of streets, almost lost in the bristle of leafless trees. The quad was clearly visible, the interior walks, the tiny speck of red that was Morale Hall. He'd had roughly this view every time they flew back from the farm, but now . . . there was nothing around him. It was just Hamid and the Blab . . . and the air stretching away forever beneath them. Hamid gulped, and didn't look down for a while.

They were still rising. The breeze came straight down upon them—and it seemed to be getting stronger. Hamid shivered uncontrollably, teeth chattering. How high up were they? Three thousand meters? Four? He was going numb, and when he moved he could hear ice crackling in his jacket. He felt dizzy and nauseous—five thousand meters was about the highest you'd want to go without oxygen on Middle America. He *thought* he could stop the rise; if not, they were headed for space, along with the rest of the agravs.

But he had to do more than slow the rise, or descend. He looked up at the Lothlrimarre's barge. It was much nearer—and two hundred meters to the east. If he couldn't move this thing sideways, he'd need the slug's active cooperation.

It was something he had thought about—for maybe all of five seconds—back in the warehouse. If the agrav had been an ordinary lighter-than-air craft, there'd be no hope. Without props or jets, a balloon goes where the wind says; the only control comes from finding the *altitude* where the wind and you want the same thing. But when he grabbed that first carpet, it really had slid horizontally toward the side he was holding. . . .

He crept toward the edge. The agrav yielded beneath his knees, but didn't tilt more than a small boat would. Next to him, the Blab looked over the edge, straight down. Her head jerked this way and that as she scanned the landscape. "Wow," she kept saying. Could she really understand what she was seeing?

The wind shifted a little. It came a bit from the side now, not straight from above. He really did have control! Hamid smiled around chattering teeth.

The carpet rose faster and faster. The downward wind was an arctic blast. They must be going up at fifteen or twenty klicks per hour. The Lothlrimarre barge loomed huge above them . . . now almost beside them.

God, they were *above* it now! Hamid pulled out his knife, picked desperately at the blade opener with numbed fingers. It came open abruptly—and almost popped out of his shaking hand. He trimmed small pieces from the edge of the carpet. The wind from heaven stayed just as strong. Bigger pieces! He tore wildly at the cloth. One large strip, two. And the wind eased . . . stopped. Hamid bent over the edge of the carpet, and stuffed his vertigo back down his throat. *Perfect.* They were directly over the barge, and closing.

The nearest of the four pressure spheres was so close it blocked his view of the others. Hamid could see the human habitat, the conference area. They would touch down on a broad flat area next to the sphere. The aiming couldn't have been better. Hamid guessed the slug must be maneuvering too, moving the barge precisely under his visitor.

There was a flash of heat, and an invisible fist slammed into the carpet. Hamid and the Blab tumbled—now beneath the agrav, now above. He had a glimpse of the barge. A jet of yellow-white spewed from the sphere, ammonia and hydrogen at one thousand atmospheres. The top pressure sphere had been breached. The spear of superpressured gas was surrounded by pale flame where the hydrogen and atmospheric oxygen burned.

The barge fell out of view, leaving thunder and burning mists. Hamid held onto the Blab and as much of the carpet as he could wrap around them. The tumbling stopped; they were upside down in the heavy swaddling. Hamid looked out:

"Overhead" was the brown and gray of farmland in late autumn. Marquette was to his left. He bent around, peeked into the sky. There! The barge was several klicks away. The top pressure vessel was spreading fire and mist, but the lower ones looked okay. Pale violet flickered from between the spheres. Moments later, thunder echoed across the sky. The slug was fighting back!

He twisted in the jumble of cloth, trying to see the high sky. To the north . . . a single blue-glowing trail lanced southwards . . . split into five separate, jigging paths that cooled through orange to red. It was beautiful . . . but somehow like a jagged claw sketched against the sky. The claw tips dimmed to nothing, but whatever caused them still raced forward. The attackers' answering fire slagged the north-facing detail of the barge. It crumpled like trash plastic in a fire. The bottom pressure vessels still looked okay, but if the visitors' deck got zapped like that, Larry would be a dead man.

Multiple sonic booms rocked the carpet. Things swept past, too small and fast to clearly see. The barge's guns still flickered violet, but the craft was rising now—faster than he had ever seen it move.

After a moment, the carpet drifted through one more tumble, and they sat heads up. The morning had been transformed. Strange clouds were banked around and above him, some burning, some glowing, all netted with the brownish-reds of nitrogen oxides. The stench of ammonia burned his eyes and mouth. The Blab was making noises through her mouth, true coughing and choking sounds.

The Tourists were long gone. The Lothlrimarre was a dot at the top of the sky. All the other agravs had passed by. He and the Blab were alone in the burning clouds. *Probably not for long.* Hamid began sawing at the agrav fabric—tearing off a slice, testing for an upwelling breeze, then tearing off another. They drifted through the cloud deck into a light drizzle, a strange rain that burned the skin as it wet them. He slid the carpet sideways into the sunlight, and they could breathe again. Things looked almost normal, except where the clouds cast a great bloody shadow across the farmland.

Where best to land? Hamid looked over the edge of the carpet . . . and saw the enemy waiting. It was a cylinder, tapered, with a pair of small fins at one end. It drifted through the carpet's shadow, and he realized the enemy craft was *close.* It couldn't be more than ten meters long, less than two meters across at the widest. It hung silent, pacing the carpet's slow descent. Hamid looked up, and saw the others—four more dark shapes. They circled in, like killer fish nosing at a possible lunch. One slid right over them, so slow and near he could have run his palm down its length. There were no ports, no breaks in the dull finish. But the fins—red glowed dim from within them, and Hamid felt a wave of heat as they passed.

The silent parade went on for a minute, each killer getting its look. The Blab's head followed the craft around and around. Her eyes were wide, and she was making the terrified whistling noises of the night before. The air was still, but for the faint updraft of the carpet's descent. Or was it? . . . The sound grew, a hissing sound like Tines had made during his phone call. Only now it came from all the killers, and there were overtones lurking at the edge of sensibility, tones that never could have come from an ordinary telephone.

"Blab." He reached to stroke her neck. She slashed at his hand, her needle-teeth slicing deep. Hamid gasped in pain, and rolled back from her. The Blab's pelt was puffed out as far as he had ever seen it. She looked twice normal size, a very large carnivore with death glittering in her eyes. Her long neck snapped this way and that, trying to track all the killers at once. Fore and rear talons dragged long rips through the carpet. She climbed onto the thickest folds of the carpet, and *shrieked* at the killers . . . and collapsed.

For a moment, Hamid couldn't move. His hand, the scream: razors across his hand, icepicks jammed in his ears. He struggled to his knees and crawled to the Blabber. "Blab?" No answer, no motion. He touched her flank: limp as something fresh dead.

In twenty years, Hamid Thompson had never had close friends, but he had never been alone, either. Until now. He looked up from the Blabber's body, at the circling shapes.

Alone at four thousand meters. He didn't have much choice when one of the killer fish came directly at him, when something wide and dark opened from its belly. The darkness swept around them, swallowing all.

Hamid had never been in space before. Under other circumstances, he would have reveled in the experience. The glimpse he'd had of Middle America from low orbit was like a beautiful dream. But now, all he could see through the floor of his cage was a bluish dot, nearly lost in the sun's glare. He pushed hard against the clear softness, and rolled onto his back. It was harder than a one-handed pushup to do that. He guessed the mothership was doing four or five gees . . . and had been for hours.

When they had pulled him off the attack craft, Hamid had been semiconscious. He had no idea what acceleration that shark boat reached, but it was more than he could take. He remembered that glimpse of Middle America, blue and serene. Then . . . they'd taken the Blab—or her body—away. *Who?* There had been a human, the Ravna woman. She had done something to his hand; it wasn't bleeding anymore. And . . . and there had been the Blabber, up and walking around. No, the pelt pattern had been all wrong. *That must have been Tines.* There had been the hissing voice, and some kind of argument with Ravna.

Hamid stared up at the sunlight on the ceiling and walls. His own shadow lay spread-eagled on the ceiling. In the first hazy hours, he had thought it was another prisoner. The walls were gray, seamless, but with scrape marks and stains, as though heavy equipment was used here. He thought there was a door in the ceiling, but he couldn't remember for sure. There was no sign of one now. The room was an empty cubical, featureless, its floor showing clear to the stars: surely not an ordinary brig. There were no toilet facilities—and at five gees they wouldn't have helped. The air was thick with the stench of himself. . . . Hamid guessed the room was an airlock. The transparent floor might be nothing more than a figment of some field generator's imagination. A flick of a switch and Hamid would be swept away forever.

The Blabber gone, Pop gone, maybe Larry and the slug gone. . . . Hamid raised his good hand a few centimeters and clenched his fist. Lying here was the first time he'd ever thought about killing anyone. He thought about it a lot now. . . . It kept the fear tied down.

"Mr. Thompson." Ravna's voice. Hamid suppressed a twitch of surprise: after hours of rage, to hear the enemy. "Mr. Thompson, we are going to free fall in fifteen seconds. Do not be alarmed."

So, airline courtesy of a sudden.

The force that had squished him flat these hours, that had made it an exercise even to breathe, slowly lessened. From beyond the walls and ceiling he heard small popping noises. For a panicky instant, it seemed as though the floor had disappeared and he was falling through. He twisted. His hand hit the barrier . . . and he floated slowly across the room, toward the wall that had been the ceiling. A door had opened. He drifted through, into a hall that would have looked normal except for the intricate pattern of grooves and ledges that covered the walls.

"Thirty meters down the hall is a latrine," came Ravna's voice. "There are clean clothes that should fit you. When you are done . . . when you are done, we will talk."

Damn right. Hamid squared his shoulders and pulled himself down the hall.

She didn't look like a killer. There was anger—tension?—on her face, the face of someone who has been awake a long time and has fought hard—and doesn't expect to win.

Hamid drifted slowly into the—conference room? bridge?—trying to size everything up at once. It was a large room, with a low ceiling. Moving across it was easy in zero gee, slow bounces from floor to ceiling and back. The wall curved around, transparent along most of its circumference. There were stars and night dark beyond.

Ravna had been standing in a splash of light. Now she moved back a meter, into the general dimness. Somehow she slipped her foot into the floor, anchoring herself. She waved him to the other side of a table. They stood in the half crouch of zero gee, less than two meters apart. Even so, she looked taller than he had guessed from the phone call. Her mass might be close to his. The rest of her was as he remembered, though she looked very tired. Her gaze flickered across him, and away. "Hello, Mr. Thompson. The floor will hold your foot, if you tap it gently."

Hamid didn't take the advice; he held onto the table edge and jammed his feet against the floor. He would have something to brace against if the time came to move quickly. "Where is my Blabber?" His voice came out hoarse, more desperate than demanding.

"Your pet is dead."

There was a tiny hesitation before the last word. She was as bad a liar as ever. Hamid pushed back the rage: if the Blab was alive, there was something still possible beyond revenge. "Oh." He kept his face blank.

"However, we intend to return you safely to home." She gestured at the star fields around them. "The six-gee boost was to avoid unnecessary fighting with the Lothlrimarre being. We will coast outwards some farther, perhaps even go into ram drive. But Mr. Tines will take you back to Middle America in one of our attack boats. There will be no problem to land you without attracting notice . . . perhaps on the western continent, somewhere out of the way." Her tone was distant. He noticed that she never looked directly at him for more than an instant. Now she was staring just to one side of his face. He remembered the phone call, how she seemed to ignore his video. Up close, she was just as attractive as before—more. Just once he would like to see her smile. *And somewhere there was unease that he could be so attracted by a murderous stranger.*

If only. "If only I could understand *why*. Why did you kill the Blab? Why did you kill my father?"

Ravna's eyes narrowed. "That cheating piece of filth? He is too tricky to kill. He was gone when we visited his farm. I'm not sure I have killed anyone on this operation. The Lothlrimarre is still functioning, I know that." She sighed. "We were all very lucky. You have no idea what Tines has been like these last days. . . . He called you last night."

Hamid nodded numbly.

"Well, he was mellow then. He tried to kill me when I took over the ship. Another day like this and he would have been dead—and most likely your planet would have been so too."

Hamid remembered the Lothlrimarre's theory about the tines's need. And now that the creature had the Blab. . . . "So now Tines is satisfied?"

Ravna nodded vaguely, missing the quaver in his voice. "He's harmless now and very confused, poor guy. Assimilation is hard. It will be a few weeks . . . but he'll stabilize, probably turn out better than he ever was."

Whatever that means.

She pushed back from the table, stopped herself with a hand on the low ceiling. Apparently their meeting was over. "Don't worry. He should be well enough to take you home quite soon. Now I will show you your—"

"Don't rush him, Rav. Why should he want to go back to Middle America?" The voice was a pleasant tenor, human sounding but a little slurred.

Ravna bounced off the ceiling. "I thought you were going to stay out of this! Of course the boy is going back to Middle America. That's his home; that's where he fits."

"I wonder." The unseen speaker laughed. He sounded cheerfully—*joyfully*—drunk. "Your name is shit down there, Hamid, did you know that?"

"Huh?"

"Yup. You slagged the Caravan's entire shipment of fusion electrics. 'Course you had a little help from the Federal Police, but that fact is being ignored. Much worse, you destroyed most of the agrav units. *Whee.* Up, up and away. And there's no way those can be replaced short of a trip back to the Outsi—"

"Shut up!" Ravna's anger rode over the good cheer. "The agrav units were a cheap trick. Nothing that subtle can work in the Zone for long. Five years from now they would all have faded."

"Sure, sure. I know that, and you know that. But both Middle America and the Tourists figure you've trashed this Caravan, Hamid. You'd be a fool to go back."

Ravna shouted something in a language Hamid had never heard.

"English, Rav, English. I want him to understand what is happening."

"He is going back!" Ravna's voice was furious, almost desperate. "We *agreed!"*

"I know, Rav." A little of the rampant joy left the voice. It sounded truly sympathetic. "And I'm sorry. But I was different then, and I understand things better now. . . . Hey, I'll be down in a minute, okay?"

She closed her eyes. It's hard to slump in free fall, but Ravna came close, her shoulders and arms relaxing, her body drifting slowly up from the floor. "Oh, Lord," she said softly.

Out in the hall, someone was whistling a tune that had been popular in Marquette six months ago. A shadow floated down the walls, followed by . . . *the Blab?* Hamid lurched off the table, flailed wildly for a handhold. He steadied himself, got a closer look.

No. Not the Blab. It was of the same race certainly, but this one had an entirely different pattern of black and white. The great patch of black around one eye and white around the other would have been laughable . . . if you didn't know what you were looking at: at last to see Mr. Tines.

Man and alien regarded each other for a long moment. It was a little smaller than the Blab. It wore a checkered orange scarf about its neck. Its paws looked no more flexible than his Blab's . . . but he didn't doubt the intelligence that looked back from its eyes. The tines drifted to the ceiling, and anchored itself with a deft swipe of paw and talons. There were faint sounds in the air now, squeaks and twitters almost beyond hearing. If he listened close enough, Hamid guessed he would hear the hissing, too.

The tines looked at him, and laughed pleasantly—the tenor voice of a minute before. "Don't rush me! I'm not all here yet."

Hamid looked at the doorway. There were two more there, one with a jeweled collar—the leader? They glided through the air and tied down next to the first. Hamid saw more shadows floating down the hall.

"How many?" he asked.

"I'm six now." He thought it was a different tines that answered, but the voice was the same.

The last three floated in the doorway. One wore no scarf or jewelry . . . and looked very familiar.

"Blab!" Hamid pushed off the table. He went into a spin that missed the door by several meters. The Blabber—it must be her—twisted skillfully around and fled the room.

"Stay away!" For an instant the tines's voice changed, held the same edge as the night before. Hamid stood on the wall next to the doorway and looked down the hall. The Blab was there, sitting on the closed door at the far end. Hamid's orientation flipped . . . the hall could just as well be a deep, bright-lit well, with the Blab trapped at the bottom of it.

"Blab?" He said softly, aware of the tines behind him.

She looked up at him. "I can't play the old games anymore, Hamid," she said in her softest femvoice. He stared for a moment, uncomprehending. Over the years, the Blab said plenty of things that—by accident or in the listeners' imagination—might seem humanly intelligent. Here, for the first time, he knew that he was hearing sense. . . . And he guessed what Ravna meant when she said the Blab was dead.

Hamid backed away from the edge of the pit. He looked at the other tines, remembered that their speech came as easily from one as the other. "You're like a hive of roaches, aren't you?"

"A little." The tenor voice came from somewhere among them.

"But telepathic," Hamid said.

The one who had been his friend answered, but in the tenor voice: "Yes, between myselves. But it's no sixth sense. You've known about it all your life. I like to talk a lot. Blabber." The squeaking and the hissing: just the edge of all they were saying to each other across their two-hundred-kilohertz bandwidth. "I'm sorry I flinched. Myselves are still confused. I don't know quite who I am."

The Blab pushed off and drifted back into the bridge. She grabbed a piece of ceiling as she came even with Hamid. She extended her head toward him, tentatively, as though he were a stranger. *I feel the same way about you*, thought Hamid. But he reached out to brush her neck with his fingers. She twitched back, glided across the room to nestle among the other tines.

Hamid stared at them staring back. He had a sudden image: a pack of long-necked rats beadily analyzing their prey. "So. Who is the real Mr.

Tines? The monster who'd smash a world, or the nice guy I'm hearing now?"

Ravna answered, her voice tired, distant. "The monster tines is gone . . . or going. Don't you see? The pack was unbalanced. It was dying."

"There were five in my pack, Hamid. Not a bad number: some of the brightest packs are that small. But I was down from seven—two of my-selves had been killed. The ones remaining were mismatched, and only one of them was female." Tines paused. "I know humans can go for years without contact with the opposite sex, and suffer only mild dis-comfort—"

Tell me about it.

"—but tines are very different. If a pack's sex ratio gets too lopsided, especially if there is a mismatch of skills, then the mind disintegrates. . . . Things can get very nasty in the process." Hamid noticed that all the time it talked, the two tines next to the one with the orange scarf had been nib-bling at the scarf's knots. They moved quickly, perfectly coordinated, un-tying and retying the knots. *Tines doesn't need hands.* Or put another way, he already had six. Hamid was seeing the equivalent of a human playing nervously with his tie.

"Ravna lied when she said the Blab is dead. I forgive her: she wants you off our ship, with no more questions, no more hassle. But the Blab-ber isn't dead. She was *rescued* . . . from being an animal the rest of her life. And her rescue saved the pack. I feel so . . . happy. Better even than when I was seven. I can understand things that have been puzzles for years. Your Blab is far more language-oriented than any of my other selves. I could never talk like this without her."

Ravna had drifted toward the pack. Now she had her feet planted on the floor beneath them. Her head brushed the shoulder of one, was even with the eyes of another. "Imagine the Blabber as the verbal hemisphere of a human brain," she said to Hamid.

"Not quite," Tines said. "A human hemisphere can almost carry on by itself. The Blab by itself could never be a person."

Hamid remembered how the Blab's greatest desire had often seemed just to *be* a real person. And listening to this creature, he heard echoes of the Blab. It would be easy to accept what they were saying. . . . Yet if you turned the words just a little, you had enslavement and rape—the slug's theory with frosting.

Hamid turned away from all the eyes and looked across the star clouds. *How much should I believe? How much should I seem to believe?* "One of the Tourists wanted to sell us a gadget, an 'ftl radio.' Did you know that we used it to ask about the tines? Do you know what we found?" He told them about the horrors Larry had found around the galactic rim.

Ravna exchanged a glance with the tines by her head. For a moment the only sound was the twittering and hissing. Then Tines spoke. "Imagine the most ghastly villains of Earth's history. Whatever they are, whatever holocausts they set, I assure you much worse has happened elsewhere. . . . Now imagine that this regime was so vast, so effectively *evil* that no honest historians survived. What stories do you suppose would be spread about the races they exterminated?"

"Okay. So—"

"Tines are not monsters. On average, we are no more bloodthirsty than you humans. But we are descended from packs of wolf-like creatures. We are deadly warriors. Given reasonable equipment and numbers, we can outfight most anything in the Slow Zone." Hamid remembered the shark pack of attack boats. With one animal in each, and radio communication . . . no team of human pilots could match their coordination. "We were once a great power in our part of the Slow Zone. We had enemies, even when there was no war. Would you trust creatures who live indefinitely, but whose personalities may drift from friendly to indifferent—even to inimical—as their components die and are replaced?"

"And you're such a peach of a guy because you've got the Blab?"

"*Yes!* Though you liked . . . I know you would have liked me when I was seven. But the Blab has a lovely outlook; she makes it fun to be alive."

Hamid looked at Ravna and the pack who surrounded her. So the tines had been great fighters. That he believed. So they were now virtually extinct, having run into something even deadlier. That he could believe, too. Beyond that . . . he'd be a fool to believe anything. He could imagine Tines as a friend, he wanted Ravna as one. But all the talk, all the seeming argument—it could just as well be manipulation. One thing was sure: if he returned to Middle America, he would never know the truth. He might live the rest of his life safe and cozy, but he wouldn't have the Blab, and he would never know what had really happened to her.

He gave Ravna a lopsided smile. "Back to square one then. I want passage to the Beyond with you."

"Out of the question. I-I made that clear from the beginning."

Hamid pushed nearer, stopped a meter in front of her. "Why won't you look at me?" he said softly. "Why do you hate me so much?"

For a full second, her eyes looked straight into his. "I *don't* hate you!" Her face clouded, as if she were about to weep. "It's just that you're such a God *damned* disappointment!" She pushed back abruptly, knocking the tines out of her way.

He followed her slowly back to the conference table. She "stood" there, talking to herself in some unknown language. "She's swearing to her ancestors," murmured a tines that drifted close by Hamid's head. "Her kind is big on that sort of thing."

Hamid anchored himself across from her. He looked at her face. Young, no older than twenty it looked. But Outsiders had some control over aging. Besides, Ravna had spent at least the last ten years in relativistic flight. "You hired my—you hired Hussein Thompson to adopt me, didn't you?"

She nodded.

"Why?"

She looked back at him for a moment, this time not flinching away. Finally she sighed. "Okay, I will try but . . . there are many things you from the Slow Zone do not understand. Middle America is close to the Beyond, but you see out through a tiny hole. You can have even less concept of what lies beyond the Beyond, in the Transhuman reaches." She was beginning to sound like Lazy Larry.

"I'm willing to start with the version for five-year-olds."

"Okay." The faintest of smiles crossed her face. It was everything he'd guessed it would be. He wondered how he could make her do it again. " 'Once upon a time,' "—the smile again, a little wider!—"there was a very wise and good man, as wise and good as any mere human or human equivalent can ever be: a mathematical genius, a great general, an even greater peacemaker. He lived five hundred years subjective, and half that time he was fighting a very great evil."

The Tines put in, "Just a part of that evil chewed up my race for breakfast."

Ravna nodded. "Eventually it chewed our hero, too. He's been dead almost a century objective. The enemy has been very alert to keep him dead. Tines and I may be the last people trying to bring him back. . . . How much do you know about cloning, Mr. Thompson?"

Hamid couldn't answer for a moment; it was too clear where all this was going. "The Tourists claim they can build a viable zygote from almost any body cell. They say it's easy, but that what you get is no more than an identical twin of the original."

"That is about right. In fact, the clone is often *much* less than an identical twin. The uterine environment determines much of an individual's adult characteristics. Consider mathematical ability. There is a genetic component—but part of mathematical genius comes from the fetus getting just the right testosterone overdose. A little too much and you have a *dummy.*

"Tines and I have been running for a long time. Fifty years ago we reached Lothlrimarre—the back end of nowhere if there ever was one. We had a clonable cell from the great man. We did our best with the humaniform medical equipment that was available. The newborn *looked* healthy enough. . . ."

Rustle, hiss.

"But why not just raise the—child—yourself?" Hamid said. "Why hire someone to take him into the Slow Zone?"

Ravna bit her lip and looked away. It was Tines who replied: "Two reasons. The enemy wants you permanently dead. Raising you in the Slow Zone was the best way to keep you out of sight. The other reason is more subtle. We don't have records of your original memories; we can't make a perfect copy. But if we could give you an upbringing that mimicked the original's . . . then we'd have someone with the same outlook."

"Like having the original back, with a bad case of amnesia."

Tines chuckled. "Right. And things went very well at first. It was great good luck to run into Hussein Thompson at Lothlrimarre. He seemed a bright fellow, willing to work for his money. He brought the newborn in suspended animation back to Middle America, and married a woman equally bright, to be your mother.

"We had everything figured, the original's background imitated better than we had ever hoped. I even gave up one of my selves, a newborn, to be with you."

"I guess I know most of the rest," said Hamid. "Everything went fine for the first eight years," the happy years of a loving family, "till it became clear that I wasn't a math genius. Then your hired hand didn't know what to do, and your plan fell apart."

"It didn't have to!" Ravna slapped the table. The motion pulled her body up, almost free of the foot anchors. "The math ability was a big part, but there was still a chance—if Thompson hadn't welshed on us." She glared at Hamid, and then at the pack. "The original's parents died when he was ten years old. Hussein and his woman were supposed to disappear when the clone was ten, in a faked air crash. *That was the agreement!* Instead—" she swallowed. "We talked to him. He wouldn't meet in person. He was full of excuses, the clever bastard. 'I didn't see what good it would do to hurt the boy any more,' he said. 'He's no superman, just a good kid. I wanted him to be happy!' " She choked on her own indignation. *"Happy!* If he knew what we have been through, what the stakes are—"

Hamid's face felt numb, frozen. He wondered what it would be like to throw up in zero gee. "What—what about my mother?" he said in a very small voice.

Ravna gave her head a quick shake. "She tried to persuade Thompson. When that didn't work, she left you. By then it was too late; besides, that sort of abandonment is not the trauma the original experienced. But she did her part of the bargain; we paid her most of what we promised. . . . We came to Middle America expecting to find someone very wonderful, living again. Instead, we found—"

"—a piece of trash?" He couldn't get any anger into the question.

She gave a shaky sigh. ". . . No, I don't really think that. Hussein Thompson probably did raise a good person, and that's more than most can claim. But if you were the one we had hoped, you would be known all over Middle America by now, the greatest inventor, the greatest mover since the colony began. And that would be just the beginning." She seemed to be looking through him . . . remembering?

Tines made a diffident throat-clearing sound. "Not a piece of trash at all. And not just a 'good kid,' either. A part of me lived with Hamid for twenty years; the Blabber's memories are about as clear as a tines fragment's can be. Hamid is not just a failed dream to me, Rav. He's different, but I like to be around him almost as much as with . . . the other one. And when the crunch came—well, I saw him fight back. Given his background, even the original couldn't have done better. Hitching a ride on a raw agrav was the sort of daring that—"

"Okay, Tiny, the boy is daring and quick. But there's a difference between suicidal foolishness and calculated risk-taking. This late in life, there's no way he'll become more than a 'good man.' " Sarcasm lilted in the words.

"We could do worse, Rav."

"We *must* do far better, and you know it! See here. It's two years subjective to get out of the Zone, and our suspension gear is failed. I will *not* accept seeing his face every day for two years. He goes back to Middle America." She kicked off, drifted toward the tines that hung over Hamid.

"I think not," said Tines. "If he doesn't want to go, I won't fly him back."

Anger and—strangely—panic played on Ravna's face. "This isn't how you were talking last week."

"Heh heh heh." Lazy Larry's cackle. "I've changed. Haven't you noticed?"

She grabbed a piece of ceiling and looked down at Hamid, calculating. "Boy. I don't think you understand. We're in a hurry; we won't be stopping any place like Lothlrimarre. There is one last way we might bring the original back to life—perhaps even with his own memories. You'll end up in Transhuman space if you come with us. The chances are that none of us will surv—" She stopped, and a slow smile spread across her face. Not a friendly smile. "Have you not thought what use your body might still be to us? You know nothing of what we plan. We may find ways of using you like a—like a blank data cartridge."

Hamid looked back at her, hoping no doubts showed on his face. "Maybe. But I'll have two years to prepare, won't I?"

They glared at each other for a long moment, the greatest eye contact yet. "So be it," she said at last. She drifted a little closer. "Some advice. We'll be two years cooped up here. It's a big ship. Stay out of my way." She drew back and pulled herself across the ceiling, faster and faster. She arrowed into the hallway beyond, and out of sight.

Hamid Thompson had his ticket to the Outside. Some tickets cost more than others. What much would he pay for his?

Eight hours later, the ship was under ram drive, outward bound. Hamid sat in the bridge, alone. The "windows" on one side of the room showed the view aft. Middle America's sun cast daylight across the room.

Invisible ahead of them, the interplanetary medium was being scooped in, fuel for the ram. The acceleration was barely perceptible, perhaps a fiftieth of a gee. The ram drive was for the long haul. That acceleration would continue indefinitely, eventually rising to almost half a gravity—and bringing them near light speed.

Middle America was a fleck of blue, trailing a white dot and a yellow one. It would be many hours before his world and its moons were lost from sight—and many days before they were lost to telescopic view.

Hamid had been here an hour—two?—since shortly after Tines showed him his quarters.

The inside of his head felt like an abandoned battlefield. A monster had become his good buddy. The man he hated turned out to be the father he had wanted . . . and his mother now seemed an uncaring manipulator. *And now I can never go back and ask you truly what you were, truly if you loved me.*

He felt something wet on his face. One good thing about gravity, even a fiftieth of a gee: it cleared the tears from your eyes.

He must be very careful these next two years. There was much to learn, and even more to guess at. What was lie and what was truth? There were things about the story that . . . how could one human being be as important as Ravna and Tines claimed? Next to the Transhumans, no human equivalent could count for much.

It might well be that these two believed the story they told him—*and that could be the most frightening possibility of all.* They talked about the Great Man as though he were some sort of messiah. Hamid had read of similar things in Earth history: twentieth-century Nazis longing for Hitler, the fanatics of the Afghan Jihad scheming to bring back their Imam. The story Larry got from the ansible could be true, and the Great Man might have been accomplice to the murder of a thousand worlds.

Hamid found himself laughing. *Where does that put me?* Could the clone of a monster rise above the original?

"What's funny, Hamid?" Tines had entered the bridge quietly. Now he settled himself on the table and posts around Hamid. The one that had been the Blab sat just a meter away.

"Nothing. Just thinking."

They sat for several minutes in silence, watching the sky. There was a wavering there—like hot air over a stove—the tiniest evidence of the fields that formed the ram around them. He glanced at the tines. Four of them were looking out the windows. The other two looked back at him, their eyes as dark and soft as the Blab's had ever been.

"Please don't think badly of Ravna," Tines said. "She had a real thing going with the almost-you of before. . . . They loved each other very much."

"I guessed."

The two heads turned back to the sky. These next two years he must watch this creature, try to decide. . . . But suspicions aside, the more he saw of Tines, the more he liked him. Hamid could almost imagine that he had not lost the Blab, but gained five of her siblings. And the bigmouth had finally become a real person.

The companionable silence stretched on. After a moment, the one that had been the Blab edged across the table and bumped her head against his shoulder. Hamid hesitated, then stroked her neck. They watched the sun and the fleck of blue a moment more. "You know," said Tines, but in the femvoice that was the Blab's favorite, "I will miss that place. And most of all . . . I will miss the cats and the dogs."

Janet Kagan

THE RETURN OF THE KANGAROO REX

Janet Kagan made her first short fiction sale in 1989, but has rapidly built a large and enthusiastic audience for her work, and has become a figure of note in the nineties. Although her debt to earlier writers of the offworld adventure tale, particularly James H. Schmitz (on whose work she is something of an authority, having contributed the introduction for the collection *The Best of James H. Schmitz*), is clear, she quickly developed a characteristic and flavorful voice of her own, and always brings her own quirky and individual perspective to whatever she's writing about, here breathing new life into the Exploring-a-Frontier-Planet story, a subgenre most commentators would have thought to be played out decades before. In fact, her linked series of stories about Mama Jason, of which "The Return of the Kangaroo Rex" is an example, later collected in book form as *Mirabile*, has proved to be one of the most popular series to run in *Asimov's Science Fiction* in recent years, with several of the stories winning the *Asimov's* Reader's Award Poll by large margins. Her first novel, a Star Trek novel called *Uhura's Song* was a nationwide bestseller, and her second novel *Hellspark* (*not* a Star Trek novel) was also widely acclaimed, and has been recently reissued. She is a frequent contributor to *Asimov's Science Fiction,* and has also sold to *Analog, Pulphouse,* and *Absolute Magnitude*. Her story "The Nutcracker Coup" won her a Hugo Award in 1993. She lives in Lincoln Park, New Jersey, with her husband, Ricky, several computers, and *lots* of cats, and is at work on a new novel.

In the wry and suspenseful story that follows, she takes us along to the frontier planet Mirabile to meet a woman whose job it is to cope with some very dangerous and very odd creatures, and follows her as she unravels a compelling biological mystery.

I'd been staring at the monitor so long all the genes were beginning to look alike to me. They shouldn't have, of course—this gene-read was native Mirabilan, so it was a whole new kettle of fish.

That's an American Guild expression, but it's the right one. At a casual look, had the critter been Earth-based, we'd have classed it as fish and left it at that. The problem was that it had taken a liking to our rice crop, and, if we didn't do something quick, nobody on Mirabile'd see a chow fun noodle ever again. So I went back to staring, trying to force those genes into patterns the team and I could cope with.

Moving the rice fields didn't guarantee we'd find a place free of them. In the first place, it encysted in dry ground, meaning you never knew where it'd pop up until you flooded the area. In the second place, it could leap like a salmon from the first place *to* the second place. It had already demonstrated its ability to spread from one field to the next. Susan had measured a twelve-foot leap.

The prospect got dimmer when Chie-Hoon caught them making that same leap from dry ground. Their limit was some five or six leaps until they hit water again, but that gave them quite a range.

It was as pretty a piece of native bioengineering as I've seen, one I could appreciate even if the rice growers couldn't. Wiping 'em out wholesale was not an option on *my* list, but I knew the farmers would be thinking along those lines if we didn't come up with something by next growing season.

I don't mess with the Mirabilan ecology any more than I have to. We don't know enough about it to know what we're getting into. Even if I thought we could do it, we'd be fools to try to wipe out any native species. The Earth-authentic species we've imported have played havoc enough with the Mirabilan ecology.

I wasn't paying much attention to anything but the problem at hand, so when Susan exclaimed, "Noisy! You look *awful*," I practically jumped out of my skin and busted my elbow turning my chair.

"Noisy" is Susan's pet name for Leonov Bellmaker Denness, and he *did* look awful. His white hair looked like something had nested in it; he was bleeding—no, *had* bled profusely—across the cheek; his shirt hung in tatters from the shoulder and there were raking claw-marks along his upper arms. Mike went scrambling for the emergency kit.

The only thing that spoiled the impact of all this disaster was that Leo was grinning from ear to ear. "Now, is that any way to greet an old friend?" he said to Susan. "Especially one who's come courting?"

He turned the grin on me and it got broader and brighter. Then he made me a deep formal bow and started in: "Ann Jason Masmajean, I, Leonov Bellmaker Denness, beg you to hear my petition."

I got to my feet and bowed back, just as deeply and formally, to let him know I'd be glad to hear him out. He made a second bow, deeper than the first, and went on: "I have brought you a gift in symbol of my intentions . . ."

Mike had the medical kit but he stood frozen. Chances were neither he nor Susan had ever seen a ship's-formal proposal except in the old films. The novelty of it kept either from interrupting. Just as well. I was enjoying the performance: Leo has flair.

Besides, I wouldn't dream of interrupting a man in the process of cataloguing my virtues, even if some of those "virtues" would have raised eyebrows in a lot of other people. I especially liked being called "reasonably stubborn."

At last Leo got to the wrap-up. "It is my hope that you will accept my gift and consider my suit." He finished off with yet another bow.

Seeing he was done spurred Mike and Susan into action. Susan held Leo down while Mike worked him over with alcohol swabs. "No respect for ritual," Leo complained, "Back 'em off, Annie, can't you? I'm not senile yet! I *did* clean the wounds."

Leo had spent years as a scout, so I didn't doubt his good sense. He'd hardly have lived to the ripe old age he had if he hadn't been cautious about infection in the bush.

To the two of them, he protested, "The lady hasn't answered yet."

"Back off," I told the kids.

They didn't until I advanced on them. Mike took two steps away from Leo, put his hands behind his back, and said to Susan, *"Now* he's going to get it." Susan nodded.

Leo just kept grinning, so I gave him a huge hug hello to make sure nothing was broken. The rest of him looked just fine, so I stepped back and bowed once more to meet the requirements of the ritual. "Leo Bellmaker Denness, I, Ann Jason Masmajean, am sufficiently intrigued to view your gift."

He crooked a finger and led me outside, Mike and Susan right behind. "In the back of the truck. *Don't* open that door until you've had a good look!"

So we climbed the back bumper and all crowded to the window for a good look. We didn't get one at first. Whatever it was was mad as all hell, and launched itself at the door hard enough to rattle the window and make the three of us jump back en masse. The door held.

Leo said, "It's been doing that all the way from Last Edges. Hasn't gotten through the door yet, but I'm a little worried it might hurt itself."

"It's not itself it wants to hurt," Susan said.

"You'd be pissed, too, if somebody wrestled you away from your mama and shoved you into the back of a truck headed god-knows-where," Leo said.

The door stopped rattling. I got a foot on the back bumper and hoisted myself up for a second try. Leo's present glared at me through the window and snarled. I snarled back in the same tone.

Since it was a youngster and I was an unknown, it backed off with a hop, letting me get a good look. In overall shape, it was kangaroo, but it had the loveliest set of stripes across the hips I'd ever seen—and the jaw! Oh, the jaw! It opened that jaw to warn me to keep back, and the head split almost to the ear, to show me the sharpest set of carnivore teeth in history.

"Oh, Leo," I murmured, stepping down from my perch. "That's the nicest present anybody's ever brought me." I gave him another big hug and a thorough kiss for good measure. "Leonov Bellmaker Denness, I accept both your gift and your suit."

He beamed. "I knew I got it right."

"Oh, shit!" said Mike, from behind me. "Susan! It's a goddam kangaroo rex!" He stared at Leo in disbelief. "Are you telling me this man brought you a *kangaroo rex* as a courting present?"

Susan, in turn, looked at *Mike* in disbelief. "It's perfect, you idiot! It means Noisy knows exactly what kind of person she is, and how to please her. Don't you understand *anything*?"

That would have devolved into a squabble—let a twenty-four-year-old and a sixteen-year-old discuss any subject and that's the usual outcome—but the kangaroo rex slammed against the door of the truck again and brought them both back to their senses.

"Leo," I said, "go on over to my house and get yourself cleaned up. We'll wrestle the thing into a cage. Then I want to hear all about it."

He nodded. "Sure. Two things first, though. Pick the right cage—I saw that thing jump a six-foot fence—then contact Moustafa Herder Kozlev or Janzen Herder Lizhi in Last Edges. I told Moustafa I'd make the official report on his Dragon's Tooth but I doubt he believes me." He examined a set of skinned knuckles. "Not when I punched him to keep him from shooting it."

"My hero," I said, meaning it.

He kissed my hand and vanished in the direction of my house. I turned to my available team-members and said, "Don't just stand there with your eyes hanging out of your heads. Let's get to work."

By the time we'd gotten an enclosure ready for the creature, Chie-Hoon and Selima had returned from up-country, where they'd been watching those damned hopping fish in the act. Just as well, because it took all five of us to maneuver the kangaroo rex safely out of the truck and into captivity.

Most of us wound up with bruises. It was still mad as all hell. It slammed each side of the fence in turn (didn't take it but two hops to cross the enclosure either) and once shot up and cracked its head on the overhead wire. That settled it down a bit. I sent Selima to get it some meat.

I couldn't take my eyes off the thing. I hadn't seen one for nine years.

"Another outbreak of kangaroo rexes," said Chie-Hoon. "Just what we needed. I assume it sprang from the kangaroos around Gogol?"

"Last Edges," I said. That didn't surprise me, the EC around Last Edges being almost identical to that around Gogol. "Contact Herders Kozlev and Lizhi up there. Tell them we've been notified. Find out if they've seen any more—"

"The usual drill," said Chie-Hoon.

"The usual drill."

Selima came back. She'd brought one of the snaggers Mike invented—let him do the honors of getting the cell sample while she distracted it with the meat. Or tried to. The snagger doesn't do more than pin-prick, but that was enough to rile the rex into slamming against the fence again, trying to get at Mike while he reeled the sample through the chain-link.

Mike jerked back but the sample came with him. He held it out to me. "Hardly necessary," he said. "I know what we're gonna find."

So did I. There was no doubt in my mind that the sample would match those from the last outbreak gene for gene. The kangaroo rex had settled down, wolfing at the meat Selima had tossed it. "It eats gladrats," said Selima, looking surprised. "It can't be all bad."

Not as far as I was concerned, it couldn't be all bad. If it was a Dragon's Tooth, it was a beautifully constructed one—completely viable.

That may need a word of explanation. . . . You see, when they shipped us off to colonize Mirabile, they were into redundancy. We got cold-storage banks of every conceivable species. (I use the "we" loosely; I'm third-generation Mirabilan myself.) But on top of that we also got the redundancy built right into the gene helices of all the stored species. Some bright-eyed geneticist back on Earth had apparently gotten *that* idea just before the expedition set off: genes within genes, helices tucked away inside other helices.

It was a good idea in theory. If we lost a species (*and* lost the ability to build it ourselves), sooner or later it would pop up spontaneously—all it needed was the right environmental conditions. Given the right EC, every hundredth turtle would lay an alligator egg.

In practice, it was a rotten idea. We'll never lack for alligators, not on Mirabile. They didn't tell us how to turn off those hidden helices, or if they did, the technique was only described in that part of ship's files we'd lost. So we Jasons have a running battle with cattle that are giving birth to reindeer and daffodils seeding iris (or worse—cockroaches).

Meanwhile, in the manner of all genes, the hidden genes *mixed.* While the turtle genes were reproducing turtles, the alligator genes tucked in with the turtle genes were mixing with god-knows-what. So given the right EC, we got chimera—familiarly known as Dragon's Teeth.

It was possible that the kangaroo rex was just an intermediate, a middle step between a kangaroo and anything from a gerbil to a water buffalo. Right now, however, it was a kangaroo rex, and impressive as all hell.

"You watch it, Mama Jason," Susan said. "I'll do the gene-read." She reached for the sample as if she had a vested interest in the beast herself. *She* figured she did, at least. Must have been all the times she'd made me tell the story of the first outbreak.

She may be the youngest and newest member of the team, but she can do a gene-read with the best of us. I handed the sample over.

Then I just stood there quietly and appreciated it. About three feet tall (not counting the tail, of course), it was already quite capable of surviving on its own. Which meant, more than likely, that its mama would very shortly move its sibling out of storage and into development. Chances were pretty good that one would be a kangaroo rex, too. Since the mama hadn't abandoned this one, it seemed unlikely she'd abandon another. I wondered if there were enough of them for a reliable gene pool.

The rex had calmed down now that it had eaten—now that most of the excitement was over. It was quietly investigating the enclosure, moving slowly on all fours. Hunched like that, it looked a lot like a mythological line-backer about to receive. With those small front legs, you never expect the thing (even a regulation kangaroo) to have the shoulders it does.

As it neared the side of the fence that I was gaping through, it yawned—the way a cat does, just to let you know it has weapons. I stayed quiet and still. It didn't come any closer and it didn't threaten any further.

That was a good sign, as far as I was concerned. Either it was full or it didn't consider me prey. I was betting it didn't consider me prey. Still, it *was* nasty-looking, which wasn't going to help its case, and it was still a baby. Adult, if it were a true kangaroo rex, it would stand as high as its kangaroo mother—six or seven feet.

In the outbreak of them we'd had nine years back near Gogol, they'd been herd animals. There had been some twenty-odd, with more on the way, of course. Chie-Hoon tells me kangaroos come in "mobs," which seemed appropriate for the kangaroo rexes as well, if a little weak-sounding. And we'd wiped out the last group wholesale.

Oh, I'd yelled and screamed a lot. At the very least, I'd hoped we could stash the genes so we could pull them out if we ever needed the creature for some reason. I got voted down, and I got voted down, and finally I got shouted down.

This time would be different.

The kangaroo rex sat back on its tail and began to wash, using its tongue and paws as prettily as any cat. In the midst of cleaning its whiskers, it froze, glanced up briefly, then went back to preening.

That was the only warning I had that Leo was back. He hadn't lost the ability to move softly with the passage of years. He put his arm around me and I leaned into him, feeling a little more than cat-smug myself, though I hadn't done anything to deserve it. Maybe *because* I hadn't done anything to deserve it.

"Pretty thing," Leo said softly, so as not to startle it. "Now I understand why you wanted to keep them."

"This time we *are* keeping them," I said.

There was a clatter of the door behind me. The kangaroo rex bounced to the farthest side of the enclosure, hit the fence on the second bounce, and froze, jaws agape and threatening.

"I know what you're thinking, Annie," Mike said. "You'd better come talk to these guys first. You're not going to like what you hear."

Herders Jarlskog and Yndurain were not inclined toward leniency, especially not Jarlskog, who had worked himself up into a fine sense of outrage. To hear him tell it, you'd have thought a mob of rexes had eaten his entire flock, plus several of his children. So the entire town was already in an uproar.

I halfway agreed with their sentiments. I like the occasional lamb chop just as much as the next guy—especially the way Chris cooks them up at Loch Moose Lodge—and this was one of only seven flocks on all of Mirabile. Sheep here are labor-intensive. They can't be trusted to graze unattended: forever eating something native that'll poison them. So we keep only the seven flocks and we keep them on a strict diet of Earth fodder.

All this means that they have to be kept behind fences and that the plant life in there with 'em has to be policed regularly. That's one of the reasons all the flocks are on the fringes of the desert—it's easier to irrigate the plant life into submission.

The result of all this is that we eat a lot more kangaroo tail soup than we eat lamb curry. The kangaroos fend for themselves quite nicely, thank you, and there's no shortage of them.

Jarlskog wanted me to arrange an instant shortage of kangaroo rexes. So did Yndurain. In an hour's time, the rest of the town would start calling in with the same demand. I soothed them by telling them I'd have a team up there by the end of the day. In the meantime, they were to shoot only if they saw a rex actually in with the sheep.

They grumbled some but agreed. When I canceled the call, I turned to Leo. "What do you think? Will they go right out and shoot every kangaroo in sight?"

"No," he said. "Janzen and Moustafa are good kids. I think they can put a damper on the hysteria. Once I convinced Moustafa the rex was mine, he was even willing to help me catch it."

"It took a bit of convincing, though." I glanced significantly at his skinned knuckles.

He grinned and shrugged. "In the heat of passion." His face turned serious and he added, "He *will* shoot any roo that jumps that fence today, though, so if you want to head up there, now's the time."

Mike handed me a sheaf of hard copy. It was the list of everybody who lived in a hundred-mile radius of the spot where the rex had turned up. "Good news," he said. "We only have to worry about twenty families."

That is the only advantage I know of being underpopulated. For a moment, I considered not issuing a general alert. After all, for all we knew, there was only *one* kangaroo rex and it was in our backyard.

Mike read my mind and shook his head. "If you want to keep them, Annie, you better not risk having one of them eat some kid."

"It was only an idle thought," I told him. "Put out a notification. Keep the kids in, keep the adults armed. But add that I don't want them shot unless it's absolutely necessary."

Chie-Hoon said, "Annie, we're not going to go through this *again*, are we?"

"Damn straight, we are," I said, "and this time I intend to win! Who's coming with me?"

"Me," said Leo.

"And me," said Susan, looking up from her monitor. "It *is* the same kangaroo rex as last time, Mama Jason, only I've got two secondary helices here. They're both marsupial, but more than that I can't tell you offhand. It'll take the computer all night to search."

"Let me have a look first," Chie-Hoon said. "Maybe I'll recognize something. I have a vested interest in marsupials, after all."

Everybody's got to have a hobby. Chie-Hoon's is the Australian Guild, meaning Chie-Hoon knows more than anybody could ever want to know about the customs and wildlife of Earth's "Australia," which includes about ninety percent of the marsupials found in ship's records.

"Help yourself," I said. I'd never found the time to join any of the

Earth Authentic Guilds myself—if I were looking for a hobby I rather thought I'd make it Leo—but this was the sort of thing that came in handy. "Since Leo volunteers to come along, we'll leave you to it."

We're habitually short-handed, and since I'd worked with Leo once before I knew he and I could handle just about anything that came up. As for Susan, well, Earth-authentic wild horses couldn't have kept her away.

Mike looked glum. "I get stuck with the fish, right?"

"And Selima," I pointed out, which brightened him up considerably. (I'm rather hoping those two will decide to help alleviate our underpopulation problem one of these fine days. I'm giving them every opportunity.) "We'll be in touch."

"We'll argue," Mike assured me.

We took my skimmer. Leo, being retired (hah!), no longer rates up-to-date equipment. We let Susan drive and scandalized her by necking in the back seat. When we'd caught up a bit on old times, we broke the clinch.

"Why will you argue?" Leo asked.

"You remember, Noisy. Mama Jason wanted to keep the kangaroo rexes the last time they cropped up. Mike and Chie-Hoon didn't."

"A *lot* of people didn't want them kept," I said. "I lost that round."

"It's not going to be any easier this time," Leo said. "Both those herders were—if you'll pardon the expression—hopping mad."

Susan giggled. So did I.

"I know. But I'm older and meaner this time around."

" 'Meaner'?" That was Susan. "Mama Jason, *last* time one of the damn things almost chewed your foot off!"

"D'you think I could forget something like that?" I leaned on the back of the seat and glared at her in the mirror. "That has nothing to do with it."

" 'You never know what might be useful in the long run.' I know," Susan said. "It's not as if we're going to pick up and go back to Earth if we run out of sheep, either."

I gave a sidelong glance at Leo. "Just what I needed; somebody who quotes my own words back at me. . . ."

"You've only yourself to blame," he said.

"Thanks," said Susan, to let us both know she took this little routine as a compliment. "Now tell me who took what side last time around, and what you expect them to do this time."

"It was me against them," I admitted. When Susan whistled, I stuck in, "I almost got Mike to go along with me, but in the end, that wouldn't have made any difference. Mike didn't have much pull then."

"Meaning he was about the same age I am now," said Susan, "so my opinion won't swing much weight either."

"I had intended to be tactful."

Leo raised an eyebrow at me. "That's not like you, Annie. Do you need the allies that badly? It occurs to me that you swing a bit more weight these days yourself."

"Oh, considerably. But that won't do me a lot of good unless I can convince people like Jarlskog and Yndurain that the rexes are worth keeping. For god's sake, Leo! What's to stop them from simply shooting down every one they see? *We* certainly haven't the hands to police every last bit of territory, especially not Last Edges or Gogol or the like."

Last Edges has a total population of fifty. That's minute, but it's five times the number of people I've got to work with.

"Most people understand enough about ecological balance to follow the guide-lines you folks set," Leo said, but with a bit of a rising inflection.

"If I tell them it's 'Earth-authentic,' sure. But this one isn't. Furthermore, nobody in his right mind likes it."

"*I* like it," Susan said. When I didn't respond to that, she said in a small amused voice, "Oh," then giggled, then sighed in resignation. "So what do we do?"

"Nothing, until we check out the situation locally."

The local situation hadn't simmered down while it waited for our arrival. Not that I'd expected it to, but I could see that both Susan and Leo had. A third of the adults were guarding the sheep field with guns. Another third, I imagine, was guarding the kids likewise. The rest turned out to be a combination welcoming committee and lynch mob. Read: *we* were welcome, the kangaroo rexes were most emphatically not.

I listened to the babble without a word for all of twenty minutes, motioning for Susan and Leo to do the same. Best to let them get as much of it out of their systems as possible while we waited for a couple of leaders to sort themselves out of the crowd—then we'd know who and what we were actually dealing with.

In the end, there were two surprises. The first was that someone was dispatched to "Go get Janzen. Right now." When Janzen arrived, Janzen got thrust to the fore. Janzen was about Susan's age. He looked at me, cocked an eyebrow at Leo, who nodded and grinned, then he grinned at me and stuck out his hand. That was when I noticed the striking resemblance the kid had to Leo. I cocked an eyebrow at Leo, whose grin got wider.

Janzen took care of shutting down the general noise level and introducing us to the population at large. Leo got introduced by his previous job description—as Leonov *Opener* Denness—and yes, Leo was Janzen's grandad. Both of which upped our status exactly the way Janzen had intended them to. At a bet, a lot of the local kids had been through a survival course or two with Leo.

The second surprise wasn't nearly as pleasant. The other speaker for the populace—read "loudmouth" in this case—was none other than Kelly Herder Sangster, formerly a resident of Gogol. She'd wanted the kangaroo rexes near Gogol wiped out and she wanted the same thing here and *now*.

I knew from experience how good she was at rousing rabble. She'd done it at Gogol. I could talk myself blue in the face, put penalties on the shooting of a rex, but I'd lose every one of them to "accidental" shootings if I couldn't get the majority of the crowd behind me.

Sangster squared off, aimed somewhere between me and Janzen, shoved back her hat, bunched her fists on her hips, and said, "They eat sheep. Next thing you know they'll be eating our kids! And Cryptobiology sends us somebody who loves Dragon's Teeth!"

She pointed an accusing finger at me. "When they attacked us in Gogol, *she* wanted to keep them! Whaddaya think about that?" The last was to the crowd.

The crowd didn't think much of that at all. There was much muttering and rumbling.

"I think," I said, waiting for the crowd to quiet enough to listen, "I'd like to know more about the situation before I make any decisions for or against."

I looked at Janzen. "You were the first to see it, I'm told. Did it eat your sheep?"

"No, it didn't," he said. That caused another stir and a bit of a calm. "It was in the enclosure—but it was chasing them, all of them, the way a dog does when it's playing. To be fair, I don't know what it would have done when it caught them. We caught it before we could find out." He looked thoughtful. "But it seems to me that it had plenty of opportunity to catch a sheep and didn't bother. Moustafa? What do you think?"

Moustafa rubbed his sore jaw, glowered at Leo, and said, very grudgingly, "You're right, Janzen. It was like the time Harkavy's dog got into the sheep pen—just chased 'em around. Plenty of time to catch 'em but didn't. Just wanted to see them run." He glowered once more. "But for a kangaroo, it's an adolescent. Maybe it hasn't learned to hunt yet. That might have been practice."

"I concede the point," I said, before Sangster could use it to launch another torpedo. "The next thing I need to know is, how many of them are there?"

As if prompted (perhaps he was, I hadn't been watching Leo for the moment), Janzen said, "For all I know, only the one." He looked hard at Sangster. "You see any?"

Sangster dropped her eyes. "No," she muttered, "not since Gogol." She raised her eyes and made a comeback, "No thanks to Jason Masmajean here."

Janzen ignored that. "Anybody else?"

"That doesn't mean a damn thing, Janzen, and you know it," someone said from the crowd. "For all we know, the entire next generation of kangaroos will be Dragon's Teeth—and *that* would be a shitload of kangaroo rexes!"

"I say we get rid of them while there's only one," Sangster put in. "I'm for loading my shotgun and cleaning the roos out *before* they sprout Dragon's Teeth!"

"Now I remember!" I said, before the crowd could agree with her, *"You're* the one that's allergic to roo-tail soup!"

"I'm not allergic—I just don't like it," she snapped back, before thinking it through.

"Well," said Janzen, *"I* like roo-tail soup, so I'd just as soon consider this carefully before I stick myself with nothing but vegetable for the rest of my life."

"Rest of your life . . ." Sangster sneered at him. "What the hell are you talking about?"

"I'll take that question," I said. "If you've a genuine outbreak of kangaroo rexes here, instead of a one-shot, then you'll have to destroy all the kangaroos. That's what was done at Gogol. Gogol can never let the kangaroo herds—"

" 'Mobs,' " corrected Sangster. "Kangaroos come in mobs, not herds."

"Gogol can never let the kangaroos *mob* again. Any kangaroo found in that EC is shot. The environmental conditions there are such that sooner or later any kangaroo around Gogol will produce a kangaroo rex." I gave a long look through the crowd. "I won't lie to you: Last Edges has roughly the same EC as Gogol did. Which means you may have to face the same decision. As for me, I'd wait to find out if the rexes eat sheep before I decide to kill off all the roos."

"Sounds fair," said Janzen, almost too promptly. "How do we go about this?"

"First, I want a good look at your EC. I want to see, if you haven't scuffed it up too much, where you spotted the rex. Then we do a little scouting of the surrounding area." I grinned over my shoulder at Leo. "Luckily, we have somebody who's an old hand at that."

"Luckily," agreed Janzen.

"But I could also use some additional help." I looked straight at Sangster—I wanted her where I could keep an eye on her and where she couldn't rabble-rouse while I was busy. "What do you say, Sangster? Willing to put in a little effort?"

What could she say? She just said it with all the bad grace she could muster.

"Take Janzen, too," came a voice from the crowd. Aha! there were two factions already. "Yes," agreed another voice. "You go with 'em, Janzen. *You* like roo soup."

"In the meantime," I said, "stick to the precautions we already discussed. However—if anyone spots a rex, I want you to notify us immediately. Don't shoot it."

"Oh, yes, right. Don't shoot it," Sangster mocked.

I looked at her as if she were nuts. "Look," I said, "if there *are* more than one, it can lead us to the rest of the mob. Or would you rather just hunt them by guess and by golly? I don't have the time myself. Are *you* volunteering?"

That was the right thing to say, too. So I added one last filip. "Susan?" Susan edged forward. "Susan will be in charge of collecting the gene samples from each sheep, simply as a precaution."

This did not make Susan happy—she wanted to go haring off after the kangaroo rexes—but I knew she wouldn't argue with me in public. "Sample each?" she said.

"That's right. I don't want a single one lost. After all, who knows what genes they've got hidden in those? Might be, one of them can sprout the Shmoo."

That brought a bit of laughter—the Shmoo's a legendary creature that tastes like everything good and drops dead for you if you look at it hungry. The ultimate Dragon's Tooth, except that Sangster would never use that derogatory term for something she *approved* of.

The crowd approved our plan, especially the part about collecting gene samples from each sheep. It was a nuisance to do, but I knew it would settle them down. Herders know as well as anybody how desperately we need diversity within a species. I was offering to clone any sheep we lost to the rexes in the process of my investigation. That meant they'd lose the time it took to bring the sheep back to breeding age, but that they wouldn't lose any genetic variation.

Moustafa volunteered to help Susan with the sampling. So did a handful of others. Then the rest of the crowd dispersed, leaving us to get down to business at last.

Moustafa led the way to the sheep pen where Janzen and Leo had bagged my baby rex. The enclosure looked like every single one I've ever seen, identical to those at Gogol, identical to every other one in Last Edges as well, no doubt. It *sounded* like the crowd had—lots of milling, scuffling, and bleating.

The moment we rounded the corner and saw the sheep, I had to clamp my jaw hard to keep from laughing. The sheep were an eye-popping sky-blue, every single one of them! Susan *did* burst into laughter. I elbowed her hard in the ribs. "Don't you dare laugh at Mike's sheep," I told her.

Mike had been trying for a breed that could eat Mirabilan plant life without killing itself. What he'd gotten was a particularly hardy type that tasted just as good as the original, but sprouted that unbelievable shade of blue wool. Mike had promptly dubbed them "Dylan Thomas sheep," and offered them out to the herders. Janzen and Moustafa had obviously taken him up on the offer.

Susan simmered down, just barely, to giggles. "But, Mama Jason," she said, "all this fuss because a Dragon's Tooth might eat a Dragon's Tooth. . . ."

And at that Janzen laughed too. He looked at Susan. "I hadn't thought of it that way, but, now that you mention it, it is funny." He cocked an eyebrow at Moustafa, who sighed and said, "You always were nuts, Janzen. Yeah. It's funny."

Moustafa looked at me more seriously, though. "But we can't afford to lose many. It's not as if we've got a high population to play around with. We don't even dare interbreed them with the Earth-authentics until we've built up the flock to twice this size or more."

I nodded. The kid was as sensible as Janzen. I wasn't surprised he'd taken a shot at the rex. In his position, I probably would have too. Hell, I'd have done it if they'd been the Earth-authentics. Why mess around? "Okay, Susan," I said. "Start with this flock. Make sure you get one of each."

If the artificial wombs were free this winter, I'd see Mike's pet project doubled, whether we needed them or not. Pretty damn things once you got over the initial shock. They smelled godawful, of course, but what sheep doesn't? The wool made beautiful cloth and even more beautiful rugs. It was already something of a posh item all over Mirabile.

"All yours," I said to Susan, and she and Moustafa set to work.

I followed Leo along the fence, watching where I put my feet. When you've got an expert tracker, you stay out of his way and let him do his job. Janzen knew this just as well as I did, so he was the one, not me, who grabbed Sangster to keep her from overstepping Leo and messing up any signs of the rex.

It wasn't long before Leo stopped and pointed us off across the sheep field. I shouldered my gear and we set out to track the kangaroo rex.

Tracking a kangaroo isn't as easy as you might think, even with the help of a world-class tracker like Leo. (I'm not so bad at it myself. Neither is Janzen, as it turns out.) These kangaroos were reds (I don't mean the warning-light red that signals that some critter is about to chain up to something else; I mean a lovely tawny animal red) and *they* are world-class distance jumpers, especially when they're panicked. They had been by Moustafa's rifle shot, which meant they'd been traveling in leaps of fifteen to twenty feet. So it was check the launch spot, then cast about for the landing and subsequent relaunch.

It was only guesswork that we were following the rex's mother anyway. We wouldn't know her to look at her. Only a full gene-read could tell us that. I'd have to sample most of the roos in the mob to find out how many of them were capable of producing baby rexes.

Sangster bent down to uproot a weed or two. When I frowned at her for taking the time, she held out the plant to me and said, "That'll kill a sheep as sure as a kangaroo rex will."

Janzen looked over. "Surer," he said. "I still don't know if kangaroo rexes eat sheep." To me, he added, "But that will poison one. That's lamb-kill."

I almost laughed. Like any Mirabilan species we've had occasion to work with, it has a fancy Latin name, but this was the first I'd heard its common name. The fancy Latin name is an exact translation. Sounded like Granpa Jason's work to me.

Sangster stooped to pull another. Curious how small they were. Must mean they policed the fields *very* carefully. These were newly sprouted. I spotted one and pulled it myself, then stuck my head up and looked for Leo again. He'd found the next set of footprints.

Good thing the roos have such big feet. In this kind of wiry, springy scrub we wouldn't have had much chance otherwise. Leo wiped sweat from his forehead and pointed toward the oasis in the distance. "Chances are they'll be there, including our rex's mother. In this heat, they'll be keeping to the shade to conserve water." He glanced at Janzen. "Is that the only natural source of water in the area?"

Janzen nodded.

I squinted into the shimmer. The plants had that spiky look of Mirabilan vegetation. There was a distinct break between the Earth-authentic lichens and scrub, then a fence, then a broad strip of desert, then the dark green of the Mirabilan oasis. The broad strip of desert was maybe twenty hops for a roo, or looked that way from this angle.

"Even the roos are a problem," Sangster observed. "They can hop the fence—they bring the lambkill seeds in on their fur."

"It'd blow in from there," I said. "Same as it did at Gogol." I couldn't help it. I'd been wondering ever since I first spotted her in the crowd. "Herder Sangster, what made you leave Gogol?"

Sangster scowled, not exactly at me. "It's Crafter Sangster now. I lost my flock, seventy percent of it anyway."

Leo said, "To the kangaroo rexes?"

She just about glared him into the ground. "To the lambkill," she said. "After we got rid of the rexes and the roos that bred them, the lambkill was still there. Worse than ever, it seemed."

"Yes," Janzen put in. "When Moustafa and I were deciding where to raise Mike's flock of Thomas sheep, I did some checking in the various areas available. Something in the EC here makes the lambkill less prevalent . . . or less deadly perhaps. The death count attributable to it isn't nearly as high here as it is around Gogol." He cocked his head, which made his resemblance to Leo all the stronger. "Say! Maybe you could find out what the difference is?"

"Maybe I could," I said, making it clear I would certainly look into the problem. "But for now let's find those roos. I'll put Susan on soil and vegetation samples as soon as she's done with sheep."

To my surprise, he frowned. "Isn't she a little young . . . ?"

"When's *your* birthday?" I asked him. When he told me, I said, "Yeah, I guess from your point of view she is a little young. You've got two months on her."

"Oops," said Janzen. "Sorry."

"No skin off my nose," I told him.

Leo grinned and slapped Janzen on the shoulder. "Would be skin off *his* if Susan had heard him, though. Rightly, too." Leo put an easy arm around Janzen's shoulder. "Susan's the one who developed the odders, Janz. You know, the neo-otters that keep the canals around Torville free of clogweed?"

Janzen looked rightly impressed. Good for Leo, I thought, rub it in just enough so the lesson takes.

"Besides," Leo said, "if age had any bearing on who gets what job, Annie and I would be sitting in the shade somewhere sipping mint juleps and fanning ourselves. Now, could we get on with this before we all, young and old alike, melt?"

So we did. The strip of desert was wider than I'd thought. We'd need that spring as much as the roos did. Of course, they were quite sensibly lying in the shade (drinking mint juleps, no doubt, whatever *they* were—

I'd have to remember to ask Leo about that later), going nowhere until the cool of evening.

We'd lost our specific roo (if we'd ever had her) on the broad rocky flat that lay between the strip of desert and the oasis. We paused in the first bit of welcoming shade.

Without a word, Leo signed the rest of us to wait while he moved farther in to scout the location of the mob without panicking it. I handed him the cell-sampler. If he saw anything that looked like a rex, I wanted an instant sample. I needed to know if more than one mother was breeding them.

For a long while, it was quiet, except for the sound of running water and the damned yakking of the chatterboxes. Every planet must have something like this—it's simply the noisiest creature in the EC. It keeps up a constant racket unless something disturbs it. When the chatterboxes shut up, you know you're in trouble. Most people think the chatterboxes are birds, and that's good enough most ways—they fly, they lay eggs, what more could you ask of birds?

I, for one, prefer that my birds have feathers. Technically speaking, feathers are required. The chatterboxes are a lot closer to lizards. I guess the closest Earth-authentic would be something like a pterodactyl, except that all the pterodactyl reconstructions in ship's files showed them brown or green. I wonder what the paleontologists back on Earth would have made of ours.

The chatterboxes, besides being noisy, are the most vivid colors imaginable—blues and reds and purples and yellows—and in some of the most tasteless combinations you can imagine. They make most Mirabilan predators violently ill, which shouldn't come as much of a surprise. The eggs are edible, though, and not just to *Mirabilan* predators.

We watched and listened to the chatterboxes, thinking all the while, I'm sure, that we ought to bring home some eggs if we lucked onto a nest.

Then Leo was back.

He leaned close and spoke in a quiet voice. The chatterboxes kept right on. "Annie, I've found the mob, but I didn't see anything that looked like a rex—nothing out of the ordinary at all. Just browsing kangaroos."

"Chances are, mine is the first one, then. Do you think we can all get a look without sending them in all directions?"

"Depends on *your* big feet."

"Thanks," I told him.

The whole bunch of us headed out as quietly as we knew how. I'd been worried about Sangster, but she'd obviously taken the kids' training course to heart—she was as quiet as the rest of us.

We worked our way through sharpscrub, dent-de-lion, careless weed, spurts, and stick-me-quick. It was mostly uphill. The terrain here was mostly rock with a very slender capping of soil. Leo brushed past a stand of creve-coeur and collected a shirtful of its nasty burrs, saving us all from a similar fate. I didn't envy him the task of picking them out.

At last Leo stopped us. Kneeling, he slid forward, motioning me to follow. Our faces inches apart, we peered through a small stand of light-enme.

There was the tiny trickle of stream that fed this oasis. In the shade of the surrounding trees lolled the mob of kangaroos, looking for the moment not so much like a mob as like a picnic luncheon. There were perhaps twenty in clear view, and not a striped hip among them. Still, that meant there were plenty more we couldn't see.

It was also quite possible that the mother of our rex had been ostracized because of her peculiar offspring. That happened often enough with Dragon's Teeth.

Beside me there was an intake of breath. The chatterboxes paused momentarily, then, to my relief, went right back to their chattering. Sangster pointed into the sharpscrub to my left.

I caught just the quickest glimpse of stripes, followed it to the end of its bound. As it knelt on its forepaws to drink from the stream, I could see it had the face and jaw of a red kangaroo, but the haunches were very faintly striped. I nodded to her. Good bet, that one. Different enough to be worth the first check.

Taking the cell-sampler back from Leo, I backed up—still on my hands and knees—and skinned around to get as close as I could. (Skinned being the operative word in that EC. My palms would never be the same.) Just at that moment, two of the adolescents started a kicking match.

Their timing was perfect. I took advantage of the distraction, rose, tiptoed forward, and potted Striped Rump with the sampler. It twitched and looked around but wasn't in the least alarmed. All it did was lean back on its tail and scratch the area with a forepaw, for all the world like a human slob.

Very slowly, I reeled in the sample. (I've startled too many creatures reeling in samples not to be aware of that problem.) Once I had it, I stashed it in my pack, reloaded, and popped a second roo, this time a male—all chest and shoulders, a good seven-footer. If the rexes got that big, I would be awfully hard put to convince anybody they should be kept.

Not that it looked menacing now. It was lying belly-up in the deep shade, with its feet in the air. Just now, it looked like some kid had dropped a stuffed toy.

I knew better: Mike had gotten into an altercation with a red that size once, and it had taken three hundred and forty-one stitches to repair the damage. Roos use their claws to dig for edible roots. They panic, those claws'll do just as efficient a job digging holes in your face.

Two sampled. I figured the best thing to do was keep sampling as long as I could. I got eleven more without incident. Then I almost walked into the fourteenth.

Its head jerked up from the vie-sans-joie it and its joey were browsing. The joey dived headfirst into mama's pouch.

I knew it was all over, so I shot the sampler at the mother point-blank, as the joey somersaulted to stare at me wide-eyed between its own hind feet. Mama took off like a shot.

Next thing I knew, the chatterboxes were in the air, dead silent except for the sound of their wings, and every kangaroo was bounding every which way.

Janzen and Leo were on their feet in the same moment, dragging Sangster to hers as well. Less chance of being jumped on if the roos were stampeding *away* from you. Leo bellowed at them, just to make sure.

Trouble is, you can't count on a roo to do anything but be the damn dumb creature it is—so three of them headed straight *for* Leo and company.

Janzen dived left. Still bellowing, Leo dived right. And there stood Sangster, right in the middle, unable to pick a direction. She took one step left, a second right—that little dance that people do in the street just before they bump into each other.

Striped Rump was still aimed straight for her.

I raised my shotgun and aimed for Striped Rump. "No, Annie!" Leo shouted. But I was thinking of Mike—I sighted.

Three things happened at once: Leo hooked a foot at Sangster's ankle and jerked her out of the path of the roo, Janzen bellowed louder than ever I'd heard Leo manage, and I squeezed the trigger.

Striped Rump touched one toe to the ground and reversed direction in mid-leap. My shot passed over its shoulder as it bounded away from Sangster. By the time the shot had finished echoing off the rocks, there wasn't a roo to be seen anywhere.

I charged over to where Leo was picking Sangster up and dusting her off. Polite full-body-check, that was. From his nod, she was just fine, so I spared a glance for Janzen, who seemed likewise.

"Dammit, woman!" Leo said. "What happened to 'Don't shoot unless it's absolutely necessary'? That was your likeliest prospect."

"The hell with you, Leo. *You've* never seen anybody mangled by a roo." It came out tired. The adrenaline rush was gone and the heat was suddenly unbearable. "I'm not in the mood to be scolded right now. You can do it later, when I'm ready to thank you for saving old Striped Rump."

I glared at Sangster. "If you're fit to travel, I vote we get the hell out of this sun and let me process my samples."

She opened her mouth, a little round O of a shape, as if to say something. Then she just nodded.

We slogged our way back across the sheep range. By the time we reached the shade of Janzen's digs, I was unpissed enough to growl at Leo, "What's a mint julep? Maybe I could use one."

Leo shot a sidelong glance at Janzen, who grinned and said, "You *know* I keep the mixings. You also know you're all welcome to stay at my place." He cocked his head slightly to the side, "If you don't tell Susan what an idiot I am."

"We'll let her find out on her own," Leo said.

Which settled that—and us as well.

I was almost into the welcome shade of Janzen's house when Sangster grabbed at my arm. I turned—the look on her face was downright ferocious. Here it comes again, I thought. Death to the kangaroo rex!

Instead, she demanded, "Why?" That ferocious look was still there.

I blinked. "Why *what,* dammit?"

"Why did you shoot at that damned roo?"

Some people just don't get it, ever. I shook my head and sighed. "Humans are the most endangered species on Mirabile," I said, "and you want to know why I fired?"

That was all I had the patience for. I turned on my heel, yanked away from her, and fairly dived into the coolness of Janzen's house, letting the door slam behind me as my final word on the subject.

The mint julep improved my outlook no end, so I keyed into Janzen's computer (rank hath its privileges) and entered the samples I'd picked up. While I was waiting for my readout, I checked my office files to see what the rest of the team had come up with.

First thing I got was a real pretty schematic of my kangaroo rex. It was an even neater bit of engineering than I'd thought at first—the teeth at the side of the jaws (they were two inches long!) worked across each other, like butchers' shears. What with the 180-degree jaw span, that would give it an awesome ability to shear bone. Sheep bone was well within its capabilities.

That still didn't mean it ate sheep, but it didn't help the cause any.

Next I got the gene-reads on the secondary helices. Didn't recognize either worth a damn. Neither had Chie-Hoon, because there was a note appended that said simply, "Annie: Sorry, neither of these looks familiar to me. We're checking them against ship's records now. Let you know what we find."

That'd be sometime the next day. A search and match takes entirely too much time, always assuming that there *is* a match. Lord only knew what was in those portions of ship's records we'd lost in transit.

The gene-read on Striped Rump was about what I'd expected, just a few twists off normal red kangaroo.

"Roo stew?" said a voice behind me.

"Sure," I said, without looking up, "still perfectly edible, despite those." I tapped the offending genes on the monitor.

"Janzen," said Leo's voice. "No point talking to her when she's reading genes. She's not talking about the same thing you are."

That was enough to make me turn away from the screen. I looked at Janzen. "Sorry," I said. "What was it you wanted to know?"

"I just asked if you'd mind having roo stew for dinner. I intend to eat a lot of roo while I still have the option."

"Say yes, Annie." That was Leo again. "Janzen and Moustafa make the best roo stew I've ever had. Even Chris couldn't beat their recipe."

Chris is the best chef on Mirabile. Like Susan, she's one of Elly's kids. She's one of the reasons Loch Moose Lodge is my favorite vacation spot.

"That's some recommendation! Can I get in on this?" That was Susan. "I put the sheep samples in the truck, Mama Jason; all set for in vitro in case we need them. Is that your rex breeder? Sangster won't talk about what you guys found—what did you do to her? Threaten her with a corn crop that sprouts cockroaches?"

"One thing at a time," I said. "Janzen, yes, thank you. I'm extremely fond of roo myself. Will there be enough for Susan too, or shall I make her eat rations?"

Susan threatened to punch me. Janzen grinned at her and said, "Plenty enough, Susan. Now I know why Leo wants to hook up with Annie. Just his type."

To change the subject, I tapped the monitor again and said, "That's our most likely candidate for rex breeder. I was just about to check for secondary helices. You can watch over my shoulder—unless you want to watch how Janzen and Moustafa make stew. The recipe'd make a good birthday present for Chris . . . ?"

Susan looked horribly torn for a brief moment. Janzen grinned at her again and said, "I'll write out our recipe for you, Susan. You stick here and tell me what I need to know about the kangaroo rexes." The kid had a *lot* in common with his granddad.

While Susan pulled up a chair, I turned back to the monitor and started reading genes again. Yup, there was a secondary helix, all right. I split the screen, called up the gene-read on my kangaroo rex, and compared the two. No doubt about it. "Thanks for saving old Striped Rump, Leo. She's it."

I stored that to send back to the lab and called up the next sample. "Let's see how many other rex breeders we've got."

By the time Moustafa dished out the roo stew, I'd found two more rex breeders in the sample of thirteen. And they were all remarkably consistent about it.

"Hell," said Leo.

"Not exactly, Noisy," Susan said. "That means most likely the kangaroo rex is an intermediate for an Earth-authentic."

I was momentarily more interested in the stew than in anything else. It lived up to Leo's billing. I was still trying to place the spices Janzen and Moustafa used when Leo laid a hand on my arm to get my attention. "Mmmph?" I said, through a mouthful.

"You've got to train your assistants to use less jargon," he said.

I scooped up another forkful of stew and simply eyed Susan.

"Oops," she said. "Sorry, Noisy. A true Dragon's Tooth is usually a chimera—bits and pieces of the genetic material of two very different species. Even a plant-animal combination's possible. But it's not consistent.

"If we've got three roos that are going to at some time produce rexes, all of which are close enough genetically to interbreed, then most likely it's *not* a Dragon's Tooth. Most likely it's the first visible step on the chain up to another Earth-authentic." She waited anxiously to see if he'd gotten it this time. When he nodded, she dived back into her own dinner. "Great stew, Moustafa, Janzen. I'd sure hate it if we have to kill off the roos."

"Any idea just how big the roo population is?" I asked the two local kids.

They exchanged a glance. Moustafa said, "Couple hundred, maybe. It never occurred to me to count."

Janzen shook his head, meaning it hadn't occurred to him either, then he said, "You can get some idea after dinner. Once the sun goes down, most of them will be out in the pasture, browsing. If it were crops we were raising instead of sheep, they'd be a much bigger nuisance than they are now."

Susan raised a querying brow at him.

"Given any kind of a choice, the roos prefer their food tender, which means they go for young shoots. That'd play havoc with any food crop.

Sheep will browse tough stuff that's inedible to most Earth-authentics, and they'll do it right down to the ground."

"Yeah," said Moustafa. "And they're too stupid to know what's poisonous and what isn't."

That reminded me. "Excuse me a minute," I said—but I took my bowl of stew with me while I went to the computer to call up the home team.

I got Mike, which was good luck, and there were no emergencies in the offing, which was better. "I need an EC workup on Gogol. Can you get me one by tomorrow evening?" At his look, I said, "It doesn't have to be complete—just a preliminary: quick and dirty is fine. We'll do a complete if anything interesting shows up." His look hadn't improved, so I added, "Take Selima. With two of you, it'll go faster and won't be quite as dirty."

That fixed the look right up. Ah, young love . . . ain't it handy? "Anything new I should know about?"

"Yeah." This time he grinned. "Your kangaroo rex didn't recognize lamb as edible."

Behind me, someone said, "All *right!*" on a note of triumph. I ignored that to eye Mike suspiciously. When he said nothing further, I voiced his implied, "But . . . ?"

"But it could learn that trick. Right now its idea of superb cuisine is chatterboxes, grubroots, and gladrats."

Interesting. Those were all Mirabilan, and all pests from our point of view. "That's certainly in its favor," I said. "They're all of a size too—nowhere near the size of sheep."

"Means nothing. There's only one rex on the premises. Who knows what size prey a mob of them will take on."

"I know," I said, "but that gives me more breathing space here." I thought about it a moment, then got an inspiration. "Mike? Try it on those damn jumping fish next time it looks hungry."

That brought a grin from Mike. "Annie," he said, "our luck's not *that* good this summer. Besides, the rexes wouldn't do well in that EC."

"Just try it. And shoot me that EC report as soon as you can." I broke the connection, picked up my bowl, and—still thinking about it—headed back for the dinner table. I almost ran Leo down. I looked around me. The whole troop had been looking over my shoulder. "Sit," I said, "my apologies. We will now give the stew the attention it deserves."

Which we did, and when we were done, it was time for Janzen and Moustafa to see to their sheep for the evening . . . and for me and Leo to place ourselves strategically in the fields to see how many roos showed up to browse—and how many of them were breeding rexes.

We ran into half a dozen of the locals and enlisted three. Susan dug out two more samplers, but those went to Leo and Susan herself. (We're short of equipment. I put that on the docket for winter, making more samplers or finding somebody who wanted the job.)

Sangster was nowhere to be seen. Despite Susan's earlier comment, I had no doubt she was off somewhere raising the level of hysteria. I could have kicked myself for not dragging Sangster in with us that afternoon, just to keep her out of trouble.

It would have been a lovely evening for hanky-panky. Too bad Leo was on the opposite edge of the field. With the sun going down, there was a bit of nip in the air. Dew had started to condense and I was wet to the knees, but I laid out a bit of tarp to sit on and to drag around my shoulders and settled down to count roos.

They weren't much worried about humans, as it turned out. At the moment, that was a plus. If the rexes had the same inclination, though, it would be just one more thing to worry about.

Susan I'd stationed roughly in eye-shot—at least, with the help of a good flashlight. But pretty soon I was so busy taking samples that I had no time for more than an occasional check on her. She was taking samples just as furiously as I was.

Moustafa's estimate had been in the hundreds, by which he'd meant maybe two hundred. I'd have guessed more. I counted nearly a hundred within the ring of light my flashlight produced. The flashlight bothered them not at all. They placidly munched at this, that, and the other. About as peaceful as a herd of cows and about as bright: one of the youngsters nibbled my tarp before I tapped its nose. Then it hopped back into mama's pouch and glared at me. Mama went on chewing, while I got samples of both.

In the cool of the evening, they were much more active. The youngsters chased and kicked each other and a lot of mock battles went down, reminding me of nothing so much as the way Susan and Mike behaved.

More than one of the youngsters had striped hips, so I crept as close as I dared while they were occupied with each other, to get samples specifically from them. Once again, a mock battle—great leaps in the air and powerful kicks from those hind legs—covered my movement.

Three older kangaroos paused to look up from their eating but they looked up at the antics of the youngsters with the same kind of wearied eye I had been known to turn on activities of that sort from our younger contingent. Satisfied that the kids weren't getting into any trouble, they went back to what they'd been doing—which was grubbing in the ground, presumably for roots.

You wouldn't believe those claws unless you saw them in action.

Once again, I appreciated the muscular shoulders. I frankly didn't see why a kangaroo rex should seem any more ferocious—at first glance, anyhow—than a basic kangaroo. Watching them, I got a tickle in the back of my skull. The stuff they were grubbing up looked familiar. Nova-light is romantic, but not as good for some things as for others. I debated the wisdom of turning my flashlight on them for a better look.

Being old hands, *they* would not be so likely to take my intrusion as lightly as the joey had. I didn't want to start a stampede. There were just too many of them in the general neighborhood. I didn't relish the thought of being run down by several hundred pounds of panicked roo.

The elder roos looked up, suddenly wary. I abandoned my plan and followed their point. Some sort of disturbance at the edge of the mob, very near where I'd last seen Susan. And damned if I could see her now—there were too many adult roos between my position and hers.

The nearby roos got a bit skittish. Two of the adult males bounced once in Susan's direction, froze, and watched. A new mob had joined the browsing.

This was a smaller group. Dominant male, two females, and two matching joeys. Damned if the male didn't have that striped rump. I didn't dare edge closer, not with the nearby roos nervous already. I held my ground and hoped the quintet of likelies would pass near enough to Susan for her to get a safe shot at sampling them.

But they skirted Susan (now that my brain was working again, I decided I was glad they had) and headed in my direction. Closer examination told me that papa was a roo. Neither of the mamas was, though. To hell with the striped rump—these two were plain and simple kangaroo rexes—and most of the nearby roos didn't like it any more than I did.

Their movements were different. (Well, let's face it—they would be.) Except for the male, they weren't grazing. They were searching the grass for whatever small prey the rest of the roos startled into motion. I could see why they liked to hang around with the browsers. The browsing roos gave them cover and, as often as not, sent gladrats and grubroots right into those waiting jaws.

I couldn't recall when I'd ever heard anything eaten with a snap quite that impressive, either. I eased back down in the grass, hoping they'd get close enough that I could get shots at both the mothers and the joeys. I laid my rifle where I could reach it at a moment's notice and raised my sampler.

To my surprise, the roos around me, after whiffling the air a few times, settled back to their browsing. When the rexes came close, the roos eased away, but didn't panic. Not quite acceptable in polite society, I could see, but nothing to worry about so long as they kept to their own table.

One of the rex joeys pounced after something small in the grass. In the excitement of the chase, it headed straight for me. I popped it with the sampler on the spot and it jumped straight up in the air, came down bouncing the opposite direction, headed for mama. It made a coughing bark the like of which I never heard from a roo.

Mama made the same coughing sound, bounded *over* the joey, and the next thing I knew I was face to face with several hundred pounds of angry rex. The jaws snapped as I brought up my gun. Then something hit me in the shoulder with the force of a freight train. The gun went in one direction, I went in the other, rolling as best I could to keep from being kicked a second time by the papa roo.

A brilliant flash of light struck in our direction, illuminating the mama rex as she came after me. There was a yell and a shot from somewhere behind me. I may have imagined it, but I swear I felt that bullet pass inches from my right ear.

The mama rex stopped in her tracks—stunned, not shot. The rest of the mobs, roos and rexes alike, took off in all directions. The ground shook from their thundering kick-offs and landings.

I scrambled to my feet, the better to dodge if dodging was possible in that chaos. It was only then that I realized that some damn fool of a human had the kangaroo rex by the tail, hauling it back as it tried to bound away.

A second damn fool of a human grabbed for the rex's feet, dragging them out from under it so it couldn't kick.

Dammit! They'd forgotten the teeth!

I was moving before I even put a thought to it. Dived, landed roughly on the rex's head and grabbed it about the throat, pulling the jaw closed toward my chest and hanging on for dear life while the thing struggled for all it was worth. It had the worst damn breath of any creature I'd ever gotten that foolishly close to.

Through the haze and the brilliance of the artificial light, I saw somebody race up and plunge a hypodermic needle into the upturned haunch. The rex coughed its outrage and struggled twice as hard. I almost suffocated. I don't even want to think how close its snap came to my ear.

Somebody else was trying to loop a rope around those thrashing hind legs and not being very successful about it. I'd have let go, if I could have thought of a safe way of doing it.

Then all at once the struggle went out of the rex. It kicked weakly a few more times, then went limp, for all the world as if it were too hot a day to do anything but lie around in the shade.

The fellow with the rope said, "Took long enough!" and finished his tying—as neat as any cowboy on ship's film. He whipped another length of rope off his hip, came round to me, and wrapped the length about the jaw, sealing it temporarily shut. Then he stood up, dusted off his hands, and said, "Kelly, you're gonna have to come up with a better mousetrap. Damned if I'm gonna do *that* again!"

Sangster uncrimped herself from the rex's tail and stood to face him. "Thought the Texan Guild would be a damn sight better at hog-tying." The challenge in her voice was unmistakable. "I guess the Australian Guild will have to handle the rest alone."

"Hell," said the Texan, in that peculiar drawl that identifies members of the guild, "just give us a chance to practice. These things move a sight different than a longhorn."

"You're on," said Sangster. "Now let's get this into the cage before the valium wears off." She turned to me and said, "We'll catch the rest of them for you."

Four of them hefted the limp rex onto their shoulders and started back toward town.

None of it was making sense, least of all Sangster's parting shot. Maybe that roo's kick had caught me in the side of the head after all and I just didn't know it. I felt like walking wounded.

Must have been stunned, because it wasn't until Leo and Susan picked up my gun and my cell sampler and caught my elbows on either side that I even remembered to make sure they were okay themselves.

Leo looked about like I felt. Susan was fine, bounding along, half in front of us, half trying to carry me by my elbow, as if she'd caught the bounds from the roos. "Mama Jason," she caroled as she bounced, "I'm so glad you're okay! That was about the most exciting thing that's ever happened to me, *ever!* Wasn't it, Noisy? Have you ever *seen* anything like that in your *life?* Just wait until I tell Chris and Elly and Mike. . . ."

None of that seemed to require any response from me, so I saved my breath for walking.

"*Are* we going to catch the rest of them?" she demanded at last. "What about the rex's joey? Shouldn't we find it? Maybe it wasn't weaned yet."

From the brief look I'd gotten at the joeys, chances were Susan was right. If the rex they'd shot full of valium lived, we'd still lose the rex joey.

But when we rounded the corner, we found a makeshift cage—a big one, much to my relief—built onto a transport trailer that sat right next to Sangster's house. In it was the mama rex, still groggy but unmuzzled now, *and* her joey. At least, I *hoped* it was hers. It was pretty damned angry, but was expending most of its energy to try to get a response out of mama.

The entire town of Last Edges and then some had turned out to gawk. Sangster lounged against the cage like she owned 'em both. When she saw us coming, she nodded and took a few steps to meet us.

"Earth used to have zoos," she said, with no preamble. Glancing at the Texan Guilder, she added, "Ramanathan checked out the references for us in ship's log." She folded her arms across her chest and, with an air of pronouncement, finished, "We've decided we don't mind if you keep them in a zoo. We'll catch the rest of them for you."

That was not what I'd had in mind at all. Still, I wasn't going to make any objection as long as it kept Sangster and her crew from shooting them on sight. "Who's funding this zoo," I said, "and who's going to catch the grubroots and gladrats to feed them?"

Sangster and the Texan exchanged glances. "We'll talk about it later," she said.

I'll just bet, I thought, but didn't say it. I shrugged and turned to plod back to Janzen's place. I needed a hot soak to get the kinks out. My shoulder was beginning to stiffen from the bruises I'd gotten. (At least, I hoped it wasn't worse than bruises.) "Get that joey something to eat," I said. "They were hunting when you interrupted them. Grubroots will do just fine. That's what it was after."

I left. Somebody would see to it—probably Janzen.

Sangster caught up with me at the door to Janzen's place. "I talked the Australian guild into cooperating. I can talk them into funding the zoo, too. Marsupials are *our* jurisdiction. Maybe the rex is an Earth-authentic that got lost with the missing ship's files."

"Maybe," I said, stopping to consider her. Damned strange woman. I was sure from her manner that she was still mad as all hell at me, so none of this made sense. "More likely an intermediate, ready to chain up to an Earth-authentic."

"We want them *off* the sheep range," she said. "It's this or kill the roos again. We talked the Texan Guild into helping us. We can get them all for your zoo."

What could I say? "Until the next batch chains up from the roos." I shrugged one more time.

Sangster scowled deeper. "I saved this pair for you. I talked them into making a zoo. Now we're even."

She practically spat that last at me, then she turned on her heel and stamped away, raising dust with her fury.

Even for *what?* I wondered. *Damn* strange woman, like I said before.

I woke up stiff all over. Susan was balanced on the edge of my cot, barely able to contain herself. "What?" I said.

"They caught the other mama rex and her joey last night, Mama Jason. We get to keep them after all."

"Zoo is *not* my idea of keeping them, dammit. Just sheer luck they haven't killed any of them yet, between the valium and beating them into submission." I tried to get coherent but I'm not ready for mornings, ever. "Read up on zoos—and I don't mean the cursory reading Sangster and her mates did. Zoos always held the *last* individuals of the species: they were a death sentence."

"Oh," she said. "Mike called. He and Selima are up at Gogol, doing that EC check you wanted. He'll have it this evening."

"Good. I want you to do the same here. That I want this evening, too."

"Betcha I'm faster than Mike."

"Better be cleaner, too," I said, "or faster doesn't count."

She grinned at me, bounded off the cot, and was out the door without another word. Guaranteed her report would be both faster and cleaner than Mike's—unless I called Mike and issued the same challenge, that is. I dragged myself out of bed. Breakfast first, to get the mind moving, then to the computer to see what, if anything, was new from the lab.

What was new was a note from Chie-Hoon. "Skipped an emergency meeting of the Australian Guild for this, Annie, so you'd better appreciate it." Appended were reconstructions of the two critters our rexes were planning to chain up to.

Chie-Hoon had a gift for that: take the gene chart and draw from it a picture of what the resulting animal would look like. There were no Latin names for 'em, which meant Chie-Hoon hadn't been able to find a gene-read for either in ship's records.

The first one was just a variant on roo. The second was, well, as weird a thing as I'd *ever* seen, including the Mirabilan jumping fish. It had the same jaw and jaw-span as the rexes, but it was a quadruped. The tail wasn't as thick (well, it didn't need the tail for balance the way the roos did) and the hip stripes continued up to the shoulders, narrowing as they went. Basic predator with camouflage stripes.

The pouch opening aimed toward the tail, instead of toward the head. Took me a moment to figure that out—kept the baby from falling out while the critter chased prey, probably also kept it from getting scratched up on creve-coeur in the same circumstances. What it boiled down to was a marsupial version of a wolf. Probably wouldn't stack up too well against the mammalian wolf (a species I'm rather partial to), but it was a fine off-the-wall bit of work nonetheless.

Then I went on to the note from Mike. As Susan had said, he and Selima were on their way. Susan *had* forgotten to pass along the final message . . . which was that my courting present thought the jumping fish were great toys but showed not the slightest interest in eating them. As Mike said, our luck's not *that* good this summer.

"How's the shoulder this morning, Annie?" Leo looked like he'd been up and around for hours already.

"Stiff," I said—and bless his sweet soul, he came right in to massage it—"I appreciate your courting gift all the more, now that I know what kind of fight you went through to catch it for me."

"All in the name of love," he said and I could feel his grin light up the room all around me even if I couldn't see it. "What can I do for you today?"

"Join me on a long, probably useless, but definitely exhausting walk around the sheep fields. Unless you could pick out the spot the Australian Guild grabbed the rex in the daylight?" Probably too much to hope for.

"I can pick it out," he said. "That big a scrabble left signs—and I know about where you were a few moments before."

"What would I do without you?"

So we headed out. The route took us past the caged rexes. Some fifteen people were still standing about staring in at them—some tourist attraction, all right. Safe but scary, as Leo had said once in another context.

I wanted to see how they were faring myself, so I shoved through the crowd. One of the gawkers had a stick and was using it to poke at the baby rex through the bars of the cage. Just to rile it and make its mother charge him.

As I got there, the mother was just rebounding off the wire. I snatched the stick out of the bastard's hand and slapped him a good one alongside the head with it. "You like that?" I demanded.

"Hell, no!" he said.

"Then what makes you think that creature does?"

"I—" He looked sheepish for a moment, then defiant. "I just wanted to see them move around some. They weren't doing anything."

"Roos don't do anything in this heat, either. That's their way of conserving water, you damn fool. Who raised you?"

Stunned, he told me.

"Well, they ought to be ashamed of themselves. They damn sure didn't teach you the sense god gave the rexes there."

"Hey! You can't talk about my raisers—"

"Then you oughta stop doing stupid things that lead me to believe they raised you wrong."

That did it. I watched him go all embarrassed.

"Sorry," he said at last. "Everybody else was doing it."

"Then prove to me that you're a cut better. First, you get the rexes some water, so they can replace what they've lost. Then you get that damned Australian Guild to move this into the shade. Then you can stand here and make sure nobody else beats up on the rexes. Then I'll revise my opinion of your raisers. Got that?"

"Yes, *ma'am!*"

Yes, *ma'am,* and he'd do it, too. I was satisfied he'd keep them from being harassed further.

Then I got a chance to look at the rexes. The other joey was dragging a foot. Hellfire and damnation, they'd broken its leg catching it. I roared at Leo, "Get Sangster and her damned Australians down here right now!"

So we spent most of the afternoon coaxing the injured joey out of the cage so we could splint its leg. Zoos, just love 'em. Hope the guy that invented 'em wound up in a cage all his own—in the sun.

Sangster and her mates were apologetic but clearly had no intention of giving up their plan to catch any more rexes that turned up for their zoo. Oughta be a damned law to protect animals from people.

It was cooling toward evening when Leo and I finally set out to look for the spot I had in mind. Something was still niggling me about that, but the whole struggle with the rex had shoved it completely out of my head. I was hoping if I saw the spot again, the same thought might come back.

Leo found it for me in record time. Would have taken me twice as long. He stood in the middle of the spot where the first rex had been when that blinding light and stunning shot hit it all at once. "Now you see if you can reconstruct your position from that," he said. "Just pretend I'm a kangaroo rex."

"You haven't got the jaw for it, Leo." I cast about and made some good guesses. They were good enough that I found bits of the broken cell sampler there. I flopped down next to the bits and glanced around. Nothing jogged my memory, so I closed my eyes and tried to see it again.

That worked: the roos (not the rexes) had been digging up plants just *there.* I hauled myself to my feet and went over to look.

The plants the roos had been grubbing up were still there, shriveled in the heat and utterly unrecognizable. Fine. I could still do a gene-read on them if I did it *now.* "Okay," I said. "Back to Janzen's. You can make me a mint julep. If this is what I hope it is, we'll toast Mirabile."

What with one thing and another, I didn't get my gene-read on the withered plants until after dinner. It was just what I expected it to be, so I put in a call to Mike out at Gogol. Mike and Selima couldn't be found for me (aha!) but they'd left their EC run in my file.

"Susan!" I yelled and she came running. "You finish that EC check for me?"

She looked smug. "On file," she said. "Did I beat Mike out?"

I cued up her file. "Mike's was filed roughly the same time as yours but then he had extra hands—Selima was with him."

"Oh," said Susan. "Well, it's only fair to say I had extra hands, too. Janzen helped me." That made her look smugger and set off a second *aha!*, which I did not voice, as much as I enjoyed it.

I read through Susan's EC on Last Edges, then went to Mike's from Gogol a second time, then pulled hard copy on both. "Gotcha," I said, as the reports stacked up in the printer. "Mint juleps all around, Leo!"

I handed Susan the sheaf of reports and said, "Read 'em. Then tell me how this EC differs from the EC at Gogol." I leaned back in my chair, accepted the mint julep from Leo, and waited to see if Susan would see it too.

After a while, Susan's head came up. She stared at me and her mouth worked, but nothing came out. She handed the sheaf of papers to Janzen, went to the computer, and called up the EC we'd done on Gogol all those years ago, the first time the kangaroo rexes had reared their ugly little heads. She nodded to herself, then pulled hard copy on that too.

She came back with it and added it to the pile Janzen was reading. Then she sat down and said, "To kill the rexes, they have to kill the roos—but if they kill the roos, the *sheep* die."

"What?" said Moustafa and tried to wrest the reports from Janzen, who didn't cooperate. "I don't see it, Susan. I don't know how to read these things."

She gave him a pitying look but explained: "There are only two significant differences between the EC here and the EC at Gogol. The first is that Gogol has no roos—or very few; they're shot on sight—and the second is that Gogol is awash in lambkill."

Moustafa made a stifled noise deep in his throat. Janzen said, "Does this mean I don't have to give up my roo-tail soup?"

"It means," I said, "that the roos eat the lambkill, which prevents your *sheep* from eating it. You may be willing to give up your roo-tail soup, but how many people in Last Edges are willing to give up their sheep—the way Sangster did after the roos were killed in Gogol?"

I raised my glass. "To Mirabile," I said.

It was Janzen who rang the meeting bell. And what with the Australian Guilders and the Texan Guilders—all of whom were antsy to be back on the range rounding up kangaroo rexes—we had a much larger turnout than expected. There was a lot of jostling and more than one case of bad manners. I had to wonder if the Texan Guild went so far as to call each other out for gunfights, but apparently not, as nobody did.

When they finally all simmered down, I explained the situation to them. I guess I expected them to forgive the rexes on the spot. I should know better at my age.

Sangster said, "Of *course,* the roos eat lambkill! They grub it out right down to the root—*anybody* could have told you that, for god's sake!"

"You don't get it," Janzen shot back. "Kill the roos and the *lambkill* kills the sheep! That's why you lost your flock at Gogol. D'you want the same thing to happen here? *I* sure as hell don't!"

There was a good loud mutter of agreement from the crowd on that one. Sangster stamped her foot and yelled for attention. After a while she got it, but it was a lot more hostile than she was used to.

"Stabilize the roos, then," she said. She glared at me. "You've done it before with domestic herds. Those guernseys that were dropping deer every other generation. You got those stabilized to where they chain up only once every ten years. Are you telling me you can't do the same for our roos—or can't you be bothered? Might mess up your beloved kangaroo rexes."

I didn't get a chance to answer. From the very back of the crowd came an agonized shout: *"No,* Annie! You can't stabilize them! You don't know what the rexes are chaining up to! I do! And you *can't* stabilize the roos!"

I peered over heads and could just barely make out a mop of straight black hair and piercing black eyes. By this time I'd recognized Chie-Hoon's voice, even though I'd never heard the kid quite so worked up about anything.

Before anybody'd had time to react to this, Chie-Hoon was standing on a chair, waving a banner-sized picture. I recognized it even from that distance: Chie-Hoon's own reconstruction of the weirder of the two critters our rexes were chaining up to, the one with the jaws.

"Mates!" shouted Chie-Hoon, and had the instant attention of every Australian Guild member there. (When one of the locals made to object to this interruption from a nonresident, he was swiftly stifled by a menacing look from a guilder.) "D'ya recognize this?" Chie-Hoon spread the picture wide and turned, slowly, on the chair to let every one of them have a good look.

"It's a Tasmanian wolf," said somebody—to which there was general agreement—then a swift reshuffling of the Australian Guild to get closer.

"Good on you, mate," said Chie-Hoon. "That's exactly right! *That's* what our rexes are chaining up to! It was extinct on Earth, but that doesn't make it any the less Earth-authentic. Speaking as a member of the Australian Guild, Annie, I won't have you stabilizing the rexes. Save the Tasmanian wolf!"

With that, Chie-Hoon raised a fist, dramatically, then shouted a second time, "Save the Tasmanian wolf!"

And before I knew what was happening, pandemonium reigned. The entire Australian Guild was chanting, "Save the Tasmanian wolf!" as if their own lives depended on it, with Kelly Crafter Sangster herself leading the chant.

Twenty minutes later, they released the uninjured rex and its mother, with promises to release the other pair as soon as the joey's leg had healed, and I was being threatened with dire consequences if I didn't return Leo's courting gift to the fields within the week.

"They won't let me keep my present," I said to Leo, grinning through my complaint.

"I know," he said, grinning just as much. "But they'll let you keep your kangaroo rexes. That's what counts."

"It was a great courting gift, Leo."

"I know."

"We'll have to see about re-establishing the kangaroos at Gogol, too, before we lose the rest of the sheep there to the lambkill."

"Don't you ever think about anything but work, woman?"

"Occasionally. Call Loch Moose Lodge and book us a room for the week. I need a vacation."

He started off to do just that. I had another thought. "Leo!"

"You're not changing your mind." That was an order.

"No, I'm not changing my mind. But it occurs to me that Chris always wanted to be a member of my team, if she could be the official cook. Tell her I'm bringing her a brace of fish." It was those damned jumping fish I had in mind. "If she can find a way to cook them that'll make them the hot item of the season, she's on the team."

He laughed. "You've just made Chris's day."

He turned to go again, but I caught him and gave him a good long kiss, just so he wouldn't forget to book the room while he was at it. "You made my year, Leo."

Now all I had to do was think of an appropriate courting present for *him*. Which wasn't going to be easy. What do you give a guy who gives you a kangaroo rex?

I'd think of something.

Walter Jon Williams

PRAYERS ON THE WIND

Walter Jon Williams was born in Minnesota and now lives in Albuquerque, New Mexico. His short fiction has appeared frequently in *Asimov's Science Fiction*, as well as in *The Magazine of Fantasy & Science Fiction, Wheel of Fortune, Global Dispatches, Alternate Outlaws*, and in other markets, and has been gathered in the collections *Facets* and *Frankensteins and Foreign Devils*. His novels include *Ambassador of Progress, Knight Moves, Hardwired, The Crown Jewels, Voice of the Whirlwind, House of Shards, Days of Atonement*, and *Aristoi*. His novel *Metropolitan* garnered wide critical acclaim in 1996 and was one of the most talked-about books of the year. His most recent book is a sequel to *Metropolitan, City on Fire*.

Williams is a highly eclectic writer, and the fact is, one Walter Jon Williams story is rarely much like any *other* Walter Jon Williams story. He's written a wider range of different *kinds* of stuff than almost any other writer of his generation, ranging from some of the best Alternate History stories of the eighties (including the deeply moving Alternate Civil War novella, following Edgar Allan Poe's career as a Confederate general, "No Spot of Ground," and the compassionate and melancholy look at the alternate and alternately entangled lives that might have been lead by Mary Wollstonecraft Shelley, Percy Bysshe Shelley, and Lord Byron, "Wall, Stone, Craft") to stories featuring scenarios quirky enough to rank with the most off-the-wall Waldropian stuff (sending H. G. Wells's invading Martians striding into the bizarre, ritualized, and mannered world of the Forbidden City in nineteenth-century China in "Foreign Devils," and, in "Red Elvis," presenting us with an Elvis Presley who grows up to become an inspirational socialist leader whose influence changes the course of modern history); he's written gritty Mean Streets hard-as-nails cyberpunk, in stories such as "Wolf Time" and "Video Star" and "Flatline," and in novels such as the *Hardwired* and *Voice of the Whirlwind;* he's written with depth and real ingenuity about the interaction of humankind with aliens, in the brilliant "Surfacing," as well as in novels such as *Angel Station;* he's written lighthearted, wryly amusing, socially satirical novels of manners, featuring the adventures of a Raffles-like thief in a future society, in *The Crown Jewels* and *House of Shards;* he's written dark, moody, intricate, involuted Machiavellian studies of Realpolitik in action, full of betrayals and counter-betrayals and counter-*counter* betrayals, such as "Solip:System" and "Erogenoscape." Williams also mixes genres with audacity and daring, mixing classical Chinese mythology with the chop-sockey fantasy of Hong Kong martial arts movies in the droll "Broadway Johnny," mixing sword and sorcery with the Hornblower-like sea story in "Consequences," having costumed superheroes grilled by the House Committee on Un-American Activities in the McCarthy–era America of the 1950s in "Witness," and mixing fantasy with technologically oriented "hard" science fiction in books such as *Metropolitan* and *City on Fire* successfully enough to be counted as one of the progenitors of an as yet nascent subgenre sometimes called "Hard Fantasy."

This breadth of range sometimes obscures the fact that Williams has also written some of the most inventive and Wide Screen Space Opera of recent times, including the monumental novel *Aristoi,* one of the most successful of Modern Space Operas. But then, Williams is a great fan of adventure writing, and even his most introspective stories are usually crammed with action; in this he strongly recalls his mentor, Roger Zelazny, and it's no accident that Walter was selected by Roger Zelazny himself to write a sequel to Zelazny's famous story "The Graveyard Heart"—and ended up producing by far the most successful Zelazny homage I've ever read, the complex and eloquent novella "Elegy for Angels and Dogs."

Zelazny's influence is also clear in the vivid and gorgeously colored story that follows, with Williams taking us deep into the far future and across the galaxy to a distant planet to detail the intricate workings of a *very* strange future society . . . a society caught at a moment of crisis that may destroy the very foundations of its civilization forever. . . .

Hard is the appearance of a Buddha.

—Dhammapada

Bold color slashed bright slices out of Vajra's violet sky. The stiff spring breeze off the Tingsum glacier made the yellow prayer flags snap with sounds like gunshots. Sun gleamed from baroque tracework adorning silver antennae and receiver dishes. Atop the dark red walls of the Diamond Library Palace, saffron-robed monks stood like sentries, some of them grouped in threes around ragdongs, trumpets so huge they required two men to hold them aloft while a third blew puff-cheeked into the mouthpiece. Over the deep, grating moan of the trumpets, other monks chanted their litany.

Salutation to the Buddha.
In the language of the gods and in that of the Lus,
In the language of the demons and in that of the men,
In all the languages which exist,
I proclaim the Doctrine.

Jigme Dzasa stood at the foot of the long granite stair leading to the great library, the spectacle filling his senses, the litany dancing in his soul. He turned to his guest. "Are you ready, Ambassador?"

The face of !urq was placid. "Lus?" she asked.

"Mythical beings," said Jigme. "Serpentine divinities who live in bodies of water."

"Ah," !urq said. "I'm glad we got that cleared up."

Jigme looked at the alien, decided to say nothing.

"Let us begin," said the Ambassador. Jigme hitched up his zen and began the long climb to the Palace, his bare feet slapping at the stones. A line of Gelugspa monks followed in respectful silence. Ambassador Colonel !urq climbed beside Jigme at a slow trot, her four boot heels rapping. Behind her was a line of Sangs, their centauroid bodies cased neatly in blue-and-gray uniforms, decorations flashing in the bright sun. Next to each was a feathery Masker servant carrying a ceremonial parasol.

Jigme was out of breath by the time he mounted the long stairway, and his head whirled as he entered the tsokhang, the giant assembly hall. Several thousand members of religious orders sat rigid at their stations, long lines of men and women: Dominicans and Sufis in white, Red Hats and Yellow Hats in their saffron zens, Jesuits in black, Gyudpas in complicated aprons made of carved, interwoven human bones. . . . Each sat in the lotus posture in front of a solid gold data terminal decorated with religious symbols, some meditating, some chanting sutras, others accessing the Library.

Jigme, !urq, and their parties passed through the vast hall that hummed with the distant, echoing sutras of those trying to achieve unity with the Diamond Mountain. At the far side of the room were huge double doors of solid jade, carved with figures illustrating the life of the first twelve incarnations of the Gyalpo Rinpoche, the Treasured King. The doors opened on silent hinges at the touch of equerries' fingertips. Jigme looked at the equerries as he passed—lovely young novices, he thought, beautiful boys really. The shaven nape of that dark one showed an extraordinary curve.

Beyond was the audience chamber. The Masker servants remained outside, holding their parasols at rigid attention, while their masters trotted into the audience chamber alongside the line of monks.

Holographic murals filled the walls, illustrating the life of the Compassionate One. The ceiling was of transparent polymer, the floor of clear crystal that went down to the solid core of the planet. The crystal refracted sunlight in interesting ways, and as he walked across the room Jigme seemed to walk on rainbows.

At the far end of the room, flanked by officials, was the platform that served as a throne. Overhead was an arching canopy of massive gold, the words AUM MANI PADME HUM worked into the design in turquoise. The platform was covered in a large carpet decorated with figures of the lotus, the Wheel, the swastika, the two fish, the eternal knot, and other holy symbols. Upon the carpet sat the Gyalpo Rinpoche himself, a small man with a sunken chest and bony shoulders, the Forty-First Incarnation of the Bodhisattva Bob Miller, the Great Librarian, himself an emanation of Avalokitesvara.

The Incarnation was dressed simply in a yellow zen, being the only person in the holy precincts permitted to wear the color. Around his waist was a rosary composed of 108 strung bone disks cut from the forty skulls of his previous incarnations. His body was motionless but his arms rose and fell as the fingers moved in a series of symbolic hand gestures, one mudra after another, their pattern set by the flow of data through the Diamond Mountain.

Jigme approached and dropped to his knees before the platform. He pressed the palms of his hands together, brought the hands to his forehead, mouth, and heart, then touched his forehead to the floor. Behind him he heard thuds as some of his delegation slammed their heads against the crystal surface in a display of piety—indeed, there were depressions in the floor worn by the countless pilgrims who had done this—but Jigme, knowing he would need his wits, only touched his forehead lightly and held the posture until he heard the Incarnation speak.

"Jigme Dzasa. I am pleased to see you again. Please get to your feet and introduce me to your friends."

The old man's voice was light and dry, full of good humor. In the seventy-third year of his incarnation, the Treasured King enjoyed good health.

Jigme straightened. Rainbows rose from the floor and danced before his eyes. He climbed slowly to his feet as his knees made popping sounds—twenty years younger than the Incarnation, he was a good deal stiffer of limb—and moved toward the platform in an attitude of reverence. He reached to the rosary at his waist and took from it a white silk scarf embroidered with a religious text. He unfolded the khata and, sticking out his tongue in respect, handed it to the Incarnation with a bow.

The Gyalpo Rinpoche took the khata and draped it around his own neck with a smile. He reached out a hand, and Jigme dropped his head for the blessing. He felt dry fingertips touch his shaven scalp, and then a sense of harmony seemed to hum through his being. Everything, he knew, was correct. The interview would go well.

Jigme straightened and the Incarnation handed him a khata in exchange, one with the mystic three knots tied by the Incarnation himself. Jigme bowed again, stuck out his tongue, and moved to the side of the platform with the other officials. Beside him was Dr. Kay O'Neill, the Minister of Science. Jigme could feel O'Neill's body vibrating like a taut cord, but the minister's overwrought state could not dispel Jigme's feeling of bliss.

"Omniscient," Jigme said, "I would like to present Colonel !urq, Ambassador of the Sang."

!urq was holding her upper arms in a Sang attitude of respect. Neither she nor her followers had prostrated themselves, but had stood politely by while their human escort had done so. !urq's boots rang against the floor as she trotted to the dais, her lower arms offering a khata. She had no tongue to stick out—her upper and lower palates were flexible, permitting a wide variety of sounds, but they weren't as flexible as all that. Still she thrust out her lower lip in a polite approximation.

"I am honored to be presented at last, Omniscient," !urq said.

Dr. O'Neill gave a snort of anger.

The Treasured King draped a knotted khata around the Ambassador's neck. "We of the Diamond Mountain are pleased to welcome you. I hope you will find our hospitality to your liking."

The old man reached forward for the blessing. !urq's instructions did not permit her to bow her head before an alien presence, so the Incarnation simply reached forward and placed his hand over her face for a moment. They remained frozen in that attitude, and then !urq backed carefully to one side of the platform, standing near Jigme. She and Jigme then presented their respective parties to the Incarnation. By the end of the audience the head of the Gyalpo Rinpoche looked like a tiny red jewel in a flowery lotus of white silk khatas.

"I thank you all for coming all these light-years to see me," said the Incarnation, and Jigme led the visitors from the audience chamber, chanting the sutra *Aum vajra guru Padma siddhi hum, Aum the diamond powerful guru Padma,* as he walked.

!urq came to a halt as soon as her party had filed from the room. Her lower arms formed an expression of bewilderment.

"Is that all?"

Jigme looked at the alien. "That is the conclusion of the audience, yes. We may tour the holy places in the Library, if you wish."

"We had no opportunity to discuss the matter of Gyangtse."

"You may apply to the Ministry for another interview."

"It took me twelve years to obtain this one." Her upper arms took a stance that Jigme recognized as martial. "The patience of my government is not unlimited," she said.

Jigme bowed. "I shall communicate this to the Ministry, Ambassador."

"Delay in the Gyangtse matter will only result in more hardship for the inhabitants when they are removed."

"It is out of my hands, Ambassador."

!urq held her stance for a long moment in order to emphasize her protest, then relaxed her arms. Her upper set of hands caressed the white silk khata. "Odd to think," she said, amused, "that I journeyed twelve years just to stick out my lip at a human and have him touch my face in return."

"Many humans would give their lives for such a blessing," said Jigme.

"Sticking out the lip is quite rude where I come from, you know."

"I believe you have told me this."

"The Omniscient's hands were very warm." !urq raised fingers to her forehead, touched the ebon flesh. "I believe I can still feel the heat on my skin."

Jigme was impressed. "The Treasured King has given you a special blessing. He can channel the energies of the Diamond Mountain through his body. That was the heat you felt."

!urq's antennae rose skeptically, but she refrained from comment.

"Would you like to see the holy places?" Jigme said. "This, for instance, is a room devoted to Maitreya, the Buddha That Will Come. Before you is his statue. Data can be accessed by manipulation of the images on his headdress."

Jigme's speech was interrupted by the entrance of a Masker servant from the audience room. A white khata was draped about the avian's neck. !urq's trunk swiveled atop her centaur body; her arms assumed a commanding stance. The clicks and pops of her own language rattled from her mouth like falling stones.

"Did I send for you, creature?"

The Masker performed an obsequious gesture with its parasol. "I beg the Colonel's pardon. The old human sent for us. He is touching us and giving us scarves." The Masker fluttered helplessly. "We did not wish to offend our hosts, and there were no Sang to query for instruction."

"How odd," said !urq. "Why should the old human want to bless our slaves?" She eyed the Masker and thought for a moment. "I will not kill you today," she decided. She turned to Jigme and switched to Tibetan. "Please continue, Rinpoche."

"As you wish, Colonel." He returned to his speech. "The Library Palace is the site of no less than twenty-one tombs of various bodhisattvas, including many incarnations of the Gyalpo Rinpoche. The Palace also contains over eight thousand data terminals and sixty shrines."

As he rattled through the prepared speech, Jigme wondered about the scene he had just witnessed. He suspected that "I will not kill you today" was less alarming than it sounded, was instead an idiomatic way of saying "Go about your business."

Then again, knowing the Sang, maybe not.

• • • •

The Cabinet had gathered in one of the many other reception rooms of the Library Palace. This one was small, the walls and ceiling hidden behind tapestry covered with appliqué, the room's sole ornament a black stone statue of a dancing demon that served tea on command.

The Gyalpo Rinpoche, to emphasize his once-humble origins, was seated on the floor. White stubble prickled from his scalp.

Jigme sat cross-legged on a pillow. Across from him was Dr. O'Neill. A lay official, her status was marked by the long turquoise earring that hung from her left ear to her collarbone, that and the long hair piled high on her head. The rosary she held was made of 108 antique microprocessors pierced and strung on a length of fiberoptic cable. Beside her sat the cheerful Miss Taisuke, the Minister of State. Although only fifteen years old, she was Jigme's immediate superior, her authority derived from being the certified reincarnation of a famous hermit nun of the Yellow Hat Gelugspa order. Beside her, the Minister of Magic, a tantric sorcerer of the Gyud School named Daddy Carbajal, toyed with a trumpet made from a human thigh bone. Behind him in a semireclined position was the elderly, frail, toothless State Oracle—his was a high-ranking position, but it was a largely symbolic one as long as the Treasured King was in his majority. Other ministers, lay or clerical, sipped tea or gossiped as they waited for the Incarnation to begin the meeting.

The Treasured King scratched one bony shoulder, grinned, then assumed in an eyeblink a posture of deep meditation, placing hands in his lap with his skull-rosary wrapped around them. "Aum," he intoned. The others straightened and joined in the holy syllable, the Pranava, the creative sound whose vibrations built the universe. Then the Horse of the Air rose from the throat of the Gyalpo Rinpoche, the syllables *Aum mane padme hum,* and the others reached for their rosaries.

As he recited the rosary, Jigme tried to meditate on each syllable as it went by, comprehend the full meaning of each, the color, the importance, the significance. *Aum,* which was white and connected with the gods. *Ma,* which was blue and connected with the titans. *Ne,* which was yellow and connected with men. *Pad,* which was green and connected with animals. *Me,* which was red and connected with giants and demigods. *Hum,* which was black and connected with dwellers in purgatory. Each syllable a separate realm, each belonging to a separate species, together forming the visible and invisible universe.

"Hri!" called everyone in unison, signifying the end of the 108th repetition. The Incarnation smiled and asked the black statue for some tea. The stone demon scuttled across the thick carpet and poured tea into his golden bowl. The demon looked up into the Incarnation's face.

"Free me!" said the statue.

The Gyalpo Rinpoche looked at the statue. "Tell me truthfully. Have you achieved Enlightenment?"

The demon said nothing.

The Treasured King smiled again. "Then you had better give Dr. O'Neill some tea."

O'Neill accepted her tea, sipped, and dismissed the demon. It scuttled back to its pedestal.

"We should consider the matter of Ambassador !urq," said the Incarnation.

O'Neill put down her teacup. "I am opposed to her presence here. The Sang are an unenlightened and violent race. They conceive of life as a struggle against nature rather than search for Enlightenment. They have already conquered an entire species, and would subdue us if they could."

"That is why I have consented to the building of warships," said the Incarnation.

"From their apartments in the Nyingmapa monastery, the Sang now have access to the Library," said O'Neill. "All our strategic information is present there. They will use the knowledge against us."

"Truth can do no harm," said Miss Taisuke.

"All truth is not vouchsafed to the unenlightened," said O'Neill. "To those unprepared by correct study and thought, truth can be a danger." She gestured with an arm, encompassing the world outside the Palace. "Who should know better than we, who live on Vajra? Haven't half the charlatans in all existence set up outside our walls to preach half-truths to the credulous, endangering their own Enlightenment and those of everyone who hears them?"

Jigme listened to O'Neill in silence. O'Neill and Daddy Carbajal were the leaders of the reactionary party, defenders of orthodoxy and the security of the realm. They had argued this point before.

"Knowledge will make the Sang cautious," said Jigme. "They will now know of our armament. They will now understand the scope of the human expansion, far greater than their own. We may hope this will deter them from attack."

"The Sang may be encouraged to build more weapons of their own," said Daddy Carbajal. "They are already highly militarized, as a way of keeping down their subject species. They may militarize further."

"Be assured they are doing so," said O'Neill. "Our own embassy is kept in close confinement on a small planetoid. They have no way of learning the scope of the Sang threat or sending this information to the Library. We, on the other hand, have escorted the Sang ambassador throughout human space and have shown her anything in which she expressed an interest."

"Deterrence," said Jigme. "We wished them to know how extensive our sphere is, that the conquest would be costly and call for more resources than they possess."

"We must do more than deter. The Sang threat should be eliminated, as were the threats of heterodox humanity during the Third and Fifth Incarnations."

"You speak jihad," said Miss Taisuke.

There was brief silence. No one, not even O'Neill, was comfortable with Taisuke's plainness.

"All human worlds are under the peace of the Library," said O'Neill. "This was accomplished partly by force, partly by conversion. The Sang will not *permit* conversion."

The Gyalpo Rinpoche cleared his throat. The others fell silent at once. The Incarnation had been listening in silence, his face showing concentration but no emotion. He always preferred to hear the opinions of others before expressing his own. "The Third and Fifth Incarnations," he said, "did nothing to encourage the jihads proclaimed in their name. The Incarnations did not wish to accept temporal power."

"They did not speak against the holy warriors," said Daddy Carbajal.

The Incarnation's elderly face was uncommonly stern. His hands formed the teaching mudra. "Does not Shakyamuni speak in the *Anguttara Nikaya* of the three ways of keeping the body pure?" he asked. "One must not commit adultery, one must not steal, one must not kill any living creature. How could warriors kill for orthodoxy and yet remain orthodox?"

There was a long moment of uncomfortable silence. Only Daddy Carbajal, whose tantric Short Path teaching included numerous ways of dispatching his enemies, did not seem nonplussed.

"The Sang are here to study us," said the Gyalpo Rinpoche. "We also study them."

"I view their pollution as a danger." Dr. O'Neill's face was stubborn.

Miss Taisuke gave a brilliant smile. "Does not the *Mahaparinirvanasutra* tell us that if we are forced to live in a difficult situation and among people of impure minds, if we cherish faith in Buddha we can ever lead them toward better actions?"

Relief fluttered through Jigme. Taisuke's apt quote, atop the Incarnation's sternness, had routed the war party.

"The Embassy will remain," said the Treasured King. "They will be given the freedom of Vajra, saving only the Holy Precincts. We must remember the oath of the Amida Buddha: 'Though I attain Buddhahood, I shall never be complete until people everywhere, hearing my name, learn right ideas about life and death, and gain that perfect wisdom that will keep their minds pure and tranquil in the midst of the world's greed and suffering.' "

"What of Gyangtse, Rinpoche?" O'Neill's voice seemed harsh after the graceful words of Scripture.

The Gyalpo Rinpoche cocked his head and thought for a moment. Suddenly the Incarnation seemed very human and very frail, and Jigme's heart surged with love for the old man.

"We will deal with that at the Picnic Festival," said the Incarnation.

From his position by the lake, Jigme could see tents and banners dotting the lower slopes of Tingsum like bright spring flowers. The Picnic Festival lasted a week, and unlike most of the other holidays had no real religious connection. It was a week-long campout during which almost the entire population of the Diamond City and the surrounding monasteries moved into the open and spent their time making merry.

Jigme could see the giant yellow hovertent of the Gyalpo Rinpoche surrounded by saffron-robed guards, the guards present not to protect the Treasured King from attackers, but rather to preserve his tranquility against invasions by devout pilgrims in search of a blessing. The guards—monks armed with staves, their shoulders padded hugely to make them look more formidable—served the additional purpose of keeping the Sang away from the Treasured King until the conclusion of the festival, something for which Jigme was devoutly grateful. He didn't want any political confrontations disturbing the joy of the holiday. Fortunately Ambassador !urq seemed content to wait until her scheduled appearance at a party given by the Incarnation on the final afternoon.

Children splashed barefoot in the shallows of the lake, and others played chibi on the sward beside, trying to keep a shuttlecock aloft using the feet alone. Jigme found himself watching a redheaded boy on the verge of adolescence, admiring the boy's grace, the way the knobbed spine and sharp shoulders moved under his pale skin. His bony ankles hadn't missed the shuttlecock yet. Jigme was sufficiently lost in his reverie that he did not hear the sound of boots on the grass beside him.

"Jigme Dzasa?"

Jigme looked up with a guilty start. !urq stood beside him, wearing hardy outdoor clothing. Her legs were wrapped up to the shoulder. Jigme stood hastily and bowed.

"Your pardon, Ambassador. I didn't hear you."

The Sang's feathery antennae waved cheerfully in the breeze. "I thought I would lead a party up Tingsum. Would you care to join us?"

What Jigme wanted to do was continue watching the ball game, but he assented with a smile. Climbing mountains: that was the sort of thing the Sang were always up to. They wanted to demonstrate they could conquer anything.

"Perhaps you should find a pony," !urq said. "Then you could keep up with us."

Jigme took a pony from the Library's corral and followed the waffle patterns of !urq's boots into the trees on the lower slopes. Three other Sang were along on the expedition; they clicked and gobbled to one another as they trotted cheerfully along. Behind toiled three Maskers-of-burden carrying food and climbing equipment. If the Sang noticed the incongruity demonstrated by the human's using a quadruped as a beast of burden while they, centauroids, used a bipedal race as servants, they politely refrained from mentioning it. The pony's genetically altered cloven forefeet took the mountain trail easily, nimbler than the Sang in their heavy boots. Jigme noticed that this made the Sang work harder, trying to outdo the dumb beast.

They came to a high mountain meadow and paused, looking down at the huge field of tents that ringed the smooth violet lake. In the middle of the meadow was a three-meter tower of crystal, weathered and yellow, ringed by rubble flaked off during the hard winters. One of the Sang trotted over to examine it.

"I thought the crystal was instructed to stay well below the surface," he said.

"There must have been a house here once," Jigme said. "The crystal would have been instructed to grow up through the surface to provide Library access."

!urq trotted across a stretch of grass, her head down. "Here's the beginning of the foundation line," she said. She gestured with an arm. "It runs from here to over there."

The Sang cantered over the ground, frisky as children, to discover the remnants of the foundation. The Sang were always keen, Jigme found, on discovering things. They had not yet learned that there was only one thing worth discovering, and it had nothing to do with old ruins.

!urq examined the pillar of crystal, touched its crumbling surface. "And over eighty percent of the planet is composed of this?" she said.

"All except the crust," Jigme said. "The crystal was instructed to convert most of the planet's material. That is why our heavy metals have to come from mined asteroids, and why we build mostly in natural materials. This house was probably of wood and laminated cloth, and it most likely burned in an accident."

!urq picked up a bit of crystal from the ring of rubble that surrounded the pillar. "And you can store information in this."

"All the information we have," Jigme said reverently. "All the information in the universe, eventually." Involuntarily, his hands formed the teaching mudra. "The Library is a hologram of the universe. The Blessed Bodhisattva Bob Miller was a reflection of the Library, its first Incarnation. The current Incarnation is the forty-first."

!urq's antennae flickered in the wind. She tossed the piece of crystal from hand to hand. "All the information you possess," she said. "That is a powerful tool. Or weapon."

"A tool, yes. The original builders of the Library considered it only a tool. Only something to help them order things, to assist them in governing. They did not comprehend that once the Diamond Mountain contained enough information, once it gathered enough energy, it would become more than the sum of its parts. That it would become the Mind of Buddha, the universe in small, and that the Mind, out of its compassion, would seek to incarnate itself as a human."

"The Library is self-aware?" !urq asked. She seemed to find the notion startling.

Jigme could only shrug. "Is the universe self-aware?"

!urq made a series of meditative clicking noises.

"Inside the Diamond Mountain," Jigme said, "there are processes going on that we cannot comprehend. The Library was designed to be nearly autonomous; it is now so large we cannot keep track of everything, because we would need a mind as large as the Library to process the information. Many of the energy and data transfers that we can track are very subtle, involving energies that are not fully understood. Yet we can track some of them. When an Incarnation dies, we can see the trace his spirit makes through the Library—like an atomic particle that comes apart in a shower of short-lived particles, we see it principally through its effects on other energies—and we can see part of those energies move from one place to another, from one body to another, becoming another Incarnation."

!urq's antennae moved skeptically. "You can document this?"

"We can produce spectra showing the tracks of energy through matter. Is that documentation?"

"I would say, with all respect, your case remains unproven."

"I do not seek to prove anything." Jigme smiled. "The Gyalpo Rinpoche is his own proof, his own truth. Buddha is truth. All else is illusion."

!urq put the piece of crystal in her pocket. "If this was our Library," she said, "we would prove things one way or another."

"You would see only your own reflection. Existence on the quantum level is largely a matter of belief. On that level, mind is as powerful as matter. We believe that the Gyalpo Rinpoche is an Incarnation of the Library; does that belief help make it so?"

"You ask me questions based on a system of belief that I do not share. How can you expect me to answer?"

"Belief is powerful. Belief can incarnate itself."

"Belief can incarnate itself as delusion."

"Delusion can incarnate itself as reality." Jigme stood in his stirrups, stretching his legs, and then settled back into his saddle. "Let me tell you a story," he said. "It's quite true. There was a man who went for a drive, over the pass yonder." He pointed across the valley, at the low blue pass, the Kampa La, between the mountains Tampa and Tsang. "It was a pleasant day, and he put the car's top down. A windstorm came up as he was riding near a crossroads, and his fur hat blew off his head into a thorn bush, where he couldn't reach it. He simply drove on his way.

"Other people walked past the bush, and they saw something inside. They told each other they'd seen something odd there. The hat got weathered and less easy to recognize. Soon the locals were telling travelers to beware the thing near the crossroads, and someone else suggested the thing might be a demon, and soon people were warning others about the demon in the bush."

"Delusion," said !urq.

"It *was* delusion," Jigme agreed. "But it was *not* delusion when the hat grew arms, legs, and teeth, and when it began chasing people up and down the Kampa La. The Ministry of Magic had to send a naljorpa to perform a rite of chöd and banish the thing."

!urq's antennae gave a meditative quiver. "People see what they want to see," she said.

"The delusion had incarnated itself. The case is classic: the Ministries of Science and Magic performed an inquiry. They could trace the patterns of energy through the crystal structure of the Library: the power of the growing belief, the reaction when the belief was fulfilled, the dispersing of the energy when chöd was performed." Jigme gave a laugh. "In the end, the naljorpa brought back an old, weathered hat. Just bits of fur and leather."

"The naljorpa got a good reward, no doubt," said !urq, "for bringing back this moldy bit of fur."

"Probably. Not my department, actually."

"It seems possible, here on Vajra, to make a good living out of others' delusions. My government would not permit such things."

"What do the people lose by being credulous?" Jigme asked. "Only money, which is earthly, and that is a pitiful thing to worry about. It would matter only that the act of giving is sincere."

!urq gave a toss of her head. "We should continue up the mountain, Rinpoche."

"Certainly." Jigme kicked his pony into a trot. He wondered if he had just convinced !urq that his government was corrupt in allowing fakirs to gull the population. Jigme knew there were many ways to Enlightenment and that the soul must try them all. Just because the preacher was corrupt did not mean his message was untrue. How to convince !urq of that? he wondered.

"We believe it is good to test oneself against things," !urq said. "Life is struggle, and one must remain sharp. Ready for whatever happens."

"In the *Parinibbana-sutra,* the Blessed One says that the point of his teaching is to control our own minds. Then one can be ready."

"Of course we control our minds, Rinpoche. If we could not control our minds, we would not achieve mastery. If we do not achieve mastery, then we are nothing."

"I am pleased, then," Jigme smiled, "that you and the Buddha are in agreement."

To which !urq had no reply, save only to launch herself savagely at the next climb, while Jigme followed easily on his cloven-hoofed pony.

The scent of incense and flowers filled the Gyalpo Rinpoche's giant yellow tent. The Treasured King, a silk khata around his neck, sat in the lotus posture on soft grass. The bottoms of his feet were stained green. Ambassador !urq stood ponderously before him, lower lip thrust forward, her four arms in a formal stance, the Incarnation's knotted scarf draped over her shoulders.

Jigme watched, standing next to the erect, angry figure of Dr. O'Neill. He took comfort from the ever-serene smile of Miss Taisuke, sitting on the grass across the tent.

"Ambassador Colonel, I am happy you have joined us on holiday."

"We are pleased to participate in your festivals, Omniscient," said !urq.

"The spring flowers are lovely, are they not? It's worthwhile to take a whole week to enjoy them. In so doing, we remember the words of Shakyamuni, who tells us to enjoy the blossoms of Enlightenment in their season and harvest the fruit of the right path."

"Is there a season, Omniscient, for discussing the matter of Gyangtse?"

Right to the point, Jigme thought. !urq might never learn the oblique manner of speech that predominated at the high ministerial levels.

The Incarnation was not disturbed. "Surely matters may be discussed in any season," he said.

"The planet is desirable, Omniscient. Your settlement violates our border. My government demands your immediate evacuation."

Dr. O'Neill's breath hissed out at the word *demand*. Jigme could see her ears redden with fury.

"The first humans reached the planet before the border negotiations were completed," the Incarnation said equably. "They did not realize they were setting in violation of the agreement."

"That does not invalidate the agreement."

"Conceded, Ambassador. Still, would it not be unjust, after all their hard labor, to ask them to move?"

!urq's antennae bobbed politely. "Does not your Blessed One admit that life is composed of suffering? Does the Buddha not condemn the demon of worldly desires? What desire could be more worldly than a desire to possess a world?"

Jigme was impressed. Definitely, he thought, she was getting better at this sort of thing.

"In the same text," said Jigme, "Shakyamuni tells us to refrain from disputes, and not repel one another like water and oil, but like milk and water mingle together." He opened his hands in an offering gesture. "Will your government not accept a new planet in exchange? Or better yet, will they not dispose of this border altogether, and allow a free commerce between our races?"

"What new planet?" !urq's arms formed a querying posture.

"We explore constantly in order to fulfill the mandate of the Library and provide it with more data. Our survey records are available through your Library access. Choose any planet that has not yet been inhabited by humans."

"Any planet chosen will be outside of our zone of influence, far from our own frontiers and easily cut off from our home sphere."

"Why would we cut you off, Ambassador?"

"Gyangtse is of strategic significance. It is a penetration of our border."

"Let us then dispose of the border entirely."

!urq's antennae stood erect. Her arms took a martial position. "You humans are larger, more populous. You would overwhelm us by sheer numbers. The border must remain inviolate."

"Let us then have greater commerce across the border than before. With increased knowledge, distrust will diminish."

"You would send missionaries. I know there are Jesuits and Gelugspa who have been training for years in hopes of obtaining converts or martyrdom in the Sang dominions."

"It would be a shame to disappoint them." There was a slight smile on the Incarnation's face.

!urq's arms formed an obstinate pattern. "They would stir up trouble among the Maskers. They would preach to the credulous among my own race. My government must protect its own people."

"The message of Shakyamuni is not a political message, Ambassador."

"That is a matter of interpretation, Omniscient."

"Will you transmit my offer to your government?"

!urq held her stance for a long moment. Jigme could sense Dr. O'Neill's fury in the alien's obstinacy. "I will do so, Omniscient," said the Ambassador. "Though I have no confidence that it will be accepted."

"I think the offer will be accepted," said Miss Taisuke. She sat on the grass in Jigme's tent. She was in the butterfly position, the soles of her feet pressed together and her knees on the ground. Jigme sat beside her. One of Jigme's students, a clean-limbed lad named Rabjoms, gracefully served them tea and cakes, then withdrew.

"The Sang are obdurate," said Jigme. "Why do you think there is hope?"

"Sooner or later the Sang will realize they may choose any one of hundreds of unoccupied planets. It will dawn on them that they can pick one on the far side of our sphere, and their spy ships can travel the length of human-occupied space on quite legitimate missions, and gather whatever information they desire."

"Ah."

"All this in exchange for one minor border penetration."

Jigme thought about this for a moment. "We've held onto Gyangtse in order to test the Sangs' rationality and their willingness to fight. There has been no war in twelve years. This shows that the Sang are susceptible to reason. Where there is reason, there is capability for Enlightenment."

"Amen," said Miss Taisuke. She finished her tea and put down the glass.

"Would you like more? Shall I summon Rabjoms?"

"Thank you, no." She cast a glance back to the door of the tent. "He has lovely brown eyes, your Rabjoms."

"Yes."

Miss Taisuke looked at him. "Is he your consort?"

Jigme put down his glass. "No. I try to forsake worldly passions."

"You are of the Red Hat order. You have taken no vow of celibacy."

Agitation fluttered in Jigme's belly. "The *Mahaparinirvana-sutra* says that lust is the soil in which other passions flourish. I avoid it."

"I wondered. It has been remarked that all your pages are such pretty boys."

Jigme tried to calm himself. "I choose them for other qualities, Miss Taisuke. I assure you."

She laughed merrily. "Of course. I merely wondered." She leaned forward from out of her butterfly position, reached out, and touched his cheek. "I have a sense this may be a randy incarnation for me. You have no desire for young girls?"

Jigme did not move. "I cannot help you, Minister."

"Poor Jigme." She drew her hand back. "I will offer prayers for you."

"Prayers are always accepted, Miss Taisuke."

"But not passes. Very well." She rose to her feet, and Jigme rose with her. "I must be off to the Kagyupas' party. Will you be there?"

"I have scheduled this hour for meditation. Perhaps later."

"Later, then." She kissed his cheek and squeezed his hand, then slipped out of the tent. Jigme sat in the lotus posture and called for Rabjoms to take away the tea things. As he watched the boy's graceful movements, he gave an inward sigh. His weakness had been noticed, and, even worse, remarked on.

His next student would have to be ugly. The ugliest one he could find. He sighed again.

A shriek rang out. Jigme looked up, heart hammering, and saw a demon at the back of the tent. Its flesh was bright red, and its eyes seemed to bulge out of its head. Rabjoms yelled and flung the tea service at it; a glass bounced off its head and shattered.

The demon charged forward, Rabjoms falling under its clawed feet. The overwhelming smell of decay filled the tent. The demon burst through the tent flap into the outdoors. Jigme heard more shrieks and cries of alarm from outside. The demon roared like a bull, then laughed like a madman. Jigme crawled forward to gather up Rabjoms, holding the terrified boy in his arms, chanting the Horse of the Air to calm himself until he heard the teakettle hissing of a thousand snakes followed by a rush of wind, the sign that the entity had dispersed. Jigme soothed his page and tried to think what the meaning of this sudden burst of psychic energy might be.

A few moments later, Jigme received a call on his radiophone. The Gyalpo Rinpoche, a few moments after returning to the Library Palace in his hovertent, had fallen stone dead.

"Cerebral hemorrhage," said Dr. O'Neill. The Minister of Science had performed the autopsy herself—her long hair was undone and tied behind, to fit under a surgical cap, and she still wore her scrubs. She was without the long turquoise earring that marked her rank, and she kept waving a hand near her ear, as if she somehow missed it. "The Incarnation was an old man," she said. "A slight erosion in an artery, and he was gone. It took only seconds."

The Cabinet accepted the news in stunned silence. For all their lives, there had been only the one Treasured King. Now the anchor of all their lives had been removed.

"The reincarnation was remarkably swift," Dr. O'Neill said. "I was able to watch most of it on the monitors in real time—the energies remained remarkably focused, not dissipated in a shower of sparks as with most individuals. I must admit I was impressed. The demon that appeared at the Picnic Festival was only one of the many side effects caused by such a massive turbulence within the crystal architecture of the Diamond Mountain."

Miss Taisuke looked up. "Have you identified the child?"

"Of course." Dr. O'Neill allowed herself a thin-lipped smile. "A second-trimester baby, to be born to a family of tax collectors in Dulan Province, near the White Ocean. The fetus is not developed to the point where a full incarnation is possible, and the energies remain clinging to the mother until they can move to the child. She must be feeling . . . elevated. I would like to interview her about her sensations before she is informed that she is carrying the new Bodhisattva." Dr. O'Neill waved a hand in the vicinity of her ear again.

"We must appoint a regent," said Daddy Carbajal.

"Yes," said Dr. O'Neill. "The more so now, with the human sphere being threatened by the unenlightened."

Jigme looked from one to the other. The shock of the Gyalpo Rinpoche's death had unnerved him to the point of forgetting political matters. Clearly this had not been the case with O'Neill and the Minister of Magic.

He could not let the reactionary party dominate this meeting.

"I believe," he said, "we should appoint Miss Taisuke as Regent."

His words surprised even himself.

The struggle was prolonged. Dr. O'Neill and Daddy Carbajal fought an obstinate rearguard action, but finally Miss Taisuke was confirmed. Jigme had a feeling that several of the ministers only consented to Miss Taisuke because they thought she was young enough that they might manipulate her. They didn't know her well, Jigme thought, and that was fortunate.

"We must formulate a policy concerning Gyangtse and the Sang," Dr. O'Neill said. Her face assumed its usual thin-lipped stubbornness.

"The Omniscient's policy was always to delay," Miss Taisuke said.

"This sad matter will furnish a further excuse for postponing any final decision."

"We must put the armed forces on alert. The Sang may consider this a moment in which to strike."

The Regent nodded. "Let this be done."

"There is the matter of the new Incarnation," Dr. O'Neill said. "Should the delivery be advanced? How should the parents be informed?"

"We shall consult the State Oracle," said Miss Taisuke.

The Oracle, his toothless mouth gaping, was a picture of terror. No one had asked him anything in years.

Eerie music echoed through the Oracular Hall of the Library, off the walls and ceiling covered with grotesque carvings—gods, demons, and skulls that grinned at the intent humans below. Chanting monks sat in rows, accompanied by magicians playing drums and trumpets all made from human bone. Jigme's stinging eyes watered from the gusts of strong incense.

In the middle of it all sat the State Oracle, his wrinkled face expressionless. Before him, sitting on a platform, was Miss Taisuke, dressed in the formal clothing of the Regency.

"In old Tibetan times, the Oracle used to be consulted frequently," Jigme told Ambassador !urq. "But since the Gyalpo Rinpoche has been incarnated on Vajra, the Omniscient's close association with the universe analogue of the Library has made most divination unnecessary. The State Oracle is usually called upon only during periods between Incarnations."

"I am having trouble phrasing my reports to my superiors, Rinpoche," said !urq. "Your government is at present run by a fifteen-year-old girl with the advice of an elderly fortune-teller. I expect to have a certain amount of difficulty getting my superiors to take this seriously."

"The Oracle is a serious diviner," Jigme said. "There are a series of competitive exams to discover his degree of empathy with the Library. Our Oracle was right at the top of his class."

"My government will be relieved to know it."

The singing and chanting had been going on for hours. !urq had long been showing signs of impatience. Suddenly the Oracle gave a start. His eyes and mouth dropped open. His face had lost all character.

Then something else was there, an alien presence. The Oracle jumped up from his seated position, began to whirl wildly with his arms outstretched. Several of his assistants ran forward carrying his headdress while others seized him, holding his rigid body steady. The headdress was enormous, all hand-wrought gold featuring skulls and gods and topped with a vast array of plumes. It weighed over ninety pounds.

"The Oracle, by use of intent meditation, has driven the spirit from his own body," Jigme reported. "He is now possessed by the Library, which assumes the form of the god Yamantaka, the Conqueror of Death."

"Interesting," !urq said noncommittally.

"An old man could not support that headdress without some form of psychic help," Jigme said. "Surely you must agree?" He was beginning to be annoyed by the Ambassador's perpetual skepticism.

The Oracle's assistants had managed to strap the headdress on the Oracle's bald head. They stepped back, and the Oracle continued his dance, the weighty headdress supported by his rigid neck. The Oracle dashed from one end of the room to the other, still whirling, sweat spraying off his brow, then ran to the feet of Miss Taisuke and fell to his knees.

When he spoke it was in a metallic, unnatural voice. "The Incarnation should be installed by New Year!" he shouted, and then toppled. When the assistant monks had unstrapped the heavy headdress and the old man rose, back in his body once more and rubbing his neck, the Oracle looked at Miss Taisuke and blinked painfully. "I resign," he said.

"Accepted," said the Regent. "With great regret."

"This is a young man's job. I could have broken my damn neck."

Ambassador !urq's antennae pricked forward. "This," she said, "is an unusually truthful oracle."

"Top of his class," said Jigme. "What did I tell you?"

The new Oracle was a young man, a strict orthodox Yellow Hat whose predictive abilities had been proved outstanding by every objective test. The calendar of festivals rolled by: the time of pilgrimage, the week of operas and plays, the kite-flying festival, the end of Ramadan, Buddha's descent from Tishita Heaven, Christmas, the celebration of Kali the Benevolent, the anniversary of the death of Tsongkhapa. . . . The New Year was calculated to fall sixty days after Christmas, and for weeks beforehand the artisans of Vajra worked on their floats. The floats—huge sculptures of fabulous buildings, religious icons, famous scenes from the opera featuring giant animated figures, tens of thousands of man-hours of work—would be taken through the streets of the Diamond City during the New Year's procession, then up onto Burning Hill in plain sight of the Library Palace where the new Incarnation could view them from the balcony.

And week after week, the new Incarnation grew, as fast as the technology safely permitted. Carefully removed from his mother's womb by Dr. O'Neill, the Incarnation was placed in a giant autowomb and fed a diet of nutrients and hormones calculated to bring him to adulthood. Microscopic wires were inserted carefully into his developing brain to feed the memory centers with scripture, philosophy, science, art, and the art of governing. As the new Gyalpo Rinpoche grew the body was exercised by electrode so that he would emerge with physical maturity.

The new Incarnation had early on assumed the lotus position during his rest periods, and Jigme often came to the Science Ministry to watch, through the womb's transparent cover, the eerie figure meditating in the bubbling nutrient solution. All growth of hair had been suppressed by Dr. O'Neill and the figure seemed smooth perfection. The Omniscient-to-be was leaving early adolescence behind, growing slim and cat-muscled.

The new Incarnation would need whatever strength it possessed. The political situation was worsening. The border remained unresolved—the Sang wanted not simply a new planet in exchange for Gyangtse, but also room to expand into a new militarized sphere on the other side of human space. Sang military movements, detected from the human side of the border, seemed to be rehearsals for an invasion, and were countered by increased human defense allotments. As a deterrent, the human response was made obvious to the Sang: Ambassador !urq complained continually about human aggression. Dr. O'Neill and Daddy Carbajal grew combative in Cabinet meetings. Opposition to them was scattered and unfocused. If the reactionary party wanted war, the Sang were doing little but playing into their hands.

Fortunately the Incarnation would be decanted within a week, to take possession of the rambling, embittered councils and give them political direction. Jigme closed his eyes and offered a long prayer that the Incarnation might soon make his presence felt among his ministers.

He opened his eyes. The smooth, adolescent Incarnation hovered before him, suspended in golden nutrient. Fine bubbles rose in the liquid, stroking the Incarnation's skin. The figure had a fascinating, eerie beauty, and Jigme felt he could stare at it forever.

Jigme saw, to his surprise, that the floating Incarnation had an erection.

And then the Incarnation opened his eyes.

The eyes were green. Jigme felt coldness flood his spine—the look was knowing, a look of recognition. A slight smile curled the Incarnation's lips. Jigme stared. The smile seemed cruel.

Dry-mouthed, Jigme bent forward, slammed his forehead to the floor in obeisance. Pain crackled through his head. He stayed that way for a long time, offering prayer after frantic prayer.

When he finally rose, the Incarnation's eyes were closed, and the body sat calmly amid golden, rising bubbles.

· · ·

The late Incarnation's rosary seemed warm as it lay against Jigme's neck. Perhaps it was anticipating being reunited with its former owner.

"The Incarnation is being dressed," Dr. O'Neill said. She stepped through the doors into the vast cabinet room. Two novice monks, doorkeepers, bowed as she swept past, their tongues stuck out in respect, then swung the doors shut behind her. O'Neill was garbed formally in a dress so heavy with brocade that it crackled as she moved. Yellow lamplight flickered from the braid as she moved through the darkened counsel chamber. Her piled hair was hidden under an embroidered cap; silver gleamed from the elaborate settings of her long turquoise earring. "He will meet with the Cabinet in a few moments and perform the recognition ceremony."

The Incarnation had been decanted that afternoon. He had walked as soon as he was permitted. The advanced growth techniques used by Dr. O'Neill appeared to have met with total success. Her eyes glowed with triumph; her cheeks were flushed.

She took her seat among the Cabinet, moving stiffly in the heavy brocade.

The Cabinet sat surrounding a small table on which some of the late Incarnation's possessions were surrounded by a number of similar objects or imitations. His rosary was around Jigme's neck. During the recognition ceremony, the new Incarnation was supposed to single out his possessions in order to display his continuance from the former personality. The ceremony was largely a formality, a holdover from the earlier, Tibetan tradition—it was already perfectly clear, from Library data, just who the Incarnation was.

There was a shout from the corridor outside, then a loud voice raised in song. The members of the Cabinet stiffened in annoyance. Someone was creating a disturbance. The Regent beckoned to a communications device hidden in an image of Kali, intending to summon guards and have the disorderly one ejected.

The doors swung open, each held by a bowing novice with outthrust tongues. The Incarnation appeared between them. He was young, just entering late adolescence. He was dressed in the tall crested formal hat and yellow robes stiff with brocade. Green eyes gleamed in the dim light as he looked at the assembled officials.

The Cabinet moved as one, offering obeisance first with praying hands lifted to the forehead, mouth, and heart, then prostrated themselves with their heads to the ground. As he fell forward, Jigme heard a voice singing.

Let us drink and sport today,
Ours is not tomorrow.

Love with Youth flies swift away,
  Age is nought but Sorrow.
  Dance and sing,
    Time's on the wing,
Life never knows the return of Spring.

In slow astonishment, Jigme realized that it was the Incarnation who was singing. Gradually Jigme rose from his bow.

Jigme saw that the Incarnation had a bottle in his hand. Was he drunk? he wondered. And where in the Library had he gotten the beer, or whatever it was? Had he materialized it?

"This way, boy," said the Incarnation. He had a hand on the shoulder of one of the doorkeepers. He drew the boy into the room, then took a long drink from his bottle. He eyed the Cabinet slowly, turning his head from one to the other.

"Omniscient—" said Miss Taisuke.

"Not yet," said the Incarnation. "I've been in a glass sphere for almost ten months. It's time I had some fun." He pushed the doorkeeper onto hands and knees, then knelt behind the boy. He pushed up the boy's zen, clutched at his buttocks. The page cast little frantic glances around the room. The new State Oracle seemed apoplectic.

"I see you've got some of my things," said the Incarnation.

Jigme felt something twitch around his neck. The former Incarnation's skull-rosary was beginning to move. Jigme's heart crashed in his chest.

The Cabinet watched in stunned silence as the Incarnation began to sodomize the doorkeeper. The boy's face showed nothing but panic and terror.

This is a lesson, Jigme thought insistently. This is a living Bodhisattva doing this, and somehow this is one of his sermons. We will learn from this.

The rosary twitched, rose slowly from around Jigme's neck, and flew through the air to drop around the Incarnation's head.

A plain ivory walking stick rose from the table and spun through the air. The Incarnation materialized a third arm to catch the cane in midair. A decorated porcelain bowl followed, a drum, and a small golden figurine of a laughing Buddha ripped itself free from the pocket of the new State Oracle. Each was caught by a new arm. Each item had belonged to the former Incarnation; each was the correct choice.

The Incarnation howled like a beast at the moment of climax. Then he stood, adjusting his garments. He bent to pick up the ivory cane. He smashed the porcelain bowl with it, then broke the cane over the head of the Buddha. He rammed the Buddha through the drum, then threw both against the wall. All six hands rose to the rosary around his neck; he ripped at it and the cord broke, white bone disks flying through the room. His extra arms vanished.

"Short Path," he said, turned and stalked out.

Across the room, in the long silence that followed, Jigme could see Dr. O'Neill. Her pale face seemed to float in the darkness, distinct amid the confusion and madness, her expression frozen in a racking, electric moment of private agony. The minister's moment of triumph had turned to ashes.

Perhaps everything had.

Jigme rose to comfort the doorkeeper.

"There has never been an Incarnation who followed the Short Path," said Miss Taisuke.

"Daddy Carbajal should be delighted," Jigme said. "He's a doubtob himself."

"I don't think he's happy," said the Regent. "I watched him. He is a tantric sorcerer, yes, one of the best. But the Incarnation's performance frightened him."

They spoke alone in Miss Taisuke's townhouse—in the lha khang, a room devoted to religious images. Incense floated gently in the air. Outside, Jigme could hear the sounds of celebration as the word reached the population that the Incarnation was among them once again.

A statue of the Thunderbolt Sow came to life, looked at the Regent. "A message from the Library Palace, Regent," it said. "The Incarnation has spent the evening in his quarters, in the company of an apprentice monk. He has now passed out from drunkenness."

"Thank you, Rinpoche," Taisuke said. The Thunderbolt Sow froze in place. Taisuke turned back to Jigme.

"His Omniscience is possibly the most powerful doubtob in history," she said. "Dr. O'Neill showed me the spectra—the display of psychic energy, as recorded by the Library, was truly awesome. And it was perfectly controlled."

"Could something have gone wrong with the process of bringing the Incarnation to adulthood?"

"The process has been used for centuries. It has been used on Incarnations before—it was a fad for a while, and the Eighteenth through Twenty-Third were all raised that way." She frowned, leaning forward. "In any case, it's all over. The Librarian Bob Miller—and the divine Avalokitesvara, if you go for that sort of thing—has now been reincarnated as the Forty-Second Gyalpo Rinpoche. There's nothing that can be done."

"Nothing," Jigme said. The Short Path, he thought, the path to Enlightenment taken by magicians and madmen, a direct route that had no reference to morality or convention. . . . The Short Path was dangerous, often heterodox, and colossally difficult. Most doubtobs ended up destroying themselves and everyone around them.

"We have had carnal Incarnations before," Taisuke said. "The Eighth left some wonderful love poetry behind, and quite a few have been sodomites. No harm was done."

"I will pray, Regent," said Jigme, "that no harm may be done now."

It seemed to him that there was a shadow on Taisuke's usual blazing smile. "That is doubtless the best solution. I will pray also."

Jigme returned to the Nyingmapa monastery, where he had an apartment near the Sang embassy. He knew he was too agitated to sit quietly and meditate, and so called for some novices to bring him a meditation box. He needed to discipline both body and mind before he could find peace.

He sat in the narrow box in a cross-legged position and drew the lid over his head. Cut off from the world, he would not allow himself to relax, to lean against the walls of the box for support. He took his rosary in his hands. *"Aum vajra sattva,"* he began, Aum the Diamond Being, one of the names of Buddha.

But the picture that floated before his mind was not that of Shakyamuni, but the naked, beautiful form of the Incarnation, staring at him from out of the autowomb with green, soul-chilling eyes.

"We should have killed the Jesuit as well. We refrained only as a courtesy to your government, Rinpoche."

Perhaps, Jigme thought, the dead Maskers' souls were even now in the Library, whirling in the patterns of energy that would result in reincarnation, whirling like the snow that fell gently as he and !urq walked down the street. To be reincarnated as humans, with the possibility of Enlightenment.

"We will dispose of the bodies, if you prefer," Jigme said.

"They dishonored their masters," said !urq. "You may do what you like with them."

As Jigme and the Ambassador walked through the snowy streets toward the Punishment Grounds, they were met with grins and waves from the population, who were getting ready for the New Year celebration. !urq acknowledged the greetings with graceful nods of her antennae. Once the population heard what had just happened, Jigme thought, the reception might well be different.

"I will send monks to collect the bodies. We will cut them up and expose them on hillsides for the vultures. Afterward their bones will be collected and perhaps turned into useful implements."

"In my nation," !urq said, "that would be considered an insult."

"The bodies will nourish the air and the earth," said Jigme. "What finer kind of death could there be?"

"Elementary. A glorious death in service to the state."

Two Masker servants, having met several times with a Jesuit acting apparently without orders from his superiors, had announced their conversion to Buddhism. !urq had promptly denounced the two as spies and had them shot out of hand. The missionary had been ordered whipped by the superiors in his Order. !urq wanted to be on hand for it.

Jigme could anticipate the public reaction. Shakyamuni had strictly forbidden the taking of life. The people would be enraged. It might be unwise for the Sang to be seen in public for the next few days, particularly during the New Year Festival, when a large percentage of the population would be drunk.

Jigme and the Ambassador passed by a row of criminals in the stocks. Offerings of flowers, food, and money were piled up below them, given by the compassionate population. Another criminal—a murderer, probably—shackled in leg irons for life, approached with his begging bowl. Jigme gave him some money and passed on.

"Your notions of punishment would be considered far from enlightened in my nation," !urq said. "Flogging, branding, putting people in chains! We would consider that savage."

"We punish only the body," Jigme said. "We always allow an opportunity for the spirit to reform. Death without Enlightenment can only result in a return to endless cycles of reincarnation."

"A clean death is always preferable to bodily insult. And a lot of your flogging victims die afterward."

"But they do not die during the flogging."

"Yet they die in agony, because your whips tear their backs apart."

"Pain," said Jigme, "can be transcended."

"Sometimes," !urq said, antennae twitching, "you humans are terrifying. I say this in absolute and admiring sincerity."

There were an unusual number of felons today, since the authorities wanted to empty the holding cells before the New Year. The Jesuit was among them—a calm, bearded, black-skinned man stripped to the waist, waiting to be lashed to the triangle. Jigme could see that he was deep in a meditative trance.

Suddenly the gray sky darkened. People looked up and pointed. Some fell down in obeisance, others bowed and thrust out their tongues.

The Incarnation was overhead, sitting on a wide hovercraft, covered with red paint and hammered gold, that held a small platform and throne. He sat in a full lotus, his elfin form dressed only in a light yellow robe. Snow melted on his shoulders and cheeks.

The proceedings halted for a moment while everyone waited for the Incarnation to say something, but at an impatient gesture from the floating throne things got under way. The floggings went efficiently, sometimes more than one going on at once. The crowd succored many of the victims with money or offers of food or medicine. There was another slight hesitation as the Jesuit was brought forward—perhaps the Incarnation would comment on, or stay, the punishment of someone who had been trying to spread his faith—but from the Incarnation came only silence. The Jesuit absorbed his twenty lashes without comment, was taken away by his cohorts. To be praised and promoted, if Jigme knew the Jesuits.

The whipping went on. Blood spattered the platform. Finally there was only one convict remaining, a young monk of perhaps seventeen in a dirty, torn zen. He was a big lad, broad-shouldered and heavily-muscled, with a malformed head and a peculiar brutal expression—at once intent and unfocused, as if he knew he hated something but couldn't be bothered to decide exactly what it was. His body was possessed by constant, uncontrollable tics and twitches. He was surrounded by police with staves. Obviously they considered him dangerous.

An official read off the charges. Kyetsang Kunlegs had killed his guru, then set fire to the dead man's hermitage in hopes of covering his crime. He was sentenced to six hundred lashes and to be shackled for life. Jigme suspected he would not get much aid from the crowd afterward; most of them were reacting with disgust.

"Stop," said the Incarnation. Jigme gaped. The floating throne was moving forward. It halted just before Kunlegs. The murderer's guards stuck out their tongues but kept their eyes on the killer.

"Why did you kill your guru?" the Incarnation asked.

Kunlegs stared at him and twitched, displaying nothing but fierce hatred. He gave no answer.

The Incarnation laughed. "That's what I thought," he said. "Will you be my disciple if I remit your punishment?"

Kunlegs seemed to have difficulty comprehending this. His belligerent expression remained unaltered. Finally he just shrugged. A violent twitch made the movement grotesque.

The Incarnation lowered his throne. "Get on board," he said. Kunlegs stepped onto the platform. The Incarnation rose from his lotus, adjusted the man's garments, and kissed him on the lips. They sat down together.

"Short Path," said the Incarnation. The throne sped at once for the Library Palace.

Jigme turned to the Ambassador. !urq had watched without visible expression.

"Terrifying," she said. "Absolutely terrifying."

Jigme sat with the other Cabinet members in a crowded courtyard of the Palace. The Incarnation was about to go through the last of the rituals required before his investiture as the Gyalpo Rinpoche. Six learned elders of six different religious orders would engage the Incarnation in prolonged debate. If he did well against them, he would be formally enthroned and take the reins of government.

The Incarnation sat on a platform-throne opposite the six. Behind him, gazing steadily with his expression of misshapen, twitching brutality, was the murderer Kyetsang Kunlegs.

The first elder rose. He was a Sufi, representing a three-thousand-year-old intellectual tradition. He stuck out his tongue and took a formal stance.

"What is the meaning of Dharma?" he began.

"I'll show you," said the Incarnation, although the question had obviously been rhetorical. The Incarnation opened his mouth, and a demon the size of a bull leapt out. Its flesh was pale as dough and covered with running sores. The demon seized the Sufi and flung him to the ground, then sat on his chest. The sound of breaking bones was audible.

Kyetsang Kunlegs opened his mouth and laughed, revealing huge yellow teeth.

The demon rose and advanced toward the five remaining elders, who fled in disorder.

"I win," said the Incarnation.

Kunlegs' laughter broke like obscene bubbles over the stunned audience.

"Short Path," said the Incarnation.

"Such a shame," said the Ambassador. Firelight flickered off her ebon features. "How many man-years of work has gone into it all? And by morning it'll be ashes."

"Everything comes to an end," said Jigme. "If the floats are not destroyed tonight, they would be gone in a year. If not a year, ten years. If not ten years, a century. If not a century . . ."

"I quite take your point, Rinpoche," said !urq.

"Only the Buddha is eternal."

"So I gather."

The crowd assembled on the roof of the Library Palace gasped as another of the floats on Burning Hill went up in flames. This one was made of figures from the opera, who danced and sang and did combat with one another until, burning, they came apart on the wind.

Jigme gratefully took a glass of hot tea from a servant and warmed his hands. The night was clear but bitterly cold. The floating throne moved silently overhead, and Jigme stuck out his tongue in salute. The Gyalpo Rinpoche, in accordance with the old Oracle's instructions, had assumed his title that afternoon.

"Jigme Dzasa, may I speak with you?" A soft voice at his elbow, that of the former Regent.

"Of course, Miss Taisuke. You will excuse me, Ambassador?"

Jigme and Taisuke moved apart. "The Incarnation has indicated that he wishes me to continue as head of the government," Taisuke said.

"I congratulate you, Prime Minister," said Jigme, surprised. He had assumed the Gyalpo Rinpoche would wish to run the state himself.

"I haven't accepted yet," she said. "It isn't a job I desire." She sighed. "I was hoping to have a randy incarnation, Jigme. Instead I'm being worked to death."

"You have my support, Prime Minister."

She gave a rueful smile and patted his arm. "Thank you. I fear I'll have to accept, if only to keep certain other people from positions where they might do harm." She leaned close, her whisper carrying over the sound of distant fireworks. "Dr. O'Neill approached me. She wished to know my views concerning whether we can declare the Incarnation insane and reinstitute the Regency."

Jigme gazed at Taisuke in shock. "Who supports this?"

"Not I. I made that clear enough."

"Daddy Carbajal?"

"I think he's too cautious. The new State Oracle might be in favor of the idea—he's such a strict young man, and, of course, his own status would rise if he became the Library's interpreter instead of subordinate to the Gyalpo Rinpoche. O'Neill herself made the proposal in a veiled manner—*if* such-and-such a thing proved true, how would I react? She never made a specific proposal."

Anger burned in Jigme's belly. "The Incarnation cannot be insane!" he said. "That would mean the Library itself is insane. That the Buddha is insane."

"People are uncomfortable with the notion of a doubtob Incarnation."

"What people? What are their names? They should be corrected!"

Jigme realized that his fists were clenched, that he was trembling with anger.

"Hush. O'Neill can do nothing."

"She speaks treason! Heresy!"

"Jigme . . ."

"Ah. The Prime Minister." Jigme gave a start at the sound of the Incarnation's voice. The floating throne, its gold ornaments gleaming in the light of the burning floats, descended noiselessly from the bright sky. The Incarnation was covered only by a reskyang, the simple white cloth worn even in the bitterest weather by adepts of tumo, the discipline of controlling one's own internal heat.

"You *will* be my Prime Minister, yes?" the Incarnation said. His green eyes seemed to glow in the darkness. Kyetsang Kunlegs loomed over his shoulder like a demon shadow.

Taisuke bowed, sticking out her tongue. "Of course, Omniscient."

"When I witnessed the floggings the other day," the Incarnation said, "I was shocked by the lack of consistency. Some of the criminals seemed to have the sympathy of the officials, and the floggers did not use their full strength. Some of the floggers were larger and stronger than others. Toward the end they all got tired, and did not lay on with proper force. This does not seem to me to be adequate justice. I would like to propose a reform." He handed Taisuke a paper. "Here I have described a flogging machine. Each strike will be equal to the one before. And as the machine is built on a rotary principle, the machine can be inscribed with religious texts, like a prayer wheel. We can therefore grant prayers and punish the wicked simultaneously."

Taisuke seemed overcome. She looked down at the paper as if afraid to open it. "Very . . . elegant, Omniscient."

"I thought so. See that the machine is instituted throughout humanity, Prime Minister."

"Very well, Omniscient."

The floating throne rose into the sky to the accompaniment of the murderer Kunlegs' gross bubbling laughter. Taisuke looked at Jigme with desperation in her eyes.

"We must protect him, Jigme," she said.

"Of course."

"We must be very, very careful."

She loves him, too, he thought. A river of sorrow poured through his heart.

Jigme looked up, seeing Ambassador !urq standing with her head lifted to watch the burning spectacle on the hill opposite. "Very careful indeed," he said.

. . .

The cycle of festivals continued. Buddha's birthday, the Picnic Festival, the time of pilgrimage . . .

In the Prime Minister's lha khang, the Thunderbolt Sow gestured toward Taisuke. "After watching the floggings," it said, "the Gyalpo Rinpoche and Kyetsang Kunlegs went to Diamond City spaceport, where they participated in a night-long orgy with ship personnel. Both have now passed out from indulgence in drink and drugs, and the party has come to an end."

The Prime Minister knit her brows as she listened to the tale. "The stories will get offworld now," Jigme told her.

"They're already offworld."

Jigme looked at her helplessly. "How much damage is being done?"

"Flogging parties? Carousing with strangers? Careening from one monastery to another in search of pretty boys? Gracious heaven—the abbots are pimping their novices to him in hopes of receiving favor." Taisuke gave a lengthy shudder. There was growing seriousness in her eyes. "I'll let you in on a state secret. We've been reading the Sang's despatches."

"How?" Jigme asked. "They don't use our communications net, and the texts are coded."

"But they compose their messages using electric media," Taisuke said. "We can use the Library crystal as a sensing device, detect each character as it's entered into their coding device. We can also read incoming despatches the same way."

"I'm impressed, Prime Minister."

"Through this process, we were kept informed of the progress of the Sang's military buildup. We were terrified to discover that it was scheduled to reach its full offensive strength within a few years."

"Ah. That was why you consented to the increase in military allotments."

"Ambassador !urq was instructed not to resolve the Gyangtse matter, in order that it be used as a *casus belli* when the Sang program reached its conclusion. !urq's despatches to her superiors urged them to attack as soon as their fleet was ready. But now, with the increased military allotments and the political situation, !urq is urging delay. The current Incarnation, she suspects, may so discredit the institution of the Gyalpo Rinpoche that our society may disintegrate without the need for a Sang attack."

"Impossible!" A storm of anger filled Jigme. His hands formed the mudra of astonishment.

"I suspect you're right, Jigme." Solemnly. "They base their models of our society on their own past despotisms—they don't realize that the Treasured King is not a despot or an absolute ruler, but rather someone of great wisdom whom others follow through their own free will. But we should encourage !urq in this estimation, yes? Anything to give impetus to the Sang's more rational impulses."

"But it's based on a slander! And a slander concerning the Incarnation can never be countenanced!"

Taisuke raised an admonishing finger. "The Sang draw their own conclusions. And should we protest this one, we might give away our knowledge of their communications."

Anger and frustration bubbled in Jigme's mind. "What barbarians!" he said. "I have tried to show them truth, but . . ."

Taisuke's voice was calm. "You have shown them the path of truth. Their choosing not to follow it is their own karma."

Jigme promised himself he would do better. He would compel !urq to recognize the Incarnation's teaching mission.

Teaching, he thought. He remembered the stunned look on the doorkeeper's face that first Cabinet meeting, the Incarnation's cry at the moment of climax, his own desperate attempt to see the thing as a lesson. And then he thought about what !urq would have said, had she been there.

He went to the meditation box that night, determined to exorcise the demon that gnawed at his vitals. Lust, he recited, provides the soil in which other passions flourish. Lust is like a demon that eats up all the good deeds of the world. Lust is a viper hiding in a flower garden; it poisons those who come in search of beauty.

It was all futile. Because all he could think of was the Gyalpo Rinpoche, the lovely body moving rhythmically in the darkness of the Cabinet room.

The moan of ragdongs echoed over the gardens and was followed by drunken applause and shouts. It was the beginning of the festival of plays and operas. The Cabinet and other high officials celebrated the festival at the Jewel Pavilion, the Incarnation's summer palace, where there was an outdoor theater specially built among the sweet-smelling meditative gardens. The palace, a lacy white fantasy ornamented with statues of gods and masts carrying prayer flags, sat bathed in spotlights atop its hill.

In addition to the members of the court were the personal followers of the Incarnation, people he had been gathering during the seven months of his reign. Novice monks and nuns, doubtobs and naljorpas, crazed hermits, looney charlatans and mediums, runaways, workers from the spaceport . . . all drunk, all pledged to follow the Short Path wherever it led.

"Disgusting," said Dr. O'Neill. "Loathsome." Furiously she brushed at a spot on her brocaded robe where someone had spilled beer.

Jigme said nothing. Cymbals clashed from the stage, where the orchestra was practicing. Three novice monks went by, staggering under the weight of a flogging machine. The festival was going to begin with the punishment of a number of criminals, and any who could walk afterward would then be able to join the revelers. The first opera would be sung on a stage spattered with blood.

Dr. O'Neill stepped closer to Jigme. "The Incarnation has asked me to furnish him a report on nerve induction. He wishes to devise a machine to induce pain without damage to the body."

Heavy sorrow filled Jigme that he could no longer be surprised by such news. "For what purpose?" he asked.

"To punish criminals, of course. Without crippling them. Then his Omniscience will be able to order up as savage punishments as he likes without being embarrassed by hordes of cripples shuffling around the capital."

Jigme tried to summon indignation. "You should not impart unworthy motives to the Gyalpo Rinpoche."

Dr. O'Neill only gave him a cynical look. Behind her, trampling through a hedge, came a young monk, laughing, being pursued by a pair of women with whips. O'Neill looked at them as they dashed off into the darkness. "At least it will give *them* less of an excuse to indulge in such behavior. It won't be as much fun to watch if there isn't any blood."

"That would be a blessing."

"The Forty-Second Incarnation is potentially the finest in history," O'Neill said. Her eyes narrowed in fury. She raised a clenched fist, the knuckles white in the darkness. "The most intelligent Incarnation, the most able, the finest rapport with the Library in centuries . . . and look at what he is doing with his gifts!"

"I thank you for the compliments, Doctor," said the Incarnation. O'Neill and Jigme jumped. The Incarnation, treading lightly on the summer grass, had walked up behind them. He was dressed only in his white reskyang and the garlands of flowers given him by his followers. Kunlegs, as always, loomed behind him, twitching furiously.

Jigme bowed profoundly, sticking out his tongue.

"The punishment machine," said the Incarnation. "Do the plans move forward?"

Dr. O'Neill's dismay was audible in her reply. "Yes, Omniscient."

"I wish the work to be completed for the New Year. I want particular care paid to the monitors that will alert the operators if the felon's life is in danger. We should not want to violate Shakyamuni's commandment against slaughter."

"The work shall be done, Omniscient."

"Thank you, Dr. O'Neill." He reached out a hand to give her a blessing. "I think of you as my mother, Dr. O'Neill. The lady who tenderly watched over me in the womb. I hope this thought pleases you."

"If it pleases your Omniscience."

"It does." The Incarnation withdrew his hand. In the darkness his smile was difficult to read. "You will be honored for your care for many generations, Doctor. I make you that promise."

"Thank you, Omniscient."

"Omniscient!" A new voice called out over the sound of revelry. The new State Oracle, dressed in the saffron zen of a simple monk, strode toward them over the grass. His thin, ascetic face was bursting with anger.

"Who are these people, Omniscient?" he demanded.

"My friends, minister."

"They are destroying the gardens!"

"They are *my* gardens, minister."

"Vanity!" The Oracle waved a finger under the Incarnation's nose. Kunlegs grunted and started forward, but the Incarnation stopped him with a gesture.

"I am pleased to accept the correction of my ministers," he said.

"Vanity and indulgence!" the Oracle said. "Has the Buddha not told us to forsake worldly desires? Instead of doing as Shakyamuni instructed, you have surrounded yourself with followers who indulge their own sensual pleasures and your vanity!"

"Vanity?" The Incarnation glanced at the Jewel Pavilion. "Look at my summer palace, minister. It is a vanity, a lovely vanity. But it does no harm."

"It is nothing! All the palaces of the world are as nothing beside the word of the Buddha!"

The Incarnation's face showed supernal calm. "Should I rid myself of these vanities, minister?"

"Yes!" The State Oracle stamped a bare foot. "Let them be swept away!"

"Very well. I accept my minister's correction." He raised his voice, calling for the attention of his followers. A collection of drunken rioters gathered around him. "Let the word be spread to all here," he cried. "The Jewel Pavilion is to be destroyed by fire. The gardens shall be uprooted. All statues shall be smashed." He looked at the State Oracle and smiled his cold smile. "I hope this shall satisfy you, minister."

A horrified look was his only reply.

The Incarnation's followers laughed and sang as they destroyed the Jewel Pavilion, as they toppled statues from its roof and destroyed furniture to create bonfires in its luxurious suites. "Short Path!" they chanted. "Short Path!" In the theater the opera began, an old Tibetan epic about the death by treachery of the Sixth Earthly Gyalpo Rinpoche, known to his Mongolian enemies as the Dalai Lama. Jigme found a quiet place in the garden and sat in a full lotus, repeating sutras and trying to calm his mind. But the screams, chanting, songs, and shouts distracted him.

He looked up to see the Gyalpo Rinpoche standing upright amid the ruin of his garden, his head raised as if to sniff the wind. Kunlegs was standing close behind, caressing him. The light of the burning palace danced on his face. The Incarnation seemed transformed, a living embodiment of . . . of what? Madness? Exultation? Ecstasy? Jigme couldn't tell, but when he saw it he felt as if his heart would explode.

Then his blood turned cold. Behind the Incarnation, moving through the garden beneath the ritual umbrella of a Masker servant, came Ambassador !urq, her dark face watching the burning palace with something like triumph.

Jigme felt someone near him. "This cannot go on," said Dr. O'Neill's voice, and at the sound of her cool resolution terror flooded him.

"*Aum vajra sattva,*" he chanted, saying the words over and over, repeating them till the Jewel Pavilion was ash and the garden looked as if a whirlwind had torn through it, leaving nothing but tangled ruin.

Rising from the desolation, he saw something bright dangling from the shattered proscenium of the outdoor stage.

It was the young State Oracle, hanging by the neck.

"!urq's despatches have grown triumphant. She knows that the Gyalpo Rinpoche has lost the affection of the people, and that they will soon lose their tolerance." Miss Taisuke was decorating a Christmas tree in her lha khang. Little glowing buddhas, in their traditional red suits and white beards, hung amid the evergreen branches. Kali danced on top, holding a skull in either hand.

"What can we do?" said Jigme.

"Prevent a coup whatever the cost. If the Incarnation is deposed or declared mad, the Sang can attack under pretext of restoring the Incarnation. Our own people will be divided. We couldn't hope to win."

"Can't Dr. O'Neill see this?"

"Dr. O'Neill desires war, Jigme. She thinks we will win it whatever occurs."

Jigme thought about what interstellar war would mean; the vast energies of modern weapons deployed against helpless planets. Tens of billions dead, even with a victory. "We should speak to the Gyalpo Rinpoche," he said. "He must be made to understand."

"The State Oracle spoke to him, and what resulted?"

"You, Prime Minister—"

Taisuke looked at him. Her eyes were brimming with tears. "I have *tried* to speak to him. He is interested only in his parties, in his new punishment device. It's all he will talk about."

Jigme said nothing. His eyes stung with tears. Two weeping officials, he thought, alone on Christmas Eve. What more pathetic picture could possibly exist?

"The device grows ever more elaborate," Taisuke said. "There will be life extension and preservation gear installed. The machine can torture people for *lifetimes!*" She shook her head. Her hands trembled as they wiped her eyes. "Perhaps Dr. O'Neill is right. Perhaps the Incarnation needs to be put away."

"Never," Jigme said. "Never."

"Prime Minister." The Thunderbolt Sow shifted in her corner. "The Gyalpo Rinpoche has made an announcement to his people. 'The Short Path will end with the New Year.' "

Taisuke wiped her eyes on her brocaded sleeve. "Was that the entire message?"

"Yes, Prime Minister."

Her eyes rose to Jigme's. "What could it mean?"

"We must have hope, Prime Minister."

"Yes." Her hands clutched at his. "We must try to have hope."

Beneath snapping prayer flags, a quarter-size Jewel Pavilion made of flammable lattice stood on Burning Hill. The Cabinet was gathered inside it, flanking the throne of the Incarnation. The Gyalpo Rinpoche had decided to view the burning from inside one of the floats.

Kyetsang Kunlegs, grinning with his huge yellow teeth, was the only one of his followers present. The others were making merry in the city.

In front of the sham Jewel Pavilion was the new torture machine, a hollow oval, twice the size of a man, its skin the color of brushed metal. The interior was filled with mysterious apparatus.

The Cabinet said the rosary, and the Horse of the Air rose up into the night. The Incarnation, draped with khatas, raised a double drum made from the tops of two human skulls. With a flick of his wrist, a bead on a string began to bound from one drum to the other. With his cold green eyes he watched it rattle for a long moment. "Welcome to my first anniversary," he said.

The others murmured in reply. The drum rattled on. A cold winter wind blew through the pavilion. The Incarnation looked from one Cabinet member to the other and gave his cruel, ambiguous smile.

"On the anniversary of my ascension to the throne and my adoption of the Short Path," he said, "I would like to honor the woman who made it possible." He held out his hand. "Dr. O'Neill, the Minister of Science, whom I think of as my mother. Mother, please come sit in the place of honor."

O'Neill rose stone-faced from her place and walked to the throne. She prostrated herself and stuck out her tongue. The Treasured King stepped off the platform, still rattling the drum; he took her hand, helped her rise. He sat her on the platform in his own place.

Another set of arms materialized on his shoulders; while the first rattled the drum, the other three went through a long succession of mudras. Amazement, Jigme read, fascination, the warding of evil.

"My first memories in this incarnation," he said, "are of fire. Fire that burned inside me, that made me want to claw my way out of my glass womb and launch myself prematurely into existence. Fires that aroused lust and hatred before I knew anyone to hate or lust for. And then, when the fires grew unendurable, I would open my eyes, and there I would see my mother, Dr. O'Neill, watching me with happiness in her face."

Another pair of arms appeared. The Incarnation looked over his shoulder at Dr. O'Neill, who was watching him with the frozen stare given a poison serpent. The Incarnation turned back to the others. The breeze fluttered the khatas around his neck.

"Why should I burn?" he said. "My memories of earlier Incarnations were incomplete, but I knew I had never known such fire before. There was something in me that was not balanced. That was made for the Short Path. Perhaps Enlightenment could be reached by leaping into the fire. In any case, I had no choice."

There was a flare of light, a roar of applause. The first of the floats outside exploded into flame. Fireworks crackled in the night. The Incarnation smiled. His drum rattled on.

"Never had I been so out of balance," he said. Another pair of arms materialized. "Never had I been so puzzled. Were my compulsions a manifestation of the Library? Was the crystal somehow out of alignment? Or was something else wrong? It was my consort Kyetsang Kunlegs who gave me the first clue." He turned to the throne and smiled at the murderer, who twitched in reply. "Kunlegs has suffered all his life from Tourette's syndrome, an excess of dopamine in the brain. It makes him compulsive, twitchy, and—curiously—brilliant. His brain works too fast for its own good. The condition should have been diagnosed and corrected years ago, but Kunlegs' elders were neglectful."

Kunlegs opened his mouth and gave a long laugh. Dr. O'Neill, seated just before him on the platform, gave a shiver. The Incarnation beamed at Kunlegs, then turned back to his audience.

"I didn't suffer from Tourette's—I didn't have all the symptoms. But

682 THE GOOD STUFF

seeing poor Kunlegs made it clear where I should look for the source of my difficulty." He raised the drum, rattled it beside his head. "In my own brain," he said.

Another float burst into flame. The bright light glowed through the wickerwork walls of the pavilion, shone on the Incarnation's face. He gazed into it with his cruel half-smile, his eyes dancing in the firelight.

Dr. O'Neill spoke. Her voice was sharp. "Omniscient, may I suggest that we withdraw? This structure is built to burn, and the wind will carry sparks from the other floats toward us."

The Incarnation looked at her. "Later, honored Mother." He turned back to the Cabinet. "Not wanting to bother my dear mother with my suspicions, I visited several doctors when I was engaged in my visits to town and various monasteries. I found that not only did I have a slight excess of dopamine, but that my mind also contained too much serotonin and norepinephrine, and too little endorphin."

Another float burst into flame. Figures from the opera screamed in eerie voices. The Incarnation's smile was beatific. "Yet my honored mother, the Minister of Science, supervised my growth. How could such a thing happen?"

Jigme's attention jerked to Dr. O'Neill. Her face was drained of color. Her eyes were those of someone gazing into the Void.

"Dr. O'Neill, of course, has political opinions. She believes the Sang heretics must be vanquished. Destroyed or subdued at all costs. And to that end she wished an Incarnation who would be a perfect conquering warrior-king—impatient, impulsive, brilliant, careless of life, and indifferent to suffering. Someone with certain sufficiencies and deficiencies in brain chemistry."

O'Neill opened her mouth. A scream came out, a hollow sound as mindless as those given by the burning floats. The Incarnation's many hands pointed to her, all but the one rattling the drum.

Laughing, Kyetsang Kunlegs lunged forward, twisting the khata around the minister's neck. The scream came to an abrupt end. Choking, she toppled back into his huge lap.

"She is the greatest traitor of all time," the Incarnation said. "She who poisoned the Forty-First Incarnation. She who would subvert the Library itself to her ends. She who would poison the mind of a Bodhisattva." His voice was soft, yet exultant. It sent an eerie chill down Jigme's back.

Kunlegs rose from the platform holding Dr. O'Neill in his big hands. Her piled-up hair had come undone and trailed across the ground. Kunlegs carried her out of the building and into the punishment machine.

The Incarnation's drum stopped rattling. Jigme looked at him in stunned comprehension.

"She shall know what it is to burn," he said. "She shall know it for many lifetimes."

Sparks blew across the floor before the Incarnation's feet. There was a glow from the doorway, where some of the wickerwork had caught fire.

The machine was automatic in its function. Dr. O'Neill began to scream again, a rising series of shrieks. Her body began to rotate. The Incarnation smiled. "She shall make that music for many centuries. Perhaps one of my future incarnations shall put a stop to it."

Jigme felt burning heat on the back of his neck. O'Neill's screams ran up and down his spine. "Omniscient," he said. "The pavilion is on fire. We should leave."

"In a moment. I wish to say a few last words."

Kunlegs came loping back, grinning, and hopped onto the platform. The Incarnation joined him and kissed him tenderly. "Kunlegs and I will stay in the pavilion," he said. "We will both die tonight."

"No!" Taisuke jumped to her feet. "We will not permit it! Your condition can be corrected."

The Incarnation stared at her. "I thank you, loyal one. But my brain is poisoned, and even if the imbalance were corrected I would still be perceiving the Library through a chemical fog that would impair my ability. My next Incarnation will not have this handicap."

"Omniscient!" Tears spilled from Taisuke's eyes. "Don't leave us!"

"You will continue as head of the government. My next Incarnation will be ready by the next New Year, and then you may retire to the secular life I know you wish to pursue in this lifetime."

"No!" Taisuke ran forward, threw herself before the platform. "I beg you, Omniscient!"

Suddenly Jigme was on his feet. He lurched forward, threw himself down beside Taisuke. "Save yourself, Omniscient!" he said.

"I wish to say something concerning the Sang." The Incarnation spoke calmly, as if he hadn't heard. "There will be danger of war in the next year. You must all promise me that you won't fight."

"Omniscient." This from Daddy Carbajal. "We must be ready to defend ourselves!"

"Are we an Enlightened race, or are we not?" The Incarnation's voice was stern.

"You are Bodhisattva." Grudgingly. "All know this."

"We are Enlightened. The Buddha commands us not to take life. If these are not facts, our existence has no purpose, and our civilization is a mockery." O'Neill's screams provided eerie counterpoint to his voice. The Incarnation's many arms pointed at the members of the Cabinet. "You may arm in order to deter attack. But if the Sang begin a war, you must promise me to surrender without condition."

"Yes!" Taisuke, still facedown, wailed from her obeisance. "I promise, Omniscient."

"The Diamond Mountain will be the greatest prize the Sang can hope for. And the Library is the Buddha. When the time is right, the Library will incarnate itself as a Sang, and the Sang will be sent on their path to Enlightenment."

"Save yourself, Omniscient!" Taisuke wailed. The roar of flames had drowned O'Neill's screams. Jigme felt sparks falling on his shaven head.

"Your plan, sir!" Daddy Carbajal's voice was desperate. "It might not work! The Sang may thwart the incarnation in some way!"

"Are we Enlightened?" The Incarnation's voice was mild. "Or are we not? Is the Buddha's truth eternal, or is it not? Do you not support the Doctrine?"

Daddy Carbajal threw himself down beside Jigme. "I believe, Omniscient! I will do as you ask!"

"Leave us, then. Kyetsang and I wish to be alone."

Certainty seized Jigme. He could feel tears stinging his eyes. "Let me stay, Omniscient!" he cried. "Let me die with you!"

"Carry these people away," said the Incarnation. Hands seized Jigme. He fought them off, weeping, but they were too powerful: he was carried from the burning pavilion. His last sight of the Incarnation was of the Gyalpo Rinpoche and Kunlegs embracing one another, silhouetted against flame, and then everything dissolved in fire and tears.

And in the morning nothing was left, nothing but ashes and the keening cries of the traitor O'Neill, whom the Bodhisattva in his wisdom had sent forever to Hell.

Jigme found !urq there, standing alone before O'Neill, staring at the figure caught in a webwork of life support and nerve stimulators. The sound of the traitor's endless agony continued to issue from her torn throat.

"There will be no war," Jigme said.

!urq looked at him. Her stance was uncertain.

"After all this," Jigme said, "a war would be indecent. You understand?"

!urq just stared.

"You must not unleash this madness in us!" Jigme cried. Tears rolled down his face. "Never, Ambassador! Never!"

!urq's antennae twitched. She looked at O'Neill again, rotating slowly in the huge wheel. "I will do what I can, Rinpoche," she said.

!urq made her lone way down Burning Hill. Jigme stared at the traitor for a long time.

Then he sat in the full lotus. Ashes drifted around him, some clinging to his zen, as he sat before the image of the tormented doctor and recited his prayers.

Maureen F. McHugh

THE MISSIONARY'S CHILD

Born in Ohio, Maureen F. McHugh spent some years living in Shijiazhuang in the People's Republic of China, an experience that has been one of the major shaping forces on her fiction to date. Upon returning to the United States, she made her first sale in 1989, and has since made a powerful impression on the SF world of the nineties with a relatively small body of work, becoming a frequent contributor to *Asimov's Science Fiction*, as well as selling to *The Magazine of Fantasy & Science Fiction*, *Alternate Warriors*, *Aladdin*, and other markets.

Not prolific by the high-production sausage-factory standards of the field, McHugh has nevertheless enjoyed the distinction of publishing some of the very best stories of the late eighties and nineties, especially such profound and disturbing stories as "Protection," "Nekropolis," and "The Lincoln Train," which won her a Hugo Award in 1996, although even her "second-string" stories such as "Baffin Island," "The Queen of Marincite," "Whispers" (with David B. Kisor), "In the Air," "The Beast," and "A Coney Island of the Mind" would be the envy of many another writer. Many of these stories take her into territories far beyond the range of the Planetary Adventure, but she can write those too when she sets her mind to it, as well or better than it's ever been done by anybody, as shown by stories such as "Strings," the recent Nebula finalist "The Cost to Be Wise," and the suspenseful, sly, and sardonic adventure that follows, "The Missionary's Child," a story with strong echoes of Ursula K. Le Guin, Joanna Russ, James Tiptree, Jr., and others, but one which demonstrates a voice and vision that are McHugh's alone. A story that shows us that sometimes even when you are determinedly minding your own business, it's hard to stay out of trouble . . . and that sometimes it's when you're *not* looking for anything that you find something that's the most worth finding. . . .

Although she's expert at shorter lengths, much of McHugh's reputation has been made with her novels. In 1992 she published one of the year's most widely acclaimed and talked-about first novels, *China Mountain Zhang*, which won the Locus Award for Best First Novel, the Lambda Literary Award, and the James Tiptree Jr. Memorial Award, and which was named a *New York Times* Notable Book as well as being a finalist for the Hugo and Nebula awards. Her most recent book, the novel *Half the Day Is Night*, received similar critical acclaim. Upcoming is a new novel, *Mission Child*, set on the same world as "The Missionary's Child" and "The Cost to Be Wise." She lives in Twinsburg, Ohio, with her husband, her son, and a golden retriever named Smith.

"Are you blind?" the woman asks.

I'm looking right at her. "No," I say, "I'm foreign."

Affronted, the woman straightens up in a swirl of rose-colored robe and chouli scent, clutching her veil. Here in the islands, they don't see very many blond-haired, blue-eyed barbarians; people have asked me if I can see normally, if all northerners are blue-eyed. But this is the first time someone has ever asked me that. Maybe she thinks that my eyes are filmed, like the milky-white of old people.

She thought I was begging—I must look pretty tattered. I should have said yes, then I could go get something to drink, get out of the sun. I'm sitting down by the water. I'm broke, and I've been hungry for awhile, and I'm listless and a little stupid from the heat and lack of food. I feel fifty instead of thirty-one.

I should go back to the hiring area, wait around with a couple of other thugs for some sort of nasty work. I should oil my sword. It's a waste of time; no one needs a mercenary here, the Celestial Prince doesn't hire foreigners in his army.

But I don't want to go back. Up in the market, some yammerhead had been rattling on about our Cousins from the stars. The Cousins haven't come to the islands in any numbers yet, and I'll wager he's never met any. Listening to this stonker gave me a headache. Wouldn't he be surprised if he knew that the Cousins think of us all about the way the woman who asked me if I was blind thinks of me. They think that we're barbarians. They think that we're stupid because we call what they do magic instead of *science*. Or they feel sorry for us.

I know better than thinking bitter; time to head back to the market, see if anybody will hire a tokking foreigner to dig ditches or something.

But I sit, my head aching with hunger and heat, too stupid to do anything about it. And I'm still sitting there a dine later, the sun is still high in the sky baked the color of celedon. Not awake, not asleep.

I'm going to have to start selling my gear, the slow road to starvation.

I open my eyes and watch a ship come in on the deep green sea. It has red eyes rimmed in violet and violet sails; from far away, I can see a person wearing dark clothes that are all of one piece. A Cousin, standing at the prow. On the boathouse there is a light, star-magic, like a third eye, blind and white. Here in the islands, when you see Cousins, they are with the rich and the powerful.

What would the Cousin think if I spoke a little of his/her language? I only remember a few phrases. "Hello," "My name is," and a phrase from my lessons, "Husband and wife Larkin have three children, a boy and two girls." Would the Cousin be curious enough to take me aboard? Recognize the debt for what the Cousins did to my kin, help me get back to the mainland?

The ship docks, three guildmen and a Cousin disembark, and come down the quay. Southerners will stare at any foreigner, but they stare double at a Cousin, and who can blame them? The Cousin is a woman, with her hair uncovered, dressed like a man, but not looking like a man, no. That amuses me. Southern women pull their veils around their mouths and stop to watch.

She comes down the quay with studied indifference. I can understand that; what does one do when people stare day after day? Pretend not to notice.

She is tall, taller than me, but Cousins are usually tall, and I'm shorter than many men. She looks up directly at me while I am smiling, by chance. The length of a man between us. I can see that she has light eyes.

"Hello," I say in the trade language of the Cousins. The word just pops out.

It stops her, though, like a roped stabros calf. "Hello," she says, in the same tongue. Consternation among the guildmen; two in dark red and one in green, all with shaven heads dull with the graphite sheen of stubble. "You speak lingua?" she says.

"A little," I say.

Then she rattles on, asking me something, "where da-da da-da da."

I shrug. Search my memory. My lessons in lingua were a lifetime ago; I remember almost nothing. Something comes to me that I often said in class: "I don't understand," I say, "I speak little."

"Where did you learn?" she says in Suhkhra, the language of the southerners. "Starport?"

"Up north." No real answer. Already I'm sorry I spoke. Bad *enough* to be a tokking foreigner; worse to be a spectacle. And my head aches, and I am tired from three days' lack of food.

"Did you work at the port?" she asks, probing.

"No," I say. Flat.

She frowns. Then, like a boat before bad winds, she comes across in another direction. She speaks in my own language, the language of home. "What is your name?" She is careful and stilted in that one phrase.

"Jahn," I say, probably the commonest name among northern men. "What is yours?" I ask, without regard for courtesy.

"Sulia," she says. "Jahn, what kin-kind?"

"My kin are all dead," I say, "Jahn no-kin-kind."

But she shakes her head. "I'm sorry," she says in Suhkhra, "I don't understand. I speak very little Krerjian. What did you say your name was?"

"Jahn Sckarline," I say. And then, in my own tongue, "Go away." Because I am tired of her, tired of everything, tired of starving.

She isn't listening, and probably doesn't understand anyway. "Sckarline," she says. "I thought everyone from Sckarline—"

"Is dead," I say. "Thank you, Cousin. I am pleased you keep my kinname." It's awkward to say in Suhkra. The Suhkra aren't good at irony anyway.

"Sulia Cousin," one of the guildmen says deferentially, "they are waiting for us."

She shakes him off. "I know about the settlement at Sckarline," she says to me. "You're a mission boy. You have an education. Why don't you work at a port?"

"And live in a *ghetto?*" The word comes back to me in her trade lingua. "With the other *natives?*"

"Isn't it better to get a tech job than to live like this?" she asks.

Better than a shantytown, I think, huddled together while the starships come screaming overhead, making one's teeth ache and one's goods rattle?

I look at her, she looks at me. I search my memory for the words in lingua, but my mind isn't sharp and it was too long ago. "Go away," I finally say in Suhkhra, "people are waiting."

She stands there hesitant, but the guildman does not. He strides forward and smacks me hard in the side of my head for my disrespect. I know better than to defend myself. Oh, Heth, my poor head! Southerners are a bad lot, they have no concept of a freeman.

So, having been knocked over, I stay still, with my nose near the stones, waiting to see if he'll hit me again, smelling dust, and sea, and the smell of myself, which is probably very distasteful to everyone else.

He crouches down, and I wait to be smacked again, empty-headed. But it isn't him, it's her. "What are you doing here?" she asks. She probably means how did you come here, but I find myself wondering, what am I doing here? Looking for work. Trying to get passage home. But home is gone, should never have existed in the first place.

What does any person do in a lifetime? I give her an answer out of the Proverbs. "Putting off death," I say. "Go away, before you complicate my task—you people have done enough to me."

She looks unhappy. Cousins are like that, a sentimental people. "If I could help you, I would," she says.

"I know," I say, "but your help would make me *need* you. And then I would be just one more local on one more backward world." Everywhere the Cousins go across the sky, it's the same. Wanji used to tell us about her people, about the Cousins. About other worlds like ours. Where two cultures meet, she said, one of them usually gives way.

The Cousin searches through her pockets, puts a coin, a rectangular silver piece, in the dust. I wait, not moving, until they go on.

I pick up the coin. A proud person would throw it after her. I'm not proud, I'm hungry. I take it.

In the market, it's rabbit and duck day—kids herding ducks with long switches, cages of rabbits for sale, hanging next to that cheap old staple, thekla lizard drying in strips. I dodge past tallgrass poles with craken-dyed cloth hanging startling yellow, and cut through between two vegetable stands. Next to the hiring area, they're grilling stabos jerky on sticks, and selling pineapple slices dipped in saltwater to make them sweeter.

I use the Cousin's silver to buy noodles and red peanut paste, spicy with proyakapiti, and I eat slowly. I'm three days empty of food, and if I eat too fast, I'll be sick. I learned about going without food during a campaign, when I first started soldiering. On the long walk to Bashtoy. I know all about the different kinds of hunger; the first sharp stabs of appetite, then the strong hunger, how your stomach hurts after awhile, and then how you forget, and then how hunger comes back, like swollen joints in an old woman. And how it wears you down, how you become tired and stupid, and how then finally it leaves you altogether, and your jaw bone softens until your teeth rock in their sockets, and you have been hungry so long you don't know what it means anymore.

The yammerhead is on the other side of the hiring area, still going on about how the guilds monopolize the Cousins. How the guilds were nothing until ten years ago, when the Cousins came and brought magic, and then no one could trade without permission of the guild. I close my eyes, feeling sleepy after food, and I can see the place where I grew up. I was born in Sckarline, a magic town. I remember the white houses, the power station where Ayuedesh taught boys to cook stabos manure and get swamp air from it, then turned that into power that sang through copper and made light. At night, we had light for three or four dine after sunset. Phrases in the lingua the Cousins speak, *Appropriate Technology*.

I am lost in Sckarline, looking for my mother, for kin. I see Trevin, and I follow him. He's way ahead, in leggings, in dark blue with fur on his shoulders. But the way he leads me is wrong, the buildings are burned, just blackened crossbeams jutting up, he is leading me toward—

"I'm looking for a musician." I jerk awake.

A flat-faced southerner waiting for hire says, "Musicians are over there." People who wait here are like me, looking for anything.

A portly man with a wine-colored robe says, "I'm looking for a musician who knows a little about swords."

"What kind of musician?" I ask. I always talk quietly, it's a failing, and the portly man doesn't hear me. He cocks his head.

"What kind of musician?" the flat-faced southerner repeats.

"Doesn't matter." The portly man shrugs, hawks so loudly it sounds as if he's clearing his tokking head, and spits.

Tokking southerners. They spit all the time, it drives me crazy. I hear them clear their throat, and I cringe and start looking to step out of the way. Heth knows I'm not squeamish, but they *all* do it, men, women, children.

"Sikha," the portly man offers. A sikha is a kind of southern lute, only they pick the strings on the neck as well as the ones on the body.

"How about flute?" I offer.

"Flute?" the portly man says. His robe is of good quality, but stained, and he has a negligent air. The robe gapes open to the belted waist, showing his smooth chest and the soft flab like breasts. "You play the flute, northerner?"

No, I want to say, I just wanted to help us think of some instruments. Patience. "Yes," I say, "I play the flute."

"Let's hear you."

So I dig out my wooden flute and make pretty sounds. He waves his hands and says, "How good are you with a sword?"

I dig into my pack and pull my cloak out of the bottom. It's crushed and wrinkled, people don't wear cloaks much in the south, but I spread it out so that he can see the badge on the breast: a white mountain against a red background. The survivors of the March to Bashtoy got them—that, and sixty gold coins. The sixty gold coins have been gone for a couple of years, but the badge is still on the cloak.

People murmur. The portly man doesn't know badges, he's not a fighter, but the flat-faced southerner does, and it shows in the sudden respect in his face, and that ends any question of my swordplay—which is fine because, badge or no badge, I'm only mediocre at swordplay. I'm just not tall enough or big enough.

Surviving a campaign is as much a matter of luck and cleverness as skill with a sword, anyway.

But that's why Barok hires me to play flute at his party.

He offers me twenty in silver, which is too much money. He pays me five right away. He must want me to be a bodyguard, and that means that he thinks that he'll *need* one. I like guard duty, or, better than that, something like being a sailor. But I didn't realize until I jumped ship that, here in the Islands, not just *anybody* can be a sailor. I shouldn't take this job, it sounds like trouble, but I've got to do something.

All boat trade except local fishing is controlled by the four Navigation Orders, all the Cousins's magic by the two Metaphysical Orders. I don't pay much attention to Magic; I'm just a whistler, a mercenary. I have three spells myself (but simple ones), that Ayuedesh Engineer, the old Cousin, wired into my skull when we knew that Scathalos High-on was going to attack Sckarline. A lot of good spells did us in the end, with all of two twenties of us and four Cousins, everybody in Sckarline who could fight at all, against the Scathalos High-on, Kin-leader's army.

I am supposed to report my spells to the Metaphysical Orders, but I'm not *that* stupid. Just stupid enough to come *here*.

A man who hires a sword to play music must have unusual parties, and I wait to hear what he wants of me.

"You'll need better clothes," he says. "And bathe, would you?"

I promise to meet him in the market in three dine or so. And then I finger the coppers left from the Cousin's silver and the five silver coins he's given me. First I go to the bath house, and I pay for a private bath. I hate bath houses. It is not, as the southerners all think, that northerners hate to bathe; I just find bath houses . . . uncomfortable. Even in a private room, I strip furtively, keeping my back to the door. But Heth, it is good to be clean, to not itch! I even wash my clothes, wring them out as best I can. The water runs black, and I have to put on wet clothes, but I imagine they'll dry fast enough.

Back at the market, I find a stall that sells used clothes. I go through piles until I find a black jacket with a high neck, fairly clean. And I have my hair trimmed.

I use much of my three dine and about half of the Cousin's silver, but when the time comes, I am back at the hiring area, cleaner, neater, with Barok's five silver still in my pocket, and ready to earn the other fifteen silver. And I don't wait long for my employer, who looks me over and spits, by which he means I have passed inspection.

I assume from his lavish way with silver and his manner that we will head to one of the better parts of town. After all, a lot of silver went into the feeding of that smooth belly and flaccid chest. But we head down toward where the river meets the ocean. It's a wide, tame river, enclosed by stone walls and arched—so they claim—by fourteen stone bridges. But this far down, all poor. The closer we get, the more rank it smells. We go down a stone stairs to the water, past women washing clothes, and out onto a small city of permanently moored boats.

The sunbleached boats have eyes painted on the prows, even though they never go anywhere. They're homes to families, each living the length of my arm from the next, all piled up together with brown dusty chickens, laundry flapping, brown children running from boat to boat, wearing nothing but a yellow gourd on a rope tied around their waist (if they fall overboard, the gourd floats, holding them up until some adult can fish them out of the water).

I've never been out here before; it's a maze, and it would be worth my life to step on these boats alone. Even walking with Barok, I feel the men's eyes follow me with hard gazes. We cross from boat to boat, they rise and fall under our feet. The boats bob, the green river stinks of garbage and rotting fish, and my poor head swirls a bit. I've been here two and half years, I speak the language, but only southerners can live piled up on top of each other this way.

Out near where the middle is kept clear for river traffic, we climb a ramp up onto a larger boat, maybe the length of five men head to foot, the home of Barok. A tiny brown woman wrapped in blue is shoving charcoal into a tampis jar, a jar with a place in the bottom to put fuel to heat the stuff cooking in the top. It's a big tampis jar. I smell meat; there's smooth creamy yogurt in a blue and white bowl next to her. I'm hungry again. She glances up, and looks back down. Barok ignores her and steps over a neat pyramid of pale lavender boxfruit, one split to show the purple meat. As I step over them, I reach down and hook one.

"Hie!" she snaps, "that is not for you!"

Barok doesn't even look back, so I wink at her and keep walking.

"Yellow-haired dog-devil!" she shrieks. I follow Barok down into the hold, now a good-sized apartment, if rather warm, and get my first surprise. There's a young girl, bare-armed and bare-haired, sitting at the table, drawing with brush and paper.

"Shell-sea," Barok growls.

So intent she is that she ignores him for a moment, and I get a chance to see what she's drawing—a long squiggling line that she's tracing as if every twist and curve has meaning. Which it clearly doesn't, since it meanders all over the page.

"Shell-sea! Take it in the back!"

She says sullenly, "It's too hot back there," and then looks up. I'm blond and sunburned, quite a sight for a southern girl who has probably never seen someone who didn't have dark hair in her life. She stares at me as she gathers her papers, and then walks to the back, her eyebrows knit into a dark line, clumping her feet heavily, like someone whose wits aren't right.

Barok watches her go as if he doesn't like the taste of something. "My guests will be here later. Wait on deck."

"What am I supposed to do?" I ask.

"Play music and watch the guests," he says.

"That's all?" I ask. "You're paying me twenty in silver to watch?" He starts to answer sharply, and I say, "If you tell me what to watch *for*, I might do a better job."

"You watch for trouble," he says. "That's enough."

This is bad, my stomach knows. An employer who doesn't trust his guests or his employees is like a dog with thrum—*everyone* gets bitten. I could quit, hand him back the five silvers, take the boxfruit, and go. I still have a little less than half of the Cousin's silver; I can do fine on that for a week, if I sleep down on the docks.

"There's food on the stern deck; help yourself, and ignore the woman if she complains."

So I keep the job. Stomach-thinking. Heth says in the Proverbs that our life hinges on little things. That's certainly true for me.

I eat slowly and carefully; I know that if I eat too much, I'll be sleepy. But I fill my pack with boxfruit, pigeon's egg dumplings, and red peanuts. Especially red peanuts—a person can live a long time on red peanuts. While I'm eating, Shell-sea comes up and sits on the stern to watch me. As I said, I'm not tall, most men have a bit of reach on me, and she's nearly my height. She's wearing a school uniform, the dark red of one of the orders, and her thick hair is tied back with a red cord. The uniform would be fine on a young girl, but only emphasizes that she's not a child. She's too old for bare arms, for uncovered hair, too old for the cord that belts the robe high under her small breasts. She is probably just past menses.

After I eat, I use a bucket to rinse my hands and face. After awhile she says, "Why don't you take off your shirt when you wash?"

"You are a forward child," I say.

She has the grace to blush, but she still looks expectant. She wants to see how much hair I have on my chest. Southerners don't have much body hair.

"I've already bathed today," I say. Southerners waiting to see if I look like a hairy termit make me very uncomfortable. "Why do you have such an unusual name?" I ask.

"It's not a name, it's a nickname." She stares at her bare toes and they curl in embarrassment. I thought she was a bit of a half-wit, but away from Barok she's quick enough, and light on her feet.

I wonder if she's his fancy girl. Most southerners don't take a pretty girl until they already have a first wife.

"Shell-sea? Why do they call you that?"

"Not 'Shell-sea'," she says, exasperated, *"Chalcey.* What kind of name is 'Shell-sea'? My name is Chalcedony. I bet you don't know what that is."

"It's a precious stone," I say.

"How did you know?"

"Because I've been to the temple of Heth in Thelahckre," I say, "and the Shesket-lion's eyes are two chunks of chalcedony." I rinse my bowl in the bucket, then dump the water over the side; the soap scums the green water like oil. I'd been to a lot of places, trying to find the right place. The islands hadn't proven to be any better than the city of Lada on the coast. And Lada no better than Gibbun, which was supposed to be full of work, but the work was all for the new star port that the Cousins were building. My people forgetting their kin, living in slums. And Gibbun no better than Thelahckre.

"Why don't you have a beard?" she asks. Southerners can't grow beards until they're old, and then only long, bedraggled, wispy white things. They believe that all northerner men have them down to their belts.

"Because I don't," I say, irritated. "Why do you live with Barok?"

"He's my uncle."

We both stop then to watch a ship come down the river to the bay. Like the one the Cousin came in on, it has red eyes rimmed in violet, and violet sails. " 'Temperance,' " I read from the side.

Chalcey glances at me out of the corner of her eye.

I smile. "Yes, some northerners can even read."

"It's a ship of the Brothers of Succor," she says. "I go to the school of the Sisters of Clarity."

"And who are the Sisters of Clarity?" I ask.

"I thought you knew everything," she says archly. When I don't rise to this, she says, "The Sisters of Clarity are the sister order to the Order of Celestial Harmony."

"I see," I say, watching the ship glide down the river.

Testily, she adds, "Celestial Harmony is the first Navigation Order."

"Do they sail to the mainland?"

"Of course," she says, patronizing.

"What does it cost to be a passenger? Do they ever hire cargo-handlers or bookkeepers or anything like that?" I know the answer, but I can't help myself from asking.

She shrugs, "I don't know, I'm a student." Then, sly again, "I study drawing."

"That's wonderful," I mutter.

Passage *out* of here is my major concern. No one can work on a ship who isn't a member of a Navigational Order, and no order is likely to take a blond-haired northerner with a sudden vocation. Passage is expensive. Even food doesn't keep me from being depressed.

The guests begin to arrive just after sunset, while the sky is still indigo in the west. I'm in the hold with two food servers. I'm sweltering in my jacket, they're (both women) serene in their blue robes. I play simple songs. Barok comes by and says to me, "Sing some northern thing."

"I don't sing," I say.

He glares at me, but I'm not about to sing, and he can't replace me now, so that's that. But I feel guilty, so I try to be flashy, playing lots of trills, and some songs that I think might sound strange to their ears.

It's a small party, only seven men. Important men, because five boats clunk against ours. Or rich men. It's hard for me to make decisions about southerners, they act differently and I don't know what it means. For instance, southerners never say "no." So at first, I decided that they were all shifty bastards, but eventually I learned how to tell a "yes" that meant *no* from a "yes" that meant *yes*. It's not so hard—if you ask a shopkeeper if he can get you ground proyakapiti, and he says, "yes," then he *can*. If he giggles nervously and then says "yes," he's embarrassed, which means that he doesn't want you to know that he *isn't* able to get it, so you smile and say that you will be back for it later. He knows you are lying, you know he knows; you are both vastly relieved.

But these men smile and shimmer like oil, and Barok smiles and shimmers like oil, and I don't know what's cast, only that if tension were food, I could cut thick slices out of the air and dine on it.

There are no women except servers. I don't know if there are ever women at southern parties, because this is my first one. If a southern man toasts another, he cannot decline the toast without looking like a gelded stabos, so they drink a great deal of wine. After awhile, it seems to me that a man in green, ferret-thin, and a man in yellow are working together to get Barok drunk. If one of them toasts Barok, a bit later the other one does too. Barok would be drinking twice as much as they are, except that Barok himself toasts his guests, especially the ferret, a number of times, so it's hard to say. Besides, Barok is portly and can drink a great deal of wine.

But the servers are finished and cleaning up on deck, and Barok is near purple himself when he finally raps on the table for silence. I stop playing, and tap the bare sword under the serving table behind me with my foot, just to know where it is.

Barok clears a space on the long thin banquet table and claps his hands. Chalcey comes in, dressed in a robe the color of her school uniform, but with her arms and hair decently covered. The effect is nice, or would be if she didn't have that sullen, half-wit face she wears around her uncle.

She puts two rolled papers on the table, and then draws her veil close around her chin and crouches down like a proper girl. Barok opens one of the rolls, and I crane my head before the men close around it. All I get is a glimpse of one of Chalcey's squiggly-line drawings, with some writing on it. The men murmur. The man in yellow says, "What is this?"

"Galgor coast," Barok points, "Lesian and Cauldor Islands, the Liliana Strait."

Charts? Navigation charts of the Islands? How could Barok have gotten . . . or rather, how could Chalcey have drawn . . . She is studying drawing with an Order, though, isn't she? *Chalcey* drew the charts? But the Cousins have sold magic to the Navigational Orders to make sure students *can't* take out so much as a piece of paper. How does she get them out of the school?

The ferret spits on the wooden floor and I wince. "What else have you got?" the ferret asks, brusque, rude.

"Only the Liliana Straits and the Hekkhare Cove," Barok says.

"Hekkhare!" the man in blue says, "I can buy *that* off any fisherman."

"Ah, but you can compare this chart with your own charts of Hekkhare to see how my source is. And there are more coming, I can assure you." Barok fairly oozes.

"These look as if they were drawn by an amateur," ferret says. Chalcey sticks out her lower lip and beetles her eyebrows. She needs a mother around to tell her not to do that.

"If you want pretty, go to the market and buy a painting," Barok says.

"I'm not interested in artistry, I'm interested in competence," ferret snaps. "What's to say you didn't copy Hekkhare from some fisherman?" A black market in navigation charts! Maybe Barok would be able to steer me to someone who smuggled, or whatever they did with them. I might be able to work my passage out of here. "I'd like to know a little more about this source," ferret says, tapping his teeth.

"It's within one of the Orders," Barok says, "that's all I can tell you."

Yellow robe says, "You're telling me that a member of the order would sell charts? That they can counter the spellbind?"

"I didn't say a 'member of the order,' " Barok says, "I said someone *within* the order."

"This stinks," ferret says, and silently I agree.

Barok shrugs. "If you don't want them, don't take them." But the dome of his forehead is slick and shining in the lamplight.

Ferret looks at Barok. The ferret is the power in this room; the others wait on him, Barok talks to him, yellow is his flunky. These men came in boats; boats that *go* somewhere in these islands mean money, and maybe some influence with the Navigational Order. And Barok—Barok lives in a slum. A two-bit nothing trying to sell to the big lizards. Oh, Heth, I am in trouble!

Ferret contemplates, and the others wait. "All right, I'll take these to verify their validity. If these prove accurate, we'll see about the next set."

"No," Barok says, "I'm giving you Hekkhare; you pay me the 200 for Liliana."

"What if I just take the charts?" ferret asks.

"You don't know my source," Barok says, desperate.

"So? Who *else* would you sell them to? The Orders?" the ferret says, bored.

"Two hundred for Liliana," Barok says stubbornly.

Ferret rolls the charts up. "I don't think so," he says blandly.

My knees turn to water. I've fought in battle, scared off a thief in a warehouse once, but never done anything like this. Still, I start to crouch for my sword.

"Tell your barbarian to be still," ferret snaps. Yellow has a knife, so do the others. I don't need to be told again.

"These aren't free!" Barok says, "I have expenses, I—I owe people money, Sterler. I don't pay people, you'll never get another chart! They're good, I swear they're good!"

"We'll negotiate the next ones," the ferret says, and nods at the rest. They rise and start to go.

I know that Barok is going to lunge, although it is a tokking stupid thing to do. But he does it, his hands hooked to claw at ferret. I think he only wants the charts, that he can't bear to see them go, but yellow reacts instantly. I see the flash of metal from under his robe, but I don't think Barok does. It isn't a good blow, they are all drunk, and Barok is a fleshy man. The knife handle stands out of his belly at about his liver, and Barok staggers back against the table. For a moment, he doesn't know about the knife—sometimes a knife-wound feels just like a punch.

"You can't have it," he says, "I'll tell them about you!" Then he sees the knife, and the wine-colored stain on his dark robe, and his mouth opens, pink and wet and helpless.

"Find out his source," the ferret says.

Chalcey is staring, blank-faced. I do not want her to see. I remember what it is like to see.

Yellow robe takes the knife handle and holds on to it, his face only a foot or so from Barok's. I smell shit. Barok looks at him, his face slack with disbelief, and starts to blubber. Some men's minds snap when they die.

"Who gets them for you?" yellow robe asks.

Arterial blood, dark and mixed with stomach blood, pumps out around the knife. Barok is silent. Maybe Barok is refusing to betray his niece, but I think the truth is that he has lost his wits. He has certainly voided his bowels. When yellow robe twists the knife, he screams, and then blubbers some more, his saliva not yet bloodied. He wants to go to his knees, but yellow robe has the knife handle, and Barok's hung on that blade like meat on a hook.

Chalcey is crouched, wrapped in her veil. She edges backward away from the men, her hands behind her, scooting backward like a crab until she bumps into my legs and stifles a little scream.

Ferret turns to us. "What do you know?"

I shrug casually, or as casually as I can. "I was hired today; he wouldn't tell me what he hired me for."

He looks down at Chalcey. I say, "He hired her right after he hired me."

Barok begins to say, over and over again, "Stop it, stop it, please stop it," monotonously, his hands making little clutching motions at his belly, but afraid of the knife.

"Tell me your source," yellow robe says.

Barok doesn't seem to understand. "Stop it, please stop it," he whimpers. *Die,* I think. Die before you say anything, you fat old man!

"Tok it," ferret says. "You've ruined it."

I whisper to Chalcey, "Scream and try to run up the stairs."

She rolls her eyes at me, but doesn't move.

Yellow robe shouts in Barok's face, "Barok! Listen to me!" He slaps the dying man. "Who is your source? You want it to stop? Tell me your source!"

"Help me," Barok whispers. There is blood in his mouth, now. The shadows from the lamps are hard, the big red-robed belly is in the light, and he is starting to spill flesh and bowels. The smell is overwhelming; one of the men turns and vomits, and adds that to the stench.

"Tell me where you get the charts, we'll get you a healer," yellow robe says. A lie, it's too late for a healer. But a dying man has nothing to lose by believing a lie. His eyes flicker toward Chalcey. Does he even know what is happening, understand what they are demanding? He licks his lips as if about to speak. I can't let him speak. So I whistle, five clear discordant notes, to waken one of the spells in my skull, the one that eats power, light and heat, and all the lights go out.

Black. Star-magic is easy to do, hard to engineer.

"TOK!" someone shouts in the dark, and Barok screams, a high, white noise. Things fall, I push Chalcey toward the stairs and grab my sword. I'm almost too frightened to move myself; maybe if it wasn't for Chalcey, I wouldn't, but sometimes responsibility lifts me above my true nature.

I collide with someone in the dark, slap at their face with my sword, and feel something hook in my jacket, tear at my shirt and the bindings I wear under it, then burn in my side. Then the person is gone. Ferret is screaming, "The stairs! Block the stairs!" when I fall over the bottom step.

The darkness only lasts a handful of heartbeats. It's a whistler spell, better against real power like the Cousin's lights than against natural things like a lamp, and it always makes me tired later. I turn at the stairs just as the lights come back. Blinded for a moment, I slap with my sword for the flame and knock it flying. Burning oil sprays across the room, I see blue robe cover his face, and, gods help him, poor Barok squirming on the floor.

The boat is tinder dry, and instantly the pools of oil from the lamp are full of licking blue flames. I run up the stairs. Chalcey is standing—not by the gangplank but next to the rail. My pack is there, and in the pack the cloak with the badge, and my chain vest and bracers—all I own in the world. I go for the girl and the pack, my shield arm clenched against my burning side. Ferret and the others will come boiling out of the hold like digger bees at any moment. I look down over the railing and see one of the sailboats, a soft Cousins' light clipped to the mast, and, in the glow, a green-robed adolescent with a cleric's shaven head, looking up at me. I grab Chalcey's arm and shout, "Jump!" and we land on top of the poor bastard, Chalcey's shrieking and my oomph! drowning the boy's bleat of surprise. Chalcey tumbles, but I have aimed truer, breaking his arm and probably his collar bone, so that he lies stunned and wide-eyed. I pitch him out of the boat. He is struggling in the water as I shove us off. I hope to Heth he can swim; I can't.

Our boat has a simple, single sail; it's a pleasure boat rather than a real fisherman's boat, but it will have to do. I run the sail up awkwardly. The wind will drive us downriver, toward the harbor. I don't see the boats of the others.

There is no pursuit. I think that ferret and the others have cut across the gangplank rather than make for the sailboats. I crouch next to the tiller and gingerly explore my injury with my fingers, a long flat scrape that crossed the ribs before the shirt and bindings and jacket hung it up. It bleeds freely, but it's not deep.

Chalcey curls in the prow of the boat, looking back toward her uncle's boat. The fire must have eaten the wood in huge bites. When we reach the bridge, I look back and see that the boat has been cut away and floats free in the river, burning bright and pouring out black, oily smoke. Two sailboats skitter away like dragonflies, silhouettes against the flames. Then we are enveloped in black smoke and ash which hides the boat from us, and hides us from everyone else.

Coughing and hacking, and, Heth forgive me, spitting, I keep us in the smoke as long as I can.

When we are almost out of the harbor, Chalcey asks, "Where are we going?"

"I don't know," I say. "I wish we had one of your charts."

It's a clear night, we have a brisk breeze and no moon yet. A good night to escape. I follow the coast, away from the city. On the shore, dogs bark at us, and to each other, distant and lonely. The sound chains along the coast as we sail.

"Was that magic?" Chalcey says.

"Was what magic," I say absently. I'm tired and not feeling well; it is painful to cough and spit ash and soot when your side is cut open.

"When it got dark. When you whistled."

I nod in the darkness, then realize she can't see it. "Yes, that was a little magic."

"Are you a mage?"

Do I *look* like a mage? Would I be living this way if I could smelt metal, and make starstuff in bright colors, and machines and lights? "No, littleheart," I say, talking sweet because my thoughts are not nearly so patient, "I'm just a whistler. A fighter with no money and only a little skill."

"Do you think they'll get a healer for my uncle?"

No answer to give but the truth. "Chalcey, your uncle is dead."

She doesn't say anything for a long time, and then she starts to cry. It's chilly, and she's tired and frightened. It doesn't hurt her to cry. Maybe I cry a little, too; it wouldn't be the first time.

We bob along, the waves going *chop, chop, chop* against the prow of the little boat. Dogs bark, to us and to each other. Along our left, the lights from the city are fewer and fewer, the houses darker and smaller. It smells like broom trees out here, not city. In the wake of our little sailboat, craken phosphoresce. I wonder, since their light is blue, why is craken dye yellow?

Chalcey speaks out of the dark, "Could we go to my grandmother?"

"I don't know, sweet, where is your grandmother?"

"Across the Liliana Strait. On Lesian."

"If I knew where it was, I could try, even without a chart, but I'm a foreigner, littleheart."

"I can draw a chart. I drew those charts."

She sounds like a little girl. I smile tiredly into the darkness. "But I don't have anything for you to copy."

"I don't need to copy," she says. "They're in my *head*. If I have drawn a chart, even once, I never forget it. That's why my Uncle Barok brought me to the Order to go to school. But we've only practiced with Hekkhare and now Liliana Strait."

"So you drew those charts from your head?" I ask.

"Of course." She tosses her hair, her veil around her shoulders, and I can see her against the sky, just for the moment the imperious and sly girl who tried to impress the northern barbarian. "Everybody thinks that the charts are safe, all the paper and everything is spellbound. But I don't carry any papers or anything; it's all in my head."

"Chalcey," I breathe. "Can you draw one?"

"We don't have any paper, and it's dark."

"We'll land in a few hours and get some sleep. Then you can use my knife and draw it on the bottom of the boat."

"On the bottom of the boat?" She is diffident.

But I'm elated. Two people hiding from the rest of the island, in a small sailboat not meant for the open sea, going on a young girl's memory of a chart. But it's better than *Barok*'s choices.

We have a fair breeze, the little sailboat is quiet except for the slap of the sail. The water is close, right at my hand. Chalcey says she's cold. I tell her to dig my cloak out of my pack and see if she can get some sleep.

I think she sleeps awhile. I keep pushing us on, thinking to go a little farther before we rest, passing places to pull the boat up, until I see the line of gray that means dawn and take us into a stream that cuts down to the ocean.

"Chalcey," I say, "when the boat stops, jump out and pull."

We come aground, and I try to stand up, and nearly fall over. My legs are numb from crouching, and my side has stiffened in the night.

"What's wrong?" Chalcey says, holding the prow to get out.

"Nothing," I say, "be careful when you get out of the boat."

The cold water is up to my waist and makes me gasp, but at the prow, Chalcey is in water only to her shins. I grit my teeth and push, sliding against the uneven bottom, and she pulls, and together we get the boat well aground. I lash it to a tree, the tide is still coming in and I don't want to lose it, and then I grab my pack and stumble up the bank.

I should check the area, but I ache and I'm exhausted, so tired. I'm a little dizzy, so I promise myself I'll only rest for a minute. I prop my head against the pack and close my eyes. The world swirls. . . .

• • •

Some tokking hero, I think, and then laugh. That's one quality to which I have never aspired.

We're in heavy trees, tall pale yellow fronds of broom trees, heavily tasseled at this time of year. I'm covered with chukka bites, and the cut in my side is hot; I can feel my pulse beating in it.

There's no sign of Chalcey.

I lever myself painfully up on my elbow and listen. Nothing. Could she have wandered off and gotten lost?

"Chalcey," I hiss.

No answer.

"Chalcey!" I say, louder.

"Here!" comes a voice from over the bank, and then her head pops up, floating above the soft lemon brush as if it had been plopped on a bush. Maybe I'm feverish.

"Are you in the water?" I ask.

"No," she says, "I'm in the boat. What's your name, anyway?"

"Jahn," I say.

"I took your knife, but you didn't wake up. Are you—" she hesitates, wide-eyed, and my heart lurches, "I mean, is your hurt bad?"

"No," I say, attempting to sit up naturally and failing.

"I drew a chart in the bottom of the boat, and then I used mud to make the lines darker." She shakes her head, "Drawing with a knife isn't the same as drawing with a pen."

She comes up on the bank, and we breakfast on boxfruit and red peanuts out of my pack. Breakfast and water improve my spirits immensely. I check Chalcey's drawing. She clenches her hands nervously while I look at it. As soon as a wave puts a little water in the bottom of the boat, the mud will wash out of the lines, and I have no way of judging how accurate it might be anyway, but I tell her it looks wonderful.

To hide her pleasure, she turns her head and spits matter-of-factly into the stream. I wince, but don't say anything.

We have nothing to store water in.

"How far is it to Lesian?" I ask.

She thinks it's about two days. "Jahn," she says, self-conscious about my name, "where did you learn your magic?"

"One of the Cousins put copper and glass in the bones of my head," I say. Not exactly true, but close enough.

That silences questions for awhile.

We get some good drinks of water and relieve ourselves, and maybe she prays to her deities, I don't know. Then we raise our pineapple-green sail, and we are off.

She chatters awhile about school. I like listening to her chatter. When it gets hot at midday, I have her spread my cloak across the prow and crawl into the shade underneath it. I stay with the tiller and wish for a hat. I've been browned by the sun, but the light off the green water is blinding and bright, and my nose suffers.

She sleeps during the heat of the day, and I nod. We are headed for a promontory which marks where we cut across the strait. In the afternoon, we have some bruised boxfruit out of my pack, which helps our thirst a bit. The way west is suddenly blocked by a spit of land; if Chalcey's drawing can be trusted, that's our promontory. Chalcey's chart indicates that it's not good to go ashore here, otherwise I'd stop for fresh water. We head for open sea, and I pray that the breeze holds up. I'm stiff, and tacking accurately all the way across is probably beyond my navigational skills.

I'm thirsty; Chalcey must be, too. She doesn't complain, but she gets quiet. The farther we go into the strait, the smaller the land behind us gets; the smaller the land, the quieter she gets. Once I ask her what the crossing was like when she came to live with her uncle. "It was a big boat," is all she'll say.

I'm light-headed from sun and thirst and fever by the time evening comes, and the cool is a relief. The sun goes down with the sudden swiftness of the south. I dig the pigeon's egg dumplings out of my pack, but they're too salty and just make me thirstier. Chalcey is hungry, though, and eats hers and half of mine.

"Jahn?" she says.

"Yes?"

"The Cousins—why do they call them that?"

"Because we are all kin," I say. "It is like in my home, when a place gets too big, and there isn't enough land to let all the stabos graze, part of the kin go somewhere else, and start a new home. Our many times elders were the Cousins. The stars are like islands for them. Some came here to live, but there was a war and the ships no longer came, and our elders' ships grew too old, and we forgot about the Cousins except for stories. Now they have found us again."

"And they help us?" she asks.

"Not really," I say. "They help the high-ons, mostly."

"What are 'high-ons'?" she asks. Southern doesn't have a word for high-ons, so I always just use the two southern words.

"High-ons, the old men who run things and have silver. Or the guilds, they are like high-ons."

"Were you a high-on?" she asks.

I laugh, which hurts my side. "No, littleheart," I say. "I am the unlucky child of unlucky parents. They believed that some of the Cousins would help us, would teach us. But the high-ons, they don't like it if anyone else has strength. So they sent an army and killed my kin. Things were better before the Cousins came."

"The Order says that the Cousins are good; they bring gifts."

"We *pay* for those gifts," I say. "With craken dye and ore and land. And with our own ways. Anywhere the Cousins come, things get bad."

It gets darker. Chalcey wraps herself in my cloak, and I hunch over the tiller. It isn't that the boat needs much sailing; there's a light wind and the sea is blessedly calm (someone seems to favor us, despite our attack on the green-robed boy to get this boat), but the boat is too small for me to go anywhere else, so I sit at the tiller.

The spray keeps the back of my left shoulder damp, and the breeze seems to leach the warmth out of me. My teeth start chattering.

"Chalcey?"

"What?" she murmurs sleepily from the prow.

"I am feeling a bit under, littleheart. Do you think you could sit with me and we could share the cloak?"

I can feel her hesitation in the dark. She's afraid of me, and that pains me. It's funny, too, considering. "I don't want anything other than warmth," I say gently.

She feels her way slowly from the prow. "It's *your* cloak," she says, "you can have it if you want."

"I think we can share it," I say. "Sit next to me, the tiller will be between us, and you can lean against me and sleep."

Gingerly, she sits down next to me, the boat rocking gently with her movements, and throws the cloak around our shoulders. She touches my arm on the tiller and jerks back. "You're hot," she says. Then she surprises me by touching my forehead. "You have a fever!"

"Don't worry about it," I say, oddly embarrassed. "Just sit here." She curls against me, and, after a few minutes, she leans her head on my shoulder. Her hair smells sweet. It's soothing to have her there. I try to keep the constellation southerners call the Crown to my right.

"How old are you?" she asks.

"Thirty-one," I say.

"That's not so old."

I laugh.

"Well," she is defensive, "you have white hair, but your face isn't old."

Sometimes I feel very old, and never more than now.

I jerk awake from scattered dreams of being back on Barok's boat. It's dawn. Chalcey stirs against my shoulder and settles again. I think about the sea, about our journey. Celestial navigation is not my strong point; I hope we haven't drifted too much. I hope that Chalcey's chart is good, and I wonder how much Barok will get paid for a boat with a chart carved on it, even if the chart isn't very good, but blue flames lick the chart, and I'm on Barok's boat again. . . .

I jerk awake. My fever feels low; because it's morning, I'm certain. I try to open my pack without disturbing Chalcey, but she's asleep against my right shoulder, and I'm awkward with my left hand and my side is stiff, so after a moment she straightens up. We have five boxfruit left, so we split one. I'm too thirsty for red peanuts, but Chalcey eats a few.

As the sun climbs, so does my fever, and I start dreaming even when my eyes are open. At one point, Trevin is in the boat with us, sitting there in his blue jerkin with the gray fur low on the shoulders, and I must be talking to him, because Chalcey says, "Who is Trevin?"

I blink and lean over the side and splash cold water on my sunburned face. When I sit up, I'm dizzy from the blood rushing to my head, but I know where I am. "Trevin was a friend," I say. "He's dead now."

"Oh," she says, and adds, with the callousness of youth, "How did he die?"

How did Trevin die? I have to think. "The flux," I say. "We were marching to Bashtoy, we were retreating, Trevin and I had decided to fight against Scalthalos High-on since he'd burned out Sckarline. It was winter, and we didn't have much to eat, and the people who got sick, many of them died." I add, "I joined the fight because of Trevin." I don't add, "I was in love."

When it gets hot, Chalcey soaks her veil in water and covers my head with it. I clutch the tiller. It seems that I am not sailing the boat so much as it is sailing me. She doles out the boxfruit, too, peeling them and splitting the purple segments.

"I think," she says, "that maybe I should look at your side."

"No," I say.

"Don't worry," she says, moving toward me in the boat.

"No," I snap.

"I could put some cool seawater on it," she says. "Saltwater is good for an injury."

"I don't take off my shirt," I say. I'm irrational and I know it, but I'm not going to take off my shirt. Not when someone is around. We were finally in Bashtoy and almost everyone I knew was dead, and the Militia-Master said, "Boy, what's your name?" and I didn't know that he was talking to me. "Boy!" he shouted, "what's your name!" and I stuttered "Jahn, sir." "We'll call you Jahn-the-clever," he said, "you're in my group now," and the others laughed, and after that I was Jahn-the-clever until they discovered that I was really clever, but I still wasn't going to take off my shirt.

My thoughts run like squirrels in a cage, and sometimes I talk out loud. Trevin comes back. He asks, "Would you rather have grown up anywhere but Sckarline?"

Chalcey soaks her veil in water and tries to keep my face cool.

"Wanji taught us about the cities," I say, "and she was right. I've been there, Trevin." My voice is high. "Wherever the Cousins come, they use us, they live like Scalthalos High-on, and we clean their houses and are grateful for light and giz stick on Sixth-day night. People don't care about kin anymore, they don't care about anything. Wanji told us about culture clash, that the weaker culture dissolves."

"Wanji and Aneal, Ayuedesh and Kumar, they dedicated their lives to helping us," Trevin says.

"Aneal *apologized* to me, Trevin!" I say. "She apologized for the terrible wrong they had done! She said it would be better if they never came!"

"I know," he said.

"Jahn," Chalcey says. "Jahn, there's nobody here but *me!* Talk to me! Don't die!" She is crying. Her veil is wet, and so cold it takes my breath away.

Trevin didn't know. I never told him about Aneal apologizing, I never told anyone. I blink and he wavers, and I blink and blink and he goes away. "You're not Trevin," I say, "I'm arguing with myself."

It's bright and hot.

I have my head on my arm.

The sky is lavender and red, and there is a dark stripe across the water that I can't make go away, no matter how hard I blink. I think that the fever is making my vision go, or that the sun has made me blind, until Chalcey, crying, says that it is Lesian.

There is no place to land, so we head up the coast northeast until we come to a river. "Go up here!" Chalcey says. "I know this place! I know that marker!" She is pointing to a pile of stone. "My grandmother lives up here!"

The night comes down around us before we see a light, like a cooking fire. I call instructions to shift the sail in a cracked voice; Chalcey has quick hands, thank Heth.

I run the boat aground, and Chalcey leaps out, calling and pulling at the boat, but I can't move. People come down and stand looking at us, and Chalcey says that her grandmother is Llasey. In the village they know her grandmother, although her grandmother lives a long walk away. I have a confused sense of being helped out of the boat, and I tell them,

"We have silver, we can pay." Blur of people in the dark, and then into a place where there is too much light.

Then they are forcing hot seawater between my teeth, I can't drink it, then I think, "It's broth." The fire flickers off a whitewashed wall, and a bareheaded woman says, "Let me help you."

I don't want them to take off my shirt. "Not my shirt!" I say, raising my hands. They are talking and I can't follow what they are saying, but with gentle persistent hands they deftly hold my wrists and peel off the torn jacket and the shirt. The gentle voice says, "What's *this?*" and cuts the bindings on my chest.

Chalcey says, startled, "What's *wrong* with him!" I turn my face away.

A woman smiles at me and says, "You'll be all right, dear." Chalcey stares at me, betrayed, and the woman says to her (and to me), "She's a woman, dear. She'll be all right, there's nothing wrong with her except a bit of fever and too much sun."

And, so, stripped, I slide defenseless into sleep, thinking of the surprise on Chalcey's face.

I sleep a great deal during the next two days, wake up and drink soup, and sleep again. Chalcey isn't there when I wake up, although there is a pallet of blankets on the floor. And perhaps if I wake up and hear her, I pretend to be asleep and soon sleep again. But eventually I can't sleep anymore. Tuwle, the woman with the gentle hands who has given me a bed, asks me if I want a shirt or a dress, and, running my hand over my cropped hair, I say a shirt. But I tell her to call me Jahnna.

They bring me my shirt, neatly mended. And they won't take my silver.

Finally, Chalcey comes to see me. I am sitting on the bed where I have slept so long, shucking beans. It embarrasses me to be caught in shirt and breeches, shucking beans, although I've shucked beans, mended clothes, done all manner of woman's work in men's clothes. But it has been a long time since I've felt so self-conscious.

She comes in, tentative as a bird, and says, "Jahn?"

So I say, "Sit down," and immediately regret it, since there is no place to sit but next to me on the bed.

We go through the old routine of "how are you feeling?" and "what have you been doing?" She holds her veil tightly, although the women here don't go veiled for everyday.

Finally she says, in a hurt little voice, "You could have *told* me."

"I haven't told anyone in years." In a way, I almost didn't think I *was* a woman anymore.

"But I'm not just *any*one!" She is vexed. And how could she know that in a fight you become close comrades, yes, but that we know nothing about each other?

The snap of beans seems very loud. I think of trying to explain, about cutting my hair off to fight with Trevin, and learning long before Trevin died that fighting makes people strangers to themselves. Heth says life hinges on little things, like the fact that I am tall for a woman and flat-chested, and when the MilitiaMaster at Bashtoy saw me, half-starved and shorthaired, he thought that I was a boy, and so after that I *was*. Snap. And I run my thumb down the pod and the beans spill into the bowl.

To break the silence, she says, "Your sunburn is almost gone," and, amazingly, she blushes scarlet.

I realize then how it is with her. She had fancied herself in love. "I'm sorry, littleheart," I say, "I didn't intend to hurt or embarrass you. I'm embarrassed, too."

She looks at me sideways. "What do you have to be embarrassed about?"

"It's a little like having no clothes on, everybody knowing, and now that my kin are gone, I am always a stranger, wherever I go—" but she is looking at me without comprehension, so I falter and say lamely, "It's hard to explain."

"What are you going to do now?" she asks.

I sigh. That is a question that has been on my mind a great deal. Here there is no chance of saving passage money to get back to the mainland. "I don't know."

"I told my grandmother about you," Chalcey says. "She said you could come and stay with us, if you would work hard. I said you were very strong." Again she blushes scarlet, and hurries on, "It's a little farm, it used to be better, but there's only my grandmother, but we could help, and I think we could be friends."

As I learned during the long walk to Bashtoy, you may be tokked, but if you just look to the immediate future, sometimes, eventually, you find the way.

"I'd like that, littleheart," I say, meaning every word. "I'd like to be friends."

The future, it seems, does indeed hinge on little things.

G. David Nordley

POLES APART

G. David Nordley is a retired air force officer and astronautical engineer who has become a frequent contributor to *Analog* in the last few years, winning that magazine's Analytical Laboratory readers' poll in 1992 for his story "Poles Apart"; he also won the same award for his story "Into the Miranda Rift" in 1993. He has also sold stories to *Asimov's Science Fiction, Tomorrow, Mindsparks,* and elsewhere. He lives in Sunnyvale, California.

Like Varley, Nordley is another writer who finds the solar system an exotic enough setting for adventures just as it is, as he's demonstrated with stories of exploration and conflict on a grand scale, such as "Into the Miranda Rift," "Crossing Chao Meng Fu," "Out of the Quiet Years," "Dawn Venus," "Comet Gypsies," "Alice's Asteroid," "The Day of Their Coming," "Messengers of Chaos," and others; many of these stories make effective use of the latest astronomical and space probe data, data that shows just how bizarre, complex, surprising, and mysterious a place our solar system really is, a far cry from the conception of the solar system as a dull collection of rock, ice, and cinders that was common in the seventies. He's also moved out of the solar system to the strange alien planet Trimus, a planet settled by three radically different alien races working in concert, for stories such as "Network," "Final Review," and the swashbuckling story of cultures and racial attitudes in conflict that follows, "Poles Apart," a story that owes much to the tradition of writers such as Hal Clement, James H. Schmitz, and H. Beam Piper, and yet which has been filtered through a wry, shrewd, hardheaded sensibility that's Nordley's alone.

Nordley has yet to publish a novel, although a fix-up of the "Trimus" stories shouldn't be that hard to produce. A story collection is also long overdue, although none is forthcoming. Until then, you'll just have to look for him in the magazines, where he will surely continue to deliver solid and suspenseful science fiction adventures, based in accurate science but with a strong Sense of Wonder kick, for years to come.

. . . to establish a single planetary society in which all three spacefaring races take
equal part: to find and develop common standards of civilized behavior, which may
serve as a model for galactic civilizations to come.

—Compact and Charter of the Planet Trimus, Preamble

The human ship, almost four Charter units long with a huge square
cloth sail, was new to Lieutenant Drinnil'ib. What, he wondered, were
primitivists doing this far north? He hailed the ship, but instead of a verbal response, his voice brought a scurrying of the small two-legged beings around its deck. Before he could repeat the hail, a sharp, explosive,
report split the air and something with a singing line attached went
"thwunk" into the sea beside him.

What in the name of the Compact? he thought. The line brushed over
his nose and he stuck his tongue out to grab and examine it. The line
came under tension, and he let it slide through his manipulators until the
end came along.

Pollution! The thing was sharp. It nicked the muscular fingers on one
fork of his tongue before he clamped down on the line with the other,
forcing the humans to try to reel him in with it. That should slow things
down a bit, he thought. He raised a front claw and wrapped the line
around it to ease the strain on his tongue. Then he held the object in front
of his eyes. It was solid metal of some sort, and barbed: something that
could have killed him if it had hit him in the wrong spot.

The thought and his reaction were almost simultaneous; he snapped
his tail and bent his body downward. Not an eighth of a heartbeat later a
tinny pop reached him through the water and another of the things zapped
by. They *were* trying to kill him!

He let go, pulled a knife from his pouch, and slashed the line between
the barbed missile and his foot. Then he swam first toward and then away
from the ship, holding the line with his foot, and felt a satisfying give in
the line after it jerked taut. He had some momentary misgivings—humans were fragile and he might have hurt one. But perhaps not: the tension on the line resumed quickly. Another slash of the knife took care of
that. Drinnil'ib shook the remains of the rope from his claw, dove beneath
the ship, and kept pace just below its hull.

Reaching back to his pouch, he replaced the knife with his gun and contemplated the plank belly of the offending vessel. Two, he thought, could play perforation. It took ten explosive rounds to put a fair-sized hole in the hull; the layers of polluting timbers were a twelfth of a Charter unit thick. But when he was finished, the ship was leaking so badly it would have to head for port too quickly to bother any other Do'utian.

Satisfied, he breached the surface immediately behind the ship, fired a shot in the air and roared a challenge: "I am planetary monitor Lieutenant Drinnil'ib and you have just assaulted me. What in the name of eternal repudiation do you think you are doing?"

Shouts sounded and sails rose. He grabbed the rudder of the ship with his front foot and wiggled it vigorously. Finally a face surrounded by reddish hair appeared over the railing on the rear of the boat.

"What in hell are you doing here, Monitor?" it shouted at him. "This is primitive territory—you damn techs are supposed to leave us alone."

"Not when people start getting killed," Drinnil'ib replied in a more conversational tone. "You can play your games but you have to observe the limits."

"Don't screw around in what you techs can't understand," it yelled. "Just leave us alone!"

Drinnil'ib rocked the ship again. "You're going to sink right here if you don't acknowledge that you can't sail around shooting people wherever you are. It's against the Compact."

"All right, all right, I hear you. Shooting at you was a big mistake. But next time, stay out of human whaling waters, Fish-man."

The polluting idiot didn't seem to show a trace of remorse, however Drinnil'ib thought he might be misinterpreting their body language. Just to be sure they didn't misinterpret *his,* Drinnil'ib gave the harpoonists something very easy to understand: he emptied his lungs of moisture-filled air right at them, soaking the speaker and sails. Then he kicked the ship away in disgust and sounded. Ten Charter units deep Drin put the barb in an evidence wrap, exchanged his gun for his communicator, and filed his report. He'd just gotten an object lesson on how some of the killings might have happened, but he would need human help to get to the bottom of it. A good excuse to look up an old colleague. With measured beats of his muscular tail, he headed for the northern reaches of the western continent.

As the tide-locked satellite of a superjovian infrared primary, Trimus has three symmetry axes: north-south, east-west, and inner-outer. This gives it three sets of geographic poles and three distinct climatic regions that allow for all three species to live in comfort. The arctic and antarctic match similar regions on Do'utia. The cool region surrounding the far pole matches the climate of the most populated areas of Kleth. The Earth-like near hemisphere is warmed both by Aurum and Ember, and ranges from temperate near the east and west poles to tropical directly beneath Ember. Trimus's close orbit about Ember gives it an effective day which is about twice the day of the Kleth homeworld, one and a half times that of Earth, and three times that of Do'utia. For the last, however, what counts is the 407–day polar season cycle produced by the half-radian inclination of Trimus's orbit to the local ecliptic, and this is almost the same as on Do'utia.

—Planet Monitor's Handbook, Introduction

The morning sun was a tiny red ball in the mists next to the great ruddy crescent of Ember, as Drinnil'ib propelled himself upstream toward the human city with powerful tail strokes. The murders, he thought, struck at the purpose of Trimunian civilization by pitting one species against another.

Trimus was supposed to be the galactic laboratory for peaceful interspecies cooperation. But Ember had circled Aurum eight-cubed times since its settlement, and only the collective memory of the Kleth and the mechanical memories of the Humans went back that far. Some, he knew, felt this purpose had faded along with the need for experiment; preempted by distances of time and space so great that the residents of Trimus no longer represented the cultures that sent them. If they ever had, he thought wryly. Beings who would leave their home worlds forever to take part in an idealistic interstellar experiment may have had more in common with each other than with their various contemporaries.

But as far as Drin was concerned, the millennial-old civilization of Trimus had become its own reason for existence. Forget the rest of the galaxy and their occasional starships: to survive in peace with each other and their planet, its residents had to put the discipline of reason ahead of the natural inclination to group things by shape. To be a monitor was a calling, and he had no greater loyalty than to his world and its ideals, except, perhaps, to reason itself.

Headquarters said that Mary Pierce would be waiting for him at the marina landing past the watchtower at the base of the main channel bar, wherever that was . . . there! He caught the echo and eased himself to the right and into the deep cool channel. The harbor bottom was a backwater fairyland of human bubbles and Earth-life reefs, and the channel led through that like a wide black road. At its end, the cigar shapes of human submarines lay in a neat row, safe on the bottom from the winter ice. He put his legs down, released a bubble to settle himself firmly on the concrete, and with even measured strides hoisted his body into the warm air of the eastern continent.

A tiny tailless being, much smaller than the arrogant, hairy-faced barbarian that had cursed him earlier, waited for him at the end of the ramp, covered with a form-hugging cloth that Drinnil'ib knew was an even better insulator than his doci-thick blubber.

"Afternoon, Drin?" it called, the high pitch indicating it was a human female.

"Greetings," he rumbled and reached forward with one of the branches of his tongue to shake her hand. The familiar taste of the air around her put him at ease. "Mary? I'm sorry but it must be eight years since we last met. It's really good to see you again."

Now that he knew it was her, it was easy to pick out the subtle individual characteristics of her almost naked simian face and match them to his memory; the slight bend in the cartilaginous growth that housed her nostrils, the upturned angle of the hair on the upper ridge of her eye sockets, and its yellow-white color framing her face. It was a clean face, unmarred by any unnatural growth or scar, and he knew other humans considered her beautiful. He would agree, judging from the esthetics of functionality, and also from the esthetics of the curve.

"You look pretty magnificent yourself, chum," she responded, but then shook her head. "I only wish the occasion was a happier one."

He bobbed his massive head in the planetary convention of assent. "Five more dead, four Do'utian and one human."

"Butchered?"

"Neatly, intelligently, as last time, except the human. The sea left too little of him to tell. But this," he held up the barbed projectile, "may be at the bottom of it."

"Primitivist hunters?"

Drinnil'ib hooted. "Not primitive enough, it seems. This was propelled by chemical explosives."

There were always some from every species, from every generation, romantics who wanted to live in the reserved areas by their instincts without having to learn the science and culture that got their ancestors to Trimus. A disease of the character, he thought, which could not be eliminated without eliminating character itself.

"I am sorry, Drin," Mary said, "for what our children have done. They form communities, the communities evolve, get recruits, and no one seems to care. Some of those places haven't been visited in a century."

Drin gave a sigh of toleration. "It is in your nature to hunt and in ours to endure the hazards of the sea. But without a trained intellect to guide, any race . . ."

She shook her tiny head in negation. "Some things are *wrong,* and always have been. Everywhere for everyone. Killing is one. They know the Compact, that's a minimum for letting them go out there. So it's up to us to find which 'they' are responsible and take corrective action." She shrugged her shoulders and spread her arms. "A policeman's lot is not a happy one."

A quote he didn't recognize, but one that fit. Lieutenant Drin bobbed his head again.

"Oh, the duty can be interesting."

"Ha! Well, my sub's ready to go; we can leave any time," she said. "But I thought you might like to try Cragun's sushi before we head out." She bared the exquisite miniature ivory chisels of her teeth to him in a human gesture of good feeling. Was there, he wondered, some art in this reminder that both of them were occasional carnivores? He would have to ask her on the journey. Meanwhile, the sushi sounded most pleasant. He hoped they could find a cubic doci of their rice wine to go with it. About one of their traditional "gallons," if he recalled: "And a, um, gallon or two of, um, sake? To go with it?"

She laughed. "Just what I was thinking, Drin. Let's go."

The "Charter unit" is identical to the Kleth "glide," precisely eight to the eighth times the wavelength of the strongest line of neutral sodium (also approximately the peak wavelength of Aurum's spectrum). This is about a traditional Do'utian "tail," once related to the length of the average Do'utian, or almost ten human "meters," once defined as 1/23,420 (1/10,000, base 10) the distance from the equator of Earth to its north pole. The common "doci" (from duo-octi) is 1/100 of this, about the size of the adult hand of any of the three races.

—Planet Monitor's Handbook, Appendix C

Glensville, on the northing Graham River, was easily cool enough in winter to be a congenial tropical vacation spot. He just had to remember to move slowly to avoid building up too much body heat. Great banks of melting snow lined the road, and ice covered the dozen park lakes scattered among the stone and wood human hives. Cheerful humans sliding on long flat boards attached to their feet waved to him as he ambled down the main road with Mary.

Cragun's was one of the few above-water taverns on the eastern continent that was set up to serve Do'utians. There were two there when he arrived with Mary: the poet Shari'inadel and a large Do'utian man with fresh white scars on his flukes and a deep, raw crescent behind his blowhole. Those were unusual wounds for this area—the sort of wound that one got in a beak fight with another Do'utian. So, Drin thought, this Do'utian must be a primitivist of sorts—the kind that got his jollies on the southern beaches and came back every now and then to partake of the benefits of civilization.

The other turned its head, saw him, and hissed. Most impolite, and for what reason? Drin's lack of scars? His civilized bearing? His human companion? But this was a human town!

"I do not know you," Drin stated formally. "I am Monitor Lieutenant Drinnil'ib and I ask respect."

"Gota'lannshk. The sea has been generous with you, pretty monitor. But don't press your luck, beachmeat." The voice was a slurring, low-pitched rumble.

Drunk. Spoiling for a fight. Drin gave the other a sharp warning hiss, then turned away to ignore the reaction and cool his own rising irritation. He heard no response.

"You don't like him, do you?" Mary whispered.

"I've never met the man," Drin replied, beak shut, letting the words escape softly through the fleshy corner of his mouth. "But what he is does not swim well in my thoughts. His companion is a poet, named Shari. I know the family—she's their first egg in two centuries, and quite indulged. She could be just the sort of dissatisfied romantic that runs off for glandular adventures in the south, and then lives to regret it. I think she is being 'offered' a place in that ogre's harem."

"Her choice, isn't it?" Mary asked.

"Choice implies an intellectual process, but he's playing on her instincts. Look at that one, and do not judge human rustics so harshly. He appears to have engaged in mortal combat for the fun of it."

Mary coughed. "Drin, Cragen's has some giant squid fresh from the farm. I'll split it with you, 999 parts to you, 1 to me."

"Can you eat that much?" Drin rumbled. After his journey, a meal ashore would be welcome.

"Try me!"

"You're on." Drin made the order. "Someday I'd like to try this squid in its native ocean, though." A fantasy of his; when would he ever find time in his life for a round trip of ninety years?

"That's where you'd have to eat it. You're too fat to walk around on Earth." She had a point. Twice the gravity of Trimus would have disadvantages, and he had been gaining a bit lately. Well, he'd swim that off on this trip.

"Maybe you underestimate me," he rumbled. Cragen's did not, however. The squid arrived—more than enough for even his appetite.

They talked strategy. The nearest concentration of humans who might know something lived on the islands near the warm inner pole. Whether or not these folk pinpointed the murderers, Drin made clear that he would need to talk to the Do'utian exiles near the south pole; to placate, to gather evidence, or both. Then would come the older human communities on the southern edge of the undeveloped West Continent.

"Cities of stone, ships of wood. Reports of warfare and slavery."
Mary shook her head. "At the very least, they need to be reminded of the
Compact."

"That was certainly my experience," Drin agreed.

A common civilization requires a common language, common measurements, and
places where all three species can meet comfortably. Human English shall be the
common language because it is the only language all three races can pronounce ac-
ceptably. Numbers and measurements shall be in the Kleth octal system, which is
easiest to learn, is compatible with cybernetic binary systems, and is more widespread than human base ten or Do'utian base twelve. Common architecture will follow Do'utian proportions, so that Do'utians will not be excluded from the social
interaction needed for a common civilization.

—The Compact and Charter of Planet Trimus, Article 6

The journey to the inner pole archipelago left Drin fit and trim, and
he enjoyed the taste of the exotic tropical fish. But to reach the island,
they left the cold south-flowing bottom current and he felt like he was
gliding through a hot bath. He looked forward to the south polar waters,
and sent an almost joyful greeting to Mary when he caught the wake-
sound of her submarine returning from her inquiries.

Nominally, the archipelago would have been reserved for Kleth primitivists, but they were very few and needed little land, so warm-loving
human refugees from technological civilization had gradually spread
among the islands. Here, near the inner pole, the infrared radiation from
Ember came in almost directly overhead, almost doubling the distant orange sun's modest daily contribution. The more or less permanent high-
pressure system kept skies clear unless the night fog rolled in. But it was
clear tonight, and the gibbous, pink-belted almost-star dominated the
zenith.

"Were there any witnesses?" Drin asked as Mary came alongside.
She was lounging on the deck behind the submarine's pilot house, and the
last rays of setting Aurum painted her a rich gold. She had no need for
her insulating garment, and he watched muscles play under her thin epi-
dermis as she got up to greet him. A strange shape, yet one that fit its
owner as well as any in nature.

"No witnesses—not really that many people around. I found one man
who heard about some whalers and got him to tell me he's seen them even
in tropical waters. Says they're operating out of a city on a half-flooded
volcanic island off the southern edge of the West Continent reserve. I
checked the recon and there *is* some sort of primitive city there. Hasn't
been visited by monitors for years."

"Were the people forthcoming?"

She shook her head. "There aren't many people here, and those who are here act frightened. I had to offer, well, an incentive to the only person who admitted knowing anything."

"I'm surprised the area isn't more heavily populated. This must be close to the original human climate, you don't seem to need artificial insulation here."

"No, we don't. And it does feel good!" She shook herself and her flesh rippled in a way that reminded him of a jellyfish, but much faster. "But it's enervating. Most people's minds need more stimulation from their environment. The people who live here don't even ask to replace the occasional death—children are too much work. They just live for pleasure."

Ages ago, Drin remembered, humans had arranged their genes to be infertile without deliberate medical intervention as a population-control measure to go along with anti-aging measures. The idea of being constantly driven to act out the reproduction process horrified him, but humans apparently enjoyed it. Of course it wasn't as messy with them.

Mary shook herself again. "Cooling off now, though. Time to kiss lotus land good-bye."

She waved and vanished down the submarine's hatch. They sounded together and slanted west toward the cold current and their joint adventure.

Half a day later his dorsal ganglia were running things while he was deep in thought about just how primitive things could get. He understood much of the attraction of the undeveloped areas. All space-faring people were descendants of those for whom the unbuilt beach and the untrod planet exerted an irresistible call. But his last trip had been eye-opening in other ways.

He had little basis for comparing what he'd seen to the depth of cultural degeneration Mary said she had experienced on her hothouse island, but all the same, he shuddered to think of what she would find on the shores of the south polar continent. At least humans without machines could still construct buildings. Ancient Do'utian women had mated and calved on the open beach. Without shelter, their retrogressing descendents would have no choice but to do the same. Despite himself, a shudder of prurient interest ran from his chest through his tail at the thought of beaches of nubile young mothers, blatantly receptive in the free air.

"Lieutenant Drin?" Daydreaming! How long had Mary been calling him?

With the flick of the tail, he glided over to the submarine and brought his right eye up to the center of the diamond hull. Its electric drive fields made him tingle as they pushed seawater toward its tail.

"Lost in thought, I'm afraid. What do you have?"

Mary was back in her artificial skin and all business. "Here's the recon on that primitive city." A relief map appeared on the holoscreen next to her. The flooded caldera surrounded a lagoon on three sides, and the fourth appeared to be filled in by a simple stone dike. Large and small masonry buildings lined the shore of the lagoon.

"Mary, I think the cold current must flow by there, see the trench to the south?"

"Yes. Good eating?"

"It should be, and if so, we should find some Do'utian primitives nearby. I suggest we stay with the plan, head south first and gain what intelligence we can from the victim population before confronting this set of potential perpetrators. . . . Mary?"

"Yes, Drin?"

"In our early days, there were tests for reproductive rights. Death swims and beach fights. Bloodlust beyond reason. These occasional hunting deaths seem, in a way, like some of those old tests. I fear I will not be proud of how some of the Do'utian back-to-nature crowd might be living."

"Do you fear more than embarrassment?"

Yes, he needed to say. Yes I fear my own primitive instincts. So why did he hesitate to tell her? Mary was a friend and colleague, and any infirmity on his part could affect the mission.

"Mary . . . we have never needed to revise our mating instincts. In our cities, with the privacy of our rooms, there is no need. In fact, we must make an effort to replace those of our colony who are lost by accident—an embarrassing and very private effort for both beings concerned. But with everything out in the open . . . I'm not sure how I will—"

Peals of musical laughter twinkled like bells from the hull of her ship, for so long that Drin became concerned for her health. Finally, she pressed herself to the transparent hull.

"Drin, my friend . . . look, don't tell what I'm going to tell you to any other human, especially the other monitors, OK?"

"My word on it," Drin said, curiosity clawing at him.

"Well," she laughed, "in order to be accepted and get information I kind of went native. I allowed—hell, Drin, I enticed—my source to perform our mating act with me. I mean I was all there, and he was all there, and it just felt like the natural thing to do. In the line of duty, I told myself."

Drin swam in silence for a while thinking that to say the wrong thing would be harmful to his friend. But he soon realized that to say nothing at all could seem even worse. He reviewed what he knew of human mating. "Was this person physically suitable?"

This occasioned more laughter. "He was. Oh, yes. Exceedingly so."

"And you left this pleasure to return to your duty with me? I find this very admirable and hope, to the extent that we can compare our temptations, that I shall be able to exhibit similar moral strength."

"Moral strength? Drin, you are a forked-tongued devil."

After a moment, he realized this was a compliment. He gently pressed a shoulder to the window so that only the eighth of a doci or so of diamond hull separated their bodies. He easily felt the warmth of her flesh through this transparent, uninsulated section. This communication of friendship had no intellectual hazards.

But his mind returned to duty. "Perhaps," he rumbled after a while, "we should ask the Kleth Monitors for backup in case we find we need eyes overhead when we visit this city. I know a certain Officer Do Tor who has a sense of humor and does not dump everything into their racial memory."

"Perhaps," Mary laughed again. "I think I met him when the last starship visited, six years ago. Gold wings, silver crest? Flighty little yellow thing under his claw?"

"The very one."

"Why not? The more the merrier."

Following planetary engineering, only the north, east, and outer poles will be intensively settled. The remainder of the planet will be reserved for biological study and kept free of large settlements or significant technological effluents. The primary objective will be to observe how the three merged ecosystems evolve from their original design point. Low-intensity visitation, consistent with these objectives, may be tolerated by those who wish to experience life in the wild.

—The Compact and Charter of Planet Trimus, Article 12

"I have never seen such a cold, desolate wasteland of rocks in my life," Mary remarked as they approached an outrageously voluptuous antarctic beach. A fish for every taste, Drin thought.

She had parked the submarine and rode on his neck toward the shoreline, her warm thighs smooth against his sandy outer skin. The idea that she often had eggs, of a sort, waiting in a part of her body so near to him gave him ridiculous and perverted thoughts—thoughts that unwontedly stimulated certain secretory organs below the tips of his fingers. Some, he had heard, had experimented with interspecies stimulation and considered it a form of art. Thank providence, he thought, that such thoughts on his part could remain private. But if Mary ever said that *she* wanted . . . No, *no.* Consign that idea to the abyss. Too much chance of giving offense.

It didn't help at all, as they neared the beach, that he could see at least four unabashedly pregnant young Do'utian women lolling thick-necked on the smooth pebbles in the sun. The beachmaster was nowhere to be seen, a circumstance that ran his biological thermometer well past its set point. He wondered if Mary understood how hard this would be for him?

"That beach is an indolent paradise for us, I'm afraid. I'd much rather talk to the head man than that naked harem, but he's left them unprotected. This isn't good. Uh, Mary, if they become aggressive with me, it might be best if I just let nature . . ."

She patted the top of his head, firmly enough for him to notice.

"I'll never say a thing. Promise." She put her arms around his neck, as far as they would go, and pressed the soft parts of her body against the back of his head, laughing. It was not at all unpleasant. Then, suddenly, she stopped.

"Drin," she spoke quickly, "to your left. What is that in the—DRIN!"

Instantly, he rolled his eyes around and slipped his tongue into his pouch, triggering his sonar with one manipulator and grabbing his weapon with the other. Then he saw, and knew instantly that it was too late to do anything.

A tall pole, perhaps half a Charter unit high, supported a white pennant at its end, snapping in the offshore breeze. The other end was firmly buried in the side of the corpse of a Do'utian man, bloated, floating in the swell. He shuddered as the wind shifted and brought the scent of death to him.

"Are you OK?" asked Mary.

"Yes. But I would prefer to approach this upwind. How are you?"

She was a trained monitor, and, he hoped, not as affected due to the difference in species. Fortunately for him, the wind shifted again.

"I'm fine. Look, why don't I check out the victim and the murder weapon while you interview?"

It made sense, but he was hoping for her presence to bolster his resolve not to be swept away by instinct on the beach. He belched in self-disgust; was he not master of himself?

"Very well, Mary. I'll take you over to it, I need to get closer anyway. I suspect the victim was the beachmaster here, and if so, these women have been widowed. I should be able to tell from his scent—he will have marked them. Widowing can be a very painful death sentence in primitive circumstances; an unbirthed egg turns poisonous in a month or so."

"So my human primitives kill five Do'utians with one harpoon?"

"Mary, they are not *your* primitives," he rumbled. "Don't take so much on yourself. It's not very professional." He extended his tongue behind him and placed manipulators on both her shoulders. "Besides, there are no reports of harems dying because of the other murders." The thought struck him: why not? "We don't know the whole story," he finished. No, indeed.

He felt her five thin bony fingers cover his three thick muscular ones. She grasped tightly, and he could feel some warmth, though not taste her skin, through her water suit. He could not fathom what feelings ran through that alien mind nor what awful images from her past this fresh corpse might conjure. But he could recognize sadness in her, and try to give sympathy.

His own feelings were proving harder to manage. There was a primal urge in his species to avoid their dead, and thus, the evolutionists believed, avoid whatever circumstances might have led to death. Then there was what waited for him on the beach. He shuddered.

"I can tell you'd rather not go any closer, Drin." A splash surprised him, and Mary swam in front of his left eye. Humans, in general, were clumsy in the water. But they were fearless and some like Mary were competent, if slow. "I'll take it from here. Looks like about as far to the corpse as to the beach. No problem; I'll just swim in when I'm done, or I'll buzz for you if I need backup. OK?"

He rumbled an assent, she bared her teeth to him, flipped and started pulling herself through the water toward the victim, climbing through the waves with steady pulls of her front limbs. The wonder, he reflected, was not that his simian friends were slow in the water, but that they could swim at all, and even appear graceful, in their own way, while doing so.

"I'll be expecting you. Take care," he called after her. Then, with mixed feelings, he sent himself toward the beach.

The approach was not the simple landing of a human boat ramp. Jagged rocks were all over. The beachmaster had chosen well: an adult Do'utian needed care to reach the shore. Drin exhaled and settled firmly on the bottom to ignore the random swells. Legs extended, he picked his way carefully along, a Charter unit below the surface, while holding his sonar transceiver high over his head, hearing the image it received through his earphones. There! A sandy path opened through the rocks. He followed it. It zigzagged to an open gravelly area under the breakers that seemed safe enough, but he chose to pick his way through the smooth stones along its side just in case. Carefully, he emerged onto the beach.

The women crowded together as soon as they saw him. Very well, he'd take it slowly.

First though, he traced his route with a sharp tongue tip on his comset's screen and sent the resulting image to Mary. While she could float over larger outlaying rocks that would disembowel him, there seemed to be only one place where the breakers might not dash her to pieces. He also sent a brief report to Monitor Central and inquired about the status of his request for Kleth support. Scheduled, they told him.

Chores done, he returned his attention to the widowed harem. Widowed because they had been very clearly scented by the dead beachmaster, and the deceased's neobarbarism seemed to have extended to marking them physically as well as with his scent—some of the scars were still unhealed.

A medical team would be needed. While, contrary to his initial assessment, only two of them were gravid; with the beachmaster gone they would both be needing egg relief soon. Also, all four were clearly undernourished.

He filed a quick report for Do Tor on his comm unit, then walked forward to them slowly, mouth politely open, tongue and manipulators spread to signal peaceful intent. Still, they cowered. They were young, very young, despite scars and abrasions on their hides that most of his people wouldn't acquire in eight times eight times eight years, and would probably remove if they did.

"I'm Lieutenant Drinnil'ib from the Monitors. I don't mean any harm," he said. "I'd just like you to answer some questions."

It must be the smell of the beachmaster's death that frightened them into silence. He had come close enough to carry some of it, and they probably thought he was responsible.

They keened and backed away as he approached. But a cliff surrounded the beach, and soon they could back up no farther.

If they could smell the death, then there was no reason to try to keep it a secret. He was hoping to avoid the legendary consequences. Nonsense, he told himself. These must be at least semi-educated people, living in primitive conditions by choice.

"I'm sorry to have to bring you this news. I've come from the North Pole colony investigating the reported deaths of several people in this back-to-nature area. I'm afraid I have one more to investigate. By what I smell, the latest victim was your husband. I'm sorry. I assure you I had nothing to do with his death before the fact." Lieutenant Drinnil'ib reached into his pouch and produced his badge, a holoprint two docis on edge—big enough for them to see easily. It gave off his scent as well.

The smallest of the harem, with deep black scars on her forelimbs, finally walked forward, then lowered herself to her belly in supplication.

"No," he protested. "I don't want you to do that. Stand up! Speak to me, please."

She keened again, then opened her mouth wide. It took him a few heartbeats to register what he saw, and then a few more for the horror of it to sink in. Where the two branches of her tongue should have been, where the manipulators that signified their species' rise from the beach should have curled, was nothing but a blackened stump, so short it would be useless for feeding or speaking.

He quickly pulled in his own tongue and lowered his belly to the gravel, to be on her level. Then he gently touched his beak to hers in sympathy. She shut her eyes and lowered her beak in sadness, and he did the same. When he looked up again, the other three had joined them. The gravid ones were looking at him expectantly. Oh-oh.

"Look," he explained, "I'm not part of your culture. I'm a Monitor. This is strictly a professional visit." Their eyes showed no comprehension, and their bodies began to sway back and forth on their legs. They came closer, swaying and keening. The first female kept nuzzling him. He tried to back away, but froze.

From then on, he noted his body's response with what was almost detachment. Body temperature up. A tightness at the base of his tail. He wanted to keep his mouth shut to avoid tasting whatever chemicals they were putting out, but a groan worked its way out from deep inside him, his beak yawned open involuntarily as reason left his brain. The women were beside him, keening, holding him between their bodies, their beaks locked wide open, pressing his most private areas. The need to give overwhelmed him. He let his tongue caress their tails, almost as if it were someone else's.

He never saw the eggs emerge from their throats, but rather felt the smooth bumps against his underside, an emptying feeling in the base of his tail, and a slight coolness in that area as his consciousness slowly faded back in.

Afterward, of course, he remembered everything with the humiliating clarity of a terapixel hologram. Especially when he looked back at two white eggs covered with sticky yellow goo. And especially when he looked up and saw little Mary Pierce standing about eight Charter units away, mouth open in what must have been a look of horror.

Setting aside his embarrassment and disgust, he tried to remember what needed to be done. Back home, in a hospital, the eggs would be sprayed clean and anointed with all sorts of healthy fluids, wrapped in germicidal barriers, and placed in an incubator. The nearest thing to an incubator they had here was a Do'utian pouch. His was full of other things, but the women had pouches, too.

It was then that he realized that since none of the women had tongues, he would have to place the eggs in their pouches himself. He shut his eyes, moaned, and buried his beak in the sand again. He couldn't do this.

"It's OK," he heard Mary say. "I'm afraid I don't remember what the handbook says about Do'utian midwifery, but if there's anything I can do, just tell me."

He lifted his head up. "The handbook doesn't say anything. It's supposed to be too private. But . . . but the eggs need to be cleaned off and placed in the women's pouches. They can't do it themselves because their former husband disabled them. I'm . . . I'm afraid I'm not up to it."

"No problem, buddy. I think they accept me. Must be your scent all over me. Is it OK if I wash the eggs in the sea?"

"Yes, I think so."

She did this quickly and efficiently, taking each egg in turn, cradling and talking to it as if it was a fresh-born human. Drin refrained from telling her that there would be nothing inside the eggs to hear her for eight-squared days. Done with the washing, Mary took the smaller egg and approached one of the formerly gravid women, who looked accusingly at Drin and backed away. Then a strange thing happened. The smaller Do'utian woman quickly moved in front of Mary and offered her own pouch.

When that member of the harem had accepted both eggs, she came over to Drin and slowly scratched the sand with her beak. It soon became clear that she was writing. When she backed away, Drin could read, fairly clearly. "I GRI'IL."

"You can understand me?" Drin asked, wonderingly. Obviously, she could not speak.

She nodded.

"Your name is Gri'il?"

She nodded again.

"Do you want to leave?"

Gri'il did nothing, then nodded slowly, followed by a vigorous head shake. Something wrong.

"Will you follow me back to the North Pole? To civilization?"

She was still a very long time. Then she began painfully scratching the gravel again. What she wrote was "DANGR HUNTRS."

Mary saw this, went up to Gri'il, wrapped herself around the Do'utian woman's foreleg, and began her own type of keening. Soon, they had all joined in.

"I'm going to get some fish for everyone," Drin said to no one in particular, and trotted back to the shore. The mutilated Do'utian's were ill nourished and couldn't feed themselves. Besides, he needed something to do alone. Away from all women of whatever species.

Individuals who wish to visit or reside in the wild regions, alone or in small groups, may do so without interference so long as they respect the rights of others and do not significantly disturb the environment. Introduction of chemical industry is specifically prohibited. Alternative societies are permitted so long as the individuals who join such societies are free to leave such when they wish. Do not interfere with suicide, or risk-taking that amounts to such. However, murder will be treated no differently than in the civilized areas.

—Planet Monitor's Handbook
Law In Reserved Areas

"Gri, Ohghli, Donota, Notri, do I have it right?" Mary asked. Human memories, Drin thought, were amazingly poor considering their technological prowess—on the other hand, perhaps necessity had made them superlative inventors.

Drin rocked her submarine by putting a little extra into his next propulsive tail-stroke. "Your memory is either much worse than I think or you find a certain humor in my situation. I think I would rather not have my thoughts in that current so often."

"My apologies." The comset relayed the drop of pitch in her voice that Drin associated with increasing concern. "But they're your wives now, aren't they?"

"No! I have made no commitment. There is no registration. Except for Gri'il, none of them seems to have any intellectual understanding of their lives, or that of the broader race. None of them is a suitable mate."

"I'd guess it will be hard for them to understand that," Mary suggested, more right than she could know.

"Very hard. I approached them under circumstances that make biological bonding almost inevitable in nature. And Gri'il took the eggs. . . ."

"She seems the responsible type, and educated somehow."

"She will have a tale to tell. I suspect she is a truant who dove into the back-to-nature business just a little deeper than her inherent depth. The others, I think, must have been born here. They seem virtually feral."

"What will happen to them?"

"I think Gri'il will return to civilization, sadder but wiser. The feral women . . . I don't know. The experts will have to decide—they may be happier as they are."

"Mutilated?"

"No, we'll fix that. But, they may be unable to adapt to civilization now. I cannot know their minds, or even if they have developed what you and I would recognize as a mind."

"That's heartless," Mary accused. "They love you."

"You don't understand the biology. I think our conversation should find different currents now."

But it didn't. Mary's attempt at matchmaking left him in no mood for conversation at all. There was silence instead, a silence that should have been filled with plans as they approached the primitivist human settlement.

It was shockingly big, even by his standards. Primitivism in humans, Drin realized at the sight, didn't really mean living without technology. It meant living with a technology so primitive that it could be sustained without any meaningful education at the expense of ceaseless, boring labor; a technology of hand-hewn planks, poles, and rough-cut stones in huge piles, piles made all the larger by beings who evolved with twice the local gravity.

The entrance to their harbor had been choked down to a canal by massive stone walls and guarded by massive wooden gates. The stream that issued from this was putrid. Drin turned away.

"Pollution! Mary, I think I would prefer to walk in."

"Understood. There must be two thousand people in this place, and that's the only outlet. The air isn't a whole lot better—lots of smoke. It's a couple of degrees over freezing; cool enough for you?"

"A nice balmy day."

"Why don't you try riding on top of the sub? You'll have to keep your tail off the rear electrodes."

Drin released a bubble of humor; the idea of him riding on a human submarine was indeed bizarre. But the water stunk like rotting carrion. "If you can steer without your forward fins, I could hang onto those with my forelegs. Then my tail wouldn't reach the electrodes."

"The sub says that's no problem. Climb aboard."

He swam into position, curled his front toes around the rounded edge of the flexidiamond fins and released some buoyancy gas to hold himself down. The submarine rose under him and broke the surface. The air stank as advertised, but only when he opened his mouth.

Soon Mary climbed out of the nose hatch to join him. She'd put her monitor uniform jumpsuit on over her insulated tights and looked academy sharp. Remembering that humans relied almost exclusively on visual identification, he pulled his monitor badges out of his pouch and stuck them on his front shoulders.

In front of them across the harbor entrance lay the top of the harbor wall, with an opening just a little wider than the submarine, the massive wooden gate was solid above water and dwarfed even Drin. It was guarded by heavyset humans in thick-belted robes around which were buckled long, heavy, cutting tools; called swords, if he remembered correctly.

"Open the gate," Mary yelled. The men did nothing. Drin tapped her on the shoulder with his tongue to warn her, and she covered her ears. He took a large breath.

"PLANET MONITORS. OPEN THE GATE!" Drin yelled, two oc-taves lower than Mary, pouring air from his bladder as well as his lungs. The human guardhouse resonated nicely with his undertones and a satis-fying crash emerged from its open door. Various stones and pieces of rot-ten mortar came clattering down the sides of the wall. One of the men extended his hands, palms out as if to plead for patience, while the other dipped into the now-steady guardhouse and emerged with a pair of col-ored flags. He faced the harbor and started waving them in various in-comprehensible patterns.

Soon, they heard a screeching and groaning of hidden wheels and levers as the left gate swung ponderously open. From aerial holos, Drin knew the breakwater was eight squared Charter units thick, but even so, the narrow canyon revealed by the opening gate made him shudder a bit. He slipped a branch of his tongue out the corner of his mouth into his pouch, and wrapped its fingers around his weapon. When the noises stopped, the submarine nosed through the half-opened gate. It had only a few doci's of clearance on either side, but it maintained this clearance with mathematical precision as it moved smartly into the channel.

About halfway through, a red-robed human man jumped onto the hull from a ladder just inside the gate, landing without stumbling despite the vessel's speed. He looked at Drin, then at Mary, apparently unsure of whom was in charge; the male Do'utian or the female human.

"Who are you?" Drin rumbled. The man shook and looked around, as if for somewhere to jump, and finding nowhere, finally faced Drin.

"Yohin Bretz a Landend. I'm . . . I'm your harbor pilot. We've got to go to city gate. Lord Thet will talk to you there."

"Yohin Bretz a Landend," Mary said, "I'm Mary Pierce from the monitor bureau. This is Lieutenant Drinnil'ib, my colleague. This is my boat; Lieutenant Drin doesn't need one. We are here to investigate the deaths of several Do'utian primitivists in this region."

"Huh? Whalers playing games with the fish-people, I'd guess." Bretz looked down at the submarine. "What do you draw?"

"Draw?" Mary clearly didn't recognize the term. Drin did, from his readings in human nautical literature, but kept silent so as not to embar-rass his partner.

"Yeah, *draw*. How far down is the bottom of this thing?"

"About a third of a Charter unit," she answered.

"What's that in meters?" A human chauvinist, Drin thought.

"It's a little over three of the old meters."

"Uh-huh. So the keel's about twice your height below the waterline?"

"Yes."

The pilot shook his head. "You'd displace thirty ton less without the fish-man on board, I'd guess, and ride a meter higher. Well, no problem, the channel's deep enough, but you'll have to stay in it. You've got to go hard aport as soon as you're out of the dike canal and steer for the big stone mill you'll see on the shore. Bear a bit to the port of it to lead the current, if I were you."

Drin rumbled a bit, and Mary smiled, recognizing his laugh. The submarine could follow the channel on sonar or with blue light without any help from the pilot.

"We'll do just fine," Mary said, "thank you. Now you can call me Mary, what can I call you?"

"Yohin, or Mr. Bretz to be polite."

They emerged into the harbor, a roughly circular body of fetid water. The air was thick with the smell of fish and dark with wood smoke. Now and then a flake of white ash would fall on them. Rough wooden human buildings lined the shore except for the far end. There, across the middling stream that struggled to flush the place, was a large stone wall, more vertical and smoothly finished than the dike across the harbor entrance.

Against this dock were tied wooden ships including several small round vessels not much longer than Drin himself, set with triangular sails, and a massive square-sailed ship—perhaps ten Charter units long. The last also had a strange, forward-projecting bow and two rows of oars with which it could presumably maneuver without wind.

"Hey, we're in the harbor!" Yohin shouted. "Don't you have to do something to turn this boat? How the . . . ?" His eyes went wide as the submarine turned to the channel without Mary doing anything. Drin rumbled again.

"Tell me, Mr. Bretz," Mary laughed, "are you happy here?"

"It puts bread on the table. Feeds me and my wife, gets me some respect. Even got a couple of slaves. I've been doing it 150 years. Yeah, I'm happy. Don't need any fancy stuff."

"Slaves?" Mary asked. "You have slaves?"

"Sure," Yohin said. "Someone's got to do the work while I'm out piloting. Be a shame if my wife had to, and I'm too tired after a day of this."

"Are the slaves happy?"

"I feed 'em well. They don't know anything else, so why shouldn't they be?"

Drin hissed. This manifestation of disgust, he realized, was wasted on this human pilot. "Do your slaves want to be slaves?" he asked. Yohin turned to him in surprise.

"They were captured fair and square. They know the game. What business is it of yours, Mister, excuse me, *Lieutenant* fish-man?"

"The primitive lifestyle is supposed to be voluntary. No one should be compelled to live like this."

"Look, I didn't set this up. But if you come after my slaves, you got an argument with me. Maybe from them, too. What would you do with them? Send them to some machine school so they can contemplate their navels for the rest of eternity? They're better off working for me."

"Now, lady," the pilot waved his hand at the other side of the harbor, "you've got to turn this tub sharp starboard and make dead on for the flagpole on the end of the fort . . . however you do it."

The submarine turned as if to the pilot's command, and he nodded judiciously.

"Never knew a woman could run a boat. But you do OK."

"I've got a lot of help," Mary said. "Yohin, I can imagine you doing this in one of those sailing ships with the wind blowing, using only your judgment and what you can see from the surface. I respect the skill you need to do that."

The pilot nodded his head and bared his teeth again. Mary, Drin realized, was gaining trust.

This human, Drin thought, had found whatever Gri'il had been seeking when she left civilization for the beach. The question was whether the failures should be allowed with the successes, particularly if the failures were involuntary.

"You said something about the whalers playing games with the Do'utians. What kind of games?"

"I heard there's a deal where the fishmen try to outfox the whalers. Them that lose are meat, but word is that's how they want it."

Drin rumbled his skepticism.

"Who sets up these games?" Mary asked.

"How the hell should I know? Maybe Lord Thet does. You can ask him, we're almost there."

The submarine's hull was well below the level of the dock, due in part to Drin's massive presence. From sea level, he couldn't see the rest of the top of the dock. The angle got worse as they fetched up next to the stones.

Carefully, using the wall as an additional point of balance, he swung his tail over the side and reared up on his hind legs, hooked the rippled pads of his front toes over the edge of the stone wall, bringing his head above dock level.

The man waiting for them on the dock by the city gate was probably Lord Thet. He was a head taller than Mary, gray-robed, and had thick black hair all over his face so that only the eyes and the nostril wattle showed when his mouth was shut. His robe covered either armor or what would, for a human, be an exceptionally large body. Others of his kind, holding metal-tipped spears, stood beside him. Perhaps fifty humans carrying some sort of primitive wood and cord weapons stood well back of the primitivist leader.

Mary was able to scramble up his back and jump from his shoulder to the stone platform. Undignified, but it got the job done. There was a fair amount of wind and harbor noise, but Mary left her comset on her belt, where it could see and record everything. Drin listened through his earphone.

"Hello, I'm Mary Pierce, Planetary Monitor."

"You are not wanted here," Lord Thet stated—with aggressive impoliteness, Drin thought.

"Your name?" Mary asked.

The man remained silent, but the comset camera got a good look at him and the Monitor net quietly relayed the information through their earphones. He'd left civilization early in life and, despite his commanding presence, was largely ignorant of things beyond what he controlled.

"You are Jacob Lebbretzky, otherwise known as 'Lord Thet' according to your voice and features. I'll be gone fairly quickly if you answer my questions," she told him.

"Don't overestimate your authority, Monitor. Your superiors are not that interested in us and your charter is open to interpretation."

Wishful thinking on his part, Drin felt—while the Monitors would bend over backward not to be overbearing, there was no question about the final outcome.

But only he and Mary were here right now, things were nowhere near final, and if this egomaniac idiot had talked himself into believing he could get away with minor violence . . . or if someone else had talked him into believing . . .

Drin spoke quickly with his beak shut so that only Mary could hear him on her earphone. "Mary, this fool could be dangerous. He's gotten so big he's forgotten what's backing us up."

She raised a hand to acknowledge him, but continued to face Lord Thet. "Someone's killed at least four Do'utian primitivists," she told him.

"Have the fish-men accused us?"

"We found the bodies."

"Death happens. Only the untested live forever."

An ancient Do'utian philosophy, Drin thought. Why was he hearing it from an ignorant human primitivist? Do'utians did not die of old age, but reproduced slowly enough that in the natural state, mating battles, disease, and accidents of the hostile sea were enough to maintain a population balance. But humans had eliminated aging and limited fertility with genetic engineering in historic times.

"You hunt them, don't you?" Mary pressed. "Your people hunt them in ships, as if they were animals."

Lebbretzsky was silent for a heartbeat or so, then said, "The contest is more even than that. There is no opportunity for heroism on either side without the opportunity for death. And the deaths let us raise new children uncontaminated by your machine culture."

This made Drin hiss as he thought of the stinking harbor, the human slaves, and the feral Do'utian women in his "harem." The sound got the momentary attention of the human, who probably had no idea of what it signified.

"Mr. Lebbretzsky," Mary responded, "I take your statement to mean that you know what I'm talking about. It has to stop, and the persons responsible must be reeducated. If you attempt to conceal them, then you will be a candidate for reeducation yourself."

Drin saw the man raise his arm as if to strike Mary, then put it down. Lebbretzsky, Drin realized, might be so ignorant and so deeply into these murders that he felt he had nothing to lose in an attack on a Monitor. Drin slipped a manipulator into his pouch holster for the second time. The movement of his tongue seemed to go unnoticed, or at least uncomprehended.

"Woman. Tell your superiors that your presence is an insult. Tell them that their interference with our culture is an interference of our rights to live and die the way we want. Tell them that we have not murdered anyone, and that the next time they want questions answered, not to send women and fish to ask them."

"Pollution!" Drin sent. "The victims were stabbed and butchered! But be careful, Mary."

The man continued: "There are no murders, woman Monitor. Now get out of here, or we will do what we can to eject you. You may have better weapons, but we are not afraid to die."

"Drin, better call that Kleth backup," Mary said aloud. Drin almost rejoined that he had done that hours ago—then realized that Mary was saying that for Lebbretzsky's benefit.

"Lebbretzsky," she continued, "I don't care what you think it is; attacking and killing Do'utians with harpoons is murder just as much as if you did it to me. The cultural group can deal with the whys later, but my job is to stop it, now. Who has been doing it? Where are they?"

Drin tensed. Mary, in her fearless eagerness to erase what she saw as a blot on her race, was pushing a bull on its own beach. Wrong species, but in this case, Drin feared some convergent evolution. As if to confirm his thoughts, the big human drew a long knife. Mary backed quickly away from him and got her gun out. Drin put a manipulator in his pouch and keyed his comset by feel. He dumped everything they had so far into the Monitor net—just in case he and Mary didn't survive her abuse of Lord Thet's hospitality.

"All right," Mary yelled. "Lebbretzsky, drop the weapon and lie down. You are in custody. You can arrange representation after you've been secured."

"Mary . . ." Drin sent. Too late. Lebbretzsky's hand seemed to flick and the knife flew at Mary. Her gun got it on doppler, flashed, and a smart bullet locked on the thing and knocked it out of the air. The two humans stared at each other in silence for a few seconds as if in a momentary stalemate. But here and now Lebbretzsky had overwhelming numbers. He made some kind of a signal and a hundred darts flew at Mary, some at Drin. He and Mary both fired as fast as their weapons could, but Mary was hit.

"Got my leg," she said with professional calmness. "Drin, let's get out of here."

Drin roared and with the occasional supreme effort his race could summon, pulled himself over the edge of the dock and scrambled toward Mary. The human archers paused in surprise and he flung his tongue out to his injured partner. He was just able to grab her leg with one manipulator and was pulling her to him when the primitivists started shooting again. He reeled Mary in with one manipulator while the other sent smart bullets at the legs of the crossbow archers.

Mary, a small moving target, wasn't hit again. But despite both their guns knocking dozens of darts off their trajectories, he was hit himself. The darts irritated like the spines of the giant dagger snail, but none seemed to reach below his layer of fat, and none had hit his eyes.

Some of the men with swords charged at him. He waited until they were too close, then quickly turned and swept the polluting snailbrains over the side of the dock with his tail. Then, with Mary firmly in his beak, he leapt into the harbor after them.

"Hold your breath," he said on the way down. He landed so as to spray as much water around as possible.

Momentarily sheltered by confusion and the high wall, he had time to help Mary into the submarine hatch. Then, thinking of the large harpoon he'd seen in the erstwhile beachmaster, Drin headed, fast and direct, for the harbor entrance. He sprinted through the harbor with a surface-racing tail-stroke, and used his legs to help him over the shallow spots. This time, he didn't even notice the dirty water.

A look back told him the human primitivists were busy with their colored flags again, and when he ducked under water he could hear the sound of the harbor gate creaking shut. Another look above water showed him that the large ship with oars was underway and pursuing them.

He reached the canal through the harbor wall well before the submarine, and sped to its end. But the massive gate was already closed and locked. He put his beak against it and pressed as hard as he could, and the thrusts of his tail sent waves of brackish brown water back down the channel. The gates hardly noticed.

He surfaced and scouted the channel walls. They were not quite vertical, perhaps widening half a Charter unit over two Charter units of rise, and the cobbled surface provided plenty of claw holds. It would not be out of the question to attempt to climb it.

But first he tried bellowing at the watchmen to open the gate. Not to his surprise, they refused. He did, however, have the satisfaction of seeing their little guardhouse collapse from resonance. Looking back, he saw the submarine enter the channel with the oar ship in hot pursuit.

"Mary, what's your status?" he sent.

"I got the dart out, patched the wound and patched the suit. Hurts like hell. I won't be running around for a while. I'm a little worried about that ram."

"Ram?"

"That rowboat with the solid nose that's chasing me. It's got to weigh a cube, it's moving fast, it's built to bash things, and it doesn't have any brakes. How are you doing on that gate?"

Weigh a cube? That was about eight-times-four as much as his body. Pollution!

"No luck at all," he sent. "Any chance your submarine can ram it open?"

"I'll try the underwater grate. That has to be the weak point."

Drin moved to the side of the canal and watched the humped deck of the submarine flow by him. Its wake grew, then disappeared. There was silence for a heartbeat, than a muffled boom. The gate held.

"Mary?" he asked.

"I'm OK, considering. Might have done some damage. Going to back off for another try."

She did, but that was no more successful than the first.

"Drin, if you can climb out of this, you'd better get going."

The primitivist ram had entered the canal at full speed. Clearly, they were going to try to crush both Drin and the submarine between the ram and the gate, regardless of what damage that did to the latter two. The slaves rowing the ram, he realized, probably didn't know their ship was charging at a locked gate. And its officers must believe, wrongly, that destroying Drin and Mary gave them a chance to avoid reeducation.

But there was no chance to discuss it with them now. Drin threw himself at the canal wall and his legs found claw holds on the rocks under water. Carefully, he heaved himself up the near vertical embankment. But as soon as he tried to put any weight at all on his forelegs, claws slipped on the damp mossy covering of the stones near the waterline, and he tumbled back into the canal. He tried it once more, then saw the submarine break the surface and start accelerating backward at the ram.

"Mary!" he bellowed, forgetting the comset.

"I got us into this, I baited them. I'd rather go down fighting." Despite the brave words, her voice trembled. "Good luck, friend."

He clung half in and out of the water like a paralyzed lungfish and watched the two human vessels collide. There was a tremendous thundering boom as they hit, followed by cracking and splintering sounds. In seeming slow motion, the ram rode up over the submarine and the rock walls transmitted an eerie hollow grating sound to him as the submarine's keel scraped along the canal's stone bottom. The combined wreck grated down the channel with scarcely diminished speed like a piston toward the massive gate.

There was too little room for him to remain where he was. He released his hold, slipped back into the water, and swam for the gate. Maybe everything would grind to a halt before it got there.

Underwater, Drin heard a sudden, ear-piercing crack. Pollution! he thought, the hull of the submarine must have broken. He surfaced and looked back. Both ends of the submarine stuck out of the water. The primitivist ship rode farther up on one of the pieces and then fell off to the side, gouging its ram into the side of the canal. Its stern hit the other side and, with a great screeching and rending, the keel of the ram snapped, leaving the broken human ship stopped sideways in the channel. Men, some of them skewered by splintered oars, tumbled from the broken vessel like fish from a torn net. The mess ground to a halt just a Charter unit from the gate.

"Mary?" he sent. There was no answer. Flames, from spilled heating fires aboard the ram, or discharging power leads on the submarine, began spreading in the above-water wreckage.

Drin threw himself into the devastation, prying blood-stained pieces of the ram away from the broken submarine hull. There was movement all around him, and he saw that the human survivors were having no better luck than he in climbing the slippery canal sides. Hoping that the time it took would not prove critical, Drin seized the still upright mast in his beak, snapped it with a vicious twist of his body, and let it fall so that its top rested on the dike above.

"CLIMB!" he roared to anyone who would listen.

Some of the astonished humans caught on and began scrambling up the mast to safety above. One was a large red-bearded man—the same one, he realized, that had mocked him from the decks of another ship only weeks ago. They stared at each other in a frozen moment of recognition, but Drin had more than an arrest on his mind.

Ignoring minor burns and lacerations, Drin clawed away the remains of a lower deck to expose the broken pressure hull of the submarine. It was filled with water. Drin stuck his tongue in and located the cockpit from feel and memory. Mary was not in the seat, but he could scent her blood. He felt around the tiny compartment, using both branches. He found her underwater gear, and, presuming success, grabbed it. A few more precious seconds, and he found Mary motionless in a small air pocket near the back of the cockpit.

With both branches wrapped around her, he strained to pull her up like a hatchling, into his mouth. With her legs sticking painfully down his throat, he was just able to close his beak over her head. Then he smashed his way out of the wreck, inhaled an hour's worth of air, and dove back into the putrid water. Over-buoyant, he swam down to the wooden grid and held on with his legs.

There was hardly room for both Mary and his tongue, so, with the skill of a contortionist, he managed to slip a loop of the tongue out the fleshy corner of his mouth, leaving the ends of the manipulator branches inside. Drin lowered his head and squeezed water from her lungs. They reinflated on their own as he forced the water from his mouth with air from his bladder. He squeezed again. She moved. Conscious? He hoped she would understand quickly enough not to panic.

He felt her hand pat one of his fingers. It seemed a controlled, understanding, gesture. He turned his attention to his external predicament.

With gloom and debris in the water, and Aurum low in the antarctic sky, he should be invisible from above. He began exploring the bottom of the gate where the submarine had smashed into it. Here and there, an outer buffer of great tree trunks had been smashed to kindling. But nothing behind had broken enough to let him through.

There was purposeful movement inside his mouth. "Drin, I've got my gills on. You can let me out now." Mary's voice in his ear was the best news he'd had since he'd come into the primitivist cesspool. Using his tongue to keep her from bobbing to the surface, he expelled the bubble of air from his mouth, then let her float free.

"How do you feel?" he asked.

"Lousy. No broken bones, I think. Tired. I've still got a little fluid in

THE GOOD NEW STUFF

my lungs." She drifted slowly over to the grate and surveyed the damaged gate. "I guess I didn't put a hole in this thing."

"It appears not."

Trapped. They were both silent.

"Uh, Drin? Can you think of any way we could make them think I did break through? If they think we're already gone maybe they'll open the gate to come after us, or to clear the floating debris."

The grate was too fine for even Mary to squeeze through—it was probably designed with human sappers in mind. His tongue could just fit, but wasn't long enough. But maybe . . .

"I could try to blow a bubble with some debris through the grate and out the other side."

"Hey, go for it!"

He did it, placing his blowhole against one of the spaces between the beams of an undamaged section and blew. Some of it escaped on their side, but not much—some must have gone through. They waited for a subjective eternity. He was on the point of suggesting another frontal assault when they heard a hideous, hollow, creak.

They waited. Nothing.

Then another creak. Drin thought he could detect a slight shudder.

"I think they're trying to open it," he said. "You might have jammed it a bit when you rammed it. That's a case of an emotional, spur of the moment action that did exactly the opposite of—"

"Drin, your folk's eyes are built for hindsight. Why don't you stop philosophizing and just try to help them open the gate?"

Of course. With a firm clawhold on the bottom stones, and not having to fight gravity, Drin could apply his full strength. He waited until a creak signified another attempt to open the gate, then *pushed.* Slowly it began to move. There was a crack and a grind as something let go. Drin released his hold immediately, and the gate began to swing open on its own.

Hiding on the bottom beneath flotsam from the wreck, they drifted with the current out through the opening. Then, with Mary hanging onto a leg, he swam hard for clear water until he judged they were well over Lord Thet's horizon. He surfaced, turned on his back and sheltered Mary between his legs as he would a hatchling, and let horizon-grazing Ember and Aurum do what they could to warm her, while he took great breaths through his mouth to rid himself of heat and to pay his oxygen debt.

Mary was quiet for a while, exhausted, Drin surmised. So it startled him when she suddenly sat up and yelled: "Look, Drin, contrails!"

Do Tor had finally arrived.

Among all races, when violence is obviously futile, reason is encouraged. For this reason, where there is the likelihood of an irrational physical confrontation, the inclusion of a large Do'utian Monitor is highly recommended. Humans excel where strength is needed in confined places. And, where overhead intelligence and logistic agility are required, the Kleth can make a major contribution—but care should be taken to avoid endangering Kleth individually.

—Planet Monitor's Handbook,
Team Composition

. . . their mating bond is such that individuals become physiologically dependent on each other. A Kleth seldom survives the death of a mate, nor is their any record of one wanting to do so. Efforts to sustain life in these circumstances are always futile and should not be attempted.

—Planet Monitor's Handbook,
Medical Appendix

The Kleth aircraft met them just over the horizon from Lord Thet's city, on the beach of an uninhabited island dominated by a huge granite crag that gave shelter from the circumpolar wind. After greetings, Team Leader Do Tor and his mate started unloading supplies.

Mary was exhausted, so Drin scraped a deep pit in the sand for her, gathered wood, and lit a fire. Then, despite her exhaustion, and still limping from her wound, she insisted on washing her clothes and body in the frigid polar water, and turned an amazing shade of blue before she got back to the fire.

"D-don't worry," she told him as she shook convulsively under a blanket in front of the fire. "It's-s h-how we get our b-body heat b-back up."

Do Tor and his mate stretched their wings to catch some fish for her, and jibbered with amusement as she threw away all the good parts and heated the remaining muscle almost to the point of decomposition on a flat stone she put by the fire. Drin looked forward to having a good long feed later that night, in his own manner, on his way back to Gri'il's beach.

"Sorry late. Assumed you'd just leave Thet and wait for us," the Klethan said in a guttural, sing-song English that was actually lower pitched than Mary's, despite his being less than half her mass.

"We tried," Mary laughed. "Things got in the way. We surface dwellers have certain problems about just flying away when things turn sour."

"Don't understand why primitivists had so much technology."

"Lack of interest on our part. Ignorance of the Charter and evolutionary pressure on theirs," Drin offered. "The best fighters end up in charge, and the best fighters are, more often than not, those with the best weapons. Also, if you can't make it clever, make it big." It would be a long while before he would forget the huge ram bearing down on him. "I doubt that Lord Thet or many of his people even understand why the Charter prohibits development in these areas; they've rebelled against anything resembling a scientific education."

"For humans, there is an inherent contradiction between 'back to nature' and 'no technology,' " Mary contributed, "because human nature *is* to make and use tools. So what happens is that the primitivists reinvent the wheel using primitive technology that, per capita, pollutes unmercifully and requires gobs of labor." Mary picked up a stone and threw it out of sight. "So then you get leadership dominance games that the most ruthless win, with slave labor of one sort or another for the losers. That works well long enough for the glandular bullies to start assembling miniature empires, and then . . ." She shook her head. "Allowing this Lord Thet set-up was taking noninterference too far, in my view. But that's up to the council. Anyway, we have our killers."

"Maybe," Drin demurred. "But I don't think this is a one-species issue." From a philosophical standpoint he certainly didn't want it to be human versus Do'utian, but something more than that was bothering him. "I'm not sure we have the whole story. In defending his hunting, the human Jacob Lebretzsky seemed to include the Do'utian primitivists in his defense."

"Do'utians help get selves butchered?" Do Tor clucked. "Strange thing, I think."

"If you think in groups, yes. But that isn't the natural Do'utian way to think." Drin moved his head slightly from side to side in mild negation. "I want to ask Gri'il some questions and learn more about this murdered beachmaster and his harem. I may have made some unfair assumptions about the last victim."

"Name was Glodego'alah, by the way," Do Tor added. "Left the north pole as a disillusioned student eight cubed great revolutions ago. Not happy as primitivist, either, but responsible. Took care of harem. Good being. We did our homework." The Kleth held its hard translucent wings out in a gesture of pride.

"Oh yes," his mate said, the first words she uttered, surprising Drin. Until now, Go Ton had been inert, folded up. One partner or the other might dominate, but they were always together. Divorce was unknown, as were widows or widowers. Go Ton's contribution was unusually forward, for a subordinate Klethan. But Monitor couples were known to be more independent.

"Did you bring the Do'utian interface coronet?" Drin asked.

"Not so late, otherwise." Do Tor rummaged in the pile of unloaded supplies and found a glasscloth package the size of a folded human tent. "Here."

Drin placed it in his pouch. Its woven-in antennae picked up and decoded motor nerve impulses—even those sent to absent peripheries. Now, not only could he ask questions of Gri'il; she would be able to answer.

There were also a tent and collapsible kayak for Mary. The tent fit nicely in the hollow he had dug, and she opened it up with its door to the fire. As it resumed its memorized shape, she turned to her fellow monitors.

"This," she said, "is camping. It's what most of us have in mind when we think of going back to nature, or living in a primitive situation. But, as you see, it's not primitive at all. And it's not social, we usually try to get away from other people when we do this. What's happened back at Thet just hasn't really registered with my people. I—"

"Mary, why should it register with you any more than with the rest of us?" Drin interrupted. "You have no special responsibility for them just because they happen to be human. There is no need to apologize."

"Oh yes, Go Ton agrees," Do Tor's mate spoke up. "We are one civilization on this world. Whole purpose of Planet Trimus. Eight-cubed years of lives meaningless if not. Eyes of Trimus we are. We should have noticed violations before dead bodies appear."

"Any Do'utian can smell that place in currents an eighth of the way around the planet. We ignored it," Drin said.

"Th-thanks," Mary said. "I just . . ." She shook her head and made sounds of human sadness, though Drin thought it was more in relief. He flicked out his tongue and wrapped his fingers around her hand, and she rewarded the gesture by squeezing him gently back, and baring her teeth in a big smile.

"We all go to the beach tomorrow, and gain more understanding," Do Tor said. "Now rest."

"You rest," Drin answered, reminding him that Do'utians didn't sleep in the eternal days of a polar summer. "I need to eat, feed the harem, and keep my injuries in water until they heal more. I will see you there at the beach. Take care, Mary."

She hugged his fingers to her, careless of her wrap, and his most sensitive organs were pressed into the alien heat and smell of her. He was overwhelmed for a moment, then she released him. "Yeah, you too," she said.

He backed away from the fire carefully, to avoid upsetting anything. Clear, he turned. And as his body turned toward the water, his mind followed, thinking ahead to his duties. His cuts and bruises were beginning to hurt, true. But something in the back of his mind was pushing him, something perhaps as powerful as the instinctual desire to join with the harem that chose him as their provider and their protector. It did not make sense to him that humans—even as degenerate as Lord Thet and his gang—would or could suddenly start preying on Do'utians, even given the sort of general philosophical license primitivism in both species seemed to grant. Something less random and more evil was happening. Perhaps Gri'il could help him.

The Planetary Civilization must be permitted to evolve, and experiments must be encouraged, for only through change is knowledge expanded.
—The Compact and Charter of Planet Trimus, Article 5

Aurum stood high above Ember when Drin returned to the harem beach with his mouth full of fish, and the star had moved a dociradian west by the time he finished the simple duty of placing the fish into throats. Once done, he unpacked the neural interface cap and approached Gri'il.

Even now she hesitated, putting her nose to the beach. Despite everything that had happened, her distaste for this artificiality was evident. But then, apparently recognizing the necessity, she raised her head and came to him. He fitted the cap over her.

"It will take a while to calibrate itself. There will be a bit of a delay to start with, but you'll get used to it. Now, just tell me your name, as if you were whole again. Repeat it until the computer in the cap gets it right."

It produced an intelligible "Gri'illaboda" after about six tries, and she got used to it in a few more. Finally, she could speak through the device more or less naturally.

"OK," Drin said. "I'm going to record this, so why don't we start by having you say who you are?"

"I am Gri'illaboda, co-mate of Drinnil'ib."

Great. Just great. "I am sorry, Gri'il. I am a planetary monitor, and not a primitivist. I care for you, yes—but more as a senior family member, not as a mate."

"You replaced our beachmaster, mated with my co-mates."

"It was not my choice. I did not seek you or them to mate."

She was silent for a few heartbeats. He could hear the waves and the sea birds.

"Drinnil'ib, I was the daughter of Slora'analta and Broti'ilita. Did you know either of those?"

"The historian."

"Who told the old tales of the free seas and made a romantic out of his daughter. I was bored with school. I met a free rover. He took me here, quickened my ovaries . . . then took my tongue."

"Glodego'alah?"

"Never. Glodego'alah was a tourist who saw what had happened, fought the free rover for us, then took us here to be safe. But he paid for his charity in a way that happens all too often here."

"Then I am sorry for what I thought about Glodego'alah. We are seeking the humans who killed him, and four others who were killed. Did you know any of them? Did they have families here?"

"Glodego'alah remarked once that harems change masters easily because of such human predation. Their ships come in the channels between the islands and the ice pack where beachmasters gather fish."

Drin nodded. "I came close to being a victim myself on my way back from my initial investigation. It is easy enough for them—I suspected nothing until they shot at me. I would think someone down here would warn the humans not to do this."

Gri'il huffed in derision. "The sea lords don't interfere. They say the humans take the weak and the race gets stronger, and that the inbred softness of civilization is thus cleansed from our blood. But Glodego'alah was not soft."

"No, I'm sure he wasn't. Who are these 'sea lords'?"

"They are the free rovers, the ones who take from both poles what they want. They live like beachmasters at the south pole, then swim north and have all the luxuries of civilization. They are . . . the human word is hypocrites."

"And if they don't come back?"

"A harem doesn't stay unmastered long here. A sea lord shows up soon enough to claim a missing master's family. They seem to know, somehow, when one isn't coming back."

Her passiveness disturbed him, but perhaps it was simply adjustment. Early Do'utian history wasn't any prettier than early human history. Less so, in some respects. And the Kleth, of course, were cannibals well into their spacefaring days. Drin shuddered, wondering at his fascination with such things. But he had to ask; it might be important.

"Gri'il, how was your tongue to be taken?" Did she just submit to such an amputation?

"The sea lord who ran off my first mate, said it was traditional. He demanded this after the first mating, then he said he would not take my egg unless I submitted. Also . . . I can't explain. I sometimes feel a need to surrender myself, to let the tides of providence have their way with my flesh. At any rate, I did not resist. In my state at the time, he was God."

Submit to mutilation, or die. Such was her natural paradise. What polluting monster would . . .

"His name?"

"Gota'lannshk." The same ruffian he encountered at Cragen's? Drin hissed in disgust.

"You know of him?"

"We met. Look, Gri'il, will you come back to the North with me? For treatment."

"We are bound to you. I need to stay with you, to submit to you. And I have the eggs, remember? Or are you so civilized that that doesn't matter?"

The eggs probably shouldn't be hatched, Drin thought. Two fathers. No tests. No family. No birth allocation.

"Gri'il, compulsions are subject to medical intervention. My duty is to try to right the wrongs done so far, if I can, and prevent others from being done. Can you get the others to come?" And how many more were there out in those islands? Should they save them all? By force if needed?

"If it is clear that we are leaving, they will come, for whatever good it will do them."

"We'll regenerate their tongues, teach them to speak, send them to school."

"They were hatched out here. Their minds were untrained during the crucial years."

Truly feral. He feared as much. "Still, we have to try. We can find a deserted northern island for your co-mates, and arrange for them to be watched. But what about you? Now that this has happened, can't you see your way back to—"

"To what? We live with the humans and the Kleth on this planet at the expense of ceasing to live like Do'utians, at the expense of always pulling against our own inner nature. And the stars are too far apart for it to matter. I showed my tail to all of that. Say what you want. I lived. I swam in the wild currents. I did it on the beach. You want me to go back to that northern emotional straitjacket and listen to all those proper titters and I told you so's? I'd rather die!"

And her present state was not a humiliation? But her age-old argument, Drin thought, was unanswerable. The civilization of Trimus was for those who thought it mattered.

"We don't want to tell you how to live. I'm sure your privacy would be respected, and protected."

"Like in a zoo! Drinnil'ib, you rescued us, fed us. Don't you want us? Don't you feel the need to own and protect us? Or in the name of your Compact have you let the humans reengineer your sex?"

Drin groaned. He wanted her enough, but he did not *want* to want her. At least not as she was now. The whine of fans reached him before he could find a suitable way to explain that. Mary! Relief flowed through him. The aircraft settled on its fans, the hatch popped, and Drin walked over to greet his partner, leaving Gri'il with her beak in the gravel.

But Mary was nowhere in sight.

"Mary?" he called, worried.

Do Tor opened the canopy, jibbered to his machine, and the cargo door popped open. Of course, Drin realized. There was no room in the Kleth cockpit for a human, and indeed, it took Mary a while to unfold herself from the cramped space.

"I'm here, Drin."

"It's good to see you!" He explained about the sea lords. "So I think your human hunters have Do'utian accomplices, at least in principle. But things still don't swim well in my mind."

"The strongest, fastest, or most clever survive. I can see that, I guess. You think the Sea Lords were using Lord Thet to cull their herd, so to speak?"

"That seems to fit."

"Well, Lord Thet's gang of wannabe barbarians seems to be only too happy to help. Your people are the most challenging hunt in the ocean, they probably think."

"Brings up the question of whether we have right to interfere," Do Tor observed.

"To save lives?" Drin protested. "Of course we do."

Mary sighed and gestured to the sky. "Drin, there are now many beings out there who can trace their origins to our home worlds, but who have engineered so much into themselves that they look on *us* as primitivists. They could make a problem like Lord Thet vanish in an instant with no loss of life—but would we want that?"

"Those who didn't get killed might appreciate it."

Mary shook her head. "The parts of our natures that lead to this mess could easily be changed, but then what would we be? Death, even random death, may have a justifiable role in society that transcends individual needs. Perhaps, to keep our identity, we need to learn to accept that."

"I think," Drin asserted, perhaps a little more loudly than necessary, "that such issues should be debated by the planetary council and that *our* job is to not let anyone else get killed until they do and decide . . . whatever. Now, I have four physically mutilated and three of them intellectually mutilated—Do'utian women to bring back to where they can be properly protected and cared for. Let's do that and sort the rest out later."

"Agreed," Do Tor chuckled. Mary nodded quietly.

"Gri'il," Drin said, "is there any way the others can be told of how long a journey this will be?"

"They will follow you if I do," she said, coldly, it seemed. "But the hunters will be watching."

"And the planet will be watching them!" Drin proclaimed. "They won't dare do anything."

"I will ride with you," Mary said. "In full uniform. At least they'll know what they're playing with."

Drin didn't remind her of how persuasive her uniform and submarine were at Thet harbor.

"We'll fly cover with loud voices and guns," Do Tor said, spreading his wings. "Aircraft can fly itself, so that makes three above."

"Oh yes," his mate chimed. So it was decided. A convoy North.

Drin led the way into the water the next morning with Mary's warm legs and arms comfortably around his neck. They'd fashioned a light glasscloth collar for him that she could grasp and so hold her position in the current of his passage. This was no irritation, but the bulge of an appliance she had constructed to protect her wounded knee was a noticeable reminder of their vulnerability in these waters—many more monitors would be needed to handle Lord Thet and his allies without loss of life.

Gri'il came quietly after him, and as predicted, the harem followed.

It was a fine gray day with favorable surface winds, and light, cooling surface squalls. A brackish current flowed north here from the ice cap on the largest southern island, overlying warmer saline water flowing from an inner pole drainage basin, and so the Do'utians had made good time without becoming overtired.

By the morning of the second day, Lord Thet's domain was well behind them, and they glided through the waves halfway into reef-crowded tropical waters. A volcanic island with wide black beaches lay to their left, and a reef to their right, but the channel was fairly deep. Drin was just beginning to relax and enjoy the scenery when the human ships appeared.

"Don't think they're hunters," Do Tor sent. "Big Do'utian male right with them, no shooting."

"Can you describe him?" Drin asked.

"One and three-eighths Charter unit long. Big white crescent-shaped scar behind the blowhole. Do you know him?"

"If it's who I think it is, I've smelled him before. A harem-coveting sea lord with his tail across two beaches. It's time to ask that rogue a few questions."

Gri'il and her co-mates keened as if they were being mortally wounded.

"It sounds like our refugees have smelled him before as well," he continued. "I'd better let those humans know what we're about. Ready, Mary?"

"Gills on." He felt her arms as well as her legs encircle his neck, and her hands grasp the collar. She was secure. He dove and, slamming the ocean back and forth with his tail, headed toward the lead human ship much faster than he could manage on the surface.

About ten Charter units from the hull, he broke water again. So did his harem—he'd forgotten to tell Gri'il to stay back. It shouldn't be necessary, but he was uneasy.

"Mary, I'm not sure how much comfort we should take from Gota'lannshk being present."

"Why would they shoot at us and not him?"

"Why is there a sea lord always ready to inherit the harem of a victim? Why did Gota'lannshk seem to know that I'd had a close call with these hunters when we met him at Cragen's?"

"Lord Thet—"

"Mary, I don't want to insult your species, but I don't think that idiot has been running this atrocity."

"Huh? Why?"

"Later. I just hope these people have sense enough to keep out of this." Drin inhaled and boomed as authoritatively as he could, "Human ship, we are Planet Monitors escorting citizens on an official mission. We need to ask your companion some questions. Please do not interfere. I say again, do not interfere."

Mary waved at them and smiled.

The report of the harpoon gun reached him first, then Mary's scream and the sharp, deep pain in his neck.

"Look out!" Do Tor yelled over the radio link.

The taste of blood was in his throat. He dove and heard a sharp smack on the water over him. Instinct said to head for the very bottom, but Mary, if she were still alive—he could no longer feel any pressure from her legs—wouldn't survive that. Despite the pain, he pushed water hard and got about eight-squared Charter units away from the ship before he surfaced again.

"Mary?" he called. If those polluting, suicidal, feral idiots had killed her . . .

There was no answer. Oblivious of his wound, he turned back toward the ship, rage building.

"Do Tor, I can't see behind my head. What's happened to Mary?" Did the Kleth follow him?

"Drin. Long spear in your neck. Went through Mary first, through her leg. Not necessarily fatal wound, but suggest you make for nearest island. Go Ton will go with you. West, Drin, *now*. I've called aircraft down. That ship will not fire again. Go!"

As if to contradict the Kleth, the harpoon gun fired again and the lance slapped the water beside him. He could hear warning blasts from the aircraft and Go Ton squawking at the top of her lungs, telling the human ship to stop shooting. In the name of eternal repudiation, the murderers would pay for this! He started swimming toward the ship.

He felt, more than saw, a Do'utian charge under him directly at the human vessel.

"GRI'IL, NO!" he bellowed hopelessly, much too late.

The impact boomed out, sound reaching him underwater before through the air. Then, beneath, he heard the creaking and cracking of wood and the screams of humans underwater.

"Drin!" Do Tor screamed. "Get to that island, now. I take care of this. I will mark them. They will not escape, not melt into primitivist population. I mark. Go, now, save yourself. Save Mary."

"Drin," a soft voice called. "I'm awake. It hurts like hell, but if you have to go back for her, I understand. I can take it."

Reason returned. "Mary. No. I'll have to trust Do Tor." There was no way Gri'il could have survived that impact. No way that he would have. And the eggs . . . it was better that way. Perhaps Gri'il had known that. But his wound had little to do with the effort it took to push himself toward the island.

A whistle and some kind of explosion sounded behind him. Then another. He could hear loudspeakers. Killing for killing—perhaps they would understand *that*. Then, somewhere from the back of his mind, between the currents of pain and grief, a thought formed in an eddy of cold fear. Gota'lannshk had disappeared when the shooting started. To where?

The island was a long swim on the surface and he gagged on his blood by the time he got there. Go Ton was waiting at water's edge, alone, with a med kit that must have weighed as much as she did.

"Come on, just a few steps farther, above the tide line," she urged.

He did that, then he was on his belly, his tail still in moist sand. Go Ton fluttered to the top of his head, out of sight. He heard the buzz of a bone saw, and the shaft of the harpoon soon tumbled to the ground. There was a yelp, quickly stifled, from Mary. Then a numbness started spreading through the wound. Soon he felt as if he didn't know what had happened to him, that all that was wrong with him was a stiff neck.

"Now, Mary," Go Ton said, "I know it looks awful, but I think it best to leave that piece in your leg alone until help arrives. Human aircraft will be here in eight-fourth beats. Might do more harm than good if I try to remove it now."

"I understand," she said, "this sounds ridiculous, but right now I feel OK, except my leg is dead to the world. I'll be all right as long as I don't look at it. Can you help me down?"

"Not alone. Lieutenant Drin, can you lend a tongue?"

His tongue still worked; the barb had not gone in that deeply, perhaps in part because Mary's leg had slowed its entry. He reached back, and between the three of them, they were able to lower Mary down to the sand.

"Where's Do Tor?" she asked.

Pollution! She'd forgotten, Drin realized, and he couldn't warn her with his tongue extended so far.

"He's with the aircraft cleaning up the mess with the human ships," Go Ton responded, shakily. "He should have everything well in hand and be back with us soon."

"You've been too busy helping us to check!" Mary said. "I'll contact him, let him know we made it, and find out how things are."

"Please do not do that," Go Ton pleaded.

Just a little farther, Drin thought. There! Mary was safely down, and he could speak again.

"But, I know how much he means to you—" Mary started, oblivious to the danger.

"That's *why,* Mary," Drin interrupted, "for the sake of providence, think!" The Kleth team had taken the ultimate risk for them, and Go Ton's position was precarious. She would live as long as she believed her mate was alive. But if everything was *not* fine with Do Tor, that would effectively eliminate Go Ton as well. "We need Go Ton just now."

"Oh!" Mary said. Everyone was quiet for a heartbeat. Then Mary continued, her voice with a certain forced steadiness. "Go Ton. Uh, that human garbage doesn't have any weapon that can hurt Do Tor. He'll be fine."

That human garbage shouldn't, Drin thought, have had any weapon that could have hurt him or Mary. But here they were.

"Drin, I am stiff-winged on Do'utian first aid," Go Ton said, firmly changing the subject, "but I think the spear should come out of you now. It is the sort that works its way in deeper every time you move, and without Mary's body holding it back . . ."

"Do it." Before the anesthetic, Drin could sense how close the barb had worked itself toward his central nervous column. He had arteries and blood to spare, but didn't want to stop breathing just yet.

"If you could roll on your side . . ." Go Ton asked. He complied, then lay silently, feeling little tugs and tears in his flesh and tried to imagine one of Go Ton's tiny thin horny arms deep in his flesh with knives, cutting a passage for the barbed spearhead.

Then the Kleth said: "Mary, need help. The strength of your arms."

Using the discarded shaft of the spear as a crutch, Mary hobbled around behind him, patting him on the beak as she went by.

A little later, he heard her say "oof," felt a sharp pull, and saw Mary fall backward into his field of view again—her arms bloody up to the elbows, her hands clutching the cruel barbed spearhead. Go Ton remained behind him; little tugs and pulls continued for another eight-cubed heartbeats.

"Now that's all closed as well as I can do it," Go Ton said.

"Thank you," Drin said, and rolled slowly back onto his belly. "Did the harem follow us here?" The thought of them reminded him of Gri'il. He shut his eyes and let the empty feeling pass.

"Yes, they're huddled together in shallows behind you," Go Ton answered. "They seem very sad, beaks in sand, but are unhurt, I think."

Drin was thinking that Do Tor should have been back by now, and searching his memory for any kind of convention for handling the worst-case situation. There would come a point when, if the news were bad, Go Ton would have to be told, and nature would have to take its course. To do otherwise would be to not respect the decision her people had made to not change this part of their genetic make up. Perhaps the best thing would be to wait until she asked herself. If . . .

The challenge roar echoed off the lava cliffs and caught them all by surprise.

In an instant, before he even realized what it meant, Drin's heart doubled the strength of its beats and he could feel the effects of various body chemicals, not greatly different from those that had hit him when he fertilized the feral eggs. That primordial insult deserved an equally primitive response. But he made himself stay still, and without moving his injured neck, he swiveled an eye to the direction of the noise. Far down the beach, a big, scarred male.

"Same Do'utian we saw with the human hunting ships," Go Ton said from above.

"Gota'lannshk," Drin rumbled, in no shape or mood to play primitive beachmaster games. "His beak is dripping with this. Tell that idiot to stay away from us, before I kill him!"

"Drin," Mary whispered, almost inaudibly, "he's bigger than you, and with your wound you'll kill yourself before you get to him. Try to calm down. Think. If he inherited Glodego'alah's harem, and he was connected with the human hunters—"

"*Precisely,* Mary. A lot easier to get Lord Thet's people to eliminate his rivals than fighting for a harem on the beach the old-fashioned way. These murders were no game of survival of the fittest, or even of macabre chance. Those polluting idiot sea rovers carefully selected the hunting victims and no doubt led Lord Thet's ships right to them. Lord Thet probably lost a few selected men as well, just to keep things even, gain birth allocations, and reduce the number of his political rivals." Drin's anger increased. He should turn the murderer into snail meat. His breath came faster.

"So," Mary said, "the whalers get their hunt, their flesh, and think they're just playing by some tough rules. But it's all fixed ahead of time. Premeditated. Drin, stay down, please. Drin? Drin! Give me your gun."

The Do'utian sea rover bellowed again and blind rage started working its way through Drin. The nerve of that cow stealer! He heaved himself to his feet, oblivious of the wound.

"DRIN!" Mary screamed. "Give me your gun! Drin. Your gun! Now!"

In some small corner of his consciousness, Mary's words got through. Somehow, as he began to rock back and forth on his legs, he sent his tongue into his pouch and retrieved the weapon for Mary, dropping it almost absentmindedly on the sand next to her. That popgun was never, he thought with a last wisp of clarity, meant to stop a charging Do'utian.

He got a whiff of the challenger, ripe with arrogance. He heard his cows keen and smelled their fright. Dimly, he remembered there were things one was supposed to do in beak-to-beak combat, things that used the opponent's charge against him. Ways to use the tail as well as the head to put the other on the sand, but that all seemed very fuzzy and far away just now. All he wanted was to charge and bite the throat.

Hardly even aware that he was doing it, Drin lifted a clawed front leg, dug it deep into sand, and bellowed. The sun was high; it was a good time to taste blood.

The other began its charge. He stomped forward to meet it. Somewhere behind him he heard a series of sharp, high-frequency sounds begin at regular intervals. He didn't care, his body was aflame, producing heat many times faster than he could lose it. He didn't care. It felt good. He felt the wind of his passage build up, giving him some relief. Somehow, both hind legs moved together while both front legs hit slightly apart. The beach shook beneath him. He fixed his eyes on the other's neck, looking for an opening, looking for where the cycle of its charging stride exposed the throat to Drin's beak.

But its neck kept getting lower to the beach. Its charge seemed to become unbalanced and slow. His opponent screamed now in protest and its scent changed from challenge to fear and danger. It keened and shrieked and wavered from side to side.

With the danger call, a bit of consciousness returned to Drin, and he swerved at the last heartbeat, avoiding a collision that could have ripped open his stitched-up insides and left him to bleed to death.

The sea lord collapsed into the sand in front of him, plowing a furrow two Charter units long with its gaping beak. He passed by the hulk in an instant and into an eerie silence. The bellows and the sharp sounds had ended; only the surf and the thunder of his own mad rush sounded on the beach.

Burning inside, Drin exhaled gales, bent his path into the sea and let momentum carry him into the cold water, sliding forward until it covered him. A very gentle bend of his tail brought his head back to the shore.

The drama was not over. The fallen sea lord groaned and snapped at sand. Its right foreleg was covered with blood and bent at a wrong angle. Its hind legs pushed sand uselessly, trying to propel it somewhere. Then it used its tail to turn itself over, trying to roll to the cooling waters of the sea. Once, twice, it rolled. But, as Drin settled himself into the life-giving cold water, the sea rover stopped rolling. Its tail rose majestically and thudded into the sand. Once, twice.

At the last, it threw its tongue at Mary, falling far short. "Dirty human cow," Gota'lannshk screamed at her. Then . . . nothing.

Heat death.

Drin lay in the shallows panting. Fiery pain shot through him. He could taste his own blood again; some of Go Ton's handiwork had come loose. He saw Mary prone, the shaft of the harpoon still projecting bloodily from her leg, her elbows in the sand, his gun in her hands, still aimed at the sea rover. She must have put a hundred bullets in his opponent's knee, but now she shook and moaned. He knew that killing a Do'utian over this was the very last thing she had wanted.

He wished to comfort her, but he was tired. Very, very tired.

His next awareness was of a hotness on his neck. He opened his right eye and looked back. Mary was there, flattened against his neck, gently calling his name.

"Mary," he managed to say, as softly as he had ever said anything, "I'm awake. I'll be OK."

She was apparently having trouble breathing, but turned to his eye and said, "Oh, Drin. Oh, Drin. It's—it's so hard to get my arms around you." Despite her appearance, he somehow knew she was happy.

Noise and smell intruded. The sky over the island beach was filled with both aircraft and Kleth. The death smell of Glodego'alah was there, among the smell of many beings, and the sound of many voices, Kleth, human, and Do'utian. He recognized Do Tor's and Go Ton's among them, and took a ragged but deep breath of satisfaction. Everyone had come through, and, like rational, civilized beings, they were all discussing what was to be done next.

Robert Reed

GUEST OF HONOR

Robert Reed sold his first story in 1986, and quickly established himself as a frequent contributor to *The Magazine of Fantasy & Science Fiction* and *Asimov's Science Fiction,* as well as selling many stories to *Science Fiction Age, Universe, New Destinies, Tomorrow, Synergy, Starlight,* and elsewhere.

Reed may be one of the most prolific of today's young writers, particularly at short-fiction lengths, seriously rivaled for that position only by authors such as Stephen Baxter and Brian Stableford. And—also like Baxter and Stableford—he manages to keep up a very high standard of quality while being prolific, something that is not at all easy to do. Almost every year throughout the mid-to-late nineties, he has produced at least two or three stories that would be good enough to get him into a Best of the Year anthology under ordinary circumstances, and some years he has produced four or five of them, and so often the choice is not whether or not to use a Reed story, but rather which Reed story to use—a remarkable accomplishment. Reed stories such as "The Utility Man," "Birth Day," "Blind," "A Place With Shade," "The Toad of Heaven," "Stride," "The Shape of Everything," "Guest of Honor," "Decency," "Waging Good," and "Killing the Morrow," among at least a half-dozen others equally as strong, count as among some of the best short work produced by anyone in the eighties and nineties. Nor is he non-prolific as a novelist, having turned out eight novels since the end of the eighties, including *The Leeshore, The Hormone Jungle, Black Milk, The Remarkables, Down the Bright Way, Beyond the Veil of Stars, An Exaltation of Larks,* and, most recently, *Beneath the Gated Sky.*

In spite of this large and remarkable body of work, though, Reed remains largely ignored and overlooked when the talk turns to the hot new writers of the nineties, and only recently is he beginning to get on to major award ballots with stories like "Chrysalis," which is on the final Nebula ballot as I type these words. Like Walter Jon Williams and Bruce Sterling, no one Robert Reed story is ever much like another Robert Reed story in tone or subject matter, and it may be that this versatility counts against him as far as building a reputation is concerned. John Clute, in *The Encyclopedia of Science Fiction,* noting that none of Reed's novels "share any background material or assumptions whatsoever," suggests that "today's sf readers tend to expect a kind of brand identity from authors, and it may be for this reason that Reed has not yet achieved any considerable fame."

It seems unfair that the range of an artist's palette should count against him—but Reed's name *is* slowly percolating into the public awareness here at the end of the nineties, and I suspect that he will become one of the big names of the first decade of the new century coming up on the horizon.

Much of Reed's output takes him beyond our purview here, into fantasy, horror, and other types of science fiction (including some stuff strongly reminiscent of *Galaxy*-era social satire), but a great deal of his output *is* strongly centered within the traditions of the Space Adventure. In fact, like some other young writers of the nineties, including Paul J. McAuley and Stephen Baxter, Reed is producing some of the most inventive and colorful of Modern Space Opera, stuff set on a scale so grand and played out across such immense vistas of time that it makes the "Superscience" stuff of the thirties look pale and conservative by comparison: his sequence of novellas for *Asimov's*, for instance, "Sister Alice," "Brother Perfect," and "Mother Death," detailing internecine warfare and intricate political intrigues between families of Immortals with powers and abilities so immense that they are for all intents and purposes gods, or the sequence of stories unfolding in *F&SF, Science Fiction Age,* and *Asimov's,* including "The Remoras," "Aeon's Child," and "Marrow," involving the journeyings of an immense spaceship the size of Jupiter, staffed by dozens of exotic alien races, that is engaged in a multimillion-year circumnavigation of the galaxy.

And in the poignant and haunting story that follows, he shows us that while being the guest of honor at an important and high-powered function is usually a position to be desired, in Reed's decadent future world of ultrarich immortals, it's an honor you might be well advised to avoid—if you *can*.

Reed lives in Lincoln, Nebraska, where he's at work on a novel-length version of his 1997 novella, "Marrow."

One of the robots offered to carry Pico for the last hundred meters, on its back or cradled in its padded arms; but she shook her head emphatically, telling it, "Thank you, no. I can make it myself." The ground was grassy and soft, lit by glowglobes and the grass-colored moon. It wasn't a difficult walk, even with her bad hip, and she wasn't an invalid. She could manage, she thought with an instinctive independence. And as if to show them, she struck out ahead of the half-dozen robots as they unloaded the big skimmer, stacking Pico's gifts in their long arms. She was halfway across the paddock before they caught her. By then she could hear the muddled voices and laughter coming from the hill-like tent straight ahead. By then she was breathing fast for reasons other than her pain. For fear, mostly. But it was a different flavor of fear than the kinds she knew. What was happening now was beyond her control, and inevitable . . . and it was that kind of certainty that made her stop after a few more steps, one hand rubbing at her hip for no reason except to delay her arrival. If only for a moment or two . . .

"Are you all right?" asked one robot.

She was gazing up at the tent, dark and smooth and gently rounded. "I don't want to be here," she admitted. "That's all." Her life on board the

Kyber had been spent with robots—they had outnumbered the human crew ten to one, then more—and she could always be ruthlessly honest with them. "This is madness. I want to leave again."

"Only, you can't," responded the ceramic creature. The voice was mild, unnervingly patient. "You have nothing to worry about."

"I know."

"The technology has been perfected since—"

"I know."

It stopped speaking, adjusting its hold on the colorful packages.

"That's not what I meant," she admitted. Then she breathed deeply, holding the breath for a moment and exhaling, saying, "All right. Let's go. Go."

The robot pivoted and strode toward the giant tent. The leading robots triggered the doorway, causing it to fold upward with a sudden rush of golden light flooding across the grass, Pico squinting and then blinking, walking faster now and allowing herself the occasional low moan.

"Ever wonder how it'll feel?" Tyson had asked her.

The tent had been pitched over a small pond, probably that very day, and in places the soft, thick grasses had been matted flat by people and their robots. So many people, she thought. Pico tried not to look at any faces. For a moment, she gazed at the pond, shallow and richly green, noticing the tamed waterfowl sprinkled over it and along its shoreline. Ducks and geese, she realized. And some small, crimson-headed cranes. Lifting her eyes, she noticed the large, omega-shaped table near the far wall. She couldn't count the place settings, but it seemed a fair assumption there were sixty-three of them. Plus a single round table and chair in the middle of the omegao—*my table*—and she took another deep breath, looking higher, noticing floating glowglobes and several indigo swallows flying around them, presuambly snatching up the insects that were drawn to the yellow-white light.

People were approaching. Since she had entered, in one patient rush, all sixty-three people had been climbing the slope while shouting, "Pico! Hello!" Their voices mixed together, forming a noisy, senseless paste. "Greetings!" they seemed to say. "Hello, hello!"

They were brightly dressed, flowing robes swishing and everyone wearing big-rimmed hats made to resemble titanic flowers. The people sharply contrasted with the gray-white shells of the robot servants. Those hats were a new fashion, Pico realized. One of the little changes made during these past decades . . . and finally she made herself look at the faces themselves, offering a forced smile and taking a step backward, her belly aching, but her hip healed. The burst of adrenaline hid the deep ache in her bones. Wrestling one of her hands into a wave, she told her audience, "Hello," with a near-whisper. Then she swallowed and said, "Greetings to you!" Was that her voice? She very nearly didn't recognize it.

A woman broke away from the others, almost running toward her. Her big, flowery hat began to work free, and she grabbed the fat, petalish brim and began to fan herself with one hand, the other hand touching Pico on the shoulder. The palm was damp and quite warm; the air suddenly stank of overly sweet perfumes. It was all Pico could manage not to cough. The woman—what was her name?—was asking, "Do you need to sit? We heard . . . about your accident. You poor girl. All the way fine, and then on the last world. Of all the luck!"

Her hip. The woman was jabbering about her sick hip.

Pico nodded and confessed, "Sitting would be nice, yes."

A dozen voices shouted commands. Robots broke into runs, racing one another around the pond to grab the chair beside the little table. The drama seemed to make people laugh. A nervous, self-conscious laugh. When the lead robot reached the chair and started back, there was applause. Another woman shouted, "Mine won! Mine won!" She threw her hat into the air and tried to follow it, leaping as high as possible.

Some man cursed her sharply, then giggled.

Another man forced his way ahead, emerging from the packed bodies in front of Pico. He was smiling in a strange fashion. Drunk or drugged . . . what was permissible these days? With a sloppy, earnest voice, he asked, "How'd it happen? The hip thing . . . how'd you do it?"

He should know. She had dutifully filed her reports throughout the mission, squirting them home. Hadn't he seen them? But then she noticed the watchful, excited faces—no exceptions—and someone seemed to read her thoughts, explaining, "We'd love to hear it *firsthand*. Tell, tell, tell!"

As if they needed to hear a word, she thought, suddenly feeling quite cold.

Her audience grew silent. The robot arrived with the promised chair, and she sat and stretched her bad leg out in front of her, working to focus her mind. It was touching, their silence . . . reverent and almost childlike . . . and she began by telling them how she had tried climbing Miriam Prime with two other crew members. Miriam Prime was the tallest volcano on a super-Venusian world; it was brutal work because of the terrain and their massive lifesuits, cumbersome refrigeration units strapped to their backs, and the atmosphere thick as water. Scalding and acidic. Carbon dioxide and water made for a double greenhouse effect. . . . And she shuddered, partly for dramatics and partly from the memory. Then she said, "Brutal," once again, shaking her head thoughtfully.

They had used hyperthreads to climb the steepest slopes and the cliffs. Normally hyperthreads were virtually unbreakable; but Miriam was not a normal world. She described the basalt cliff and the awful instant of the tragedy; the clarity of the scene startled her. She could feel the heat seeping into her suit, see the dense, dark air, and her arms and legs shook with exhaustion. She told sixty-three people how it felt to be suspended on an invisible thread, two friends and a winch somewhere above in the acidic fog. The winch had jammed without warning, she told; the worst bad luck made it jam where the thread was its weakest. This was near the mission's end, and all the equipment was tired. Several dozen alien worlds had been visited, many mapped for the first time, and every one of them examined up close. As planned.

"Everything has its limits," she told them, her voice having an ominous quality that she hadn't intended.

Even hyperthreads had limits. Pico was dangling, talking to her companions by radio; and just as the jam was cleared, a voice saying, "There . . . got it!", the thread parted. He didn't have any way to know it had parted. Pico was falling, gaining velocity, and the poor man was ignorantly telling her, "It's running strong. You'll be up in no time, no problem. . . ."

People muttered to themselves.

"Oh my," they said.

"Gosh."

"Shit."

Their excitement was obvious, perhaps even overdone. Pico almost laughed, thinking they were making fun of her storytelling . . . thinking, *What do they know about such things? . . .* Only, they were sincere, she realized a moment later. They were enraptured with the image of Pico's long fall, her spinning and lashing out with both hands, fighting to grab anything and slow her fall any way possible—

—and she struck a narrow shelf of eroded stone, the one leg shattered and telescoping down to a gruesome stump. Pico remembered the painless shock of the impact and that glorious instant free of all sensation. She was alive, and the realization had made her giddy. Joyous. Then the pain found her head—a great nauseating wave of pain—and she heard her distant friends shouting, "Pico? Are you there? Can you hear us? Oh, Pico . . . *Pico?* Answer us!"

She had to remain absolutely motionless, sensing that any move would send her tumbling again. She answered in a whisper, telling her friends that she was alive, yes, and please, please hurry. But they had only a partial thread left, and it would take them more than half an hour to descend . . . and she spoke of her agony and the horror, her hip and leg screaming, and not just from the impact. It was worse than mere broken bone, the lifesuit's insulation damaged and the heat bleeding inward, slowly and thoroughly cooking her living flesh.

Pico paused, gazing out at the round-mouthed faces.

So many people and not a breath of sound; and she was having fun. She realized her pleasure almost too late, nearly missing it. Then she told them, "I nearly died," and shrugged her shoulders. "All the distances traveled, every imaginable adventure . . . and I nearly died on one of our last worlds, doing an ordinary climb. . . ."

Let them appreciate her luck, she decided. *Their luck.*

Then another woman lifted her purple flowery hat with both hands, pressing it flush against her own chest. "Of course you survived!" she proclaimed. "You wanted to come home, Pico! You couldn't stand the thought of *dying.*"

Pico nodded without comment, then said, "I was rescued. Obviously." She flexed the damaged leg, saying, "I never really healed," and she touched her hip with reverence, admitting, "We didn't have the resources on board the *Kyber.* This was the best our medical units could do."

Her mood shifted again, without warning. Suddenly she felt sad to tears, eyes dropping and her mouth clamped shut.

"We worried about you, Pico!"

"All the time, dear!"

". . . in our prayers . . . !"

Voices pulled upon each other, competing to be heard. The faces were smiling and thoroughly sincere. Handsome people, she was thinking. Clean and civilized and older than her by centuries. Some of them were more than a thousand years old.

Look at them! she told herself.

And now she felt fear. Pulling both legs toward her chest, she hugged herself, weeping hard enough to dampen her trouser legs; and her audience said, "But you made it, Pico! You came home! The wonders you've seen, the places you've actually touched . . . with those hands. . . . And we're so proud of you! So proud! You've proven your worth a thousand times, Pico! You're made of the very best stuff—!"

—which brought laughter, a great clattering roar of laughter, the joke obviously and apparently tireless.

Even after so long.

They were Pico; Pico was they.

Centuries ago, during the Blossoming, technologies had raced forward at an unprecedented rate. Starships like the *Kyber* and a functional immortality had allowed the first missions to the distant worlds, and there were some grand adventures. Yet adventure requires some element of danger; exploration has never been a safe enterprise. Despite precautions, there were casualties. People who had lived for centuries died suddenly, oftentimes in stupid accidents; and it was no wonder that after the first wave of missions came a long moratorium. No new starships were built, and no sensible person would have ridden inside even the safest vessel. Why risk yourself? Whatever the benefits, why taunt extinction when you have a choice.

Only recently had a solution been invented. Maybe it was prompted by the call of deep space, though Tyson used to claim, "It's the boredom on Earth that inspired them. That's why they came up with their elaborate scheme."

The near-immortals devised ways of making highly gifted, highly trained crews from themselves. With computers and genetic engineering, groups of people could pool their qualities and create compilation humans. Sixty-three individuals had each donated moneys and their own natures, and Pico was the result. She was a grand and sophisticated average of the group. Her face was a blending of every face; her body was a feminine approximation of their own varied bodies. In a few instances, the engineers had planted synthetic genes—for speed and strength, for example—and her brain had a subtly different architecture. Yet basically Pico was their offspring, a stewlike clone. The second of two clones, she knew. The first clone created had had subtle flaws, and he was painlessly destroyed just before birth.

Pico and Tyson and every other compilation person had been born at adult size. Because she was the second attempt, and behind schedule, Pico was thrown straight into her training. Unlike the other crew members, she had spent only a minimal time with her parents. Her sponsors. Whatever they were calling themselves. That and the long intervening years made it difficult to recognize faces and names. She found herself gazing out at them, believing they were strangers, their tireless smiles hinting at something predatory. The neat white teeth gleamed at her, and she wanted to shiver again, holding the knees closer to her mouth.

Someone suggested opening the lovely gifts.

A good idea. She agreed, and the robots brought down the stacks of boxes, placing them beside and behind her. The presents were a young tradition; when she was leaving Earth, the first compilation people were returning with little souvenirs of their travels. Pico had liked the gesture and had done the same. One after another, she started reading the names inscribed in her own flowing handwriting. Then each person stepped forward, thanking her for the treasure, then greedily unwrapping it, the papers flaring into bright colors as they were bent and twisted and torn, then tossed aside for the robots to collect.

She knew none of these people, and that was wrong. What she should have done, she realized, was go into the *Kyber*'s records and memorize names and faces. It would have been easy enough, and proper, and she felt guilty for never having made the effort.

It wasn't merely genetics that she shared with these people; she also embodied slivers of their personalities and basic tendencies. Inside Pico's sophisticated womb, the computers had blended together their shrugs and tongue clicks and the distinctive patterns of their speech. She had emerged as an approximation of every one of them; yet why didn't she feel a greater closeness? Why wasn't there a strong, tangible bond here?

Or was there something—only, she wasn't noticing it?

One early gift was a slab of mirrored rock. "From Tween V," she explained. "What it doesn't reflect, it absorbs and reemits later. I kept that particular piece in my own cabin, fixed to the outer wall—"

"Thank you, thank you," gushed the woman.

For an instant, Pico saw herself reflected on the rock. She looked much older than these people. Tired, she thought. Badly weathered. In the cramped starship, they hadn't the tools to revitalize aged flesh, nor had there been the need. Most of the voyage had been spent in cold-sleep. Their waking times, added together, barely exceeded forty years of biological activity.

"Look at this!" the woman shouted, turning and waving her prize at the others. "Isn't it lovely?"

"A shiny rock," teased one voice. "Perfect!"

Yet the woman refused to be anything but impressed. She clasped her prize to her chest and giggled, merging with the crowd and then vanishing.

They look like children, Pico told herself.

At least how she imagined children to appear . . . unworldly and spoiled, needing care and infinite patience. . . .

She read the next name, and a new woman emerged to collect her gift. "My, what a large box!" She tore at the paper, then the box's lid, then eased her hands into the dunnage of white foam. Pico remembered wrapping this gift—one of the only ones where she was positive of its contents—and she happily watched the smooth, elegant hands pulling free a greasy and knob-faced nut. Then Pico explained:

"It's from the Yult Tree on Proxima Centauri 2." The only member of the species on that strange little world. "If you wish, you can break its dormancy with liquid nitrogen. Then plant it in pure quartz sand, never anything else. Sand, and use red sunlight—"

"I know how to cultivate them," the woman snapped.

There was a sudden silence, uneasy and prolonged.

Finally Pico said, "Well . . . good . . ."

"Everyone knows about Yult nuts," the woman explained. "They're practically giving them away at the greeneries now."

Someone spoke sharply, warning her to stop and think.

"I'm sorry," she responded. "If I sound ungrateful, I mean. I was just thinking, hoping . . . I don't know. Never mind."

A weak, almost inconsequential apology, and the woman paused to feel the grease between her fingertips.

The thing was, Pico thought, that she had relied on guesswork in selecting these gifts. She had decided to represent every alien world, and she felt proud of herself on the job accomplished. Yult Trees were common on Earth? But how could she know such a thing? And besides, why should it matter? She had brought the nut and everything else because she'd taken risks, and these people were obviously too ignorant and silly to appreciate what they were receiving.

Rage had replaced her fear.

Sometimes she heard people talking among themselves, trying to trade gifts. Gemstones and pieces of alien driftwood were being passed about like orphans. Yet nobody would release the specimens of odd life-forms from living worlds, transparent canisters holding bugs and birds and whatnot inside preserving fluids or hard vacuums. If only she had known what she couldn't have known, these silly brats . . . And she found herself swallowing, holding her breath, and wanting to scream at all of them.

Pico was a compilation, yet she wasn't.

She hadn't lived one day as these people had lived their entire lives. She didn't know about comfort or changelessness, and with an attempt at empathy, she tried to imagine such an incredible existence.

Tyson used to tell her, "Shallowness is a luxury. Maybe the ultimate luxury." She hadn't understood him. Not really. "Only the rich can master true frivolity." Now those words echoed back at her, making her think of Tyson. That intense and angry man . . . the opposite of frivolity, the truth told.

And with that, her mood shifted again. Her skin tingled. She felt nothing for or against her audience. How could they help being what they were? How could anyone help their nature? And with that, she found herself reading another name on another unopened box. A little box, she saw. Probably another one of the unpopular gemstones, born deep inside an alien crust and thrown out by forces unimaginable . . .

There was a silence, an odd stillness, and she repeated the name.

"Opera? Opera Ting?"

Was it her imagination, or was there a nervousness running through the audience? Just what was happening—?

"Excuse me?" said a voice from the back. "Pardon?"

People began moving aside, making room, and a figure emerged. A male, something about him noticeably different. He moved with a telltale lightness, with a spring to his gait. Smiling, he took the tiny package while saying, "Thank you," with great feeling. "For my father, thank you. I'm sure he would have enjoyed this moment. I only wish he could have been here, if only . . ."

Father? Wasn't this Opera Ting?

Pico managed to nod, then she asked, "Where is he? I mean, is he busy somewhere?"

"Oh no. He died, I'm afraid." The man moved differently because he was different. He was young—even younger than I, Pico realized—and he shook his head, smiling in a serene way. Was he a clone? A biological child? What? "But on his behalf," said the man, "I wish to thank you. Whatever this gift is, *I* will treasure it. I promise you. I know you must have gone through hell to find it and bring it to me, and thank you so very much, Pico. Thank you, thank you. Thank you!"

Death.

An appropriate intruder in the evening's festivities, thought Pico. Some accident, some kind of tragedy . . . something had killed one of her sixty-three parents, and that thought pleased her. There was a pang of guilt woven into her pleasure, but not very much. It was comforting to know that even these people weren't perfectly insulated from death; it was a force that would grasp everyone, given time. Like it had taken Midge, she thought. And Uoo, she thought. *And Tyson.*

Seventeen compilated people had embarked on *Kyber*, representing almost a thousand near-immortals. Only nine had returned, including Pico. Eight friends were lost. . . . *Lost* was a better word than *death*, she decided. . . . And usually it happened in places worse than any Hell conceived by human beings.

After Opera—his name, she learned, was the same as his father's—the giving of the gifts settled into a routine. Maybe it was because of the young man's attitude. People seemed more polite, more self-contained. Someone had the presence to ask for another story. Anything she wished to tell. And Pico found herself thinking of a watery planet circling a distant red-dwarf sun, her voice saying, "Coldtear," and watching faces nod in unison. They recognized the name, and it was too late. It wasn't the story she would have preferred to tell, yet she couldn't seem to stop herself. Coldtear was on her mind.

Just tell parts, she warned herself.

What you can stand!

The world was terran-class and covered with a single ocean frozen on its surface and heated from below. By tides, in part. And by Coldtear's own nuclear decay. It had been Tyson's idea to build a submersible and dive to the ocean's remote floor. He used spare parts in *Kyber*'s machine shop—the largest room on board—then he'd taken his machine to the surface, setting it on the red-stained ice and using lasers and robot help to bore a wide hole and keep it clear.

Pico described the submersible, in brief, then mentioned that Tyson had asked her to accompany him. She didn't add that they'd been lovers now and again, nor that sometimes they had feuded. She'd keep those parts of the story to herself for as long as possible.

The submersible's interior was cramped and ascetic, and she tried to impress her audience with the pressures that would build on the hyperfiber hull. Many times the pressure found in Earth's oceans, she warned; and Tyson's goal was to set down on the floor, then don a lifesuit protected with a human-shaped force field, actually stepping outside and taking a brief walk.

"Because we need to leave behind footprints," he had argued. "Isn't that why we've come here? We can't just leave prints up on the ice. It moves and melts, wiping itself clean every thousand years or so."

"But isn't that the same below?" Pico had responded. "New muds rain down—slowly, granted—and quakes cause slides and avalanches."

"So we pick right. We find someplace where our marks will be quietly covered. Enshrouded. Made everlasting."

She had blinked, surprised that Tyson cared about such things.

"I've studied the currents," he explained, "and the terrain—"

"Are you serious?" Yet you couldn't feel certain about Tyson. He was a creature full of surprises. "All this trouble, and for what—?"

"Trust me, Pico. Trust me!"

Tyson had had an enormous laugh. His parents, sponsors, whatever—an entirely different group of people—had purposefully made him larger than the norm. They had selected genes for physical size, perhaps wanting Tyson to dominate the *Kyber*'s crew in at least that one fashion. If his own noise was to be believed, that was the only tinkering done to him. Otherwise, he was a pure compilation of his parents' traits, fiery and passionate to a fault. It was a little unclear to Pico what group of people could be so uniformly aggressive; yet Tyson had had his place in their tight-woven crew, and he had had his charms in addition to his size and the biting intelligence.

"Oh Pico," he cried out. "What's this about, coming here? If it's not about leaving traces of our passage . . . then *what?*"

"It's about going home again," she had answered.

"Then why do we leave the *Kyber?* Why not just orbit Coldtear and send down our robots to explore?"

"Because . . ."

"Indeed! Because!" The giant head nodded, and he put a big hand on her shoulder. "I knew you'd see my point. I just needed to give you time, my friend."

She agreed to the deep dive, but not without misgivings.

And during their descent, listening to the ominous creaks and groans of the hull while lying flat on their backs, the misgivings began to reassert themselves.

It was Tyson's fault, and maybe his aim.

No, she thought. It was most definitely his aim.

At first, she thought it was some game, him asking, "Do you ever wonder how it will feel? We come home and are welcomed, and then our dear parents disassemble our brains and implant them—"

"Quiet," she interrupted. "We agreed. Everyone agreed. We aren't going to talk about it, all right?"

A pause, then he said, "Except, I know. How it feels, I mean."

She heard him, then she listened to him take a deep breath from the close, damp air; and finally she had strength enough to ask, "How can you know?"

When Tyson didn't answer, she rolled onto her side and saw the outline of his face. A handsome face, she thought. Strong and incapable of any doubts. This was the only taboo subject among the compilations— "How will it feel?"—and it was left to each of them to decide what they believed. Was it a fate or a reward? To be subdivided and implanted into the minds of dozens and dozens of near-immortals . . .

It wasn't a difficult trick, medically speaking.

After all, each of their minds had been designed for this one specific goal. Memories and talent; passion and training. All of the qualities would be saved—diluted, but, in the same instant, gaining their own near-immortality. Death of a sort, but a kind of everlasting life, too.

That was the creed by which Pico had been born and raised.

The return home brings a great reward, and peace.

Pico's first memory was of her birth, spilling slippery-wet from the womb and coughing hard, a pair of doctoring robots bent over her, whispering to her, "Welcome, child. Welcome. You've been born from *them* to be joined with *them* when it is time. . . . We promise you . . . !"

Comforting noise, and mostly Pico had believed it.

But Tyson had to say, "I know how it feels, Pico," and she could make out his grin, his amusement patronizing. Endless.

"How?" she muttered. "How do you know—?"

"Because some of my parents . . . well, let's just say that I'm not their first time. Understand me?"

"They made another compilation?"

"One of the very first, yes. Which was incorporated into them before I was begun, and which was incorporated into me because there was a spare piece. A leftover chunk of the mind—"

"You're making this up, Tyson!"

Except, he wasn't, she sensed. Knew. Several times, on several early worlds, Tyson had seemed too knowledgeable about too much. Nobody could have prepared himself that well, she realized. She and the others had assumed that Tyson was intuitive in some useful way. Part of him was from another compilation? From someone like them? A fragment of the man had walked twicè beside the gray dust sea of Plicker, and it had twice climbed the giant ant mounds on Proxima Centauri 2. It was a revelation, unnerving and hard to accept; and just the memory of that instant made her tremble secretly, facing her audience, her tired blood turning to ice.

Pico told none of this to her audience.

Instead, they heard about the long descent and the glow of rare life-forms outside—a thin plankton consuming chemical energies as they found them—and, too, the growing creaks of the spherical hull.

They didn't hear how she asked, "So how does it feel? You've got a piece of compilation inside you . . . all right! Are you going to tell me what it's like?"

They didn't hear about her partner's long, deep laugh.

Nor could they imagine him saying, "Pico, my dear. You're such a passive, foolish creature. That's why I love you. So docile, so damned innocent—"

"Does it live inside you, Tyson?"

"It depends on what you consider life."

"Can you feel its presence? I mean, does it have a personality? An existence? Or have you swallowed it all up?"

"I don't think I'll tell." Then the laugh enlarged, and the man lifted his legs and kicked at the hyperfiber with his powerful muscles. She could hear, and feel, the solid impacts of his bootheels. She knew that Tyson's strength was nothing compared to the ocean's mass bearing down on them, their hull scarcely feeling the blows . . . yet some irrational part of her was terrified. She had to reach out, grasping one of his trouser legs and tugging hard, telling him:

"Don't! Stop that! Will you please . . . quit!?"

The tension shifted direction in an instant.

Tyson said, "I was lying," and then added, "About knowing. About having a compilation inside me." And he gave her a huge hug, laughing in a different way now. He nearly crushed her ribs and lungs. Then he spoke into one of her ears, offering more, whispering with the old charm, and she accepting his offer. They did it as well as possible, considering their circumstances and the endless groaning of their tiny vessel; and she remembered all of it while her voice, detached but thorough, described how they had landed on top of something rare. There was a distinct *crunch* of stone. They had made their touchdown on the slope of a recent volcano—an island on an endless plain of mud—and afterward they dressed in their lifesuits, triple-checked their force fields, then flooded the compartment and crawled into the frigid, pressurized water.

It was an eerie, almost indescribable experience to walk on that ocean floor. When language failed Pico, she tried to use silence and oblique gestures to capture the sense of endless time and the cold and darkness. Even when Tyson ignited the submersible's outer lights, making the nearby terrain bright as late afternoon, there was the palpable taste of endless dark just beyond. She told of feeling the pressure despite the force field shrouding her; she told of climbing after Tyson, scrambling up a rough slope of youngish rock to a summit where they discovered a hot-water spring that pumped heated, mineral-rich water up at them.

That might have been the garden spot of Coldtear. Surrounding the spring was a thick, almost gelatinous mass of gray-green bacteria, pulsating and fat by its own standards. She paused, seeing the scene all over again. Then she assured her parents, "It had a beauty. I mean it. An elegant, minimalist beauty."

Nobody spoke.

Then someone muttered, "I can hardly wait to remember it," and gave a weak laugh.

The audience became uncomfortable, tense and too quiet. People shot accusing looks at the offender, and Pico worked not to notice any of it. A bitterness was building in her guts, and she sat up straighter, rubbing at both hips.

Then a woman coughed for attention, waited, and then asked, "What happened next?"

Pico searched for her face.

"There was an accident, wasn't there? On Coldtear . . . ?"

I won't tell them, thought Pico. Not now. Not this way.

She said, "No, not then. Later." And maybe some of them knew better. Judging by the expressions, a few must have remembered the records. Tyson died on the first dive. It was recorded as being an equipment failure—Pico's lie—and she'd hold on to the lie as long as possible. It was a promise she'd made to herself and kept all these years.

Shutting her eyes, she saw Tyson's face smiling at her. Even through the thick faceplate and the shimmering glow of the force field, she could make out the mischievous expression, eyes glinting, the large mouth saying, "Go on back, Pico. In and up and a safe trip to you, pretty lady."

She had been too stunned to respond, gawking at him.

"Remember? I've still got to leave my footprints somewhere—"

"What are you planning?" she interrupted.

He laughed and asked, "Isn't it obvious? I'm going to make my mark on this world. It's dull and nearly dead, and I don't think anyone is ever going to return here. Certainly not to *here*. Which means I'll be pretty well left alone—"

"Your force field will drain your batteries," she argued stupidly. Of course he knew that salient fact. "If you stay here—!"

"I know, Pico. I know."

"But why—?"

"I lied before. About lying." The big face gave a disappointed look, then the old smile reemerged. "Poor, docile Pico. I knew you wouldn't take this well. You'd take it too much to heart . . . which I suppose is why I asked you along in the first place. . . ." and he turned away, starting to walk through the bacterial mat with threads and chunks kicked loose, sailing into the warm current and obscuring him. It was a strange gray snow moving against gravity. Her last image of Tyson was of a hulking figure amid the living goo; and to this day, she had wondered if she could have wrestled him back to the submersible—an impossibility, of course—and how far could he have walked before his force field failed.

Down the opposite slope and onto the mud, no doubt.

She could imagine him walking fast, using his strength . . . fighting the deep, cold muds . . . Tyson plus that fragment of an earlier compilation—and who was driving whom? she asked herself. Again and again and again.

Sometimes she heard herself asking Tyson, "How does it feel having a sliver of another soul inside you?"

His ghost never answered, merely laughing with his booming voice.

She hated him for his suicide, and admired him; and sometimes she cursed him for taking her along with him and for the way he kept crop-ping up in her thoughts. . . . "Damn you, Tyson. Goddamn you, goddamn you . . . !"

No more presents remained.

One near-immortal asked, "Are we hungry?", and others replied, "Famished," in one voice, then breaking into laughter. The party moved toward the distant tables, a noisy mass of bodies surrounding Pico. Her hip had stiffened while sitting, but she worked hard to move normally, managing the downslope toward the pond and then the little wooden bridge spanning a rocky brook. The waterfowl made grumbling sounds, angered by the disturbances; Pico stopped and watched them, finally asking, "What kinds are those?" She meant the ducks.

"Just mallards," she heard. "Nothing fancy."

Yet, to her, they seemed like miraculous creatures, vivid plumage and the moving eyes, wings spreading as a reflex and their nervous motions lending them a sense of muscular power. A vibrancy.

Someone said, "You've seen many birds, I'm sure."

Of a sort, yes . . .

"What were your favorites, Pico?"

They were starting uphill, quieter now, feet making a swishing sound in the grass; and Pico told them about the pterosaurs of Wilder, the man-sized bats on Little Quark, and the giant insects—a multitude of species—thriving in the thick, warm air of Tau Ceti I.

"Bugs," grumbled someone. "Uggh!"

"Now, now," another person responded.

Then a third joked, "I'm not looking forward to *that*. Who wants to trade memories?"

A joke, thought Pico, because memories weren't tradable properties. Minds were holographic—every piece held the basic picture of the whole—and these people each would receive a sliver of Pico's whole self. Somehow that made her smile, thinking how none of them would be spared. Every terror and every agony would be set inside each of them. In a diluted form, of course. The *Pico-ness* minimized. Made manageable. Yet it was something, wasn't it? It pleased her to think that a few of them might awaken in the night, bathed in sweat after dreaming of Tyson's death . . . just as she had dreamed of it time after time . . . her audience given more than they had anticipated, a dark little joke of her own. . . .

They reached the tables, Pico taking hers and sitting, feeling rather self-conscious as the others quietly assembled around her, each of them knowing where they belonged. She watched their faces. The excitement she had sensed from the beginning remained; only, it seemed magnified now. More colorful, more intense. Facing toward the inside of the omega, her hosts couldn't quit staring, forever smiling, scarcely able to eat once the robots brought them plates filled with steaming foods.

Fancy meals, Pico learned.

The robot setting her dinner before her explained, "The vegetables are from Triton, miss. A very special and much-prized strain. And the meat is from a wild hound killed just yesterday—"

"Really?"

"As part of the festivities, yes." The ceramic face, white and expressionless, stared down at her. "There have been hunting parties and games, among other diversions. Quite an assortment of activities, yes."

"For how long?" she asked. "These festivities . . . have they been going on for days?"

"A little longer than three months, miss."

She had no appetite; nonetheless, she lifted her utensils and made the proper motions, reminding herself that three months of continuous parties would be nothing to these people. Three months was a day to them, and what did they do with their time? So much of it, and such a constricted existence. What had Tyson once told her? The average citizen of earth averages less than one off-world trip in eighty years, and the trends were toward less traveling. Spaceflight was safe only to a degree, and these people couldn't stand the idea of being meters away from a cold, raw vacuum.

"Cowards," Tyson had called them. "Gutted, deblooded cowards!"

Looking about, she saw the delicate twists of green leaves vanishing into grinning mouths, the chewing prolonged and indifferent. Except for Opera, that is. Opera saw her and smiled back in turn, his eyes different, something mocking about the tilt of his head and the curl of his mouth.

She found her eyes returning to Opera every little while, and she wasn't sure why. She felt no physical attraction for the man. His youth and attitudes made him different from the others, but how much different? Then she noticed his dinner—cultured potatoes with meaty hearts— and that made an impression on Pico. It was a standard food on board the *Kyber.* Opera was making a gesture, perhaps. Nobody else was eating that bland food, and she decided this was a show of solidarity. At least the man was trying, wasn't he? More than the others, he was. He was.

Dessert was cold and sweet and shot full of some odd liquor.

Pico watched the others drinking and talking among themselves. For the first time, she noticed how they seemed subdivided—discrete groups formed, and boundaries between each one. A dozen people here, seven back there, and sometimes individuals sitting alone—like Opera—chatting politely or appearing entirely friendless.

One lonesome woman rose to her feet and approached Pico, not smil-

ing, and with a sharp voice, she declared, "Tomorrow, come morning . . .
you'll live forever . . . !"

Conversations diminished, then quit entirely.

"Plugged in. Here." "She was under the influence of some drug, the
tip of her finger shaking and missing her own temple. "You fine lucky girl
. . . Yes, you are . . . !"

Some people laughed at the woman, suddenly and without shame.

The harsh sound made her turn and squint, and Pico watched her
straightening her back. The woman was pretending to be above them and
uninjured, her thin mouth squeezed shut and her nose tilting with mock
pride. With a clear, soft voice, she said, "Fuck every one of you," and then
laughed, turning toward Pico, acting as if they had just shared some glorious joke of their own.

"I would apologize for our behavior," said Opera, "but I can't. Not in
good faith, I'm afraid."

Pico eyed the man. Dessert was finished; people stood about drinking, keeping the three-month-old party in motion. A few of them stripped
naked and swam in the green pond. It was a raucous scene, tireless and
full of happy scenes that never seemed convincingly joyous. Happy
sounds by practice, rather. Centuries of practice, and the result was to
make Pico feel sad and quite lonely.

"A silly, vain lot," Opera told her.

She said, "Perhaps," with a diplomatic tone, then saw several others
approaching. At least they looked polite, she thought. Respectful. It was
odd how a dose of respect glossed over so much. Particularly when the
respect wasn't reciprocated, Pico feeling none toward them. . . .

A man asked to hear more stories. Please?

Pico shrugged her shoulders, then asked, "Of what?" Every request
brought her a momentary sense of claustrophobia, her memories threatening to crush her. "Maybe you're interested in a specific world?"

Opera responded, saying, "Blueblue!"

Blueblue was a giant gaseous world circling a bluish sun. Her first
thought was of Midge vanishing into the dark storm on its southern hemisphere, searching for the source of the carbon monoxide upflow that effectively gave breath to half the world. Most of Blueblue was calm in
comparison. Thick winds; strong sunlight. Its largest organisms would
dwarf most cities, their bodies balloonlike and their lives spent feeding on
sunlight and hydrocarbons, utilizing carbon monoxide and other radicals in
their patient metabolisms. Pico and the others had spent several months living on the living clouds, walking across them, taking samples and studying
the assortment of parasites and symbionts that grew in their flesh.

She told about sunrise on Blueblue, remembering its colors and its astounding speed. Suddenly she found herself talking about a particular morning when the landing party was jostled out of sleep by an apparent quake. Their little huts had been strapped down and secured, but they found themselves tilting fast. Their cloud was colliding with a neighboring cloud—something they had never seen—and of course there was a rush to load their shuttle and leave. If it came to that.

"Normally, you see, the clouds avoid each other," Pico told her little audience. "At first, we thought the creatures were fighting, judging by their roaring and the hard shoving. They make sounds by forcing air through pores and throats and anuses. It was a strange show. Deafening. The collision point was maybe a third of a kilometer from camp, our whole world rolling over while the sun kept rising, its bright, hot light cutting through the organic haze—"

"Gorgeous," someone said.

A companion said, "Quiet!"

Then Opera touched Pico on the arm, saying, "Go on. Don't pay any attention to them."

The others glanced at Opera, hearing something in his voice, and their backs stiffening reflexively.

And then Pico was speaking again, finishing her story. Tyson was the first one of them to understand, who somehow made the right guess and began laughing, not saying a word. By then everyone was on board the shuttle, ready to fly; the tilting stopped suddenly, the air filling with countless little blue balloons. Each was the size of a toy balloon, she told. Their cloud was bleeding them from new pores, and the other cloud responded with a thick gray fog of butterflylike somethings. The somethings flew after the balloons, and Tyson laughed harder, his face contorted and the laugh finally shattering into a string of gasping coughs.

"Don't you see?" he asked the others. "Look! The clouds are enjoying a morning screw!"

Pico imitated Tyson's voice, regurgitating the words and enthusiasm. Then she was laughing for herself, scarcely noticing how the others giggled politely. No more. Only Opera was enjoying her story, again touching her arm and saying, "That's lovely. Perfect. God, precious . . . !"

The rest began to drift away, not quite excusing themselves.

What was wrong?

"Don't mind them," Opera cautioned. "They're members of some new chastity faith. Clarity through horniness, and all that." He laughed at them now. "They probably went to too many orgies, and this is how they're coping with their guilt. That's all."

Pico shut her eyes, remembering the scene on Blueblue for herself. She didn't want to relinquish it.

"Screwing clouds," Opera was saying. "That is lovely."

And she thought.

He sounds a little like Tyson. In places. In ways.

After a while, Pico admitted. "I can't remember your father's face. I'm sure I must have met him, but I don't—"

"You did meet him," Opera replied. "He left a recording of it in his journal—a brief meeting—and I made a point of studying everything about the mission and you. His journal entries; your reports. Actually, I'm the best-prepared person here today. Other than you, of course."

She said nothing, considering those words.

They were walking now, making their way down to the pond, and sometimes Pico noticed the hard glances of the others. Did they approve of Opera? Did it anger them, watching him monopolizing her time? Yet she didn't want to be with *them,* the truth told. Fuck them, she thought; and she smiled at her private profanity.

The pond was empty of swimmers now. There were just a few sleepless ducks and the roiled water. A lot of the celebrants had vanished, Pico realized. To where? She asked Opera, and he said:

"It's late. But then again, most people sleep ten or twelve hours every night."

"That much?"

He nodded. "Enhanced dreams are popular lately. And the oldest people sometimes exceed fifteen hours—"

"Always?"

He shrugged and offered a smile.

"What a waste!"

"Of time?" he countered.

Immortals can waste many things, she realized. But never time. And with that thought, she looked straight at her companion, asking him, "What happened to your father?"

"How did he die, you mean?"

A little nod. A respectful expression, she hoped. But curious.

Opera said, "He used an extremely toxic poison, self-induced." He gave a vague disapproving look directed at nobody. "A suicide at the end of a prolonged depression. He made certain that his mind was ruined before autodocs and his own robots could save him."

"I'm sorry."

"Yet I can't afford to feel sorry," he responded. "You see, I was born according to the terms of his will. I'm 99 percent his clone, the rest of my genes tailored according to his desires. If he hadn't murdered himself, I wouldn't exist. Nor would I have inherited his money." He shrugged, saying, "Parents," with a measured scorn. "They have such power over you, like it or not."

She didn't know how to respond.

"Listen to us. All of this death talk, and doesn't it seem out of place?" Opera said, "After all, we're here to celebrate your return home. Your successes. Your gifts. And you . . . you on the brink of being magnified many times over." He paused before saying, "By this time tomorrow, you'll reside inside all of us, making everyone richer as a consequence."

The young man had an odd way of phrasing his statements, the entire speech either earnest or satirical. She couldn't tell which. Or if there was a *which*. Maybe it was her ignorance with the audible clues, the unknown trappings of this culture. . . . Then something else occurred to her.

"What do you mean? 'Death talk . . .' "

"Your friend Tyson died on Coldtear," he replied. "And didn't you lose another on Blueblue?"

"Midge. Yes."

He nodded gravely, glancing down at Pico's legs. "We can sit. I'm sorry; I should have noticed you were getting tired."

They sat side by side on the grass, watching the mallard ducks. Males and females had the same vivid green heads. Beautiful, she mentioned. Opera explained how females were once brown and quite drab, but people thought that was a shame, and voted to have the species altered, both sexes made equally resplendent. Pico nodded, only halfway listening. She couldn't get Tyson and her other dead friends out of her mind. Particularly Tyson. She had been angry with him for a long time, and even now her anger wasn't finished. Her confusion and general tiredness made it worse. Why had he done it? In life the man had had a way of dominating every meeting, every little gathering. He had been optimistic and fearless, the last sort of person to do such an awful thing. Suicide. The others had heard it was an accident—Pico had held to her lie—but she and they were in agreement about one fact. When Tyson died, at that precise instant, some essential heart of their mission had been lost.

Why? she wondered. Why?

Midge had flown into the storm on Blueblue, seeking adventure and important scientific answers; and her death was sad, yes, and everyone had missed her. But it wasn't like Tyson's death. It felt honorable, maybe even perfect. They had a duty to fulfill in the wilderness, and that duty was in their blood and their training. People spoke about Midge for years, acting as if she were still alive. As if she were still flying the shuttle into the storm's vortex.

But Tyson was different.

Maybe everyone knew the truth about his death. Sometimes it seemed that, in Pico's eyes, the crew could see what had really happened, and they'd hear it between her practiced lines. They weren't fooled.

Meanwhile, others died in the throes of life.

Uoo—a slender wisp of a compilation—was incinerated by a giant bolt of lightning on Miriam II, little left but ashes, and the rest of the party continuing its descent into the superheated Bottoms and the quiet Lead Sea.

Opaltu died in the mouth of a nameless predator. He had been another of Pico's lovers, a proud man and the best example of vanity that she had known—until today, she thought—and she and the others had laughed at the justice that befell Opaltu's killer. Unable to digest alien meats, the predator had sickened and died in a slow, agonizing fashion, vomiting up its insides as it staggered through the yellow jungle.

Boo was killed while working outside the *Kyber,* struck by a mote of interstellar debris.

Xon's lifesuit failed, suffocating her.

As did Kyties's suit, and that wasn't long ago. Just a year now, ship time, and she remembered a cascade of jokes and his endless good humor. The most decent person on board the *Kyber.*

Yet it was Tyson who dominated her memories of the dead. It was the man as well as his self-induced extinction, and the anger within her swelled all at once. Suddenly even simple breathing was work. Pico found herself sweating, then blinking away the salt in her eyes. Once, then again, she coughed into a fist; then finally she had the energy to ask, "Why did he do it?"

"Who? My father?"

"Depression is . . . should be . . . a curable ailment. We had drugs and therapies on board that could erase it."

"But it was more than depression. It was something that attacks the very old people. A kind of giant boredom, if you will."

She wasn't surprised. Nodding as if she'd expected that reply, she told him, "I can understand that, considering your lives." Then she thought how Tyson hadn't been depressed or bored. How could he have been either?

Opera touched her bad leg, for just a moment. "You must wonder how it will be," he mentioned. "Tomorrow, I mean."

She shivered, aware of the fear returning. Closing her burning eyes, she saw Tyson's walk through the bacterial mat, the loose gray chunks spinning as the currents carried them, lending them a greater sort of life with the motion. . . . And she opened her eyes, Opera watching, saying something to her with his expression, and her unable to decipher any meanings.

"Maybe I should go to bed, too," she allowed.

The park under the tent was nearly empty now. Where had the others gone?

Opera said, "Of course," as if expecting it. He rose and offered his hand, and she surprised herself by taking the hand with both of hers. Then he said, "If you like, I can show you your quarters."

She nodded, saying nothing.

It was a long, painful walk, and Pico honestly considered asking for a robot's help. For anyone's. Even a cane would have been a blessing, her hip never having felt so bad. Earth's gravity and the general stress were making it worse, most likely. She told herself that at least it was a pleasant night, warm and calm and perfectly clear, and the soft ground beneath the grass seemed to be calling to her, inviting her to lie down and sleep in the open.

People were staying in a chain of old houses subdivided into apartments, luxurious yet small. Pico's apartment was on the ground floor, Opera happy to show her through the rooms. For an instant, she considered asking him to stay the night. Indeed, she sensed that he was delaying, hoping for some sort of invitation. But she heard herself saying, "Rest well, and thank you," and her companion smiled and left without comment, vanishing through the crystal front door and leaving her completely alone.

For a little while, she sat on her bed, doing nothing. Not even thinking, at least in any conscious fashion.

Then she realized something, no warning given; and aloud, in a voice almost too soft for even her to hear, she said, "He didn't know. Didn't have an idea, the shit." Tyson. She was thinking about the fiery man and his boast about being the second generation of star explorers. What if it was all true? His parents had injected a portion of a former Tyson into him, and he had already known the early worlds they had visited. He already knew the look of double sunrises on the desert world orbiting Alpha Centauri A; he knew the smell of constant rot before they cracked their airlocks on Barnard's 2. But try as he might—

"—he couldn't remember how it feels to be disassembled." She spoke without sound. To herself. "That titanic and fearless creature, and he couldn't remember. Everything else, yes, but not that. And not knowing had to scare him. Nothing else did, but that terrified him. The only time in his life he was truly scared, and it took all his bluster to keep that secret—!"

Killing himself rather than face his fear.

Of course, she thought. Why not?

And he took Pico as his audience, knowing she'd be a good audience. Because they were lovers. Because he must have decided that he could convince her of his fearlessness one last time, leaving his legend secure. Immortal, in a sense.

That's what you were thinking . . .

. . . wasn't it?

And she shivered, holding both legs close to her mouth, and feeling the warm misery of her doomed hip.

She sat for a couple more hours, neither sleeping nor feeling the slightest need for sleep. Finally she rose and used the bathroom, and after a long, careful look through the windows, she ordered the door to open, and stepped outside, picking a reasonable direction and walking stiffly and quickly on the weakened leg.

Opera emerged from the shadows, startling her.

"If you want to escape," he whispered, "I can help. Let me help you, please."

The face was handsome in the moonlight, young in every fashion. He must have guessed her mood, she realized, and she didn't allow herself to become upset. Help was important, she reasoned. Even essential. She had to find her way across a vast and very strange alien world. "I want to get back into orbit," she told him, "and find another starship. We saw several. They looked almost ready to embark." Bigger than the *Kyber,* and obviously faster. No doubt designed to move even deeper into the endless wilderness.

"I'm not surprised," Opera told her. "And I understand."

She paused, staring at him before asking, "How did you guess?"

"Living forever inside our heads . . . That's just a mess of metaphysical nonsense, isn't it? You know you'll die tomorrow. Bits of your brain will vanish inside us, made part of us, and not vice versa. I think it sounds like an awful way to die, certainly for someone like you—"

"Can you really help me?"

"This way," he told her. "Come on."

They walked for an age, crossing the paddock and finally reaching the wide tube where the skimmers shot past with a rush of air. Opera touched a simple control, then said, "It won't be long," and smiled at her. Just for a moment. "You know, I almost gave up on you. I thought I must have read you wrong. You didn't strike me as someone who'd go quietly to her death. . . ."

She had a vague, fleeting memory of the senior Opera. Gazing at the young face, she could recall a big, warm hand shaking her hand, and a similar voice saying, "It's very good to meet you, Pico. At last!"

"I bet one of the new starships will want you." The young Opera was telling her, "You're right. They're bigger ships, and they've got better facilities. Since they'll be gone even longer, they've been given the best possible medical equipment. That hip and your general body should respond to treatments—"

"I have experience," she whispered.

"Pardon me?"

"Experience." She nodded with conviction. "I can offer a crew plenty of valuable experience."

"They'd be idiots not to take you."

A skimmer slowed and stopped before them. Opera made the windows opaque—"So nobody can see you"—and punched in their destination, Pico making herself comfortable.

"Here we go," he chuckled, and they accelerated away.

There was an excitement to all of this, an adventure like every other. Pico realized that she was scared, but in a good, familiar way. Life and death. Both possibilities seemed balanced on a very narrow fulcrum, and she found herself smiling, rubbing her hip with a slow hand.

They were moving fast, following Opera's instructions.

"A circuitous route," he explained. "We want to make our whereabouts less obvious. All right?"

"Fine."

"Are you comfortable?"

"Yes," she allowed. "Basically."

Then she was thinking about the others—the other survivors from the *Kyber*—wondering how many of them were having second or third thoughts. The long journey home had been spent in cold-sleep, but there had been intervals when two or three of them were awakened to do normal maintenance. Not once did anyone even joke about taking the ship elsewhere. Nobody had asked, "Why do we have to go to Earth?" The obvious question had eluded them, and at the time, she had assumed it was because there were no doubters. Besides herself, that is. The rest believed this would be the natural conclusion to full and satisfied lives; they were returning home to a new life and an appreciative audience. How could any sane compilation think otherwise?

Yet she found herself wondering.

Why no jokes?

If they hadn't had doubts, wouldn't they have made jokes?

Eight others had survived the mission. Yet none were as close to Pico

as she had been to Tyson. They had saved each other's proverbial skin
many times, and she did feel a sudden deep empathy for them, remembering how they had boarded nine separate shuttles after kisses and hugs
and a few careful tears, each of them struggling with the proper things to
say. But what could anyone say at such a moment? Particularly when you
believed that your companions were of one mind, and, in some fashion,
happy. . . .

Pico said, "I wonder about the others," and intended to leave it at that.
To say nothing more.

"The others?"

"From the *Kyber*. My friends." She paused and swallowed, then said
softly, "Maybe I could contact them."

"No," he responded.

She jerked her head, watching Opera's profile.

"That would make it easy to catch you." His voice was quite sensible
and measured. "Besides," he added, "can't they make up their own
minds? Like you have?"

She nodded, thinking that was reasonable. Sure.

He waited a long moment, then said, "Perhaps you'd like to talk
about something else?"

"Like what?"

He eyed Pico, then broke into a wide smile. "If I'm not going to inherit a slice of your mind, leave me another story. Tell . . . I don't know.
Tell me about your favorite single place. Not a world, but some favorite
patch of ground on any world. If you could be anywhere now, where
would it be? And with whom?

Pico felt the skimmer turning, following the tube. She didn't have to
consider the question—her answer seemed obvious to her—but the pause
was to collect herself, weighing how to begin and what to tell.

"In the mountains on Erindi 3," she said, "the air thins enough to be
breathed safely, and it's really quite pretty. The scenery, I mean."

"I've seen holos of the place. It is lovely."

"Not just lovely." She was surprised by her authority, her self-assured
voice telling him, "There's a strange sense of peace there. You don't get
that from holos. Supposedly it's produced by the weather and the vegetation. . . . They make showers of negative ions, some say. . . . And it's the
colors, too. A subtle interplay of shades and shadows. All very one-of-a-
kind."

"Of course," he said carefully.

She shut her eyes, seeing the place with almost perfect clarity. A
summer storm had swept overhead, charging the glorious atmosphere
even further, leaving everyone in the party invigorated. She and Tyson,

Midge, and several others had decided to swim in a deep-blue pool near their campsite. The terrain itself was rugged, black rocks erupting from the blue-green vegetation. The valley's little river poured into a gorge and the pool, and the people did the same. Tyson was first, naturally. He laughed and bounced in the icy water, screaming loud enough to make a flock of razor-bats take flight. This was only the third solar system they had visited, and they were still young in every sense. It seemed to them that every world would be this much fun.

She recalled—and described—diving feet first. She was last into the pool, having inherited a lot of caution from her parents. Tyson had teased her, calling her a coward and then worse, then showing where to aim. "Right here! It's deep here! Come on, coward! Take a chance!"

The water was startlingly cold, and there wasn't much of it beneath the shiny flowing surface. She struck and hit the packed sand below, and the impact made her groan, then shout. Tyson had lied, and she chased the bastard around the pool, screaming and finally clawing at his broad back until she'd driven him up the gorge walls, him laughing and once, losing strength with all the laughing, almost tumbling down on top of her.

She told Opera everything.

At first, it seemed like an accident. All her filters were off; she admitted everything without hesitation. Then she told herself that the man was saving her life and deserved the whole story. That's when she was describing the lovemaking between her and Tyson. That night. It was their first time, and maybe the best time. They did it on a bed of mosses, perched on the rim of the gorge, and she tried to paint a vivid word picture for her audience, including smells and the textures and the sight of the double moons overhead, colored a strange living pink and moving fast.

Their skimmer ride seemed to be taking a long time, she thought once she was finished. She mentioned this to Opera, and he nodded soberly. Otherwise, he made no comment.

I won't be disembodied tomorrow, she told herself.

Then she added, *Today, I mean today.*

She felt certain now. Secure. She was glad for this chance and for this dear new friend, and it was too bad she'd have to leave so quickly, escaping into the relative safety of space. Perhaps there were more people like Opera . . . people who would be kind to her, appreciating her circumstances and desires . . . supportive and interesting companions in their own right. . . .

And suddenly the skimmer was slowing, preparing to stop.

When Opera said, "Almost there," she felt completely at ease. Entirely calm. She shut her eyes and saw the raw, wild mountains on Erindi

3, storm clouds gathering and flashes of lightning piercing the howling winds. She summoned a different day, and saw Tyson standing against the storms, smiling, beckoning for her to climb up to him just as the first cold, fat raindrops smacked against her face.

The skimmer's hatch opened with a hiss.

Sunlight streamed inside, and she thought: *Dawn. By now, sure . . .*

Opera rose and stepped outside, then held a hand out to Pico. She took it with both of hers and said, "Thank you," while rising, looking past him and seeing the paddock and the familiar faces, the green ground and the giant tent with its doorways opened now, various birds flying inside and out again . . . and Pico most surprised by how little she was surprised, Opera still holding her hands, and his flesh dry, the hand perfectly calm.

The autodocs stood waiting for orders.

This time, Pico had been carried from the skimmer, riding cradled in a robot's arms. She had taken just a few faltering steps before half-crumbling. Exhaustion was to blame. Not fear. At least it didn't feel like fear, she told herself. Everyone told her to take it easy, to enjoy her comfort, and now, finding herself flanked by autodocs, her exhaustion worsened. She thought she might die before the cutting began, too tired now to pump her own blood or fire her neurons or even breathe.

Opera was standing nearby, almost smiling, his pleasure serene and chilly and without regrets.

He hadn't said a word since they left the skimmer.

Several others told her to sit, offering her a padded seat with built-in channels to catch any flowing blood. Pico took an uneasy step toward the seat, then paused and straightened her back, saying, "I'm thirsty," softly, her words sounding thoroughly parched.

"Pardon?" they asked.

"I want to drink . . . some water, please . . . ?"

Faces turned, hunting for a cup and water.

It was Opera who said, "Will the pond do?" Then he came forward, extending an arm and telling everyone else, "It won't take long. Give us a moment, will you?"

Pico and Opera walked alone.

Last night's ducks were sleeping and lazily feeding. Pico looked at their metallic green heads, so lovely that she ached at seeing them, and she tried to miss nothing. She tried to concentrate so hard that time itself would compress, seconds turning to hours, and her life in that way prolonged.

Opera was speaking, asking her, "Do you want to hear why?"

She shook her head, not caring in the slightest.

"But you must be wondering why. I fool you into believing that I'm your ally, and I manipulate you—"

"Why?" she sputtered. "So tell me."

"Because," he allowed, "it helps the process. It helps your integration into us. I gave you a chance for doubts and helped you think you were fleeing, convinced you that you'd be free . . . and now you're angry and scared and intensely alive. It's that intensity that we want. It makes the neurological grafts take hold. It's a trick that we learned since the *Kyber* left Earth. Some compilations tried to escape, and when they were caught and finally incorporated along with their anger—"

"Except, I'm not angry," she lied, gazing at his self-satisfied grin.

"A nervous system in flux," he said. "I volunteered, by the way."

She thought of hitting him. Could she kill him somehow?

But instead, she turned and asked, "Why this way? Why not just let me slip away, then catch me at the spaceport?"

"You were going to drink," he reminded her. "Drink."

She knelt despite her hip's pain, knees sinking into the muddy bank and her lips pursing, taking in a long, warmish thread of muddy water, and then her face lifting, the water spilling across her chin and chest, and her mouth unable to close tight.

"Nothing angers," he said, "like the betrayal of someone you trust."

True enough, she thought. Suddenly she could see Tyson leaving her alone on the ocean floor, his private fears too much, and his answer being to kill himself while dressed up in apparent bravery. A kind of betrayal, wasn't that? To both of them, and it still hurt. . . .

"Are you still thirsty?" asked Opera.

"Yes," she whispered.

"Then drink. Go on."

She knelt again, taking a bulging mouthful and swirling it with her tongue. Yet she couldn't make herself swallow, and after a moment, it began leaking out from her lips and down her front again. Making a mess, she realized. Muddy, warm, ugly water, and she couldn't remember how it felt to be thirsty. Such a little thing, and ordinary, and she couldn't remember it.

"Come on, then," said Opera.

She looked at him.

He took her arm and began lifting her, a small, smiling voice saying, "You've done very well, Pico. You have. The truth is that everyone is very proud of you."

She was on her feet again and walking, not sure when she had begun moving her legs. She wanted to poison her thoughts with her hatred of these awful people, and for a little while, she could think of nothing else.

She would make her mind bilious and cancerous, poisoning all of these bastards and finally destroying them. That's what she would do, she promised herself. Except, suddenly she was sitting on the padded chair, autodocs coming close with their bright, humming limbs; and there was so much stored in her mind—worlds and people, emotions heaped on emotions—and she didn't have the time she would need to poison herself.

Which proved something, she realized.

Sitting still now.

Sitting still and silent. At ease. Her front drenched and stained brown, but her open eyes calm and dry.

George Turner

FLOWERING MANDRAKE

An Australian writer and critic of great renown, the late George Turner was for many years that country's most distinguished science fiction writer, and one of the few Australian SF writers to have established an international reputation that transcended parochial boundaries. Although he also published six mainstream novels, he was best known in the genre for the string of unsentimental, rigorous, and sometimes acerbic science fiction novels that he began to publish in 1978, including *Beloved Son, Vaneglory, Yesterday's Men, Brain Child, In the Heart or in the Head, Destiny Makers,* and the widely acclaimed *Drowning Towers,* which won the Arthur C. Clarke Award. His most recent novel was *Genetic Soldier.* His short fiction was collected in *A Pursuit of Miracles,* and he was the editor of an anthology of Australian science fiction, *The View from the Edge.*

During his lifetime Turner may have been considered to be the Grandmaster of Australian science fiction, and, true, he was decades older than his next most talked-about compatriot, Greg Egan . . . but even toward the end of his life he had lost none of his imagination or intellectual vigor, as he proved with the powerful and ingenious story that follows, a tale unsurpassed by any young Turks anywhere for the bravura sweep and daring of its conceptualization.

Turner died in 1997, at the age of eighty-two.

> Go, and catch a falling star,
> Get with child a mandrake root . . .
> —From the song, "Go, and catch," by John Donne

Four stars make Capella: two G-type suns sharing between them five times the mass of Terra's sol and two lesser lights seen only with difficulty from a system so far away.

Two of the fifteen orbiting worlds produced thinking life under fairly similar conditions but the dominant forms which evolved on each bore little resemblance to each other save in the possession of upright carriage, a head, and limbs for ambulation and grasping.

When, in time, they discovered each other's existence, they fought with that ferocity of civilized hatred which no feral species can or need to match.

The Red-Bloods fought at first because they were attacked, then because they perceived that the Green Folk were bent not on conquest but on destruction. The Green Folk fought because the discovery of Red-Blood dominance over a planet uncovered traits deep in their genetic structure. Evolution had been for them a million-year struggle against domination by emerging red-blooded forms and their eventual supremacy had been achieved only by ruthless self-preservation—the destruction of all competition. They kept small animals for various domestic and manufacturing purposes, even ate them at times for gourmet pleasure rather than need and feared them not at all, but the ancient enmity and dread persisted in racial defensiveness like a memory in the blood.

The discovery of a planet of Red-Bloods with a capacity for cultural competition wreaked psychological havoc. Almost without thought the Green Folk attacked.

Ships exploded, ancient cities drowned in fresh-sprung lava pits, atmospheres were polluted with death.

Beyond the Capellan system no sentient being knew of species in conflict. Galactic darkness swallowed the bright, tiny carnage.

Capella lay some forty-seven light-years from the nearest habitable planet, which its people called, by various forms of the name, Terra.

Only one member of crew, a young officer of the Fifth Brachiate, new to his insignia and with little seniority, but infinitely privileged over the Root-kin of his gunnery unit, escaped the destruction of *Deadly Thorn.* His name (if it matters, because it was never heard anywhere again) was Fernix, which meant in the Old Tongue, "journeying forest father."

When the Triple Alert flashed he was in the Leisure Mess, sucking at a tubule of the stem, taking in the new, mildly stimulating liquor fermented from the red fluid of animals. It was a popular drink, not too dangerously potent, taken with a flick of excitement for the rumor that it was salted with the life-blood of enemy captives. This was surely untrue but made a good morale boosting story.

Triple Alerts came a dozen a day and these bored old hands of the war no longer leapt to battle stations like sprouts-in-training. Some hostile craft a satellite's orbit distant had detected *Deadly Thorn* and launched a missile; deflector arrays would catch and return it with augmented velocity and the flurry would be over before they reached the doorway.

There was, of course, always the unlucky chance. Deflector arrays had their failings and enemy launchers their moments of cunning.

Fernix was still clearing his mouth when an instant of brilliant explosion filled space around *Deadly Thorn* and her nose section and Command Room blew out into the long night.

He was running, an automation trained to emergency, when the sirens screamed and through the remaining two-thirds of the ship the ironwood bulkheads thudded closed. He was running for his Brachiate Enclave, where his Root-kin waited for orders, when the second missile struck somewhere forward of him and on the belly plates five decks below.

A brutal rending and splintering rose under him and at his running feet the immensely strong deck-timbers tore apart in a gaping mouth that he attempted uselessly to cross in a clumsy, shaken leap. Off balance and unprepared, he felt himself falling into Cargo Three, the Maintenance Stores hold.

At the same moment ship's gravity vanished and the lighting system failed. *Deadly Thorn* was Dead Thorn. Fernix tumbled at a blind angle into darkness, arms across his head against crashing into a pillar or bulkhead at speed. In fact his foot caught in a length of rope, dragging him to a jarring halt.

Spread arms told him he had been fortunate to land on a stack of tarpaulins when it might as easily have been the sharp edges of tool boxes. Knowledge of the Issue Layout told him precisely where he was in the huge hold. There was a nub of escape pods in the wall not far to his left. He moved cautiously sideways, not daring to lose contact in null-gravity darkness but slithering as fast as he safely might.

Bulkheads had warped in the broken and twisted hull; both temperature and air pressure were dropping perceptibly.

He found the wall of the hold at the outer skin and moved slowly towards the vanished fore section until he felt the swelling of the nub of pods and at last the mechanism of an entry lock. Needing a little light to align the incised lines which would spring the mechanism, he pumped sap until the luminescent buds of his right arm shed a mild greenish radiance on the ironwood.

He thought momentarily, regretfully, of his Root-kin crew able to move only a creeper-length from their assigned beds, awaiting death without him. In this extremity he owed them no loyalty and they would expect none but they would, he hoped, think well of him. They were neuters, expendable and aware of it whereas he, Officer Class free-moving breeder, carried in him the gift of new life. There could be no question of dying with them though sentimental ballads wept such ideas; they, hard-headed pragmatists, would think it the act of an idiot. And they would be right.

He matched the lock lines and stepped quickly in as the fissure opened. As he closed the inner porte the automatic launch set the pod drifting gently into space.

He activated fresh luminescence to find the control panels and light switch. A low-powered light—perhaps forty watts—shone in the small space. To his eyes it was brilliant and a little dangerous; to a culture which made little use of metals, the power-carrying copper wires were a constant threat to wood, however tempered and insulated.

To discover where he was with respect to *Deadly Thorn,* he activated an enzyme flow through the ironwood hull at a point he judged would offer the best vision. As the area cleared he was able to see the lightless hulk occulting stars. The entire forward section was gone, perhaps blown to dust, and a ragged hole gaped amidships under the belly holds. If other pods floated nearby he could not see them.

Poised weightless over the controls, he checked the direction of the three-dimensional compass point in its bowl and saw that the homing beam shone steadily with no flicker from intervening wreckage. His way was clear and his duty certain, to return to the Home World carrying his spores of life.

A final, useless missile must have struck *Deadly Thorn* as he stretched for the controls and never reached them. A silent explosion dazzled his eyes, then assaulted his hearing as the shock wave struck the pod. A huge plate of *Deadly Thorn*'s armor loomed in the faint glow of his light, spinning lazily to strike the pod a glancing blow that set it tumbling end over end.

He had a split second for cursing carelessness because he had not strapped down at once. Then his curled up, frightened body bounced back and forth from the spinning walls until his head struck solidly and unconsciousness took him.

He came to in midair with legs bunched into his stomach and arms clasped around his skull. There was no gravity; he was falling free. But where?

Slow swimming motions brought him to a handhold but he became aware of a brutal stiffness in his right side. He pumped sap to make fingerlight, bent his head to the ribplates and saw with revulsion that he was deformed; the plates had been broken and had healed while he floated, but had healed unevenly in a body curled up instead of stretched. Surgery would rectify that—but first he must find a surgeon.

He was struck unpleasantly by the fact that even his botched joining would have occupied several months of the somatic shutdown which had maintained him in coma while the central system concentrated on healing. (He recalled sourly that the Red-Bloods healed quickly, almost on the run.)

Deity only knew where in space he might be by now.

But what had broken his body?

There were no sharp edges in the pod. Something broken, protruding spikes?

Shockingly, yes. The compass needle had been wrenched loose and the transparent, glassy tegument, black with his sap, lay shattered around it.

He thought, *I am lost,* but not yet with despair; there were actions to be taken before despair need be faced. He fed the hull, creating windows. Spaces cleared, opening on darkness and the diamond points of far stars. He found no sign of *Deadly Thorn;* he might have drifted a long way from her after the blast. He looked for the Home world, palely green, but could not find it; nor could he see the bluer, duller sister-world of the red-sapped, animal enemy.

Patiently he scanned the sky until a terrifying sight of the double star told him his search was done. It was visible still as a pair but as the twin radiances of a distant star. Of the lesser companions he could see nothing; their dimness was lost in the deep sky.

He had drifted unbelievably far. He could not estimate the distance; he remembered only from some long ago lecture that the double star might appear like this from a point beyond the orbit of the outermost planet, the dark fifteenth world.

The sight spoke not of months of healing but of years.

Only a brain injury . . .

Every officer carried a small grooming mirror in his tunic; with it Fernix examined the front and sides of his skull as well as he was able. Tiny swellings of healed fractures were visible, telling him that the brain-case had crushed cruelly in on his frontal lobes and temples. Regrowth of brain tissue had forced them out again but the marks were unmistakable. In the collision with the wreckage of *Deadly Thorn* he had crashed disastrously into . . . what?

The whole drive panel was buckled and cracked, its levers broken off or jammed down hard in their guides. They were what had assaulted him. Acceleration at top level had held him unconscious until the last drops in the tank were consumed, releasing him then to float and commence healing.

Fearfully he examined the fuel gauges. The Forward Flight gauge was empty, its black needle flush with the bottom.

The Retro fuel gauge still showed full, indicating precisely enough to balance the forward gauge supply and bring the pod to a halt—enough, he realized drearily, to leave him twice as far from home as he now was, because the buckled panel had locked the steering jet controls with the rest. He could not take the pod into the necessary end for end roll. Only the useless deceleration lever still seemed free in its guides. The linkages behind the panel might still be operable but he had no means of reaching them and no engineering skill to achieve much if he did.

He was more than lost; he was coffined alive.

Something like despair, something like fear shook his mind as he eased himself into the pilot's seat, bruises complaining, but his species was not given to the disintegrative emotions. He sat quietly until the spasm subsided.

His actions now were culturally governed; there could be no question of what he would do. He was an officer, a carrier of breeding, and the next generation must be given every chance, however small, to be born. Very small, he thought. His pod could drift for a million years without being found and without falling into the gravity field of a world, let alone a livable world, but the Compulsion could not be denied. The Compulsion had never been stated in words; it was in the genes, irrevocable.

Calmly now, he withdrew the hull enzymes and blacked out the universe. He started the air pump and the quiet hiss of intake assured him that it was operative still. As the pressure tank filled with the withdrawn atmosphere he made the mental adjustment for Transformation. As with the Compulsion, there were no words for what took place. Psychologists theorized and priests pontificated but when the time and the circumstance came together, the thing happened. The process was as intangible as thought, about whose nature there was also no agreement. The thought and the need and the will formed the cultural imperative and the thing happened.

Before consciousness left him, perhaps for ever, Fernix doused the internal heating, which was not run from the ruined drive panel.

Resuscitation he did not think about. That would take place automatically if the pod ever drifted close enough to a sun for its hull to warm appreciably, but that would not, could not happen. Deity did not play at Chance-in-a-Million with His creation.

Consciousness faded out. The last wisps of air withdrew. The temperature fell slowly; it would require several days to match the cold of space.

The Transformation crept over him as a hardening of his outer skin, slowly, slowly, until his form was sheathed in seamless bark. Enzymes clustered at the underside of his skin, fostering a hardening above and below until tegument and muscle took on the impermeability of ironwood. Officer of the Fifth Brachiate Fernix had become a huge, complex spore drifting in galactic emptiness.

He was, in fact, drifting at a surprising speed. A full tank expended at full acceleration had cut out with the pod moving at something close to six thousandths of the speed of light.

The pod's automatic distress signal shut down. It had never been heard amidst the radio noise of battle fleets. The interior temperature dropped towards zero and the vegetal computers faded out as ion exchange ceased. The pod slept.

Nearly eight thousand Terrestrial years passed before the old saying was disproved: Deity did indeed play at Chance-in-a-Million with His creation.

Vegetal computers were more efficient than a metal-working culture would readily believe, though they could not compete in any way with the multiplex machines of the animal foe—in any, that is, except one.

The pod's computers were living things in the sense that any plant is a living thing. They were as much grown as fashioned, as much trained as programmed, and their essential mechanisms shared one faculty with the entity in Transformation who slept in his armor: They could adopt the spore mode and recover from it in the presence of warmth.

They had no way of detecting the passage of millennia as they slept but their links to the skin of the pod could and did react to the heat of a G-type sun rushing nearer by the moment.

As the outer temperature rose, at first by microscopic increments, then faster and faster, the computer frame sucked warmth from the hull and, still at cryogenic levels, returned to minimal function.

At the end of half a day the chemical warming plant came silently into operation and the internal temperature climbed towards normal. Automatically the Life Maintenance computer opened the air tank to loose a jet of snow that evanesced at once into invisible gases.

The miracle of awakening came to Fernix. His outer tegument metamorphosed, cell by cell, into vegetal flesh as his body heat responded;

first pores, then more generalized organs sucked carbon dioxide from the
air and return from Transformation began.

Emergence into full consciousness was slow, first as an emptiness in
which flashes of dreams, inchoate and meaningless, darted and vanished;
then as a closer, more personal space occupied by true dreams becoming
ever more lucid as metabolism completed its regeneration; finally as an
awareness of self, of small pressures from the restricted pilot's seat, of
sap swelling in capillaries and veins, of warmth and the sharp scent of
too-pure air. His first coherent thought was that a good life caterer would
have included some forest fragrance, mulch or nitrate, in the atmosphere
tank.

From that point he was awake, in full muscular and mental control,
more swiftly than a Red-Blood could have managed. (But the Red-Blood
had no Transformation refuge that the scientists could discover; in deep
cold or without air they died and quickly rotted. They were disgusting.)

He knew that only rising warmth could have recalled him.

A sun?

The Great Twin itself?

That was not possible.

Thanking Deity that the computers were not operated from the drive
panel, he directed them to provide enzyme vision and in a moment gazed
straight ahead at a smallish yellow sun near the center of the forward
field.

So Deity did . . . He wasted no time on that beyond a transient
thought that every chance must come to coincidence at some time in the
life of the universe—and that he might as well be winner as any other.

He asked the navigating computer for details: distance, size, luminescence. Slowly, because vegetal processes cannot be hurried, the thing
made its observations and calculations and offered them. Obediently it
unrolled the stellar chart and almanac—and Fernix knew where he was.

And, he thought, little good *that* brings me.

This was a star not easily naked-eye visible from the Home world,
but the astronomers had long ago pinpointed it and its unseen planets. He
was forty-seven light-years from home (his mind accepted without understanding the abyss of time passed) on a course plunging him into the
gravity well of an all-too welcoming star at some thirty-two miles per
second. The computer assured him that on his present course this yellow
sun, though a child by comparison with the Great Twin, was powerful
enough to grasp him and draw him into its atmosphere of flame.

But he had not come so far across time and space to die sitting still,
eaten alive by a pigmy star.

He needed to buy time for thought. Deceleration alone was not enough for useful flight.

There was a blue-green planet, the almanac told him, which might possibly offer livable conditions. The hope was small in a universe where minute changes of temperature, orbit or atmosphere composition could put a world for ever beyond life, but the Deity which had guided him so finely and so far could surely crown His miracle with a greater one.

If he could achieve steering . . .

He was tempted to jimmy the cover off the Drive Panel and expose the linkages but common sense suggested that he would merely cause greater damage. He was coldly aware of ignorance and lack of mechanical talent; the maze of linkages would be to him just that—a maze, impenetrable.

Because he was untrained he failed for several hours to hit on the possibility that the the computer, once programmed to act rather than simply inform the pilot, might operate directly on the machine structures, bypassing linkages and levers. The entertainment media had imprinted him and all but those who actually operated space craft with a mental picture of pilots working by manual control, whereas it might be necessary only to tell the computer what he wanted.

That turned out to be anything but simple. As a gunnery officer he considered himself computer competent but he slept several times before he penetrated the symbols, information needs and connections of the highly specialized machine. Like most junior officers he had been rushed through an inadequate basic training and sent into space innocent of the peacetime auxiliary courses, with no expertise in other than visual navigation.

But, finally, the steering jets turned the pod end for end, the main jet roared triumphantly and the little craft slowed at the limit of deceleration his consciousness could bear. Held firmly in his straps with an arm weighing like stonewood, he questioned the computer about trajectories and escape velocities and how it might take him to the third planet of the yellow star.

It balanced distance against fuel and calculated a slingshot rounding of the central sun which would bring him economically to his goal, his destiny. There would be, Fernix knew, only a single chance and choice.

A Miner's Mate is, more correctly, an Asteroid Mining Navigational and Mass Detection Buoy. One of them sat sedately above a group of fairly large iridium-bearing "rocks" in the Belt, providing guidance for the occasional incoming or outgoing scow and warning against rogue intruders—meteorites or small asteroids in eccentric orbits. It carried a considerable armament, including two fusion bombs capable of shattering a ten-million-ton mass, but large wanderers were rare and collision orbits rarer still. Its warnings commonly did little more than send miners scurrying to the sheltered side of their rock until the danger passed.

Since space debris travels at speeds of miles per second, the sensitivity radius of the Mate's radar and vision systems was necessarily large. It registered the incoming pod at a million kilometers. Being fully automatic, it had no intelligence to find anything peculiar in the fact that it saw the thing before the mass detectors noted its presence. It simply radioed a routine alert to the mines and thereafter conscientiously observed.

The Shift Safety Monitor at the communication shack saw the tiny, brilliant point of light on his screen and wondered briefly what sort of craft was blasting inwards from the outer orbits. Scientific and exploratory probes were continuously listed and there were none due in this area of the System. Somebody racing home in emergency? Automatically he looked for the mass reading and there was none. What could the bloody Mate be doing? The mass of metal that put out such a blast must be easily measurable.

The Monitor's name was John Takamatta; he was a Murri from Western Queensland. This particular group of mines was a Murri venture and he was a trained miner and emergency pilot, now taking his turn on the dreary safety shift. Like most of his people he rarely acted without careful observation first; he waited for the Mate to declare or solve its problem.

The Mate's problem was that it could not recognize timber or any substance that let most of its beam through and diffused it thoroughly in passage. There was metal present but not enough to contain the tubes for such a drive blast and there was ceramic, probably enough for linings, but the amorphous mass surrounding these was matter for conjecture and conjecture was outside its capacity.

However, it tried, feeding back to the Mines computer a flicker of figures which mimicked a state of desperate uncertainty and gave the impression of a large, fuzzy thing of indefinite outline secreting within it some small metal components and ceramic duct lining.

Takamatta tried to enlarge the screen image but the size of the light did not change. It was either very small or far away or both.

The Mate's hesitant figures hovered around something under a ton but no mass so slight could contain such brilliance. Yet it could only be a ship and there were no ships of that nursery size. He rang the dormitory for the off-duty, sleeping Computer Technician. Albert Tjilkamati would curse him for it but they were related, men of the same Dreaming, and the curse would be routinely friendly.

Albert came, cursed, watched, sent a few test orders to the Mate and decided that it was not malfunctioning, yet the oscillating, tentative figures suggested a human operator floundering with an observation beyond his competence. Once the analogy had occurred to him, he saw the force of it.

"Something it can't recognize, John. Its beam is being diffused and spread from inner surfaces—like light shining into a box of fog. The receptors don't understand. John, man, it's picked up something new in space! We'll be in the newscasts!"

He called Search and Rescue's advance base in the Belt.

The Search and Rescue Watch Officer knew Albert Tjilkamati; if he said "strange" and "unusual," then strange and unusual the thing was.

"OK, Albert; I'll send a probe. Get back to you later."

He eased a torpedo probe out of its hangar, instructed its computers and sent it to intercept the flight path of the stranger. The probe was mainly a block of observational and analytical equipment in a narrow, twelve-meter tube, most of which was fuel tank; it leapt across the sky at an acceleration that would have broken every bone in a human body.

Starting from a point five million kilometers retrograde from the orbit of the Murri Mines, it used the Miner's Mate broadcast to form a base for triangulation and discovered at once that the incoming craft was decelerating at a g-number so high that the probe would have to recalculate its navigating instructions in order to draw alongside. It would, in fact, have to slow down and let the thing catch up with it.

The Watch Officer asked his prime computer for enhancement of the fuzzy mass/size estimates of the Mate, but the machine could not decide what the craft was made of or precisely where its edges were.

At this point, as if aware of observation, the craft's blast vanished from the screen.

The Watch Officer was intrigued but not much concerned; his probe had it on firm trace and would not let go. He notified HQ Mars, which was providentially the nearest HQ to him, of an incoming "artificial object of unknown origin," accompanied by a full transcript of the Mate's data, stated: "Intelligence probe despatched" and sat back to contemplate the probable uproar at HQ Mars. The lunatic fringe would be in full babble.

The computer, not Fernix, had cut the pod's blast because its velocity had dropped to the effective rate for rounding the system's sun. There would be corrections later as approach allowed more accurate data on the star's mass and gravity but for two million kilometers the pod would coast.

Fernix drifted into sleep. Transformation sleep conferred no healing, being essentially a reduction of metabolism to preservative zero; nothing was lost or gained during the hiatus. So he had awakened still in reaction to the stress of escape from *Deadly Thorn* and now needed sleep.

He woke again to the stridency of an alarm. The computer flashed characters in urgent orange, proclaiming the presence of a mass in steady attendance above and to the right of the pod and no more than twice its length distant.

He realized sluggishly that the mass must be a ship; only a ship equipped with damping screens could have approached so closely without detection.

The thought brought him fully alert. He opened a narrow vision slit and at first saw nothing; then he observed the slender occulting of stars. The thing was in darkness and probably painted black, else the central sun should have glinted on its nose.

If this was an artifact of the local life, he needed to find out what he could about it, even at the risk of exposing himself—if that was indeed a risk. The crew might well be friendly. He primed a camera for minimum exposure and, to aid it, turned the pod's lighting up full and opened the vision slit to his head's width for a tenth of a second.

It was enough for the camera to take its picture. It was enough, also, for the other to shoot through the gap a beam of intense light to take its own picture and blind Fernix's weak eyes. He flung his arms across his face and grunted with pain until his sight cleared. He stayed in darkness with the slit closed. He reasoned that he had been photographed by a race whose vision stretched farther into the shortwave light spectrum than his and not so far into the gentler infrared.

When the ache in his eyes subsided he examined his own infra-red picture. It showed a slender needle of nondescript color, dull and non-reflective, without visible ports. The small diameter of the craft inclined him to think it was an unmanned reconnaissance probe. His evolutionary teaching dictated that an intelligent life form must perforce have its brain case and sensory organs raised well above ground level, and no such entity could have stood upright or even sat comfortably in that projectile.

He considered what action he might take.

He had been outplayed at the observation game and could do nothing about that. His weaponless pod was not equipped to fight, which was perhaps as well; nothing would be gained by antagonizing these unknown people. Evasive action was out of the question. His fuel supply was low and his computer's decisions had been made on limits too tight for any but last-ditch interference from himself; there was none for ad hoc maneuver.

He could take no action. The next move must come from outside.

Conclusion reached, he slept.

The Search and Rescue call sign squealed in the shack, the screen cleared and Takamarra looked up from his novel as the Watch Officer hailed him, "John, oh John, have we got something here! This one will puncture holes in your Dreaming!"

John said coldly, "Indeed." He was no traditionalist but did not appreciate light handling of his cultural mores by a white man.

Some fifteen seconds would pass before his reply reached S & R and fifteen more for the Watch Officer's response. In that time he digested the message and concluded that the unlikely was true, that the intruding craft was extra-systemic. Alien. And that the existence of life among the stars *could* have some effect on the credibility of Murri Dreaming.

Then he decided that it would not. Incursion of the white man and knowledge of a huge world beyond the oceans had altered most things in his people's lives but not that one thing, the Dreamings around which the Murri cultures were built. Science and civilization might rock on their foundations as the word went out, *We are not alone,* but the ancient beliefs would not shift by the quiver of a thought.

Willy Grant's voice said, "Get this carefully, John. Make notes. We need the biggest scow you've got because yours is the nearest mining group. We want to pick this little ship out of the sky but we can't get a magnetic grapple on it because what little metal there is appears to be shielded. The best bet is to clamp it in the loading jaws of your Number Three scow if it's available. The thing is only ten meters long and three wide, so it will fit in easily. The scow can dawdle sunwards and let the outsider catch up with it until they are matched for speed. Forty-eight hours at one point five-g should do it. This is an Emergency Order, John, so time and fuel compensation will be paid. Relay that to your Manager, but pronto. The scow's computer can talk to mine about course and speed and we'll have your Manager's balls in a double reef knot if he raises objections. Got it?"

"Got it, Willy." He repeated the message for check. "Hang on while I pass it." Minus the threat; the Elder might not appreciate blunt humor.

The Murri Duty Manager preserved the Old Man routine of unimpressed self-possession, which fooled nobody. He turned his eyes from his screen, contemplated infinity in his fingernails for a respectable sixty seconds, raised his white-bearded head with an air of responsible decision-making and said, "Number Three scow is empty and available. It shall be floated off. The S & R computer can then take over." He would not have had the nerve to say otherwise; nobody in space flouted S & R.

Grant, on the other screen, heard the message and beat down the temptation to wink at John; the tribal old dear would be outraged and so would his miners. The Murri were good blokes but in some areas you had to tread carefully. When the Manager had cut out, he said, "Now, John, this'll rock you from here to Uluru. Look!"

He displayed a picture of the intruder illuminated by the probe's beam. It was shaped roughly like an appleseed, symmetrical and smooth, its line broken only by what must be a surprisingly narrow jet throat. Its color seemed to be a deep brown, almost ebony.

"Now, get this!" He homed the viewpoint to a distance of a few inches from the hull. "What do you make of it?"

What John saw surprised him very much. The hull surface was grained like wood; there was even a spot where some missile (sand-grain meteoroid?) had gouged it to expose a slightly lighter color and what was surely a broken splinter end.

Willy carried on talking. You do not wait for an answer across a thirty-second delay. "Looks like wood, doesn't it? Well, see this!" The view roved back and forth from nose to tail, and the wave pattern of the grain flowed evenly along the whole length. "You'd think they grew the thing and lathed it out of a single block. And why not? A ship doesn't have to be built of steel, does it? I know timber couldn't stand the take-off and landing strains but how about if they are ferried up in bulk in a metal mother ship or built on asteroids and launched at low speed? Or there could be means of hardening and strengthening timber; we don't know because we've never needed to do it. But a race on a metal-poor world would develop alternative technologies. I'd stake a month's pay the thing's made of wood, John."

In John's opinion he would have won the bet.

Willy did not display the other picture, the shocker taken when the alien tried to photograph the probe. Under instruction he had given Taka-matta enough to satisfy immediate curiosity without providing food for the idiot fantasy that flourishes when laymen are presented with too much mystery and too few answers.

Alone he studied the startling hologram, at life size, which his computer had built for him.

It seemed that the alien had also taken a shot of the probe just as the automatic camera took advantage of the widening slit in the intruder's hull. The thing's face—"face" for want of a word—stared at him over what was surely a camera lens.

The alien—being, entity, what you would—seemed generally patterned on an anthropoid model with a skin dappled in gray and green. The head and neck protruded above shoulders from which sprang arms or extensions of some kind—probably arms, Willy thought, because on the thing's camera rested what should be fingers, though they looked more like a bunch of aerial roots dropped by some variety of creeper but thicker and, judging by their outlandish grasping, more flexible than fingers.

In the narrow head he could discern no obvious bone structure under thick—flesh? The face was repulsive in the vague fashion of nightmare when the horror is incompletely seen. There was a mouth, or something in the place of a mouth—an orifice, small and round with slightly raised edges where lips should have been. He thought of a tube which would shoot forward to fix and suck. Nose there was none. The eyes—they had to be eyes—were circular black discs with little holes at their centers.

He guessed hazily that black eyes, totally receptive of all wavelengths of light, could be very powerful organs of vision, given the outlandish nervous system necessary to operate them. Or, perhaps the central holes were the receptors, like pinhole cameras.

Ears? Well . . . there were flaps on the sides of the head, probably capable of manipulation since the hologram showed one raised and one nearly flush with the gray and green flesh. A third flap, partly open, in what must be called the forehead and revealing under it an intricately shaped opening reminiscent of the outer ear, suggested all-around hearing with a capacity for blocking out sound and/or direction finding. A useful variation.

Hair there seemed to be none but on the crown of the bud-shaped skull sat a plain, yellowish lump like a skittish party hat, a fez six inches or so high and four wide. Yet it seemed to be part of the head, not a decoration. He could make nothing of it.

There remained the faintly purplish cape around the thing's shoulders. Or was it a cape? It hung loosely over both shoulders and its lower edges fell below the rim of the vision slit, but it was parted at the throat and he had an impression that what he saw at the parting was dappled flesh rather than a garment. On closer examination he thought that the "cape" was actually a huge flap of skin, perhaps growing from the back of the neck. He thought of an elephant's ears, which serve as cooling surfaces.

An idea that had been knocking for expression came suddenly into the light and he said aloud, "The thing's a plant!"

At once he was, however unwarrantably, certain that he looked on the portrait of a plant shaped in the caricature of a man. The "cape" was a huge leaf, not for cooling but for transpiration. The seemingly boneless skull and tentacular hands made vegetable sense; the thing would be infinitely flexible in body, acquiring rigidity as and where needed by hydrostatic pressure. He pondered root systems and acquired mobility as an evolutionary problem without a glimmer of an answer, but his impression would not be shifted.

The thing from out there was a motile vegetable.

The setting up of ore refineries on asteroids which were usually worked out in a few years would have been prohibitively expensive, so the main refinery had been located on Phobos, and there the output of all Belt companies was handled without need for the scows to make planetfall. The saving in expensive fuel was most of what made the ventures profitable. Nor was there any waste of manpower on those lonely voyages; the scows were computer-directed from float-off to docking.

An empty scow, not slowed by several hundred ton mass of ore, could accelerate at a very respectable g-rate. Number Three scow from the Murri outfit caught its prey dead on time, forty-eight hours after float-off. Forty-eight hours of silent flight, accompanied by a probe which made no move, took toll of nerves. Fernix slept and wondered and theorized from too little knowledge and slept again. At the second waking he fed, sparsely, not knowing how long his supplies must stretch; he injected a bare minimum of trace elements into the mulch tray with just enough water to guarantee ingestion, and rested his feet in it. The splayed pads protruded their tubules like tiny rootlets as his system drew up the moisture. He preferred mouth feeding but in the pod he had no choice.

The brief euphoria of ingestion passed and his mood flickered between fear and hope. Did the probe accompany him for a purpose unknown or did its controllers watch and wait to see what he would do?

He would do nothing. The vacillations of mood rendered him unfit to decide with proper reason. He writhed internally but sat still, did nothing.

His people, slow-thinking and phlegmatic, did not slip easily into neurosis but he was muttering and twitching when new outside action came. He switched into calm observation and appraisal.

The alarm indicated a new presence in space, ahead of him but drawing close. He chanced a pinhole observation in the direction of the new mass but could see nothing. Whatever the thing was, either he was closing on it or it waited for him. His computer reported that the mass was losing some speed and he decided that it intended to match his course.

His instruments described it as long in body and large in diameter but not of a mass consistent with such size. An empty shell? Such as a cargo vessel with cleared holds?

Shortly he found that the probe had vanished and a quite monstrous ship was slipping back past him; the light of the system's sun shone on its pitted, blue-painted nose. It was old in space and about the size of a raiding destroyer but showed no sign of armament.

It slipped behind him and took up a steady position uncomfortably close to him. He was tempted to discover what it would do if he accelerated or changed course, then thought of his thin-edge supply of fuel. Do nothing, nothing; pray for friendly beings.

He saw with a frisson of tension that it was moving swiftly up to him.

Looming close to collision point, it opened its forward hull in a vast black mouth and gullet, like the sea monsters of his baby tales.

Its forward surge engulfed his pod, swallowed it whole and closed about it as something (grasping bands?) thudded on the pod's shell and held captor and prey to matched speeds. He was imprisoned in a vast, empty space, in darkness.

After a while he cleared the pod's entire shell, turning it into a transparent seed hanging in a white space illuminated by his interior lights. White, he thought, for optimum lighting when they work in here.

The space was utterly vacant. At the far end, roughly amidships he calculated, vertical oblong outlines were visible against her white paint—entry hatches. So the entities stood upright; he had expected no less. Evolutionary observation and theory (formulated so long ago, so far away) suggested that an intelligent, land-based being must stand erect, that it should carry brain and major sensory organs at its greatest height, that it should possess strong limbs for locomotion and grasping in limited number according to the law of minimum replication, that it—

—a dozen other things whose correctness he should soon discover in fact.

He saw that his pod was clamped above and below in a vise powerful enough to hold it steady in a turbulent maneuver. It was, his instruments told him, basically iron, as was the hull of the ship.

He was not sure whether or not he should envy a race which could be so prodigal of metal. Their technologies would be very different from those of the Home World.

He waited for them but they did not come.

Could their ship be unmanned, totally remote-controlled? His people had a few such—had had a few such—but their radio-control techniques had been primitive and doubtful. Given unlimited iron and copper for experiment . . .

He waited.

Suddenly the pod was jerked backward as the captor vessel decelerated at a comfortable rate; he could have withstood twice as much.

Homing on a world nearby? He could not tell; his instruments could not penetrate the metal hull.

He thought, I am learning the discipline of patience.

The crew of a ship approaching Phobos would have seen few surface installations though the moonlet housed the HQ Outer Planets Search and Rescue, an Advanced College of Null-Gravity Science, the Belt Mining Co-Operative Ore Refineries, a dozen privately owned and very secretive research organizations and, most extensive of all, the Martian Terraforming Project Laboratories and Administrative Offices.

All of these were located inside the tunnelled and hollowed rock that was Phobos.

It had been known for a century or more that the moonlet was slowly spiralling inwards for a long fall to Mars and Martian Terraforming did not want some six thousand cubic kilometers of solid matter crashing on the planet either before or after its hundred-year work was completed. So the interior had been excavated to the extent of nearly twenty per cent of the total mass (the engineers had vetoed more less stress changes break the rock apart) and the detritus blasted into space at high velocity. The change in mass, even after the installation of men and machinery, had slowed the inward drift but more brutal measures would eventually have to be taken, and one College research unit was permanently engaged in deciding what such measures might be (brute force is easily said) and how they might be applied (less easily said).

Phobos, swinging six thousand kilometers above the Martian surface, was a busy hive where even gossip rarely rose above the intellectual feuds and excitements of dogged dedication—

—until a junior ass in S & R cried breathlessly, careless of eager ears, "Bloody thing looks like a lily pad with head and chest. A plant, bejesus!"

After that, S & R had trouble preventing the information being broadcast throughout the System, but prevent if they did. The last thing a troubled Earth needed as it emerged from the Greenhouse Years and the Population Wars was the political, religious and lunatic fringe upheaval expectable on the cry of *We are not alone.*

· · ·

Possum Takamatta, John's younger brother, a Communications Operative with S & R, pondered the hologram transmitted from the Belt and asked, "Just what sense do they think an ecologist might make of that?"

"God knows," said ecologist Anne Spriggs of Waterloo, Iowa, and Martian Terraforming, who was as pink-and-white as Possum was deep brown-black, "but I know some botany, which is more than anyone else around here does, so I just might make a useful contribution, read guess."

"With no tame expert at hand, they're desperate?"

"Possum, wouldn't you be desperate?"

"Why? I'm just interested. My people knew that 'more things in heaven and earth' line twenty thousand years before Shakespeare. You got any ideas?"

"No, only questions."

"Like?"

"Is it necessarily a plant because it reminds us of a plant? If it is, how does a rooted vegetable evolve into a motile form?"

"Who says it's motile? We've only got this still picture."

"It has to be to go into space. It couldn't take a garden plot with it."

"Why not? A small one, packed with concentrates, eh? And why should it have to become motile? Might have descended from floating algae washed up in swamplands with plenty of mud. Developed feet instead of roots, eh?'

Anne said with frustration, "So much for the ecologist! The local screeneye has more ideas than I do."

He tried soothing because he liked Anne. "You're hampered by knowledge, while I can give free rein to ignorance."

She was not mollified. "Anyway, is it plant or animal? Why not something new? Who knows what conditions formed it or where it's from?"

"From at least Alpha Centauri; that's the nearest. It came in at thirty k per second, and decelerating; if that was anything like its constant speed it's been on its way for centuries. That's a long time for one little lone entity."

"Why not FTL propulsion?"

"Come off it, girl! Do you credit that shit?"

"Not really."

"Nor does anyone else. If it came from anywhere out there, then it's an ancient monument in its own lifetime."

"In the face of that," she said, "I feel monumentally useless. What in hell am I good for?"

"Marry me and find out."

"In a humpy outside Alice Springs?"

"I've a bloody expensive home in Brisbane."

"And I've a fiancé in Waterloo, Iowa."

"The hell you say!"

"So watch it, Buster!" She planted a kiss on the tip of his ear. "That's it. Everything else is off limits."

"In Australia we say out of bounds."

"In Australia you also say sheila when you mean pushover."

Not quite right but near enough and she certainly made better viewing than the mess on the screen.

In another part of the cavern system the Base Commander S & R held a meeting in an office not designed to hold thirteen people at once—himself and the twelve managers of the moonlet's private research companies. Commander Ali Musad's mother was Italian, his father Iraqi and himself a citizen of Switzerland; S & R took pride in being the least racially oriented of all the service arms.

He had set the office internal g at one-fifth, enough to keep them all on the floor, however crowded; it is difficult to dominate a meeting whose units sit on walls and ceiling and float away at a careless gesture.

He said, "I have a problem and I need your help. As Station senior executive I can give orders to service groups and enforce them; of you ladies and gentlemen representing civilian projects I can only ask."

They resented his overall authority. They remained silent, letting him wriggle on his own hook, whatever it was. Then they might help, cautiously, if advantage offered.

"Some of you will have heard of a . . . presence . . . in space. A foolish boy talked too loudly in a mess room and no doubt the whisper of what he said has gone the rounds."

That should have produced a murmur but did not. Only Harrison of Ultra-Micro asked, "Something about a green man in a sort of lifeboat?"

"Something like that."

"I didn't pay attention. Another comedian at work or has someone picked up a phantom image from a dramacast?"

"Neither. He's real."

Someone jeered softly, someone laughed, most preferred a skeptical lift of eyebrows. Chan of Null-G Germinants suggested that managers had low priority on the rumor chain. "Ask the maintenance staff; they're the slush bearers."

Musad told them, "It isn't silly season slush; it's real; I've seen it. Talk has to be stopped."

Still they did not take him too seriously. "Can't stop gossip, Commander."

"I mean: Stop it getting off Phobos."

"Too late, Commander. If it's a little green men story it's gone out on a dozen private coms by now."

He said stiffly, "It hasn't. I've activated the censor network." The shocked silence was everything he could have desired. "Every com going out is being scanned for key words; anything containing them is being held for my decision."

He waited while anger ran its course of outrage and vituperation. They didn't give a damn about little green men but censorship was an arbitrary interference guaranteed to rouse fury anywhere across the System. The noise simmered down in predictable protests: ". . . abuse of power . . . justifiable only in war emergency . . . legally doubtful on international Phobos . . ."

Melanie Duchamp, the Beautiful Battleaxe of Fillette Bonded Aromatics, produced the growling English that browbeat boardrooms: "You will need a vairy good reason for this."

No honorific, he noted; Melanie was psyching herself for battle. "It was a necessary move. Now I am asking you to ratify it among your company personnel."

"Fat chance," said one, and another, "We'd have mutiny on our hands."

He had expected as much. "In that case I shall order it as a service necessity and take whatever blame comes." And leave them to accept blame if events proved his action the right one. "I can promise worse than mutiny if the news is not controlled."

At that at least they listened. He told them what he knew of the intruding ship, its contents and the speculation about its origin, and then: "Let this news loose on Earth and Luna and we'll have every whining, power-grabbing, politicking ratbag in the System here within days. I don't mean just the service arms and intelligence wood-beetles and scientists and power-brokers; I mean the churches and cults and fringe pseudo-sciences and rich brats with nothing better to do. I also mean your own company executives and research specialists and the same from your merchant rivals—to say nothing of the print and electronic media nosing at your secrets. How do you feel about it?"

It was Melanie who surrendered savagely. "I will support you— under protest."

"You don't have to cover your arse, Melanie. I'll take the flack."

"So? There will be lawsuits, class actions that will cost the companies millions."

"No! I will declare a Defense Emergency."

"Then God or Allah help you, Commander."

Harrison said, "You can't do it. You say the thing seems to be un-armed; how can you invoke defense?"

"Possible espionage by an alien intruder. If that won't do, the Legal Section will think up something else."

In the end they agreed if only because he left them no choice. Satis-fied that they would keep the lid on civilian protest, he threw them a bone: He would call on them to supply experts in various fields not im-mediately available among the service personnel on Phobos, because he intended to bring the thing inside and mount as complete an examination as possible before allowing a squeak out of Phobos Communications.

They brightened behind impassive agreement. With their own men at the center of action they would be first with the news as history was made in their particular corners . . . with profit perhaps . . . and Wily Musad was welcome to the lawsuits.

When they had gone he summoned his secretary. "All on record?"

"Yes, sir."

"Am I covered?"

"I think so. They will cooperate in case you retaliate by leaving them out of the selection of expert assistance. Which means that you must take at least one from each firm, however useless."

"Yes. Many messages intercepted?"

"Seven for your attention. Three to media outlets. It seems we have some unofficial stringers aboard."

"The buggers are everywhere. I don't want media complaints when they find out that their lines were stopped. They stir up too much shit." He recalled too late that Miss Merritt was a Clean Thinker. "Sorry."

She was unforgiving. "Nevertheless there will be complaints." Her tone added, And serve you right. Clean Thinkers held that censorship was unnecessary in a right-minded community—and so was crude language.

"I think the courts will uphold me."

"No doubt, sir. Will that be all?"

"Yes, Miss Merritt." And to hell with you, Miss Merritt, but you are too efficient to be returned to the pool.

The Number Three scow drifted down through darkness to hover over the moonlet's docking intake, a square hole like a mineshaft, that came suddenly alive with light.

The docking computer took control, edged the huge scow, precisely centered, through the intake and closed the entry behind it.

A backup computer waited, ready to take over in the event of malfunction, and a human operator waited with finger on override, prepared to assume manual control at an unpredictable, unprogrammable happening. This was a first in the history of the human race and almost anything, including the inconceivable, might occur.

Nothing did.

The computer took the scow evenly through the second lock, closed it, moved the vessel sideways through the Repair and Maintenance Cavern to the largest dock and set it smoothly belly-down on the floor. Then, because nobody had thought to tell it otherwise, it followed normal procedure and switched on one-eighth g in the floor area covered by the vessel, sufficient to ensure cargo stability.

Watching in his office screen, Musad cursed somebody's thoughtlessness—his own, where the buck stopped—and opened his mouth for a countermanding order. Then he thought that any damage was already done. Anyway, why should there be damage? No world with an eighth g would have produced a life form requiring an atmosphere, and the probe had certainly reported an atmosphere of sorts. Whatever lived inside the . . . lifeboat? . . . should be comfortable enough.

He shut his mouth and called Analysis. "Full scan, inside and out. There is a living being inside; take care."

Analysis knew more than he about taking care and had prepared accordingly. The first necessity was to establish the precise position of the thing inside—being, entity, e-t, what you would—and ascertain that it was or was not alone. So: a very delicate selection of penetrating radiation in irreducibly small doses, just enough to get a readable shadow and keep it in view.

Analysis had far better instrumentation than the comparatively crude probe and established at once that the thing was alive and moving its . . . limbs? . . . While remaining in seated position facing the nose of the vessel. Able now to work safely around the thing, visitor, whatever, Analysis unleashed its full battery of probe, camera, resolution and dissection.

The results were interesting, exciting, even breathtaking, but no scrap of evidence suggested where the little ship might have come from.

Musad was an administrator, not a scientist; Analysis gave him a very condensed version of its immensely detailed preliminary report—blocked out, scripted, eviscerated, rendered down and printed for him in under three hours—highlighting the facts he had called for most urgently:

The living entity in the captive vessel would be, when it stood, approximately one and a half meters tall. It showed the basic pentagonal structure—head and four limbs—which might well represent an evolutionary optimum design for surface dwellers in a low-g Terrene range. There was a rudimentary skeletal structure, more in the nature of supportive surface plates than armatures of bone, and the limbs appeared tentacular rather than jointed. This raised problems of push-pull capability with no answers immediately available.

Spectroscopic reading was complicated by the chemical structure of the vessel's hull, but chlorophyll was definitely present in the entity as well as in the hull, and the bulky "cape" on its shoulders showed the visual characteristics of a huge leaf. It was certainly a carbon-based form and seemed to be about ninety per cent water; there was no sign of hemoglobin or any related molecule.

The atmosphere was some forty per cent denser than Terrene air at sea level, a little light in oxygen but heavy with water vapor and carbon dioxide.

Tentative description: Highly intelligent, highly evolved, motile plant species.

We always wondered about aliens and now we've got one. What does he eat? Fertilizer? Or does that snout work like a Venus fly trap?

The small amounts of iron in the vessel—tank linings and a few hand tools—argued a metal-poor environment, ruling out any Sol-system planet as a world of origin.

As if they needed ruling out!

The ceramic lining of the jet would require longer evaluation but appeared to be of an unfamiliar crystalline macro-structure. All the other parts of the vessel, including the hull, were timber. There was nothing unusual about the composition of the various woods but a great deal unusual about about the treatments they had undergone, presumably for hardening and strengthening; no description of these could be hazarded without closer examination. (There followed a dissertation on the possible technology of a timber-based culture. Musad skipped over it.)

Dating procedures were at best tentative on materials whose isotopic balance might not match Terrene counterparts, but guesstimates gave a pro tem figure of between seven and ten thousand Terrene years. The signatories declined to draw any conclusions as to the age of the vegetal pilot or where he might have originated.

And all it does is sit there, sit there, sit there, occasionally moving a tentacle in some unguessable activity. So: What next?

He was taken by an idea so absurd that it would not go away, an idea which might, just might stir the creature into some action. It was a sort of "welcome home" idea—rather, an introduction . . .

He called the Projection Library.

Fernix slept and woke while the deceleration held him comfortably in his seat. He slept again and woke, nerves alert, when deceleration ceased.

He opened a tiny vision hole but saw only his prison still closed around him.

Shortly there was a perceptible forward motion and the slightest of centrifugal effects as the direction changed several times. Then his captor ship settled, gently for so large a transport. His pod shook momentarily and was still.

Suddenly there was gravity, not much of it but enough to aid balance and movement.

Not that he had any intention of moving; he could not afford movement. He needed energy. Food alone was not enough; his thousands of chloroplasts needed sunlight for the miracle of conversion to maintain body temperature, muscle tone, even the capacity to think effectively. There was a spectrum lamp aboard but its batteries would operate for only a limited time; a pod was not intended for pan-galactic voyaging.

Yet full alertness could be demanded of him at any moment; he must pump his body resources to a reasonable ability for sustained effort. He used a third of the lamp's reserve, switched it off and continued at rest in the pilot seat.

There was little assessment he could make of his position. His captors had demonstrated no technological expertise (beyond a squandering of metal) which could not have been duplicated on the Home World, nor had they attempted to harm him. So they were civilized beings, reasonably of a cultural status with which he could relate.

On the panel, radiation detectors flickered at low power. He was, he guessed, being investigated. So, this race was able to operate its instruments *through* the metal hull outside. That proved little; a race evolving on a metal-rich world would naturally develop along different lines of scientific interest from one grown from the forests of Home. Different need not mean better.

It was an exciting thought, that on another world a people had emerged from the nurturing trees to conquer the void of space.

The thought was followed by another, more like a dream, in which his people had traversed the unimaginable distance between stars to colonize this faraway system, facing and overcoming the challenges of worlds utterly variant from their own, inventing whole new sciences to maintain their foothold on the universe.

The open-minded intelligence can contemplate the unfamiliar, the never conceived, and adapt it to new modes of survival.

He had arrived by freakish accident; could not his people have made the crossing during the eons while he crept through space in free fall? The idea of using Transformation for survival while a ship traversed the years and miles had been mooted often.

His reverie was broken by a squealing hiss from outside the pod.

Outside. They were supplying his prison with an atmosphere.

Chemist Megan Ryan was the first to curse Musad for mishandling the approach to the alien ship. Suited up and ready to examine the hull, she heard someone at the closed-circuit screen ask, "What the hell's going on? They've let air into the scow."

She clawed the man out of the way and punched Musad's number to scream at him, "What do you think you're bloody well doing?"

"And who do you think you're talking to, Captain-Specialist?"

She took a deep, furious breath. "To you . . . sir. Who ordered air into the scow?"

"I did." His tone said that if she objected, her reason had better be foolproof.

"But why, why, why?" She was close to stuttering with rage.

His administrative mind groped uneasily at the likelihood of an error of unscientific judgment and decided that this was not a moment for discipline. "To provide air and temperature for the investigating teams to work in. What else?"

She swallowed, conscious of a red face and tears of frustration. "Sir, that ship has been in space for God only knows how long, in the interstellar deep. Its timber hull will have collected impact evidence of space-borne elements and zero-temperature molecules. That evidence will by now have been negated by temperature change and highly reactive gases. Knowledge has been destroyed."

She was right and he would hear about it later from higher echelons; he simply had not thought from a laboratory standpoint. "I'm sorry, Meg, but my first priority for investigation is the traveller rather than the ship. He represents more urgent science than a little basic chemistry."

The wriggling was shameful and he knew it; he had forgotten everything outside the focus of his own excitement, the alien.

She was glaring still as he cut her off.

He spoke to the Library: "Have you got much?"

"A good representative selection, sir. Vegetable environments from different climates. As you requested, no human beings."

"Good. I don't want humans presented to him in stances and occupations he—it—won't understand. Get a computer mockup ready—a naked man, good physique, in a space suit. Set it up so that the suit can be dissolved from around him. I want a laboratory effect, emotionally distancing, to reduce any 'monster' reaction."

"Yes, sir," the screen murmured.

"He's put out a probe of some sort," said another screen. "Sampling the air maybe."

Musad turned to screen 3 and the alien ship. The temperature in the hold had risen to minus thirty Celsius and vapor was clearing rapidly from the warming air. Visibility was already good.

When the air reached normal temperature and pressure for their planet, Fernix reasoned, they would come for him.

They did not come, though temperature and pressure levelled off. He was disappointed but accepted that there would be circumstances which he could not at present comprehend.

He extended a hull probe for atmosphere analysis, to find the outside pressure very low while the water vapor content hovered at the "dry" end of the scale and the carbon dioxide reading was disturbingly light. He could exist in such an atmosphere only with difficulty and constant re-energizing. Acclimatization would take time.

Through the generations, he reasoned, his people would have made adaptation, for the vegetal germ was capable of swift genetic change. There would be visible differences by now—of skin, of stature, of breathing areas—but essentially they would be his people still. . . .

He saw a flash of colored movement outside his spyhole and leaned forward to observe.

In the prison space, a bare armslength from the pod's nose, a silver-green tree flickered into existence, took color and solidity to become a dark, slender trunk rising high before spreading into radiating fronds. His narrow field of vision took in others like it on both sides and beyond, ranged at roughly equal distances. Beyond them again, a broad river. The palmate forms were familiar (mutations, perhaps, of ancestral seeds carried across the void?) as was the formal arrangement on a river bank, the traditional files of the rituals of Deity.

As he watched, the scene changed to a vista of rolling highlands thickly covered with conical trees of the deep green of polar growths, and in the foreground a meadow brilliant with some manner of green cover where four-legged, white beasts grazed. Their shape was unfamiliar, but his people had used grazing beasts throughout historical time; children loved them and petted them and wept when they were slaughtered. Only the anthropoid monsters from the sister world could terrify the young and rouse the adults to protective fury.

As the picture faded he wondered had the man-beasts been utterly destroyed. Some would have been preserved for study . . . mated in zoos . . . exhibited . . .

A new view faded in and the hologram placed him at the edge of a great pond on whose surface floated green pads three or four strides across their diameter. He recognized water-dwelling tubers though the evolved details were strange, as were the flitting things that darted on and above them. Forms analogous to insects he guessed, thinking that some such line was an almost inevitable product of similar environment.

Cautiously he opened the vision slit wider and saw that the huge picture extended away and above as though no walls set limits to it. He looked upwards to an outrageously blue, cloudless sky that hurt his eyes. This world, without cloud cover, would be different indeed.

He realized with a burst of emotion, of enormous pride and fulfilment, that he was being shown the local planet of his people, accentuating the similarities that he would recognize, welcoming him Home as best they could.

The picture changed again and this time he wept.

His pod lay now in the heart of a jungle clearing, brilliant-hued with flowers and fungi that stirred memory though none were truly familiar. Tall, damp trunks lifted to the light, up to the tight leaf cover where the branching giants competed for the light filtered down through cloud cover. For there was cloud cover here, familiarly gray, pressing down and loosing its continuous drizzle to collect on the leaves and slide groundwards in silver-liquid tendrils. Bright insect-things darted, and larger things that flapped extensions like flattened arms to stay aloft in surprisingly effective fashion. These were strange indeed as were the four-legged, furry things that leapt and scurried on the ground, chewing leaves and grubbing for roots.

The whole area could have been a corner of his ancestral estate, transformed yet strangely and truly belonging. He had been welcomed to a various but beautiful world.

With the drunken recklessness of love and recognition he activated the enzyme control and cleared the entire hull of the pod for vision. It was as though he stood in the heart of a Home playground, amid surroundings he already loved.

Soon, soon his people of these new, triumphant years must show themselves . . .

. . . and as though the desire had triggered the revelation, the jungle faded away and a single figure formed beyond the nose of the pod, floating in darkness as only a hologram could, hugely bulky in its pressure suit, face hidden behind the filtering helmet plate but wholly human in its outward structure of head and arms and motor limbs.

He left the seat to lean, yearning, against his transparent hull, face pressed to the invisible surface, arms spread in unrestrained blessing.

The figure spread its arms in a similar gesture, the ancient gesture of welcome and peace, unchanged across the void and down the centuries.

The outlines of the pressure suit commenced to blur, to fade, revealing the creature within.

The naked body was white, stiff-limbed, fang-mouthed, bright-eyed with recognition of its helpless, immemorial foe.

It floated, arms outstretched, in mockery of the ritual of peace.

The Red-Blood.

The enemy.

When the first hologram appeared—the Nile-bank scene of the planting program for binding the loosening soil—Musad watched for reaction from the ship but there was none.

The Swedish panorama, its forest of firs contrasted with the feeding sheep, pleased him better. On any habitable world there must be some environment roughly correlating with this, some scene of bucolic peace.

Then came the Victoria lilies and their pond life— A screen voice said, "It's opened the vision slit a little bit. It's interested."

It? Too clinical. Musad would settle for he. Could be she, of course, or some exotic gender yet unclassified.

The fourth scene, the jungle display, brought a dramatic result. The entire hull of the ship became cloudy, then translucent and—vanished. The interior was revealed from nose to jet.

Musad did not bother scanning the internal fittings; a dozen cameras would be doing that from every angle. He concentrated on the alien.

It—*he* rose swiftly out of his chair, head thrust forward in the fashion of a pointing hound and stepped close to the invisible inner hull. He was not very tall, Musad thought, nor heavily muscled but very limber, as though jointless. (But how could a jointless being stand erect or exert pressure? His basically engineering-mind thought vaguely of a compartmentalized hydrostatic system, nerve-operated. Practical but slow in reaction time.) He lifted his tentacular arms, spreading the great "cape" like

a leaf to sunlight, and raised them over his head in a movement redolent
of ecstasy.

Could jungle, or something like it, be the preferred habitat? *He* was
plainly enthralled.

The jungle scene faded and the hold was in darkness save for the low-
level radiance of the little ship's interior lighting.

The computer's creation, man-in-space-suit, appeared forward of the
ship, floating a meter above the floor. *He* leaned, in unmistakable fascination, close against the inner hull. *He* pressed his face against the invisible timber like a child at a sweetshop window and slowly spread his
arms. His "hands" were bunches of gray-green hoses until the fingers
separated and stiffened. Musad could see that the tubular members
straightened and swelled slightly; he could detect no muscle but they had
plainly hardened as they pressed against the wood. It seemed to Musad
that he stood in a posture of unrestrained, longing welcome.

The Library operator must have caught the same impression and in a
moment of inspiration had the space-suited figure duplicate the outspread
stance of friendship. Then he began to fade the armor, baring the symbolic man within.

He remained perfectly still.

Musad advanced his viewpoint until the alien's face dominated his
screen. The face changed slowly. Thin folds of skin advanced across the
huge black eyes, closing until only small circles remained. The mouth
tube retracted and simultaneously opened wide in another circle, a great
"Oh!" of wonder and surprise. The face resembled nothing more than a
child's drawing of a happy clown.

Musad pulled back the view and saw that the "cape" was now fully
raised behind the head, like some vast Elizabethan jewelled collar, save
that the leaf veins shone bright yellow.

"He's happy," Musad said to anyone who might hear him. "He's
happy!"

He stepped slowly back from the hull, lowered an arm to one of the
panels—and the dark hull was there again, lightless, impenetrable.

Musad could not, never did know that what he had seen was a rictus
mask more deeply murderous than simple hatred could rouse and mold.

For Fernix recognition of the Red-Blood was more than a cataclysm;
it was a trigger.

On the Home world, when the end came it was recognized.

An end was an end. Intellect lost overriding control and biological forces took over. Genetically dictated reactions awoke and the process of Final Change began.

Pollination, initiated in the peak years of adolescence and suspended until the Time of Flowering, was completed in a burst of inner activity. At the same time stimulant molecules invaded his cerebrum, clarifying and calming thought for the Last Actions. In the domed crown of his skull the bud stirred; the first lines of cleavage appeared faintly on the surface as the pressure of opening mounted. His people flowered once only in life— when, at the moment of leaving it, the pollen was gathered by exultant young partners while the dying one's children were born.

There would be none to gather pollen from Fernix but his salute should be as royal as his lineage.

The initial burst of killing rage against the Red-Blood ebbed slowly. Had the projection been indeed a physical Red-Blood he would have been unable to master the urge to murder; he would have been out of the pod and in attack without conscious thought, obeying an impulse prehistorically ancient. The fading of the thing helped return him to reason.

It had shown him in the opening of its mouth, in what the things called a "smile," that he was the helpless captive of enemy cruelty. The display of fangs had been the promise of the last insult to honorable extinction, the eating of his body before Final Change could translate him to Deity.

It did not seem to him irrational that he had so simply projected as fact his people's conquest of space and the new worlds; his psychology carried no understanding other than that the vegetal races were naturally dominant in the intellectual universe. The Home World scientists found it difficult to account for the evolution of thinking Red-Bloods on the neighbor planet; such things, they reasoned, could only be sports, the occasional creations of a blind chance, having no destiny.

Fernix, orthodox because he had no training beyond orthodoxy, could only grasp that his people must have been totally destroyed in that long ago war, overwhelmed by unimaginable disaster. Not they had conquered interstellar space but the Red-Bloods. He, Fernix, was alone in a universe empty of his kind.

He knew, as he regained mental balance, that Final Change had begun. There was no fear of death in his people's psychology, only an ineradicable instinct to perpetuate the species; Fernix felt already the changes in his lower limbs heralding the swift growth of embryonic offspring, motile units in one limb, rooted slave-kin in the other.

That they would be born only to die almost at once did not trouble him; he could not abort births governed by autonomic forces and he was not capable of useless railing against the inevitable. He had seen the terror of Red-Bloods as death came to them and been unable to comprehend the working of brains which in extremity rendered their possessors useless and demented. How could such creatures have mastered the great void?

He settled again into the pilot's seat and with quick actions emptied the whole store of trace elements into the feeding bed and thrust his feet deep into the mulch.

With triumphant pleasure he opened the emergency carbon dioxide cock and drained the tank into the pod's atmosphere. His death would be such a flowering of insult as few had ever offered the Red-Bloods. The burst of mocking blossom, in the color of their own life fluid, would take his people out of history in a blaze of derisive laughter at their barbarian destroyers.

That was not all. One other gesture was possible—the winning of a last battle although the war was long over.

The alien had shut himself in. The shortwave team reported that he had resumed the pilot seat and as far as they could determine had moved little in several hours.

Anne Ryan blamed Musad and was careless who heard her. "It's a vegetable form and he lulls it into euphoria with holograms of arboreal paradise, then confronts it with a bone-and-meat structure as far outside its experience as it is outside ours! It's probably half-paralyzed with shock. It needs time to assimilate the unthinkable. We need a brain here, not a bloody bureaucrat."

Melanie's contribution seemed more vicious for being delivered in a strong Breton accent. "The thing showed its teeth! The plant was terrified. It has no teeth, only a sucking tube! So you bare teeth at it and it runs to hide! Who would not?"

Musad thought the woman had a point and that he had acted with more authority than prudence. But, what should be done on first contact with the unknowable? The only certainty had been that he must take some action; if he had ordered the scientists to leave the thing alone he would have had rebellion on his hands and eventually questions asked in political arenas; if he had given them their heads they would have mauled each other in battles for priority and he would have ended up cashiered for inefficient management of an undisciplined rabble.

Now, when he had no idea what to do, help came from his own S & R, from the shortwave investigation team. "Something's going on inside, sir, but we don't know what it means. In the first minutes after it closed off the vision we could see it—the shadow of it, that is—gesturing like an angry man. Then it went back to the seat and made motions like pressing little buttons or flicking small levers—maybe. We can't be sure because with so much wood it's hard to get even a shadow picture. At any rate it made some adjustments because the carbon dioxide component in its air went up to eight per cent. The water vapor content seems to have increased, too, and the temperature has risen from thirty-five degrees to forty-six."

"Hothouse conditions!"

"Super-hothouse, sir."

"What's he up to? Forcing his growth?"

"We think more likely some other growth it carries in there. Maybe it has seeds in that thing like a tub at its feet. That's if the things make seeds."

Seeds or sprouts or tubers or buds . . . What do you do when you don't know what you're dealing with? How do you even think?

The diffident, careful tones of the radiographer said, "Sir, it doesn't want any part of us."

"Seems so."

"If it won't come to us, sir, shouldn't we go to it?"

Musad had no false pride. "You have a suggestion, Sergeant?"

"We could put a duroplastic tent round its ship, sir, big enough to allow a bunch of scientists to work in space suits, and fill it with an atmosphere matching the alien's."

"Then?"

"Cut a hole in the hull, sir, and get it out. Cut the ship in half if necessary."

That should at least keep everybody quiet until the next decision—except, perhaps, the alien—and anything he did would be marginably preferable to stalemate. And—oh, God!—he would have to decide who to allow into the tent and who must wait his or her turn.

He noted the Sergeant's name; one man at least was thinking while the rest boiled and complained. Yet he hesitated to give a command which in itself would be controversial.

He was still hesitating when the Analysis team gave an update: "It hasn't moved from the chair in two hours. Now chest movement has ceased; it is no longer breathing. It is probably dead."

That settled it. He ordered positioning of the tent and matching of atmospheres. That done, they must recover the body before serious deterioration set in.

Fernix was not dead. Not quite. The complex overlapping of birth and death made the passing of his kind a drawn-out experience.

Fully aerated, he had ceased to breathe. The new ones in his lower limbs drew their nourishment from the mulch and no longer needed him, were in the process of detaching themselves. When they dropped free his life's duty, life's story, life's meaning would be complete . . .

. . . save for the one thing more, planned and prepared.

Now he could only wait with tentacle/finger curled for tightening, remaining perfectly still, having no reason to move, conserving strength for the final action.

His quietly sinking senses told him dully of sounds outside the pod and a fading curiosity wondered what they did out there. He thought of activating hull vision but the thought slipped away.

A sword of white fire cut a section from the hull alongside the control panels a long armslength from him and he was aware, without reacting as alertness ebbed (only the last command holding strength for its moment) of a suited figure entering the pod, followed by another. And another.

Red-Bloods. He no longer hated or cared. They would be dealt with.

One knelt by his lower limbs and unintelligible sounds dribbled from the grille in its helmet. He could not tell what it did.

Came the Last Pain, the splitting of cleavage lines in his bud sheath as the death flower swelled and bloomed from his ruined head.

At the moment of brain death his body obeyed the command stored in its nervous system for this moment. The curled tentacle/finger retracted, giving the computer its last command.

Under the tent the science teams went at it with a will. A small piece of timber was carved, with unexpected difficulty, from the alien craft's hull and rushed to a laboratory. The preliminary report came very quickly: ". . . a technique of molecular fusion—everything packed tight in cross-bonded grids. Not brittle but elastic beyond anything you'd believe. Take a real explosive wallop to do more than make it quiver and settle back."

The ceramic jet lining seemed impervious to common cutting methods and nobody wanted to use force at this stage. Soft radiation told little and they agreed that hard radiation should not be risked until they had found a means of excising small samples.

Chemanalysis had managed to create a computer mockup of the contents of the fuel tank, derived from hazy shortwave and sonar pictures, and was excited by a vision of complex molecular structures which promised incredible power output but must remain illogical until their catalysts were derived.

Carbon Dating, on safer ground with a piece of timber more or less analyzed, certified the ship eight thousand years old, give or take a hundred, which made no sense at all of the presence of a living thing within.

Well, it had been living, in some fashion, perhaps still was—in some fashion. But, centuries?

Then the section of hull was cut out and the first group went in. There was surprisingly little to see. The cabin was small because most of the vessel's volume was fuel storage and the living space was parsimoniously uncluttered. There was a timber panel with wooden keys mid-mounted like tiny seesaws, which might be on-off controls, another console-type installation that could reasonably be a keyboard and clusters of incomprehensible recording instruments—some circular, some square and some like bent thermometers. There was also a sort of dashboard set with small levers, badly smashed.

Ecologist Anne Spriggs of Waterloo, Iowa, surveyed the alien with the despair of a preserver arrived too late. The creature was an unpleasant sight, its gray and green skin muted in death to patched and streaky brown, its slender body collapsed upon itself until it resembled nothing so much as a stick-figure doll. It had died with a tentacle resting loosely around one of the on-off seesaw controls.

A tiny movement, low down, brought her kneeling cumbersomely to scrutinize the container of mulch on the floor beneath the creature's lower limbs. The limbs hung oddly above it, their exposed, footless termini lighter-colored than the body, as if only recently exposed. Broken off? Cut off? How and why?

Several brown sticks lay on the surface of the mulch. One of them wriggled. Despite an instant revulsion she reached a gloved hand to pick it up. It was a tuber of some kind, like a brown artichoke formed fortuitously with nubs for vestigial arms and legs and head, and spots for eyes.

Musad spoke in her helmet. "What have you there, Anne?"

"I think it's an embryo alien. It's like—" She shrugged and held it up. He suggested, "A mandrake."

That was a somehow nasty idea, smelling of small evil.

A rending crack from the dead creature itself startled the suited figures crowding into the hull and those who watched through screens.

They were offered a miracle. The excrescence on the thing's skull opened flaps like huge sepals and a blood-red crimson bolt shot a meter's length of unfolding bloom free of the body. It unfurled not a single flower but a clustered dozen packed in and on each other, each opening the flared trumpet of a monstrous lily.

The flowers expanded in a drunken ecstasy of growth, bending down and over the dead thing that fed them until it was wrapped in a shroud of blood. From the hearts of the trumpets rose green stamens like spears, each crowned with a golden magnet of pollen.

And not another, Anne thought, for such a flourish of procreation to attract and join.

In the surprised stillness someone, somewhere, whistled softly and another hissed an indrawn breath of wonder. Melanie's voice spoke from her office deep in the moonlet, Breton roughness smoothed in awe; "I have never seen so lovely a thing."

An unidentified voice said, "Like a salute from somewhere out there."

And that, Musad thought, would be the line the media would fall on with crocodile tears: A Dying Salute from Infinity . . .

Then Anne Spriggs said with a touch of panic, "It moved!"

"What moved?"

"The body. It moved its hand. On the lever."

"A natural contraction," Musad said. "The whole external form appears to have shrunk."

Fernix had placed a slight delay on the ignition. He wanted the Red-Bloods to see his derisive flowering but he also wanted to be decently dead before the fury struck.

When the fuel spark finally leapt the ignition gap his life was over; he had timed his going with dignity. Home world would have honored him.

The jet roared, filling the scow's hold with a sea of fire before the craft skidded across the floor to crash through the soft steel of the imprisoning hull.

Those outside the scow had a microsecond's view of death in a blinding, incandescent torpedo that struck the rock wall of the Maintenance Cavern and disintegrated. The cloudburst of fuel from the shattered tank burgeoned in a twenty-thousand-degree ball of fire, engulfing and destroying the watchers in a hell-breath and licking its tongues of bellowing flame into the adjoining corridors and tunnels, a monstrous blast of heat driving death before it.

Thirty-seven scientists died and more than three hundred general personnel. Nearly a thousand others suffered serious burns.

The material damage ran to the total of a dozen national debts and the lawsuits of the private companies on Phobos made the fortunes of the lawyers on both sides.

Heads fell on the political chopping block, Musad's first among the offerings to the smug virtue of scapegoating.

First contact between intelligent cultures had been made.

Stephen Baxter

CILIA-OF-GOLD

Stephen Baxter made his first sale to *Interzone* in 1987, and since then has become one of that magazine's most frequent contributors, as well as making sales to *Asimov's Science Fiction, Science Fiction Age, Zenith, New Worlds,* and elsewhere. He's one of the most prolific of the new writers of the nineties, particularly at short lengths. In 1997, for instance, he probably published more short work in the genre than any other author (rivaled only by writers such as Robert Reed and Brian Stableford), at least eleven stories that I'm aware of, plus two or three non-genre stories—and, in spite of this prodigious output, managed to keep the overall quality amazingly high. His first novel, *Raft,* was released in 1991 to wide and enthusiastic response, and was rapidly followed by other well-received novels such as *Timelike Infinity, Anti-Ice, Flux,* and the H. G. Wells pastiche—a sequel to *The Time Machine*—*The Time Ships,* which won both the Campbell Memorial Award and the Philip K. Dick Award. His most recent books are the novels *Moonseed, Voyage,* and *Titan,* and the collections *Vacuum Diagrams: Stories of the Xeelee Sequence* and *Traces.*

Like many of his colleagues here in the late nineties—Greg Egan comes to mind, as do people like Paul J. McAuley, Michael Swanwick, Iain M. Banks, Bruce Sterling, Pat Cadigan, Brian Stableford, Gregory Benford, Ian McDonald, Gwyneth Jones, Vernor Vinge, Greg Bear, Geoff Ryman, and a half-dozen others—Stephen Baxter is busily engaged with revitalizing and reinventing the "hard-science" story for a new generation of readers.

And, like a few of those colleagues—Paul J. McAuley, for instance, or Walter Jon Williams—Baxter has a range that's broad enough to encompass several different styles of story, from Alternate History (in stories such as "Moon Six" and "Zemyla" and "War Birds," and novels such as *Voyage,* where he works out sometimes drastically different variants on how the space program would have turned out under different historical circumstances), to retro "Victorian SF" such as "Voyage to the King Planet," "The Ant-Men of Tibet," and *The Time Ships,* from the hardest of hard science fiction in stories such as "Planck Zero" and "Soliton Star" and *Raft,* to wide-screen Modern Space Opera of stunning scope and audacity of concept, such as the stories and novels of the "Xeelee Sequence." The influence of writers such as Wells, Larry Niven, and (especially) Arthur C. Clarke are clear enough in his work, but he is also involved in forging a new voice that's all his own.

Here he takes us to a mining colony on Mercury, in company with a troubleshooting mission that runs into troubles *considerably* more bizarre than anyone could ever have *anticipated* having to deal with. . . .

The people—though exhausted by the tunnel's cold—had rested long enough, Cilia-of-Gold decided.

Now it was time to fight.

She climbed up through the water, her flukes pulsing, and prepared to lead the group farther along the Ice-tunnel to the new Chimney cavern.

But, even as the people rose from their browsing and crowded through the cold, stale water behind her, Cilia-of-Gold's resolve wavered. The Seeker was a heavy presence inside her. She could *feel* its tendrils wrapped around her stomach, and—she knew—its probes must already have penetrated her brain, her mind, her *self.*

With a beat of her flukes, she thrust her body along the tunnel. She couldn't afford to show weakness. Not now.

"Cilia-of-Gold."

A broad body, warm through the turbulent water, came pushing out of the crowd to bump against hers: it was Strong-Flukes, one of Cilia-of-Gold's Three-mates. Strong-Flukes's presence was immediately comforting. "Cilia-of-Gold. I know something's wrong."

Cilia-of-Gold thought of denying it; but she turned away, her depression deepening. "I couldn't expect to keep secrets from you. Do you think the others are aware?"

The hairlike Cilia lining Strong-Flukes's belly barely vibrated as she spoke. "Only Ice-Born suspects something is wrong. And if she didn't, we'd have to tell her." Ice-Born was the third of Cilia-of-Gold's mates.

"I can't afford to be weak, Strong-Flukes. Not now."

As they swam together, Strong-Flukes flipped onto her back. Tunnel water filtered between Strong-Flukes's carapace and her body; her cilia flickered as they plucked particles of food from the stream and popped them into the multiple mouths along her belly. "Cilia-of-Gold," she said. "I *know* what's wrong. You're carrying a Seeker, aren't you?"

". . . Yes. How could you tell?"

"I love you," Strong-Flukes said. *"That's* how I could tell."

The pain of Strong-Flukes's perception was as sharp, and unexpected, as the moment when Cilia-of-Gold had first detected the signs of the infestation in herself . . . and had realized, with horror, that her life must inevitably end in madness, in a purposeless scrabble into the Ice over the world. "It's still in its early stages, I think. It's like a huge heat, inside me. And I can feel it reaching into my mind. Oh, Strong-Flukes . . ."

"Fight it."

"I can't. I—"

"You can. You *must.*"

The end of the tunnel was an encroaching disk of darkness; already Cilia-of-Gold felt the inviting warmth of the Chimney-heated water in the cavern beyond.

This should have been the climax, the supreme moment of Cilia-of-Gold's life.

The group's old Chimney, with its fount of warm, rich water, was failing; and so they had to flee, and fight for a place in a new cavern.

That, or die.

It was Cilia-of-Gold who had found the new Chimney, as she had explored the endless network of tunnels between the Chimney caverns. Thus, it was she who must lead this war—Seeker or no Seeker.

She gathered up the fragments of her melting courage.

"You're the best of us, Cilia-of-Gold," Strong-Flukes said, slowing. "Don't ever forget that."

Cilia-of-Gold pressed her carapace against Strong-Flukes's in silent gratitude.

Cilia-of-Gold turned and clacked her mandibles, signaling the rest of the people to halt. They did so, the adults sweeping the smaller children inside their strong carapaces.

Strong-Flukes lay flat against the floor and pushed a single eyestalk toward the mouth of the tunnel. Her caution was wise; there were species who could home in on even a single sound-pulse from an unwary eye.

After some moments of silent inspection, Strong-Flukes wriggled back along the Ice surface to Cilia-of-Gold.

She hesitated. "We've got problems, I think," she said at last.

The Seeker seemed to pulse inside Cilia-of-Gold, tightening around her gut. "What problems?"

"This Chimney's inhabited already. By *Heads.*"

Kevan Scholes stopped the rover a hundred yards short of the wall-mountain's crest.

Irina Larionova, wrapped in a borrowed environment suit, could tell from the tilt of the cabin that the surface here was inclined upward at around forty degrees—shallower than a flight of stairs. This "mountain," heavily eroded, was really little more than a dust-clad hill, she thought.

"The wall of Chao Meng-Fu Crater," Scholes said briskly, his radio-distorted voice tinny. "Come on. We'll walk to the summit from here."

"Walk?" She studied him, irritated. "Scholes, I've had one hour's sleep in the last thirty-six; I've traveled across ninety million miles to get here, via tugs and wormhole transit links—and you're telling me I have to *walk* up this damn hill?"

Scholes grinned through his faceplate. He was AS-preserved at around physical-twenty-five, Larionova guessed, and he had a boyishness that grated on her. *Damn it,* she reminded herself, *this "boy" is probably older than me.*

"Trust me," he said. "You'll love the view. And we have to change transports anyway."

"Why?"

"You'll see."

He twisted gracefully to his feet. He reached out a gloved hand to help Larionova pull herself, awkwardly, out of her seat. When she stood on the cabin's tilted deck, her heavy boots hurt her ankles.

Scholes threw open the rover's lock. Residual air puffed out of the cabin, crystallizing. The glow from the cabin interior was dazzling; beyond the lock, Larionova saw only darkness.

Scholes climbed out of the lock and down to the planet's invisible surface. Larionova followed him awkwardly; it seemed a long way to the lock's single step.

Her boots settled to the surface, crunching softly. The lock was situated between the rover's rear wheels: the wheels were constructs of metal strips and webbing, wide and light, each wheel taller than she was.

Scholes pushed the lock closed, and Larionova was plunged into sudden darkness.

Scholes loomed before her. He was a shape cut out of blackness. "Are you okay? Your pulse is rapid."

She could hear the rattle of her own breath, loud and immediate. "Just a little disoriented."

"We've got all of a third of a gee down here, you know. You'll get used to it. Let your eyes dark-adapt. We don't have to hurry this."

She looked up.

In her peripheral vision, the stars were already coming out. She looked for a bright double star, blue and white. There it was: Earth, with Luna.

And now, with a slow grandeur, the landscape revealed itself to her adjusting eyes. The plain from which the rover had climbed spread out from the foot of the crater wall-mountain. It was a complex patchwork of crowding craters, ridges and scarps—some of which must have been miles high—all revealed as a glimmering tracery in the starlight. The face of the planet seemed *wrinkled,* she thought, as if shrunk with age.

"These wall-mountains are over a mile high," Scholes said. "Up here, the surface is firm enough to walk on; the regolith dust layer is only a couple of inches thick. But down on the plain the dust can be ten or fifteen yards deep. Hence the big wheels on the rover. I guess that's what five billion years of a thousand-degree temperature range does for a landscape. . . ."

Just twenty-four hours ago, she reflected, Larionova had been stuck in a boardroom in New York, buried in one of Superet's endless funding battles. And now this . . . wormhole travel was bewildering. "Lethe's waters," she said. "It's so—desolate."

Scholes gave an ironic bow. "Welcome to Mercury," he said.

Cilia-of-Gold and Strong-Flukes peered down into the Chimney cavern.

Cilia-of-Gold had chosen the cavern well. The Chimney here was a fine young vent, a glowing crater much wider than their old, dying home. The water above the Chimney was turbulent, and richly cloudy; the cavern itself was wide and smooth-walled. Cilia-plants grew in mats around the Chimney's base. Cutters browsed in turn on the cilia-plants, great chains of them, their tough little arms slicing steadily through the plants. Sliding through the plant mats Cilia-of-Gold could make out the supple form of a Crawler, its mindless, tube-like body wider than Cilia-of-Gold's and more than three times as long. . . .

And, stalking around their little forest, here came the Heads themselves, the rulers of the cavern. Cilia-of-Gold counted four, five, six of the Heads, and no doubt there were many more in the dark recesses of the cavern.

One Head—close to the tunnel mouth—swiveled its huge, swollen helmet-skull toward her.

She ducked back into the tunnel, aware that all her cilia were quivering.

Strong-Flukes drifted to the tunnel floor, landing in a little cloud of food particles. *"Heads,"* she said, her voice soft with despair. "We can't fight Heads."

The Heads' huge helmet-skulls were sensitive to heat—fantastically so, enabling the Heads to track and kill with almost perfect accuracy. Heads *were* deadly opponents, Cilia-of-Gold reflected. But the people had nowhere else to go.

"We've come a long way to reach this place, Strong-Flukes. If we had to undergo another journey"—*through more cold, stagnant tunnels*—"many of us couldn't survive. And those who did would be too weakened to fight.

"No. We have to stay here—to *fight* here."

Strong-Flukes groaned, wrapping her carapace close around her. "Then we'll all be killed."

Cilia-of-Gold tried to ignore the heavy presence of the Seeker within her—and its prompting, growing more insistent now, that she *get away* from all this, from the crowding presence of people—and she forced herself to *think*.

Larionova followed Kevan Scholes up the slope of the wall-mountain. Silicate surface dust compressed under her boots, like fine sand. The climbing was easy—it was no more than a steep walk, really—but she stumbled frequently, clumsy in this reduced gee.

They reached the crest of the mountain. It wasn't a sharp summit: more a wide, smooth platform, fractured to dust by Mercury's wild temperature range.

"Chao Meng-Fu Crater," Scholes said. "A hundred miles wide, stretching right across Mercury's South Pole."

The crater was so large that even from this height its full breadth was hidden by the tight curve of the planet. The wall-mountain was one of a series that swept across the landscape from left to right, like a row of eroded teeth, separated by broad, rubble-strewn valleys. On the far side of the summit, the flanks of the wall-mountain swept down to the plain of the crater, a full mile below.

Mercury's angry sun was hidden beyond the curve of the world, but its corona extended delicate, structured tendrils above the far horizon.

The plain itself was immersed in darkness. But by the milky, diffuse light of the corona, Larionova could see a peak at the center of the plain, shouldering its way above the horizon. There was a spark of light at the base of the central peak, incongruously bright in the crater's shadows: that must be the Thoth team's camp.

"This reminds me of the Moon," she said.

Scholes considered this. "Forgive me, Dr. Larionova. Have you been down to Mercury before?"

"No," she said, his easy, informed arrogance grating on her. "I'm here to oversee the construction of Thoth, not to sightsee."

"Well, there's obviously a superficial similarity. After the formation of the main System objects five billion years ago, all the inner planets suffered bombardment by residual planetesimals. That's when Mercury took its biggest strike: the one which created the Caloris feature. But after that, Mercury was massive enough to retain a molten core—unlike the Moon. Later planetesimal strikes punched holes in the crust, so there were lava outflows that drowned some of the older cratering.

"Thus, on Mercury, you have a mixture of terrains. There's the most ancient landscape, heavily cratered, and the *planitia:* smooth lava plains, punctured by small, young craters.

"Later, as the core cooled, the surface actually shrank inward. The planet lost a mile or so of radius."

Like a dried-out tomato. "So the surface *is* wrinkled."

"Yes. There are *rupes* and *dorsa:* ridges and lobate scarps, cliffs a couple of miles tall and extending for hundreds of miles. Great climbing country. And in some places there are gas vents, chimneys of residual thermal activity." He turned to her, corona light misty in his faceplate. "So Mercury isn't really so much like the Moon at all. . . . Look. You can see Thoth."

She looked up, following his pointing arm. There, just above the far horizon, was a small blue star.

She had her faceplate magnify the image. The star exploded into a compact sculpture of electric blue threads, surrounded by firefly lights: the Thoth construction site.

Thoth was a habitat to be placed in orbit close to Sol. Irina Larionova was the consulting engineer contracted by Superet to oversee the construction of the habitat.

Thoth's purpose was to find out what was wrong with the Sun.

Recently, anomalies had been recorded in the Sun's behavior; aspects of its interior seemed to be diverging, and widely, from the standard theoretical models. Superet was a loose coalition of interest groups on Earth and Mars, intent on studying problems likely to impact the longterm survival of the human species.

Problems in the interior of mankind's only star clearly came into the category of things of interest to Superet.

Irina Larionova wasn't much interested in any of Superet's semi-mystical philosophizing. It was the work that was important, for her: and the engineering problems posed by Thoth were fascinating.

At Thoth, a Solar-interior probe would be constructed. The probe would be one Interface of a wormhole terminal, loaded with sensors. The Interface would be dropped into the Sun. The other Interface would remain in orbit, at the center of the habitat.

The electric-blue bars she could see now were struts of exotic matter, which would eventually frame the wormhole termini. The sparks of light moving around the struts were GUTships and short-haul tugs. She stared at the image, wishing she could get back to some real work.

Irina Larionova had had no intention of visiting Mercury herself. Mercury was a detail, for Thoth. Why would *anyone* come to Mercury, unless they had to? Mercury was a piece of junk, a desolate ball of iron and rock too close to the Sun to be interesting, or remotely habitable. The two Thoth exploratory teams had come here only to exploit: to see if it was possible to dig raw materials out of Mercury's shallow—and close-at-hand—gravity well, for use in the construction of the habitat. The teams had landed at the

South Pole, where traces of water-ice had been detected, and at the Caloris Basin, the huge equatorial crater where—it was hoped—that ancient impact might have brought iron-rich compounds to the surface.

The tugs from Thoth actually comprised the largest expedition ever to land on Mercury.

But, within days of landing, both investigative teams had reported anomalies.

Larionova tapped at her suit's sleeve-controls. After a couple of minutes an image of Dolores Wu appeared in one corner of Larionova's faceplate. *Hi, Irina,* she said, her voice buzzing like an insect in Larionova's helmet's enclosed space.

Dolores Wu was the leader of the Thoth exploratory team in Caloris. Wu was Mars-born, with small features and hair grayed despite AntiSenescence treatments. She looked weary.

"How's Caloris?" Larionova asked.

Well, we don't have much to report yet. We decided to start with a detailed gravimetric survey. . . .

"And?"

We found the impact object. We think. It's as massive as we thought, but much—much—too small, Irina. It's barely a mile across, way too dense to be a planetesimal fragment.

"A black hole?"

No. Not dense enough for that.

"Then what?"

Wu looked exasperated. *We don't know yet, Irina. We don't have any answers. I'll keep you informed.*

Wu closed off the link.

Standing on the corona-lit wall of Chao Meng-Fu Crater, Larionova asked Kevan Scholes about Caloris.

"Caloris is *big,*" he said. "Luna has no impact feature on the scale of Caloris. And Luna has nothing like the Weird Country in the other hemisphere. . . ."

"The what?"

A huge planetesimal—or *something*—had struck the equator of Mercury, five billion years ago, Scholes said. The Caloris Basin—an immense, ridged crater system—formed around the primary impact site. Whatever caused the impact was still buried in the planet, somewhere under the crust, dense and massive; the object was a gravitational anomaly which had helped lock Mercury's rotation into synchronization with its orbit.

"Away from Caloris itself, shock waves spread around the planet's young crust," Scholes said. "The waves focused at Caloris' antipode—the

point on the equator diametrically opposite Caloris itself. And the land
there was shattered, into a jumble of bizarre hill and valley formations.
The Weird Country . . . Hey. Dr. Larionova."

She could *hear* that damnable grin of Schole's. "What now?" she
snapped.

He walked across the summit toward her. "Look up," he said.

"Damn it, Scholes—"

There was a pattering against her faceplate.

She tilted up her head. Needle-shaped particles swirled over the wall-
mountain from the planet's dark side and bounced off her faceplate,
sparkling in corona light.

"What in Lethe is that?"

"Snow," he said.

Snow . . . On Mercury?

In the cool darkness of the tunnel, the people clambered over each
other; they bumped against the Ice walls, and their muttering filled the
water with crisscrossing voice-ripples. Cilia-of-Gold swam through and
around the crowd, coaxing the people to follow her will.

She felt immensely weary. Her concentration and resolve threatened
continually to shatter under the Seeker's assault. And the end of the tunnel, with the deadly Heads beyond, was a looming, threatening mouth, utterly intimidating.

At last the group was ready. She surveyed them. All of the people—
except the very oldest and the very youngest—were arranged in an array
which filled the tunnel from wall to wall; she could hear flukes and carapaces scraping softly against Ice.

The people looked weak, foolish, eager, she thought with dismay;
now that she was actually implementing it her scheme seemed simple-
minded. Was she about to lead them all to their deaths?

But it was too late for the luxury of doubt, she told herself. Now,
there was no other option to follow.

She lifted herself to the axis of the tunnel, and clacked her mandibles
sharply.

"Now," she said, "it is time. The most important moment of your
lives. And you must *swim!* Swim as hard as you can; swim for your
lives!"

And the people responded.

There was a surge of movement, of almost exhilarating *intent.* The
people beat their flukes as one, and a jostling mass of flesh and carapaces
scraped down the tunnel.

Cilia-of-Gold hurried ahead of them, leading the way toward the tunnel mouth. As she swam she could feel the current the people were creating, the plug of cold tunnel water they pushed ahead of themselves.

Within moments the tunnel mouth was upon her.

She burst from the tunnel, shooting out into the open water of the cavern, her carapace clenched firm around her. She was plunged immediately into a clammy heat, so great was the temperature difference between tunnel and cavern.

Above her the Ice of the cavern roof arched over the warm Chimney mouth. And from all around the cavern, the helmet-skulls of Heads snapped around toward her.

Now the people erupted out of the tunnel, a shield of flesh and chitin behind her. The rush of tunnel water they pushed ahead of themselves washed over Cilia-of-Gold, chilling her anew.

She tried to imagine this from the Heads' point of view. This explosion of cold water into the cavern would bring about a much greater temperature difference than the Heads' heat-sensor skulls were accustomed to; the Heads would be *dazzled,* at least for a time: long enough—she hoped—to give her people a fighting chance against the more powerful Heads.

She swiveled in the water. She screamed at her people, so loud she could feel her cilia strain at the turbulent water. *"Now!* Hit them now!"

The people, with a roar, descended toward the Heads.

Kevan Scholes led Larionova down the wall-mountain slope into Chao Meng-Fu Crater.

After a hundred yards they came to another rover. This car was similar to the one they'd abandoned on the other side of the summit, but it had an additional fitting, obviously improvised: two wide, flat rails of metal, suspended between the wheels on hydraulic legs.

Scholes helped Larionova into the rover and pressurized it. Larionova removed her helmet with relief. The rover smelled, oppressively, of metal and plastic.

While Scholes settled behind his controls, Larionova checked the rover's data desk. An update from Dolores Wu was waiting for her. Wu wanted Larionova to come to Caloris, to see for herself what had been found there. Larionova sent a sharp message back, ordering Wu to summarize her findings and transmit them to the data desks at the Chao site.

Wu acknowledged immediately, but replied: *I'm going to find this hard to summarize, Irina.*

Larionova tapped out: *Why?*

We *think we've found an artifact.*

Larionova stared at the blunt words on the screen.

She massaged the bridge of her nose; she felt an ache spreading out from her temples and around her eye sockets. She wished she had time to sleep.

Scholes started the vehicle up. The rover bounced down the slope, descending into shadow. "It's genuine water-ice snow," Scholes said as he drove. "You know that a day on Mercury lasts a hundred and seventy-six Earth days. It's a combination of the eighty-eight-day year and the tidally locked rotation, which—"

"I know."

"During the day, the Sun drives water vapor out of the rocks and into the atmosphere."

"What atmosphere?"

"You really don't know much about Mercury, do you? It's mostly helium and hydrogen—only a billionth of Earth's sea-level pressure."

"How come those gases don't escape from the gravity well?"

"They do," Scholes said. "But the atmosphere is replenished by the solar wind. Particles from the Sun are trapped by Mercury's magnetosphere. Mercury has quite a respectable magnetic field: the planet has a solid iron core, which . . ."

She let Scholes' words run on through her head, unregistered. *Air from the solar wind, and snow at the South Pole . . .*

Maybe Mercury was a more interesting place than she'd imagined.

"Anyway," Scholes was saying, "the water vapor disperses across the planet's sunlit hemisphere. But at the South Pole we have this crater: Chao Meng-Fu, straddling the Pole itself. Mercury has no axial tilt— there are no seasons here—and so Chaos's floor is in permanent shadow."

"And snow falls."

"And snow falls."

Scholes stopped the rover and tapped telltales on his control panel. There was a whir of hydraulics, and she heard a soft crunch, transmitted into the cabin through the rover's structure.

Then the rover lifted upward through a foot.

The rover lurched forward again. The motion was much smoother than before, and there was an easy, hissing sound.

"You've just lowered those rails," Larionova said. "I knew it. This damn rover is a sled, isn't it?"

"It was easy enough to improvise," Scholes said, sounding smug. "Just a couple of metal rails on hydraulics, and Vernier rockets from a cannibalized tug to give us some push. . . ."

"It's astonishing that there's enough ice here to sustain this."

"Well, that snow may have seemed sparse, but it's been falling steadily—for five billion years . . . Dr. Larionova, there's a whole frozen ocean here, in Chao Meng-Fu Crater: enough ice to be detectable even from Earth."

Larionova twisted to look out through a viewport at the back of the cabin. The rover's rear lights picked out twin sled tracks, leading back to the summit of the wall-mountain; ice, exposed in the tracks, gleamed brightly in starlight.

Lethe, she thought. *Now I'm skiing. Skiing, on Mercury. What a day.*

The wall-mountain shallowed out, merging seamlessly with the crater plain. Scholes retracted the sled rails; on the flat, the regolith dust gave the ice sufficient traction for the rover's wide wheels. The rover made fast progress through the fifty miles to the heart of the plain.

Larionova drank coffee and watched the landscape through the viewports. The corona light was silvery and quite bright here, like moonlight. The central peak loomed up over the horizon, like some approaching ship on a sea of dust. The ice-surface of Chao's floor—though pocked with craters and covered with the ubiquitous regolith dust—was visibly smoother and more level than the plain outside the crater.

The rover drew to a halt on the outskirts of the Thoth team's sprawling camp, close to the foothills of the central peak. The dust here was churned up by rover tracks and tug exhaust splashes, and semi-transparent bubble-shelters were hemispheres of yellow, homely light, illuminating the darkened ice surface. There were drilling rigs, and several large pits dug into the ice.

Scholes helped Larionova out onto the surface. "I'll take you to a shelter," he said. "Or a tug. Maybe you want to freshen up before—"

"Where's Dixon?"

Scholes pointed to one of the rigs. "When I left, over there."

"Then that's where we're going. Come on."

Frank Dixon was the team leader. He met Larionova on the surface, and invited her into a small opaqued bubble-shelter nestling at the foot of the rig.

Scholes wandered off into the camp, in search of food.

The shelter contained a couple of chairs, a data desk, and a basic toilet. Dixon was a morose, burly American; when he took off his helmet there was a band of dirt at the base of his wide neck, and Larionova noticed a sharp, acrid stink from his suit. Dixon had evidently been out on the surface for long hours.

He pulled a hip flask from an environment suit pocket. "You want to drink?" he asked. "Scotch?"

"Sure."

Dixon poured a measure for Larionova into the flask's cap, and took a draught himself from the flask's small mouth.

Larionova drank; the liquor burned her mouth and throat, but it immediately took an edge off her tiredness. "It's good. But it needs ice."

He smiled. "Ice we got. Actually, we have tried it; Mercury ice is good, as clean as you like. We're not going to die of thirst out here, Irina."

"Tell me what you've found, Frank."

Dixon sat on the edge of the desk, his fat haunches bulging inside the leggings of his environment suit. "Trouble, Irina. We've found trouble."

"I know that much."

"I think we're going to have to get off the planet. The System authorities—and the scientists and conservation groups—are going to climb all over us, if we try to mine here. I wanted to tell you about it, before—"

Larionova struggled to contain her irritation and tiredness. "That's *not* a problem for Thoth," she said. "Therefore it's not a problem for me. We can tell Superet to bring in a water-ice asteroid from the Belt, for our supplies. You know that. Come on, Frank. Tell me why you're wasting my time down here."

Dixon took another long pull on his flask, and eyed her.

"There's *life* here, Irina," he said. "Life, inside this frozen ocean. Drink up; I'll show you."

The sample was in a case on the surface, beside a data desk.

The thing in the case looked like a strip of multicolored meat: perhaps three feet long, crushed and obviously dead; shards of some transparent shell material were embedded in flesh that sparkled with ice crystals.

"We found this inside a two-thousand-yard-deep core," Dixon said.

Larionova tried to imagine how this would have looked, intact and mobile. "This means nothing to me, Frank. I'm no biologist."

He grunted, self-deprecating. "Nor me. Nor any of us. Who expected to find life, on Mercury?" Dixon tapped at the data desk with gloved fingers. "We used our desks' medico-diagnostic facilities to come up with this reconstruction," he said. "We call it a *mercuric,* Irina."

A Virtual projected into space a foot above the desk's surface; the image rotated, sleek and menacing.

The body was a thin cone, tapering to a tail from a wide, flat head. Three parabolic cups—*eyes?*—were embedded in the smooth "face," symmetrically placed around a lipless mouth. . . . No, not eyes, Larionova corrected herself. Maybe some kind of sonar sensor? That would explain the parabolic profile.

Mandibles, like pincers, protruded from the mouth. From the tail, three fins were splayed out around what looked like an anus. A transparent carapace surrounded the main body, like a cylindrical cloak; inside the carapace, rows of small, hairlike cilia lined the body, supple and vibratile.

There were regular markings, faintly visible, in the surface of the carapace.

"Is this accurate?"

"Who knows? It's the best *we* can do. When we have your clearance, we can transmit our data to Earth, and let the experts get at it."

"Lethe, Frank," Larionova said. "This looks like a fish. It looks like it could *swim.* The streamlining, the tail—"

Dixon scratched the short hairs at the back of his neck and said nothing.

"But we're on Mercury, damn it, not in Hawaii," Larionova said.

Dixon pointed down, past the dusty floor. "Irina. It's not all frozen. There are *cavities* down there, inside the Chao ice-cap. According to our sonar probes—"

"Cavities?"

"Water. At the base of the crater, under a couple of miles of ice. Kept liquid by thermal vents, in crust-collapse scarps and ridges. Plenty of room for swimming . . . We speculate that our friend here swims on his back"—he tapped the desk surface, and the image swiveled—"and the water passes down, between his body and this carapace, and he uses all those tiny hairs to filter out particles of food. The trunk seems to be lined with little mouths. See?" He flicked the image to another representation; the skin became transparent, and Larionova could see blocky reconstructions of internal organs. Dixon said, "There's no true stomach, but there is what looks like a continuous digestive tube passing down the axis of the body, to the anus at the tail."

Larionova noticed a thread-like structure wrapped around some of the organs, as well as around the axial digestive tract.

"Look," Dixon said, pointing to one area. "Look at the surface structure of these lengths of tubing, here near the digestive tract."

Larionova looked. The tubes, clustering around the digestive axis, had complex, rippled surfaces. "So?"

"You don't get it, do you? It's *convoluted*—like the surface of a brain. Irina, we think that stuff must be some equivalent of nervous tissue."

Larionova frowned. *Damn it, I wish I knew more biology.* "What about this thread material, wrapped around the organs?"

Dixon sighed. "We don't know, Irina. It doesn't seem to fit with the rest of the structure, does it?" He pointed. "Follow the threads back. There's a broader main body, just here. We think maybe this is some kind of parasite, which has infested the main organism. Like a tapeworm. It's as if the threads are extended, vestigial limbs. . . ."

Leaning closer, Larionova saw that tendrils from the worm-thing had even infiltrated the brain-tubes. She shuddered; if this was a parasite, it was a particularly vile infestation. Maybe the parasite even modified the mercuric's behavior, she wondered.

Dixon restored the solid-aspect Virtual.

Uneasily, Larionova pointed to the markings on the carapace. They were small triangles, clustered into elaborate patterns. "And what's this stuff?"

Dixon hesitated. "I was afraid you might ask that."

"Well?"

". . . We think the markings are artificial, Irina. A deliberate tattoo, carved into the carapace, probably with the mandibles. Writing, maybe: those look like symbolic markings, with information content."

"Lethe," she said.

"I know This fish was smart," Dixon said.

The people, victorious, clustered around the warmth of their new Chimney. Recovering from their journey and from their battle-wounds, they cruised easily over the gardens of cilia-plants, and browsed on floating fragments of food.

It had been a great triumph. The Heads were dead, or driven off into the labyrinth of tunnels through the Ice. Strong-Flukes had even found the Heads' principal nest here, under the silty floor of the cavern. With sharp stabs of her mandibles, Strong-Flukes had destroyed a dozen or more Head young.

Cilia-of-Gold took herself off, away from the Chimney. She prowled the edge of the Ice cavern, feeding fitfully.

She was a hero. But she couldn't bear the attention of others: their praise, the warmth of their bodies. All she seemed to desire now was the uncomplicated, silent coolness of Ice.

She brooded on the infestation that was spreading through her.

Seekers were a mystery. Nobody knew *why* Seekers compelled their hosts to isolate themselves, to bury themselves in the Ice. What was the point? When the hosts were destroyed, so were the Seekers.

Perhaps it wasn't the Ice itself the Seekers desired, she wondered. Perhaps they sought, in their blind way, something *beyond* the Ice. . . .

But there *was* nothing above the Ice. The caverns were hollows in an infinite, eternal Universe of Ice. Cilia-of-Gold, with a shudder, imagined herself burrowing, chewing her way into the endless Ice, upward without limit. . . . Was that, finally, how her life would end?

She hated the Seeker within her. She hated her body, for betraying her in this way; and she hated herself.

"Cilia-of-Gold."

She turned, startled, and closed her carapace around herself reflexively.

It was Strong-Flukes and Ice-Born, together.

Seeing their warm, familiar bodies, here in this desolate corner of the cavern, Cilia-of-Gold's loneliness welled up inside her, like a Chimney of emotion.

But she swam away from her Three-mates, backward, her carapace scraping on the cavern's Ice wall.

Ice-Born came toward her, hesitantly. "We're concerned about you."

"Then don't be," she snapped. "Go back to the Chimney, and leave me here."

"No," Strong-Flukes said quietly.

Cilia-of-Gold felt desperate, angry, confined. "You know what's wrong with me, Strong-Flukes. I have a *Seeker.* It's going to kill me. And there's nothing any of us can do about it."

Their bodies pressed close around her now; she longed to open up her carapace to them and bury herself in their warmth.

"We know we're going to lose you, Cilia-of-Gold," Ice-Born said. It sounded as if she could barely speak. Ice-Born had always been the softest, the most loving, of the Three, Cilia-of-Gold thought, the warm heart of their relationship. "And—"

"Yes?"

Strong-Flukes opened her carapace wide. "We want to be Three again," she said.

Already, Cilia-of-Gold saw with a surge of love and excitement, Strong-Flukes's ovipositor was distended: swollen with one of the three isogametes which would fuse to form a new child, their fourth. . . .

A child Cilia-of-Gold could never see growing to consciousness.

"No!" Her cilia pulsed with the single, agonized word.

Suddenly the warmth of her Three-mates was confining, claustrophobic. She had to get away from this prison of flesh; her mind was filled with visions of the coolness and purity of *Ice:* of clean, high *Ice.*

"Cilia-of-Gold. Wait. Please—"

She flung herself away, along the wall. She came to a tunnel mouth, and she plunged into it, relishing the tunnel's cold, stagnant water.

"Cilia-of-Gold! *Cilia-of-Gold!*"

She hurled her body through the web of tunnels, carelessly colliding with walls of Ice so hard that she could feel her carapace splinter. On and on she swam, until the voices of her Three-mates were lost forever.

We've dug out a large part of the artifact, Irina, Dolores Wu reported. *It's a mash of what looks like hull material.*

"Did you get a sample?"

No. We don't have anything that could cut through material so dense. . . . Irina, we're looking at something beyond our understanding.

Larionova sighed. "Just tell me, Dolores," she told Wu's data desk image.

Irina, we think we're dealing with the Pauli Principle.

Pauli's Exclusion Principle stated that no two baryonic particles could exist in the same quantum state. Only a certain number of electrons, for example, could share a given energy level in an atom. Adding more electrons caused complex shells of charge to build up around the atom's nucleus. It was the electron shells—this consequence of Pauli—that gave the atom its chemical properties.

But the Pauli principle *didn't* apply to photons; it was possible for many photons to share the same quantum state. That was the essence of the laser: billions of photons, coherent, sharing the same quantum properties.

Irina, Wu said slowly, *what would happen if you could turn off the Exclusion Principle, for a piece of baryonic matter?*

"You can't," Larionova said immediately.

Of course not. Try to imagine anyway.

Larionova frowned. What if one could lase mass? "The atomic electron shells would implode, of course."

Yes.

"All electrons would fall into their ground state. Chemistry would be impossible."

Yes. But you may not care . . .

"Molecules would collapse. Atoms would fall into each other, releasing immense quantities of binding energy."

You'd end up with a superdense substance, wouldn't you? Completely non-reactive, chemically. And almost unbreachable, given the huge energies required to detach non-Pauli atoms.

Ideal hull material, Irina . . .

"But it's all impossible," Larionova said weakly. "You *can't* violate Pauli."

Of course you can't, Dolores Wu replied.

Inside an opaqued bubble-shelter, Larionova, Dixon and Scholes sat on fold-out chairs, cradling coffees.

"If your mercuric was so smart," Larionova said to Dixon, "how come he got himself stuck in the ice?"

Dixon shrugged. "In fact it goes deeper than that. It looked to us as if the mercuric burrowed his way up into the ice, deliberately. What kind of evolutionary advantage could there be in behavior like that? The mercuric was certain to be killed."

"Yes," Larionova said. She massaged her temples, thinking about the mercuric's infection. "But maybe that thread-parasite had something to do with it. I mean, some parasites change the way their hosts behave."

Scholes tapped at a data desk; text and images, reflected from the desk, flickered over his face. "That's true. There are parasites which transfer themselves from one host to another—by forcing a primary host to get itself eaten by the second."

Dixon's wide face crumpled. "Lethe. That's disgusting."

"The lancet fluke," Scholes read slowly, "is a parasite of some species of ant. The fluke can make its host climb to the top of a grass stem and then lock onto the stem with its mandibles—and wait until it's swallowed by a grazing sheep. Then the fluke can go on to infest the sheep in turn."

"Okay," Dixon said. "But why would a parasite force its mercuric host to burrow up into the ice of a frozen ocean? When the host dies, the parasite dies too. It doesn't make sense."

"There's a lot about this that doesn't make sense," Larionova said. "Like, the whole question of the existence of life in the cavities in the first place. There's no *light* down there. How do the mercurics survive, under two miles of ice?"

Scholes folded one leg on top of the other and scratched his ankle. "I've been going through the data desks." He grimaced, self-deprecating. "A crash course in exotic biology. You want my theory?"

"Go ahead."

"The thermal vents—which cause the cavities in the first place. The vents are the key. I think the bottom of the Chao ice-cap is like the mid-Atlantic ridge, back on Earth.

"The deep sea, a mile down, is a desert; by the time any particle of food has drifted down from the richer waters above it's passed through so many guts that its energy content is exhausted.

"But along the Ridge, where tectonic plates are colliding, you have hydrothermal vents—just as at the bottom of Chao. And the heat from the Atlantic vents supports life: in little colonies, strung out along the mid-Atlantic Ridge. The vents form superheated fountains, smoking with deep-crust minerals that life can exploit: sulphides of copper, zinc, lead, and iron, for instance. And there are very steep temperature differences, and so there are high energy gradients—another prerequisite for life."

"Hmm." Larionova closed her eyes and tried to picture it. *Pockets of warm water, deep in the ice of Mercury; luxuriant mats of life surrounding mineral-rich hydrothermal vents, browsed by Dixon's mercuric animals. . . . Was it possible?*

Dixon asked, "How long do the vents persist?"

"On Earth, in the Ridge, a couple of decades. Here we don't know."

"What happens when a vent dies?" Larionova asked. "That's the end of your pocket world, isn't it? The ice chamber would simply freeze up."

"Maybe," Scholes said. "But the vents would occur in rows, along the scarps. Maybe there are corridors of liquid water, within the ice, along which mercurics could migrate."

Larionova thought about that for a while.

"I don't believe it," she said.

"Why not?"

"I don't see how it's possible for life to have *evolve* here in the first place." In the primeval oceans of Earth, there had been complex chemicals, and electrical storms, and . . .

"Oh, I don't think that's a problem," Scholes said.

She looked at him sharply. Maddeningly, he was grinning again. "Well?" she snapped.

"Look," Scholes said with grating patience, "we've two anomalies on Mercury: the life forms here at the South Pole, and Dolores Wu's artifact under Caloris. The simplest assumption is that the two anomalies are connected. Let's put the pieces together," he said. "Let's construct a hypothesis. . . ."

Her mandibles ached as she crushed the gritty Ice, carving out her tunnel upward. The rough walls of the tunnel scraped against her carapace, and she pushed Ice rubble down between her body and her carapace, sacrificing fragile cilia designed to extract soft food particles from warm streams.

The higher she climbed, the harder the Ice became. The Ice was now so cold she was beyond cold; she couldn't even feel the Ice fragments that scraped along her belly and flukes. And, she suspected, the tunnel behind her was no longer open but had refrozen, sealing her here, in this shifting cage, forever.

The world she had left—of caverns, and Chimneys, and children, and her Three-mates—were remote bubbles of warmth, a distant dream. The only reality was the hard Ice in her mandibles, and the Seeker heavy and questing inside her.

She could feel her strength seeping out with the last of her warmth into the Ice's infinite extent. And yet *still* the Seeker wasn't satisfied; still she had to climb, on and up, into the endless darkness of the Ice.

. . . But now—impossibly—there was something *above* her, breaking through the Ice. . . .

She cowered inside her Ice-prison.

Kevan Scholes said, "Five billion years ago—when the solar system was very young, and the crusts of Earth and other inner planets were still subject to bombardment from stray planetesimals—a ship came here. An interstellar craft, maybe with FTL technology."

"Why? Where from?" Larionova asked.

"I don't know. How could I know that? But the ship must have been massive—with the bulk of a planetesimal, or more. Certainly highly advanced, with a hull composed of Dolores's superdense Pauli construction material."

"Hmm. Go on."

"Then the ship hit trouble."

"What kind of trouble?"

"I don't *know.* Come on, Dr. Larionova. Maybe it got hit by a planetesimal itself. Anyway, the ship crashed here, on Mercury—"

"Right." Dixon nodded, gazing at Scholes hungrily; the American reminded Larionova of a child enthralled by a story. "It was a disastrous impact. It caused the Caloris feature. . . ."

"Oh, be serious," Larionova said.

Dixon looked at her. "Caloris *was* a pretty unique impact, Irina. Extraordinarily violent, even by the standards of the system's early bombardment phase. . . . Caloris Basin is *eight hundred miles* across; on Earth, its walls would stretch from New York to Chicago."

"So how did anything survive?"

Scholes shrugged. "Maybe the starfarers had some kind of inertial shielding. How can we know? Anyway the ship was wrecked; and the density of the smashed-up hull material caused it to sink into the bulk of the planet, through the Caloris puncture.

"The crew were stranded. So they sought a place to survive. Here, on Mercury."

"I get it," Dixon said. "The only viable environment, long term, was the Chao Meng-Fu ice cap."

Scholes spread his hands. "Maybe the starfarers had to engineer descendants, quite unlike the original crew, to survive in such conditions. And perhaps they had to do a little planetary engineering too; they may have had to initiate some of the hydrothermal vents which created the enclosed liquid-water world down there. And so—"

"Yes?"

"And so the creature we've dug out of the ice is a degenerate descendant of those ancient star travelers, still swimming around the Chao sea."

Scholes fell silent, his eyes on Larionova.

Larionova stared into her coffee. "A 'degenerate descendant.' After *five billion years?* Look, Scholes, on Earth it's only three and a half billion years since the first prokaryotic cells. And on Earth, whole phyla—groups of species—have emerged or declined over periods less than a *tenth* of the time since the Caloris Basin event. Over time intervals like that, the morphology of species flows like hot plastic. So how is it possible for these mercurics to have persisted?"

Scholes looked uncertain. "Maybe they've suffered massive evolutionary changes," he said. "Changes we're just not seeing. For example, maybe the worm parasite is the malevolent descendant of some harmless creature the starfarers brought with them."

Dixon scratched his neck, where the suit-collar ring of dirt was prominent. "Anyway, we've still got the puzzle of the mercuric's burrowing into the ice."

"Hmm." Scholes sipped his cooling coffee. "I've got a theory about that, too."

"I thought you might," Larionova said sourly.

Scholes said, "I wonder if the impulse to climb up to the surface is some kind of residual yearning for the stars."

"What?"

Scholes looked embarrassed, but he pressed on: "A racial memory buried deep, prompting the mercurics to seek their lost home world. . . . Why not?"

Larionova snorted. "You're a romantic, Kevin Scholes."

A telltale flashed on the surface of the data desk. Dixon leaned over, tapped the telltale and took the call.

He looked up at Larionova, his moon-like face animated. "Irina. They've found another mercuric," he said.

"Is it intact?"

"More than that." Dixon stood and reached for his helmet. "This one isn't dead yet. . . ."

The mercuric lay on Chao's dust-coated ice. Humans stood around it, suited, their faceplates anonymously blank.

The mercuric, dying, was a cone of bruised-purple meat a yard long. Shards of shattered transparent carapace had been crushed into its crystallizing flesh. Some of the cilia, within the carapace, stretched and twitched. The cilia looked differently colored from Dixon's reconstruction, as far as Larionova could remember: these were yellowish threads, almost golden.

Dixon spoke quickly to his team, then joined Larionova and Scholes. "We couldn't have saved it. It was in distress as soon as our core broke through into its tunnel. I guess it couldn't take the pressure and temperature differentials. Its internal organs seem to be massively disrupted. . . ."

"Just think." Kevan Scholes stood beside Dixon, his hands clasped behind his back. "There must be millions of these animals in the ice under our feet, embedded in their pointless little chambers. Surely none of them could dig more than a hundred yards or so up from the liquid layer."

Larionova switched their voices out of her consciousness. She knelt down, on the ice; under her knees she could feel the crisscross heating elements in her suit's fabric.

She peered into the dulling sonar-eyes of the mercuric. The creature's mandibles—prominent and sharp—opened and closed, in vacuum silence.

She felt an impulse to reach out her gloved hand to the battered flank of the creature: to *touch* this animal, this person, whose species had, perhaps, traveled across light-years—and five billion years—to reach her. . . .

But still, she had the nagging feeling that something was wrong with Scholes' neat hypothesis. The mercuric's physical design seemed crude. Could this really have been a starfaring species? The builders of the ship in Caloris must have had some form of major tool-wielding capability. And Dixon's earlier study had shown that the creature had no trace of any limbs, even vestigially. . . .

Vestigial limbs, she remembered. *Lethe.*

Abruptly her perception of this animal—and its host parasite—began to shift; she could feel a paradigm dissolving inside her, melting like a Mercury snowflake in the Sun.

"Dr. Larionova? Are you all right?"

Larionova looked up at Scholes. "Kevan, I called you a romantic. But I think you were almost correct, after all. *But not quite.* Remember we've suggested that the *parasite*—the infestation—changes the mercuric's behavior, causing it to make its climb."

"What are you saying?"

Suddenly, Larionova saw it all. "I don't believe this mercuric is descended from the starfarers—the builders of the ship in Caloris. I think the rise of the mercurics' intelligence was a *later* development; the mercurics grew to consciousness *here,* on Mercury. I *do* think the mercurics are descended from something that came to Mercury on that ship, though.

A pet, or a food animal—Lethe, even some equivalent of a stomach bacteria. Five billion years is time enough for anything. And, given the competition for space near the short-lived vents, there's plenty of encouragement for the development of intelligence, down inside this frozen sea."

"And the starfarers themselves?" Scholes asked. "What became of them? Did they die?"

"No," she said. "No, I don't think so. But they, too, suffered huge evolutionary changes. I think they did devolve, Scholes; in fact, I think they lost their awareness.

"But one thing persisted within them, across all this desert of time. And that was the starfarers' vestigial will to *return*—to the surface, one day, and at last to the stars. . . ."

It was a will which had survived even the loss of consciousness itself, somewhere in the long, stranded aeons: a relic of awareness long since transmuted to a deeper biochemical urge—*a will to return home,* still embedded within a once-intelligent species reduced by time to a mere parasitic infection.

But it was a home which, surely, could no longer exist.

The mercuric's golden cilia twitched once more, in a great wave of motion which shuddered down its ice-flecked body.

Then it was still.

Larionova stood up; her knees and calves were stiff and cold, despite the suit's heater. "Come on," she said to Scholes and Dixon. "You'd better get your team off the ice as soon as possible; I'll bet the universities have their first exploratory teams down here half a day after we pass Earth the news."

Dixon nodded. "And Thoth?"

"Thoth? I'll call Superet. I guess I've an asteroid to order. . . ."

And then, she thought, *at last I can sleep. Sleep and get back to work.*

With Scholes and Dixon, she trudged across the dust-strewn ice to the bubble shelters.

She could feel the Ice under her belly . . . but above her *there was no Ice,* no water even, an infinite *nothing* into which the desperate pulses of her blinded eyes disappeared without echo.

Astonishingly—impossibly—she *was,* after all, above the Ice. How could this be? Was she in some immense upper cavern, its Ice roof too remote to see? Was this the nature of the Universe, a hierarchy of caverns within caverns?

She knew she would never understand. But it didn't seem to matter.

And, as her awareness faded, she felt the Seeker inside her subside to peace.

A final warmth spread out within her. Consciousness splintered like melting ice, flowing away through the closing tunnels of her memory.

R. Garcia y Robertson

GONE TO GLORY

R. Garcia y Robertson made his first sale in 1987, and since has become a frequent contributor to *Asimov's Science Fiction* and *The Magazine of Fantasy & Science Fiction,* as well as selling several stories to *Amazing, Pulphouse,* and *Weird Tales,* and other markets.

Robertson has made something of a specialty of adventure writing and, in fact, may be one of the very best in the business when it comes to turning out vivid, headlong, fast-paced, colorful, inventive, swashbuckling, and yet keenly *intelligent* adventure stories. Since adventure writing is still widely considered to be synonymous with "junk" or throwaway writing by many genre critics, stuff not really worth considering (although a really good adventure story is actually harder to write in some ways than more introspective fiction), this may help to explain why Robertson's work, like Robert Reed's, has been largely and undeservedly ignored, and why he's rarely mentioned among the ranks of good new writers of the eighties and nineties—although a good case could be made that he's delivered more pure first-rate entertainment pound for pound than almost any other new writer of the last ten years.

L. Sprague de Camp was clearly one of the major influences on Robertson (although I suspect that George MacDonald Fraser, author of the *Flashman* series, was a strong influence as well), and, like de Camp, even the most swashbuckling of his adventures contains a generous measure of sly humor; also like de Camp, he makes intensive use of authentic and intensively researched historical settings, and clearly has a love for obscure and little-known corners of history. He's taken us to the bitter days of the Indian Wars on the American frontier in stories such as "The Moon of Popping Trees" and "The Other Magpie," to San Francisco's Chinatown during the Gold Rush days in "Four Kings and an Ace," to the turmoil of the French Revolution in "The Great Fear," to the Cretaceous period to stalk hungry dinosaurs in "The Virgin and the Dinosaur," to ancient Scandinavia in "The Wagon God's Wife," on a trip on a Mississippi paddle wheeler with Mark Twain in "Down the River," to London during the Blitz in "Wendy Darling, RFC," and to Greece in the days *before* history to deal with a fractious Hercules in "The Moon Maid"—among many other historical milieus that he has made his own.

Some of these stories are fantasy, and so outside our purview here, but his stories about the misadventures of Jake Bento and Peg and their bumbling crew of time-traveling documentary filmmakers—which includes the aforementioned "The Virgin and the Dinosaur" and "Down the River," as well as "On the Way to Gaugamela" and "Seven Wonders," as well as his recent novel *The Virgin and the Dinosaur*—have been extremely popular with *Asimov's* readers, as were his non-series time-travel stories "Gypsy Trade" and "Not Fade Away." He's also written baroque and inventive Space Opera or Space Adventures of various sorts, including "The Werewolves of Luna," "Into a Sunless Sea," "The Siren Shoals," "Cast on a Distant Shore," "Fair Verona," "Starfall," and the exuberant picaresque adventure that follows, "Gone to Glory," which takes us out across the boundless prairies of an exotic and dangerous alien world, in search of answers that it would be safer *not* to find. . . .

Robertson's books include, *The Spiral Dance, The Virgin and the Dinosaur, Atlantis Found,* and, most recently, *American Woman.* His most recent book is his first short-story collection, *The Moon Maid and Other Stories.* Several of his recent stories, including "Gypsy Trade," have been optioned for the movies, although none of them have made it to the screen as yet. He was born in Oakland, California, has a Ph.D. in the history of science and technology, and, before becoming a full-time writer, taught those subjects at UCLA and Villanova. He lives in Mt. Vernon, Washington.

Let's hope that as the years to come take us into the new century, Robertson gets some of the respect and attention he deserves. In the meantime, if you're looking for first-class adventure fiction, watch for his name—you're unlikely to be disappointed.

THE SAD CAFE

Defoe sat at one of the Sad Cafe's outdoor tables, soaking up gin slings and watching an energetic couple attempting to mate in midair, wearing nothing but gossamer wings and happy smiles. This pair of human mayflies had to be used to the exercise—neither showed a gram of fat or a bit of shame.

The four-hundred-year-old bistro stood in an open-air park on the Rue Sportif near Spindle's main axis, where g forces were low and the fun never slowed. Holodomes and hanging gardens arched overhead. Beyond the mating couple, halfway up Spindle's curve, nude bathers raised slow-motion splashes in a low-g pool. Not a shoddy spot for doing nothing. Defoe ordered his third (or maybe sixth) sloe gin sling from a roving cocktail bar, a barrel-shaped dispenser doing a lazy drunkard's walk between the tables, happily doling out drinks. Never asking for credit or expecting a tip. Human service was rarer than saber-tooth's teeth on Spindle.

Sipping his sloe gin, Defoe listened with mild disinterest to priority beeps coming over the comlink clipped to his ear. The first calls weren't for him, but they were coming fast and close together. Always a sad sign. Hoping not to be dragged too deeply into other people's troubles, he had his navmatrix decode the binary signals. The pilot's navmatrix grafted into the back of his skull was immune to alcohol. Defoe could down a dozen gin slings and still pilot a tilt-rotor VTOL in a blinding sandstorm or rendezvous with a starship—if the need arose. Only the need never arose. Not here. Not now.

First came a distress bulletin, direct from dirtside.

Then a standby alert.

Followed by a formal AID action request.

The final call was for him. Defoe answered in his off-duty voice.

Salome, his section head, came on-line. Her parents had been ultra-orthodox Satanists (who believed John the Baptist had it coming), and her strict religious upbringing made Salome controlled and precise, with barely a wayward impulse. Except for her hair, which tumbled in untamed curls and wild midnight-blue ringlets past her hips, almost to the floor. She sounded soft and winsome over the comlink, a sure sign HQ was in second-degree alarm—Salome never courted underlings unless she needed something. "There's an AID team down in Tuch-Dah country. They want us to send someone."

Defoe snickered. "Who's the lucky sucker?"

"AID wants an 'experienced surface hand.' Someone who knows the Tuch-Dah. You've been fortunate with them."

"Fortunate? Not hardly. Incredibly lucky would be nearer the mark." Not the sort of luck Defoe aimed to lean on.

Salome persisted. "But you have come through intact—always a plus—and saved us a lot of trouble." And saved the Tuch-Dah a lot of trouble, thought Defoe, not that the ungrateful bastards ever seemed to notice. "Besides, you're fresh up from the surface; it won't be so much of a shock."

"Right. With four months up-time coming." Up-time as in up here—on Spindle—where it was too perfect a day to contemplate work. Defoe had just done a solid eighteen weeks on Glory. Great-aunt Tillie in Alpha C would do duty dirtside before he went back early. "Last time AID lost a team, the problem solved itself—Tuch-Dahs sent their heads back in a leather bag."

"Marvelously considerate. But we can't always count on it. Take a couple of weeks," Salome suggested. "Clear this up, and we'll make it five months." That was double time. A rare offer. AID had to be in a fine panic.

"Make it six months," Defoe countered. *Every* day in paradise is perfect—so one is as good as another. He was demanding four days of up-time for every day dirtside—a splendid deal if he was so awfully essential.

"Find the team first," Salome told him primly. "Four weeks for going down to Glory. Four more for getting the job done." Defoe would get the extra days only if he delivered.

Bargaining with a Satanist was like dealing with the Devil. Centuries of persecution had turned a diabolically carefree sect into overcompensating overachievers. But it was always a comfort knowing that in the bad old days decent folk would have tied his boss to a stake and had her barbecued.

"I'll need a free hand," Defoe told her. "No interference from AID."

"That's your lookout. AID will be there—it's their team that's down. The way to avoid them is to get going and keep going."

"Sure thing." Defoe was already up and moving. "See you in Hell, Salome."

"Not unless you convert." He could hear her wicked smile. Another sign things were serious. Normally, Salome would never kid about religion.

Sloe gin and low gravity made the sidewalk seem to float in front of him. Rooftops and tree-lined arcades curved upward, vanishing into the light streaming down the length of the rotating habitat, reflected inward from mirrors set in the spinning well of stars. Spindle could amaze even sober senses.

Kids flashed past on the sidewalk, tanned young bodies in overdrive. Defoe passed feelie spas and low-g saunas. Happy holos invited him in. No more. Not now. Sorry, guys. Got to sober up and go to work.

Temptation abounded. And it was all free, from gaming orgies to organic feasts. Free as air to anyone who set foot on Spindle. Like an ancient Greek polis, Spindle made its own laws—but without the polis's slavery and infanticide—computers and birth lotteries took their place. No money. No credit. No theft, graft, or taxes. And like the ancient polis, Spindle had only two punishments that mattered. Death and exile. Now Defoe had to face both of these fates, for nothing except the right to return. Hardly fair, but the system lacked honest work.

At Port Orifice—the cavernous lock that let ships enter and exit—he drew emergency rations, heat caps, a thermal parka, bedroll, camp knife, folding mattock, climbing rope, canteen, and medikit. Telling the medikit to sober him up, he ticketed himself for the surface.

A call came through with his clearance. Salome's assistant, a pretty little catamite with painted lids and pierced nipples, purred into the comlink. "Hey, big boy. Is it true the Tuch-Dahs are cannibals?"

"No such luck." Defoe doubted Salome's kept boy had ever seen the surface. "They only eat people." Given conditions on Glory, Defoe thought cannibalism should at least be legal. Maybe even mandatory. If people were like hyenas, compelled to eat everything they killed, dirtside would be a safer place.

Salome's pet laughed wickedly. "Old Battle-ax wants to talk with you."

"Who?" The lock door dilated, cheerily welcoming Defoe aboard.

"Ellenor Battle. Boss dragon lady at AID."

Defoe stepped through the lock into the shuttle. "Tell 'em I've gone to Glory."

The oxyhydrogen shuttle lacked g-fields and cabin service; in-flight entertainment was a pair of tiny portholes. Defoe felt the backward jolt of retros. Spindle seemed to leap ahead; the sole fleck of civilization in this very outback system dwindled rapidly.

He had his navmatrix tap into the shuttle's moronic guidance system. Nerve endings merged with avionics—sensors, astrogation, and stabilization became extensions of sight, sound, and kinesthetics. A modest thrill. Pretty dry compared to real piloting. Defoe's previous employer had been an overprivileged idiot who wracked up a Fornax Skylark, stranding Defoe in-system. Delta Eridani was a dead end, producing nothing the wider universe needed. Traffic was all incoming. Subsidized AID shipments came in cosmic packing crates—robofreighters cannibalized at their destination.

Only a knack for steering through trouble (and putting up with Thals) earned Defoe part-time privileges on Spindle.

At the top of the stratosphere, the shuttle shifted her angle of attack. Acceleration gave way to the gentle persistent push of gravity. Through the near porthole Defoe saw the green-brown limb of the planet rising to greet him, edged by a thin corona of atmosphere. Cloud puffs hung over blue splotches—large lakes or inland seas. Knocking around the Near Eridani, he had seen worlds aplenty, some good, some bad, some merely uninhabitable. When humans first arrived, Glory had been an airless husk, pitted with craters. Relentless terraforming had made her almost livable. No worse than New Harmony, Elysium, Bliss, or any of a half-dozen made-to-order worlds. Either a shining success story, or a case of hideous ecocide. As a pilot, Defoe had to believe in terra-forming; starships needed places to go.

The shuttle came screeching in for a horizontal landing. Millions of kilometers of steppe, savanna, and lava desert allowed landing strips to be as long as needed. A groundhand undogged the hatch with a gleeful "Welcome to dirtside, land of enchantment—where falls can kill you, beasts can eat you, and Thals will snap your spine just to hear it pop. Watch your step, you are in two-thirds g."

Defoe nodded. He was used to gaining thirty kilos every time he went down to Glory. The strip was a study in spasmodic activity. Cargo pallets came dropping down from orbit, braked by big silver chutes, raising yellow clouds of dust. Semirigids landed and departed. SuperChimps sat like rows of sad monkeys, ready to help with the unloading. It had been cocktail time on Spindle; here it was early morning. Dun-colored hills stretched north and west of the field. Beyond the electrified perimeter, a solitary male moropus dug for steppe tubers. Hyenas trotted past, giving the moropus wide leeway—behind them, the Camelback Steppe disappeared into endless distance.

Waiting at the bottom of the landing ladder was a uniformed woman. Tall and athletic, with her steel-gray hair cut down to stubble, Ellenor Battle could easily have looked half her age—but she did not go for biosculpt or hair toner. Taking life as it came, she expected the universe to do the same. Defoe had dealt with Ellenor before, finding her as proud as Lucifer's aunt, a no-nonsense reminder that AID stood for the Agency for *Imperial* Development.

She gave him a liquid hydrogen greeting. "Welcome to Glory. You missed your briefing." Defoe confessed as much. Full-blown AID briefings were full of glaring oversights and ass-backward assumptions—besides, if the problem was solvable from orbit, AID would not have asked him down. But he listened dutifully to the facts as Ellenor saw them. "We have a semirigid and crew more than forty hours overdue. Orbital recon spotted the crash site in the TransAzur, Tuch-Dah territory. . . ."

"How many in the crew?"

"Three."

"All human?" A normal enough question, but Ellenor Battle took it badly, replying with a curt nod. Defoe never knew what was about to bother her. She was very like a Thal in that way—moody and demanding. Salome might worship Satan, but you at least knew where you stood.

A bang and a wail cut off conversation. SuperChimps were refueling the shuttle for her return to Spindle. Boiling LOX filled the collapsed tanks, screaming through the safety valves. With an irritated wave, Ellenor led him away from the ladder. Defoe matched her swift sure strides.

Two huge airship hangars dwarfed the clutter of buildings edging the strip. Outside the electrified perimeter sprawled Shacktown, one of those shameful slums-cum-animal-pens that sprang up around an Outback landing field. Cook smoke climbed lazily over dirty-naked Thal children searching through dung heaps for breakfast. Plastic honeycomb, narrow alleys, and open sewers gave Shacktown the look and smell of a slave labor camp—lacking only the camp's energy fences and city services.

The howl of liquid oxygen faded, and Ellenor went on, "A Thal came into Azur Station with a ship's recorder—hoping to trade it for booze. When the ship crashed, the survivors were attacked by Tuch-Dahs."

It had been a long time coming, Defoe decided, but all hell had finally broken out.

The main hangar was packed with nervous armed humans. Defoe was welcomed aboard by the Port Master, a local worthy who doubled as Mayor of Shacktown, charged with neglecting sanitation and handing out beer and bhang on election day. The hangar canteen had been opened for the duration. Drunk vigilantes brandished riot pistols, pepper grenades, and scoped sporting lasers—as though they could not decide whether they were faced with a prison break or a big game hunt. A Tuch-Dah uprising had the worst elements of both.

The quarter-kilometer hangar housed a giant rigid airship, the *Joie de Vivre,* belonging to a rancher named Helio from the Azur. Ellenor Battle pushed through the jittery throng with Defoe in tow, making for the control car. The gangway was guarded by a brace of armed Thals, meaner than normal Neanderthals, nearly as tall as Defoe, and twice as wide. They wore standard airship harnesses, supporting stubby grenade launchers and bandoliers of gas grenades. A pair of dire wolves strained on electronic leashes.

The liquored-up posse, loudly aiming to take on the entire Tuch-Dah nation, gave the two Thals ample space. It was easier to talk of annihilating ten thousand Neanderthals somewhere out on the steppe than to face down a couple of them sporting grim looks and civilized weapons.

What the Thals thought, Defoe could hardly guess. Heavy browridges hid their deep-set eyes.

A rigger appeared at the top of the gangway—a *Homo sapiens* with dark skin and a drooping mustache trained to blend into trim whiskers. Giving a sloppy sarcastic salute, he led them to the control car's lounge. He had a gasman's easy grace, accustomed to balancing on a catwalk in any sort of wind and weather. Crepe overshoes kept him from raising sparks. RIG'EM RIGHT was scrawled across the back of his bull-hide flight jacket, and he had the veteran gasman's grin—the small ironic smile that said he savored the insanity of making his living aboard a flying bomb.

Helio had that smile too. He sat by an open lounge window, eyes hidden by blue wraparound shades. Broad-shouldered as a Thal, the rancher was reckoned to be a dead shot. Surrounded by a breakfast buffet of cold capon and Azur caviar, he still looked deadlier than any dozen men outside.

Defoe pulled up a handwoven wicker seat, admiring the gold pattern in his plate.

Ellenor Battle tried to decline brunch, but Helio insisted. "It's no advantage to be uncomfortable."

No advantage indeed. Defoe let his host pour him some off-planet champagne. Relaxing under six tons of explosive hydrogen did not stop Helio from doing himself up right. Silk paneling framed slender lacquered columns.

"The first thing," Helio told his guests, "is to see this recorder—and the Thal who found it. We have the transmission from Azur Station. But what is that? A bunch of digital blips." He smiled behind his blue shades, kissing off the tips of his fingers. Electronic evidence was notoriously manipulatable—inadmissible in honest courts.

"So long as we get going." Ellenor Battle glared out the open window at the panicky mob scene below.

Defoe agreed. He too wanted to see the recorder—and the Thal who found it. But most immediately he had to get out of this idiotic atmosphere with its infectious panic. Once underway, things were bound to be better. Helio was supposed to understand Thals—and conditions in Tuch-Dah country—as well as anyone could pretend to. Besides, if there was any answer to the disappearance of the AID team, it was going to be "out there." Somewhere in the endless unknown that lay beyond the fringes of settlement, even on human-made planets. Defoe was fairly at peace with that. Hell, at the moment he made a dubious living off it.

Helio gave orders from the table, speaking through the open window and into the ship's comlink, letting the Port Master's young assistant come aboard, along with a couple of sober gunmen. The rest of the mob would be more of a threat to themselves than to the Tuch-Dahs. A gang of SuperChimps hauled on the ground lines, and the cabin began to move.

As they cleared the hangar, Defoe had his navmatrix lock into the onboard systems. Everything read right. Gas pressure. Wind speed. Elevator alignment. Keel angle. When Helio gave the order to "up ship," the champagne in Defoe's glass did not so much as quiver. The sign of a good crew.

Shacktown and the landing strip fell away to windward. There was a hesitation as the big props started to turn, biting into thin air. Then airspeed picked up and they plowed along, powered by a cold-fusion reactor driving four paired propellers. The Camelback Steppe rolled placidly along a few hundred meters below. Springbok bounded off, alarmed by the airship's shadow.

Defoe decided he should see the recorder transmission from Azur Station, subjecting it to his own prejudices before hearing about it from others. Helio gave an airy wave. "Use my cabin. I have flying to do."

Ellenor Battle followed Defoe to the cabin, bent on seeing the recording again. Helio's private quarters were a sumptuous reminder of the good things to be had on Glory—hand-carved ivory and fine embroidery—luxuries that people on Spindle were too busy enjoying themselves to produce. And there was power to be had as well. Snappy service from human and semihuman attendants. Naked authority over Chimps, Thals, and Shacktown whores who would do nearly anything for next to nothing. Exotic animals roamed the endless veldt, ready to be hunted, killed, and butchered—the cabin was carpeted with a giant moropus hide, its head and claws attached. Defoe knew Dirtsiders who were not even tempted by the tame pleasures of Spindle, who snickered when he boarded a shuttle to go back.

The 3V imager made use of one whole bulkhead, turning curios and tapestries into a stereo tank.

Images leaped out. Defoe saw at once that the transmission wasn't a proper flight recording. The transmission had to come from an AID team member's personal recorder. First came establishing scenes—the semirigid taking off, steppe wildlife, a couple of male team members. Then came a terrible swift pan of breathtaking intensity. The recorder was sited on a small rise, aiming downslope. A low cairn of charred stones poked out of the steppe grass. Defoe flinched as rocket grenades and recoilless projectiles roared right at the recorder, a barrage so real that he almost dived out of his wicker seat, expecting to be showered with exploding shrapnel and shattered bric-a-brac. A ragged line of Thals came screaming out of the long grass, waving steel hatchets and hideous spiked clubs. They were Tuch-Dahs—no doubt there—Defoe recognized the garish paint and blood-freezing cries.

Willungha himself led the charge, atop a full-grown moropus—a tremendous horse-headed, long-necked beast with rhino-sized shoulders and tree-trunk limbs. Like Tars Tarkas aboard a wild thoat, the Neanderthal chieftain brayed commands, wielding a long thin lance. A grenade launcher in his rein hand looked like a tiny toy pistol.

Willungha's mount reared, waving clawed forefeet, and the recorder swung crazily, focusing for a second on the scene atop the knoll. Defoe could clearly make out the crash site. Kneeling among blackened girders and burnt grass was a woman, the third member of the AID team. She was small and brown-haired, in a rumpled uniform, taking painstaking aim with a recoilless pistol. Brown eyes stared intently over the sights, seeming to look right at Defoe. She squeezed off shot after shot as death stormed toward her.

The recorder jerked upward. Swaying grass tops framed empty blue sky. A superbly ugly Tuch-Dah appeared, swinging a hideous curved club. The transmission ceased, replaced by braided hangings and a case of bone china.

Defoe turned to Lady Ellenor, saying, "That was fairly ghastly." Shutting her eyes, she gripped her wicker seat with white knuckles, letting out a short sharp gasp. He had thought Ellenor Battle would be fairly shockproof, especially on a second viewing—but without any warning, her feelings were showing. The woman was full of surprises.

Helio was in the lounge. Any flying he had done had not taken him away from the table. Breakfast had disappeared, but his glass still held champagne. Broken highlands had replaced the Camelback Steppe. Defoe's navmatrix knew the country; beyond these mesas lay the Sleeping Steppe. Then the Azur.

"Enjoy the show?" Helio's eyes were still hidden by blue shades, so it was hard to tell how he meant it.

Defoe nodded. A full-blown Tuch-Dah massacre. No wonder everyone from the Port Master on down was potted and praying. There were a thousand or so bona fide *Homo sapiens* on Glory. Plus maybe twice as many on Spindle who weren't much inclined to come down. Willungha could field twenty thousand club-wielding Tuch-Dah, if he cared to. There were ten million Thals spread over the planet.

Helio twirled the stem of his champagne glass. "Glory might have been a new Eden for ambitious youngsters from the Home Systems—but the task of terraforming was too real for them." Helio did not have to say that *he* had come here, giving up the easy life to raise bison and horses, risking his neck with archaic technology, making the planet not merely habitable but semi-inviting.

He clearly relished the irony of how hard it was to get people just to come down from Spindle. Yet the habitat was built as an interstellar slowboat, launched ages ago to seed the Delta Eridani system. A home for humans while Glory was being terraformed. But by the time Glory had a biosphere and a semibreathable atmosphere, the in-system humans had become perfectly adapted—to life on Spindle.

So AID had to go for Thals. Retrobred Neanderthals were shipped direct to Glory, to do the drudge work, overseeing SuperChimps, leveling landing strips, digging canals, tending great herds of herbivores. And the brutes had done a sterling job. Hell, they were still doing it. While backward types—like the Tuch-Dahs—bred like lemmings out on the vast steppes.

Defoe glanced over at Ellenor Battle. AID had planned this fiasco, from the first slowboats to the retrobreeding program that produced not just the Neanderthals, but a ready-made Cenozoic ecology as well.

She gave him a defiant glare, daring him to say that AID's multithousand-year program was a disaster. "The first colonists are on their way—ten thousand settlers, headed straight from Epsilon Eridani at near light speed. And a hundred thousand more are set to follow. And a million after that."

Epsilon E was less than twenty light-years away.

"Excellent." Helio emptied his champagne glass with an evil chuckle. "Willungha will have them for breakfast."

The rancher was right. Even a Navy cruiser with antimatter warheads could hardly cope with ten million Thals spread over an entire planet. (Currently the Navy had not so much as a captain's gig in-system.) The colonists could be armed, of course—but the Tuch-Dahs knew all about modern weapons. Dumping an armed mob of city-bred humans on a strange world, outnumbered ten thousand to one, with no way of telling the "good" Thals from the "bad" ones, would be a first-magnitude disaster. They might as well ship the weapons straight to Willungha, compliments of AID.

Ellenor Battle looked angrily out the lounge window, staring stiff-necked and imperious at the endless veldt. "There is room enough for humans and Neanderthals." As she saw it, AID was doing everyone a favor, bringing life to a dead world, making space for settlement, resurrecting a lost race, perhaps partly atoning for some ancient Cro-Magnon genocide.

Helio laughed heartily. "Tell that to Willungha. Maybe there is room. If the wild ones can be tamed, or pushed back. And the colonists kept near the strips. But no one is planning for that, eh?" He clearly thought someone should be.

"We have plans," Ellenor retorted.

Defoe thought of the lone AID woman in the recording, backed against the burnt-out wreck, coolly firing at the oncoming Thals. Whatever plans AID was hoarding had to beat that—in fact, they had better be damned slick.

The great blue-green ink blot of the Azur hove into sight. Azur Station stood at the near end, a small circle of dugouts and stock pens between the Blue Water Canal and an east-west fence line. All along the canal the Sleeping Steppe had been made to bloom, growing rice, melons, and sugarcane.

Azur's station chief met the airship. She was a big weatherbeaten woman named Cleo with flaming red hair, and scoped Centauri Special tucked under her arm—a sign of the times. A caravan was leaving her station, headed west along the fence line. The beasts of burden were low-humped retrobred camels, *Camelops hesternus,* as strong as Bactrians but more docile, with finer wool, also better eating.

Cleo had the recorder, and the Thal who had brought it, guarded by armed SuperChimps. The Thal did not understand Universal, or at least pretended not to—staring dumbly at the ring of narrow Cro-Magnon faces.

Helio tried signs. Grudgingly the Thal responded enough to indicate that he was *not* Tuch-Dah. He was Kee-too-Hee, from the marshes. He had found the recorder in a salt pan and trekked down to the station, hoping to get a reward. Instead he was being held prisoner and insulted. This did not altogether surprise him, but did not please him, either.

Ellenor Battle studied the recorder, then passed it to Defoe with a grim "What do you think?" The first time she had asked his opinion. Touched, he had his navmatrix go over the recorder. No sign of tampering. But this was an idiot box with sensors, playing back what was put in.

Defoe nodded at the Thal. "He's telling the truth. At least about not being Tuch-Dah. That circle and dot on his cheek is a Kee-too-Hee clan mark. Any right-thinking Tuch-Dah would cut his throat with a dull clamshell before claiming to be a Kee-too-Hee."

"But what was the recorder doing, sitting on a salt pan?" Ellenor sounded unconvinced. Rightly, so far as Defoe could see. "Give him his reward," she decided. "AID will pay. But don't let him go until we come back from the crash site."

The crash site lay across the Azur. Defoe watched the approach from the control car's foredeck, standing before wide wraparound windows. He felt Helio's firm hand on the elevators, anticipating changes in trim, keeping the keel angle constant. North of Azur Station, the shoreline became a maze of salt marsh teeming with spoonbills and wild boar. Then came the Azur itself, bright green in the shallows, deep blue in the center.

Helio pointed out his plantation, a great green delta thrust out into the sea. On the landward side, a long straight north-south fence kept his domestic herds from straying into Tuch-Dah country. West of the fence line was a knoll topped with a black smear left by the burned semirigid. Helio descended, dodging tall columns of vultures. Never a good sign.

Ellenor told Helio to turn out the *Joie*'s crew. "Have them go through the long grass around the knoll."

"Looking for what?" The rancher sounded skeptical.

"Whatever they find."

On the ground, Defoe was struck by how peaceful it seemed. This was the Saber-tooth Steppe, a silent mysterious savanna, its mystique as solid and tangible as a patch of unterraformed bedrock. The semirigid's small control car was intact, showing no sign of having come down hard. Blackened girders formed big looping curves. They might have been spares ready to be assembled into another ship.

Dire wolves sniffed out two bodies. "Burned beyond recognition" hardly conveyed the horror of the charred skeletons, jaws agape in final agony, held together by shreds of cooked flesh. Riggers watched Ellenor Battle go over the corpses with cool intensity, calling down DNA signatures and dental data from orbit. "This guy's kinda short," someone suggested. "Maybe he's a Thal."

"I don't know. Might be human."

"Human as you anyway."

"Just bein' hopeful."

Glad not to be needed, Defoe conducted his own search, using his navmatrix to find the low black cairn and the fold the Tuch-Dah had burst from. A rigger was down in the grass on his knees, a strip of gasbag fabric tied around his head like a bandanna holding his hair back. Defoe recognized RIG'EM RIGHT on the back of the man's jacket.

Seeing Defoe, he got up. His name was Rayson, which everyone shortened to Ray. He held up a small finned and pointed object. "There's a mess of these in the grass." Defoe recognized the spent projectile from a recoilless pistol. The young AID woman had been firing downslope from up by the wreck. Had she hit anything? Defoe looked for bloodstains.

Ray glanced upslope to where Ellenor Battle was working over the bodies, then walked around behind the fire-blackened cairn, opening his pants.

Defoe called out softly, "That's a shrine."

Taking a sharp step back, Ray zipped his pants. "Shit, I thought it was a barbecue pit." Just the sort of thing that got people in trouble in Tuch-Dah country—you could get brained by a Thal and never know why.

Finding no blood on the grass tops, Defoe stood up, studying the shoreline. The colder north shore marshes were thin, broken by shimmering white pans. Wind whipped fine dry grit off the pans, stinging his eyes, settling in skin creases. He licked the corners of his mouth, tasting tiny bits of the Saber-tooth Steppe. It was salty.

A dark object lay between the steppe and the sea, as still as the shrine. Defoe walked toward it, brittle shore grass crunching underfoot. The big still object was a bison, down on its knees. Vultures flapped off as Defoe approached. Tail, ears, eyes, and testicles were gone, but the bison was hideously alive, managing to lift its head, turning bloody sightless sockets toward Defoe.

"Damn." Ray was right behind him, letting out a low whistle. "I'll fix him." He produced a recoilless pistol with a folding stock. Shouldering it like a rifle, he fired.

The bison jerked at the impact, his head dropping, one horn gouging into the sandy pan. Defoe bent down, examining the dead beast; the tongue was torn out, the muzzle white with salt. There was more salt beneath the sand, where the horn had gone in. Looking east and west along the shore, Defoe saw spiraling columns of vultures.

Ellenor Battle pronounced the bodies to be *Homo sapiens sapiens*. Male. Two members of the AID team were accounted for. Cause of death unknown. "We should start a slow search, standard pattern, centered on the crash site."

Helio nodded and they set off again. As Glory's tight ten-hour day ended, Defoe sat in the lounge, trying to fit together everything he had seen—the mob scene in the hangar, the recording, the silent Thal, the crash site, and the dying bison. Delta Eridani had sunk down almost to the level of the steppe. The *Joie* was making gentle sweeps at less than thirty kph, twenty meters or so above the grass tops. He doubted they would turn up anything. That would be far too easy.

Gathering his things, Defoe climbed up to the keel. Tall hydrogen-filled gasbags swayed in semidarkness. A rigger with CATWALK CHARLIE on his jacket bossed a gang of SuperChimps.

Defoe made his way to the empty tail, unsealing an inspection hatch. Grass tops slid by less than twenty meters below. Unreeling a dozen meters of cable from a nearby winch, he swung his legs through the open hatch, letting the cable drop.

"Hope it wasn't something we said." Rigger Ray was standing on the keel catwalk.

Defoe shrugged. "I need room to work."

Ray sat down on a girder, eyeing the open hatch. This close to dusk, shaded by the giant tail, the hatch looked like a black hole whipping along in midair. "There's room aplenty down there. Just don't end up at the bottom of the food chain."

Defoe nodded. "I'll do my damnedest."

"Well, good-bye, an' good luck." Ray made it sound like, "Hope to hell you come back."

Defoe dropped through, slid down the cable, and let go. He had ample time to position himself. The most charming thing about Glory was the lazy falls at two-thirds g.

Steppe floated up to meet him.

Defoe hit, bounced, and scrambled to his feet. He stood staring up at the big tail of the dwindling airship. The *Joie de Vivre* kept to her search pattern, straining to complete the last leg before nightfall. When she dipped below a rise, he was alone.

Hip-high grass tops ran in every direction, prowled by tawny killers with knife-sized fangs. A cold undertaker's wind sent waves of color sweeping over the twilight steppe—deep blue, rust brown, old gold, and a dozen shades of green. Hyenas chuckled in the deepening gloom.

As Delta Eridani slid beneath the horizon, darkness rose up out of the grass roots, devouring the light. Night birds keened. Whoever said humans were the meanest animals—"the most dangerous game"—undoubtedly said it in daylight. Certainly it was never said at night, alone and unarmed on the Saber-tooth Steppe. Orienting himself by the strange stars of Eridani Sector, Defoe set out walking toward the distant fence line.

THE SABER-TOOTH STEPPE

Dew clung to the grass tops by the time Defoe found the fence line. He had slept once, to be roused stiff and sore by the cough of a saber-tooth. Throughout the dark morning hours, he heard the catlike predators that gave the steppe its name calling to each other. Dawn wind carried their smell, like the odor of a ship's cat in a confined cabin. At first light the calls ceased; he supposed the pride had made its kill.

The energy fence cut a shimmering line across the steppe, carrying a hefty neural frequency shock. Domestic herds grazed beyond it. Overgrazed, in fact. The far side looked like a low-cut lawn.

Defoe walked along the fence until he found a knot of horses, *Equus occidentalis,* tall as Arabians but heavier, with slender feet, reminding Defoe of zebras or unicorns. The lead mare even had zebra stripes across her withers.

The horses lifted their heads as he approached, staring at him and at the hip-high steppe grass. Defoe told his navmatrix to bypass the fence's gullible software. The air between the nearest pylons ceased to shimmer, but still carried the signal saying the fence was intact. Ripping up some long grass, Defoe stepped through, offering it to the lead mare. They were immediate friends. She took the grass, letting him mount.

Riding bareback, he guided her through the break in the fence. Her little herd trotted after them. Defoe set a leisurely course deeper into Tuch-Dah country. As his navmatrix moved out of range, the fence reestablished itself.

He saw springbok and pronghorn, but no bison or Tuch-Dahs. Steppe thinned into shortgrass prairie broken by black knobs of basalt. Curious antelope came right up to him, heads held high, showing off tiny horns and white throats. Brown somber eyes studied him intently. Defoe doubted they had ever been hunted by humans.

Seeing a spiraling column of vultures, Defoe made for it. It marked a bison kill, a lone bull set upon by hyenas. He got down to study the kill site. Drag marks mapped the struggle. The bison had been hit once and ripped completely apart, probably in seconds. Nothing remained but rags of hide and white bone-rich dung. Hyenas were more to be feared than overgrown cats; their bite was better than a panther's, and they weren't as picky as a saber-tooth pride.

A shadow swept over him, a gigantic condor-sized shape among the vultures, circling downward, parting the smaller birds, boring toward Defoe in a tight spiraling dive, hiding in the orange glare of Delta Eridani. Almost on top of him, the big shape sideslipped, spilling air. He recognized Ellenor Battle, wearing an ornithopter harness—a powered version of the wings people flew with on Spindle. She flew like she had been born with them, doing a low-level stall and landing feetfirst.

Never let down your guard on Saber-tooth Steppe. Defoe had been blissfully alone, sharing the day with vultures and a dead bison. Now without warning Ellenor Battle was standing over him, demanding an explanation. What excuse could he have for jumping ship, cutting fences, and stealing horses?

Defoe shrugged. "No one needed me just to fly around in circles aboard the *Joie de Vivre.*"

What fascinated him was her wings. A really fine pair. Falcoform Condors, solar assisted, seven-plus meters of extendible wingspan, with autoflaps and fingertip trim tabs. An energy pack in the small of her back powered the harness.

He nodded at the horses. "These are my tickets into Tuch-Dah country. What's your excuse for being here?" When it came to unwanted company, Glory could be more crowded than Spindle.

Ellenor slowly reached behind her back, taking the AID recorder from between her wings—it must have been strapped alongside the power pack. "I'm here because of this." She weighed it in her hands, then held it out. "It's my daughter's."

Defoe shooed aside some vultures and sat down. So, the woman on the AID team was another Battle. They did not look much alike, except perhaps in the shape of the face. But maybe Ellenor's hair used to be brown. More important, this explained her readiness to listen to reason.

"What *is* her name?" Defoe bore down lightly on the verb; no reason to assume she was dead.

"Lila. It's Hindu, and means the playful will of Heaven."

He took the recorder, turning it over in his hands. "So, why didn't your daughter have this with her during the attack?"

"I've been wondering. There might be some simple explanation."

"Might be." But Defoe doubted it. "That makes another strange circumstance about the crash and recording."

"What are the others?" Ellenor folded her wings, settling down across from him.

"First—no crash. That semirigid landed intact, then burned on the ground. Second, what sort of shot is Lila?"

"I taught her myself." There was pride in her voice and a recoilless pistol on her hip.

"So I supposed." He remembered how cool and unflinching Lila had looked—a lot like her mother. "But there was no blood on the grass. It is hard to believe every shot was a miss."

Ellenor nodded grimly.

Defoe got up, handed back the recorder, and dusted fine grains off his lap. The soil felt thin and silty. "Can you ride bareback?" Ellenor was not his first choice as a traveling companion, or even his fiftieth, but that was Glory for you.

"I was doing it before you were born." She fixed up a loop bridle, selected a mount, and they set off.

The prairie thinned further. Sandy patches showed between tufts of shriveled grass. More buzzards appeared, over more dead bison. More than even hyenas could eat. Defoe reined in, asking, "What do you make of this?"

Ellenor dismissed the apocalyptic scene. "A local die-off. We saw it from orbit. Lila's team was investigating."

Defoe shook his head. "I've been seeing signs of major drought ever since crossing the Azur. And real overgrazing as well. Helio's horses were frantic to cross the fence line."

Ellenor sniffed. "Is that a pilot's opinion, or are you a xenoecologist as well?"

"You don't have to be a xenoecologist to know a dead buffalo. The water table is falling. You can see the steppe salting up. Springbok and pronghorns are filtering in from out of the wild, replacing the bison."

Ellenor denied the Azur was in any trouble. "The sea is stabilized."

"Stabilized?" He reminded her the planet was still terraforming. "Shouldn't the Azur be growing?"

"A local shortfall," she insisted, shrugging off the buzzards and dead bison. "Another wet season and this will all be forgotten."

It did not seem that local to Defoe. Kilometers north of the Azur he could still smell salt on the breeze. Nor would the Tuch-Dah take a "local condition" so calmly—they had to live here. And they were not the types to forget and forgive. Anyone who endured a two-day Naming Fast knew Thals had god-awful long memories.

From time to time Ellenor took off, soaring aloft to do a turn around the landscape, looking for water. Near to dusk she found a dry bed winding through a sandy bottom. Dismounting, Defoe attacked the damp sand with his mattock. An hour of digging produced a small hole full of brackish liquid. He refilled his canteen, then let the horses drink.

Ellenor alighted on a cutbank, saying a rider was coming.

Defoe nodded. Dusk was when they could expect company. Gathering dry grass and brushwood, he made a bed for a fire. Then he took out a heat cap, a capsule the size of an oral antibiotic, breaking it and tossing it on the wood. It burned with an intense flame and acrid odor.

He watched the rider trot warily into camp, separating from the red-orange disk of Delta Eridani. It was Willungha, atop a giant male moropus. Thals did not have aerial recon and orbital scans, but not much that went on in Tuch-Dah country escaped Willungha's attention.

Despite rumors about him being a half-breed, or even *Homo sapiens*, the Tuch-Dah chieftain was pure Neanderthal, with bulging browridges, buckteeth, and a receding chin. That chin was the only weak thing about him. Willungha's huge head and shoulders topped a meter-wide chest; arms the size of Defoe's calves ended in hands strong enough to strangle a hungry saber-tooth (a perennial party-pleaser at Tuch-Dah fetes). An old scar ran along one gigantic thigh. In his youth, Willungha had been gored by a wounded bison, the horn going through his thigh. Hanging head down, with the horn tearing at his leg, Willungha had clamped his good leg and left arm around the beast's neck. Calmly drawing a sheath knife, he cut the bison's throat. Willungha's mount was an ancient cousin of the horse and rhino, intended to be a browser and pruner—recycling plant material into the soil. AID had never thought a moropus could be ridden.

He grunted a greeting.

Defoe did not attempt to answer. Instead he unhobbled the horses, laying the lead mare's halter rope ceremoniously before the Tuch-Dah. He kept back only a pair of mounts and a led horse for himself and Ellenor.

Willungha responded with a series of snorts. Wild Thals spoke a hideous concoction of clicks, hoots, and grunts, which some *Homo sapiens* claimed to understand, but none could imitate. To the Tuch-Dah, *Homo sapiens* were overwhelmingly deaf and totally dumb, hardly even a thinking species. Powerful and unpredictable maybe, able to tear up the landscape like a mad moropus. But reasoning? Even Willungha reserved judgment. He was tolerably familiar with "man the wise"—which explained his mixed opinion.

Having given gifts, Defoe moved to the next stop in the evening's entertainment, setting up the recorder by the fire so it would play on the cutbank. Using the eroded rock as a 3V screen, he had his navmatrix sort through the recorder's memory for the final images, including the Tuch-Dah attack. When Willungha himself materialized atop his charging moropus, the chieftain gave a hoot and whistle. For all Defoe knew, it merely meant, "Hello." Or, "Handsome fellow, what?"

Lila appeared next, pistol in hand. Defoe froze the image. Walking up to the scene, he stabbed a finger at her, then made as if to look about—hopefully telling Willungha that he was looking for her.

The Tuch-Dah's eyes fixed him from within their deep sockets. Defoe repeated the signs. Wild Thals were not much impressed with off-planet marvels unless they could put them to use. Without as much as a grunt, Willungha headed off into the dark with his gift horses in tow.

Defoe leaped up, telling Ellenor, "We've got to follow." Willungha was the best lead they were likely to get.

They trekked through most of the short night. Badlands gave way to savanna. Tangerine dawn outlined the tops of black acacias.

Twenty-odd hours without sleep had Defoe dizzy with fatigue—wishing to God he could glaze over for a while. From upwind came the smell of burning dung, denoting a nomad camp.

Beneath the acacias stood a dark circle of yurts, surrounded by lowing herds. A crowd of Thals emerged to click and whistle their leader into camp. Defoe and Ellenor got no such cheery greetings, facing stony indifference leavened by the occasional dirty look.

While Ellenor sat with folded wings, Defoe listened to a lively exchange among the Thals, seeing fists waved in their direction. The discussion narrowed to a debate between Willungha and a tall brute with a broken nose and bold red-ocher tattoos. He must have outweighed Willungha by a couple of stone, but lacked the chieftain's sangfroid.

Plug-ugly's part in the conversation consisted of low growls and grim looks.

Willungha ended the exchange, turning abruptly and striding over to where Defoe and Ellenor sat waiting. Squatting on his haunches, he made his position plain with signs and finger jabbing. They were free to search for their stray female, with a single exception. Defoe explained to Ellenor, "The only yurt we cannot enter belongs to Mean and Ugly over there." He nodded toward the tall Thal with the broken nose and ocher tattoos.

Ellenor frowned. "Logically that is the yurt we most want to examine."

Defoe nodded. Thals could be amazingly unsubtle. He fished out his medikit, knowing he would need a boost. Strapping the kit to his calf, he told it to give him the chemical equivalent of a week's rest. "I'll see what I can do about getting Plug-ugly's permission."

Stimulants hummed through his blood. The morning got brighter. A two-thirds-g bounce came back to his step. But Defoe hated relying on chemical imbalance; you could fool your body only so long. The Thal stood planted in front of his yurt, a skin hovel on wheels trimmed with camel tails. A bison hide hung over the doorway. Defoe strolled up with a hearty "How ya doin'?"

The Tuch-Dah merely spat. Since neither could speak the other's language, there was no need for formal insults. Defoe slid silently into migi game, arms hanging loose, spine aligned, right foot leading. Out the corner of his eye, he could see Willungha and the boys settling down to watch the fun.

Giving a roar, the Thal rushed at him, arms raised, bent on snapping the spindly Cro-Magnon in half. Defoe was well outweighed, and his sparring partner would be immune to any sort of body blow. He seized the big right wrist with his left hand. Pivoting sideways, he used the Neanderthal's momentum to sling the ogre over his hip, hacking as hard as he could at the immobilized right wrist. Mean and Ugly went butt-over-browridge into a heap against one wheel of his yurt.

Willungha's boys applauded with pant hoots.

The Thal bounded right back up, snarling like a wounded lion. Favoring his right hand, he lashed at Defoe with his left. Defoe parried with his forearm. A bad mistake—the glancing blow staggered him.

Grinning with feral glee, the Thal circled leftward, not even winded. The bastard had probably gotten his beauty sleep. Defoe's right forearm felt numb, and his lungs rasped—a sign the medikit had reached its limits. Much more of this, and the Thal would wear him down. Then stomp him into oblivion.

The Tuch-Dah lunged at Defoe with his left. This time Defoe ducked under the blow, grabbing the Thal's left hand with both of his, ignoring the injured right. Lacking the strength to go the distance, Defoe held grimly to the Tuch-Dah's good hand. He sent the bellowing ogre cart-wheeling over his shoulder, letting the Thal's own weight and momentum bend the left wrist until it snapped.

The Neanderthal lay dazed, one wrist badly sprained, the other bro-ken. A firm believer in kicking a fellow when he was down, Defoe brought his boot heel sharply on the Thal's tattooed instep, to discourage the brute from getting up. Mean and Ugly moaned.

Dusting himself off, Defoe glanced over at Willungha. The Tuch-Dah chieftain gave a congratulatory grunt. Defoe was free to search the yurt. He hoped to hell he'd find something.

As soon as he lifted the bison hide, Defoe knew that whatever was in the yurt stank all the way to Spindle. Urine, sweat, and burning dung mixed with moldy leather. Worming his way in, he startled a gaggle of Thal children playing beside the central fire. They piled out past him, ter-rified by a *Homo sapiens* bogeyman turned real.

The yurt was dank and smoky, walled with soot and skins; aside from body paint and tattoos, Thals did not bother with decoration. What he was looking for sat in the back, amazingly alive. Alert brown eyes ringed with fatigue stared back at him, hardly believing what they were seeing. "Lila Battle, I presume?"

She managed a nod. Tuch-Dah methods were crude and pitiless. To keep Lila in place, a long yoke was fitted around her neck, made from two heavy lengths of wood lashed together with leather. Her hands were free, but the ends of the yoke were out of reach, anchored to the bed of the yurt. She could move enough to feed herself and attend to body functions, but could not reach the knots holding the yoke in place.

As he cut Lila loose, Ellenor Battle came crawling in, dragging her wings. She hurriedly strapped her medikit around Lila's forearm. Mother and daughter were reunited in the fetid interior of a Tuch-Dah yurt, a touching moment lasting about a nanosecond. Lila was clearly Ellenor's daughter, and neither was given to excess sentiment. Before they had fin-ished hugging, Ellenor wanted to know what had happened, and Lila was telling them.

"Helio did it. The bastard flagged us down for a face-to-face. The next thing I knew, I was being bundled up and given to the Tuch-Dahs."

Defoe had suspected something of the sort—it wasn't in Willungha's nature to mix with *Homo sapiens,* either as friends or as enemies. Full-fledged humans had to be behind this. But he was sorry to find out it was Helio. He had liked the arrogant asshole.

Hauling out the recorder, he gave Lila a look at her "last stand." She shook her head. "I wish I had put up that fight, but I never saw it coming." She knew nothing about the fate of her ship and team.

"Dead and burned," Ellenor told her daughter bluntly. Everything else had been digitally programmed straight into the dimwitted recorder's memory. A decent scheme, but not foolproof. The chance selection of Lila's recorder had made her mother suspicious, while Defoe was always willing to believe the worst.

"Why didn't he just kill me?" Lila wondered. Having spent the last few days bound in the back of a Tuch-Dah yurt, she was in many ways the most amazed.

"You are his insurance shot." Defoe set the recorder next to his knee. "A good hunter always has an extra charge handy, to insure his prey is nailed. The crash and fake recording were not enough to thoroughly implicate the Tuch-Dahs. But by the time your body turned up, it would be obvious who had you." Willungha's people probably had no idea why Helio wanted one of his females carted about against her will. But the Thal he had made the deal with fought to keep up his end. Touching in a terrible way.

"But why do this at all?" For once Ellenor looked at a loss. "Why wipe out our team? Why blame it on the Tuch-Dahs?"

"Because Azur is dying." Lila spoke softly. "The sea is overloaded. The steppe is salting up." From the way Ellenor scowled, Defoe guessed this was an old argument.

Lila matched her mother's stubbornness, insisting, "Sea and grass aren't returning water to the air as fast as the canals are draining it away. The thin layer of soil atop this cinder and bedrock cannot absorb new arrivals. We saw it. Helio sees it. Willungha must know as well. Helio wants the Azur closed off to settlement. So do I. But he apparently thinks it will take a war to do it."

Ellenor gave Lila a sour to-think-I-suckled-you look. But as far as Defoe could see, Helio might be right, even AID wouldn't dump settlers into a war zone. With the colonists diverted and the Tuch-Dah pushed back, Helio would have the Azur to himself.

Hearing hoots outside, Defoe lifted the bison hide for a peek. Thals were looking up. From over the steppe came the beat of paired propellers, announcing more unwanted company. The *Joie de Vivre* was approaching.

Ellenor swore. Her daughter began to gather her strength for a getaway. No one was burning to confront the guilty culprit. Defoe had pictured them sending a signal to Spindle, then lying low until AID organized a rescue operation. Armed and reckless felons should be cared for by the pros.

While Ellenor hustled her daughter out, Defoe scooped up the recorder. Telling his navmatrix to turn the recorder on, he pointed the business end at the yurt fire, getting a long shot of the flames.

By the time Defoe tumbled out, the *Joie de Vivre* was poking her nose over the nearest rise, looming larger as she descended. Mother and daughter were disappearing into the long grass beyond the yurt circle. When he caught up with them, Ellenor had her wings on and communicator out, preparing to punch through a call to Spindle. He grabbed her hand, stopping her from opening the channel. "Wait."

"Why?" Ellenor looked angry, annoyed, and scared. Her recoilless pistol was out and armed.

"Helio will be listening," he reminded her. Ellenor might be absolutely ready to sacrifice everything just to see justice done, but Defoe was not near as determined to die for the law. "Give us a chance to get away first."

"How?" she demanded. Running was ridiculous. Helio would swiftly spot them. Nor was there any reason for Willungha to take their side.

"Start by lying down," Defoe insisted, "so we don't disturb the grass tops. Right now we can see him, but Helio can't see us." He had to make the most of that.

The *Joie* settled down on a hillock near camp, close enough to cover the exits, but not so close as to disturb the Tuch-Dahs. SuperChimps swarmed down the ground lines and anchored the airship to the hilltop. Helio and his gunmen trooped down the control-car gangway, sporting rifles tucked under their arms, fanning out as they approached the yurts.

"Get ready to run." Defoe aimed the recorder at the airship. "I'm going to create a diversion."

Lila nodded gamely. Ellenor remained unconvinced. "What sort of a diversion?"

"Fire and panic." Defoe told his navmatrix to set the recorder on playback, projecting a continuously expanding loop using the most recent image in memory. "No matter what you see, run straight for the *Joie de Vivre,* and up that gangway. Got it?" Both women nodded. "Then go," he hissed, triggering the recorder.

They broke cover as a red glow appeared on the hull of the airship—the image of the yurt fire magnified by the recorder—growing into a terrible circle of fire. SuperChimps hooted in terror, scattering away from the ship. In seconds the image covered half the hull, looking for all the world like a trillion cubic centimeters of hydrogen bursting into flame. The control-car crew dived out the gondola windows.

Defoe topped the hill. Shoving Ellenor and Lila toward the gangway, he began releasing ground lines. Lightened by the loss of men and chimps, the airship strained at her anchors, heaving about above him like a whale in labor.

Someone yelled stop. Without bothering to answer, Defoe leaped on the last line, pulling the anchor pin, letting the line hoist him up and away. The airship tore off downwind, wallowing drunkenly, her control gondola empty. Dangling cables rattled through the stand of acacias.

Seeing he could not clear the trees, Defoe had his navmatrix send a frantic call to the *Joie*'s emergency system, releasing the landing ballast. Tons of water cascaded past. The ship shot upward, out of Helio's range and reach.

His navmatrix ticked off altitude increases. One thousand, two thousand, three thousand meters. Savanna spun below him. Time he hauled himself aboard. Holding on with his left hand, Defoe reached up with his right, grasping the taut line. Getting a good grip, he let go with his left.

He fell, steel line sliding through his fingers. His right hand would not hold. Making a frantic grab with his left, he managed to catch the line.

Dangling left-handed, Defoe realized his right arm was useless. It would no longer support him. The medikit strapped to his leg had masked his pain, and the damage done by the Thal. Betraying him into trying too much.

Swinging silently, several kilometers in the air beneath a bucking airship, he pondered his next move. Unable to climb one-handed, Defoe kicked at the end of the line with his boot. If he could snag the anchor loop, he could hang safely until someone hauled him up.

Too far. His foot would not reach. Grass tops whirled dizzily below him. The *Joie de Vivre* topped four kilometers, still rising.

Loosening his left hand, he slid down the line, feeling with his boot for the loop. His toe went in. He gave a silent cheer. He had made it.

Just as his boot settled in, the line jerked—the *Joie* had reached her pressure height, automatically venting hydrogen. Nosing down, she took a drunken dip, porpoising out of control.

Defoe fought to regain his grip. Fatigued fingers weren't quick enough. The line snapped away. Two sleepless nights, the fight with the Thal, the struggle on the line, had all taken too much out of him.

Arms flailing, he fell slowly backward, his booted foot twisting in the loop. Two-thirds g gave him enough time to make a last lunge at the line. And miss.

Dangling upside down, holding on by his boot, he could feel his foot slipping. Doubling up, Defoe made a grab at the boot with his good hand. He got it. Fingers gripped the boot as his foot slipped free and the line bounded away.

He was falling. Holding tight to the useless boot, Defoe shrieked in fright and exasperation. He could see the snaking line above him and the shadowy form of the airship starting to dwindle. Five kilometers away, ground rushed silently up to greet him.

Defoe felt none of the dreamy complacency the dying were supposed to enjoy. Even in two-thirds g, onto soft grass, he knew he would hit hard, bounce badly, and not get up. Ever. His navmatrix ticked off the fall. Slow at first. A few meters per second—but ever faster. Numbers began to blur.

The horrible silence was broken by the rush of wings. Hands seized him. Primaries beat frantically. He could feel flaps straining against the sky.

Ellenor Battle had him. Pulling out of her stoop, she was trying to brake, wings beating against better than twice her weight. Good shot, thought Defoe. But the wing loading was way too high. He could feel her stalling, about to tumble into a spin—unless she let go.

But she dug in instead, spreading her wings, defiant to the end, her contorted face centimeters from his.

Then came a miraculous jerk, and the impossible happened. Defoe bounded to a dead stop in midair.

A line stood taut between Ellenor's shoulders. She had clipped a cable to her harness before diving after him. Staring up at the skyline, Defoe tried to cheer, getting out a grateful croak. The woman was a pig-headed genius, and he wanted to kiss her. But then Ellenor might really drop him.

Meter by meter he felt himself being hauled to safety. The AID woman was grinning.

As they were drawn aboard the galloping airship, Defoe saw Rigger Ray working the winch. Lila lay full out on the deck, reaching down to help her mother. Catwalk Charlie was holding tight to a girder, eyes shut, still waiting for the flaming crash. Defoe could hear him mumbling:

Our Satan that art in Hell,
Damned be thy name.
Lead us into temptation,
And encourage our trespasses . . .

Defoe was shocked. Charlie had never *looked* religious. But a brush with death will bring out the Devil in anyone.

Gingerly sliding his boot on, Defoe told his navmatrix to take control of the airship. The *Joie* righted herself, turning back toward Shacktown.

Hearing Ellenor put in her call to Spindle, Defoe wondered how Helio was doing with Willungha. After murdering two AID workers, trying to frame the Tuch-Dahs, then bungling the cover-up, Helio had serious problems ahead. But so did everyone on Glory. And the first ten thousand colonists were already on their way, leaving Epsilon Eridani at near light speed.

Defoe for one did not want to be there when trouble arrived. Right now he was headed back for Spindle, to spend long lazy hours of enjoying himself and looking for a ship headed out-system. AID could deal with the mess they had made. More people meant more traffic, and one day dirtside and all its dangers would be a batch of not-too-pleasant recollections. The sort of memories you were free to file and forget.

Tony Daniel

A DRY, QUIET WAR

One of the fastest-rising new stars of the nineties, Tony Daniel grew up in Alabama, lived for a while on Vashon Island, in Washington state, and in recent years, in the best tradition of the young bohemian artist, has been restlessly on the move, from Vashon Island to Europe, from Europe to New York City, from New York City to Alabama, and, most recently, back to New York City again. He attended the Clarion West Writers Workshop in 1989, and since then has become a frequent contributor to *Asimov's Science Fiction,* as well as to markets such as *The Magazine of Fantasy & Science Fiction, Amazing, SF Age, Universe, Full Spectrum,* and elsewhere.

Like many writers of his generation, Tony Daniel first made an impression on the field with his short fiction. He made his first sale, to *Asimov's,* in 1990, "The Passage of Night Trains," and followed it up with a long string of well-received stories both there and elsewhere throughout the first few years of the nineties, stories such as "The Careful Man Goes West," "Sun So Hot I Froze to Death," "Prism Tree," "Death of Reason," "Lost in Transmission," "God's Foot," "Candle," "Aconguaca," and others. His first novel, *Warpath,* a lush, baroque Planetary Romance full of deliberately over-the-top tropes such as superpowered Indians "paddling" birch-bark canoes across the gulfs of interstellar space, was released simultaneously in America and England in 1993, and he subsequently won two thousand dollars and the T. Morris Hackney Award for his unpublished mountain-climbing novel *Ascension,* based on his story "Aconguaca."

Daniel's career seemed to be well launched at this point, with his short stories receiving a lot of attention and *Warpath* getting largely positive reviews, but then he was unable to find a publisher for *Ascension* (it remains unpublished to this day), he stalled on his second novel, and his career abruptly seemed to run out of steam. Little would be heard from him during the middle years of the decade, while he moved restlessly around the world, from one minor job to another. In 1995, though, he returned suddenly to the field with a string of new stories, work even stronger and at a higher level of literary accomplishment than his previous stuff, including "Life on the Moon," which was a finalist for the Hugo Award in 1996, "No Love in All of Dwingeloo," "The Joy of the Sidereal Long-Distance Runner," "A Dry, Quiet War," and a highly impressive novella called "The Robot's Twilight Companion." In 1997, he published a major new novel, *Earthling,* which has gotten enthusiastic reviews everywhere from *Interzone* to the *New York Times.* His career seems to be firmly back on track again, knock wood, and I have a feeling he'll be one of the major players in SF in the opening decades of the new century.

Like George R.R. Martin, Daniel is a lushly romantic writer, and his characters also tend toward Byronism, although Daniel's brooding Byronic heroes tend to be darker, more cynical, and more violent than Martin's are, and also tend to possess Zelaznyesque superpowers and abilities of a sort that Martin's usually do not. One of the major influences on Daniel's work, of course, is clearly that of his one-time mentor, Lucius Shepard, although the impact of Zelazny, van Vogt, Walter M. Miller, Jr., and, oddly, Ray Bradbury can also be demonstrated fairly clearly. Like some of his other young colleagues, though, Daniel's other influences spread far beyond the boundaries of the genre, and even beyond the print world itself; the influence of Japanese samurai movies and spaghetti Westerns on the vivid, violent story that follows are pretty clear, for instance, and Daniel himself has specifically said that one of his direct inspirations for the story was the movies of John Ford.

In "A Dry, Quiet War," he spins a colorful and exotic story of a battle-weary veteran who returns from a bewilderingly strange high-tech future war only to face his greatest and most sinister challenge right at *home.* . . .

I cannot tell you what it meant to me to see the two suns of Ferro set behind the dry mountain east of my home. I had been away twelve billion years. I passed my cabin to the pump well, and taking a metal cup from where it hung from a set-pin, I worked the handle three times. At first it creaked, and I believed it was rusted tight, but then it loosened, and within fifteen pulls, I had a cup of water.

Someone had kept the pump up. Someone had seen to the house and the land while I was away at the war. For me, it had been fifteen years; I wasn't sure how long it had been for Ferro. The water was tinged red and tasted of iron. Good. I drank it down in a long draft, then put the cup back onto its hangar. When the big sun, Hemingway, set, a slight breeze kicked up. Then Fitzgerald went down and a cold, cloudless night spanked down onto the plateau. I shivered a little, adjusted my internals, and stood motionless, waiting for the last of twilight to pass, and the stars—my stars— to come out. Steiner, the planet that is Ferro's evening star, was the first to emerge, low in the west, methane blue. Then the constellations. Ngal. Gilgamesh. The Big Snake, half-coiled over the southwestern horizon. There was no moon tonight. There was never a moon on Ferro, and that was right.

After a time, I walked to the house, climbed up the porch, and the house recognized me and turned on the lights. I went inside. The place was dusty, the furniture covered with sheets, but there were no signs of rats or jinjas, and all seemed in repair. I sighed, blinked, tried to feel something. Too early, probably. I started to take a covering from a chair, then let it be. I went to the kitchen and checked the cupboard. An old malt-whiskey bottle, some dry cereal, some spices. The spices had been my mother's, and I seldom used them before I left for the end of time. I considered that the whiskey might be perfectly aged by now. But, as the saying goes on Ferro, we like a bit of food with our drink, so I left the house and took the road to town, to Heidel.

It was a five-mile walk, and though I could have enhanced and covered the ground in ten minutes or so, I walked at a regular pace under my homeworld stars. The road was dirt, of course, and my pant legs were dusted red when I stopped under the outside light of Thredmartin's Pub. I took a last breath of cold air, then went inside to the warm.

It was a good night at Thredmartin's. There were men and women gathered around the fire hearth, usas and splices in the cold corners. The regulars were at the bar, a couple of whom I recognized—so old now, wizened like stored apples in a barrel. I looked around for a particular face, but she was not there. A jukebox sputtered some core-cloud deak, and the air was thick with smoke and conversation. Or was, until I walked in. Nobody turned to face me. Most of them couldn't have seen me. But a signal passed and conversation fell to a quiet murmur. Somebody quickly killed the jukebox.

I blinked up an internals menu into my peripheral vision and adjusted to the room's temperature. Then I went to the edge of the bar. The room got even quieter. . . .

The bartender, old Thredmartin himself, reluctantly came over to me. "What can I do for you, sir?" he asked me.

I looked over him, to the selection of bottles, tubes, and cans on display behind him. "I don't see it," I said.

"Eh?" He glanced back over his shoulder, then quickly returned to peering at me.

"Bone's Barley," I said.

"We don't have any more of that," Thredmartin said, with a suspicious tone.

"Why not?"

"The man who made it died."

"How long ago?"

"Twenty years, more or less. I don't see what business of—"

"What about his son?"

Thredmartin backed up a step. Then another. "Henry," he whispered. "Henry Bone."

"Just give me the best that you do have, Peter Thredmartin," I said. "In fact, I'd like to buy everybody a round on me."

"Henry Bone! Why, you looked to me like a bad 'un indeed when you walked in here. I took you for one of them glims, I did," Thredmartin said. I did not know what he was talking about. Then he smiled an old devil's crooked smile. "Your money's no good here, Henry Bone. I do happen to have a couple of bottles of your old dad's whiskey stowed away in back. Drinks are on the house."

And so I returned to my world, and for most of those I'd left behind it seemed as if I'd never really gone. My neighbors hadn't changed much in the twenty years local that had passed, and of course, they had no conception of what had happened to me. They knew only that I'd been to the war—the Big War at the End of Time—and evidently everything turned out okay, for here I was, back in my own time and my own place. I planted Ferro's desert barley, brought in peat from the mountain bogs, bred the biomass that would extract the minerals from my hard ground water, and got ready for making whiskey once again. Most of the inhabitants of Ferro were divided between whiskey families and beer families. Bones were distillers, never brewers, since the Settlement, ten generations before.

It wasn't until she called upon me that I heard the first hints of the troubles that had come. Her name was Alinda Bexter, but since we played together under the floorplanks of her father's hotel, I had always called her Bex. When I left for the war, she was twenty, and I twenty-one. I still recognized her at forty, five years older than I was now, as she came walking down the road to my house, a week after I'd returned. She was taller than most women on Ferro, and she might be mistaken for a usa-human splice anywhere else. She was rangy, and she wore a khaki dress that whipped in the dry wind as she came toward me. I stood on the porch, waiting for her, wondering what she would say.

"Well, this is a load off of me," she said. She was wearing a brimmed hat. It had a ribbon to tie under her chin, but Bex had not done that. She held her hand on it to keep it from blowing from her head. "This damn ranch has been one big thankless task."

"So it was you who kept it up," I said.

"Just kept it from falling apart as fast as it would have otherwise," she replied. We stood and looked at one another for a moment. Her eyes were green. Now that I had seen an ocean, I could understand the kind of green they were.

"Well then," I finally said. "Come on in."

I offered her some sweetcake I'd fried up, and some beer that my neighbor, Shin, had brought by, both of which she declined. We sat in the living room, on furniture covered with the white sheets I had yet to remove. Bex and I took it slow, getting to know each other again. She ran her father's place now. For years, the only way to get to Heidel was by freighter, but we had finally gotten a node on the Flash, and even though

Ferro was still a backwater planet, there were more strangers passing through than there ever had been—usually en route to other places. But they sometimes stayed a night or two in the Bexter Hotel. Its reputation was spreading, Bex claimed, and I believed her. Even when she was young, she had been shrewd but honest, a combination you don't often find in an innkeeper. She was a quiet woman—that is, until she got to know you well—and some most likely thought her conceited. I got the feeling that she hadn't let down her reserve for a long time. When I knew her before, Bex did not have many close friends, but for the ones she had, such as me, she poured out her thoughts, and her heart. I found that she hadn't changed much in that way.

"Did you marry?" I asked her, after hearing about the hotel and her father's bad health.

"No," she said. "No, I very nearly did, but then I did not. Did you?"

"No. Who was it?"

"Rall Kenton."

"Rall Kenton? Rall Kenton whose parents run the hops market?" He was a quarter-splice, a tall man on a world of tall men. Yet, when I knew him, his long shadow had been deceptive. There was no spark or force in him. "I can't see that, Bex."

"Tom Kenton died ten years ago," she said. "Marjorie retired, and Rall owned the business until just last year. Rall did all right; you'd be surprised. Something about his father's passing gave him a backbone. Too much of one, maybe."

"What happened?"

"He died," she said. "He died too, just as I thought you had." Now she told me she would like a beer after all, and I went to get her a bottle of Shin's ale. When I returned, I could tell that she'd been crying a little.

"The glims killed Rall," said Bex, before I could ask her about him. "That's their name for themselves, anyway. Humans, repons, kaliwaks, and I don't know what else. They passed through last year and stayed for a week in Heidel. Very bad. They made my father give over the whole hotel to them, and then they had a . . . trial, they called it. Every house was called and made to pay a tithe. The glims decided how much. Rall refused to pay. He brought along a pistol—Lord knows where he got it— and tried to shoot one of them. They just laughed and took it from him." Now the tears started again.

"And then they hauled him out into the street in front of the hotel." Bex took a moment and got control of herself. "They burnt him up with a p-gun. Burned his legs off first, then his arms, then the rest of him after they'd let him lie there a while. There wasn't a trace of him after that; we couldn't even bury him."

I couldn't take her to me, hold her, not after she'd told me about Rall. Needing something to do, I took some tangled banwood from the tinder box and struggled to get a fire going from the burnt-down coals in my hearth. I blew into the fireplace and only got a nose full of ashes for my trouble. "Didn't anybody fight?" I asked.

"Not after that. We just waited them out. Or they got bored. I don't know. It was bad for everybody, not just Rall." Bex shook her head, sighed, then saw the trouble I was having and bent down to help me. She was much better at it than I, and the fire was soon ablaze. We sat back down and watched it flicker.

"Sounds like war-ghosts," I said.

"The glims?"

"Soldiers who don't go home after the war. The fighting gets into them and they don't want to give it up, or can't. Sometimes they have . . . modifications that won't let them give it up. They wander the timeways— and since they don't belong to the time they show up in, they're hard to kill. In the early times, where people don't know about the war, or have only heard rumors of it, they had lots of names. Vampires. Hagamonsters. Zombies."

"What can you do?"

I put my arm around her. It had been so long. She tensed up, then breathed deeply, serenely.

"Hope they don't come back," I said. "They are bad ones. Not the worst, but bad."

We were quiet for a while, and the wind, blowing over the chimney's top, made the flue moan as if it were a big stone flute.

"Did you love him, Bex?" I asked. "Rall?"

She didn't even hesitate in her answer this time. "Of course not, Henry Bone. How could you ever think such a thing? I was waiting to catch up with you. Now tell me about the future."

And so I drew away from her for a while, and told her—part of it at least. About how there is not enough dark matter to pull the cosmos back together again, not enough mass to undulate in an eternal cycle. Instead, there *is* an end, and all the stars are either dead or dying, and all that there is is nothing but dim night. I told her about the twilight armies gathered there, culled from all times, all places. Creatures, presences, machines, weapons fighting galaxy-to-galaxy, system-to-system, fighting until the critical point is reached, when entropy flows no more, but pools, pools in endless, stagnant pools of nothing. No light. No heat. No effect. And the universe is dead, and so those who remain . . . inherit the dark field. They win.

"And did you win?" she asked me. "If that's the word for it."

The suns were going down. Instead of answering, I went outside to the woodpile and brought in enough banwood to fuel the fire for the night. I thought maybe she would forget what she'd asked me—but not Bex.

"How does the war end, Henry?"

"You must never ask me that." I spoke the words carefully, making sure I was giving away nothing in my reply. "Every time a returning soldier tells that answer, he changes everything. Then he has two choices. He can either go away, leave his own time, and go back to fight again. Or he can stay, and it will all mean nothing, what he did. Not just who won and who lost, but all the things he did in the war spin off into nothing."

Bex thought about this for a while. "What could it matter? What in God's name could be worth fighting *for?*" she finally asked. "Time ends. Nothing matters after that. What could it possibly matter who won . . . who wins?"

"It means you can go back home," I said. "After it's over."

"I don't understand."

I shook my head and was silent. I had said enough. There was no way to tell her more, in any case—not without changing things. And no way to *say* what it was that had brought those forces together at the end of everything. And what the hell do *I* know, even now? All I know is what I was told, and what I was trained to do. If we don't fight at the end, there won't be a beginning. For there to be people, there has to be a war to fight at the end of things. We live in that kind of universe, and not another, they told me. They told me, and then I told myself. And I did what I had to do so that it would be over and I could go home, come back.

"Bex, I never forgot you," I said. She came to sit with me by the fire. We didn't touch at first, but I felt her next to me, breathed the flush of her skin as the fire warmed her. Then she ran her hand along my arm, felt the bumps from the operational enhancements.

"What have they done to you?" she whispered.

Unbidden the old words of the skyfallers' scream, the words that were yet to be, surfaced in my mind.

They sucked down my heart
to a little black hole.
You cannot stab me.

They wrote down my brain
on a hard knot of space.
You cannot turn me.

Icicle spike
from the eye of a star.
I've come to kill you.

I almost spoke them, from sheer habit. But I did not. The war was over. Bex was here, and I knew it was over. I was going to *feel* something, once again, something besides guile, hate, and rage. I didn't yet, that was true, but I *could* feel the possibility.

"I don't really breathe anymore, Bex; I pretend to so I won't put people off," I told her. "It's been so long, I can't even remember what it was like to *have* to."

Bex kissed me then. At first, I didn't remember how to do that either. And then I did. I added wood to the fire, then ran my hand along Bex's neck and shoulder. Her skin had the health of youth still, but years in the sun and wind had made a supple leather of it, tanned and grained fine. We took the sheet from the couch and pulled it near to the warmth, and she drew me down to her on it, to her neck and breasts.

"Did they leave enough of you for me?" she whispered.

I had not known until now. "Yes," I answered, "there's enough." I found my way inside her, and we made love slowly, in a way that might seem sad to any others but us, for there were memories and years of longing that flowed from us, around us, like amber just at the melting point, and we were inside and there was nothing but this present with all of what was, and what would be, already passed. No time. Finally, only Bex and no time between us.

We fell asleep on the old couch, and it was dim half-morning when we awoke, with Fitzgerald yet to rise in the west and the fire a bed of coals as red as the sky.

Two months later, I was in Thredmartin's when Bex came in with an evil look on her face. We had taken getting back together slow and easy up till then, but the more time we spent around each other, the more we understood that nothing basic had changed. Bex kept coming to the ranch and I took to spending a couple of nights a week in a room her father made up for me at the hotel. Furly Bexter was an old-style McKinnonite. Men and women were to live separately and only meet for business and copulation. But he liked me well enough, and when I insisted on paying for my room, he found a loophole somewhere in the Tracts of McKinnon about cohabitation being all right in hotels and hostels.

"The glims are back," Bex said, sitting down at my table. I was in a dark corner of the pub. I left the fire for those who could not adjust their

own internals to keep them warm. "They've taken over the top floor of
the hotel. What should we do?"

I took a draw of beer—Thredmartin's own thick porter—and looked
at her. She was visibly shivering, probably more from agitation than
fright.

"How many of them are there?" I asked.

"Six. And something else, some splice I've never seen, however
many that makes."

I took another sip of beer. "Let it be," I said. "They'll get tired, and
they'll move on."

"What?" Bex's voice was full of astonishment. "What are you saying?"

"You don't want a war here, Bex," I replied. "You have no idea how
bad it can get."

"They killed Rall. They took our *money.*"

"Money." My voice sounded many years away, even to me.

"It's muscle and worry and care. You know how hard people work on
Ferro. And for those . . . *things* . . . to come in and take it! We cannot let
them—"

"—Bex," I said. "I am not going to do anything."

She said nothing; she put a hand on her forehead as if she had a sickening fever, stared at me for a moment, then looked away.

One of the glims chose that moment to come into Thredmartin's. It
was a halandana, a splice—human and jan—from up-time and a couple
of possible universes over. It was nearly seven feet tall, with a two-foot-
long neck, and it stooped to enter Thredmartin's. Without stopping, it
went to the bar and demanded morphine.

Thredmartin was at the bar. He pulled out a dusty rubber, little used,
and before he could get out an injector, the halandana reached over, took
the entire rubber and put it in the pocket of the long gray coat it wore.
Thredmartin started to speak, then shook his head, and found a spray
shooter. He slapped it on the bar, and started to walk away. The halandana's hand shot out and pushed the old man. Thredmartin stumbled to
his knees.

I felt the fingers of my hands clawing, clenching. Let them loosen;
let them go.

Thredmartin rose slowly to one knee. Bex was up, around the bar,
and over to him, steadying his shoulder. The glim watched this for a moment, then took its drug and shooter to a table, where it got itself ready
for an injection.

I looked at it closely now. It was female, but that did not mean much
in halandana splices. I could see it phase around the edges with dead,

gray flames. I clicked in wideband overspace, and I could see through the halandana to the chair it was sitting in and the unpainted wood of the wall behind it. And I saw more, in the spaces between spaces. The halandana was keyed in to a websquad; it wasn't really an individual anymore. Its fate was tied to that of its unit commander. So the war-ghosts—the glims—were a renegade squad, most likely, with a single leader calling the shots. For a moment, the halandana glanced in my direction, maybe feeling my gaze somewhere outside of local time, and I banded down to human normal. It quickly went back to what it was doing. Bex made sure Thredmartin was all right, then came back over to my table.

"We're not even in its timeline," I said. "It doesn't think of us as really being alive."

"Oh God," Bex said. "This is just like before."

I got up and walked out. It was the only solution. I could not say anything to Bex. She would not understand. I understood—not acting was the rational, the *only,* way, but not *my* way. Not until now.

I enhanced my legs and loped along the road to my house. But when I got there, I kept running, running off into the red sands of Ferro's outback. The night came down, and as the planet turned, I ran along the length of the Big Snake, bright and hard to the southwest, and then under the blue glow of Steiner, when she rose in the moonless, trackless night. I ran for miles and miles, as fast as a jaguar, but never tiring. How could I tire when parts of me stretched off into dimensions of utter stillness, utter rest? Could Bex see me for what I *was,* she would not see a man, but a kind of colonial creature, a mash of life pressed into the niches and fault lines of existence like so much grit and lichen. A human is anchored with only his heart and his mind; sever those, and he floats away. Floats away. What was I? A medusa fish in an ocean of time? A tight clump of nothing, disguised as a man? Something else?

Something damned hard to kill, that was certain. And so were the glims. When I returned to my house in the star-bright night, I half expected to find Bex, but she was not there. And so I rattled about for a while, powered down for an hour at dawn and rested on a living-room chair, dreaming in one part of my mind, completely alert in another. The next day, Bex still did not come, and I began to fear something had happened to her. I walked partway into Heidel, then cut off the road and stole around the outskirts, to a mound of shattered, volcanic rocks—the tailings of some early prospector's pit—not far from the town's edge. There I stepped up my vision and hearing, and made a long sweep of Main Street. Nothing. Far, far too quiet, even for Heidel.

I worked out the parabolic to the Bexter Hotel, and after a small adjustment, heard Bex's voice, then her father's. I was too far away to make out the words, but my quantitatives gave it a positive ID. So Bex was all right, at least for the moment. I made my way back home, and put in a good day's work making whiskey.

The next morning—it was the quarteryear's double dawn, with both suns rising in the east nearly together—Bex came to me. I brought her inside, and in the moted sunlight of my family's living room, where I now took my rest, when I rested, Bex told me that the glims had taken her father.

"He held back some old Midnight Livet down in the cellar, and didn't deliver it when they called for room service." Bex rubbed her left fist with her right fingers, expertly, almost mechanically, as she'd kneaded a thousand balls of bread dough. "How do they know these things? How do they know, Henry?"

"They can see *around* things," I said. "Some of them can, anyway."

"So they read our thoughts? What do we have left?"

"No, no. They can't see in *there,* at least I'm sure they can't see in your old man's McKinnonite nut lump of a brain. But they probably saw the whiskey down in the cellar, all right. A door isn't a very solid thing for a war-ghost out of its own time and place."

Bex gave her hand a final squeeze, spread it out upon her lap. She stared down at the lines of her palm, then looked up at me. "If you won't fight, then you have to tell *me* how to fight them," she said. "I won't let them kill my father."

"Maybe they won't."

"I can't take that chance."

Her eyes were blazing green, as the suns came full through the window. Her face was bright-lit and shadowed, as if by the steady coals of a fire. You have loved this woman a long time, I thought. You have to tell her something that will be of use. But what could possibly be of use against a creature that had survived—*will* survive—that great and final war—and so must survive *now?* You can't kill the future. That's how the old sergeants would explain battle fate to the recruits. If you are meant to be there, they'd say, then nothing can hurt you. And if you're not, then you'll just fade, so you might as well go out fighting.

"You can only irritate them," I finally said to Bex. "There's a way to do it with the Flash. Talk to that technician, what's his name—"

"Jurven Dvorak."

"Tell Dvorak to strobe the local interrupt, fifty, sixty tetracycles. It'll cut off all traffic, but it will be like a wasp nest to them, and they won't want to get close enough to turn it off. Maybe they'll leave. Dvorak better stay near the node after that too."

"All right," Bex said. "Is that all?"

"Yes," I said. I rubbed my temples, felt the vague pain of a headache, which quickly receded as my internals rushed more blood to my scalp. "Yes, that's it."

Later that day, I heard the crackle of random quantum-tunnel spray, as split, unsieved particles decided their spin, charm, and color without guidance from the world of gravity and cause. It was an angry buzz, like the hum of an insect caught between screen and windowpane, tremendously irritating to listen to for hours on end, if you were unlucky enough to be sensitive to the effect. I put up with it, hoping against hope that it would be enough to drive off the glims.

Bex arrived in the early evening, leading her father, who was ragged and half-crazed from two days without light or water. The glims had locked him in a cleaning closet, in the hotel, where he'd sat cramped and doubled over. After the buzz started, Bex opened the lock and dragged the old man out. It was as if the glims had forgotten the whole affair.

"Maybe," I said. "We can hope."

She wanted me to put the old man up at my house, in case the glims suddenly remembered. Old Furly Bexter didn't like the idea. He rattled on about something in McKinnon's "Letter to the Canadians," but I said yes, he could stay. Bex left me with her father in the shrouds of my living room.

Some time that night, the quantum buzz stopped. And in the early morning, I saw them—five of them—stalking along the road, kicking before them the cowering, stumbling form of Jurven Dvorak. I waited for them on the porch. Furly Bexter was asleep in my parents' bedroom. He was exhausted from his ordeal, and I expected him to stay that way for a while.

When they came into the yard, Dvorak ran to the pump and held to the handle, as if it were a branch suspending him over a bottomless chasm. And for him it was. They'd broken his mind and given him a dream of dying. Soon to be replaced by reality, I suspected, and no pump-handle hope of salvation.

Their leader—or the one who did the talking—was human-looking. I'd have to band out to make a full ID, and I didn't want to give anything away for the moment. He saved me the trouble by telling me himself.

"My name's Marek," he said. "Come from a D-line, not far downtime from here."

I nodded, squinting into the red brightness reflected off my hardpan yard.

"We're just here for a good time," the human continued. "What you want to spoil that for?"

I didn't say anything for a moment. One of Marek's gang spat into the dryness of my dirt.

"Go ahead and have it," I said.

"All right," Marek said. He turned to Dvorak, then pulled out a weapon—not really a weapon, though, for it is the tool of behind-the-lines enforcers, prison interrogators, confession extractors. It's called an algorithmic truncheon, a *trunch,* in the parlance. A trunch, used at full load, will strip the myelin sheath from axons and dendrites; it will burn up a man's nerves as if they were fuses. It is a way to kill with horrible pain. Marek walked over and touched the trunch to the leg of Dvorak, as if he were lighting a bonfire.

The Flash technician began to shiver, and then to seethe, like a teapot coming to boil. The motion traveled up his legs, into his chest, out his arms. His neck began to writhe, as if the corded muscles were so many snakes. Then Dvorak's brain burned, as a teapot will when all the water has run out and there is nothing but flame against hot metal. And then Dvorak screamed. He screamed for a long, long time. And then he died, crumpled and spent, on the ground in front of my house.

"I don't know you," Marek said, standing over Dvorak's body and looking up at me. "I know *what* you are, but I can't get a read on *who* you are, and that worries me," he said. He kicked at one of the Flash tech's twisted arms. "But now you know *me.*"

"Get off my land," I said. I looked at him without heat. Maybe I felt nothing inside, either. That uncertainty had been my companion for a long time, my grim companion. Marek studied me for a moment. If I kept his attention, he might not look around me, look inside the house, to find his other fun, Furly Bexter, half-dead from Marek's amusements. Marek turned to the others.

"We're going," he said to them. "We've done what we came for." They turned around and left by the road on which they'd come, the only road there was. After a while, I took Dvorak's body to a low hill and dug him a grave there. I set up a sandstone marker, and since I knew Dvorak came from Catholic people, I scratched into the stone the sign of the cross. Jesus, from the Milky Way. Another glim. Hard to kill.

It took old-man Bexter only a week or so to fully recover; I should have known by knowing Bex that he was made of a tougher grit. He began to putter around the house, helping me out where he could, although I ran a tidy one-man operation, and he was more in the way than anything. Bex risked a trip out once that week. Her father again insisted he was going back into town, but Bex told him the glims were looking for him. So far, she'd managed to convince them that she had no idea where he'd gotten to.

I was running low on food and supplies, and had to go into town the following Firstday. I picked up a good backpack load at the mercantile and some chemicals for treating the peat at the druggist, then risked a quick look-in on Bex. A sign on the desk told all that they could find her at Thredmartin's, taking her lunch, should they want her. I walked across the street, set my load down just inside Thredmartin's door, in the cloakroom, then passed through the entrance into the afternoon dank of the pub.

I immediately sensed glims all around, and hunched myself in, both mentally and physically. I saw Bex in her usual corner, and walked toward her across the room. As I stepped beside a table in the pub's middle, a glim—it was the halandana—stuck out a long, hairy leg. Almost, I tripped—and in that instant, I almost did the natural thing and cast about for some hold that was not present in the three-dimensional world—but I did not. I caught myself, came to a dead stop, then carefully walked around the glim's outstretched leg.

"Mind if I sit down?" I said as I reached Bex's table. She nodded toward a free chair. She was finishing a beer, and an empty glass stood beside it. Thredmartin usually had the tables clear as soon as the last drop left a mug. Bex was drinking fast. Why? Working up her courage, perhaps.

I lowered myself into the chair, and for a long time, neither of us said anything to the other. Bex finished her beer. Thredmartin appeared, looked curiously at the two empty mugs. Bex signaled for another, and I ordered my own whiskey.

"How's the ranch," she finally asked me. Her face was flush and her lips trembled slightly. She was angry, I decided. At me, at the situation. It was understandable. Completely understandable.

"Fine," I said. "The ranch is fine."

"Good."

Again a long silence. Thredmartin returned with our drinks. Bex sighed, and for a moment, I thought she would speak, but she did not. Instead, she reached under the table and touched my hand. I opened my palm, and she put her hand into mine. I felt the tension in her, the bonework of her hand as she squeezed tightly. I felt her fear and worry. I felt her love.

And then Marek came into the pub looking for her. He stalked across the room and stood in front of our table. He looked hard at me, then at Bex, and then he swept an arm across the table and sent Bex's beer and my whiskey flying toward the wall. The beer mug broke, but I quickly reached out and caught my tumbler of scotch in midair without spilling a drop. Of course, no ordinary human could have done it.

Bex noticed Marek looking at me strangely and spoke with a loud voice that got his attention. "What do you want? You were looking for me at the hotel?"

"Your sign says you're open," Marek said in a reasonable, ugly voice. "I rang for room service. Repeatedly."

"Sorry," Bex said. "Just let me settle up and I'll be right there."

"Be right there *now,*" Marek said, pushing the table from in front of her. Again, I caught my drink, held it on a knee while I remained sitting. Bex started up from her chair and stood facing Marek. She looked him in the eyes. "I'll *be* there directly," she said.

Without warning, Marek reached out and grabbed her by the chin. He didn't seem to be pressing hard, but I knew he must have her in a painful grip. He pulled Bex toward him. Still, she stared him in the eyes. Slowly, I rose from my chair, setting my tumbler of whiskey down on the warm seat where I had been.

Marek glanced over at me. Our eyes met, and at that close distance, he could plainly see the enhancements under my corneas. I could see his.

"Let go of her," I said.

He did not let go of Bex.

"Who the hell are you?" he asked. "That you tell *me* what to do?"

"I'm just a grunt, same as you," I said. "Let go of her."

The halandana had risen from its chair and was soon standing behind Marek. It-she growled mean and low. A combat schematic of how to handle the situation iconed up into the corner of my vision. The halandana was a green figure, Marek was red, Bex was a faded rose. I blinked once to enlarge it. Studied it in a fractional second. Blinked again to close it down. Marek let go of Bex.

She stumbled back, hurt and mad, rubbing her chin.

"I don't think we've got a grunt here," Marek said, perhaps to the halandana, or to himself, but looking at me. "I think we've got us a genuine skyfalling space marine."

The halandana's growl grew deeper and louder, filling ultra and subsonic frequencies.

"How many systems'd you take out, skyfaller?" Marek asked. "A couple of galaxies worth?" The halandana made to advance on me, but Marek put out his hand to stop it. "Where do you get off? This ain't nothing but small potatoes next to what *you've* done."

In that moment, I spread out, stretched a bit in ways that Bex could not see, but that Marek could—to some extent at least. I encompassed him, all of him, and did a thorough ID on both him and the halandana. I ran the data through some trans-d personnel files tucked into a swirl in n-space I'd never expected to access again. Marek Lambrois. Corporal of a back-line military-police platoon assigned to the local cluster in a couple of possible worlds, deserters all in a couple of others. He was aggression enhanced by trans-weblink anti-alg coding. The squad's fighting profile was notched to the top level at all times. They were bastards who were now *preprogrammed* bastards. Marek was right about them being small potatoes. He and his gang were nothing but mean-ass grunts, small-time goons for some of the nonaligned contingency troops.

"What the hell?" Marek said. He noticed my analytics, although it was too fast for him to get a good glimpse of me. But he did understand something in that moment, something it didn't take enhancement to figure out. And in that moment, everything was changed, had I but seen. Had I but seen.

"You're some bigwig, ain't you, skyfaller? Somebody that *matters* to the outcome," Marek said. "This is your actual, and you don't want to fuck yourself up-time, so you won't fight." He smiled crookedly. A diagonal of teeth, straight and narrow, showed whitely.

"Don't count on it," I said.

"You won't," he said, this time with more confidence. "I don't know what I was worrying about! I can do anything I want here."

"Well," I said. "Well." And then I said nothing.

"Get on over there and round me up some grub," Marek said to Bex. "I'll be waiting for it in room forty-five, little lady."

"I'd rather—"

"Do it," I said. The words were harsh and did not sound like my voice. But they were my words, and after a moment, I remembered the voice. It was mine. From far, far in the future. Bex gasped at their hardness, but took a step forward, moved to obey.

"Bex," I said, more softly. "Just get the man some food." I turned to Marek. "If you hurt her, I don't care about anything. Do you understand? Nothing will matter to me."

Marek's smile widened into a grin. He reached over, slowly, so that I could think about it, and patted my cheek. Then he deliberately slapped me, hard. Hard enough to turn my head. Hard enough to draw a trickle of blood from my lip. It didn't hurt very much, of course. Of course it didn't hurt.

"Don't you worry, skyfaller," he said. "I know exactly where I stand now." He turned and left, and the halandana, its drugs unfinished on the table where it had sat, trailed out after him.

Bex looked at me. I tried to meet her gaze, but did not. I did not look down, but stared off into Thredmartin's darkness. She reached over and wiped the blood from my chin with her little finger.

"I guess I'd better go," she said.

I did not reply. She shook her head sadly, and walked in front of me. I kept my eyes fixed, far away from this place, this time, and her passing was a swirl of air, a red-brown swish of hair, and Bex was gone. Gone.

They sucked down my heart
to a little black hole.
You cannot stab me.

"Colonel Bone, we've done the prelims on sector eleven sixty-eight, and there are fifty-six class-one civilizations along with two-hundred seventy rationals in stage-one or -two development."

"Fifty-six. Two hundred seventy. Ah. Me."

"Colonel, sir, we can evac over half of them within thirty-six hours local."

"And have to defend them in the transcendent. Chaos neutral. Guaranteed forty percent casualties for us."

"Yes, sir. But what about the civs at least. We can save a few."

They wrote down my brain
on a hard knot of space.
You cannot turn me.

"Unacceptable, soldier."

"Sir?"

"Unacceptable."

"Yes, sir."

All dead. All those millions of dead people. But it was the end of time, and they had to die, so that they—so that we *all,* all in time—could live. But they didn't know, those civilizations. Those people. It was the end of time, but you loved life all the same, and you died the same hard way as always. For nothing. It would be for nothing. Outside, the wind had kicked up. The sky was red with Ferro's dust, and a storm was brewing for the evening. I coated my sclera with a hard and glassy membrane, and unblinking, I stalked home with my supplies through a fierce and growing wind.

That night, on the curtains of dust and thin rain, on the heave of the storm, Bex came to my house. Her clothes were torn and her face was bruised. She said nothing, as I closed the door behind her, led her into the kitchen, and began to treat her wounds. She said nothing as her worried father sat at my kitchen table and watched, and wrung his hands, and watched because there wasn't anything he could do.

"Did that man . . ." her father said. The old man's voice broke. "Did he?"

"I tried to take the thing, the trunch, from him. He'd left it lying on the table by the door." Bex spoke in a hollow voice. "I thought that no-

body was going to do anything, not even Henry, so I had to. I had to."
Her facial bruises were superficial. But she held her legs stiffly together,
and clasped her hands to her stomach. There was vomit on her dress.
"The trunch had some kind of alarm set on it," Bex said. "So he caught
me."

"Bex, are you hurting?" I said to her. She looked down, then carefully
spread her legs. "He caught me and then he used the trunch on me. Not
full strength. Said he didn't want to do permanent damage. Said he
wanted to save me for later." Her voice sounded far away. She covered her
face with her hands. "He put it in me," she said.

Then she breathed deeply, raggedly, and made herself look at me.
"Well," she said. "So."

I put her into my bed, and he sat in the chair beside it, standing watch
for who knew what? He could not defend his daughter, but he must try,
as surely as the suns rose, now growing farther apart, over the hard pack
of my homeworld desert.

Everything was changed.

"Bex," I said to her, and touched her forehead. Touched her fine,
brown skin. "Bex, in the future, we won. I won, my command won it. Really, really big. That's why we're here. That's why we're all here."

Bex's eyes were closed. I could not tell if she'd already fallen asleep.
I hoped she had.

"I have to take care of some business, and then I'll do it again," I said
in a whisper. "I'll just have to go back up-time and do it again."

Between the first and second rising, I'd reached Heidel, and as Hemingway burned red through the storm's dusty leavings, I stood in the
shadows of the entrance foyer of the Bexter Hotel. There I waited.

The halandana was the first up—like me, they never really slept—
and it came down from its room looking, no doubt, to go out and get another rubber of its drug. Instead, it found me. I didn't waste time with the
creature. With a quick twist in n-space, I pulled it down to the present,
down to a local concentration of hate and lust and stupidity that I could
kill with a quick thrust into its throat. But I let it live; I showed it myself,
all of me spread out and huge, and I let it fear.

"Go and get Marek Lambrois," I told it. "Tell him Colonel Bone
wants to see him. Colonel Henry Bone of the Eighth Sky and Light."

"Bone," said the halandana. "I thought—"

I reached out and grabbed the creature's long neck. This was the halandana weak point, and this halandana had a ceramic implant as protection. I clicked up the power in my forearm a level and crushed the collar
as I might a tea cup. The halandana's neck carapace shattered to platelets
and shards, outlined in fine cracks under its skin.

"Don't think," I said. "Tell Marek Lambrois to come into the street and I will let him live."

This was untrue, of course, but hope never dies, I'd discovered, even in the hardest of soldiers. But perhaps I'd underestimated Marek. Sometimes I still wonder.

He stumbled out, still partly asleep, onto the street. Last night had evidently been a hard and long one. His eyes were a red no detox nano could fully clean up. His skin was the color of paste.

"You have something on me," I said. "I cannot abide that."

"Colonel Bone," he began. "If I'd knowed it was *you*—"

"Too late for that."

"It's never too late, that's what you taught us all when you turned that offensive around out on the Husk and gave the Chaos the what-for. I'll just be going. I'll take the gang with me. It's to no purpose, our staying now."

"You knew enough *yesterday*—enough to leave." I felt the rage, the old rage that was to be, once again. "Why did you do that to her?" I asked. "Why did you—"

And then I looked into his eyes and saw it there. The quiet desire—beaten down by synthesized emotions, but now triumphant, sadly triumphant. The desire to finally, finally *die*. Marek was not the unthinking brute I'd taken him for after all. Too bad for him.

I took a step toward Marek. His instincts made him reach down, go for the trunch. But it was a useless weapon on me. I don't have myelin sheaths on my nerves. I don't have nerves anymore; I have *wiring*. Marek realized this was so almost instantly. He dropped the trunch, then turned and ran. I caught him. He tried to fight, but there was never any question of him beating me. That would be absurd. I'm Colonel Bone of the Skyfalling 8th. I kill so that there might be life. *Nobody* beats me. It is my fate, and yours too.

I caught him by the shoulder, and I looped my other arm around his neck and reined him to me—not enough to snap anything. Just enough to calm him down. He was strong, but had no finesse.

Like I said, glims are hard to kill. They're the same as snails in shells in a way, and the trick is to draw them out—way out. Which is what I did with Marek. As I held him physically, I caught hold of him, all of him, *over there,* in the place I can't tell you about, can't describe. The way you do this is by holding a glim still and causing him great suffering, so that they can't withdraw into the deep places. That's what vampire stakes and Roman crosses are all about.

And, like I told Bex, glims are bad ones, all right. Bad, but not the worst. *I* am the worst.

Icicle spike
from the eye of a star.
I've come to kill you.

I sharpened my nails. Then I plunged them into Marek's stomach, through the skin, into the twist of his guts. I reached around there and caught hold of something, a piece of intestine. I pulled it out. This I tied to the porch of the Bexter Hotel.

Marek tried to untie himself and pull away. He was staring at his insides, rolled out, raw and exposed, and thinking—I don't know what. I haven't died. I don't know what it is like to die. He moaned sickly. His hands fumbled uselessly in the grease and phlegm that coated his very own self. There was no undoing the knots I'd tied, no pushing himself back in.

I picked him up, and as he whimpered, I walked down the street with him. His guts trailed out behind us, like a pink ribbon. After I'd gotten about twenty feet, I figured this was all he had in him. I dropped him into the street.

Hemingway was in the northeast and Fitzgerald directly east. They both shone at different angles on Marek's crumple, and cast crazy, mazy shadows down the length of the street.

"Colonel Bone," he said. I was tired of his talking. "Colonel—"

I reached into his mouth, past his gnashing teeth, and pulled out his tongue. He reached for it as I extracted it, so I handed it to him. Blood and drool flowed from his mouth and colored the red ground even redder about him. Then, one by one, I broke his arms and legs, then I broke each of the vertebrae in his backbone, moving up his spinal column with quick pinches. It didn't take long.

This is what I did in the world that people can see. In the twists of other times and spaces, I did similar things, horrible, irrevocable things, to the man. I killed him. I killed him in such a way that he would never come to life again, not in any possible place, not in any possible time. I wiped Marek Lambrois from existence. Thoroughly. And with his death the other glims died, like lights going out, lights ceasing to exist, bulb, filament and all. Or like the quick loss of all sensation after a brain is snuffed out.

Irrevocably gone from this timeline, and that was what mattered. Keeping this possible future uncertain, balanced on the fulcrum of chaos and necessity. Keeping it *free,* so that I could go back and do my work.

I left Marek lying there, in the main street of Heidel. Others could do the mopping up; that wasn't my job. As I left town, on the way back to my house and my life there, I saw that I wasn't alone in the dawn-lit town.

Some had business out at this hour, and they had watched. Others had heard the commotion and come to windows and porches to see what it was. Now they knew. They knew what I was, what I was to be. I walked alone down the road, and found Bex and her father both sound asleep in my room.

I stroked her fine hair. She groaned, turned in her sleep. I pulled my covers up to her chin. Forty years old, and as beautiful as a child. Safe in my bed. Bex. Bex. I will miss you. Always, always, Bex.

I went to the living room, to the shroud-covered furniture. I sat down in what had been my father's chair. I sipped a cup of my father's best barley-malt whiskey. I sat, and as the suns of Ferro rose in the hard-iron sky, I faded into the distant, dying future.

Paul J. McAuley

ALL TOMORROW'S PARTIES

Born in Stroud, England, in 1955, Paul J. McAuley now makes his home in London. A professional biologist for many years, he sold his first story in 1984, and has gone on to be a frequent contributor to *Interzone,* as well as to markets such as *Amazing, The Magazine of Fantasy & Science Fiction, Asimov's Science Fiction, When the Music's Over,* and elsewhere.

Like his friend and colleague Stephen Baxter, McAuley has a foot in several different camps of science fiction writing, being considered to be one of the best of the new breed of British writers (although a few Australian writers could be fit in under this heading as well) who are producing that brand of rigorous hard science fiction with updated modern and stylistic sensibilities that is sometimes referred to as "radical hard science fiction," but he also writes Dystopian sociological speculations about the very near future, and he *also* is one of the major young writers who are producing that revamped and retooled widescreen Space Opera that has sometimes been called the New Baroque Space Opera, reminiscent of the Superscience stories of the thirties taken to an even higher level of intensity and scale (wait a minute! how many feet does he *have,* anyway?). His first novel, *Four Hundred Billion Stars,* one of the earliest examples of the New Space Opera, was published in 1988, and won the Philip K. Dick Award. It was followed by sequels, *Secret Harmonies* and *Eternal Light,* and by one of the most vivid of the recent spate of Martian novels, *Red Dust.* With his next novel, *Pasquale's Angel,* he put yet another foot down in yet another camp, producing an ingenious and gorgeously colored Alternate History where Leonardo di Vinci brings modern technology to Europe centuries before its time. His next novel, 1996's *Fairyland,* perhaps his best-known novel and perhaps also his best performance to date at novel length, took us to a troubled future Europe thrown into chaos by fractional politics and out-of-control biotechnology, only a few years into the next century; it won the Arthur C. Clarke Award and the John W. Campbell Award. With his next novel project, though, he is plunging back into Space Opera territory, on an even more ambitious scale, with a major new trilogy, *Confluence,* set ten million years in the future, the first volume of which, *Child of the River,* has just been published.

McAuley is not as prolific at shorter lengths as Baxter, having built most of his reputation to date on his novels, but has produced some memorable short work over the last fourteen years, with stories such as "The Temporary King," "Jacob's Rock," "Exiles," "Inheritance," "Karl and the Ogre," "Gene Wars," and others. In the last couple of years, his stories seem to have increased in impact and complexity, and recent stories such as "Slaves," "Children of the Revolution," "Prison Dreams," "Recording Angel," "Second Skin," "17," and "Sea Change, With Monsters" strike me as being even better than his already distinguished previous work, and I look forward with anticipation to see what he produces in the years to come.

A wide range of influences can be seen in McAuley's work, from Cordwainer Smith and Brian Aldiss to Roger Zelazny and Larry Niven, topped off with a dash of Samuel R. Delany, with perhaps some H. G. Wells to give a bottom to the mixture. All of which and more are evident in the evocative, supercharged, and intense little story that follows, packed with enough new ideas to fuel many another author's six hundred-page novel, that takes us far into the future and thousands of light-years from home for a very odd sort of family reunion. . . .

McAuley's other books include two collections of his short work, *The King of the Hill and Other Stories* and *The Invisible Country,* and an original anthology co-edited with Kim Newman, *In Dreams.*

And with exactly a year left before the end of the century-long gathering of her clade, she went to Paris with her current lover, racing ahead of midnight and the beginning of the New Year. Paris! The Premier Quartier: the early Twentieth Century. Fireworks bursting in great flowers above the night-black Seine, and a brawling carnival which under a multicolored rain of confetti filled every street from the Quai du Louvre to the Arc de Triomphe.

Escorted by her lover (they had been hunting big game in the Pleistocene–era taiga of Siberia; he still wore his safari suit, and a Springfield rifle was slung over his shoulder), she crossed to the Paleolithic oak woods of the Ile de la Cité. In the middle of the great stone circle naked druids with blue-stained skins beat huge drums under flaring torches, while holographic ghosts swung above the electric lights of the Twentieth Century shore, a fleet of luminous clouds dancing in the sky. Her attentive lover identified them for her, leaning against her shoulder so she could sight along his arm. He was exactly her height, with piercing blue eyes and a salt-and-pepper beard.

An astronaut. A gene pirate. Emperor Victoria. Mickey Mouse.

"What is a mouse?"

He pointed. "That one, the black-skinned creature with the circular ears."

She leaned against his solid human warmth. "For an animal, it seems very much like a person. Was it a product of the gene wars?"

"It is a famous icon of the country where I was born. My countrymen preferred creatures of the imagination to those of the real world. It is why they produced so few good authors."

"But you were a good author."

"I was not bad, except at the end. Something bad always happened to all good writers from my country. Sometimes slowly, sometimes quickly, but without exception."

"What is it carrying?"

"A light saber. It is an imaginary weapon that is authentic for the period. They were obsessed with weapons and divisions. They saw the world as a struggle of good against evil. That was how wars could be called good, except by those who fought in them."

She didn't argue. Her lover, a partial, had been modelled on a particular Twentieth Century writer, and had direct access to the appropriate records in the Library. Although she had been born just at the end of the Twentieth Century, she had long ago forgotten everything about it.

Behind them, the drums reached a frenzied climax and fell silent. The sacrificial victim writhed on the heel stone and the chief druid lifted the still beating heart above his head in triumph. Blood that looked black in the torchlight ran down his arms.

The spectators beyond the circle clapped or toasted each other. One man was trying to persuade his companion to fuck on the altar. They were invisible to the druids, who were merely puppets lending local color to the scene.

"I'm getting tired of this," she said.

"Of course. We could go to Cuba. The ocean fishing there is good. Or to Afrique, to hunt lions. I think I liked that best, but after a while I could no longer do it. That was one of the things that destroyed my writing."

"I'm getting tired of you," she said, and her lover bowed and walked away.

She was getting tired of everything.

She had been getting tired of everything for longer than she could remember. What was the point of living forever if you did nothing new? Despite all her hopes, this *faux* Earth, populated by two billion puppets and partials, and ten million of her clade, had failed to revive her.

In one more year, the fleet of spaceships would disperse; the sun, an ordinary G2 star she had moved by the pressure of its own light upon gravity tethered reflective sails, would go supernova; nothing would be saved but the store of information which the Library had collected and collated. She had not yet accessed any of that. Perhaps that would save her.

She returned to the carnival, stayed there three days. But despite use of various intoxicants she could not quite lose herself in it, could not escape the feeling that she had failed after all. This was supposed to be a great congress of her own selves, a place to share and exchange memories that spanned five million years and the entire Galaxy. But it seemed to her that the millions of her selves simply wanted to forget what they were, to lose themselves in the pleasures of the flesh. Of course, many had assumed bodies for the first time to attend the gathering; one could perhaps excuse them, for this carnival was to them a genuine farewell to flesh they would abandon at the end of the year.

On the third day she was sitting in cold dawn light at a green café table in the Jardin des Tuileries, by the great fountain. Someone was sculpting the clouds through which the sun was rising. The café was crowded with guests, partials and puppets, androids and animals—even a silver gynoid, its face a smooth oval mirror. The air buzzed with the tiny machines which attended the guests; in one case, a swirling cloud of gnat-sized beads *was* a guest. After almost a century in costume, the guests were reverting to type.

She sipped a *citron pressé,* listened to the idle chatter. The party in Paris would break up soon. The revelers would disperse to other parts of the Earth. Except for a clean-up crew, the puppets, partials and all the rest would be returned to store. At another table, a youthful version of her erstwhile lover was talking to an older man with brown hair brushed back from his high forehead and pale blue eyes magnified by the thick lenses of his spectacles.

"The lions, Jim. Go to Afrique and listen to the lions roar at night. There is no sound like it."

"Ah, and I would love that, but Nora would not stand it. She needs the comforts of civilization. Besides, the thing we must not forget is that I would not be able to see the lions. Instead I think we will drink some more of this fine white wine and you will tell me about them."

"Aw hell, I could bring you a living lion if you like," the younger man said. "I could describe him to you and you could touch him and smell him until you got the idea." He was quite unaware that there were two lions right there in the park, accompanying a naked girl child whose feet, with pigeon's wings at the ankles, did not quite touch the ground.

Did these puppets come here every day, and recreate a conversation millions of years dead for the delectation of the guests? Was each day to them the same day? Suddenly, she felt as if a cold wind was blowing through her, as if she was raised up high and naked upon the pinnacle of the mountain of her millions of years.

"You confuse the true and the real," someone said. A man's voice, soft, lisping. She looked around but could not see who amongst the amazing people and creatures might have said such a thing, the truest realest thing she had heard for . . . how long? She could not remember how long.

She left, and went to New Orleans.

Where it was night, and raining, a soft warm rain falling in the lamp-lit streets. It was the Twentieth Century here, too. They were cooking crawfish under the mimosa trees at every intersection of the brick-paved streets, and burning the Maid of New Orleans over Lake Pontchartrain. The Maid hung up there in the black night sky—wrapped in oiled silks and shining like a star, with the blue-white wheel of the Galaxy a back-drop that spanned the horizon—then flamed like a comet and plunged into the black water while cornet bands played *"Laissez le Bon Temps Rouler."*

She fell in with a trio of guests whose originals were all less than a thousand years old. They were students of the Rediscovery, they said, al-though it was not quite clear what the Rediscovery was. They wore green ("For Earth," one said, although she thought that odd because most of the Earth was blue), and drank a mild psychotropic called absinthe, bitter white stuff poured into water over a sugar cube held in silver tongs. They were interested in the origins of the clade, which amused her greatly, be-cause of course she was its origin, going amongst the copies and clones disguised as her own self. But even if they made her feel every one of her five million years, she liked their innocence, their energy, their openness.

She strolled with her new friends through the great orrery at the wa-terfront. Its display of the lost natural wonders of the Galaxy was derived from records and memories guests had deposited in the Library, and changed every day. She was listening to the three students discuss the possibility that humans had not originally come from the Earth when someone went past and said loudly, looking right at her, "None of them look like you, but they are just like you all the same. All obsessed with the past because they are trapped in it."

A tall man with a black, spade-shaped beard and black eyes that looked at her with infinite amusement. The same soft, lisping voice she had heard in the café in Paris. He winked and plunged into the heart of the white-hot whirlpool of the accretion disc of the black hole of Sigma Draconis 2, which drew matter from the photosphere of its companion blue-white giant—before the reconstruction, it had been one of the won-ders of the Galaxy. She followed, but he was gone.

She looked for him everywhere in New Orleans, and fell in with a woman who before the gathering had lived in the water vapor zone of a gas giant, running a tourist business for those who could afford to down-load themselves into the ganglia of living blimps a kilometer across. The woman's name was Rapha; she had ruled the worlds of a hundred stars once, but had given that up long before she had answered the call for the gathering.

"I was a man when I had my empire," Rapha said, "but I gave that up too. When you've done everything, what's left but to party?"

She had always been a woman, she thought. And for two million years she had ruled an empire of a million worlds—for all she knew, the copy she had left behind ruled there still. But she didn't tell Rapha that. No one knew who she was, on all the Earth. She said, "Then let's party until the end of the world."

She knew that it wouldn't work—she had already tried everything, in every combination—but because she didn't care if it worked or not, perhaps this time it would.

They raised hell in New Orleans, and went to Antarctica.

It was raining in Antarctica, too.

It had been raining for a century, ever since the world had been made.

Statite sails hung in stationary orbit, reflecting sunlight so that the swamps and cycad forests and volcanic mountain ranges of the South Pole were in perpetual day. The hunting lodge was on a floating island a hundred meters above the tops of the giant ferns, close to the edge of a shallow viridescent lake. A flock of delicate, dappled *Dromiceiomimus* squealed and splashed in the shallows; great dragonflies flitted through the rainy middle air; at the misty horizon the perfect cones of three volcanoes sent up threads of smoke into the sagging clouds.

She and Rapha rode bubbles in wild loops above the forests, chasing dinosaurs or goading dinosaurs to chase them. Then they plunged into one of the volcanoes and caused it to erupt, and one of the hunters overrode the bubbles and brought them back and politely asked them to stop.

The lake and the forest were covered in a mantle of volcanic ash. The sky was milky with ash.

"The guests are amused, but they will not be amused forever. It is the hunting that is important here. If I may suggest other areas where you might find enjoyment . . ."

He was a slightly younger version of her last lover. A little less salt in his beard; a little more spring in his step.

She said, "How many of you have I made?"

But he didn't understand the question.

They went to Thebes (and some of the hunting party went with them), where they ran naked and screaming through the streets, toppling the statues of the gods. They went to Greenland, and broke the rainbow bridge of Valhalla and fought the trolls and ran again, laughing, with Odin's thunder about their ears. Went to Troy, and set fire to the wooden horse before the Greeks could climb inside it.

None of it mattered. The machines would repair everything; the puppets would resume their roles. Troy would fall again the next night, on schedule.

"Let's go to Golgotha," Rapha said, wild-eyed, very drunk.

This was in a bar of some Christian–era American town. Outside, a couple of the men were roaring up and down the main street on motorcycles, weaving in and out of the slow-moving, candy-colored cars. Two cops watched indulgently.

"Or Afrique," Rapha said. "We could hunt man-apes."

"I've done it before," someone said. He didn't have a name, but some kind of number. He was part of a clone. His shaved head was horribly scarred; one of his eyes was mechanical. He said, "You hunt them with spears or slings. They're pretty smart, for man-apes. I got killed twice."

Someone came into the bar. Tall, saturnine, black eyes, a spade-shaped beard. At once, she asked her machines if he was a partial or a guest, but the question confused them. She asked them if there were any strangers in the world, and at once they told her that there were the servants and those of her clade, but no strangers.

He said softly, "Are you having a good time?"

"Who are you?"

"Perhaps I'm the one who whispers in your ear, 'Remember that you are mortal.' Are you mortal, Angel?"

No one in the world should know her name. Her true name.

Danger, danger, someone sang in the background of the song that was playing on the jukebox. *Danger,* burbled the coffee pot on the heater behind the counter of the bar.

She said, "I made you, then."

"Oh no. Not me. You made all of this. Even all of the guests, in one way or another. But not me. We can't talk here. Try the one place which has any use in this *faux* world. There's something there I'm going to take, and when I've done that I'll wait for you."

"Who are you? What do you want?"

"Perhaps I want to kill you." He smiled. "And perhaps you want to die. It's one thing you have not tried yet."

He walked away, and when she started after him Rapha got in the way. Rapha hadn't seen the man. She said the others wanted to go to Hy Brasil.

"The gene wars," Rapha said. "That's where we started to become what we are. And then—I don't know, but it doesn't matter. We're going to party to the end of the world. When the sun explodes, I'm going to ride the shock wave as far as I can. I'm not going back. There's a lot of us who aren't going back. Why should we? We went to get copied and woke up here, thousands of years later, thousands of light-years away. What's to go back for? Wait! Where are you going?"

"I don't know," she said, and walked out.

· · ·

The man had scared her. He had touched the doubt which had made her organize the gathering. She wanted a place to hide so that she could think about that before she confronted him.

Most of the North American continent was, in one form or another, modeled after the Third Millennium of the Christian Era. She took a car (a red Dodge as big as a boat, with fins and chrome trim) and drove to Dallas, where she was attacked by tribes of horsemen near the glittering slag of the wrecked city. She took up with a warlord for a while, poisoned all his wives, grew bored and seduced his son, who murdered his father and began a civil war. She went south on horseback through the alien flower jungles which had conquered Earth after humanity had more or less abandoned it, then caught a *pneumatique* all the way down the spine of Florida to Key West.

A version of her last lover lived there, too. She saw him in a bar by the beach two weeks later. There were three main drugs in Key West: cigarettes, heroin, and alcohol. She had tried them all, decided she liked alcohol best. It helped you forget yourself in an odd, dissociative way that was both pleasant and disturbing. Perhaps she should have spent more of her long life drunk.

This version of her lover liked alcohol, too. He was both lumbering but shy, pretending not to notice the people who looked at him while he drank several complicated cocktails. He had thickened at the waist; his beard was white and full. His eyes, webbed by wrinkles, were still piercingly blue, but his gaze was vague and troubled. She eavesdropped while he talked with the barkeep. She wanted to find out how the brash man who had to constantly prove himself against the world had turned out.

Badly, it seemed. The world was unforgiving, and his powers were fading.

"I lost her, Carlos," he told the barkeep. He meant his muse. "She's run out on me, the bitch."

"Now, Papa, you know that is not true," the young barkeep said. "I read your article in *Life* just last week."

"It was shit, Carlos. I can fake it well enough, but I can't do the good stuff any more. I need some quiet, and all day I get tourists trying to take my picture and spooking the cats. When I was younger I could work all day in a café, but now I need . . . hell, I don't know what I need. She's a bitch, Carlos. She only loves the young." Later, he said, "I keep dreaming of lions. One of the long white beaches in Afrique where the lions come down at dusk. They play there like cats, and I want to get to them, but I can't."

But Carlos was attending to another customer. Only she heard the old man. Later, after he had gone, she talked with Carlos herself. He was a puppet, and couldn't understand, but it didn't matter.

"All this was a bad idea," she said. She meant the bar, Key West, the Pacific Ocean, the world. "Do you want to know how it started?"

"Of course, ma'am. And may I bring you another drink?"

"I think I have had enough. You stay there and listen. Millions of years ago, while all of what would become humanity lived on the nine worlds and thousand worldlets around a single star in the Sky Hunter arm of the Galaxy, there was a religion which taught that individuals need never die. It was this religion which first drove humanity from star to star in the Galaxy. Individuals copied their personalities into computers, or cloned themselves, or spread their personalities through flocks of birds, or fish, or amongst hive insects. But there was one flaw in this religion. After millions of years, many of its followers were no longer human in form or in thought, except that they could trace back, generation upon generation, their descent from a single human ancestor. They had become transcendents, and each individual transcendent had become a clade, or an alliance, of millions of different minds. Mine is merely one of many, but it is one of the oldest, and one of the largest.

"I brought us here to unite us all in shared experiences. It isn't possible that one of us could have seen every wonder in the Galaxy, visit every world. There are a hundred billion stars in the Galaxy. It takes a year or two to explore the worlds of each star, and then there is the travel between the stars. But there are ten million of us here. Clones, copies, descendants of clones and copies. Many of us have done nothing but explore. We have not seen everything, but we have seen most of it. I thought that we could pool all our information, that it would result in . . . something. A new religion, godhead. Something new, something *different*. But it seems that most just want to party, and I wonder how much I have changed, for they are so little like me. Many of them say that they will not return, that they will stay here until the sun ends it all. Some have joined in the war in China—a few even refuse regeneration. Mostly, though, they want to party."

"There are parties every night, ma'am," the barkeep said. "That's Key West for you."

"Someone was following me, but I lost him. I think he was tracing me through the travel net, but I used contemporary transport to get here. He frightened me and I ran away, but perhaps he is what I need. I think I will find him. What month is this?"

"June, ma'am. Very hot, even for June. It means a bad hurricane season."

"It will get hotter," she said, thinking of the machine ticking away in the core of the sun.

And went to Tibet, where the Library was.

For some reason, the high plateau had been constructed as a replica of part of Mars. She had given her servants a lot of discretion when building the Earth; it pleased her to be surprised, although it did not happen very often.

She had arrived at the top of one of the rugged massifs that defined the edge of the vast basin. There was a shrine here, a mani eye painted on a stone pillar, a heap of stones swamped with skeins of red and blue and white and yellow prayer flags raveling in the cold wind. The scarp dropped away steeply to talus slopes and the flood lava of the basin's floor, a smooth, lightly cratered red plain mantled with fleets of barchan dunes. Directly below, nestling amongst birches at the foot of the scarp's sheer cliff, was the bone-white Library.

She took a day to descend the winding path. Now and then pilgrims climbed past her. Many shuffled on their knees, eyes lifted to the sky; a few fell face-forward at each step, standing up and starting again at the point where their hands touched the ground. All whirled prayer wheels and muttered their personal mantra as they climbed, and few spared her more than a glance, although at noon while she sat under a gnarled juniper one old man came to her and shared his heel of dry black bread and stringy dried yak meat. She learned from him that the pilgrims were not puppets, as she had thought, but were guests searching for enlightenment. That was so funny and so sad she did not know what to think about it.

The Library was a replica of the White Palace of the Potala. It had been a place of quiet order and contemplation, where all the stories that the clade had told each other, all the memories that they had downloaded or exchanged, had been collected and collated.

Now it was a battleground.

Saffron-robed monks armed with weaponry from a thousand different eras were fighting against man-shaped black androids. Bodies of men and machines were sprawled on the great steps; smoke billowed from the topmost ranks of the narrow windows; red and green energy beams flickered against the pink sky.

She walked through the carnage untouched. Nothing in this world could touch her. Only perhaps the man who was waiting for her, sitting cross-legged beneath the great golden Buddha, which a stray shot from some energy weapon had decapitated and half-melted to slag. On either side, hundreds of candles floated in great bowls filled with water; their lights shivered and flickered from the vibration of heavy weaponry.

The man did not open his eyes as she approached, but he said softly, "I already have what I need. These foolish monks are defending a lost cause. You should stop them."

"It is what they have to do. They can't destroy us, of course, but I could destroy you."

"Guests can't harm other guests," he said calmly. "It is one of the rules."

"I am not a guest. Nor, I think, are you."

She told her machines to remove him. Nothing happened.

He opened his eyes. He said, "Your machines are invisible to the puppets and partials you created to populate this fantasy world. I am invisible to the machines. I do not draw my energy from the world grid, but from elsewhere."

And then he leaped at her, striking with formal moves millions of years old. The Angry Grasshopper, the Rearing Horse, the Snapping Mantis. Each move, magnified by convergent energies, could have killed her, evaporated her body, melted her machines.

But she allowed her body to respond, countering his attacks. She had thought that she might welcome death; instead, she was amused and exhilarated by the fury of her response. The habit of living was deeply ingrained; now it had found a focus.

Striking attitudes, tangling in a flurry of blows and counterblows, they moved through the battleground of the Library, through its gardens, moved down the long talus slope at the foot of the massif in a storm of dust and shattered stones.

At the edge of a lake which filled a small, perfectly circular crater, she finally tired of defensive moves and went on the attack. The Striking Eagle, the Plunging Dragon, the Springing Tiger Who Defends Her Cubs. He countered in turn. Stray energies boiled the lake dry. The dry ground shook, split open in a mosaic of plates. Gradually, a curtain of dust was raised above the land, obscuring the setting sun and the green face of the Moon, which was rising above the mountains.

They broke apart at last. They stood in the center of a vast crater of vitrified rock. Their clothes hung in tatters about their bodies. It was night, now. Halfway up the scarp of the massif, small lightnings flashed where the monks still defended the Library.

"Who are you?" she said again. "Did I create you?"

"I'm closer to you than anyone else in this strange mad world," he said.

That gave her pause. All the guests, clones or copies or replicants, were of her direct genetic lineage.

She said, "Are you my death?"

As if in answer, he attacked again. But she fought back as forcefully as before, and when he broke off, she saw that he was sweating.

"I am stronger than you thought," she said.

He took out a small black cube from his tattered tunic. He said, "I have what I need. I have the memory core of the Library. Everything anyone who came here placed on record is here."

"Then why do you want to kill me?"

"Because you are the original. I thought it would be fitting, after I stole this."

She laughed. "You foolish man! Do you think we rely on a single physical location, a single master copy? It is the right of everyone in the clade to carry away the memories of everyone else. Why else are we gathered here?"

"I am not of your clade." He tossed the cube into the air, caught it, tucked it away. "I will use this knowledge against you. Against all of you. I have all your secrets."

"You say you are closer to me than a brother, yet you do not belong to the clade. You want to use our memories to destroy us." She had a sudden insight. "Is this war, then?"

He bowed. He was nearly naked, lit by the green light of the Moon and the dimming glow of the slag that stretched away in every direction. "Bravo," he said. "But it has already begun. Perhaps it is even over by now; after all, we are twenty thousand light-years above the plane of the Galactic disc, thirty-five thousand light-years from the hub of your Empire. It will take you that long to return. And if the war is not over, then this will finish it."

She was astonished. Then she laughed. "What an imagination I have!"

He bowed again, and said softly, "You made this world from your imagination, but you did not imagine me."

And he went somewhere else.

Her machines could not tell her where he had gone; she called upon all the machines in the world, but he was no longer on the Earth. Nor was he amongst the fleet of ships which had carried the guests—in suspended animation, as frozen embryos, as codes triply engraved in gold—to the world she had created for the gathering.

There were only two other places he could be, and she did not think he could have gone to the sun. If he had, then he would have triggered the machine at the core, and destroyed her and everyone else in the subsequent supernova.

So she went to the Moon.

She arrived on the farside. The energies he had used against her suggested that he had his own machines, and she did not think that he would have hidden them in full view of the Earth.

The machines which she had instructed to recreate the Earth for the one hundred years of the gathering had recreated the Moon, too, so that the oceans of the Earth would have the necessary tides; it had been easier than tangling gravithic resonances to produce the same effect. It had taken little extra effort to recreate the forests which had cloaked the Moon for a million years, between the first faltering footsteps and the abandonment of the Earth.

It was towards the end of the long Lunar night. All around, blue firs soared up for hundreds of meters, cloaked in wide fans of needles that in the cold and the dark had drooped down to protect the scaly trunks. The gray rocks were coated in thin snow, and frozen lichens crunched underfoot. Her machines scattered in every direction, quick as thought. She sat down on top of a big rough boulder and waited.

It was very quiet. The sky was dominated by the triple-armed pinwheel of the Galaxy. It was so big that when she looked at one edge she could not see the other. The Arm of the Warrior rose high above the arch of the Arm of the Hunter; the Arm of the Archer curved in the opposite direction, below the close horizon. Star clusters made long chains of concentrated light through the milky haze of the galactic arms. There were lines and threads and globes and clouds of stars, all fading into a general misty radiance dissected by dark lanes which barred the arms at regular intervals. The core was knitted from thin shells of stars in tidy orbits concentrically packed around the great globular clusters of the heart stars, like layers of glittering tissue wrapped around a heap of jewels.

Every star had been touched by humankind. Existing stars had been moved or destroyed; millions of new stars and planetary systems had been created by collapsing dust clouds. A garden of stars, regulated, ordered, tidied. The Library held memories of every star, every planet, every wonder of the old untamed Galaxy. She was beginning to realize that the gathering was not the start of something new, but the end of five million years of Galactic colonization.

After a long time, the machines came back, and she went where they told her.

It was hidden within a steep-sided crater, a castle or maze of crystal vanes that rose in serried ranks from deep roots within the crust, where they collected and focused tidal energy. He was at its heart, busily folding together a small spacecraft. The energy of the vanes had been greatly depleted by the fight, and he was trying to concentrate the remainder in the motor of the spacecraft. He was preparing to leave.

Her machines rose up and began to spin, locking in resonance with the vanes and bleeding off their store of energy. The machines began to glow as she bounded down the steep smooth slope towards the floor of the crater, red-hot, white-hot, as hot as the core of the sun, for that was where they were diverting the energy stored in the vanes.

Violet threads flicked up, but the machines simply absorbed that energy too. Their stark white light flooded the crater, bleaching the ranks of crystal vanes.

She walked through the traps and tricks of the defenses, pulled him from his fragile craft and took him up in a bubble of air to the neutral point between the Moon and the Earth.

"Tell me," she said. "Tell me why you came here. Tell me about the war."

He was surprisingly calm. He said, "I am a first generation clone, but I am on the side of humanity, not the transcendents. Transcendent clades are a danger to all of the variety within and between the civilizations in the Galaxy. At last the merely human races have risen against them. I am just one weapon in the greatest war ever fought."

"You are my flesh. You are of my clade."

"I am a secret agent. I was made from a single cell stolen from you several hundred years before you set off for this fake Earth and the gathering of your clade. I arrived only two years ago, grew my power source, came down to steal the memory core and kill you. Although I failed to kill you before, we are no longer in the place where you draw your power. Now—"

After a moment in which nothing happened, he screamed in frustration and despair. She pitied him. Pitied all those who had bent their lives to produce this poor vessel, this failed moment, although all the power, the intrigues and desperate schemes his presence implied were as remote from her as the politics of a termite nest.

She said, "Your power source is not destroyed, but my machines take all its energy. Why did your masters think us dangerous?"

"Because you would fill the Galaxy with your own kind. Because you would end human evolution. Because you will not accept that the Universe is greater than you can ever be. Because you refuse to die, and death is a necessary part of evolution."

She laughed. "Silly little man! Why would we accept limits? We are only doing what humanity has always done. We use science to master nature just as man-apes changed their way of thinking by making tools and using fire. Humanity has always striven to become more than it is, to grow spiritually and morally and intellectually, to go up to the edge and step over it."

For the first time in a million years, those sentiments did not taste of ashes. By trying to destroy her, he had shown her what her life was worth.

He said, "But you do not change. That is why you are so dangerous. You and the other clades of transhumans have stopped humanity evolving. You would fill the Galaxy with copies of a dozen individuals who are so scared of physical death that they will do any strange and terrible thing to themselves to survive."

He gestured at the blue-white globe that hung beneath their feet, small and vulnerable against the vast blackness between galaxies.

"Look at your Earth! Humanity left it four million years ago, yet you chose to recreate it for this gathering. You had a million years of human history on Earth to choose from, and four and a half billion years of the history of the planet itself, and yet almost half of your creation is given over to a single century."

"It is the century where we became what we are," she said, remembering Rapha. "It is the century when it became possible to become transhuman, when humanity made the first steps beyond the surface of a single planet."

"It is the century you were born in. You would freeze all history if you could, an eternity of the same thoughts thought by the same people. You deny all possibilities but your own self."

He drew himself up, defiant to the last. He said, "My ship will carry the memory core home without me. You take all, and give nothing. I give my life, and I give you this."

He held up something as complex and infolded as the throat of an orchid. It was a vacuum fluctuation, a hole in reality that when inflated would remove them from the Universe. She looked away at once—the image was already burned in her brain—and threw him into the core of the sun. He did not even have a chance to scream.

Alone in her bubble of air, she studied the wheel of the Galaxy, the ordered pattern of braids and clusters. Light was so slow. It took a hundred thousand years to cross from one edge of the Galaxy to the other. Had the war against her empire, and the empires of all the other transcendents, already ended? Had it already changed the Galaxy, stirred the stars into new patterns? She would not know until she returned, and that would take thirty-five thousand years.

But she did not have to return. In the other direction was the limitless

Universe, a hundred billion galaxies. She hung there a long time, watching little smudges of ancient light resolve out of the darkness. Empires of stars wherever she looked, wonders without end.

We will fight the war, she thought, and we shall win, and we will go on forever and ever.

And went down, found the bar near the beach. She would wait until the old man came in, and buy him a drink, and talk to him about his dream of the lions.

Peter F. Hamilton

ESCAPE ROUTE

Prolific new British writer Peter F. Hamilton has sold to *Interzone, In Dreams, New Worlds, Fears,* and elsewhere. He sold his first novel, *Mindstar Rising,* in 1993, and quickly followed it up with two sequels, *A Quantum Murder* and *The Nano Flower.* Hamilton's first three books managed to slip into print without attracting a great deal of attention, on this side of the Atlantic, at least, but that changed dramatically with the publication of his next novel, *The Reality Dysfunction,* a huge modern Space Opera (it needed to be divided into two volumes for publication in the United States) that is itself only the start of a projected trilogy of staggering size and scope. *The Reality Dysfunction* has been attracting the reviews and the acclaim that his prior novels did not and has suddenly put Hamilton on the map as a writer to watch, perhaps a potential rival for writers such as Dan Simmons, Iain M. Banks, Paul J. McAuley, Gregory Benford, C. J. Cherryh, Stephen R. Donaldson, Colin Greenland, and other major players in the expanding subgenre of Modern Baroque Space Opera, an increasingly popular area these days. The second novel in the trilogy, *The Neutronium Alchemist,* is just out and generating the same kind of excited critical buzz. Upcoming is the third novel in the trilogy, *The Naked God,* and Hamilton's first collection, *A Second Chance at Eden.*

In the pyrotechnic novella that follows, one as packed with intriguing new ideas and fast-paced action and suspense as many another author's four-hundred-page novel, he unravels the mystery of an enigmatic object found in deep space, one that may prove to be harder—and considerably more dangerous—to get *out* of than it was to get *in.* . . .

Marcus Calvert had never seen an asteroid cavern quite like Sonora's before; it was disorientating even for someone who had spent 30 years captaining a starship. The center of the gigantic rock had been hollowed out by mining machines, producing a cylindrical cavity twelve kilometers long, five in diameter. Usually, the floor would be covered in soil and planted with fruit trees and grass. In Sonora's case, the environmental engineers had simply flooded it. The result was a small freshwater sea that no matter where you were on it, you appeared to be at the bottom of a valley of water.

Floating around the gray surface were innumerable rafts, occupied by hotels, bars, and restaurants. Taxi boats whizzed between them and the wharfs at the base of the two flat cavern walls.

Marcus and two of his crew had taken a boat out to the Lomaz bar, a raft which resembled a Chinese dragon trying to mate with a Mississippi paddle steamer.

"Any idea what our charter is, Captain?" asked Katherine Maddox, the *Lady Macbeth*'s node specialist.

"The agent didn't say," Marcus admitted. "Apart from confirming it's private, not corporate."

"They don't want us for combat, do they?" Katherine asked. There was a hint of rebellion in her voice. She was in her late forties, and like the Calverts her family had geneered their offspring to withstand both freefall and high acceleration. The dominant modifications had given her thicker skin, tougher bones, and harder internal membranes; she was never sick or giddy in freefall, nor did her face bloat up. Such changes were a formula for blunt features, and Katherine was no exception.

"If they do, we're not taking it," Marcus assured her.

Katherine exchanged an unsettled glance with Roman Zucker, the ship's fusion engineer, and slumped back in her chair.

The combat option was one Marcus had considered possible. *Lady Macbeth* was combat-capable, and Sonora asteroid belonged to a Lagrange-point cluster with a strong autonomy movement. An unfortunate combination. But having passed his sixty-seventh birthday two months ago he sincerely hoped those kind of flights were behind him.

"This could be them," Roman said, glancing over the rail. One of Sonora's little taxi boats was approaching their big resort raft.

The trim cutter curving around towards the Lomaz had two people sitting on its red leather seats.

Marcus watched with interest as they left the taxi. He ordered his neural nanonics to open a fresh memory cell, and stored the pair of them in a visual file. The first to alight was a man in his mid-thirties, dressed in expensive casual clothes; a long face and a very broad nose gave him a kind of imposing dignity.

His partner was less flamboyant. She was in her late twenties, obviously geneered; Oriental features matched with white hair that had been drawn together in wide dreadlocks and folded back aerodynamically.

They walked straight over to Marcus's table, and introduced themselves as Antonio Ribeiro and Victoria Keef. Antonio clicked his fingers at the waitress, and told her to fetch a bottle of Norfolk Tears.

"Hopefully to celebrate the success of our business venture, my friends," he said. "And if not, it is a pleasant time of day to imbibe such a magical potion. No?"

Marcus found himself immediately distrustful. It wasn't just Antonio's phony attitude; his intuition was scratching away at the back of his skull. Some friends called it his paranoia program, but it was rarely wrong. A family trait, like the wanderlust which no geneering treatment had ever eradicated.

"The cargo agent said you had a charter for us," Marcus said. "He never mentioned any sort of business deal."

"If I may ask your indulgence for a moment, Captain Calvert. You arrived here without a cargo. You must be a very rich man to afford that."

"There were . . . circumstances requiring us to leave Ayachcho ahead of schedule."

"Yeah," Katherine muttered darkly. "Her husband."

Marcus was expecting it, and smiled serenely. He'd heard very little else from the crew for the whole flight.

Antonio received the tray and its precious pear-shaped bottle from the waitress, and waved away the change.

"If I may be indelicate, Captain, your financial resources are not optimal at this moment," Antonio suggested.

"They've been better."

Antonio sipped his Norfolk Tears, and grinned in appreciation. "For myself, I was born with the wrong amount of money. Enough to know I needed more."

"Mr Ribeiro, I've heard all the get-rich-quick schemes in existence. They all have one thing in common, they don't work. If they did, I wouldn't be sitting here with you."

"You are wise to be cautious, Captain. I was, too, when I first heard this proposal. However, if you would humor me a moment longer, I can assure you this requires no capital outlay on your part. At the worst you will have another mad scheme to laugh about with your fellow captains."

"No money at all?"

"None at all, simply the use of your ship. We would be equal partners sharing whatever reward we find."

"Jesus. All right, I can spare you five minutes. Your drink has bought you that much attention span."

"Thank you, Captain. My colleagues and I want to fly the *Lady Macbeth* on a prospecting mission."

"For planets?" Roman asked curiously.

"No. Sadly, the discovery of a terracompatible planet does not guarantee wealth. Settlement rights will not bring more than a couple of million fuseodollars, and even that is dependant on a favorable biospectrum assessment, which would take many years. We have something more immediate in mind. You have just come from the Dorados?"

"That's right," Marcus said. The system had been discovered six years earlier, comprising a red dwarf sun surrounded by a vast disc of rocky particles. Several of the larger chunks had turned out to be nearly pure metal. Dorados was an obvious name; whoever managed to develop them would gain a colossal economic resource. So much so that the governments of Omuta and Garissa had gone to war over who had that development right.

It was the Garissan survivors who had ultimately been awarded settlement by the Confederation Assembly. There weren't many of them. Omuta had deployed twelve antimatter planetbusters against their homeworld. "Is that what you're hoping to find, another flock of solid metal asteroids?"

"Not quite," Antonio said. "Companies have been searching similar disc systems ever since the Dorados were discovered, to no avail. Victoria, my dear, if you would care to explain."

She nodded curtly and put her glass down on the table. "I'm an astrophysicist by training," she said. "I used to work for Forrester-Courtney; it's a company based in the O'Neill Halo that manufactures starship sensors, although their speciality is survey probes. It's been a very healthy business recently. Consortiums have been flying survey missions through every catalogued disc system in the Confederation. As Antonio said, none of our clients found anything remotely like the Dorados. That didn't surprise me, I never expected any of Forrester-Courtney's probes to be of much use. All our sensors did was run broad spectrographic sweeps. If anyone was going to find another Dorados cluster it would be the Edenists. Their voidhawks have a big advantage; those ships generate an enormous distortion field which can literally see mass. A lump of metal 50 kilometers across would have a very distinct density signature; they'd be aware of it from at least half a million kilometers away. If we were going to compete against that, we'd need a sensor which gave us the same level of results, if not better."

"And you produced one?" Marcus inquired.

"Not quite. I proposed expanding our magnetic anomaly detector array. It's a very ancient technology; Earth's old nations pioneered it during the twentieth century. Their military maritime aircraft were equipped with crude arrays to track enemy submarines. Forrester-Courtney builds its array into low-orbit resource-mapping satellites; they produce quite valuable survey data. Unfortunately, the company turned down my proposal. They said an expanded magnetic array wouldn't produce better results than a spectrographic sweep, not on the scale required. And a spectrographic scan would be quicker."

"Unfortunate for Forrester-Courtney," Antonio said wolfishly. "Not for us. Dear Victoria came to me with her suggestion, and a simple observation."

"A spectrographic sweep will only locate relatively large pieces of mass," she said. "Fly a starship 50 million kilometers above a disc, and it can spot a fifty-kilometer lump of solid metal easily. But the smaller the lump, the higher the resolution you need or the closer you have to fly, a fairly obvious equation. My magnetic anomaly detector can pick out much smaller lumps of metal than a Dorado."

"So? If they're smaller, they're worth less," Katherine said. "The whole point of the Dorados is that they're huge. I've seen the operation those ex-Garissans are building up. They've got enough metal to supply their industrial stations with specialist microgee alloys for the next 2,000 years. Small is no good."

"Not necessarily," Marcus said carefully. Maybe it was his intuition again, or just plain logical extrapolation, but he could see the way Victoria Keef's thoughts were flowing. "It depends on what kind of small, doesn't it?"

Antonio applauded. "Excellent, Captain. I knew you were the right man for us."

"What makes you think they're there?" Marcus asked.

"The Dorados are the ultimate proof of concept," Victoria said. "There are two possible origins for disc material around stars. The first is accretion; matter left over from the star's formation. That's no use to us, it's mostly the light elements, carbonaceous chondritic particles with some silica aluminum thrown in if you're lucky. The second type of disc is made up out of collision debris. We believe that's what the Dorados are, fragments of planetoids that were large enough to form molten metal cores. When they broke apart the metal cooled and congealed into those hugely valuable chunks."

"But nickel iron wouldn't be the only metal," Marcus reasoned, pleased by the way he was following through. "There will be other chunks floating about in the disc."

"Exactly, Captain," Antonio said eagerly. "Theoretically, the whole periodic table will be available to us, we can fly above the disc and pick out whatever element we require. There will be no tedious and expensive refining process to extract it from ore. It's there waiting for us in its purest form; gold, silver, platinum, iridium. Whatever takes your fancy."

Lady Macbeth sat on a docking cradle in Sonora's spaceport, a simple dull-gray sphere 57 meters in diameter. All Adamist starships shared the same geometry, dictated by the operating parameters of the ZTT jump, which required perfect symmetry. At her heart were four separate life-support capsules, arranged in a pyramid formation; there was also a cylindrical hangar for her spaceplane, a smaller one for her Multiple Service Vehicle, and five main cargo holds. The rest of her bulk was a solid intestinal tangle of machinery and tanks. Her main drive system was three fusion rockets capable of accelerating her at eleven gees, clustered around an antimatter intermix tube which could multiply that figure by an unspecified amount; a sure sign of her combat-capable-status. (By a legislative quirk it wasn't actually illegal to have an antimatter drive, though possession of antimatter itself was a capital crime throughout the Confederation.)

Spaceport umbilical hoses were jacked into sockets on her lower hull, supplying basic utility functions. Another expense Marcus wished he could avoid; it was inflicting further pain on his already ailing cash-flow situation. They were going to have to fly soon, and fate seemed to have decided what flight it would be. That hadn't stopped his intuition from maintaining its subliminal assault on Antonio Ribeiro's scheme. If he could just find a single practical or logical argument against it . . .

He waited patiently while the crew drifted into the main lounge in life-support capsule A. Wai Choi, the spaceplane pilot, came down through the ceiling hatch and used a stikpad to anchor her shoes to the decking. She gave Marcus a sly smile that bordered on teasing. There had been times in the last five years when she'd joined him in his cabin, nothing serious, but they'd certainly had their moments. Which, he supposed, made her more tolerant of him than the others.

At the opposite end of the spectrum was Karl Jordan, the *Lady Mac*'s systems specialist, with the shortest temper, the greatest enthusiasm, and certainly the most serious of the crew. His age was the reason, only twenty-five; the *Lady Mac* was his second starship duty.

As for Schutz, who knew what emotions were at play in the cosmonik's mind; there was no visible outlet for them. Unlike Marcus, he hadn't been geneered for freefall; decades of working on ships and spaceport docks had seen his bones lose calcium, his muscles waste away, and his cardiovascular system atrophy. There were hundreds like him in every asteroid, slowly replacing their body parts with mechanical substitutes. Some even divested themselves of their human shape altogether. At sixty-three, Schutz was still humanoid, though only twenty per cent of him was biological. His body supplements made him an excellent engineer.

"We've been offered a joint-prize flight," Marcus told them. He explained Victoria's theory about disc systems and the magnetic anomaly array. "Ribeiro will provide us with consumables and a full cryogenics load. All we have to do is take *Lady Mac* to a disc system and scoop up the gold."

"There has to be a catch," Wai said. "I don't believe in mountains of gold just drifting through space waiting for us to come along and find them."

"Believe it," Roman said. "You've seen the Dorados. Why can't the elements exist in the same way?"

"I don't know. I just don't think anything comes that easy."

"Always the pessimist."

"What do you think, Marcus?" she asked. "What does your intuition tell you?"

"About the mission, nothing. I'm more worried about Antonio Ribeiro."

"Definitely suspect," Katherine agreed.

"Being a total prat is socially unfortunate," Roman said. "But it's not a crime. Besides, Victoria Keef seemed levelheaded enough."

"An odd combination," Marcus mused. "A wannabe playboy and an astrophysicist. I wonder how they ever got together."

"They're both Sonora nationals," Katherine said. "I ran a check through the public data cores, they were born here. It's not that remarkable."

"Any criminal record?" Wai asked.

"None listed. Antonio has been in court three times in the last seven years; each case was over disputed taxes. He paid every time."

"So he doesn't like the tax man," Roman said. "That makes him one of the good guys."

"Run-ins with the tax office are standard for the rich," Wai said.

"Except he's not actually all that rich," Katherine said. "I also queried the local Collins Media library; they keep tabs on Sonora's principal citizens. Mr Ribeiro senior made his money out of fish breeding; he won the franchise from the asteroid development corporation to keep the biosphere sea stocked. Antonio was given a 15 per cent stake in the breeding company when he was twenty-one, which he promptly sold for an estimated 800,000 fuseodollars. Daddy didn't approve, there are several news files on the quarrel; it became very public."

"So he is what he claims to be," Roman said. "A not-very rich boy with expensive tastes."

"How can he pay for the magnetic detectors we have to deploy, then?" Wai asked. "Or is he going to hit us with the bill and suddenly vanish?"

"The detector arrays are already waiting to be loaded on board," Marcus said. "Antonio has several partners; people in the same leaky boat as himself, and willing to take a gamble."

Wai shook her head, still dubious. "I don't buy it. It's a free lunch."

"They're willing to invest their own money in the array hardware. What other guarantees do you want?"

"What kind of money are we talking about, exactly?" Karl asked. "I mean, if we do fill the ship up, what's it going to be worth?"

"Given its density, *Lady Mac* can carry roughly 5,000 tons of gold in her cargo holds," Marcus said. "That'll make maneuvering very sluggish, but I can handle her."

Roman grinned at Karl. "And today's price for gold is three and a half thousand fuseodollars per kilogram."

Karl's eyes went blank for a second as his neural nanonics ran the conversion. "Seventeen billion fuseodollars worth!"

He laughed. "Per trip."

"How is this Ribeiro character proposing to divide the proceeds?" Schutz asked.

"We get one third," Marcus said. "Roughly five point eight billion fuseodollars. Of which I take 30 per cent. The rest is split equally between you, as per the bounty flight clause in your contracts."

"Shit," Karl whispered. "When do we leave, Captain?"

"Does anybody have any objections?" Marcus asked. He gave Wai a quizzical look.

"Okay," she said. "But just because you can't see surface cracks, it doesn't mean there isn't any metal fatigue."

The docking cradle lifted *Lady Macbeth* cleanly out of the spaceport's crater-shaped bay. As soon as she cleared the rim her thermo-dump panels unfolded, sensor clusters rose up out of their recesses on long booms. Visual and radar information was collated by the flight computer, which datavised it directly into Marcus's neural nanonics. He lay on the acceleration couch at the center of the bridge with his eyes closed as the external starfield blossomed in his mind. Delicate icons unfurled across the visualization, ship status schematics and navigational plots sketched in primary colors.

Chemical verniers fired, lifting *Lady Mac* off the cradle amid spumes of hot saffron vapor. A tube of orange circles appeared ahead of him, the course vector formatted to take them in towards the gas giant. Marcus switched to the more powerful ion thrusters, and the orange circles began to stream past the hull.

The gas giant, Zacateca, and its moon, Lazaro, had the same apparent size as *Lady Mac* accelerated away from the spaceport. Sonora was one of fifteen asteroids captured by their Lagrange point, a zone where their respective gravity fields were in equilibrium. Behind the starship, Lazaro was a grubby gray crescent splattered with white craters. Given that Zacateca was small for a gas giant, barely 40,000 kilometers in diameter, Lazaro was an unusual companion. A moon 9,000 kilometers in diameter, with an outer crust of ice 50 kilometers deep. It was that ice which had originally attracted the interest of the banks and multistellar finance consortia. Stony iron asteroids were an ideal source of metal and minerals for industrial stations, but they were also notoriously short of the light elements essential to sustain life. To have abundant supplies of both so close together was a strong investment incentive.

Lady Mac's radar showed Marcus a serpentine line of one-ton ice cubes flung out from Lazaro's equatorial mass-driver, gliding inertly up to the Lagrange point for collection. The same inexhaustible source which allowed Sonora to have its unique sea.

All the asteroids in the cluster had benefited from the plentiful ice, their economic growth racing ahead of equivalent settlements. Such success always bred resentment among the indigenous population, who inevitably became eager for freedom from the founding companies. In this case, having so many settlements so close together gave their population a strong sense of identity and shared anger. The cluster's demands for autonomy had become increasingly strident over the last few years. A situation agitated by numerous violent incidents and acts of sabotage against the company administration staff.

Ahead of the *Lady Mac,* Marcus could see the tidal hurricane Lazaro stirred up amid the wan amber and emerald stormbands of Zacateca's upper atmosphere. An ocean-sized hypervelocity maelstrom which followed the moon's orbit faithfully around the equator. Lightning crackled around its fringes, 500-kilometer-long forks stabbing out into the surrounding cyclones of ammonia cirrus and methane sleet.

The starship was accelerating at two gees now, her triple fusion drives sending out a vast streamer of arc-bright plasma as she curved around the bulk of the huge planet. Her course vector was slowly bending to align on the star which Antonio intended to prospect, 38 light-years distant. There was very little information contained in the almanac file other than confirming it was a K-class star with a disc.

Marcus cut the fusion drives when the *Lady Mac* was 7,000 kilometers past perigee and climbing steadily. The thermo-dump panels and sensor clusters sank down into their jump recesses below the fuselage, returning the ship to a perfect sphere. Fusion generators began charging the energy-patterning nodes. Orange circles flashing through Marcus's mind were illustrating the slingshot parabola she'd flown, straightening up the farther the gas giant was left behind. A faint star slid into the last circle.

An event horizon swallowed the starship. Five milliseconds later it had shrunk to nothing.

"Okay, try this one," Katherine said. "Why should the gold or anything else congeal into lumps as big as the ones they say it will? Just because you've got a planetoid with a hot core doesn't mean it's producing the metallic equivalent of fractional distillation. You're not going to get an onion-layer effect with strata of different metals. It doesn't happen on planets, it won't happen here. If there is gold, and platinum and all the rest of this fantasy junk, it's going to be hidden away in ores just like it always is."

"So Antonio exaggerated when he said it would be pure," Karl retorted. "We just hunt down the highest-grade ore particles in the disc. Even if it's only 50 per cent, who cares? We're never going to be able to spend it all anyway."

Marcus let the discussion grumble on. It had been virtually the only topic for the crew since they'd departed Sonora five days ago. Katherine was playing the part of chief skeptic, with occasional support from Schutz and Wai; while the others tried to shoot her down. The trouble was, he acknowledged, that none of them knew enough to comment with real authority. At least they weren't talking about the sudden departure from Ayachcho any more.

"If the planetoids did produce ore, then it would fragment badly during the collision which formed the disc," Katherine said. "There won't even be any mountain-sized chunks left, only pebbles."

"Have you taken a look outside recently?" Roman asked. "The disc doesn't exactly have a shortage of large particles."

Marcus smiled to himself at that. The disc material had worried him when they arrived at the star two days ago. *Lady Mac* had jumped deep into the system, emerging three million kilometers above the ecliptic. It was a superb vantage point. The small orange star burned at the center of a disc 160 million kilometers in diameter. There were no distinct bands like those found in a gas giant's rings; this was a continuous grainy copper mist veiling half of the universe. Only around the star itself did it fade away; whatever particles were there to start with had long since evaporated to leave a clear band three million kilometers wide above the turbulent photosphere.

Lady Mac was accelerating away from the star at a twentieth of a gee, and curving around into a retrograde orbit. It was the vector which would give the magnetic arrays the best possible coverage of the disc. Unfortunately, it increased the probability of collision by an order of magnitude. So far, the radar had only detected standard motes of interplanetary dust, but Marcus insisted there were always two crew on duty monitoring the local environment.

"Time for another launch," he announced.

Wai datavised the flight computer to run a final systems diagnostic through the array satellite. "I notice Jorge isn't here again," she said sardonically. "I wonder why that is?"

Jorge Leon was the second companion Antonio Ribeiro had brought with him on the flight. He'd been introduced to the crew as a first-class hardware technician who had supervised the construction of the magnetic array satellites. As introverted as Antonio was outgoing, he'd shown remarkably little interest in the arrays so far. It was Victoria Keef who'd familiarized the crew with the systems they were deploying.

"We should bung him in our medical scanner," Karl suggested cheerfully. "Be interesting to see what's inside him. Bet you'd find a whole load of weapon implants."

"Great idea," Roman said. "You ask him. He gives me the creeps."

"Yeah, Katherine, explain that away," Karl said. "If there's no gold in the disc, how come they brought a contract killer along to make sure we don't fly off with their share?"

"Karl!" Marcus warned. "That's enough." He gave the open floor hatch a pointed look. "Now let's get the array launched, please."

Karl's face reddened as he began establishing a tracking link between the starship's communication system and the array satellite's transponder.

"Satellite systems on line," Wai reported. "Launch when ready."

Marcus datavised the flight computer to retract the satellite's holddown latches. An induction rail shot it clear of the ship. Ion thrusters flared, refining its trajectory as it headed down towards the squally apricot surface of the disc.

Victoria had designed the satellites to skim 5,000 kilometers above the nomadic particles. When their operational altitude was established they would spin up and start to reel out 25 gossamer-thin optical fibers. Rotation insured the fibers remained straight, forming a spoke array parallel to the disc. Each fiber was 150 kilometers long, and coated in a reflective, magnetically-sensitive film.

As the disc particles were still within the star's magnetosphere, every one of them generated a tiny wake as it traversed the flux lines. It was that wake which resonated the magnetically-sensitive film, producing fluctuations in the reflectivity. By bouncing a laser pulse down the fiber and measuring the distortions inflicted by the film, it was possible to build up an image of the magnetic waves writhing chaotically through the disc. With the correct discrimination programs, the origin of each wave could be determined.

The amount of data streaming back into the *Lady Macbeth* from the array satellites was colossal. One satellite array could cover an area of 250,000 square kilometers, and Antonio Ribeiro had persuaded the Sonora Autonomy Crusade to pay for 15. It was a huge gamble, and the responsibility was his alone. Forty hours after the first satellite was deployed, the strain of that responsibility was beginning to show. He hadn't slept since then, choosing to stay in the cabin which Marcus Calvert had assigned to them, and where they'd set up their network of analysis processors. Forty hours of his mind being flooded with near-incomprehensible neuroiconic displays. Forty hours spent fingering his silver crucifix and praying.

The medical monitor program running in his neural nanonics was flashing up fatigue toxin cautions, and warning him of impending dehydration. So far he'd ignored them, telling himself discovery would occur any minute now. In his heart, Antonio had been hoping they would find what they wanted in the first five hours.

His neural nanonics informed him the analysis network was focusing on the mass-density ratio of a three-kilometer particle exposed by satellite seven. The processors began a more detailed interrogation of the raw data.

"What is it?" Antonio demanded. His eyes fluttered open to glance at Victoria, who was resting lightly on one of the cabin's flatchairs.

"Interesting," she murmured. "It appears to be a cassiterite ore. The planetoids definitely had tin."

"Shit!" He thumped his fist into the chair's padding, only to feel the restraint straps tighten against his chest, preventing him from sailing free. "I don't care about tin. That's not what we're here for."

"I am aware of that." Her eyes were open, staring at him with a mixture of contempt and anger.

"Sure, sure," he mumbled. "Holy Mother, you'd expect us to find some by now."

"Careful," she datavised. "Remember this damn ship has internal sensors."

"I know how to follow elementary security procedures," he datavised back.

"Yes. But you're tired. That's when errors creep in."

"I'm not that tired. Shit, I expected results by now; some progress."

"We have had some very positive results, Antonio. The arrays have found three separate deposits of pitchblende."

"Yeah, in hundred-kilogram lumps. We need more than that, a lot more."

"You're missing the point. We've proved it exists here; that's a stupendous discovery. Finding it in quantity is just a matter of time."

"This isn't some astrological experiment you're running for that university which threw you out. We're on an assignment for the cause. And we cannot go back empty handed. Got that? Cannot."

"Astrophysics."

"What?"

"You said astrological, that's fortune-telling."

"Yeah? You want I should take a guess at how much future you're going to have if we don't find what we need out here?"

"For Christ's sake, Antonio," she said out loud. "Go and get some sleep."

"Maybe." He scratched the side of his head, unhappy with how limp and oily his hair had become. A vapor shower was something else he hadn't had for a while. "I'll get Jorge in here to help you monitor the results."

"Great." Her eyes closed again.

Antonio deactivated his flatchair's restraint straps. He hadn't seen much of Jorge on the flight. Nobody had. The man kept strictly to himself in his small cabin. The Crusade's council wanted him on board to ensure the crew's continuing cooperation once they realized there was no gold. It was Antonio who had suggested the arrangement; what bothered him was the orders Jorge had received concerning himself should things go wrong.

"Hold it." Victoria raised her hand. "This is a really weird one."

Antonio tapped his feet on a stikpad to steady himself. His neural nanonics accessed the analysis network again. Satellite eleven had located a particle with an impossible mass-density ratio; it also had its own magnetic field, a very complex one. "Holy Mother, what is that? Is there another ship here?"

"No, it's too big for a ship. Some kind of station, I suppose. But what's it doing in the disc?"

"Refining ore?" he said with a strong twist of irony.

"I doubt it."

"Okay. So forget it."

"You are joking."

"No. If it doesn't affect us, it doesn't concern us."

"Jesus, Antonio; if I didn't know you were born rich I'd be frightened by how stupid you were."

"Be careful, Victoria my dear. Very careful."

"Listen, there's two options. One, it's some kind of commercial operation; which must be illegal because nobody has filed for industrial development rights." She gave him a significant look.

"You think they're mining pitchblende?" he datavised.

"What else? We thought of the concept, why not one of the black syndicates as well? They just didn't come up with my magnetic array idea, so they're having to do it the hard way."

"Secondly," she continued aloud, "it's some kind of covert military station; in which case they've tracked us from the moment we emerged. Either way, we're under observation. We have to know who they are before we proceed any further."

"A station?" Marcus asked. "Here?"

"It would appear so," Antonio said glumly.

"And you want us to find out who they are?"

"I think that would be prudent," Victoria said, "given what we're doing here."

"All right," Marcus said. "Karl, lock a communication dish on them. Give them our CAB identification code, let's see if we can get a response."

"Aye, sir," Karl said. He settled back on his acceleration couch.

"While we're waiting," Katherine said. "I have a question for you, Antonio."

She ignored the warning glare Marcus directed at her.

Antonio's bogus smile blinked on. "If it is one I can answer, then I will do so gladly, dear lady."

"Gold is expensive because of its rarity value, right?"

"Of course."

"So here we are, about to fill *Lady Mac*'s cargo holds with 5,000 tons of the stuff. On top of that you've developed a method which means people can scoop up millions of tons any time they want. If we try and sell it to a dealer or a bank, how long do you think we're going to be billionaires for, a fortnight?"

Antonio laughed. "Gold has never been that rare. Its value is completely artificial. The Edenists have the largest stockpile. We don't know exactly how much they possess because the Jovian Bank will not declare the exact figure. But they dominate the commodity market, and sustain the price by controlling how much is released. We shall simply play the same game. Our gold will have to be sold discreetly, in small batches, in different star systems, and over the course of several years. And knowledge of the magnetic array system should be kept to ourselves."

"Nice try, Katherine," Roman chuckled. "You'll just have to settle for an income of a hundred million a year."

She showed him a stiff finger, backed by a shark's smile.

"No response," Karl said. "Not even a transponder."

"Keep trying," Marcus told him. "Okay, Antonio, what do you want to do about it?"

"We have to know who they are," Victoria said. "As Antonio has just explained so eloquently, we can't have other people seeing what we're doing here."

"It's what *they're* doing here that worries me," Marcus said; although, curiously, his intuition wasn't causing him any grief on the subject.

"I see no alternative but a rendezvous," Antonio said.

"We're in a retrograde orbit, 32 million kilometers away and receding. That's going to use up an awful lot of fuel."

"Which I believe I have already paid for."

"Okay, we rendezvous."

"What if they don't want us there?" Schutz asked.

"If we detect any combat wasp launch, then we jump outsystem immediately," Marcus said. "The disc's gravity field isn't strong enough to affect *Lady Mac*'s patterning node symmetry. We can leave any time we want."

For the last quarter of a million kilometers of the approach, Marcus put the ship on combat status. The nodes were fully charged, ready to jump. Thermo-dump panels were retracted. Sensors maintained a vigilant watch for approaching combat wasps.

"They must know we're here," Wai said when they were 8,000 kilometers away. "Why don't they acknowledge us?"

"Ask them," Marcus said sourly. *Lady Mac* was decelerating at a nominal one gee, which he was varying at random. It made their exact approach vector impossible to predict, which meant their course couldn't be seeded with proximity mines. The maneuver took a lot of concentration.

"Still no electromagnetic emission in any spectrum," Karl reported. "They're certainly not scanning us with active sensors."

"Sensors are picking up their thermal signature," Schutz said. "The structure is being maintained at 36 degrees Celsius."

"That's on the warm side," Katherine observed. "Perhaps their environmental system is malfunctioning."

"Shouldn't affect the transponder," Karl said.

"Captain, I think you'd better access the radar return," Schutz said.

Marcus boosted the fusion drives up to one and a half gees, and ordered the flight computer to datavise him the radar feed. The image which rose into his mind was of a fine scarlet mesh suspended in the darkness, its gentle ocean-swell pattern outlining the surface of the station and the disc particle it was attached to. Except Marcus had never seen any station like this before. It was a gently curved wedge-shape structure, 400 meters long, 300 wide, and 150 meters at its blunt end. The accompanying disc particle was a flattened ellipsoid of stony iron rock, measuring eight kilometers along its axis. The tip had been sheared off, leaving a flat cliff half a kilometer in diameter, to which the structure was clinging. That was the smallest of the particle's modifications. A crater four kilometers across, with perfectly smooth walls, had been cut into one side of the rock. An elaborate unicorn-horn tower rose 900 meters from its center, ending in a clump of jagged spikes.

"Oh Jesus," Marcus whispered. Elation mingled with fear, producing a deviant adrenaline high. He smiled thinly. "How about that?"

"This was one option I didn't consider," Victoria said weakly.

Antonio looked round the bridge, a frown cheapening his handsome face. The crew seemed dazed, while Victoria was grinning with delight. "Is it some kind of radio astronomy station?" he asked.

"Yes," Marcus said. "But not one of ours. We don't build like that. It's xenoc."

Lady Mac locked attitude a kilometer above the xenoc structure. It was a position which made the disc appear uncomfortably malevolent. The smallest particle beyond the fuselage must have massed over a million tons; and all of them were moving, a slow, random three-dimensional cruise of lethal inertia. Amber sunlight stained those near the disc's surface a baleful ginger, while deeper in there were only phantom silhouettes drifting over total blackness, flowing in and out of visibility. No stars were evident through the dark, tightly packed nebula.

"That's not a station," Roman declared. "It's a shipwreck."

Now that *Lady Mac*'s visual-spectrum sensors were providing them with excellent images of the xenoc structure, Marcus had to agree. The upper and lower surfaces of the wedge was some kind of silver-white material, a fuselage shell which was fraying away at the edges. Both of the side surfaces were dull brown, obviously interior bulkhead walls, with the black geometrical outline of decking printed across them. The whole structure was a cross-section torn out of a much larger craft. Marcus tried to fill in the missing bulk in his mind; it must have been vast, a streamlined delta fuselage like a hypersonic aircraft. Which didn't make sense for a starship. Rather, he corrected himself, for a starship built with current human technology. He wondered what it would be like to fly through interstellar space the way a plane flew through an atmosphere, swooping around stars at a hundred times the speed of light. Quite something.

"This doesn't make a lot of sense," Katherine said. "If they were visiting the telescope dish when they had the accident, why did they bother to anchor themselves to the asteroid? Surely they'd just take refuge in the operations center."

"Only if there is one," Schutz said. "Most of our deep space science facilities are automated, and by the look of it their technology is considerably more advanced."

"If they are so advanced, why would they build a radio telescope on this scale anyway?" Victoria asked. "It's very impractical. Humans have been using linked baseline arrays for centuries. Five small dishes orbiting a million kilometers apart would provide a reception which is orders of magnitude greater than this. And why build it here? Firstly, the particles are hazardous, certainly to something that size. You can see it's been pocked by small impacts, and that horn looks broken to me. Secondly, the disc itself blocks half of the universe from observation. No, if you're going to do major radio astronomy, you don't do it from a star system like this one."

"Perhaps they were only here to build the dish," Wai said. "They intended it to be a remote research station in this part of the galaxy. Once they had it up and running, they'd boost it into a high-inclination orbit. They had their accident before the project was finished."

"That still doesn't explain why they chose this system. Any other star would be better that this one."

"I think Wai's right about them being long-range visitors," Marcus said. "If a xenoc race like that existed close to the Confederation we would have found them by now. Or they would have contacted us."

"The Kiint," Karl said quickly.

"Possibly," Marcus conceded. The Kiint were an enigmatic xenoc race, with a technology far in advance of anything the Confederation had mastered. However, they were reclusive, and cryptic to the point of obscurity. They also claimed to have abandoned starflight a long time ago. "If it is one of their ships, then it's very old."

"And it's still functional," Roman said eagerly. "Hell, think of the technology inside. We'll wind up a lot richer than the gold could ever make us." He grinned over at Antonio, whose humor had blackened considerably.

"So what were the Kiint doing building a radio telescope here?" Victoria asked.

"Who the hell cares?" Karl said. "I volunteer to go over, Captain."

Marcus almost didn't hear him. He'd accessed the *Lady Mac*'s sensor suite again, sweeping the focus over the tip of the dish's tower, then the sheer cliff which the wreckage was attached to. Intuition was making a lot of junctions in his head. "I don't think it is a radio telescope," he said. "I think it's a distress beacon."

"It's four kilometers across!" Katherine said.

"If they came from the other side of the galaxy, it would need to be. We can't even see the galactic core from here there's so much gas and dust in the way. You'd need something this big to punch a message through."

"That's valid," Victoria said. "You believe they were signaling their homeworld for help?"

"Yes. Assume their world is a long way off, three-four thousand light-years away if not more. They were flying a research or survey mission in this area and they have an accident. Three quarters of their ship is lost, including the drive section. Their technology isn't good enough to build the survivors a working stardrive out of what's left, but they can enlarge an existing crater on the disc particle. So they do that; they build the dish and a transmitter powerful enough to give God an alarm call, point it at their homeworld, and scream for help. The ship can sustain them until the rescue team arrives. Even our own zero-tau technology is up to that."

"Gets my vote," Wai said, she gave Marcus a wink.

"No way," said Katherine. "If they were in trouble they'd use a supralight communicator to call for help. Look at that ship, we're centuries away from building anything like it."

"Edenist voidhawks are pretty sophisticated," Marcus countered. "We just scale things differently. These xenocs might have a more advanced technology, but physics is still the same the universe over. Our understanding of quantum relativity is good enough to build faster than light starships, yet after 450 years of theoretical research we still haven't come up with a method of supralight communication. It doesn't exist."

"If they didn't return on time, then surely their homeworld would send out a search and recovery craft," Schutz said.

"They'd have to know the original ship's course exactly," Wai said.

"And if a search ship did manage to locate them, why did they build the dish?"

Marcus didn't say anything. He knew he was right. The others would accept his scenario eventually, they always did.

"All right, let's stop arguing about what happened to them, and why they built the dish," Karl said. "When do we go over there, Captain?"

"Have you forgotten the gold?" Antonio asked. "That is why we came to this disc system. We should resume our search for it. This piece of wreckage can wait."

"Don't be crazy. This is worth a hundred times as much as any gold."

"I fail to see how. An ancient, derelict, starship with a few heating circuits operational. Come along. I've been reasonable indulging you, but we must return to the original mission."

Marcus regarded the man cautiously, a real bad feeling starting to develop. Anyone with the slightest knowledge of finance and the markets would know the value of salvaging a xenoc starship. And Antonio had been born rich. "Victoria," he said, not shifting his gaze. "Is the data from the magnetic array satellites still coming through?"

"Yes." She touched Antonio's arm. "The captain is right. We can continue to monitor the satellite results from here, and investigate the xenoc ship simultaneously."

"Double your money time," Katherine said with apparent innocence.

Antonio's face hardened. "Very well," he said curtly. "If that's your expert opinion, Victoria, my dear. Carry on by all means, Captain."

In its inert state the SII spacesuit was a broad sensor collar with a protruding respirator tube and a black football-sized globe of programmable silicon hanging from it. Marcus slipped the collar around his neck, bit on the tube nozzle, and datavised an activation code into the suit's control processor. The silicon ball began to change shape, flattening out against his chest, then flowing over his body like a tenacious oil slick. It enveloped his head completely, and the collar sensors replaced his eyes, datavising their vision directly into his neural nanonics. Three others were in the preparation compartment with him; Schutz, who didn't need a spacesuit to EVA, Antonio, and Jorge Leon. Marcus had managed to control his surprise when they'd volunteered. At the same time, with Wai flying the MSV he was glad they weren't going to be left behind in the ship.

Once his body was sealed by the silicon, he climbed into an armored exoskeleton with an integral cold-gas maneuvering pack. The SII silicon would never puncture, but if he was struck by a rogue particle the armor would absorb the impact.

When the airlock's outer hatch opened, the MSV was floating 15 meters away. Marcus datavised an order into his maneuvering pack processor, and the gas jets behind his shoulder fired, pushing him towards the small egg-shaped vehicle. Wai extended two of the MSV's three waldo arms in greeting. Each of them ended in a simple metal grid, with a pair of boot clamps on both sides.

Once all four of her passengers were locked into place, Wai piloted the MSV in towards the disc. The rock particle had a slow, erratic tumble, taking 120 hours to complete its cycle. As she approached, the flattish surface with the dish was just turning into the sunlight. It was a strange kind of dawn, the rock's crumpled gray-brown crust speckled by the sharp black shadows of its own rolling prominences, while the dish was a lake of infinite black, broken only by the jagged spire of the horn rising from its center. The xenoc ship was already exposed to the amber light, casting its bloated sundial shadow across the featureless glassy cliff. She could see the ripple of different ores and mineral strata frozen below the glazed surface, deluding her for a moment that she was flying towards a mountain of cut and polished onyx.

Then again, if Victoria's theory was right, she could well be.

"Take us in towards the top of the wedge," Marcus datavised. "There's a series of darker rectangles there."

"Will do," she responded. The MSV's chemical thrusters pulsed in compliance.

"Do you see the color difference near the frayed edges of the shell?" Schutz asked. "The stuff's turning gray. It's as if the decay is creeping inwards."

"They must be using something like our molecular binding force generators to resist vacuum ablation," Marcus datavised. "That's why the main section is still intact."

"It could have been here for a long time, then."

"Yeah. We'll know better once Wai collects some samples from the tower."

There were five of the rectangles, arranged in parallel, one and a half meters long and one meter wide. The shell material below the shorter edge of each one had a set of ten grooves leading away down the curve.

"They looks like ladders to me," Antonio datavised. "Would that mean these are airlocks?"

"It can't be that easy," Schutz replied.

"Why not?" Marcus datavised. "A ship this size is bound to have more than one airlock."

"Yeah, but five together?"

"Multiple redundancy."

"With technology this good?"

"That's human hubris. The ship still blew up, didn't it?"

Wai locked the MSV's attitude 50 meters above the shell section. "The micropulse radar is bouncing right back at me," she informed them. "I can't tell what's below the shell, it's a perfect electromagnetic reflector. We're going to have communication difficulties once you're inside."

Marcus disengaged his boots from the grid and fired his pack's gas jets. The shell was as slippery as ice; neither stikpads nor magnetic soles would hold them to it.

"Definitely enhanced-valency bonds," Schutz datavised. He was floating parallel to the surface, holding a sensor block against it. "It's a much stronger field than *Lady Mac*'s. The shell composition is a real mix; the resonance scan is picking up titanium, silicon, boron, nickel, silver, and a whole load of polymers."

"Silver's weird," Marcus commented. "But if there's nickel in it our magnetic soles should've worked." He maneuvered himself over one of the rectangles. It was recessed about five centimeters, though it blended seamlessly into the main shell. His sensor collar couldn't detect any seal lining. Half way along one side were two circular dimples, ten centimeters across. Logically, if the rectangle was an airlock, then these should be the controls. Human back-ups were kept simple. This shouldn't be any different.

Marcus stuck his fingers in one. It turned bright blue.

"Power surge," Schutz datavised. "The block's picking up several high-voltage circuits activating under the shell. What did you do, Marcus?"

"Tried to open one."

The rectangle dilated smoothly, material flowing back to the edges. Brilliant white light flooded out.

"Clever," Schutz datavised.

"No more than our programmable silicon," Antonio retorted.

"We don't use programmable silicon for external applications."

"It settles one thing," Marcus datavised. "They weren't Kiint, not with an airlock this size."

"Quite. What now?"

"We try to establish control over the cycling mechanism. I'll go in and see if I can operate the hatch from inside. If it doesn't open after ten minutes, try the dimple again. If that doesn't work, cut through it with the MSV's fission blade."

The chamber inside was thankfully bigger than the hatch: a pentagonal tube two meters wide and 15 long. Four of the walls shone brightly, while the fifth was a strip of dark-maroon composite. He drifted in, then flipped himself over so he was facing the hatch, floating in the center of the chamber. There were four dimples just beside the hatch. "First one," he datavised. Nothing happened when he put his fingers in. "Second." It turned blue. The hatch flowed shut.

Marcus crashed down onto the strip of dark composite, landing on his left shoulder. The force of the impact was almost enough to jar the respirator tube out of his mouth. He grunted in shock. Neural nanonics blocked the burst of pain from his bruised shoulder.

Jesus! They've got artificial gravity.

He was flat on his back, the exoskeleton and maneuvering pack weighing far too much. Whatever planet the xenocs came from, it had a gravity field about one and a half times that of Earth. He released the catches down the side of his exoskeleton, and wriggled his way out. Standing was an effort, but he was used to higher gees on *Lady Mac;* admittedly not for prolonged periods, though.

He stuck his fingers in the first dimple. The gravity faded fast, and the hatch flowed apart.

"We just became billionaires," he datavised.

The third dimple pressurized the airlock chamber; while the fourth depressurized it.

The xenoc atmosphere was mostly a nitrogen-oxygen blend, with one per cent argon and six per cent carbon dioxide. The humidity was appalling, pressure was lower than standard, and the temperature was 42 degrees Celsius.

"We'd have to keep our SII suits on anyway, because of the heat," Marcus datavised. "But the carbon dioxide would kill us. And we'll have to go through biological decontamination when we go back to *Lady Mac.*"

The four of them stood together at the far end of the airlock chamber, their exoskeleton armor lying on the floor behind them. Marcus had told Wai and the rest of the crew their first foray would be an hour.

"Are you proposing we go in without a weapon?" Jorge asked.

Marcus focused his collar sensors on the man who alleged he was a hardware technician. "That's carrying paranoia too far. No, we do not engage in first contact either deploying or displaying weapons of any kind. That's the law, and the Assembly regulations are very specific about it. In any case, don't you think that if there are any xenocs left after all this time they're going to be glad to see someone? Especially a space-faring species."

"That is, I'm afraid, a rather naive attitude, Captain. You keep saying how advanced this starship is, and yet it suffered catastrophic damage. Frankly, an unbelievable amount of damage for an accident. Isn't it more likely this ship was engaged in some kind of battle?"

Which was a background worry Marcus had suffered right from the start. That this starship could ever fail was unnerving. But like physical constants, Murphy's Law would be the same the universe over. He'd entered the airlock because intuition told him the wreck was safe for him personally. Somehow he doubted a man like Jorge would be convinced by that argument.

"If it's a warship, then it will be rigged to alert any surviving crew or flight computer of our arrival. Had they wanted to annihilate us, they would have done so by now. *Lady Mac* is a superb ship, but hardly in this class. So if they're waiting for us on the other side of this airlock, I don't think any weapon you or I can carry is going to make the slightest difference."

"Very well, proceed."

Marcus postponed the answer which came straight to mind, and put his fingers in one of the two dimples by the inner hatchway. It turned blue.

The xenoc ship wasn't disappointing, exactly, but Marcus couldn't help a growing sense of anticlimax. The artificial gravity was a fabulous piece of equipment, the atmosphere strange, the layout exotic. Yet for all that, it was just a ship; built from the universal rules of logical engineering. Had the xenocs themselves been there, it would have been so different. A whole new species with its history and culture. But they'd gone, so he was an archaeologist rather than an explorer.

They surveyed the first deck, which was made up from large compartments and broad hallways. The interior was made out of a pale-jade composite, slightly ruffled to a snake-skin texture. Surfaces always curved together, there were no real corners. Every ceiling emitted the same intense white glare, which their collar sensors compensated for. Arching doorways were all open, though they could still dilate if you used the dimples. The only oddity were 50-centimeter hemispherical blisters on the floor and walls, scattered completely at random.

There was an ongoing argument about the shape of the xenocs. They were undoubtedly shorter than humans, and they probably had legs, because there were spiral stair-wells, although the steps were very broad, difficult for bipeds. Lounges had long tables with large, rounded stool-chairs inset with four deep ridges.

After the first 15 minutes it was clear that all loose equipment had been removed. Lockers, with the standard dilating door, were empty. Every compartment had its fitted furnishings and nothing more. Some were completely bare.

On the second deck there were no large compartments, only long corridors lined with gray circles along the center of the walls. Antonio used a dimple at the side of one, and it dilated to reveal a spherical cell three meters wide. Its walls were translucent, with short lines of color slithering around behind them like photonic fish.

"Beds?" Schutz suggested. "There's an awful lot of them."

Marcus shrugged. "Could be." He moved on, eager to get down to the next deck. Then he slowed, switching his collar focus. Three of the hemispherical blisters were following him, two gliding along the wall, one on the floor. They stopped when he did. He walked over to the closest, and waved his sensor block over it. "There's a lot of electronic activity inside it," he reported.

The others gathered around.

"Are they extruded by the wall, or are they a separate device?" Schutz asked.

Marcus switched on the block's resonance scan. "I'm not sure, I can't find any break in the composite around its base, not even a hairline fracture; but with their materials technology that doesn't mean much."

"Five more approaching," Jorge datavised. The blisters were approaching from ahead, three of them on the walls, two on the floor. They stopped just short of the group.

"Something knows we're here," Antonio datavised.

Marcus retrieved the CAB xenoc interface communication protocol from a neural nanonics memory cell. He'd stored it decades ago, all qualified starship crew were obliged to carry it along with a million and one other bureaucratic lunacies. His communication block transmitted the protocol using a multispectrum sweep. If the blister could sense them, it had to have some kind of electromagnetic reception facility. The communication block switched to laser-light, then a magnetic pulse.

"Nothing," Marcus datavised.

"Maybe the central computer needs time to interpret the protocol," Schutz datavised.

"A desktop block should be able to work that out."

"Perhaps the computer hasn't got anything to say to us."

"Then why send the blisters after us?"

"They could be autonomous, whatever they are."

Marcus ran his sensor block over the blister again, but there was no change to its electronic pattern. He straightened up, wincing at the creak of complaint his spine made at the heavy gravity. "Okay, our hour is almost up anyway. We'll get back to *Lady Mac* and decide what stage two is going to be."

The blisters followed them all the way back to the stairwell they'd used. As soon as they started walking down the broad central hallway of the upper deck, more blisters started sliding in from compartments and other halls to stalk them.

The airlock hatch was still open when they got back, but the exoskeletons were missing.

"Shit," Antonio datavised. "They're still here, the bloody xenocs are here."

Marcus shoved his fingers into the dimple. His heartbeat calmed considerably when the hatch congealed behind them. The lock cycled obediently, and the outer rectangle opened.

"Wai," he datavised. "We need a lift. Quickly, please."

"On my way, Marcus."

"Strange way for xenocs to communicate," Schutz datavised. "What did they do that for? If they wanted to make sure we stayed, they could have disabled the airlock."

The MSV swooped over the edge of the shell, jets of twinkling flame shooting from its thrusters.

"Beats me," Marcus datavised. "But we'll find out."

Opinion on the ship was a straight split; the crew wanted to continue investigating the xenoc ship, Antonio and his colleagues wanted to leave. For once Jorge had joined them, which Marcus considered significant. He was beginning to think young Karl might have been closer to the truth than was strictly comfortable.

"The dish is just rock with a coating of aluminium sprayed on," Katherine said. "There's very little aluminium left now, most of it has boiled away in the vacuum. The tower is a pretty ordinary silicon-boron composite wrapped around a titanium load structure. The samples Wai cut off were very brittle."

"Did you carbon-date them?" Victoria asked.

"Yeah." She gave her audience a labored glance. "Give or take a decade, it's 13,000 years old."

Breath whistled out of Marcus's mouth. "Jesus."

"Then they must have been rescued, or died," Roman said. "There's nobody left over there. Not after that time."

"They're there," Antonio growled. "They stole our exoskeletons."

"I don't understand what happened to the exoskeletons. Not yet. But any entity who can build a ship like that isn't going to go creeping around stealing bits of space armor. There has to be a rational explanation."

"Yes! They wanted to keep us over there."

"What for? What possible reason would they have for that?"

"It's a warship, it's been in battle. The survivors don't know who we are, if we're their old enemies. If they kept us there, they could study us and find out."

"After 13,000 years, I imagine the war will be over. And where did you get this battleship idea from anyway?"

"It's a logical assumption," Jorge said quietly.

Roman turned to Marcus. "My guess is that some kind of mechanoid picked them up. If you look in one of the lockers you'll probably find them neatly stored away."

"Some automated systems are definitely still working," Schutz said. "We saw the blisters. There could be others."

"That seems the most remarkable part of it," Marcus said. "Especially now we know the age of the thing. The inside of that ship was brand new. There wasn't any dust, any scuff marks. The lighting worked perfectly, so did the gravity, the humidity hasn't corroded anything. It's extraordinary. As if the whole structure has been in zero-tau. And yet only the shell is protected by the molecular bonding force generators. They're not used inside, not in the decks we examined."

"However they preserve it, they'll need a lot of power for the job, and that's on top of gravity generation and environmental maintenance. Where's that been coming from uninterrupted for 13,000 years?"

"Direct mass to energy conversion," Katherine speculated. "Or they could be tapping straight into the sun's fusion. Whatever, bang goes the Edenist He3 monopoly."

"We have to go back," Marcus said.

"NO!" Antonio yelled. "We must find the gold first. When that has been achieved, you can come back by yourselves. I won't allow anything to interfere with our priorities."

"Look, I'm sorry you had a fright while you were over there. But a power supply that works for 13,000 years is a lot more valuable than a whole load of gold which we have to sell furtively," Katherine said levelly.

"I hired this ship. You do as I say. We go after the gold."

"We're partners, actually. I'm not being paid for this flight unless we strike lucky. And now we have. We've got the xenoc ship, we haven't got any gold. What does it matter to you how we get rich, as long as we do? I thought money was the whole point of this flight."

Antonio snarled at her, and flung himself at the floor hatch, kicking off hard with his legs. His elbow caught the rim a nasty crack as he flashed through it.

"Victoria?" Marcus asked as the silence became strained. "Have the satellite arrays found any heavy metal particles yet?"

"There are definitely traces of gold and platinum, but nothing to justify a rendezvous."

"In that case, I say we start to research the xenoc wreck properly." He looked straight at Jorge. "How about you?"

"I think it would be prudent. You're sure we can continue to monitor the array satellites from here?"

"Yes."

"Good. Count me in."

"Thanks. Victoria?"

She seemed troubled by Jorge's response, even a little bewildered, but she said: "Sure."

"Karl, you're the nearest thing we've got to a computer expert. I want you over there trying to make contact with whatever control network is still operating."

"You got it."

"From now on we go over in teams of four. I want sensors put up to watch the airlocks when we're not around, and start thinking about how we communicate with people inside. Wai, you and I are going to secure *Lady Mac* to the side of the shell. Okay, let's get active, people."

Unsurprisingly, none of the standard astronautics industry vacuum epoxies worked on the shell. Marcus and Wai wound up using tether cables wrapped around the whole of the xenoc ship to hold *Lady Mac* in place.

Three hours after Karl went over, he asked Marcus to join him.

Lady Mac's main airlock tube had telescoped out of the hull to rest against the shell. There was no way it could ever be mated to the xenoc airlock rectangle, but it did allow the crew to transfer over directly without having to use exoskeleton armor and the MSV. They'd also run an optical fiber through the xenoc airlock to the interior of the ship. The hatch material closed around it forming a perfect seal, rather than cutting through it.

Marcus found Karl just inside the airlock, sitting on the floor with several processor blocks in his lap. Eight blisters were slowly circling around him; two on the wall were stationary.

"Roman was almost right," he datavised as soon as Marcus stepped out of the airlock. "Your exoskeletons were cleared away. But not by any butler mechanoid. Watch." He lobbed an empty recording flek case onto the floor behind the blisters. One of them slid over to it. The green com-

posite became soft, then liquid. The little plastic case sank through it into
the blister.

"I call them cybermice," Karl datavised. "They just scurry around
keeping the place clean. You won't see the exoskeletons again, they ate
them, along with anything else they don't recognize as part of the ship's
structure. I imagine they haven't tried digesting us yet because we're
large and active; maybe they think we're friends of the xenocs. But I
wouldn't want to try sleeping over here."

"Does this mean we won't be able to put sensors up?"

"Not for a while. I've managed to stop them digesting the communication block which the optical fiber is connected to."

"How?"

He pointed to the two on the wall. "I shut them down."

"Jesus, have you accessed a control network?"

"No. Schutz and I used a micro SQUID on one of the cybermice to
get a more detailed scan of its electronics. Once we'd tapped the data-
bus traffic it was just a question of running standard decryption programs. I can't tell you how these things work, but I have found some
basic command routines. There's a deactivation code which you can
datavise to them. I've also got a reactivation code, and some directional codes. The good news is that the xenoc program language is
standardized." He stood and held a communication block up to the
ceiling. "This is the deactivation code." A small circle of the ceiling
around the block turned dark. "It's only localized, I haven't worked out
how to control entire sections yet. We need to trace the circuitry to find
an access port."

"Can you turn it back on again?"

"Oh yes." The dark section flared white again. "The codes work for
the doors as well; just hold your block over the dimples."

"Be quicker to use the dimples."

"For now, yes."

"I wasn't complaining, Karl. This is an excellent start. What's your
next step?"

"I want to access the next level of the cybermice program architecture. That way I should be able to load recognition patterns in their memory. Once I can do that I'll enter our equipment, and they should leave it
alone. But that's going to take a long time; *Lady Mac* isn't exactly heavily stocked with equipment for this kind of work. Of course, once I do get
deeper into their management routines we should be able to learn a lot
about their internal systems. From what I can make out the cybermice are
built around a molecular synthesizer." He switched on a fission knife, its

ten-centimeter blade glowing a pale yellow under the ceiling's glare. It scored a dark smoldering scar in the floor composite.

A cybermouse immediately slipped towards the blemish. This time when the composite softened the charred granules were sucked down, and the small valley closed up.

"Exactly the same thickness and molecular structure as before," Karl datavised. "That's why the ship's interior looks brand new, and everything's still working flawlessly after 13,000 years. The cybermice keep regenerating it. Just keep giving them energy and a supply of mass and there's no reason this ship won't last for eternity."

"It's almost a Von Neumann machine, isn't it?"

"Close. I expect a synthesizer this small has limits. After all, if it could reproduce anything, they would have built themselves another starship. But the principle's here, Captain. We can learn and expand on it. Think of the effect a unit like this will have on our manufacturing industry."

Marcus was glad he was in an SII suit; it blocked any give-away facial expressions. Replicator technology would be a true revolution, restructuring every aspect of human society, Adamist and Edenist alike. And revolutions never favored the old.

I just came here for the money, not to destroy a way of life for 800 star systems.

"That's good, Karl. Where did the others go?"

"Down to the third deck. Once we solved the puzzle of the disappearing exoskeletons, they decided it was safe to start exploring again."

"Fair enough, I'll go down and join them."

"I cannot believe you agreed to help them," Antonio stormed. "You of all people. You know how much the cause is depending on us."

Jorge gave him a hollow smile. They were together in his sleeping cubicle, which made it very cramped. But it was one place on the starship he knew for certain no sensors were operational; a block he'd brought with him had made sure of that. "The cause has become dependent on your project. There's a difference."

"What are you talking about?"

"Those detector satellites cost us a million and a half fuseodollars each; and most of that money came from sources who will require repayment no matter what the outcome of our struggle."

"The satellites are a hell of a lot cheaper than antimatter."

"Indeed so. But they are worthless to us unless they find pitchblende."

"We'll find it. Victoria says there are plenty of traces. It's only a question of time before we get a big one."

"Maybe. It was a good idea, Antonio, I'm not criticizing. Fusion bomb components are not easily obtainable to a novice political organization with limited resources. One mistake, and the intelligence agencies would wipe us out. No, old-fashioned fission was a viable alternative. Even if we couldn't process the uranium up to weapons-quality, we can still use it as a lethal large-scale contaminate. As you say, we couldn't lose. Sonora would gain independence, and we would form the first government, with full access to the Treasury. Everyone would be reimbursed for their individual contribution to the liberation."

"So why are we mucking about in a pile of xenoc junk? Just back me up, Jorge, please. Calvert will leave it alone if we both pressure him."

"Because, Antonio, this piece of so-called xenoc junk has changed the rules of the game. In fact we're not even playing the same game any more. Gravity generation, an inexhaustible power supply, molecular synthesis, and if Karl can access the control network he might even find the blueprints to build whatever stardrive they used. Are you aware of the impact such a spectrum of radical technologies will have upon the Confederation when released all together? Entire industries will collapse from overnight obsolescence. There will be an economic depression the like of which we haven't seen since before the invention of the ZTT drive. It will take decades for the human race to return to the kind of stability we enjoy today. We will be richer and stronger because of it; but the transition years, ah . . . I would not like to be a citizen in an asteroid settlement that has just blackmailed the founding company into premature independence. Who is going to loan an asteroid such as that the funds to re-equip our industrial stations, eh?"

"I . . . I hadn't thought of that."

"Neither has the crew. Except for Calvert. Look at his face next time you talk to him, Antonio. He knows, he has reasoned it out, and he's seen the end of his captaincy and freedom. The rest of them are lost amid their dreams of exorbitant wealth."

"So what do we do?"

Jorge clamped a hand on Antonio's shoulder. "Fate has smiled on us, Antonio. This was registered as a joint-venture flight. No matter we were looking for something different. By law, we are entitled to an equal share of the xenoc technology. We are already trillionaires, my friend. When we get home we can *buy* Sonora asteroid; Holy Mother, we can buy the entire Lagrange cluster."

Antonio managed a smile, which didn't quite correspond with the dew of sweat on his forehead. "Okay, Jorge. Hell, you're right. We don't have to worry about anything any more. But . . ."

"Now what?"

"I know we can pay off the loan on the satellites, but what about the Crusade council? They won't like this. They might—"

"There's no cause for alarm. The council will never trouble us again. I maintain that I am right about the disaster which destroyed the xenoc ship. It didn't have an accident. That is a warship, Antonio. And you know what that means, don't you? Somewhere on board there will be weapons just as advanced and as powerful as the rest of its technology."

It was Wai's third trip over to the xenoc ship. None of them spent more than two hours at a time inside. The gravity field made every muscle ache; walking around was like being put on a crash exercise regimen.

Schutz and Karl were still busy by the airlock, probing the circuitry of the cybermice, and decrypting more of their programming. It was probably the most promising line of research; once they could use the xenoc program language they should be able to extract any answer they wanted from the ship's controlling network. Assuming there was one. Wai was convinced there would be. The number of systems operating— life-support, power, gravity—had to mean some basic management integration system was functional.

In the meantime there was the rest of the structure to explore. She had a layout file stored in her neural nanonics, updated by the others every time they came back from an excursion. At the blunt end of the wedge there could be anything up to 40 decks, if the spacing was standard. Nobody had gone down to the bottom yet. There were some areas which had no obvious entrance; presumably engineering compartments, or storage tanks. Marcus had the teams tracing the main power lines with magnetic sensors, trying to locate the generator.

Wai plodded after Roman as he followed a cable running down the center of a corridor on the eighth deck.

"It's got so many secondary feeds it looks like a fishbone," he complained. They paused at a junction with five branches, and he swept the block around. "This way." He started off down one of the new corridors.

"We're heading towards stairwell five," she told him, as the layout file scrolled through her skull.

There were more cybermice than usual on deck eight; over 30 were currently pursuing her and Roman, creating strong ripples in the composite floor and walls. Wai had noticed that the deeper she went into the ship the more of them there seemed to be. Although after her second trip she'd completely ignored them. She wasn't paying a lot of attention to the compartments leading off from the corridors, either. It wasn't that they were all the same, rather that they were all similarly empty.

They reached the stairwell, and Roman stepped inside. "It's going down," he datavised.

"Great, that means we've got another level to climb up when we're finished."

Not that going down these stairs was easy, she acknowledged charily. If only they could find some kind of variable gravity chute. Perhaps they'd all been positioned in the part of the ship that was destroyed.

"You know, I think Marcus might have been right about the dish being an emergency beacon," she datavised. "I can't think of any other reason for it being built. Believe me, I've tried."

"He always is right. It's bloody annoying, but that's why I fly with him."

"I was against it because of the faith gap."

"Say what?"

"The amount of faith these xenocs must have had in themselves. It's awesome. So different from humans. Think about it. Even if their homeworld is only 2,000 light-years away, that's how long the message is going to take to reach there. Yet they sent it believing someone would still be around to receive it, and more, act on it. Suppose that was us; suppose the *Lady Mac* had an accident a thousand light-years away. Would you think there was any point in sending a lightspeed message to the Confederation, then going into zero-tau to wait for a rescue ship?"

"If their technology can last that long, then I guess their civilization can, too."

"No, our hardware can last for a long time. It's our culture that's fragile, at least compared to theirs. I don't think the Confederation will last a thousand years."

"The Edenists will be here, I expect. So will all the planets, physically if nothing else. Some of their societies will advance, possibly even to a state similar to the Kiint; some will revert to barbarism. But there will be somebody left to hear the message and help."

"You're a terrible optimist."

They arrived at the ninth deck, only to find the doorway was sealed over with composite.

"Odd," Roman datavised. "If there's no corridor or compartment beyond, why put a doorway here at all?"

"Because this was a change made after the accident."

"Could be. But why would they block off an interior section?"

"I've no idea. You want to keep going down?"

"Sure. I'm optimistic enough not to believe in ghosts lurking in the basement."

"I really wish you hadn't said that."

The tenth deck had been sealed off as well.

"My legs can take one more level," Wai datavised. "Then I'm going back."

There was a door on deck 11. It was the first one in the ship to be closed.

Wai stuck her fingers in the dimple, and the door dilated. She edged over cautiously, and swept the focus of her collar sensors around. "Holy shit. We'd better fetch Marcus."

Decks nine and ten had simply been removed to make the chamber. Standing on the floor and looking up, Marcus could actually see the outline of the stairwell doorways in the wall above him. By xenoc standards it was a cathedral. There was only one altar, right in the center. A doughnut of some dull metallic substance, eight meters in diameter with a central aperture five meters across; the air around it was emitting a faint violet glow. It stood on five sableblack arching buttresses, four meters tall.

"The positioning must be significant," Wai datavised. "They built it almost at the center of the wreck. They wanted to give it as much protection as possible."

"Agreed," Katherine replied. "They obviously considered it important. After a ship has suffered this much damage, you don't expend resources on anything other than critical survival requirements."

"Whatever it is," Schutz reported. "It's using up an awful lot of power." He was walking around it, keeping a respectful distance, wiping a sensor block over the floor as he went. "There's a power cable feeding each of those legs."

"Is it radiating in any spectrum?" Marcus asked.

"Only that light you can see, which spills over into ultraviolet, too. Apart from that, it's inert. But the energy must be going somewhere."

"Okay." Marcus walked up to a buttress, and switched his collar focus to scan the aperture. It was veiled by a gray haze, as if a sheet of fog had solidified across it. When he took another tentative step forward the fluid in his semicircular canals was suddenly affected by a very strange tidal force. His foot began to slip forwards and upwards. He threw himself backwards, and almost stumbled. Jorge and Karl just caught him in time.

"There's no artificial gravity underneath it," he datavised. "But there's some kind of gravity field wrapped around it." He paused. "No, that's not right. It pushed me."

"Pushed?" Katherine hurried to his side. "Are you sure?"

"Yes."

"My God."

"What? Do you know what it is?"

"Possibly. Schutz, hang on to my arm, please."

The cosmonik came forward and took her left arm. Katherine edged forward until she was almost under the lambent doughnut. She stretched up her right arm, holding out a sensor block, and tried to press it against the doughnut. It was as if she was trying to make two identical magnetic poles touch. The block couldn't get to within 20 centimeters of the surface; it kept slithering and sliding through the air. She held it as steady as she could, and datavised it to run an analysis of the doughnut's molecular structure.

The results made her back away.

"So?" Marcus asked.

"I'm not entirely sure it's solid in any reference frame we understand. That surface could just be a boundary effect. There's no spectroscopic data at all; the sensor couldn't even detect an atomic structure in there, let alone valency bonds."

"You mean it's a ring of energy?"

"Don't hold me to it, but I think that thing could be some kind of exotic matter."

"Exotic in what sense, exactly?" Jorge asked.

"It has a negative energy density. And before you ask, that doesn't mean antigravity. Exotic matter only has one known use, to keep a wormhole open."

"Jesus, that's a wormhole portal?" Marcus asked.

"It must be."

"Any way of telling where it leads?"

"I can't give you an exact stellar coordinate; but I know where the other end has to emerge. The xenocs never called for a rescue ship, Marcus. They threaded a wormhole with exotic matter to stop it collapsing, and escaped down it. That is the entrance to a tunnel which leads right back to their homeworld."

Schutz found Marcus in the passenger lounge in capsule C. He was floating centimeters above one of the flatchairs, with the lights down low.

The cosmonik touched his heels to a stikpad on the decking beside the lower hatch. "You really don't like being wrong, do you?"

"No, but I'm not sulking about it, either." Marcus molded a jaded grin. "I still think I'm right about the dish, but I don't know how the hell to prove it."

"The wormhole portal is rather conclusive evidence."

"Very tactful. It doesn't solve anything, actually. If they could open a wormhole straight back home, why did they build the dish? Like Katherine said, if you have an accident of that magnitude then you devote yourself completely to survival. Either they called for help, or they went home through the wormhole. They wouldn't do both."

"Possibly it wasn't their dish, they were just here to investigate it."

"Two ancient unknown xenoc races with FTL starship technology is pushing credibility. It also takes us back to the original problem: if the dish isn't a distress beacon, then what the hell was it built for?"

"I'm sure there will be an answer at some time."

"I know, we're only a commercial trader's crew, with a very limited research capability. But we can still ask fundamental questions, like why have they kept the wormhole open for 13,000 years?"

"Because that's the way their technology works. They probably wouldn't consider it odd."

"I'm not saying it shouldn't work for that long, I'm asking why their homeworld would bother maintaining a link to a chunk of derelict wreckage?"

"That is harder for logic to explain. The answer must lie in their psychology."

"That's a cop out; you can't simply cry alien at everything you don't understand. But it does bring us to my final query, if you can open a wormhole with such accuracy across God knows how many light-years, why would you need a starship in the first place? What sort of psychology accounts for that?"

"All right, Marcus, you got me. Why?"

"I haven't got a clue. I've been reviewing all the file texts we have on wormholes, trying to find a solution which pulls all this together. And I can't do it. It's a complete paradox."

"There's only one thing left then, isn't there?"

Marcus turned to look at the hulking figure of the cosmonik. "What?"

"Go down the wormhole and ask them."

"Yeah, maybe I will. Somebody has to go eventually. What does our dear Katherine have to say on that subject? Can we go inside it in our S11 suits?"

"She's rigging up some sensors that she can shove through the interface. That gray sheet isn't a physical barrier. She's already pushed a length of conduit tubing through. It's some kind of pressure membrane, apparently, stops the ship's atmosphere from flooding into the wormhole."

"Another billion-fuseodollar gadget. Jesus, this is getting too big for us, we're going to have to prioritize." He datavised the flight computer, and issued a general order for everyone to assemble in capsule A's main lounge.

Karl was the last to arrive. The young systems engineer looked exhausted. He frowned when he caught sight of Marcus.

"I thought you were over in the xenoc ship."

"No."

"But you . . ." He rubbed his fingers against his temples. "Skip it."

"Any progress?" Marcus asked.

"A little. From what I can make out, the molecular synthesizer and its governing circuitry are combined within the same crystal lattice. To give you a biological analogy, it's as though a muscle is also a brain."

"Don't follow that one through too far," Roman called.

Karl didn't even smile. He took a chocolate sac from the dispenser, and sucked on the nipple.

"Katherine?" Marcus said.

"I've managed to place a visual-spectrum sensor in the wormhole. There's not much light in there, only what soaks through the pressure membrane. From what we can see it's a straight tunnel. I assume the xenocs cut off the artificial gravity under the portal so they could egress it easily. What I'd like to do next is dismount a laser radar from the MSV and use that."

"If the wormhole's threaded with exotic matter, will you get a return from it?"

"Probably not. But we should get a return from whatever is at the other end."

"What's the point?"

Three of them began to talk at once, Katherine loudest of all. Marcus held his hand up for silence. "Listen, everybody, according to Confederation law if the appointed commander or designated controlling mechanism of a spaceship or free-flying space structure discontinues that control for one year and a day then any ownership title becomes null and void. Legally, this xenoc ship is an abandoned structure which we are entitled to file a salvage claim on."

"There is a controlling network," Karl said.

"It's a sub-system," Marcus said. "The law is very clear on that point.

If a starship's flight computer fails, but, say, the fusion generators keep working, their governing processors do not constitute the designated controlling mechanism. Nobody will be able to challenge our claim."

"The xenocs might," Wai said.

"Let's not make extra problems for ourselves. As the situation stands right now, we have title. We can't not claim the ship because the xenocs may return at some time."

Katherine rocked her head in understanding. "If we start examining the wormhole they might come back, sooner rather than later. Is that what you're worried about?"

"It's a consideration, yes. Personally, I'd rather like to meet them. But, Katherine, are you really going to learn how to build exotic matter and open a wormhole with the kind of sensor blocks we've got?"

"You know I'm not, Marcus."

"Right. Nor are we going to find the principle behind the artificial gravity generator, or any of the other miracles on board. What we have to do is catalogue as much as we can, and identify the areas that need researching. Once we've done that we can bring back the appropriate specialists, pay them a huge salary, and let them get on with it. Don't any of you understand yet? When we found this ship, we stopped being starship crew, and turned into the highest-flying corporate executives in the galaxy. We don't pioneer any more, we designate. So, we map out the last remaining decks. We track the power cables and note what they power. Then we leave."

"I know I can crack their program language, Marcus," Karl said. "I can get us into the command network."

Marcus smiled at the weary pride in his voice. "Nobody is going to be more pleased about that than me, Karl. One thing I do intend to take with us is a cybermouse, preferably more than one. That molecular synthesizer is the hard evidence we need to convince the banks of what we've got."

Karl blushed. "Uh, Marcus, I don't know what'll happen if we try and cut one out of the composite. So far we've been left alone; but if the network thinks we're endangering the ship. Well . . ."

"I'd like to think we're capable of something more sophisticated than ripping a cybermouse out of the composite. Hopefully, you'll be able to access the network, and we can simply ask it to replicate a molecular synthesizer unit for us. They have to be manufactured somewhere on board."

"Yeah, I suppose they do. Unless the cybermice duplicate themselves."

"Now that'd be a sight," Roman said happily. "One of them humping away on top of the other."

His neural nanonics time function told Karl he'd slept for nine hours. After he wriggled out of his sleep pouch he airswam into the crew lounge and helped himself to a pile of food sachets from the galley. There wasn't much activity in the ship, so he didn't even bother to access the flight computer until he'd almost finished eating.

Katherine was on watch when he dived into the bridge through the floor hatch.

"Who's here?" he asked breathlessly. "Who else is on board right now?"

"Just Roman. The rest of them are all over on the wreck. Why?"

"Shit."

"Why, what's the matter?"

"Have you accessed the flight computer?"

"I'm on watch, of course I'm accessing."

"No, not the ship's functions. The satellite analysis network Victoria set up."

Her flat features twisted into a surprised grin. "You mean they've found some gold?"

"No way. The network was reporting that satellite seven had located a target deposit three hours ago. When I accessed the network direct to follow it up I found out what the search parameters really are. They're not looking for gold, those bastards are here to get pitchblende."

"Pitchblende?" Katherine had to run a search program through her neural nanonics encyclopedia to find out what it was. "Oh Christ, uranium. They want uranium."

"Exactly. You could never mine it from a planet without the local government knowing; that kind of operation would be easily spotted by the observation satellites. Asteroids don't have deposits of pitchblende. But planetoids do, and out here nobody is going to know that they're scooping it up."

"I knew it! I bloody knew that fable about gold mountains was a load of balls."

"They must be terrorists, or Sonora independence freaks, or black syndicate members. We have to warn the others, we can't let them back on board *Lady Mac*."

"Wait a minute, Karl. Yes, they're shits, but if we leave them over on the wreck they'll die. Even if you're prepared to do that, it's the captain's decision."

"No, it isn't, not any more. If they come back then neither you, me, nor the captain is going to be in any position to make decisions about anything. They knew we'd find out about the pitchblende eventually when *Lady Mac* rendezvoused with the ore particle. They knew we wouldn't take it on board voluntarily. That means they came fully prepared to force us. They've got guns, or weapons implants. Jorge is exactly what I said he was, a mercenary killer. We can't let them back on the ship, Katherine. We can't."

"Oh Christ." She was gripping the side of her acceleration couch in reflex. Command decision. And it was all hers.

"Can we datavise the captain?" he asked.

"I don't know. We've got relay blocks in the stairwells now the cybermice have been deactivated, but they're not very reliable; the structure plays hell with our signals."

"Who's he with?"

"He was partnering Victoria. Wai and Schutz are together; Antonio and Jorge made up the last team."

"Datavise Wai and Schutz, get them out first. Then try for the captain."

"Okay. Get Roman, and go down to the airlock chamber; I'll authorize the weapons cabinet to release some maser carbines . . . Shit!"

"What?"

"I can't. Marcus has the flight computer command codes. We can't even fire the thrusters without him."

Deck 14 appeared no different to any other as Marcus and Victoria wandered through it. The corridors were broad, and there were few doorways.

"About 60 per cent is sealed off," Marcus datavised. "This must be a major engineering level."

"Yeah. There's so many cables around here I'm having trouble cataloguing the grid." She was wiping a magnetic sensor block slowly from side to side as they walked.

His communication block reported it was receiving an encrypted signal from the *Lady Mac*. Sheer surprise made him halt. He retrieved the appropriate code file from a neural nanonics memory cell.

"Captain?"

"What's the problem, Katherine?"

"You've got to get back to the ship. Now, Captain, and make sure Victoria doesn't come with you."

"Why?"

"Captain, this is Karl. The array satellites are looking for pitchblende, not gold or platinum. Antonio's people are terrorists, they want to build fission bombs."

Marcus focused his collar sensors on Victoria, who was waiting a couple of meters down the corridor. "Where's Schutz and Wai?"

"On their way back," Katherine datavised. "They should be here in another five minutes."

"Okay, it's going to take me at least half an hour to get back." He didn't like to think about climbing 14 flights of stairs fast, not in this gravity. "Start prepping the ship."

"Captain, Karl thinks they're probably armed."

Marcus's communication block reported another signal coming on line.

"Karl is quite right," Jorge datavised. "We are indeed armed; and we also have excellent processor blocks and decryption programs. Really, Captain, this code of yours is at least three years out of date."

Marcus saw Victoria turn towards him. "Care to comment on the pitchblende?" he asked.

"I admit, the material would have been of some considerable use to us," Jorge replied. "But of course, this wreck has changed the Confederation beyond recognition, has it not, Captain?"

"Possibly."

"Definitely. And so we no longer require the pitchblende."

"That's a very drastic switch of allegiance."

"Please, Captain, do not be facetious. The satellites were left on purely for your benefit; we didn't wish to alarm you."

"Thank you for your consideration."

"Captain," Katherine datavised. "Schutz and Wai are in the airlock."

"I do hope you're not proposing to leave without us," Jorge datavised. "That would be most unwise."

"You were going to kill us," Karl datavised.

"That is a hysterical claim. You would not have been hurt."

"As long as we obeyed, and helped you slaughter thousands of people."

Marcus wished Karl would stop being quite so blunt. He had few enough options as it was.

"Come now, Captain," Jorge said. "The *Lady Macbeth* is combat-capable; are you telling me you have never killed people in political disputes?"

"We've fought. But only against other ships."

"Don't try and claim the moral high ground, Captain. War is war, no matter how it is fought."

"Only when it's between soldiers; anything else is terrorism."

"I assure you, we have put our old allegiance behind us. I ask you to do the same. This quarrel is foolish in the extreme. We both have so much to gain."

And you're armed, Marcus filled in silently. Jorge and Antonio were supposed to be inspecting decks 12 and 13. It would be tough if not impossible getting back to the airlock before them. But I can't trust them on *Lady Mac.*

"Captain, they're moving," Katherine datavised. "The communication block in stairwell three has acquired them, strength one. They must be coming up."

"Victoria," Jorge datavised. "Restrain the captain and bring him to the airlock. I advise all of you on the ship to remain calm, we can still find a peaceful solution to this situation."

Unarmed combat programs went primary in Marcus's neural nanonics. The black, featureless figure opposite him didn't move.

"Your call," he datavised. According to his tactical analysis program she had few choices. Jorge's order implied she was armed, though a scan of her utility belt didn't reveal anything obvious other than a standard fission blade. If she went for a gun he would have an attack window. If she didn't, then he could probably stay ahead of her. She was a lot younger, but his geneered physique should be able to match her in this gravity field.

Victoria dropped the sensor block she was carrying, and moved her hand to her belt. She grabbed the multipurpose power tool and started to bring it up.

Marcus slammed into her, using his greater mass to throw her off balance. She was hampered by trying to keep her grip on the tool. His impact made her sway sideways, then the fierce xenoc gravity took over. She toppled helplessly, falling *fast.* The power tool was swinging around to point at him. Marcus kicked her hand, and the unit skittered away. It didn't slide far, the gravity saw to that.

Victoria landed with a terrible thud. Her neural nanonics medical monitor program flashed up an alert that the impact had broken her collar bone. Axon blocks came on line, muting all but the briefest pulse of pain. It was her program again which made her twist around to avoid any follow-on blow; her conscious mind was almost unaware of the fact she was still moving. A hand scrabbled for the power tool. She snatched it and sat up. Marcus was disappearing down a side corridor. She fired at him before the targeting program even gave her an overlay grid.

"Jorge," she datavised. "I've lost him."

"Then get after him."

Marcus's collar sensors showed him a spray of incendiary droplets fizzing out of the wall barely a meter behind him. The multipurpose tool must be some kind of laser pistol. "Katherine," he datavised. "Retract

Lady Mac's airlock tube. Now. Close the outer hatch and codelock it. They are not to come on board."

"Acknowledged. How do we get you back?"

"Yes, Captain," Jorge datavised. "Do tell."

Marcus dodged down a junction. "Have Wai stand by. When I need her, I'll need her fast."

"You think you can cut your way out of the shell, Captain? You have a fission blade, and that shell is held together by a molecular bonding generator."

"You touch him, shithead, and we'll fry that wreck," Karl datavised. *"Lady Mac*'s got maser cannons."

"But do you have the command codes, I wonder. Captain?"

"Communication silence," Marcus ordered. "When I want you, I'll call."

Jorge's boosted muscles allowed him to ascend stairwell three at a speed which Antonio could never match. He was soon left struggling along behind. The airlock was the tactical high ground; once he had secured that, Jorge knew he'd won. As he climbed his hands moved automatically, assembling the weapon from various innocuous-looking pieces of equipment he was carrying on his utility belt.

"Victoria?" he datavised. "Have you got him?"

"No. He broke my shoulder, the bastard. I've lost him."

"Go to the nearest stairwell, I expect that's what he's done. Antonio, go back and meet her. Then start searching for him."

"Is that a joke?" Antonio asked. "He could be anywhere."

"No, he's not. He has to come up. Up is where the airlock is."

"Yes, but—"

"Don't argue. And when you find him, don't kill him. We have to have him alive. He's our ticket out. Our only ticket, understand?"

"Yes, Jorge."

When he reached the airlock, Jorge closed the inner hatch and cycled the chamber. The outer hatch dilated to show him the *Lady Macbeth*'s fuselage 15 meters away. Her airlock tube had retracted, and the fuselage shield was in place.

"This is a no-win stand-off," he datavised. "Captain, please come up to the airlock. You have to deal with me, you have no choice. The three of us will leave our weapons over here, and then we can all go back on board together. And when we return to a port none of us will mention this unfortunate incident again. That is reasonable, surely?"

Schutz had just reached the bridge when they received Jorge's datavise.

"Damn! He's disconnected our cable from the communication block," Karl said. "We can't call the captain now even if we wanted to."

Schutz rolled in mid air above his acceleration couch and landed gently on the cushioning. Restraint webbing slithered over him.

"What the hell do we do now?" Roman asked. "Without the command codes we're bloody helpless."

"It wouldn't take that long for us to break open the weapons cabinet," Schutz said. "They haven't got the captain. We can go over there and hunt them down with the carbines."

"I can't sanction that," Katherine said. "God knows what sort of weapons they have."

"Sanction it? We put it to the vote."

"It's my duty watch. Nobody votes on anything. The last order the captain gave us was to wait. We wait." She datavised the flight computer for a channel to the MSV. Wai, status please?"

"Powering up. I'll be ready for a flight in two minutes."

"Thank you."

"We have to do something!" Karl said.

"For a start you can calm down," Katherine told him. "We're not going to help Marcus by doing anything rash. He obviously had something in mind when he told Wai to get ready."

The hatchway to the captain's cabin slid open. Marcus air-swam out and grinned around at their stupefied expressions. "Actually, I didn't have any idea what to do when I said that. I was stalling."

"How the hell did you get back on board?" Roman yelped.

Marcus looked at Katherine and gave her a lopsided smile. "By being right, I'm afraid. The dish is a distress beacon."

"So what?" she whispered numbly.

He drifted over to his acceleration couch and activated the webbing. "It means the wormhole doesn't go back to the xenoc homeworld."

"You found out how to use it!" Karl exclaimed. "You opened its other end inside the *Lady Mac*."

"No. There is no other end. Yes, they built it as part of their survival operation. It was their escape route, you were right about that. But it doesn't go somewhere; it goes some*when*."

Instinct had brought Marcus to the portal chamber. It was as good as any other part of the ship. Besides, the xenocs had escaped their predicament from here. In a remote part of his mind he assumed that ending up on their homeworld was preferable to capture here by Jorge. It wasn't the kind of choice he wanted to make.

He walked slowly around the portal. The pale violet emanation in the air around it remained constant, hazing the dull surface from perfect observation. That and a faint hum were the only evidence of the massive quantity of power it consumed. Its eternal stability a mocking enigma.

Despite all the logic of argument he knew Katherine was wrong. Why build the dish if you had this ability? And why keep it operational?

That factor must have been important to them. It had been built in the center of the ship, and built to last. They'd even reconfigured the wreck to ensure it lasted. Fine, they needed reliability, and they were masters of material science. But a one-off piece of emergency equipment lasting 13,000 years? There must be a reason, and the only logical one was that they knew they would need it to remain functional so they could come back one day.

The SII suit prevented him from smiling as realization dawned. But it did reveal a shiver ripple along his limbs as the cold wonder of the knowledge struck home.

On the *Lady Mac*'s bridge, Marcus said: "We originally assumed that the xenocs would just go into zero-tau and wait for a rescue ship; because that's what we would do. But their technology allows them to take a much different approach to engineering problems."

"The wormhole leads into the future," Roman said in astonishment.

"Almost. It doesn't lead anywhere but back to itself, so the length inside it represents time not space. As long as the portal exists you can travel through it. The xenocs went in just after they built the dish and came out again when their rescue ship arrived. That's why they built the portal to survive so long. It had to carry them through a great deal of time."

"How does that help you get here?" Katherine asked. "You're trapped over in the xenoc wreckage right now, not in the past."

"The wormhole exists as long as the portal does. It's an open tube to every second of that entire period of existence; you're not restricted which way you travel through it."

In the portal chamber Marcus approached one of the curving black buttress legs. The artificial gravity was off directly underneath the doughnut so the xenocs could rise into it. But they had been intent on traveling into the future.

He started to climb the buttress. The first section was the steepest; he had to clamp his hands behind it, and haul himself up. Not easy in that gravity field. It gradually curved over, flattening out at the top, leaving him standing above the doughnut. He balanced there precariously, very aware of the potentially lethal fall down onto the floor.

The doughnut didn't look any different from this position, a glowing ring surrounding the gray pressure membrane. Marcus put one foot over the edge of the exotic matter, and jumped.

He fell clean through the pressure membrane. There was no gravity field in the wormhole, although every movement suddenly became very sluggish. To his waving limbs it felt as if he was immersed in some kind of fluid, though his sensor block reported a perfect vacuum.

The wormhole wall was insubstantial, difficult to see in the meager backscatter of light from the pressure membrane. Five narrow lines of yellow light materialized, spaced equidistantly around the wall. They stretched from the rim of the pressure membrane up to a vanishing point some indefinable distance away.

Nothing else happened. Marcus drifted until he reached the wall, which his hand adhered to as though the entire surface was one giant stikpad. He crawled his way back to the pressure membrane. When he stuck his hand through, there was no resistance. He pushed his head out.

There was no visible difference to the chamber outside. He datavised his communication block to search for a signal. It told him there was only the band from one of the relay blocks in the stairwells. No time had passed.

He withdrew back into the wormhole. Surely the xenocs hadn't expected to crawl along the entire length? In any case, the other end would be 13,000 years ago. Marcus retrieved the xenoc activation code from his neural nanonics, and datavised it.

The lines of light turned blue.

He quickly datavised the deactivation code, and the lines reverted to yellow. This time when he emerged out into the portal chamber there was no signal at all.

"That was ten hours ago," Marcus told his crew. "I climbed out and walked back to the ship. I passed you on the way, Karl."

"Holy shit," Roman muttered. "A time machine."

"How long was the wormhole active for?" Katherine asked.

"A couple of seconds, that's all."

"Ten hours in two seconds." She paused, loading sums into her neural nanonics. "That's a year in 30 minutes. Actually, that's not so fast. Not if they were intending to travel a couple of thousand years into the future."

"You're complaining about it?" Roman asked.

"Maybe it speeds up the further you go through it," Schutz suggested. "Or more likely we need the correct access codes to vary its speed."

"Whatever," Marcus said. He datavised the flight computer and blew the tether bolts which were holding *Lady Mac* to the wreckage. "I want flight-readiness status, people, please."

"What about Jorge and the others?" Karl asked.

"They only come back on board under our terms," Marcus said. "No weapons, and they go straight into zero-tau. We can hand them over to Tranquillity's serjeants as soon as we get home." Purple course vectors were rising into his mind. He fired the maneuvering thrusters, easing *Lady Mac* clear of the xenoc shell.

Jorge saw the sparkle of bright dust as the explosive bolts fired. He scanned his sensor collar around until he found the tethers, narrow gray serpents flexing against the speckled backdrop of drab orange particles. It didn't bother him unduly. Then the small thrusters ringing the starship's equator fired, pouring out translucent amber plumes of gas.

"Katherine, what do you think you're doing?" he datavised.

"Following my orders," Marcus replied. "She's helping to prep the ship for a jump. Is that a problem for you?"

Jorge watched the starship receding, an absurdly stately movement for an artifact that big. His respirator tube seemed to have stopped supplying fresh oxygen, paralyzing every muscle. "Calvert. How?" he managed to datavise.

"I might tell you some time. Right now, there are a lot of conditions you have to agree to before I allow you back on board."

Pure fury at being so completely outmaneuvered by Calvert made him reach automatically for his weapon. "You will come back now," he datavised.

"You're not in any position to dictate terms."

Lady Macbeth was a good 200 meters away. Jorge lined the stubby barrel up on the rear of the starship. A green targeting grid flipped up over the image, and he zeroed on the nozzle of a fusion drive tube. He datavised the X-ray laser to fire. Pale white vapor spewed out of the nozzle.

"Depressurization in fusion drive three," Roman shouted.

"The lower deflector coil casing is breached. He shot us, Marcus, Jesus Christ, he shot us with an X-ray."

"What the hell kind of weapon has he got back there?" Karl demanded.

"Whatever it is, he can't have the power capacity for many more shots," Schutz said.

"Give me fire control for the maser cannons," Roman said. "I'll blast the little shit."

"Marcus!" Katherine cried. "He just hit a patterning node. Stop him."

Neuroiconic displays zipped through Marcus's mind. Ship's systems coming on line as they shifted over to full operational status, each with its own schematic. He knew just about every performance parameter by heart. Combat sensor clusters were already sliding out of their recesses. Maser cannons powering up. It would be another seven seconds before they could be aimed and fired.

There was one system with a faster response time.

"Hang on," he yelled.

Designed for combat avoidance maneuvers, the fusion drive tubes exploded into life two seconds after he triggered their ignition sequence. Twin spears of solar-bright plasma transfixed the xenoc shell, burning through deck after deck. They didn't even strike anywhere near the airlock which Jorge was cloistered in. They didn't have to. At that range, their infrared emission alone was enough to break down his SII suit's integrity.

Superenergized ions hammered into the wreck, smashing the internal structure apart, heating the atmosphere to an intolerable pressure. Xenoc machinery detonated in tremendous energy bursts all through the structure, the units expending themselves in spherical clouds of solid light which clashed and merged into a single wavefront of destruction. The giant rock particle lurched wildly from the explosion. Drenched in a cascade of hard radiation and subatomic particles, the unicorn tower at the center of the dish snapped off at its base to tumble away into the darkness.

Then the process seemed to reverse. The spume of light blossoming from the cliff curved in on itself, growing in brightness as it was compressed back to its point of origin.

Lady Mac's crew were straining under the five-gee acceleration of the starship's flight. The inertial guidance systems started to flash priority warnings into Marcus's neural nanonics.

"We're going back," he datavised. Five gees made talking too difficult. "Jesus, five gees and it's still pulling us in." The external sensor suite showed him the contracting fireball, its luminosity surging towards violet. Large sections of the cliff were flaking free and plummeting into the conflagration. Fissures like black lightning bolts split open right across the rock.

He ordered the flight computer to power up the nodes and retract the last sensor clusters.

"Marcus, we can't jump," Katherine datavised, her face pummelled into frantic creases by the acceleration. "It's a gravitonic emission. Don't."

"Have some faith in the old girl." He initiated the jump.

An event horizon eclipsed the *Lady Macbeth*'s fuselage.

Behind her, the wormhole at the heart of the newborn micro-star gradually collapsed, pulling in its gravitational field as it went. Soon there was nothing left but an expanding cloud of dark snowdust embers.

They were three jumps away from Tranquillity when Katherine ventured into Marcus's cabin. *Lady Mac* was accelerating at a tenth of a gee towards her next jump coordinate, holding him lightly in one of the large blackfoam sculpture chairs. It was the first time she'd ever really noticed his age.

"I came to say sorry," she said. "I shouldn't have doubted."

He waved limply. "*Lady Mac* was built for combat, her nodes are powerful enough to jump us out of some gravity fields. Not that I had a lot of choice. Still, we only reduced three nodes to slag, plus the one dear old Jorge damaged."

"She's a hell of ship, and you're the perfect captain for her. I'll keep flying with you, Marcus."

"Thanks. But I'm not sure what I'm going to do after we dock. Replacing three nodes will cost a fortune. I'll be in debt to the banks again."

She pointed at the row of transparent bubbles which all held identical antique electronic circuit boards. "You can always sell some more Apollo command module guidance computers."

"I think that scam's just about run its course. Don't worry, when we get back to Tranquillity I know a captain who'll buy them from me. At least that way I'll be able to settle the flight pay I owe all of you."

"For Heaven's sake, Marcus, the whole astronautics industry is in debt to the banks. I swear I never could understand the economics behind starflight."

He closed his eyes, a wry smile quirking his lips. "We very nearly solved human economics for good, didn't we?"

"Yeah. Very nearly."

"The wormhole would have let me change the past. Their technology was going to change the future. We could have rebuilt our entire history."

"I don't think that's a very good idea. What about the grandfather paradox for a start? How come you didn't warn us about Jorge as soon as you emerged from the wormhole?"

"Scared, I guess. I don't know nearly enough about quantum temporal displacement theory to start risking paradoxes. I'm not even sure I'm the Marcus Calvert that brought this particular *Lady Macbeth* to the xenoc wreck. Suppose you really can't travel between times, only parallel realities? That would mean I didn't escape into the past, I just shifted sideways."

"You look and sound pretty familiar to me."

"So do you. But is my crew still stuck back at their version of the wreck waiting for me to deal with Jorge?"

"Stop it," she said softly. "You're Marcus Calvert, and you're back where you belong, flying *Lady Mac.*"

"Yeah, sure."

"The xenocs wouldn't have built the wormhole unless they were sure it would help them get home, their true home. They were smart people."

"And no mistake."

"I wonder where they did come from?"

"We'll never know, now." Marcus lifted his head, some of the old humor emerging through his melancholia. "But I hope they got back safe."

Mary Rosenblum

THE EYE OF GOD

One of the most popular and prolific of the new writers of the nineties, Mary Rosenblum made her first sale, to *Asimov's Science Fiction,* in 1990, and has since become a mainstay of that magazine, and one of its most frequent contributors, with more than twenty-five sales there to her credit. She has also sold to *The Magazine of Fantasy & Science Fiction, Science Fiction Age, Pulphouse, New Legends,* and elsewhere.

Rosenblum has produced some of the most colorful, exciting, and emotionally powerful stories of the nineties, earning her a large and devoted following of readers. Her linked series of "Drylands" stories have proved to be one of *Asimov's* most popular series, but she has also published memorable stories such as "The Stone Garden," "Synthesis," "Flight," "California Dreamer," "Casting at Pegasus," "Entrada," "Rat," "The Centaur Garden," and many, many others. Her novella "Gas Fish" won the *Asimov's* Readers Award Poll in 1996, and was a finalist for that year's Nebula Award. Her first novel, *The Drylands,* appeared in 1993 to wide critical acclaim, winning the prestigious Compton Crook Award for Best First Novel of the year; it was followed in short order by her second novel, *Chimera,* and her third, *The Stone Garden.* Her most recent book was her first short-story collection, *Synthesis and Other Stories,* widely hailed by critics as one of the best collections of 1996. She recently sold a trilogy of mystery novels under a pseudonym, and has just finished the first book in the series, *The Devil's Trumpet.*

Most of Rosenblum's work has a strong adventure element, but only recently has she started taking us away from future Earths of one sort or another and out among the stars, in stories such as "Gas Fish" and the exciting and exotic adventure that follows, "The Eye of God." In it she takes us to a remote and hostile planet where human and alien antagonists must fight a battle of wits and will and nerve with the lives of the contestants literally hanging by a thread (over a thousand-foot drop!), with the destiny of the human race and the redemption of an individual's soul at stake. . . .

Rosenblum is another young and prolific writer who works very hard and with great discipline, and if she doesn't vanish into the mystery world completely to become the new Agatha Christie, it will be very interesting to see what directions she moves in and what she produces in the years to come; whatever it is, I'm sure it will be as vivid and compulsively readable as the rest of her work has been. A graduate of Clarion West, Mary Rosenblum lives with her family in Portland, Oregon.

The coral-reeds' agitation alerted her. Etienne came out onto the porch of her cottage to watch three Rethe wade through the thick blue-green stems. From this distance, they could have been three tall women, as human as herself. The coral-reeds stirred at their passage, the anxious rasp of their stems like distant whispering—words at the bare edge of comprehension.

She had never expected to see Rethe here. Etienne swallowed, fighting back memories that she had banished years ago. For a moment she entertained the hope that this visit was a mistake, or some kind of minor bureaucratic ritual.

She knew better.

Abruptly, she turned on her heel, and went inside to make tea. The Rethe would drink tea. That much at least humanity knew about them.

Etienne filled the teapot and arranged fruit-flavored gels on a plate. She had bought them in the shabby squatter village that had grown up around the Gate. Vat-grown in someone's back yard as masses of amorphous cells, the orange and ruby cubes bore no resemblance to apricot or cherries except taste. The plants on this world—or sessile animals that photosynthesized—did not bear fruit. She missed apples the most—crisp and tart after a frost. Vilya had bought her a miniature apple tree in a pot. For their balcony. It was a winesap—a true genetic antique. She had never gone back for it.

Etienne realized that she was arranging and rearranging the gels on their plate, and took her hand away. Outside, the reeds rustled softly. The squatters ate them—cracked their silicaceous stems and sucked out the flesh inside. They turned your urine orange, but they didn't make you sick.

She had never eaten one. Sometimes Etienne entertained the fantasy that that was the reason for the whispering meadow of the creatures that had formed around her cottage. Anthropomorphism, she thought. A seductive danger, in her profession as interpreter of aliens.

Her former profession.

Angry at herself for this lapse into yesterday, Etienne picked up the tray of tea, gels, and utensils. The Rethe were waiting for her on the shaded porch. Politely. Patiently. They nodded in unison as she came through the door, and Etienne froze. Memory was optional. Life went on for a long time, and yesterdays gathered like dust in the cramped vault of the human skull. You could go to a reputable body shop and have a well-trained tech in sterile greens sweep it all away. Or, for more money, you could have them sweep out only selected bits. Memory could be tucked, tightened, and tailored, as easily as any other part of the body.

She had never chosen to excise Vilya from her memory. Etienne set the tray down on the small table so hard that tea slopped over beneath the pot's lid. Staring at the smallest of the Rethe—the one who stood at the rear, right on the boundary between shade and searing sun—Etienne wished suddenly that she had done so.

First real contact with an alien species, the Rethe disturbed humanity. Not because they were creepy nightmares or incomprehensible monsters. That might have been easier to take. But they looked utterly human. And utterly female, although each individual possessed three X and three Y chromosomes. Gender was one of the many things about themselves that the Rethe refused to discuss. All humans and Rethe were referred to as "it" in translated conversation.

The small Rethe whose wide face was slashed by sun and shadow looked utterly like Vilya.

Etienne looked down at the amber puddle soaking into the napkins she had laid out on the tray. "Would you care for tea?"

The oldest of the Rethe—at least her . . . his? . . . face looked oldest—extended a hand, palm up. A small iridescent vial lay on her . . . his? . . . palm.

She, Etienne decided as she scowled at the vial. They were all *she,* and to hell with their chromosomal makeup. The vial contained a fungus that would infiltrate her ear canal, growing mycocelia through her skull within minutes to interface directly with her brain. A translator, it was a bit of Rethe bio-tech, and as yet incomprehensible. But necessary. Because the Rethe weren't about to share their language, or waste their time learning humanity's dialects. The Rethe was waiting silently, *her* eyes on Etienne's face, smiling.

Impatient behind that smile. "No need." Etienne arched an eyebrow. "I was infected nearly two decades ago. As you must surely know, if you checked me out at all."

The eldest Rethe bowed, still smiling. Dropped the vial into a pocket in her loose robe. "I hope you will pardon our intrusion."

"You're pardoned." Etienne began to fill mugs. "So why are you here?"

"Retirement from public service must provide many benefits." The Rethe lifted her steaming mug in a small salute. "Not the least of which is the privilege to be rude."

"I didn't retire. I quit. Yes, I'm rude." Etienne sat down in the only chair and smiled up at the Rethe. Waiting.

For several minutes the Rethe sipped their tea, their expressions relaxed and appreciative, as if they had come all this way in the hot sun to savor her cheap tea, bought from the squatters. But their impatience hummed in the air and made the nearest coral-reeds shiver.

At last, the eldest Rethe sank gracefully to the fabbed-wood planks of the porch and folded her legs into lotus position. "I am Grik." She nodded at the two Rethe behind her. "Rynn and Zynth."

Zynth was the one who might have been Vilya's twin. Etienne turned her eyes away as that one sat down. The loose garments that the Rethe wore hinted at solid bone and sleek, thickly muscled bodies. Peasant body, Vilya used to say of her stocky form. Etienne clenched her teeth and made a show of arranging her caftan. "Since I am entitled to be rude, why *are* you here?"

"To hire you." Grik reached for a cherry gel. "It is a matter of rescue."

"I . . . am no longer a registered empath. As you obviously know. And I retired from Search and Rescue last year." Etienne offered the plate of gels to the other two Rethe. The one called Rynn declined with a smile and nod. Zynth gave her boss a quick apprehensive look and took an orange cube.

"And I'm not for hire in any case." Etienne put the plate down on the table with a decisive thump. The girl's diffident air annoyed her. "I'm sorry you wasted your time coming here."

Grik lifted her left hand, palm up, tilted it in a pouring gesture.

Etienne interpreted a shrug from the emotional context. As she reached for her mug of tea, she noticed that Zynth had closed her hand into a fist. Orange gel leaked between her white-knuckled fingers, and the reeds rustled at her anguish.

Basic emotion seemed to be such a universal language, Etienne thought bitterly. Pleasure, anger, pain, and fear. Reeds, and humans, and Rethe. Etienne looked at Grik, who was smiling gently.

"Your superior at the Interface Center referred us to you," she said. "It told us that you were the best empath it had worked with."

"That was long ago." It jolted her that he would remember. He had been angry when she had quit to work for Search and Rescue.

"It said that it was time someone reminded you." She shrugged. "I do not understand what it meant."

Anton. Colonel Xyrus Anton, chief of the Interface Team—the euphemism for the human negotiators with the aloof Rethe. Etienne looked out at the reeds bathing and feeding in the planet's young hot sun. *We need you,* he had yelled at her when she had turned in her resignation. *We need every edge we can get against the Rethe. We never really believed that we'd meet a species more advanced than us. Not in our gut. Look what it's doing to us. Our morale as a race is eroding all over the planet. This is a war, and we need to win.* "I don't understand either," she murmured. "But it doesn't matter."

"One of your . . . creators of art became a friend to one of our people." Grik went on as if Etienne hadn't spoken. "Its sincerity was apparently impressive. So that one offered it access to a world we have not opened to your species."

"You haven't opened many worlds to us."

The Rethe did the pouring-gesture again. "The art-creator was lost there in a tragic accident."

"There are several registered empaths working for Search and Rescue." Etienne watched the Rethe narrowly. "Why *me?* We are back to that question."

"According to your datafile, you are a very intelligent human." Grik placed her hands palm up on her thighs, her eyes shifting very slightly toward the young Zynth. "Do I truly need to answer this question for you?"

Zynth sat with her head bowed, pale, her anguish an almost palpable mist. The reeds had inched away from her, leaving a semicircle of clear soil beyond her. Etienne knew suddenly who had invited the artist onto a forbidden world.

"You closely control the Gates—allow us onto only a few poor planets. Like this one. Only the culls for us humans, eh? And you won't transport extraction technology for us—in the name of environmental concern." Etienne turned back to Grik, teeth bared. "We accept that limitation because you awed us. And because we can't operate the Gates without you." She smiled. "If you go to a registered empath, the media will surely find out about this . . . art-creator. And interview him or her. The grass is always greener in someone else's pasture, and now you've let one of us through the fence. We're quite an envious bunch, and we don't stay awed very long." She grinned and reached for a cherry gel. "A species trait, I'm afraid. People will begin to clamor for admittance to these wonderful forbidden worlds and there will be friction. Since our treaty with you is up for renewal this year, friction could be . . . a problem. Thus, you come to an unregistered empath, hoping to keep the media out of it."

The Rethe turned her hands palm down. "We will pay you well," she said. "Ending a life—even accidentally—is no trivial matter to us."

Etienne stole a glance at Zynth. She was looking at Etienne now, fear and desperate hope like a violin note humming on the hot, dusty air. The reeds quivered to its song, and Etienne sighed. "I will not take any money," she said, and wondered how much she was going to regret this.

A synskin habitat had been anchored to a wide terrace cut into a cliff. Below, dark water lapped at the roots of worn ancient mountains. They were capped and streaked with a white deposit that looked more like guano than snow. But it wasn't the severely beautiful landscape that held

Etienne's attention. It was the moon. Huge, bloated, haloed by a pink mist, it floated above the horizon. An irregular brown blotch in the center of the blue and white orb gave it the appearance of a giant, unwinking eye. Beautiful, she thought. Unforgiving. And she shivered, although her light thermal suit kept her warm enough. The habitat shivered too, straining against its anchors.

Behind her, invisible and undetectable to any human tech, lay a Rethe Gateway. Zynth had brought them through. A dozen steps could take Etienne back to summer heat and whispering coral-reeds. But only if Zynth escorted her. The bio-engineering of the Gates didn't work for humans.

This was humanity's humiliation. That the Rethe could walk across the galaxy unhindered and in moments. Human technology didn't so much lag behind—it was as extinct as the dinosaurs. And it left humanity obedient to the Rethe—for the price of the Gateways that the Rethe opened for them. Once, she had been one of the negotiators. They had staffed the Interface Team with empaths, hoping for an edge, a clue as to how the Rethe could be met as equals. It hadn't yet happened. With each renewed Treaty, humanity lost a little more ground, granted a few more concessions. Eventually, they'll own us, Etienne thought cynically. For the price of a few mediocre planets.

Vilya had been fascinated by the Rethe. She had understood them far better than Etienne ever would.

A sudden gust of wind shoved Etienne so that she staggered. That invisible doorway behind her seemed less than real beneath the inhuman scrutiny of that planetary eye. I do not want to be here, she thought.

"The Eye of God." Zynth's voice was clear and high.

She would sing mezzo. Like Vilya. "I wish it would close." Etienne tensed as Zynth laid a gentle hand on her arm. "Please don't touch me." She shook her off.

"Are you well?" Zynth's dark eyes were full of concern.

"Yes, yes, I'm fine." Etienne let her breath out in a rush. "Why couldn't we have come here at the beginning of the day?" She glowered at the girl, needing to be angry at her, because no emotion except anger was safe. "It's too dark to search. Why spend the night here?"

"I . . . am required to be here." Zynth's eyes evaded hers. "Until the artist is found. All life is sacred, and I permitted it to be put at risk. This is a place of truth. Beneath the Eye of God, I must face my failure. Can you understand?" She spread her fingers wide. "But I can open the Gateway for you. You may go back to your home and return in fifteen hours. It will be dawn then. I am thoughtless." She raised her face to the bloated moon. "There is no need for you to be here."

"I'll stay." Etienne turned her back on that unsettling orb, realizing that she had offered to stay because Zynth was afraid. "Who named that thing, anyway? I'd call it the Dead Eye, myself." Etienne stomped over to their habitat, ignoring Zynth's shocked silence. "Why don't you tell me how this person got lost—and where?" She knelt and shoved her way into the sphinctered opening. The transparent smart-plastic squeezed her body gently as she crawled through, blocking out the wind, but not the judgmental stare of the Eye. It's a *moon,* she told herself. A planetoid with weird coloring. But she couldn't deny her relief as she touched the light strip and warm yellow light subdued its glare. "We need to plan our search for the morning," she said as Zynth crawled through the sphincter after her.

As the Rethe began to take off her thermal suit, Etienne pulled a sleeping bag over against the wall and wrapped it around her. Like armor. The sculpted curves of Zynth's muscled arms and shoulders showed through her undershirt. It was warm in here. Thermal fibers were woven into the shell, and Etienne was sweating in her own suit. But she was damned if she'd strip, too.

"I will tell you," Zynth said in a low voice. "It is my shame." She flung herself onto her own bag with a grace so much like Vilya's that Etienne's throat closed.

"So I guessed," she managed, felt immediately guilty as Zynth flinched.

"I met him at our embassy in New Amsterdam." Propped on her elbows, she kept her eyes on the floor. "He had been hired to create several visual environments for the conference center there. The environments . . . moved me. We talked a lot. And one evening I told him about the Eye of Truth, and the song of this place. He . . . asked me to bring him here. The seeing mattered to his soul, so I did." She clenched one fist slowly. "I returned to find this camp empty. Duran was gone. I do not know. . . ."

"Shit!" Etienne slammed her fist down on the synskin floor.

Zynth's eyes widened. "I . . . I am sorry," she stammered, her cheeks flaming. "Grik said that you were . . . friends."

This was *Duran's* bloody camp! He had slept here, breathed the air in here. Etienne got abruptly to her feet, afraid she might catch his scent, some trace of his physical presence. I hope he fell over the damn cliff! she thought savagely. She lifted her head to face the bloated eye staring at her through the shuddering walls of the habitat. That's the truth, she told it silently.

"Etienne, please. I apologize." The anguish in Zynth's voice pierced her.

"Apologize?" Etienne laughed, winced at the cracked sound, and stared down at the kneeling Rethe. "What for?"

Tears streaked Zynth's face and she looked frightened. "For referring to its . . . status," she whispered. "He . . . it . . . told me that it had been the *giver* for a child. And I thought that because you were its friend, you must know." She bowed from the waist until her forehead rested on the floor at Etienne's feet. "I was wrong to be so familiar."

"Sit up. I knew *he* . . . fathered a child." Tight-lipped, Etienne turned away, met the Eye's stare. "I knew very well, thank you. You can call *him* he, or it, or whatever you want. It was his name that startled me. That's all."

"But he is a friend?" Zynth asked eagerly. "That will make it easier for you to find him, perhaps?"

The Eye's stare prodded her and Etienne licked her lips. "I didn't expect to run into him again," she said shortly. Not if she could help it anyway. Interesting that Grik hadn't mentioned his name, since she obviously knew of Etienne's connection to Duran. "So Duran talked you into bringing him here, and you got in trouble for it. That sounds like Duran. Always the opportunist."

"It wasn't . . . like that." Zynth stared at the floor between her knees, her face stricken.

Almost without volition, Etienne reached across the space between them to brush wisps of dark hair from her face. "I'm not angry at you." She let her breath out in a slow sigh. "Really."

"I should never have told it about . . . the Eye."

"Him." Etienne's lips were tight. "Say *him.*"

"Him." Head bowed, Zynth spoke so softly that Etienne could barely make out her words. "He . . . said that he would translate the Eye into sound and vision . . . so that you might know it, too. And . . . I could see the light of the Eye shining in his face as he spoke. So I . . . opened the door for him, even though it is forbidden. And then I came back for him and . . . he was no longer here." She raised her head at last, and her face was composed now. "He could not have passed the Gateway, so he must have fallen. I told Grik."

"Because the Eye was watching?"

"Because life is sacred." Zynth drew herself up straight, then hesitated. "And yes." She bowed her head. "Because the Eye watches."

Etienne sighed. "Will you be punished?"

"This *is* my punishment."

She was afraid. Fear was such a universal. Even the coral-reeds felt fear. "It's just a moon." Etienne put her arm around Zynth's shoulders. "Duran is careless." Careless enough to have cost Vilya her life. "If he fell, it's his own fault."

Zynth flinched at her tone. "I just . . . I have never been . . . in danger."

She began to tremble. "That is one of the things I like most about your race. There are so *many* of you," she said in a nearly inaudible voice. "Is that why you can all walk down the street, have jobs, *do* things? It . . . he . . . Duran told me how he climbed up the sides of mountains. He *risked* himself!"

"Huh?" I should have a recorder, Etienne thought dizzily. We don't know any of this. "I don't understand," she said.

"He is a . . . giver." She blushed. "A breeder? Is that your word? Grik said that because so many of you can create life, none of you really matter to each other." She eyed Etienne apprehensively. "But you can go with anyone you wish, do anything you want, even risk yourself—just like any it of our people. True?"

"We matter to each other. Some of us matter a lot." Was love a universal, like fear? Etienne touched Zynth's cheek lightly. "Can't your people go with anyone they wish?"

"The ones who are *it* can." She hunched her shoulders. "The . . . few who are *he* or *she* . . ." She blushed. ". . . We love. But we can love only one of the cooperative expression. It can be no other way. We . . . are the jewels of our people, treasured by all. We are tomorrow."

We. Etienne was beginning to understand. "What you're saying is that very few of you can breed?" Secretive as they were about their culture, the Rethe were more than open about their physical attributes. They seemed to be potentially hermaphroditic for all their feminine form. Which troubled humanity even more than their female appearance, Etienne thought cynically. Etienne's blush had deepened. Obviously, reproduction was not a topic of casual conversation.

"I'm sorry. I don't mean to embarrass you." Etienne ruffled her hair lightly, then took her hand quickly away. That was how she had touched Vilya when she needed to be teased from one of her dark moods. Beyond the flimsy wall, the Eye glared, reminding her that Duran was here and that this was not Vilya. Did *she* know that he was lost? Etienne wondered suddenly. Duran's daughter?

Vilya's daughter, too.

As if that thought had conjured Duran, she felt him. Or someone. The jagged note of human pain and despair pierced her briefly, then faded, dissipating like smoke in a breeze. Etienne turned, automatically groping to pinpoint the source, responding with years of search and rescue practice. But it had been too brief, too weak, for her to be sure of more than a vague direction.

"What is it? Do you sense him?" Zynth's hands came up, fingers stiffly together. "He is alive? Oh please, he is still alive?"

"Yes." Etienne looked up to meet the Eye's stark gaze. "He's alive. And injured. I don't know how badly."

"He must live." Zynth leaned forward to clutch Etienne's hand. "Your biotechnology is quite good, really. We will find him, and your people will heal him. Where is he?"

"Out there." Etienne nodded at the cliff edge. "I couldn't get an accurate position," she said stiffly. Zynth smelled of cinnamon, with a musky undertone that was unfamiliar, but not repulsive. Not like Vilya at all.

"We will climb down, and then you can hear him better." Zynth began to rummage urgently in the pack she had brought through the Gateway. "Here." She handed Etienne a tangle of neon blue webbing. "You know how to put this on, yes?"

A climbing harness. "You've pried into my entire damn life, haven't you?" Etienne clenched her fingers around the supple webbing, wanting to throw it across the chamber. "I don't climb any more," she said between clenched teeth.

"Grik did the research." Zynth put on her thermal suit, and began to don a second harness. She moved clumsily. "You know *how*. I do not. We cannot use a floater because of the wind."

"If you don't know how to climb, then no way you go over that edge." Etienne crossed her arms.

"It will be safe." Zynth reached for the pack. "We will anchor the line to the top of the cliff. And you will be with me. So I am not afraid at all." Her smile filled her face with beauty. Vilya's face had been filled with the same beauty on that long ago morning when she had propped herself on one elbow in Etienne's bed and whispered *I think I love you.* They had both been so young. So sure.

"No." Etienne swallowed, fighting the images. "Open the Gate for me. I'm leaving. I won't be responsible for your death. Life is sacred to me, too, damn it!"

For a moment, Zynth faced her, head thrown back, face burning with defiance and Vilya's beauty. Then her shoulders slumped, and she turned away. "All right, I'll stay," she whispered, and her hands quivered with defeat. "I am afraid to go without you. Will you go down?"

Etienne nodded and crawled out of the habitat, with Zynth on her heels. Bending into the gusty wind, she snapped the clasps on her harness. Her fingers were trembling. I will get you for this night, she promised Grik silently. Somehow, some day, I will pay you back for doing this to me. Lips tight, she took the anchor drill that Zynth handed her.

"Can you hear him?" Zynth peered over her shoulder as Etienne drilled the anchor into the gray stone well back from the cliff edge.

The rock wanted to fracture. Bad stone for an anchor point, but there wasn't anything better. "I'll listen when I can concentrate." Satisfied at last that the anchor would hold, she threaded the tough thin rope through it and tied it off to her harness.

It moved in her hands and she almost dropped it. Bio-fibers, she realized. Another bit of Rethe biotechnology. The rope was woven of thousands of living fibers that could heal minor injuries and responded to direct stimuli such as stress. She tugged once on the rope, then stepped deliberately to the lip of the chasm. For a heartbeat she hesitated, reluctant to trust herself to this alien rope. Then the wind gusted fiercely, and she swayed with it, leaning outward, with her feet planted firmly on the lip of stone. The rope tensed in her fingers. And held her.

Your small-act-of-defiance ritual, Vilya had dubbed this preliminary testing. Couldn't she have found a better climbing partner? Etienne asked the staring orb of the Eye. Why *Duran?* Just because he had provided chromosomes for her daughter? Or had she been trying to wound Etienne—replacing the expert partner with the novice?

It had cost her her life.

There are a hundred labs that can put a kid together for you, she had yelled during their last fight. They could recombine your own gametes. They could use my DNA and . . . fix what's wrong. Her voice hadn't given her away when she had said that. *Wrong,* because that was how Vilya thought of her empathic talent. As a burden—too much for a child to have to bear.

Vilya had refused to get angry. If we create her, she had said implacably, if some technician snips out sections of your code and replaces them, then what is she? Not you—not me—but our *construct.* I don't want that. I want her to be her own person—not our creation.

You're in love with this Duran, aren't you? Etienne's angry words had scalded her throat. Don't give me that artificial insemination song again either. Maybe I'm a failure, a genetic mutation, but that's not really the issue, is it? You just want to fuck him!

Vilya had walked out of their condo and closed the door gently behind her. That had hurt the worst—that she hadn't even slammed the damn door. Etienne had packed and left that afternoon. She didn't know if Vilya had ever come back to the apartment.

Far below, still water filled the fjord-like channel between this cliff and the rounded mountains beyond. Their blue-white images reflected in water that gleamed purple beneath the baleful glare of the Eye. No wind down there? Maybe the Eye was just trying to blow them off the cliff, she thought bitterly.

She turned around in time to see Zynth lift her face to the Eye, hands weaving a graceful pattern in the air.

Acceptance? Reverence? Worship?

A human empath could read only a few universal emotions. Beyond that, you guessed what the Rethe were really feeling. Zynth's head was bowed now, and Etienne caught the gleam of tears on her face, within the shadow of her thermal suit's hood. Her grief she could be sure of. Without another word, Etienne began to rappel cautiously down the cliff. When you trust your rope, your life seeps into it and it becomes part of you. You feel the solid mass of the anchoring stone, feel the quivering strain in the rope as if it is your own tendon and ligament straining, your fingers wrapped around that ring of steel far above. The biofiber rope tensed like muscle in her gloved hands.

The wind snatched at her, trying to smash her against the wall. Teeth clenched, Etienne fought it. The cliff face was sheer, polished to a smoothness that was eerie. It made her wonder if the damned wind blew forever up here. Grit stung her face and she regretted that she hadn't asked for goggles. The only holds were tiny cracks and uneven protrusions. It would be a bad climb back up.

And he was down there. Duran. She had picked the wrong place to go over—he was off to the right. She wondered if he had tried to climb down—if he was that stupid. From above, Zynth's flash beam probed the darkness, a weak finger of light that didn't penetrate much below Etienne's position.

An eye for an eye. The words shivered through her and Etienne paused for a moment, looked up to meet the Eye's stare. She remembered those words most clearly from her childhood brush with religion: An eye for an eye. A life for a life.

Duran's consciousness was like a whisper in the darkness. His lack of skill had cost Vilya her life. It had cost Vilya's infant daughter a mother. Etienne's groping foot came down hard on a ledge and the shock jarred up through the top of her skull. Standing on the bare meter of polished stone, Etienne listened to the wind and the faint murmur of Duran's dying. Maybe Zynth's flash beam would find him. Maybe not. He wouldn't live much longer. Until daylight?

"Zynth?" She raised her voice. "I hear only wind." Only truth beneath the Eye's stare. She met it, cold inside, maybe cold forever—but everything has a price. "I'm coming back up."

"No." The determination in Zynth's voice pierced Etienne with memory.

You can't quit the team, Vilya had said, again and again, when Etienne got tired of the endless meetings, the familiar boring dance of diplomat circling diplomat. We need to understand the Rethe, we need to learn that we are their equals. If we don't, our spirit will die.

Throat tight, she threaded the loose end of the rope through the auto-brake, and searched the rock face in front of her for a toehold. The living rope quivered and she looked upward. "Stop!" she cried as the dark shape of Zynth backed out over the cliff edge. "Zynth, go back up!"

"I cannot." Zynth's voice was calm. "This is my punishment—that I should risk my life."

"That anchor won't hold us both!" Etienne's fingers clenched uselessly around her own rope. "Zynth! Stop!"

Zynth's foot slipped on the polished stone face. Etienne sucked in a gasping breath as the Rethe skidded downward, but the rope jerked her to a bouncing stop before she had fallen more than three meters. Either she had managed to use the auto-brake but not properly, or this living rope had the ability to stop a fall. "Climb back up," she croaked. "Before the anchor goes. If you have to come down here, I'll put in another anchor. Do it *now.*"

Too late. A gust of wind slammed along the cliff face, striking Etienne like a giant fist. Staggering, gasping for breath, Etienne skidded across the narrow ledge. The rope was stretching, thinning as it took up the strain. Then stone crumbled beneath her, and she dangled briefly over the void. The rope gave. Etienne threw her weight forward, clawing her way onto the ledge.

The anchor was breaking loose. "Climb up!" she screamed into the howling wind. "Damn it, Zynth, climb *up."*

Another hammering fist struck them. A vague shape flapped along the edge of the cliff, stooping like an alien bird of prey. The habitat had torn loose from its anchors. For a moment Zynth was obscured by the twisting folds of plastic. Then the rope convulsed in Etienne's hands and went slack. Zynth's scream echoed from the walls as Etienne flung herself against the face of the cliff. Zynth's falling body was directly above her—seeming to drift downward in slow motion. In another moment, she would hit, would smash her downward and outward, and they would both fall into that dark void beneath the Eye's mocking stare.

Because I lied, Etienne thought.

Zynth's wide eyes met hers for a second, sharing fear, sharing death. Then her body twisted convulsively, and she hit the wall, rebounding as she clawed for a hold.

She missed Etienne, hit the widest part of the narrow ledge. Etienne threw herself on top of her, knowing that it was a stupid thing to do, that they would both go over. Her toes dug into the slippery stone as Zynth's momentum torqued them both toward the lip of darkness.

They stopped, poised on the brink, still alive. Etienne inched her way backward, arms around Zynth, pulling her away from that dark drop. "Zynth?" she breathed, her heart pounding in her chest. "Are you hurt?"

Zynth sobbed once deep in her throat, burrowed her face against Etienne's shoulder. "Yes," the whisper was a breath of terror. "It hurts so bad. Inside." Her body tensed convulsively within Etienne's arms. "What if I'm damaged? Etienne? I . . . I can't be damaged."

She was so young—perhaps too young yet to have learned she was mortal. It could come as such a shock to you to realize that you could really die. "It's all right. It's going to be all right." She stroked Zynth's hair, holding her close, smothering her own fear. "I'm going to climb up," she murmured. "I'll get Grik. She'll bring help." Oh God. The Gateway. The Rethe could come and go, but not humans. Not without a Rethe.

"I'm afraid," Zynth whispered. "Don't leave me?"

Don't leave me. The words echoed through the black tunnel of the past, and Etienne raised her face to the Eye, remembering the image of Vilya's pale face on her e-mail screen. Don't leave me, Etienne. I love you. Why can't you understand? When Etienne hadn't answered, she had sent no more mail. "I may not be able to leave you." The words caught in her throat, choking her. "The Gate . . ."

"It's all right." Zynth drew back a little, her face clearing, pain lines smoothing into an expression of peace. "Etienne . . . I need to tell you . . ." She lifted her hand, fingers opening like the petals of a flower. Gently she touched Etienne's face. "I wish . . . you could have been . . . other than what you are." She closed her eyes, her fingers exploring the planes of Etienne's face as if to commit it to memory. "You can go and I won't be afraid." She opened her eyes, her smile making her beautiful. "You will need to take the key. It's just below my collarbone. On the left."

"Key?"

"To the Gate. You will have to take it out." She shuddered. "But it is just beneath the skin, so it should not hurt much."

So, the Rethe's ability to manipulate the Gateways was *not* an inborn psychic ability, as they had claimed! They used tech after all! Even as these thoughts were running through her head, Etienne had clicked on her flesh and was opening the neck of Zynth's suit, feeling beneath her shirt. Her flesh was clammy and her skin had gone pale. Shock? Internal bleeding? Her pain was seeping shrilly into Etienne's head, as she found a tiny subdermal lump just below the knob of Zynth's left collarbone. She looked into Zynth's wide eyes, brushed sweaty hair back from her forehead. "I'll be quick," she said softly.

"Thank you." Zynth swallowed. Her eyes followed Etienne's hand as it slid into the pocket of her suit to retrieve her laser blade. As Etienne thumbed it on, Zynth shuddered and closed her eyes.

Etienne placed a restraining hand on her shoulder, but Zynth lay utterly still as the tiny beam of energy sliced neatly through the skin just above the sphere. She caught her breath as Etienne pinched the embedded sphere free of the surrounding tissue, but made no other sound. "Press." Etienne placed Zynth's fingers over the gash. "It's not bleeding much." Fingers red with Zynth's blood, she studied the sphere. It was made of a matte black material, was about the size of a garden pea. Carefully, Etienne slipped it into an inside pocket on her suit, sealed the pocket closed. "I'm going to climb up. It shouldn't take me too long. We'll be back soon." She leaned down to kiss Zynth gently on the forehead. "I promise."

Zynth's eyes opened and she reached up to cup Etienne's face between her palms. "I know you'll come back." She kissed Etienne slowly, sensuously, on the lips. "Be careful."

"I will." Etienne got stiffly to her feet. The damned wind had died, as if the Eye had accomplished what it had wanted to accomplish. Or maybe it thought that they were trapped. You've never watched me climb, Etienne told it silently. When I come back, I will come back for them both. She bowed slowly, formally to the Eye, then turned and searched for the first holds.

You never look down. You look up, to the sides, focus on that next crevice or ledge where you might jam fingers or toes. You don't think about wind or the seconds ticking by as a girl dies.

And a man, too. She caught a whisper of Duran's delirium, pressed her lips together, and eased her weight upward.

You don't look at the top, either. Not after your muscles start to shake and your fingers are numb and you know that you can't do this a whole lot longer. So when she reached up, groping blindly, and her hand slapped down on level ground, she almost lost her grip and fell. With a final spasm of exhausted muscles, she shoved herself upward, lunging over the edge to flop belly-down onto the blessed stone. For awhile she simply lay there, panting and shaking. Then she forced herself to her feet.

It was still dark—didn't dawn ever come here?—and the habitat was gone, of course. Etienne staggered to her feet and stumbled away from the cliff edge. Clutching the tiny key, she headed for the place where the Gate had been. For a moment she thought that it wasn't going to work—there was still nothing to see. Then, in an eyeblink of time, she stepped through into the dusty square near the squatter village. The shacks and pre-fab cottages drowsed in the hot afternoon sun, and Grik sat beneath a tower of branching turquoise silicate that housed a native hive creature.

Asleep, her head leaning back against the stem of the structure,

Grik's face was carved into gaunt lines of worry, or exhaustion. She jerked awake as Etienne approached.

"Where is . . . it." She bolted to her feet.

"Hurt." Etienne took a single step toward her, fists clenching. "Are you satisfied? Has she been punished enough, or does she have to die there?"

"You mean . . . injured?" Grik's face had gone pinched and white. "She needed to risk herself, yes . . . but to be *injured* . . ." Outrage filled her voice. "How could you let that happen? Impossible!"

"I was right," Etienne said coldly. "About why you hired me."

"Enough." Grik was already striding toward the gate. "How badly is she injured?"

"I don't know." Etienne had to trot to keep pace with her. "She said it hurt inside."

Grik made a short ugly chopping gesture with both hands. "Remain here."

She took a single long stride into the air and vanished.

How the hell did they know where the damn Gates *were?* Etienne wondered. More buried hardware? She wasn't buying the "higher evolution" explanation any more. She looked toward the cottages. A girl peeped at her from the sparse reed bed that grew along the south side of the square. She ducked out of sight when she saw Etienne looking. Her excited curiosity came to Etienne like the bright smell of rain on summer dust. Etienne smiled at her, closed her fist around the black sphere, and stepped through the Gateway.

A dozen Rethe clustered at the top of the cliff. Light globes mounted on long poles flooded the area with blue-white radiance and four of the Rethe lowered a stretcher. Another Rethe was just clipping herself to an anchor. Fast response time, Etienne thought cynically. They must have been waiting at another Gate for just such an emergency. This whole escapade felt more and more orchestrated. She didn't see Grik, but another anchor and rope suggested that she might be below. Etienne walked over to the small red-haired Rethe who was about to climb over the edge and put a hand on her shoulder. The Rethe recoiled with a sharp clap of her cupped palms, but Etienne ignored her as she unclipped the rope from her harness.

They had researched her well enough to give Zynth a rope without a clip, knowing that Etienne always tied off. With an angry snap, she secured the clip to the harness she still wore. The Rethe was saying something, but Etienne ignored her. Grabbing the ropes, she stepped over the edge. No time for small defiances now. She was going for a big one. The Eye stared down impassively as she bounced fast down the wall, ignoring caution, eyes fixed on the single figure crouched beside Zynth's curled body.

"What are you doing here?" Grik barely looked up as Etienne knelt beside her.

Zynth's eyes were closed. Fine blue veins webbed the pale skin of her eyelids, and for a terrible instant, Etienne thought she wasn't breathing. She touched her throat, felt the reassuring twitch of a pulse before Grik shoved her hand away.

"Don't touch me again," Etienne said carefully. "Or I will throw you off this ledge." Only truth beneath the Eye of God. She smiled thinly as Grik recoiled. "You have used me very thoroughly." She kept her eyes on Grik's face. "What did you do? Review the personal profiles of every empath on the planet? Until you found someone who would be highly motivated to keep your breeder safe? She *is* fertile, isn't she? One of your national treasures?" Her lips drew back from her teeth. "And you needed to punish her properly so as to satisfy your evolved sense of *ethics.*" She spat the word. "But you didn't really want to *risk* her, eh? An eye for an eye? You haven't really evolved beyond us, have you? You've just learned how to cheat." She looked down at Zynth. "Well, I took care of her—for her own sake," she said softly.

"I thank you for the risk you assumed." Grik's nostrils flared slightly, but whatever her emotions were, they were too complex for Etienne to read. "That is a difficult climb." She inclined her head at the sheer cliff face behind her.

"Why did you make her do this?" Etienne asked softly.

"Your race is sated with fertility. The creation of new life has little value to you." Her face looked as smooth and hard as marble in the Eye's cold glare. "For us . . . there are very few who can rightfully claim the pronouns you so casually toss around. We have avoided the internal strife that has weakened you as a race, but everything has its price. Continuation of our species is a privilege and an obligation that involves the species—above and beyond the individual. You cannot comprehend." She made a chopping gesture. "The rule that Zynth broke was not a minor infraction. In our society, the failure of the individual is the failure of us all. The punishment—the risk of her loss—was inflicted upon us all." She stood and looked beyond Etienne. Two more Rethe were descending, guiding the stretcher downward. In a moment, it was going to get very crowded on the ledge.

"The creation of new life isn't always a casual thing for us, either." Etienne looked down at Zynth, remembering the trust in her voice. She didn't look so much like Vilya now. "I care about her," she said softly. "For herself, not for her face."

"Do not fantasize, Empath." Grik's tone was icy. "Love is only possible with another . . . appropriate Rethe. That is the way it is."

Etienne smiled at her. "What is the penalty for lying beneath the Eye?"

Grik turned abruptly away to speak to the descending Rethe. Etienne moved back as far as she could along the diminishing ledge. Duran's dying whispered in her mind. It strengthened suddenly, and a murky image formed in her head—a girl with dark hair, pale, with a spare, elegant face. Etienne felt a piercing grief. Duran's vision, Duran's grief. For a rending moment, she thought he was remembering Vilya, but he hadn't known Vilya when she was that young. And then she realized . . .

His daughter. Terane.

His daughter. That was how she had thought of the child. She had been a baby when Vilya had died, and Duran had laid legal claim to her. So Etienne had never seen her. Not because Duran had forbidden it. She herself had forbidden it. *His* daughter. She closed her eyes, but his love and grief beat in her head, filling her brain with the merciless image of the girl who was Vilya's daughter, too.

Grik believed that Zynth could not love anyone who couldn't father a child for her. Etienne looked up into the Eye, met its cold stare. "So did I," she murmured. "Grik!" She raised her voice and the Rethe paused as she was about to begin her climb to the top of the cliff. "Send the stretcher back down," she called.

"Why?"

"For Duran," she said shortly. "You sent me here to find him, didn't you?"

The two Rethe with the stretcher paused and looked down, too, and for a moment there was only the sound of wind across the ledge. "You are correct." Grik sounded reluctant. "I will . . . send the stretcher down."

"How is she doing?" Etienne forced out the question. Brown and green blobs like fat slugs clung to Zynth's forehead, chest, arms, and belly. More Rethe biotech? "Grik?"

"She may live." Grik shrugged and began to climb. After a second, the two other Rethe continued to ease the stretcher up the cliff face.

Go to hell, Etienne thought, but she was too weary to say it aloud. Taking a deep breath, she leaned out over the void. One more small defiance. The living rope quivered in her hands as she turned around, found a toe hold, and began to follow Duran's grief for his daughter, crevice by crevice, across the face of polished stone.

He lay on another ledge, similar to the one Zynth had landed on. It occurred to Etienne, as she pulled some slack into the rope and knelt beside his huddled body, that they were remarkably regular. Perhaps too regular to be natural, but she was too exhausted to worry about it. In the light of her flash, she saw that Duran's hair was beginning to go gray, and his face had thinned a bit in twenty years. He was no youth any more, but he looked pretty much as she remembered him. Blood stained the fabric of his thermal suit, red and fresh in one place. That arm was crooked, and a touch confirmed her diagnosis. Compound fracture, and he had bled a lot. Broken leg, too, and probably more damage that wasn't so obvious. There was no sign of a climbing harness.

His eyelids fluttered as she started to get up. "Wh . . . who?" he mumbled, squinting up at her. "E . . . tienne?" Dried blood crusted his lips, and one side of his face was scraped and bruised from the fall. *"You?"*

She was surprised that he recognized her. She had been older than Duran, when he and Vilya had first been friends. Older, verging on old. Twenty years of search and rescue work had changed her a lot. "It's me, Duran. Help is on the way." Maybe. She looked up at the cliff top, yanked on the rope. A part of her half expected it to come loose and fall around her in writhing living coils. Who would know if the Rethe left both of them to die here?

"Hang on," she said to him. Conscious, his pain beat at her, bad enough to get in past her barriers. She fumbled in her belt pack, took out a couple of pain patches. Two would put him out, or nearly so. She peeled the protective backing from the first patch, smoothed it onto his throat.

She didn't want any more of his grieving images. But he fumbled a hand up to stop her before she could apply the second patch. "Etienne?"

"Yes, it's me. Help is on the way."

"Can you hear it?" His eyes were ringed with white, mundane gray turned to a clear blue by the Eye's glare. "The voice of God, of *their* God. It shaped them, hear it? The wind is its breath. It sings to them, Etienne. This is their soul. Zynth told me, and it's true. This is where they . . . were born."

Their soul? Their God? Etienne remembered Zynth, her hands weaving worship on the lip of the cliff. *The* Eye of God. Not just a casual name dubbed onto an alien landmark then. Their God. Their . . . homeworld. She looked out into the purple darkness and shivered. No wonder Grik had spoken of Zynth's transgression as a sin. And it occurred to her suddenly that perhaps Grik *hadn't* been searching for an empath who would protect a precious breeder.

Perhaps she had been searching for an empath who would kill.

"I wanted . . . to tell you . . . how she died." Duran was losing consciousness as the drugs hit him. "It was my fault. I . . . tried to stop her fall, but she . . . had too much rope. She . . . cut it. So I wouldn't fall, too. I . . . tried to tell you. I'm . . . so sorry, Etienne. I should have stopped her fall. So . . . sorry . . ." His eyes closed and his hand fell away from her wrist.

So Vilya had fallen, not he. And she had relinquished her last chance of life, in order to save Duran. So that her daughter would have a parent?

And if *you* had been there, Etienne? To be a parent? That was what Vilya wanted.

The whisper in her head was in her own voice, but she looked up at the Eye. Slowly, she got to her feet. The accident report was public record. She could have looked it up any time in the last twenty years. If she had wanted to know.

Only truth beneath the Eye of God?

Something scraped loudly behind her and she started. It was the stretcher bumping down the face, followed closely by the two Rethe. "He has a broken arm and leg," she called up to them. "Maybe internal injuries. I'll help you move him."

She wasn't sure how flexible Rethe ethics might be, after all.

But the team was efficient and careful. They helped her strap Duran into the stretcher, and guided him silently up the face of the cliff. The wind eased off again, as if this god was willing to let them depart in peace now. At the top of the cliff, the remaining two Rethe unhooked the stretcher from the ropes, and carried it silently through the Gateway. Grik and Zynth had disappeared. Etienne trudged after them, exhaustion dragging at her. The two Rethe who had climbed with her flanked her. Oh yeah. Operating the Gateway, because she was a mere human. They didn't realize yet that she had a key. Etienne blinked as they emerged from night into bright day. The same girl was still at the edge of the plaza, playing some game with a ball and bits of empty reed shell.

The girl leaped to her feet as the Rethe set the stretcher down in the dust and went running barefoot across the dusty ground, her shift flapping around her thighs. She was heading for the small medical clinic.

Etienne sighed as her Rethe escort made identical wiping motions with their left hands. Good riddance? Farewell? Still silent, they walked back through the Gateway and vanished. Wanting only to drag herself home and climb into bed, Etienne squatted beside the stretcher. She was already sweating in her thermal suit, and she unsealed it. Duran was still alive. She held his wrist, his pulse faltering beneath her fingertips. "I don't like you," she said softly. "I don't think I can change that." Three of the squatters came running toward her, dust rising from their feet. "But I don't blame you anymore," Etienne said. And she looked up automatically, as if the Eye would be there in the off-blue sky.

It wasn't, of course. The squatters—two men and a woman in cut-offs and grimy shirts—arrived. "I'm the med-tech," said the woman.

"Pick up an end and give us a hand," she snapped at Etienne. "Then you can tell me what's going on here."

The reeds swayed and rattled, happy in the morning sun. Etienne kneaded bread dough in her small hands-on kitchen, listening to the familiar susurration. The reed-song soothed her as the dough stretched and flattened beneath her palms. But as she shaped a round loaf, the reeds' song changed to a scattered rattle. A visitor? Etienne wiped her hands on a towel, scrubbing briefly and vainly at the drying dough on her fingers.

She hoped it wasn't Duran, come to thank her for saving his life. But it had only been three days since the accident. The med-tech at the squatters' clinic had told her it would be at least a week before Duran could be released. Medical technology was less than cutting-edge out here.

Tossing the towel onto the counter, she crossed the small living room in three strides and flung the door open. She had tried to hide it from herself—how much she wanted it to be Zynth waiting on the porch. The sight of her actually standing there took Etienne's breath away, and made her blush, because she felt about as transparent as a teenager in the throes of true love.

"May I come in?" Zynth sounded as uncertain as Etienne felt. Her hand lifted in the direction of her shoulder, and Etienne followed its movement. Ah yes. Grik was hovering. Of course.

"Please do." Etienne was impressed with the cool graciousness of her tone. What a lie! She backed, held the door open as Zynth walked through, then closed it firmly, before Grik could follow. "Would you care for tea?"

"We began here." Zynth stood in the middle of the floor, her arms at her sides. "It seems like a long time ago, but it was not."

"You're all right," Etienne said softly.

"Yes." Zynth's smile faltered. "If you had not climbed . . ." She shook her head, her hair sliding forward to hide her expression. "I don't think Grik believed that . . . I would climb down. I think it believed that I would be too afraid, that I would humiliate myself in sight of the Eye."

The Eye. Etienne heard all the nuance now. Maybe you could begin to understand another race once you caught a glimpse of their soul. "Your homeworld," she said softly.

"Is it such a sin, for you to know?" Her hands lifted in a fragile, pleading gesture. "We hide so much from you. Why?"

"Because I think we are too much alike," Etienne said softly.

Zynth smiled. "On that ledge, I was not afraid. I knew that you would not let me die."

The words made her shiver, and Etienne clenched her fists at her sides. She averted her head as Zynth stepped close.

"I will remember you forever." Her breath tickled Etienne's throat, warm as summer. "Please realize how much I . . . care."

"You're saying goodbye." Etienne's voice was harsh.

"I do not think that we will meet again." Zynth's voice trembled. "It is . . . a tremendous sorrow."

"Grik won't let it happen, you mean. Grik is afraid of me." Etienne clasped her hands behind her back, resisting the urge to grab Zynth by the shoulders and kiss her, or shake her. "I . . . love you." And she bit her lip because she hadn't meant to say those words out loud. Not ever.

"No," Zynth whispered. She was trembling. "It is *my* choice, not Grik's. *I* am afraid of you. Because I can forget that you are . . . other."

"That's right." Etienne didn't try to soften the bitterness in her voice. "You can only love another breeder. I forgot."

"You do not understand," Zynth said softly. "Grik says you would not, and I think now, that it is right." Her fingers were gentle on Etienne's face.

"I wish you a wonderful life," Etienne said through clenched teeth. "I hope you find a nice fertile *he.*"

Zynth's sigh touched her like the last warm wind of fall. "I am a giver, not the one who nurtures the life within." She laughed softly, sadly. "A *he,* as you say."

Anthropomorphism, Etienne thought dizzily. Look at a child with the face of a girl you once loved, and what do you see? Not a man. The irony was so wonderful. She laughed.

"I am sorry." Zynth stepped back, affront in the stiff posture of her body.

"I'm laughing at *me,* not you." Etienne held out her hand, didn't let herself flinch as Zynth took it. "Don't mind me. I'm old and bitter, and I see ghosts. I really do wish you . . . love. And children."

"Thank you." Zynth's smile was beautiful, but still tinged with sadness. He paused with his hand on the door, looked back over his shoulder. "I love you, too," he said. "For all that it is wrong."

Then the door closed behind him and he was gone. Etienne sat down on a floor cushion and listened to the reeds whisper their contentment to the summer heat. Love was another universal. Like pain, and fear. And grief. She rested her forehead on her knees and didn't cry. After a time—when the Rethe had had plenty of time to leave—she got up. Her joints still ached from her climb, and she felt suddenly old—as old as she really was.

Outside, the sun was high. The reeds brushed her thighs as she waded through them, touching her like a lover's fingers. The girl wasn't at the plaza today. Etienne strode across the open space and stepped onto the unmarked patch of ground that should be a Gate.

Her foot landed on gray stone, and the Eye stared dispassionately down. Slowly, Etienne walked over the broken remains of the habitat's anchor, and stopped on the lip of the chasm. Far below, blue-white mountains reflected in still water like purple ink. Duran had heard the soul of a people in the song of this world. Is that what you loved about him, Vilya? Braced against the gusts, Etienne lifted her face to the Eye. Duran's ability to *hear*—like her empathic sense, but different? Safer?

Truth only, beneath the Eye of God. She bent her head and the first tears spotted the cracked stone where her anchor had pulled loose. Tears for Vilya, because she had never cried for her—no—she had never let herself cry. And for herself, because Terane could have been her daughter, as well as Duran's and Vilya's.

And for Zynth who would find someone to love who was as fertile as she . . . he . . . was. Because he had to.

Etienne wondered if Terane had inherited Duran's ability to image a soul in light and music. She turned her back on the cliff and the Eye, trudged slowly back across the gray stone. At the edge of the Gateway, she paused, her fingers curling around the sphere that was the key to this technology. "You want truth?" Etienne looked up at the Eye. "Our awe is wearing thin. It's time for us to look you in the eye." Courtesy of Duran. "We're good at unraveling tech." As she stepped forward, she wondered if her old boss Anton would be surprised to hear from her. Maybe not.

Her foot landed in sun and dust, and her ears filled with the whisper of reeds. She didn't turn toward home. Instead, she began to trudge past the squatters' shacks toward the clinic. She didn't want to know how much Duran might have loved Vilya, but she needed to talk to him. She needed to ask about . . . their daughter. She needed an address. Too late to be a mother, maybe she could be a friend, offer another version of Vilya. Maybe not, but she could try.

The reeds sang contentment, and the dust puffed up from beneath her feet to blow away on the wind.

About the Editor

Gardner Dozois has been the editor of *Asimov's Science Fiction* magazine for more than a decade, during which time he has won many Hugo Awards for Best Editor. He is the author of the novels *Nightmare Blue* (with George Alec Effinger) and *Strangers*, and his short fiction (which has earned him two Nebula Awards) has been collected in *Geodesic Dreams*. Another collection, *Slow Dancing Through Time*, contains his collaborative work with such writers as Jack Dann, Michael Swanwick, and Susan Casper. Born in Salem, Massachusetts, he resides in Philadelphia, Pennsylvania.